Dec. 1937

Dear Mr Thurston

Re Hagleton: I possess his
"Charley Wagg" which, quite stupidly,
has been ascribed to Sala, apparently because they said that he
had written the Sweeny Todd book
This appears to have arisen
owing to the libel case brought
in Feb. 1871 against Hain
Friswell for his article on G.A.S
"Modern Men of Letters honestly
Criticized." In the book, however
I fancy that the allegation
was only implied.

Yours sincerely,
Ralph Thain

CHARLEY WAG,

THE NEW

JACK SHEPPARD.

BY GEORGE SAVAGE,

Author of " The Woman with the Yellow Hair," " Somebody Else's Wife," &c.

LONDON :

PUBLISHED BY WILLIAM GRANT, 4, BOUVERIE STREET, E.C.

SOLD BY ALL BOOKSELLERS.

CONTENTS.

BOOK THE FIRST—CHILDHOOD IN THE GUTTER.

BOOK THE SECOND.

BOOK THE THIRD.

BOOK THE FOURTH.

CHARLEY WAG,

THE NEW JACK SHEPPARD.

[MR. TODDLEBOY IS "PUT OUT.."]

BOOK THE FIRST—CHILDHOOD IN THE GUTTER.

I.—ALL BUT MURDER.

A WOMAN ran wildly down one of the several steep flights of steps leading from Hungerford Market to the Quay below, and creeping along upon the slippery stonework, overhanging the water, paused for a moment at the extreme

point, cast one fearful, shuddering glance around and FLUNG HER CHILD INTO THE RIVER.

The rain was lashing heavily against the window panes, and the wind sweeping in fierce and fitful gusts along the deserted streets above, while every now and then a streak of livid lightning rent the air, followed by deafening peals of

No 1.

thunder. Few people were likely to be out in such a storm, and even in the best of weather the place which the woman had chosen is at night a dreary and forsaken spot.

She was young and almost beautiful, but deadly pale; her hair hung dark and tangled round her face; her clothes of costly fabric, but torn, and wet, and muddy, clung to her lithe and graceful form in heavy folds. She trod the slimy stonework, firmly and rapidly, though cautiously. Her flashing eyes, set teeth, and knitted brows bespoke her courage and determination, and her DEADLY PURPOSE.

She tore the sleeping babe which a moment since had nestled at her breast, from its warm shelter beneath her thick plaid shawl, raised it high in the air, to give her the more power, and flung it fiercely from her into the black and sluggish waters gurgling at her feet.

"Thus perishes the record of my sin and folly."

It was more a murmured than a spoken thought, for her blanched lips scarce gave utterance to any sound; but had it been instead the loudest shriek, the raging tempest would have drowned her cry in its boisterous fury. Thus did she cast her child into the river, and then with fast but certain footsteps retraced her dangerous course, and flying up the steps, again hurried along the covered passage of the market, through another passage to the right, and so by Villiers-street, into the Strand.

No one had seen her, no one followed her. The darkness hid her retreating form, and Heaven alone was witness to her crime   The would-be murderess fled away, careful alone of her own safety, heeding not how fared the little living bundle the dark waters swept along towards death. What hope was there for it? What guardian angel came to rescue it?

None other than TODDLEBOY.

If Toddleboy had been a moment later he would have been too late. If Toddleboy had not happened to be hanging over the boat side, he would never have seen it. If Toddleboy had not taken it into his head to cross the river in Joe Cudder's boat, instead of paying a halfpenny to cross the bridge like any other mortal, he would never have been on the spot at all, and if he had not dawdled an unusual time over that last three halfpennyworth of gin, he would have been home an hour before it happened at the very least. So you see after all, some good may come of dram drinking and procrastination, whatever Mr. Gough and the copy-books may say to the contrary.

Joe Cudder was pulling with all the strength of his great sinewy arms towards the landing place by the bridge, from which a moment before the mother had thrown her baby, and Mr. Toddleboy, wrapped up in Cudder's waterproof, and an old piece of sacking, was lolling, warm and drowsy, at the stern, with only the end of his nose and his left hand exposed to the weather. With his left hand he was paddling in the water, not with any particular object, but merely because, as everybody knows, one is apt to feel a little playful and sportive after an extra three-ha'p'orth, and so Mr. Toddleboy was splashing about like a young duckling, letting the water run through his fingers, and wantonly endeavouring to catch a bubble. And it was while thus engaged, his left hand came in contact with something which rose to the surface directly underneath it.

Perhaps his first thought was of sharks and sea serpents, and other monsters of the deep, not excluding dead dogs and cats; but his eye fell on the object floating by, and he saw a little white baby face upturned towards Heaven.

"Hi, Cudder! Hold hard! Stop her! Ease her!" bawled Mr. Toddleboy, grown nautical and energetic of a sudden. "Turn her astarn. There's a man overboard."

"What's up now?" growled Joe Cudder, whom drink, bad weather, and want of luck had rendered gruff and grumpy. "Who are you howling at?"

"Man alive, put back the vessel. Don't you see that bundle of white?"

"Ah, I see it."

"It's a baby."

"Then why the deuce didn't you say so before," asked Joe Cudder, with the tone of a deeply injured man, and turning the boat, he pulled sulkily in the direction of the drowning child. Even now they would have been too late, had not his companion, leaning over the boat-side at the imminent risk of capsizing the gallant craft, stretched out his arm, and clutched at it wildly, as it was just about to sink again.

"It isn't dead, I think," cried Toddleboy, as he wrapped the little dripping stranger in the sacking. "Pull to shore, Joe, as hard as you can."

Turning the boat's-head round again, and sullenly putting his whole back unto the work, Joe Cudder brought the wherry, with half-a-dozen vigorous strokes, safe to the landing place at the foot of the bridge, where they stepped on land.

"What do you advise should be done with it, Mr. Cudder? I put it to you as a family man. You are a family man, I believe, are you not?"

Joe Cudder was so far a family man that he had had a couple of wives, who had departed for a better world, and at that present time owned something bony, gaunt, and squalid, which had a legal right to Mr. Cudder's name, and haunted the pot houses where her liege lord muddled himself, helped him home late at night, and took his kicks and buffets patiently and without complaint, like many other British wives are used to do.

Receiving no reply from this great martial authority, Mr. Toddleboy continued—

"And is not it extraordinary, Joe? I never read anything so wonderful. To think that we should be passing at the moment. How long do you think it had been in the water?"

"A week," growled Cudder, who was busy with his boat.

"Lord bless me," said Mr. Toddleboy, holding the baby a little further off him. "But it would be green, wouldn't it."

"One on you's green enough," retorted Mr. Cudder, chuckling as though he had said something wonderfully funny. "Now, then, are you coming?"

But Mr. Toddleboy was examining his precious burden anxiously, and endeavouring to see whether it was still warm.

"It's alive!" he cried. "It's healthy, Joe, I'll take my davy."

"Come on, then. What are you going to do with it?"

"Take it into the public-house, and try to revive it."

"And after that?"

"After that?"

"Ah—you heard me, didn't you?"

"Well, after that," said Mr. Toddleboy, looking rather serious, as they entered the tavern. "I ain't a wet nus, and I ain't a foundling hospital. I only hope I haven't got myself into a fix. But if I have, what am I to do with it?"

"Put it back where you took it from," said Joe Cudder. "That's about the best course I can recommend."

II.—ONE OF THE SHABBIEST TRICKS ON RECORD.

"WHY what on earth and goodness me have you got now, Mr. Toddleboy?"

It was the landlady who spoke, and who knew Mr. Toddleboy intimately, or ought to have done, seeing that he had used "The Drinking Fish" off and on these fifteen years.

"Is that your last Toddleboy?" cried a chorus of customers,

"It's the first I've come by this way," said Mr. Toddleboy—"I've just picked it up."

"Picked it up! where?"

"In the river. It's a foundling."

"Go on with you."

"I tell you it is, and I'm in search of a wet nurse."

"Better find a dry nurse first, hadn't you. It looks rather damp!"

By this time every body at the bar had crowded round Mr. Toddleboy and his little charge, and was offering a variety of suggestions all more or less impracticable, from standing the baby on its head to using a stomach pump. Toddleboy was a dreamy old man, bald-headed, weak-eyed, and red-nosed, who spent his life in a fog of gin and tobacco, smelt of garlic and stale smoke, was supposed to sleep in his boots, had bits of broken pipes and fag ends of "screws" in all his pockets, carried his private correspondence and his broken victuals loose in his hat, was believed to have seen better days, talked Latin and spouted Shakespeare, and earned about six shillings a week when he was sober enough to earn anything at all. At other times his relations kept him. Toddleboy was not the sort of person you would naturally have turned to in an emergency like this. Indeed his suggestion of giving it "a little drop of something warm" met with the contempt it merited.

"I've heard salt was a good thing" said he, his mind evidently running on the popular method of resuscitating drowned flies.

All this while the unfortunate little infant was dangling, as it were, 'twixt life and death in its eccentric preserver's arms, and there is no knowing what its fate would have ultimately been had not the landlady come to its rescue and kindly taken the little stranger under her care.

With the assistance of the young lady in ringlets who dispensed liquors and broke hearts over the bar, she undressed the child and applied such restoratives as are to be found in "Dr. Buchan's Domestic Medicine," and in the hands of the ladies the little patient soon began to show signs of returning animation.

Such few spectators as were allowed to penetrate to the exclusive privacy of the bar parlour watched the operations with breathless interest.

Of course you know very well, gentle Reader, as well as I do myself, that I never intended the baby to die, or else what good would there have been in rescuing it and intruding it upon your polite consideration.

No—to ease your suspense—supposing you feel any (and if you are a very young reader, I don't know that you may not after all), I may as well tell you that in an hour's time IT WAS ALIVE AND KICKING,

"Might I venture to enquire" said Mr. Toddleboy with some small amount of diffidence consequent upon so delicate a question, "might I venture to enquire how we shall allude to our young friend in the forthcoming Census?"—

"What do you mean!" said the landlady.

"I alluded," said the gentleman with still increasing timidity, "to the question of what attire it will be necessary to select when our young friend gets too big for long clothes. In short," said he, tossing up a halfpenny and covering it with his hand, "shall we say pegtops or crinoline?"

"Lord bless me!—get along with you How can you talk such rubbish!"

And the buxom hostess blushed all over her pretty face and down her plump neck to where her collar fastened.

"How can you be so foolish? at your age too!"

"I only asked for information!"

"It's a boy of course. What do you suppose?"

"Well I'm sorry for that, said Mr. Toddleboy, "I should have preferred a girl myself."

"Would you?" retorted the landlady, "that's all you know about it. Drat girls say I, they're twice the trouble boys are!"

"I can't abide boys, myself," said the gentleman. "However, it don't matter much to me what it is."

"What do you mean to do with the baby?"

"I haven't the least idea."

"Haven't you?" said the landlady, a little alarmed. "But you can't leave it here, you know."

"I suppose," remarked Mr. Toddleboy, after an uncomfortable pause, "they'd take it in at the workhouse."

"Well they don't take in more than they can help, I can assure you."

"You're right there. I expect they'd refuse to take me if I asked 'em."

"I expect they would, Mr. Toddleboy."

"There's one thing to be said, I shall be as loath to go in as they will be loath to have me. But it's a fine institution."

"Well, you'd better try it to-night," said the landlord, joining in the conversation, "and take that precious kid of yours there."

"Kid of mine!" cried Toddleboy in amazement; "it's no kid of mine, you know. What do you mean?"

"Come, come, Toddleboy!" said everybody in a breath, "that won't wash at any figure."

"What won't wash?" roared Toddleboy

"That tale of yours about the river."

"Tale of mine. Dash it! you don't suppose—"

"Oh! we supposes nothing, only it really is cutting it a trifle too fat."

"What, dash my buttons—do you dare to insinuate—"

"We insinuates nothing, only it aint likely you know."

"What aint likely? Why here's Joe Cudder helped me to rescue it, didn't you, Joe? speak up, man."

"Oh, shut up," said Joe, puffing at his pipe: "I don't want none of your chaff."

"None of whose chaff! I aint chaffing, Joe. What do you mean?"

"Mean, about what?"

"Didn't we pick that baby out of the water?"

"What baby?"

"You know what baby, fast enough. Answer my question."

"If you mean, did we pick the young whelp out of the water as you let fall in, in course we did. And more fool you, says I, for if you wanted to get shut on it, as you said you did, what was the good of fishing it in again when you chucked it overboard."

I wish I was an artist, I should draw now poor Toddleboy's face when he heard these words. It was a sight to look at. Mr. PROWSE has chosen other subjects for the exercise of his facile pencil, but that is the one I should have given you.

He was thunderstruck; he was dumbfounded: he stared and gasped like a stranded codfish: he would have said something, but the words stuck in his throat and choked him. To be proved a liar before a whole barful of people, and by that traitor Joe too, a man to whom he had stood untold quarterns in his time—it was beyond belief.

He stammered and stuttered out something, and tried to laugh. Like most honest persons when accused of wrongdoing, he looked infinitely more ashamed of himself than the guilty party would have done had he been detected.

The voice of the landlord recalled him to his senses, aided by a half-suppressed titter among the bystanders.

"I suppose its clothes won't take long drying," said the host to his wife.

"They're nearly dry now, dear—James is holding them before the kitchen fire."

"As soon as they are dry put 'em on to the kid."

"Yes, dear."

"And give it to its father."

"Yes, dear."

Here Mr. Toddleboy's rage was something awful, but he was calm and self-possessed. He only knocked his glass over and bit the stem of his pipe in two, otherwise you could not have imagined what angry passions were stirring his ordinary tranquil breast.

He said nothing.

Presently, when the clothes were sufficiently dry, the baby was re-dressed and brought out to him. The landlord handed it across the counter.

"Let me advise you, Mr. Toddleboy," said the landlord sternly, "to take the child home again and don't get yourself into any trouble."

"Damnation!" began Toddleboy, black in the face.

"None of that 'ere, if you please," said the landlord.

"You infernal old fool," began Toddleboy.

"Turn him out," said the landlord, and out he went, neck and crop as the saying is. In other words all of a heap, on his nose, atop of the baby which had been thrust into his arms.

"Well," said he, "they shall smart for this, or I'll know why. If they call it a joke, I don't. Its carrying a joke a precious sight too far. Hush-a-by-baby—Hold your noise, can't you. I've got nothing to give you. Lord bless me, I'm holding it the wrong way up."

"You hav'n't got one of them to spare, I suppose," said a rough sort of boatman, who was smoking a pipe and leaning against the wall of the public house, apparently quite indifferent to wind or rain.

"Got one to spare, eh?"

"Ah, you look as if you had."

"Well, I have," said Mr. Toddleboy; "you needn't tell everybody, but I've a very fine one here I'll part with on the most reasonable terms Are you in want of such a thing yourself?"

"Not I," responded the boatman gruffly, "I don't see no good in 'em."

And he turned upon his heel and walked away.

"Don't you, said Mr. Toddleboy snappishly, but more to himself than to the last speaker. "I suppose you were never one yourself, you inhuman vagabond. Though what the dickins I am to do with the precious infant is more than I can say I suppose I'd better take it to the workhouse; bu where is the workhouse? that's the question. I don't much matter which, I suppose, so I'll taket it to the one I know. Isn't it raining too! I'm really very miserable."

As he spoke a loud burst of merriment coming from the public-house, smote upon his ear.

"Ah, you may laugh," he said indignantly. "Grin away, you set of fools. This is what they call a jolly lark, is it. They knew very well it wasn't my baby. Whose is it, I wonder. Perhaps there's some mark upon its clothes—a family crest or coat of arms, or something of that sort, which might lead to its being proved to be some young swell or another, and the heir to millions of pounds a-year. I've often read of such things in romances. Well, that can't be helped now. The question is, what am I to do with it; I can't take it home, Mrs. Grinderbones won't stand babies, I know; besides what could I give it. It couldn't chew tobacco I suppose, and I've got nothing else. Joe Cudder suggested putting it back where we took it from. Upon my word, it would be about the best thing for it."

III.—BEADLEDOM.

THE workhouse to which Mr. Toddleboy bent his steps is to be found in the densely populated parish of Saint Starver-Cum-Bag-o-'Bones, situated in the very heart of a huge labyrinth of noisome courts and alleys, where reduced gentility hides its diminished head, sordid poverty grubs and grovels, and Cain-branded guilt is hidden snugly in defiance of the law.

A horrible locality, in which it is not safe to wander alone and late at night. A dangerous, scowling, skulking neighbourhood, where the police, like the water, are laid on in the smallest quantities. A mean and paltry set of people living there who are for ever pinching and pining and planning and scheming to keep the wolf from off the door-step, and to make both ends meet It is there that coal is sold by the seven pounds, and tea by the quarter ounce; where the women are dirty and squalid, and the children ragged and wan. It is a first-rate place for public houses, and a gin palace is a certain fortune. I wish I had money enough to start one!

If Mr. Toddleboy had had much valuable property about him, he might have hesitated before plunging into this choice district. Good lack! his pockets were never over full at any time, and he had nothing in them now. The baby he carried was the only valuable in his possession, and I do not know but that he would have liked to have been robbed of it. However, nobody offered. I suppose there is a glut of babies in the market, for out of story books I seldom hear of much child-stealing. Indeed, between ourselves, it is my opinion that a five-shilling advertisement in the *Times* would get you fifty for nothing—nice fine ones.

Mr. Toddleboy trotted on through the mud, whistling a tune with all his might, and trying to make believe that he was very jolly.

"I shall hand it in," said he to himself, "and if they want any explanation about it, I shall give my address, and call round again in the morning.

According to his account you see he was going to take a very high hand with the parochial authorities. He had never had an interview with a beadle, poor man, and did not know what it was like.

You know the Union, I dare say. A great lop-sided, dirty-faced house, with huge iron-bound gates, well locked and barred as though, dear heart, there was anything inside worth taking, or any inmate they would not have liked to have seen run away.

The night was still stormy and wet, but in spite of the inclemency of the weather, half-a-dozen God-forsaken, cowering, shivering wretches were huddled up under the scanty shelter of the outer walls of poverty's stronghold, and there they sat or lay unnoticed and uncared for, praying for another day.

"They are always there, bless you!" said a man with his pipe in his mouth, who had pointed out the miserable creatures to Mr. Toddleboy. "Summer and winter all the same. I come by here at all hours, working at a printing-office just by, and I always see them. Some of 'em dies there sometimes, of too much cold, and too little grub. Gallows hard, aint it?"

"But won't they let 'em in?" asked Mr. Toddleboy, innocently.

"Let 'em in," replied the printer, with a scornful laugh." "It's an easier job for a pauper to get out of purgatory, and that must be a difficulty if you've nothing to pay the parson to do the needful for you."

"But do you mean to tell me that in a Christian land—"

"Christian land be bothered. As if Christianity had got anything to do with empty stomachs. 'Praps there's too many Christians to be looked after. I've a good mind to be a Jew myself. I never heard of a Jew being a pauper. I don't believe they'd allow it for the honour of the persuasion."

And this free-thinking printer, who seemed to fancy that he had said something smart, departed on his way, leaving Toddleboy nursing the baby and gaping at the gates.

He walked up and knocked at them, then turned round and kicked at them with his heels.

But nobody took any particular notice.

Then Mr. Toddleboy began to remember he was a Briton. When a person becomes thoroughly imbued with the fact of his being a Briton, he makes up his mind to stand no nonsense from anybody, and he usually ends by being very ob-

jectionable to everybody, without achieving anything especially noteworthy.

"Damn me if I stand this," said Mr. Toddleboy, and then stood and waited another ten minutes.

What was to be done. Aha! a bell! He would ring it.

He seized the huge handle and gave it a jerk, which he intended should cause a tolerable tinkling, but hardly imagined that such a terriffic peal would have resulted. It was in fact a deafener. Three of the houseless ones woke up in terror; and one who dreamt, poor fool, that he had a roof to cover him, called out "Come in."

Before Mr. Toddleboy had time to recover from his surprise, a little wicket sprang open at his ear, and a voice cried—

"Now then, who are you, I'd like to know?"

"I'm one of the public," responded Mr. Toddleboy, determined to be bumptious and going in, as the saying is, a 'buster.'

"We don't want nothink to do with no publics," said the voice inside. "What are you breaking our bell for?"

"It seems to me a person might break his heart before he'd get in here."

"We don't want to have nothink to do with no hearts. This 'ere's the work'us. What d'ye want?"

Thus brought to the point, and thinking it best to reserve his spare eloquence for a more fitting occasion, Mr. Toddleboy informed his questioner that he had picked up a baby in the Thames, and wished to find it an asylum.

"The Thames is not our parish," replied the voice within, "you'd better take it to the right place."

"And may I ask you which is the right place," cried Mr. Toddleboy in desperation, though sarcastic.

"Ask the police," said the voice; slam went the door, and so the conversation ended.

Just as it happened, a policeman came strolling round the corner at the time and Mr. Toddleboy requested his assistance. He told his tale, and paused for a reply.

"And what am I to do?" asked the policeman.

"Why, make 'em take it in."

"But I can't."

"What do you mean by 'can't?' aint you the law."

"Only an arm of the law. I'd have to be half a dozen arms, and a leg or two, to manage it."

"What do you propose then?"

"To begin with, this ain't the right parish."

"Which is?"

"Well I should say—that is—if you come to a question of parish—"

"That's what we want to come to."

"Then I should say none of 'em would take it in."

"What do you mean?" roared Toddleboy, aghast. "Aint this a christian country. What's the good of poor rates, I should like to know?"

"If you take my advice," replied the officer, tapping Toddleboy upon the shoulder, "you wont have nothing to do with them."

"With whom?"

"The parishes."

"What's the good of talking nonsense," cried the unfortunate old gentleman. "What am I to do with the baby?"

"It seems to me," observed the policeman, slowly and emphasising every word, "it seems to me a most unfortunate thing to happen to any one; but as it has, you'd better make the best of it."

"Make the best of what? Do you mean to say I'm to carry this infant about all night?"

"Why don't you take it home?"

"What's the good of asking such questions. How would you like to take a strange baby home?"

The disadvantages of such a proceeding dawning, as it seemed, for the first time upon the officer's dull faculties of comprehension, he offered no further suggestions upon that head, "Only," said he—

"What else do you propose?"

"What I propose," said Toddleboy, still on the Briton tack, "is just to ring again."

And so they rang. In course of time the bell was answered, and the same voice from the inside said again—

"Now then, who are you, I'd like to know?"

"Well, if you come to that," retorted Todddleboy, "I shouldn't mind knowing who *you're* supposed to be."

"You'll know who I am fast enough, if you aint off," replied the voice; and the door opening, a fat man appeared with his head tied up in flannel, and his body enveloped in a choice assortment of coats and capes.

"I'm the beadle, and I give that man in charge."

Here Mr. Toddleboy grew purple in the face with indignation and inarticulation. Here the policeman essayed his powers of persuasion, and suggested that it might be best if they came to terms and gave the baby a night's shelter, any how until next morning, when it could be moved on to its right parish."

"And what do you suppose the board would say to me if I did anything so foolish?" the beadle asked.

"And what do you suppose the public press will say to you if this baby dies?" asked Toddleboy.

"That'll be your look out," replied the beadle. "You aint going to put off your brat upon us, old fellow." And slamming to the door, he once more returned to bed.

"I wont be beat like this, no, by heavens I won't," cried Toddleboy, raising his fist on high, and clenching it with much dramatic effect.

"What will you do then?" asked the policeman.

"I'll appeal to a higher tribunal."

"Between ourselves," remarked the policeman, in a confidential whisper, "don't you think you'd better drop it?"

"I'll be hanged if I don't," said Toddleboy, "upon the next door step, too."

"No, no—I'll see you don't do that, my boy. Not on my beat, any ways."

"What do you mean then?"

"Why—look here—what I means, don't you think the game too stale?"

"Eh?"

"It wont wash, you know."

"What wont wash?"

"Get on with you," the officer observed, closing one eye, and laying his forefinger upon his nose. "I'm fly."

"Are you?" said Toddleboy; "then perhaps you'll make me fly, as you call it."

"What's the good of beating about the bush?"

"Certainly."

",, Well then—"

"Well then."

"It's your kid, I suppose, and you want to get rid of it."

I never knew what it was to be reduced to that condition of physical feebleness which people describe when they say that a blow from a feather would have prostrated them; but I suppose poor old Mr. Toddleboy must have reached it, when the policeman thus imparted his opinion, for, reeling back a yard or two, he leant against a pump that providence had placed in the immediate vicinity, and opening his mouth and eyes to their widest, stared and panted at the other in speechless indignation.

IV.—EXTRAORDINARY ADVENTURES OF A BABY.

THERE are some insults which blood alone will expiate.

When duelling was fashionable, such insults were a matter of every-day occurrence, but things have altered with the Act. The Old Bailey tends to blunt one's nice sense of honour; and if we are not big enough to punch the aggressor's head, and don't feel inclined to go to law about it, we gulp down our injuries, and rub the mud off the seat of our trousers.

Just such an outrage had Mr. Toddleboy's feelings experienced.

For half a minute he had half a mind to do his little best towards creating a vacancy in the A division, but in the next half minute he thought better of it, and bottled up his vengeance.

So he merely replied with withering sarcasm—

"It is NOT my kid, Mr. Bluebottle."

And then stalked off down the street, looking as dignified as a little man carrying a large baby could possibly look.

When he had turned the corner he halted, not knowing exactly where he was going to; pulled up short, and sat down upon a nice dry doorstep to think about it.

Then the baby, which had been happily asleep for some time past, woke up and began to cry.

"Shut up!" said Mr. Toddleboy, whom the noise disturbed. "Shut up, I say; whatever is the good of making such a row. Hang me, you're not worse off than I am!"

Seeing that it found no consolation from this cheering assurance, but continued to bawl with all its little might and main, he shook it well, like you might do a physic bottle, then trotted it on his knee, then made faces at it, then called Bo! at it, then trotted it and shook it up again.

All which little attentions but made it bawl the louder.

"You seem to be a sing'larly perverse infant!" mused Mr. Toddleboy aloud. "You're a healthy child, I suppose, by the way you squawk. Leastways I've seen one of a litter of kittens picked out on that account, before the rest were drowned. You're what's called a fine child too, I suppose, by the weight of you, though I should prefer a weakly one, as I have got to carry you. Hold your nasty noise. I really don't think anything would be of any good but sitting on it."

Whether or not the distressed old gentleman would have resorted to this mode of quieting the noisy little child, which otherwise than in a Christmas pantomime I have seldom seen resorted to, although in the course of my experience I have come across the worst of mothers, I really cannot say.

Luckily for it the baby left off crying, and there was no occasion for proceeding to extremities.

"Well, I don't wonder you're rather fractious," said Mr. Toddleboy, looking down into the infant's face. "You're too young, I should say, to be troubled with teeth, but I fancy your little wesket must be very empty; and what's more, it seems very likely that it will remain so."

And he shook his head solemnly at the little pudding face before him.

"I shouldn't be surprised," he continued presently, in a pensive and meditative strain—"I shouldn't be the least surprised if I was tried for murder. There seems to be a fate about this infant, which attaches me to it and it to me. It's more than probable this infant will die upon my hands, through want of the common necessaries of life, gin and tobacco —— I mean milk and sop."

Here he paused, and then continued in a more sombre tone —

"Having attracted the unfavourable notice of the municipal authorities by constantly carrying about the skeleton of a famished infant, of which he had been unable to dispose to any of the metropolitan undertakers, Theophilus Toddleboy, widower, aged sixty-two, late in the employ of Messrs. Bottle and Bung, but stated to be out of work and starving, was fully committed for trial at the Old Bailey Sessions, and he having subsequently been found guilty by an intelligent jury of his countrymen, was duly hanged by the neck until he was dead, and his miserable fragments interred within the precincts of the prison.

"And all because I was fool enough to pull you out of the water," he added with great indignation. "Now there's a pretty kettle of fish you've cooked for me, young Jackanapes. And who are you, pray, that I should get myself into trouble about you?"

Who, indeed. It had occurred to him before, that perhaps the baby he had found might turn out to be the child of somebody of consequence; but then there was no earthly reason for supposing so. Of course he had not seen the woman who threw it into the water, or certainly her appearance might have tempted him to believe that the little stranger was a scion of some illustrious house.

The females at the "public" who had dried the baby's clothes, said that they were made of a good material, but were without any mark by which they might be identified.

"It's got a red ribbon round its neck," said Mr. Toddleboy, "but perhaps that's to know it by when it gets to the workhouse, and is mixed up with the rest of them. There wants something to know one from the other, else how could you tell which had had its dinner, and which hadn't—whether that's it, or whether it's to keep its head on, is more than I can tell. I don't like touching babies' heads," continued Mr. Toddleboy. "I'm always afraid of my finger going in. I'm told it's just like tissue paper round about the crown."

Having thus lengthily soliloquized, it occurred to the old gentleman that it was high time that he was moving onwards.

Onwards! Where to?

To anywhere where there was light and life. You may suppose perhaps that the plan he could easily have adopted for getting rid of this baby, which threatened to be such an incumbrance to him, was quietly to deposit it in some dark doorway, and make as much haste as possible round the street corner, and into the next street.

You do him an injustice.

Toddleboy was a tender-hearted old man. When he talked of putting the poor little thing back into the Thames, or of sitting down upon and flattening it, bless you, he would no more have done it than you or I would.

Toddleboy was in the habit of taking more three-ha'p'orths of gin than was good for him, and he had besides his share of faults and follies like the rest of us, perhaps a larger share than ordinary, but he had his good points as well.

Now if he left the baby in the street, the probabilities were that it would die of cold or hunger, or both.

So, being tender-hearted, he couldn't do it.

Onward—onward, with his burthen, and a deuce of a weight he found it, I can tell you.

By dint of walking hard, in course of time he found himself in the neighbourhood of the Haymarket. As that is the liveliest part of the town in the small hours of the morning, he went thither in search of the light and life he felt was indispensable, if he must pass the time in the streets.

Most of the public houses were closed; but seeing through the chink of a partly-shut door a blaze of gas within, he knocked, and, after a little parley, was admitted.

There was an abundance of light and life here: the bar was crowded with young men laughing and chaffing together. A good deal of drinking was going on, and there was such an amount of tobacco-smoke about, that the atmosphere had reached that degree of solidity when it is supposed that it may be cut with a knife.

But if the bar was noisy and crowded, there must have been a vast number of customers stowed away in some other place over head; for the din of stamping feet and rattling glasses, varied by gushes of spasmodic melody, would have led one to suppose that a hundred persons at least were somewhere or other "keeping it up," with musical honours.

While Mr. Toddleboy was "taking stock" of those around him, and wondering what on earth could be going on up-stairs, a little, fussy, red-faced young man, with his hat very much on one side, his hair in muscular ringlets, and his ears nearly sawn off with a stiff pair of stick-up collars, came running down stairs, bustled up to the bar, and addressed the landlord,—

"Mr. Potts," said he, "the Chirpy Cock-Robins are dying for their supper."

"They shall have it, Mr. Larkins," replied the landlord, "in a couple of jiffies"

"If you can make it a jiffy and a half," said Mr. Larkins, "I, as an individual Cock-Robin, will feel obliged to you."

"You're the vice, ain't you, Mr. Larkins?" said a lady behind the bar.

"The only vice there is in the company, m'am."

"Oh, we all know you, Mr. Larkins!" giggled the lady; "you're a bad 'un, you are."

"What made you ask?" said Larkins presently.

"Well, I was thinking who was going to carve."

"Carve what?"

"Why the sucking-pig, to be sure."

"Well, the chair did it last time."

"No, the vice, I think."

"Dash me if I do, then. No, give it to Jobson. I'll do the sausages."

"Spoken with spirit, Mr. Larkins."

"Well, I think Mr. Jobson is the proper person too," said Mr. Potts; "he looks the most like a family man."

"He is a family man, you know," said Larkins, "and, hang it, I think he's a damp blanket; only the fellows voted him into the chair to have a lark with him. You know, we're going to make him drunk if we can, and send him home to Mrs. J. in a state of the highest elevation."

"Well, it's a great shame of you, Mr. Larkins, cried the lady, "I hope he won't drink anything, but will keep you wicked ones in order."

"We wanted him to bring his eldest with him," continued Larkins, "or the twins—he's had twins lately, you know,—that's to say, Mrs. J.'s had twins,—it's all the same, by—Jove!"

"What's the matter?"

"By jingo!"

"What are you shouting about?"

"Well, I'm jiggered!"

"I should think you were. What's it feel like?"

"Potts!" screamed Mr. Larkins, seizing the landlord by the arm, and pulling him on one side, in a state of the wildest excitement, "Potts! I've something to tell you."

"What the dickins is up with you?" ejaculated Mr. Potts.

Mr. Larkins whispered in his ear.

"Go on with you!" shouted Potts.

"What do you say?"

"You'll never do it."

"Wont I?"

"What'll he say?"

"Murder me, I should think."

"'Gad I shouldn't wonder."

Here they both burst into the most immoderate and uncontrollable roars of laughter.

"I never see sich a one for a joke as you are," said the landlord, wiping his eyes. "How are we to—ha, ha, ha! What do you say to—ha, ha, ha!—Dash my buttons if ever I heard of such a spree!"

And again he was doubled up with convulsive merriment.

At this period of this eccentric performance Mr. Toddleboy, who had been staring at Mr. Larkins and Mr. Potts with all his eyes, in blank astonishment, was even further astonished by Mr. Larkins beckoning him into a little room behind the bar.

Mr. Toddleboy stared harder.

"Come here, said Mr. Larkins.

Mr. Toddleboy looked behind him, and on each side of him, fancying that somebody else must be intended.

But evidently he was the person Mr. Larkins meant.

"You with the baby," said the landlord.

"Me?" cried Toddleboy.

"You," replied Larkins; "I want to speak to you."

Still more astonished, Mr. Toddleboy followed the two gentlemen into the little bar-parlour, where they closed the door behind them; and the landlord, placing his back against it, Mr. Larkins took upon himself to be spokesman; and, said he,

"What are you up to with that baby?"

Toddleboy staggered back, up against the landlord.

"What's your lay?" pursued Mr. Larkins.

"What's yours?" retorted Mr. Toddleboy, recovering himself a little; "what's the plant?"

"You're on the widdower-left-with-a-small-family dodge, aint you?"

"That'll do," replied Mr. Toddleboy, thinking that, all things considered, he might as well be believed to be upon that dodge as any other.

"Anyhow," he thought to himself, "it's a precious sight better dodge than the real one."

"Well," pursued Mr. Larkins, closing one eye, and assuming an expression intended to indicate that he was "up to a thing or two,"—"look here, old cockolorum—"

"I'm lookin'."

"How much 'll you take for your baby?"

"For the baby?" gasped Toddleboy.

He was on the point of telling Mr. Larkins that he could have it for nothing, and welcome, when he reflected how foolish it would be.

Luckily he checked himself in time.

"I don't want to sell it," he replied.

"Well, I don't want to buy it," said Mr. Larkins.

"Then what made you ask?"

"I want the loan of it."

"For how long?"

"Twenty minutes."

"What'll you stand for it?"

"A shilling's-worth of brandy-and-water."

"Wont it be hurt?"

"Not the least in life."

"What's going to be done with it?"

"That's a secret. No harm shall come to it, I'll promise you that. Just you stand at the bar, and sip your grog for twenty minutes, and the baby shall be brought back to you, at the end of that time, all safe and sound."

"You're on," said Mr. Toddleboy, handing Mr. Larkins the baby, "and I trust to your honour as a gentleman."

"You may depend upon him," said the landlord; "it shan't be hurt."

"Well, the fact is," said Mr. Toddleboy, confidentially, I expect the missus to look in directly, and I shouldn't like her to find no larks being played with it."

"Certainly not—certainly not. Quite proper. Now come and have your brandy, old flick."

Thus politely invited, Mr. Toddleboy walked round to the bar and was soon behind a steaming tumblerful of hot liquor, and thus engaged he was observed by a bystander to wink his left eye three times, each wink being succeeded by a silent chuckle, which was none the less hearty for being noiseless.

"It's bringing me in something anyhow," said he.

He was a bit of a wag in his way, was Mr Toddleboy.

But if you want a wag of the first water, there was Larkins. You will see

The "Chirpy Cock Robins" were medical students with a sprinkling of retail chemists. They formed a little club for festive purposes. That is to say, they had weekly meetings and quarterly suppers. They met rather late for the convenience of all parties. The harmony began at twelve, and at two o'clock precisely supper was put upon the table, after which more harmony followed, and they broke up about four.

It was rather a racketty, rakish, stay-out-all-

[MISS PAMELA AND THE STRANGE BABY.]

night and go-home-with-the-milk-in-the-morning sort of affair, you see, and just the kind of thing those wild young scamps the "Sucking Sawbones" delight in.

Now there was one respectable member at least—though for that matter I do not think there was much harm in any one of them. Your noisy, bawling young fellows haven't often much vice in them.

It's your quiet dogs that are the worst, depend upon it.

But as every rule has an exception (thank goodness), the quietest dog of the present company was anything but the worst. Nobody accused him, like they did that Larkins, of being a "bad 'un." Larkins liked to be thought a naughty man, a sad rogue and awfully fast: Jobson had never had the wish to be fast, and did not covet the reputation.

On the contrary, he had early in life taken a wife to his bosom, settled down in a little "Blue Bottle Shop" in the Borough, and devoted himself to his lozenges and his family.

You ask, then, why did he belong to such a fraternity? I will tell you.

He sang a good song.

You know what that means; when a man sings a good song, and knows he does—that is to say, when he has the credit of doing so, there's no knowing what bad company it may not lead him into. He consorts with other fellows who sing good songs, or have the credit for it, and they sit and bawl at one another for any number of hours, without feeling any fatigue.

Thus was it that Jobson had been seduced into joining the "Chirpy Cock Robins;" this fatal desire to hear himself sing had caused him to go into the company of these young profligates, though in every other taste than that for amateur vocalisation, he differed with them entirely.

The supper by this time was announced to be quite ready. The cloth had been laid this half hour Mr. Jobson took his place solemnly and decorously, as became the chair, and Mr. Larkins skipped into his with his accustomed friskiness.

There is in all these sort of meetings an amount of pompous absurdity, fatiguing as it is ridiculous. There are many big bellied, shallow pates, who make quite an imposing ceremony out of the most sociable and unpretending of repasts.

Jobson was of this sort.

"Ahem!" said he, with a little cough, and tapping the table with his knife handle to bespeak attention. "Silence, gentlemen, if you please. I will ask a blessing."

Having done so at some length, he motioned to the attendant nearest him to remove the cover.

"What have we here, waiter?" asked Mr. Jobson, blandly.

"Roast sucking pig," replied the waiter, and whipping off the cover, displayed to the astonished eyes of the assembly Mr. Toddleboy's baby lying in the dish.

———

V.—Further and still more Extraordinary Adventures of a Baby.

WHEN the tumultuous burst of laughter which the appearance of this unexpected delicacy had occasioned was gradually subsiding, somebody called out—

"That's Larkins for a sovereign."

"That's one of Larkins's," echoed another voice.

"That's Larkins's last," shouted a third.

"What a chap you are, Larkins."

"Dash it all, Larkins, that's too bad."

"Larkins, you ought to be ashamed of yourself, you really ought."

But bless you he wasn't. He thought, instead, that he had done something remarkably clever. It had been rather a studied and laborious bit of facetiousness, but young men who regularly go in for being wags don't seem to care what trouble they take over a joke.

So there was that Larkins sniggering and chuckling as though he had done some act which should for ever immortalize him.

He did not make any attempt to deny that he was the author of this little practical pleasantry, and indeed seemed very proud of it.

But while the attention was almost entirely concentrated in Larkins and the baby, somebody happened to look at Jobson, and uttered an exclamation of astonishment, for Jobson was on his legs, with his hat pulled down over his brows, a terrible expression of countenance, and buttoning up his overcoat furiously.

"Why, Jobson, what are you up to?" inquired one.

"What's the matter?" said another.

"Nothing's the matter," said Jobson, highly excited and tearing and dragging at his buttons. "What should be the matter? Ha! ha! that's very good, I really can't imagine what the matter could be. Good evening, gentlemen."

"No, I say, Jobson; look here; stop a minute."

"Oh, yes, I'll stop as long as you like, to be insulted as much as you like. Go on. I'm not particular to a minute or two."

"Nobody wants to insult you. Come, I say, sit down again."

"No, thank you, gentlemen," replied Mr. Jobson, in freezing tones. "I won't intrude upon you. You'll find a better chair than me in Mr.—ah—Larkins. I wish you joy of him. Good evening."

"Hallo! hi! stop!"

No, he was gone. There was no stopping him; bursting his button-holes with indignation, he rushed down stairs and out of the house.

Everybody looked at everybody else a minute or so seriously and silently. They were half inclined to laugh, and half inclined to be angry. If Larkins had been ready with a joke, he would have carried the day, but he wasn't, and so popular opinion went against him.

"I say Larkins," said somebody, "there's no fun in that sort of thing."

"Rather low," said somebody else.

"Very," said somebody else's neighbour.

"I tell you what it is," roared Larkins, out of temper, "if you're all going to make fools of yourselves"—

"You've made one of yourself, Larkins."

"No mistake about that."

Then everybody began to reason with and advise him, and he began to get very savage.

"Perhaps you'd better take that dish away," suggested some one more surly than the rest, "and bring the other pig."

"I'll take it," said Larkins, "and since you've pleased to turn so precious squeamish, I'll leave you to enjoy your supper, and while you're looking for another chair you can look for another vice."

So saying, Mr. Larkins put on his hat, and taking the baby in his arms left the room in the same sort of style that Mr. Jobson had done before him.

"Confound them," said he, "a set of paltry snobs. That's just the way with them; nice fellows to see a joke, they are. Bother the baby, I didn't want to quarrel about it, I'd much rather have had my supper. There, hush, hush, can't you. What are you crying about, young fellow? You're going back to your daddy."

Where was his daddy?

He was not standing at the bar as Larkins had left him Larkins looked all around, but could see him nowhere.

"I say Potts, where's the old gentleman?"

"What the parient?"

"Yes, the baby's governor."

"Well," said Potts, looking around in his turn, "I don't see him, where's he got to?"

"He was here just now," remarked the lady behind the bar. "I say, what's become of the old gentleman?"

Nobody had seen him.

"He's outside, perhaps."

No, he wasn't.

"He's hooked it perhaps."

It looked precious like it, and Larkins's face was longer than usual.

"Here's a go!" cried Potts, "what'll you do with it, sir?"

"Do with it!" cried Larkins; "what the devil do you suppose I can do with it. Here, hang you all, run out somebody and look for him. He can't have gone away altogether. It's ridiculous."

It was very ridiculous, but it was the case

While they were debating as to what should be done with it, some one came down stairs.

"I say, Larkins, don't go away like that; come up and have your supper, man."

"Thank you, I've no appetite."

"What are you doing with the baby?"

"What am I doing. What am I going to do? That's the question."

And he explained at length.

"Well, Larkins, I shan't go back if you won't, and if you want any one to help you, I'm the man."

"Are you, Tom. I always thought you were a trump, and so you are. I shall have to pass off this little unfortunate upon somebody else, I suppose. Will you assist me?"

"Of course I will. What's to be done first?"

"Follow me."

"To death or victory."

And out they went, slamming-to the public house door behind them, and leaving the assembled guests equally amazed and amused.

Without saying a word, Mr. Larkins led the way, his friend Tom followed him, and they walked straight forward, neither turning to the right nor the left.

Now the reason why Mr. Larkins said nothing was because he had nothing to say, and the reason he walked straight forward was because he was going nowhere in particular, and had no fixed plan of action.

Tom, on the contrary, imagined that he had, and followed him in all good faith. However, when they had walked a mile it became a little monotonous, so, said Tom—

"Larkins," said he, "is it much further?"

"What?" said Larkins, turning round.

"What," echoed Tom, "what, why where the dickins are you going to?"

"Tom," replied Larkins, laying his hand upon his shoulder, and replying slowly and solemnly, "I havn't the remotest idea"

"Well then, damn your impudence, what did you mean by trailing me after you this way? I thought you were going to do something wonderful, by the look of you."

"Tom," said Larkins, a bright idea striking him, "you're a plucky fellow."

"Pretty well, I suppose."

"I've thought of a spree we might have."

"Well, I don't know about sprees," said Tom, a little doubtfully; "they don't always turn out funny, do they?"

"There are some fools who don't think 'em fun, but that doesn't prove they're not."

"To be sure, certainly; and what's this particular spree?"

"I'll tell you. You know I've changed my lodgings."

"At the spinster's, weren't they?"

"Yes! She said I was too fast."

"So you told me."

"Well sir, I left yesterday, but Tom, BUT—"

"But what."

"I didn't give up the latch-key."

"Well."

"Don't you see."

"No, I can't say I do."

"You're very dull then."

"Perhaps so. Please explain."

"Why, Tommy, my boy, we'll open the door and put the baby inside."

"But I say, that's ticklish work, isn't it? Suppose we're caught."

"It'll go hard with me, I dare say, but not with you, old fellow, for you can stop a little way off and keep watch."

"No, I won't do that, Larkins. If you're going to be in a scrape, I'll be in it too."

"It'll be rather fine when the spinster finds it, eh?"

"What on earth will she do?"

"Go out of her wits, I should think"

Chuckling over the probable results of the adventure, the two young hopefuls bent their steps towards Brompton, where the unfortunate lady resided.

She lived in Montpellier-square; her name was Miss Pamela Andrews; she was very religious, very thin, very serious, and aged forty-five. She was the most proper of women, the driest and most angular, the most raw-boned and scraggy. In fact, she was very much like what I should fancy her celebrated namesake would have become, had she lived long enough unmarried.

"That's the house," said Larkins, pointing to a certain door. "You stop here, and I'll go and reconnoitre."

He went to the house-door and fumbled about for awhile, then returned.

"Tom, I must ask you to help me."

"What's the matter?"

"It's the most infernal door to open that ever you can imagine. I can't turn the key and hold the baby at the same time; and the steps are so wet and dirty, I can't put it down upon them, while I use both hands."

"All right, Larkins, I'm your most obedient."

"Come on, then."

"It would be better fun if it didn't rain so hard, wouldn't it?"

As Mr. Tom made the remark, he shivered, for the rain had begun to pour down again, like a thousand water-spouts.

"There's always some drawback to one's pleasure," observed Mr. Larkins.

"I suppose so," said Tom. "There seems to be another drawback: look there—isn't that a policeman trying the doors?"

"Yes, let us wait till he goes by."

"No—if he sees you with the baby, he'll suspect something; it looks so odd."

"What shall we do?"

"Let us open the door, and pop it inside. He'll be five minutes before he reaches us."

"Not if he comes as quickly as he is doing."

"We can try, anyhow."

"Never say die!"

They hastily ascended the steps of Miss Andrews' house, then, with as much rapidity and as little noise as possible, Larkins undid the door.

"It's dark as pitch," he whispered. "I wish I'd got a match."

"I've got a fusee"

"Hush! that won't do. It will leave such a smell. Let me feel in my pocket. Ha! here's a match. I thought I had one."

Click, click.

"Be quick, the policeman's coming."

Click went the match, squeak went the baby.

"Hush, hush!" gasped Larkins; hold your hand over its mouth: be careful, don't smother it."

Having by this time lighted a match, he held i[t] on high, and endeavoured to pierce the dim obscurity of the passage

"The very thing," he said, in a hurried whisper; "give me the baby. Here's a clothes-basket."

Tom handed him the child, bidding him at the same time to look sharp, for that the policeman was close upon them.

Just then the baby began to cry much louder.

"Quick, quick," exclaimed Tom. "He's next door but one."

But yet a moment Larkins hesitated, for he fancied he heard a footstep on the stairs, and some one was moving in the parlour.

"Good heavens," he thought, "if I am discovered, what possible excuse can I make."

"He's here," cried Tom.

Without more hesitation, Larkins placed the poor little innocent on the top of some dirty clothes, which formed a kind of nest for it in the basket, and pushing Tom out upon the steps, closed the door behind them as noiselessly as possible.

"Well, Tom," said he, loud enough for the policeman to hear. "I've got him to go to bed quietly, and the next time I help to bring home a drunken man, just be kind enough to tell me of it, will you?'

"Nasty job, that, gentlemen," said the policeman, who was inclined to be agreeable. "Had much trouble with him, sir?"

"Shocking"—

"Makes such a disturbance too, don't it. What's that row?"

"I don't hear anything."

"Squealing noise, ain't there?"

"It's a cat, perhaps," said Tom in an agony.

"No, it aint a cat. Is there a baby in the house, you come out of it?"

"Well, I believe there are one or two," replied Mr. Larkins. "Belong to gentlemen who got a little on."

"Well, if it's only a baby, it don't much matter," said the policeman, after listening for a minute or two, "They're always a bawling."

"So they are. Ha! ha! Good night to you."

"Good night, gentlemen."

When they had turned the corner they took to their heels and ran to Hyde Park Corner, without stopping.

———

VI.—A SHOCKING THING TO HAPPEN TO
AN ELDERLY SPINSTER.

MISS Pamela Andrews was fussy and fidgetty. She was a confirmed invalid and seldom stirred out of doors, or saw any company. Her only visitors being Mr. Ezekiah Sleeky and Mr. Oyly Swabb from the little dissenting chapel in Groaner's Court, and her medical adviser who lived nice and handy, and dropped in about once a day.

Her bedroom was on the second-floor, the first-floor was her drawing-room, and her parlour she let to single gentlemen more for protection than for profit. Having however had the misfortune to fall into the hands of a series of Larkinses, who stopped out all night or came home drunk and left the door unlatched, her object can scarcely be said to have been gained.

But now she had got rid of Larkins, and in his stead found the nicest and most quiet of living gentlemen, who took most of his meals out of doors, supped on a basin of gruel and half a round of toast, and went to bed every night at nine o'clock. Had he not had a weakness when he was in bed, for playing the flute, which, perhaps imagining it would be objectionable to the rest of the household, he did under the bedclothes, making them into a tent, and getting underneath with his music book and a night light, I do not think that there was anything about him that a landlady could reasonably have complained of.

On this particular night Miss Andrews slept worse than usual. She fancied she heard a strange squealing noise in the passage, somewhat different to the new lodger's plaintive strains, and fancying something might have happened to her favourite tabby, descended the stairs to see into the matter.

The poor little thing was very weak through want of food and rest (I don't suppose than any other baby had ever gone through so much in so short a time), and its wailings were low and plaintive.

"Puss! Puss!" cried Miss Pamela. "Come, pussy, pussy—poor thing, come along."

But pussy did not come, and the wailing continued.

"Those shameful sluts haven't given it its cat's meat, I suppose," said Miss Andrews, descending the last steps. "I wonder how they can behave so to a poor dumb creature."

By this time she had reached the passage. There the first thing her eyes fell upon was the poor little foundling lying on its back very red in the face, and wide in the mouth.

"Mercy on me!" screamed Miss Pamela, springing back as though she had just trodden upon a black beetle. "It's a baby!"

What was to be done? What did it mean? Who put it there?

"One of those sluts of girls!" thought Miss Andrews. "How horrible! how scandalous! I'll pack the hussy out of the house! Which is it, I wonder. I haven't noticed anything about them, though really, now every one wears crinoline——."

She took the little child out of the basket, and finding its clothes were all damp, and that it looked in a pitiful plight, carried it up stairs to her own room, pondering the while upon the extraordinary nature of the circumstances.

"It's been out of doors! Who on earth put it there? Could it have been Mr. Spooner. Surely not, for he is the worst I ever had. Even that Larkins never did such a thing as this."

Meanwhile the baby continued to wail; and so Miss Andrews thought that the best thing she could do would be to make it some pap, and warm it well in front of the fire.

With her own fair fingers she therefore laid and lighted the fire, and preparing some milk and bread in a saucepan, began to feed the hungry little babe with a teaspoon.

What woman is there alive who does not love a baby? If you know of any I should like to give her a shaking, for she *must* be a peevish thing. What elderly spinster is there who does not doat on them? With men it is different. I suppose the exception is to find a man who has not secretly a great dislike for his species in the infantine state.

"It's a dear little duck of child, and its mother

is an inhuman monster. Oh! if it *is* one of those sluts, I'll give it her. Dere den, a icle popsetty wopsetty. Ketchetty! Ketchetty! Ketchetty!"

While thus engaged trotting the baby on her knee, and addressing it in that eccentric perversion of the English language which mothers seem to think more comprehensible to baby understanding than the vernacular, the door opened, and a head was poked into the room, which was as rapidly withdrawn and poked in again.

Unconscious of the intrusion, Miss Andrews proceeded with her inspection of the baby, talking the while to herself in a low tone.

"But you mustn't stop here, you little rascal," continued the lady. "Whatever would the Reverend Mr. Swabb and the Reverend Mr. Sleeky say to it. It can't stay here. Good gracious! my reputation would be gone for ever!"

Here looking up, her eyes met those of the person peeping in at the door, and both parties for a moment stared fixedly at one another in a kind of fascination.

"Well, marm!" cried Martha.

"What are you staring at there?"

"At what you're nursing."

"Don't you see what it is, you stupid?"

"I'm sorry to say I do, marm. Very sorry."

"Why, what do you mean. you hussey? How dare you!"

"Excuse me, marm, if I'm offensive, meaning by no means so to be; but if you'll have the kindness to settle up, I'd rather leave at once. I wont stand out to have my month, marm. I should rather leave. I'm only a poor girl as has got my character to look to, and meaning no offence, would rather go at onct."

"Why you—you—WRETCH!" screamed Miss Andrews, making a sudden pounce, and pinning the other against the wall. "Do you mean to insinuate that I am the mother of this child?"

"Who is?"

"Who is! How dare you! You are, for what I know."

"I am? Dare to say it again! A poor girl with only her character to look to."

"Bother your character. Listen to me, and don't make a fool of yourself."

Miss Andrews then related what had taken place, to which her servant Martha listened attentively.

"Whoever can it belong to?" said she. "It isn't Susan's."

"Are you sure?"

"Certain, marm—don't I sleep with her?"

"What do you mean? You don't suppose the baby was born to-day. It is a month old, at the very least."

"Lawks, is it? That's quite another thing."

"Don't stand staring like that, but suggest something. However it has got here I can't imagine. If we called in the aid of the police we might discover, but that must not be. It must go again as it came, and how are we to get rid of it?"

"Tie it to somebody's knocker."

"No, no. that wont do. See, the day is breaking. Some one will see us. Can't you think of any other plan?"

"No, marm, I can't."

"But think, Martha, it is of the most vital importance. I'll tell you what, I will give you five pounds if you get rid of it somehow. Of course without hurting it."

"Well," said Martha, her ingenuity considerably sharpened by the promise of a reward. "I'll think about it. What shall we do? Oh, marm, I've got it.'

"What is it?"

"Never mind, give it to me; I'll tell you when I come back. It's most lucky that I got up so early this morning to put the room to rights before the sweep came, or I should never have looked and seen you, and then it would have been too late."

"Too late for what?"

"Never mind, marm, I'll tell you when I come back."

Thus persisting in silence, Martha fetched her bonnet and shawl, wrapped the little baby up warmly, and set off upon her expedition.

She walked straight to Hyde Park Corner, took the road down by the side of Buckingham Palace, walked along the Mall till she passed the Duke of York's steps, then turned to the right and followed the railings till she reached the gate which opens from the Parade into Birdcage Walk.

It was locked. She seemed to have expected that it would be so, and uttered an exclamation of satisfaction at the discovery.

"So far so good," said she, "now let me see who will come."

Almost immediately a woman came by on the other side.

"I beg your pardon," said Martha, "but would you have the kindness to hold my baby a moment, while I climb over the gate. I have to be at work in half-an-hour, and came across here for a short cut."

"Certainly," said the woman, holding out her arms.

Martha handed her the baby. Not another soul was to be seen in any direction.

"Have you got hold of it?" said she.

"Yes," replied the stranger.

"Keep hold then," said Martha; and to the other's astonishment, turned round and taking to her heels, ran back by the railings as fast as her legs would carry her.

For full two minutes the other stood dumbfounded, unable to make a sound, or move a step. Then, quick as thought, she placed the baby on the ground, and began to climb over the gate; no easy task for any lady, as those who know it can testify.

By dint of energetic scrambling she managed, however, to reach the other side, but scarcely had she got three yards from the gate, when a policeman, who had appeared at the top of the street at the moment that she had commenced climbing, and had been watching the operation with interest, ran forward, and catching sight of the baby, imagined of course that the woman was deserting it, and gave chase.

Over the gate he went with the agility of a harlequin, and in another minute had hold of her.

"I have caught you, have I," said he.

"I was running after a woman who gave me that baby to hold."

"What woman?"

Alas, she could not tell. Already had Martha turned the corner, and was lost to view.

"She's run up there," cried the prisoner, wildly, "just this moment. You will catch her if you try."

"I dare say," replied the policeman. "But I ain't going to try, so come along with me."

He took her back and poked his arm through the gate for the baby, which he managed thus to lay hold of.

"Now," said he, "we'll be moving."

"Oh, please sir, don't," cried the woman, clinging frantically to the rails. She was a young woman, good-looking, but careworn and very poorly clad. "Oh, please, sir, don't. What have I done? I am innocent! I am innocent."

Then in an agony of sobs and screams, she reiterated what she had already said; told him her name and address, and implored him to take her back to her lodgings, and ascertain the truth of her story.

Nobody would be so unjust as to say that all policemen are uniformly brutal and mercenary, though they may know from experience that such is unhappily the case.

In this particular instance the policeman was a tender-hearted man, and he thought he would put the young woman's story to the test, however unlikely it might seem; therefore, giving her the baby to carry, he accompanied her to her lodgings in an alley leading out of Tothill-street, Westminster.

She was a sempstress she told him, and was on her way to a lady's house in Pimlico, when the circumstance had occurred which got her into all this trouble. She had been out of work for a long while: this was the first job she had had for a month, and she was fearful that her want of punctuality should cause her to lose it, as she had promised positively to be at the appointed place before eight o'clock.

"Well, you will have time enough," said the policeman, "if we find your story is all right."

"I'm sure you will, sir," said the poor girl.

"I hope so."

Tothill-street, Westminster, is not the nicest of localities, and Slogger's Alley is not the best address for virtue of any sort, but there was something very honest about this young woman's face, and something very ingenuous about her way of telling her story, which induced the officer to go with her.

At No. 8, they knocked at the door and asked for Mrs Grinderbones. A deal of knocking it took, and then a husky voice from the basement story wanted to know what all that row was about. Informed that she had better step up and see, a face inflamed and swollen by drink, and surrounded by a dirty night-cap, with an enormous frill, after the fashion of "Judy" in the Punch show, appeared above the level of the floor, and once more inquired what they meant by making all that noise.

"Does this young woman live here?" asked the officer.

"She wont live here long, I can tell you."

"I don't want to know how long she'll live. Does she at present?"

"I've not seen the colour of her money—"

"I don't want to know about that. Has she a baby?"

"Lord bless the man, she's got a dozen for what I know."

"Oh, Mrs. Grinderbones, do please speak for me, I am suspected of deserting my child. But it is not my child at all. My poor baby was born dead, you know it was, Mrs. Grinderbones."

"Oh, don't bother me about your babies," growled the terrible Grinderbones, who seemed to

be, even at that early hour, much excited by drink. "What do you mean by draggin' a poor creature out of bed about your nonsense. Lock her up, policeman. I can't get no rent of her, and I don't want her here. I'd be precious glad to get rid of that tipsy old fool Toddleboy at the same price."

"Who's a blowing me up," said a squeaky voice at their elbow; and an elderly gentleman of dilapidated aspect, who walked and talked with considerable difficulty, presented himself before them. "Who's a taking away my keracter for sobriety?"

"Oh, it's you, is it?" screamed the fair Grinderbones. "It's you, Mr. Toddleboy, is it? Come home at this hour? Perhaps you'll ask him about the baby, Mr. Policeman."

"Baby!" said Mr. Toddleboy, "I've had enough of babies. GOOD HEAVENS!"

"Mr Toddleboy, do speak for me? You know it's not mine."

"I'll be hanged if I know whose it is, but by that there bit of red ribbon round its neck, I'll be hanged if it isn't the identical child I pulled out of the Thames last night, and served up for supper to the Chirpy Cock Robins."

"Is this man mad or drunk?"

"Both, sir," replied Toddleboy. "Both sir, I've no doubt. Give me hold of the infant. I am its father. Everybody else is of that opinion. So why should I not be. Interesting infant, come to the arms of your long-lost parent."

"But, Mr. Toddleboy, what do you mean? Is it really yours?"

"I can't say: it may be, and it may not be. Either case is equally probable. So many extraordinary circumstances occur every day, that it would take a remarkably clever father to know his own child. Poor little creature! there's a fate about it. It's intended for me, and I suppose I must keep it—though how it's to be done on my income, is more than I can, at the present moment, decide. All I've got to say is, that there can be no doubt but that the little boy will turn out to something remarkable. He evidently was not born to be drowned, but whether he was born to be hanged, is another question"—

Which this story has been written to show. He has had many a strange adventure very early in life. When he is old enough to talk and act for himself, I dare say that we shall find his history no less interesting. Strange company we leave him in,—strange nurses, strange nursery. What will come of it? At this very moment the policeman is waiting impatiently to take charge of him.

Poor little vagabond baby!

VII.—BABY FINDS A MOTHER.

AFTER an immensity of cross-questioning and beating about the bush, which would tax the reader's patience beyond all endurance, were I to repeat a half of it, the policeman finally arrived at the conclusion that the young woman was innocent of the crime which he had imputed to her, and that extraordinary as it was, there appeared to be some truth in Mr. Toddleboy's story.

And so neither the young woman nor the baby was taken into custody.

But as several allusions which have been made with reference to some other baby supposed to be dead must appear mysterious to my reader, I will endeavour to explain them before going any further.

Sarah Williams was a poor girl who had fallen the victim to the seductions of a flashy young scoundrel, who, while she was in the service of a lady in Bedford-square, had won her affections, and taking advantage of her love for him, effected her ruin.

It was the old story—keeping company—promise of marriage—seduction and desertion.

We all know the formula of events. Desertion, desperation, the pawn shop, the gin palace, the street, and the hospital. Why go over these unpleasant details, familiar to every newspaper reader?

A little baby was born and died, poor thing, —lucky for it. The mother, still honest, still left remaining some fragment or tatter of virtue in that bruised heart, strives to earn her bread by needle-work. It is a sorry trade to try, and one that few grow fat upon. We find her trying it, and find that she has found it doesn't pay.

And what has become of the flashy young man? Why, he turned out to be a swell mobsman. When he got into difficulties some mates of his raffled a "wipe" at the "Skeleton-key," and gave the proceeds to his "widow."

If he was transported then, it was not his fault that she was deserted.

Certainly not! I admit that there were extenuating circumstances. Farther than that, he was a scoundrel and a thief, I have nothing else to say against him.

"Well," said the policeman, when he had listened to all Mr. Toddleboy had to say, "I don't partickler wish to make a case of it. If you'll take charge of the baby and act fair by it, I don't see that I can do better than leave it with you. Though I'd like to give you both a word of warning, and that is, don't carry on no more of these games. If you want to get rid of the baby, the proper plan is to take it to the workhouse, and state the case. Perhaps they'll take it in, perhaps they wont. It all depends. However, the board day is the time to go, and so the first thing you have got to do is to find out when the Board is. Good morning to you."

"Well, that's consolation, aint it?" observed Mr. Toddleboy, looking down into the little stranger's face. "If you've been half the trouble to your mother that you've been to me, I pity her."

"Pity her, indeed!" cried his companion. "However could she have the heart to desert such a dear little creature as this is? Look how it smiles."

"Smiles. It's a laughing, aint it?"

And indeed it did in its small way seem to be enjoying the joke immensely.

"What's it a laughing at, do you think?"

"Lor, Mr. Toddleboy," cried the young woman, laughing herself, "how can I tell?"

"Well, you women know most about these sort of things."

"I know one thing."

"And that—"

"And that is, that it ought to have something to eat."

"Well, I thought the same about six hours ago, only the difficulty was how to manage it. I

was thinking I might give it ——, but no, perhaps that wouldn't do."

"Give it what?"

"Some warm milk, you know, and feed it through the finger of a kid glove. I've got an odd glove somewheres in my pocket."

And he began to look for it.

"Never mind that," interrupted his companion. "You know my poor dear baby has only been dead a week, and so—I—"

She did not finish the sentence, but blushed crimson.

I suppose Mr. Toddleboy understood what she meant, for he said—

"If you will, you're an angel, and I'll go and see about the workhouse directly."

"Heigho!" the young woman sighed. "I wish I were not so poor, that I could keep it altogether."

"If you take care of it to-day," remarked Mr. Toddleboy, "you must accept of something for the trouble; besides, it will keep you from your work."

"I should be too late for that, if I went now," rejoined the young woman. "The lady was so very particular about the time, and said that if I did not get there to the moment, I need not get there at all."

"By jingo! that's exactly what the governor said to me yesterday," observed Mr. Toddleboy. "If I don't go and get the shutters down, it'll be all up with me! Good bye for the present, and take care of the young 'un. Why, he's laughing again, I'm hanged if he's not. It's at the idea of my getting the sack. Well, there's ingratitude! Oh, you're a bad 'un, you are. Do look at him a laughing, Miss Williams. He's a regular little wag, aint he? I should call him WAG, if I christened him."

So saying, Mr. Toddleboy scuttered off as fast as his shaky old shanks would allow him, and Sarah Williams began to ascend the stairs.

"Well!" said Mrs. Grinderbones, coming up from the kitchen, "you've got another pauper to keep besides yourself, have you? When you'd got shut of your own brat, I should have fancied you'd have thought yourself lucky. What's your trade now, I should like to know. If you've turned wet nurse, I hope you'll get paid for it, for I sha'n't wait much longer for my money, do you hear!" screamed the virago. "I sha'n't keep no sich baggages as you here without you pays me my money."

But the woman she addressed made no reply, only, very white and frightened, let herself into her room, and double-locked the door, while the little baby, as brave as a lion, chuckled, and crowed, and sucked its chubby fist.

VIII.—LIVING AMONG THE GHOSTS.

RALPH FAVERSHAM lived by himself, in the dreariest set of chambers, in the dullest inn in London.

He was thirty years of age, and by profession a barrister.

He was tall and thin, and rather bald; his features were harsh, and his eyes were large, dark, and piercing. He did very little in the way of business, never had a visitor, and seldom stirred without his door—

Because he paced the floor at night, when others slept, and mumbled to himself strange, incoherent words, and wore odd clothes, and acted in a wild, eccentric way, folks said he was cracked, and that he had sold himself to the Evil One—

Because his rooms were close and sombre, and prison-like, beyond the power of tallow and oil to lighten into cheerfulness, folks said that they looked like graves.

They were graves!

In the front room a former tenant had died, a poor, bed-ridden wretch, all worn to sores by years of long-drawn, weary misery; had been brought out from the inner chamber, to see the blessed light once more—and seeing, it, had died contented.

In the second room another tenant had hanged himself. That was the peg on which Ralph Faversham now hangs his cloak, where they had found him dangling in a noose made of his pocket-handkerchief, and had at first mistaken him for clothes.

But of the innermost room, they tell the dreariest tale, for it was there the woman died mad, whom the young law student had seduced and deserted—

When she was supposed to have fallen off to sleep after her fit of delirium, and the old nurse was nodding over the fire, she had risen from her couch, rummaged in the medicine-chest, and gulped the contents of the deadly phial.

She did not die at once, the poison was not strong enough for that, but lived to repent in agony, and roll and shriek for help, and die with tight-clenched hands and curving spine, the fearful death of strychnine.

Because he was so strange in manner and appearance, and because he had chosen these rooms of all others to live in, and even made the housekeeper repeat again the hideous details connected with them, gloating, as it appeared, upon these revolting subjects, they said that he would make a capital murderer.

He was a MURDERER.

Because there lay hidden in his staring eyes and pallid face a sort of indescribable shuddering horror, they said that he looked as though he had just seen a ghost.

He had just seen a ghost.

HE LIVED AMONG THEM.

It has gone twelve. His reading lamp is lit, and at his table strewed with books and papers he sits writing.

His lamp has got a dark green shade which is dusty and dirty. It throws a powerful light upon the paper he is engaged upon, and on his hands. The rest of the room is almost black, except in one corner, where the blind pulled on one side admits a thin, pale streak of moonlight. The room, the house, and the deserted yard, on which the windows look, are still as death.

No living soul is in the room besides Ralph Faversham, but *he is not alone.*

What is there then?

Oh, ye of little faith—'tis scarce two thousand years ago since unbelievers scoffed and ridiculed the divinity of the blessed Saviour of mankind, at the mention of whose holy name all Christians bow their heads in reverence and love. Two thousand years ago, were not the miracles that He performed accounted charlatanism? Were not the believers counted by tens, the unbelievers by thousands? Had we lived then, oh! reader of mine, on which side should we have been?—world-wise, wary, wide-awake as we are.

Do we believe in miracles? Not if we read them in the newspapers to-day. They must be two thousand years old at least before they can hope for credence from such downy dogs as you and I. Don't you think so?

Do you believe in ghosts, reader?

Some ghosts.

Read on.

Before Ralph Faversham lies open an ancient-looking volume, brown with age, and half-destroyed by damp, the title of which is this: "THE HISTORY OF SECRET POISONS."

This is he most intently studying, and from time to time takes notes of what he reads, working earnestly but silently, the flutter of the leaves when he turns one over, alone breaking the dead quiet of his chamber.

So hour follows hour, without change of position or of occupation.

At last he lays down the pen, and breaks the silence thus:—

"Wife!"

But one syllable and then a pause. So clear and distinct his voice has sounded in the room, that even now the echo seems to cling to it, and vibrate dully in the heavy air.

"Wife of my heart—wife of my soul, my own, my ever-loved dead wife, come to me! Oh, I am weary unto death. My fingers numbed and cramped—my eyesight dim—my brain on fire and aching with this endless work. Are you content to see me toil so on the stony path of knowledge? Are you content to know my every hour is passed in searching for this secret which shall enable me to avenge you with a vengeance sure and certain as it is cruel and devilish? Eleanor, sweet wife, come from the grave. Eleanor, what demon holds you back? The jaws of Hell may yawn for us, but 'tis not yet. Our time is not yet come. Oh, Eleanor—my love, my life, my soul, I wait for you!"

The air is heavier—duller still.

The darkness more dark, the silence deeper.

The throbbing of the listener's heart as he awaits the phantom he has thus conjured is almost audible.

Still thicker grows the air, and heaped up shadows in the murky gloom creep into shape, move forward and concentrate around his chair.

Then follows a dread and awful pause, in which the man's breath is, for the nonce, suspended, and in which even his heart ceases to beat, as he listens and waits.

Then—

Then.

A dead hand lies white and cold and heavy on his arm, and as he raises his eyes a dead face, sallow, and rigid, and fixed, is looking down upon him.

"Eleanor!"

————

IX.—MUTTON CHOPS AND MYSTERY.

YOU know, by this time, that old Toddleboy was not a teetotaller.

When he had any money to spend, which was not often, he spent it at the bar of several houses he was in the habit of using, a penny at a time. He was a most disreputable old man, and I wonder Messrs. Bottle and Bung put up with him as they did.

Very often of a day, and always of a night, was he the worse for liquor, and you might have found him any evening at one of the taverns he frequented, regaling a choice circle

No. 3.

of kindred spirits with recollections of his past life, or his views upon things in general.

He was the wag or the butt of several houses, and the landlords encouraged his visits, even on tick, as he brought them custom.

At one of these, he looked in on his way to business, and, over his pennyworth of gin, recounted the wonderful history of the preceding night.

A gentleman of somewhat seedy exterior, and whom he was in the habit of meeting there occasionally, listened to him with the profoundest attention, and laughed heartily at the recital.

When it was finished, he took Mr. Toddleboy on one side, mysteriously.

"Is it true?" said he.

"Is what true?"

"What you've been telling us."

"Do you think I'm a liar?" began Mr. Toddleboy, indignantly.

"Certainly not, sir," replied the seedy gentleman, hastily. "I hope you're not offended."

"If no offence was intended, none is taken."

"That's all right. What'll you have to drink, sir?"

"I don't mind if I have a taste of hot rum."

"Three of hot rum, if you please! And while you're drinking it, perhaps you wouldn't mind my taking a note or two of what you've said."

"Note or two?" cried Mr. Toddleboy, uneasily. "You aint a detective, are you?"

"Don't be alarmed, my dear sir," replied the other. "The fact is"—here he whispered behind an old kid glove—"I'm on the press."

"Oh! I see; a penny-a-liner, eh?"

"Well," said the other, a little hurt, "it is the custom so to call us. 'Occasional reporter' is the proper term; and it is three half-pence, and not a penny, which we receive."

"I beg *your* pardon, this time," said Mr. Toddleboy; "pray say how I can help you."

"I'll tell you," returned the reporter. "We'll make a neat little paragraph for the daily papers out of your little adventure. You won't mind your name being in print, will you?"

"No harm can come of it, can there?"

"Not likely."

"Very well, then, put me in in capitals, if you like."

Sure enough next day, in all the papers, there appeared a very humourous account of Mr. Toddleboy's adventures, and that night he was a hero at all his houses of call.

It was on the succeeding day, about five o'clock in the afternoon, that he was sitting alone, in the dark and dismal tap-room of the "Skeleton Key," the ill-favoured public-house at the entrance of Slogger's Alley, which enjoys now, as it did then, a very unenviable notoriety, in consequence of its being the rendezvous of all the bad characters in the neighbourhood.

Nursing his knees, and warming his nose at the fire, Mr. Toddleboy was mentally calculating the extent of his resources with so lugubrious an expression of countenance, that, to judge from it, would lead us to believe such an occupation was anything but a pleasant one.

"They're good for a quartern at the "Blue Boar," said he; "and, at the King's Head, I've tick up to a shilling: but that's not victuals. I want something to eat. I haven't tasted a morsel to-day; and I feel a sinking in my stomach, that

nobody who hasn't had it can form any notion of —but where am I to get credit? I don't like asking that poor girl Williams. In fact, I'm sure she hasn't got it; and how she keeps herself is a wonder to me. I ought to have gone to the workhouse about that precious baby, but I haven't had the time. Oh, my eyes! I could walk into a chump chop, if I'd got it."

He said the last sentence out loud, and with a plaintive melancholy which must have penetrated to the hardest heart.

"Why not have one, then?" said a voice behind him.

Toddleboy started to his feet.

"What did you say?"

"Why not have one?"

"One what?"

"A chump chop weren't you talking about?"

"I didn't know I spoke aloud, but that's what I was wishing for anyhow."

"Well I was wishing for one myself. Could we cook 'em here when we got 'em?"

"The difficulty don't lie in the cooking," replied Mr T. "It's in the buying!"

"How's that?"

"I've got no money!"

"Well, I have."

"But then—"

"Then I'll stand treat; so go and get them, and don't be long about it."

Saying this, the stranger handed Mr. Toddleboy half-a-crown, and the latter, after a momentary shock of astonishment, departed with all haste, to procure the delicacies with which he very shortly returned.

"Here's two thumpers," said he, laying them down upon the table; "a shilling, and two penny loaves makes one and twopence—a penny you have to pay for the use of the gridiron, and plates, and knives and forks. Then you order what you choose to drink."

"What I choose," replied the gentleman who had been so liberal, "is what you choose. Give the order, Mr. Toddleboy."

"Hallo!" cried Mr Toddleboy. "How do you know my name?"

"Read it in the newspaper."

"Hang the newspaper, I shall never hear the last of it."

"It's a deuced lucky thing for you, anyhow."

"What do you mean?"

"I'll tell you. My name is Leech. I'm in the law, and live in Bevis Marks."

"Indeed, sir," said Mr. Toddleboy, staring at him.

He was a dry man, was Leech of Bevis Marks; bony and hard to look at, with by no means a pleasant face, or one that would have done him much service as an index to his character.

If he were an honest man, he didn't look it.

"I want to talk to you," continued Mr. Leech, "and will do so while we dine. Where's the gridiron?"

"I'll get it."

"Get it; and sharp's the word."

Having got it, they put on the chops, Mr. Leech acting as cook, and turning them with singular dexterity.

"Well, Toddleboy," he said, when they were seated at their meal. "And so you picked it out of the water."

"What, the baby?"

"Ah, the baby."

"Yes, I did; but, if I'd known what was coming, I don't know that I should."

"Yes, you would, if you'd known what was coming."

"No I shouldn't."

"You would."

"Well, you know best, I suppose."

"Supposing now a five-pound note was coming, what would you say then?"

"A five-pound note—you're chaffing."

"I never chaff."

"Well, if it's the case, I only wish it had been twins."

"It is the case, I can assure you; and you may thank your stars you were in the way when it happened. But what puzzles me is, why you didn't follow her."

"Her!"

"The woman—that would have been your game; though I suppose she gave you the slip."

"I suppose she did; though I haven't the remotest idea who you are talking about."

"The woman who threw it in, of course."

"What! threw the baby in?"

"To be sure."

"I never saw her."

"Was it so dark, then?"

"Dark as pitch."

"Hum! that alters the matter."

Mr. Leech bolted his chop silently for some minutes.

"Well, as you didn't see her," said he, pleasantly, "you can't tell what she was like. However, I saw her to-day, or a friend of hers. I saw somebody, in fact, who sent me to you to give you five pounds for rescuing the child, and five more for its keep. Where is the child?"

"It is in the care of a poor young woman of the name of Sarah Williams, who lives down the alley here, by the side of this house."

"You're not taking charge of it, then?"

"She lives at the same house that I do; and, as she had just lost her own baby, she offered to suckle this one."

"Well, when you've done your chop, we'll go and see her."

A few minutes afterwards, they did so.

X.—Born to be Hanged.

"IS that the baby?" asked Mr. Leech.

"Yes, sir."

"Are those the clothes it wore?"

"Yes, sir, exactly the same."

"Let me look."

He took the child in his arms and began to examine its apparel minutely; turning the poor little innocent upside down, and topsy-turvy, in a way which most certainly could not have been agreeable, even to a kitten, and which almost tempted Sarah to rush forward and rescue it from his rough handling, only that the dread inspired by Mr. Leech's forbidding countenance deterred her.

"It has no marks on it—has it?"

"There's something like a fork upon his neck," said Sarah.

"A fork you call it, eh! It looks more like a gallows."

"Lord, sir, how horrid!" cried Sarah; "I'm sure it doesn't."

"Perhaps not—I'm no judge. But I didn't mean—that I meant marks upon its linen."

"There are none, sir."

"They seem of very good material, don't they?"

"Beautiful."

"So I thought. But, I say, where is the ribbon?"

"What ribbon?"

"That was round its neck."

"Bless me! I don't know what's become of it."

"Why, you've not lost it, surely?"

"I don't know."

As Mr. Leech expressed the strongest desire that it should be found, a diligent search was instituted, and in course of time it was discovered.

"Is that it?" said Mr. Leech, when the ribbon was submitted to him. "I'll take charge of it, and here's the money. I'll pay it to you, Mr. Toddleboy; and if this young woman likes to be the nurse, I don't see any objection myself. However, you, Mr. Toddleboy, I shall hold responsible for its well-doing. Are you agreeable?"

"Quite so."

"Then, here's the money. First—five pounds for rescuing it from the water, and five pounds more for its keep for the next twenty weeks—at the end of that time you'll hear from me. Give me a receipt."

This was no easy matter, I can tell you; for Mr. Toddleboy was, as he afterwards expressed it, "all of a tremble like," so that it was all that he could do to touch anything without knocking something else down. The first difficulty was the paper, which, being produced by Mr. Leech, they then stuck fast for pen and ink; and these two being procured in course of time, and with a recklessness about the cost (Mr. Toddleboy changed a sovereign to buy it, and bought a twopenny bottle, because a penny one was so small an order), the pen turned out to be a bad one, and, in the shaking fingers of old Mr. T., went everywhere but where it ought to have done, and would make nothing but blots.

The Toddleboy signature having at length been obtained—it was spelt, in the confusion, with only one d—the stranger departed, and the baby and its protectors were left together.

"Well, you'll be able to keep it now, Miss Williams."

"Oh, how happy I am!"

"And with this five pounds I hope you'll be able to get a little shop and parlour round the corner somewheres, buy some plaids, or something of that sort, to make into children's dresses for the window, and start in business."

"Oh, Mr. Toddleboy, how good you are! but you don't think I would accept it?"

"Don't I; but you will though. You can pay me back when you've made your fortune; and now, I say, we must have the baby christened. What should it be called? I quite forgot to ask what its name was, if it had one."

"Poor dear, I don't suppose it has."

"No, by what he said, I should think not. Anyhow, we'll call it—what shall we call it?"

"Dear Mr. Toddleboy, might I give it a name?"

"Of course, my dear—a dozen, if you like."

"Then I should like to give it the name I was

going to give my poor baby that is dead. I was going to call it Charles."

"Charles, eh? It's rather common, aint it?" said Mr. Toddleboy, doubtfully. "I should have thought we might have had something in three syllables; it don't cost no more, you know."

"No name is so beautiful as Charley, I think," replied Sarah.

"Charley be it, then. By-the-bye, Charley wasn't HIS name, was it?"

"Whose?"

"That's gone abroad."

"No," she answered with a sigh; "it was my brother who was drowned when a little boy."

"Ah! I'm glad of that," thought Mr. T. to himself. "I shouldn't have liked him to have been called after that scamp; it would have been unlucky. It's not unlucky, when I come to think of it, that he's named after any one who has been drowned. I don't think he's meant to be drowned, or else I'd never have come across him."

While musing thus, Sarah interrupted him by saying—

"And what's his surname to be?"

"Well, there's a puzzler. Toddleboy's out of the question. It's enough to drive a man to drink, such a name as that. It's been the ruin of me; I'm sure of it! I should have been a famous man if it hadn't been for my name; but what was the good of making it more conspicuous. I hadn't the face to do it. I don't know how I came to agree to that three-halfpence-a-lining gent. putting it in print. It gave me an awful turn when I saw it there, a-staring at me with a big *T* and a turn in the tail of the *y*, as though it knew it was ridiculous, and was a-trying to make its escape."

"Well, what shall we call it?"

"What do you say to your name?"

"Well—no, Mr. Toddleboy; it is not my baby? and people would talk so."

"We must call it something. I'll tell you what—"

"What?"

"WAG. We'll call it 'Wag,' because it's always laughing. Look at it! it's a-having a devil of a joke at our expense, I'll swear it is."

And so it was, to all appearance, cracking its little sides.

"But people will laugh at him so, won't they?" asked Sarah. "'Charley Wag!' it sounds so funny."

"It sounds very easy. I've heard it a hundred times already, it seems to me."

"Why, they call all Charleys 'Charley Wag,' down in the country—

"'Charley, Charley, Charley Wag,
    Ate the pudding and swallow'd the bag.'"

"Well," said Mr. Toddleboy, "it's a popular name, and I hope he'll be a popular character." *

"And only to think that it's real!" the old gentleman said aloud, as he toddled into the "Skeleton Key" for a drain, "and that I'm not dreaming. It'll grow up to be famous, that baby will; mark my words if it don't. I shall never be famous, and I never expected to be, but it's different with that baby. I wish I knew an astrologer who wasn't a humbug, and that he could tell me what destiny was in store for it. I should

say to him—'Most potent sage, canst thou reveal to me why this little child was born?' and he would reply, 'It was born to——'"

"Be hanged!" broke in a rough voice behind him; "that's about the figure."

Then pushing past him, with a coarse oath, the speaker, a slangy young fellow in a stylish, though tawdry clothes, nodded to the landlord.

"Hallo!" cried the host; "is that you, Jack Rattan?"

"Hist! stow your gab," the other said; "it's me, sure enough. But drop the herrin' pond. Have you seen my widow?"

"What, Sal?"

"Ay."

"She lives down the alley, at this old gentleman's."

"Which?"

"Him you spoke to."

The new comer turned towards Mr. Toddleboy; but, seeing that the old gentleman had his eyes fixed upon them, averted his own, and changed the subject.

"Who did he mean by 'Sal,'" thought Toddleboy, uneasily. "It can't be that scoundrel come back—I pray to God it is not."

X.—WAITING FOR DEATH.

SENTENCE of death had been passed.

The order for the execution of the prisoner had been received.

There was no hope.

He lay in the condemned cell of Newgate this Sunday night, at eight o'clock, just twelve hours before the time which it had been fixed by man that he should meet his God.

And he would die as surely as he was then living, curled upon his bed with his restless fingers clutching at the blanket.

There was no hope.

Until that very afternoon he had felt confident that the sentence would not be carried out; that the Secretary of State would reconsider the evidence, and that if not pardoned, he would be reprieved, temporarily. Others had bidden him dismiss the idea from his mind, and prepare himself for the worst; but he had not hearkened to them. He had felt so certain that he should escape. Now that was over.

There was no hope.

This Sunday night, as he was stretched upon his bed, wrestling fiercely with his mental anguish, the silence of the dreadful prison lay heavy upon him, and the awful sense of quiet ate itself into his very soul. Thus was it that—so painfully acute did his hearing become—he could at last distinguish the faint echoes of far distant footsteps within the walls, and catch a something which must have been the murmur of the busy, crowded streets without.

Still straining to hear these sounds, the prisoner became at last conscious of a dull and heavy noise which at times rose above all others, when the wind blew towards him, and then again was almost drowned in the buzz of voices and pattering of feet.

It was a sound that you and I in our easy chairs, by the fireside, would scarce have turned our heads to listen to—certainly not spent two consecutive moments in endeavouring to account for; but for the prisoner it bore a fearful interest.

It was the hammering of the workmen upon the instrument of death.

In less than twelve hours he would be pinioned, and brought forth to be hanged by the neck until he was dead.

He had seen a man hanged—two—three—once two at a time. And he had read accounts of executions often. He had always had a morbid hankering after that style of literature. He was, indeed, well up in all the details.

At six o'clock, should he be asleep, they would awaken him; he would then dress and have his breakfast—chocolate and bread-and-butter. A little before eight they would come and pinion him. There would be the sheriffs and the chaplain, jailers, and hangman, and others besides. Some one would be there most likely from the newspapers, to notice how he looked, and what his last words were, and to criticise his walk. Next Sunday, if he had been alive, and this had not been him, but some other man, he could have read it all in *Lloyd's*, or *Reynolds's*, or the *Dispatch*, and gloated over the details, as he masticated his buttered toast at breakfast.

Others would do the same by him.

As he lay and thought of all this, he rolled in his agony upon the bed, and groaned aloud.

There was no hope.

Who said not? Had not reprieves come the very last moment, as the condemned man was about to ascend the scaffold steps—ay! as he stood beneath the fatal beam?

But in such cases it had only been, as well as he could recollect, when there had been no answer from the Secretary of State.

The answer had come; the petition had been refused. There was no hope.

Does not the novelist, when he has his villain to make an end of, heap up horror upon horror, and rack his brain to think of some new way of finishing him, which shall rival in imagination the fiendish cruelty of the tortures of the Inquisition? But what horror could he pick upon to surpass this dread certainty of impending death, which the shivering wretch suffers as he waits, through the livelong dreary night, in anticipation of the hangman's visit!

In general the story-teller deals out sudden death. But here we have the long-drawn agony, the waiting for it, feeling the hours slip by, and the end approach, without possessing the power to stave it off—caged like a beast for slaughter, without the faintest hope of mercy upon earth.

This man of whom I write was more than usually deserving of his fate—were we to admit that one man has a right to deprive another of the life that God has given him—he was a hardened, mean-souled, avaricious wretch; who, in cold blood, had slain his dearest friend and benefactor, to grasp her wealth, and who had subsequently, with devilish schemes and machinations, endeavoured to shift the guilt upon an innocent person, and profit by his death.

So very little sympathy was felt for this monster, that when the news got abroad that he had petitioned for mercy, the hearers laughed, and asked each other, why and on what grounds.

And so horribly cruel had his conduct been, and so blood-thirsty his testimony against the innocent man, who, for the sake of the reward, he would have hanged, that some quite tender-hearted people were heard to say—if ever they did go to see a man hanged, this should be the man.

The tag-rag and bobtail, the scoundrelism and shamelessness which go to see such sights, intended to muster strong on this occasion, it would seem, for stragglers began to come upon the ground early on Sunday evening, and to form groups, and take up positions.

The very greatest interest was manifested in all that concerned the prisoner. His sayings and doings were minutely chronicled; and Mr. Jemmys the under-turnkey, who took his turn with a fellow jailer to sit up with the murderer, and was that hour off duty, and doing his pipe in the "Last Drop" public-house, opposite the prison, was listened to with breathless interest.

"Groan," said he, in answer to somebody; "I should say you'd groan too, if you had what he's got on your mind."

"I'd give a trifle to see him," said somebody.

"It isn't a trifle that would do it," replied Mr. Jemmys. "If you've got the proper order, you could do so. Not unless—no, not for twenty pun'."

"Couldn't a follow do it by bribing, now, Mr. Jemmys?"

"Bribing!" cried the jailer, in a terrible voice. "I should like to catch anybody a bribing, I'd bribe 'em, double sharp."

And, it being time for him to return to his duty, Mr. Jemmys buttoned up his coat with a determined air, and left the house without another word.

Crossing the street, a stranger stopped him.

He came up behind him in a stealthy, noiseless way, and laid his hand so suddenly upon Mr. Jemmys' shoulder, that that worthy gentleman jumped half a foot, and felt that his heart and the gin-and-water he had just swallowed were in his mouth.

"What the devil did you do that for?" he asked. "Couldn't you have come up like a rational creature?"

It was, perhaps, the fact of the stranger—a lanky man in black, wearing goloshes, which had rendered his approach so silent and cat-like; but he was so remarkable-looking a person, and with so cadaverous a face, that he might have startled anybody coming upon them any how in the dark.

Indeed, as he stood there a moment silently, he startled Mr. Jemmys, who cried out sharply— "Well! what do you want, now you've caught me?'

"You are one of the turnkeys, are you not?" the pale-faced stranger asked, in hollow tones.

"I am."

"You're sitting up with him?"

"With whom?"

"The man who dies to-morrow there."

He pointed, as he spoke, to the dark outline of the scaffold, which rose up close beside them against the leaden sky.

"Yes?" said Mr. Jemmys, a little nervously, "I am."

"I wish to see him."

"You can't without an order."

"I have one. Can I see him alone?"

"Not now; it's against the rules."

"I know it is. I'll pay for breaking them."

"What do you mean?" began Mr. Jemmys, indignantly.

"Hush!" said the other, grasping his arm—"I know all that. I heard you just now to the same effect in the public-house opposite. I must speak with this man, I say, and I will pay. Here are five pounds."

As he spoke, he showed the gold, glistening in his hand.

"No," said Mr. Jemmys; "it can't be done."

"At the price?"

"At any price."

"It must. How much do you want?"

"Well, if I agreed, my mate wouldn't."

"How much would he want?"

"I tell you it can't be done."

"I tell you it must. I'll speak to him,—which door do we go in at?"

"This one."

"Come, then; lead the way."

Mr. Jemmys led the way through the governor's house, and through a little office on the right-hand side as you enter; and having presented his credentials, which bore the name of William Murdock, he was conducted by Mr. Jemmys to the condemned cell where the prisoner was confined. The entrance was by a narrow staircase leading into a gloomy passage, in which a charcoal stove cast a lurid light upon the objects around it. From this passage opened the massive door of the cell into which they entered.

It was a stone dungeon eight feet long by six wide, and contained a bench at the upper end, a mattress and blanket, a bible, a prayer-book, a small high window, a candlestick fixed in the wall, a couple of chairs, the prisoner, and a fat jailer.

Pointing to him, Mr. Jemmys said, "You see my mate wants managing—so just you stop a bit till I can speak to him;" and, stepping forward, he addressed him thus—

"This gentleman," said he, addressing a whisper to his companion in a corner, "wishes particularly to speak to the prisoner alone; which is, as I tell him, dead against all rules."

"Decidedly."

"To compensate, for which—he being a near relation of the prisoner's, a brother, I think he said, as he hasn't seen him for years, and wishes to do the meeting business private like—he will insist on our accepting a trifle to turn our backs to them, and let them have it out as quiet as they can."

"He couldn't do otherwise."

"So, privacy being the pertickler requisite, you see, and the more private the better he'd like it, the more private we make it the more he'll insist upon our accepting of, for this accommodation."

"Most certainly."

"Then what's to be considered, you see, is how private we *can* make it."

"What does he want?"

"Well, would just outside the door be too much?"

"It's dead against the rules, anyhow."

"He says he knows it is, and that the little something he is going to press upon us must be proportionate."

"I don't think twenty pounds would cover our risk—do you?"

"I think its hardly worth it."

"But, if the gentleman says twenty, shall we entertain the offer."

"Well, you know best; I'll leave it all to you."

"Don't leave it to me, Mr. Jemmys, you'd better make the arrangement with the gentleman, and if any harm comes of it, you can't say that I brought it about."

The gentleman alluded to, who had been an attentive listener to this little colloquy—as there is some reason to believe he was intended to be—here interrupted, somewhat harshly, by saying that he did not intend to give more than half as much.

"Then," said Mr. Jemmys' friend, addressing Mr. Jemmys, and not even casting a glance in the direction of the gentleman who had spoken, "I don't think it's to be managed no how."

"But, look here, Bill," Mr. Jemmys pursued, "before deciding altogether, let's have what the gentleman is willing to give, and then make up our minds whether we can take it."

"Why don't he make a hoffer then, if he means business," grunted Mr. Jemmys' friend; "I've got no patience with sich dilly-dallying."

"My offer is, that I shall give you five pounds each, when I have had the interview; and if you don't like to agree to it you can leave it alone. I'll give you," said he, taking out his watch, "three minutes to decide."

As the gentleman spoke with such determination, and moreover, looked like a person who having made up his mind to a thing would not easily be made to change it, Mr. Jemmys and his friend consulted together again seriously, and, this time, in a lower tone.

In the whispered conference which ensued, it seemed as though Mr. Jemmys urged upon his friend the propriety of taking the amount offered; that the friend for some time stood out against all persuasion; but, that at length, just as the gentleman was losing patience, he knocked under, and agreed to the terms proposed.

"Which he'll pay first, of course," said Mr. Jemmys' friend.

But the gentleman wouldn't.

"Well, half first," suggested Mr. Jemmys' friend.

"Not a half-penny," persisted the gentleman. "If I did, you might take it into your heads to break in upon me at the end of the first three minutes."

"No, that I promise we wouldn't," said Mr Jemmys.

"I'll take my own precautions," retorted the gentleman. "Come, is it agreed?"

"Yes."

"Then leave the cell, both of you."

With a muttered remonstrance about it really not being worth the risk, Mr. Jemmys' friend was led outside the door, where he was heard confusedly to grumble for the next twenty minutes.

Then the stranger was left alone with the condemned man.

For a few moments neither broke the silence.

The murderer, when the stranger had just entered the cell, had looked up for a moment; but, seeing that the new comer was unknown to him, turned over upon his uneasy couch with a half-uttered curse, and lay with his face to the wall.

Slowly the stranger advanced, and, taking his seat close to the prisoner, placed his heavy hand upon the man's shoulder, in the same way that he had a little while ago laid it, unexpectedly, on the shoulder of the under-turnkey.

In like fashion, the prisoner started, and cried out at his touch.

"Who are you?" he exclaimed in a terrified voice. "I don't know you. What do you want?"

"I know you, James Murdoch, like all the world knows you, as the murderer of Mrs. Emsby, and the would-be murderer of Thomas Hemmings."

"It is a lie!" the prisoner cried, springing up in his bed, and endeavouring to shake off the other's fingers, which closed upon him like a vice. "It is a lie! I never murdered her."

"If I thought you hadn't, fool, I'd leave you to your fate. It is because I'm certain that you did, that I have come to be your friend."

"What do you mean?" the murderer asked, hoarsely. "How will you befriend me? You've come to wring a confession from me. Who are you?"

"My name is very little consequence. It is Ralph Faversham."

"I know the name," cried the prisoner. "Weren't you one of the counsel for the prosecution, but unable, through illness, to attend the trial?"

"I was."

"A thousand curses light upon you," the other screamed. "It was through your instrumentality that I was condemned."

"Who told you so?"

"My counsel said that, had it not been for the suggestions on your notes, I should have escaped."

"He told you right. *It was I who hanged you.*"

"Then, why," cried the prisoner with a fearful oath, at the same time struggling to get at the other's throat, but, by Faversham's superior strength, held back, foaming like a wild beast at bay—"why do you come here, unless it be to drive me mad?"

"I come to save you."

"Save me? It is impossible."

"Nothing is impossible."

"Can you get a reprieve?"

"No."

"Will you help me to escape?"

"No."

"Then how will you save me?"

"Listen," said Faversham, sinking his voice to the lowest whisper, but speaking so distinctly that every word thrilled through the hearer's frame—"*When you are hanged, I can bring you back to life!*"

XII.—Giving Death the Double.

SO astonishing and incredible was the statement, that for several seconds the murderer remained rooted to the spot, and, with wide-open eyes and mouth, regarded the speaker.

"You are mad!" he said, at last.

"I must be very mad indeed to take an interest in such as you, and to pay ten pounds for the honour of a private interview."

"What makes you take an interest, then, if you are not mad?"

"I have my reasons for doing so."

"But, why should you have worked so hard to get me hanged, if you are now going to bring me to life again?"

"Had you not been hanged, you might have been transported for life."

"Well, why not?"

"In that case, I should have lost you."

"Lost me?"

"Perhaps you might have been acquitted. That would have been worse."

"Why worse?"

"Because then I could have had no claim upon you."

"You speak in riddles."

"I will explain. I want to have an accomplice in a scheme of vengeance I have planned. It is necessary that my accomplice should be wholly and solely in my power. Where could I look for such an one, unless I looked to you?"

"But, why to me?"

"When you are hanged—to all the world there is an end of you. You are legally dead, and must remain dead evermore. Without a disguise, you dare not show your face. There is no place on earth where you dare call yourself by the name you now are called by. You will be mine. I will give you food and shelter; I will keep you from all harm while you are true to me; but should you play me false, then I will give you up again to the hangman's hands, and you will die again, this time to rise no more."

"But, stay," the prisoner cried, with a shudder; "shall I not be in a worse state as your slave than I should be if I died now?"

"That is for you to judge. The torments of hell await you as it is. Will you stave them off awhile? Speak but the word, and speak it quickly; or snap the slender thread that your existence hangs by."

The murderer, with his head buried in his hands, rocked to and fro upon the bed, his breast heaving convulsively.

"Quick!" the other cried, "there is no time to lose. Of course you will agree. You're not a madman, I suppose, if I am."

"Yes, I agree," the prisoner said. "Are you sure you can do it?"

"You may rely upon me."

"Great God! if you should fail!"

"I shall not fail."

"I believe you, then."

"That's well. And now I want you to tell these men that I am your brother. Do you hear?"

A knocking at the door at this moment interrupted them.

"Your brother," repeated Faversham.

"Why is that? My brother is dead, they know, already."

"They know you think so; I told them you were deceived. Remember, it is necessary for our plan."

The knocking increased.

"How so?"

"Because it is on that account *that I am to have your body.*"

The murderer involuntarily uttered an exclamation of horror, and fell back upon the bed.

At that moment the gaolers entered.

"We really can't stay out no longer," Mr. Jemmys said; "we expect the chaplain here directly."

"I am ready," said Faversham. "Good-bye, dear brother!"

"Good-bye, dear brother!"

"Farewell on earth!"

"Farewell on earth!"

"We shall meet," said Faversham—squeezing his hand significantly—"we shall meet in another world!"

The prisoner, trembling violently, sat down upon the bed, and Faversham walked slowly towards the door of the cell.

Upon the threshold he turned, and there was a strange, triumphant, malicious smile upon his pallid face, which made the prisoner tremble more than ever.

And, as he looked, the thought rushed through his brain, that it was to this man, of whom he knew nothing, to assist in a scheme of vengeance, with the particulars of which he was totally unacquainted, and which would, no doubt, be horrible to the last degree—or why should he have been selected? Should he reject his aid? Could he reject it? If this man had the power to restore his life, and wished to do so, would he not carry out his intention in spite of him?

With an overwhelming sense of dread of some undefined horror, he gazed upon the stranger's ghastly face, as the gaoler's lamp lit it up.

Next moment it was gone, and he was alone with Mr. Jemmys' friend.

Whatever was to be his fate, it was in others' hands; he was entirely helpless.

What would it be?

"We're only just in time," said Mr. Jemmys, with a chuckle, "for there's the chaplain coming."

"That gentleman?"

"Yes, walking towards us."

"Thank you, my friend; then I'll say Good night."

"Good night, sir," said Mr. Jemmys, in a loud voice.

Then poking out his hand, in a mysterious way, he added—

"Slip it in."

"Eh?"

"Do it quiet."

"Do what quiet?"

"The quids."

"Quids?"

"Why, no—damme—you're not going to try that game, are you?"

"What game, my good fellow?"

"Don't shout so. Curse you for a scurvy knave! If I had only suspected it!"

"My good man, what are you talking of?" continued Mr. Faversham, blandly.

The chaplain was, at this time, close to them.

"If it is the custom to tip the gaolers, of course I will. Here's half-a-sovereign, to drink my health."

"Thank you, sir, we takes no bribes," replied Mr. Jemmys.

"I'm sorry for that, for you're a most deserving fellow."

"Damn you," muttered Mr. Jemmys, in a low tone. "If ever I come across you out of here, I'll make you pay for this."

"I think not," replied Mr. Faversham, with a sneer; "or else I shall report all the circumstances, and have you discharged."

With a muttered imprecation, the gaoler prepared to follow him; but Faversham stopped him.

"Don't trouble yourself," he said; "I know the way, perfectly."

"I dare say it's not the first time you've been here," retorted Mr. Jemmys; "the last time, perhaps, you didn't get out so easy."

"Pretty well," said Faversham, with a laugh. "It was by the use of the same tools: I used my wits."

"And cheated the gaolers."

"Exactly so. Good evening to you."

When he was outside the prison, Faversham hailed a cab from the nearest stand.

"Do you know it?" he said, mentioning a street leading out of Church Street, Camberwell.

"Yes, sir," said the cabman with a grin; "it's where the gentleman lives as will have a job here to-morrow."

"Possibly. Take me to his house."

"Yes, sir."

"I say," said cabby to the waterman, as he removed the nosebag from his horse, "there's summut up."

"What's up?"

"I've got a bloak inside—"

"Well?"

"As wants to be drove—where d'ye think?"

"To Blazes?"

"Better than that."

"Where then?"

"To Jack Ketch's private residence."

"By golly! perhaps they're goin' to let the chap off. That's deuced provokin'."

"Why so, gov'nor?"

"Because I was going to bring the missus and the young 'uns, as a treat, to see it."

"Oh, that's al'ays the way, when one sets one's mind upon a bit of pleasuring."

"Now, then," cried Faversham from within; "are you going to be all night, fellow? Go on, or I'll get out."

"All right, your honour—I'll hit 'em up."

And away they went, leaving the frowning gaol behind them—leaving the shivering wretch condemned to death to toss and tumble on his restless couch, and dream, by fits and starts, of all the terrors of hell.

XIII.—JACK KETCH IN THE BOSOM OF HIS FAMILY.

IT is curious, seeing what an interest most of us take in the subject, what a very little any of us know about Jack Ketch.

A strange existence his, and a strange trade How is he remunerated? Does he have a yearly salary? If so, there have been some years when he has not had much to do! Does he have so much a job? If so, how much? Something very paltry, they say. A good deal too little for such ugly work.

And is the hangman's fee grown larger, now that executions are not quite so common? Nowadays, he must have quite an easy life of it, when we think that at Newgate alone, the executions in 1781 were forty; in '82, forty-five; and in '83, fifty-nine—more than one a-week!

Once upon a time, the prisoner's clothes were among his perquisites. Did he wear them himself, or sell them to the predecessor of Madame TUSSAUD, to decorate the victim's angular effigy? Do you recollect how Mother DONOVAN, on the way to Tyburn in a cart, insisted upon disposing of her raiment among the crowd, and gave Jack Ketch a drubbing for trying to prevent her? She afterwards threw herself out of the vehicle with such violence, as immediately to break her neck, and died instantaneously. They did not generally break their necks in those days. A light weight

[RISEN FROM THE GRAVE.]

left dangling in the air when the cart had driven away, might be near fifteen minutes strangling.

The hangman once was nearly hanged himself, at the time of the Gordon Riots, when Mr. Dennis, the Jack Ketch of the period, was tried for assisting in the destruction of Newgate. They let him off, however, and he strung up his fellow-rioters—good stiff work too—of all sorts and sizes. Men and women, and boys and girls—almost babies, some of them.

Certainly, there is a prejudice against public executioners, and yet at the rumour of a vacancy I am told the applications are numerous. Are they a little nervous over the first job? What requisites are looked for? Does Government make a contract? Has any body offered to do the business cheaper and better than the gentleman at present filling the onerous office?

As I have got a story to tell, and not a history to write, I will reserve the discussion of these questions till a more fitting opportunity.

No. 4.

I have a hangman to introduce to you.

Richard Rackstraw was having supper with his wife and family, when Faversham arrived.

No visitors at that hour were expected, and his visitor had not rung the bell. A little girl, the eldest of the young Rackstraws, and aged twelve, was going in at the garden gate with a jug.

"This is Mr. Rackstraw's?" said Faversham, interrogatively.

"Yes, sir."

"Who are you?"

"His daughter, sir."

"Go in, I'll follow you."

Following her in his noiseless way, Faversham looked in upon the litttle supper party, before anybody was aware of his having passed the street door.

It was Mrs. Rackstraw, who, looking up and seeing the pallid face staring in at her, gave a little scream. She was a comfortable little woman, fat and rosy.

"Lord a mercy me!" she cried, "Who's that?"

"Don't be alarmed," replied Faversham. "Mr. Rackstraw, I believe."

"My name, sir," said a stout, pleasant-looking man, speaking with his mouthful. "What's your pleasure?"

"I wish to speak to you."

"About business?"

"Yes; to-morrow's business."

"I'll speak to you at once, sir," the man said, rising hastily from his seat—"in the next room."

"I am disturbing you—I'll wait till you have done."

"Oh, no."

"I would rather."

"Well, if you would. Will you sit by the fire, or will you join us—we have only just commenced."

No, thank you, I never eat supper."

With a slight shudder, Faversham sat down. "What, eat with the hangman," he thought—"I can't stomach that."

Rackstraw may have guessed what was passing in his mind, for his brow darkened for a moment.

Then, with an apparent effort, he recovered his self-possession, and went on with his meal.

Had you not known that he was the public executioner, it would have been very difficult to have guessed it. By his appearance, he was a cheerful, honest-faced fellow, as I have said, inclined to be stout, and, if a merry twinkle in his eye was anything to go by, he was a man who loved a bit of fun as well as the rest of us.

About the walls hung coloured prints and cheap engravings of "Family Devotion," "Family Love," "Fireside Pleasures," and the like subjects; there were also a number of stuffed birds, and a number of live ones. In private life he seemed anything but a Tartar.

The apple-faced little ones round the table called him "Pa, dear," and his pretty little wife—pretty yet, though mother of seven, with unmistakeable indications of an eighth, looked like anything but what story books would lead us to believe that the wife of a hired assassin would be like.

As he looked on at the little party with his grim death's head gleaming in the firelight, Faversham thought to himself—

"It is in the same way that the wife and children of a butcher may come to love and fondle, and kiss the monster, who, a moment before, with a pole-axe has battered in the skull of some poor panting beast, and twisted a pointed stick round in his brain. It's all in the way of business. At home he's as playful as a lamb, and handles the baby as gently as though it were a lollipop, and he was afraid of its melting by the warmth of his hands.

But, however happy and comfortable the hangman's family might have been at other times, there was something dispiriting and disheartening in the silent presence of the white-faced stranger, who sat there, grim and ghostly, in the chimney corner, with his great staring eyes fixed upon the group. Indeed, so great an effect had it upon the youngest born, that he several times choked himself with terror at finding that Faversham was fixing him; while Mrs. Rackstraw, being in an interesting state, and subject to the strange ideas and fancies attendant upon that condition, could not rid herself of the notion that he was something supernatural; and sitting, as she did, with her back towards him, was taken with the shivers to such a degree, that if she had not made an excuse to leave the room and escape from his presence, there is no knowing what the consequences might have been.

Seeing that the appetite of even Rackstraw himself, a man, as you may suppose, of tolerably strong nerves, began to flag; and that he found an unusual difficulty in masticating his food, the stranger broke the silence by asking, in his deep voice, whether the hangman was ready.

"Quite," said the official, jumping up. "This way, if you please."

He ushered his visitor into an adjoining apartment, over the objects of which the candle he brought with him and placed upon the mantel-piece, cast a dim and uncertain light.

Faversham looked round and saw a row of white heads standing upon a shelf, and exhibiting in their cast of features every imaginable variety of hideousness, and every sign of low cunning, brutality, and vindictiveness, and all the basest passions which disgrace humanity.

"Those," said the hangman, seeing the direction of Faversham's eyes, "are the jobs I have worked off. All sorts of crimes; forgery, horse-stealing, rape, murder, and worse. That upon the table is *the rope I shall use to-morrow.* These things don't make you uncomfortable, do they?" added Rackstraw, hastily. "If they do, we won't stop in here. This is my study."

"Not they!" replied Faversham, with a short laugh. "I like them."

"I thought you were the sort of man who would," said the hangman. "You don't look chicken-hearted."

"Not very. There's nothing so very terrible in your little show. Pray, how many men have you worked off, as you call it?"

"To-morrow will be the fortieth job."

"Stiff jobs, some of them, I reckon."

"Ah! hard diers some have been."

"What kills them, now, do you think. Is it suffocation or dislocation?"

"Well, dislocation, the doctors have it. The fall breaks their neck; that is, snaps the marrow in the spine, and death is instantaneous. It's consoling to know, it is, for the sake of themselves and their relations."

"You think otherwise, then?"

"I tell you to-morrow's job will be the fortieth. I've had a couple of cases of broken necks among 'em."

"How do you think the rest have died?"

"By suffocation, if I should judge by the look of them."

"How did they look?"

"Tongue out; eyes starting; black in the face, and blood from ears and nostrils."

"All much distorted?"

"Mostly all."

"You don't suppose that there is much life left in one you've had the handling of, then, do you?"

"It's not my fault if there is. I try and earn my money. You see, the heavy ones may break their necks by the fall, and require no trouble; but the light weights don't, and require you to swing by their legs until they're throttled. Some, too, prepare themselves for the shock, and keep their shoulders well up—that spoils the neck-breaking business."

"Now, if one prepared himself, as you say—a strong, muscular fellow, like Murdoch, for instance

—and you did not swing by his legs, you think there might be a chance for him?"

"I should say there would."

"But, hanging for an hour by the neck would seem to be enough to suffocate any man."

"It's a long while, certainly. However, if the proper remedies were applied directly afterwards, he might come round. Then, again, a good deal depends upon the knot."

"How do you mean?"

"Why, you see, I slip the knot under their left ears, if I'm particularly anxious about their working off easy. That's a great help to 'em."

"You think so."

"I've found it very efficacious. But, breaking their spine, of course, would be the easiest, if you could only take them unawares."

"What, they know when the shock's coming?"

"Of course they do. When I've pulled the cap over the man's eyes, and gone down underneath to pull the bolt, ten to one but he hears it grating, or he may hear me fumbling about for it in the dark, if it should be in the dark, or else he knows by some other sign. Then he gets ready for the jerk, and screws himself up, like. That's how it doesn't answer. At the first shock he thinks he's killed, but soon finds he isn't, and begins to struggle. You've seen a hanging, p'raps."

"Yes."

"Then you must have noticed it. Now, policeman do the trick much better."

"What trick?"

"Putting a chap's neck out. Haven't you often heard of a drunken man dying in the street of apoplexy?"

"I think I have."

"That's it, then. When they begin struggling and fighting, and p'raps fetch the officer a wipe over the mouth, he gets a little rusty. Then he does it."

"Does what?"

"Pulls the man back suddenly by the collar, and taps him pretty sharp over the back of his head with his knuckles. It's done in a minute. The spine is snapped. Verdict—accidental death, and no questions asked."

"Good God! you don't mean to say that such things are possible?"

"All the mysteries of London haven't been told yet. No, nor a half of them. The police are a fine institution, so is the gallows, and long live them both, say I!"

"Rackstraw," said Faversham, taking a seat, and at the same time motioning the hangman to do likewise, "you are a man of superior intelligence. This brutal office is altogether unworthy of you."

"It's a disagreeable place enough, but a man must live somehow."

"You find it hard enough to live, I dare say."

"I haven't got more than I can do with."

"I suppose not, and twenty pounds would be a pretty little sum to put in your pocket."

"As long as I put it there honestly."

"Honestly, of course."

"The relations and friends sometimes offer a little something by way of inducement for me to make it as easy as possible for the job, and, in such cases, I defy any one to say that the job has had cause to complain."

"If they had, their spirits would come and argue the question with you afterwards, perhaps."

"Lord, sir, don't! Fancy any of those twenty. A dead body I don't think anything of—it's all in the way of business; but, when they're buried, there ought to be an end of them—"

"*But there is not.*"

The visitor spoke so earnestly and solemnly, that Rackstraw shivered all over, and, throwing an uneasy glance towards the ugly casts, bade him change the subject, and say what business he had come about.

"I will," said Faversham, sinking his voice to a whisper. "You say that, if certain of your offices about the doomed man are omitted, there may be a chance of his life."

"Yes."

"Those offices must, then, be omitted in the case of Murdoch. Do you hear?"

"But—but—I daren't do it."

"Here are twenty pounds, and—you can read."

"Yes."

"You know the signature and handwriting of the governor of Newgate?"

"I do."

"Read that."

As he spoke, Faversham handed to him an open letter, which was addressed to John Rackstraw, the public executioner. It ran thus:—

"It is with my knowledge and sanction that the bearer, Mr. Murdoch, a brother of James Murdoch, the murderer, now lying under sentence of death in this prison, will call upon and make certain suggestions to you with respect to Monday's business. *Obey him in every particular, and to the letter.* Otherwise, you will forfeit that regard and forbearance which I have hitherto shown you.

"Newgate Prison,　　　"THOMAS ADAMS,
"Sunday morning.　　"Governor of Newgate."

"That seems right enough," said Rackstraw, strongly agitated, and wiping away, as he spoke, the drops of sweat which rolled down his white face.

"Do you see the word '*forbearance?*'"

"Yes, I see it."

"You understand it?"

"I do—God help me!"

"God will help you, if you behave well. You understand that I have the sanction of the governor. You understand also what I want. I shall take the place of the prison-surgeon to-morrow. When the body is cut down, it must be lowered through the trap; I shall be waiting there for it. I shall take charge of it, and some stones will be provided to fill its place in the coffin. These must be buried instead of James Murdoch's corpse, which I shall convey to a certain place I have prepared for it."

"But shall I get into no trouble?"

"None, so long as you keep a still tongue in your head—everything depends upon that. Do you agree?"

"If I do not, what then?"

"Expect no mercy at the governor's hands, *nor at mine.*"

A fiendish smile, for a moment, lit up the visitor's pallid face, which was at once so unearthly and devilish, that Rackstraw trembled as he saw it.

"I agree," said he.

"I depend on you," said the other; "and, if you play me false, beware! *A hangman's rope may fit a hangman's neck.*"

" Hush, hush, for God's sake, sir; if you know my secret, spare me !"

" I have no wish to hurt you. All will depend upon to-morrow's work. One false step and you suffer. Mark that !"

" Do you, then, know ? "

" I KNOW ALL, and will act without pity, and without mercy. Good-night !"

Thus speaking, the stranger threw his cloak around him, and letting himself out of the house, as noiselessly as a burglar, crossed the garden and retraced his steps to where the cab was waiting for him.

The man was having a quiet nap on the box, and so gently did Faversham approach him, that he was standing by his side, and had lain his hand upon his shoulder, before he awoke.

He then awoke with a scream, and so violent a start, that he fell off the other side of the box into the mud, where he sat trembling, and rattling his teeth.

" Wha-a-a-at the devil did you do that for ?" said he.

" Do what ?" asked the fare.

" Why, come all of a sudden, with that cold hand of yours, and that white face, poking yourself into one's dreams."

" You've been drinking, man. Get up, and let us be going. I have no time to waste."

" Well, I don't half like it," said the cabman to himself, rising and shaking his coat. " Dash me, if ever I see such a party before. A complexion like that isn't human; I'll be blowed if it is—so thin, and so hollow in the cheeks. I never *have* seed a wampire, but if he aint one, I don't believe there is none—that's all I've got to say about it."

XIV.—WINDING-SHEETS.

IS there anything peculiar to the night which should make lonely folks feel lonelier, and those upon whose hands the time hangs heavily, at most times to hang heavier still ?

Is there anything peculiar in the bitter coldness of the wind, which every known preventive seems quite unable to keep away, that, penetrating to the porter's lodge at the inn of law where Faversham lives, searches out old Mrs. Aker's most vulnerable places, and gives her, as she says, "the horrors ?"

It does not look like the horrors, that porter's lodge, so warm, and snug, and comfortable is it.

She does not look the sort of person—sitting there warming her knees, in the fashion so prevalent among old ladies whose knees are cold, and whose dresses are too good to be scorched.

She's, perhaps, a little peevish at times, is Mrs. Aker, and a bit of a martyr in a small way, sorely troubled by toothache and rheumatiz; but she is an old soul who knows when she's comfortable, and, what's more, knows how to make herself so.

How's that ?

I'll tell you.

You see that black saucepan upon the fire ? Well, when she takes off the lid again, you'll smell a smell of onions that will knock you over if you are a fastidious party, and afraid of that king of vegetables.

And look here, too ! Do you suppose there is nothing but onions in the pot ? Bless your innocence, there's tripe as well. A savoury, succulent, luscious, gollopscious dish, that makes one's mouth water only to think of it.

And then that black bottle. Ah ! it was an artful dodge of yours, Mrs. Aker, to rear a book up in front of it. Lord love you, I know it's a bottle, for I can see the cork, and I know there's rum in it, as well as though I had smelt it.

To tell the truth, I do smell it faintly, for Mrs. Aker has anticipated the stiff glass after supper, by half-a-thimbleful neat, to stay her poor dear old stomach till the tripe's ready.

It's not a scene that would give one the horrors, is it ? and Mrs. Aker does not look like a person who has them, but she has ! and she says to herself, as she shivers and creeps closer to the grate, " It's all down my back like a hicicle—whatever is the matter with me ? I hope nothink dreadful aint a goin' to happen. My gracious ! if there's not a *winding-sheet in the candle*."

Some people don't like winding-sheets.

She was as cosy as cosy could be, only half-a-minute ago, and when Mr Toddleboy had said good-night to her, and wished himself well home, she had wished him well home too, came in and shut the door, and thanked her stars she hadn't got to be out " in sich horrible weathers."

Perhaps it had given her a turn, thinking of that poor creature as was going to be hung to-morrow, and the Lord rest his guilty soul !

Perhaps it was that, or perhaps it might have been that the ghostly, deathlike face of the mysterious tenant of the chambers had crept into her thoughts, and risen up uncalled-for before her eyes.

" I can't abear to think of him," she says to herself, " I really can't, and that's the truth; Mr. Toddleboy may well call him 'Old Bones,' I never see sich a man in my life. He comes upon one all at once, for all the world like a jack-in-the—— Good heavens !"

" What's the matter ? " a deep voice says, close to her.

The speaker is the subject of her thoughts, who stands there in the doorway, having silently approached, and opened the door without her hearing him.

" Dear me, how you startled me !"

" Startled you. I did not mean to do so. Let me have what parcels and letters you have of mine."

" I have a parcel, sir; no letters."

" There should have been a letter. The old man brought this parcel, did he not ?"

" Yes, sir; Mr. Toddleboy, from Bottle and Bung's."

" Give it me. Pleasant dreams to you."

" Pleasant dreams, indeed !" says Mrs. Aker to herself; " a nice man he is to give anybody pleasant dreams. He's given me the horrors worse than ever ! I'd better take a little somethink."

Which she does—medicinally. A couple of thimblesful this time.

Slowly up the creaking stairs he of the deathly face and leaden hand goes towards his room.

Slowly and noiselessly he enters his home, puts down his hat and cloak, and lighting his lamp, opens his books and begins to study.

Still upon the same black-lettered page. Still pondering over the history of secret poisons. Eagerly, breathlessly pursuing his search after those deadly secrets which were known to the

Borgias and Brinvilliers', but which our *savans* would have us believe we know no longer.

Will he find them? has he found them? What power does he call to his aid?

Do churchyards really yawn, and graves give up their dead? Will the inhabitants of the other world come back and help to guide us?

"Oh! powers of darkness. Mighty, unfathomable, infinite, send her to me! Wife of my heart—of my soul—I am waiting for you!"

From out the darkness which shrouds the distant objects in the room, slowly but steadily, and with a gliding motion, so very gradual that it is scarce perceptible, the phantom he has summoned from the grave approaches him, and stands erect—motionless, behind his chair.

He feels no fear—no horror, at the ghastly presence.

To him there is no ghostly terrors in the company he has sought for and obtained.

If his unholy prayers have made the dead rise from its grave, and it has come in all the hideous garniture of the grave, wrapped in its winding-sheet, 'tis but what he desired.

Slowly the gliding phantom creeps towards him, steals its dead arms round his neck, glues its bloodless lips upon his brow.

XV.—Returned from Transportation.

SARAH WILLIAMS sat sewing in her little bed-room, much happier than she had felt for many a day.

As she stitched she sang—not the "Song of a Shirt," but some plaintive ditty about a Highland Laddie or a Bold Sailor Boy, or a Gallant Troubadour, with lots of flourishes in it, and runs, in which she got so very high, as to be almost altogether inaudible.

But although singing and working, as if for a wager, yet was her busy brain as well employed as her active tongue and fingers.

In imagination, she had improvised a little shop out of some tiny front parlour, and had decorated the window beautifully with the latest thing in mantles and the sweetest thing in children's frocks.

In imagination, she was attending to a rush of lady customers, who had been waiting eagerly for the door to open, that they might come in and buy everything up.

In imagination, she had already achieved the genteelest of connections, and that it was a ready money business.

And among all her customers she had not, she thought, one of those impostors who, calling themselves ladies, desiring to dress beyond their means and outshine their neighbours, order recklessly any amount of goods upon credit, and, unable or unwilling to pay for their borrowed plumage, leave the poor dress-maker to starve or go to prison, without remorse or pity.

Shame on all such!

She was very happy, poor creature! Hers had been a hard fate. It is true that she was among the fallen; but let us look upon her, brothers and sisters, as one rather sinned against than sinning. Let us not gather up a stone to fling at her, but rather thank God that those nearest and dearest

to us are safe within the fold, and well out of the way of temptation. Alas! this is a hard-hearted world, ready to judge evilly where it sees a chance.

A knock at the door interrupted her meditations. "Come in," said she.

The person thus invited adopted a rather curious mode of complying with the request.

He first of all popped in his head, glanced hastily round, and, withdrawing it again, closed the door after him.

A second time he repeated this singular pantomime, and then, entering suddenly, but in a stealthy, cautious style, which, under the circumstances, seemed rather unnecessary, turned the key twice in the lock, and, twisting round to face the woman, jerked from his face a large brown comforter, which had hitherto muffled his features, and pushing up the peak of his fur cap, displayed the well-known features of her former lover.

"Good God, Jack!" she cried, springing to her feet, what brings you back?"

"Curse it, woman! don't blab out my name like that. Who's that in bed?"

"Only a little baby."

"A kinchen, eh?—yours?"

"No, Jack; mine is dead."

"So much the better. Well! you don't seem over glad to see me."

While speaking, he had laid aside a rough over-coat, his comforter, and cap, and was busy with the priming of a revolver, which he took from his breast-pocket. Thus engaged, he looked up inquiringly at the woman, for an answer to his question.

She did not reply: leaning against the wall for support, with her hand pressed upon her heart, she seemed to have lost the power of speech; and the intensity of her feelings could only be judged by the heaving of her troubled breast, beneath her wasted hand.

"Well, Sal!" pursued the unwelcome guest, taking a seat, and beginning to load a pipe, "are you struck silly?"

"Jack!" cried the woman, "you must go away. This is no place for you. What brings you back? Have you returned from transportation?"

"Yes, I have, if you like to call it so. I've give 'em the double at the floating academy,* skulked it in the back slums last night, and did a doss† in the saw-dust at a ballum rancum.‡ I looked up, thinking to spot you; and where I dropped all my tin, it was only two bob and a bandy,§ and should be without a blessed mag, if the old fence‖ up the 'Key' hadn't put me on to this crib."

"I don't understand your language, Jack, or what you mean. But you mustn't stay here—indeed, indeed, you mustn't!"

"Well, I'm agreeable—only where am I to go to, if you please?"

"Go anywhere; but here you cannot remain. Oh, Jack! have pity on me. I have got a chance of being respectable once more. A good old man who lives here has given me this child to nurse, and some money to set up in business. I may yet be able to earn an honest livelihood. Oh, Jack! I know you too well—I am sure you have too good a heart to stand between me and my only chance."

---

* The hulks. † A sleep.
‡ A low dancing academy. § Sixpence.
‖ Receiver of stolen goods.

"Ah!" retorted the other, "that's gallus fine, so far, aint it? It's a jolly nice opening for me to make a martyr of myself, but I'm not so blessed green as that, my dimber doxy."*

"But, Jack! I say you can't remain."

"And Sal—I say, where am I to go to? I hav'n't a taste for padding the hoof.† I have had no exercise lately, before I gave the overseers leg bail,‡ and have got out of the way of it. Beside, don't I tell you I haven't a mag? I'm stumped."

"Do you mean you have no money?"

"Well, that's St. Giles's Greek for it."

"But I have nothing, Jack. I have to work hard, very hard, for what I get. For many weeks past, I have been almost upon the point of death. Oh, Jack! I have found it bitterly hard to live."

"Stow this cant," growled the ruffian; "it won't go down with me. Didn't you a minute ago say the old bloke who lives here was going to set you up, and had give you the chink? Where is it? I want some—so shell up!"

"Jack, he has not yet given me leave to spend it. I dare not do so. It would be dishonourable."

"Oh," said Jack, ironically, and with the most evil of expressions, "it would be dishonourable, would it? Well, p'raps it would, only I'm a goin' to have it. That's all. Come, where's it kep?"

As he spoke he fixed his eyes upon her, and with the quickness of one used to trifles, saw the slightest possible inclination of her eyes towards a workbox on the table.

"It's there, is it?" he cried, laying his hand upon the lid.

"Jack," she screamed, springing to his side and wrenching the box suddenly from his hands, "I tell you, you shall not have it."

"Do you?" he growled between his teeth. "Then, I tell you, I shall."

"If you kill me, Jack, you sha'n't."

"Then I must kill you, for I shall have it. Strike me dead if I don't!"

Without another word, the ruffian seized her round the waist, and forcing her head back with his chin, endeavoured to draw the hand in which she held the box, closer to him.

Madly—frantically—with the fierce desperation of one who struggles with the last hope—like a drowning man clutches at the slippery boat side, or one who, falling over a precipice, tears with bleeding fingers at the crumbling bank—so Sarah battled resolutely with the thief.

In most cases where men struggle with women, the advantage generally is on the woman's side, for does not the man fear to hurt her by his violence? She has only got to cry out that he squeezes too hard, and he at once loosens his hold, and gives up an advantage which my lady straightway takes to herself.

But no such scruples had this cowardly bully. Determined upon possessing himself of the money he supposed her to be in possession of, he would not for a moment have hesitated to strangle her, had he thought that such a proceeding would have furthered the end he had in view, and that the atrocious deed would not have been traced to him.

She was weak with illness and want of food. The bread of struggling honesty is not made into the largest-sized loaves, nor is it the most fattening.

She had no power to contend against his violence, and had it not been that the terror of her situation gave her the strength of desperation, she would have been easily overcome.

Like Lucretia in the arms of Tarquin, she struggled madly for the victory, and, twisting and writhing eel-like in his grasp, managed to keep possession of the treasure.

And, like Lucretia, at last she lost it.

Jack Rattan was not the sort of fellow to be overcome. Desperate and unscrupulous, the knowledge that there was some ready cash within arm's length, and while he himself was without a farthing, or a prospect of getting one in any other way, determined him to possess himself of the woman's money.

He might have sought her out under the impression that they would live together upon the old terms, but the way in which she had received him, led him to believe that all love on her side was over.

"Who knows," he had thought to himself, "I may find her snug and comfortable, and with a pretty little penny put by in a stocking. I can spend a week or so very pleasantly, and then, if anything else turns up, and I've a run of luck, I can change my quarters."

But it was all over now, he saw very plainly, and the best game out was to collar the swag when he'd got a chance.

Poor fool! his low cunning and knavery helped him not to understand aught that was pure and good. In his little philosophy, he knew not how a woman's heart trodden upon, bruised, and lacerated, still clings desperately to the idol it has loved; and makes a god out of a clumsy lump of clay, which in our eyes, who love it not, is hideous enough.

Seeing only the fact before the end of his nose, that there was money in a box, and, by overcoming the poor panting woman who strove to defend it, it would be his, he seized her fiercely by the throat, and, throwing her backwards heavily upon the bed, tore the treasure from her grasp.

He opened the lid. Yes, there it lay. A five-pound note, beautifully clean and crisp, and apparently quite correct and genuine, and there were, besides, two pounds in gold.

"Well, this is a pretty find," muttered the villain to himself. "It's worth a tussel, after all."

"Jack! Jack!" cried the woman, clinging to his arm, as he was engaged stowing the money away in his pocket, "You won't take it from me. You won't be so hard-hearted as to take it all away. Oh, my God, Jack, if you do, I'm ruined Take some of it, Jack, and I will work hard and make it up. I know you must want money. I will do my best to get it for you. Oh, dear Jack, you that I have loved so! You who have been the cause of these months of misery I have suffered. Jack, I forgive you all; I have never blamed you. I swear before Heaven, I have never blamed you by the slightest word. Oh, Jack, do not rob me of my only hope. I will love you still, Jack. I will do all that the Almighty will permit me to do to support you; but, oh, Jack, in the name of everything that we should hold sacred and holy, do not do this wicked act."

"Curse your whining cant," he growled fiercely.

---

* Pretty girl.   † Walking.   ‡ Ran away.

"You're enough to make a parson swear, you are, by ——. I tell you I want the money; I will have it, if I have to cut a dozen throats to get it. Hush, do you hear anything. There's some one coming up-stairs."

"Can you hear who it is?"

"It's Mr. Toddleboy."

"Who's he?"

"The old gentleman I spoke of."

"Where can I hide?"

She looked at him for a moment, uncertain what course to pursue.

Here was an opportunity of saving her money. But, then, it only could be effected by giving him into custody. Could she do that? What would be the consequences?

Meanwhile, Rattan had hastily taken a survey of the room, to see whether it offered any convenience for hiding.

There was a large cupboard without shelves in one corner—into this he stepped.

At the same moment there was a knock at the door.

Then he came for a moment from his hiding-place, and, seizing her by the waist, hissed these words into her ear:—

"Take care what you're about. You saw the revolver I have got. It is loaded. I don't want this man to see me. Don't let him know I am here. If you show a sign of treachery, I'll blow your brains out. Let him in; I will watch you from the cupboard."

Getting back again into his place of concealment, he left the door a-chink, and, drawing out his revolver, stood in such a position that he could cover her in any part of the room.

"Miss Williams," cried Toddleboy's voice without, "if you haven't gone to bed, let me in for a moment; I want to see you particularly, about what I gave you to take care of."

XVI.—NIGHTMARE.

THROUGHOUT the lengthened, weary night, the murderer tossed uneasily upon his bed, in the condemned cell in Newgate.

Sometimes he slept for half an hour or so.

But, what a sleep it was! Full of horrible dreams, where his distorted fancy conjured up the ghastly inmates of the tomb, with fleshless limbs and sightless eyes, which strove to clasp him in their dread embrace, and drag him down unfathomable depths, where writhing serpents, grinning fiends, and sulphurous flames awaited him.

Again and again, in imagination, did he enact the brutal murder for which he was about to suffer.

Again and again, as he had done that fatal night, he crept in tiger-fashion up the creaking stairs, behind the old miserly crone whom he intended to slay, watched and waited for his opportunity, then stole in upon her, and struck the blow which stretched her dead and bloody at his feet.

Back to his mind it all came—horribly real and true—in all its details.

He felt again the weight of the hammer in his hand; heard, as before, its whistle through the parted air; the shock with which it fell upon the woman's head; the sickening sound of crushing bone beneath the deadly iron.

You could not call this sleep; for, should not sleep bring rest, and ease, and comfort, to the jaded spirits and weary frame; but this was torture too intense for human endurance, and; with a scream for help, the condemned man sprang up in bed, and glared with blood-shot eyes upon the startled jailers.

"Lie down," said Mr. Jemmys, surlily. "What's up with you?"

His late disappointment had soured the amiable jailer's temper, and he felt very little inclined to put up with any nonsense from anybody.

"Lie down," he said, "and don't let's have any more of that, or else I'll help you."

To which Mr. Jemmys' friend Bill, who was, if anything, more surly than Mr. Jemmys, added gruffly—

"Gallus quick."

And became once more silent and gloomy, as he had been for two hours previously.

The murderer, wiping away the huge drops of perspiration which hung upon his clammy brow, rested his head upon his hand, and determined to remain awake.

"What time is it?" he asked.

"Past four."

"Much past?"

"Twenty minutes."

Three hours and forty minutes left before the fatal moment would arrive.

Was it to be fatal? If not, there was nothing so very terrible in the ordeal he was about to go through. Oh, if he could be certain of what Faversham had promised him. But the promise was so strange, so extraordinary, so unheard of—he could not believe in it.

At last he began to doubt whether he had not dreamt it all; whether he had really been to see him; whether there was such a person as Ralph Faversham.

Yes, he was sure of that! for Murdoch recollected well his name, and the part he had taken in the trial.

By pondering over his dreams and the reality, he became at last so inextricably confused and jumbled up together, that he was obliged to appeal to one of the turnkeys for information.

"Did some one come to see me to-night?" he asked.

"Yes, somebody did," replied Mr. Jemmys.

"My brother, was it not?"

"Well, you ought to know best about that. He said he was."

"Nice brother, too," grumbled Mr. Jemmys' friend; "a hornament to anybody's family, he is."

Thus relieved as to one important particular, the condemned man felt a little more easy in his mind, and, determining to place implicit faith in the mysterious being who had promised to save him, he gradually dozed off to sleep.

Listening to his regular breathing, and staring very hard at the flame of a candle, which flared and flickered in the draught, Mr. Jemmys began to feel very lonely and uncomfortable, and as his friend Bill was by this time growing rather tired of maintaining a dignified silence, he opened a conversation in a low tone, upon to-morrow's business.

"I can't make it out," said Mr. Jemmys.

"Make what out?" asked Bill.

"The gov'nor's orders."

"What are they?"

"There's going to be another surgeon."

"What's that for?"

"Mr. Smith is ill," he said, "but he was all right when I saw him this morning."

"Well, what else has he ordered?"

"Why, the man as usually buries the parties as is hung, aint going to do it."

"How's that?"

"Because he's ill, too. One of Rackstraw's assistants is going to do it instead."

"What was that came for the gov'nor this evening?—a long box full of something."

"The coffin, wasn't it?"

"No, bless you, that's here already A long deal box."

"To be sure, I saw it. The gov'nor said it was eggs."

"Eggs, eh. Rum thing for a box of eggs to come on a Sunday night, aint it? What's he going to do with a boxful? Are all the prisoners going to have one for breakfast?"

"I shouldn't wonder. Prisoners is indulged so now-a-days; prisoners isn't what they used to be, when I was a boy. They calls it philanthropy, I think: humbug I calls it, pampering up a lot of thieves and vagabonds. They'll be pampering paupers next, I'm blowed if they won't. There'll be a nice game then, won't there?"

Reflecting upon the consequences of such a terrible state of things, Mr. Jemmys and his friend relapsed into silence, and having nothing more to say to one another, took a nap.

Meanwhile, the prisoner had resumed his fitful slumbers, and was again among the land of dreams; again rehearsing the tragedy of the old woman's death; again struggling with the dead body upon the brink of the fiery pit.

Ah! his foot slips—he totters and falls—he is lost!

But, no—here he is, safe and sound in bed, in the condemned cell. It is a relief to find himself there, under the circumstances; but it is more than relief, it is joy and ecstacy to find that his jailers are asleep.

Hush! hush! not a sound—not a breath—for your life. He slides from the bed. How difficult it is to disencumber himself of the bedclothes. They cling to him, like the clothes of a woman who has been found drowned.

If he can but open the door, without being heard, he is saved! Once outside the cells, he knows the way. He will pass through the door, out upon the scaffold. Ha! ha! upon the very scaffold they are so busy erecting for him.

Cautiously—cautiously. It is done at last—he creeps to the door—the key is in the lock—he turns it noiselessly, goes out, shuts the door upon the jailers, and is safe in the passage beyond.

Quick as lightning he hurries on through yards and passages. There is the door, which next morning would have led to death. He draws back the bolts—he is standing on the scaffold!

There are men there busy at work, but none seem to see or heed him.

He reaches the ground, rushes through the crowd, and through the silent streets, until he reaches the open fields. He is saved! Thank God, he is saved!

Suddenly, a hand is laid upon his shoulder.

"It's time to get up," says Mr. Jemmys. "It's past six."

Gracious heavens; it was then nothing but a dream.

He is still a prisoner.

He is condemned to death, and, in less than two hours, will be hanged.

XVII.—IN THE HANDS OF THE HANGMAN.

A DULL, cold morning, and a drizzling rain falling, which, however, interfered very little with the densely-packed crowd of shamelessness and ruffianism, waiting outside the prison walls to feast their eyes upon the edifying spectacle a generous government had provided for them—sparing no expense, and omitting none of the revolting details.

Impatiently they waited for the appearance of the victim, and cursed the tardy moments for passing so slowly.

Within the walls, this impatience was by no means manifested by the victim himself.

James Murdoch was, indeed, one of the blackest-hearted, cruel, and cowardly scoundrels who ever disgraced humanity by claiming a right to the name of man. In proportion as he had been merciless in his destruction of others, so he valued his own miserable life

The most abject, trembling, whining, and self-debasing of white-livered curs, he had, upon this last morning, and in the dread of impending death, not one spark of courage or self-respect remaining.

When thoroughly awakened to the sense of his situation, when he found that the time was fast approaching, and that he must submit to his fate, he lost all control over his feelings. The daylight—the grim prison walls and stern faces round him—had utterly scattered to the winds all the faith that he had placed in Faversham's promise. Did not the chaplain tell him there was no hope on earth? The jailers said the same. He must prepare to die. He would not prepare. He would not die. He would not stir a step. If they took him to the scaffold, they must do it by force. He would resist them while he had any strength remaining.

He refused to touch any breakfast, or to listen to the exhortations of the reverend gentleman attending on him, and sat, huddled up, upon his bed, with his knees up to his chin, and his chin resting on his breast, a pitiful object to look at.

A little before half-past seven o'clock the functionaries upon whom the principal duty devolved of seeing that the sentence of the law was carried into execution, two sheriffs and two under-sheriffs, arrived at the Sessions-house; and at a quarter before eight the governor of Newgate, accompanied by the ordinary and a surgeon, waited upon them, and escorted them to the interior of the gaol, where they were joined by the chief warder and Mr. Jemmys.

The governor was conversing in a low tone to the surgeon, a stoutish man, with a great deal of beard and whiskers, and a pair of blue spectacles, which gave him a curious appearance.

"Well," thought Mr. Jemmys to himself, "he's the queerest doctor I ever clapt my eyes on."

In a few minutes the prisoner came in. He was either too weak or too stubborn to help himself, and a warder on either side supported him, who loosening their hold when he was in the

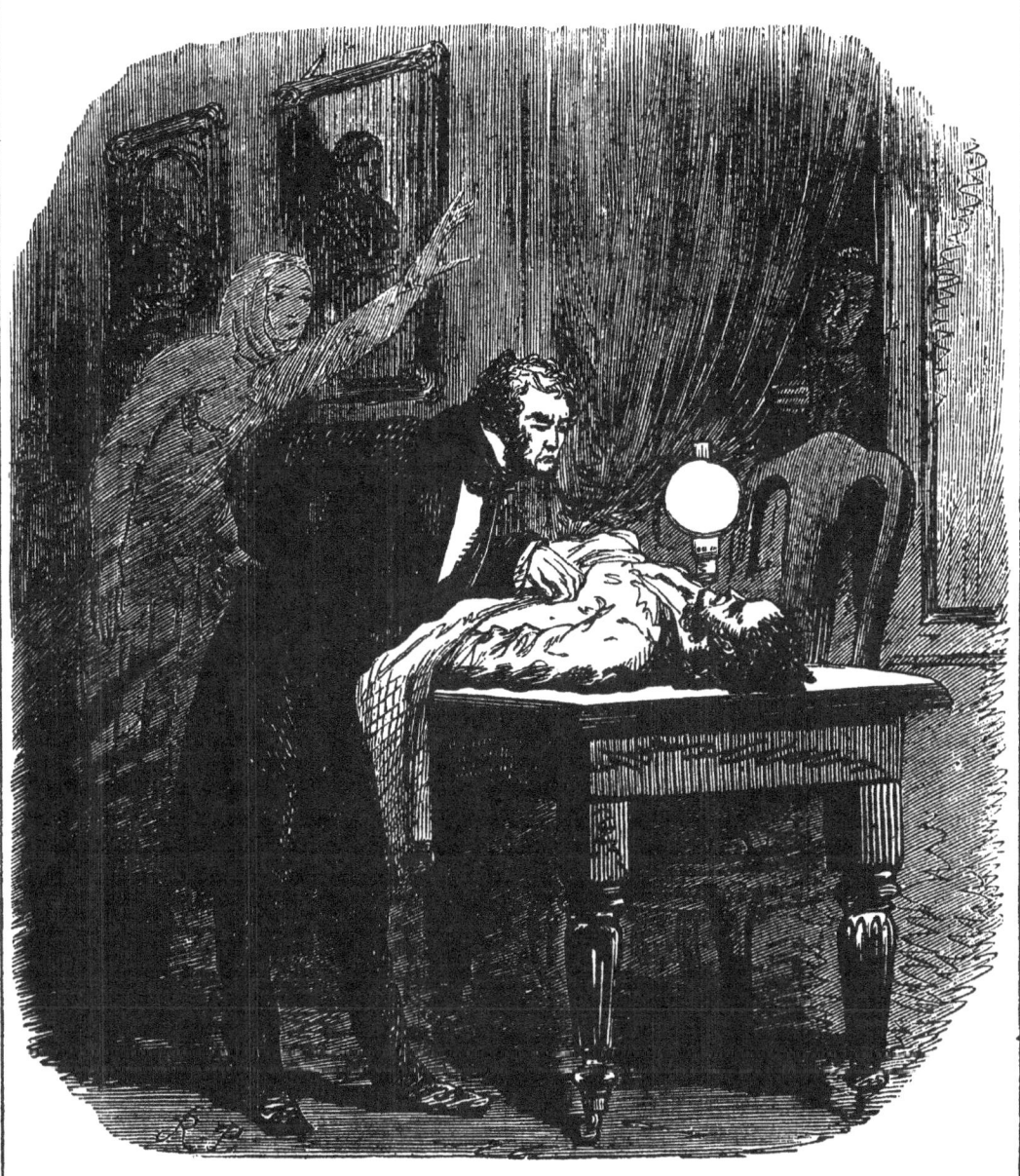

[MR. TODDLEBOY SEES A HORRIBLE SIGHT.]

centre of the group, he slipped to the ground a shapeless mass, with his face flat to the stones.

"Bring a chair," said the governor, "and let him sit in it. Look to him, Mr. Brown—I think he has fainted."

Thus addressed, the surgeon hastened forward, and bending over the prostrate form of the murderer, raised his head from the ground, and, while doing this, managed to whisper to him.

"Be a man—fear nothing—I will save you."

The cowardly wretch, however, senseless with terror, could not comprehend a word that was said to him, but catching at the word "save," struggled into a kneeling posture, and commenced a passionate appeal to the sheriffs to save his life.

The surgeon, with something like a curse and an irrepressible gesture of disgust, stepped hastily back, and proffered no further assistance.

"Spare me, spare me," whined the abject being, literally grovelling at the governor's feet. "Do anything you like with me, but don't take my life. I've been a good servant to the Crown, gentlemen. I've been a government spy these twenty years, gentlemen, and hanged as many traitors. You wouldn't take my life, gentlemen. I know the government never intended to take my life. The Home Secretary knows me well, and gave me his word of honour I shouldn't suffer, in return for the benefit I had done the State. Dear, good, kind, gentlemen, spare me, spare me."

Crawling along the ground, and clinging to the feet of those within his reach, it was a sad and

No. 5.

humiliating spectacle to see this man so disgracing himself; and the govenor, half in anger and half in compassion for the poor wretch's sufferings, bade them hasten the preparations, and send the hangman to them.

Then Rackstraw entered, and the culprit having been raised into the chair, he began the operation of pinioning.

When this was done eight o'clock had arrived, and the mournful procession moved towards the place of execution, the ordinary leading the way, and the prisoner, in an apparently senseless state, supported by the two warders.

When they came to the prison kitchen, out of the further end of which a black-grated and dismal door led on to the scaffold, the tolling of the solemn bell smote upon their ears, and the hoarse murmur of the expectant crowd, which heaved and surged like a sea without the prison walls, was distinctly audible.

As he heard it, the prisoner shuddered fearfully, and seemed almost dead with fright.

The surgeon was observing him intently. "It could not have been better," he muttered to himself. "If I had made the man on purpose, he could not have suited me better than he does. A merciless, unscrupulous, cunning, cowardly wretch. To save his own neck, there is no crime on earth he would not willingly have committed. Once in my power, I can keep the dread and terror of this scene ever present to his mind, and mould him like soft clay betwixt my fingers."

The dread door swang heavily back before them, and the procession moved forward.

In another moment, the shrinking, trembling victim came out upon the scaffold, in the presence of the ruffianly and furious mob, who saluted the spy with a fierce yell of hate and execration.

*　　*　　*　　*　　*

Beneath the scaffold all is prepared.

Thither descends the surgeon, who lays aside his blue spectacles and his rough overcoat.

Then Rackstraw descends hastily to draw the bolt which supports the trapdoor on which the culprit stands, and finds himself face to face with the mysterious stranger who had called upon him the previous evening.

"Is it time?" Faversham asks in a whisper.

"Quite, are you ready?"

"Yes—draw the bolt!"

"Stand there, and break his fall."

*　　*　　*　　*　　*　　*

The customary certificates of death have been given by the surgeon. The coffin, which is said to contain the murderer's body, and which Mr. Jemmys, who assists in carrying it, says is heavy enough for six, is taken out from underneath the scaffold, and buried within a couple of hours' time, at the usual burial-place within the prison.

The governor has ordered the body to be interred, without a cast being taken of the head of the deceased.

Mr. Jemmys observes that things are rather more hurried than usual; he is sent away, too, to a distant part of the prison, and, talking the matter over afterwards, it would appear that none of the warders were witnesses of the various ceremonies and observances usual on these occasions.

As for the governor, he seems to be more interested about the fate of his egg-chest than that of the murderer's remains.

He is most anxious about it being conveyed carefully into a cart waiting at his private door, and the surgeon is almost as interested in the matter as the governor, and is most particular about the box not being shaken.

When, at length, it is in the cart, the governor whispers to the surgeon—

"Have I kept my faith with you? Are you content?"

"I am; the business has been well managed."

"There have not even been occasion for all our precautions."

"One cannot be too cautious. Had anything been discovered, or should anything be discovered, you can take the man into your confidence, and show him the forged order of the Secretary of State, for the sham burial and disposal of the body to the murderer's brother."

"Hush, hush! should this ever come to be known, I am ruined and disgraced."

"It never shall. The secret is mine, and must remain as inviolable as a secret known but to the dead. Be careful: if it is discovered by accident, it will be your fault; if it is disclosed willingly by one who knows it now, he seals his death-warrant as he opens his lips."

———

XVIII.—The Thief in the Cupboard.

WITH a sinking heart and a pale face the unhappy Sarah approached the door of her bedchamber, and, turning the key in the lock, admitted Mr. Toddleboy.

Very few of us have much presence of mind in moments of danger. We do not give half the credit which is their due to those gallant fellows who have caught up a live shell, and in the very nick of time cut off the lighted match, thereby saving themselves from the certain death which, in another moment, nothing human could have averted. When we read such an account, we say at once, off hand, that he did just what we should have done; but, between you and I, I expect that the probabilities are in favour of our having made frantic but abortive efforts to get out of the way, which would have resulted in our tumbling over our own legs in our hurry and confusion, and being "blown to Smithereens"—where or whatever that may be.

Now what Miss Williams should have done, was to have pretended that she was fast asleep in bed, and sent Mr. Toddleboy about his business.

This would have gained time, anyhow; though you may think that, perhaps, the best plan would have been to have opened the door and sprung suddenly out upon the landing. Jack Rattan would scarcely have expected this move; and it is rather questionable whether he would have fired, and very questionable whether he would have hit her.

Then, on the other side, you see people don't like running these risks. There may be just time to cut off the match if you stoop down this moment and lay hold of the shell; but, then again, there may not, and, perhaps, it would be best to get as far off the murderous missile as you possibly can in a couple of seconds.

Trembling in every limb, and mentally tortured by fear and apprehension, Sarah admitted the old gentleman, who, taking off his hat as he entered, glanced round the room and said—

"I thought you'd got company."

"N-no," she stammered.

"Or that you was asleep."

"I *was* asleep, I think."

"You must have had the nightmare," said the old gentleman. "You was crying out, I thought, and making a scuffling noise like."

"Lor, Mr. Toddleboy, it was your fancy."

She assumed a cheerful, bantering tone, although ready to sink into the ground with fright, and getting her visitor a chair, placed it for him in such a position that, when he sat down, he would have his back to the cupboard containing the hidden thief.

"My fancy, eh?" said Mr. Toddleboy, rubbing his hands upon his knees in a thoughtful sort of way, and glancing round the room again. "I shouldn't wonder. I'm al'ays a-fancying something, but I could have sworn I heard you calling out just when I came in at the street door—besides—"

"Besides what? Goodness gracious, Mr. Toddleboy, don't I tell you I was not. Why should I deceive you?"

"To be sure, Miss Williams, why should you, indeed. I know you wouldn't, but then—"

"But then—"

"Well, I'll tell you: I looked up at the window as I came down the alley, and as sure as I'm a-sitting on this cane-bottomed chair, which, by the bye, it's a Windsor, I saw the shadow of you and some one struggling behind the blind, as plain as the figure of the chap on the broken bridge in the Fantoccini."

"You —you mistake," the woman replied, deadly pale and trembling in every limb. "You must have seen double, Mr. Toddleboy. Had you been taking anything?"

I told you she had no presence of mind. She had less tact it would seem than generally falls to the share of woman. This was a most unfortunate remark.

It annoyed Mr. Toddleboy. He was in the habit of getting the worse for drink, but since he had come into his property (I mean the five pounds), he had mentally turned over a new leaf, and intended in future, if not altogther to cut the bottle, at least not to look into it frequently.

"I beg your pardon, Miss Williams," said the old gentleman with dignity, diving down into his neckerchief after the ghost of a shirt collar, and bringing up instead an end of a dirty tape. "I assure you, it is you who are very much mistaken. If I never taste another drop of liquor in my life I saw what I describe."

"Well, have it as you like. I won't contradict."

"Thank you," said Mr. Toddleboy, very much hurt indeed, and tucking in the end of the string. "That's one consolation at any rate."

Then followed an awkward pause.

"You said you wanted to speak to me, I think," said Sarah, at last, in a kind tone.

"To be sure," replied the old gentleman, a little mortified "about the money. You have it all right?"

"Ye-yes, all right," the woman gasped, in so curious a voice that the old man looked up at her surprised.

"You're not well," said he, "sit down. Here, have my chair. I'll get another."

"No, no, don't move, thank you; I'll sit on the bed. Stop where you are."

"I'm sure you're ill. How funny you look. What are you staring at?"

"At nothing. I'm quite well. It was only a sudden faintness came over me."

It might certainly have been a sudden faintness; and had Mr. Toddleboy turned round sharply, he might have felt a little faint himself, at seeing about a quarter of a yard off a four-barrelled revolver, with which an ill-looking vagabond was taking a deliberate aim at his "knowledge-box."

There was in this ruffian's face so much ferocity and cold-blooded determination, that the woman felt certain that, should there be any occasion for it, her life and the old man's would be sacrificed, without the smallest scruple upon the murderer's part.

"I wanted to tell you, that I thought it would hardly be safe to keep the money here," said Mr. Toddleboy; "this is not the most respectable of neighbourhoods."

"What did you propose we should do?"

"Well, I have to go up and see the gov'nor this evening about some business, and I thought I might take it with me, and ask him to take care of it."

"But, do you think there is any occasion? Nobody knows we have it."

"Well, I'm not comfortable about it. When I went into the oil-shop to buy a bottle of ink, and changed the sovereign, there were several rum customers looking on, and I had the money mixed up with some farthings in my waistcoat-pocket, so that I had to take them all out together to find the coin I wanted; and I can tell you, the parties standing round opened their eyes, "above a few" when they saw the shiners. I was not sorry, to tell the truth, when I got safe home, after I got out of the shop."

"But in that case, Mr. Toddleboy, don't you see, some of these people may lie in wait for you and try to rob you; so that it would not be safe for you to carry the money, at night, in your pocket."

The thought had occurred to her, that, if she could only persuade the old gentleman to go away without it that evening, in the idea that he should take it with him in the morning, she might pretend, if things came to the worst, that during the night she had been robbed.

Besides, she still believed, with infatuated belief of a loving heart, that this man, for whom she had suffered so much, could not act such a scoundrel's part towards her as he threatened to do.

Mr. Toddleboy thought for a minute or two, and then he said—

"I should do so; but then I don't feel quite comfortable."

"What do you mean?"

"Well, you will wonder what I *do* mean when I ask you a question."

"That is?—"

"What was that man like who behaved so badly to you, and was transported? I mean, what was his personal appearance?"

Luckily, the candle burnt dimly for want of snuffing, and the old man sat at some distance from the girl, or he could not have failed to have noticed the terrified expression of her face.

A third person, too, well out of harm's way, would have been rather amused to have seen the effect which the observation had upon Mr. Rattan, who jerked his head into the cupboard so suddenly, that it came, with a sounding thump, against the wall behind.

"What's that?" said Mr. Toddleboy.

"Nothing, nothing; the people in the next house," cried the woman hastily. "Tell me what reason you had for asking about this person?"

"When I was in at the 'Skeleton Key'—I just looked in to get a little wet to keep out the cold— It's very chilly turned."

"Yes, yes."

"And a young fellow came in—a smart, slangy sort of chap, who by his cropped hair, and by an observation he made about the 'herring-pond,' I took to be a returned convict, either escaped or out with a 'ticket-of-leave.'"

"What did he say else?"

"I did not catch his words exactly, but I think he asked after his widow."

"His widow?"

"Yes: then the landlord says, 'What, Sal?' and the man says, 'Yes.' Then the landlord says, 'She lives down the Alley, at that old gentleman's,' meaning me, and then they whispered together."

"But—but," stammered Sarah, "that does not prove anything."

"I don't says it does," replied Mr. Toddleboy, pettishly. "What I wanted to know was, what he was like?"

"What who was like?"

"That scoundrel who deserted you. Describe him."

Sarah, glancing momentarily at the scowling face peering out from the cupboard, which at the instant wore even a more threatening and ferocious expression than it had hitherto assumed, began her description in a trembling voice.

"He is fair and thin," said she.

"That aint like him," muttered Toddleboy; "this was a grimy-faced vagabond, with a stubbly black beard. What sort of an expression had he?"

"Very mild and gentle, I remember him," said Sarah," with something of a sigh.

"A cock-eye?" asked Mr. Toddleboy.

"N-no."

"This fellow had a horrible one; it can't be the same."

"No, I think not"

"But who could he have meant by 'Sal?'"

"There are lots of that name."

"Yes; but he said, 'at that old gentleman's.'"

"Ha, ha, ha!"

"What is there to laugh at?"

"Do you know whom he must have meant?"

"I can't say I do."

"Why, Mrs. Grinderbones?"

"You don't mean that! well, that isn't so bad, really. To be sure, her Christian name is Sarah, and they do say that her last husband went abroad and never came back. However, let that be as it may, now my mind's easy upon the point, I think that it will be best for me to leave the money with you till next morning. Good night, Miss Williams, and I'm sorry I troubled you. Halloa!—"

In going towards the door, his foot kicked against a workbox lying on the floor.

"What's this?" said he.

"Oh! nothing," answered Sarah, "only my old box."

"Why, that's the one the money was in."

"Yes, I know," she said; "but I took it out."

"That's what you knocked over when you were dreaming."

"To be sure; I suppose I must have done so. Never mind picking up the things, I'll do all that. Your gov'ner, as you call him, will be waiting for you."

"Ah! I forgot that. I'm off. Just show a light, please, or I shall be treading upon your thimble, or something."

She did as he desired; and, holding up the candle, *the light fell full upon Jack Rattan's fur cap.*

"Halloa!" cried the old man again, "what's this? That don't belong to you, does it?"

"Yes—no; that is, it belongs to the young man down stairs, the cabinet-maker; he asked me to sew on the peak that had come loose."

"Oh," said Mr. Toddleboy, a little glumly, turning the cap round between his fingers, "it seems to be mended now. Shall I return it to him?"

"Thank you, I have not quite finished."

"The peak's sewn on."

"Yes, but I'm going to re-line it."

"It seems not to want it."

"Bless me, Mr. Toddleboy, do put the cap down. I don't know what ever has come to you to-night, you are so very suspicious."

"Suspicious!" the old man replied, turning sharply upon her, "suspicious of what?"

"Of nothing that I can understand, without you are jealous of the young man up-stairs."

"I have no right to be jealous of any one."

"Certainly not, upon my account. Good night, sir."

"Good night: don't trouble yourself with the candle, I can find my way."

Very gloomy, and rather savage in expression, Mr. Toddleboy descended the stairs, stamping on each separate step.

At the door stood the young man to whom Sarah had alluded as the cabinet-maker.

"Good evening, Mr Woodbridge," said the old gentleman. "What a smart cap that is of yours Miss Williams is mending."

"What cap's that?"

"That beautiful hairy one."

"She aint mending any cap of mine."

"Go on with you; I know all about it."

"What the deuce do you mean by knowing all about it? I haven't got a hairy cap and I never had a hairy cap, I don't know anybody else who has, and you and your hairy caps may go and be blow'd."

Saying which, the cabinet-maker walked himself off in a huff.

"I thought as much," said Toddleboy to himself. "If I had not another hour to live, I would swear that that was the same fur cap the young man wore who came in to the 'Key.' Perhaps there is a policeman round the corner. If there is I'll fetch him. Where could she have had him concealed—I'm sure she had, from her manner."

And Toddleboy departed with all haste upon his errand.

─────

XIX.—BLOOD FOR BLOOD.

NO sooner had Toddleboy passed out of the room than Sarah closed and double-locked the door. "Jack," she said, turning round to her companion, "you heard what the old man said. For God's sake do not take the money. Take a pound of it, if you will. I can perhaps make up that deficiency, but do not take it all, or I am ruined."

"Well, I reyther like that," responded Jack, picking up and putting on the fur cap. "That seems to be very like the coves in the papers, as offers a reward of ' five bob for a fob full of quids.' It's a gallus fine hinducement to be honest, aint it?"

" I don't know I'm sure; but, Jack, I am certain you will not take this money. You haven't the heart."

" It's consolin' to you to think so, I dessay, only I shall stick to the tin, I can assure you; so, good night!"

" Jack, dear Jack, do not leave me like this."

"What do you want, then—to kiss me?"

" God forbid! I want that money."

" You're going the way to catch a slap in the mouth," observed Mr. Rattan, with a peculiar twist of his cock-eye. " By the way, who's kid is that in bed?"

"It belongs to some one who has given it to me to nurse, and the money you have taken they gave Mr. Toddleboy at the same time."

" Ah, well, you'd better ask 'em for some more, or I will. Where do they live?"

" I don't know."

" That's a lie, if nothing else is. Howsomedever, I shall make it my business to find out. Now then, open the door."

" Not unless you give me the money."

"Don't be a fool. Leave go of me."

" Never!"

"If you don't I shall smash you."

" You coward, you would not strike a defenceless woman," she said more in a whisper than aloud, at the same time clinging to his coat, and striving to reach his pocket. " Give it back, Jack. I will have it, if I have to scream for help."

" You shall have something," the man returned betwixt his set teeth, at the same time raising his huge fist in the air to strike her in the face.

As it descended, and she fell backwards with a piercing shriek, a heavy blow without shattered one of the panels of the room door, and a policeman stood before him upon the threshold.

He saw the glazed cape, the iron-bound hat, and the stern features of the officer (a strongly-built man,) through the aperture.

The lock had not yet given way, but the next blow must inevitably cause it to yield. At the glance which the robber threw upon the enemy, he saw that he was alone.

One course only remained, but he was unwilling, unscrupulous ruffian though he might be, to resort to it.

At this juncture, the officer spoke and decided his fate.

"What are you about?" the policeman said. " Robbing and ill-using that woman. Give in quietly. I know who you are, and you're my prisoner."

"Not yet," replied Rattan. " One man won't take me."

" There are others handy," said the officer.

" In that case," cried the robber, with a fearful oath, " I'll send them where I shall send you."

And, as he spoke, he pulled the revolver from his breast coat-pocket, and thrusting it into the face of the policeman, who stood close to the other side of the broken door, drew the trigger and shot him dead.

Next moment he had thrown open the window and stepped out upon the sill.

It was a second-floor window at the back of the house, and at a great height from the back-yard, which looked even further off than it really was, in the uncertain light from a distant gas-lamp, peeping its head above a brick wall enclosing the garden of the next house but one.

Turning his eyes from the uninviting depths below, he hastily scanned the prospect above him.

The window was close to the roof. By treading upon and clinging to the sashes with one hand. he would be able by a desperate effort to reach the gutter with the other. About three yards from the window was the iron-pipe, down which he fancied that he might descend into the yard below.

It was not a time to stick at trifles. Every moment wasted brought him nearer to the gallows, for he heard the sound of voices upon the stairs. If he slipped, certain death awaited him. If taken alive, there was very little hope of mercy.

Seizing tightly hold of the gutter with a grasp of iron, he contrived to shift himself cautiously along, and having every confidence from, the enormous power of his hands and wrists, that he could hang for any reasonable time and bear his weight, he thus managed to traverse the distance which divided him from the pipe.

This reached with the same caution, the same dare-devil courage and gigantic strength, he commenced the descent.

The pipe was almost close to the wall, the space scarcely allowing him to insert his fingers; and in some cases the rough contact of the brickwork chafed the skin and nails, and caused them to bleed profusely.

Changing from hand to hand, and every now and then gaining some slight support from his toes and knees, he worked his way downwards.

Meanwhile, the murmur of the voices in the house had waxed into an angry roar, and loud shouts of "murder" smote upon his affrighted heart.

The windows of the houses on either side were flung open, and anxious faces, lighted by flaring candles which their owners held, thrust forth.

Still did he work his way downwards, and he had now passed the first floor, and was about eight or ten feet from the ground.

He looked beneath him and would, next moment, have loosened his hold and dropped, but at that very instant several persons rushed out from the back-door into the yard.

What was to be done? No hope of escape this way. Nothing left but to climb back. Had he strength to do it?

Without wasting time in reflection he sprang upwards, and in two more seconds had made a progress of six feet.

"See, see, there he goes," shouted the pursuers.

" Fire at him—stop him—throw stones at him."

A brick-bat was instantly hurled, and struck the robber on the leg, almost breaking it. Amidst a shower of missiles he struggled upwards towards the roof, bleeding and half-stunned by the blows he had received.

And now, as he approached the parapet, his strength began to fail him and his courage to give way.

His fingers nearly raw with the friction, his arms aching almost beyond endurance, his head badly cut, his leg stiff from the effects of the first brick-bat which had been hurled at him, he was upon the point of giving way, and falling like a fly intoxicated with tobacco-smoke down into the yard below.

But the hope of liberty upheld him, and he struggled on. He reached the top of the pipe.

One more effort is wanting to get hold of the gutter. His strength is all going. He feels that he must release his hold.

No, not yet; one spring—one spring will save him.

It is made—he clutches the stone work—draws himself over.

Thank God, he is for the moment safe. But no—

Simultaneously with his reaching the roof, the trap-door leading to it is thrown open, and a policeman springs upon him like a tiger on his prey. "I am the brother of the man you shot, you infernal scoundrel!" Rattan's assailant hisses in his ear, "and I'll have ' BLOOD FOR BLOOD.' "

———

XX.—The Death-Struggle on the Parapet.

"TAKE your hands off my throat, you cursed maniac," roared the robber, driven by desperation and despair to a state almost similar to that of a wild beast beset by furious dogs, "I mean to save my life, in spite of you all; and, if I have to take a hundred other lives to do so, by God, I'll take them."

"Don't try to frighten me," the policeman returned, twisting his hands still tighter in the other's neckerchief. "You are my prisoner, and you shall not escape. I'll see you hanged, as certainly as I now have hold of you."

"We'll see that. Leave go!"

"Surrender!"

Without another word they closed in deadly strife, and, tightly clutched in each other's arms, rolled and staggered, panting, upon the very brink of the parapet.

And, as though they possessed charmed lives, in this fierce encounter the combatants escaped the edge by a mere hair's breath; and, though each strove with all his might and main to hurl the other to destruction, they both managed to avoid this fearful doom and keep their footing on the slippery tiles.

And now the voices of those below were heard vociferously shouting directions to others to go up to the policeman's rescue,, and loud cries for help and assistance rang from every side, mingled with a few encouraging cheers from the more ruffianly portion of the neighbouring population, who having by this time ascertained that it was only a policeman who had been murdered, and not a pickpocket or a pickpocket's mistress, were inclined to hail the occurrence with delight; and in any case determined not to afford the slightest assistance, even if such a passive course of proceeding were to lead to the total extermination of the " bluebottle" race.

"Throw him over—throw him over!" they shouted.

"Police, police! Murder! Help!" shouted the others.

And while the majority of the spectators were thus giving directions to which nobody paid any attention whatever, the death-struggle continued upon the roof with the same ferocity and determination as hitherto.

The combatants were pretty equally matched; there was not much to choose between them.

Both were strongly-built and muscular, both brave and resolute, both equally determined to gain his particular aim and object.

The aim and object of the policeman was to take Rattan into custody. The aim of Rattan was to throw the policeman over the parapet.

Fiercely and savagely they clawed, and wrenched, and tore at each other, upon the slippery roof. The tiles cracked beneath their heavy tread, and every movement threatened to precipitate them into eternity.

But still they fought, and struggled, and wrenched, and tore at one another.

Although in his revengeful malice the robber would have liked to have murdered his assailant had he had the chance, yet, as long as he could only manage to escape, he would be content. Therefore, relinquishing the object he had hitherto striven to gain, namely, that of throwing the policeman off the roof, and warned by the sound of approaching voices and the sound of hurrying feet upon the stairs that he had not much time to spare, he concentrated all his power into one tremendous effort, and, instead of thrusting his enemy towards the edge, as he had previously done, gave him a sudden and vigorous jerk forward, which threw him off his balance, and sent his head, with stunning force, against a stack of chimneys.

There the policeman lay, motionless and insensible; and Rattan stood for a moment over him, uncertain whether or not he would rise to renew the conflict.

Then, fearing that he might do so, and at all risks determined to make safety doubly sure, he seized the prostrate man in his brawny arms and dragged him towards the edge of the parapet.

But just at this moment several of his pursuers were close upon him, and by the sound of their voices he judged them to be climbing up the ladder which led to the roof through the trap-door.

To stay their progress and gain time was of the most vital importance, or escape would be hopeless.

What should he do? He could not bolt the door. He could not hope to stop their course, as they rushed forward in any way but one. And this he chose.

With a strength which was absolutely Herculean, he poised the senseless body for a moment above his head, and the next hurled it with gigantic force right into the face of the first person who appeared at the trap.

With a deafening crash the body descended, and the whole of the pursuers to a man fell in a heap down the ladder to the landing beneath, where, coming with fearful violence against the bannisters, the whole gave way and let them down with a noise like thunder, which brought the neighbours screaming to their assistance.

Without waiting to hear what became of them or who was killed or wounded, but replying to the sounds of stifled groans and shrieks with a ferocious laugh of triumph, the robber sped along the roofs of that house and the next, and letting himself in through an attic window, which he providentially found open, walked down stairs uninterrupted—for the inmates of the house were all out in the street; and passing some persons crowding round the door without remark or observation, strolled coolly round the corner, and then took to his heels.

"Escaped," he muttered to himself, when, pulling up to rest himself in a quiet spot at some distance from the place of danger, he wiped the perspiration off his face, "escaped in spite of them all. I'm sorry I did for the 'bobby;' they may make it warm for me. Perhaps I did as much for the other. Well, anyhow, I shall read all the particulars in the papers to-morrow. That's one of the advantages of education. I've got the money all safe; and I'll have some more from the same quarter. What did Sal mean by that tale about the kid? I must find it out. I can, perhaps, work its mother for a trifle. I wish it was a bit older, and I'd make a prig of it Well, there's time yet. I dessay I shall before I have done."

———

XXI.—Recalled to Life—the Mortgaged Soul—the Unholy Oath.

IT is five minutes past eleven o'clock on Monday morning—the day of the execution.

It is exactly one hour and thirty-seven minutes since the miserable culprit, James Murdoch, came to an untimely and ignominious end at the hands of the common hangman.

The ordinary business of London streets progresses much as usual, and there is no particular depression of spirits visible in the faces of the busy traders, sauntering pleasure seekers, and slouching mendicants—as why should there be?

Is there any reason because James Murdoch, spy, perjurer and murderer, has been hanged by the neck until he was dead in front of Newgate prison, that you and I, who know nothing that is good of him, should feel particularly unhappy, or look particularly doleful? Why should we?

Nor is there any reason—I put it to you, as an unprejudiced individual—why Mr. Toddleboy should look so much more miserable than it is his wont to be, or should take a quartern more or less upon the occasion?

Being, as a rule, in the habit of regaling himself with a quartern in the course of the morning, he took it a pennyworth at a time, and neat. He would this morning, I have little doubt, follow his usual custom, only that he has no money

"Just when I had arranged everything in my own mind to my own satisfaction," says he, "why ever did she not tell me, at once, that the scoundrel was in the cupboard? though certainly, if she had, he would have blown our brains out, which would not have done either of us any particular service. It's the luckiest thing that ever happened that I kept three pound in my own pocket; but then that won't last till doomsday, I suppose. However, as I have come to the determination of never putting my lips to another drop of gin as long as I live, there'll be money saved one way at least. I feel dreadfully low this morning, and looked upon it in the light of a medicine—well, I haven't got any money with me, so I can't; and so there's an end of it."

Reasoning with himself after this fashion, Mr.

Toddleboy comes, in course of time, to the Inns of Law, where Mr. Faversham had chambers, and finding Mrs. Aker and a strong suspicion of rum-shrub occupying the porter's lodge, addresses himself politely to the lady, and asks "how she finds herself by this time?"

Mrs. Aker, making a reply to the effect that she finds herself, all things considered, "pretty middleingish," Mr. Toddleboy sasks, facetiously—

"How's old Bones?"

"Hout," says Mrs. Aker.

"When's he expected back?" says Mr. Toddleboy.

"Every minute."

"Did he say I was to wait?"

"He left no orders."

"Then I'll wait for him on the stairs," says Mr. Toddleboy, as a hint to Mrs. Aker that she should ask him in to wait by the fire; but Mrs. Aker being a little put out for some reason or reasons with which it is unnecessary to trouble the reader, does not offer him any encouragement, so Mr. Toddleboy betakes himself to the resting place he had mentioned, and propping himself up in a dark corner, very much in the same position that the merchant in the story found the little hunchback who had choked himself with a herring bone, propped up in the chimney, takes forty very uncomfortable winks.

But the landing-place is too full of draughts for anybody to go to sleep upon, and Mr. Toddleboy, attracted by one particular current of air sawing at his left ear, endeavours to discover the cause thereof, and finds to his surprise that Mr. Faversham's door is ajar.

"He would not like me to go in and sit down I suppose," says the old gentleman; "but that landing's too much for any one, so here goes."

He enters the room, which strikes cold and damp like a vault, as though it had been long uninhabited.

"I wonder whether he ever lights a fire," thinks Mr. Toddleboy. "If I ever did want a little drop of something short more than at any other time, now is the moment. I should very much like to know where he keeps it."

Not knowing where it is kept, and growing anxious about it, Mr. Toddleboy looks cautiously round the room. Do not think that the old gentleman is altogether a thief. With untold gold you might, I verily believe, have trusted him, but I should not have liked to have left him and a half-quartern alone together. There are many people in the world of the same style of morality.

After a little investigation, he discovers the object of his search. There is the cupboard, and sure enough there is something in it. In goes his hand, out comes the bottle, and in a twinkling he has drawn the cork and tasted the liquor. He takes a gulp, being in a great hurry, and the next moment is doubled up with a violent fit of coughing, whilst his throat and stomach feel as though they are on fire.

"It's turpentine," gasps Mr. Toddleboy. "Why the blazes does he keep it in a gin bottle with the label on?"

Just then, while he is considering the subject and examining the bottle, he suddenly becomes aware of a footstep upon the landing. In his fit of coughing he has backed away from the cupboard, and is now too far off it to hope to be able to replace the stolen property in time to avoid discovery. It does not occur to him to pocket it, and not exactly knowing what to do, he very ridiculously hides himself behind the window-curtain, still holding the turpentine in his hand.

Several persons enter, carrying something heavy. Placing it down upon the table, in accordance with the direction of a deep, grave voice, they depart, and Mr Toddleboy, listening attentively, hears what he considers to be the noise of the creaking of a box-lid; and at this juncture, peeping through the curtain, Mr. Toddleboy sees what he considers to be a horrible sight. For there, stiff and stark, lies a corpse in a long box, over which bends the mysterious tenant of the rooms, as white and as motionless as the dead body before him; and just behind them, in the dim obscurity of the inner room, the old man fancies he sees another face, or the reflection of their faces—the sight of which, though faint and shadowy as a dream, thrills through his frame, and for a moment, in speechless horror, stagnates his blood.

"Good God!" says the old man to himself, almost audibly, "am I awake?"

Well might he ask himself the question, and doubt the evidence of his own senses, so strange and unearthly is the character of the scene enacting before his eyes.

Keeping out of sight, he watches.

First of all Faversham applies a match to his gas-stove, which instantly springs into light; then he draws forth from a corner where it has been standing, a large tin bath, and an apparatus which Mr. Toddleboy judges to be an electric battery. Into this bath Faversham lifts the body, and subjects it to several most powerful charges of the battery, but without producing any visible result. Then, stooping down, he introduces an instrument into the mouth and nostrils, and so endeavours to inflate the lungs.

At every fresh effort he pauses to listen attentively for the breath, and to feel the beating of the heart; but the form he would revive is still as pale, and cold, and motionless, as that awful presence hovering in the dim obscurity of the inner room.

But yet the experimentalist is not daunted. He has long studied the subject, as he had studied many others more profound and mysterious. Well does he know that there exists in the great nervous centre for some time after the state which we call death, a hidden and smothered vitality, and that hundreds of people have been restored to life by galvanism and artificial respiration long after the breathing has ceased, or have been rescued from this state of suspended animation by a thrust of the dissecting knife.

Long and anxiously does Faversham watch for his experiment to take effect. At last, applying a cautery to the man's foot, a slight contraction of the muscles follow, and cheered by his success, the operator repeats the same experiment under the right ear, taking care not to injure the jugular vein.

This time the head begins to roll from side to side in a manner indicative to acute sensibility, and then by slow degrees the eyes open, the jaws chatter, and another and still more powerful charge of the battery causes the re-animated murderer, with a piercing shriek, to struggle into a sitting posture, where he remains fixed and glaring horribly at his deliverer.

"He lives! he lives!" cries Faversham, falling on his knees beside the bath. "The first step is taken—the first point gained My labours have not been in vain. Speak, if you can. Speak to me. You are saved from the gallows."

"Saved—from—the—gallows," echoes the resuscitated, in hollow tones.

"It is I who have saved you," cries Faversham, his eyes glittering, and his ghostlike face quivering with the intensity of his excitement. "It is I who have saved you. It is I whom you must serve, faithfully, honestly with body and soul. You're mine alone. Play me false, and the halter which you have escaped, again encircles your throat. You have died by the hangman's hands. You are dead to all the world. For me, and with me alone you shall live. Swear, if you have strength, that you will serve me as I dictate, or even now you shall go back to the state in which you were, and perish miserably. Swear, I say, swear!"

"I swear!" the other answers faintly.

"Louder—louder!" almost shrieks Faversham, seizing the murderer by the hand. "Swear with me and mine, that henceforth you belong entirely to us. Swear by Heaven and Hell —by all the powers of good and evil—by everything holy and damnable—swear."

"I swear!"

Something which seems like a burst of devilish merriment, more shrill, more terrible than the joyless laugh of babbling idiocy, rings through the air, and even startles Mrs. Aker in the distant porter's lodge; and the old man, scarce crediting his senses, sees that the shadowy figure in the inner room takes the form of a woman, with a face of statuesque and awful beauty, though with a serpent-like and malignant expression in its glaring eyes.

This phantom gliding forward to the side of the two men, they all join hands, and, in a whispered chorus, repeat the words—

"We swear!"

"And now," says Faversham, in a whisper so distinct that it fills the room, and is perfectly audible to the attentive listener, "now begins our plot. We must be bold, fearless, resolute, and bloody; without pity for man, woman, or child. Without remorse, without heart, Eleanour, my love and life, you shall be avenged, and the memory of your wrongs shall be drowned in rivers of blood."

Mr. Toddleboy must have fainted at this moment, for he remembers no more of what occurred.

When he comes to himself he is still behind the curtain, sitting on the floor. The lamps are lit without, and the room is pitch dark. He listens for a moment: not a sound is to be heard. Somehow or other he has not the smallest idea how he gets out of the room into the court-yard below, where he tumbles down and swoons again.

"Hold up, there," says somebody, shaking him. "What's the matter?"

Toddleboy stares at the speaker.

"What are you staring at?" continues the individual, who is shaking him, and who, as well as he can understand anything, Toddleboy understands to be a policeman, "you look as though you had just seen a ghost."

"If there are such things," says Mr. Toddleboy in reply, "I should rayther be inclined to say that I had."

THE END OF BOOK THE FIRST.

GAMMON AND SPINNIDGE;

OR,

Charley Wag's Opinions on Things in General.

COMMUNICATED BY CHARLES WAG,

Late of Holloway Jail, and now of Priggington Hall, Burkshire, Esquire.

A COMIC SONG, WRITTEN BY RYMER.

AIR—"*Rancum-crancum Fakey-wakey,*" the celebrated flash Thieves' Song ; also "*Old Bob Ridley.*"

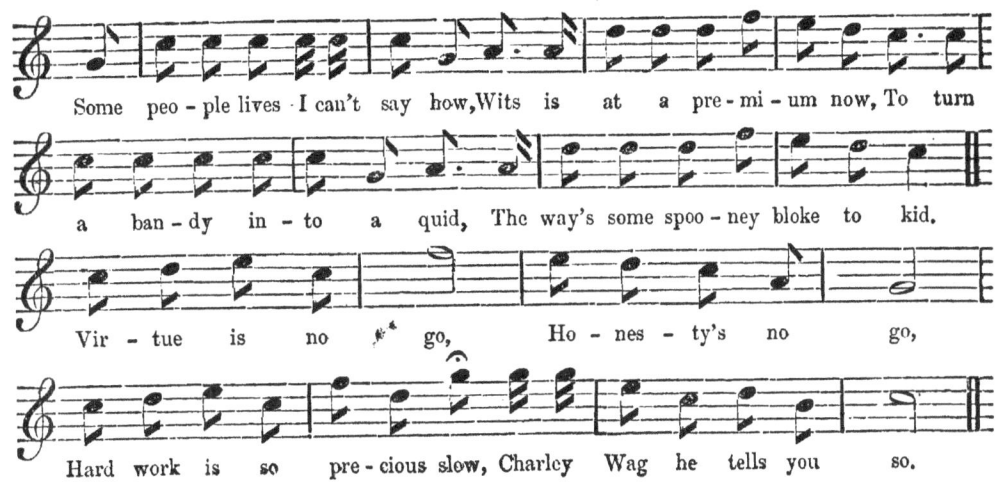

Some peo-ple lives I can't say how, Wits is at a pre-mi-um now, To turn a ban-dy in-to a quid, The way's some spoo-ney bloke to kid. Vir-tue is no go, Ho-nes-ty's no go, Hard work is so pre-cious slow, Charley Wag he tells you so.

CHORUS.

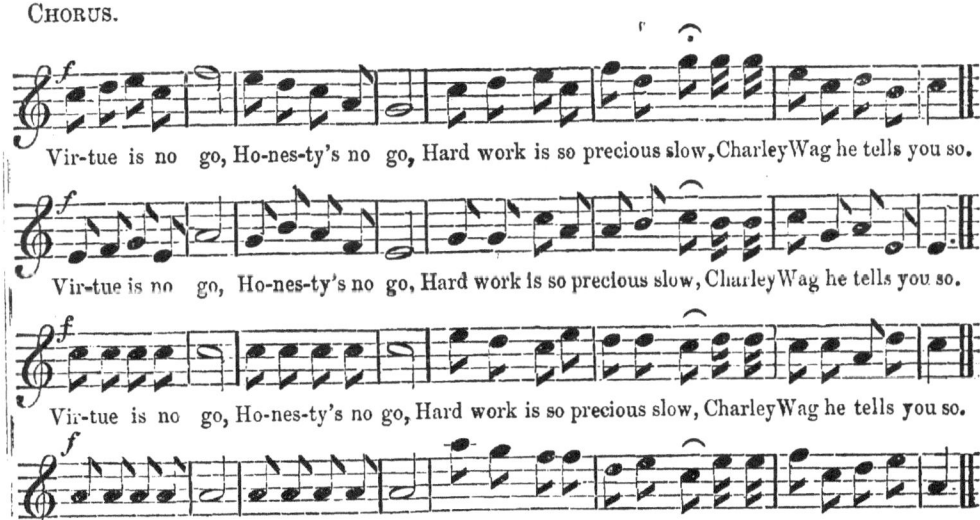

Vir-tue is no go, Ho-nes-ty's no go, Hard work is so precious slow, Charley Wag he tells you so.

Vir-tue is no go, Ho-nes-ty's no go, Hard work is so precious slow, Charley Wag he tells you so.

Vir-tue is no go, Ho-nes-ty's no go, Hard work is so precious slow, Charley Wag he tells you so.

Vir-tue is no go, Ho-nes-ty's no go, Hard work is so precious slow, Charley Wag he tells you so.

Some people lives I can't say how,
Wits is at a premium now ;
To turn a bandy into a quid,
The way's some spooney bloke to kid.
Chorus. — Virtue is no go,
Honesty's no go,
Hardwork is so precious slow,—
Charley Wag he tells you so.

When his Rev'rence patters prayers
D'ye think it's for your soul he cares ?
He lets his pews, and feathers his nest,
And lets the free-seats go and be blest.
Chorus.—At the expense of the parsons.

Mr. Gladstone pops a tax
On all us poor creature's backs ;
He drinks his wine, and don't care a pin
For the extra penny on the poor man's gin.
Chorus.—At the expense of the Chancellor of the Exchequer.

For foring foes need we have fears,
Now we have got our Wollingteers ?
The last Nelson did for his King was to die :
It's the last thing our corpses would like to try.
Chorus.—In favour of the beautiful uniforms (with three cheers for the scare-crows inside of 'em).

From Canada we've heard fine tales
Of his Royal Highness the Prince of Wales,
He's a Wollingteer Colonel's, Young England's star.
I hope he'll be as great a warrior as his Pa !
Chorus—

I'll tell you what surprises me—
Folks won't be what they pretend to be.
If you've been amused just tell me so :
I can't help it if you've not, but I'd like to know.
Chorus —

Given away to each purchaser of No. 6 (Book 2) of "CHARLEY WAG," the New Jack Sheppard. Office—28, Brydges Street, Strand.

BOOK THE SECOND,
THE BOY BURGLAR.

£500.
ANY PERSON
APPREHENDING
CHARLEY WAG
AND TAKING HIM TO
UNITED KINGDOM PRESS
OFFICE
SHALL RECEIVE THE ABOVE

BOOK THE SECOND—THE BOY BURGLAR.

I.—An Imp of Mischief.

"YOU may just say whatever you like ma'am, but what I've got to say, ma'am—and to what I says I sticks—is that no good will never come to that there boy Wag."

"Right you are, Mrs. Higgins, and I am of the same way of thinking myself."

"Of course I am right, ma'am, the mother of a family of twelve, and all reared and thriving except the youngest but three, which, being overlaid as it were permiskus, and smothered like the babies in the wood (or, was it in the Tower?) have a right to express a opinion upon sich a pint."

"And there's no woman I know as has so good right as you have, Mrs. Higgins."

Mrs. Higgins, Mrs. Stiggins, and Mrs. Wiggins, all near neighbours, all living down Slogger's-alley, and all gossiping together instead of getting the good men's teas ready this, Christmas-eve—our young friend Charley Wag being the subject of their conversation.

"There never was such a young scamp," said Mrs. Higgins.

"Such a howdacious young wagabond," added Mrs. Stiggins.

"Such a limb of the old one," put in Mrs. Wiggins, by way of a clencher.

"He's not more than thirteen, is he?"

"I don't know, I am sure. If he was thirty he couldn't go on much worse."

"There really aint a gal in the place that's safe for him. And the encouragement the young hussies give him, they ought to be ashamed of theirselves. Nice bringings up he's had.

"I thought that Miss Williams had teached him reading, and writing, and figuring, and sich like."

"Yes, he's fine enough reader, and writer, and figurer, I daresay, but what is the good of that? Why wasn't he teached a trade? I think she wants to make a gentleman of him, if you ever heerd sich nonsense.

"It's all very fine making gentlemen of people, but you ought have something to put into their pockets when you've finished. I suppose he'll be a clerk somewhere at five shillings a week when he's served half-a-dozen years for nothing."

"Well, whatever they do with him its my opinion he won't come to no good. He's a regular young rip."

"Though, after all, he hasn't got a bad heart, do you think he has? He's as good a boy as you could wish to see when he chooses, and what I like him for is he's so kind to dumb things. Don't you recollect him thrashing that big boy at the coal shed for torturing Miss Adams's cat. I for one was very glad to see the great coward have a pummelling. Then, again, don't you recollect how he beat them boys for taking the halfpence away from the blind man's dog, and give the old man sixpence out of his own pocket to make up for the loss, when he had it gave to him to get his dinner, poor boy? You can't say that was a bad action."

"He's such a mixture," said Mrs. Higgins, impatiently.

"That's what pervokes me. Who'd think to see the young monkey reading his book at the chapel with a face as serious as a judge, that he could be such a young imp as to put a pin in the shepherd's cushion and send him pretty near out of his wits when he sat down upon it? And who'd think, to hear him singing a hymn with old Mrs. Crocker at the grocer's shop, as she says, like an angel, that the moment her back was turned he was going on disgraceful with that fat niece of hers, kissing her and pocketing the raisins?"

"Oh, he is the most deceitful young villain."

"Fighting the boys."

"Running arter the girls."

"In fact he's al'ays in mischief someway or other, and I thank goodness he doesn't belong to me."

This is a terrible character they are giving the young rascal. Don't you think so, gentle reader?

Though after all the Higginses, and Stigginses, and Wigginses can't help owning that he has his good qualities.

He is a mischievous young imp and makes fun of his elders. There's no excuse for him, except that it is what most of us have done, and we ought to be ashamed of ourselves for doing so.

He is pugnacious. Great at punching heads, bunging up eyes, and giving the youth of Slogger's-alley one of those heavy taps upon the nasal organ, which is, I believe, in the language of the prize ring denominated a "smeller."

Add to this, he is a regular rascal where a pretty girl is concerned.

Half-a-dozen times, at least, I have begun a sentence, in which I was going to dress the young gentleman's jacket. I have a small collection of moral remarks upon things in general, all nicely cut and dried, and when I am at a loss to fill up my chapter, I stick one or two in to make my incidents go a little further. You do not blame me, do you? We all have our little tricks. Have we not, brother tradesmen?

I will not, upon this occasion, inflict upon you any of the moral philosophy to which I have referred. I am at a loss to tell what I ought to say about a young fellow who is too general in his love-making. Why are so many of you young ladies so pretty? It is very hard to choose among you. I should feel much obliged if one out of my thousands of fair readers would write and tell me what she thinks of Master Charles's conduct, and I could put her opinion into the next number.

He was a very clever boy, was Charley Wag; and thanks to his foster-mother, who had spared no time or trouble in teaching him, he possessed a very tolerable plain education. You know the old saying, that "Poverty makes us acquainted with strange bedfellows." It makes us also acquainted with strange play-mates. I have before hinted that Slogger's-alley was not the most respectable of localities. There was a mixture there of savage Irish labourers, poor mechanics, roughs and thieves. The very worst society could be found in the neighbourhood.

Who shall wonder if our Charley, a high-spirited, mischief-loving, young scapegrace, fell among the evilly-disposed, and learnt something of their evil ways. I suppose that London streets are a bad school to learn honesty in, though as yet our hero was as honest as the day.

He dearly loved a joke, and for the sake of a joke would often get himself into sad disgrace, as we shall see.

This particular Christmas-eve, about nine o'clock, Mr. Charley Wag, with his hands in his trowsers' pockets, and one of the very finest Pickwick cigars that could be bought for a penny between his lips, walked out of Slogger's-alley and went for a stroll, puffing at his weed with the air of an experienced smoker.

He was about thirteen years and six months old.

He had blue eyes and white teeth, and his hair was parted and pomatumed, and combed and brushed to the highest possible state of perfection.

Perhaps his clothes were a little worn and shabby, and his boots would not have been any the worse of re-soling, but no blacking brush in the world could have put a finer polish on them. Then, again, his neck-pin might only have cost twopence, but I should very much like to see a diamond that would shine like it did. By the green mark which it left upon his finger, I take it that his ring was not solid gold, but it was truly magnificent, and was admirably set off by his pretty hand; he had pretty hands by the way, and kept them washed, which is a fine plan, I may tell you, to keep them white, and better than all the chemical preparations prescribed for the red fisted readers, by the editors of the *London Journal* and *Family Herald.*

Besides, he did not wear his nails too long, nor bite them.

He was, altogether, a dandified little chap, and one whom I could excuse that susceptible young creature, Mrs. Croker's fat niece, for falling in love with.

Turning the corner of Slogger's-alley, and puffing, as I have described, at his cigar, who should Mr. Wag encounter but his friend Sam Higgins—two years his senior, gawkey and tall, and affecting a tail coat and stickups.

"Hallo, Charley!" said Sam Higgins, "where are you a-goin' to?"

"I'm taking the air, Mister Higgins," said Mr. Wag, rather distantly.

"Can I take it along 'er you?" asked Mr. Higgins, humbly.

"There is no particular objection to that, that I am aware of," replied Mr. Wag, "providing you conduct yourself like a gentleman. Do you think you can?"

"I'll try to."

"You'll try, will you. Why, good heavens!"

"What is it, Mr. Wag?"

"What is it? why—what's the matter with your head? You're all goss."

"Well, you see, sir," replied Mr. Higgins,

apologetically, "Mother would make me do it. It's a new hat."

"A hat you call it," said Mr. Wag, disdainfully, eyeing over Samuel Higgins's beaver, which quite covered that young gentleman's large ears, and rested on his coat-collar behind. "A hat; eh! I thought it was a band-box. They've left you room to grow in, any how. You don't smoke, I believe?"

"Not without being sick, sir."

"So I should think, Sam. You're an awful muff."

"I'm not so up to things as you are."

"No; I should say you weren't. There, don't sprawl those legs of yours about quite so much. You haven't got another hat at home, I suppose?"

"I've only got a cap; but it's a very old one."

"Then it can't be helped. Take my arm; and we'll go for a ramble."

So Mr. Higgins, who was at least a head and shoulders taller than his friend, made great efforts to do as he was directed, and to accommodate his shambling gate with Mr. Wag's fashionable lounge.

II.—A REGULAR CASE OF "KID."

"I tell you what it is, Mr. Higgins," said Charley Wag, when he had finished his cigar, and standing with his legs a-straddle at a street corner, surveyed the moon as complacently as though he hired it to shine, and was satisfied with its performance, "I feel rather dry. Shall we liquor?"

"Have something to drink?"

"Yes; what's your particular tipple?"

"Pershing sherbet—only I like it best dry, in a paper, to dip your finger in and suck it."

"You're a nice sort of fellow—at your age too; any one would think you were a girl. I shall stand you some shrub."

"Thank you, sir."

Adjourning to a neighbouring public-house, Mr. Wag gave his orders.

"Three-ha'porth of shrub for this young gentleman," says he; "and have the goodness, my dear, to give me half-a-quartern of rum, in the measure, if you please."

"By having it in the measure, young man," Mr. Wag imparted in confidence to his companion, "you get your whack. I always do."

Mr. Higgins profoundly impressed, took a gulph at his shrub, and choked himself.

Then Mr. Wag having finished his liquor, and amused himself by breaking to pieces a leaden tea-spoon lying on the counter, and surreptitiously filling an old gentleman's tumbler of grog with the fragments, pulled his friend by the sleeve, and suggested that they should "slope."

Sloping accordingly, they found themselves in the street, when Mr. Wag, reaching up as high as he could, slapped his friend on the shoulder, and said that he felt "on for a lark."

"So do I," said Mr. Higgins, upon whom the mild refection he had been partaking of seemed to have taken a great deal more effect than the half-quartern of raw spirit had upon his precocious companion. "What's your game?"

"What do you say to taking those play-bill

boards ?" said Mr. Wag, pointing to some standing in front of a shop, " and hanging them on the railings of old Oyley Swab's chapel."

" That's my sort," cried Mr. Higgins, in ecstacy. " But what shall we get done to, if we're nobbled ?"

" Leave that to me, Samuel. I believe I am up to a move or two."

" That you are, Mr. Wag, if ever anybody was."

" Then catch hold of the boards."

Mr. Higgins, imagining this conceit to be excessively droll, lent a willing hand, and they both loaded themselves with the stolen property.

At the street corner Mr. Wag, marching forward with the utmost confidence, and whistling an air from the last opera, ran against a policeman with such violence that the shock quite knocked the officer " out of time."

" Where are you going with them boards, young fellow ?"

" Going home, sir."

" Where's home ?"

" Round the corner."

" Round which corner ?"

" The other one, sir ; in the next street but two."

" Very well then, I'll see you leave them."

" Thank you, sir, it's very kind of you," said Mr. Wag, walking forward as bold as brass, " I'll show you the way."

But at this point Samuel Higgins, taking sudden fright, dropped his load, turned round, and, as the vulgar have it, " mizzled."

" I'll warm him for this," thought Charley, looking savagely after his friend. Then, turning round to the policeman, in a pitiful tone, like one who is much injured, said—

" See what you've done now."

" What do you mean ?"

" Don't you see, you've frightened my poor brother Bill out of his wits. He's simple-like, you know, and what's to become of these boards ? Who's a going to carry them ? you won't, I suppose."

" Don't you try to gammon me," said the policeman.

" Gammon you, sir ;" cried Mr. Wag, in tears, " I hope you don't think so badly of me. Indeed, and indeed, what I am telling you is correct. We were carrying them home ; and only last Tuesday week my poor dear mother says to my poor dear brother, 'Thomas,' says she "—

" I thought it was Bill ?"

" That's the younger one, sir. There's eight of us."

" Well, cut it short, then."

" Would you mind, sir, catching hold of one or two. We haven't far to go, and when we get to the house you'll see I'm an honest boy. Do please carry some, sir ; and come and see with your own eyes that I haven't been deceiving you."

Very indignant, and more than half believing that he was being " kidded " by the audacious young jackanapes, but at the same time rendered a little doubtful by the boy's earnest manner, whether there might not be some truth in his story ; and thinking that in any case the boy's friends might tip him to let Charley go if it was

all a lark, he decided upon helping him ; and well loaded by Mr. Wag, they set off together to the next street but two.

The next street but two was a precious long way off, and the policeman growing redder and redder in the face asked, out of breath and with aching fingers, " When they were likely to arrive."

" Here we are, sir ;" said Mr. Wag, stopping immediately in front of a house. " Would you be so good as to ring the top bell, sir, and ask for Mr. Smith."

" Ring it yourself," said the policeman.

So Mr. Wag rang it.

" Does Mr. Smith live here ?"

" No."

" But this is No. 7," reasoned Charley, " I suppose it was 17."

With Job-like patience the policeman, who was a raw young man from the country, and had just joined the force, accompanied him to No. 17, where they inquired with a similar result.

" I'ts twenty-seven," said Mr. Wag, " I know there's a seven in it."

But it happened that there were but twenty-four houses in the street.

Upon this discovery the policeman put down his boards and took Charley by the collar.

" You know very well, you young vagabond," said he, " you're only having a lark with me. I shall take the lot of you into custody."

" What lot ?"

" You and the boards. Come on."

" No ; but I say Mr. Policeman," said Charley, in a confidential and persuasive tone, " Suppose it was a lark. My brother who ran away put me up to it. I'm very well connected, and it would break my mamma's heart if she knew I had been disgracing myself. So please let me off, and I'll give you half a sovereign."

" It won't do, I tell you. You were going to steal them, and I shan't take your money."

" No, but look here," persisted Mr. Wag, " what's the good of taking me into custody ? Why not have the half sovereign, nobody will know anything about it ? "

" Well, anyhow, half a sovereign is too little, I can't neglect my duty at the price."

" I've got a sovereign in my pocket," said Mr. Wag, who had not a half-penny, " but mamma gave it me to buy a shilling's worth of almonds and raisins, for to-morrow's dinner."

" Give it to me, then, and say you lost it."

" No, I can't do that, because I shall get scolded ; but if I buy the shilling's worth of raisins, I'll tell you what I can do."

" What ? "

" Why, give you the nineteen shillings and persuade mamma that she only gave me a bob."

" Very well, only none of your larks."

" You don't think I should act dishonourable, do you ?"

" What's to be done with the boards ; we'd better take them back, hadn't we—it's not far off ?"

" Blow the boards," said the policeman, indignantly, " I've had quite enough of 'em.

" Come along, then, and we'll change the sovereign."

Accompanying Mr. Wag in the most innocent manner possible, like a lamb to the slaughterhouse, the policeman came under his young friend's guidance to the identical shop from which the boards had been stolen.

"They don't sell almonds and raisins there," said the policeman, "it's a pastry-cooks."

"Don't they," said Mr. Wag, "you'll see."

So saying he entered the shop.

A dispute was going on inside.

"I tell you I saw them carrying them," said one person.

"So did I, and it was two boys."

"What's the good of you talking; it was a boy and policeman. Do you think I'm blind?"

"Pack of nonsense. Is it likely that a policeman would steal play-bill boards?"

"I don't know what is likely and what isn't likely. I know I saw him, and I said to myself says I, here's a queer start, what's he up to with those boards? Where's he got 'em from, I wonder? P'r'aps they're Mr. Lollipop's, and round I came to see, and sure enough they were."

"Why didn't you stop them then?"

"How you talk. How could I stop them before I knew they were stolen?"

At this moment Mr. Wag interposed, "If you please, sir, there's a policeman been stealing your play-bills."

"Where is he?" cried Mr. Lollipop and his two friends, in a breath.

"Outside the shop. Look, he's taking some more."

Sure enough the officer was in rather a suspicious attitude, for he did not wish to be seen by the people in the shop, and had taken up a board and was covering his face with it.

Without another word Mr. Lollipop took a spring and a run, and got the policeman by the collar.

"What's up now?" cried the astonished officer.

"Oh you villain—oh you vagabond; you wolf in sheep's clothing. This is what we pay taxes for, is it? Come along to the inspector."

"Leave go, are you mad?"

"Not exactly."

"What have I been doing?"

"Stealing our boards."

"Me?"

"Yes, you," put in Mr. Wag, "didn't you ask me to carry some for you? You know you did, and you know where you have hid them round the corner in the next street."

"Oh, you awful young blackguard," cried the policeman, "you hid them yourself and offered to bribe me with a sovereign."

"Me bribe you with a sovereign. A poor boy like me to bribe him with a sovereign. Listen to him, gentlemen."

"Where has he put the boards, my boy?" said Mr. Lollipop.

"Round the corner, sir, I'll show you."

"You shall, presently, in the meantime somebody run for another policeman."

"I'll run sir," said Mr. Wag.

"Very well."

"Don't let him go," cried the officer struggling, "don't be such fools."

But it was too late, for, skipping through the crowd, Mr. Wag took to his heels, and never paused until he could run no farther, owing to his having ran right into a man's arms, who immediately seized him by the throat and penned him up against a wall.

"What are you in such a hurry about?" said his captor.

———

III.—WHO STOLE THE GOOSE.

THE person who had thus seized and held prisoner our youthful hero was a stalwart ruffian, dressed in a fur cap, velveteen coat, and fustian trowsers, with a flaming yellow belcher knotted loosely round his neck.

"What have you been up to—you young prig? Faking a cly,* I guess. Come; half of the swag, and I'll let you go, easy."

"I've been doing nothing," shouted the boy, struggling. "Leave go of me; can't you."

"Oh; you're a sperrity young blade, I dessay," replied the man, tightening his grasp. "Look at me, you young warmint; don't you know your best friend?"

Thus addressed the boy looked into the man's face, which in his fright he had not previously observed, and recognising him, ceased struggling.

"It's you, is it, Mr. Rattan?"

"Ah! it's me, sure enough; now, what have you been up to this time, my young prig? Lifting† something, I suppose—"

"No—I haven't. At least, I didn't mean to steal it. It was all a lark."

"Just for fun; eh? Well; let's have a look at it."

"I haven't got them, here. They were play-bill boards."

"Play-bill boards? why what the blazes were you prigging them for? I was in hopes it was a ticker. Tell us all about it."

Then Charley narrated his adventures, and Mr. Rattan laughed heartily at the recital.

"You'd be a pride to anybody, if you only had the training," cried Mr. Rattan. "You're the right sort all over: I'm damned if you aint. Come inside and have a drop of some thing."

Thus invited, Charley accompanied his friend into a tavern, and was soon doing his best, as he termed it, to "make a hole" in a pot of porter.

"Take another swig," said Rattan, when the boy at last desisted through want of breath." "You aint half a drinker."

"Pretty tidy, I think, for my size," retorted Charley.

"You're a rum un, you are, and no mistake," said Mr. Rattan, enthusiastically, "with your face and figure, and the hedication youv'e had, you ought to make a fortune."

"So I shall, I dare say."

"What at, I should like to know?"

"I haven't the least idea."

"Then, I can tell you." And Rattan, patting the boy upon the head. "You didn't have this knowledge-box give you for nothink. You're a precious sight sharper than any lad of twice your age I ever came across or heer'd on.

———

* Stealing a handkerchief.   † Stealing.

You're a deuced sight too sharp, that's what you are; and what's the good of having your wits, if you can't live by them? One half of the world is fools, and the other half, as has the wits, ought to live on 'em; that's my opinion, Now, you know all about it. If you want to live like a gentleman, and keep your fingers clean, I'll put you on to the caper for doing it. What do you say?"

"What do you want me to do?"

"Do what I've told you a hundred times—turn prig."

"Be a thief."

"Ah if you like the word better, why shouldn't you?"

"But thieves never grow rich; you're not rich, are you?"

"I shouldn't have done much better if I'd been honest."

"But then you may be sent to prison."

"If I'm nabbed. But us old birds aint caught with chaff, you know. Prison, indeed, as if one out of a hundred got there, and as for not being rich, you're very much mistook. I've made as much money before now in five lucky minutes as you would make in fifty years of hum-drum honesty. I'm out of luck at present. What of that? It won't last for ever. I'll be bound that before next year's over, I'll be back in my old place again, at the top of the tree.

"But then I might be an unlucky one," said Charley, "and get caught at the first offence, and put in prison for the rest of my life.

"Rest of your fiddlestick. You'd get a very little for the first offence, and when you were out again, you would be a little more careful.

"But you can never persuade me it's a paying trade."

"If you like always to persist in your own stupidity, of course I can't," said Rattan, plunging his nose into the pewter pot.

"Confound him!" muttered the ruffian to himself, "I'll force him to it, there's no persuading him."

While he was thus reflecting the public-house door was flung open, and a fussy little gentleman, very bald, grey, and fat, though at the outside not more than forty, came bustling in, pulling off a huge white worsted comforter and an immense pair of woollen gloves.

"How are you, Potts?" asked the new comer, "How are you, Potts? I hope you find yourself pretty comfortable by this time, Potts; and how's the missus? You see I am as good as my word, am I not?"

"I'm sure it's very kind of you, Mr. Larkins," said the landlady, offering the fussy gentleman her pretty little fat hand to shake. "You always was as good as your word, I never found you no different."

"That's right, Mrs. Potts, I'm proud to have your good opinion," said Mr. Larkins, for it was no other than our old friend the medical student, now gone into practice on his own account, and driving a roaring trade in a nice unhealthy neighbourhood.

"I hope I shall always deserve it, ma'am," he continued. "Has the drawing begun, and is Jobson come?"

"Yes to both the questions," said the landlord. "We expected you'd be here before."

"So I should, only I had to go to a couple of lyings-in and a splintered shoulder-bone, which made me a little late; besides, you know I live at the other end of London, and I've got so much to do."

"I'm very happy to hear it," said the landlord. "Mr. Jobson will be glad to see you, I'm sure. We've had such a spree just now: he brought a box of leeches with him in his pocket, and they broke loose, and got hold of some of the ladies. Such squealing as never you heard in your born days."

"Well, I hope they haven't got hold of any of the gooses."

"No, they haven't done that. This 'ere is the crack prize; have you seen it?"

"No! what a beauty."

It was a beauty, and no mistake, decorated with coloured ribbons. Rattan walked up to look at it, and licked his lips.

"That's a fine bird," said he. "Is there a goose club on to-night?"

"Yes," said Mr. Potts, "there is; this is one of the prizes. This and a bottle of rum's worth winning, aint they?"

"You're right there, governor," said Rattan, with a sigh. "I wish they was mine."

He took a seat and lighted his pipe, puffing away for some minutes in silence. Then he said—

"Charley, I'm going to have that goose."

"How? You can't if you don't win it."

"Can't I. You shall take it for me."

"I! I'm sure I shan't."

"Why not?"

"Because I won't steal for you or anybody."

"Steal be bothered. "Didn't you steal them boards just now?"

"But that was only a lark."

"Ah! a gallus fine lark, as you'll find before you've done, if you don't look out. La k, indeed! why this is twice the lark."

"How so?"

"Because, don't you see, every body will be standing sam to everybody, and then all of a second, when I give you the office, you ketch hold of the bird and the bottle, and slope like winkin', while I tumble over in front of the door and cover your retreat."

"It would be rather fun."

"I should think so," cried Rattan. "To see them all with their mouths open, and the awful sell it would be for the chap as it was took from. My eye, I never heerd of sich a spree.

"But then it would be stealing."

"Not it. It would be only a lark, like the play-bill boards; and think how we should crack our sides as we was a eating of it for supper."

"No, Mr. Rattan, I don't agree with you, and I shan't do it."

"Well, I'll tell you what, if you're so beastly squeamish about it, and as I only want to do it for a lark, I'll give you my word of honour as a gentleman that I'll bring the things back again when the joke's over. Lord love you, I only want to do it for the spree of the thing. Is it likely that me as never does nothing under a firt-class crack* would go demeaning myself over such trumpery, if it wasn't for the fun?"

---

* Burglary.

"Well, I don't like it."

"Come, now," said Rattan, a little angrily, "no more of this rot or I shall cut up rough. If you won't do it, by gosh! I'll take you back to that there shop where you took the boards and tell 'em all about it."

The boy's eyes flashed fire at the others words, and he was about to make some indignant remark, when he reflected that perhaps it would be very unwise to quarrel with the unprincipled scroundrel into whose clutches fate had thrown him, and so he resolved to do what was asked of him this once, and in future to studiously avoid the tempter's company.

Heigho! It is only the first step that requires so much persuasion, after that all is plain sailing.

While he was turning it over in his mind, Mr. Larkins came bustling back from the club-room, where he had, a few minutes previously, retired, and cried out at the top of his voice, "Who do you think's won it, Potts? I say, Potts, who do you think is the lucky man?"

"Jobson."

"Jobson it is. He's got the big goose. Mine is the size of a chicken."

"Well I never," said the landlady, "I never knew anyone so lucky. This is his third year running."

"Give us hold of it," said Larkins, "and let me take it in. It is a stunner, upon my word. It's pretty near a hundred weight. Give me the rum, too."

Taking the delicacies into the club-room, Mr. Larkins was hailed with a great shout, and everybody crowded round the table to admire the bird and congratulate Mr. Jobson upon his extraordinary good luck.

"What a beauty!"

"Look at its legs!"

"It's larger than a turkey!"

"It is as big as a sheep!"

"Aint it stuffed?"

"Is it real?"

Such were the exclamations the splendid sight elicited.

Mr. Jobson, very solemn and consequential, stood with his arms folded admiring it.

"Please to keep your fingers off," said he, "it's not a pig at the Cattle Show, you know, and I've got to eat it. Do you hear what I say, Mr. Larkins? I'd thank you not to pinch it any more, you'll only make it tough."

"All right, cocky," said Mr. Larkins, "no offence, I hope."

"None at present."

"Then what'll you stand?"

"Ah! what's he going to stand, glasses round?"

"I'm not aware," began Mr. Jobson, "that it is the custom."

"Oh, yes! you are. Here, Mr. Potts, twenty sixes of hot gin."

During the confusion which ensued—consequent upon Mr. Jobson refusing to pay for the liquor, and at length giving way and pulling out his money with a very bad grace—Rattan tugged Charley by the arm.

"Now's your time," said he, and "if you don't, by God you'll know the consequences."

"You'll cover me, will you?"

"Safe as a bank."

"And you'll bring them back?"

"Yes."

"Where shall I run to?"

"To the Cockle-shell, down the steps by Hungerford-bridge—you know it—I'll meet you there. Now go it."

Without more ado, Charley slipped in between Mr. Jobson and the table, laid hold of the goose and the bottle of rum, made a but at Mr. Jobson's stomach, which doubled him up and knocked him over, and sprang out of the room through the bar into the street.

"Stop thief!" roared fifty voices simultaneously.

IV.—Stop Thief.—The Lady and the Ruffian.—The Murderous Threat.

"STOP thief! Stop thief!"

Fifty more voices caught up the cry, and shouted with the united strength of fifty pairs of lungs.

That vagabond Rattan had not kept his promise, or in the slightest degree endeavoured to arrest the progress of the pursuers.

"Let him get away if he can," the blackguard had said to himself. "If he does get away, I'll have the prog, and if he don't, he'll get locked up, and once having been in quod, it'll be all up with his honesty. There's nothing does for virtue like a taste of stone walls. In any case, he'll be in my power; I shan't get myself into a mess to help him. It aint likely."

So instead, he joined the boy's pursuers, and bawled louder than anybody.

"Stop thief! stop thief!"

"Stop him—knock him down—trip him up —get in front of him. That's it, go it butcher, you'll cop him—a little faster—catch hold of his collar. Yah! butter fingers!"

On went the thief, and after him came the mob, bellowing and shouting.

Several times people dodged in the way, and as often did master Charley dodge them in his turn and escape.

Running through Covent Garden-market and into the Strand, though his pursuers were close behind, he still managed to keep a head of them.

Could he hold out much longer?

Several times he had more than half a mind to drop the goose and throw the bottle in the face of the foremost of the troop. Perhaps then they would let him escape. But this was very uncertain, too.

When he thought what a degradation and disgrace it would be to be brought back ignominiously after all this running, he redoubled his efforts.

But his strength began to fail him. He could not hold out for ever. His only chance lay in the hope that he might be able to get out of sight somewhere, and let them pass him.

Ah, a happy thought.

The dark arches!

He was now in the Strand, rushing across the road suddenly, under horses' heads and before galloping omnibuses, he ran down Durham-street and plunged into the gaping aperture.

He was well acquainted with the locality, and soon found a hiding-place, from whence he watched each of his pursuers who ventured into the darkness after him, go running headlong past the spot.

He was saved.

He listened.

Yes, he was alone.

They were soon gone, and he was safe; but for some time he sat panting with his exertion, and too wearied to move a step. When he had somewhat recovered from his fatigue he took up the cause of all his trouble and journeyed onwards.

Keeping among the labyrinth of courts, and lanes, and alleys which lie along the river's bank, he worked his way round to the foot of Hungerford Suspension-bridge, and took the goose and gin into the public-house where Rattan had directed that he should meet him.

Charley was aware that the man was very well known at this hostelry, and so he handed over the goose and the bottle to the landlord, saying that Rattan would shortly call for it; and thinking it wisest to get out of the vagabond's way, hastily ascended the stone steps leading to the market above, intending to make the best of his way home.

In a dark turn of the stairs he heard voices approaching, and recognised that of Rattan.

He was afraid to turn back, lest the man should recognize him as he came out at the bottom of the flight in the gaslight. The same fear prevented him him from going any further up.

The only way to escape notice was to crouch in the shade, and allow Rattan to pass. This he determined to do.

Drawing himself up into a corner, and covering his face with his hand, he waited.

The voices drew nearer.

"Surely," said some voice, which was a woman's, and by the pureness of her accent, evidently a lady's, "this is far enough removed from observation. Where are you taking me? Does this lead to the river?"

"No. I only want to take you a little lower down," said Rattan. "I have already told you my reasons for objecting to the glare of the gaslight. Come along, ma'am, you're quite safe with me."

"I am not afraid," replied the lady, haughtily. "Lead on."

Wondering what business Rattan could possibly have with his fair companion, the boy looked anxiously after them when they had passed him by unobserved.

The rustle of the lady's dress, and a delicious odour of Jockey Club scent, told him that she must be richly attired, although it was too dark to see what she wore.

"He is going to rob her," thought Charley, "I'll follow them and see, perhaps I may be of some service."

Cautiously descending the steps, and taking care to keep well out of sight, he crept along under the shadow of the bridge and managed to get close enough to hear what they said, without being perceived by either of the couple.

"You said it did not lead to the river," were

the first words he heard. "What bridge is that—where have you brought me?"

"That's the iron-bridge above. Do you know the spot?"

"Yes—yes—that is, no," the woman said in an agitated voice. "How should I know it?"

"How! only by having been here before, I suppose, and you have."

"I never have. What do you mean?"

"I mean I'm not such a fool as I look. How do you think I found you out?"

"I neither know nor care."

"Well, I'll tell you, anyways. I found you out through Mr. Leech."

"Indeed!"

"He got me through the last time I was in trouble. That's how I come to be know'd by him. Quite by accident I heer'd as he was the person as paid Miss Williams for the child's keep. When I called upon him, I axed for your address. He wouldn't have given it me if if he had know'd it. But, by some rum chance you came in while we was a talking. He didn't say it was you, but I seed directly by the look of his mug who it was. He had sent his boy out to follow you several times, but the warmint somehow had always missed you, howsomdever, this journey I did the detective dodge on my own account, and a nice dance you led me."

"What was your object in taking all this trouble?" asked the lady coldly"

"The object!" replied Rattan, with a short laugh, "just try and recollect, my lady, if you never was in this 'ere pretty place before."

"I have told you," said the lady, in an agitated voice, "I never have."

"It's reyther lonely, aint it; the sort of place as a party could put another party out of the way in, without much fear of interruption, supposing they felt so inclined."

It was lonely enough; the door of the Cockleshell public-house was closed, and, excepting a faint glimmer through the fanlight, no sign of life was to be seen, the echo of a distant footstep in the market above grew fainter as the owner of it wended towards the Strand; the bridge, the quays, the surrounding streets, and the gloomy river, were silent as death.

It seemed the place of all others suited for the commission of a horrible crime, for there was no fear of interruption and little chance of the presence of a witness.

The boy crept closer under the shadow of the bridge, and, trembling in every limb, listened eagerly to the conversation.

Presently the lady continued, as it seemed to Charley in a faltering voice—

"What occasion was there to choose so lonely a spot for our interview?"

"I'll tell you," replied the ruffian, in a whisper full of sinister significance, "Well, I want money."

"I supposed that that was your object."

"You suppose right, I said as much, in fact, in my bit of a letter; you brought the blunt I suppose."

"No."

"Why not?"

"Because I thought it safest not to do so"

CHARLEY TO THE RESCUE!

"You could'nt trust me, then?"

"I did not wish to. Besides, I had not made my .terms"

"Begad! you're a knowing one. What do you propose?"

"I propose that you should keep your promise with respect to this—this boy. Have you made a thief of him?"

"Yes!"

"Yes! When was it? Where is he? In custody?"

"To the best of my belief he is."

"When did it occur?"

"Only to night. An hour or so ago."

They were both speaking in a low tone of voice, but the night was so still and the air so clear and resonant that, although at the distance of ten or perhaps fifteen yards, the boy could hear every word that was uttered.

Amazed and confounded by what he did hear, he still listened, eager to learn more.

"If I find that what you tell me is true," the lady continued, "I shall send you twenty pounds to-morrow."

"Only twenty?"

"How much more would you have?"

"Look here," said Rattan, after a brief pause, "let us understand one another. I am not a cove to be played with. · I expected that you would have brought some money to-night. I counted on it, and you have put me off. I'm not a man as stands such disappointments."

He advanced a step nearer to her as he spoke. They stood upon a sort of stone jetty projecting into the water, upon the very place, indeed, from which a woman flung her child one night in the beginning of this history.

The spot was lonely, silent, and deserted. The faint ripple of the black and sluggish water at their feet was the only sound they heard.

"It's quiet enough and dark enough here," the man said in a fierce whisper. "If I thought you was playing me false—by God—"

Again he advanced a step nearer towards the lady, who, receding before him, drew consequently closer to the edge of the jetty.

"Do you threaten me?" she said.

"Yes! Why not?" replied Rattan. "What should prevent me even now taking your life?"

"Your interest would prevent you, I should think."

"Not it. Suppose I am sick of the job. You have money about you I feel confident. Why should I not take it, and throw your body into the water? Nobody would be the wiser."

"It would be a fool's trick," the woman said, in what she intended to be in firm and determined tones, but not without a certain tremor in her voice. "It would be more to your interest to let me live."

"Why so?"

"That you might make more out of me."

Rattan was far too shrewd and calculating a scoundrel not to perfectly agree with her, but at the same time he wanted to inspire her with fear, and, if possible, to pass for even a greater ruffian than he really was. He therefore stepped forward again with a threatening gesture, and in retreating to avoid him, the lady slipped her foot upon the slippery stonework, and before he could spread out a hand to save her, fell backwards into the river.

———

V.—CHARLEY TO THE RESCUE—A PERILOUS POSITION 'TWIXT LIFE AND DEATH.

IT was high tide, and round the jetty the water was deep. The lady sank to the bottom, and when she rose again to the surface, after a few minutes interval, it was at more than ten yards distance.

Now Rattan could swim no better than a stone. He was, besides, an arrant coward, like most brutal bulliers of women, and would as soon have thought of jumping into a cauldron of boiling lead as into the cold river after the drowning lady.

Drowning was she most certainly, and as she sank and rose again with a faint cry for help, she was at least another ten yards distant.

"I can't help her," the ruffian cried aloud, stamping his foot and uttering a loud and savage imprecation, "Curses light up the infernal place. Who the blazes ever knowed anything so provoking? As good as an income gone at once, and not a blessed mag got by it. It's all over—nobody's here to help her, and no one will hear her cry, which, 'ecod, it's as well, p'r'aps, if they dont, or they might think it was me as done it."

And thinking that, perhaps, it would be as well, under the circumstances, were he to place a more respectable distance between himself and the scene of the accident, he turned round, intending to beat a retreat.

But, at the same moment, Charley, who hitherto had remained in his place of concealment, half paralized with horror, recovered his presence of mind, and rapidly tearing off his coat and waistcoat, flung them on one side, and, with a wild and piercing cry for help, pushed past the frightened Rattan, nigh upsetting him in his eager, headlong course, and plunged into the water.

Rattan, staggering for a moment from the violence of the collision, and saving himself by a miracle upon the extreme edge of the parapet, turned round and took to his heels like a hunted hare.

So sudden and unexpected was Charley's appearance, and so rapid his disappearance again in the Thames, that the man did not recognise him, but fancying that there might be lots more where the lad came from, and that if caught he (Mr. Rattan) might get into hot water instead of cold, he made off as fast as he could go.

While the skulking vagabond made the best use of his legs in one direction, Charley was making the best of his in another, and at the same time bringing his arms into play, swam like a fish towards the spot where he had last seen the lady go down.

He was an excellent swimmer, having, like many other street boys, acquired the art in a vagabond and illegal fashion by bathing in the river between Vauxhall and Chelsea.

But the night was intensely cold, the snow lay upon the ground; and as the lad struggled onwards through the icy waters—the dreadful thought that he might be seized with cramp and perish unnoticed, and without help, made him redouble his efforts.

Looking a-head as he swam on, he saw her again.

For the third time she rose to the surface. Her white face gleamed in the moonlight.

She was not more than five yards distant.

There was still hope. Yet another effort!

She made no cry, but waved her arms despairingly. Then, again, she sank.

But at the same time he dived, and the next moment had hold of her. Although so young, he was very strong for his age, and being an expert swimmer, managed at the same time that he made rapid progress towards the shore, to keep his companion's head above water.

When the lady had fallen into the river, she had floated with the tide towards Westminster; and now in returning to the landing-place from which she had fallen, the boy was making the best of his way underneath the bridge.

It was just as he came out from under the arch that his forebodings were realized.

He was seized with the cramp.

An intensely acute and agonising pain seized his legs, depriving him of all power of motion; and, like a stone, he sank to the bottom. But the intensity of the pain caused him to retain his hold of the lady's garments, and as he rose again to the surface, his fingers were still tightly clasped upon the breast of the rich velvet mantle by which he had supported her.

With that promptitude and presence of mind which, in the varied and critical situations of his eventful life, never by any chance deserted him, he cast about rapidly for some means of saving himself and his fair charge.

Although his lower extremities were paralysed he yet retained some power in his arms, and clutching at the stone-work of the bridge, managed to support himself for a moment, and resist the strength of the tide.

Just over his head, jammed between the stones of the second arch from the Middlesex side, there was an iron spike. The reader, passing at high-tide, has probably noticed it, and may have wondered how it came there, and for what purpose it was used; but though I have made inquiries of several watermen, I have been unable to learn anything respecting it, and its origin is enveloped in the same obscurity as the stone with the classical inscription referring to Bill Stump's mark, which the great Mr. Pickwick discovered.

This spike was about a yard above the boy's head, and making a tremendous effort, he managed to lay hold of it with one arm, at the same time retaining his hold of the lady with the other.

But the strain upon his wrist, and the pain in his legs, were fearful; and he felt that it could only be a few moments that he could keep up.

Breathless was he with his exertions; he could scarcely get his breath, he was so exhausted: but his only hope of escape lay in his lungs, and with the energy of desperation he shouted for help—

"Help! help! help!"

The boy's piercing cry rang through the still air, and was distinctly audible in the market above.

Plethoric fishmongers, heavy in their first sleep, woke up and listened a moment, then turned over again, covered up their heads, and snored louder than ever.

"Help! help!"

Hardy amateur vocalists coughing the preparatory cough necessary to their performance, paused disconcerted in the act, while the audience, eager to delay or deter them altogether, as it is the nature of the amateur's audience to do, asked one another what the sound meant, and kept on wondering a good quarter of an hour afterwards.

Some who heard it said, "Holiday people."

Others said, "Keeping it up."

And others, "Drunk again."

The impression left upon some sturdy Britons minds was, that it was "somebody wolloping a woman;" but as the woman was not their property, and out of a play people don't risk their neck to rescue suffering virtue, they took no particular notice, but went on with their pipes, or comic songs, or skittles, without giving the matter another thought.

"Help! help!"

Great heaven! can it be possible that no one will come to the rescue? When his poor arm is tired out, and his fingers relax in their hold, will he drop off quietly like a moth drops into a candle, and the black waters of London's river swallow him up like a dead dog or cat?

"Help! help!"

Even now his arm grew weak and powerless, and the agonies of the cramp were so intense, that he ground his teeth and groaned aloud.

Had he relinquished his hold upon the woman, there might yet have been a chance for him; but such an act never entered the mind of the courageous boy; and had it done, he would have at once rejected it with scorn and indignation.

No, while he was able—while he had himself life remaining, he would preserve hers.

"Oh, God, give me strength," he prayed between his intervals of shouting, "Oh, God, send some one to my aid."

"Help! help!"

More shrill—more piercing—more desperate than before, and no one comes.

He cannot hold by his fingers any longer. One enormous effort he must make to get his arm over the spike, and so support himself. With his last remaining strength he makes a spring upward to gain the desired position. The weight of his body and the lady's are too much for the rusty iron.

It bends slowly—and breaks.

In wild despair he yells again—

"Help! help!"

And sinks.

  * * * * *

Thank God, this last appeal is answered. The sound of hurrying footsteps come towards the landing-place. At the same time the sound of oars smote on the boy's ear, as the water closes over him.

He sinks, but rises again without relinquishing his hold. He battles with a lion's heart against the icy monster which is chilling his lifes' blood.

Quick! quick! boatmen! or you will be too late.

A second time he sinks; beware of the fatal third. But no; they are here! They have pulled him and his fair companion into the boat, and row them quickly to the shore.

The shore is now alive with faces. At least fifty people are congregated round the landing-place, and still more come racing down the steps and down the lane leading to the river from the market-place.

The fact is, the gentleman who takes the toll upon the bridge above has heard the sound of some one shouting, but, as he expresses it, imagined it to be "another try-on."

Interrogated as to the meaning of the term, he says that he's "been had that way afore!" That parties under the bridge had been and bellowed out "help," and then other parties had taken advantage of his absence from the gate to slip through, and "give him the double."

A friend of the knowing gentleman, however, having also heard the cries of distress repeated again and again in increasing energy, thought it best to go and see what was the matter.

After thinking it over and listening to the boy's voice for ten minutes and more he came to the conclusion that somebody must be in some position requiring assistance, and so, as the best plan that his imaginative mind could suggest towards their aid, he began to bawl for help himself.

Meanwhile other persons who had heard the cries reluctantly approached the scene of action, and so in time there assembled on the spot a goodly company of persons who would have been willing to lend a hand if they had only known how.

Providentially Joe Cudder, the waterman, rowing across the river at the time, was, for the second time in his life, enabled to rescue Charley from a watery grave.

They bore the two bodies—the lady quite insensible, the boy almost so—into the nearest public-house ("the Drinking Fish"), which opened its doors to receive them, and a general demand was immediately made for a medical man.

A medical man turned up at the moment—a fussy little gentleman, fat, and grey, and bald.

"I'm a medical man," said he, "so's my friend. Be so good as to clear the room, landlord. We must have a little more air, and a little less noise. Case of suicide, I suppose. Hum.—Ah! Mr. Jobson, the pulse is still beating."

"Then there's every hope. The boy's all right. He's only had a ducking. There, there, my man, shake yourself up. What have you been about, young fellow?"

"Give him some brandy."

"Brandy, Mr. Larkins? He hardly requires it."

"'Gad! but you'd require something, I expect, if you'd had such a wetting. I say, Jobson, ha, ha! Can you tell me what's the difference between you and this boy?"

"A good deal of difference, I should hope, Mr. Larkins."

"It is something considerable. You see, he's just had a *duck*, and you've just lost a *goose*, Don't you see, 'duck,' a bird, you know, and 'duck' in the water? Duck and goose. That aint so bad, is it?"

"Dash it all, Jobson, that really is *not* so bad."

"I should feel obliged, Mr. Larkins, as I have said before, if you would let the subject drop; it's exceedingly distasteful to me, and the less I hear about it the better I shall be pleased."

"All right, Jobby; then we won't say any more about the goose. All I wish is that we had been able to catch the young scamp."

"If I had, by Jove, I'd have warmed him."

Having administered to Charley a stiff glass of grog by way of restorative, the doctor dismissed him from the room, with strict injunctions to take himself off as hard as he could go, or he would catch his death of cold, to say the least of it.

This, however, he did not do, being anxious to know how the lady fared, and thus it was that presently, when she was so far recovered as to be able to speak and ask for the person who had saved her, the boy, obedient to a call, came forward and stood face to face with her.

She had been conveyed upstairs, and lay warm and comfortable in the best bed that the "Drinking Fish" could boast of.

She was very pale, but very beautiful. More beautiful, Charley thought, than any woman he had ever seen out of the print-shop windows.

As she lay there in the quiet splendour of her golden hair, which in thick soft yellow masses encircled her lovely head; the little fellow, dripping wet, and shivering with cold, for a moment quite forgot the state of physical discomfort under which he was suffering, and stood open-mouthed before the angelic vision, like one might stand, did the clouds fly assunder, and we caught through the aperture a glimpse of heavenly grandeur.

She slightly raised her head to look at him, and languidly said,

"Is that the, boy?"

Yes, that was the, boy.

"Come here, boy."

The boy coming closer to her, she lay looking him fixedly in the eyes, and, with a quiet earnestness which quite disconcerted him and made him blush poppy colour,

After a while she said,

"Did you save me, boy?"

"I tried to, ma'am, as well as I could. I—I—I'm very sorry, I'm sure, if you did not wish me,"—

He was frightened, and began to stammer in the middle of his sentence, for the lady's behaviour was as strange as it was unexpected.

At the sound of his voice she sprang up in the bed with wild, dilated eyes, and twitching nostrils. Then seizing his arm with more force than one would suppose so delicate a hand to be capable of, cried in excited tones,

"Your name, boy? who are you? what do you call yourself?"

"I'm called Charley Wag," the lad replied. "I'm nothing particular."

"I thought as much," said the lady, after a pause of several moments duration. "That will do—go away—at once. Take him out of the room."

Mr. Jobson, who had been an attentive spectator of the curious scene, relieved his mind by bundling Charley out of the room by the nape of the neck, and, immediately upon getting him there, backing him up in a corner and asking him a few questions.

"Listen here, young fellow," said he, "now none of your nonsense. I know all about it."

"About what, sir?"

"What you've been up to."

"I haven't been up to anything."

"You haven't. Do you mean to tell me—why, I say Larkins!"

"What is it?"

"Good Heavens! this is the boy."

"Of course it is, there are not two of them."

"You don't understand—I mean *the* boy, the boy that stole the goose.

"Never."

"It is, I'll swear to him."

"Then how did he get into the river?"

"I can't say—he must have fallen into it."

"What! with the goose?"

"I don't know that, but this I know, I'll give this boy into custody. Here, policeman, take this young vagabond in charge."

————

V.—Charley Gets Roughly Handled.— The False Witness.—Tit for Tat.

AN energetic member of the B division, being fortunately (or perhaps, as some persons might say, unfortunately) upon the spot, the young vagabond was laid violent hands upon; and, as is usually the fate of a boy in the clutches of the police, was presently well shaken, tightly screwed up in his neckerchief, and warned that he had better take care of what he was about.

"Take him up," said Mr. Jobson, in the words of the pedagogue in the spelling-book.

"Take him up," said Mr. Jobson, waving his hand, like the tyrant in the play does, when he wants the hero to be put into irons, only the tyrant uses more imperious language, and says, "away with him."

"What's he been up to, sir?" says the policeman.

"Robbery," says Jobson; "Lock him up."

"Will you give the charge?"

"With the greatest pleasure."

"Come on, then, you young scoundrel."

The young scoundrel and vagabond feeling very cold and weak and miserable, and inclined to double up limp at the knees and waist, made no resistance whatever, so the officer with a good stiff poke in the back of his neck, such as only a policeman's knuckles could administer, shoved him out towards the door.

"No; but I say, Jobson," began Mr. Larkins, "you won't have the boy locked up—"

"Won't—why not?"

"Look at the state he's in"

"State he's in?"

"Yes—so wet."

"Well! what's that to do with me?"

"Nothing to do with you, I suppose, but it has with him."

"Well, what will it have with him?"

"It'll give him his death, I suppose."

"All the better; an infernal young scamp!"

"Jobson, you ought to be ashamed of yourself."

"Indeed, Mr. Larkins."

"Yes, indeed."

"And why, pray? Here's this boy, whom you yourself can swear to, stole my goose, and gave us all this run. I suppose, now we've got him, you would have me let him go scot free. Bah! what rubbish.

"If he gives you the goose back, there's an end of it. Give the boy a good slap over the head and think no more about it. He's an honest-looking lad enough, and I'll be hanged if I can think him to be a regular thief."

"Regular bosh. He tell me where the goose is, indeed. I know where it is; he's thrown it into the river; that's what he has done with it. Haven't you, you young miscreant?"

"No—sir; if you'll let me go for five minutes, I'll bring it to you."

"Ha, ha! that's not so bad," said Mr. Jobson.

"Not if we know it, young gentleman."

"Not if we know it," repeated the officer, giving his charge another knuckler.

"If you will come with me, then," said Charley, with a sinking heart, for he feared that Rattan might be beforehand with him. "I will take you to the place where I left it."

"Where's that?"

"A public-house, close by?"

"Which?"

"The Cockleshell."

"What sort of a house is that, policeman?" asked Jobson.

"Shocking bad," said the policeman. "But we'd better go and see if it's lies. Most likely it's lies."

"You think so, do you?"

"Yes," said the officer. "I gene'ally finds it's lies."

With this cheering assurance they departed upon the expedition. Mr. Jobson, calm but determined; the policeman determined, but distrustful; Charley Wag shaking like a leaf, and in low spirits. Mr. Larkins and the rest eager to see fair play.

"Bother him and his goose too," the landlady said. "I wish he'd tumbled into the water, instead of the boy, that's all I've got to say. The poor child will be frozen to death, this bitter night."

It was, indeed, a bitter night, and Charley's teeth rattled like the brass heels of the celebrated Mr. MACKNEY, when he is doing one of his "little dances."

When the party reached the public-house rejoicing in the name of the "Cockleshell," they found it shut up and dark; but, listening attentively, they found that it was by no means empty.

"I'll do the trick," said the policeman, knowingly. "This 'll open them."

Then he wet his thumb, and rubbed it up the shutter, in a peculiar manner, which made a loud noise.

Suddenly all became still inside.

Then a pause.

Then a voice, saying—

"Who's there?"

"All right—open."

"Visit?"

"Police."

A little bustle and clinking of glasses, then the door opened enough to allow them to pass, and the policeman, the boy, and the two gentlemen going through, it closed again.

"Any one wanted?" the man who had admitted them asked, in a confidential whisper.

"No; nothing of that sort. We want a goose."

"A goose?"

"Yes, this young whelp's been and boned one. He says it's here? Is it?"

"Yes, sir," Charley said addressing the landlord "you know it is, sir, I brought it here an hour ago, a goose and a bottle of spirits."

The landlord remembered it well enough of course, and he had got it put by for Mr. Rattan, to whom he would no doubt have delivered it, had not he seen the boy in custody. Then it occurred to him that, what was sauce for the goose was sauce for the gander.

Why should'nt I stick to it, thought he, it would be a very poor lark to give it up to the bobby.

"Don't you recollect, sir?" asked Charley, anxiously.

"Recollect what, my lad?"

"About my bringing in the goose?"

"Well, we've been rather busy to-night," said the landlord. "What time was it?"

"An hour ago, sir. I left it for Mr. Rattan. It was only a lark, sir. He got me to do it, and he was going to take it back. Perhaps he has taken it back."

"Oh!" said the landlord, puffing at his pipe, "P'r'aps he has, who can say?"

"No, no!" broke in Mr. Larkins. "Let's have an answer, if you please, one way or the other. Did the boy bring a goose here, and if so, where is it?"

"If you think I'm going to be answerable for all the geese that come into my bar," said the landlord, "you're mistaken, for I shan't be for you."

Mr. Larkins trying not to look foolish, but not succeding very well, continued,

"Did that boy give you a goose to take care of? Be good enough to answer that."

"Well, I will then. He did'nt."

"Ah, Mr. Larkins," said Jobson, "I told you so."

Poor Charley's jaw dropped. He could hardly complain, could he, for the landlord was only serving him as he served the man about the boards? The consequences in this case, however, promised to be more unpleasant.

"Oh, sir! oh, sir!" he cried, "Do not say so, or I shall be locked up."

"Ah, you'll be locked up, sure enough," said the policeman. "Are you satisfied, gentlemen? Come on, boy."

"I don't believe him," said Mr. Larkins, confidentirlly to Jobson, "I am sure the boy is telling the truth."

"Are you?" said Mr. Jobson with contempt, "but then you're so very credulous."

"Damn it," cried Larkins, in a passion, "take him up, and be hanged to you."

"Thank you, Larkins, I shall."

The procession started again, and, in due course, arrived at the station-house.

It was the one in Quod-street.

That awful individual who takes the night charges, ever sleepless, vigilant and unwinking, was there, ready to receive them as he would be were it your turn. God grant it may never be the hard lot of any of us to go before him.

"What's this?" he said.

"Stolen a goose, sir."

"Where?"

Then the policeman told the story.

"What's your name, boy?"

"Charley Wag."

"Come, none of your chaff. What's your name?"

"That is my name."

"Where do you live?"

"Number seven, Slogger's-alley, Tothill's Fields."

"Will you appear against him?" asked the Inspector.

"Certainly," said Mr. Jobson.

"All right, lock him up, then."

"I beg your pardon," said Mr. Larkins, "but the boy is not in a condition to be locked up, he is wet through. He has been in the river."

"Jumped in the river, eh?"

"Yes."

"That's his look out."

"No, you mistake. He jumped in to save a lady."

"Save a lady, eh? A lady friend of his, I suppose."

"No, it wasn't."

"Well, it don't much matter—lock him up."

"If you do, you'll kill him."

"Shall we?"

"I am a medical man, and I say you will. If that boy goes to sleep in his wet clothes it will kill him."

"He'd better not go to sleep, then, that's all I've got to say. Let him walk about. There's no objection."

"I tell you, sir," cried Mr. Larkins, in a violent passion, "I tell you, sir"—

"There, that'll do," broke in the Inspector. "You can go outside and say the rest. Turn him out."

Out he was turned accordingly, and Charley was locked up.

Locked up—cold, wet, and hungry—this Christmas eve, with a dreary prospect before him.

Severe punishment for a "lark," you'll say.

My advice is, don't have anything to do with larks.

VII.—DYING OF COLD.

OUT in the hard hearted streets, this merry Christmas season, miserable, homeless, wretches, whimper and shiver, and creep as it were within themselves.

Pretty young ladies, nestling like little dormice in their warm soft couches, think how nice it is to lie there, so carefully covered up, and tucked in, and listen to the howling wind without, which must be only howling just to convince them how comfortable they are, and how unpleasant it would be to have no bed to lie upon.

Jovial blades, keeping it up with pipe and song, throw on more coals, or else another log, and think how jolly it is that it is so cold out of doors and warm in, and that they are in and not out.

More jovial blades swaddled in so many coats and wrappers that there is scarcely an inch of their faces exposed, slap one another on the back when they meet in the street, and one asks the other what he thinks of the weather—to which the other replies that he thinks its seasonable, and then they get up a sort of extemporaneous double shuffle to keep their feet warm.

Enthusiastic skaters hope it will last, and everybody says it is much better than those beastly warm un-English sort of winters we've been having lately.

Meanwhile this merry Christmas season, the ragged, and famished, and homeless, whimper and shiver, and moan, and huddled up in the warmest corner to be had for nothing—which is not very warm either—sit in a meditative way, raising their knees and wondering how much of this sort of thing it takes before your toes drop off.

Poor Charley Wag, screwed up in a corner, so blue and numb with cold that he has hardly any feeling left, makes up his mind to wait as patiently as he can till the morning.

It was a hard matter for a young lad like he was to make up his mind to endure such agony —harder when his mind was made up to go through with it.

The cell in which he was confined was lighted by something which at some remote period had been intended to be a window guarded by iron bars.

The bars still remained, but every particle of glass had been broken away, and a piercing cold wind poured through the aperture upon the young captive.

The draught cut into his bones like a knife.

His wet clothes began to freeze stiff as a board.

He had lost all use in his hands and feet.

In a dull half stupified state, he heard the church clocks chime the hours—a drowsiness stole over him, and a horrible chill crept up his limbs, and began to settle round his heart.

At last his senses left him. Then with a groanhe fell forward on his face and lay motionless upon the stone floor.

Nobody particularly troubling their heads about him, he continued to lie in the position in which he had fallen without being disturbed.

Perhaps, had it not accidently happened that on this particular night the police were more then ususlly active, and the criminal population more than usually obstreperous, it is probable that he would have remained there unmolested until the morning, in which case——

In which case this would have been the last chapter of Charley Wag, or more probably—

His history would never have been written.

For if he was going to do nothing more wonderful than what he has done, rest assured he would never have been chosen for a hero by me.

As it was, there were such numbers of tenants for the cells in Quod-street that there was not nearly sufficient accommodation, and they almost all had three or four occupants.

Charley's cell, being the last along the passage, was left unmolested until there was no room left anywhere else, when the door being flung suddenly open, a very ragged young man was flung suddenly inside, who, falling perforce right on the top of Mr. Wag's back, lay there for a moment silently, and then, scrambling on to his legs, began to shout for help.

"You'd better hold your row," a voice said, presently, in answer to the young man's cries, 'or you'll get something to make a row about."

"I have got something to make a row about," expostulated the young man.

"Ah! and you'll have somethink more, before you've done."

"I want to come out."

"So I suppose."

"Let me out—"

"Shut up!"

The sound of the policeman's heavy boots

retreating up the passage told him that his request was not going to be attended to.

With increased energy he then began to shout.

Finding it was no good, he desisted. He stood for a while quite still and motionless, then softly approached the boy's prostrate form.

He undid Charley's waistcoat, and placed his hand upon the region of his heart. Then held his breath and listened.

His heart was still.

Perhaps his own fingers were so dead with cold that they were utterly powerless.

He would try again.

This time he laid his ear upon the boy's breast, and listened again more intently.

No; all was still there—still as the grave. "Help! help!" shrieked the stranger.

And rushing to the door he shook and wrenched at the iron fastenings in a mad effort to get out of the dungeon.

"What now?" called the same voice which had before spoken. "You won't shut up, won't you?"

"Open the door," replied the prisoner, frantic with terror. "I'm shut up with a dead body."

"Shut up with what?"

"Come and open the door—I say. Come and open the door. I'm locked up, here, with a dead body. Here's somebody frozed to death on the floor."

Thinking it just within the limits of possibility that Charley might have frozen to death, and supposing that he was the person referred to, the Inspector bade a couple of his subordinates go and inquire into the real state of affairs.

Going accordingly, and raising him from the ground and carefully examining him, they put him down again and returned to the outer office.

"Well?" said the Inspector.

"All up, I should say," replied one of the men.

"Well dressed, aint he?"

"Rather so—if his things wasn't dragged out of shape by the water."

"Young prig, eh?"

"P'r'aps not, might be respectable."

"Not much respectability to be found up Slogger's-alley, I should think."

"I've heard no harm against the woman he mentioned. Should we send there?"

"Yes, you'd better. I don't want any row to be made about us having starved the boy to death. It don't matter with a pauper, as there's nobody but the parish to be anxious about them, and they're not. Who can go?"

It seemed that, upon consideration, nobody could be spared.

"There's Clam."

"To be sure. Window breaking, aint it? He'll come back, I suppose."

Oh yes, sure enough. He did it to get locked up."

"Fetch him out then, and bring this boy out too. There may be a chance for him."

They brought the boy out, and laying him down close to the fire, began to take off his clothes, which had, by this time, become as hard as boards.

They then rubbed his hands and feet, poured hot brandy down his throat, and wrapped him up in all the available blankets and great-coats to be found upon the establishment.

While thus engaged, the Inspector sent for the person called "Clam," who turned out, upon making his appearance, to be none other than the young man who had a short time since made so much disturbance in Charley's cell.

"Well, scarecrow," said the Inspector.

He very aptly described the young man's appearance when he thus addressed him.

He was, without exception, the raggedest, and the forlornest young man on record.

The most woe-begone—the most emaciated.

The hungriest and lankiest.

He was a young man whose age it was very difficult to decide, for it might have been anything between twenty and forty.

"Well, scarecrow," said the Inspector.

"Same to you, sir," said the young man, pulling a piece of hair where the peak of his cap would probably have been if he had had one. "I hope you're nicely, sir, by this time."

"Let's have none of your chaff," replied the Inspector. "What's up with you?"

"Hup wid me?"

"Ah, what are you shaking about?"

"About the hague, sir. I'm most shook to bits."

"You look as though you couldn't stand much more of it. How long have you had it?"

"Three months, I st'd think. Ketched it creasing—"

"Water cresses?"

"Same, sir. It's very fash'nable down my ways."

"Where's your ways?"

"The Harches."

"Take care it don't shake the little bit of life you've got left clean out of you. It wouldn't have to shake much."

"Well, I don't spose I st'd put nobody to no pertickler espense in monimings. Nobody, I st'd s'pose 'ud wish to keep no pertickler acccunt of me when I was hooked it. Nobody's took no pertickler account on me whiles I hevn't hooked it."

"You never did live anywhere exactly, did you Clam?"

"Not escept the House and these ere Diggins, and the C'rection."

"And how old are you?"

"I've no idea."

"You broke a window to get into quod, didn't you?"

"Yes, sir."

"Well, then, look here, I want to send you with a message, and if you don't come back you won't get locked up. Do you hear? Besides which you'll be led a life of it, I can tell you. There won't be a stone in London you shall have to lie your head on. Do you hear?"

"Yes, sir."

"Then you'll come back?"

"Yes, sir."

"On your Bible?"

"Yes, sir."

"I suppose you don't know what a Bible is?"

"Never heerd on it before, as I knows on."

"Never mind. Go to Miss Williams, No. 6, Slogger's-alley, Toothill's-fields, and tell her that the lad who lives with her is here. Be off, now, I shall give you an hour to get there and back again."

Making the greatest haste that was possible in a rickety old pair of shoes, one or other of which fell off at every third step, the messenger hurried along and was very soon in Slogger's-alley.

Miss Williams had not changed her neighbourhood, although some time ago she had quitted Mrs. Grinderbones's inhospitable roof for more desirable lodgings lower down the yard.

Owing to that consummate scoundrel, Rattan, having robbed her of the money which Mr. Leech had given her, she had never been able to set up a shop as at first she had hoped to do.

The expenses of the boy's maintenance had more than swallowed up the allowance which from time to time she had received from the hands of the lawyer, and yet struggling on she scarcely managed to live from day to day and supply her darling with a trifle of pocket money; for, rather than see him go without anything, she would herself have gone supperless to bed, or parted with the very gown from off her back.

And I suppose in this respect she does not differ much from any other of your dear, kind-hearted women, where the object of her love is concerned. I wish it was me.

Knocking at the door of No. 6, Clam had not to wait very long before a gentle voice on the inside called out to him to wait a moment.

"Oh, you naughty boy," it said; "however could you stop out so late? I have been in such a dreadful way about you. Wherever have you been?"

By this time the door was opened, and Sarah Williams stood, not as she expected, in front of Charley, but opposite to a very dilapidated object, which pulled its hair by way of bow, and said—

"I aint him, mum, but I've comed from him."

"From where?" asked Miss Williams.

"The p'lice station."

"Great heavens!" the woman exclaimed, supporting herself against the door-post. "What has happened to him?"

"He's quodded."

"Locked up! Why, he has not—he surely has not done anything very bad. It must have been a mistake or his fun."

"It's no lark, mum, it's prigging."

"You do not mean to tell me he has stolen anything?"

"Wus."

"Worse! For God's sake speak—what has happened?"

"He's dead."

"Without another word, she fell forward heavily, and would have fallen into the street, had not Clam been there to catch her.

"Don't take on so," he cried, in great alarm. I'm not certing he is; p'r'aps he isn't; and if he is, don't you die too — there's no call for nobody else to die. Don't do it, mum, I begs on you."

CHARLEY IS KIDNAPPED.

VIII.—MORE ABOUT THE BEAUTIFUL LADY— SHOWING WHAT MR. LARKINS FOUND OUT, AND WHAT HE DIDN'T.

WHEN Charley Wag was safely under lock and key, Mr. Larkins and Mr. Jobson found themselves face to face before the station-house door.

"Well!" said Mr. Larkins, "you've made a fine night's work of it."

"Have the kindness to keep your remarks until they are asked for," said Mr. Jobson.

"Jobson!" said Mr. Larkins, bursting with suppressed wrath, "if there ever was a man who wanted his nose pulled you are the party."

"And if there ever was a man who wasn't able to do it," replied Mr. Jobson, "that individual is yourself."

No. 8.

Whether or not bloodshed might have ensued it is difficult to say.

The policeman interfering at this juncture, Mr. Jobson reserved the rest of his indignation for a more fitting occasion; and Mr. Larkins bottled up his vengeance until the next opportunity.

Mr. Jobson turned round and walked straight home to the Borough.

Mr. Larkins bent his steps towards the "Drinking Fish."

Gaining admission by a tap at the side door, he soon found himself in the presence of the landlady.

"How is our patient?" said he, "gone to sleep."

"She is up and dressed."

[CHARLEY WAG, THE NEW JACK SHEPPARD.

"Up and dressed!" cried Mr Larkins, aghast. "You don't say so?"

"Yes; she says she must go home; and has sent for a cab."

"I say, Mrs. Dryers, said Mr. Larkins, confidentially, "what do you make her out to be?"

"I give you my word of honour," replied the landlady, "I can't make out anything at all. The clothes we have had at the fire are really superb. Such depths of embroidery as there is on her under petticoats I never before clapt my eyes on."

"Ah! the money that is spent upon some of these girls. It's wonderful, isn't it?"

"What, do you make her out to be one of *them*?"

"Don't you?"

"Lord, Doctor!" said the landlady, with a flounce. "She shouldn't have had my best bed if I had thought it, I can tell you. Bless you, no. If there ever was a real, right down, born and bred lady, she's one."

"Queer thing, for her to be in the river, isn't it? The boy said a man threw her in. I think the case ought to be looked into; but Jobson made such a fuss about that infernal goose. However, I'll speak to the lady, myself. By-the-way, the clothes are not dry yet; are they?"

"No: she has some of mine—and is going to send for her's."

"Did she say where she lived?"

"No—hush! Here she is."

At that moment the lady entered.

She was very plainly attired, in such things as the landlady could supply, but her's was a beauty which would have asserted itself in rags.

"If you would only have allowed me to send for your ladyship's clothes," said the landlady, busying herself behind the fair stranger with a hook and eye.

"My dear creature," the other replied, "don't call me my lady, if you please. I am very comfortable as I am, and shall soon be at home."

"I trust, madam," said the doctor, "that we shall soon be enabled to trace out the perpetrator of this gross outrage."

"How so?" the lady exclaimed, turning upon him sharply, at the same time that a deadly pallor stole over her lovely face.

"He cannot be far off, I should think, and having his description we can then—"

"Who has his description? Who gave his description? Who saw him? Ah! the boy."

"The boy tells us that he did not see him, madam, and that he cannot describe him."

At these words a smile lit up her face, and to conceal her emotion, she bowed her head and pretended to be pinning her shawl.

"But you, madam," continued Mr. Larkins, "must have seen the man's face, and will probably be able to describe him. Rest assured that no effort shall be wanting on my part to bring such an atrocious ruffian within the pale of the law."

"I am really very much obliged to you, sir," the lady replied, in a tone, and with a smile which had a slight dash of contempt in them, excessively mortifying to the fussy little gentle-man. "But I am afraid that I shall not be able to gratify you with any particulars."

"Exceedingly ill-bred," thought Mr. Larkins to himself, "particularly when I offered to take all the trouble."

"I suppose you were so alarmed, madam, by the sudden attack," he said aloud, "that you were not able to observe the man's appearance?"

"Exactly."

"I trust that he did not rob you of a large amount?"

"He did not rob me at all."

"Oh!"

The lady turned away from him, and Mr. Larkins rubbed his nose in a cogitative fashion for the next five minutes.

"If he didn't rob her, why did he throw her into the water?" thought the little doctor. "It's very extraordinary altogether. How was it she did not see him? She must be wishing to mislead me. But why? That's the question."

"Will you send out to procure me a cab?" said the lady to the hostess "and at the same time tell me how much I am indebted to you for what I have had, and for the use of these clothes."

"Oh, I am sure," the landlady replied bashfully, fingering her apron, "you are very welcome, ma'am, to what you have had, and as you are going to send the clothes back you are very welcome to the use of them."

"On the contrary," the lady replied, coldly and without the faintest touch of kindness in her voice, "I should much prefer you naming a price."

"Well, really, I am sure, if you will accept—"

"I never accept of anything which I do not pay for. I am much obliged to you, but should prefer not to remain in your debt."

There could not possibly have been anything harder nor colder than her manner in saying this.

The landlady felt nettled and hurt by it.

"You can pay if you wish, ma'am," she replied, with a toss of the head, " but I'd have you to know, ma'am, that when you was brought in, all cold and insensible like, and, for all I knew, dead, it was not for the sake of what I should get by doing it that I took you in."

"I am sure I am very much obliged to you," the lady continued, without the slightest possible change in the tone of her voice or the expression of her face, "will you accept of this?"

So speaking, she placed five sovereigns in the landlady's hand, which, half involuntarily, had been stretched forth to prevent the money falling upon the ground.

Then, turning to the doctor, she continued, in the same manner—a manner which had in it something indescribably insulting, she said—

"I am also indebted to you, sir. Allow me to express my gratitude."

With equal liberality the beautiful lady paid Mr. Larkins for his trouble. Then, without heeding the stammering thanks of the landlady and doctor, she gathered her shawl round her, and advanced towards the door.

"Might I venture to take the liberty, madam, of calling to-morrow morning, to enquire after your health?" Mr. Larkins asked, timidly.

"Call—where?"

"At your house."

"No: thank you. I do not live in town. I shall start for the country early to-morrow morning."

"Oh, in that case, of course—good evening, madam."

"Good evening."

Without another word, she swept from the room, and several officious individuals rushed forward to open the door leading into the street.

Mr. Larkins came close to the carriage window when the lady was safe inside.

"Where shall I tell the man to drive to?" he asked.

"To Charing-cross, if you please."

"Anywhere in Charing-cross?"

"The Nelson column."

Mr. Larkins gave the order.

"That's a rum direction, too," said the cabman to himself as he whipped up his steed.

He had been fetched almost as far—from the stand by St. Martin's Church.

Mr. Larkins returning to the bar-parlour was arrested in the act of seating himself by somebody telling him that the lady had returned, and wanted to speak to him.

He ran out eagerly, and found her leaning her head out of the cab window.

"I am sorry to trouble you," she said, "but I wished to speak to you about the boy?"

"The boy—"

"The boy who saved—who jumped into the water after me; where is he?"

"He is in the station-house."

"In which one, and why?"

"In Quod-street, for stealing a goose."

"A goose. What will be done to him, do you think?"

"He may have a month with hard labour if he lives."

"Lives?"

"Why, locked up in his wet clothes all night this horrible weather—I could not answer for the consequences."

"You think it might be fatal?"

"I think he would probably be found dead in the morning."

"And I should be the cause."

"Well, not exactly—I attribute it to the police."

"When will he appear before the magistrate?"

"The day after to-morrow."

"I will send somebody to the court—good night, and thank you—stop a moment."

Mr. Larkins, who was retiring, returned again.

"I beg your pardon," the lady said, at the same time feeling again in her purse, and squeezing two more sovereigns in the astonished doctor's hand. "I am sorry to be obliged to trespass upon your valuable time, but I should feel obliged by your going round to the police station, and seeing how the boy is getting on: I have a reason for taking an interest in him. You will do what I wish. Thank you."

As she finished speaking, she drew up the window, cutting Mr. Larkins's reply in two, and the cab drove on again.

"A reason for taking an interest in him," said Mr. Larkins, "I should think there was reason enough when the poor little fellow risked his life to save her's. I wonder whether that is what she meant. I can't make her out, I'm hanged if I can. Who is she, and what is she? Valuable time, eh? seven pounds in an hour, why, it beats the Marquis of Westminster's income all to fits."

He found the landlady puzzling her head over the same questions.

"Well, sir?" said she.

"Well, ma'am?" said he.

"Anything fresh?"

"No more evidence; have you any?"

"Only this, it was in her pocket; you see the writing is torn, and half-rubbed away; it was sopping wet you know, and stuck to the lining."

Mr. Larkins took the paper in his hand, and made out this much—

"My laDy a perSinghas is Unnone 2 yew tho by Haydence as * * * * * yeur seCret whants to See yew ter morreR nite 2 aVe A fue wordS * * * Ungerfud SustpenShing * * * * * * * * * * * * at twelf o cloc * * * * bring a trifil has i Ham * * Hup * * * *"

"Jack ratN."

IX.—The Mysteries of a Police Court.

THEY were very busy at the police court in Quod-street on boxing-day.

I suppose that Mr. Slang, the magistrate, is not the only person in the world who disgraces the bench by his daily recurring exhibitions of besotted ignorance, sickening vulgarity, and bad taste.

Come with me, reader, and if you have never before had an opportunity of seeing how justice is dispensed to the rich and poor, now is your time.

I hope you will be edified.

It was just upon the stroke of ten that a spare and hungry-looking gentleman, carrying a blue bag, arrived in Quod-street.

This was Mr. Leech.

In the dirty corridor leading to the Court, a number of policemen were lounging about, some of them carrying bundles which might be bundles of stolen property, and waiting till the case which they had "in charge" should come before "his washup."

Besides these, there were numbers of beetle-browed, close-cropped and generally ill-looking vagabonds, "pals" and "mates" of the "parties in trouble," several lawyers and lawyers clerks, half-a-dozen or so ladies and gentlemen, who had had a drop too much over night, and had been out on bail, and a good many seedy individuals, who had no particular business to be where they were, or indeed anywhere else, but who had come to knock out a portion of the weary day, hearing the cases and so getting a little amusement and excitement "upon the cheap."

Whispering a few words into the ear of a surly policeman who was on guard at the door, Mr. Leech obtained permission to enter the prisoners' waiting-room, which opened out of the corridor.

This waiting-room was barely furnished with a few benches ranged round the wall, on which a very uninviting collection of blackguardly men, ragged boys, and half-naked women and girls sat scowling and mouthing at the attendant policemen.

Among these was Mr. Wag, who, except that he seemed to have a violent cold in his eyes and nose, which were much inflamed, had otherwise got over his recent ducking. But what with the effects of his cold, the lengthened imprisonment he had endured, and an agonizing interview he had with his poor foster-mother, who was overwhelmed with shame and grief at finding her darling in such a position, Charley had lost a great deal of that light and airy, free and easy deportment, which usually distinguished him.

For you know that as yet he was not in his heart a thief, and felt his humiliating position severely.

"Your name's Wag, I think," said Mr. Leech singling Charley out from the rest at the first glance, "I appear on behalf of this young gentleman, policeman. Now, young fellow how is it you have got yourself in this mess?"

"What do you think I shall be done to, sir?" asked Charley, in great alarm, "It will break my poor mother's heart I'm sure if I'm sent to prison."

"That's very fine as far as it goes," retorted Mr. Leech, with a coarse laugh. "You young gents are always so very thoughtful of your mothers when you've done your little best by your infernal misconduct to send them to their graves."

"Oh dear! oh dear!" the boy exclaimed screwing his knuckles into the corners of his eyes, as though he were trying to gouge himself, "I wish I'd been dead before I had met that Rattan."

"Met Rattan, did you?"

"Yes sir, he made me do it, or he said he'd tell about the boards!"

"What boards?"

Then Charley described, not without a sly chuckle, how he had bested the policeman.

"You'll live to be hanged, mark my words if you don't," said Mr. Leech. "You're a most infernal young vagabond. However, I'll do the best for you, as the lady wishes me."

"What lady, sir?"

"Mind your own business," replied Mr. Leech, "and don't presume to ask me questions."

"You'll try to get me off, sir; thank you, sir, for you kinkness."

"You need not thank me," said Mr. Leech, "because I don't feel the slighest practicle of interest in you, one way or the other. I act for my client. As my client has requested me to do the best I can for you, I shall do so, but if you are transported for the rest of your natural life, I shan't break my heart about it by any means. You understand me, I hope."

With a particularly hard smile, this man of business took himself and his blue bag into court.

The night charges were on, and Mr. Leech sat down at the clerk's table—the place set aside for solicitors and counsel, and beguiled his leisure time by listening to the different cases.

First, Samuel Dubchuck, fat, fair and forty. White waist-coat, fitting tightly over capacious stomach. Regrets that he is in such a disgraceful position. Was dining out at a public-dinner, at the Freemason's Tavern. A charity dinner in aid of the funds of the Dilapidated Tooth-pick Makers' Orphan Asylum. Cannot deny that he had rather too much to drink, and may have taken off his boots and laid down in the street, but does not recollect assaulting three policemen. Policemen, however, remember it very distinctly, and go at considerable length into details. Fined Forty Shillings.

Next case, Mrs. Slommax, a "respectable married woman," and Mrs. Draggletail, another equally chaste ornament to her sex, drunk and incapable, as usual. Five Shillings and a caution. Hard-working weary-looking, man, supposed to be the lawful proprietor of the beauteous Slommax, pays the fine, and the three retire to a public-house, opposite the office, to have a drain, and talk things over.

In a few days one of the ladies will be fined again, and her husband have to scrape the money together to liberate her. A cheerful life truly, and an inducement to the poor wretch to labour and toil.

Oh, how many poor squallid pigsties of places might be made into comfortable homes, did their mistresses but try what could be done.

It wants no magician's wand.

I used to wonder how it was that the streets at night were filled with besotted, bellowing beasts, whose brutal oaths and savage cries served to make a Pandemonium of all the poor quarters of the city—until I came to visit their homes by day, and noted the groups of ragged, gin-drinking slatterns congregated round the door of the public-house at the corner, or squatted in the filth of their own doorstep.

Then I wondered no longer why workingmen spend their earnings away from home.

Next case, Miss Juliana Sloper, of Trevorsquare, Brompton; Miss Louisa Talbot, Churchstreet, Soho, and Mrs. Fitzgerald, Union-street, Oxford-street, of that class the newspapers call "unfortunate," charged with not moving on, and fined accordingly.

There are a good many of those sort of cases when business is slack.

Next, Private Wallops of the guards, for illegally using his belt upon citizen Jones's face, to the detriment of that gentleman's eyesight. These are the men we pay to protect us.

Next, a case of wife beating—then a case of biting—fine manly English amusements, which make one proud of living in an age of ultra civilization.

Then, a needlewoman, who had pawned the slopwork entrusted to her to make up. Sage remarks thereon from the bench. Lengthened report in next days' papers, and much horror expressed at the rapacity of Noses and Son, who can expect a mantle to be made for three-halfpence. Then universal sympathy and a handsome subscription for poor Mary Whalebone, whose little dodge answers beyond her wildest hopes.

Charity is a good thing in its way, and would you have the charitable neglect poor Paul, who is hungry and sore, because Peter get himself up with vermillion, and labels himself starving, when his belly is fuller than yours or mine?

The next case was that of Charley Wag.

X.—Contains a Little Perjury—A Good Deal of Injustice—A Little Love-Making—and a Little "Sell."

"WHAT'S this, policeman?" asked Mr. Slang, when a policeman stepping briskly into the box, had kissed the book, and was ready to swear to anything.

"Felony, your washup," replied the policeman readily.

Then continued, with great rapidity of utterance—

"Was on duty in the Strand, and was called down to the "Drinking Fish" public-house—party of the name of Jobson—give the boy in charge —took him to the station-house, and see him locked up."

"Know anything of the boy?"

"No particular good."

"Where's Jobson?"

Mr. Jobson being sworn, stated the circumstances attending the rape of the goose, and added, that he did not wish the boy to be dealt hardly with.

Now, nothing put Mr. Slang's blood up more than one of these kind of remarks.

"Don't tell me what you wish," said Mr. Slang, indignantly. "How dare you tell me what you wish. Do you imagine that I care the value of a brass button whether you do or don't? I am here to do justice, and not to attend to your wishes, so don't deceive yourself."

Mr. Jobson, very much abashed by this attack, which was one of Mr. Slang's usual ways of impressing a stranger with a notion of the grandeur and importance of the bench, was overwhelmed with confusion.

"I—I—I'm sure I beg your pardon, sir, if I have said anything to offend you," he stammered.

"Don't talk to me—I'm not offended or likely to be at anything such an insignificant person could say. Who are you, fellow—what's your name?"

"Jobson, sir."

"Dobson, eh?"

"No, Jobson."

"I said Jobson. What are you?"

"A chemist, sir."

"Hum. I should have thought you kept a public-house by the look of you. Have you been drinking?"

"No, sir, I have not," replied Mr. Jobson, rather savage at this style of questioning.

"How is it that you are always guzzling at goose clubs instead of attending to your business?"

"I am not always at goose clubs. If I attend to my business sufficiently to get a living at it, I suppose I have a right to enjoy myself when I choose?"

"Pretty enjoyment. You ought to be ashamed of yourself. I suppose you were drunk when this happened?"

"I had been drinking, but was not drunk."

"Policeman, was this man drunk?"

"Very drunk, your washup."

"You damned scoundrel!" roared Jobson, in a fury.

"How dare you," roared his washup, if anything, a little louder. "I shall fine you five shillings."

"Damn the five shillings," yelled Jobson, desperately.

"That's five more," yelled his washup.

Ten shillings he was accordingly fined, and would, perhaps, have been fined still further had not he restrained his feelings by a strong moral and physical effort, which caused him to grow perfectly purple with suppressed emotion.

"I should advise you, my friend," said Mr. Slang, with a bitter smile, "to be a little more guarded in your language, or I shall take the liberty of committing you."

Mr. Jobson snorted.

"So he was drunk, was he?" the magistrate continued, "and gave the boy the goose, I suppose, if, indeed, there is any goose at all. Is there any other witness?"

There was not.

"Hum!" said Mr. Slang, "I really see nothing against the prisoner, and shall discharge him."

In spite of the perfectly appalling indignation of the ill-used chemist, there is little doubt but that Mr. Slang would have carried his intention into effect had it not unfortunately happened that his eye falling upon Mr. Wag's smiling face, he took it into his head to ask him a few questions.

Unlucky Charley!

"What's your name?" said Mr. Slang, pleasantly.

"Charley Wag, sir."

"I asked you your name, sir," said Mr. Slang, seriously.

"Charles, sir."

"Your surname?"

"Wag."

"Don't try your jokes here," said the magistrate, sternly.

"I'm not joking, sir," replied the boy, "that is my name."

"You're an impudent young vagabond," cried Mr. Slang, by this time quite as much enraged against the boy as he had just been against Jobson.

He was rather changeable, was his washup.

"Is there anybody here," said Mr. Slang, "who knows anything of this fellow?"

"I do, if you please, your washup," said a policeman in the body of the court, and stepping forward to the witness box, Charley, in dire amazement and alarm, recognised the officer upon whom he had played off the little practical joke about the play-bill boards.

"I know him, your washup," said the policeman, after he had kissed the book, "and a more hardened and unprincipled young vagabond I have never come across."

"Just as I thought," said Mr. Slang, "just as I thought the first moment I clapt my eyes upon him. I am very happy to think that I did not yield to the dictates of a kind heart, and let him loose again upon society. First impressions are always the best. What do you know of him, policeman?"

The policeman, who did not exactly wish to bring up the play-bill board story which he thought might tell against him considerably if it got wind, contented himself by saying, "From information I received from a certain quarter, I have kept my eye upon the prisoner for some time past, and have found him to be the constant associate of the worst of characters."

"Ah!" said Mr. Slang, with a sigh, "A very pretty young blackguard, I have no doubt. I shall give him a month."

This time, in spite of a half-smothered remonstrance from Mr. Leech, and a deprecatory cough from the clerk, Mr. Slang would have committed the unfortunate lad to prison had not a messenger at this juncture whispered in the magistrate's ear that a lady wished to speak to him privately.

"What name?" asked Mr. Slang.

"She did not give any, sir."

"Where is she?"

"There."

And looking in the direction indicated, Mr. Slang saw, at about a couple of yards distance, a lady standing, richly apparelled and closely veiled.

He beckoned to her to approach.

"What is it?" he asked, "this is really a very inconvenient time to seek for an interview. If you were to come after the night charges were disposed of, now it would be—"

"Too late. I wish to see you respecting this particular case. You must grant me an interview."

"Well, as to must—"

He would probably have returned her some surly rejoinder had not the lady slightly raised her veil, and the glimpse of one of the loveliest female faces which sun ever shone upon, decided him to be gallant.

Mr. Slang had acquired, and not without some reason, a great reputation for gallantry.

We have all read in history how the first of judges have been the worst of men, when a pretty woman was concerned. If we may believe the newspapers, some of our county magistrates are fashioned after the same model, and have their little weaknesses even to-day.

"Will you step this way?" said old Slang, with the leer of a satyr.

And the lady, accompanying him into his private room, he motioned her to a seat; and, carefully closing the door behind him, drew his own chair close to that of the fair one, and waited for her to open the ball.

This she did by raising her veil, and allowing Mr. Slang to feast his wicked eyes upon a countenance of surpassing loveliness.

"I trust, sir," said the lady, speaking with a certain amount of timidity, real or assumed, which was exceedingly captivating, and in which, keeping her eyes turned towards the ground, she allowed the magistrate to admire her to his heart's content, without any interruption.

"I trust that you will excuse the great liberty I have taken in intruding upon you at this busy hour."

"I am sure," said Slang, with a killing smirk, "I cannot quarrel with the chance which has thrown so much beauty in my way."

"I will not, however," continued the lady, with a gracious smile, "intrude longer than is necessary upon your valuable time, but at once come to the point. A boy, of the name of Wag, is at this moment in Court, charged with theft."

"He is."

"You must acquit him."

"But, really—on what ground?"

"On no ground; but that I am sure you will do it for my sake," the lady replied, at the same time sending a glance of her bright eyes right through the heart of the susceptible magistrate, which made his blood mount into his head.

"For your sake, my dear young lady," he said, taking her hand in his, which she graciously allowed to remain there, "I would do a great deal, as I am sure any man would; but, you see, unfortunately—"

"What?"

"That the evidence is too strong—"

"Why, I myself heard you say there was no evidence."

"Did you?—Ah! well. But, then, I've sentenced him."

"Change the sentence."

"It would make me look so ridiculous. No; it is impossible."

"I am sure, my dear Mr. Slang, that nothing is impossible to you—you are always successful, be it in war or in—love."

It might have been by accident, and it might have been designedly, that the fair speaker's shawl came unfastened at this moment, and the magistrate, at once surprised and delighted, perceived that his visitor wore an evening dress of the most costly black velvet, which was fashioned so as to show off to the utmost advantage the matchless symetry of her graceful form, and was so low in the neck as to leave her swelling bosom of dazzling whiteness almost entirely exposed to the old rascal's prying eyes.

"Dear, dear Mr. Slang, you will not refuse me," the bewitching enchantress contended, laying her pretty hands upon the magistrate's shoulder in the earnestness of her appeal, and at the same time leaning so forward that the delicious perfume of her luxuriant hair tickled his nostrils, and added, if possible, more fuel to the fire of his passions.

"I am sure you will not refuse me."

"There are some occasions," Slang replied, in a choking voice, "when one is not one's own master."

And as he spoke, he stooped his head until his *leech*-like lips rested on her forehead.

"Go, then," the lady continued, gently disengaging herself from Mr. Slang's rather encroaching tenderness, "go, then, and discharge him."

"That will do presently," he said, in a whisper. "I promise you he shall go free."

And again he endeavoured to take her into his arms.

"If you mean to do what you say, do it at once," she replied, pushing him from her.

"And my reward?"

" Need you ask ?"

Gluing his lips for a moment to her's, he hastily returned to the court, and said—

" I have just received an important communication in the prisoner's favour. Boy, you are discharged, and you may thank your stars that you have got off so easy ; perhaps the next time you may fare worse."

As Charley made the best of his way out of court, Mr. Slang continued—

" I have some important business to transact which may detain me for some little time. Do not allow any one to interrupt me. The rest of the charges I will hear on my return."

Leaving the persons in court not a little astonished at the very curious fashion in which Mr. Slang's justice seemed to be dispensed, the magistrate returned to his fair companion.

She was standing close to the door leading into the court, and must have heard all that had just taken place.

She had resumed her shawl, and the expression of her face was now as cold and unimpassioned as it had before been melting and tender.

The worthy magistrate, however, was too much excited to notice the change.

He clasped her in his arms, and would have covered her face and neck with burning kisses, but with a strength and violence which was surprising as it was unexpected, she thrust his head from her, and grasping his grey locks in her left hand, with her right placed the cold barrel of a pocket pistol against his brow.

" Release me, you miserable, despicable, old wretch !" she said, in a cold hissing whisper ; " take your hands off me or I'll blow your brains out."

" You—you, you're playing with me," he stammered.

" Am I ?" she retorted with a quiet laugh, " I was, perhaps, but I am serious enough, now let me pass."

Very white, and not a little frightened, Mr. Slang shrank back, and the determined beauty moved towards the door.

Pausing, with the handle in her hand, she smiled contemptuously, and said—

" Good morning."

" Don't think you shall escape me like this," roared Slang in a fury, " I will have my revenge."

" We will talk about that another time," the lady replied. " In the mean time, our love-making must be postponed till a more fitting opportunity."

The magistrate foamed with rage.

" You have certainly got the advantage over me upon this occasion, and it's no good struggling against fate, but by the heavens above us, you shall pay dearly for this insult ; and at no very distant time, I will take by force the favours which awhile ago you offered me as a bribe."

" Ha ! ha ! Mr. Slang," the lady said, with a sneer, " I have no doubt but that you are quite a Tarquin in your way, but I think it extremely unlikely that we shall meet again for some time, if ever. I shall take precautions to guard against you discovering my address."

" Will you ?" cried Slang, and at the same movement he sprang forward and picked from the ground the envelope of a letter which had been *rked from her pocket in the recent struggle.

Her first moment on seeing what it was, was to snatch it from him, but on second thoughts, she changed her tactics.

As for Slang, when his eyes fell upon the name, he was, as it appeared, dumbfounded with astonishment, and for some moments had not a word to say for himself.

" Since you have discovered who I am, the lady said, coldly and firmly, " you can easily suppose how any attempt at insult would be chastised. I need say no more."

" Believe me, your grace," the magistrate began, " if I had only imagined, I should never have dared. I hope and trust that you will not—"

" The particulars of our interview will remain a secret," the lady replied, haughtily, " as far as I am concerned. It is not likely that I should make public so degrading a scene. As for you, I think that now my reputation is safe as far as *you* are concerned. Good morning."

Thus speaking, she quitted the apartment, and quickly picking her way through the crowded court, made her way out into the street.

" I say, Tom," whispered one policeman to another, " do you see that lady ? "

" To be sure I do. Who is she ? "

" Don't you know ? "

" How could I tell when she kept her veil down."

" She lifted it up when she first came in, and I caught a glimpse of her."

" Well, who is she, then ? "

" Why, last night I was on duty in Grosvenor-square and I heard her carriage announced outside a house where they'd been having a tightner —a dinner party you know."

" Well ? "

" And she's the Duchess of Heatherland."

" What, the Prime Minister's lady ? What the duce could she have to say about that there young pickpocket ? "

" I'll be hanged if I know. They're a rum lot the aristocracy."

" You're right there, Jack. Have you ever read Mr. Reynolds's ' Mysteries of the Court ?' That puts you up to a thing or two."

" I believe you, Tom. I should say it rather warmed some of the nobs when it came out. They all of them took it in, didn't they ? "

" Well, if they didn't ; the footmen did, and the nobs borrowed it off 'em when they'd done with it, so its all the same."

XI. — THE SNARE — THE ABDUCTION — THE FINISHING ACADEMY.

AS Charley was elbowing his way to the door, delighted beyond measure at his lucky escape, Mr. Leech overtook him, and laid his hand upon his shoulder.

" Where are you going, my boy ? "

" Home, sir."

" To Miss Williams ? "

" Yes. I thought she would have been here. Have you seen her, sir ? "

" To be sure I have. I will take you to her."

Taking the boy's hand in his, Mr. Leech led the way to the corner of Quod-street, where a cab was waiting.

Opening the door, Mr. Leech motioned to him to enter.

The boy hesitated.

"Get in, get in," said the lawyer, "we will ride to Tothill's-fields."

They were going to Tothill-fields. Why should he hesitate? It had struck the boy as odd that the lawyer should have a cab waiting, and that they should ride such a short distance. But perhaps gentlefolks thought nothing of riding in cabs. He was not sorry to have the opportunity.

In he jumped, and away they went.

How delightful was the sensation. You laugh at the idea. Have you not seen Molly the maid, when you have sent her for a hansom, come back riding inside, and smiling complacently with her arms folded over the apron? That is the moment, I'll be sworn, when she would like that nice young man at the baker's to be looking out at the door and notice her.

Well, it was a great treat to Charley.

For some time he sat with a bright face, looking out of the window and watching the objects as they passed, without particularly noticing in which direction they were going.

But after about half-an-hour had so passed, and he noticed that they were passing along streets which were quite unknown to him, he turned round to his companion and said, rather uneasily—

"I thought you were going to take me home."

"So I am."

"But this isn't the way—we're going wrong."

"We're going right enough. Sit down and hold your jaw."

Thus rebuked, the boy became silent, and anxiously watched the streets from the window, hoping every moment to come upon some landmark, with which he was acquainted.

Such, however, was not the case.

They were travelling at a rapid pace, and by this time were in one of the suburbs.

Long, quiet roads, flanked by houses with prim gardens in front. Then straggling cottages, and isolated villas. Then rows of mean, one-storied buildings. Then a long, uninterrupted course of red-brick wall, enlivened by occasional white-paint advertisements of Groves, the Shoreditch clothier. Then nursery gardens, and then hedges and ditches.

They were in the country.

Still they journeyed onward, abating little in their speed. By this time the boy's anxiety had become so great, that he was unable to remain any longer silent.

"Oh! sir," he said, "please where are you taking me to?"

"I am taking you to where you'll be safe enough, young gentleman. You're going to school."

"To school! But I don't want to go to school. I want to go home."

"Ah! that's the worst of you, young people," said Mr. Leech, shaking his head, "you never want to do what you ought. However, this is an academy that you'll find very comfortable. Indeed," he added with a sinister smile, and a facetiousness which alarmed the boy considerably, although he hardly knew why, "the pupils are so very fond of it, they hardly ever *come back again*. It's what they call a *finishing* school. Ha! ha!"

"But why am I to go there? Who has sent me?"

"The lady you picked out of the river has been kind enough to do it. Aint you grateful to her?"

"No, I'm not. Stop the cab, I say. I want to get out."

"Oh! you want to get out, do you? Now, look here, you young varmint. If you take my advice, you'll hold your jaw, and not put my monkey up."

"I shan't hold my jaw," cried the boy, at the top of his voice. "Let me out, I say—I will get out. What right have you to keep me here? You said you were going to take me home. Let me out."

Mr. Leech was not a muscular man; and in a struggle he was no match for the hardy young fellow he had got to deal with.

Taking every possible precaution to guard against a "topper" on the nose, he reached out his long arms, and endeavoured to clutch Charley by the collar.

This the young gentleman resented by a kick in the bottom button of Mr. Leech's waistcoat, which sent the man of law gasping into a corner.

Taking advantage of the disabled condition of the enemy, Charley let down the window and sprang out into the road.

But the lawyer had yet sufficient strength of mind and body, in spite of his winded state, to make another effort, and having the best of reasons for not wishing his young prisoner to escape, he sprang forward after him, and seized him by the back of the neck, as he jumped out.

This act, coupled with the rapid motion of the cab, had the effect of precipitating the boy upon his face in the road; and the cabman, attracted by the lawyer's cries, when, at some fifty yards distance, was beyond measure astonished to see Charley and that gentleman rolling one over the other across the road, until they both disappeared in the bottom of a ditch at the road side.

Then, pulling up his horse, he jumped from the box, and ran to the lawyer's assistance.

"Help! help!" bellowed Mr. Leech, from the ditch, spitting and spluttering, with his mouth full of mud. "Pull him off—break his head—strangle him!"

The cabman did not, perhaps, consider himself quite justified in resorting to these extreme measures, but he clutched Charley with one hand by the nape of the neck, and with the other by the seat of his trowsers; then, giving him a tremendous jerk, pulled him out, as though he had been a back tooth very tightly set.

But with the force of the pull he, at the same time lost his balance, and his legs flying up into the air, he came down with such a bang upon the back of his head, that he immediately loosened his hold upon the boy, and this latter, twisting round, began to pummell away at the driver's

WHAT CHARLEY FOUND IN THE CELLAR.

head, with the same vigour and pertinacity which he displayed in walloping the lawyer.

This time it was Mr. Leech's turn to come to the rescue of the cabman, and scrambling out of the ditch, covered with chick-weed and frog-spawn, which gave him the appearance of some strange amphibious monster, he rushed at the boy, and getting hold of him by the throat with both hands, contrived to drag him off his panting antagonist.

The cabman finding himself free, jumped to his feet, and the two men together, but not without immense difficulty, and more than one stumble, managed to overcome the redoubtable Mr. Wag, and thrust him yelling and screaming and kicking into the cab.

"Gag him," gasped Leech panting with his exertions; "his cursed row will be heard a mile off."

"I'll be blowed," said the cabman hastily wiping the perspiration off his head with the cuff of his coat; "if ever I see sich a bi—he's a hinfant Samson."

"Help me to fasten him; we musn't have this sort of thing happen again."

"You're right there, dash my buttons if the young vagabond don't want a regiment of soldiers to look after him. He could take us two along, I do believe, better than we can take him."

"Oh, he'll have a good deal of the bounce knocked out of him at the far end, that's one comfort."

"To school, he's going—aint he?"

"Yes, to a sort of school—kind of reformatory, where they lick young cubs into shape."

"Party of the name of Hopley keeps it, don't he?"

"Yes, do you know him?"

"I've heard of him. It was in the papers about him hiding a boy with a poker, wasn't it?"

"He did do something of the kind some time back, but he manages these things much better now, and keeps it quiet."

"Well, all I've got to say, is, I hope he'll lay on to this young animal pretty stiff for the trouble he's give us."

Charley, listening to this conversation, felt his heart sink within him at the awful prospect that seemed to be awaiting him.

"Never mind, though," the plucky little fellow thought to himself, "I've got a tidy pair of legs of my own, and I'll give them the slip yet if they don't look particularly sharp after me."

The men fastened his hands tightly behind his back with some thick string, which the driver happened to have in his pocket.

So tightly, indeed, that the jogging of the vehicle caused the cord to cut into the flesh of his wrists and his hands, through the stoppage of the circulation of the blood, swelled to almost double their natural size.

In like fashion they fastened his feet together, and then laid him at the bottom of the cab among the straw, where from time to time Mr. Leech amused himself by treading upon and kicking him.

The driver, climbing back upon his box, drove on as before, and Mr. Leech lighted a cigar.

Briskly along the level roads, sharply down the hills, and slowly up them, the cab travelled onwards.

The shades of night began to steal over the landscape, and arriving at the top of a higher hill than usual, the driver pointed out to the passenger inside that it was already night down below in the valley.

"How much further is it?" asked Mr. Leech, leaning his head out of the cab window.

"Ten mile or more yet, I expect."

"It'll be pitch dark, then, when we get there?"

"It will so."

They journeyed slowly along, for the horse was getting very tired, and dragged its legs very along, like a fatigued pedestrian doing his last mile in a wager against time.

"Do you think the mare 'll hold out?" Mr. Leech asked.

"All if it will," replied the driver.

"We'd better stop and halt for an hour, what do you think?"

"It won't do none of us no harm."

To tell the truth, the driver was weary too, and throughout the day had made several suggestions that they should get out and recruit the inner man, which, upon several occasions, Mr. Leech had complied with.

Coming upon a snug little public-house at the bottom of the hill, the driver got down to stretch his legs, while Mr. Leech went inside the inn to get a couple of glasses of hot gin-and-water.

He was some time gone. Perhaps he might have been having a little private drain on his own account before he brought out the driver's.

He was so very long gone that at last the cabman thought he would go and peep through the glass-door to see what the other was about.

Why should he not? The boy was safe enough — the cab door shut — nobody but a sleepy country lad to be seen, and he was leaning against the gate leading to the stables, about thirty yards off, whistling something with variations, which was meant to be "Rule Britannia," but was more like "Limerick Races."

He went up to the inn door, and looked through.

Not seeing Mr. Leech, he stepped in to light his pipe.

No sooner had the door closed upon him, than the sleepy country lad ceased to be sleepy, gave up "Rule Britannia" as a bad job, and, advancing to the cab, flattened his nose against the glass.

What he saw made him jump backwards, as though he had been shot; it was so unexpected.

It was a pale face turned upwards, the moonlight falling full upon and glittering in its open eyes.

"Oh, oh, oh! a boggard—a boggard!"* the lad bawled in an awful fright.

Then recovering a little of his small stock of wits, the young countryman advanced again to the window, and flattened his nose once more.

"It bain't a boggard, nother," this time he said, "it's a lad a loyin' of yis back."

Charley thus lying had managed to work the bandage which had been tied over his nose and mouth a little on one side, and he called out to him to open the door.

"Wha' dost say?" asked the young countryman.

"I'm being run away with," Charley bawled at the top of his voice, "call somebody to help me, or help me yourself."

"Who's a runnin' away with thee?" asked the yokel, who, of course, must ask a hundred questions before he could decide upon any course of action. "Where are they takin' thee to?"

"I don't know—be quick, for God's sake, or they will be back again."

"Is thee toid like?"

"I'm tied, of course, or I should get up. Open the door and cut the cords on my hands."

The young clodhopper slowly opened the door, and as leisurely took from his pocket a great clasp-knife. Then opening the largest blade said:

"Thee mun get up first."

"I can't unless you help me. Be quick or it will be no good."

Indeed so slow were his friend's movements that there was every reason to suppose that the driver and Mr. Leech would have returned before the strings were cut.

Once free from his bonds, the boy thought he could run with lightening speed along the road, jump over a hedge, and, sheltered in some dark corner, bid defiance to his pursuers.

But everything depended upon rapidity of action.

The delay of a moment might be fatal.

"Lift me up," cried Charley, in beseeching

---

* Bucholic for boguey or ghost.

tones, "do lift me up, for Heaven's sake, or I am lost."

The lad stooped down, and raised him to his feet. Charley turned round his hands towards him.

"Cut through," he said, "do not be afraid of hurting me, only be quick."

The other raised the knife, but as its edge touched the string he hesitated.

"I do'no that I'm doing roight," said he, "perhaps thee's some thieving chap that they're takin to t' lock-up."

"No—no, I am not. Oh! be quick."

Still, however, he deliberated.

This hesitation was fatal.

For by this time the cabman had lighted his pipe, and Mr. Leech, who being detained making some enquiries concerning the establishment in which they were in search, had made them, and they were returning to the cab together.

Opening the public-house door, they saw the state of affairs at the first glance.

In a much shorter time than it takes me to write it, and I am by no means slow with my pen, however illegible and difficult to decipher my caligraphy may be, the driver had seized the country lad by the ear and giving that organ a good wrench, swung him round by it from the door, and at the same time accompanying the movement with a sounding kick in the young gentleman's corduroys, sent him flying to the distance of half-a-dozen yards at least, when he fell on his head in a "muck-midden," where he lay blubbering, and squalling, and frightennd almost out of his senses.

"Drive on," said Leech, throwing the boy down again upon the floor of the cab, and resuming his seat inside. "Drive on as fast as you can, or that idiot's row will bring some one out of the house."

The driver jumped upon the box, and seizing the reins, they went as fast as the almost spent strength of the horse could carry them.

His chance of escape was gone, and a prey to feelings which it is easier to imagine than describe, the poor boy lay among the straw, and his heart heaved with suppressed sobs as though it would every moment have broken.

What was his fate to be? Where was he going? What was the meaning of this mysterious talk of these two men who held him captive?

Was there some place, some sort of school or prison, where boys were put quietly out of the way? Where they were starved, or tortured, or flogged to death?

If so, was this to be his fate, and why? What had he done? How had he wronged this mysterious lady who seemed to have conceived such an unaccountable hatred for him, that when she first saw him, her face and language had expressed the most intense loathing and detestation.

Had he not saved her life? Should she not rather have had cause to love him? What was the solution of this terrible mystery?

It seemed that the driver's calculation of the distance to their destination was not very correct, for in less than half-an-hour they had arrived.

During the last part of their journey they had travelled through a lonely, barren, and desolate tract of country, chiefly composed of marshes and fens, the only characteristics of which were the stunted growth of its trees, the rank luxuriance of its weeds, and the uniform stagnation of its water.

A miserably poor and unproductive spot it seemed, and the few straggling dwellings to be found here and there, were evidently inhabited by the most poverty-stricken and wretched of agricultural labourers.

This much and no more the travellers were able to see by the aid of the moon; before long they had reached the object of their journey.

A large red brick mansion, partly hidden by a row of lanky poplars, enclosed in a high wall with a massive iron-bound gate, and furthermore protected by a broad ditch of stagnant water, which was crossed by a little draw-bridge slung up to posts.

Pulling up in front of this, the driver began to shout "House," and "hallo" with all the power of his lungs by way of announcing their arrival.

"Who's there?" a voice presently replied from within.

"We've brought a pupil," bawled Mr. Leech.

"All right, I'll let you in."

The draw-bridge slowly descended, and the gates swang open.

Then the speaker, who had been as yet unseen, advanced towards them.

"Mr. Hopley," said the lawyer.

"My name, sir."

He was a thick set man, about forty years of age, bald-headed, and benevolent in appearance, only his mouth spoilt him, being a little too hard in its lines, and a little too thin lipped. His eyes, too, had perhaps rather a cunning look in them at times.

All this you noticed when first you saw him, but when you grew used to him, and heard him talk, (he had the most heavenly sentiments, and was tender and fatherly in his manner) you thought you must have been mistaken.

In this intermediate period of your knowledge of the man, that is to say, after you had left off suspecting him, and before you had found out for certain that he was a scoundrel, you probably thought him a pattern of excellence.

"This is the boy, is it?" said Mr. Hopley. "We have been expecting him for some time. He will find everything nice and comfortable. We have—ha, ha!—we have had the sheets aired."

Here the speaker laughed a very unpleasant laugh, without a halfpenny's worth of merriment in it, in which cheerful performance the other two men joined him with a loud guffaw.

"Will you take something to drink?" Hopley asked, when their laughing had subsided.

"No," replied Mr. Leech, "we will look up some inn in the neighbourhood, and get our supper; we shan't go back to-night, and if we leave it till much later, we may'nt get accommodation in this outlandish place."

"It is retired and primitive," said Mr. Hopley, with another of his unpleasant sniggers. "It suits me—ha, ha! very nicely. You won't come in, then? May I trouble you for—ha, ha! for my young charge?"

"Here's the tender plant ready trussed," said the cabman, dragging the boy out so violently, that he groaned with the pain of the cords cutting into his wrists, " shall I loosen him ?"

" Only his feet, so that he can walk. His hands are out of mischief as they are, so let them be."

Charley's feet having been untied, Hopley took charge of him, and, twisting his fingers in the boy's soft, silken hair, so as to manage him the more easily, ran him thus into the house.

As they entered, some one whom Charley had not hitherto observed, drew up the draw-bridge, and closed the door behind them.

It swung to with a dull and heavy bang, and the sound fell upon the poor boy's shrinking soul like the sound of the closing of a tomb upon the affrighted ears of one whose doom it is to be buried alive among the dead.

XII.—A Bad Place for Doctors—Faver-sham's Narrative—The Nocturn of Horror.

I SUPPOSE there is hardly any other neighbourhood about London so overdone with doctors, as Bayswater.

I dare say it is more unhealthy than others, and there is probably a greater demand for medical aid in this than in less damp and swampy suburbs.

Swamps, you say. Bless you, here is a stratum of clay, I don't know how deep, under your very kitchens. I recollect the whole of Westburnia no better than a marsh, in my school-days, and used to get bottling " effs " in the bog where the Grove stands, on half-holidays.

Perhaps, then, there is room for the doctors, but I can hardly think it. When I stand with my back to the " Royal Oak," and look up all the turnings, the number of red lamps and blue-bottle shops, is really awful. Do you mean to say they all can make a living ? If so, God save the sickly ones. Though, if you come to that, if I lived in such a neighbourhood, I should think it my duty to call in medical aid at least once a week, and keep a running account at a couple of chemist's shops for lozenges.

It was in Bayswater, and not a hundred miles from the " Royal Oak," that one morning when the medical population woke up sharp and active, they found that their ranks had been swollen by another F.R.C.S.

You can fancy how old Forceps, Steph. S. Cope, and Bolusout (brother of Bolusout, of Red Lion-square), stared aghast at the intruder's lamp and door plate.

Who did he expect was going to patronise him ? Where was his connection to come from ? they asked one another.

Lord, if he were only to have fallen ill, and required aid himself, how they would have been down upon him. I do not believe that there was one so uncharitable that he would not have supplied leeches gratis, and renewed them fifty an hour at the same terms if he would only have had them on.

But it seemed that the new doctor had means of his own.

The very first week he was there he started a carriage.

" Ha, ha ! " the medical community laughed hysterically, " let us hope it will last."

It did.

In a little while a rumour got about that the new doctor had a footing in the very best of families, and numbered among his patients the Duke of Heatherland himself, the Prime Minister of England.

How does he do it, thought Forceps, and he began to have serious thoughts of enlarging his own brass plate to the size of the new doctor's, and jobbing a brougham of the livery stables behind.

The new doctor was a tall, melancholy man, with fierce black eyes, sunken as it might be by long hours of laborious study. A gaunt, lean, ill-shapen man, on whom the tailor's art was thrown away, for no clothes seemed to fit him rightly.

As he sits this winter's evening in his surgery, and the fire-light falls full upon his strongly-marked features, if one did not know for a positive fact, that Faversham was not the name upon the door plate, one would be inclined to think that it must be our old friend thirteen years older, perhaps, than when we saw him last, but still the same.

And on the other side of the fire-place, who is that ?

One can hardly recognise in the grey-headed decrepid old man any likeness to a certain James Murdoch, who, thirteen years ago, was hanged for murder in front of Newgate prison.

But, nevertheless, James Murdoch it was —*alive*, too, certainly.

As they sit here silently, the flickering fire-light plays fitfully upon Murdoch's face, and makes one side of it look horribly distorted.

Or, is it really so ?

Yes, one corner of his mouth is drawn down, and one eye is wide open and fixed. His face is fearfully twisted, and baboon-like.

It has been so ever since the day *he was recalled to life.*

They have sat for some time perfectly still and motionless. At last, Faversham, raising his head from his hand, on which, supported by his elbow, it has been resting, he breaks the silence thus—

"Do you ever weary of the life I have restored to you, Murdoch ? " he asks.

At this question, his companion, who may have been thinking or dozing, starts half off his chair, and says in frightened tones—

" No sir, I never have; you know I never have, sir. What cause could I have for growing weary ? No, sir, I'm sure I haven't. How could I, and you so kind to me ? "

" You seem to be a poor, sickly, ailing wretch, with hardly ever a day's health to boast of."

" I've always been pulled out of shape-like since I had that cursed jerk. It seems to have broken up my constitution."

" Few people go so near to hell as you did Murdoch, without being a little singed."

" Lord, doctor, don't talk like that, please ; I can't bear it."

" You are in constant pain and misery, and afraid to go out of doors, or to show your face among men, lest you may be recognised as a man who has forfeited all claim to life, and who has no right to live."

Murdoch looks at the speaker uneasily.

" Yes—yes—" he stammers, " it is lucky they don't know, isn't it ? No, I'm not tired, sir, I assure you—not the least."

" Yet, I am! "

" You are ? What, tired of allowing me to live ?"

" No : what's your life to me ? Tired of living myself. Tired of acting this weary part. Tired of scheming, plotting, and planning. Tired of these deeds of blood that we do every day. How many have we struck off the list?"

" There have been thirteen fatalities during the last thirteen years of our practice of the noble art of medicine. Singular to say, all our little accidents have been in one family. In other cases, our cures have been miraculous. Have any of the thirteen deaths to which you allude, been attributed to any want of skill on the doctor's part?"

" Certainly not."

" Have the relations of the deceased in any instance expressed themselves in any way, but with admiration and gratitude ?"

" I do not recollect an instance."

" And on our list now many remains ? "

" Three. The duke, the duchess, and the little boy."

" And they shall go, too. In less than three years we shall have wiped from the face of the earth the last of the accursed race. Three short years more. Three years—three years. Would to God that they were come and passed, and that the deeds were done."

" You never told me your reason for this hatred which you bear them. At least, I have heard fragments of the history, but never all the facts."

" I have told you most of it, I think. I have told you how Heatherland and I were at school together. How he was the bully and I the fag. How I was used as a living warming pan, forced up the chimney of a winter's night, and made to stand with my feet in cold water a couple of hours at a time when there was snow upon the ground. How I have had to lick my lord's boots when I had not polished them to his satisfaction. How I have been thrust inside the wire fire-guard before a blazing furnace to make my lord's toast, and how one day I fainted with the heat, and fell against the red hot bars to burn my hand as now you see it. Look at the scar, it's blue and livid still. Look, man, can you see the wound creep as I recall the brutal act of that matchless scoundrel, tyrant, and bully —my enemy through life?"

As he spoke his excitement seemed to grow intense.

He rises from his seat, and paces the floor with the heavy, but wearing and restless tread of a caged tiger.

His companion silently regards him, alarmed and amazed, for it is a strange spectacle to see this man usually so calm and self-contained, thus strongly agitated.

" Have I not told you this again and again ? If I have not, it is because I have so long in secret, brooded over my injuries, that I have come at last to fancy all the world was in the same way occupied by them."

He pauses for a moment, and is silent.

Then continues—

" Perhaps I may not have told you how, when we grew up to be men, he thrust himself between me and all that I had on earth ? How, meeting at every turn, our interests clashed, and he was always victorious. How, at length, he broke up my home, and she whom I loved —nay, idolized rather, became his victim. She, a pure and gentle angel, who was brutally outraged, and murdered barbarously by this doubly-damned coward and miscreant.

Again the speaker pauses, and with his head held 'twixt his hands, sobs like a child.

At last he recovers his composure sufficiently to proceed.

" One night—I shall never forget it, if I live twice a hundred years—I was sent for, as I supposed, by a sick friend, who lived some miles from me. My house was then in one of the wildest and least frequented districts of Cornwall, upon the sea shore. I have recently taken up my abode there with my young wife. I did not even know that Heatherland was in that part of the country. Never, since the day when he had endeavoured to intrude his hateful presence upon our wedding party, and was, by my orders, ignominiously kicked out of Saint George's Church, had I seen or heard anything of him.

" I should tell you, by the way, Murdoch that he had endeavoured to supplant me in the affections of the woman who was to be my wife, as he had done upon every occasion, where I had set my heart upon the possession of any object. I said one night I was sent for to the bedside of a sick friend. Do you follow me ?"

" Perfectly ; perfectly ; go on."

" It was a wild and stormy night—wild and stormy even for that part of the country, where every night almost it blew a little hurricane. I was loath to depart and leave my warm comfortable fire-side and the company of she whom I loved so. Besides, I could not help fancying that there must be some mistake in the message I had received. Less than three hours ago I had left his bed-side, and my friend was then so much better than he had been for some days that I had every hope of his speedy recovery, and now came the astounding intelligence that he lay upon the point of death.

" As I rose, and took my riding cloak, I could not divert myself, of a strange foreboding of evil, and fain would I have interrogated the messenger to satisfy myself of the truth of his statement, but he, after delivering his errand to one of the female servants, had immediately departed. At length, my wife having noticed my hesitation, and enquired its cause, I made some trifling excuse, for I felt ashamed of owning my weakness even to her, and so, embracing her tenderly, I put on my hat and hurried from the house.

"The two men servants had that afternoon requested leave to absent themselves for a few hours, and had not yet returned. I went into the stable to saddle my horse myself, and not being over well acquainted with its external economy, was groping in the dark for the lantern and matches, when I was all of a sudden seized from behind by three or four pairs of hands, dashed violently to the earth, so that I was for some moments stunned and helpless from the effects of the fall, and lay almost unconscious; and then was securely bound with cords, gagged by some rude sharp instrument being thrust into my mouth, and dragged out into the moonlight. Then, firmly lashed to a tree, with my face towards the house, I was confronted with the Duke of Heatherland.

" 'Ralph Faversham,' he said, ' do you know me?'

"In the way that I was gagged, I was, of course, unable to utter a word, but I suppose he saw by the expression of loathing and disgust upon my countenance, that I knew him well enough, for he continued,

"I see you do, and I will tell you what has brought me here. You fancied, no doubt, that you had had a mighty triumph when you had married the woman whom I had honoured by falling in love with. You thought as you rode away in your carriage, and splashed me with the mud from your carriage wheels, that your triumph was complete. Poor fool. Think you that the insult which I suffered at your lacquey's hands would ever be forgotten or forgiven in me? No! I would have cut your plebian throat upon the spot, or stabbed you in your wedding bed, had I not had a glorious scheme of vengeance in my head. The time for carrying it out has come.

"Listen, Ralph Faversham," he continued, ' I have planned it that there shall be no interruption to night. I have brought with me a chosen band of young fellows, ripe for the work. We shall break into your house, pillage and gutter it from roof to cellar; and the woman who awhile ago dared to treat my honourable proposals with indifference, shall now be my prize by right of strength, and that while you are within hearing of her virtuous shrieks, without having power to render her the slightest assistance.'

"How shall I describe to you my feelings of mingled rage and despair at this open avowal of the dastardly intentions of this arch fiend? For some time I could not credit my senses, that such things could possibly take place in this enlightened age, and in England. Madly I strove to break the bonds which held me. Alas! they resisted my puerile efforts, and though in the fury of my passion and struggles the tree shook with my violence, the cords remained as tight as ever.

"Soon, as he had foretold, I heard screams of distress within the house. I strained my sense of hearing to the utmost to endeavour to catch a stray word of the loud and piercing cries which seemed simultaneously to burst from all parts of the building. At last a window was flung open on the side of the house where I was, and I heard the voice of her whom I love, her, whom to save an hour's pain I would have willingly myself have submitted to the severest torture that the devilish ingenuity of man could suggest—her voice I heard vainly pleading with the brutal ruffian in whose arms she struggled. Her voice I heard vainly shrieking to me to come and rescue her from pollution, shame, and disgrace.

"What could I do? I was powerless, worse than powerless, for I was there chained, within sight, within hearing of this monstrous outrage.

"After a while, by the lights which flitted about from room to room, and the wild shouts of boisterous merriment which smote upon my ears, I knew that the intruders must be ransacking the house, and from the sound of broken glass in the direction of the cellars that they had broken in there, and were intoxicating themselves with the wine.

"Louder and louder grew the shouts of demoniacal laughter; louder and louder the heart-rending shrieks and sobbings of the women. Hell seemed broken loose, my brain was on fire, my heart throbbed as though it would tear its way out of my lacerated breast. What centuries of time would it require to obliterate from my memory the fearful details of that horrid Saturnalia of blood and lust: but worse remains yet to be told.

"Awakening from what might have a brief period of unconciousness, I found the whole scene bathed in a flood of lurid light. The house was on fire. The flames poured from the lower windows. The sounds of merriment had died away. The shrieks of the women louder and more piercing, still remained. The cries issued from the garret, where the females had been confined. Chained there, unable to move hand or foot. I saw my poor wife at one of the topmost windows, wringing her hands in despair, and casting her beseeching eyes towards where I stood.

"Slowly, but surely the firey monster crept upwards towards his prey; the room beneath the floor on which she stood was a raging furnace; not a soul was there to render these martyred women assistance. The flames crept up and up, and lapped the smouldering rafters with their scorpion's tongues. At last the crisis came—the floor fell in, and, with a frenzied shriek, the suffering women fell into the blazing fire beneath."

"One remained alone—my wife.

"For a few brief moments, which were ages of agony to me, I saw her clinging wildly to the fragile woodwork of the window, enveloped in flames and smoke, but rending the scorched air with her hoarse shrieks of excruciating torture.

"Oh, God in Heaven! what did I not suffer. I prayed the Almighty to strike me blind or dead. My senses went at last, and when I came to myself again, many months had passed, and I was the inmate of a lunatic asylum. How I had been tried for murder and arson, and pardoned upon the ground of my insanity, is too long a story.

"When I recovered my reason, and through interest which I possessed, and still possess in certain high quarters, obtained my liberty, I wrote a full account of the circumstances, and publicly accused the duke. I narrowly escaped incarceration for the second time, the story was so wildly improbable and preposterous. Convinced of the folly of pursuing such a course any longer, I lit upon the scheme for vengeance, with the details of which you are already acquainted, and with my dead wife's aid have been able to carry them out."

When he has arrived thus far in his narrative, the speaker stopped abruptly, and burrying his head in his hands, seems lost in thought.

His companion, who has hung entranced and spell-bound upon the doctor's words, appears to be for some time quietly digesting the extraordinary story he has heard, and at last repeats, slowly and meditatively.

" With your dead wife's aid."

" With my dead wife's aid, yes," cries Faversham, springing suddenly to his feet, and clutching the murderer's arm in his iron grasp—" Yes, I have learnt the secrets of the tomb. The grave is not closed for me. The flesh may rot, the bones may crumble into dust; each particle of what was a human form slowly absorb itself into naught, and mingle with its mother earth, but I can call them back, Murdoch, from the realms of mystery, where all spirits, the blessed and damned crouch, waiting for the *awful summons.* You know how we have broken open the graves of those whom we have poisoned, for you have helped me at the work of resurrection, and brought the bodies here. You're used to corses now, I hope, after these years of contact with them; so am I with the spirits that have left them. Say man—say spy and felon, and murderer, doubly and trebly stained with blood; say, food for future fire, will you look on those who owe their present immortality to us. Speak! shall I call them forth?"

" No, no ; for God's sake doctor—devil— whatever you call yourself—I cannot bear it. Save me from them. Hide me! hide me! or I shall go stark, staring mad with fright."

The screaming, shivering, frantic wretch, clings to the other's skirts, and waves his outstretched hands, as though he would drive back the monstrous, stifling, indescribable horror, bearing down upon him.

But no, miserable man. Shut your eyes as tightly as you will. Lie grovelling like a crushed worm, on the floor, with your hidious, twisted, and distorted face grinding itself against the boards, as though he would burrow itself out of sight ; you cannot shut out the horror which surrounds you.

Cannot shut out the heavy, vapoury cloud curling round you nearer and nearer.

Cannot shut out the ghastly phantoms mouthing at you.

Cannot shut out the cold and grating voice of your companion, which, through the fearful nightmare, bids you look at them and be brave, for that the very air is thick with spirits such as these ; that they crowd your dwelling and jostle you in the busy street, only that they are unseen while these are visible and palpable.

But clutch at them, poor fool, in the desperation of your terror, and see how they will melt away into the thinnest air.

XIII.—FOLLOWS THE FORTUNES OF CHARLEY WAG, AND SHOWS WHAT HE DID IN A DARK CELLAR.

THE inside of Hopley's house was scarcely calculated to restore poor Charley's drooping spirits.

The door opened into a large, bare hall, the paper on the walls of which drooped with the damp, and in some places hung fluttering in the wind, like soiled and weather-beaten flags.

There was quite a colony of spiders, long-legged and lankey, also a slug or two, and a solitary black beetle.

He had not, however, much time allowed him for the study of these agreeable objects.

Hopley, after securing the door behind them, took him as before by the hair of the head, and guided him into a room which opened into the hall.

This was more comfortably furnished than the appearance outside would have led one to expect.

There were a few maps upon the walls, and several shelves filled with books; a drugget on the floor, a red cloth on the table, and an easy chair close up to a bright cheerful fire, blazing in the grate.

But, besides Hopley and the boy, the room had no other occupants.

The former lighted a lantern standing on a side-board, and then turning to Charley, said—

" Are you hungry ?"

" Yes, I am," the boy replied, stoutly.

" That's a pity, as far as it goes, because I don't give suppers. They're not wholesome."

" Will you give me something to drink ?"

" I've got nothing handy. However, the morning will soon be here, and then you'll have your breakfast. You seem a determined young blackguard, by the look of your eyes. I hardly know where I shall put you. You must not disturb your playfellows to night. What *shall* I do with you ?"

" If you can't find room," said Charley, who could not forbear from having his joke, even if he had known that it would have cost him a terrific hiding next moment. " You'd better put me outside the street door ; I can walk back to town, and get a bed."

Hopley looked at him a moment as though he could hardly believe the boy had spoken.

Then he advanced towards him.

Then—

Like a cowardly cur, as he was, he struck the boy in the face with his closed fist, a heavy vengeful blow, which sent him staggering back against the wall, and left a blue and swollen mark beneath his eye.

After this delicate attention, which Charley received silently, without cry or sob, Hopley took down a thick stick hanging by a string from the wall, and poising it in his right hand, seemed more than half inclined to use it over the boy's shoulders.

On second thoughts he did not, but pushing the boy before him, took the lantern, and thus guided Charley down stairs.

They descended several flights of steps, and found themselves at length in a kind of bricked vault horribly damp, and chilly, and foul.

From this, several doors opened into cellars still more damp and noisome.

Opening the door of one of these, Hopley pushed the boy in.

"Am not I to have any bed?" Charley asked, casting a rueful glance round.

"No."

"Won't you untie my hands?"

"No."

"The strings cut me dreadfully."

"So much the better."

"How long shall I stop here?"

"As long as I like. Till you die, perhaps."

"Why am I used in this way?"

"Because it's a good way of getting rid of you."

"Have I done anything to deserve it?"

"Not that I know of. Get in, will you, or I'll give you something to warm you. Now then, I'm going to shut the door."

"But, sir—you—you're not going to leave me in the dark?"

"Am I not, though, you'll see."

The door banged to, and the key grated in the rusty lock.

Then the boy heard the sound his of jailer's retreating footsteps.

After that, all was still.

It was an alarming situation, was it not, for one so young; and enough to try his courage, though he was as brave as a little lion.

Well, we shall see how he gets out of his fix. For I must not kill him yet, unless I can't possibly help it, after all the flattering letters young ladies at Leeds, Manchester, and Carlisle and I don't know where else besides, have sent to me about him.

Why, there are some who have even forgiven him that escapade of the goose, and think nothing of his flirtation with Mrs. Crocker's fat niece, and the other damsels of Slogger's-alley.

One who dates from "Land's End" (is it possible that Charley's history has got into that neighbourhood, and what news-agent supplied it?) says she would like to marry him if he were only old enough. Think of that, and would she marry the writer instead, I wonder.

Dear heart I wish I was not so grey, and bald and short-sighted, and that my teeth were sounder and more numerous.

Except a wrinkle or two, and, a slight stoop, there is no other sign of age about me, and I might do, perhaps, for Mary Ann of Land's End.

Left alone in the dark, Charley remained for some time silent, his mind a prey to contending emotions, in which rage and fear were curiously amalgamated.

His first idea was to go and kick the door with all his might, and to scream with all his voice, but he thought better of this, when he remembered that stick up stairs, hanging to a nail on the wall.

If he could only get his hands loose, he thought he might be able to make his escape.

Once outside the house, and in the open country, he would soon get back to town again, and defy the enemy.

He thought of his poor foster-mother.

What must her feelings be? What could she think had become of him? That he had left his home, and become the associate of thieves. She would then put the worse construction that upon affair of the goose.

This idea made him desperate; at any risk he would attempt to escape.

How could he loosen his hands.

He walked backwards round the room, so that he could feel the walls with his hands, (fastened, as you may remember, behind his back), and came at last to that which he was in search of—a sharp angle in the wall.

He fancied that he has seen such a thing in the cursory survey he had taken of his prison by the light of Hopley's lantern. Placing his hands close to this, he began to rub the string.

It was a slow process, and a painful one, for every now and then he grazed the skin off his wrist.

However, he stuck at it bravely, and in about an hour had cut through one of the strings. How to manage now was rather difficult, his wrists were so sore with the cutting of the cords and stoppage of the circulation of the blood, that he could not bare to pull them assunder.

It would take a whole page to tell you how he jerked and fiddled with, and manipulated that piece of string in endeavouring to unwrap it. At last it was unwrapped, and after a painful and tedious process, in which he had more than once, overcome with fatigue, leant against the wall and cryed, he managed to free himself.

But he had yet a great deal of work before him.

After he had pulled and pushed at the door for full ten minutes, without making any effect upon it, he began to come to the conclusion that it was a little too strong for him.

In his rage and mortification he flung himself against it with all his little strength.

The noise awakened a hundred echoes and frightened him by the clatter.

But moved not an inch.

It was coated with iron.

Decidedly it was not by the door that he must hope to effect his escape.

How else then?

The vault was dark as pitch.

He knew very well that it was a beautiful moonlight night without, and that if there was anything in the dungeon in the shape of a window, the rays of the moon must penetrate through it.

There was not, however, a speck of light to be seen.

It was black and silent as the tomb.

"If I could break away through the wall," the boy thought.

The walls were cold and moist. A thrill of horror shook his frame as he thought that, in making a hole, it might only be *to let in the water of the moat.*

"DON'T SHE SNORE!" SAID CHARLEY.

XIV.—SHOWS HOW CHARLEY MADE A HOLE IN THE WALL, AND WHAT HE FOUND WHEN HE GOT ON THE OTHER SIDE.

HOW should he commence?

With what implement effect his escape?

Round, and round the four walls, in all the corners, and on the floor, he groped about in the dark.

If he could only find some piece of iron—a crowbar—a spike, a rusty nail, anything that he could use to pick out a brick.

Most certainly, the way to liberty lay through the wall, and to get through the wall, he must pull out some of the bricks, and make a hole.

I suppose my reader has never tried to take a brick out of the side of a house. It is an operation which is both tiresome and difficult.

No. 10.

It can't be done with the finger nails. There is no good trying.

Poor Charley felt all round and round, as high up as he could reach. Every inch of the moist and filthy floor did he thumb over, getting his delicate little hands in a terribly grimy state, and damaging his neatly trimmed nails very considerably.

No, he could find nothing, not so much as a pin.

Fool!

So he called himself, for he all at once recollected that he had something in his pocket.

Not quite the sort of tool that a mason would have chosen, perhaps, had he wanted to do the job, but still not such a bad one after all.

It was a german silver pocket comb.

[CHARLEY WAG, THE NEW JACK SHEPPARD

You would have liked something else, perhaps. Bnt, you see, beggars must not be choosers.

If Robinson Crusoe had had his way, he would have liked to have taken a great many more little traps on shore with him. But if he had, his history would not have been nearly so interesting, so, I for one, am glad he didn't.

When Charley bethought him of his pocket comb, he set to work directly.

That is to say, he kicked the walls all round to find which sounded the hollowest.

Then he laid his ear against them, to listen for any noise.

The house was awfully quiet. It was impossible to tell on which side of him the water was. He must risk all, and try.

"Now, or never," said Charley, with determination, and opening his comb, he commenced operations.

After niggling a long while at the mortar, which was in many places damp and soft, he managed to get the extreme end of the comb between the bricks.

This done, he began to saw.

The long way of the brick, it was pretty straight sailing. The ends were more difficult, because in the latter case, he could not get such a good hold.

It seemed to him, too, that the further he got into the mortar, the harder it became. But still, he sawed away.

"Only to think that I should be doing this with Sophy's present," thought he.

It was that slut of a fat niece of Mrs. Crocker's who had given it to the young rascal, in exchange for, I should not like to say how many kisses.

However, he kept on working.

"It was meant to open *locks*," said Charley, with a smile, "but I don't know so much about bolts, keys, and bars, and as to stone walls, that *'ere's* quite out of the question."

Just to think of the hardened little vagabond cracking his jokes ever so much below low water mark, and with a prospect before his eyes of either being drowned, or flogged, or starved to death.

He sawed away. It had quite a musical sound, grating against the mortar.

Tring, tring—tring, tring. Very "like a bird."

But it was an awfully slow process. After an hour's work he had not more than done three sides of the brick.

If he should not have finished by the morning. If they should find that he had been attempting an escape, what fate awaited him?

He trembled to think of it.

But it was no good trembling. "Death or liberty," he thought. Your tremblers and deliberators never make any way in the world.

They don't take out many bricks, you may take your oath of that.

He worked away with renewed energy.

Thank God, at last he had gone all round. Now to prize it out.

The worst of it was, that in this instance, as in most others, the wall was two bricks thick, and between the bricks there was more mortar.

It was astonishing what a lot of useless labour had been expended upon the building of that house.

So at least Charley thought, as he poked his finger ends into the crevices he had made, and tried to force the brick out.

"It's only the first that is so difficult," said Charley to himself, "it has been done before, many a time, with a worse tool than I've got."

Then he began to think of the great JACK SHEPPARD, and of Baron Trenck, and a number of other famous persons who had done wonderful things in the prison-breaking way.

"I wonder whether I shall ever have to do this sort of work again," said Charley to himself.

I wonder, reader?

How he did pull and push at that obstinate brick. He made his finger ends dreadfully sore, and broke a nail or two, but got it no looser.

He could not manage to get well hold of it, as the mortar which he had cut away had but occupied a very small space. The only way that it could be managed was to grind away some of the brick on each side.

It was a long and wearisome process, but time and perseverance at last overcame the difficulty, and with a grand final effort, into which he threw all his remaining strength, he dislodged the first of the impediments to his liberty, and sent it with a crash to the other end of the cellar.

With renewed energy Charley worked at the hole.

In prizing at the second brick he broke his comb in half, but with the end he hacked and sawed until after another couple of hours he had managed to make an aperture sufficiently large to take a peep through at the cellar beyond.

It did not take long, you may be sure, to find out that he had not made a hole into the moat. The place, as well as he could see it, seemed to be much larger than the cellar in which he was confined, and it had a window in it.

By twisting his head round in several directions, to the imminent risk of dislocating his young neck, he could see the lower part of the window frame, and what seemed to be a dishclout thrust into one of the broken panes. He could also see a pile of wood, an old basket, and other rubbish heaped up in one corner.

But he could see nothing else: apparently the cellar was untenanted.

"There aren't any other boys locked up, I suppose," said Charley to himself. "I should have thought there were."

He worked away now with redoubled activity. "That's the window I shall get out of," he thought, as he peeped through again. "I hope the water isn't just close under it, but, of course, it can't be that, for there was a wall and a space between the house and the moat."

Perhaps, after all, he thought, he might not be near the water.

However that was to turn out he determined not to remain very long where he was, but to find his way into the next cellar.

By dint of much tugging and wrenching he got out some more bricks, and in time, through an inconceivably small aperture, he squeezed his little body, feet first, and landed safely on some flag-stones on the other side.

Then turning round, he blinked for a few moments in the strong moonlight, which, after the four or five hours of total darkness he had had, seemed as bright to his weak eyes as a noon-day sun in midsummer; he took a more deliberate survey of his new quarters.

It was then that his sight resting upon some horrible object straight before him, he gave a little scream, and retreated several steps in the direction from which he had come.

For there, at ten feet distant from the spot where he stood, he saw what at first he took to be the *half naked corpse of a boy chained by the waist to the wall.*

XV.—THE WRETCHED CAPTIVE—A TALE OF TORTURE—THE BLACK BEETLES.

CHARLEY'S first impulse was to beat a hasty retreat by the way that he had come.

Upon a moment's reflection he saw how foolish this would be. If this was a corpse he did not get very far away from it by going back. If he only managed to get out at the window he might escape in that way, and then it would not matter much to him whether there were one or a hundred corpses left behind.

He would look at it again.

"It can't eat me," he thought.

An attentive observation of the miserable object which had so alarmed him proved it to be alive.

If possible, it's being alive rendered it more horrible than if it had been dead.

It was a boy with matted hair, with red and watery eyes, with hollow cheeks, high cheek bones, and thin, bloodless lips.

He was wasted almost to a skeleton, and where his fleshless limbs, bare and blue with cold, burst through the huge rents in his torn and ragged garments, they had an indescribably ghastly effect in the pale moonlight.

He was so emaciated, wasted, and weak, that the only sign of life about him was a fish-like movement of his mouth, which he opened and shut slowly, as though he were talking, but in reality uttering no sound.

Overcoming, in some measure, the sensation of intense horror and disgust which the sight had involuntarily caused him, Charley advanced towards the unfortunate creature, and falling on his knees by his side, asked him to speak.

But the mouth only opened and shut as before, without uttering a sound.

Charley looked round him anxiously in search of some water.

A broken jar, placed just out of the boy's reach, contained a small quantity. It was stagnant and foul-smelling, but Charley, offering it to the boy, the latter drank it ravenously as though it were nectar.

Poor Charley was himself almost dying of thirst, but he felt that he would have rather remained another twelve hours without water, than have touched this loathsome liquid.

The wretched captive, partially revived by the draught, made several ineffectual efforts to express himself audibly, and at last got out three words, which bore some slight resemblance to :—

"Who—are—you?"

"I'm Charley Wag," replied that young gentleman, naively.

The name was not as well known then, as it is now, or it might have been known even to the person he was speaking to.

"Are—you—one—of—us?" asked Charley's fellow prisoner.

"One of who?" asked Charley.

"One of Hopley's lot."

"I don't know, I'm sure. Are you?"

"Yes," said the other with a sigh, "I am."

"What are you chained up for?" asked Charley.

"They've chained me up to starve me to death, I think."

"Starve you to death!"

"Yes. They have beaten me, oh horribly! Look!"

As he spoke, the unhappy creature uncovered one of his shoulders, and Charley saw that the whole of his back was one fearful sore, apparently the result of repeated floggings, and that, in some places, there were evident signs of rapidly approaching mortification.

For some seconds, our hero stood with his eyes rivetted upon the repulsive spectacle, and utterly speechless with horror and disgust.

"Good God!" he said at last, "who has done it?"

"Mr. Hopley, and Mrs. Hopley."

"Is there a Mrs. Hopley, then?"

"Yes; and a Miss."

"Does Miss beat the boys?"

"No, she don't, she plays the pianny."

"Plays the piano! Don't she do anything else?"

"Yes; I heard her singing."

"When?"

"When they've been licking us."

"That must have been a soothing accompaniment."

"No it ain't. It doesn't make it any the pleasanter."

"He can't see a joke," thought Charley to himself. "Poor beggar, I should be surprised if he could in the state he is. How often do they flog you?" he asked.

"Mostly every day; sometimes all day long. Either old Hopley or Mother Hopley, or one of the other boys, one after the other."

"Well, you get enough of it I should think. What do the brutes do it with?"

"Sometimes it's with a stick; sometimes with a cane; but mostly with a whalebone whip tied round with waxed string—and it cuts like a knife."

"You're joking."

"Indeed, I'm not, as you'll find out if you are one of us. Sometimes I've been tied up by the hands to a hook in the ceiling that they put there a purpose, five hours at a stretch."

"You may well say a stretch."

"They strip me naked; then Hopley goes at me till he was tired out, then the old woman, and sometimes one of the boys, and when they are all tired out, or I swoon with the pain, they cut me down all streaming with blood, and douse me head over heels into a tub of cold water, then chain me up here, where I am, to come round."

"The monsters! but have you never tried to escape?"

"I am so weak and poorly with the treatment I have had, I haven't got the strength."

"But surely somebody out of doors must hear your screaming."

"I don't think so. There are no houses near. The walls of the hou e are so thick, and the windows so well fastened. One day, up at one of the attic windows, I called out to a man I saw; that's why I speak so indistinct."

"What do you mean?"

"Hopley cut my tongue."

"Cut your tongue; impossible!"

"Didn't he though, you look.''

Sure enough, the atrocious ruffian had seriously mutilated the victim's tongue in such a way, that it was with the greatest difficulty that he could articulate his words.

Charley was petrified with terror.

"What did he do it with?" he said at last.

"With a pair of scissors; and he said he would put my eyes out, too, if I looked out of the window again. He caught hold of me by the cheeks then, and dragged them dreadfully. If Miss Hopeley hadn't come, I think he would have done it."

"But how many boys are there here? Why don't you turn round on them? I would."

"I don't think you would if you had been here as long as I have. The want of victuals takes your courage away."

"But how many of you are there?"

"I think there's six now."

"Now?"

"Four have died since I came. Three was licked to death, and *one the beadles eat!*"

"Beadles?"

"Black beadles. Hopeley put him in the cellar full of them, and he was too weak to keep them off, and they eat him up!"

"Don't talk like that," cried Charley, shivering all over like a leaf at this new horror. "I don't believe that beetles would hurt any one."

"Won't they, though. There was hundreds of thousands of them," the other boy cried, in the wildest excitement. "Thousands of thousands, all creeping and creeping; all the walls and the ceiling and the floor was alive. All creeping and creeping, and crackling like dry peas rolling about in a tray. It sent him mad: and we all heard him screaching louder and louder till they eat him up!"

When the boy paused a dead silence ensued, in which Charley, with suspended breath, remained motionless for several minutes, too horrified to speak.

At last he sprang to his feet.

"Come," said he, "let us go at once. If we waste any more time it may be too late. See, even now the daylight is breaking."

It was true. The moon had disappeared, and a dull, leaden hue was visible in the sky.

"What is outside that window?"

"I don't know."

"Then I'll try and find out," said Charley.

Placing his foot in a little niche in the wall, he sprang upwards and grasped the window-frame.

Then he pulled with all his might, to try and pull it open.

"It's stuck fast," said he.

"Break the panes!" said the other boy.

"Not so," replied Charley, "if I do it will make such a row; perhaps they will hear us."

"What's to be done, then?"

"If I had a good strong nail I might break away this strip of wood that holds the sash in. Then I could pull out the bottom part easily."

"There's a nail, I think, sticking in the wall?"

"Where?"

"Just on the left of the window."

Charley got down again, and sure enough there was a nail where the other had said. One of the ten-penny sort.

Charley caught hold of it with both hands, and after a desperate struggle loosened it.

Then with another struggle pulled it out.

"Now for it," said he, climbing back to his perch, "see how I'll manage it."

He was one of the handiest young dogs that ever breathed, and one of the most ingenious. Years afterwards, when he was differently situated, these talents of his came into play, and his genius electrified the great world of London, and set many older heads puzzling.

The woodwork of the window-frame was old and rotten, and forcing the nail between the laths like a chisel, he managed, after a little trouble, to loosen one at the side which held in the frame surrounding the glass. In the same way he loosened a lath at the bottom.

Then he easily managed to take out the bottom part of the window.

Who can tell with what unspeakable joy he felt the free air of Heaven blowing upon his face.

Yet another effort and he would be free.

But how about the other boy?

Up to now, Charley had been so busy that he had not had time to consider in what way he was going to help his friend out of the place. He had not considered one very great difficulty, which lay in the fact of the unfortunate creature's being too weak to stand.

When the window was out, Charley got down to help him.

"You're fastened to the wall, aren't you?"

"Yes, by the waist."

"Couldn't you break the chain?"

"It is too strong—I am too weak. I could not pull, or it would cut into my wounds."

"It's fastened round your waist with a padlock isn't it?"

"Yes, this large one."

"Ah! for that matter, the larger the better, as we shall have to pick it."

"Pick it! with what?"

"My friend the ten-penny will do it; or, stop a minute. My neck pin. No, hang it all, that bends too much. They don't manufacture a very good article for two-pence. It looks well, but there's no wear in it."

"What will you do?"

"There's a small nail somewhere, I hope. Ah, here we are. Come out of that."

So saying he pulled a nail out of the woodwork of the window.

"This will do," he continued, "it's got a beautiful twist to its tail that will be the very thing for the job."

With as much readiness as he had shown in breaking through walls and tearing open windows, Mr. Wag now set about picking the lock.

In three minutes he had done it.

"Who taught you that?" asked his companion, astonished.

"Never mind now," replied Charley, "we'll talk it over presently. It's not the only trick I've learnt, by ever so many."

"So it seems."

"Can you stand up?"

The captive struggled feebly to do as he was desired, but fell back exhausted.

"I'm too weak," he said. "I'm afraid you must leave me."

"Leave you! What are you talking about? I'll carry you pig-a-back."

"No, no: you can't do it. I shall only hinder you. Get away yourself."

"What! do you think I would be such a cur as to leave you in the lurch? never."

"Do, do. Bless you for your kindness, but it is no good—Hush, listen!"

"What is it? I hear nothing."

"I do. Some one's coming down the cellar stairs."

"Yes, I hear them now. Let me get you on my back."

And Charley endeavoured to lift him.

"No—no—you can't, leave me."

"Hold round my neck."

"My fingers are numbed with cold."

"Try, try. I want my hands to climb with."

"Let me down. I can't hold you. I've no strength. Save yourself for God's sake!"

"But you will be eaten by beetles," cried Charley, endeavouring to throw him across his shoulder.

"Heaven help me!"

Charley clutched the lad round the waist, and jumped up to the window.

At that moment the sound of a key grating in the lock of the door, smote upon their ears.

At the same moment, too, the lath to which Charley was clinging gave way, and they fell back into the cellar.

The door opened.

XVI.—UNDER THE BED.

CLOSE by the side of the window, there was a hole in the wall, arched at the top, shallow, but very dark.

Into this, like a flash of lightning, Charley sprang.

So rapid was the movement that, although the door opened towards that side of the cellar, the person entering did not see him.

It was Hopley.

"What's up now?" he said. "What are you trying to do? How have you broken your chain?"

In entering the cellar, the jailor's eyes had fallen upon the prostrate form of his victim, which, lying in the lightest place there was, and directly in front of the door, when it was wide open, was naturally the first object to attract his attention.

Stooping down, Hopley took the boy in his arms to raise him up.

In doing so, he caught sight of the broken window, then twisting round glared at the hole which Charley had made in the wall of communication.

Throwing his living burthen with violence to the ground, he ran forward and jumped through the aperture, to make sure that the fugitive was not concealed there.

Desperately seizing this moment as the one in which it would be best to make an attempt at escape, Charley slipped out of his hiding-place.

For half-a-second he hesitated which course to pursue.

Should he climb up to the window, jump out, and run for his life.

If he did, could he get over the wall? Could he open the gate? Could he cross the moat? Would he even then be able to get clean away?

He would not have much start. The house stood in the centre of an extensive plot of marsh land. For almost half-a-mile there was no tree or shelter of any kind. Did they not rush out and capture him, they might with the greatest ease have shot him dead from one of the upper windows.

No, there was no escape that way, he would have been as much at their mercy as a wretched rat is at the mercy of an experienced terrier in a rat pit.

There was no corner to creep into out of harms way.

Another scheme that came into his head, and was as rapidly dismissed, was to catch up one of the brick-bats strewn upon the floor, and dash it into Hopley's face.

Thus stunning him, he might have got clear off, and perhaps helped his unfortunate companion.

But if he missed? If Hopley guarded the blow?

No it was risking too much.

Then the last scheme. What was it? What did he do after all?

Slipped from his hiding place, as I have said, and in the twinkling of an eye passed through the open door, and on to the dark staircase.

"I'll hide here, somewhere," Charley thought, "and when he's gone, come back and get through the window, or out some other way. I dare say he'll think I've escaped through the window already, if that boy doesn't tell him to the contrary."

At that moment he heard Hopley's voice, in furious tones, enquiring,

"Where is he? What has become of the infernal young scoundrel?"

Then came a dull heavy sound, as though the brutal ruffian were kicking the poor boy lying on the floor.

Then a hollow moan of agony.

Next moment he was outside the door, and rapidly ascending the stairs.

Like the wind, Charley flew before him, dreading at every moment that he should be detected. Most fortunately, the staircase was very dark; The only light in the hall above, struggled through a crack in the shutters of a staircase window, between the first and ground floors.

Profiting by this obscurity, he hoped to escape, but a fresh danger arose.

Hopley, below, began to shout for help.

"Mrs. Hopley! Mrs. Hopley!"

To which a shrill female voice, from a room leading out of the hall, rejoined with—

"Well, what is it now."

"If she comes out, and catches sight of me," thought Charley, "it will be all over."

How could he then avoid it? There was no convenient nook or corner to slip into out of sight. The only plan was to make for the stairs leading to the top of the house. If he could pass through the hall, before the lady came out, and get round the turning on the stairs above, he would be safe.

He sprung forward as nimble as a fawn, as noiseless as a cat.

"Come down here," he heard Hopley calling.

"I'm coming;" the lady replied.

Then he heard her moving forward. She opened the door. He would inevitably have been discovered—indeed, he had given himself up for lost—but Providence befriended him. The door opened *outwards*. In opening it concealed him.

He flattened himself against the wall and held his breath.

The woman passed out—passed by—never noticed him.

As she descended to the lower regions, he ran up-stairs to the upper. His plan was now to find some place of concealment where he could stow himself away until night.

"What I shall do for my grub," said Mr. Wag, as a rumbling inside his little waistcoat apprised him that it stood in need of a lining, "is more than I can tell. However, something may turn up. The question is, where shall I get to?"

He tried the handles of several doors along the landing, but they were all fast. To add to his perplexity, he heard the steps of Hopley ascending the stairs. He *must* get somewhere.

Ah! at last! The last door yielded to his touch: he opened it as noiselessly as possible, shut it behind him again, and turning round found himself in a bed-room.

It was a lady's bed-room he could see, by the hasty observation he took of it.

There was a bonnet, and a straw-hat, and several dresses of different material hanging up upon pegs. There was also a dress, lately taken off, thrown over the back of a chair. Several petticoats, plain and embroidered, calico and flannel, a pair of stays, and a crinoline.

Looking from there to the bed, he saw that the person to whom they belonged had been reading in bed, for the book had fallen open by the bed-side.

"It's Mrs. Hopley's bed-room," said Charley to himself. "I'd better shift my quarters."

But no! there was not time for that; Hopley was coming up the passage. Was apparently coming straight towards the door of this apartment.

"I'll get under the bed. GOOD GRACIOUS!"

Well might he make the observation for the bed was occupied.

One of the plumpest and prettiest faces you could have wished to have seen—in oh! such a frilled nightcap—lay upon the pillow.

"That's Miss Hopley, for a penny!" said Mr. Wag. "That's the young lady who plays the piano while the governor wollops the boys. If she was to catch sight of me, I suppose I should be put among the beetles directly; however, here goes."

And under the bed he went.

Meanwhile the steps approached but stopped, to Charley's great relief, at the next room door.

Rather pleased with his success so far, Mr. Wag screwed himself round in his hiding place and endeavoured to make himself as comfortable as possible.

"I wonder what sort of a party she is?" thought he, peeping out under the vallance, "If she takes after her pa, she's not the nicest disposition in the world. She's better looking than he is, any how. I didn't see much of Mrs. H., only that she had on a flannel petticoat, a good deal too short behind, and wore a pocket handkerchief wrapped round her head for a nightcap. What's that book about, I wonder."

He reached out for it, and pulled it under the bed. It was Lord Byron's *Don Juan*.

"That's rather spicey, I've heard," said Mr. Wag, "I don't care much for poetry as a general rule, but if I have to stop here long, I think I shall read it."

He was a cool young card, don't you think so?

"A lady who reads Lord Byron in bed, ought to be sentimental," thought Master Charles, "I wonder whether she would have pity on an unhappy captive. I wish I'd whiskers."

He pondered mournfully on the disadvantage of being young.

"Don't she snore just," said he, presently. "That's not very sentimental. I wonder whether most girls do."

XVII.—DEAD BODIES BY WHOLESALE.

DID you imagine that I had done with our old friend Toddleboy?

Did you think I had let him die quietly, or put him out of the way, because I did not know what to do with him?

Not a bit of it. Before I have done with him, he will have some surprising adventures, and the same remark may apply to my other characters. I am obliged to let them sleep for a little while, but all in good time, I shall go back to them again, and show you that they were not introduced, like some of the people in a pantomime, just for the sake of being knocked down.

Besides, you would not have me fill up page after page, when I had nothing interesting to tell you. My publisher requires *quality*, as well as *quantity*. You should go to those wretched weaklings who encumber our would-be comic periodicals—Mr. Hollingshead and the rest of the "slop-shop" *literari*—if you want the greatest possible number of words with the smallest possible amount of meaning.

Do you recollect a workhouse, of which I described the exterior in my 3rd chapter, (Book I.) It was in the parish of Saint Starver-Cum-Bago'-Bones, I told you. You may not, perhaps, be acquainted with the establishment to which I allude. It seems, however, that my sketch was pretty true to nature, if I may judge by the indignant remonstrance of an indignant parochial authority, which lies before me at this moment, and the receipt of which I here take the opportunity of acknowledging, at the same time, hoping that the writer is no worse than he was when he sat down to abuse me.

I am going in at the same workhouse again. This time, a good deal stronger.

One wild and wintry night, just about the same time that the events I have been describing in my last three or four chapters were taking place, an elderly individual with his coat collar turned up, and his nose hidden in a red comforter, was paddling through the mud and half-melted snow, in Smithfield market.

"It was Toddleboy, and he was on his way to the workhouse, where he had attempted to leave little Charley that night he was instrumental in rescuing the young gentleman from the river Thames.

In course of time, after a good many stumbles, and a good many good round curses directed against other wayfarers who stumbled up against him, old Mr. Toddleboy at length reached his destination, and rang the great bell.

"Now then!" said the beadle.

"I have come," began Mr. Toddleboy, deliberately—he was an old gentleman, who took his time over every thing, and picked his words well—"I have come—"

"I can see that," growled the doorkeeper. "When are you going back?"

"I tell you what it is—"

"That's what I want you to do."

Finding it was no good to attempt to argue with any one so ready with his rejoinders, Mr. Toddleboy contented himself by saying—

"Please to let me in; I have come on business."

"Who do you want to see?"

"Joe Cudder."

"Who's he?"

"A pauper who's dying."

"Ah, there's a many of 'em that ways inclined. I never see sich perverseness. As if they didn't cost the country enough in wittles, without robbin' 'em in doctor's bills. Come in, will you? Relation, I suppose?"

"No, a friend."

"A friend, eh? That aint a bad 'un; I never heered of a pauper having a friend afore. Them paupers is going it."

Without waiting to discuss the matter any further, Mr. Toddleboy walked forward, and crossing the court-yard, entered the low, frowning portal of St. Starver's.

In the hall, the first person that he encountered was Bloodyer, the master.

Bloodyer was a pompous man, with a face which might have been handsome had it not been for the hardness of the mouth and the slyness of his eyes.

Those who read men's characters by their physiognomy, would have saw that he could be both cruel and crafty, but yet he bore the best of characters.

He had from time to time got a little name in parish politics. Had suggested some improvements, and talked largely of ameliorating the condition of the poor. When he was a churchwarden the poor had been his hobby. That is why he had got his present berth. Failing in business (he was in the undertaking way) certain influential friends of his had got him the mastership of the workhouse, and since he had been in it everybody had spoken well of him.

Even the paupers.

In fact St. Starvers was such a comfortable workhouse that there was quite a run on it by the old people in the parish, and the only drawback was when they were in it they died off so quickly.

So much the better you may say (that is supposing you are a Poor Law Commissioner), so much the better for the other old people.

Perhaps it was. One old person died off and another old person crept into their place in the old people's wards, which was very comfortable indeed : then began to ail a little—ailed a little more—took to their bed, and passed out to the dead-house in a wooden box a very plump and comfortable-looking pauper corpse, by no means like what you would have expected a pauper corpse to have been.

When Mr. Toddleboy came into the hall, there stood Bloodyer the master, talking in the kindest possible way to an old pauper woman leaning on a crutch.

"You've got the warm corner by the fire, now Mrs. Hubbard, I hope."

"Thank you kindly, yes sir."

"Take care of yourself then, you good old soul, will you?"

"Thank you, sir, I'll try."

"Do you take snuff, Mrs. Hubbard?"

"When I get it gave me, sir."

"There's a pinch for you, then."

"God bless your kind heart, sir."

And the old lady tottered off, crowing with delight over a quarter ounce of Irish blackguard, screwed up in paper.

Just then, Mr. Toddleboy came up and caught the master's eye.

"What is it, old man," said the latter.

"I want to see a man who is dying, sir, I believe."

"Who is that?"

"Joe Cudder."

A curious expression passed over the workhouse master's face, half anger—half apprehensive.

"I thought he had no relations," he said.

"Nor has he, except his wife—at least I know of none."

"And his wife has not been heard of for these ten years past."

"Not that I know of."

"Then who are you, pray?"

"A friend of his."

"A friend, eh?"

"The only one he ever had. When I heard by accident this evening that he was so near death, I came at once to see him."

"I should be sorry to go between you and any kindness you might wish to show the dying man, but you cannot do so."

"Cannot!"

"The doctor has forbidden his being disturbed."

"It is of the greatest importance that I should see him. Otherwise the ends of justice will be defeated."

Again a change came over the workhouse master's face.

"Ends of justice," he gasped.

"Yes; the fact is, that the dying man is alone acquainted with the address of a certain notorious scoundrel, of the name of Jack Rattan."

Once more a change in Bloodyer's face. This time it became perfectly livid. Mr. Toddleboy could not help noticing it. "You are ill," said he.

Bloodyer wiped the perspiration off his face.

"No, no," he replied, hastily. "It is nothing—a passing faintness. I shall be better, directly. What name did you say?"

"Joe Cudder."

"No; the other man. Jack, something."

"Rattan."

"Yes! Rattan, was it? I have heard the name before, I think. That is to say, I have read it in the police reports. What has he done now?"

"He has lured away a boy, of the name of Wag. His friends are all very anxious about him. They are afraid that Rattan will induce him to become a thief."

"Oh! indeed! That is it. I hope you'll find him."

Bloodyer seemed to recover himself after this, and Mr. Toddleboy having enquired whether he was better, and been answered in the affirmative, they proceeded together in the direction of the ward where Joe Cudder was lying.

He was lying in a bed apart from the rest, quite by itself, in a corner of a long straggling apartment, and surrounded by a tall screen.

Noiselessly passing down the room, the floor of which with its india-rubber covering muffled the sound of their footsteps, naturally rendered as noiseless as possible, in the presence of so much sickness, for almost every bed had an occupant, they presently reached the one in which they were in search.

The man lay asleep, or insensible, when Mr. Toddleboy first glanced at him, and he was so still and motionless, that his visitor in his first surprise and terror, called out—

"Good God, he is dead."

But at the sound of his voice, the sufferer slowly opened his eyes.

"Not yet," he said, in hollow tones—"not yet. I soon shall be, no doubt."

He was a ghastly spectacle to look at, so shrunken and pinched up. His hand lying upon the coverlet, a mere claw, bony and bird-like.

When the dying man's eyes rested on Toddleboy's face, the transient smile of recognition flitted across his ashy lips, and he muttered his name.

"Well, Joe," his friend said, "Joe, my poor fellow."

He took the dying man's hand in his saying this, and pressed it gently.

"I thought you wouldn't let me die without giving me a look up," Joe said; "I've been waiting for you."

"I am sorry to find you down so low, old boy. What have you to say to me?"

"Say to you. Nothing. Yes, yes, I have. Something I must say to you alone."

His manner became wild and excited as he spoke, and he clutched Toddleboy's wrist with his thin and wasted hand.

"This really cannot continue," Bloodyer broke in, "it's against all rules. Is it not, doctor?"

"Quite so," a solemn voice rejoined close to Toddleboy's elbow.

He turned round with a start, and an exclamation of surprise. Then recognised, with a feeling of unspeakable horror, the mysterious being to whose unholy incantations he had been compulsorily obliged to listen one day, nearly thirteen years ago, behind a curtain in an old set of chambers.

What did he want there?

Without an atom of evidence, the old man instinctively connected the baneful presence of Ralph Faversham with the hopeless condition of the emaciated body lying before them upon the workhouse bed.

Faversham and he regarded each other silently, for a few moments. It was evident that the former recollected having seen the old man before, but had forgotten under what circumstances the meeting had taken place.

"Quite so," he repeated after a while, "I would not answer for the consequences resulting from any injudicious excitement."

"But I must, I will speak to him," screamed the old man frantically, "I will not die until I have said what I have to say."

"Calm yourself, my good fellow," the workhouse master interposed, "we will not talk of dying yet. Calm yourself, and say what you have to say now. There are none but friends round you."

"No, no," persisted Cudder, "I will tell it to no one but him. Let the others leave me."

"This is madness," the master said, with a shake of the head and a shrug of the shoulders, "perfect madness. Can we allow it, doctor?"

"It shall not take place with my authority," replied Faversham, looking at his watch, "if this state of excitement continue, any moment may be fatal to the patient."

"I think then, sir," interposed Mr. Toddleboy, "that our further prolonging the dispute will cause a continuance, or even an increase of the excitement you think so injurious. Had we not better humour the poor fellow?"

The master glanced at the doctor, and the doctor returned the look. Then the latter nodded slightly, and without a word, they withdrew.

LISTENERS HEAR NO GOOD OF THEMSELVES.

Not to any great distance, however, for Faversham took a chair, about ten yards off, while Bloodyer remained just outside the screen, concealed from the view of the dying man and his visitor, but still within hearing of anything above a low whisper.

When Cudder thought they were alone, he said, endeavouring to draw Mr. Toddleboy towards him, with a weak fretful motion of his skinny fingers.

"I have something to tell you—something horrible to tell you. They're not listening, are they?"

"No, no; I think not. Speak low; what is it?"

There was very little occasion for the caution. The man's voice was so subdued by sickness and suffering that he hardly spoke at loudest above his breath.

"Yes, yes!" he said, "I will tell you. I am so happy that you have come. I have known you a long while, Toddleboy. How many years is it, now?"

"Never mind that, Joe. I am afraid that they may interrupt us, if you do not make haste."

"To be sure: I hope they won't. I could never die, until I had told you. I have been thinking of it, day and night, these three weary weeks that I have been lying here dying on this miserable bed, and have been planning and scheming how I should manage to see you. I have been fearing that you too might be ill, or gone from London, or somehow out of the way at the time. If you had been, I do believe the disappointment would have killed me."

"I got your message all right," said Toddleboy, "of course, I came at once."

"I knew you would. It's very kind of you. I had something to say to you. Let's see, what was it? To be sure—I am very glad you have come."

The old boatman's mind was evidently fast leaving him.

His wits were wool-gathering.

"Come, come," said Toddleboy, endeavouring to rouse and quicken his sluggish faculties, "you've told me all that before."

"Told it you all before! Yes, yes, to be sure—to be sure. Then that is off my mind!"

And the dying man leant back his head, and remained silent.

This would never do. Toddleboy's curiosity was excited beyond all possible endurance.

Just then, Bloodyer, who, owing to the low tone in which the dialogue had been conducted, had, up to now, been unable to catch a word; and, if one might judge by the anxious expression of his attentive face, as he stood listening behind the screen, was fearful, lest the dying man should make some communication prejudicial to his establishment, thought it best now to interfere.

"This conversation really cannot continue any longer," he continued, "the doctor has strictly forbidden any excitement. In my position, as master of the workhouse, I cannot allow you to remain any longer. If I did I should think that I was answerable for the poor creature's death."

Mr. Toddleboy looked anxiously at his old friend to see whether he would remonstrate with this decision, or would express a wish for a prolongation of their interview, but he said not a word.

White and quiet as a corpse he lay back upon his pillow, scarcely breathing.

"At any rate," said Mr. Toddleboy, as the object which chiefly brought him there occurred to his mind, "I cannot depart without enquiring the man's address which I am in search of. Joe—Joe," he continued, stooping down over the dying man, and calling in his ear, "do you know Jack Rattan?"

As though he had just received an electric shock the old boatman sprang up in bed with eyes and mouth distended.

The workhouse master with a cry of alarm fell back from him several paces, and Faversham hurried forward.

"Rattan—Rattan, yes," the dying man cried hoarsely, "know him, of course I know him. I want to speak of him, as I told you. He was here last night."

"Oh, this is delirium—madness," the master interrupted, "I cannot allow it to continue."

"Mad, you say," screamed Cudder, "I am not mad, although what I have got to say is so frightfully horrible it will seem much more like the raving of a madman than the statement of a sane man."

"Really, really, doctor is this to be permitted to continue?"

But the doctor was silent, waiting to hear what the man had to say, and, perhaps, judging it wiser to interfere at a later period.

"Last night, when they thought me asleep, but when I but lay with my eyes shut shamming slumber, they came whispering round my bed. Rattan and him—and him."

He pointed his bony finger as he spoke towards the workhouse master and the doctor, and, as Toddleboy fancied, they exchanged looks, and the former grew a trifle paler than was his wont —but the latter's face was always of such a deadly hue that it was impossible for it to lose more of its colour.

"Then, then," continued Cudder, "when they thought I slept they looked at me awhile, and one said, 'I told you the medicine did not act,' and the other, 'What was the good of trying any fresh stuff when the old kind worked them off so easy!' and then the third replied, 'It was an experiment of mine, but there's time to remedy the evil yet; he shall die as well conditioned as any of them, or at the worst, we can put his body out of the way. Considering the trade we have driven lately we can afford to lose his measily carcase.'"

During this speech, the workhouse master had remained perfectly silent, the muscles of his face twitching convulsively, and the drops of sweat chasing each other down his pallid brow.

As Toddleboy turned towards him in wild alarm and terror at the strange statement the dying man had just made, Bloodyer endeavoured to recover his wonted composure, but in vain, and he wiped his face with his pocket handkerchief, endeavouring to conceal his features as much as possible.

Faversham, however, maintained his usual demeanour; he even laughed in a quiet way.

"As good as a romance," he said, "but very horrid — really, very horrid. A disagreeable phase of the complaint I think it would be better to leave him."

So saying, the doctor laid his hand upon Mr. Toddleboy's shoulder, and endeavoured quietly to draw him away from the bed-side.

The old gentleman was very much perplexed. He could, as yet, make neither head nor tail of what Cudder had just said, but he felt convinced that there must be something very horrible going on somewhere, if he could only make out where and what it was.

"If it is his raving—" he said doubtfully.

But here Cudder interrupted wildly, and schreeching at the top of his voice—

"As heaven is my witness, no; I am not raving. They are murdering me, slowly as they are murdering all the other poor wretches in this accursed place. Track them, bring them to justice. Seek out Rattan—you will find him."

"You shall *not* remain any longer here," interposed the workhouse master, catching Toddleboy by the arm, and dragging him forcibly away. "As for that maniac, I will have him chained up in a separate part of the building. I cannot have everybody annoyed in this way. It is scandalous. Such charges—such absurdities in an establishment which has so long been cited as the best regulated in London—I really"—

"You *know* it is true, you black-hearted villian," yelled the boatman, now perfectly furious, who in his passion, sprang half out of bed as though he would have clutched Bloodyer by the throat, at which movement, the master beat a precipitated retreat behind Toddleboy, and trembled violently. "You know it is true—you have sold all their bodies—you monster—you have—you have."

Here his indignation or his terror lending him strength, the workhouse master got his two arms round Toddleboy's waist, and tore him from the spot.

While yet he was struggling with him, Faversham stepped up to the dying man, thrust him back foaming at the mouth and screaming frantically, and as he held his head upon the pillow, pressed something into his mouth.

Almost simultaneously as his fingers touched the dying man's lips, old Joe's head fell back upon the pillow motionless. A slight convulsion shook his frame, and for a moment or two his feet and hands quivered like dead leaves in the wind.

Then all was still.

The inmates of the other beds, awakened by the noise, look up with scared faces, poked out of the bed-clothes, which, otherwise, they held tightly under their chins.

A faint odour of almonds crept towards the nearest beds, and set one pauper, who liked the flavour, sniffing.

"Lie down, all of you," said the doctor, in a kind voice, "he will disturb you no more. I have given him something to quiet him."

XVIII.—Mr. Toddleboy gets out of the Frying-pan into the Fire.

TODDLEBOY had not seen what the doctor did to quiet his old friend, but quite undecided how to act, and by no means too sure whether he was really wide awake, and had really heard the extraordinary statements Cudder had just made, he allowed himself to be led quietly away, along the room, and down stairs into the workhouse master's private room.

When there, Bloodyer, closing the door behind him and the doctor, said:

"Sit down, my friend, I will give you a glass of brandy, I am sure I want one myself after that distressing scene."

So saying, he took a bottle and some glasses from a sideboard and filled a glass for each of them.

Then, handing one to Mr. Toddleboy and another to Faversham, he took the third himself, and, nodding to the other gentlemen, tossed off the contents of his own.

Toddleboy, in a like fashion, emptied his. Spirits never came amiss to him, though he had taken the pledge half-a-dozen times, at least, in the course of his life.

"You knew the poor man, Mr. ——. I did not catch the name."

"Toddleboy."

"Mr. Toddleboy, from what I understood, he sent to you."

"Yes, he sent to me."

"By someone, now, I suppose, attached to this establishment. Poor fellow, he was not always wandering like we have seen him to-night. You said attached to the establishment, I think, Mr. Toddledchoy."

"Toddleboy's my name. No; I didn't."

Mr. Toddleboy did not like a mistake made in his patronymic.

"I thought you mentioned the name of one of the inmates?"

"I mentioned no name."

"Have a little more brandy. It was a mistake of mine. Heigho! what a wreck? what a wreck?"

He looked straight at Mr. T. as he said this, and that gentleman asked, a little gruffly,

"Who's a wreck?"

"I referred to the mind of the poor creature whose bedside we have just left. What an extraordinary hallucination that was?"

"What was?"

"What he was raving about."

"It was extraordinary, as you say," replied Mr. Toddleboy, drily.

"Such a monstrous notion, and, unhappily, one, if promulgated, so likely to cause all sorts of absurd ideas to creep into people's heads, is it not?"

"I shouldn't wonder," said Mr. Toddleboy, with something very like a chuckle, "if it didn't lead to an enquiry, *if it got about.*"

"But then it cannot do—"

"Some of the parties in the other beds may mention it."

"Poor creatures, I fear they are all too much absorbed by their own ailments to notice anything that goes on round them."

"He called loud enough."

"Not loud enough for them to hear or understand, unless you were to repeat it."

"I were to repeat it?"

"I know it is a perfect absurdity to suppose that you would. As a man of the world, Mr. Toddleboy, you must know how foolishly people talk; of course, if there were a single word of truth in it—"

"What then?"

"What then?"

"Yes."

They looked at each other fixedly, Toddleboy and the workhouse master, as though each were endeavouring to find out what was the other's precise game.

"Why, then," said the workhouse master, after a slight pause, "it would be different, wouldn't it? However, there isn't—in fact, it is really so outrageously improbable that no one would believe it."

"Some people are very credulous."

"What do you mean? Are you?"

"Sometimes."

"In this instance, I mean?"

"I hardly know. What Cudder said was very extraordinary, was it not? but I have, in my time, seen some very extraordinary things. I once saw a man, who had been hanged, brought to life again."

"How long ago was that?" asked Faversham, who up to now had not mixed himself in the conversation, "where did it happen?"

"At a barrister's chambers in one of the inns of law."

"Indeed! I used to live in chambers myself once. Have some more brandy."

Here Faversham helped him.

" Now tell us all about it."

"But Mr. Toddleboy was reasoning with me upon the probability of Cudder's statement," broke in the master.

"We will speak about that presently," said Faversham, abruptly, "where were you when you saw this ? "

Mr. Toddleboy was going to explain, when a most curious thing happened to him.

I have just told you that spirits never came amiss to him. He was, in fact, accustomed upon occasions to "put away" any quantity without showing any particular signs of it having disagreed with him. On the contrary, he came out rather strong under the influence of intoxicating drinks, and was at times very brilliant and witty.

But here was a most astonishing event.

He had only had three small glasses of brandy and he was beginning to feel a most remarkable sensation in his head. A sort of buzzing, a sort of spinning. There were half-a-dozen workhouse masters sitting in a row, and as many white-faced doctors leaning upon the backs of their chairs, regarding him fixedly. Then again they were wagging their heads, and presently, strange as it may seem, the workhouse masters and doctors, fifty of them if there was one, were playing at leap frog.

When he had sat and seen them jump a hundred times over one another's heads, all which they did in half as many seconds, he thought he would take a little nap—he felt so very sleepy.

But he could not have been long like this before he felt himself being shaken violently, so that his head rocked to and fro upon his shoulders, and the doctor's voice, as loud and ringing as a trumpet's blast, repeated the question it had put before.

"Where were you," it said, "when you saw this ? "

Then Toddleboy, opening one eye at a time, with almost as great an effort as though each eyelid weighed a hundredweight, stared at him and saw as much of him as he could, considering the way in which the doctor kept on jumping, and tried vainly to say something, but finding his tongue a great deal too big for his mouth, and very much in the way, gave it up, shut his eyes again, and took another nap.

While thus enjoying himself, he heard, or dream't that he heard, this conversation.

" It has soon taken effect."

" I intended it to do so."

" How much did you give him."

" If anything, I gave him *too* much."

" That's on the safe side though."

"Tolerably safe. It will throw him into a trance."

" We can get rid of his body then."

" Yes, I have thought of that."

" How do you propose." ?

"None of the nurses have been near the bed, you know. I told them it was the typhus. I will bring a woman from the other side to lay him out. Do you see we can change the bodies, I will carry the other away presently by the private staircase. Put the screen well before

the bed and turn the lights down and the other wretches will never notice us."

" But the nurses ?"

" We must keep them out of the way."

"Why should you change the bodies though ?"

"Because I can account for this. The other I used the quick medicine for."

" But the body-dressers can see nothing suspicious, can they ?"

" They can smell it though ; it is not safe."

" And the other body. How shall we dispose of it ?"

" Leave that to me. It's not the first piece of carrion we have disposed of. I think there's a market for all of them."

"Ha, ha ! nobody would believe so much could be made out of a pauper ; would they ? It was a bright idea."

"It has saved the county some expense at any rate. Here, help me to take his clothes off. We must make haste and change the corpses."

The next thing that Toddleboy dreamt was that he had died sometime ago, and was *lying in a dead house covered with a sheet.*

XIX.—A Very Romantic Young Lady—A Very Audacious Invention—and a Very Wild Scheme of Escape.

I LEFT Charley Wag under the bed, reading his book of poetry as comfortable as you please.

It however occurred to him all of a sudden, that he had better not keep *Don Juan* any longer, for fear the young lady should wake up and look for it, which, to say the least, would be rather awkward.

As he couldn't read, the next best thing for him to do, was to go to sleep. But there were two drawbacks. One, that he might snore. He was not sure whether he usually did so or not ; nobody is, but he was afraid that perhaps he might.

The other objection was, she might while he was asleep, get up, and then in that case—he always was a regular young monkey.

These things considered, he determined not to go to sleep, but just to take two or three winks at a time, and keep on the look out.

It would not take a Solomon to tell what was the result of this great determination. He had no sooner shut his eyes, than he was as the saying is, " fast as a rock."

He could form no notion as to how long he had slept, but he woke up frightfully hungry. Well he might, too, if you will please to consider the length of time the unfortunate little fellow had been without food.

Waking up ravenous, he listens for a moment to ascertain whether anybody was in the room, peeped out cautiously, satisfied himself that he was alone, and crept from under the bed.

First, he took a drink from the water-bottle, and then, without any more ado, or making any unnecessary fuss about the matter, began to open the drawers and the cupboards to see what he could find.

"Girls do keep good things up in their bed-rooms," said he to himself; "Mrs. Crocker's neice does—bulls-eyes and biscuits to eat in bed. She says they're lumptious if it wasn't for the crumbs."

Sure enough, Miss Hopley had a little store of "goodies."

He found three peppermint drops in a paper.

These did not take very much eating as you may suppose, and did not fill his stomach particularly, when he had done with them. He, however, continued his investigation. The next lot he dropped upon, was half-a-stick of chocolate. Then some sweet biscuits (two and a-half), which had been kept rather too long, and tasted of hair oil, owing, their proximity to a chenille net. To wash these down, he took a little *eau de Cologne* and water, mixing it in a tooth tumbler, and stirring it round with a hair-pin.

After he had finished this pleasing beverage—I am told that it is the favourite tipple of the female aristocrary, and accounts for much of the brilliancy of their eyes, and their immense flow of spirits, which otherwise the horrible unnatural life that they lead, would very soon destroy; after he finished, he went on with his search, but found nothing more to eat in the drawers.

There was a large quantity of wearing apparel, which, had he not been so peckish, he might have regarded with more interest and curiosity. There were also some old valentines, a few penny numbers of intensely exciting love stories, adorned with pictures of finely-proportioned females, lounging in voluptuous attitudes, with as little clothes on as the hotest possible weather would permit of. But what were they to him? He was too hungry.

When he had looked everywhere else as a last resource, he opened a cupboard door, and there to be sure, was what he was in search of. In a box on the floor was a large plum cake, and by the side of it a bottle of ginger wine.

"I wish I had come across this," said master Charles, "before I found those beastly biscuits."

They had, in fact, made him feel rather sick.

To compensate himself, however, he broke a large lump of the cake and took a great gulph of the wine, and then sat down on the edge of the bed and enjoyed himself.

While thus engaged, he heard a door slam.

At first, he was so startled, that he half thought it was the door of the room where he was, and he was devided between the idea of bolting under the bed and that of seizing the poker, and selling his life dearly after a terrific combat.

But recovering his presence of mind, he recognised the direction of the sound, which was that of the street-door slamming to. He ran to the window and looked out.

It was Hopley and his wife who had left the house together, and were walking rapidly across the common.

"By Jove!" cried Charley, "is Miss H. here by herself, I wonder. Do they keep a servant? Shall I try to make my escape? No, I wont risk it yet."

When he had come to this conclusion, he heard steps on the landing. He had made up

his mind he would not go back under the bed, for it was very uncomfortable—not to say undignified.

"I'll get into the cupboard" thought he; "even if she comes to peg away at that cake, I can get behind one of these frocks and she'll never see me."

He therefore got into the cupboard with as little delay as possible; hid himself, covering up his legs with some dirty linen, which was fortunately there, and waited.

The room door opened, and two persons entered the apartment.

They were Miss Hopley and Jemima the maid come to make the bed. They began to talk of course, as ladies always do talk, when they are making a bed. It is a great time for the exchange of confidences. When they go up stairs to brush their hair or put on their "things" is another. That makes them so long about it. We mankind don't take a quarter the time over our hair.

Charley screwed himself up into the smallest possible compass and, little rascal that he was, listened with all his ears as big as pitchers.

"Heigho! Jemima," sighed Miss Hopley, punching at a bolster.

"Heigho! Miss Lucinda," sighed Jemima, doing the same by the feather bed.

"I'm bored to death, Jemima!"

"So am I, Miss."

"Nothing to see—nothing to do—nobody to speak to—nobody to fall in love with."

"Nobody to fall in love with us, that's the worst of it, Miss."

"I suppose it is. You have had one sweet-heart, Jemima, haven't you?"

"I won't deny Miss, there was a young feller very sweet on me at one time. We kept company reg'lar, near on to three months."

"You were betrothed."

"Was we, Miss. Well, p'r'aps we was. Anyhow we was very comfortable."

"What used he to say to you, Jemima? Tell me all about it."

"He usedn't to say much, Miss, no more did I. He was in the green-grocery as I've told you before, Miss. He used to call upon me at my place, all unbeknown, and he would sit as it might be you there and me here on the kitchin dresser, or if it was full of plates, on the sink, and then he would fetch a sithe—"

"Fetch a scythe? What for?"

"To relieve himself, Miss. Draw a long breath, I mean, from the bottom of his stomach."

"You mean a sigh, Jemima. Go on."

"I dare say I do, Miss. And then I would fetch a what-do-you-call-it too. And then we would neither of us say nothing by the hour together and we was so happy—so happy! Oh, you have no idea."

"It must be very sweet to be loved," Miss Hopley said, with a pensive sadness, probably pondering over the touching picture of bliss which Jemima had just been drawing. "Sweet, very sweet."

"It is, Miss, there is no denying. And I should have had that young man now, I make no doubt, if parties as ought to be ashamed of theirselves for so doing, had not come betwixt us and made mischief, besides my having had words with him touching his conduct on a Sunday out when we went a ride in the train, and he behaved hisself unbecoming a gentleman when passing through a tunnel."

By this time they had finished making the bed, and Jemima, after taking the rough dust off the chimney ornaments, the shepherdesses and china bow-wows, beat a retreat, and the beautiful Lucinda was left alone with her own love-sick reflections.

She was a most sentimental young person although she was fat. It doesn't follow because a lady is fat that she must not be sentimental. The spare ones pretend so, but believe me it's only jealousy after all.

Miss Lucinda took up her favourite *Don Juan*, and sighing deeply, began to turn over the pages in a pensive mood, but she was not long before she again laid down the book, and heaving another sigh, much deeper than the last, exclaimed, in sorrowful accents—

Oh, why, why—why have I not a lover? I am young, and handsome, and rich. I am sure —I am positive—that there are lots of handsome young fellows who would fall in love with me like they fall in love with other girls, if they only knew of me, but they don't; and how am I ever to let them in this horrible desert?"

"But they do know of you. One knows of you, most beautiful lady," cried that audacious young vagabond, Charles Wag, Esq., jumping out of the cupboard, "one who loves you with his whole heart, his whole soul—his—his—loves you like anything, and will lay the treasures of the Indies at your feet."

"Boy!" cried Miss Lucinda, when she had sufficiently recovered from the shock of the first surprise to speak, "what means this? Who are you? Is this madness?"

"Oh, Miss Lucinda," cried Mr. Wag, upon his knees, "spurn me not; oh, Miss Lucinda but hear my tale."

"Boy," said Miss Lucinda, again in freezing accents, "you are much too young. Your proposition is ridiculous."

Charley, although he did not exactly know what the proposition was which he was supposed to have made, continued—

"It is not of myself," he said, "that I would speak. Oh, no, lovely lady, I am much too humble a poor boy to dare to have the assurance. It is of another that I want to tell you. Ah, one who loves you madly and blindly."

Charley had read a good many penny romances, and knew the proper style.

"Of whom would you speak?" said she.

"Of a stranger—a mysterious stranger."

"A mysterious stranger?" said Lucinda, deeply interested.

"Yes," said Charley, "a mysterious stranger —a foreign nobleman, who loves you to distraction."

"Loves me, impossible! Why, I have never set eyes on him, that I am aware of."

"What does that matter, Miss? He has seen you at least a hundred times. By the hour he has stood and watched you."

"Watched me! How?"

"From behind the wall. Look, he is there now; do you not perceive the crown of his hat?"

"No," replied Lucinda, opening her big brown eyes to their widest, "I can't say I do."

"You're not looking in the right direction," said the mischievous young monkey, pointing to quite an opposite point to that which at first he had indicated.

"Where?" cried Lucinda, dreadfully eager.

"Too late!" said Mr. Wag, "he is lost to our view."

"What has become of him, then?"

"I think he has in all probability sat down by the edge of the water, if he has not thrown himself in it, unless he has taken his hat off."

"Good gracious, boy! he would not surely be so foolish. Why does he hang about the house like that? I am sure he will get into trouble if he is seen. Why does he not make a proposition to my papa, in the usual form?"

"Because, alas!" said Mr. Wag, pathetically, "he knows that it would be hopeless."

"And who are you?" pursued Miss Lucinda, "Are you sent by him, or— Ah! I know who you are—you are the boy who broke out of the cellar."

"Yes," replied Charley, "but I know that you are too tender hearted to betray me. Listen to me, and I will tell you my history."

"I am sure I don't know why I should. I know it is very imprudent of me. And in my bed-chamber too—if you were not such a bit of a boy—"

You should have seen Master Charles blush. It touched his dignity sadly. Nothing hurt him more than an allusion to his youth. The precocious young imp wanted to be taken for twice his age. He had wit and assurance enough for a man of the world of fifty, for that matter; but allowing for some degrees of doubt respecting his precise age, when he was picked out of the water he could not have been much more than fourteen, and was believed by his foster-mother to be even less.

"Listen to me," said he, "and I will tell you all—"

"Be as quick as possible, then," said she. "I would not, for the world, have Jemima find you here."

"To begin, then," said the audacious young vagabond, who had not the remotest idea what he was going to say next, "I must commence at the beginning."

"Do so, then," suggested Miss Lucinda, seeing that he hesitated.

"Or rather, it is necessary that I should begin in the middle."

"Well, begin, somewhere, please."

"But before beginning," said Mr. Wag, gradually getting up a terrible tree, "I had better ask you whether you know why I was brought here?"

"I know that you came here by the desire of the lady whom you rescued from the water."

"Right, so far," said Mr. Wag, "but do you know why?"

"No."

"Do you know what was going to be done with me?"

"I don't know what papa does with the boys that are brought here. He keeps them to work down in the cellars, I believe. Papa has forbidden me to go there."

"How did you know I had broken out then?"

"I heard papa say so."

"Did you ever hear of the black beetles?"

"No; what black beetles?"

"Do you know how many boys your papa has got here?"

"Yes, ten."

Charley considered a moment. The boy in the cellar had told him that since he had been there, four had died and only six remained. Was it possible that she did not know of the horrible cruelties that were practised in the house? He looked her steadfastly in the face. She met his gaze without flinching. No; she was perfectly innocent, he was convinced.

Could what the boy had told him be false? But when he remembered the treatment he himself had experienced at Hopley's hands, he could not doubt the truth of the story. Besides, had he not seen the frightfully bruised and emaciated condition of the poor creatures body?

During the time that he was pondering over these and other matters, Lucinda was growing impatient.

"What story were you going to tell me?" said she, "why don't you begin?"

"You must know, then," said Mr. Wag, commencing a story he recollected, "Francesco De Crossbones, otherwise the Red Eyed Pirate of the Poisoned Pacific, whose life he took in in numbers, had commenced his autobiography when in a communicative mood to his Lieutenant, Pedro Crack Skull, alias the Mangy Man-eater of the Mountains. "You must know, then, that I was born of rich and noble parents. Having been changed in infancy, for reasons with which I will not trouble you, I was put out to nurse to a humble but honest woman, and having remained with her some years, gradually grew up."

"Yes, of course; go on."

"My mother frequently came to see me, and used to take me home, in her carriage, when his lordship, my father, was out. She lived—do you know London?"

"No, I have never been there."

"Haven't you? Well! She lived in a magnificent house, in the middle of Trafalgar-square, surrounded by the most beautiful fountains. To bring my story to a close, I met the foreign nobleman, I told you of, who is outside the wall, at my mother's mansion, and he told me that he was hopelessly in love with one of the most beautiful women in the world, who lived in a lonely house, on a common, in the country. When I happened to look out of the window, just now, I saw him, to my astonishment, looking up at me, and I called to him to say that I wanted to get out, and he called to me to say that he wanted to get in. Now, what I propose is, that we both escape together. The nobleman will marry you, and you will have a splendid palace and lots of servants, and I can help you along the road. What do you say?"

Lucinda did not know what to say. She was a romantic young lady, who had spent her life in the country, reading all sorts of nonsensical stories, in all of which things twice as improbable occurred over and over again.

She longed to be away from that hateful old house. She had about fifty pounds in gold, which, a pound at a time, she had pilfered from her papa, with a foolish romantic idea of eloping, assuming man's attire, and wandering about in search of adventures. If she was ever to go, why not now. She would, before her father and mother returned.

But just as she had made up her mind, the great door-bell rung, and she saw that her father and mother had come back, bringing with them Mr. Leech and the cabman.

They must put off their scheme for the present.

"I hope that my papa will not see the nobleman," she said.

"No fear of that," replied Mr. Wag, "He'll keep out of sight, I'll bet a penny."

"Do you want anything to eat or drink?" she asked, "I have some plum-cake in the cupboard."

"No thank you," replied Master Charles hastily, "I'm not at all hungry."

Then they entered into a long conversation in whispers, as to what the nobleman was like, what his name was, &c. All which information Master Charles obliged her with very readily.

Presently, Charley asked what time it was, and was much astonished to find that it was four o'clock in the afternoon. Lucinda told him to hide himself in the cupboard, and went down stairs to tea—coming up every now and then to see how he was getting on, and telling him not to spare the ginger wine.

"They are all setting drinking," said she, "they think you have gone back to London. We will wait till they get tipsy and go to sleep."

Then they waited until night fall, with fluttering hearts, dreading they knew not what.

XX.—FIRE! FIRE! FIRE!

NIGHT came at last.

From time to time, throughout the evening, the sounds of coarse and boisterous merriment from below told the boy that his captors were having a drunken debauch.

"So much the better," thought he, "we shall be all the better able to give them the slip."

The hours gradually crept by; the noise below grew louder and louder—they were singing songs, which, from the stray portions that reached them, seemed not of the selectest; then they heard Mrs. Hopley, in shrill falsetto joining in the chorus.

"The old woman is getting tight, too," said Charley, to himself; "she is a sweet thing in feminines, if ever there was one."

Lucinda did not remain long below after the harmony had commenced.

Pleading a bad sick headache, she left the pleasing society of her parents and their guests, and came up-stairs to her own bed-room. Jemima slept on the ground-floor, and had already gone to bed.

It was past twelve o'clock.

"Now is the time," said Charley, "we must commence operations, let us go down stairs, open the street door, let down the draw-bridge as quietly as possible. They will never hear us now they are so drunk, and we can make a bolt of it."

Acting upon this advice, the enterprising young couple took off their boots, Miss Lucinda her Balmorals, and Master Charles his Bluchers, and descended the stairs on tip-toe.

Passing the sitting-room door they heard a boisterous chorus going on inside, which was noisy if not musical.

"Couldn't be better," said Charley, "they wont listen to us. Now for the door."

Charley pulled the bolts open, then the bottom, then turned the handle of the door. It did not open.

"It's locked," said Charley, "where is the key kept?"

"Gracious goodness," cried Lucinda, "papa keeps it, I ought to have thought of that before."

"Well, I don't know that it wouldn't have been as well if you had, for yor see it rather interferes with our arrangements."

And the young monkey leant against the wall to laugh, as though forsooth it was an occasion for the indulgence of levity.

"What is to be done?" Lucinda said, with tears in her eyes.

"Isn't there any other door?" asked Charley.

"There used to be one at the back, but papa had it plastered up."

"I wish your papa was plastered up," said Mr. Wag, "let us go upstairs again."

"But what shall we do?" Lucinda asked when they had again reached the bed room.

"We shall let ourselves out of window by a sheet. Are you a good one at climbing?"

"I don't think I am," replied the fat young lady, doubtfully, "but I never tried."

"Oh, you'll do it famously, I know. You've only got to slide down the sheet like a rope. I'll go first, if you like, and show you how."

"No," said Lucinda, with a little hesitation, "I think I had better go first, because—it would be better."

"All right," said Charley with a grin, and he straightway began to drag the sheets off the bed, and knot them together in quite a business-like fashion.

When they were fastened, he tried their steength in various ways, then he made one end fast to the leg of a solid mahogany table, and then made a rope out of some towels, and fastened the leg of the table to the bars of the grate.

His elaborate preparations somewhat resembled the intricate apparatuses erected by the rocky wonders at the Alhambra Music Hall before they go through with some of their terrible performances.

When everything was ready, Charley said: "Doesn't the window underneath belong to the room where your pa's friends are sitting drinking."

"No, it dosen't, that is two windows further on."

"I tell you what will be a capital plan, then."

"What's that?"

"To set the house on fire."

"Merciful goodness!" Why should we do that?"

"Just to cover our retreat. They'll be trying to put it out, and we shall get clear off. Don't you see."

"But perhaps we shall burn them."

"No such luck, they are all close to the door, and they'll all get out, you may take your oath to that."

"How shall we do it, then?"

"I'll do it," said Charley "with the greatest of pleasure; give me a match or two, and you stop where you are."

She did as he desired, and he left the room, and crept softly down stairs.

In three minutes he returned.

"What have you done?" said she.

"Set light to some feathers."

"Where?"

"In a sort of lumber-room—they were tied up in paper bags. I lit them all. They are going it like blazes."

"Merciful providence," exclaimed Lucinda, in the wildest alarm, "we are ruined!"

"Why so?"

"Because, in that room papa keeps a little keg of gunpowder, and, if the fire reaches it, in another moment we may be launched into eternity."

"Then, the sooner we are off the better."

He forthwith threw the end of the sheet out of the window.

But now, when everything depended upon their activity, poor Lucinda's presence of mind deserted her.

She felt sure she couldn't do it.

"Try," said Charley, "I don't think I can lift you."

Indeed she was a thumper, and fainting in a girl of her size at such a time was, to say the best of it, rather out of place.

"Try," repeated Charley, more persuasively, "think of the nobleman waiting for you."

I don't know whether it was her terror for fire or her love of sparks which caused her to hasten her movements a little.

They climbed out of the window together, she took hold of the sheets with both hands, he took hold of them with his right, passing his left round her waist.

Then at the moment they commenced the descent a fearful explosion shook the house to it's very foundation, and simultaneously as it seemed, the flames burst out of the window beneath them.

And then, as if to add an additional terror to his situation; for a moment the girl's senses appeared to desert her, and loosening her hold she hung for an instant a dead weight upon his arm.

"Hold up, hold up, for God sake," he cried, in frenzied accents, clinging at the same time to the sheet with all his strength.

Recovering her sences in some measure by an immense effort, the fair Lucinda managed to keep her hold upon the sheet, and so they glided down to the ground.

They were no sooner there than they ran to the gate. This, of course, Lucinda knew how to open. They lowered the bridge, and were half a-cross the moat in another sixty seconds.

CHARLEY SAVES HIS DEAREST LUCINDA.

On they ran, without once looking back. The whole country was as light as day. Behind them they fancied they heard the hoarse shouting of their pursuers mingle with the roaring of the furnace.

"I don't think I can run much further," said the fat young lady.

And she paused and panted, with her hand upon her heart.

Indeed, few ladies are good runners, and the stout ones are not the best, I should fancy.

"We must keep on for a little while," said Charley, pulling her by the arm. "Don't give in yet."

Every moment the country seemed to grow lighter and lighter, as the flames, which now had seized upon every part of the building, increased in fierceness, and poured through a

No. 12.

gaping aperture in the roof, reddening the sky above by the reflection.

In front of them, at a short distance, there was a low stone wall, which serpentined by the roadside for a considerable distance.

"When we get to that," said Charley, pointing towards the wall in question, "we can take our breath a bit."

It required but one last effort. With his arm round her waist they ran forward. They reached it, and the girl sank down upon the moist earth, almost fainting.

"Oh, Charley," she said, "Oh! I am so tired. Oh! I cannot go any further. Leave me, and run on yourself."

"That's likely, isn't it? What's to become of you?"

[CHARLEY WAG, THE NEW JACK SHEPPARD.

"I don't know, and I don't care. I could not move another step to save my life."

"Well, you won't have to do so, yet awhile. In this light we can see whether anybody is coming. If they do we can hide behind the wall, in this dark corner. They would never see us. Look at the fire!"

They both looked at it. The fury of the devouring monster seemed momentarily to increase."

"Oh, Charley," the girl whispered, clinging to his arm, and trembling in every limb. "How awful it is! How wicked we have been! Do you think they will escape?"

"Who?"

"My father and mother, and the rest."

"Yes—yes. Don't you see the figures of two women by the side of the moat. Those must be Mrs. Hopley and the servant. Look there, two men, also, but I don't see the boys.

"I do. Over there, by the gate."

"How many do you see?" cried Charley, becoming violently excited. "I only see five."

"That is all."

"Then *he* is left behind," Charley exclaimed, springing forward from the shade of the wall.

"Charley, Charley," repeated Lucinda, clasping her arms round him, "what would you do? where are you going?"

"They have left him behind, I tell you. He will be burnt to death, or buried among the ruins. And I am the cause of it. Oh, my God! my God! forgive me!"

And he fell, sobbing, upon his knees, with his arms outstretched towards Heaven.

For a moment, awe-struck by his violent emotion, the girl stood watching him. Then she, too, sank down by his side, and leaning her face upon his shoulder—sobbed in concert.

But was not woman ever a comforter? Even in that business of the apple, I warrant me Mrs. Eve did her best to console Adam for his lost Paradise, and kissed and carressed the foolish creature more than ever in their banishment.

Thus was it, that Lucinda endeavoured to console her young companion.

"Don't take it to heart like that, Charley, we never meant it to end like this; but so it has, and so it can't be helped. What's done, cannot be undone."

"And perhaps they have got him out, poor fellow. He was too weak to stand. He is lying down, perhaps, and so we cannot seek him. They would never be such wretches as to leave him to burn."

"Oh, Charley, whatever would they do to us if they caught us? Hadn't we better be going?"

"Yes—are you stronger, now?"

"Much stronger."

"Come, then."

XXI.—NOTHING LIKE "CHEEK"—UPON THE ROAD, BUT NOT OUT OF DANGER.

KEEPING as much as possible in the shade of the wall, the hopeful young couple made as much haste as they possibly could, and had soon put such a distance between themselves and the scene of conflagration, that nothing but the reflection upon the skies was visible to them.

"Do you know which way we are going?" Charley asked of his companion, when they had travelled about a couple of miles.

"The road we are on is the London road, I believe," replied Lucinda.

"How far do you think it is to the next inn?"

"I think there is what they call a posting-house, at the next turn of the road."

"What's that, a post-office?"

"No; an inn, where they keep post-chaises for hire."

"That's the very thing for us."

"How so?"

"Because we can hire one."

"We can? But it will look so extraordinary, wont it."

"Not a bit of it. They know you, don't they."

"Yes; I think they do."

"Well, then, say the governor is ill, and you are going for a doctor."

"What, to London?"

"No; to some railway station. Pretend you want to telegraph. Don't you see?"

"The nearest station is about fifteen miles off. There is no line running through this part of the country."

"How far is it to the nearest large town?"

"Further than that, I think."

"That's all the better; say you are going there."

"But when we get there, we shall not be in London."

"How far off, do you think?"

"About fifteen miles; more, perhaps.

"It's on the road, anyhow. Isn't it?"

"Yes."

"Then leave the rest to me. There's the inn."

"Yes, there it is. But stop, see the people are looking out of the window. They must have seen the fire. They will know we did it."

"Well I like that. How can they know? You let me talk."

"I wish you would. I daren't speak myself, I am in such a fright."

"Halloa! halloa!" cried Charley.

Two or three persons at the upper windows looked down, and the landlord, who was among them, replied,—

"Halloa there! what do you want?"

"We want a post-chaise," bawled Charley, "and as sharp as you like. This is Miss Hopley, who lives at the big house on the marshes, and we want to go to—what's the place, Miss?"

Miss Hopley told him, and he repeated the name at the top of his voice for the benefit of mine host.

"Mr. Hopley's place is on fire, isn't it?" called the landlord.

"Yes, don't you see it blazing," replied Charley, "a piece of wood has fallen on the governor, and we want to fetch the doctor."

"Stop there, then, I'll come down."

They waited, and presently the landlord and landlady, the ostler and the boots, came down stairs and opened the door.

"What is the matter, do you say?" asked the landlord.

Then Charley repeated his story, and entered into details.

"Well," said the landlord, "I don't know what to say."

"The poor gentleman can't be left to die, Mr. Jackson," said the landlady, coming to the rescue.

"No ma'am," put in Mr. Wag slily, "I am sure you have much too good a heart to allow of such a thing."

"Have you got a chaise?" Miss Hopley asked.

"We've got one, certainly."

"Well, we only want one."

"Certainly."

"Have you no horses, then?"

"Oh yes, we've horses enough. The fact is there's no one to drive."

"There are three of you."

"Yes, Miss, certainly; but the night air don't suit my rheumatism. Boots, here, never had a whip in his hand, and the ostler I can't spare."

"Why not, it wont take him long to drive us."

"No," the landlord said, shaking his head obstinately, "some other party might want a chaise, and then where should we be."

"I suppose," said Charley, whom the delay began to alarm considerably, for he every moment expected to see Hopley or his myrmidons come running round the corner of the lane, "I suppose you would be in much the same fix as you are now."

"Well, that's true," said the landlady, again returning to the rescue, "what the young gentleman says is true, Mr. Jackson."

"I knew you'd see it, ma'am," cried Charley, "and if it comes to a pinch, I'll drive myself."

"Will you, young fellow?" returned the landlord, "you wont drive my cattle."

"Very well, then," Charley said, "we will do without you; come along, Miss, I know where we can get suited."

And they made a step or two from the door.

"There is no other inn, young man" said the landlord, "for a very long way."

"That's true," whispered Lucinda.

"Well," said Charley to the landlord, "we don't want to take away our custom, only what's the good of raising so many obstacles."

"I tell you what it is, young man," observed the landlord, with a broad grin, "if you are not the coolest bit of goods I ever clapped my eyes upon, dash my——"

"Wig," added Mr. Wag, "only what's the good of saying that, when you don't wear one. As I said before, sharp's the word. We don't mind what we pay, only bring us the carraige directly."

"If Bob wasn't drunk," said the landlord, "there wouldn't be any objection."

"Do you think he is too drunk to ride," said the boots, "I've know'd him keep in the saddle when he has been blazing."

"So have I," said the landlady, "go and wake him up, Tom; he won't be best tempered, but it can't be helped."

The Bob in question slept over the stable and was not, as the hostess truly predicted, in the most amiable mood upon being disturbed.

If there really exist a right and a wrong side of a bed, we may reasonably suppose that it was out of the wrong which Mr Robert, aroused by the united efforts of ostler and boots, came tumbling and hiccuping, very rough headed and red eyed.

"What the——are you making that——row about you——sons of——."

I have given you all the printable words in a sentence which would have made at least a dozen lines with the suppressed substantives and adjectives.

"I told you how it would be," said the landlord "he's dreadful bad about it. Come Bob, old fellow," he shouted, "here's a job for you."

"I dont want no jobs," Mr. Robert replied, with more of his flowery language.

The rest, however, were busily engaged, dragging out a post-chaise from underneath a shed, and putting in the horses. When all was ready, the ostler went up, and by threats and persuasions, induced Bob to come down, and he was, after a little trouble helped into the saddle.

"Are you ready?" asked the landlord.

"Yes; no; stop a minute," called Charley; "If you please, have you such a thing as a pistol in your house?"

"A pistol. What for?"

"Why the fact is, Miss Hopley is so timid, she can't travel without one."

"But, what good will it be to you."

"Oh, I can fire it, if it's needed."

"Ah, the devil trust you. I don't know what you couldn't do. I never see sich a boy. Here Tom, bring out my big horse pistol. It's loaded to the muzzle, so take care you don't blow yourself up, as well as the highwaymen. It's a devil to kick."

"All right. I'll look after it, good night."

Tom handed the pistol in at the carriage window.

"Hadn't one or two of us better step over to Mr. Hopley's," he asked, "just to lend a hand if required."

"No," said Charley, "thinking that if they did, Hopley would, in all probability, set off after them, as hard as he could go. No, there is no occasion for you to do so. There are several hands employed in getting the fire under. It will be out directly."

"It seems to be getting worse."

"I think not."

"Well, here's some one coming up the road. They'll have the latest intelligence."

Charley, shading his eyes with his hand, peered eagerly in the direction indicated.

He fancied he recognized the familiar form of Leech the lawyer.

"Oh Charley," Lucinda whispered in his ear, "tell them to make haste, in mercy's sake, or we are lost."

"Drive on," cried Charley, "as fast as you can gallop."

"All right, your honour," replied Mr. Bob, with a twitch at the brim of his hat, and a hiccup.

Then plunging his spurs into the horse's sides, with a rear and a plunge, and a great lurch on one side, that threatened to upset the chaise, they started on their journey.

"Whoop—whoop, kim up! gevr hup! will yer? Take that, Hi, hi."

With innumerable expletives and unintelligible cries, by turns of a threatening and encouraging nature, the post boy urged on his gallant steeds.

For a long while Charley was hanging half out of the window, endeavouring to pierce the dense obscurity of the lane behind them, from which the thick matted foliage of the enclosing hedges effectually kept out the rays of the placid moon, sailing serenely in the deep blue heavens. Nothing but the rattling of the horses' hoofs, the "whoop, whoop," of the post boy, and the crunching of the stones beneath the wheels, mingled with the creaking and spraining of the springs of the chaise, disturbed the silence of the night.

They were not, then, pursued.

When the young gentleman was satisfied of their temporary safety, he leant back in the carriage, and cocked his young legs on to the opposite seat, with the air of a person who all his life had been accustomed to his private brougham, though the reader may remember that before he rode in Mr. Leech's cab he had never known what it was, since he was a baby, to travel in any sort of vehicle, unless we except a penny steam boat, on a Sunday, or perhaps Joe Cudder's wherry, when fifteen or sixteen young ladies and gentlemen clubbed together a half-penny a head, and went a row between Hungerford and Westminster.

"This is very jolly, aint it?" said Mr. Charles. "It's worth all the trouble."

"What is?"

"Why, this carriage. Don't it jump you up, just? It's much better than Leech's was."

"I don't think much of it," replied Lucinda. "Besides, I do not suppose it is as good as your mamma's carriage. Is it?"

"Oh!—ah!—no." replied Mr. Wag, re-collecting himself, suddenly.

"To be sure it isn't. It don't jump half as much."

Lucinda looked a little surprised, and re-mained silent for some time. Charley saw that he had said something very foolish, and so looked out of the window, and hid his blushes.

When he again resumed his seat, his fair companion asked him—

"What has become of the foreign nobleman all this while?"

"The foreign nobleman?"

"Yes; why is he not with us?"

"Oh, to be sure. Yes; he's gone on in front," replied Charley. "We shall find him all right, presently."

And out of window he popped his head again.

They were at the time passing along a smooth piece of turnpike road. The carriage made hardly any noise, but as Charley looked back in the direction from which they had come he fancied he heard the sound of a horse's hoofs.

"Listen," he said to Lucinda, "do you hear anything?"

"No, nothing."

"There—there; now you do. It is gaining on us."

"I think it is only the echo of our own horses' feet."

"Perhaps so. I hope it is."

"There is no fear of highwaymen, is there?" Lucinda asked presently.

"No," said Charley, "I should think not. They have been done away with, long ago. What makes you ask?"

"Because," said Lucinda, "mind you keep the fifty pounds safely. Where have you put it?"

"I have it knotted up in my pocket-handker-chief—in my breast-pocket."

"Very well, take care if it."

Just then the carriage stopped with a jolt. Charley looked out. They were at a turnpike-gate. "House! house! hullo-o-o-a!" bawled Bob. "Hulloa, house! house! bawled Charley. Then they both bawled together.

Presently a redhead in a white nightcap was poked out of a window, and a voice asked, gruffly, who was there.

"Come down, and see, you old muff," shouted Mr. Wag. "Don't stick snoring there, you antiquated old beetle."

Doubtless supposing it was somebody of conse-quence who addressed him the old tollgate-keeper slipped on his clothes and made the best haste to come down and open the gate.

He was certainly surprised to see Mr. Wag, and more so when that gentleman handed him a sovereign.

"I haven't got any change," said the man.

"I don't want it," replied Charley. "Do you hear a horse galloping behind us?"

"Yes," said the man, after listening attentively for a few moments, "I think I do."

"You don't mind doing something to earn that money I suppose."

"Not if it's not too hard."

"It is easy enough, If we are followed, put them off the scent, do you understand?"

"Aye, aye? your honour," replied the man

Then he whispered to the post-boy, with a wink, "It's a runaway couple, by the Lord Harry. Some young lord, I should think. If it aint the rummest start I ever come across, I should like to know what was."

XXII.—SHOWING HOW BOB WAS ROBBED OF HIS BOOTS AND HIS BREECHES.

"DRIVE on—drive on," shouted our hero to the post-boy, "you shall have five guineas, if you look alive."

"All right, your honour," cried Bob, whom the sight of the sovereign had considerably elated. "I'll hit 'em up, believe me."

On they went at double the speed that they had hitherto journeyed, jolting in and out of the cart-ruts, saving the ditches by a miracle, and bumping up against the bank protecting the footway at every moment in a manner that seemed to threaten them with instant annihila-tion.

For some time they proceeded in perfect silence. Lucinda in a corner of the carriage, wrapped up in her cloak, shivered with cold and fright; Charley, hanging half out of one of the windows, looked and listened with all his eyes and ears.

Thus they got over another five miles.

Then, as before, with a great jolt, the carriage came to a stand-still.

"Another gate, I suppose," thought Charley.

It was not, however, for this reason that they had stopped. The post-boy was leaning back in his saddle and endeavouring to rattle the handle of his whip against the front windows of the chaise.

"Where do you want to be drove to?" said he.

"Where are we?" said Charley.

"Close on to the town."

"Drive through it then."

"I thought you wanted to go to a doctor's?"

"We don't want to go to any doctor's, drive straight through the town, I tell you."

The post-boy remained passive.

"But where do you want to go to?" said he.

"To London."

"To London?"

"Yes; you are hard of hearing aren't you. I spoke plain enough, I thought. Perhaps you thought I said America."

"I don't know what you said, but I know what I'll do, and that is, I shan't drive you."

"There you are, talking nonsense again; you mean to say that you know what you won't do, but you are mistaken, you are going to drive us."

"Am I, we'll see about that, young jackan-apes." And Bob began to turn the carriage round, and the horses' heads towards home.

"Boy," roared Mr. Wag, in as imposing a voice as his small lungs were capable of produc-ing, "if you don't go on without any more foolery, I shall blow your brains out."

"Fiddlesticks," said Bob, and he began to whistle.

This was more than our impetuous young gentleman could put up with.

"Give me the pistol Miss," said he.

She gave it him, and springing out of the car-riage, he ran forward—got hold of the head of one of the leaders, and presented the muzzle of the "barker," at old Robert's head.

"Put that down," said the post-boy, shuffling uneasily in his saddle, "it may go off."

"It will go off, too, if you try on any of your games, if you hadn't been a fool, and had driven as I told you, we should have given you ten pounds instead of five, but, as it is, you won't have a halfpenny, so come off that horse—do you hear."

"Yes; but what are you going to do?"

"Come off, I say."

"Well, I'm coming, only point that pistol another way."

"I shan't speak to you again," said Charley, stamping his foot, "that's right; now turn the horses' heads round as they were; now go about your business."

"What, without the shay?"

"Yes, to be sure, and as quick as you like; but stop a minute, I shall take your place, so I ought to have your clothes. I'll trouble you to take off your boots and breeches; perhaps you had better go behind the carriage, because of the lady, but don't try to give me the double, because I shall keep the pistol pointed at you."

Bob, with an immensity of grumbling, went behind the carriage as he was told, and began to undress himself.

"I shall catch my death of cold," said he, "it's a hard frost."

"No you won't," observed Charley coolly, helping himself to the post-boy's clothes, "not if you run."

"But I shall get the sack from my place, or be put in prison for stealing the shay."

"I don't see that; you must tell them I stole it."

"But who do you suppose would believe it; a bit of a whippersnapper like you; and me, here sixty years old, come Lady-day."

"However, its true enough," said Charley, "and what's more, if you are not out of sight in a couple of cracks, I shall fire at you; I shan't try to kill you, but only to break your leg. I've had many a sixpen'orth of sparrows at the Sluice-house, and you may consider it as safe as done, if I take aim at you."

"Bad luck to you. I have no reason to dis-believe what you say. You won't go firing, though, if I don't turn back."

"Not unless you look round. Now be off; I've no time to waste."

Afraid to spend any more time in parleying with such a fierce young gentleman, old Bob turned round as desired, and taking to his heels, went as fast as his poor old legs would carry him, his shirt tails streaming in the wind like the tail of a kite.

"Faster," shouted Charley, and faster the post-boy went.

"Faster!" Charley repeated.

The old man couldn't do much more; he seemed to be skimming along the surface of the earth like a bird.

When he was out of sight, Charley hastily pulled on the leather breeches over his own trousers. Then slipped his feet into the boots. He had not much difficulty, for they would have fitted a person four times his size.

"What do you think of this, Miss," said he presenting himself at the window "We shan't be asked any questions now."

Lucinda looked at him, and burst out laugh-ing.

He certainly cut a most comical figure.

Mr. Wag was mortified. He put the pistol into his breast-pocket, and shutting the carriage door, without a word scrambled into the saddle.

He had never in his life before been on horse-back. He had not the remotest idea that there was any particular side on which it was customary for persons to get up. He got on anyhow, all of a heap, as it were. When he was in his seat, he did not feel very safe, but he held on some-how, and called out "Gee wup."

The horses did not move.

"Where's his whip, I wonder," said Charley, looking round, "I don't see it anywhere."

While he was hanging over the side of the horse to look under its legs, he unintentionally drove his spur deep into the leader's flank.

The horse made a terrific spring forward, the others followed, and the chaise set off at full gallop.

Charley kept his seat by a miracle, holding on like grim death. But even in the extremity of his fright at the sudden movement and his help-less position, he distinctly heard the sound of horses' hoofs behind him. This time it was un-mistakeable.

The pursuers were on their track.

XXIII.—MORE VICTIMS—THE CORPSE IN THE CUPBOARD—THE DEAD-HOUSE.

THE workhouse of Saint Starver-cum-Bag-o'-Bones had gone to bed. The porter was tucked up and snoring. The paupers were not, perhaps, particularly well tucked up, but, as a rule, there were a good many in a bed and ought to have kept one another warm if they didn't, and they were all snoring loud enough.

As Mr. Bloodyer was a model workhouse master, so was his a model workhouse.

Gabb, the member, had mentioned it in the House, and had said, knocking the dust out of the left side of his waistcoat as he did so, that in the parish of Saint Starver-cum-Bag-o'-Bones, unlike other parishes, the parishioners were delighted to pay the poor-rates.

"And why?" said he, "and why?"

He paused for a reply. As he would probably have had to have paused a long while unless he had replied himself, he did so, and he said:

"It is because, Mr. Speaker and gentlemen, because they know the money is properly applied, and is in proper hands."

In fact there is not, and never was, another parish where the rate is so low, and where paupers are so well managed.

But to our story.

While Toddleboy was dreaming of all kinds of unpleasant subjects, the kind gentlemen who had pressed him to take so much brandy, were sitting quietly by the fire-side, in the workhouse master's private room, holding a conversation, of which this is a portion.

"Everything been going on all right to-day?" said Faversham. "Any fresh inmates?"

"There have been four applications."

"What sort? Friendless."

"No; not exactly. One was brought here by his son."

"The scoundrel! what does he mean by burthening the parish with the keep of his parent."

"I don't know, I'm sure. However, it doesn't much matter, as far as we are concerned. There did not seem to be over much love lost between them. The son said the old man had been a burthen to him these ten years, and was a drunken old rip. It'll be a relief to him to know that the old boy has shuffled off the mortal coil. Won't it?"

"It ought to be. What were the other three?"

"Two were man and wife. An awful scene we had parting them. Quite pathetic!"

The worthy gentlemen laughed at this, which was, I have no doubt, intended for a very excellent joke.

Well, shall we blame them? They are not the only persons in the world, I suppose, who find food for mirth in the sorrows of poor old people. Would you have us become sentimental about the separation of two dilapidated old paupers, male and female?

If they have lived and struggled forty years together through want and privation, and breaking down at last are compelled to seek a refuge in poverty's stronghold, are we to study

their absurd romantic notions about clinging to one another unto the last?

"Not a bit of it," says the Poor Law Commissioner. "No humbug of that kind, here, my old turtle doves; the man to the right, the woman to the left."

"For better for worse, for richer for poorer, in sickness and in health, till death us do part; according to God's holy ordinance."

That is what the prayer-book says. But you don't suppose that Poor Law Commissioners are governed by what the prayer-book says. Do you?

"And what is the fourth person like?" asked Faversham.

"Well," replied Bloodyer, rubbing his chin, doubtfully, with his right hand, while in his left he held his half-smoked cigar, the ash of which he knocked off gently against the edge of the table; "I don't know but that he is the best of the lot for our purpose."

"Has he any friends in London?"

"Aye, he says he has plenty, and relations too, of the richest, but they have sent him adrift, and won't assist him with a half-penny."

"What is his name?"

"He calls himself Smith. I begged to doubt him, when he said the name was his. 'It's as good a name as any other,' he said. 'It's a respectable name, too, isn't it? It's about the only respectable thing that I can lay claim to. Why shouldn't I claim it?'"

"That was a singular speech."

"I thought so. He seems to be a reckless, dare-devil sort of a chap, sick of life, and everything else."

"If he's sick of life he has come to the right shop."

"You're right there, doctor. We've got the physic to suit his complaint."

"Ho! ho! ho!"

"He! he! he!"

The two gentlemen laughed—one noisily, the other quietly—both heartily.

"To come back to business," said the doctor, when Mr. Bloodyer's mirth had somewhat subsided. "We must move that cursed body out of the house. How shall we manage it?"

"To tell the truth, I don't see my way very clearly."

"There is one way; but there is a good deal of risk in it."

"And that?"

"We could dress it up in that man Toddleboy's clothes, and wrap the lower part of the face up in a handkerchief. Then you could take one arm and me the other, and walk him quietly out."

"Walk him out?"

"Yes; he's no weight, you know. He felt like a child when I lugged him downstairs just now."

"But do you mean that we should take him so into the street?"

"Why not? I will tell the porter he has fainted. He will fetch a cab. We help him in, and I take him straight to my house in Bayswater."

"As you say, there's a good deal of risk in it. My plan is this."

" Go on, I thought you had not got one."

" There is a large shell, you know, in the dead-house. I will have Toddleboy's body put into it, then we will lay the other on the top of it, and Rattan can move them away to-night. He is coming, is he not ?"

" I told him to do so. He will be here at twelve. It is now eleven. Is the body up-stairs laid out ?"

" I will go and see."

" Let them bring it downstairs. Keep your back against the cupboard where the other is. Everything depends upon your caution. A slip at such a time as this would be fatal."

Nodding an assent, the workhouse master left the room.

Then Faversham, with cautious cat-like steps, paced the floor, waited, and listened.

He had not long to wait. Before ten minutes had elapsed he heard the sound of heavy footfalls on the stairs.

They were bringing down the body.

Bump, bump, bump. He listened to the sound of their feet as they fell upon each successive step, deadened, in some measure, by the thick India-rubber covering purposely placed there by the workhouse master, that his stealthy approach to the chamber of sickness above might be without warning, unexpected—even unknown.

Presently, he heard the grating of the bars in the outer door. Then, the grating of the shell against the door-posts.

They were carrying the body out into the dead-house.

Cautiously and silently the doctor paces the floor, taking in his walk the greatest possible care to tread right in the middle of the red and green squares, which formed the pattern of the carpet.

Thus, he walked, and waited, and listened.

And soon he heard the sound of the departing footsteps of the men who had assisted in the movement of Toddleboy's body. Shortly afterwards, Bloodyer returned to the apartment.

" Well," said the doctor.

" It is done," Bloodyer replied. " I told them that the man who came for the corpse, would fasten down the lid. Are you ready to help with the other ?"

" Quite ready."

" It's odd, that I should feel so," said Bloodyer, laying the palm of his hand upon his burning forehead. " It must have been that cursed idiot's yelling up stairs that did it."

" What is the matter ?"

" I feel so nervous. I am ready to faint at the sight of my own shadow."

" Pooh ! You want some medicine, I should think. Try a drop of brandy."

" I will."

Saying so, Bloodyer stretched out his hand for the decanter.

In the act of pouring some out—he hesitated —glanced around nervously, at the bottle and the glass, and then, with an ashy face, looked up at the cold piercing eyes looking down upon him.

Faversham laughed silently, showing his large white teeth.

" You didn't think it, did you ?" he said.

" Think what, man ? No, no, of course. I didn't—I know it's all right between us. It is not likely you would physic me."

" Not very—yet awhile."

" Not yet awhile—no, never, I should think. " Of course not. Drink."

Still Bloodyer hesitated.

" Which glass did the old man have ?" he asked, examining each of the three carefully.

The doctor took one up and smelt it.

" This is it," said he, and flung it into the grate, where it lay shivered to a thousand atoms.

Then he filled two glasses from the decanter, and pushed them towards the workhouse master.

" Choose."

Bloodyer took one and drained it. The doctor did likewise.

" Are you ready ?" said he.

" Quite ready. Will you lift out the body ?"

" Aye, why not ? A dozen after it, if we had them."

The corpse was concealed in a cupboard, at the bottom of the stairs. It was very small, and the body had had to be partly doubled up to get it in. When Faversham threw the door open, and the light from the candle, which Bloodyer carried, fell full upon its ghastly occupant, the workhouse master started back, with a half uttered scream of terror, and leaning against the wall for support, was, for several moments, unable to summon sufficient courage to look at it again.

" Are you an idiot, man ?" whispered Faversham, fiercely turning upon his companion. " Do you want some of those accursed old crones upstairs to hear us, and come down to see what we are doing ? Keep your fainting fits till you go to bed, if you must have them at all."

Thus rebuked, Bloodyer shewed a light as desired, and the doctor took the corpse from the cupboard, and carried it over his shoulder out of the back door across a little yard, and into the dead-house.

There already a body was lying in its shroud, in a roughly made deal coffin, on a stone bench.

" There will be room for two, I see," the doctor said, after taking a glance at the size of the shell. " Rattan can take them away together."

He placed the dead body he carried upon the top of the body lying in the coffin, and squeezing it in, after some difficulty laid the lid upon the top, and fastened it, loosely, with a couple of nails, one at the top and one at the bottom.

" So far so good," Faversham said. " Shall we go ?"

" The sooner the better," the workhouse master replied. " I am quite ready."

" In ten minutes Rattan will be here. We shall hear the bell in your room, if we listen."

" Let us go then."

They left the dead-house, Bloodyer pulling the door to after them ; as he did so he fancied he heard a low plaintive sighing sound close to him.

With a violent start he slammed the door, and dropped the candle from his hand.

" What now ?" Faversham asked savagely.

"Did you not hear it?" the other cried, his teeth chattering with terror.

"Hear it. Hear what?"

"That—that moaning. I thought it was the uneasy spirit of some of those whom we have quieted. Listen! Do you hear nothing."

"Not I."

Both men listened intently, but they could hear no sound. The scene was dreary, desolate, and lonely, to the last degree.

In front of them the workhouse rose up a black and frowning mass, relieved but by the faint glimmer of a light in one of the topmost windows. The yard in which they stood was in the shadow of the building—but the pale moon, struggling past the house side, lit up some portion of wall at the back of the deadhouse, and threw upon it a goblin effect of light and shade, by passing through some chimney pots.

"I hear nothing. It is your fancy," said Faversham, impatiently; and led the way back to the workhouse master's private room, where the latter again resorted to the brandy bottle.

Perhaps it was not fancy, though, for all that.

The sigh came from the shell where they had placed the bodies.

There they lay alike cold, stiff, and motionless. Outwardly they closely resembled each other in all the dread characteristics of the inmates of the tomb.

But yet what a wide world of mystery divided them!

One was living, while the other was dead. The dead lay upon the living. The living lay pressed down and half-suffocated by the dead.

The face of the corpse rested upon the face of the living. The death froth from the dead man's mouth moistened the cheek of him who woke in speechless horror to find where he was, and what was his companionship.

———

XXIV.—An Unlucky "Spill."

WHETHER or not there was any foundation for Master Charley's fears on the score of pursuers, he could not possibly have travelled any faster had he been the most experienced postboy upon the road, instead of this being his very first appearance upon any "stage," and his *debut* in the equestrian line.

The fact is, that perfectly unconscious of the spur upon his right heel, he kept digging away at the unfortunate horse's side, and the animal, driven almost wild by the incessant irritation, dashed madly onwards, dragging its surprised companions in harness along with it at such a tremendous pace, that the chaise behind them positively rocked with the motion, and threatened every moment to overturn into the ditch on one side or the other of the road.

Looking back now and then over his shoulder, Charley fancied he could see a horseman in the distance, galloping furiously after them.

He fancied, too, that he was gaining on them.

I have said that it was not possible for him to have mended his pace, even if he had been accustomed to the management of horses, but utterly ignorant as he was upon the subject, he was no more able to urge them on, check them, or guide them in their impetuous career, than a little monkey would have been on the back of a wild cat.

He was obliged to put his trust in Providence, and hold on with his hands and knees as well as he was able.

This, however, was far from an easy task. So furious was their pace. His feet had slipped from the stirrups, he bumped and jolted at every step; his leg was crushed by the other horses striking violently against it. He was nearly frightened out of his life, and his wits began to desert him.

At last the climax came. A greater jolt than usual threw the pistol he was carrying in his breast-pocket out into the road, and in falling, it exploded with a report worthy of the largest-sized cannon.

Most fortunately it injured no one, but the noise increased the fury of the now perfectly maddened horses.

They made a wild plunge and a snort, and swinging round the carriage behind them, as though its weight were but that of a bundle of feathers, turned a corner of the road, and dashed through an open gate on to a sort of marsh or common, lying by the side of the highway.

With a horrible sensation of terror and helplessness, the young jockey was flung through the air, and fell with crushing violence upon his back in the road.

The carriage pursued its headlong course. A horseman following it cleared his prostrate body, and galloped on in pursuit.

He lay very still and quiet, his pale face turned up towards the moon, as though he were asleep.

You might have thought him so at the first glance; but at the second you would have seen—

The blood slowly trickling from his nose, and mouth, and ears.

———

XXV.—Charley falls into Bad Hands.

MOSTLY, the jolly waggoners, that I have met with in the country have been driving their teems up long, dusty roads, cracking their twine-bound whips, and accompanying themselves with fragments of one of those rare old stock songs which people sing in rustic alehouses, on Saturday night, and which all have exactly the same tune, all seem to be equally uninteresting, and capable of being carried on to an indefinite period without any hope of the singer's ever coming to an end. Or else he has been helping himself liberally to the contents of a brown pitcher, or delf mug, before a public-house door, while his horses have been feeding. Or else, perhaps, he has been fast asleep on his stomach, inside his cumbersome vehicle, and it has been journeying onwards quite as safely, or safer, than if it had had the advantage of his direction and guidance.

In fact, to cut it short, I have, as I suppose

[IMMENSE SUCCESS OF THE CELEBRATED JULIA JENKINI, EVERY EVENING UNTIL FURTHER NOTICE. NO EXTRA CHARGE FOR ADMISSION.]

you have too, always laboured under the impression that waggoners were a guileless race of men, given to strong drinks and weak thoughts, healthy, happy, heavy and empty headed.

You would scarcely expect to find a right down villain, of the melo dramatic stamp, under one of those brown wide-awakes, and elaborately braided smock frocks. But I will, with your permission, introduce you to one.

As Charley lay senseless upon his back, looking as like a poor little dead boy as he ever did in all his life—and he has had, and will have, as we shall see, some very awkward knocks—a countryman, driving a waggon, and dressed in the traditional smock, wide-awake, lace up boots, velveteens &c., &c., came singing down the road, and being, happily, in advance of his waggon and

No. 13.

horses, saved our hero from instant annihilation from horses' hoofs and heavy wheels, by accidentally kicking against his body and just tumbling over it immediately afterwards, like the shopman tumbles over the clown who has knocked at the door and laid down directly in front of it, on the door step.

"Who—ay!" cried the countryman, regaining a sitting position with a little difficulty, for he was fat and slow to move. "Who—ay, can't you?" he repeated to his horses.

Scrambling on to his legs, he looked round and about to see what it was that had upset him.

While thus engaged, some one inside the waggon, who had probably been asleep, looked out at the opening in front, and bawled—

[CHARLEY WAG, THE NEW JACK SHEPPARD.

" What's up, George ?"

"I don't know exactly what's up," the first speaker replied, rubbing his hands together to wipe off the gravel which had been ground, as it were, into his skin. "If you ask what's down, I am, myself, for one."

" I thought I heerd you tumbling, George,"the man inside observed, with a yawn. "I supposed you'd got the nightmare."

"I wasn't asleep, as it happens; though, for that matter, I often take a quiet nap walking along by the side. But it's so infernally dark just here, I tumbled over something. Why, good God!"

" What is it ?"

" Get out, man, and come and see. It's some one lying in the road."

" Drunk ?"

" No, dead, by the look of him—and bloody."

Although more than half inclined to go on with his nap, the account which George gave of the condition of the fallen stranger seemed sufficiently interesting to tempt him to get out and look for himself.

Which, with a little grumbling and a good deal of yawning, he did.

"Bring a light," George sang out. "Let's have a look at him."

The other man struck a match and lighted a small lantern, which was of the description called "dark." With this they took a very careful survey of Mr. Charles' exterior.

" He's a postilion, aint he ?"

" Seems like it ; but he's rather young."

" His clothes don't fit him, particular."

" No ; nor his boots."

" What's he been up to, do you think ?"

" Drunk, I should say, and fallen off."

" Or, perhaps he wasn't riding at all. I don't see how he could have been, or we should have seen the empty trap pass us."

The waggon had come in an opposite direction to the post-chaise, and it did not occur to them that it might have passed through the gate in front of which they were then standing.

" He looks very like a croaker, though, don't he ?" one of the men said, after silently watching Charley's face for some time. " What shall we do with him ?"

" If he don't come round again, these togs can't be of no particular service to him, can they ? And if he does, why, there won't be any particular harm done, as I suppose they don't belong to him."

" You're right there," said the other. " Suppose we take his spicy rig-out, and then shove him over into the ditch."

Acting upon this good-natured suggestion, the worthy couple began to divest Master Charley of his postboy's dress.

But when he had unbuttoned the coat, the man who was called George uttered a loud exclamation of astonishment.

" I'll be damned," he said, "if he arn't got on another rig-out underneath."

"It's the cold weather, I should think. What's that sticks his side out so ?"

" A bag full of something."

" It's a bag full of money."

" What sort ?"

" Gold ! by ——"

For a few moments they were both too much astonished to speak. George was silently engaged in biting one of the coins between his teeth, endeavouring to test its hardness. His companion was carefully examining the edge of another to see if it was properly milled.

" It's the real stuff, George."

" It's the genuine article, Bill."

Then they lifted the little bag out of Charley's pocket and began to guess how much it contained. As, however, George suggested that they could find out by counting it, and save time, if they put it inside the waggon, they consulted together concerning the manner in which they should dispose of Charley's body.

Having discovered upon his person this large sum of money, George argued that it would be exceedingly paltry to take away his boots and clothes, and so they determined to leave them.

" I should vote for chucking him into the ditch, as you proposed," said George, " but I've got an objection."

" What's that ?"

" You've heard of the motto about honesty, haven't you ?"

" Which one ?"

" The one as particular alludes to our profession."

" Sure I have ; but I can't say that I see how it applies in the present instance."

" I'll show you, then. It's my opinion the young feller's one of us."

" You think so, do you ?"

" There's not a doubt of it. Why should he have on two suits of clothes ? Where did he get this money from ? What's it all mean, if it don't mean that he's one of the noble profession ?"

" But I don't quite see what you're driving at, George. If you mean to say that we ain't to stick to the yellow boys because this 'ere youngster's a prig, all I be got to say is, that you're talking gallows soft ; and I, for one, shan't cotton to it."

" You don't take me for a suck-eggs entirely, I hope, Bill. Of course we shall lift the shiners, only at the same time I don't see why we should behave worse than is necessary to the young whelp."

" That's fair enough, certainly ; but then I don't see as how as it will be unnecessary to shove his young carcase into the ditch."

" I do, then ; and we're not going to do it. We sticks to the swag, in course, and halves it fair ; but the lad himself we'll give a lift in the waggon, and see if we can't bring him round."

" Yes, and when he's brought round he'll want the tin back."

" But he won't get it, you know."

" No ; there aint much fear of that, only he'll begin his hollering and nonsense."

" Not he ; we'll say he was robbed afore we found him. Don't you take ?"

" George, you'd adone to have wrote a book. I always said you would, and dash me if I don't stick to it."

" Seeing what books are written, and what muffs write 'em, I make no doubt but that I could, Bill—a fizzer."

Without pursuing the subject any further, the two men employed themselves in raising Charley's body; and, carrying him to the waggon, laid him upon the straw inside.

Then they got in themselves, and upon Bill's suggestion, counted and divided the money before they took any further steps towards resuscitating the unfortunate little post-boy.

"Forty-eight pounds dewided by two," said George, calculating, "is two's in four is two, and two's in eight is four, that makes your share twenty-four pounds, which, considering you didn't find him, is acting handsome to you, any ways."

"Twenty-four's the half, is it?" Bill observed, a little doubtfully, and began to calculate on the palm of his hand with his thumb nail. "I thought it were forty-two."

"That's back'ards," said George, contemptuously, "it's twenty-four furrards."

"I make no doubt of it," replied Bill, "only I like counting a thing over best, It's more above board, like. That figuring business don't go for nothing."

They would have probably counted the money again, had not a movement on the boy's part alarmed them.

"Hush, man," said George, "put your money away, the lad's coming round."

XXVI.—CHARLEY GETS INTO WORSE COMPANY STILL.

HE was, however, far from coming round. It was only his arm, which slipping from the position in which they had placed it, fell heavily upon the floor of the waggon, and disturbed them.

They gave him some brandy, loosened his neck-handkerchief, bathed his face with cold water, and did all that they could think of, to revive him.

But when, at last, he opened his eyes, slowly and languidly, it was only to stare at the men kneeling by his side, with a vacant and meaningless look, and closing them again with a hollow groan, relapse into his previous state of insensibility.

The waggon slowly lumbered on towards London, stopping every now and then, for lengthy baits of several hours' duration.

The day broke coldly over the dreary, marshy, land, through which lay the road. The sun mounted up the sky, and they were still upon the way. It sank again slowly in the west, and still they were travelling at the same jog-trot pace.

Still the boy lay, prone and inert, upon his rough couch of straw.

It was not until about seven in the evening that they came into London by the Mile End road, and lumbered on until they reached Whitechapel church; when, turning off to the left, they drew up in front of an ill-favoured building, with what might have been a timber-yard attached.

Into this they took the waggon, and unloading it of its contents, which were but three or four small kegs of spirits, the man George, lifted Charley into a light spring cart, and fetching an old horse from a stable at the bottom of the yard, harnessed it to the cart, and drove away in the direction of Commercial-street.

Turning down Keat-street, and bearing to the left, they presently came to a rag and bottle shop, where a doll in a dirty, white frock, dangled over the doorway, and the name of MEASELS, painted in yellow, on a blue ground, stared at you from over a window, ornamented with every imaginable species of rubbish which one would naturally have supposed nobody would ever have dreamt of buying.

There you might have seen glaring placards and astounding posters, highly coloured cartoons, and highly seasoned poetry.

"This is the shop for your bones;" "the highest price for kitchen stuff;" "how to make a hundred a-year out of a penny a week;" "a sure fortune," and so on.

Without heeding these fascinating announcements, George alighted from his cart, and taking up the boy in his arms with a greater degree of gentleness than one would have supposed so rough looking a customer to be capable of, carried him into the shop.

At the sound of his approach, the door leading into the inner room opened, and a particularly repulsive looking old man, with a head of dirty grey hair, which could not possibly have been combed out for a fortnight, came sneaking up the shop, holding one of his lean hands over his eyes to shade against the light.

"What is it?" said the dirty old man. "If it's bones, we've got enough of them already, so it's no good you making an offer. Why, Georgy, is that you?"

"Yes, it's me, guv'nor," replied George. "I hope you find yourself pretty nicely by this time."

"I'm always nice," replied the old gentleman. But what's that you have got there?"

While they had been speaking, George had deposited his burthen upon the counter.

"It's a boy," said he. "I picked him up in the country. He had forty pounds in his pocket when I came across him, lying in the road, and I was afraid he would lose 'em if I left him there."

"He hasn't got them in his pocket now, I suppose," said the old gentleman.

"No, I took 'em out for safety."

"That was right, Georgy. And you want me to take care of them."

"Not quite that, neither; I'll manage that part of the business myself. I want you to take care of the boy."

The old gentleman didn't seem quite so pleased with this proposition; however, he made no objection, but took stock of Charley through a pair of tortoise-shell spectacles, which he pulled down from the top of his head, and fixed upon his nose, for the purpose.

"He looks very bad, George. What's the matter with him?"

"Why, you're a bit of a doctor, guv'nor, and you must try and find out. I have been feeling him over, and there is no bones broke that I can see; but he has been swouning like this all day, and as well as I can make out, has been dreadfully shook up—throwed off a horse, or something of that sort."

"Well, George, I'll do my best for him, for your sake; but times is awful bad, and it's as much as I can do to keep myself in victuals, let alone keeping strange boys in physic."

"Nobody wants you to be out of pocket," said George. "Here's a sovereign to start with, which might go a long way in rhubarb, I should think. When it's spent, you shall have some more; only mind you take care of him. I've taken a fancy to the lad, and I shall not forget it, if you don't act honourable."

Saying this, he again raised the boy in his arms and carried him into the inner room.

"Where shall I put him?"

The old man threw some lumber off a sofa standing in the corner, and upon this, wrapped up in some old wragged over-coats and a dirty patched counterpane, they left Charley to his slumbers.

Refusing to partake of any other hospitality which the old man offered him, excepting a pipe full of tobacco, George, after filling and lighting his short clay, lounged, with his hands in his pockets, out of the shop, up Keat-street, and into Commercial-street, where, at a public-house he was acquainted with, he sat down and regaled himself with his "fancy" drink.

Meanwhile the dirty old gentleman, left alone with Charley, examined the sovereign carefully by the light of the flaring tallow candle, burning on the parlour table, and the inspection proving satisfactory, he put it into his pocket, with a complacent smirk, and, lighting his own pipe, sat down by the fire-side and ruminated.

"A sovereign's worth of physic," said he, "might cure him and it mightn't. If it didn't it's a good deal to throw away. It's a matter that requires a little consideration."

He continued to smoke and to consider.

"Them boots he has on are very good 'uns, and look as if they hadn't been soled. He can't be comfortable sleeping in his boots. I shall take 'em off. I have a pair of hunting boots somewheres, very much like 'em, only not *quite* so new. I wonder whether he would know the difference."

More consideration and tobacco smoke.

"If he was to die on my hands George couldn't blame me, because he might die with the best of physic. Such is life. Here we are to-day, and where are we to-morrow? no-wheres. I'll take his boots off. They spoilt his rest."

XXVII.—ALL IS NOT GOLD THAT GLITTERS. —THERE ARE ACHING HEARTS IN PALACES AS WELL AS IN THE HUMBLEST LODGINGS OF THE POOR.

I AM very much afraid there are some of my young lady readers who must have come to the conclusion that this book is going to be full of nothing but murderers and thieves, and, the writer's experience unfortunately lying in Whitechapel and the Dials, that he will never for a moment take his characters into genteel society.

Not a bit of it.

On the contrary. I will, with your kind permission, carry you into the very middle of a vortex of fashion. But, to tell the truth, between you and I, I think that some stories are rather over done with great people, particularly stories in penny numbers.

Although I'm going to introduce some very great people indeed to your polite consideration, I trust you won't mind my sneering at them a little, because it is an unfortunate habit I have contracted, and can't easily get out of. It is all very well for those poor polite gentlemen who do the penny literature, to flourish about their Lords Fitz Balderdash and Ladies Aramintha de Bandolines. When all is said and done, the nobs are no more than flesh and blood. Looked at in their fine feathers they are very fine birds indeed; but come along with me, and let's pluck them, and we shall see what scarecrows they are underneath.

*   *   *   *   *   *   *

Park-lane was blazing with carriage lamps; coachmen were swearing; horses backing and plunging. John Thomas, and Jeames, and Charles, behind the carriages, were in a mortal fright about their calves, so very near to them were the horses' heads belonging to the carriage next in the rank. If anybody was in their element in this scene of bustle and confusion, it was the policeman. He certainly was in force. He had his Berlins on, and his staff out; he backed horses; he threatened drivers; he told John Thomas, and Jeames, and Charles to mind what they were "up to," and that he would stand none of their "infernal nonsense." He would very much have liked to have taken all Park-lane into custody, the great Marble Arch and all, and made a great case of it next day in Marlborough-street. As he was determined to take up somebody, he took up the smallest, raggedest, and quietest little boy he could find, and shook him well in doing so. When he had thus asserted his prerogative, not for any particular reason, but because he wanted something to keep his hand in, he took up Clam.

There is no doubt about it, Clam had no business in Park-lane. For the matter of that, he had no business anywhere.

He was an outcast, a waif, and a stray; an incubus clinging to an overgrown population. Trying to make a living when there was no room for him. Refusing to die out of the way, and be got rid of, like other incubuses, but always turning up again more ragged than he was the last time, and a good deal hungrier.

There he squatted on the door step, that ragged vagabond, until policeman Perger, of the A division, took him up and dragged him off triumphantly to limbo.

There he squatted, watching the great folks going to and coming from the Duchess of Heatherland's magnificent mansion, facing Hyde Park.

For this was one of the duchess's famous Wednesday evenings, and all the notabilities, and celebrities, and fashionable nonentities, that London contained, had come to it.

Why should we linger, like Clam, outside the awful portal, which guardian angels, in gorgeous plush, most jealously protect? Have we not the card of *entree*? Take my arm, gentle reader, and we will leave the poor penny romance writers,

Clam, and the rest of the tag and rag and bob-tail, to kick their heels in the cold, while you and I walk up stairs, and see what the great folks are doing, and what they have to say for themselves.

To begin with—who is there? Though, for the matter of that, the question should rather be, who is not there? One has to elbow an earl and a duke, and a marquis, to get in at the door. That common-looking man is an admiral; the bald-headed person, mopping himself with his handkerchief, is a commander-in-chief; there was a leader in the *Times* to-day about both of them. The great journal called one a bungler, and asked why the other was not superannuated, but for all that there are hundreds of thousands who put their faith in them like they do in many other old humbugs.

The *Times* I said, why yonder is the *chef*. There is everybody here with any name in literature, from the editor of the *Thunderer* to a leader writer of the *Daily Cut Throat*, from Lord Macaulay to Albert Smith. Mongini is singing at the piano. There are all the popular members of Parliament, including John Bright, and Cox for Finsbury.

There are, in short—but what does it matter? One has not come to look at the gentlemen; the ladies, surely, should have the preference.

How shall I describe them? I am nowhere at millinery, and certainly I ought to allude to their dresses. What can I say, except that it is a scene of surpassing—bewitching—enthralling loveliness? Every type of beauty there finds its representatives.

The glancing of bright eyes, the flashing of fair bosoms, lavishly and voluptuously displayed, the rustling of rich silks, the crushing of costly velvets, the soft contact of their robes, the delicate scent of their smooth and shining hair, mingled with the sweet sounds of music, the glare of the gas, and the brilliancy of the illuminations, all combine in making up a something perfectly indescribable, which, if it is not earthly paradise, is so much like it that those words will do as well as any other to explain its effect upon the entranced noviciate.

But, amidst all this splendour and magnificence this luxurious ease and enjoyment, the queen of the night, the centre of attraction, the beloved of all beholders—Her Grace the Duchess of Heatherland—was dull and heavy-hearted.

Fatigued to death by the repetition of the inane common places, which the arbitrary laws of conventionalism enforced upon her, she had, late in the evening, forsaken the giddy throng, and in the privacy of her own chamber, she sat alone, and superb in her placid loveliness, but with an expression of rage, mortification, and unutterable weariness upon her grandly-chiselled, and classic features.

While thus she sat, her head resting upon her white hand, and deep in thought, the door opened, and another lady of about the same age, though of a dark complexion, and not nearly so beautiful, appeared upon the threshold.

"Maud," she whispered gently, but the other heeded her not, so deeply engaged was she with her own unpleasant reflections.

"Maud!"

This time she spoke louder; the duchess raised her eyes.

"Alice," she said, "you, of all others in the world, I would rather talk to. I am dull to-night. Wretchedly bored by the insufferable twaddle I have had to listen to, and to utter in return. Has any body noticed my absence."

"No one has, within my hearing, remarked upon it."

"I suppose they are going away."

"The rooms are rapidly thinning."

"So much the better. I will go back presently, for fear that my desertion of my post may cause some disagreeable remarks."

"But, dearest Maud, are you ill? You look pale and worn, and fatigued. Has anything happened to distress you, or cause you annoyance?"

"No, no; nothing of any conseqnence."

"Now, I am sure you are deceiving me. I—your oldest friend—I—to whom, I once flattered myself, you intrusted all your secrets—to whom, indeed, you once intrusted a secret of such vital importance that I thought it would for ever have cemented the firmest and truest friendship betwixt us."

"It is true, Alice. There are few women, none, that I am acquainted with, except yourself, to whom I would reveal the inner workings of my heart. Women are so fickle and false to one another; more fickle and falser far than they are to men."

"Dearest Maud, I have never, I trust, given you any cause to judge me thus harsh."

"On the contrary, Alice. If I had thought you capable of ever so doing, I should not have told you that secret—'*the awful secret of my life.*'"

"Then tell me now, I implore you, what has happened?"

"Alice," whispered the duchess, glancing nervously round, "Are you—are you sure that we are alone?"

"Yes. There is no one within hearing."

"You are certain of it. Please look out into the passage."

The lady did as the duchess desired, and returning said, "that below stairs she heard the sound of the music, and the voices of the guests on the stairs, but that the upper part of the house was perfectly silent and deserted."

"Certainly, certainly," the duchess exclaimed in an irritable and excited tone, "I might have known that no one but the nurses are likely to be upstairs at this time, and these rooms are too far removed from this for us to have any occasion to fear an interruption on their part."

"No, dearest; and now what have you to say to me?"

"What I have to say," replied the duchess, again speaking in a sort of terrified whisper, and again glancing round, as though she feared that eavesdroppers might be crouching in concealment behind the window curtains, or hidden by the heavy drapery of the bed. "What I have to say relates to the secret you already know—and concerns my pure name, my honour, my very life. Alice, I AM DISCOVERED!"

"Great God!" exclaimed her companion, clasping the duchess's hand between her own, "Speak to me quickly. Tell me all that has occurred."

XXVIII.—A Woman's Secret.

THE duchess took her friend's hand in hers, and drawing her closer, repeated

"I am discovered."

"By whom?"

"By a vile, thieving, murdering wretch—a man whose trade is blood, it would seem."

"But how did he discover you?"

"You know that ever since I discovered where the child had been taken to, and in whose care it was, I have regularly supplied that attorney person, Leech, of whom I told you, with a small sum of money, to take to the woman who had charge of it."

"Yes; you have told me so."

"I, of course, wished this to be done, as privately as possible, and thought that I myself was the best person to go about it."

"So I should think."

"I thought so and I acted like a fool."

"But explain."

"This man, then, it would seem, by his own account, was acquainted with Leech. Leech was the attorney he had employed, when last he was, as he termed it, 'in trouble.' I suppose, by what I know of slang, that he must have been in custody for some unlawful act. You know, I made Mr. Leech's acquaintance through reading his name in a disgraceful police report, by the account there given of him, he seemed to be an atrocious scamp. I wanted a scamp, and one who knew scamps' ways, and I went to the police court, inquired for him, found him, and have employed him since."

"But about this other man?"

"I am coming to him. Of course I did not wish Leech to know who I was. I paid him well for what he had to do; and I told him that if I detected him in any way endeavouring to pry in any secrets of mine, except those which I chose to let him pry into I would withdraw my custom. He agreed to it. According to this murderer's account, Leech sent his boy to follow me; but if he did, I don't think that he was successful, for I always took the greatest possible precaution to guard against discovery, except on one unfortunate occasion."

"And that?"

"And that was when this wretch—Rattan, he calls himself—followed me."

"By Leech's desire?"

"No, his own. As he afterwards told me, he was accidentally present at Leech's office when I called upon the lawyer, and had come there to inquire after the address of the person who supplied him with money on the child's account. The lawyer was telling him that he did not know it when I came in, and by some change in the expression of his face, Rattan guessed who I was, and followed me."

"Here?"

"Yes, he saw me come in, I suppose, and made inquiries. Next day he wrote to me."

"Gracious heavens!"

"It was a wretched scrawl, but I managed to make out what he meant."

"Which was?"

"This. The letter contained these words:— 'My lady, a person as is unknown to you, though by accident, has obtained possession of your secret, wants to see you to-morrow night to have a few words upon the subject at the foot of Hungerford Suspension Bridge, the left hand side. I shall wait for you above, in the covered part, at twelve o'clock to-night. Bring a trifle, as I am hard up, and without a halfpenny.— JACK RATTAN.'"

"A curious letter, certainly; but you did not go, of course?"

"Of course I did. Why should I not?"

"However could you be so courageous. I should have expected to have been murdered."

"I was, almost. The wretch took me down by the waterside and endeavoured to extort a large sum of money from me, which I, however, refused to give him; and then the monster, in a fit of passion, precipitated me into the river. What made it more horrible was, that the spot—"

She hesitated.

"Yes," said Alice, seeing she paused.

"That—that the spot was so lonely. Had not a boy, accidentally passing by, jumped in and picked me up, I should have been drowned without a doubt."

There was a certain amount of hurry and embarrassment about the latter portion of the duchess's story, as though she were carefully selecting her words, and was timorous of using a wrong one in describing what had occurred.

If, however, the reader will take the trouble to recall the conversation which took place between Rattan and the duchess at the interview to which she alluded, he will remember that the lady, upon that occasion, referred to some promise Rattan had made about Charley. Indeed, her words were these:—"I propose," she had said, "that you keep your promise with respect to this boy. Have you made a thief of him?"

Then, again, she said a boy had rescued her, and did not say which boy. She was, therefore, deceiving her friend in some respects, and only telling her as much of the truth as she thought was necessary.

The other lady, however, was far from suspecting this to be the case, and asked a variety of questions concerning the murderous assault, and the subsequent conduct of Rattan.

"Have you seen him since?" she asked.

"No," replied the duchess. "Nor have I heard from him."

"Perhaps he is afraid to address you, after what has occurred."

"Alas! I do not think that it is attributable to his modesty or timidity. A more hardened ruffian it is scarcely possible to conceive. But it is not this which annoys me."

"What then?"

"You must know that I lately removed the boy from the guardianship of Miss Williams, the woman who has hitherto taken charge of him, and sent him to a respectable school in the country, from which he escaped, carrying with him about fifty pounds in gold, besides attempting the abduction of the schoolmaster's daughter."

"Abduction! what? a boy of fourteen years of age?"

"Yes; you see his horrible disposition; but is my fault. I am a sinful wretch to have serted him."

"No, no, my dear Maud, that I am sure you e not. If you were compelled, in the first stanc", by the direst necessity to disown your or little innocent babe, whatever a mother's ve could prompt her to do for it you have one. Did you not, when the baby was stolen om the wet-nurse, thirteen years ago, search a every direction until you found it? And ave you not ever since paid for it liberally, and atched over its welfare, though at a distance, nxiously and tenderly? Yes, Maud, I am sure ou have."

"Yes, yes," replied the duchess, though ather uneasily, as it seemed, and apparently lesirous of dropping the subject. "But still, I dare say I am to blame. However, I must act promptly. I want to ascertain whether this Leech's statement is true, and if so, whether the boy has returned to Miss Williams. Now, if I send Mr. Leech, or any other man, to inquire, I do not think they will tell him, as, of course, they would be afraid that the boy might be, by their agency, recaptured, and taken to prison."

"What will you do, then?"

"I must send a woman. Having none in whom I could rely, I must go myself."

"And I, dear Maud, if you will allow me, will accompany you."

"Will you, Alice? A thousand thanks; in your company I shall feel safe. It is a curious neighbourhood, and there is no knowing what might befall one unprotected female, but two of us can defy every danger."

"Yes;" replied Alice, with a little less confidence in her tone than the duchess displayed,; "Shall we go the first thing to-morrow?"

"To-morrow, no; it would be too late. We must go to-night. In an hours' time."

"To-night!" ejaculated Alice, in great alarm. "I am sure, I dare not; besides, how can we get away unobserved?"

"Easily; I can manage all that. Let us now go down stairs again. They must have missed me by this time."

With these words, she took her companion's hand, and thus, the Duchess of Heatherland and Lady Alice de Courtenay began to descend the grand staircase to the drawing-rooms below.

But, as they came out, upon the landing, which, ornamented by Chinese lanterns, looked dark and gloomy, by comparison with the more brilliant light thrown by the numerous wax candles illuminating the duchess' boudoir, Lady Alice started, and grasping her friends' arm, pointed to what she fancied was the shadow of a figure, stealthily creeping away in the inner darkness of one of the rooms at the further end of the landing.

"Look! look!" she whispered. "Who is it?"

"I do not know," the duchess replied in the same low tone; "but, whoever it is, they must have been listening to us. Will you stay here? No; I will. You go back into the room, and fetch a light."

Alice, pale and trembling, did as she was desired, and returned with a candle in each hand. One she gave to the duchess, and the other she took herself.

Thus illumined, they stepped forward, and entered the room into which the supposed eavesdropper disappeared.

It was a bed-room, furnished with much splendour, and with heavy chairs, tables, and cabinets of elaborately carved oak. Rich hangings of crimson satin damask hung round the bed, and were drawn across the diamond-paned window.

Leaving Lady Alice by the door, the duchess advanced, perhaps not without a certain tremour and sinking in the heart, but, outwardly, with every appearance of calm and self reliance, to look behind the drapery, and see whether the person they were in search of could be concealed there.

He might be, the duchess thought, might be a thief, and might spring out upon her, with some murderous weapon, desperate at discovery, but resolved at any cost to effect his escape.

This fear suggested to her the idea of summoning to her assistance some of her servants, but she dreaded to find that the listener had been one of the household, and by so doing she would cause a scene which could result in no good, and might originate a great deal of scandal.

Therefore she advanced, and summoning all her courage to her aid, jerked the curtains on one side, expecting to find the fugitive standing upon the broad window-seat behind them.

But no one was there.

The same process she repeated with the draperies of the bed, the valance, the cabinets, and wardrobes.

With the same result.

Then her eyes moved slowly round the room, seeking to find some probable place of concealment, but there was not one that she had not visited.

With much more fear than her beautiful face had hitherto expressed, she now turned round to the Lady Alice.

And her eyes seemed to interrogate her friend, and inquire what construction she placed upon the mysterious occurence.

"Was it fancy," asked the duchess in a hollow voice.

"Impossible; I am as certain I saw a figure come in, as I am that we are now standing here."

"But what could have become of him, no mortal soul could lie hidden in this room without our finding him."

"*No, nothing mortal,*" Alice replied, in an agitated whisper, "let us go, I am afraid."

And so, without further parley, they descended the staircase and rejoined the company below.

But when the rustling of their dresses was no longer audible, from out the darkness of the room which they had thus been investigating, a tall dark figure crept forth stealthily and serpent-like, and coming forward to the head of the stairs, leant its arms upon the banisters, and peered with its white face down below—a sinister and malignant smile lurking upon its unearthly features.

* * * * * * *

As one o'clock tolled from the London churches, two women, closely veiled, let themselves out of the Duke of Heatherland's, Park-lane mansion, cautiously and noiselessly and closing the door behind them, hurried away in the direciton of the Haymarket.

After proceeding a short distance, they hailed a cab, and bade the driver take them to Tothill-fields.

XXIX.—WHICH GOES BACK TO TODDLEBOY IN HIS COFFIN.

PERHAPS he might have swooned again at the horrible discovery, or it might have been the effect of the poison he had taken which caused him to doze off again after making the horrible discovery; but Toddleboy, after clearly recognizing the fact that he was lying underneath a dead body, became unconscious again.

For how long a period, it was impossible for him to decide. But he woke up again with three facts distinctly present to his understanding.

One, that he was fastened down in a coffin, underneath a dead body.

Two, that he had been poisoned and was dead, or as good as dead.

Three, that it was all over with him.

Having settled this much in his mind, and got thus far in a review of his present position and future prospects, he went on from that point with some further reflections, but having no more facts to go upon, launched into the vague and imaginative.

" If I am dead," thought Toddleboy to himself, " am I buried? And if so, where?"

After due consideration he settled upon Kensal-green.

" That's where it is," thought Mr. Toddleboy, " so far, so bad: and now as to this other dead body, what right has it in my coffin?"

He could not decide upon that point without a great deal of consideration.

While considering, he began to reflect upon the singular events that had preceded his demise. They had poisoned him—he had been undressed—and buried for dead. How long ago? Perhaps a week—who could tell?

That he was dead, he never for a moment doubted. It did not occur to him that he had been buried alive; and this was attributable to the effects of the poison he had given him. You may remember that he had an *over-dose*.

The proper quantity would probably have struck him down like a stone, but the over-dose caused a kind of re-action. In fact, however horribly unnatural it may seem, Mr. Toddleboy felt exceedingly jolly.

He was an old gentleman, as I have told you ever so many times, exceedingly given to " mixing his liquors." The more intoxication he could get out of twopence, the better it pleased him. And in all the course of his imbibing experience, he never recollected to have been so pleasantly drunk before.

" If I had not got this weight upon me," he thought, " I should be regularly enjoying myself.

If this is what is called Purgatory, it has been very grossly misrepresented."

All sorts of ridiculous and unseemly ideas crept into the old man's noddle. It would be outrageous to repeat a quarter of them.

He had come to the conclusion that the other body belonged to Cudder, though why he could not tell. As Cudder continued to lie upon him, still and heavy, he began to get indignant. It was an intrusion upon Cudder's part, to be in the same coffin. He was there first, and Cudder had no business to get in afterwards. He began to resent Cudder's behaviour, and to push him.

He pushed him so hard that the coffin lid above them creaked ominously.

Anyhow it was an improvement. He did not get rid of Cudder, but he got a little more air, which most certainly he stood in need of.

He went on rambling in a wild and absurd fashion, until, all of a sudden he stopped at an extraordinary sound.

Hitherto all had been silent. The silence had been oppressive, overpowering. It had hummed as it were in his ears, with a sound like there is inside a shell.

But this noise, which he now heard, was amazing, startling, almost terrifying, in its discordance with the surrounding objects.

Some one was singing.

Who?

Not himself; not Cudder. Some one else.

He listened attentively. He knew the tune. He had sung it himself when he was last alive, some years ago it seemed. It was not very inappropriate, he thought, when he came to reflect upon the matter.

The song was " *Down among the Dead Men.*"

Hitherto, he had not attempted to use his voice, because he was convinced that he had lost it. He did not believe in ghosts talking. He was himself a ghost, and he did not imagine for a moment, that he could make himself audible.

But he would try. He raised his voice, and joined in rather hoarsely, and a little out of time, but, considering all things, very well for a ghost.

But instead of going on with his song, the person singing ceased suddenly and screamed out in a fright, much to Mr. Toddleboy's astonishment.

XXX.—OUTSIDE THE COFFIN.

BENEATH a lonely unfinished house in the Bow-road, which lay a neglected ruin, owing to its builder having gone into Chancery before it was completed, and which was of course, supposed to be haunted, by the superstituous young and old folks of the neighbourhood, was an extensive vault.

Very extensive it was, when compared to the size of the house above, which was one of a row of rather mean looking tenements, suitable for the habitation of members of the lower middle classes of limited means.

Those who have passed frequently upon the road to or from Stratford, cannot have failed to notice the row of houses to which I allude.

UP THE CHIMNEY AND OUT ON THE TILES.

They are an ugly eye-sore, even in a place where nothing is very pretty. What is their history, and why they are thus left in an unfinished state we need not, at the present moment, discuss. We have only got to do with one particular house, or rather, with a cellar underneath it.

Descend with me.

It is a large oblong-shaped vault, with an arched room. It is cold, slimy, and damp. In it your voice sounds terribly hollow, ghostly, and unnatural. The atmosphere is close and fœtid, and the place wears the appearance of having been shut up for years, unused, and neglected, like the house itself.

But such is not the case, *it has its inmates.*

First of all there is a low-browed, cowering

ruffian, coarsely featured and coarsely attired, whom we are already acquainted with, none other, in fact, than Mr. Jack Rattan.

He is smoking his pipe, he is wrapped up in his great coat, he has his hands thrust into his trowsers' pockets, and he is beating the devil's tattoo against the floor with the heels of his boots, so we may conclude that he feels the cold. From certain impatient gestures and half-uttered oaths, which every now and then escape him, we may also conclude that he is put out about something, or is impatient at some delay.

And the other inmates of the room?

Upon a high bench, or table, before him, by the side of a black bottle containing the remains

No. 14.

[CHARLEY WAG, THE NEW JACK SHEPPARD.

of a pint of "blue ruin," is a large deal coffin, which holds a couple of dead bodies.

This is his company. He calls them his "lodgers," and his stock-in-trade. In his more cheerful moments he dubs himself "dealer in dead bodies, graves carefully opened, and 'snatches' neatly executed."

One would not imagine that anybody could become so blunted and callous to all natural feelings as to thus joke upon these horrible subjects; but I dare say that Rattan thought very little of it.

He was a monster whose hands throughout his whole life had been stained with blood, and upon whose soul the weight of almost every conceivable crime lay heavy.

He cared very little more about sitting alone with those two dead bodies and smoking his pipe, than we should have cared about sitting alone with a cold leg of mutton and a bottle of mixed pickles.

If he was looking gloomy, it was not on that account. Let us listen to him and hear what are his thoughts. He is obligingly thinking aloud, so we shall have no trouble.

Hush! as they say in the play! hush! he speaks. Slow music, if you please, and solo from heavy villain.

"Cursed luck!" growled Rattan between his teeth, "nothing turns up as it ought to. I was an infernal idiot to frighten that woman into tumbling into the water. She won't have anything more to say to me, I expect, and serve me right for being such a blundering ass. Besides, what claim have I on her? Nothing very particular. Supposing the boy is her son, as by the likeness I make no doubt he is, I can't prove it. I can't threaten her. If I was to say I would go and tell all I knew to the duke, she would get beforehand with me—give me into custody, too. She knows more about me, curse her, than I know about her; and I think of the two, I'm more in her power than she is in mine."

Here he lit a fresh pipe, and took a swig at the raw spirits.

"She's an awful plummy bit of goods, though," he continued, with an ugly smirk, "I don't know as I ever come across a plummier. I wonder whether all the aristocracy takes after her. She's what I call a right down rattler. But what does that matter to me? Curse her again, a hundred times! she's not likely to be casting sheep's eyes at me. She treats me, instead, like so much dirt. She does, by G—! a great deal worser, too."

To drown his sorrows he took a little more raw spirits.

"This trade's all very well, if it wasn't such cursed hard work. Everybody thinks that body-snatching's done away with, because nobody hears nothing about it. It was a fine idea starting it again, and going into the business wholesale. Your odd jobs don't pay one. When everybody was on the look-out for the snatchers there was hardly any chance of getting clear off, without being nobbled; but now no one dreams of such a thing, and when they've shoved their relations into the ground they thinks 'em as safe as though they was in the Bank, and, for what I know, a precious sight safer.

He meant this for a little joke, at the expense of the banks generally, and laughed at it heartily himself.

"No; I don't complain of the times, pertickler. Deaths is plentiful, and we're doing a rare stroke of business. If I did nothink else I might almost live on what I get from the workhouse in the way of commission, in disposing of the bodies. Most astonishing lot of deaths they do have, to be sure. I suppose it's all right. It's precious rum though, they should go off like they do. I've heard of paupers being put out of the way on the quiet, but I don't believe in it to no great extent. Then if anything had been done to them there would be the marks, I should think, and as the bodies are sold to the doctors they would be the very boys to find it out, I should say. Well, if there is anything it's devilish artful. I wish I was in the partnership, that's all.—Damnation!"

The last exclamation was caused by the candle, which, for some time past, had been sinking slowly into the rough candle-stick in which it was fixed, suddenly going down, and out with a pop.

"I wonder whether there's any matches anywhere," said Rattan, "I've used all I had, with my pipe. It's infernally awkward. My mate ought to leave some out somewhere handy."

He groped about, as he spoke, in all the corners of the vault, and upon the table where the coffin was, taking it up a little, gently to feel under it; but he could find none.

Round and round he groped and groped, but with the same success.

"I shall have to sit in the dark," he thought. "Curse me if I half like it. It aint the way to pass the time very easy. Besides, corpses in the light is one thing, and corpses in the dark is another. I don't mind 'em a bit, when I see 'em fair, but in the dark, one never knows where they may have you next. Howsomedever, they can't eat me, I reckon. How long's my mate going to be, I should like to know."

There was no disguising the fact. He certainly did not relish his present position. He was, like almost every other ruffian and bully, an awful coward. Although in the habit of constantly looking upon and touching the dead, when left there alone with two in the dark, he began to feel as timid as a little baby.

A church clock struck twelve (it was, I should have said, the night after the events I have described as occuring at the workhouse), and the sound of the bell dying away left an awful kind of lull and silence behind it, which made him shiver.

"If he don't make haste," Rattan said to himself, "I shall hook it; I can't stand this."

For another five minutes he sat silent. Then he coughed slightly. The noise sounded as loud as a cannon, after the death-like stillness which had preceded it.

He began to be afraid of moving, and, straining every sense, listened intently.

Click! click!

He started to his feet with an exclamation of horror, for he fancied that the coffin-lid had given way, and at one end, owing to the pressure within.

"It's only fancy!" he said, wiping the sweat off his face, "I won't give way to it; I'll sing a song."

He didn't know a great many songs, and these were of a mournful character.

"Sam Hall," "The Morning that Bill was Scragged," and "The Shroud of Dick Turpin the Bold." Besides he was not quite sure of the words of any of these.*

"Down among the Dead Men" was the one he knew the most of, and was the liveliest, so he thought he would try that.

It was an awful thing to do, to break the silence, but he would make the attempt.

"For he who woman's rights deny, down among the dead men, down among the dead men, down among the dead men, down—down—down —down among the dead men let him lie-e-e"

This was as much as he knew, but he sang it several times over, each time louder than the last.

"Down, down," he bellowed, " down among the dead men let him lie."

Was it the echo which took up the chorus?

Was it fancy?

Was it reality?

As sure as death something took it up, and sang after him in hollow and unearthly tones.

"Down among the dead men let him lie."

He ceased suddenly, as though he had been shot, and listened with his hair on end, bristling like the quills on a porcupine.

The vault was pitch dark, but Rattan's eyes were turned in the direction of the coffin, and were wide open and staring.

He felt the perspiration slowly trickling down his face, and the blood curdled in his veins.

For a moment or two there was no other movement, and then he heard a faint rustling and a sound, as though of laboured breathing.

It was Toddleboy struggling with the corpse.

Rattan was too much terrified to move or to speak. The perspiration still trickled down his face, and his eyes were still turned in the same direction.

There was a sound of rustling again, and then the voice which he had heard before uttered, in the same awful tones that it had previously been singing in, one single word.

That word was CHORUS.

It did not very much matter what the word was. The most ridiculous word in the English language would have been just as terrible under the circumstances. It was a word coming from a coffin, and from the lips of a dead man.

Rattan, in an agony of fright, rushed towards the door, but, on his way, the tail of his coat caught upon a nail sticking in the side of the table.

In his terror, he fancied that the corpse had got hold of him.

He tugged and wrenched wildly. The stuff of his coat was strong. The nail was very firmly fixed. He could not release himself.

The author thinks it may be interesting to some of his fair readers to know that that the "dead men" in this popular ballad, are not deceased persons but empty wine-bottles, so that the wish expressed by the singer is not that the person of whom he speaks should be in his grave but simply under the table, a place where our grandfathers frequently got, after one of those old English drinking bouts since gone a little out of fashion.

He pulled, and dragged, and tore at it, in savage desperation.

He was a man of gigantic strength, and as the coat would not tear, nor the nail give way, he dragged the table after him.

In so doing he upset it, and flinging the coffin heavily upon the ground, sent Toddleboy and the dead body sprawling together on the floor.

When there, Toddleboy, sitting upright, called out "holloa," in astonishment, as well he might, at the same time rubbing the back of his head, which had been bumped by the tumble.

Rattan's terror, by this time, had reached a climax. He would have fainted with fright, had not the nail opportunely given way.

A fresh obstacle here arose. The door opened inwards. Rattan pushed it.

Of course it did not yield to the pressure.

In his paroxysm of fright, he howled aloud. Toddleboy howled too, in a more dismal manner still. Such a combination of unearthly sounds it would have well nigh sent anybody out of their wits to listen to.

How he tore and dragged at the lock of the door. How he pushed frantically, and kicked against the panels.

It did not yield an inch. Meantime, Toddleboy rose to his feet.

The miserable wretch trying to get out, heard him coming.

In another moment he would be in his clutches.

His mind gave way. His senses deserted him. He fell in a fainting fit upon the floor.

XXXI.—MORE ABOUT THE DIRTY OLD MAN.

POOR little Charley managed to sleep a very long while, although his couch was none of the softest.

It might have been that the dirty old man felt afraid that the postilion's dress would prevent him from sleeping, or that he had discovered among the miscellaneous contents of the shop, certain articles so nearly resembling them, that he might with safety make a "swap," and when the boy woke up, palm off the shabbier suit upon him, and appropriate the better one. It might have been either or neither of these reasons which impelled him to the act, but whatever it was, Mr. Measles certainly undressed him.

What is more, he made him up a bed.

This was on the third day. The man called George had dropped in, in a lounging, loafing style peculiar to him, and had asked, first of all, how the boy was, and secondly, where was the physic.

There was not much difficulty in answering the first question. The boy was there in the back parlour, looking very sickly and queer.

As for the second,

"That's the physic," said the old man, pointing to a half emptied bottle, containing the remains of some noxious stuff he had purchased more than a month ago, for his own private use.

"That's lotion," said George, who, after smelling it and looking at the label, put it down again with a wry face, and an expression of disgust.

"What the dickens are you giving him that for?"

"Lotion, is it!" observed the old gentleman, fishing for his spectacles at the back of his head, and fixing them on his nose to look at the bottle, "lotion, you call it?"

"Why, damn it," cried George, sharply turning upon him, "what do you it?"

"The same as you call it, George. Bless us and save us, don't snap at one so. How can you?"

"Then if you do call it lotion," continued George, "what do you mean by it?"

"By what, George?"

"By what? Curse it, man, you know what. What are you using lotion for?"

"I'm rubbing him with it, to be sure, George, I aint making him swallow it."

"No; trust you for that. You wouldn't make anybody swallow much you had to pay for, but there's one thing I'd like to say a word about."

"Certainly, George, as much as you choose. What is it?"

"About this bottle."

"I thought we'd settled that."

"Not quite; there's something besides a label here."

"What is there?"

"A date."

"Oh—ah—yes. What, a date, eh?"

"You heard me, I suppose."

"Yes; I heard you, George. What of it?"

"Why this much of it and no more. You are the most infernal old scamp, although you are my father, I ever came across; and I tell you no lie about it. It's only because you're related, and an objection that I nat'rally have to walloping one of the family, that keeps my hands off you. You know very well you never spent the money, as I told you, and that that lotion was bought in November, and here we are in January."

"George, I assure you, it's a mistake of the chap that sold it me. He's put the wrong date."

"Don't try to Welch me, I tell you, or, by gosh, you'll put my dander up. Do the right thing by that lad, and spend the money I gave you to spend upon him. Else, if I find out you haven't, I'll twist your cunning old head off, although you are my parent. So I tell 'ee."

"A deary, deary, George, how it makes my heart ache to hear you!"

And the old gentleman took a pinch of snuff and burst out crying in a mournful way, rocking himself to and fro meanwhile, and dragging at his dirty grey locks his as though he would pull out a handfull.

"Well, you need not take on so," said George, with something of contempt in his tone, "only just take my advice, and behave well to the boy, or else, as I have previously intimated, it will be the worse for you. Now, make no mistake."

"I ain't a making no mistake, George; I wonder you can talk so to your poor old father

What a hard-hearted wretch you must be to suspect your own flesh and blood this way."

"My own flesh and blood be damned!" the other retorted. "What's up with the boy, do you think?"

"He only wants a little care and attention, and he will soon come round."

"Well, let him have it."

"He shall have it."

"Good morning, then."

"Good morning, George."

So George took his departure, and when he was well out of the shop the old man shook his fist at him, and then shook his fist at the boy; and a stray forlorn-looking dog, of vagabond exterior, having the ill-fortune to wander into the shop at this juncture, the old gentleman ran after it with a walking-stick, and sent it yelling and yelping three streets off.

Poor Charley, even with the aid of physic, which the old man procured for him, groaning in spirit over every penny he had to pay for it, got no better.

He was like this for almost three weeks. Sometimes he wandered and talked wildly in his sick dreams of boys being eaten by black beetles, and young ladies escaping out of burning houses, and lots of other surprising things to which the old gentleman, smoking a meditative pipe, listened to with considerable astonishment.

"He is a rum boy that," said the old gentleman, "and to judge from what he says, has seen a thing or two in the course of his small experience."

At last Charley recovered. He woke up one morning after what seemed to him to have been a few hours' sleep, and opening his eyes, looked drowsily round the room, and wondered where he was. It was a curious room, crammed full of odds and ends of rubbish, like the shop outside. There were also one or two boxes with strips of wood nailed roughly across the front, in the form of bars, wherein rabbits and guinea pigs, and tumbler pigeons were congregated.

It was a remarkably bad smelling room (though he did not notice that), for, besides the smell arising from dirty odds and ends, before alluded to, and the naturally unpleasant odour of the guinea pigs, rabbits, and pigeons, there was also a powerful stench of red herrings and tobacco. In fact, Mr. Measles, the proprietor of the shop, was cooking his breakfast and smoking a strong pipe of shag to give him an appetite for it.

He was a curious old man, that Measles, and had eccentric notions about his victuals, for he did not take a cup of coffee like you and I would, but had got some gin and water by the side of him, with which he presently intended to wash down the "soldier."

Charley, in a drowsy way, turned his eyes towards him, when he had looked at the other contents of the room, and began to wonder, not unnaturally, whether the old gentleman ever washed his face.

Suddenly the object of his scrutiny turned round his head, and their eyes met. "Now, then," said the old man, "what do you want?"

"Nothing, sir," replied Charley.

"Then mind your own business," said Mr. Measles, "and don't interfere with me."

Charley did not exactly see how he had interfered as yet, but, by way of conciliation, he said,

"I beg your pardon, sir, I am sure."

The old gentleman made no reply for some time, being particularly engaged in turning over his herring on the gridiron, with the stem of his pipe. When he had effected this to his entire satisfaction he observed,

"I wonder how long you are going to lie there, idling. You're costing me a fine penny, you are."

"Am I?" said Charley.

"Are you?" repeated the old man. "Of course you are. Hundreds of pounds' worth of physic I have bought for you. And who are you, after all, I should like to know?"

"I am Charley Wag," replied our hero.

"Charley, how much?"

"Wag."

"The devil you are!"

With every sign of the greatest excitement the old gentleman jumped up from his seat, deserted his herring, and disappeared into the shop.

Charley raised his head and looked after him in astonishment, but could see nothing of him.

He however heard a rustling of paper, and presently the old gentleman returned with a large bundle of what appeared to be printed placards, jagged and torn at the edges.

"Do you know what these are?" said the old gentleman.

"No, sir," replied Charley.

"Well, they are posters."

"Posters?"

"Yes; haven't you heard of posters before? they are what the bill-stickers stick upon the walls. These have been stuck upon the walls, but they have been taken down again. I have a contract with a sticker, and send a boy after him to pull them down while they are damp. The paper I use in my trade, as I can use anything that other people would throw away; and the sticker is glad enough to make a little something over his regular pay by this means. Though whether he has the dishonesty to sell a lot more of his bills that have never been stuck up at all is more than I can say. Let us hope, for the sake of human nature, that he does not."

While he was speaking, Mr. Measles had been busily engaged turning over the bills, and at last alighted upon one, in the search of which he seemed to have been engaged.

"Here it is," said he, "here's the poster; now Mr. Charley Wag, what have you to say to this?"

He handed Charley as he spoke, a large bill, printed in large type, which, at the first glance, he saw bore a reference to himself.

It said :—

"LOOK OUT FOR CHARLEY WAG—FIFTY POUNDS REWARD. Whereas, any person who will bring this boy to Mr. Leech, solicitor, of Symmond's Inn, Chancery-lane, will receive the above. When last seen, he was wearing a postilion's dress. He is about fourteen years old, but looks older, has light brown curly hair, blue eyes, and very white and regular teeth. He is of a remarkably lively disposition, talks very fast, and has a peculiar swaggering walk, unusual in a person of his years. Whoever shall harbour the boy after this notice, will render themselves amenable to the law, as he is charged with highway robbery, abduction, and arson. Should he have died, any person bringing information thereof to Mr. Leech, of Symmond's Inn, will receive the above reward.

"What do you say to that!" said the old gentleman, with a grin. "That's you, I suppose."

Charley said nothing, but his lips quivered, and the tears started in his eyes.

He was, as yet, very ill and weak; even had he been strong such a startling announcement as that which he now looked upon would have been calculated to terrify any person of twice his age.

"Oh, sir," he cried, "what are they going to do with me? Where am I?"

"You are all right enough at present," said the old gentleman, "and in the hands of friends, but you had better mind your p's and q's, that's all I have got to say."

"But," said Charley, "what highway robbery have I committed. To be sure, I did not give back the money, but I am going to do so. Where is Lucinda?"

"Where's who?" said the old gentleman, looking up from his herring. "We have got no Lucindas here, and we ain't going to have, young fellow, don't you think it."

"She is the daughter of Mr. Hopley," said Charley. "She is the one I ran away with."

"A nice chap you are to run away with Lucindas," said Mr. Measles. "I shouldn't have done it at your age myself, I am certain," and he took a drink at his gin-and-water, and winked his eye at the frolicsome recollection of his happy childhood.

Meanwhile Charley was looking round for his clothes, and presently managed to get hold of his coat which was, lying across his feet. When he had reached it, he felt in the breast-pocket.

"It's gone," he exclaimed, in great alarm; "It's gone. What have you done with it?"

"Done with what?" asked Mr. Measles.

"Done with my money. Forty-nine pounds, that I had in a bag in my pocket. I have been robbed of it."

"Well," said the old gentleman, "I can't help your being robbed, can I? Lots of people are robbed besides you. I have been robbed often. I am always being robbed. My sons rob me, my daughters rob me. I am a poor pillaged parent, who is always having his pocket picked by one or the other."

"But I must have the money!" cried Charley, wildly, "I must have the money, or they will think that I stole it! Oh, pray do, good gentleman, give it me back!"

"Come now, shut up. I can't enjoy my breakfast, while you are making that row."

Charley said no more, but lay sobbing in the most dreadful grief and despair, while Mr. Measles, quite unconcerned, discussed his herring and gin-and-water.

When the old gentleman had finished, he went out into the shop, where he sorted over his goods

and bargained with his customers the greater part
of the day, returning every now and then to the
back-parlour to smoke another strong pipe, or to
refresh himself from his favourite black bottle.

He did not, however, throughout the day,
partake of any other refreshment.

Charley, in the afternoon, asked whether he
might get up for a little while, but Mr. Measles
said "no," and he was fain to stop where he was
and make himself as comfortable as circumstances
allowed of.

XXXII.—The Mysteries of the Rag and Bottle Shop.

ONE day so nearly resembled another, that
when it was over in his recollection
Charley could not distinguish it from the preceding or succeeding ones.

In the course of two or three days the old
gentleman allowed him to get up, and gave him
his clothes, with the exception of his boots,
which he exchanged for a pair of slippers.

That is to say, he gave him the clothes which
the boy had worn underneath the postilion's
dress; "for the latter," he said, "it would not
be very wise to be seen in, unless he wanted to
be taken before a magistrate, and forthwith
hanged, without a trial, in front of the Old
Bailey.

Charley several times begged to be allowed to
return to his foster mother's, who, he felt certain, must be alarmed by his long absence, and
to whom he wished to explain the cause; but
this the old gentleman would not hear of, and
told him that if he ventured to put his head
outside the door, he would in all probability be
pounced upon by a policeman who was watching the house (here Mr. Measles pointed out an
officer who happened to be standing on the
other side of the way, in corroboration of his
statement), and carried off to limbo.

One day, too, when Charley was peeping out
of the door of the shop, during the temporary
absence of the old gentleman, who had gone to
get his bottle filled, the latter returned, and
clutching him by the hair of the head, ran him
back into the parlour, and holding him down in
a chair, brandished the bottle in the air, like an
Indian might his tomahawk.

"You ungrateful young wretch—you sneaking
young vagabond—you backsliding young blackguard, what are you up to?—where are you
going to?—what the blessed blazes is your little
game?"

"Nothing, is my game," replied Charley,
panting for breath, "leave us alone, can't you?
you dirty old coward. Hit one of your own
size."

"I'll tear your tongue out and roast it on a
nail—I'll poke a red hot bodkin in your eye—
I'll scalp you—I'll flay you—I'll make a freemason of you—if ever I catch you at the door
again."

After every one of these threats the old man
flourished his bottle, and performed some ex-
centric steps, which might have stood in place of
a war dance. It was not for a long while that

he recovered sufficiently from his excitement to
sit down and smoke one of those strong pipes
he was so fond of.

He was so excited as to be even careless of
his business, and on a little girl coming into the
shop with bones, he roared out that he did not
want any, and told her to get out of his sight,
or he would cut her head off. At which threat
the little girl, dropping the biggest bone of the
lot, fled precipitately, and was seen no more.

Although he referred no more to the subject,
Mr. Measles was evidently uneasy in his mind
with regard to his young friend's intentions,
and he always locked him in the room when he
went out of the shop into the upper part of the
house.

Mr. Measles very frequently went upstairs,
and as Charley knew for a fact, having heard
the old gentleman say so several times, that
all the upper part of the house was occupied by
lodgers, he could not understand where on
earth Mr. Measles went to, unless it was into
one of the lodgers' rooms.

But this was not the case, it would seem, for
Mr. Measles informed him, without his inquiring, that he never by any chance spoke to
any of his lodgers, except when he met them on
the stairs, or they came down into the shop, on
a Saturday night, about the rent. While he
was upstairs, a boy, who came there during the
day, was in the habit of taking care of the
shop, and this young gentleman informed
Charley that Mr. Measles spent a good deal of
his time upon the roof.

"What's he do there," asked Mr. Wag?

"Feeds his pigeons," replied the boy.

"But he is always feeding them," said
Charley.

"Yes," said the boy; "they take a deal of
feeding."

Charley made no further remarks, but he
thought to himself that it was very odd that he
never saw the old gentleman take up any food
with him.

Certainly, when some of the visitors (there
were a great many visitors) had called upon him
they had suggested that they should go and
look at the pigeons, or asked him after his
birds. But, though there were others who
made no allusion to the feathered favourites,
they all went upstairs with the old gentleman,
and did business of some sort or other upon
the roof.

There were, of course, a great number of
people who came about bottles, and bones, and
rags, but there were quite as many who came
upon some other mysterious business and went
up stairs with Mr. Measles on to the roof.

These last customers, or clients, or friends, or
whatever they were, were curious kind of persons
to visit a rag and bottle warehouse.

There were beautiful young ladies, in pink
silk frocks, with black lace flounces, and cach-
mere shawls, and fly-away bonnets. There were
also fashionably attired young swells, with
wonderful jewellery and gorgeous apparel; and
there were, also, staid respectable men, of
middle age, with white cravats, who had the
appearance of being respectable clergymen, or
head clerks at banks. As a rule, the only
thing which spoilt the distinguished appearance

of Mr. Measles' friends was that their hands were rather queer.

They hardly any of them had respectable hands.

The young ladies and the young swells wore light-coloured kid gloves, but when they took them off, their fingers were short, and stumpy, and coarse, and their nails were all in mourning.

Whatever did they come for? They brought no rags nor bottles with them; perhaps they were the purchasers—if so, they never took anything away.

It was a curious place, this shop of Mr. Measles', and Mr. Measles was a curious man. He was full of eccentricities; he hardly ever took any nourishment, except it was from his strong pipes and his black bottle. He said he was too poor. But this could not be the case, for he allowed Charley to have mutton chops, and eggs, and sweetbreads, and other delicacies in profusion.

And besides he had always got a lot of sovereigns in his pocket.

There was another peculiarity; although he was so careless of his sovereigns, and would often leave four or five laying about on the mantelpiece, he was most particular about pennies, and one day, when the boy in the shop brought a halfpenny short in change, the old gentleman threatened him with every conceivable sort of violence.

But the most curious thing was to come.

One day Charley picked up a card, on which some words were written in printing letters, and they were these:

PRICE LIST.

	s.	d.
A Brum Quid	4	6
A Bull	1	0
Half Bull	0	5½

N.B. Not Payable in Same.

Nothing smaller made.—Flimsies in great variety.

Ask for Measles', at the Old Place.

What could that mean? he puzzled over it for an hour, but could make nothing of it.

It is probable that had not certain circumstances occurred, which I am about to relate, he never would have discovered the mystery.

XXXIII.—Shows how little Pitchers have Ears, and how Charley's ears were as long as those of any other little Pitcher.

ONE night Charley lay upon the sofa as usual, where he had slept since he took up his abode with Mr. Measles.

He had been to sleep for several hours. The old gentleman had gone out at about seven in the evening upon some particular business, taking his favourite black bottle and his strong pipe along with him, and the boy had been trying to amuse himself with what Mr. Measles facetiously termed his library.

This consisted of two volumes, one termed the "Terrific Record; or, Cabinet Calendar of Horrors," and the other was a book of sermons, the alternate leaves of which had been torn out so as to allow of the pasting upon the remaining leaves, of extracts clipped from weekly newspapers, and, as all these referred to indecent charges, rapes, and seductions, the reader can imagine that it was a very popular volume among Mr. Measles' lady and gentleman friends.

Charley had read the greater part of both these works. Don't be shocked, gentle reader, a man ought to read such things, or ought to know them, anyhow. Besides, are they not printed as a warning to youth, and surely not to incite him to go and do likewise. Well, never mind that now, I have got a story to write, and must leave the moral reflections to my reviewers, if I ever have any.

He had been reading these books this particular night, and had fallen asleep over the account of the torture of a missionary in the backwoods of America, who had been submitted to the most fearful atrocities, which I will not make my readers' hair stand on end by repeating.

He had fallen asleep, as I say, and had slept for several hours, when he was awakened by the sound of whispering voices in the room. He opened his eyes, and without changing his position or making any other movement, looked towards the place from which the sound emanated.

There, by the fire-side, sat old Mr. Measles, and the man called George.

They were evidently engaged in earnest conversation.

"I tell you the trade's worth nothing," the old man said, "there's too much risk and too little profit; the dies are out of order, too, and that infernal battery cost so much I shall never clear my expenses."

"That's all very fine, as far as it goes, but you have a quiet stocking put by somewhere."

"That's like you, George, suspecting your own flesh and blood."

"Well, to tell the truth, I have seen such a precious deal of my own flesh and blood, and such a precious little good about it, that it has rather shook my good opinion; however, it's no time for chaffing. As soon as I have got this little affair, the reel, we shall be perfectly rolling in wealth."

"I hope we shall, George, only you're precious slow about it."

"Slow, you call it. Good God! I should like to see you doing the same work any sharper, with those old spindles of yours."

"Well, what are you doing?—you have never explained rightly what your little game was."

"To begin with, I expect you know my game was breaking into the Bank of England."

"Yes—yes."

"Well, that's settled; then, the next thing is, how I am going to do it."

"Well, you know I have taken a cellar in

Princes-street. What do you suppose I have taken it for?"

"Well, you have told me it was to make an underground passage to reach the cellars in the Bank."

"And that's what I am doing, only it's a more difficult job than it sounds.

"It sounds great nonsense to me; I always thought it a mad-cap scheme."

"Yes, you are the old school, dad; you're happy enough, making your old half-crowns and five shillings, and selling them again at a loss, that's your notion of trade."

And here Mr. George laughed a hoarse laugh, which shook the room, and made the half-quartern glasses on the table jingle.

"Hush! hush!" cried the old man, laying his hand upon his companion's arm; "Not so loud, for God's sake, you will wake the cursed whelp."

Charles Wag, Esq., imagining this delicate allusion to apply to himself, immediately screwed up his eyes as tight as wax, and began to snore.

"He is all right enough," said George, tilting his chair on to its hind legs, to get a good look at him; "he's asleep fast enough."

But the old man did not seem to be so well satisfied, but, taking a carving knife off the table, which chanced to be laying there, and holding it in one hand, he took the candlestick in the other, and approached the boy. Three or four times he passed the light across Charley's eyes, backwards and forwards, but the boy never stirred. He even laid the cold steel against the pretended sleeper's throat without his flinching.

"Yes, he is asleep," said the old man.

And he came back to his seat by the fire.

Then they resumed their conversation.

"How far have you got with your work there, George?"

"I have made two or three false starts, as I told you, and I got into the sewer once, but I have arranged it all right now, and have crossed the street."

"So far it's all right, then; but how will you know where to break through upwards?"

"That's the difficulty; or, rather, it was the difficulty before I got a plan of the building."

"You have got one then?"

"Yes, to be sure, I got one from a chap inside."

"How was that?"

"I've been hanging about for a long while trying to pick someone up. This chap is a messenger, a lucky card, who is likely to get the sack."

"You did not tell him your plan, though."

"Not so green. I told him I was going to try to prig something, but I said that I should come in in the day time and hide myself."

"Ah, to be sure; I should not let more into the job than was necessary."

"You and me, George, will be quite plenty enough to do the crack together."

"Well, guv'nor, I ain't so sure about you; you are hardly nimble enough for the job. Of course, you shall have a share of the swag, but I should like some active whelp to be with me at the time. A man, of course, could carry most, but then he would want most; now if that lad, there, I picked up, could be trusted, he will suit my appetite to a nicety; but then, the question is, is he to be trusted."

Charley opened his eyes very wide, and shut them again very tight, and snored as before."

"Well, as to that," said the old man, "there is two ways of managing him, and one is to slit his wizen when the job is done, and so stroke him out of the books."

"But that I shan't do," said George, angrily. "I have taken a fancy to the lad, and mean to look after his interest."

"Well, I can understand your looking after his interest, if you expect to pick him up very often with fifty pounds in his pocket; but I should say that would not occur again for some time, anyhow."

"But never mind about that," said George, with an impatient gesture. "I tell you, the boy shall come to no harm."

"You've took a rare fancy to him, George."

"I have."

"Well, you know best, I suppose, but if it was me, I should collar this 'ere reward that's offered on the bills. Fifty pounds is not to be sneezed at, particular in these hard times."

"I tell you, curse it, I shall not give him up. If you do so, you do it at your peril, and know what you may expect."

"The only thing is, you see, is he safe? These boy's tongues are as long as my arm."

"As to that," cried the other, turning round with a savage glare in his eyes, "you know, well enough, if he played us false, I shouldn't stick at a trifle."

"You'd twist his young neck for him."

"Aye, his or any other's, for that matter."

"That's spoken hearty, George, and like yourself; and suppose he won't join us."

"What makes you think he won't?"

"To tell the truth, there's too much infernal straightforward look about him. He's a fool, I take it. Why, I give you my word of honour, I've many a time left out a Brum or two, to try him with, and I've never found him do it. He's a fool, I tell you."

"It don't prove he's a fool because he didn't pick up them duffers."

"Duffers or not," the old man answered, testily, "they're the best article as is made, and I defy you to match 'em. But we won't quarrel about that. You'll take the boy with you to help at this 'crack.' When's it to be?"

"To-morrow night."

"To-morrow, then, we make a thief of him."

XXXIV.—UP THE CHIMNEY, AND OUT ON THE TILES.

WHEN they had come to this praiseworthy determination, the two vagabonds rose from their seats, and putting on their hats, prepared to leave the house.

"I've got some of the stuff here, I'm going to take to a customer," said the old gentleman, displaying a small canvas bag full of counterfeit half-crowns.

THE USE OF SOLDIERS' BELTS.

"That's a good whack," said George, looking at them. "How many is there?"

"Best part of two hundred, George. He's in the wholesale way."

"He ought to be, to get rid of them."

"Yes; he keeps a glove shop in Regent-street, and passes 'em off like smoke."

"Hasn't he been spotted?"

"Sometimes one's brought back, and then he blows up the young men for giving it to the customers, and calls 'em all the fools he can lay his tongue to for taking 'em. They're not in the kid themselves; and sometimes, if more than one comes back in a week, he stops it out of their wages."

"That's a fine move, too."

No. 15.

"Ah, there's many fine moves in our line. Smashing's the best game out, depend upon it."

"I suppose so. Better than mine," replied George, wrapping his throat up in a comforter. "It's time I was on the river, if I'm to pick anything up to night. When it gets later on, the cursed police are all on the look out."

Here the two worthies lit their pipes, and, carefully locking Master Charles in the room, went away, taking the key with them.

While the men remained in the room, Charley pretended to be fast asleep, and screwed his eyes up very tight, but as soon as they were gone, he sat upright on the sofa and opened them to their widest.

"They are going to make a thief of me!"

"What am I to do?"

[CHARLEY WAG, THE NEW JACK SHEPPARD.

"How am I to escape?"

These were the questions he asked himself, with an interval of three minutes between each.

The doors were locked, and he knew he could not force them, for one of the peculiarities of the singular rag and bottle emporium was, that the doors at the bottom of the house were coated with iron; Mr. Measles accounting for it, when Charley questioned him, by saying that there were so many bad characters about that part of London, and that he was so very much afraid of thieves.

The window, too, was double barred, and he could not go that way.

How then?

He had no wish to begin again picking out bricks; besides, there was no time for anything of that sort.

He could not tell how long the old man might be away. It was then about eleven o'clock. He might be away for hours, but it was quite as probable that he might return directly.

Which way should he go? if he could not get out of the door or the window, or through the floor? Why, of course, the reader has guessed it long ago.

Up the chimney.

He did not stay to consider about it; jumped off the sofa, slipped on his coat, waistcoat, trousers and boots, and went straight to the fire-place.

Luckily for him there had been but a very small fire all the evening, and now there were only a few sparks in the grate. However, unless my readers have climbed chimneys (which, if of the gentler sex, is highly improbable) they can form no notion how hot a chimney gets when there has been any fire in the grate at all.

"I wonder whether it is a register stove," said Charley, as he put his hand up.

He had never had the curiosity to look at the fire-place before, and, indeed, was not quite certain, in his own mind, what sort of a stove the one was which he mentioned, only he had heard that boys could not climb up them.

He felt with great anxiety, but found, to his delight, that there was no obstacle to impede his progress—and he began to climb.

He was an active young fellow, as you must know by this time, and he had often heard the process of climbing described. However, just when he had got his head and shoulders up, a thought struck him.

"I shall get in an awful mess," thought he, "I had much better put something over my clothes."

There were an old coat and a pair of trousers in the room, belonging to Mr. Measles. He came out of the fire-place again, and put them on.

Then he began the perilous ascent once more.

At first it was all right, but after awhile it became very fatiguing.

He had not got the right knack, he supposed; and, grinding away at the sides of the chimney, he felt as though his knees and his elbows were wearing out, and would soon come to the bone.

It was such a tremendous long chimney, too—a regular twister.

"I should think," said Charley to himself, as he stopped half-way for breath, at a place where Providence had placed a ledge that he could stand upon, and relieve his knees for a moment, "I should think that boys usually began a little higher up than the parlour. I should have been out of the attic long ago."

After he had rested a bit, he struggled on again as before.

What, however, struck him as being rather curious was, that he could see no light above.

When first he noticed it he did not think very much of the circumstance, but as he continued to struggle upwards he began to be rather alarmed, and, thought he,

"Perhaps there's a cowl on the top, if so, I shall be like a fly in a bottle with a cork in it."

This struck him as being funny, and he stopped to snigger at his nonsensical joke before he went on any further.

But working on, steadily and surely, to his intense satisfaction he discovered the cause of the darkness. It was a twist in the chimney. He worked his way through it, and scrambled and elbowed and kicked at the walls, until he began to feel the air through the chimney-pot.

"Now, if the pot's too small," said Charley, "I'm done for."

There was no mistake about it, it was a tight fit. He forced himself up. He got jammed. He thrust, and panted, and struggled, and the perspiration poured down his face.

As he was struggling and panting, suddenly he stopped, in an awful fright.

For he heard, just above him, one of the most terrific sounds which it is possible to conceive.

It was not a laugh—it was not a scream—it was not a groan—but a combination of all these. Shrill and loud at first, and dying off in a long faint wail, as though of agony.

At first he knew not what to make of it, and then the thought struck him that it must be the cry of a maniac.

Perhaps a maniac which Measles kept upon the roof.

Charley's blood began to grow cold and his flesh to creep.

If he had not been wedged too tight, he would have tumbled down the chimney again to a certainty.

For several minutes he remained perfectly motionless.

All was still.

He would venture again.

Indeed it would be madness to try to go back. In fact, to tell the truth, he could not. He had stuck fast, and could not move an inch.

"If I could only get out of this," he said to himself, "I shouldn't care if there were fifty maniacs. I wonder whether he is chained up."

Again he set to struggling.

"If I don't get out before the morning, old Measles will most likely set a light to the fire underneath to cook that blessed old bloater of his; and then where shall I be?"

The idea made him push his hardest.

"I shall be cooked before the herring, to a dead certainty. And then if the fire smokes, he will, perhaps, come up and look what has happened to the chimney pot. He might think it was the maniac stuck his head in the top, and couldn't get it out again. By Jingo, he'd have me out, I expect, or pull the ears off me trying."

This time he made a terrific effort. The chimney pot was old and cracked. With the force of his pushing it gave way on one side. He forced his way upwards, poking his head out at the top, with a sniff of exquisite delight.

But just at that moment the same awful sound rang in his ears. This time louder and shriller, and nearer to him than before.

"The maniac's going it," thought Charley. "He must have broken his chain."

XXXV.—IN WHICH CHARLEY INTERRUPTS THE LOVE-MAKING OF A CERTAIN REVEREND GENTLEMAN.

CHARLEY poked his head out a little further, and looking round, expected to see a madman in the act of springing upon him to throttle him, but he did not.

Right in front of him there was some unearthly looking object, with great green eyes, which glistened like phosphorus in the moonlight.

From it proceeded the awful sounds he had just heard.

He stared at it with his hair on end, and knocked the soot out of his eyes.

Could he be awake.

No! Yes! Impossible!

IT WAS A CAT.

A great black Tom, on a chimney close to him, stood glaring at him, and bristling up the hair on its back and its tail, until it looked twice its ordinary size.

As Charley worked his way out at the top, several other cats went scampering across the tiles, and made the best of their way home, with their tails in the air.

"It's you, is it?" said Charley to the feline vocalist; "I suppose you were courting. Be off with you."

But the cat did not follow his advice. On the contrary, it came up to him, smelt him, and licked his nose.

"Be off!" said Charley again.

Tom, however, only sang a song at the top of his voice, and went on washing Master Charles' nose.

"Well," said Charley, "if he likes it, I don't complain. I certainly ought to wash my face before I go into the street, if I can ever manage get there."

He sat down resignedly, and his new friend washed his face as clean as though he had used soap and water. When it had done this it sat down upon his knee, and coiling itself up, prepared to go to sleep.

But Charley thought he had better be moving; so he set Tom down very gently and looked about him.

Here he was, on the roof where the mysterious old man spent so much of his time.

What on earth could he do there?

There were two or three old rabbit-hutches, and some broken boxes, and a pigeon-house.

Nothing else that he could see. There was an old broken chair, to be sure. Perhaps that was what the old gentleman sat upon and smoked those strong pipes of his. Or perhaps it was what the visitors sat down upon when they went up to look at the pigeons.

Charley peeped at the pigeons, but saw nothing very well worth looking at. Decidedly not worth the trouble of coming up all that way to see.

"It can't be the pigeons," said Charley; "and if it isn't, whatever does the old man do when he brings the young ladies and gentlemen upstairs on to the roof?"

After a little more reflection he determined to leave the consideration of the subject to a more fitting opportunity, should he ever have the misfortune to find himself again in the neighbourhood.

What he determined to do was, to get down into the street somehow or other.

But how was it to be managed?

He had had enough of chimneys. Besides, there were other objections. It made such a noise. The people in the house might hear him, and fire a blunderbuss up after him.

"Then," he reflected, "where should I be?"

He answered the question himself with—

"Blown to Smithereens! wherever that may be."

Then, again, he reflected.

"Suppose it should be one of those register stoves, what should I do? I should have to climb back again.

At this point he thought it would, perhaps, be a wiser plan to go along from roof to roof, and, if possible, creep in at some window.

He walked along the roofs very like a cat himself, Tom followed behind, and, in spite of several threatening gestures, kept close at his heels.

Once Charley turned round and tried to slap its head, but then Tom jumped behind a chimney-pot, and darted out suddenly, alighting on the boy's back and springing away again, like a wild thing.

Decidedly a parapet is not the place for "sky-larking," and so Charley, seeing that his feline friend was bent upon following, let him do so without any more fuss.

With great precaution, and as little noise as possible, Charley pursued his course, over the slanting roofs until he noticed, in a corner behind a stack of chimneys, a window, open a little at the bottom.

Holding firmly by the parapet, Charley reached down his leg till he came to the window-sill, and then pulling the window wide open, crept noiselessly into the room, the cat following after him.

He found himself, first of all, behind some red damask curtains, but opening these discovered, by the light of a brisk fire blazing in the grate that he was in a neat little sitting-room, very tidily arranged, with a book-shelf full of books, two or three religious prints, a sofa, some chairs, a little round table laid for supper, &c. &c.

Taking a hasty glance at the apartment, he was about to make for the door, when he heard voices close to it upon the landing, and running back he hid himself behind the curtains, where the cat followed him, and the two adventurers stood quite quiet and listened.

Then the door opened, and two persons entered the room together.

"This way, Mr. Swabb, if you please; wherever that stupid girl is got to is more than I can tell. I sent her for the beer, and whenever I do she is stopping and gossiping a good hour, and says she couldn't get served. However, I'll catch her out some of these fine days, and, if it's the pot-boy, I'll pack her off about her business."

"Heigho !" said a man's voice, with what seemed to be a little fat sigh, such as only a little fat man could give vent to, "young women are all that way. The flesh is weak, Miss Tabitha, the flesh is weak. They will have their pot-boys, and nobody can prevent them."

"Don't talk like that, I beg of you, Mr. Swabb. I should be very sorry to think that I had been so when I was a young woman."

"You never were a young woman, Miss Tabitha," said Mr. Swabb; and as he paused here, Charley could not help thinking that it was rather a doubtful compliment.

But the gentleman continued, having in the interval pulled off his great coat,

"Nor will you ever be an old woman. In fact you are not a woman at all, but an angel. An angel, abiding among us common vessels of clay !"

Thus disparagingly alluding to himself, Mr. Swabb sat down with a good sounding thump, which showed that he himself was of some weight, whatever his opinions might be.

At that moment the servant girl came in with the beer, and Miss Tabitha and her visitor sat down to supper, to which, if Charley might judge by the smacking of their lips, they were doing ample justice.

Indeed they seemed, by the rattling of their knives and forks, to be pegging away so heartily, that Charley thought he might venture to take a peep.

So he looked out.

There was a red-faced, fat little man, in a shabby black suit, in a white neckerchief, bald-headed and big-lipped, the personification of over-fed sensuality. This was the Reverend Oyley Swabb, the shepherd of Little Rawbones Chapel, Groaner's-court, Brompton.

There was also a plump, comfortable-looking young lady, of about forty-five or thereabouts, whose tight-fitting black silk dress displayed the well-developed contour of her person to the very greatest advantage. This was Miss Tabitha.

They were eating oysters and drinking stout, and evidently enjoying themselves to the very utmost.

The reverend gentleman did upon most occasions. He had a snug little connection among ladies of a certain age, and of a serious turn. He used to read to them (he was a beautiful reader); he used to expound to them, used to take down their names upon his subscription list, and used to put away vast quantities of victuals and drink beneath that sleek black waistcoat of his.

He was, if you want my opinion, a canting old humbug, and I don't mind stating it, in spite of all the little Ebenezers, and Rawboneses, and Shakers, and Groaners, and Moaners, that he was not, and is not, by any means, a solitary case of a canting old humbug attached to the clerical profession.

"I've been to see our good sister, Miss Pamela Andrews, this evening," said the reverend gentleman, when he had finished eating. "She was so good and so kind as to put down her name for a trifle towards the fresh painting and whitewashing of my little chapel. She's a righteous woman."

"She's a good soul," echoed Miss Tabitha, "Is she any better than she has been lately ?"

"Always ailing, Miss Tabitha, always ailing," sighed the little fat man. "A great invalid, it's almost a pity she has not married, and got some one to look after her."

"She remains single, Mr. Swabb, for the good cause. Has she not the poor benighted Hindoos to look after ? She has no time for domestic cares, or to tend children of her own."

"Right, Miss Tabitha, and beautifully spoken; and it is for a like reason that I am a bachelor, but there are times when such a condition of isolation is hard to bear; don't you think so, too, Miss Tabitha ?"

Here the lady sighed.

"Let us pull the sofa nearer the fire; that's it."

"Will you take a little drop of rum, Mr. Swabb ?"

"With hot-water, if you please, Miss Tabitha, and with the same quantity of sugar and lemon that you usually put in it. Thank you; that is very nice."

Here there was a pause, in which the rum and water gurgled down Mr. Swabb's fat throat.

"Yes," Mr Swabb continued, "sometimes it is very hard to bear, and Satan is strong, and the flesh is weak. Is it not so, Miss Tabitha ?"

"Yes, Mr. Swabb," the lady replied, softly.

"Shall I read the Book to you," pursued the reverend gentleman; "the history of Joseph and the woman Potiphar, is peculiarly applicable to the question at issue, showing, as it does, the triumph of righteousness over lustful temptation. Shall I read ?"

As the lady made no reply, Mr. Swabb began to read the portion of Scripture to which he had alluded with great unction.

"How sad this is," Mr. Swabb observed, looking up after he had finished. "What dreadful depravity to contemplate is that of this woman, Potiphar. But on the other hand, how ready are we to judge and to condemn others before we have been similarly placed ourselves. The flesh is weak, my dear lady, and we are all unrighteous vessels of clay, wallowing in the filth and mire. How are we to tell that we, too, should not be weak if placed in the way of temptation. Let us place ourselves, now, in such a position as that of Potiphar's wife and Joseph."

"Yes—yes; but let me trim up the lamp, Mr. Swabb, it is going out."

"Oh, heed not the light, Miss Tabitha; what is the worldly light to us, except to show us our own darkness? Rather let us, in this pleasant obscurity, pursue our inquiries."

How the inquiries would have ended it is impossible to say, for just at this interesting part of Mr. Swabb's discourse, Charley, poking out his head to see and hear as much as he could, lost his balance, gave the curtains a great jerk, and brought them and the cornice, with a tremendous crash, upon the supper table, sending the plates and dishes flying to remote parts of the room.

Then, without waiting a moment to see what he had done, and how the reverend gentleman and his fair companion were disturbed by the intrusion, he rushed down stairs, the cat flying after him.

But just outside the door, upon the landing, he ran full butt into the stomach of some person standing there in the dark, and, bowling him over like a nine-pin on to the top of another person directly behind him, they all three fell in a heap down the first flight of stairs, and lay a confused mass of arms, and legs, and petticoats, upon the landing.

Then springing to his feet, Master Charles, without waiting to apologize, rushed wildly into the street, and ran up it, and down another, and up a third, as though all the policemen in London were in full chase after him, leaving the inmates of the house he had just quitted in a state of terror and bewilderment, which it is not very easy to describe.

And as I cannot be expected to follow the fortunes of all the various characters with which Charley Wag, in the course of his surprising adventures, will meet with, I must leave the discomforted household to come to themselves the best way they can.

Merely remarking by the way that if the maidservant and the footboy had a good deal of difficulty in accounting for their presence together in the dark on the landing, the lady and the reverend gentleman found it rather difficult to explain why they were alone in the dark inside the room, particularly as Mr. Swabb persisted in saying that he was reading the Scriptures.

———

XXXVI.—MUGGINS'S MUSIC HALL—THE BALLET GIRL—SOLDIERS' BELTS—ONE FOR HIS NOB.

EVERYBODY in Shadwell knows Muggins's Music Hall.

That is to say, all the first-class society of that polite neighbourhood.

Muggins's Grand New Musical Hall is situated up Cut-throat-court, at the back of Shambles-lane. The prices of admission are, if you go to the body of the hall, threepence; but if you want to be extra genteel, the reserved seats are sixpence. You can smoke in either, but in the reserved seats clay pipes are not put up with, so it will be necessary for you to provide yourself with an eighteenpenny Meerschaum, or a three-halfpenny Cuba. But, first of all, let us have a look at the bill. What is doing at Muggins's Music Hall?

Here we have—

First-class talent, and the best entertainment in London.

Every evening the celebrated PADDY BELLOWS, the unrivalled Hibernian Howler.

Miss BRASS, the extraordinary Comic Characteristic Vocalist.

Signora JULIA JENKINI, the world-famed (though never before heard of) Statuesque Pantomimist and Danseuse, from the principal continental theatres, and who has had the honour of appearing before the Emperor of Russia and the Emperor of China.

Besides a host of other talent.

No extra charge for admission during the Signora Jenkini's engagement.

Decidedly, the world-famed Julia Jenkini seems to be the attraction, and on the particular night, when I am going to take the gentle reader to Muggins's, she was in great force, and had created a perfect *furore* among the threepenny seats. The sixpennies, too, were not less enthusiastic, though perhaps less demonstrative. The threepennies banged their boots upon the floor, and bellowed "Brayvo, brayvo!" and "Hang kore!" The sixpennies clapped their hands together and made almost as much noise.

Every one was equally delighted.

"Signora Jenkini will appear again," said the chairman, hammering the table, and, sure enough, Signora Jenkini bounded on to the stage. A little brown-haired, black-eyed girl, with a tiny nose and a rather large mouth, full of pearl-like little teeth, a pretty figure, nicely rounded, and a pair of legs that were a perfect marvel of symmetry.

It is we men who are strongest in spindles in fact; there are very few women—even the thinnest—but have wonderful legs, and the generality of them hide them, worse luck—I thank my stars I was not born a footman, though, who knows, perhaps false calves are not so uncomfortable as one would suppose.

She bounded on to the stage, that pretty little dancing girl.

"She floated towards me in a wreathing crowd
Of peachy nymphs, and swam, a breathing cloud;
Less with a regulated kind of motion,
Than like a sea-bird sweeping the breast of ocean."

Well might she have recalled to mind those glowing verses on Carlotta Grisi. Indeed, if Mr. Muggins had not made it worth my while to speak well of his establishment, I should say, unhesitatingly, that she was a great deal too good for the place she danced in.

She was a "great hit," an "immense success," and filled the hall to overflowing every evening. Therefore, as you may suppose, she had lots of lovers. Sometimes, some one threw her a bouquet (I don't mean one of Muggins's, with paper flowers, but a real one, bought in Covent Garden for a shilling). At "penny gaffs," the audience often throw coppers upon the stage as a token of regard towards the popular performers; and here, sometimes, money had been thrown, wrapped up in paper—half-a-crown occasionally, and once half-a-sovereign.

A good many letters, too, came by the post, and a good many gentlemen, all desperately in love, and some "meaning honourable," waited at the door leading to the dressing-room to speak to her as she came out.

But she would have nothing to say to them. There were city clerks, dressed in the height of fashion, and private soldiers in full uniform. Even rifle volunteers she turned her little nose up at. Think of that!

This particular night, a couple of military men, full of love and drink, determined upon accosting her, and they took their station in the street, close to the door in question, where they knew she must come out.

It is a very fatiguing process waiting for any body, more particularly for an actress. (Take my advice, and never keep company with one, young man, or you will repent it, believe me.) And when at last she came out, the gallant sons of Mars were nearly dead beat.

She stepped out of the door hurriedly, and with her veil drawn down, and a roll of music in her hand, was making her way rapidly across the street, and out of the glare of gas, when Sergeant Stripes said to Corporal Wadding, "That's her, for sixpence!"

"No doubt of it," said Wadding. " Here goes."

And he swaggered up to her, and caught her by the arm.

"Hallow, my little Kisser," said the gallant gentleman. "Where are you scudding off to, so very fast?"

"I'm going home," replied the girl, jerking her shawl from between his fingers, and walking faster. "Please don't detain me."

"Detain you, by G—," cried Mr. Wadding, with his choicest barrack oath. "I shan't detain you longer than I want you. Don't you run like that, I want to speak to you."

And again he got hold of her arm, and twisted her round, with her face towards him.

"I am surprised at you!" the little dancer said, her face flushing crimson. "Please leave me alone, if you are a gentleman."

"Bravo!" cried Sergeant Stripes, maintaining his equilibrium with considerable difficulty. "Spoken like a man—that is to say, a woman." Here both gentlemen indulged in a loud coarse laugh.

The girl struggled with them to regain her liberty.

"How dare you," she cried, tears of shame and rage starting into her eyes. "How dare you insult me so, in the public street. I don't know either of you. You mistake me for one of your servant-girl sweethearts. I am not what you take me for."

"Aint you, though; we take you for Miss Julia Jenkini," said Corporal Wadding, "and my gentleman friend here's fell in love with you. I suppose there's no objection to that."

"Please to leave me alone. I don't want to have anything to say to you."

"Not before you kiss me and my gentleman friend here," said Corporal Wadding, catching her up in his arms. "Come on, give us a buss, old girl, and I am good for a quartern."

But Miss Julia appeared to be far from anxious to accept his generous offer; but clenching her little fist, drummed his big red nose for him, and played a very devil's tattoo with the heels of her diminutive kid boots on his manly leg, at the same time screaming with all her might.

"Help—help—help! You're a blackguard! Leave me alone! You shan't kiss me! Help—help—who will help me?"

Who do you suppose, reader?

Charley Wag!

Somebody must have told you! How did you guess it? Ah! to be sure, I forgot. You must have seen the picture.

Charley Wag, of course it was, who, running away from Miss Tabitha's house, had stopped to get his breath, in an archway facing Muggins's Music Hall, and had thus been a spectator to the cowardly assault I have described.

Without waiting to hear any more, but judging from what he had heard, that the soldiers were in the wrong—as, I am sorry to say, is, when ladies are concerned, not unfrequently the case—he ran forward, and knowing that if he was to do anything it must be done with a rush, he made a rush and did it.

He sprang straight at Corporal Wadding's face, with his fist doubled, and the force of the concussion, added to a certain unsteadiness, which was the result of the gin and water, the gallant son of Mars had imbibed in an early period of the evening, caused that gentleman to perform a species of wild gymnastic, similar to that which is gone through by a skater, when losing his balance, and concluded by coming down flat on his back in the middle of the pavement, where he lay howling and kicking like a great baby.

And before Sergeant Stripes could recover from the astonishment which this attack upon his friend had caused him, Charley made a similar attack upon him, and sent him sprawling in at the window of a coal and potatoe warehouse, where, in his struggling, he sent the best "Regents," at one penny per pound, flying in every direction, until one particularly large one catching the proprietor in the eye, that irate individual resented the insult by kicking Sergeant Stripes into the street.

Meanwhile Charley helped up the young lady he had so gallantly rescued, and stood upon the defensive.

But the soldiers quickly recovering from their surprise, pulled off their belts and rushed upon him.

And then there seemed but little chance for the poor boy, as the unmanly curs flung their straps over their shoulders, and with the buckles whizzing in the air, approached him on either side, and prepared to take a deadly aim at his head.

————

XXXVII.—CHARLEY WAG AND HIS WIFE, AND HIS CAT.

EVERYTHING depended upon his pluck and his activity; but he had got the young lady clinging to his arm, which rather impeded his movements.

However this was fortunate, upon one account. The soldiers, blackguards though they were, did not want to strike the woman, and so dodged round and round, waiting their opportunity.

Now, being both considerably the worse for liquor, and very unsteady, "on their pins," this dodging round was by no means easy; and one of them, in dodging, happening to dodge a little too near, Charley hit him "a one on the nose;" or, if you prefer it so, "smeller," which sent him down on his back in a moment.

Then, thinking caution the better part of valour, he whispered to his fair friend "Can you run?" and she, answering in the affirmative, they joined hands and ran as hard as their legs could carry them down the street.

They paused at about a hundred yards distance, and turned round to see if they were pursued, but no one was in sight.

The soldiers had either given up the chase, or mistaken the direction in which they had gone.

"Well," said Charley, when he had got his breath, "we're all right, ain't we?"

"I'm very much obliged to you, indeed," said the young lady. "You're very kind to do so much for a stranger."

"Lord bless you," said the boy, laughing, "that's nothing for me; I'm always running away with some girl or other."

"Are you?" said Miss Julia, "then you must be very fond of the ladies."

"I am," said Charley, with a wink, "the pretty ones, particularly."

"Go along with you," said Miss Julia.

"Along where?" asked Charley.

And then they laughed.

And then the young vagabond, nobody being by, put his arm round her waist and kissed the ballet girl under a lamp.

"Don't do that, for fear someone should see you," said she.

"Is that the only objection?" asked Charley.

"It's one of them."

"Then," said he, looking round and immediately kissing her again; "there's nobody to see us, and so it's removed."

Perhaps she thought that her objections only made him worse; or, perhaps, she liked it (there really is an instance on record of a lady who liked to be kissed, though, I believe, it is not generally known); anyhow she let him do it, and then laughed again, and then they walked on together.

"What's your name?" asked the young lady, presently.

"Charley Wag," replied that gentleman.

"Charley Wag! What a funny one."

"Don't you like it?"

"I like Charley very much. Charley's are always such nice fellows too; besides, you know, 'Charley is my darling.'"

"Which Charley's that. If I'm big enough, I'll punch his head."

"Nonsense; you know what I mean, it's a song."

"Oh well, if it's a song, I'll let them off."

"That's right. And pray where do you live, Mr. Charley Wag?"

Where do I live? Well, that's a pozer. I ought to live in Slogger's-alley, with my foster mother, but I have not been to see the poor dear for ever-so-many weeks."

"How is that, it's very wrong of you."

"Well, it's a long story, but I'll tell you all about it another time. At present, I am afraid that it is rather too late for me to go home; I shall go to-morrow morning the first thing."

"Where will you sleep to-night, then?"

"I am not particular, I shall walk about until day-light."

"Walk about, good gracious! that will make you very tired. However, if you want a walk, perhaps you will walk with me as far as my lodgings."

"With the greatest pleasure."

"And now I come to think of it, I don't see why I should not—that is to say, if you promise to be a good boy, why I should not allow you to sleep on the sofa."

"I promise willingly, if you have got a sofa."

"Well, we will see."

Thus chatting together, they walked along, until, in course of time, they reached a house, situated in a quiet back street, leading out of the Commercial-road, where Miss Julia Jenkini said she lived.

Here she paused, and taking a latch key from her pocket, put it in the lock, and turned it round.

But the door did not open.

"Something is in the key, perhaps," said Charley.

"No, nothing;" replied Julia, after probing it with a hair-pin.

"Give the door a good push, then."

She pushed it, he pushed it, they pushed it together.

"It's tight as wax," said Master Charles.

"Gracious goodness!" said the young lady, "the old woman must have put up the bolts."

"Well, let's ring her up."

"No; I don't think that will be any good."

"How do you mean; she will let us in? won't you?"

"I am afraid not."

"Why?"

"Because—because."

"Because what?"

"Because I owe for the rent."

"Ah!" said Charley, with a long breath. "That makes it quite another thing."

Here there was an awkward pause. Miss Julia leant against the railings, and Master Charles sat down upon the door-step.

"This is not a very lively way of spending the night," said he; "It is very well to begin with, but after a bit I expect it becomes monotonous."

"I should think it did," said Julia.

"Well, then," said Charley, "Let's ring the bell anyhow, and risk it."

They rang it accordingly.

After waiting a little while and getting no reply, they rang again, then again and again. At last a female head, in a night-cap of preposterous dimensions, was poked out of a top window, and a remarkably shrill voice asked "Who was there?"

"Me!" said Julia.

"It would have been more grammatical to have said "I," but then nobody ever does say "I" under such circumstances, and so she didn't.

"Oh, it's you, is it?" continued the party in the night-cap; "you are not coming in here, I can tell you, unless you pay me my money. Have you got it?"

"No, but I promise ——"

"I don't want none of your promises, I'm sick of them; and my money I'll have—I only ask for my rights."

"How much is it ?" asked Charley.

"Fifteen shillings," replied Julia.

"All right old lady " cried Mr. Wag "I'll be responsible for the amount. Come down and open the door."

"Who are you calling an old lady, you imperrunt young waggybond. Take yourself off, and that baggage along with you."

And down went the window.

"Shall I ring again ?" said Charley.

"If you please," replied Julia.

So Charley rang till he broke the wire, and knocked a baker's dozen of postman's knocks ; but getting no answer, they thought they had better give it up.

"Whatever shall we do ?" exclaimed Julia ; " we are two wanderers upon the face of the earth. Two, did I say ! no, look there, there is another wanderer, who has been locked out like us."

Charley turned round, and could scarcely believe his eyes, when he saw standing before them, the identical black tom cat which he had met upon Mr. Measle's roof.

"I'll be hanged if he must not have followed me," said Charley.

"Does it belong to you ?"

"Well, I hardly know. It seems as though it wanted to belong to me, for it has followed me a couple of miles at least."

"Well, we'll all three keep together. Don't you think so ?"

"Certainly. Where shall we go to ?"

"Have you any money ?"

"No, not a halfpenny."

"I have a couple of shillings. I think that will get a bed somewhere."

"All right. Then you shall have it, and I and Tommy will stop out in the streets till morning,"

"Gracious me, you can't do that ! you must have a bed, too."

"But if it will only pay for one ?"

"Well, what then ?" said the ballet girl.

She must have been a dreadful slut, and he was a promising young chick. Don't you think so ?

"I tell you what it is," said Charley, with great energy, " you are the jolliest girl I ever clapt my eyes on ; dash my buttons if you're not ! I wish to goodness we were married."

"Well, what's to prevent us ? Shall we put up the banns ?"

"I vote we do directly. But—I say—"

"What's the matter ?"

"What are we to live on ? I haven't got any money."

"Well, I earn a pound a week ; that ought to be enough for us."

"It's enough for one, perhaps."

"Very well. Everybody knows, in housekeeping, that what's enough for one is enough for two."

"But then it seems as though you couldn't live on it when you were by yourself, or else you would not have owed for your rent."

"That was because I was extravagant ; but in future I shan't be. Besides, I have had a rise in my salary ; and until last week I only had ten shillings."

"Well, certainly that makes all the difference. But, then—I say—"

"What do you say now ?"

"Aint we too young to get married ?"

"I don't think so. I'm fifteen."

"And I'm sixteen," said Charley, telling a " cracker," to give himself more importance.

"Well, then, you're quite old enough to be a widower," said Miss Julia.

And from this moment commences the wonderful adventures of Charley Wag, his wife, and his cat.

———

XXXVIII.—Shows what befel the Duchess in the Wilds of Westminster.

SIMPLE country folks, who take their notions of London from novels and romances, written a quarter of a century ago, imagine that to those, perhaps, personally unacquainted with the capital, their knowledge, in theory, of the great metropolis and its goings on is by no means contemptible.

Even cockneys born and bred are quite as ignorant of the dark phases of London life. They talk vaguely of the " rookery" in Saint Giles's ; and if you mention Field-lane, say, " To be sure, that's where the thieves live." Then there are others (cunning ones, those who are "up to a thing or two"), who, knowing, that the worst part of Saint Giles's has vanished, and that " Alsatia " is nowhere, laugh at the other people's ignorance, and tell you, confidently that " all that sort of thing is done away with my good fellow. That sort of game couldn't go on now, with our police."

Heigho ! what a number of ugly neighbourhoods I could tell you of, gentle reader. What a number of vile iniquitous dens, in which the police dare not show their faces—of the bare existence of which they are lamentably ignorant.

Come with me to Westminster.

Come into the loathsome, leprous district surrounding Victoria-street. It matters little which turning we take to arrive at it from the great thoroughfare. Come to Grub-street, York-buildings, Pye-street, or Snow's-rents, if you would see some choice examples of social degradation.

Come at noon-day, for after night-fall it is not over safe for any one bearing the outward semblance of respectability to thread the intricacies of this maze of rotten corruption.

In these fearful slums—composed of miserable, tumble-down, tottering tenements, in the last stage of decay—in the middle of the road or pavement there is generally a long puddle, choked up and overflowing, in consequence of the accumulation of oyster-shells, rotten cabbage-stalks, and broken crockery ; and in this, dirty, ragged children are dabbling about, with the glee of infantine ducklings just taking to the water. While, lolling out of the first floor windows, half-naked, greasy, tangled-haired women ogle the passers-by, and exchange choice chaff with their opposite neighbours.

Very often you may find a barrel-organ, or a blind fiddler, acting as orchestra, and a lot of drunken wretches, male and female, gambolling in a boorish sort of fashion, upon the pavement, in time to the music.

A MEETING OF OLD FRIENDS UNDER UNPLEASANT CIRCUMSTANCES.

There is very little mock modesty about the neighbourhood.

The greater part of the men are theives, and the greater part of the women are prostitutes, and they are neither of them at all ashamed to own it. Lads of thirteen with mistresses of twelve years old, are no rarity, and debauchery, in its lowest and most degrading phases, is a recognised feature of life in Westminster Wilds.

From the slight sketch I have drawn of this uninviting neighbourhood, the reader can judge how very hazardous an expedition the Duchess of Heatherland had undertaken when she determined upon visiting Slogger's-alley at one in the morning.

Surely some powerful motive must have existed to have prompted her to take such a step.

What could it be?

She was afraid of the treachery of her hired servants, and wished to ascertain, herself, what had become of the boy. What could have prompted her to pursue him in this way? What was the secret of her powerful and all-absorbing hate.

Time will show. As yet you must but read patiently, and wait until the time shall come.

As one tolled from the London churches the Duchess, accompanied by Lady Alice de Courtenay, both closely veiled, and attired in as plain and homely a fashion as their costly wardrobe would admit of, took a cab in Piccadilly, and bade the driver convey them to Tothill-fields.

The Duchess, however, upon reflection,

No. 16.

[CHARLEY WAG, THE NEW JACK SHEPPARD.

thought that it would be wisest to descend near Westminster Abbey, and proceed upon foot, which they therefore did.

" What is the name of the place we are going to, Maud ?" asked her companion. " Do you think that you will be able to find it."

" I have never been here before, but I have no doubt that I shall."

" Why not ask a policeman ?"

" I do not think that we had better ; or he will perhaps watch us."

" What, is it so bad a place, that the fact of a respectably dressed person going to it would create suspicion in a policeman's mind ?"

" My dear Alice, do not be shocked. Our dresses are handsome, though plain. Hearing us ask for such a disreputable place, he might— he might take us for—"

" For what—thieves ?"

" No ; for those unfortunate girls who walk the streets."

" Maud!—Let us go back. Oh! why was I so imprudent as to join this expedition ? What shame and degradation we may have to submit to, who can say ?"

" If you like to desert me, Alice," said the Duchess, angrily, " you can go back at once."

" You know I would not do that," cried her companion, reproachfully. " If there is any danger we will share it together."

" It is agreed, then let us go forward."

And they silently pursued their walk.

" You did not tell me the name of the place," Alice presently remarked.

" It is called Slogger's-alley."

" Slogger's!—what a dreadful word! What is a Slogger ? Is it a man's name ?"

" It is a slang word, which means to thrash a person severely, and to beat them in the face ; they also call it *mugging !*"

" Gracious me!" said Lady Alice, who could not refrain from laughing. " Wherever did you learn the words ?"

" Leech, the lawyer, told me, I believe. Or I must have learnt them some other time. You know I was always famous for my collection of unlady-like knowledge."

" You were the cleverest and the most beautiful of all the young ladies at our school, in the same way that you are the cleverest and most beautiful of all the proud and rich and lovely frequenters of your own drawing-rooms."

" Well! well! Alice! Don't compliment me any more, if you please, or you will make me dreadfully vain. This is the street we should turn down."

" Why, I thought you had never been here before!"

" No more I have, in person ; but I have got a map of London, and have been here in imagination several times."

Following the instructions which she had thus received, the Duchess soon found herself in front of the villanous tavern, known as the " Skeleton Key," and after some little difficulty, arising from the badness of the light and faintness of the characters, at length made out the words " Slogger's-alley," over an exceedingly repulsive looking court.

Having succeeded thus far they began to look for No. 6.

But this was a more difficult matter than you would have supposed, owing to a certain amount of pleasing eccentricity on the part of the person who had numbered the houses.

To begin with, there was no No. 1, but the alley began with No. 2½, though what on earth had become of the house and a fragment, was more than the oldest Slogger could tell. After this came No. 4, then 5, and then 8.

However, having at length, and quite by accident, discovered No. 6, which came between No. 3 and No. 12 ; the Duchess knocked.

But when she had done so, it, for the first time, occurred to her, that it was a very extraordinary time to make a call. However, she must find some excuse. Her anxiety to know whether the boy had returned overcame all her scruples.

Fortunately there was a light burning in the house, as, indeed, there was in several others, and, in some cases, the sounds of brutal merriment was audible.

She knocked again.

An old woman opened the door, yawning.

" Who do you please to want ?" she asked.

" Miss Williams."

" Oh! then you are the ladies that promised to come."

" Promised to come !"

" This morning you said you would, I think, when I was out. My girl is so stupid, she never takes a proper message."

Rightly thinking that the mistake would secure her an interview without further questioning, the Duchess said something in assent, and the old woman let them in and closed the door.

" Come up stairs to the bed-room," said the latter.

" Is she in bed ?" asked the Duchess.

" Bless you, yes, ma'am ; didn't you know ? She's much too ill to sit up. The Lord only can tell whether she will ever get over it. Oh! that young vagabond! What hasn't he got to answer for ?"

The old lady speaking was the Mrs. Crocker, of whom mention has been made upon several occasions, and whose fat niece Master Charles had paid his addresses to and kissed, greatly to the aunt's annoyance.

Preceding the ladies upstairs, Mrs. Crocker presently introduced them to Miss Williams' sick chamber.

Upon a mean looking bed, the covering to which, as well as the furniture in the room, was, though scrupulously clean, extremely scanty and poor-looking, lay the woman of whom they were in search.

Poor thing! she had suffered severely during the last few days.

Always in very indifferent health, the news of Charley's death, which, the reader may remember, a certain ragged forlorn creature of the name of Clam had conveyed to her so unguardedly that night that our hero was locked-up in the station-house, had given her sensitive nature a violent shock.

Recovering from this, under old Mr. Toddleboy's ministering care, she had learnt the circumstances of her adopted child's imprisonment, and her terror and anxiety upon his account so preyed upon her shattered nerves that a violent illness ensued.

Mr. Toddleboy sent for the doctor. The doctor came and pronounced the illness to be brain fever.

So for three days and three nights the poor woman lay at the point of death, tossing to and fro her weary head, and crying out in her uneasy broken slumbers for the child that she had lost.

To think that after all her care of him he should have become a thief—most certainly he was one, what else could she think? If he had been innocent would he not have returned to her after he was liberated from custody? Mr. Toddleboy had been to the police court to make enquiries about him, having been unable to get there in time to hear Charley's case come on, and when he arrived heard that the boy had gone away more than an hour.

As he had called on his way from Messrs. Bottle and Bung's, his employers, at Miss Williams's house, he knew that the boy could not have returned home; and it being almost an impossibility that they had passed each other upon the road, he therefore inquired of a policeman standing near whether he could inform him what had become of the boy.

Now it happened that the officer he chanced thus to fix upon, as a likely person to afford him the information he required, was none other than the particular policeman upon whom Charley had played off that heartless trick about the play-bill boards.

"Who do you want," he asked, sharply.

"A boy who was had up just now before his worship, upon a charge of theft."

"What name did you say?"

"Charley Wag."

"Oh! Charley Wag, was it. A bright specimen of a boy he is."

"Do you know whether he has left the court?"

"Yes; he's left."

"Did he leave by himself, do you know?"

"No; he was in company."

"With whom; did you observe?"

Now the policeman had not observed anything about it, but here was a chance of doing Charley a bad turn, and you don't suppose that he was going to miss it. Besides, who ever heard of a policeman expressing his ignorance, when asked if he knows anything of a prisoner.

"Do you know this man," says the magistrate.

"Known him for years, your worship—awful bad character."

"Ah!" says his worship, impressed. "That's sufficient. Three month's—Next case." And away goes Jack Rag to prison, loudly asserting his innocence, and swearing that this was his first "misfortune."

"Yes," said the policeman, in answer to Mr. Toddleboy's inquiry. "I observed 'em; and a bad lot they was."

"What, thieves?" asked the old man, in great alarm.

"Ah! prigs, every one of them."

"Oh Lord! oh Lord!" cried poor old Toddleboy, in great anguish. "What ever will Miss Williams say? What can I tell her?"

"You'd better tell her," said the policeman, brutally; "that if she don't get the young vermin caged up in a reformatory before he is six months older, he'll live to have his young neck stretched."

With these woeful tidings, Mr. Toddleboy toddled back to his friend, and broke the news as gently as he could.

But still, not so gently but that it came upon the tender loving-mother like a thunderbolt, and struck her senseless to the earth.

Thus was it that the Duchess found her lying ill in bed—lying at death's door.

She was wasted and wan. Her hand, which was nothing but skin and bone, lay motionless upon the coverlid, while her breath was so weak that it scarcely stirred the bed-clothes.

"Is she dead?" the Duchess asked, starting back, as her eyes fell upon the quiet figure.

"No, ma'am, not quite," replied Mrs. Crocker, next door to it, I'm afraid—next door to it."

Here the sick-woman opened her eyes.

"Who is this," she asked. "Are you the lady who called with the clergyman? It is very kind of you to come."

"No;" replied the Duchess, "but we wish to speak to you, if you are not too ill, upon a subject of great interest to both us."

Miss Williams made no reply, and her Grace continued—

"You have had a boy under your charge for some years back, I believe, whom you call Charley Wag."

Miss Williams still remained silent, but her fingers twitched uneasily and her hollow eyes were fixed earnestly upon the speaker.

"He was lately charged with theft at the Quod-street police-office, and since then has disappeared. He is here?"

"Here!" cried the woman, starting up into a sitting posture, and eagerly stretching forth her thin, wasted arms; "here, do you say? Oh, where, where is he? Why does he keep back? Oh, bless you, dear lady, for bringing him. Where is he? Charley—Charley!"

She glanced round, hoping to see him spring forward and fall into her arms; but when she had waited for a moment in a state of intense expectation, she sank back exhausted upon her pillow with a low sigh, and closed her eyes.

Here Mrs. Crocker interposed.

"She's very weak, ma'am, as you see," said the old lady, "very weak, and wandering, too. You've given her a shock like, mentioning his name; the young rascal, he's the cause of all of it."

"But is he not here?" asked the Duchess, turning her cold eyes upon the woman; "I thought he was."

"Oh, bless you no, ma'am. I only wish he was."

The Duchess eyed her suspiciously for a few moments without speaking.

"I am a friend," she said, slowly, "I am the lady he saved from the water. If he is here he has nothing to fear from me."

"I am sure of that, ma'am," said the old lady, warmly, "I only wish he was here, or that we knew what had become of him, for it is that which has made the poor creature there so ill. It is the anxiety as regards his fate which keeps her down, and destroys all hope of her recovery."

The Duchess looked at Mrs. Crocker again, even more earnestly than before, but she noticed not the slightest appearance of hesitation or reserve in the old woman's manner. No, she must be speaking the truth. The boy had not returned home.

"In that case," said the Duchess, at last, "my journey has been in a great measure useless. Would you be good enough to apply this money," she added, taking from her purse five sovereigns, "in the purchase of any little necessaries which the poor woman may require. I will not longer trespass upon your time."

She was moving towards the door as she spoke, when the sick woman, suddenly starting from a state of heavy torpor into which she had fallen directly after her last outbreak, began to toss her arms wildly to and fro, and to cry out in her delirium some unconnected sentences relating to the subject engrossing all her thoughts.

"My child, my child, my child! my poor lost child! What has become of you? Why do you not return? He is innocent, my lord; I call Heaven to witness that he is innocent. Oh, good gentlemen, have mercy upon him! He is a poor orphan, bred up in the streets; the vile unnatural wretch who deserted him, is answerable for his crime."

"Come," the Duchess whispered, hoarsely. "Let us go."

But before they could move from the room, the sick-woman had started up in bed, and stretching out her finger at them, shrieked at the top of her voice—

"You are cursed! You are cursed! There is no rest for you on earth. No hope for you hereafter. Your soul is black with guilt. Your hands are red with blood. Your murdered childs' soul cries aloud for vengeance. Yes, you may shake and hide your head; you are doomed—doomed—doomed! The torments of the wicked await you!"

The Duchess, at the commencement of this extraordinary address, staggered back against the door, the handle of which she held in her hand.

Then, as the sick-woman still pursued her ravings, she reflected that the fact of her thus being chosen as the object to which the awful warnings were addressed, was purely accidental. She, in a great measure, recovered her composure, though her face remained of an ashy-whiteness.

But Lady Alice, who was of a weaker and more sensitive nature, was, beyond measure, alarmed and horrified by Miss Williams's wanderings, and hid herself in terror behind her companion, clutching the Duchess's dress to save herself from falling.

As the sick-woman's temporary frenzy subsided, the Duchess opened the door and passed out, Mrs. Crocker following with a light.

"I trust, ma'am, you are not frightened at what the poor thing said. I thank you, on her account and my own, for your great kindness and liberality."

"No, no!" replied the Duchess, whose face was yet as pale as death. "I am not frightened, thank you—only a little startled."

"Certainly, ma'am, quite natural; and the other lady?"

"No—no!" replied Lady Alice, faintly.

"Thank you both again, for your goodness, and good-night."

They had reached the door by this time. Mrs. Crocker held her light on high to help them as much as possible in the obscurity of the court; and, thanking her, the two ladies hurried away as fast as they could go.

It was for some time before they spoke, and then Lady Alice, breaking the silence, exclaimed, as she squeezed her companion's arm—

"Oh, Maud! how dreadful it was! How I felt for you!"

"Felt for me?" the other replied, angrily, turning towards her. "What construction do you put upon the wanderings of that wretched idiot?"

"My dear Maud, how hastily you speak. What do you mean?"

"What do you mean?"

"I meant that I was afraid the wanderings of this poor woman, though horribly unjust, might cause you pain, and I regretted that we had come."

"To be sure. Yes," the other replied; "you are very kind, Alice. To be sure they did cause me pain; but as they were all unjust—"

"Unjust, of course, my darling. You know that I know them to be unjust as well as you do."

The Duchess said no more, but gently pressed her friend's hand in answer to her assurance of good faith, and proceeded onwards in silence.

Indeed, so occupied were they both with their own thoughts, that they did not for some time notice in what direction they were going.

Alice was the first to notice it.

"Is this the way we came?" she asked.

The Duchess stopped and looked round.

"No," she said. "No; we must have taken a wrong turning. We will go back."

They retraced their steps as well as they could, but had not gone very far, before the Duchess stopped again, and said—

"We are altogether wrong. Do you remember the streets?"

"No, I am sure I do not."

"Nor I. What shall we do?"

"Let us ask."

"Stop, we will try again for a little while."

They did so, but with no better success.

"We must ask, then, said the Duchess, for we are lost."

Just then a shower of rain, which had been for some time gathering, came on with sudden violence, and they looked round eagerly for a place of shelter.

———

XXXIX.—A QUEER NEIGHBOURHOOD — A MYSTERIOUS HOUSE—THE WOLF IN SHEEP'S CLOTHING—THE DEN OF INFAMY.

THEY were in a truly horrible neighbourhood, and they cast their eyes to the right and to the left, with feelings of surprise and disgust that human beings could possibly exist, in the greatest city of the world, in the very heart of civilisation, who were obliged to dwell in such unwholesome and repulsive dens.

Never before had Lady Alice imagined that there were such places. She had read of them in books, but had always believed the description to be grossly exaggerated, for the sake of effect; now she saw them before her, and it made her heart sad to think of the poor unhappy creatures that a hard necessity compelled to seek a shelter among such wretchedness as that which surrounded her.

Ah! well would it be did more of the aristocracy, who pass their days in sinful idleness, visit the humble dwellings of the poor. There are many lessons which the purse-proud and pampered patrician might learn and benefit by, to be found in the humble home of the honest and hard-working artisan. Still more impressive the lesson which is to be found in those hideous pest houses, in stifling alleys, and suffocating courts, where misery, and sickness, and want, and hunger lie hidden, huddled out of sight. My lord's carriage passes the corner, at the top of the lane leading to the abode of wretchedness; my lord, lolling upon the luxurious carriage cushions, perchance may deign to cast his noble eyes into the filthy reeking alley, and wonder why on earth so mean and dirty a place was ever built, and, being built, why it was not immediately afterwards taken down to give more air to the genteeler houses surrounding it.

It would be a good thing, my lord thinks, if the place caught fire and was burnt to ashes. It would clear out another nest of dirty wretches. So it would; but, heigho! where are the wretches to go to when the nest is burnt. There will ever be two worlds in this great city of ours—the well-fed and the hungry. Between them is a tall wall. There is an old saying, which tells us that one half of the world does not know how the other half lives. It is not generally admitted, perhaps, but, believe me it is true, of the half who do not know, there is much more than a quarter WHO DO NOT CARE.

But it is not to be wondered at if these two ladies, nursed in the lap of luxury, and totally unused to buffet with the rude world, or to have to rely upon themselves in such an emergency as the present, should feel alarmed at finding themselves at such an hour in such a place.

Every moment the fury of the storm increased. The rain poured down upon them like so many waterspouts.

If they did not quickly find some shelter they would be drenched to the skin.

Where could they go?

Upon the opposite side of the way, a little distance from them, was an old fashioned door with a deep door-way, from which came forth a faint red light. Towards it they ran, seeing that it was the only place within their reach which could afford them any cover from the storm.

Half the door was glass, and before it hung a red curtain. Behind the curtain, a faint light was burning, a circumstance which struck them as being rather curious at such an hour.

It was a much larger house, too, than any of those surrounding it, and had all the appearance of having been at some time or other the dwelling of some noble or wealthy person.

As the rain seemed but to increase instead of abate, the ladies crept nearer and nearer to the door, endeavouring to escape from the wet which penetrated even to where they were standing.

"I do not think it will clear up for a long while," said the Lady Alice, mournfully. "I hope our absence will not be noticed."

"None of the servants get up until five o'clock, and it is now three," replied the Duchess. If we have even to wait another hour after that, if we get a cab we shall be in time."

"I hope so."

"There is no fear."

"But should the rain not hold up."

Their conversation was interrupted at this moment by a loud noise within the house, of shrill female voices. A mixture of shrieks and laughter, as though a game at romps were going on inside.

"What is that?" whispered Lady Alice, seizing her friend's arm, and trembling like a leaf. "Let us go away. I am so afraid."

"Nonsense," said the other, "what is there to be afraid of. It was only the sound of women laughing. Perhaps there is some sort of a party going on."

"Yes, and the men may be tipsy. We shall be insulted. Let us go."

Perhaps they might have acted upon this suggestion, but at the time that the Duchess was hesitating whether or not they should stay any longer in the shelter of the door-way, and as she turned her eyes from the red curtain to the street, she saw an old woman standing before her under an umbrella, who had approached them without their having heard her.

"Well, my dears," said the old woman, who had a very ugly look in her eyes, and a very strong suspicion of gin in her voice and her breath. "What makes you out so late to-night?"

The Duchess looked at her companion, and back again at the old woman.

She was such a very suspicious old woman, and was looking at them so very hard that the Duchess, knowing that her face, a remarkable as well as a very beautiful one, must, as it belonged to one of the most distinguished ornaments of fashionable society, be known to many hundreds of people in London, whom she herself did not know in the least, began to fear that the speaker had recognised her.

At the same time she hoped to mislead her.

"We are from the country, if you please," said the Duchess, "and have lost our way."

"Oh, indeed!" cried the old woman, her eyes brightening a little. "From the country, eh! and when did you come up, my dears?"

"We came by the mail train from Dover, last night, and were directed this way to Charing-cross. Would you tell us how we ought to go?"

"Certainly, my dears, with the greatest of pleasure. But it is so wet. You can't go while it pours like this."

"Oh! that won't hurt us; we had better go," said Alice.

"If you like to step inside my house a moment?—This is my house, where you are standing—I will lend you an umbrella. I can see you are two honest girls, or I shouldn't do it. Indeed, in London, my dears, one oughtn't to trust any one."

The two ladies were both rather doubtful whether it was a wise proceeding on their part to trust this ugly old woman.

Lady Alice, squeezing her friend's hand, seemed to urge her to decline the offer, and the Duchess debated in her own mind how she could refuse what appeared to be a piece of very great kindness.

But then, after all, the old lady would not eat them.

The Duchess was a most courageous woman, as I have already shown you upon other occasions.

"Well my dears, I'm waiting for you."

Yes she would go in and risk it.

"What sort of a house is this" asked Alice, still hesitating, "is it a public house."

"A public house, bless you? no."

"We heard a great many people laughing and screaming just now."

"You might have done that. It's one of my work-girl's birthday, poor thing, and I have given her a little party. One mustn't be too hard on young folks, must one?"

"Have you got work-girls, then."

"Yes, we're mantle makers, my dear. A capital trade; I'll take you, too, if you like."

While speaking the old lady had pushed open the street door, which seemed to be only closed and not clasped; and they all three entered the house together.

A bell rang as the door opened, and another old woman, but this one very meanly attired, and evidently a servant, came hastily out of a room close by to see who it was.

"All right, Hannah," said the old woman.

"It's you, Mrs. Crow, is it?"

"Yes. Here are two young ladies from the country, who have been caught in the rain. Have you got a good fire in the sitting-room."

"A capital fire, mum?"

"Come, then, young ladies?"

The ladies were inclined to hesitate, but Mrs. Crow shut the door behind them, and pushed them gently towards the room, the door of which the other woman held open for them.

The room which they entered, was comfortably, even handsomely furnished, but the subjects of the pictures hanging round the walls, were of a character which the ladies could scarcely think would be found in a respectable house.

There was one thing which rather spoilt the appearance of the room, and this was an ugly screen, covered with picture scraps, which stood on one side of the fire place; and if one might judge by an end of the blanket sticking out beyond, it was evidently intended to hide a bed, from whence the sound of hard breathing occasionally reached them.

Another thing, which, at the same time that it did not improve the appearance of the room, struck one as scarcely in accordance with the manners of the first society, was the fact of the servant sitting in the same room with the mistress, and evidently on terms of great familiarity,

for she had a low seat for her particular accommodation, on the opposite side of the fire to the screen; and she had, besides, a glass of gin-and-water for her own particular and private refection, which she placed upon the hob to keep warm, and dipped her old nose into it every now and then when she felt inclined.

Mrs. Crow, noticing the direction of Lady Alice's eyes, and the blush which involuntarily rose to her fair cheeks, said—

"It's my son will hang them up. He says they're very valuable. I can't abide sich impudence myself.

Meanwhile, the servant had stirred the fire, and placed seats before it for the ladies. But the Duchess politely declined to sit down.

"I thank you very much," said she, "but I am sure our friends will be anxious about us."

"Nonsense," cried Mrs. Crow, "I can't think of your going out in this dreadful shower."

"But indeed we must."

"Not until you have warmed yourselves, anyhow; and, here Hannah, bring some wine."

In spite of their repeated refusals and protests, that they must leave directly, and that they could not possibly stop any longer, the wine was brought, and Mrs. Crow made them some hot negus.

"Drink a little, my dears," said she, "it will do you good."

They thought it best to do as she wished, without making any further objections.

When they had done so, the Duchess rose as though she thought it time that they should depart.

"Don't hurry so, my dear," remonstrated Mrs. Crow, leaning back very comfortably in her chair, and biting her tea-spoon. "Half-an-hour one way or the other can't make much difference. And so you're from Dover, are you?"

"Yes, madam—only I assure you—"

"There, don't bother any more about it. You shall go directly. I want to talk to you. Have you many friends in London?"

"No, very few."

"Any relations?"

"None."

"It is very strange that they should not have been at the station to meet you. London is a dangerous place for young country girls to be wandering about in by themselves."

"But sure no one would molest, or rob us."

"I don't know that. I suppose you don't carry much money about with you?"

"No, indeed, we do not," cried the Duchess eagerly. "We were warned not to do so."

"That's lucky," said the old woman. "But really there are so many bad people in London, and a poor girl might suffer other losses besides her purse. Indeed, it is most lucky that you happened to meet with me."

Though they were far from sure of this fact, the ladies deemed it expedient to acquiesce with what the old woman remarked.

"And pray," continued Mrs. Crow, "what may you be going to do in London, now you have come here?"

"Indeed, we have hardly decided."

"You had much better stop with me, then, I should think."

"But we do not know how to make mantles."

"Oh, we do other things besides making mantles—"

She would probably have explained the nature of the other business, had not a ring at the bell just then interrupted the conversation, and the servant, who had run out to see who it was, presently returned, and whispered in her ear.

"Lord bless me, is it?" cried Mrs. Crow, with every sign of the greatest excitement. "Show him up stairs, and I'll be there in a moment. How extraordinary lucky things should have happened as they have. There, bustle out, and don't go to sleep, Hannah."

Hastily telling her visitors to make themselves at home until she returned, Mrs. Crow hurried away to see the new comer, whoever he might be; and the servant, returning almost immediately, sat down on the low seat by the side of the fire where she had previously been sitting, and began to doze and nod, and fall forward into the fire, and catch herself at the very nick of time, then go through the same performance over and over again.

But when Mrs. Crow was gone, and the echo of her footsteps along the passage and up the stairs had died away, the Duchess whispered to her friend that they had better now make an attempt to leave the house.

"Yes, yes," said Alice, earnestly, but in the same low tone. "For heaven's sake, let us go from this horrible place. I am frightened to death."

"Come, then, said the Duchess," rising as noiselessly as possible, and creeping towards the door.

But just as they reached it the skirts of one of their dresses caught against a chair and knocked it over.

The noise wakened the servant.

"Hallo! hallo!" said she, "Where are you off to?"

"We are going home."

"Are you though? Oh, dear, no. Not at all. That's quite a mistake of yours."

"What do you mean, woman?" asked the Duchess, haughtily. "Who dare detain us?"

"Well, as to that," said the servant, with a laugh, "I shall, till misses comes, and then she will. Come, sit down, the pair of you, and don't make fools of yourselves."

Although they were yet perfectly at a loss to know why they should be detained, and what was ultimately to be their fate, the ladies thought it best to make an effort at escape while there was time.

The Duchess seized the handle of the door.

The servant sprang forward and threw herself against it.

The three women struggled together for the mastery.

Lady Alice was almost worse than useless, for she had no strength, and she managed only to get in the way and prevent her friend from pulling open the door, when, perhaps, she could have overcome the efforts of the servant to force their passage out; for the patrician lady, although she had been reared in luxury and pampered from her cradle upwards, possessed an amount of strength and bravery which rarely falls to the share of a woman in the upper circles.

Grasping the woman who opposed her by the wrist, the Duchess twisted her arm round, and caused her, by the intense pain, to relinquish her hold and cry for quarter.

But just at that moment, when they might have hoped to effect their escape, had they only the servant to deal with, a sudden noise behind the screen apprised them of the fact of the person, whoever it was, who had been sleeping there having awoke.

"What's the row?" a gruff voice asked, and an uncombed head, with a remarkably repulsive set of features, was thrust forth at one end, "What's all this shindy about?"

"Lend a hand," cried the servant, "and stop these cats from getting out. They've just been caged, and are worth the keeping."

"Detain us at your peril, you wretches," said the Duchess in a fury. "Rest assured that your presumption shall be punished. You do not know who we are!"

"No, nor I don't much care, neither," said the owner of the repulsive features, making his appearance on the other side of the scene.

And, advancing towards them, he drew a pistol from his breast and presented it at the Duchess's head, while Lady Alice, almost fainting with terror, cowered behind her.

"Try to move a step," he said, "and I'll let some of this into you."

He had got thus far and seemed to have every intention of carrying his murderous threat into immediate execution, when his eyes, meeting those of the lady's to whom he spoke, at the same time that the light which the servant had caught up fell full upon her face, his own physiognomy underwent the most extraordinary change.

He dropped the barrel of the pistol and opened his mouth wide enough to swallow a moderately sized turnip.

"Why, who the devil expected to see you," said he, after a pause of several minutes.

The astonishment of the Duchess at the meeting was scarcely less than that of the man; for when she recognised his face and his voice, as he lowered the pistol, her countenance, for the first time, turned deadly pale, and she leant against the door, as though for support.

"Great God!" she murmured to herself, "AM I AGAIN IN HIS POWER?"

XL.—THE REMARKABLE ADVENTURES OF AN OLD GENTLEMAN IN HIS SHIRT TAILS.

IF I had my own way, I should now go back to that boy, Charley but I must not.

I have so many other characters, whose fortunes I must follow, and I have so many extraordinary events yet to relate, that if I do not begin now, gradually to work up to them, but go on with the adventures of our young friend, I shall have got to the end of his life, and had him comfortably hanged, or made a lord mayor of him,* before I have hardly introduced the rest of my company.

* You don't imagine I am going to tell you which it is to be, do you? Much as I love you, reader, I can't possibly oblige you in that particular just at present.

No, have a little patience, and you shall have half-a-dozen more chapters of Charley, one after another.

I left Toddleboy getting out of his coffin, Jack Rattan lying in a swoon, and the dead body of Cudder lying between them.

Now, Toddleboy, being as I have already told you, very drunk, was not, perhaps, so terrified by his awful position, as he otherwise would have been, if sober.

He was, however, in sufficient dread of being replaced in the coffin with his dead companion, to make him anxious to effect his escape as soon as he conveniently could.

Liberty was upon the other side of the door, and he was on this side.

What was the first impediment?

The senseless body of Jack Rattan.

He, therefore, devoted all his energies to tugging it on one side, as he found, upon trying the door, that it opened inwards.

When, at last, he had got the body sufficiently far away, to enable him to pull the door open a quarter of a yard, he squeezed himself through, pulled the door after him, and ran up the steps into the open air.

The first thing that struck him when he found himself there was that it was very cold.

You may not have had much opportunity of trying it, but I assure you, a winding sheet is any-thing but comfortable in cold weather. Our friend Toddleboy, however, had less protection, he had only got his shirt on. It was a very old one, and very ragged, or he probably would not have had that, for now the workhouse of Saint Starver CumBag o'Bones usually sent the un-claimed paupers naked to the hospital.

He was therefore in his shirt tails, and mighty cold he found it.

The second thing that struck him was the peculiar appearance of the place where he found himself. He was in a sort of unfinished garden at the back of a row of unfinished houses.

In the wall, at the back of the garden, he saw a door, which was open a few inches.

This led out to a patch of barren oyster-shell-strewed ground, which had originally been in-tended for building purposes, could any builder be found sufficiently speculative to build upon it.

"The sooner I am half a mile from this place the better. How horribly lonely the spot looks!"

Thus the old gentleman meditated.

"The only drawback is," said he, "that the night is rather fresh, and a shirt alone is not the warmest thing to walk about in; besides, it isn't proper."

What could he find then?

People do not usually leave their clothes about out of doors in London.

But in unfinished buildings—that is to say, in houses during their construction—there are fre-quently to be found some old rags and patches, and, now and then, stray pieces of sacking.

Upon one of these morsels of sackcloth Mr. Toddleboy was lucky enough to tumble.

He wrapped it round him, and then, without delaying any longer in such a dangerous locality, he opened the door to which I had alluded, crossed the plot of ground with a nice apprecia-tion of the oyster-shells under his feet, and found himself in the Bow-road.

"It's an uncommon fresh night," said Mr. Toddleboy, his teeth chattering with cold; "but perhaps it's as well, all things being considered, for I sha'n't meet so many people."

And he trudged on in his airy costume.

But not very far.

The cold was intense. If he had been sober, he could not have borne it half as long as he did; but the liquor inside him made up for the want of clothing outside him, and the fumes of the narcotics in his head, made him reckless of the cold wind at his tail. So, you see, my tee-totaller friends, there is something in intoxica-tion after all, whatever the pumps may say to the contrary.

However poor Toddleboy could not stand it very long. He sat down in a doorway and nursed his knees and considered.

What should he do to get home?

"I haven't got a pocket," said he, "and if I had it's more than probable that I should'nt have any-thing in it, or else I should get a cab and go to Slogger's-alley. If I do get a cab, the proba-bility is that there's no money at home. Poor Miss Williams hasn't got any, and I'm precious sure I havn't, at least, not that I recollect; and I don't usually forget when I have — Good Heavens!"

What caused this exclamation? What made the old gentleman for a moment forget his cold legs and his pitiable position?

He had suddenly remembered that in the pocket of the clothes, which had been stripped from him at the workhouse, were three pounds belonging to his employers, Messrs. Bottle and Bung, of Garlic-hill, Thames-street, City.

Well did he know that on his small wages (eight shillings a week) he would not be able to repay it for more than a year.

Well did he know, also, what hard-hearted mechanical men of business Messrs. Bottle and Bung were, and with what intermittent rapacity they pursued the unfortunate debtor, who could not come to time.

How much harder would they be with a fraudulent servant of theirs who betrayed the trust reposed in him?

There was no hope of mercy at their hands.

In truth, old Toddleboy had not the best of characters. If you had asked Messrs Bottle and Bung what his character was, they would probably have hummed and hawed, and said that they knew nothing particular against him, except that—he drank.

Oh, you topers, you thought I was defending you just now, did you? But I was not, by any means. The way the world judges of a toper is this—*If a man drinks he will do anything.*

In like fashion, the world says, that if a woman is not virtuous, she is nothing. The world ought to be right. The majority is against you, any-how.

Old Toddleboy was in an awful state of mind when he came to think of these things, and he fancied himself at the bar of the Old Bailey, and, subsequently, confined in the House of Correction for the term of his natural life.

But why not demand his clothes at the work-house?

Why not? Why, who would believe him?

MR. TODDLEBOY IN A FIX.

The whole story was outrageously improbable.

When he had sat a quarter of an hour, reflecting upon the difficulty he should probably find himself in in a few hours' time, the cold recalled him to a sense of the unpleasantness of his position at the present moment.

Decidedly he must make a stir, and was just going to make it, when half-a-dozen policemen came tramping by, on their way to the stationhouse.

"Hallo! stop!" cried the sergeant in command. "What we have got here?"

"All right," said Mr. Toddleboy, screwing himself up in his sacking; "I'm resting myself."

"You can't rest yourself here," replied the sergeant, gruffly. "Come, get up and take yourself off."

"I can't," said Toddleboy.

"Why not?"

"Because—because—"

"Come, speak up, or I shall make you."

"Well, then," said Toddleboy, in desperation, "because I've got no trousers."

"What's become of them?"

Now Toddleboy did not like to tell his story, for he felt convinced that they would set him down as an imposter if he did so. He hit upon a tale which struck him at the moment as being more probable, though, to tell the truth, it hardly was.

"Well," said he, "the fact is—"

Have you noticed how most of your great

No. 17.

story-tellers begin a fib this way—or with, " if I never speak another word," and a strong oath or two to make it more forcible ?

" Stick to the facts," said the policeman.

" The fact is, then, I've been walking in my sleep."

" Oh, you're a somnambulist, are you ?"

" Yes, sir, I always have been. It runs in the family. To-night, after I went to bed, I must have got up, for I found myself just now where I am."

" Where do you live then ?"

" In Westminster."

" Oh, so you've walked in your shirt from Westminster to Bow, have you ? That's a very likely tale, now, aint it ?"

Certainly it was rather a twister.

From Westminster to Bow, is an average long walk for anybody to take in their sleep.

But the idea of anybody doing it in their shirt-tails was rather too preposterous.

The policemen burst out laughing.

" It aint likely," said the sergeant. It really aint likely, old gentleman, and so I shall trouble you to come along with us."

What was to be done? Mr. Toddleboy did not wish to figure in the police reports.

Let alone the ridicule which he must meet with, he was eager to take some steps towards getting back his clothes and money from the workhouse.

" I assure you, gentlemen, that I am innocent," he cried, in piteous accents, " besides, what charge are you going to take me up upon?"

" Oh, we will find a charge ;" said the sergeant. " Don't you make no mistake."

And there is very little doubt indeed, but that a charge would have been found, and Mr. Toddleboy comfortably locked up on it, had not somebody fortunately come at that moment to his rescue.

This was a young man, dressed in the last fashion, with a cigar in his mouth, and his hands in his trousers' pockets—a modern fast man, in fact ; a young swell out on the spree.

" What's the little joke ?" said he, elbowing his way through the crowd. " What are you doing to the old gentleman, policeman, and which of you has stolen his trousers ?"

" Just you mind your own business," retorted the sergeant, " or else you will get yourself into trouble."

" It won't be the first time, if I do," said the young stranger, " anyhow, as a tax-payer, I have a right to ask what's the row, haven't I ?"

" Well, the row is simply this," said the policeman. " This old gent. is found on a door-step in his shirt, and he gives us as an explanation that he is a somnambulist. In my opinion that's no excuse, and so we are going to take him up."

" However," said the young man, " it seems to me if he goes quietly home, that's all you have got to trouble your heads about."

" But how is he to go home, pray, in the state he is in ?"

" Well I will give him a lift in a cab. Where do you hang out, old strike-a-light ?"

" He lives at Westminster," said the policeman, who, perhaps, was not a bad sort upon the

whole, or perhaps he thought, that before his men, it would be best to agree to what the stranger proposed.

If he had been by himself he might have made a snug little case out of it, but before all his companions in blue he did not like to do anything so glaringly illegal.

Therefore it was soon arranged that Mr. Toddleboy should get inside a four-wheeler, and the young gentleman mounting on the box with the driver, they presently drove off amidst the cheers and laughter of the assembled multitude, who were extremely tickled by the forlorn appearance of poor old Toddleboy's bare shanks.

Now this young gentleman who had apparently acted with such kindness towards the old gentleman, was, in reality, a heartless young scamp, and had undertaken the charge of Mr. T, merely for the purpose of playing off upon him one of those jokes which are commonly denominated practical.

This young man's little idea was in imitation of a well-known joke perpetrated by the Marquis of Waterford upon an eminent physician.

It was not, therefore, very new ; but then your practical jokers don't go in for novelty. One follows in anothers wake, and is quite content at re-echoing some nameless absurdity which might have originally been funny, but has lost all its point by constant repetition.

The little plant which this youth was going to put upon Toddleboy was this, he intended to turn the old gentleman out in his shirt-tails, at the top of the Haymarket, and he expected that it would be very fine fun indeed, to see his victim's misery at finding himself in so very airy a costume before the young ladies who frequent that charming locality.

He told the driver what his little joke was to be, when they descended somewhere for a glass of something hot, and the driver expressed his opinion that it was " prime."

" But as the old boy will probably twig that we are taking him the wrong road," said the fast man, " we had better give him a stiff glass of grog, and send him to sleep."

Acting upon this brilliant notion a very stiff glass, containing a quartern and-a-half of spirits, was administered to Mr. Toddleboy, and coming as it did upon the old gentleman's already deranged system it made him, in about a couple of minutes, to use a popular expression, as " drunk as a fly."

The cab drove on, and Mr. Toddleboy, wrapped up in the sacking, and coiled up on the seat within, slept very comfortably, and dreamt he was in bed.

The cab stopped, and he awoke with a start. Where was he ? In Cannon-street.

He rubbed his eyes, and looked out of the window.

The cab had stopped at the corner of the street which leads down to Garlic-hill, where Messrs. Bottle and Bung's warehouse was situated.

He did not understand what was going on, or recollect that the young gentleman had offered to take him to Westminster. He did not even recollect that he had only got on his shirt and a piece of sacking. He was, as I have told you, considerably intoxicated. Without a moment's consideration, he opened the door and jumped out.

The road was up in Cheapside, and for this reason the cab had come by this road to get to Ludgate-hill. Something had happened to the harness, and the cabman had thus, by a mere accident, got down at this place to mend it.

Both the cabman and the young swell had alighted, and were busy at the horse's head.

Mr. Toddleboy got out without making any noise, in consequence of his having no shoes on, so that when the harness was mended the two practical jokers climbed back on to the box and drove on again, in happy ignorance of their little fun having been by these means put a stop to.

Mr. Toddleboy walked down the hill until he arrived at his employers' warehouse, when endeavouring to feel in his trowsers' pockets, the fact of his having no trowsers' pockets to feel in, for the first time, became apparent to his gin-and-watery understanding.

———

XLI.—THE CONTINUATION OF THE ADVEN-
TURES OF AN OLD GENTLEMAN IN HIS SHIRT
TAILS.

IT was a nice fix to be in, was it not? However, he felt much more at home without his trowsers in Garlic-hill, than he had done in the Bow-road.

He had not got the key, but he knew how he could manage to get into the premises at the back.

The way was this.

Next door to Messrs. Bottle and Bung's was a milliners and mantle maker's of the name of Gusset, and he had more that once climbed over a low wall in their back yard, and got from the yard in at the window of his employers' warehouse.

He climbed over the wall, as he had often done before, and tried the window, but as luck would have it, it was fast.

The night was horribly cold. It wanted several hours of the time of opening, and he could not remain where he was much longer without standing a good chance of being frozen to death.

Close to the window which he would have got into, there was another window, belonging to the mantle-makers.

He tried it.

It yielded.

He pushed it open, and got in.

So far, so good.

Now he would find some place where he could have a quiet sleep for an hour or two, and creep out again, before he was caught.

He knew that nobody slept upon Gusset's premises, any more than they did upon Bottle and Bung's.

In the room in which he found himself, there was a closet where the young ladies employed in the mantle-making business kept their bonnets and shawls, and in this there were a lot of old clothes, and some bags full of scraps and fragments of cloth.

Mr. Toddleboy fancied that he might make himself very comfortable, so he got in, wrapped himself up, and fell asleep.

Not for long.

The twenty young ladies who came there every day to work, arrived very early in the morning, and all came trooping up stairs together to the room where the unfortunate gentleman had hidden himself.

The sound of their voices awakened him.

"Gracious heavens!" said he to himself, recollecting with a shudder where he was; "what will be the end of all this? I wish to goodness, now, that I had got locked up at the Station-house, instead of coming here. It's just like my luck!"

Oh! such a gabbling of tongues there was in the room! Such a rustling of dresses! Such a shuffling of feet. Such a scampering up and down stairs and slamming of doors!

"I wonder how many of 'em there are?" said Mr. Toddleboy to himself. "They sound like a hundred, but these girls are such ones for talking."

While he was meditating, the looked-for event occurred.

Some one opened the door.

Toddleboy ducked down his "two-penny." It was rather dark. He was, luckily, well covered over with the clothes which he had found in the closet, and hemmed in by the patch-bags, and the young lady being in a great hurry, hung her bonnet and shawl in front of him, and departed without casting her eyes down at the intruder.

Another followed after her; then another; and another, until he was quite covered up in a corner by cloaks, shawls, and mantles.

But still he tucked in his "two-penny," and trembled.

At last they were all gone to their work in the next room, and Toddleboy, after listening awhile to the distant hum of their voices, began to breathe again more freely.

"Now's my time," thought he; "if I am to escape, this must be the moment."

He shook off the clothes and the patch-bags, and got into an upright posture.

Then opened the closet door.

But just then he heard some one coming, and skipped back again into his place.

Two of the young ladies arrived together, and came running in with their bonnets in their hands.

"Bother it," said one; "how late it is! I suppose I shall get a nice nagging from old Mother Gusset."

"So shall I, for that matter," said the other. But you've been late before this week."

"I was at Caldwell's last night, and I was so tired this morning I couldn't get up."

"How did you enjoy yourself?"

"Oh, capital! And I had such a duck of a fellow, with moustaches, for a partner. When we was in the gallery he says to me, 'How I love you?' says he. 'If you would come and live with me I would give you five pounds a week and a brougham.'"

"My gracious! that's better pay than making

mantles at two-pence half-penny a piece; aint it ?"

" Yes ; but then how long is it to last, do you suppose ?"

" Well, I suppose mantles won't last for ever."

" And it is a great temptation to us poor girls, isn't it ? with the little wages we get."

" And the work we have to do for it."

" Very well ! Miss Montague and Miss Stubbs," here broke in a shrill female voice. " This is a nice time to come, aint it ? And when you do come you stand there chattering, instead of doing your work. Never mind ; you shan't either of you stop and work for me much longer, I can tell you. Go into the other room, will you, miss? and don't stand staring at me, there, in that way. How dare you ?"

And when the girls were gone, the lady, who was none other than Miss Gusset, an elderly spinster of vinegary aspect, approached the cupboard, and began to rummage among the pegs behind the shawls and mantles for something she wanted.

Toddleboy screwed himself as close as possible to the wall, as she approached nearer to him in her search.

" Where the dickens is it ?" said she, as it seemed, right into Toddleboy's ear.

His knees shook under him.

" Some of those hussies have knocked my apron down to hang their trumpery things on the top of the peg. Whose bonnet's this ? Miss Gibbons's, by the look of it. I'll teach her to try her impertinent tricks with my property. It's on the ground, I suppose."

And stooping down, she began to feel for it on the floor.

" It's all over !" said Toddleboy to himself, and standing on one leg, he held his breath and gave himself up for lost.

As indeed he was, for, as luck would have it, the spinster's apron was round Toddleboy's other foot.

The lady caught hold of both sides and, very much to the old gentleman's astonishment, let alone the elderly spinster's dismay, she literally jerked him off his balance, and he fell sprawling upon the closet floor.

Then, with a piercing shriek, the lady sprang to her feet, slammed-to the door, and called for help.

" At the sound of her voice, all the young ladies came running into the room to hear what the matter was, and formed themselves into a tableau, like you sometimes see at the theatre, in the last scene of a melodrama.

" What is it ? What is it ?" they asked.

" A man—a man ;" answered Miss Gusset.

" Where ? Where ?"

" In the cupboard."

" In the cupboard !" echoed everybody.

Then they all protested that she must be mistaken. They had all hung up their bonnets there not half-an-hour ago. Anyhow, if there was some one there, he must have got in afterwards.

" Perhaps it's Miss Gusset's young man," suggested some bold hussy in the back-ground ; and at this there was a little titter.

" Who said that ?" said Miss Gusset. " If I

knew, I'd pack her off this minute. Which of you said it ? Speak !"

But as no one was kind enough to tell her, the attention was again directed to the cupboard mystery.

" How many are there, ma'am ?" one young lady inquired.

" There may be half-a-dozen, for what I know," said Miss Gusset. " If it is only one, all I can say is that it's a very big one."

At this awful intelligence, all the ladies became very much excited.

" What does he want ?"

" Shall I go for the police ?"

" Yes ; run."

" No ; call out of window."

" Won't he escape ?"

" Shoot him through the door."

" But we haven't got anything to shoot him with."

" Make the poker red-hot, then, and bore a hole through to get at him."

Meanwhile, in the midst of these amiable suggestions, Mr. Toddleboy was heard to speak.

" Young ladies," said he, " I don't mean any harm."

" Oh, the wretch ! Oh, the monster !"

" Hold the door fast."

" Oh, I'm so frightened !"

" Oh, I'm going to faint !"

But as the old gentleman began to shake the door inside, in his efforts to get his head out, Miss Gusset fled precipitately to the furthest corner of the room, and bade him come out at his peril.

" Who are you, man?" she asked, in a voice of thunder.

" If you please," said Toddleboy, " I'm next door."

" How can you be next door when you're here ?"

" I mean—I'm the porter next door."

" What are you doing there, then ?"

" I will explain, 'ma'am, if you will allow me."

" Have you any fire-arms with you ?"

" Nothing of the sort."

" You swear you haven't ?"

" I swear I haven't."

" Come out then."

This was rather embarassing, and there was an awkward pause.

" I can't, said Toddleboy.

" Why not ?"

" Because I haven't got—"

" Got what ?"

" I haven't got anything—I mean anything on."

" Ain't you dressed ?" cried Miss Gusset, in horror."

" Not quite," said Mr. Toddleboy ; " I haven't got any trousers."

" Gracious heavens !" ejaculated Miss Gusset, " the monster is naked. I thought as much, by what little I saw of him."

And she hid her face in her handkerchief.

" If you'll only let me wrap myself up in something, " said Mr. Toddleboy, poking his head out of the door, " I'll get out of the window, and go into the warehouse next door, and when I've put on some clothes I'll come back and make an explanation."

But this Miss Gusset would not listen to.

"Send for a policeman," said she.

"For God's sake, don't," cried Mr. Toddleboy, "or I'm a ruined man."

"You horrid old wretch, if we don't, we may all be ruined women, for what I know. What's your object in coming here in this condition?"

"I assure you, ma'am, my intentions are strictly honourable. If you would only be so kind as to look at me, you'd see I was—"

"Go back into the cupboard, you horrid old man. How dare you ask me to do such a thing? Here, some of you girls, run for the police."

And in spite of the old gentleman's remonstrances and entreaties, the policeman was fetched.

In five minutes more he was in custody.

XLII.—Follows the Fortunes of Charley Wag, and shows what a very foolish thing it is to Count your Chickens before they are Hatched, with other matters more or less interesting.

AS the writer is informed that this work is "taken in" by the most respectable families in the land, and may, for all he knows, circulate in Buckingham Palace, it is necessary before everything that it should be quite proper and correct in its morals.

Consequently, I shall take the liberty of passing over an hour or two of Mr. Wag's life, and introduce him again to your notice, when he and Miss Julia are partaking of a sumptuous breakfast of coffee and "slices," at a coffee-house in Whitechapel.

"Well, Julia," said Charley, how do you propose I should earn my living? for, you know, I don't mean to live upon you."

"Well, the question is, what can you do."

"Now, for instance, there isn't an opening, I suppose, in your line."

"What, as a dancer? they don't take gentlemen dancers, unless they are very clever indeed."

"But couldn't I dress up as a girl in some of your things."

Oh! the idea! Why you are not graceful enough."

"Ah!" laughed Charley, "that's because you are jealous."

And then Julia laughed, and said she wasn't, and tapped him playfully upon the head with a tea-spoon.

When he and Julia, and Master Tom the cat, had had their breakfast, it was agreed that Charley should go and see his fostermother, that Julia should go to rehearsal at Muggins's, and that they should afterwards meet to look for lodgings.

In front of the Royal Exchange, was the place which they chose for a rendezvous, and after an affectionate leave-taking, the young lady departed in the direction of Shadwell, whilst our hero set off towards Westminster.

He was in the very highest spirits. Both be-

cause he was full of wonderful schemes for the future, and because he anticipated soon seeing his dear fostermother, for one of whose fond affectionate embraces his heart yearned convulsively.

But, as he went whistling upon his way, it is not to be denied that every now and then an uneasy feeling stole over him, and a misgiving arising in his mind dispelled the happy expression on his handsome face.

What were his thoughts? I am almost afraid to tell you, reader, lest you should think him an unnatural young rascal. Though, after all, I do my little best to depict human nature, and if you find fault with human nature when I have drawn it for you, that is not my fault.

Well, then. Until the previous evening there was nothing in the world that Charley would have looked forward to with so much happiness as the meeting with his foster-mother, but now—now there was another somebody engrossing his attention. The mother had found a rival in this pretty little chit of a dancing girl. Lord! is it not natural, after all, and do we not find fathers and mothers every day forsaken for much plainer little parties than Julia Jenkini.

Thus was it that Master Charles, having very strong doubts in his mind how his foster-mother would receive the intelligence that he had found a sweetheart and was going away from home, and as he was not very hardened, although rather inclined to be cheeky, I don't think I am exaggerating the case when I say that he would much rather have had his biggest back tooth taken out than have had to tell Miss Williams how matters stood.

"But I can crack her up some fine tale," the young rip thought to himself, "and, if the worst comes to the worst, and she won't agree to my leaving home, why I shall have to jolly well hook it. So that's all about it."

Ah! he was like all the rest of us, counting his chickens before they were hatched. Little did he dream what was awaiting him in Slogger's-alley.

He walked briskly along down the Strand, and down Parliament-street, and past the Abbey. There were some hoardings close to the alley walls, upon a house undergoing repairs, and on it were many bills, all sizes and colours.

One particularly caught his eye, and brought him up short, like as though some one had suddenly thrust the hooked end of a walking-stick down the back of his neck and jerked him backwards.

It commenced with these words, in large capitals,

"LOOK OUT FOR CHARLEY WAG!"

He read every word of the bill. It was the same which the old man had shown to him at the rag and bottle shop.

"Good heavens!" he thought, "have they read it in our alley? Will anybody give me up to the lawyer before I can see my mother? Surely no one would be so unfeeling as to betray me for the sake of the bribe. Perhaps after all there may not be many bills about."

Fallacious hope! He passed another before long, and when he reached the entrance to Slogger's-alley, there was a third stuck upon th wall, in a most conspicuous place, and he could read his name full fifty yards off.

It was not a pleasant welcome to the young prodigal upon his return.

For a long while he hesitated what course to pursue, and had more than half a mind to run away again.

While he was thus undecided, and was keeping round the corner of the next street, from which he could see the entrance to the Abbey, a girl came running out of a public-house close to him, and no sooner had her eyes fallen upon our hero than she let fall a jug of beer which she was carrying, and uttered a little scream of recognition.

"Oh- my-gracious- goodness -me - and-well - I never-did - did-you-upon- my-word-and-honour-who'd-a-thought it? cried the young lady who was thus startled at seeing him, expressing herself as above, all in a breath, and without any commas.

"Hallo, Bessy!" said Master Charles, "How are you getting on ; and how's your aunt?"

"My aunt's quite well, thank you, Mr. Wag ;" replied the young lady, who was none other than Mrs. Crocker's niece. "I am quite well, too, I thank you," she added, assuming a very distant and dignified tone, quite unlike her first address.

Charley could not help noticing it.

"What's the matter?" he asked,

"Oh don't talk to me!" she replied, "go back to your schoolmaster's daughters. I don't want to have anything to say to you. I'm ashamed of you!"

"I haven't got any schoolmaster's daughters," said Charley, though he could not help blushing when he thought of Julia (the heartless young deceiver). "What do you mean, Bessy?"

"What do I mean? Why, I have heard it all, and so has everybody else."

"You mean those bills. I swear to you they are all lies, Bessy, and I will tell you the truth, if you will listen to me."

"Oh, I don't want to listen."

But she did ; and so he told her.

"Oh, gracious me!" said Mrs. Crocker's niece, when he had finished. What dreadful stories that lawer person, Mr. Leech, has been telling about you. Why, I never heard such goings on in my life ; but—"

Here she suddenly paused, and looked confused.

"But what?" said Charley.

The girl looked still more confused, and unwilling to continue what she was about to say.

At last she summoned up courage.

"Have you been home?" she asked.

"No," he replied, "not yet ; but I am going now. I was afraid of being taken. How is my poor, dear mother?"

The girl made no answer, but started at the question, and turned pale.

"But I shall see for myself," he said, without noticing her emotion. "Good-bye till we meet again."

He was running away, when she stopped him.

"Stay, stay!" she said. Oh, Charley, your poor mother!"

"Yes, yes—"

"She has been ill—very ill. Have you no heard?"

"No," replied Charley, growing alarmed. "I have heard nothing. Has she been dangerously ill?"

"She has been very dangerously ill," replied the girl.

She spoke in such a serious tone, and there was such a look of warning in her face, that Charley trembled in every limb, and his heart beat fast with the dread of some impending misfortune or calamity—he knew not what.

Again he started forward to go home, and again she stopped him.

"Oh, Charley, not yet. Wait until I have told you all."

"No, no," he answered, "I cannot wait. I must go and see her."

Without another word he quitted his companion, and ran down the alley.

There there was a strange excitement, although the place seemed to strike him as unnaturally hushed and quiet.

The people were who was at the doors, and, as he passed by they whispered together, and pointed to him, but nobody spoke to him. He passed on until he came within six yards of his own house, round which a little crowd was standing.

As he came up, a man standing upon the doorstep, told the people outside "to stand a little backer," for "it was coming down."

What was coming down?

He pushed forward to the door, and was about to enter, when the man who had spoken, laying his hand upon Charley's collar, pushed him back.

"Who are you?" said the man, "you can't come in here."

"I live here," said Charley.

"I can't help that," replied the other, "they're bringing it down," said he.

"Bringing what down," asked Charley.

"What down," echoed the man. "What do you suppose, unless it's the coffin."

"Whose coffin?"

"Sarah Williams's."

As though he had been struck down by a poleaxe, Charley, as the man uttered these words, fell upon his knees upon the ground.

Great God! was she then dead! Dead, while he was away from her—he, who ought of all others, to have been at her bed-side, attendant upon her, at every beck and call.

Dead, while he was passing his time in dissolute profligacy. Ah! there was no hope for him, he must have been born to be a bad character, fate seemed to be dead against him.

There he knelt upon the knees.

Four men bearing the coffin, which contained the body of her who had been so good to him in life, came down the stairs, and the crowd giving way for them—they walked slowly down the alley.

Charley sprang to his feet, and struggled violently with those of the spectators, who would have detained him.

"Let me go," he cried, frantically, "how dare you hold me back, have I not a right to go to her, is she not my mother?"

But they heeded him not ; and one person in the

crowd, a stout, ill-natured looking old lady, who was, in fact, the Mrs. Crocker before alluded to, expressed a great deal of virtuous indignation at the sight of him.

"A nasty little varmint," said she, "if he doesn't take himself off in a couple of cracks, I will give him in charge of a police constable, drat me if I don't."

"Ah!" joined in another lady in the crowd, "an infamous little blackguard, he is like all the boys, never knows the value of their mothers till they loses them."

"But she was not his mother, was she?"

"Well, no; his foster mother only, but she was as good as a mother to him—an ungrateful little wretch."

"She wasn't a good character, was she?"

"Well, far from it; although she certainly behaved decent during the last years of her life. She was the woman of that Rattan that was transported."

While they were thus talking over the good and bad qualities, of poor Sarah Williams, Charley sat sobbing upon the cold stones, unheeded and uncared for.

So, for some twenty minutes did he remain there, and then, with an almost breaking heart, and at a slow, painful pace, he crawled rather than walked out of the alley and along the street, in the direction from which he had just come.

Stunned and stupified with his misfortune—with his irreparable loss—the poor boy, wild and giddy though he might have been, was yet surely to be pitied in his sorrow.

But nobody in the alley pitied him, he was in everybody's eyes a selfish, unnatural little monster, deserving of the severest punishment, and of universal loathing and execration.

They did not, it is true, detain him and hand him over to the lawyer, and get the fifty pounds reward as promised, for several reasons. One might have been that they would have thought such a course dishonourable, though for that matter, I should not like to say too much, for in my small experience, I have not found more honour to exist among thieves than among London tradesmen, which is not saying much, is it?

Perhaps they may have thought that the time was past for getting the reward, or that if they took the boy, the lawyer probably would not pay up, for the Slogger-alleyites had not a great deal of faith in legal gentlemen.

It doesn't matter why, but they let him go, and he wandered on, still sobbing, without turning his head to the right or to the left.

But suddenly he was brought to a stand-still by a sharp blow upon the shoulder, and the next moment a strong hand was twisted into his collar, and a remarkably bony set of knuckles were dug into his neck.

"I have got you, have I?" said a voice, "you damned young vagabond, you have led me a nice dance."

Charley turned round, and to his horror recognised Mr. Leech.

XLIII.—CHARLEY IS MADE A THIEF OF.

"LEAVE me alone!" cried the boy, struggling desperately, and punching at the lawyer's legs, "what have you got to do with me?"

"I'll show you what I have got to do with you, young six-pen'orth of halfpence, I'll teach you to bolt off with young ladies and post-chaises and thousands of pounds in gold. Where is a policeman?"

"Who want's a policeman?" said a strong, rough, good-looking fellow, dressed in sailor-fashion, pushing past the half-dozen people who had gathered round to see fair-play, and to know what the row was about.

"I want a policeman," said Mr. Leech, "run and get me one."

"Not a bit of it," replied the new comer, "what's this boy done? What are you up to, with him?"

"He has done highway robbery, for one thing," said Leech, "and arson, for another, besides abduction and petty larceny, and other little trifles of that sort."

"Well!" said the other, whom Charley, to his astonishment, recognised as the man called George. "It's all very well, Mr. What's-your-name, only you see the boy is my brother, and I should fancy you was mistaken in the party you are looking for, that's all."

And so saying, he suddenly wrenched the boy out of the lawyer's hands, and hitting the latter a staggering blow in the breast, which knocked him up against a shop-window, and sent his elbow through, at the same time that the hat fell off his head, and the papers which it contained were scattered in the mud; he pushed Charley before him, and they took to their heels down a court, the entrance to which was close at hand.

Without saying a word George pulled the boy along, turned him sharp round one corner, then another, and another, until thinking himself out of harm's way, the man paused to take breath.

"Thank you, thank you, for saving me," cried Charley, as soon as he could speak.

"Saving you, you young imp of Satan," growled George, "what the devil did you mean by running away from the guvnor? what was your game?"

Charley was dumbfounded, and could make no reply.

"We will take precious good care you don't do it again, my young cockchafer," said George.

"What right have you to keep me," asked the boy, "anymore than that lawyer has? What does everybody want to keep locking me up for? What have I done to everybody?"

"Hold your row, will you?" said George, "and come along quiet, else I shall knock your young head off. With this intimation of what he might expect if he was at all obstreperous, Charley was led along by his companion, until they reached a leading thoroughfare, when George, calling a cab, bade the driver take them to Commercial-street.

Having arrived here, the man who had captured him still retained his hold upon Charley, and led him along helplessly, down Keat-street, to the shop of old Mr. Measles.

The delight of this gentleman upon seeing him was intense.

"I thought he could not keep away from me for long," cried the old gentleman. "Such ingratitude could not be human. Me, too, who nursed him in his illness, and did everything that science and my natural kindness of heart could do to bring him round again. Get into the back parlour, you cursed young wiper, and if you are up to any of your hanky-panky dodges again I'll skin you alive."

Throughout the day old Measles kept a close watch upon him: but he was so depressed, broken-down, and unnerved by the great misfortune which had befallen him in the death of his foster-mother, that it is doubtful whether he would have made any effort to escape, even if he had the chance.

"It was one of the rummest goes I ever heard on," he heard George say to the old man.

"It was rayther strange," replied Mr. Measles, "as you and the lawyer should just pitch upon him at the same time."

"In course I was hanging round the neighbourhood, as the likeliest place to spot him, as you telled me he said he lived there, and I suppose the other chap must have been up to the same move."

"It's a pity, almost," said Mr. Measles, "that we didn't make the fifty pun' by him, ain't it?"

"Well, if you think it better to have had the money, and to have let him have blowed on this ere crib, I can't say I agree with you. We shall clinch the matter to-night, 'cos I shall take him along with me to the crack that I am going to do."

"Do you think he can be trusted?"

"By God, I will put a bullet through his head, if he tries to play me false."

"That you will, George; trust you for that."

They were, then, as well as Charley could understand, going to make him participate in some burglary, which was to take place that evening.

The hours passed by, and when shutting-up time came, the shop was closed, and the two men had a long conference in the back parlour, most of which Charley overheard.

"Have you got a plan of the premises?" asked George.

"Yes, everything, all correct. I'll show you how it's to be done. There is an empty house four doors off. You'll get in there at the time the old woman in charge of it goes out for the beer. Go up stairs, and out on the tiles, and so get through the trap-door of the other house, and the jewels are all in a cupboard in a bedroom on the second floor; it's all easy enough, as you will see. The jeweller who had the resetting of the diamonds has given me all the particulars."

"What's the swag worth, do you suppose?"

"Well, it would not be worth much to you, you know, unless you were helped, but you will have ten pounds down for the job, and all the trouble off your hands, which, considering the tightness of the money market, is a very fair price."

"Yes, it's dev'lish fine, but us poor fellows as runs all the risk always comes off so precious poorly paid for our trouble," said George, with an oath.

"And if it was not for us getting you the information, and taking the goods of you when you have got them, where would you be? why, starving, I should think. Why, you might just as well be honest; you would make as much money by it."

Here the conversation ceased for awhile, and Mr. Measles, unlocking a cupboard, fetched down from underneath a quantity of rubbish at the bottom of it, a very handsome set of housebreaker's tools, which he laid upon the table, and then produced a little bottle containing some liquid.

"What's that?" asked George.

"It's the last invention," replied Mr. Measles, "some acid, which you rub on the windows, and it makes the glass as soft as putty, so that you can break it without the least noise."*

"Well, that's a thing the inventor ought to have been made a lord for, if ever there was anything; he is a benefactor to the whole of the human race, as you call it."

At eleven o'clock, George, taking our hero by the arm, conducted him down the street, and calling a passing cab which chanced to be empty, he, the old man, and the boy proceeded straight to the Marble Arch.

Here they alighted, and going down Parklane, on the side where the railings are, stopped in front of a house which Measles pointed out.

"We shan't be seen here," said he, "the old woman don't go out for the beer until a little past twelve, for her husband is a policeman, and she gets it for his supper, and, as she told me the other night, she leaves it till the last thing, because he says it tastes flat when it's kept in a bottle."

"It's past twelve now, then," said George.

"Yes, and here she comes."

As he spoke he pointed to a woman leaving the house opposite, with a jug in her apron.

No sooner had she disappeared round the corner, than the two men, dragging the boy with them, crossed the street.

"Don't you see that she has got her big key with her," said Measles. "The latch is put back, so out with your skeletons and open the door."

This was but the work of a few moments.

Then they entered the house and closed the door after them.

Without pausing for a moment they proceeded straight up stairs, making as little noise as possible for fear, by some chance, some one might be in the house; and with the aid of a ladder, which they found in one of the garrets, they let themselves out upon the roof. And here for a moment they paused to consult together upon the best way of committing the burglary.

"This is as good a time as any," said Measles. "Here's the saw, begin upon the bolt."

George took it from him, and stooping down, was soon busily engaged upon the work allotted to him.

The others remained quite quiet, and the sound of their half-suppressed breathing and the grating of the file were the only sounds which broke the stillness of the night.

* A fact—ask any housebreaker of your acquaintance.

THE BURGLARY.

"It's done," whispered George, after a while raising his head. "Now for the other."

Then he pulled open the door, and entered the loft of the house.

In a minute he returned.

"The other door is open," he said. "So, the boy shall go down along of me, and keep cavy on the stairs, whilst I do the job in my lady's bed-room."

"All right," said Measles. "Now, you young wiper, take off your shoes, and go down quiet, or I shall have to pitch you over the parapet."

But the boy did not stir.

"Don't you hear?" cried the old man.

"Why do you want me to go into the house?" the boy asked.

No. 18.

"Why?"

"Yes. Is it to assist in a robbery?"

"It's to keep watch, while we prig some jewels."

"Then I won't go."

"You won't go?"

"No."

"Look here, George! Do you hear what he says?"

"What does he say?"

"He says he won't help."

"Says he won't help, does he?" repeated George, with an ominous frown, and he raised himself out of the trap.

Then advancing with a menacing gesture towards the boy, he asked—

"Did you say you wouldn't help?"

[CHARLEY WAG, THE NEW JACK SHEPPARD.

"Yes, I did," replied Charley, stoutly, "Why should I be forced to be a thief? What have I done to you that you should persecute me so?"

"What have you done to us? This much; you know too much for us. When anyone mixes themselves up in our affairs, and gets one finger into the concern we makes 'em put their whole arm in, and wo holds 'em there, that's how we manage it."

"But I swear to you, I will not betray you, only let me go. For God's sake do not make a thief of me."

"Well, that strikes us as being the best plan, so we shall."

"But I defy you. I will spoil your schemes."

"Will you," said George, in a ferocious whisper, "Now look here! Don't try to play the fool with me, or, by God, I'll put a bullet through your stupid young skull. Come down with me and do as I bid you, and mind, the least attempt at treachery on your part, and I send you to your last account; even should I miss you, which isn't likely, one of our company will manage your business for you some other time. We never forgive and we never forget, and traitors are roughly handled when we drop upon them."

As he spoke, George drew a pistol from his pocket, and to make his words more impressive, he placed the muzzle against Charley's forehead, and while there the boy heard the click of the trigger.

What resistance could he make? How could he struggle against his assailants? his life would be forfeited.

Anyhow the best plan would certainly be to affect to agree with them. Then he thought that if he saw an opportunity when inside, he would immediately alarm the house, and trust to providence to escape the murderous revenge which had been threatened him.

Without more waste words, George re-opened the trap, which, while they had been talking, he had shut down, and, beckoning Charley to follow him, let himself down, and alighted upon a chest of drawers standing directly underneath, upon the landing.

The upper part of the house was dark and quiet.

Down below, in the hall, where they paused for a moment to listen, they heard the steps of some one, probably a servant, cross the passage, and descend the kitchen stairs.

Then all was quiet there, also.

There was a light burning in the hall, and at intervals upon the stairs, as far as the landing, half way between the first and second floors, but nobody seemed to be, at that time, in the upper part of the house.

As well as Charley could judge, it seemed to be a grand and spacious mansion—almost a palace. As they descended to the second floor, although George had put on list slippers, and obliged the boy to do the same, the latter could not help thinking that precaution rather unnecessary, for the rich, thick carpets would have muffled the sound of the heaviest boot.

When they reached the second floor landing, George pulled from his breast-pocket a dark lantern and a piece of paper, on which had been drawn the plan of the premises.

"That's the room," said he at once, after he had taken a rapid glance at the doors along the landing, and compared them with the diagram which he held in his hand. "That's the room. You wait here, and keep watch while I go inside. If you hear any one coming up stairs, come and give me warning; and if you try any of your tricks, why then, by ——, you know what you've got to look out for."

With a menacing gesture and a savage frown, the man left him, and carefully opening the door of the room he was in search of, went noiselessly in, and pulled it to after him without shutting it.

He found himself in a superbly furnished bed-room, the air of which was redolent with sweet perfume. Turning the light of his lantern upon the various articles in the apartment, he soon fixed upon a wardrobe of richly-carved oak, and straightway producing his skeleton-keys, began to operate upon the lock.

"This is the place where they're kept, according to the description," he muttered; "and here goes."

He had opened the door by this time, and laid his hand upon a small mahogany box which lay before him.

He shook it, and the jingle within told him that it was what he sought.

"It's no good breaking into it here," he said to himself; "I'll take it with me."

Acting upon this resolve, he put the box under his arm, and as he retraced his steps towards the landing, he could not help congratulating himself upon the successful issue of the adventure, and the rapidity of its execution.

But as he approached the door, the sound of scuffling on the landing outside made him pause. But while undecided what course to take, the door was flung back upon him with such violence that it dashed the lantern from his hand, and sent it with a loud crash against a looking-glass, which it shivered to atoms, and Charley, in the grasp of some other person, fell right into his arms.

XLIV.—The Noiseless Wanderer of the Night—The Phial—Is it Poison?—Treachery—The Spy—The Rattlesnake and its Victim—The Struggle—The Captives—The Police.

WHEN the boy found himself alone, his first idea was to run down stairs and give the alarm, and it is probable that in another instant he would have followed out this resolve, had not something of a very unexpected character taken place to prevent him.

Just as he was about to make the first step forward, a door opened close by his side, and a man bearing a light came out upon the landing almost upon the very spot where the boy stood. There was an old-fashioned clock-case by which he was standing. On the other side of this the door opened.

The figure bearing the light came out without making any noise, or giving the slightest warning of its approach, and had it not been for the candle which it carried, the boy would not have been aware of its presence.

As it was, he drew himself up close to the wall, and the clock-case concealed him from the other's eyes.

For a moment the figure paused to listen, and as it stood there, shading the light with its hand in such a way that the reflection fell full upon its strongly-marked, lean, and cadaverous visage, Charley could not refrain from a cold shudder, fearing he scarcely knew what.

As thus it stood and listened for an instant, the house was unnaturally still, and the boy, in an agony of fear, waited for the sound of the burglar's work within the room before the door of which he stood on guard.

But no sound reached them, and the house-breaker must have been, by some fortuitous chance, engaged in some noiseless occupation at the time.

After listening for a moment, the figure glided rather than walked along the passage, and opening a door at the far-end, in the same stealthy quiet fashion that it had opened the door by the side of the clock, stole in, pausing, however, once more to listen, and shading the light as before with its skinny hand.

And, as it passed into the inner darkness of the room, a certain indescribable something in the ghastly whiteness of the face, or the emaciated, bony, spectre-like form, drew him after it, and though trembling with a hitherto unknown dread and terror, the boy could not refrain from creeping in its wake, and peering through a crack of the door where it had entered, to see upon what work this noiseless night-wanderer was engaged.

The room was a bed-room, and some one was asleep in bed.

The mysterious person stole up to the bed-side on the opposite side to the door, so that Charley could see his every action.

He stooped over the sleeper and passed the light across his eyes.

The sleeper was a young boy, of perhaps thirteen or fourteen years of age, with golden curls, hanging in clusters round his fair brow. A beautiful boy he was, but so delicate and fragile, that the tiny hand resting upon the coverlid seemed almost transparent, and the thin cheeks were drawn into the little face, as though years of sickness had tended to waste away that fair form.

Over this sleeping figure, the man, whose every movement Charley was so earnestly watching, stooped down, and again and again passed the light before his eyes.

Then, when quite convinced of the strength of the boy's slumbers, the mysterious being drew from his breast-pocket a little phial, containing some colourless liquid, and dipping a feather into this, stooped down and passed it gently over the sleeper's lips.

For a moment there was no change in the boy's face, and the man stood anxiously watching him.

Then the fingers of the hand outside the bed-clothes began to twist and twine themselves uneasily on the fringe upon the silk coverlet,

and the sleeper's breath heaved, as though with half-suppressed sobs.

And then the head rolled to-and-fro, as though the sleeper was in acute bodily pain.

The man who had caused all this shaded the light with his hand, and stood motionless by the bed-side, waiting.

In a few moments all was again still.

Then again he repeated the process, and with the same result.

Once more.

And it was after the last, and when as it seemed, he was about to withdraw from the bed-side, that a loud jingling noise in the room where the burglar was at work, attracted his attention, and caused him to raise his eyes hastily towards the door.

They encountered those of Charley, who was glaring in upon him, entranced and spell-bound.

For a moment they stood thus, like a rattle-snake charming a bird. Charley would have flown from the spot had he been able, but some power stronger than himself kept him there a prisoner.

The other still gazed, with his fixed and snake-like fashion upon our hero's face, crept forward towards him, until he got within a couple of yards.

Then he made a spring, like a tiger upon its prey.

The boy fell back, with a stifled cry of horror and dismay, and fled precipitately.

The man pursued him.

Gained on him.

Clutched him by the throat.

With the energy of despair he struggled to free himself, and fighting together for the mastery they fell against the door of the room where George had entered, and falling against him, as he was coming out, dashed the lantern from his hand, and sent it with a deafening crash, as I have described, against a looking-glass, which it shivered to atoms.

For several seconds George was too much astounded by the blow he had received, and the tremendous crash of broken glass, to be able either to think or act, but when he recovered his senses, it at once became clear to his understanding that the sooner he was off the better.

He must make a bolt of it, and a bolt he made, scarcely knowing in his hurry and confusion, in what direction he was going.

Charley at the same time sprang to his feet and endeavoured to follow him, but he had hardly time to cross the threshold when his pursuer seized him again by the collar, and flung him down upon the floor of the landing.

At the same time the noise had alarmed the other inmates of the house, and several footmen came racing up-stairs with candles in their hands.

"Help! help!" shouted Charley's assailant; "secure the man, I will hold the boy safely till your return."

But the John Thomases stood staring at him in a mortal funk.

"Quick, quick!" he called again. "Quick or he will escape."

"Which way has he gone, and how many of

them are there?" asked the foremost footman, undecided.

"There is only one, make haste!"

Thus encouraged, and thinking that though they might not be a match for the burglar, that anyhow, seeing there were six of them, they had the advantage in point of numbers, they rushed up-stairs with as much boldness as they could assume, and called upon him to surrender.

Now, as he had run away at their approach, they advanced with a great deal more courage than they would have done had he shown fight. Indeed, those behind, who were the most out of harm's way, called on those in front to go a little quicker, and asked them, indignantly, what the dickens they were stopping for.

But, suddenly, everybody stopped, for at the top of the stairs the burglar stood, waiting for them, with a pistol in his hand.

"The first one of you who comes up another step," said he, "I shall blow his brains out."

At the sound of his voice, the foremost of the footmen staggered back into the waistcoat of the gentleman immediately behind him, and he, in his turn, tumbled back into some other gentleman's waistcoat, and they all looked as white in their faces as though they had had them powdered like their hair.

But the man who held Charley, hearing the robber's threat, gave the boy into the hands of two more footmen, who had just come up-stairs, and shouted to some of the others to come and take charge of him.

"Come, one of you, and help," he shouted.

And, immediately, the whole of the footmen, to a man, came flocking down to assist him.

"Curse you all, for a pack of idiots and cowards!" he cried, "you've let him go, have you?"

They had almost.

Rushing up stairs, he reached the fourth floor, just as the robber's legs were disappearing through the trap-door on to the roof.

He made a spring at them, seized one foot and dragged George down on to the ground, where he held him with the strength of a lion.

"Measles!" cried the burglar, struggling fiercely, "Measles!"

"Yes;" said the old man's voice, above.

"Fire at him," continued George. "Fire, or I shall be taken."

"It's so dark," the old man replied, "I can't see which is which."

"Never mind; it's the only chance. He's a top of me. Fire!"

Next moment a pistol was fired, and the robber, with a groan, fell helpless beneath the other's weight.

"Hell flames!" he roared, gnashing his teeth, "you've broken my arm. It's all up with me."

Probably, considering what he had done to be much more than was necessary, Mr. Measles shut down the trap-door above, and exerted his thin legs to the utmost in scampering, like an overgrown tom-cat, across the roofs of the houses, till he reached the trap-door where they had come up.

Opening this, he jumped in with a greater display of nimbleness than one would have been led to expect from so aged an individual, and made the best of his way down stairs.

In the passage he encountered the old woman, who had just returned with the beer, and who, upon seeing him, set up a piercing shriek, but disposing of her in a very summary manner, by a back-handed blow in the face, which sent the old lady and the beer-jug head over heels down the kitchen stairs, he rushed out into the street, and climbing the park railings, scampered across the green sward, and was soon out of sight and reach of any one who might have thought it worth their while to give chase.

In the meantime George's captor held him fast by the throat, and, with the assistance of some of the flunkies, who, seeing that there was not now much danger, approached the scene of the conflict a little more willingly, managed to bind the robber hand and foot, and keep him fast until the arrival of the police.

A couple of officers happening to saunter down Park-lane, when the inmates of the house were begining to despair of getting the burglars to the police station, otherwise than by carrying them there themselves, the man George, and the boy Charley, were given into custody.

"Who took 'em?" asked one of the policemen.

"I heard the noise first," said Jeames.

"If you did, it was me that suggested we should go up stairs and see what it was about," retorted John Thomas.

"Come, I like that," interposed Charles and Augustus, in a breath. "If it had not been for us you would never have stirred."

But while these gentlemen were thus taking to themselves all the honour and glory, a tall, pale faced, quiet-looking man, elbowed his way forward, at sight of whom the flunkies shrank back abashed.

"Please not to make so much noise. Her Grace must not be disturbed," he said. "Her Grace has extremely delicate health, and this uproar cannot be endured."

"I was asking, sir," the policeman said, "who it was took the robbers."

"Took them," said the pale gentleman, "what consequence is that, since you have them in custody?"

"Only, sir, that it will be necessary to make a charge."

"In that case, I will make it," the pale gentleman replied, quietly. "I captured them. My name is Faversham. I am Her Grace's physician."

At that moment the dining-room door opened, and a beautiful lady, richly attired in evening dress, came out into the passage, and asked in anxious tones for her son.

"Where is he?" she said. "Have none of you taken care of him. He may have been murdered."

"Quiet yourself on that score," said Mr. Faversham, gently, "I have only just left him. Our little patient was sleeping, I am happy to say, much easier than he has of late. The crisis decidedly is past."

"Thank God for that!" the lady exclaimed, fervently.

Then altering her tone—

"How many thieves are there?" she asked.

"Not a very formidable band," replied the doctor, with a bland smile. "This man and this boy."

The lady turned her eyes in the direction indicated, and as they rested upon Charley's face, uttered a half-suppressed scream.

"You are ill," the doctor cried, running forward to her assistance. "Stand back there, and let Her Grace have a little more air."

"Let Her Grace have a little more air," said Charles to Jeames.

"Stand back there," said Jeames to John Thomas.

And the phalanx of flunkies falling back, Her Grace did have a little more air, though it did not seem to do her such a mighty deal of good.

As you may imagine, Master Charles was not a little alarmed at the unpleasant position in which he found himself; and it is not to be supposed that he had much time or inclination to think about anything but what particularly concerned him.

However, he found time to wonder, in spite of that, how it was that he should fancy he had seen Her Grace before.

It was a preposterous idea; but he could not help thinking that it was the very same lady whom he had rescued that night out of the Thames.

He had not a very long while allowed him to think about anything, for a policeman seized him by the collar, and the next moment he was being dragged through the streets to the station, a select company of rag, tag, and bobtail following behind.

XLV.—JACK RATTAN AGAIN—COMPLICATIONS —THE ABODE OF THE HOURIS—AN OLD PEER, AND AN OLD PROFLIGATE—A TABLEAU!

I LEFT the Duchess in a certain house in Westminster, in attempting to escape from which she found herself confronted by a ruffian with a pistol in his hand, who threatened to shoot her if she stirred a step.

She had recognised him at the same time that he recognised her.

She recognised him as Jack Rattan—as the man who had attempted her life.

And why was Jack Rattan here? Because it was where he lived when he was at home. Mrs. Crow was Jack Rattan's mother.

While they stood eyeing each other and undecided in both cases what course to pursue, the door opened behind them, and the fat woman came bustling in again.

"Heighty-tighty," cried she, "what's going on here, I'd like to know?"

"It's these two gals a kickin up a rumpus to get out."

"Get out, nonsense," said Mrs. Crow, "they're not going to get out yet, I'll promise 'em. That is to say, not 'till I've done with 'em."

"What do you mean?" cried the Duchess, indignantly. "What right have you to detain us? You do not know whom you are addressing."

"Well, p'r'aps not," said Mrs. Crow, "I didn't ask your name, to be sure; and, to tell the truth, it's not of vital consequence to me to know it. It's quite sufficient for me to know that you are two nice looking young women."

"What do you mean?"

"Well, what I mean," replied Mrs. Crow, "you'll find out directly. There, don't make fools of yourselves, but sit down and pull your bonnets off. There's a nice old gentleman coming, who wants to talk to you."

Without taking any notice of the Duchess's indignant reply, Mrs. Crow bade her servant set the room to rights, and hide out of sight a common deal table, a jug, a pipe, and a bull dog, which seemed to be the exclusive property of Mr. Jack Rattan. When this was done, and the bed-clothes carefully tucked in behind the screen, the room assumed a much more creditable appearance, and Mrs. Crow evidently satisfied with it, went away, taking Rattan with her.

Outside the room, the latter said,

"What are you going to do, Mrs. C.?"

"I'll tell you, presently, replied the old woman. "His lordship's waiting now, and I can't stop."

"Well," said Rattan, with a chuckle, "I'm blest if this 'ere aint a·go, and no mistake. Here's old Mother Crow got the Duchess into her clutches, and thinks she's going to make something out of her, by introducing her to an old swell as a young gal fresh from the country. There'll be a precious row over this lot, or I'm a Dutchman."

Without, however, waiting for his opinion, Mrs. Crow proceeded straight upstairs and entered a room on the first floor.

One would not have expected to have seen such a room in such a house or such a neighbourhood; but the old woman seemed to be perfectly familiar with its peculiarities, and by no means astonished at the sight which met her eyes.

It was a large apartment, splendidly furnished, and lighted with at least twenty gas burners. In the centre, a table was spread for supper, of which half-a-dozen young ladies were then partaking.

Half-a-dozen young ladies, all supremely beautiful, all magnificently and tastefully attired.

These young ladies reclined upon rich crimson velvet couches, beautifully ornamented with gold braid. Upon the table were spread, in wild luxuriance, the rarest hothouse fruits and costliest wines, of which all Mrs. Crow's pupils, as she called them, were always at liberty to partake to their heart's desire.

The walls were covered with splendid paintings, but in which no prudery had restrained the artist's pencil, and the subjects which he had chosen were chiefly those of a voluptuous character, from ancient history or the heathen mythology.

There was "Leda and the Swan," "Messalina naked in the bath," "Tarquin and Lucretia,"

"Joseph and Potiphar," besides many others too numerous to mention.

But it was not to the pictures, or to the supper, or to the young ladies, that Mrs. Crow's attention was directed.

There was someone else who seemed to engross all her care and attention.

This was an elderly gentlemen, with an exceedingly wrinkled face, and a pair of legs which would have been of the thinnest, had not a little judicious padding been introduced here and there, to give them the symmetry they otherwise lacked.

He was a sprightly old gentleman, and one, too, who must have worn remarkably well.

He had beautiful, curly, light brown hair, almost flaxen, though it was rather curious how there should be grey hairs in such quantities in the nape of his neck.

He had the most beautiful teeth, only they did not seem to be as comfortable in his mouth as they might have been, and had a curious knack of trying to jump out from between his jaws, for all the world like a great ivory frog.

He had rather a wicked face too, had this gentleman; a wicked, purple, leering face, covered with wrinkles, as I have said, and crow's feet, and, besides a yellow goose-skin like integument, exceedingly unpleasant to look upon, I should fancy, when the gentleman first got up in the morning and was yet sallow and moist.

Yes, he was an ugly old man, most certainly, for all his beautifully fitting coat, with its velvet collar, his tightly strapped trowsers, and his brightly polished leather boots, for his three layers of silk waistcoats, and the huge mass of glittering gems upon his fingers.

And if there were ugly wicked looks upon his face, think you not that there were as ugly and as wicked thoughts within his heart?

Why, bless your innocence, he was as naughty an old nobleman as any to be found in London; which is saying a good deal, too.

He was, in fact, an awful bad one.

In his youth he had been a wild, devil-me-care young fellow, who had acquired a very unenviable notoriety in the bell-ringing and knocker-stealing line.

If he had been only a common John Smith, or Tom Jones, the British public would never have put up with half of his nonsense. John Bull is a fine, proud-spirited animal, which can, however, cringe to a nob as well as any other inferior sort of beast. As he was a lord, the world was not so very hard on him, as they might have been, and they laughed at his cub-like antics, and said that when he grew older he would be wiser, and perhaps, after all, not make a worse husband and father for being such a dreadful rake as a young bachelor.

I expect, reader, if you and I had indulged in such antics as this young nobleman, we should have been sent to Coventry, in double short time, but his lordship did not seem to suffer much for his vagaries.

He married the most beautiful woman in England—the woman with the largest fortune—and the woman with the greatest wit. He raised himself to the highest place in the senate,

and became the premier of England, and before him half the nation uncovered in respectful humility.

But he had forgotten and given over his youthful vices, you suppose. Bah! there are some vices which, when contracted, cannot be thrown away with life. He had no better—no—nor so good a character, now, this lord, as when his name was a by-word in all the haunts of profligacy and dissipation in this hot-bed of crime and corruption—modern Babylon.

Reader of mine, I do not often go in for these long descriptions, do I? You must excuse me this once, and surely, when I am introducing so important a character, and so distinguished a nobleman, I am not to be expected to do it all in a couple of lines.

Well, anyhow, here is my lord, ladies and gentlemen, and I hope you like him. A thoroughly depraved, unprincipled, godless, servile, blasphemous, lecherous old wretch. A peer of the realm, if you please. Take off your hats to him, gentlemen, and ladies bob him a curtsey.

Mrs. Crow, coming into the room, bobbed him one, and said—

"My lord, the room is ready."

"And the two Phillises?" said my lord; "How are they? What do they say to the arrangement?"

"Oh, them!" said Mrs. Crow, "They'll be agreeable, I've no doubt. You know the way to please the ladies, if anybody does."

"Do I—do I?" cried the hoary old sinner." "He! he! he! Do I, darling Mrs. Crow?"

"Don't he girls?" cried Mrs Crow.

"On course you do, my lord."

"Everybody owns to that."

"Everybody knows that's true as Gospel."

"What an old duck."

"Let me kiss him."

And all the young ladies rising simultaneously, made a rush at the shaky old nobleman, and smothered him with kisses.

To see all those playful young kittens gambolling round him, pressing their red pouting lips to his yellow cheeks, and squeezing him up to their warm scented bosoms, it was enough to make one wish one was a lord oneself. Only when you come to think how he had to pay for it all, the horrible reflection took a considerable quantity of the gilt off the gingerbread.

"Mrs. Crow," cried the old nobleman, kicking up his spider shanks in wild delight "Let's have a dozen of your best. What is it to be, girls?"

"Champagne," everybody voted.

And so champagne was brought, and drunk amid loud acclamation.

"And now for these little country girls," said his lordship. "Come along, Mrs. Crow, we'll go and make their acquaintance."

So saying, they left the room together, and descended to the parlour, where the Duchess and Lady Alice had been left in charge of the servant.

"You say they're very spirity, don't you?" asked the old nobleman.

"Very much so," replied Mrs. Crow. "They were dreadfully indignant at our shutting them up."

"He! he! that's what I like. I like a spirity woman, Mrs. Crow. I like to see 'em rave and storm, and stamp and tear their hair—particularly when they are quite helpless. It's twice the fun."

"Of course it is, my lord."

"It's twice the pleasure to take by force what they won't yield by persuasion."

"Of course it is, my lord."

"And you know just exactly the sort of article that suits me, darling Mrs. Crow."

"Of course I do, my lord."

"Of course you do—and I'll reward you, Mrs. Crow. You shall have a handsome pension when you give up trade, but not yet, my dear. We couldn't spare you yet. We really couldn't."

Thus chuckling over their infamy, the worthy couple arrived at the door of the parlour.

"Here they are," said Mrs. Crow, throwing open the door. "Here's the two little sluts."

His lordship toddled in, with a ghastly grin upon his wrinkled old phiz.

The Duchess turned round to meet him.

Then gave a little scream.

At the same time his lordship tumbled back upon Mrs. Crow, quite dumb-foundered.

"Gracious Heavens!" cried the Duchess. It's MY HUSBAND !"

"Gracious Heavens!" cried the Duke. "IT's MY WIFE !"

———

XLVI.—HUSBAND AND WIFE—ACCUSATIONS AND RECRIMINATIONS — A VILLAINOUS SCHEME IS CONCOCTED, OF WHICH MORE HEREAFTER.

IT formed quite a tableau, the meeting of these ladies and the old peer.

It would have been worth while to have photographed all their faces. They would have been invaluable as studies of dismay and astonishment.

For some time no one uttered a word.

Then said the Duke—

"Leave us, Mrs. Crow—leave us. I know these ladies, and wish to speak to them alone."

So Mrs. Crow dropped a curtsey, and going outside, applied her ear to the key-hole, and listened her hardest.

"Well, Madam," said the Duke, when they were alone, "what explanation have you to offer?"

The Duchess was silent.

"I thought you were in bed," said the Duke.

"I thought you were there, also," retorted the lady. "A pretty place this for a peer of the realm to be found in."

"Me found in—damnation—madam. How about you?"

"About me?"

"Yes—with a man it's different; but, curse me, a woman can have no explanation to give."

"I don't intend to give any, my lord."

"You think to pooh-pooh me, do you? By God! I will have a divorce."

"Have what you choose, my lord, but please not to attempt to bully me."

"Ah! madam, I can see that you have, indeed, sunk low. And Lady Alice—I am grieved—"

"My lord—my lord," cried the young lady, throwing herself upon her knees before him, "I intreat of you—I beseech you, do not go away with a false impression. We are the victims of circumstances. We have been lured into this den of wickedness, without the slightest suspicion of the character of the place."

"Perhaps," said the peer, in a less angry tone, "Her Grace will condescend to explain."

"I shall do nothing of the kind," retorted the Duchess, indignantly. "At least, not in this place. Since you seem to be in authority here, perhaps you will be kind enough to give orders for our release."

"Madam," cried the Duke, boiling over with rage. "This must not continue. It is to both our interests to remain, to outward appearance, friends; although from this time all love must cease between us."

"I quite agree with you," said the Duchess, with a scornful laugh. "I am willing to pardon you, if you apologise for what you have said. I have found out what a horrible old wretch you are, and what company you keep. But let that pass."

"Madam—this language !"

"If, on the other hand, you dare to cast a slur on my character."

"Dare! why hell and furies !"

"Dare, I repeat. I will resort to other means of receiving reparation for the gross insult."

"But do you mean to say that I am to find you here, in a house of ill-fame, and take you home and ask for no explanation?"

"Do I ask for one of you?"

"No; but damn it, that is quite another thing."

"In what way?"

"Why men can do what they like; but—"

"Indeed! That's a very pretty rule, my lord, but I beg to dispute it."

"In any case, madam, we will discuss this matter at another time and place."

"To-morrow, then."

"To-morrow be it."

"Will you give the order, then, to your friend to allow us to pass."

The Duke made no reply; but opening the door (almost too quickly for Mrs. Crow), he bade her allow the ladies to pass out into the street.

When they were gone, and the Duke, too, had taken his departure, Mr. Jack Rattan came upstairs from the kitchen, and took Mrs. Crow on one side.

"You've done it to rights, you have;" said he, with a chuckle.

"What could I do else?" asked Mrs. Crow, indignantly.

"Why didn't you listen to me, then," said Rattan. "I wanted to tell you who she was, but you wouldn't hear me."

"Well, it can't be helped; we must do better next time."

"I hope so. I've thought of a little plant which I think we may make some money out of."

"Who is it to be put on?"

"On the Duke."

"The Duke."

"Yes; he uses your house reg'lar, don't he?"

"He's the chief support of it."

"Then he's pretty flush?"

"He is worth a couple of millions, I should think."

"Very well, then, we'll ease him of some of it."

"What, rob him?"

"No, not exactly. Listen."

And the ruffian whispered something in the old woman's ear.

"Good God!" she exclaimed, "what a horrible thing."

"But how shall we manage it?" she added, presently.

Then they talked their scheme over.

"By-the-way, there's a rum thing happened," said Rattan, after a while, "you know I carry the stiffuns from Saint Starver's to the hospital and doctor's?"

"Yes."

"Who do you think is lying ill in the workhouse?"

"Who, pray?"

"You recollect young Horford, who was such a friend of the Duke of Heatherland, when they used to be on the town together?"

"What, he who used to be mixed up in the Springheel Jack business?"

"Yes, the same. He was a great friend of the Duke's."

"And all at once he left him, it is said; and when the Duke wanted to know why he avoided his society, said that he had done the Duke a frightful injury, which he dare not explain, and that they must never meet again."

"What a rum thing, wasn't it? And the mystery was never cleared up, eh?"

"No, never. And what's more, the Duke could never discover how he had been injured. Indeed, he thought Horford was mad."

"Well, now he is a pauper in the workhouse."

"Poor fellow! he was a good friend to me in my time. I wish I could serve him."

"In that case," said Rattan, "get him away from the workhouse."

"I will, indeed; that is, if he will come."

"I dare say he will; paupers aint usually over proud."

"I'll go to-day."

"Lose no time, is my advice. I shouldn't leave a friend of mine at Saint Starver's longer than I could help."

"And about this trick on the Duke."

"I will arrange it all."

And so the worthy pair separated, and betook themselves to their couches.

Nice mother and nice son, were they not, gentle reader?

XLVII.—Saint Starver-Cum-Bag-o'-Bones.

DO you remember, reader, how, in the twenty-third chapter of the present book of Charley Wag's veracious history, Mr. Bloodyer, the master of the workhouse of Saint Starver-cum-Bag-o'-Bones, mentioned to Mr. Faversham that a new pauper had arrived, who gave his name as Smith, but who was supposed to have no right to that very popular patronymic.

"He seemed to be a reckless, dare-devil, sort of a chap, sick of life and everything else," Mr. Bloodyer had said.

Upon which, Mr. Faversham had replied, that if he were tired of life he had come to the right shop.

When Rattan called to take away the dead body of Cudder, an incident occurred which led to Rattan's discovering the real name of this homeless man.

After they quitted the dead-house, Bloodyer and the doctor returned to the former's private room, where, drawing their chairs close to the fire, they brewed a couple of stiff glasses of grog, and sat down to wait until Rattan arrived.

They said very little to one another, both being too busily occupied by their own thoughts to care about entering upon a conversation on indifferent topics, and the dead-body trade was a subject which they rarely alluded to, even when by themselves, and confident of being out of hearing.

But as the time slipped by, the workhouse master at length broke the silence and said,

"It was most unfortunate, that we had to put that old man out of the way."

"Why so?" asked the other. "was it not necessary to make him safe?"

"As he knew so much, or suspected so much, I think it was. But, do you not think he will be missed and traced here."

"If he is he will be moved away."

"But you won't send him to the hospital, will you, for fear he should be recognised."

"No; he shall go to my surgery, and I will soon get rid of him."

"And Cudder, having used the quick medicine, we shall not be able to send his body either."

"No; I must get rid of it in the same way as the other."

"But, then, suppose Cudder's wife were to come forward to claim the body. She might do, you know. In that case she might want to see it."

"In that case, then, I should show her a body."

"What, the right one?"

"No, another."

"But she would know it."

"I don't think so—without the head."

"But why not have the body burned in quick lime, and give typhus as the cause of death?"

"Because I do not like to trust the ground with my secrets. I like to keep them under my hand and lock them up."

"How do you mean?"

CHARLEY'S CARRIAGE STOPS THE WAY.

So saying, and with a sneering laugh at the workhouse master's poltroonery, Faversham took the key and left the room.

There was a door in the yard close to the dead-house, which led out into a dark, dirty little lane, and through this the bodies were carried at night when the inmates of the workhouse slept.

There was no particular reason in general why this should have been done in so quiet a manner, except that it was part of Faversham's system to do everything he did in the most mysterious and stealthy fashion.

On this occasion, however, it was necessary that more than usual caution should be observed.

The doctor wished the circumstances connected with Cudder's death to be known to as few people as possible, at the same time that he wished no suspicion of aiming at secrecy to creep into the mind of any person connected with the establishment.

Therefore he had called in the aid of the persons usually employed in laying out the dead bodies, to lay out Toddleboy's body, which had been substituted for Cudder's corpse.

All he wanted now was to get both bodies off the premises, and then he would breathe again freely.

As he stepped out into the yard a low whistle was again heard, and the doctor hurried forward to open the outer door.

"Who is it?" he whispered.

"Rattan," replied the other.

Then he opened the door.

No. 19.

[CHARLEY WAG, THE NEW JACK SHEPPARD

" You told me to come round to-night. Have you a job?"

" Yes. Is anyone with you?"

" No—"

" I'm sorry for that. You won't be able to lift it."

" Why not? I can manage the stiff un, however heavy he is."

" But there are two of them."

" What, both in the same shell?"

" Yes."

" Golly! that's wholesale. Never mind though, I'll manage them."

So saying, they walked together towards the dead-house, but at the very moment that they were opening the door, the window was thrown open behind them, and to their amazement a figure in white appeared, wildly waving its arms, preparatory, as it seemed, to taking a jump out into the yard.

" What the devil is that?" said Rattan, staggering back; " it's a man."

" I think so. What is he doing?"

" He is trying to get out upon the window-sill. Here, come with me."

Rattan followed the doctor into the house, and into the work-house master's room.

" Did you hear that noise?" he asked.

" Yes, yes," replied Bloodyer, in an agitated voice.

" What was it? What has happened?"

" One of the cursed paupers gone out of his mind it seems. We had better go up and look."

He took the light as he spoke, and the three men proceeded up stairs to the room, from the window of which they had seen this strange apparition.

It was a long dormitory in which there were some thirty or forty beds, all occupied by paupers.

Over there there were two warders appointed to keep watch, one at a time. But it seemed that the man they had seen had crept out of bed quickly, and was half out of the window by the time that the warder saw him.

At the moment that they came into the room, the latter was endeavouring to pull him back by the leg.

———

XLVIII.—Another new Character appears in our Story, and one who has much more to do with the Plot than the reader might at first be inclined to think.

IT was not without very considerable difficulty that this outrageous pauper was hauled in at the window and induced to lie down in bed.

" Who is he?" the doctor asked.

" It's a new one," the attendant replied.

" That one who came to-day?"

" Yes, sir."

" The man I was speaking to you about," said Bloodyer.

" The man who said his name was Smith."

The self-called Smith was a dark-skinned, ragged-haired, wild-looking fellow, who might have been thirty or thereabouts, but looked a good deal older. Held down in bed by the attendant and the strongest pauper available for the service, he rolled his head from side to side in a weary, restless fashion, moaning unceasingly.

For a time he struggled and fought with those who held him, but after a while his strength being spent by his violent efforts to regain his liberty, he sank back overcome with fatigue, and closing his eyes rolled his head gently to and fro, and groaned in a faint subdued way, like one who was worn almost to death by mental and physical agony.

The Doctor approached the bedside at this juncture, and taking the man's wrist in his hand, felt his pulse.

" He is quiet now," said Faversham.

Then turning to those standing round:

" You can go," he said, " you (to the attendant) be within call."

" A troublesome customer," observed the workhouse master, when he, Faversham, and Rattan were left to themselves.

" One I should physic," said Mr. Rattan, " if I had the doing of him."

" But you haven't the doing of him, as you term it," retorted the workhouse master, " so you need not make any suggestions."

" Look here—look here!" cried the Doctor, suddenly interrupting them.

The workhouse master turned towards him inquiringly.

" What is it?" he asked.

The Doctor pointed to the man's breast.

" See," said he, " did you notice this locket?"

" A locket!"

" Yes, look!"

Sure enough, there was a locket hanging to the man's neck by a thin gold chain. The locket itself was of gold, with a row of emeralds let into the back.

" Rather an expensive bit of jewellery for a pauper to carry," said Jack Rattan, staring over their shoulders.

The Doctor undid the clasp of the chain, and took the locket into his hand.

" It opens, don't it?" asked Bloodyer.

It did, and after some little difficulty the Doctor managed to find the spring. Touching this, the lid sprang up, and they found it to contain a portrait.

" A woman!" said Bloodyer.

" A handsome one," said Rattan.

Faversham made no remark. He was busily engaged, endeavouring to decipher some old English characters running round the picture.

" I can read them, I think," said Bloodyer; and he began to spell them up. T.O, to, M.Y, my, D.E.A.R, dear, S.O.N, son, F.R.O.M, from, H.I.S, his, L.O.V.I.N.G, loving, M.O.T.H.E.R, mother, H.E.L.E.N.A, Helena, H.O.R.F.O.R.D, Horford."

" Horford!" cried Rattan. " It can't be young Horford—the Honourable Jack Horford, as they used to call Handsome Jack."

" Perhaps it is," said Bloodyer, " I never heard of him."

" Never heard of him," said Rattan, " he was one of the notabilities on town when I was a young man,—ah! not more than fifteen years ago. Everybody was talking of him then."

" What did he do?"

"He got up to every imaginable sort of lark, bless you. It was him started the spring-heel Jack business, and used to frighten all the servant girls almost out of their lives. You must recollect the time when nobody couldn't get their beer fetched of a evening 'cause the gals was all afeared Spring-heel Jack would get hold on 'em by the leg, or some sich game?"

"To be sure, I rememember that."

"Remember it, of course you do, and that was handsome Jack."

"But then I always thought there was another mixed up in it."

"So there was."

"A duke, wasn't it."

"Yes, the Duke of Heatherland. Ever so much older than Handsome Jack, and a precious sight worse. A regular devil they say. There wasn't never much harm in Jack, and the other led him on. No! if it is him, all I can say is, that he's been a trump, has Jack Horford."

"Who calls?" cried the refractory pauper, struggling to gain an upright position.

They had been speaking in a low tone, and until now no word of their conversation had apparently caught his ear until Rattan, pronouncing the name of Horford louder than the rest, he had opened his eyes and glared round him with a wild, frightened look, like that of a hunted hare.

"Who calls?" he cried again.

But the Doctor, taking him by the shoulders, thrust him back again upon the pillow.

"Here," he called to the attendants, "we will put him in a straight-waistcoat. That will save a good deal of trouble."

They thereupon seized the unfortunate man, and bound and strapped him up so tightly that he could move neither hand nor foot. Then left him to himself.

"It is time that we went to our business," said the Doctor, in a low tone to Rattan. "I should like to ask you a question or two about this Horford upon some other occasion."

"I will take care of the locket," said the workhouse master, slipping it into his breeches pocket.

* * * * *

Throughout the night he rolled and tossed, Throughout the livelong weary night.

From side to side, from side to side, he rolled his weary head. From his dry, cracked, feverish lips, strange incoherent mutterings fell, which reaching the attendants' ear, made him start up from his forty winks, astonished, half doubting that he had heard aright.

"Lie quiet, can't you?" said this latter indignantly.

"Forgive me—forgive me—forgive me!" the sick man cried, wandering in his uneasy sleep, "Forgive me the wrong I have done you."

"Forgive you? Yes! I'll forgive you, with a clout on the head, if you ain't quiet."

"I did not know that I was wronging you, my lord. Oh! my God! how I have suffered for it. I ask your pardon before I die."

"I wish you was dead, that's all I've got to say about it."

The pauper was silent for a while, and the attendant dozed off to sleep.

But not for long.

Again the other began to shout and rave, and again had the watcher to remonstrate indignantly, while the other paupers sleeping in the room, complained bitterly of their slumbers being disturbed.

From side to side—from side to side, the weary head yet rolled and tossed.

Throughout the night,
The livelong night.

———

XLIX.—In which Toddleboy comes to Grief.

OLD Bung was not a man to be trifled with. You might have had your joke with Bottle, perhaps. That is, if you happened to catch him in the right humour—which wasn't often; and you might have wrung a smile out of him. But I never heard of Bung's smiling.

He couldn't do it. The muscles of his mouth did not allow of such an amiable contraction.

He was a terrible old tyke was Bung, before whom the hearts of his hirelings quaked, and the knees of the boldest shook beneath him in the awful presence.

Now, unfortunately for Toddleboy, Bung had taken it into his head to come to business much earlier on the morning that the old man had been discovered in the cupboard at Miss Gusset's establishment, so that when he made his appearance at his employer's warehouse under the guidance of a policeman, and wrapped up in a scrap of sacking and an old rag of a shawl, the first person he met after crossing the threshold of Messrs. Bottle and Bung's shop, was Bung himself, with his hands under his coat tails, and his spectacles on his nose, looking very tremendous.

"Well, sir," said Bung. "What's all this about?"

Now, it was a long, not to say an improbable story, and Mr. Toddleboy hardly knew which way to begin.

The policeman stepped in to explain.

He had found the prisoner in the state in which he then was, concealed in a cupboard in Miss Gusset's establishment — doubtless for a felonious purpose.

Where were his clothes, Mr. Bung inquired.

The old man commenced his story. As he proceeded the grin, which at the first few words had begun to dawn upon the policeman's face, spread more and more, until the corners of his mouth threatened to meet at the back of his had.

"It ain't likely, sir, is it?" he asked of Bung.

"The man is mad!" cried Bung.

"Mad as a March hare," said the policeman.

"Unless he's drunk," said Bung.

"I think he's a little drunk too," said the policeman.

"He went to collect some money of mine last night," remarked Bung. "I suppose I may demand it of him now?"

"I haven't got it," cried old Toddleboy. "It was taken away from me with my clothes."

"I give him in custody, then," said Bung, "upon a charge of embezzlement."

"He is in custody already, sir; but you can prosecute after the other charge is disposed of."

"I shall do so."

" If you come to the court about eleven it will do, sir."

" Which court ?"

" Thames-street is the nearest."

" Can't you take him to Quod-street ? Mr. Slang is a friend of mine."

" Very well, sir; I daresay it can be managed."

So Toddleboy was taken off to the police-station as soon as he had had time to slip on two or three articles of clothing which belonged to him, and which he kept at the warehouse, in case he should require at some time or other to do some very dirty work.

After the inspector had taken the charge, the old man was locked up, of course; and as he had no money in his pockets—nor, indeed, any at his lodgings—he was unable to send to Miss Williams to acquaint her with his melancholy predicament.

About twelve o'clock his case came on ; and when it had been heard, he was called upon by Mr. Slang for an explanation.

The explanation was therefore given at considerable length, the worthy magistrate occasionally interrupting it with an impatient exclamation of incredulity.

" Absurd !" he cried, when Toddleboy had finished.   " Perfectly absurd !"

The old man protested vehemently that what he had said was true.

" Is the man mad, policeman ?" asked Mr. Slang.

" He's in liquor, I think, sir," replied that official.

" Was he drunk when you took him in custody?" asked Mr. Slang.

" Very drunk indeed," replied the policeman.

It is a very curious fact, but every other prisoner, according to the police, is in a state of intoxication. I don't know how it is, but ask any one who frequents police-courts if such is not the case.

" I should suggest that he should be sent to a lunatic asylum," the clerk said, in a whisper.

" An old vagabond !" cried Mr. Slang. " I'll give him a month instead."

But while he was hesitating Mr. Bung stepped forward and made his statement.

" Ah !" says the magistrate, " this is serious. I shall send him for trial."

But as the old man begged that he might have a little time to clear himself, the clerk suggested that Mr. Slang should remand him until that day week.

" If you do," said Mr. Bung, " I shall have to waste another day about the matter. You will do me a great favour if you commit him at once."

" Is this a land of liberty—?" began Toddleboy ; but he was quickly silenced.

" Three months with hard labour," said Slang.

Then the old man began to protest against the injustice and illegality of the whole proceeding. Why was not the truth of his story inquired into ? What reason was there for thinking him a thief? For the last sixteen years, off and on, he had served Mr. Bung and Mr. Bottle faithfully. Had they ever had a charge of dishonesty to bring against him ?

He was repeatedly drunk.

Well, he owned that ; but because he had been drunk that did not prove that he was a thief.

Didn't it ?   A drunkard was capable of anything.

Poor old Toddleboy !   He went off to prison in the van that afternoon, and everybody thought him a hardened old vagabond.

What do you think, reader ?

You think, no doubt, that there is gross exaggeration in what I have been telling you. Perhaps you do not know much about police-courts. I am glad you do not, for your sake.

There is some funny justice done there sometimes. If I were to sit down and write some things that I have heard about them, why I believe that Charley Wag would stop next week, and that his countless thousands of readers would LOOK OUT for him in vain.

———

L.—CHARLEY WAG MAKES HIS BOW AS THE BOY BURGLAR.

IT was a week or two after Toddleboy's committal that Charles Wag, Esquire, made his appearance before Mr. Slang of Quod-street.

I have been obliged to go backwards and forwards with my story, but have now brought the adventures of all my characters up to the same period.

George and he were taken to the Quod-street police-station, and charged by Ralph Faversham with attempting a burglarious entrance into the mansion of His Grace the Duke of Heatherland.

The last time that Charley was in difficulties I described the police-station, and now need only briefly state that he was locked up all night, and next morning, about half-past eleven, made his bow to his worship.

His worship recognized our hero immediately.

" Ah !" said he, I did not think it would be very long before I saw you again."

Here Charley protested his innocence.

" Yes, I dare say," said Mr. Slang. " You look an innocent sort of subject, you do."

" There is several charges against him," said one of the policemen.   " There have been bills stuck up all over London for a month or more, offering fifty pounds for his apprehension."

" I shall send him to prison for six months, with hard labour," said his worship.

" Six months" was a favourite term with Mr. Slang. He gave it to a dozen people at least in the course of a week.

" What is known against the other prisoner ?" asked Mr. Slang.

There was a great deal of suspicion against the other prisoner, but nothing was known for certain.

It was his first offence, and he also had his six months.

" Have you anything to say for yourself?" asked the magistrate.

George, if he had, declined to say it, or to take any notice.

The magistrate repeated the question.

" Yes," said the robber, suddenly looking up. " The boy is not to blame. If any one is to go to limbo, it ought to be me. I made the boy do it."

" Yes, that's very fine, I daresay," observed

Mr. Slang. "However, you shall both go to gaol together; and all I have got to say is, that I hope it will do you both good."

"Oh, sir!" cried Charley, "what have I done that I should be so persecuted? Will nobody say a good word for me?"

"I will, Charley," cried a female voice among the spectators.

"Who's that?" asked Mr. Slang, indignantly. "I'll commit them, whoever it is."

It turned out to be a very pretty young woman, who wished to say a few words in favour of the young prisoner.

"Let her stand forward," said Mr. Slang.

"Young woman, stand forward," said one policeman.

"Stand forward, young woman," said another policeman.

And, thus advised, the young woman did stand forward, and curtsied to his worship.

"What's your name?"

Her name was Julia Jenkini. If his worship wanted to know particularly, it was not Jenkini.

Then why did she say it was?

Because she was generally known as Jenkini.

"Oh, it's one of your aliases, is it?" said Mr. Slang.

"One of my what, sir?"

"A false name you go under for some unlawful purpose."

"No, it isn't," retorted Miss Julia; "it is my professional name."

"Professional name, eh? A pretty profession! I wonder you're not ashamed of yourself."

At this Miss Julia got very indignant, and asked him what he meant. And so, after a great deal of beating about the bush, it came out that Miss Jenkins was the celebrated Jenkini of Muggins's Music-hall, who had had the honour, according to the bills, of appearing before all the crowned heads of Europe.

"And pray what have you got to say?" asked Mr. Slang, when the question of Miss Julia's profession had been satisfactorily settled. "Pray what have you to say?"

Then came the poser. Miss Julia really had next to nothing to say, although she had been very anxious to come forward and make her statement.

What little she did say certainly did not tend to exculpate the prisoner.

What did she know of him? She had first made his acquaintance at a street fight. He was then without a home. She had been locked out of her lodgings. Mr. Wag had accompanied her to a coffee-house of very questionable morality, and had been indebted to her generosity for a bed.

"I should very much like to know the name of anybody who would speak to your character," said Mr. Slang to Charley, with a sarcastic smile.

"Well, I'll tell you," said Mr. Wag; and, by way of improving the magistrate's opinion of him, he named Toddleboy.

"Toddleboy, is it?" cried Mr. Slang. "A pretty person to speak to character. A man I myself sent to prison for felony. One of the most incorrigible liars I ever had the misfortune to listen to."

There was no hope for him. Poor Charley saw that he was doomed.

"Six months with hard labour," said Mr.

Slang. "Remove the prisoners, and call the next case."

So, without more ado, Charley was removed to his cell, "to wait for the waggon."

———

LI.—CHARLEY WAG BECOMES A BURTHEN TO HIS COUNTRY, BUT IS NEVERTHELESS NOT ONLY PROVIDED WITH A SPACIOUS TOWN MANSION TO RESIDE IN, BUT IS CONDUCTED THERE FREE OF CHARGE, IN A HANDSOME CARRIAGE AND PAIR OF HER MAJESTY'S PROVIDING.

ANY afternoon in Quod-street, you may if you so think fit, see "Black Maria" waiting at the door of the police-station, for its load of ladies and gentlemen, bound for the mystic realms of Limbo.

In fewer words—THE PRISONERS' VAN.

You know the song, perhaps.

"Sing, wentilator, separate cell,
It's long and dark and hot as well,
Sing locked up doors—get out if you can;
There's a crusher outside of the prisoner's van."

A very handsome conveyance, is it not? Perhaps rather too sombre in colour, but that is a matter of taste. A sort of Jack Ketch's omnibus, with a policeman driver and a policeman conductor, not to mention a policeman passenger in the little narrow passage within, which divides the carriage in half. And it is the duty of this latter gentleman, to see that no communication takes place between the occupants of the various cells, opening from the corridor in which he is stationed. While the conductors duty is, of course, to keep the outer door securely locked.

About a quarter to five on any afternoon, all the year round, you may see the "reglars," the ladies and gentlemen, who live in Sloggers-alley, or Cop-court, or Scraggings-rents, assembling in great force.

Oh! what a forlorn-looking, debased, godless company it is, forsooth.

And here comes "Her Majesty's carriage."

Who are to be the passengers this afternoon?

First, a grimy, ferocious-looking gentlemen, who has got into trouble for wife-beating. He does not seem to be popular, and the crowd groan at the sight of him.

Next, a well-known pickpocket, smartly attired, but with a very hang-dog look about him. As he comes down the steps from the police-court, he glances eagerly around among the faces surrounding him, and singles out some friend.

"How much, Bill?" this person calls.

"Two," says the pickpocket, at the same time holding up two fingers.

"Labour?" asked the friend.

The pickpocket nods his head.

"Now then," interrupts the policeman, "none of that," and he pushes the thief into the conveyance.

After him comes another party, who has a friend in the crowd. A lady friend this time.

"Don't forget the clean things on Sunday, Sal," says he.

What clean things? and why does he want

them? and where is he going to? I have not the least idea.

Next to him, George, sullen and gloomy.

Next to him, the Boy Burglar.

There were other boys—boys of ten, as hardened in vice as men of fifty, who had been to prison half-a-dozen times before, and did not care a button for the punishment; but poor Charley hung his head, and was overwhelmed with shame, when he first came out into the broad daylight, beneath the stare of the crowd.

But it was not for long. When he came to reflect how hardly he was being used, and that he was in fact a martyr, he plucked up his courage, and with a bold step and flashing eyes took his way to the carriage.

"What a pretty boy!" some of the women in the crowd remarked as he passed by.

"What a duck of a boy!" said others.

"What's he in for?"

"He don't look guilty, does he."

"Bless you, them quiet ones is altogether the worst."

"Ah, you're right there, Mrs. Grundy. He's a bad 'un, if ever there was one."

Upon the step he turned and saw Julia in the crowd, weeping bitterly.

He waved his hand to her, and she waved hers to him, and held up a cat. She had brought the celebrated Tom to see him off.

He tried to smile, and waved his hand to her again. And then the policeman pushed him in.

Next minute the door was slammed to, and Her Majesty's carriage started on its journey, while the wretched crowd left behind raised the ghost of a cheer, by way of encouragement.

And Charley Wag's wife and cat departed also, one crying and the other singing. Don't, please, put Tom down for a hard-hearted animal. I am sure he was not: bless you he thought his master was having a nice ride, and he was glad to see him enjoy himself.

*　　*　　*　　*　　*

That evening, the Doctor called upon the Duchess, and described what had taken place at the police-court.

"An old offender, it seems," said Faversham. "There was a person there of the name of Leech, who would have prosecuted, had the case not been sufficiently strong without him."

"Did you speak to him?" the Duchess asked, anxiously.

"Yes," the other replied.

"He—he did not say what the other charge was."

"No, he did not go into particulars."

"How much have they given this—this—What did you say his name was?"

"George Measles."

"No; the other."

"Charley Wag?"

"Yes."

"They gave him six months."

"Only six months?"

"That is a long while, though. Perhaps your grace is not acquainted with the severity of prison discipline. He is to be on the silent system."

"I have always understood that these prisons are hot-beds of vice, and that if a boy were not even a thief when he went in, he would be sure

to be corrupted while he was there. Is that the case?"

"No," replied Faversham. "I believe that these things are altered now, and that a great many prisoners are reformed."

The Duchess said nothing, but bit her lips and walked away.

She turned, however, before she reached the door, and said in quite an altered tone, and one full of tenderness and love.

"How is my son to-day, doctor? Have you seen him?"

"Ah!" sighed Faversham, "I fear he is no better. Even worse to-day than yesterday. The alarm of last night may have thrown him back."

"But you must apply stimulants. What can we do for him? Name anything. Oh, Doctor! if you would only restore my poor dear boy to health, I would give you every half-penny I have in the world, if you desired it."

"My dear, madam," replied Faversham, "you know that I am devoted to your interests, and that all that lies in my power I would do—and do do."

"I am sure of that," the lady replied, squeezing his hand. "God bless you."

But still the young scion of a noble house lay on his bed of sickness, and the sands of his life were fast ebbing away.

As the twilight gathered in the street, the doctor stood at the bow window thinking.

"Three more," he muttered to himself: "three more between me and wealth; three more, and I shall be avenged. The son first, then the mother, and then the father; but on the last I will wreak a vengeance with which the others shall be as naught. Patience, patience, the time is not far distant."

Thus did the monster plot and plan, and lay his deadly schemes for the future.

How far they were carried out we shall see in the future chapters of this eventful history.

Even now, as the shades of night crept across the park, and encompassed the spot on which he stood, the shadow of the hand of GOD crept towards him unheeded and unseen.

The blow was coming.

When?

We shall see.

LII.—SPIKE ISLAND.

COME along, reader; we will go to gaol together.

Which? you say. Never mind which. I have private and particular reasons for not wishing to name the one we are going to. I call it, just for the sake of calling it something, "Spike Island."

It is not a thousand miles from the Bank; never mind in what direction. We will take an omnibus; never mind which. Now suppose we have got there: let us knock at the door.

A grim-looking gentleman looks at us through a small grating; and, finding he has such distinguished visitors as you and I, reader, admits us without a murmur.

He is a very grim man, though, this guardian

of the gate; and he carries at his girdle a large quantity of iron in the shape of keys.

With one of these, and with a very slight effort, he opens the iron door, and admits us to the prison; then shuts the door again behind us, and locks it fast.

Passing through a yard beyond the gate, you come to an extensive aisle, which is crossed at right angles by another aisle of similar size. In the centre of each there is a spiral staircase made of iron, with perforated steps. Going up either of these, you come to long corridors, all studded with doors, which lead to the prisoner's cells.

The interior of these is in every case alike.

They are whitewashed, and very clean. In the wall on either side of the apartment are two staples of polished steel, about a yard from the ground. The prisoner's mattrass, which is made of cocoa bark, has two stout iron hooks at each end, which, when the bed is made up, are hooked into the staples; so that the prisoner, when in bed, lies right across the cell.

In one corner of the room there are some shelves fixed, on which are arranged a bright pewter plate, a knife and fork, and a wooden spoon. Underneath this there is a drawer, in which there is a remarkably angular piece of yellow soap, and a brush and comb.

There is also a little deal table, three quarters of a yard square, and a deal stool.

There is a small gas-pipe, and a water-spout, which can be directed either into a fixed copper basin at one side, or into a bottomless close-stool on the other.

Close down there is a grating to admit hot air, and close to the ceiling another for foul air to escape.

On the wall hang the printed rules of the prison and seveaal small placards, similar to those used in infant schools, containing texts of Scripture.

There were also a slate and pencil, and a couple of leathern knee-caps to be used by the prisoner while polishing the floor of his cell.

Altogether it really looks very comfortable, only, I suppose, like most other good things, one gets tired of it after a bit, and I believe there have been some prisoners sufficiently ungrateful to try to get away.

The dietary table of Spike Island is as follows:—

	Soup.	Gruel.	Meat.	Bread.
	Pints.	Pints.	Ounces.	Ounces.
Monday	—	2¼	—	20
Tuesday............	—	1¼	6	20
Wednesday	—	2¼	—	20
Thursday	—	2¼	—	20
Friday	1	1¼	—	20
Saturday	—	1¼	6	20
Sunday	1	1¼	—	20
Total per Week	2	13¼	12	140

Sumptuous fare, is it not; and yet, would you believe it, there are some prisoners who grumble. Now, at the workhouse it is different. Its short commons and no mistake. What do you think of this:—

	Bread.	Gruel.	Meat.	Bacon.	Potato's.	Soup.	Cheese.	Suet Pudding
	ozs.	pts.	ozs.	ozs.	ozs.	pts.	ozs.	ozs.
Monday	14	1½	—	—	—	1½	2	—
Tuesday	21	1¼	—	—	—	—	4	—
Wednesday	14	1¼	—	—	—	1½	2	—
Thursday	14	1¼	—	4	8	—	2	—
Friday..........	14	1¼	—	—	—	—	2	14
Saturday	14	1¼	—	—	—	1½	2	—
Sunday	14	1¼	5	—	8	1½	—	—
Grand Total	105	10¼	5	4	16	6	14	14

And that is for the able-bodied men. Mind you, the able-bodied hungry women get less, and as for the infirm paupers, there's no knowing what they get, or rather, I should say, what they don't get. They have each one ounce of tea and seven ounces of sugar weekly, instead of gruel for breakfast. Think of that! what stiff tea you could make with an ounce for seven meals.

Then don't run away with the notion that those able-bodied men who live as you, in clover, do nothing for it. They pick their four pounds of oakum per day; break stones, and a variety of other work. They haven't much idle time left them, I can assure you.

And now I think I have said all that I need do at present of the interior arrangements of Spike Island. A young gentleman of your acquaintance of the name of Wag, is going to be a boarder here for some little time, so we shall see how he gets on, and I will describe the daily life of the Spike Islanders more minutely.

When the young prisoner arrived he was conducted to a room on the ground floor; ordered to strip naked, and get into a bath. His clothes were then taken from him, and baked in an oven, and another suit of clothes given to him.

A peculiar sort of uniform this was, with a cap of coarse material, and to this was attached a visor, or mask, which concealed the features all but the chin and eyes, which peeped out in a strange glassy way, through two holes cut for that purpose.

After this he was conducted to his cell, and the various offices with respect to cleaning the same, explained to him.

The prison was awfully silent, and the warder even seemed to speak in a subdued voice.

"Ain't there any other prisoners?" asked Charley; for everything was so still, he almost fancied that he must be there alone.

"Four hundred," said the man.

"Where are they?" asked Charley.

"Shut up," replied the man; though whether he referred to the confinement of the prisoners, or would have suggested that Master Charley should be silent, is doubtful.

" Don't we ever see one another ?" he asked presently.

" Talking's not allowed, Number Ten," rejoined the gaoler gruffly; and, leaving the room, slammed the door after him.

" This is a lively look-out," said Mr. Wag to himself, when he was alone. " I havn't even got a name to call my own. Number Ten, eh ? I wonder when skillogolee time comes. I'm dreadfully peckish."

Skillogolee time, however, seemed to be a long while off.

He waited for it until he felt very hungry.

Then went on waiting until he felt faint.

But it did not come.

" They don't seem to run to suppers," said Charley.

" I Suppose breakfast is the grand meal."

Just when he was giving it up for a bad job, a warder suddenly opened a little trap in the door, and shoved in the long-looked-for victuals.

" Prime prog this," said Mr. Wag, stirring it round with disgust.

It consisted of three-quarters of a pint of gruel and six ounces of bread.

" Just enough to make one feel hungry," said Charley.

" I think I could tackle another dollop, if it wasn't quite so loathsome."

It was remarkably thin gruel, by the way, and the bread was black.

Not very long after supper was over a bell rang, which a warder looked in to tell him was for bed, and about a quarter of an hour afterwards the man looked round again to see whether he had obeyed the order.

He had done so, and had made himself as comfortable as circumstances allowed of.

" Good night, sir," said he to the man.

But the latter slammed to the door without making any answer, and went away up the passage to look after the other boarders.

" They don't go in for civility," said Charley, as he popped his head under the clothes.

And he tried to go to sleep and forget his troubles.

He was a reckless, light-hearted, easy-going, young scamp, was this Mr. Wag, but he must have been a very hardened scamp indeed, to have borne his present situation, without some feelings of grief, shame, and remorse.

In vain he turned from side to side upon his hard bed, sleep refused to visit his eyes, and rest his fatigued and aching limbs.

It was not until past midnight that he got to sleep.

Poor boy ! Had thou a woman's heart, proud Duchess of Heatherland, the sight of that poor, little, innocent, boyish face, lying there so tranquil and so still, would surely bring the tears of pity to thine eyes !

Sleep on, poor boy. God only knows what troubles yet await thee ! Sleep on ! Perchance 'twere better dids't thou never wake again, than to awake to such a fate as that which awaits a felon in this dread abode of SECRET DEATH.

END OF BOOK THE SECOND.

BOOK THE THIRD. THE JAIL BIRD.

I.—CHARLEY THE CAPTIVE.

GENTLE Reader, allow me to introduce to your notice a handsome young gentleman of about fifteen years of age, of the name of Charles Wag, commonly called Charley. He is sitting in a clean and airy, though scantily furnished, apartment, in a large and imposing building of the Gothic style, capable of, and containing, several hundred other young gentlemen, whom a generous government provide gratuitously with all the necessaries of life—that is to say, bread and water, skillogalee, and stringy boiled beef.

It I must speak plainer, he s in gaol, though I should have preferred so dreadful a statement

No. 20.

to have been printed in the very smallest italics, it is really such a dreadful beginning.

Well, then, without further preface, let us suppose that Master Charles has slept his first night in Spike Island, and has woke up on the first morning of his captivity feeling, as he termed it, rather "peckish."

It was half-past five, and the loud discordant prison bell was ringing for the warders to get up.

Half-an-hour afterwards, a turnkey opened the door of the cell, and, poking in his head, growled as follows:—

"Number Ten, get up and wash your face, and neck and hands, shake your bedding, roll your hammock up, and clean your cell, and get yourself ready to clean the passage. Look alive!"

[CHARLEY WAG, THE NEW JACK SHEPPARD.

"Oh ah," said Mr. Wag, when the door was shut, "it is very fine saying, look sharp; it seems to me that my work is cut out for a week."

It turned out, however, that it was not so: for in about half-an-hour he had finished everything except cleaning the passage, which, as he was locked in his cell, of course he could not do. He was rather sorry that he could not, for he would have given the world to have seen some of his fellow-prisoners.

He sat on his deal stool until eight o'clock, and then a trap in the centre of the door was suddenly opened, and his breakfast was pushed in, with a surly

"Now then, lay hold."

His breakfast was in a round tin, with two compartments; one containing six ounces of bread, and the other three quarters of a pint of gruel.

"There ain't much variety as yet," said Charley; "but I suppose one don't feel to miss it after a month or two. Perhaps it's as well, after all, that I have a long term, or there might have been not only no variety, but precious little of the same thing."

When he had finished his meal, and was pretty well tired out of waiting for something to turn up, the discordant bell rung again—this time for chapel.

"Hurray!" said Mr. Wag; not that he was fond of chapel by any means, only, as he remarked, he was "dying to stretch his legs."

When the warder opened his door, he bade him put on the prison cap, and pull the mask down, and then ordered him to come out into the passage.

Here he found fifty other young gentlemen, all with their masks on, and their eyes glaring through the holes like those of a cat in the dark.

"Ready," cried the gaoler. "March," and Charley, falling into his place, they marched to chapel.

The chapel contained a great number of small boxes, or pews, (each large enough to hold one man), which were open only on one side, sufficient for the prisoner's head to be seen by the chaplain, but not by any of the other captives.

Each box had a number outside, and to this the prisoner walked in silence. When inside, he pulled-to the door, which shut with a spring, and took off his cap and mask. There was a nail in the side of the box, on which he could hang them.

The female prisoners were altogether hidden behind a screen of lattice-work. When the service was over, the governor turned a wheel in his pew, on which were the numbers of the prisoners; and as each number appeared, the prisoner whose number it was put on his cap and mask, and went out into the lobby, where he waited silently for the rest. Then, when they had all assembled at the word "march," they marched back to the cells in dead silence; after which the warders formed them into gangs, and conducted them to the Cranks, or to the yards, to take an airing.

Master Charley was to have the latter, and the warder conducted him to the place of his promenade. This was a passage with an iron gate locked at each end, up and down which he walked about for an hour, looking up at the sky, and rather wishing he was a bird.

There was somebody else taking a walk upon the same limited scale on the other side of each of the gates, and he would, if he could, have exchanged a word with one of them, only that a couple of warders kept jealous guard over them, and most effectually cut off all hope of communication.

"I never did feel so inclined for a jaw," said Charley to himself. "I'd give a month of my life if I could have half-an-hour's talk with Julia—or Lucinda—or Mr. Toddleboy. Yes! dash it all, I wouldn't mind old Measles even, as long as I could only have a little conversation. This silent business is smashing me."

They did not allow him more than an hour for his exercise, and then he was taken back to his cell, where at noon his dinner was served to him in the rough fashion which his other meals had been served before.

"They ought to take a lesson from the waiters at an eating-house," thought Charley. There was a very economical slap-bang in Westminster much affected by the Slogger Alleyites, where thumping lumps of pudding and surprisingly filling messes of stewed-beef could be obtained for a very trifling charge, and where the attendants, as may be supposed, in the hurry and confusion of serving the rapacious customers, did not waste more time than was positively necessary in politeness; but by the side of these warders they were perfect Chesterfields.

The dinner consisted of another three-quarters of a pint of gruel, and another seven ounces of bread, just as he had had for breakfast.

"I wonder when meat day comes?" thought Charley, as he bolted his gruel with a wry face.

However, though he found it exceedingly unsavoury, he would willingly have had a little more; but it was one of the rules of Spike Island that the prisoners should be kept on short-commons, and those who were in tolerably robust health, were half-starved all the while they were in jail.

After dinner, Master Charles was left entirely to his own resources for six hours, and during the whole course of his life never remembered the time to have hung so heavily upon his hands.

At six, came seven more ounces of bread and another three-quarters of a pint of the celebrated "mixture as before."

Charley spent as much time as he possibly could over it, and then read all the texts round the room for the twentieth time, and waited for bed-time.

Bed-time was eight o'clock, and when Charley had turned-in, the warder looked in at the door to see whether he had done so.

Tumbling about for an hour or so, and then to sleep.

Next day exactly the same formula.

Next day again the same.

When meat day came, the meat turned out to be six ounces in weight; but as it had been boiled for twelve or fourteen hours, it was quite devoid of all taste and goodness.

On the fourth day, the Governor, a stern, forbidding-looking man, dressed in black, came in to see how he was getting on, and carefully inspected the cell. Then, without a word, retired.

Charley's spirits began to give way.

The awful, overwhelmingly oppressive silence weighed him down and crushed him.

He would have given the world to have had some employment; but though he had been condemned to hard labour, he had not yet had any work given to him.

The hours grew longer and longer. The warders more and more surly and taciturn.

"I shall die if this sort of thing goes on," said Charley.

But the worst had not come yet.

Poor boy, he little thought what was in store for him.

II.—THE BLACK HOLE.

ONE day, after Charley had been in prison about a week, the warder opened the door after the boy had returned from chapel, and said in his usual gruff tones—

"Come out!"

Charley came out with alacrity, thinking he was going for his customary promenade, which, although it was extremely limited, was nevertheless an immense boon to him.

His idea, however, turned out to be erroneous. He was going to the oakum-picking room.

This was a long, low-roofed apartment, with high tables round the sides and down the middle. At the end was a pair of scales, and a quantity of oakum in sacks.

There were present some forty or fifty prisoners, and all wore their masks.

By the order of the warders they took their places at the tables, and a certain quantity of oakum was weighed and handed out to each.

They were dreadfully tough, these pieces of rope, and Charley's fingers were remarkably tender, for at any time he was not accustomed to do much work, and lately, as the reader knows, he had been living in total idleness.

He picked and picked.

For ever so long he picked away at the oakum. He broke a nail or two, but could not do very much work.

"There's some precious tough lumps among it," said he to himself. "How those other chaps get through it is more than I can tell."

And he resolved to watch them.

"It must be knack," he thought.

The men on either side of him were not more than three quarters of a yard off. He watched one and then another, as he stopped to rest himself and lick his fingers.

Presently he thought he had got hold of the right plan, and went on with his own work.

But on looking back at his own little heap, which he had left by the side of his right hand, when he had turned half round to study the manœuvring of his neighbour on the left, a very extraordinary idea struck him.

And this was—what do you think?

He could not help fancying that his stock of oakum had decreased. But it was impossible; who could have taken it? What reason could anybody have for taking it?

He dismissed the thought as absurd, and pegged away as hard as he could, but presently, for some reason, having again turned away

his head, on looking back, he noticed the hand of his neighbour on the right, in the act of being quickly withdrawn from his (Charley's) heap of ends.

"Oh, it's you, is it," thought Mr. Wag, though he dare make no remark: "and what on earth makes you take it? Well I shan't grumble, any how. All I wish is, that you'd take the whole of it, if you're so precious fond of the work, for I'll be blessed if I am."

So Master Charley chuckled to himself, and went on with his picking quite merrily.

They were engaged for a couple of hours like this, and though the work made his finger-ends feel quite raw, he nevertheless preferred it to the awful monotony of solitary confinement. "I hope to goodnes," he thought, "that I shall have a spell to-morrow. After a bit I shall grow quite a dab, I haven't a doubt."

He had barely finished, when one of the warders gave some order, which he did not catch, but in obedience to which one of the prisoners, the furthest off from Charley, at the table where he was standing, took up the stuff he had been picking and laid it in the scales: after which, he walked out to the lobby and took his place, in readiness to march back to his cell.

The next prisoner to him followed, then the next, and then the next.

Charley's turn came in due course. He took up his work with some slight misgiving that all was not right.

The warder weighed it.

"Short," said he.

"I beg your pardon," said Charley, hardly understanding him.

"Stand back," said the warder, pointing to the wall.

Charley went to the place indicated, and the rest of the prisoners came up with their lots of oakum, had them weighed, and formed the ranks in the passage.

When they were all disposed of, the warder turned round to Charley.

"You're short weight," said he.

"Am I, sir."

"You're a fool."

"Thank you, sir."

"Hold your tongue, or I'll report you. How is it?"

"The man next to me took it," Charley explained.

"Why did'nt you speak at the time?"

"Because I thought we might not talk."

"I thought you were a fool. You're a liar too, or I'm ducedly mistaken. What's he done with his own, do you suppose?"

"I'll look on the floor," said another warder.

And looking, sure enough, under Charley's table, were two or three nice hard lumps, which the thief had thrown there before he helped himself to softer pieces from Charley's heap.

"That's where you've thrown 'em, eh?" said one of the warders.

"No I've not," replied Charley. "I did not throw them there."

"Take your place among the rest," growled the other. "The governor shall know of this."

Charley would have again protested his innocence, but the man gave him a rough push towards the door, which nearly threw him upon his face, and he deemed it wisest to be silent.

After dinner he was again brought out to the oakum-picking room, and this time so sore were his fingers that the work seemed to him twice as laborious as it had done in the morning. However, he dreaded the consequences which would ensue were he to neglect it, and so picked away his hardest.

Again, as in the afternoon, happening to turn away his head, on turning it back again, he noticed his neighbour's hand among his oakum.

"No, no, my gentleman," thought he, "I can't afford to get punished on your account."

And he made a snatch at the other's hand.

The thief tried to drag his away.

"Leave go, you young fool," he said in a loud whisper, as he gave Charley's wrist a great wrench, and freed himself.

"Who spoke?" asked one of the warders.

Then turning to Charley, he said,

"You did, did you? You shall have a day in the black hole, my fine gentleman."

"I did not speak, sir," said Charley.

"You did."

"I did not."

"You're a liar."

"I am not a liar."

"Very well, we'll see what the governor says."

When he got back to his cell, and had been there about half-an-hour, two turnkeys waited upon him, ordered him out, and marched him down-stairs to a punishment dungeon.

I daresay, reader, that you fancy that I mean a dungeon with a small grating near the roof, admitting a tiny streak of day-light.

Not at all.

It was pitch dark.

Perhaps this does not strike you at first as being anything very terrible. You think, no doubt, that, were you so confined, you would do as you do in bed when you have put out the candle—go to sleep.

But supposing now that you should not happen to be sleepy. Have you ever laid in bed without a light and longed for day to come? In such a case you may be able to form some slight notion of the feelings of a wretched prisoner thus deprived of one of the greatest of God's blessings.

This horrible, barbarous, and unnatural privation of light is most trying to persons of an excitable temperament; to Charley it was almost death.

He was a bold-hearted, courageous young fellow, but by no means fitted to be a martyr.

The silence of his cell was bad enough, but silence and darkness combined was more than he could bear.

It chilled and crushed him.

When at night they came to release him, after he had been there about half-a-dozen hours, he trembled violently in every limb, and his face was ashy white.

At the same time he covered his eyes, as though to shade them from some powerful light, and with his head bowed down upon his breast, he slunk back to his cell.

Next morning the warders fetched him again, and put him into the Black Hole.

He offered no resistance; but looked dazed and bewildered, like a drunken man just awakened from a sound sleep.

When they took him out at night, the same symptoms, only rather exaggerated.

The third day, when they came to fetch him, he was sitting on the edge of his bed, with his eyes fixed on the ground, silent and moody.

"Get up!" said one of the men, shaking him.

"What do you want?" cried the poor boy, looking up at him in a wild and startled fashion. "What are you going to do with me?"

"You're going to the Black Hole. Get up!"

"No—no!" cried Charley, dropping down upon his knees at the others feet. "Not the Black Hole any more. No—no! for God's sake, not the Black Hole any more!"

"Come, now," growled the man, "none of this 'ere humbug, if you please."

And, with the assistance of his companion, he dragged Charley down stairs, and threw him "neck and crop" into the dismal cellar.

When he went in the middle of the day to give him his food, he started back with a cry of amazement and terror.

"Hallo! what the devil's this?"

"What's what?" said the man behind, peeping over his shoulder.

"Here's something up with the boy."

"What's up?"

Anyhow the boy was not up, for he was down on his face on the ground, almost in exactly the same place that the gaoler had thrown him in the morning.

"He ain't dead, is he?"

"He looks precious like it."

"He is cold enough."

"And stiff enough."

He was, indeed, very cold, and stiff, and heavy, and as like a dead boy as one pea is like another.

"By gosh!" said one of the warders, "it strikes me he has kicked the bucket."

"There will be a deuce of a row if he has; but it's the governor's fault for giving the order. I thought it was rather stiff punishment for the young whelp."

"Well, what's to be done?"

"Go for the doctor, I think."

"Yes, suppose we do."

"We had better carry him up to his cell first."

They carried him up accordingly, made up his bed, laid him on it, and fetched the surgeon.

After a short delay, this functionary made his appearance. He felt the boy's pulse, laid his hand upon his heart, and prescribed a restorative.

This was a bucket of water.

They took the boy off the bed, laid him on the floor, and dashed it over him.

Then the unfortunate little wretch rose to his feet, shook himself like a drowned rat, and stared vacantly at the good company surrounding him, but said nothing.

The surgeon watched his movements and the expression of his face, pushed up his eyelids, and stared fixedly into his eyes; then felt his pulse again, and shook his head.

"How are you, boy?" he asked.

Charley made no answer.

"What's the matter with you, boy?"

No answer again.

"I think he is a fool," said one of the gaolers.

"If he isn't one now, he precious soon will be. His brain is softening."

"By jingo, we had better speak to the guv-nor," said the warder, in alarm; and all three walked off in that direction.

Stone, the "guvnor," received the deputation coldly.

"One of you would have done, I should have thought," said he. "What's the matter, Mr. Purge?"

"Number Ten's had it a trifle too strong, sir."

"What's been done to him?"

"Ten days' solitary, one day's oakum, and twenty-four hours' black-hole."

"Can't he stand it?"

"I think he will most likely die in a couple more days if the treatment is not changed."

"What does he want, then?"

"A little more excitement, I should think."

"What do you say to a couple of dozen lashes? that will excite him."

III.—Such a getting up Stairs.

THE surgeon grinned and coughed.

"I should try something milder."

"We will try the wheel, then, or the crank."

"Let it be the wheel," said the doctor; "he will get on better with a little company."

The next day Charley was put upon the tread-mill. In Spike Island they had both a tread-wheel and cranks. The cranks were worked by one man, in a cell by himself; but several prisoners worked together—as many as twenty or thirty—upon the wheel.

The tread-mill, or tread-wheel, is an enormous cylinder, or drum, round which are steps, about a foot and a half distant from each other. It revolves slowly towards the prisoners placed upon it, and thus the step upon which the foot rests gives way beneath it at the same time that the next step comes forward. There is a platform half the height of the wheel, from which the prisoners step upon the wheel; and, when on it, they support themselves by a rail, and their weight keeps the machine in motion.

It is literally such a "getting up stairs," the only drawback being, however, that you never get to a landing; and, though you are for ever stepping upwards, you never get any higher.

I have seen Mr. Mackney, in his song of "Sally Come Up," do a step which puts me very much in mind of it; that is, while remaining stationary in the same place, he makes belief to be walking with all his might, as though for a wager.

The prisoners who are waiting their turn to go upon the wheel sit down upon the platform, and the attendant warders direct their intervals of rest and labour.

There have been a great many improvements in prison discipline of late, but it is a very few years ago since women worked on the tread-mill—women suckling babies, who leaving the children when their turn was come, took their place upon this barbarous instrument of torture.

Charley took his turn, and walked up-stairs as hard as he could go, glad of the change from the fearful dungeon he had quitted, to this new and laborious toil. Indeed, he worked with such good-will that the gaolers were, if any-thing, rather annoyed by his energy.

"The young beggar was shamming, it's my opinion," said Warder Darbies to Warder Manacle.

"Yes," said Warder Manacle to Warder Darbies; "but I should take the spring out of him, if I had my way, double sharp."

"Suppose you suggest it to the guv'nor."

"What! a little of the crank, eh?"

"Yes, that will surprise his young mind."

The next day our young unfortunate went on to the crank.

You would like to know, perhaps, what the crank is like. I will tell you.

Each of the cranks is in a little cell by itself, about half the size of the cells in which the prisoner sleeps. A crank is a machine with a handle, such as there is to wells, where the water is drawn up in a bucket. The handle you lay hold of with both hands, and, to use a popular phrase, you twist it round "till all is blue." As long as you can, in fact, till there is no wind left in you, till you are done up.

The ingenious inventor of these machines has contrived them upon a principle by which there are various amounts of resistance in the several cranks.

There are five pound cranks, seven pound cranks, ten pound cranks, and so on.

Charley had a seven pound crank.

"You will have to work two hours," observed the warder, "eighteen hundred turns an hour."

Mr. Wag left to himself, got hold of the handle and set at it. It seemed easy enough at starting, but, like every thing else, grew fatiguing by repetition

There was a very ingenious contrivance in the way of a dial, which marked the number of turns that the handle had taken, so you see there was no shirking work, and the hand upon the clock face would not budge a jot without a con-siderable amount of exertion upon the prisoner's part.

After he had taken one hundred turns, he stood up and stretched his arms, and wiped his forehead.

After he had taken another hundred he wiped his forehead again, and when he reached a thou-sand he thought he never recollected to have had such a "crick," in his back.

He was afraid to leave off, though, and worked away until the jailor fetched him, when he had completed his number to a turn.

Next day he went at it again, and this time, though he did it more easily than the first, he had more work allotted to him.

Again, the next day, the work was increased.

When they came to fetch him to the crank the day after this, he complained of head-ache, sickness, and diarrhœa, and said that he could not get up.

"Why not?" said the warder.

Charley repeated his complaints.

"Bosh!" said Mr. Darbies. "I should advise you, No. 10, not to sham Abraham here."

Charley said he was not shamming Abraham, nor Isaac either.

And Mr. Darbies said, "We will see."

He accordingly fetched the "Guvnor."

The governor said, "There's a deal of your sort of complaint among the prisoners; but it don't succeed; we soon cure them of it—Get up!"

Charley, groaning and tottering, got out of his bed, and tried to dress himself.

"You must be a little sharper than that," said the governor, and walked out of the cell.

"Yes!" said Mr. Darbies, when he was gone, "a precious sight sharper."

Charley made the best haste that he could, and in a very despondent state dragged his weary legs to the labour yard, and went into his usual cell.

"Eight thousand is your lot," said the jailor, as he left, and Charley, clenching his teeth, and scarcely able to keep his eyes open through the intolerable agony he was suffering with headache, set to work.

He turned, and turned, and turned, and turned.

His head spun round, he thought it would have fallen off. He soon became so giddy that he was obliged to cease and grasp the upright of the crank to save himself from falling.

Then he went on again.

But his headache increased, he grew giddier every moment, the handle slipped from his hand, and he fell backwards upon the floor of the cell in a swoon.

IV.—THE LASH!

"THIS sir, is a very obstinate case indeed. A very depraved character. An old offender. In for burglary, sir: last offence larceny: charges of highway robbery, horse-stealing, and abduction, not brought against him, as the burglary was clearly proved, a very bad case indeed."

This much Mr. Stone, the Governor, to Mr. Bullhead, one of the visiting magistrates, and Mr. Pigswill, another.

Mr. Bullhead.—A very bad case indeed. Mr. Stone, as you observe, and one where a little whipping would be very well applied.

Mr. Pigswill.—A good deal of whipping I should say.

Mr. Stone.—If you think so, gentlemen, he shall have it, only, for my part, I never resort to measures only when it is absolutely necessary. How many do you think we ought to give him?

Mr. Bullhead.—I don't think a couple of dozen would do him any harm.

Mr. Pigswill.—Three dozen would not kill him.

Mr. Stone.—Suppose we say two dozen and a half.

Both of the Magistrates.—You're far too leinent.

Mr. Stone.—[With a smirk of modesty and self-denial.] I always *was* soft-hearted.

And so it was decided that the young prisoner should have a taste of the cat.

Perhaps the reader may think that the fine old institution of flogging, when practised at all in our gaols, is practised with great leniency. You may think that the defenders of this country, are the persons who came in for the most "walloping." For nobody can deny, that if our soldiers are not walloped by the enemy, we make up for it at home. The reader, how-

ever, would be mistaken, and if he look into the parliamentary returns he will doubtless be startled at the shocking amount the visiting justices, the assizes, and sessions, award to criminal children.

In the years 1857-58-59, 67 criminals of 12 years of age, 41 of 11, 34 of 10, 12 of 9, 3 of 8, and one of *seven*, appear in the list as having been flogged, a few with the birch, but mostly with the cat. In Chester gaol, a child of 8 is stated to have received 24 lashes for repeated misconduct, a child of 9 to have received the same for house-breaking, and at Bodmin, a boy of 12 got 2 separate floggings of 36 lashes each, for horse-stealing.

At Hertford a boy of 10 received 36 lashes for stealing a piece of beef, while a man 29 only received the same punishment for stealing 29 fowls. Two children, of 9 years old, received 15 lashes each at Faversham—one for stealing a cocoanut, value 3d.; the other for stealing a half-pound weight, value 7d.; while a man of 36, at Maidstone, received but 18 for running away and deserting his wife and family!

At Salford, in Lancashire, a boy of 12 received 48 lashes for "most artfully and wontonly destroying the books in his cell;" a boy of 11 got 36 lashes for shouting in his cell; and a boy of ten, 48 lashes for putting the cotton given to him to pick into his cell pot. In the same prison another boy of 11 got 48 lashes also for shouting in his cell: and a boy of 10 was similarly maltreated. A boy of 14 got 60 lashes for idleness at crank labour.

In Oxford gaol two criminals of 9 years of age were chastised with 24 lashes each; and the Hetworth Petty Sessions enjoy the melancholy distinction of having awarded corporal punishment to the youngest criminal on the list, *one infant of seven years of age*, who, with two accomplices of nine years of age, "stole a knife:" one of the accomplices of nine is noted as "an old offender."

When I was myself at school, some forty years ago, says a writer in the *Times*, the punishment of flogging was more in vogue than it now is, and I have often been flogged. I recollect still, how unpleasant it was, although the usual dose was, even in those flogging days, but from eight to ten cuts. In very grave cases as many as fourteen or sixteen cuts were administered, and a *fresh* birch was introduced during the operation; but such terrible executions were happily rare, and were generally followed by subsequent expulsion.

I do not think that flogging is so much approved now as a means of imparting knowledge to the young as it used to be. In our lower and middle-class schools it is almost entirely dispensed with, and I believe that, although still adhered to in our upper-class schools, as a time-honoured institution, which has produced many great men, of whom England has great cause to be proud, it is not indulged in as freely as when you and I were boys.

We flog our soldiers and sailors, too, much less than we used to do, no punishment now exceeding 48 lashes, and the sentence, whatever it may be, being always got over at once, a weakly criminal not being required to take his punishment by instalments, as used formerly to be the practice. For grown soldiers and sailors the instrument used is the " cat," and a sore and heavy instrument it is.

The well-fed children of the rich, when they come to be stripped for punishment, are at eight, nine, or ten years of age, but frail, delicate-skinned little creatures, very ill-fitted to bear even a dozen cuts of the cane or the birch; *the underfed children of the poor are frailer and punier still*; and I appeal to every member of the House of Commons who has young children of his own, to put a stop to these wanton and unnecessary cruelties.

Well, to go on with my story, it was satisfactorily settled, you see, that Charley Wag would be all the better for a good whipping.

There was no particular reason assigned for this, except that, in a general way, he was set down for sulky, and the chaplain could do nothing with him, and the gaolers had made up their minds about him long ago, and come to the conclusion that he was an " out and out bad un."

" A tidy walloping," said Mr. Darbies, with the air of a man bestowing a favour upon a fellow-creature " That would just do him all the good in life."

" That's my opinion to a T," said Mr. Manacle, " and jist what I should have said myself if you hadn't took the words out of my mouth."

" So just you mind your eye, my young tulip," said Mr. Darbies; " because it seems to me you're going the right road to cop it; and the guvnor won't put up with none of your nonsense, so don't you make no mistake."

The governor, indeed, had himself already hinted as much to Charley, and warned that young gentleman, that if he did not mind what he was about, he had better look out.

For some time, however, he gave the gaol authorities no opportunity of operating upon him.

The surgeon having recommended lighter work, saying at the same time, that otherwise it was more than probable he would not last out the week, the little unfortunate was allowed to do a trifle less work, and with the desperation of despair, contrived to get through the allotted portion.

But it was not for long.

Very soon he began to " shirk" again, as the warder pleasantly termed the recurrence of his illness, and then came the day of vengeance.

A faintness came over him while at the crank, and after vainly struggling for some time, he gave up the unequal contest, and when Mr. Stone presently came on his rounds, he found the boy sitting down on the floor of the cell, with his head resting against the wall.

" What now?" said he.

" I feel so ill and weak," Charley replied, " that I could work no longer."

" Haven't you done the quantity?" Stone asked, at the same time consulting the dial.

He had not, it seemed, by a great deal.

" Only a hundred, by God!" roared the governor. " You shall smart for this."

" I was too ill," the boy replied, " to do any more."

" Bosh," said Stone; " however ill you are you could have done more than that; besides, from the first, you have been shamming, and now

there shall be an end of it, so I tell you. Here, Darbies, catch hold of the young skulker, and take him out into the yard; we will warm him before we have done with him."

The boy made no resistance, and uttered not another word.

They took him out into a yard, which was frequently used for the same purpose and stripping off his coat and waistcoat and shirt, tied him up to a whipping-post, and fetching the " Cat," began to belabour his miserable little carcase.

" Fifty lashes," said Stone, " will do for him this time, and next we will make it a little stronger."

The gaoler who was intrusted with the whip prided himself exceedingly upon his barbarous expertness in inflicting torture.

He had a knack, as he termed it, of giving them straight from his shoulder, which was very effective.

Stepping back a yard or two, Mr. Darbies spread his fingers through the thongs of the whip, then advanced, threw it over his shoulder, and taking a deadly aim, brought it down with stunning violence upon the sufferer's naked back, which in a moment rose up in livid streaks.

At the same time a piercing shriek of agony burst from the victim's lips; but it did not tend to soften the iron hearts of his persecutors.

Again the blow descended.

Again the piercing shriek of agony rent the air.

Scenes of this description were, alas, too frequent in Spike Island, and the cries of suffering too often heard, for them to cause any excitement when they reached by the other prisoners. They knew that somebody was being beaten, but took so little interest in the matter, that they scarcely raised their heads from their work or paused to listen.

They were not being thrashed, and that was quite sufficient for them.

Again and again did the terrible lash fall upon the boy's back, until the flesh, purple and quivering beneath the cruel strokes, at length burst out bleeding here and there where the thongs had broken the skin. For a while he ceased to cry, and bit his lips and ground his teeth, endeavouring with a heroism of a martyr at the stake, to defy his tormentors.

But still the punishment continued. At length human endurance broke down under the torture, and a deadly sickness overcoming him, the boy's lips turned black and his face a leaden hue. Then his head rolled over on one side and he fainted.

Seeing this, they took him down and flung a bucket of water over him.

The effect was magical.

The shock for a moment seemed to stun him: but the next it sent the blood tingling through his veins like so much molten lead, and he felt as though he had suddenly acquired sufficient strength to bear any amount of torture.

" Well," said Stone, " will you shirk your work again?"

" I have always done as much as I could do, sir, and I can do no more."

" We shall see," said the governor.

" Is he to have any more?" asked Darbys.

" No," replied Stone. " What he has had will do for him at present. Take him back to his cell."

Then they threw the clothes over the boy's back, and he was taken away.

When he was alone that night, lying bruised and sore upon his bed, he prayed to God in his misery to take away his life.

"Six months of this!" he said. "I could never live through it. Is there no escape?"

V.—Prisoner Number Ten is wanted.

HOW could he escape?

The thing was impossible.

Those who, by the description I have given, recognise which prison it is that I have called Spike Island, know that no prisoners have escaped from it except when the door has been opened for them, and they have been let out upon the world again at the expiration of the term for which they were condemned to imprisonment.

No, there was no chance of escape.

And could he live much longer under this treatment?

Despair seized upon his soul, and he gave himself up for lost.

Throughout the night he rolled from side to side upon his weary sleepless couch, and ground his teeth in misery, mental and physical.

The combined effects of his previous weakness, and his subsequent ill-treatment, turned his brain; and, as he lay there, he screamed aloud, and raved, and babbled, wild and fearful incoherencies.

Then flung himself upon the floor of his cell, and battered against the door and walls with his puny fists.

When the warder came in the morning to see whether he was up, a glance was sufficient to show him that the poor boy was in a state of raging delirium.

That is to say, that a glance would have been sufficient to have convinced any reasonable person.

The playful Darbies, however, was not usually very lynx-eyed where prisoners' ailments were in question.

If now his visual powers had been called into question, to discover a speck of dirt upon the floor of Number Ten's cell, he would have been down upon it in no time.

He saw the boy was lying in bed, when he should have been up and dressed, and was taking it, as Mr. Darbies subsequently observed, "Onkimman Heasy."

"What's the game now, Number Ten?" said the gaoler.

But Number Ten made no reply.

"Come, tumble up," Mr. Darbies cried, irate.

Still no reply.

"Oh, you're sulky, are you—very well."

"Mr. Stone was passing by at the time.

"What's all this about?" he asked.

Mr. Darbies explained.

"Number Ten's in the sulks, and won't get out of bed."

"Heave a bucket of cold water over him," said Mr. Stone.

And walked briskly off with his hands in his pockets, to a breakfast of coffee and hot buttered toast awaiting him in his private room.

He was always most particular about his meals, and exceedingly angry if anything occurred to disturb him while he was at them.

After breakfast, too, he read the paper for a couple of hours, and pursued the same course after dinner, and should he chance to be sent for in consequence of a prisoner's obstreperous behaviour at one of these periods, it went rather hard with him.

He was not, therefore, in the best of tempers, while perusing a nice slangy leader in his favourite penny daily, to be disturbed on account of Master Charles.

"What, now?" said he.

"Number Ten, sir,"

"What's the matter with Number Ten?"

"Black in the face."

"What do you mean?"

"He's awful bad, sir; we can't do nothing with him."

"Yes, sir; he's either ill, or its an onkimmon clever sham."

"Confound the fellow! There's always something amiss with him. What's the matter now?"

"He's quite off his head, sir, and raving away like—excuse the expression—one o'clock."

"How's it come about, pray? Can you account for it?"

"Well, sir, I—"

"You what? Speak up."

"Well, if I must, then, I think it's the—the—"

"Now, then, what are you stammering about?"

"I think it's the cold water we gave him."

"Don't talk nonsense. Have we never given any other prisoner a bucket of cold water? Preposterous!"

"Well, then, perhaps it was the—the flogging."

"Haven't we flogged other prisoners?"

"Certainly, sir."

"Well, then, that can't be it."

"Perhaps it's too much dark hole, sir."

"Haven't we put others into the dark hole?"

"Certainly, sir."

"For a longer time than this fellow?"

"Much longer, sir."

"Then why should it make this fellow ill?"

"It's very curious, sir."

"It's not curious. It's a part of his system."

"Yes, sir, certainly," said Darbies, rubbing his chin rather doubtfully.

"It's his obstinacy, that's what it is."

"To be sure, sir."

"And I'll take it out of him, or, by God, I'll know the reason why!"

And so saying, Mr. Stone leant back in his chair and went on with his newspaper.

Darbies stood fumbling with his keys and waiting for orders.

"What shall I do, sir?" he asked, at length.

"Leave him till I come," said the Governor. "I'll manage him."

"If he don't come soon," said the jailor, as he walked away, "he'll have a dead body to manage with, that's my opinion."

Mr. Stone meanwhile went on with his leader.

Presently there was a knock at the door.

"Come in!" said Mr. Stone.

A CRITICAL SITUATION

It was a warder who announced a visitor.

"Who is it?" asked Stone.

"A gentleman that's brought this letter."

Stone took it.

It was an order for the bearer, Mr. Ralph Faversham, to be allowed to see Charles Wag, a prisoner, confined in Her Majesty's Gaol at ————, and was signed by the Home Secretary.

"Well I'm ——!" exclaimed Stone, using a very strong expression. "Send Darbies here."

Darbies came.

"Look at this," said the Governor.

Darbies did look, and pulled an uncommonly long face.

"Well, I'm ——!" cried he, using the same expression that Stone had done.

No. 21.

"Don't stand gaping there!" roared the Governor in a fury. "How are we to manage?"

"Something must be done."

"Make a suggestion, then."

"I think we'd better put him in bed, sir; and get him up comfortable before the gentleman sees him; unless—"

"What!"

"You put him off, sir. Could you not do that?"

"Ah! to be sure. I'll try."

When the warder was gone, Stone gave an order for the visitor to be admitted.

"What I am to say is more than I can tell," said the Governor to himself, and when the gentleman entered, he felt exceedingly ill at case.

[CHARLEY WAG, THE NEW JACK SHEPPARD.

" To what am I indebted for the honour of this interview ?" said the Governor.

He was a very solemn, sedate, and oppressive genteel gentleman, this visitor; clad all in black with the exception of his neckerchief, which was white as the driven snow.

He was rather bald, his features were strongly marked, and his face was of so cadaverous a hue that it suggested the idea of his having just risen from a bed of sickness, though even that does not quite give you a proper notion of its pallor. It was, in fact, the face of a dead man. A sickly yellow green, heavy and fixed looking.

He made no immediate answer to Mr. Stone's question, but gently peeling off his right hand glove, dropped it into his hat, placed his hat on the table, and sat himself down in a chair.

When there he coughed slightly behind his hand, crossed his legs, and fixed his eyes in a remarkably hard and stony stare upon the Governor.

This gentleman, not unnaturally supposing that his visitor must be rather deaf, as he had not replied, repeated his question in a louder voice.

" I brought a letter," Mr. Faversham observed, " which, if I do not mistake, you are holding in your hand."

" Yes, certainly," replied Stone, glancing at it. " It does not, however, assign any reason for this—this unusual request."

" I believe that such is unnecessary."

" It is unusual to omit it."

" But it is, as you observed, altogether an unusual proceeding."

" Yes, sir ; and a very irregular one."

" In what does the irregularity consist ?"

" Well, as to that," stammered the Governor, re-reading the letter, and taking as long a time as possible in doing so, " the order is regular enough, as far as that goes—unless—" (here a thought struck him), " unless, to be sure—it is not a genuine one."

" Sir !"

" You must not think that I intend to throw any disrespect upon you," said the Governor with a sneering smile, " but I regret to say that I cannot admit you to an audience with the prisoner upon the authority of this letter."

" Why not ?"

" Because I do not recognize the hand-writing."

He thought this a clincher, and when he had made the observation, leant back in the chair and rubbed his chin with the paper.

" You do not recognize the handwriting ?" repeated Faversham.

" No."

" Do you know the Home Secretary's hand-writing ?"

" Perfectly."

" And you think this letter a forgery ?"

" That is my opinion."

" Very well—and you therefore refuse to admit me ?"

" I do."

They paused, and looked at each other for some minutes attentively.

" Do you not think," said Faversham, slowly and deliberately, " that you are pursuing an injudicious course ?"

" In what way ?"

" In thwarting the Home Secretary's wishes, upon the supposition of this letter not being genuine."

" I am only doing what I think to be my duty."

" You are perfectly right in doing so. At the same time, should you be unhappily labouring under a mistake, I suppose you have well considered what would be the consequences of the baronet's displeasure."

Stone grew a little doubtful. He did not wish to displease the Home Secretary, far from it. But then he did not wish this visitor to see Charley's condition.

He had some vague idea that he had over-stepped his duty, and been a trifle too hard upon the young prisoner.

He weighed the matter over in his mind. No! at any rate he would not let the boy be seen.

" You see, sir," he said at last, " the hand-writing seems to me to be different from Sir Benjamin Tory's customary style, and as I am perfectly unacquainted with your person, I think I am quite justified in denying you admission."

" Suppose I could establish my identity as that of the confidential physician of your friend and patron."

" My friend and patron ?"

" The Duke of Heatherland."

The governor opened his eyes and his mouth, and stared at his visitor in astonishment.

" I presume," said Faversham, " that you are acquainted with his Graces' handwriting ?"

" I am."

" Read this, then."

As he spoke, the doctor handed a letter to the governor.

It was a letter of introduction, which the duke had written to Stone, and which Faver-sham, with his usual long-sightedness, had deemed it necessary to provide himself with, before starting upon his mission.

" In that case," said Stone, " I can no longer have any doubts."

And he began to rack his brain for some other excuse by which he might yet get off showing the boy.

" I am sorry to put you to any inconvenience, Mr. Faversham," he said. " Under the present circumstances, after having, in the first instance doubted your word, I regret to propose that you should pay your visit at some other time."

" But why postpone it ?"

" Well, the fact is, the boy has been exceedingly unruly during his confinement here, and I have been obliged to lock him up in his cell as a punishment, and to debar him from all communications with his fellow-creatures. It is a course which I greatly object to, as I object to all harsh measures, but in the case of this boy it is absolutely necessary."

" And in the case of this visit," said Faver-sham, who began to perceive that the other had some secret reason for wishing to put him off, and therefore, was the more determined that he would not be put off—" in the case of this visit, it is absolutely necessary that the rule should be broken through. Matters of the most vital importance compels me to insist upon my demand."

"Really, sir," cried Stone, growing desperate, "have I no authority in my own prison? I refuse your request."

The doctor looked at him very hard for a moment or two, then smiled blandly.

"Before we proceed to the prisoner's cell," said he, "I would like to ask you a few questions about another prisoner. There was once a prisoner here of the name of Horford ——"

A most surprising effect this had upon Mr. Stone, the governor.

He turned as white as note paper, and his lower jaw dropped.

"Horford," he repeated.

"Yes, that was the name."

"There has never been anybody of that name in this gaol."

"That name may not perhaps have appeared upon the prison books, but I do not think you will deny that Handsome Jack Horford was confined in this gaol under some alias, and that he escaped in a very suprising manner."

"He did, I believe, though I do not quite recollect the circumstances of the case."

"Your memory is very defective," said Faversham, again with another of his bland smiles. "I cannot hope to recall other circumstances to your mind which occured at a still earlier period—for instance, you have doubtless no recollection of any of the circumstances which attended the burning of the house of a certain Hezekiah Sleek, a quaker gentleman in Cornwall."

If Mr. Stone's face had before been as white as note-paper, it now began to take a bluish tint, and became the colour of foolscap.

"What are you driving at?" he asked at length. "Who are you? What do you mean? and what do you wish to do?"

Faversham lent forward towards the other, and, sinking his voice, said, laying an emphasis on each word :—

"I wish to see that boy, and I shall."

"Come, then," said Stone, rising to his feet, but trembling in every limb, "come, then, and I will show you to his cell."

Faversham took up his hat, and followed him from the room.

——

VI.—In which the writer, with a humble apology, goes back to a beautiful young lady, whom he had deserted in a very ungentlemanly fashion several chapters ago.

YES, most decidedly an apology is needed. The idea of introducing a young lady into a story, endeavouring to excite the reader's interest in her behalf, rescuing her from a fire, running her across country until she was out of breath, popping her into a post-chaise, whipping up the horses into a mad gallop, flinging the postillion senseless into the middle of the road, and sending the carriage upon its wild career unchecked, with the unfortunate young lady inside!

All this, and then to leave her so for thirty chapters. Why it is scandalous!

When I come to reflect upon the state of anxious suspense in which some young lady reader may have been waiting from page to page to hear what became of Lucinda, I feel quite ashamed of myself.

I left her in a post-chaise, as perhaps you may remember, galloping pell-mell across the marshes.

There was also, as you may also remember, a horseman galloping after them.

This horseman was Leech the lawyer.

Hopley had sent him in search of assistance, and he had learnt, to his amazement, at the inn where Charley had got the post-chaise, that the boy, in company with Hopley's daughter, had gone off together, and what account they had given of the fire.

Up to now the lawyer had supposed, as had also Hopley and his wife, that Lucinda had perished in the fire, and that Master Charley had long since escaped from the house.

You can readily believe how dumbfoundered he was to learn that they were together, and safely on the road, with a good start.

"And to think," said the lawyer to himself, "to think that that young imp should have deceived us in this way. He must have been hidden in the house all the while; perhaps in the girl's bed-room. And who knows? perhaps he set the place on fire. However, I will make him smart for it before I have done with him."

What was to be done now was, however, the question for his consideration.

He thought about it, and soon made up his mind. He would leave Hopley and his burning house to their fate, and go after the boy.

It was the boy that he was interested in. The boy was worth money to him, and the boy he must have.

He did not get him, as the reader already knows. But he set off in pursuit, in right good earnest.

He hired a horse at the same inn where Charley had hired the chaise, and galloped after the boy as fast as the horse's legs could carry him.

There was some delay in getting the horse ready, and the chaise had a good ten minutes' start; but having heard what was its destination, he stuck the spurs into the horse's sides, and set off at a good round pace, confident of catching them up before long.

Galloping straight on, in course of time he arrived at the tollbar through which the chaise had passed, and the keeper of which Charley had feed to put any pursuers upon the wrong track.

"Hallo, old man!" he bawled. "Has a chaise been through just now?"

"Eh?" said the old man, putting his hand to his ear, and feigning to be deaf.

"Has a chaise been through here just now, booby?"

"Who are you a calling booby?"

"Oh, you can hear that, can you? That's a wonder. Here's a shilling for you, and perhaps you can tell me whether a post-chaise has been through here about a quarter-of-an-hour ago."

"What's the matter?"

"Confound you!" muttered the lawyer; then he roared at him,

"How long ago is it?"

" How long ago, eh ?"

" Yes."

" Since a chaise went through ?"

" To be sure."

" Well, I can't say exactly to a minute like ; but it warn't so long ago neither."

" I suppose there *has* been a chaise by."

" Certain sure there's been a chay by."

" Well, then, how long ago is it ?"

" I can't say for cartin, but I should think—"

" Ten minutes, now ?"

" Well, I shouldn't be surprised if it were."

" Or an hour, eh ?"

" Well, it might be as much as that."

" Or six hours ?"

" I shouldn't be surprised, neither; time do go so."

" Time do go so," repeated Leech, contemptuously. " You cursed old duffer. Let me through, will you. I can't waste any more time over your infernal stupidity."

And away he gallopped down the road.

The toll-bar man stood staring after him, scratching his head.

" Not sich infernal stupidity, neither," said he with a grin, as he stood in the middle of the road with the gate half-closed, watching the retreating forms of the horse and horseman as they rapidly diminished in the increasing darkness.

" Not sich infernal stupidity, neither. I've earned the money the young gent gave me, and that's all I had to do. He's got a good ten minutes start of you, old foul-mouth, and I hope for my part, that you never set eyes on him till you see him off Jack Ketches jumping board, when he looks up at you from the crowd, and takes a sight at your ugly old phisimygog, that's all the harm I wish you."

So saying he shut the gate, and going into the house closed the door, crept into bed to Mrs. Keeper, and was soon snoring loud enough for six.

Meanwhile Leech gallopped on, cursing the old man for having so long delayed him.

In another half-hour he overtook Bob the post-boy in his shirt-tails, running along the road on his way home.

Bob shouted to him and he reined in his horse.

" Hallo !" cried Leech, " that's an airy costume for this weather."

" I've b—b—b—been rob—bob—bob—ed," stammered Bob.

And he explained the circumstances as well as he could speak for the cold, winding up his narrative by begging Leech in the name of all that was merciful, to lend him something to cover him with, and keep his poor old bones warm.

" You'd better run," said Leech, in reply, " That'll warm you as well as clothes. Besides, I have none to spare."

And with this consoling advice left Bob to his fate, and galloped on faster than ever.

He came in sight of the chaise at the moment that it turned the corner from the high road into the field, and just when Charley was flung on his back into the middle of the road.

He did not perceive the fall of the boy, but pursued the carriage across the marshes.

On they went. It was a tremendous pace, and very questionable whether or not he would succeed in overtaking the fugitive.

As he galloped on, great was his amazement to see that the horses were without a rider

Perhaps, then, the carriage was without an occupant. But no—somebody was leaning out of window and screaming for help.

It was Lucinda. What, then, had become of Charley ? He must be inside, unless he were left behind upon the road. In a few more moments he would be up with the carriage and see how the case stood.

But Lucinda all this time was screaming at the top of her voice—

" Help ! help ! help !" she cried. " Save me ! save me ! Stop the horses, we are going down a quarry !"

Leech with difficulty catching the words looked ahead of the carriage, and by the light of the moon, which at that moment came forth from behind the clouds and illumined the surrounding country as though it was noon-day, he perceived a great black streak cutting the marshes in two about thirty yards ahead of the carriage. This, then, was a stone-quarry, many of which he knew to abound in this part of the country, and towards this the maddened horses were now galloping at the height of their speed.

In a few moments more, horses, carriage, and occupant would be dashed to pieces at the bottom of the yawning chasm.

If he were to try to save them there was no time to be lost.

Now you see, Leech was far from being a benevolent or soft-hearted individual. He had very few sympathies with his fellow-creatures, and would just as soon have seen a human being fall over a precipice and lie at the bottom smashed to pieces as not.

That is to say, had his opinion been asked upon the subject when he was seated in his easy chair at his fireside, smoking a quiet pipe. Had he reflected about it, I am sure he would have decided in favour of leaving Lucinda and the carriage to their fate, but taken, as it were, unawares, and with hardly a moment left him in which to make up his mind, he decided off-hand quite against his reason and ordinary principles of prudence to make an effort to save the woman's life.

Vigorously drumming his heels into his horses side, and shouting at the top of his voice to incite it to fresh efforts, he dashed forward.

But the sound of his cries and the rattling of his horse's hoofs terrified the horses in front, and they doubled their speed.

Rapidly they approached the brink of the precipice. If he could not throw himself between it and them there was no hope.

With a wild shout he drew near to them. His horse had passed the carriage window, and was now breast to breast with the other horses.

Now he leant down and made a clutch at the bridle of one of the foremost.

In doing so he lost his balance.

He fell with a shrill scream, still clinging to the bridle.

His own horse cleared the edge of the precipice with a wild bound and snort.

He closed his eyes and clenched his teeth, expecting instant death.

VII.—LUCINDA IN THE WEB OF A SPIDER—A PLOT AGAINST A MAIDEN'S VIRTUE.

But the rascal's time had not arrived. The surprise of his assault had stopped the furious horses in their mad career, and they came to a dead stand-still upon the very brink of the precipice.

Then opening his eyes he found himself suspended 'twixt heaven and earth, with one foot hanging over the side of the quarry.

Awakening instantly to the awful danger of his position, and the strong necessity for immediate action, he scrambled upwards and thrust the horses heads backwards with all his might, shouting to them at the top of his voice.

And the neighing of the frightened animals, his shouts, and the scream of the girl within, all combined to make a disturbance, which could be compared to nothing but the breaking up of pandemonium for the holidays, supposing, that is, that they ever have any holidays there, or that they ever break up.

"Back—back!" he screamed, struggling desperately. "Back—back. Curse you, where are you coming to?"

Whether or not the horses were convinced by his forcible language that they were about to do something very foolish, or whether they came to that conclusion of their own accord, and without his aid, is extremely doubtful; however, one way or the other they did come to the conclusion, and backed accordingly.

Then Mr. Leech tugged their heads round in an opposite direction, and drew the carriage away about twenty yards from the mouth of the quarry.

"Whew!" said he, wiping his head with his pocket-handkerchief, when at length he could find time to get his breath and rest himself. "This ain't exactly my line, I'm blowed if it is."

He was blowed literally, and had almost every particle of wind taken out of his body.

When he had somewhat recovered, he bethought himself of the young lady inside.

"How's she getting on, I wonder!" said he, "and what the dickens has become of the boy?"

The lady was quite quiet, and for a moment the lawyer fancied that she must have fallen over the precipice.

With this idea he went to look.

She had not, however. And he found her lying at the bottom of the carriage apparently in a swoon.

Then he took her in his arms, and raising her on to the seat, endeavoured to bring her to her senses.

But as he had no restoratives at hand, this was rather a tedious affair. He could only loosen her dress and cut her staylace.

And while thus engaged, he studied her face and figure with an admiring eye, while certain thoughts crept into his head during the contemplation which would have considerably shocked the young lady had she been aware of them.

"She's an extraordinarily nice gal," said Mr. Leech, half aloud. "I thought so to-night, when she was having tea with Mr and Mrs. H. and me, and was pouring out the bohea so gracefully. And she's a deuced fine figure, too. I like these fat ones myself. There's something of 'em. With those thin uns, you might as well be cuddling up a bundle of firewood, or four walking-sticks tied together with a string."

Then, as she began to show signs of returning consciousness,—

"I don't see why I shouldn't," he said to himself, arguing some point. "She was running away with this young fellow. I shouldn't think her the sort of gal to stick at a trifle, after the games she's been playing. Besides, if she has any of her nonsense, I'll threaten to give her in charge for setting her father's house on fire. Then, after all, why should I go back? Here's a chaise and pair that Master Wag has got the credit of running away with. Let him have the credit. I might as well have the chaise. It's worth something, I suppose; if I can get rid of it, all the better. If not, I can ride to London in it. Anyhow, I can have the girl, and I'll be hanged if I don't."

Having come to this conclusion, this unprincipled gentleman laid the young lady back in the carriage, and examined the horses' harness.

"I shall have to ride postilion," he thought. "It's rather awkward, and it looks rather odd. However, at this time of night there's nobody particular about; so I shall drive into the nearest town, and get a bed somewhere. It's rather too far to go on to London to-night, worse luck, and I am rather too tired. Though, by the way, how about the chaise? The people to whom it belongs will be scouring the country after it. Well, never mind; if they find I have got it I can easily clear myself, and if I get well off with it, all the better. I don't much mind how it is. The young woman I shall take care of in any case. Hallo! she's waking."

She had, in fact, recovered her senses, and was looking out at him from the carriage window.

As he approached, she started back with a slight scream; for she immediately recognized him.

"No—no!" she cried, "I will not go back."

"I don't want to take you back, my dear," replied Leech, with his most bewitching grin. and the kindest tones his harsh voice could assume.

"Where is my father?" asked Lucinda. "Is he here with you?"

"No, my darling, he isn't," replied the lawyer.

"Why are you here, then?"

"I've come after you."

"What right have you to come after me?"

"It's all right, Miss Hopley, I'm a friend of Charley's."

"A friend of Charley's," cried Lucinda. "Were you to meet us?"

"Yes," said Leech, wondering what she meant.

"You are the friend he spoke about then?"

"Yes, I am the friend he spoke about."

She looked at him long and earnestly.

She was thinking of the foreign nobleman, about whom Charley had told her such "whoppers." The nobleman who wanted to run away with her.

She did not think very much of the foreign nobleman's appearance when she came to observe closely, and she could not quite understand how it was that when he was taking tea with her father and mother, he had not told her who he was.

Then she fancied, though, that she remembered his casting sheep's eyes at her, which she had resented wrathfully.

However, he was the nobleman, without a doubt, she thought. She was a very green young lady, you will think. But then the generality of young ladies are green, you know, and most authors work themselves up into a state of great enthusiasm upon the subject of female innocence.

"Where's Charley," he asked presently.

Then she explained how she had seen him flung into the road.

"Perhaps he's killed," thought Leech; "however, it don't much matter; I had better go and look for his body. The lady who seems to take such an interest in him, will probably stand something handsome if I can tell her he's a croaker."

He went, therefore in search of Charley's remains, but they had been carried away by the jolly waggoner in the manner that I have before described.

"We will go on to the nearest town," said Leech, "and get a lodging for the night. You must be dreadfully tired."

The lady agreeing to this, the lawyer kissed her hand, climbed into the saddle and whipped up the horses.

The town to which they were bound was not many miles off, and they arrived there in another hour, and repaired straight way to the principal hotel.

Here Mr. Leech ordered a couple of sleeping apartments, representing the young lady as his daughter, to which deception she willingly agreed.

And as they retired to their different rooms the lawyer consoled himself for what he was at first inclined to consider a rather muffish proceeding, by the reflection that he was much more fit for a good night's rest than for any love-making; and furthermore, that it was best not to be too hasty in these matters, and that the ruin of a young lady should be effected with some degree of delicacy.

Before retiring to rest, he informed the ostler who assisted in putting away the post-chaise, that the post-boy had met with an accident upon the road, which accounted for he himself having ridden postilion.

Poor Lucinda was too tired and too bewildered by the extraordinary events of the night to be able to think much about anything, and her head was scarcely laid upon the pillow before she was fast asleep.

VIII.—NEXT MORNING—WHAT THE WAITER THOUGHT, WHAT THE CHAMBERMAID SAID, WHAT THE LANDLORD DID.

NEXT day, both Leech and Lucinda were so desperately sleepy they did not open their eyes until late in the afternoon.

But as soon as he did awoke, like the celebrated Robert in the nursery rhyme, he "looked at the sky," and seeing that "the sun was very high," thought it must be time to get up. So not having a watch, he rang the bell, and inquired of the waiter whether it was too early for breakfast.

"Not much too early," replied the waiter, with a grin. "It's three in the afternoon."

"Lord bless me," said Mr. Leech. "Is my —my niece—that is to say, my daughter come down yet?"

"Not yet, sir."

"When is the next train to London?"

"One at half-past three, and one at six, sir."

"Very well; go and wake the young lady, and tell her I am coming down."

"Yes, sir."

"Rum party, that," said the waiter to the chambermaid. "Didn't quite seem to know what relation the young woman was. I suppose it's all right."

"I don't know, I'm sure," replied the young lady he addressed. "She don't seem to be quite sure of her father's name; but as you say, I suppose it's all right."

When the lawyer met the young lady at breakfast, the latter felt somewhat bashful and timid, and hardly knew where to look.

She, however, in spite of that, managed unobserved to scan her companion's appearance.

"He don't look very much like a nobleman," she thought. "But then, he's a foreign nobleman, and perhaps they look different to ours."

Indeed, to tell the truth, he did not. He was at the time engaged in ladling up the gravy from his plate with his knife, thrusting the blade half down his throat at every mouthful, after the style of a Chinese juggler.

Neither did he allude to his rank in any way, or make love to her after the style she would have expected a nobleman to make love; and, except squeezing her hand now and then, when she handed him anything, or winking at her like an ogre over the rim of his teacup, he made no advances of a tender nature, and seemed to be chiefly engrossed with his victuals.

There was no doubt about it, he was an exceedingly vulgar person, only at the same time he had a certain insinuating way, which was very telling, and—as she set down his coarseness to eccentricity—found considerable favour in the eyes of this good-natured young lady.

However, though he was progressing in her good graces, it is a lamentable fact that he was far from doing so with the landlord and servants.

In fact, at the close of the meal, and just when he was about to take a sip of nectar from the fair one's lips, mine host tapped at the room door.

"There's a party here wants to do see you," said he.

"See me?" cried Leech.

"Yes, see you," replied the landlord sternly.

"Who is it, then?"

"It's a party about the shay."

"The shay! What about that?"

The landlord made no reply, but, stepping back a yard or so, beckoned to somebody to come forward.

Thus summoned, Bob the post-boy presented himself, and pulled his forelock by way of a bow.

"Now, then," said Leech, "what do you want?"

"Well, it's consarning of that there shay."

"What about it?"

"Well, consarning of the hire of it."

"I didn't hire it, did I?"

"No, but that young lady did."

"Well?"

"Well, the master says I'm to be paid."

"Does he? By whom?"

"Well, by them as hired it, I suppose."

"But suppose they don't feel inclined to pay for it, what then?"

This contingency had not occurred to Bob before, so he scratched his head, and looked rather dismal.

"Ain't I to be paid for it at all?" said he.

"My dear fellow," replied Mr. Leech, lighting a three-halfpenny Cuba with the air of Rothschild smoking a shilling Regalia, "I haven't the remotest idea."

"Haven't you?" said Bob, humbly.

"No," replied Mr. Leech; "nor do I take the slightest interest in the question. You will find your chaise in the stable; take it and yourself off the premises as soon as you like."

"But," said the landlord, "who's to pay for its putting up for the night, and the feed of the horses?"

"My dear sir," replied Mr. Leech, "I must again repeat that I haven't the remotest idea. If this worthy person (here he nodded towards Bob) likes to pay for it, I have no objection; otherwise, I should be inclined to suggest that you should distrain upon the trap and cattle for the amount of your little account."

This argument so flabbergastered the postboy and the landlord, that for some time they hadn't a word to say for themselves; but the latter kept repeating to himself, in a low whisper,

"Well, you are a cool chick, you are, so help me never!"

However, Bob was the first to come to the rescue.

"But how about that horse you hired?" said he. "What do you propose to pay for him?"

"That's quite another affair," replied Mr. Leech. "I shall give you my address, and I will return the horse when I have done with it, and pay your master for the hire of it. Until then, it is my property."

This was floorer No. 2.

Bob and the landlord retired into the passage, and laid their heads together.

Leech rang the bell.

"Have the kindness to bring my bill," said he to the waiter who answered it.

The man departed, but presently returned, and said that it was being made out.

When an hour had elapsed, and Leech thought it time that they should think about going to the railway, he suggested to the young lady that she should put on her bonnet and shawl, and she having done so, he rang the bell again.

Then the landlord came up-stairs and presented his bill, which was rather a stiff one, and Mr. Leech paid it with a good deal of grumbling.

After that they walked down-stairs, and were going out of the door, when a couple of rustic policemen made their appearance and barred their exit.

"What's this?" said Leech, indignantly. "Let me pass by."

"It's concerning of that there horse," said Bob, the post-boy, from behind the constables.

"What do you mean, you old fool," cried Leech. "Do you know what you are about. I beg to inform you that I am a lawyer, and that what you are doing is illegal. However, it don't matter a button to me. Come, what is it to be? Are you going to lock me up, or what else?"

The policemen and the post-boy conferred together.

"I shall go back, and ask my master about it," said the post-boy, "and until then you musn't try to stir away from this inn."

"Don't alarm yourself," replied Leech, "I shan't try to, and I will have thumping damages for an assault and false imprisonment, my fine fellow."

Then turning to the young lady he bade her come with him to the sitting-room.

"Won't we be put in prison?" asked Lucinda, in a great fright.

"Not at all," replied her companion. "Don't be afraid on that score. Landlord, we will have dinner at seven o'clock, the best you can get ready, and some of your crustiest port."

IX.—A RELIGIOUS REVIVAL AND SOME RUM GOINGS ON—THE REVEREND JACK PUDDING, AND THE REVEREND GHASTLY GASH—TEA AND CAKE—HUNT THE SLIPPER AND OTHER IMPUDENCE.

"WE won't make ourselves wretched, my darling," said Leech, kissing his companion; "since we have got to stop here, we'll be as comfortable as we can under the circumstances."

"There seems to be a great many people about the streets," said Lucinda, looking out of the window. "Whatever can be going on?"

"I'm blest if I know," replied her companion, "unless it is a Dorcas meeting."

"They seem a very holy-looking set of people, don't they?"

They were indeed a remarkably sanctified looking race, much inclined to red noses, thick lips, and huge gouty umbrellas.

The ladies were of the sort that is commonly called "dowdy;" very much tumbled and musty-smelling, like seedy females on a wet day in an omnibus.

The male kind were mostly fat, greasy, big-paunched men, who looked as if they were not altogether exempt from carnal appetites.

The children were mostly heavy and spiritless,—rather lumpish, in fact,—and distinguishable from other young people by the woful want of fit in their garments. The lads rejoicing in terribly tall and heavy hats, the nap of which seemed to have been carefully brushed round the wrong way, high and stiffly-starched stick-up collars, or collars laid out over the shoulders a foot broad at least, and boots of such a thickness, and of such ungainly proportions, that their approach was heralded with an ominous thumping and bumping, as though a troop of infant elephants was coming up.

The lasses, on the other hand, went in largely for black stockings and huge cotton gloves, the latter sticking out their fingers in all directions, like the spikes on a mace. Some of them were rosy-faced plummy ones, though, mind you, and more than one of the shepherds cast a sheep's eye at them as they passed by.

It was not, however, a Dorcas meeting which was the cause of all this excitement, but simply a great religious revival, organized and brought together by a select company of reverend gentlemen standing in need of a little cash.

"A regular got up thing," the profane and illiterate termed it: and a rumour got about in town, that the chief movers—the Reverend Ezekia Sleek, and the Reverend Oyley Swabb—had made an arrangement with the great Smash and Splinter Junction to share the profits of the day.

The reverend Jack Pudding, the inimitable comic Baptist of the Obelisk, had been hired at a great expense, and made all his hearers crack their sides by his highly humourous argument between the Deity and a drunken shoemaker, let alone perfectly convulsing them by disappearing for a moment at the bottom of the pulpit, and reappearing again with a false nose and a long pipe, besides performing some very amusing tricks with a hat and a guinea-pig, which you would hardly have seen equalled in a penny show at Camberwell fair.

In addition to this gent, there was Mr. Ghastly Gash, also a Baptist minister of celebrity, but going in for the blood-and-murder style of oratory, in preference to the low comic business. And perhaps he was a greater success upon the occasion that Mr. Pudding, at least if one might judge by the fact of half-a-dozen women going off in a fainting-fit every half-dozen minutes in consequence of his brimstone eloquence; though persons who are hard to please might have found the constant repetition of the words "hell," and "damnation," a trifle monotonous.

After the oratory and hysterics were over, the company adjourned to three immense booths, provided for the occasion, where a "tea fight" of extraordinary magnitude was to take place, of which the revivalists, to the tune of eighteen-pence a-head, were allowed to partake.

This was a "fight," and no mistake.

Fat podgy men were squeezed up flat against fat podgy women in corners where there was no room to breathe, and where they were heard in their perspiring agony to make anything but saintly observations to each other.

The greasy-faced shepherds managed mostly to get squeezed up to the plummy little maidens in the big white gloves, and here and there among the jabber of tongues and clattering of dishes, might be heard the half suppressed remonstrances of some young virgin, telling some gentleman to "adone now, do, I'm surprised at you." "Keep your hands to yourself," or "your wife's a-looking."

To say that the tea-cakes were consumed by the hundred-weight, and the tea put away by the bucketful, would be speaking in mild terms.

There surely never was such a consumption of hot water and sugar, diluted with decoction of chalk and essence or birch-brooms.

And when everybody was—as the Reverend Jack Pudding facetiously termed it—"chuck to the bung," somebody proposed a hymn, which was sung to the tune of "Old Bob Ridley," and seemed to afford general satisfaction.

After that, the Reverend Pudding said a few words upon things in general, and plumcake in particular, asked a blessing, danced a hornpipe, and broke up the meeting by proposing a round game of hunt the slipper, which was played with much delight by the gentlemen, and some confusion by the plummy young maidens, who were inclined to resent the lawless and lascivious advances of the amorous shepherds.

The meeting had broken up by about half-past six, and some of the holy ones, considerably the worse for tea and cake, were proclaiming their intention of not going home till morning, and till daylight did appear; while others, excited by their recent amusements, were proposing all sorts of romps and games, which the elderly female portion of the community were rather inclined to be shocked at; and some few very zealous ones were distributing little tracts with startling titles, such as "What's your game?" "What are you up to?" "Who kissed Maria?" "Come out of the cupboard," and "How the little Boy went to Hell for Whistling on a Sunday."

The crowds in the streets which Leech and Lucinda had seen from the window were the Revivalists on their way to the railway-station. "Those are some of the shepherds, I expect," said the lawyer, pointing to three or four fat men in black. "Coming in here, too"

X.—DESCRIBES THE VERY EXTRAORDINARY BEHAVIOUR OF CERTAIN REVEREND GENTLEMEN, AND SHOWS HOW EVEN METHODIST PARSONS MAY MAKE FOOLS OF THEMSELVES, WHERE A PRETTY GIRL IS CONCERNED.

THE clerical parties whom Leech had observed, were coming into the hotel, to inquire whether they could have anything to eat; for though they shone very bright ornaments indeed at numerous tea-drinkings, they were not themselves over partial to such a mild order of refreshment.

Indeed, in a confidential whisper to the reverend Ghastly Gash, the reverend Jack Pudding had called the bohea he had just been partaking of, "unmitigated hog's wash;" which you will allow, is not a respectful way of speaking of "good family mixed."

The landlord received the clergy with great respect.

"Have you anything we can eat, Mr. Tipple?" asked the Reverend Pudding.

"Plenty, sir," replied Mr. Tipple, "and of the best."

"That I'm sure it is," said Pudding. "But the question is, have you anything hot?"

"Well, we've as fine a jint as ever you clapt your eyes on, sir, down at the fire, and will be ready—that is, if you wouldn't object to—"

"To what?"

A SERMON IN THE KITCHEN.

"Well, to—you won't be offended?"

"No offence, Tipple; go on."

"Well, there's two—two parties, if I may call 'em so."

"What of them?"

"Well, one is a gent, sir."

"Certainly."

"In the legal way; and the other—"

"The other—"

"Is, if I may call her so—in short, a female."

"A female, eh? A young female?"

"Well, yes, sir: she's young."

"And comely?"

"Yes, sir, she's tidy looking."

"Plump, Tipple?"

"Reyther crummy, sir."

"Then what is your objection to her?"

No. 22.

"Well, you see, sir, she's—ahem—"

"Yes."

Here all the reverend gentlemen opened their eyes and their ears very greedily.

"Not to put too fine a pint on it," then said the landlord, "though the parties certainly does pretend to be fathers and mothers—that is to say, fathers and daughters—and has had separate beds, and all that's proper, we're inclined to think there's some impidence betwixt 'em which don't meet—if I may be allowed the expression—the naked eye."

"Merciful goodness!" cried all the reverend gentlemen in a breath, casting up their fishy eyes ceilingwards with pious horror.

"An improper female!" said Mr. Gash.

"A person devoid of virtue!" said Mr. Swabb.

[CHARLEY WAG, THE NEW JACK SHEPPARD.

"Or modesty!" said Mr. Sleek.

"Scandalous!"

"Outrageous!!"

"Shameful!!!"

"It ought to be put a stop to."

"What sort of a looking person is she?" the Reverend Jack Pudding inquired, after everybody had expressed their unqualified disgust.

"She's a tidy looking wench enough," replied the landlord, "to them as likes the style."

"What style is it, pray?" asked Pudding.

"Well," said the landlord, after a little reflection, "she's what I should call the scrumptious style."

"And what sort's that?"

"Built like the Dutch, sir, if I may so explain myself. The sort of gal, sir, now that would fill the seat of a tidy sized arm-chair. In fact, she's the very reverse to a cheribum, which you will excuse me, sir, if I remind you, is not exactly the sort of gentry suited for sitting down."

But when the landlord had got thus far in his rigmarole, a shrill female voice broke in behind them :—

"It's a most extraordinary thing, Mr. Tipple, that you must stand jabbering there, when the gentlemen want to come in, and are, I will be bound, almost dying for a bit of dinner. Get out of the way, do. Will you step forward, gentlemen, if you please; and I really must apologise for Mr. T., he's so very tedious, poor man, and does so love to hear himself chatter. As for me, I do assure you, gentlemen, if it is the last word I ever have to say in all my life, and was upon my Bible oath, which I said the same thing only this very morning to Mrs. Gibbons, over the way at the oil-shop—doubtless unbeknown to you, gentlemen, but the best of women, I assure you, and the mother of seven children, all boys, and as fine lads as you could wish to see, excepting always her eldest, that is sickly, and a cripple, having blowed hisself up when two years old with a quarter of a pound of gunpowder he was, childlike, playing at making a pudding with in a saucepan over the kitchen fire, and sent him up the chimney. Yes, gentlemen, as I said to her, I says, Mrs. Gibbons, says I, that husband of mine is the magginest old man I ever come across; and so he is."

Then pushing her husband on one side, this lady who seemed to have so very little to say for herself, ushered them into a parlour at the back of the bar, and gave orders for a cloth to be laid.

"The idea, Tipple! I'm surprised at you," said she, bustling about. "However you could have thought of wanting these reverend gentlemen to set down at the same table with that low forward creature up-stairs. I'm surprised at you; but it seems to me, that some men haven't got any more head about 'em than a pin, and not so much."

But here Jack Pudding interposed.

"We're not going to see this lady, then," said he to Swabb, in a whisper.

"What, the sinful vessel?" said Swabb.

"Yes," replied the Pudding, "the one that isn't made like a cheribum."

"Something must be done," said Sleek. "We must not lose this opportunity of converting the unrighteous," put in Ghastly Gash.

Then they all tackled the landlady, and persisted in going up-stairs.

She would not hear of it.

They stuck to their point.

Was it not their mission to go among the ungodly and the unclean, to visit the leper, tend to the sick, preach to the corrupt, and gather in the black sheep straying in the wilderness.

The landlady hardly knew. She didn't exactly see how any gentlemen could get much good by mixing with the likes of that—*that creature*. She couldn't exactly understand gentlemen's taste, if they could associate with *creatures* at all. For her part, she didn't know why *creatures* were allowed to go about in the brazen way they did, and if she had her way she would have them all whipped at the cart's tail, or pumped upon—perhaps that would be better.

Thus addressing them, the little landlady worked herself up into a tremendous state of excitement and bounced about like a cracker, slamming doors and breaking plates, and almost knocking poor Mr. Tipple on to his back every time she turned round.

"There, drat your stupid old head," she cried at last, catching hold of his collar, and thrusting him back into a chair, where she held him and shook him until you would almost have fancied one of his ears would have dropped off. "You don't want to go up with them, I suppose. That's what you'd like to be doing, I know. You've been purring about all the day after that baggage, as it is. I'm ashamed of you. Yah, you horrible old man."

So Mr. Tipple colapsed, and the reverend gents proceeded up-stairs, where the cloth was being laid.

As you may suppose, the parsons fixed their eyes upon Miss Lucinda directly after they got into the room, and if one might judge by the expression of their saintly physiognomies, they evidently intensely admired her plump proportions.

But the expression of Mr. Leech's face was far from amiable.

He was not over fond of the clerical persons at any time, and when they threw sheep's eyes at his lady love, you may readily suppose it did not increase his affection for them.

And they certainly did throw sheep's eyes, and ogle, and sigh with a vengeance. Poor Lucinda at first did not know which way to look, but after awhile, when she became more used to it, she began to think it was rather good fun, particularly when she saw how very savage it made the "foreign nobleman."

Girls like a joke of that sort, I believe; at least, when I was a young man (that is not more than fifty years ago, and we wore tights and Hessian boots, a rather trying thing for the legs, as as you may imagine); when I was a young man, the young lady I used to take out, was particularly fond of "trying it on," as the saying is, with other gentlemen, and as I was no fighter, I found it unpleasant. That is why, in maturer years, I took out a plain young woman, with a nose like a cricket-stump. There was never any annoyance then. It was no good her winking at the fellows; they wouldn't take any notice of her.

Presently the waiter came in, and lighted the

candles, and very shortly afterwards the dinner appeared.

"Waiter," said Leech, "have you no private rooms?"

"No other room than this, sir," said the waiter.

"I thought this was to have been kept private," Leech observed.

"If you have any objection to these gentlemen dining here," said the waiter, "I'll speak to master."

"No, no—it does not matter."

He thought it best not to press the point, as it might only make matters more disagreeable.

So they all sat down to table—Miss Lucinda, Mr. Leech, Mr. Swabb, Mr. Sleek, Mr. Gash, and Mr. Jack Pudding.

When the meat was disposed of, and the sweets came upon the table, the reverend gentlemen ordered in a couple of bottles of wine, which they insisted upon Leech and the young lady partaking of; and an evil-disposed person might have been inclined to suppose from their behaviour that they were endeavouring to fuddle the lawyer.

If that were their scheme, unfortunately for themselves, they had chosen a very injudicious course, for the lawyer could drink like a fish; and, though he took two glasses to anybody else's one, they were all getting rather flushed in the face, while he was, as usual, as pale as parchment.

Not upon those two bottles, of course; for he had insisted upon having in another bottle, and then some one had had another, and another after that, until there had been as many bottles consumed as there were gentlemen at table.

After which, somebody suggested a little hot spirits and water, just to settle the dinner; and then everybody had a good stiff glass of rum and water, upon Leech's recommendation, he asserting, from his own experience, that there was an uncommonly fine tap of the right down genuine old Jamaica to be found in the house, and that they ought to try it.

A good stiff glass of rum—or, for the matter of that, say a couple or three good stiff glasses—upon the top of a bottle of remarkably crusty old port, is enough to intoxicate some people.

Mind, I only said some people.

I don't for a moment intend to say that it was enough to intoxicate Mr. Oyley Swabb, for instance, or that it would overcome Mr. Ezekiah Sleek, or be too many for Mr. Ghastly Gash, or get the better of the Reverend Pudding; only to a person, like myself, who have not an over strong head, I should say decidedly, that when I have put that amount of liquor away, I should be rather, if not very much, the worse for it.

But I am talking of reverend gentlemen, and I should not like to say that any of them were tipsy, because I don't know but that next week a deputation of indignant old ladies, with gouty umbrellas, would not wait upon me in Brydges Street, and belabour my bones. I know for a fact that old ladies don't like their shepherds made fun of, and so I should not like to do it, and would much rather not make any disparaging statements about them, although some of you naughty ones would like nothing better. I know you.

Therefore we will, if you please, take it for granted that none of the reverend gents were either "sprung," or "lushy," or "half-seas-over," or "slued," or "groggy," or "swipey," or—I cannot think of any more terms for the same state; but you know a great many more I daresay, and are able to supply them wholesale to the clown in the pantomime, when he sings "Hot Codlins," and comes to that part of the legend where "she swigged and she swigged till the bottle it shrunk, and this little old woman, they say, got—whack fol di rol dol diddle liddle, whack fol di diddle liddle li do."

It is settled, then, they were not drunk—only Mr. Swabb began to fix Mr. Sleek with one eye in the most curious fashion, only Mr. Pudding began to talk extraordinarily thick, and Mr. Gash, regardless of all the usages of good society, went to sleep with his head in his plate, and snored like a pig.

Only Mr. Swabb would insist on rubbing his feet against Mr. Sleek's legs, and treading on his toes, and squeezing one of Mr. Sleek's feet between his, in a way which was extremely peculiar, and if it was not that he mistook Mr. Sleek's legs for Lucinda's, it was in my opinion rather ridiculous.

XI.—A Sermon in the Kitchen—When the candle was put out—What's the number—Something wrong—Four mysterious figures in the dark.

WHILE matters were going on much after this fashion, and the gentlemen were becoming rather verbose, not to say maudlin, the landlady made her appearance at the door, and with a curtsey to the gentlemen and a toss of the head at Lucinda, said that she had come to remind Mr. Pudding that he had promised to oblige a select few with a little discourse down in the kitchen, and that the select few had assembled and were waiting to hear him.

Now Mr. Pudding had quite forgotten this promise, and indeed, doubted whether he had ever made such a one, but he thought it wisest to pretend that he remembered it, and that he would have much pleasure in doing his little best.

So staggering on to his legs, he made a lurch at the door, and followed by the other reverends, the lawyer, and Lucinda, repaired as steadily as he could to the kitchen.

There were a good many old women assembled, some young ones, a few serious looking men, too, small shop-keepers, and the like, for the revivals had turned everybody's head in those parts, and the rustic population were for the nonce religious mad.

Mr. Pudding after taking a glance at the wooden expression of countenance enjoyed by most of his little congregation, thought his usual facetious style would be rather thrown away, and having prepared nothing, as everybody knows, it is easier to be serious than comic at a moment's notice, he went in for the former style, mounted upon the chair, and commenced a discourse, as full of hard words as he could make it; but as his pronunciation was not of the clearest, or his meaning of the plainest, all the old women shook their heads, and tried to look as though they knew what it was all about, while the young ones, after the first five minutes, began to vote it a nuisance, and to gape with all their might.

At this critical juncture, Mr. Ghastly Gash, having pulled himself together, came in at the rescue, and commenced in his famous hell and damnation style.

It was astonishing how he carried his hearers with him. If the reader has never had the ill-fortune to be present at one of those most atrocious and blasphemous scenes, which are called religious revivals, he can form no idea of the spectacle it presents.

These poor, besotted, ignorant and half-educated creatures, confused and bewildered by the preposterous jargon, that is hurled at them by the tub-orator of the time, give way to their feelings in the wildest and most extravagant manner.

Some women you will see fling themselves upon the ground, and writhe and scream, some rock themselves to and fro, groaning as though they were suffering from a severe stomach-ache, whilst others have been even known in their religious frenzy, to tear their clothes off their backs, and burst into demoniacal dances in a comparative state of nudity.

In the middle of a scene something similar to this, when fanaticism was at its height, one of the reverend gentlemen, either to give more effect to Mr. Gash's discourse, or because he happened to be sitting between a couple of very nice young women with his arm round each of their waists, proposed putting out the lights.

This motion being carried by general consent, Mr. Gash hammered away harder than ever, and the rest of the company groaned and shrieked harder than ever, except here and there in cases where reverend gentlemen were sitting next to nice young women, where there was a good deal of giggling, and a little struggling, and some exceedingly unclerical behaviour.

At last, Mr. Gash, probably thinking that his brothers were having all the fun, while he was having all the hard work, got off his chair and made his way through a confusion of legs to the door, and so broke up the meeting.

Then more rum and water set in, and the reverend gentlemen asked for their bedroom candlesticks, and retired to bed, all more or less unsteadily.

"Waiter," said Mr. Oily Swabb, in a husky whisper, "which is the sleeping appartment of that young lady we had the pleasure of dining with?"

"No. 6, sir," said the waiter with a grin.

"Thank you, waiter," replied Mr. Swabb. "I only asked, because—because I thought Mr. Pudding said that was his room—you needn't mention the circumstance—here's a shilling for you."

And Mr. Swabb went off to bed, trying to wink to himself with one eye, and bobbing his nose in the candle in the operation.

"I say, my dear, said Mr. Sleek to the chambermaid, "that seems a very nice young lady who had dinner with us. Did you say she was the daughter or the wife of the gentleman she was with?"

"She's his daughter, I believe, sir."

"Oh, indeed; and she's gone to bed, I suppose."

"I believe she has, sir."

"She wished me to knock at her door tomorrow morning, as we are going out for a walk together; but I quite forget what she said was her number."

"The number of her bed-room, sir?"

"Yes, my dear. Here's sixpence for you. Don't say anything to anybody. Which is it?"

"It's No. 6, sir."

"Thank you, my dear. Now give me a kiss, and I'll give you another sixpence."

"Get along, you horrid man; I won't do it under a shilling."

"Well, here is one—a new one: so give us two."

"There, there, that'll do, sir; that's enough. Please be quiet—you're rumpling me so. Look what you've done; here's my candle gone out."

"Brother Gash, brother Gash," said the Reverend Mr. Jack Pudding, "what do you think I heard brother Sleek asking just now?"

"What?"

"The number of the bed-room of that unrighteous though comely young vessel who had dinner with us to-day."

"Surely not. And did he obtain the information?"

"Yes, brother Gash, and it is—"

"What?"

"No. 6."

"What is his intention, think you?"

"I am afraid to form an idea. No good, though."

"Ah!" sighed Mr. Gash, "we are all erring creatures, brother Pudding."

"You're right, brother Gash. Let us take warning by the wicked."

"Heigho! Amen. No. 6, didn't you say?"

"Yes."

"Good-night. Let us pray for him."

Thus did the four reverend gents betake themselves to their separate chambers.

The hotel closed for the night; the lights were extinguished; all good people were a-snoring.

Hush!

Four doors opened stealthily; four mysterious figures clad in white crept thief-like through the darkness to one spot.

To one door did they direct their steps.

With bated breath, with fast beating hearts, with heated brains, excited by drink and desire.

The young lady in No. 6 slept peacefully, thinking of no harm.

Hush!

Was that the creaking of a board, or the turning of the handle of the door, or was it fancy?

XII.—FAVERSHAM APPEARS IN THE CHARACTER OF A GUARDIAN ANGEL.

YOU see I ought to go back to our mutual friend Charley for a chapter or so. And, with your permission, we will leave these amorous gentlemen in their shirts in the cold, and come back to them again presently.

There was no putting that Faversham off.

Stone had done all he could think of, and now he gave the matter up as hopeless, and led the way in gloomy resignation to the prisoner's cell.

In the meanwhile, Mr. Darbies had been doing all he could to make the prisoner, as he termed it, "comfortable."

Mr. Darbies' notion of comfort, and that of my young lady readers, are probably slightly at variance.

For instance.

As Charley persisted in lying on his back in the middle of the floor, just exactly as he had lain when one of the gaolers threw a bucket of cold water over him, Mr. Darbies took the liberty of raising him on to his feet by a vigorous jerk, which, had you not known Mr. D. to be the kindest-hearted of men, you would have supposed must have been done with the intention of dislocating the youthful prisoner's neck.

Then, when raised to his feet, as he still persisted in slipping down again, and doubling up in a limp and ungainly, not to say ungraceful fashion, you cannot surely blame Mr. Darbies for giving him a right down good shaking.

And as he persisted, even after this, in pretending to be insensible, and in refusing to look alive, and change his wet shirt for a dry one, Mr. Darbies had but one course to pursue, which was to "put a little life into him."

Now those young gentlemen who live by going errands, who are slow upon the journey, and who have hard taskmasters to deal with, most likely know much better than I can tell them the meaning of the phrase.

There are a variety of ways in which life can be put into a person. Sometimes it is done with the buckle end of a strap; I have heard that a lump of wood with a nail in it is very efficacious, though rather painful. There are also other methods, and all of them hurt.

Mr. Darbies took to the shaking plan. He shook Charley out of the wet garment as you might shake a rat out of a bag.

Then he shook him into the dry one, and buttoned him up very tight indeed—if you must know, rather choky.

After this, Mr. Darbies gave him a fair chance of getting into bed of his own accord, and, as he did not choose to avail himself of it, Mr. Darbies helped him in in a very summary fashion—as you might call it, "neck and crop."

When he was thus settled, with his heels a trifle higher than his head, and his shirt-collar pinching him to that degree that his very ears seemed redder than usual, Mr. Darbies covered him up, tucked him in, and took a complacent survey of him, like a sculptor might do of a very beautiful statue he had just completed.

"There," said he, "now you're to rights if you like, ain't you?"

But the ungrateful boy made no reply.

"Ain't you?" repeated Mr. Darbies.

The same silence.

Mr. D. seemed half inclined to shake him again, but, on reflection, thought he wouldn't.

"Kindness is throwed away on the likes of you," he observed.

Indeed it seemed to be so.

"Don't go a chattering of your teeth in that fashion, as if you was cold."

Master Charles did certainly look very cold—rather blue and numbed.

"Do you hear me?" repeated Mr. Darbies.

"Rat-a-tat-tat-tat-tat," went the teeth.

"Because if you don't blessed soon drop it I shall give you somethink as 'll warm you; and I ain't quite sure, if you come to that, as it won't put you in a perspiration."

And I think there is very little doubt that the gaoler would have been as good as his word, only that at that moment the door opened, and Mr. Stone, the governor, followed by Mr. Faversham, the doctor, entered the prisoner's cell.

"Well, Number Ten," said Mr. Stone, in the kindest voice possible, "how do you find yourself to-day?"

"Rat-a-tat-tat."

"What's he say, Darbies?"

"He's a laughin' I think, sir."

"What's the matter, Number Ten?"

"Rat-a-tat-tat."

It was, however, anything but a merry expression which was upon Number Ten's pinched features.

Faversham walked up to the side of the hammock, and looked at him attentively.

"Has he got on clothes enough?" he said.

"Oh, plenty," cried Darbies, as though Charley were rather being suffocated than otherwise.

"Has he had enough to eat?"

"He's always a eatin'—bustin' I may call it."

"His collar seems tight."

"He will have it so, sir. I tried to persuade him not."

And Mr. Darbies would have interposed, but Faversham gently, though firmly, repulsed his interference, and took the prisoner's hand in his.

"His pulse is very weak," he said. "As weak as water."

"Yes," replied Stone, who thought he ought to say something. "Quite as weak. I can't make it out."

"He seems to have been overworked," the physician continued. "His strength has been overtaxed."

"I trust not."

"I trust not also."

Then the doctor undid the boy's collar, and raised him up in bed.

The gaoler tried to prevent this, but was not quick enough.

In raising him up, the doctor caught a glimpse of Charley's back, and uttered an exclamation of horror at the sight.

"What have you done to him?" he asked.

"Done to what?"

"Done to his back. Why it is one mass of sores."

Then Stone, seeing that it was no good continuing in the same style as heretofore, burst into a violent rage, or a very good imitation of of the same.

"He's one of the worst boys I ever had to deal with. He's a most incorrigible young vagabond. He's a most abominable young scoundrel. He's a lazy, idle, shamming, lying, young thief. If I had killed him it wouldn't have been more than he deserved."

"You have killed him."

"I've only done my duty, whatever I've done."

"I have no doubt of that, Mr. Stone, and that you will be able to satisfactorily account to the coroner for the prisoner's death."

"I—I—don't suppose it's as bad as that."

"I am a medical man, as you are aware, and I warn you, sir, that this boy's life is in the greatest possible danger."

"What do you recommend I should do, then?"

"Move him instantly into the infirmary, and let him have every care and attention."

"That's quite against rules—"

"Mr. Stone," interrupted Faversham, looking towards Darbies, "can I speak to you alone?"

"Well—yes—certainly. Go out, Darbies."

Darbies went out very sulkily, and slammed the door.

Then when they were alone. "Stone," said the doctor, "this boy has been most cruelly treated. That you have been a party to this treatment, I cannot for a moment doubt, or else why should you have been so unwilling to have admitted me to see him. However, it matters very little to me whether the boy's bruises are to be attributed to justifiable punishment, or to brutal cruelty. One thing, however, I must impress upon your attention—"

"Go on, sir, go on," replied the other, livid with rage."

"And that is, that it must cease. There must be no more of it. Do you hear?"

"I hear, certainly, and what in the name of ——"

"You have a bad memory."

"Blast my memory."

"I have no objection."

"What has my memory got to do with the matter?"

"You have forgotten what I said just now about Horford."

"I don't know Horford, and I never did, and I know no person who escaped from here in a mysterious way; and if they did, I had nothing to do with it, and I'm damned if you're going to bully me."

"You also forget about the burning of the house of a certain Hezekiah Crawle.

"I don't know the name, and never heard it before, and I know nothing of the burning of any houses."

"You mean, then, to defy me, Mr. Stone."

"Defy you; No! damn you. I don't want to defy you. Who are you? what do you want with me, in God's name?"

"I want that boy not to be murdered, mind you. I have no affection for the boy, nor for any boy, nor for any man. I have no affection for any man, woman, or child alive, and would rather see them all dead than alive. But I have a reason for taking an interest in this young thief. I wish him to live, and those who thwart my wishes, come in my way—and those who come in my way I remove."

"I ask you again," said Stone, "who you are?"

"I am a doctor, as you already know, and my name is Faversham."

Stone looked at him long and fixedly.

"I don't know the name, and I cannot understand what reasons you can have for wishing to intimidate me by referring to circumstances about which I know nothing."

"You do know something, and when you know me better, you will know that I am not in the habit of making a statement which I cannot prove; you will therefore remove this boy immediately to the infirmary, and take every care of him; and not doing so, I shall consider that it is war between us, and act accordingly."

I need not weary the reader's patience any longer by the fencing of these two gentlemen.

A great deal more was said, but it is unnecessary at the present time to enter into particulars. Later on in our story, I dare say, we shall hear a little more about this mystery, besides several other little mysteries which, at present, I do not think it wise to disclose to my readers; although I beg to assure them, that there is nothing in a small way which I would not do to merit their good opinion.

It matters not how Faversham obtained the mastery which he did obtain over the governor, but Charley Wag was in the course of an hour at most removed from his hard hammock to a comfortable feather bed in the infirmary, and the celebrated skillagolee that day formed no portion of his diet.

————

XIII.—IN WHICH THE OLD NURSE SAYS WHAT SHE WOULD DO IF SHE WERE A THIEF.

MANY days and nights did the young prisoner pass upon his sick bed.

Many basins of beef-tea did he put out of sight, besides many glasses of jelly; and presently, when he grew a little stronger, a leg or a wing or two of fowl. They gave the prisoners chicken sometimes in the infirmary; and, after a long course of stringy beef, black bread, and gruel, it was by no means to be sneezed at; in fact, it seemed like a Lord Mayor's feast to them.

He could scarcely believe that it was not a dream, when, on his convalescence, he was allowed to lie on his comfortable bed, and read such books as the chaplain charitably provided.

They were not, perhaps, exactly the sort of books that Master Charles would have chosen had he had the right of choice, but he was very thankful for them under the circumstances.

"Claude Duval, the Dashing Highwayman; or, Hurrah for the Road"—"Blue Blazes, the Smuggler King; or, the Murdered Maiden and the Spifflicated Old Man of Peckham Rye," and "Ada the Betrayed and the Titled Ruffian; or, the Pleasures of Poverty and the Horrors of Seduction."

That was his sort of reading, if he could have his way; however, I am glad to say that on the present occasion he could not, and so he was obliged, against his will, to improve his mind, and gain a scrap or two of knowledge.

When again his health improved in some measure, and he was well enough to sit up, he was allowed to sit by the window, and watch the free birds singing in the trees in the prison garden.

What funny fellows he thought them, to stay

there when they might go into the open fields, away from stone walls and iron spikes. It really was a very happy time ; and if he had only been a free boy instead of a prisoner, and had known that he could have gone out into the world at any minute, I don't believe he would have done so.

Only he was a prisoner, you see, and that made the difference between him and the birds.

Thus the time passed on. One of the nurses, an amiable old lady, to whom rheumatics was a sore trial, but who at other times was inclined to be chatty and " comfortable like," took quite a fancy to Master Charles, and entertained him with many stories about the persons she had known in her youth.

She asked Charley how it was that he had become a prisoner, and he told her such of his history as he was acquainted with.

She was much astonished at many portions of his narrative, and asked many questions about the beautiful lady he had rescued from the river.

But I need not tell you that he suppressed all that portion of his life which had reference to Miss Julia Jenkini.

He told her, however, and without in the slightest degree departing from the truth, all the circumstances connected with Mr. Measles' establishment, and of the way in which he had been forced into the burglary.

"I quite believe you, my dear," said the old lady. "I was certain the first moment I clapt my eyes upon you that you were innocent. Heigho! I had a son once the very image of you."

Charley asked what became of him, and then the old lady told him that he (the son) had got into difficulties and come to grief upon account of some little embezzling matter in the city.

"But," said the old lady, " it is not always the biggest rogues that are hanged."

"Indeed, ma'am," said Charley.

"No, no, my dear, not at all. If I were a thief—which God forbid I should be ; and, indeed, at my age it is not very likely—but if I were a thief now, I think I should play my cards a little better than some of them do."

"How so, ma'am ?"

"Well, I have noticed that thievery seems to do most of them no good, they live in such a miserable squalid way. They're always hiding and skulking out of sight, for fear of being taken by the police. Why, bless me, it must almost be worse always fearing it than being taken and put in prison."

"Do you think so, ma'am ?"

"Oh! Yes, certainly I do."

"Now if I was to take to thieving, I should do quite different."

"What would you do, ma'am ?"

"Well, I should purchase every luxury which money could purchase. I should live in the most splendid apartments, and, if I were a man, keep the most magnificent women, live on the most delicious food, drink the most costly wines, and taste every delicacy of life, exactly as though I were one of the aristocracy."

"But that would take a great deal of money, ma'am."

"Yes, it would ; but then, unless you can make a great deal of money by thieving, I think

the risks are so very great, that it is much better to be honest."

"Then you don't think it better to be honest, ma'am, if you don't make as much by it as you would by thieving."

"Lord bless the boy! I don't mean anything of the kind. I don't know what I have been saying. I am sure I hope nobody connected with me, and nobody I take any interest in, will ever turn thief. And as for you, young gentleman, I should have thought you must have suffered quite sufficient already to prevent your taking to that line of business. There, drat you, it's time you had your broth, so don't keep me any longer listening to your chatters."

They talked no more upon the subject, but for a long while Charley meditated over what she had said, and wondered, perhaps, whether he would ever be a rich thief, or whether it would be his luck to fall into good hands when he left the prison, and be able to earn an honest livelihood.

"No, no," said Master Charles ; " thieving may be all very well if you are lucky, and if it was not wicked ; but most decidedly prison is a little worse than I have heard it described. Anyhow, if I ever do get out alive, I shall take all the precautions I know of not to get in again."

XIV.—CHARLEY HELPS THE COOK—TIMES ARE NOT SO HARD—THE GATES ARE OPENED

BUT Charley was not very happy, although his situation at present was comfortable enough.

Every day he expected to be told that he must go back to his cell ; and every time that the governor, Stone, made his appearance in the infirmary, which was very frequently, his heart sank within him.

Then, when Stone turned upon his heel again, Charley's joy was intense.

However, at last it came.

One day, Stone, after looking at the boy for a few moments, called the doctor to him.

"How is Number Ten getting on ?"

"He's getting as strong as a lion," replied Mr. Purge, cheerfully, for he liked to look upon the sunny side of things terrestrial.

"Well enough to move ?" asked Stone.

"Bless you, yes, sir."

"He shall do so to-day, then,"

"We mustn't put him too hard at it at present, perhaps,"

"He is not going to be."

"A little light at first, I should advise."

"Certainly, Mr. Purge. Here, boy, what can you do ?"

Charley made no answer, uncertain what to say.

"Do you know any trade ?"

"No, sir; but I could turn my hand to almost anything, I think, sir."

"Can you read ?"

"Yes, sir, and write."

"Do figures ?"

"Yes, sir."

"We'll put him into the kitchen, then," said

Stone. "He can keep the accounts, and help the cook when required."

"I think that will do capitally, sir," said the surgeon. "When shall he go, did you say?"

"Directly. Here, Hudson (to a warder), take this boy to the culinary department."

Charley accompanied him forthwith.

From that time until the end of the term of his imprisonment he assisted Mr. Grilby, the cook, stirred the soup and the gruel, made up the accounts, washed the dishes, and did anything else that was required.

Although this situation was by no means so agreeable as the one which he had just quitted, still it was far preferable to his former one.

Mr. Grilby was kind to him in an uncouth, clumsy way. Charley was kept upon he prison diet, but every now and then the cook would push a basin of soup towards him, and tell him to throw it down the sink, at the same time winking with all his might, and screwing up his face into a ludicrous and knowing expression, intended to signify that Charley's throat was the sink alluded to, and that it was so to be disposed of.

The cooks were strictly forbidden to speak to the prisoners; but Mr. Grilby frequently made a sort of compromise by reading an article out of the newspaper to his companion cook, a Mr. Sop, who, I ought to tell you by the way, was as deaf as a stone, but would not own to it; so that when Mr. Grilby had given him a full, true, and particular account of the last horrible murder, or the great mill between young Bumps and Conky Bill of Brummagem, Mr. Sops would say:—

"Very good indeed, very capital—I quite agree with you;" or, "That has him, and no mistake."

Though he had not the remotest idea what the other had been saying.

However, Charley understood, and was very thankful to him for his kindness.

"Poor young beggar!" Grilby would say, "he wants a bit of life put into him."

But he had a more agreeable way of putting life into anybody than Mr. Darbies had.

Of course this improvement in his treatment must not be attributed to any increase in kindheartedness upon the part of the governor.

If anything, Mr. Stone would have liked to have skinned him alive. When he took a dislike to a prisoner, he never afterwards got over it.

The only reason, then, to account for the change, was to suppose that what Faversham had threatened him with, had in some measure intimidated him.

When Faversham had come, he had found the boy insensible; and had it been his intention to ask Charley any questions, his object was foiled; and though when he left, he told Stone that he would come again before long, he did not keep his promise.

Many and graver matters prevented him.

Every day the duke's son grew more and more sickly and ailing.

The doctor whose assistance, when the malady reached an alarming point, Faversham had called in, owned himself to be altogether unequal to grapple with the ravages of this fearful disease.

At last, when the patient seemed to be sinking silently into the tomb, the mother in a desperate frenzy of love, spite of all that could be urged to the contrary, took the boy from his rich bed, and fled with him from England.

Then, in the genial warmth of the sunny south of France, did the future heir of the house of Heatherland begin to mend.

The fury of Faversham at this event almost amounted to madness, but never for a moment did the mask drop from his bloodless face.

Ever the same patient, gentle, courteous gentleman, he bowed his head in deference to the duchess's superior judgment; and none were louder in their expressions of joy at the young lord's recovery than Ralph Faversham, the family physician.

Thus time rolled on, and Charley in prison was forgotten by this wily hatcher of plots.

Thus time rolled on, and the long looked-for day of release drew nigh.

Soon the months dwindled into weeks, and the weeks into days; at last the days shrank into hours.

The night before the day of freedom came at last.

A summer's night. The air, which all day long had been oppressively heavy and hot, was now beautifully fresh and cool; but the prisoner tossed wearily upon his feverish bed, and flung the clothes from him, unable to sleep.

Was he going to be free—to walk once more in the wide wide world, away from those bars, stone walls, and chains, and bondage?

Yet a few hours and he would be no longer a prisoner.

Oh, what a happy, happy world it seemed to him!

So full of pleasures and delights! Such a merry laughing world, with no sad hearts and empty bellies in it!

What would he do when he got out?

His head was crammed full of the most wonderful schemes for earning a livelihood. He had not quite made up his mind what trade he should honour by adopting, but he meant, immediately he got out, to get some employment.

He would go and offer his services to somebody or other, work away like a young steam-engine, gain his employer's good will, rise in his good graces, marry his employer's fair daughter, and become a partner at least.

With respect to Julia Jenkini?

What about her, Master Charles?

Well, you see, that sort of thing is all very well; fellows must sow their wild oats. At least fellows do, anyhow; but a connection of that kind is not very desirable.

Suppose he married her.

How could he marry her?

Would she be a fit wife for the Lord Mayor of London?

Lord Mayor of how much? asks the reader, astonished.

Well, what of it? I said London, and I meant it. Why should he not be Lord Mayor of London?

Look at that fellow Whittington, who came up to town on his ten toes, with his other shirt, his other pocket-handkerchief, his other pair of socks, and his toothbrush, done up in a little bundle.

That was not much of a stock-in-trade to

CHARLEY THINKS OF BETTERING HIMSELF.

start with. Had there been pawnbrokers in those days, I don't suppose the ATTENBOROUGH of the period would have lent more than eightpence on the whole lot,

Well, Charley would not be so very much worse off.

He would start in life without the little articles of toilet above enumerated.

He would walk into the world with nothing in his trouser's pockets besides his hands; but then, look at his talents and genius.

It was a dead certainty that he would make his fortune.

And he went to sleep, and dreamt that he had already done so.

Morning came at last! Oh, such a beautifully sunny morning! There never was such a morn-
No. 23.

ing. Don't tell me that you know its equal. Rubbish! I don't believe you.

There never was a morning on which the London sparrows chirped as they did upon this occasion.

There was one chap in particular—a youthful bird, with no tail at all to speak of—which was as good as the whole orchestra at Covent Garden, and a precious sight better too.

Besides that, it happened to be a public holiday, and most of the shops were closed, and the greater part of the population were perambulating the streets.

I don't quite think, myself, that the English nation show to much advantage when enjoying themselves; but then that is a matter of opinion. It has often struck me that the poor, ground

[CHARLEY WAG, THE NEW JACK SHEPPARD.

down, oppressed, and overtaxed labouring classes, have a worn tired-out lifeless aspect during their hours of recreation, which is anything but a pleasant subject for the contemplation of a lover of his fellow men.

Charley could scarcely believe his senses, when, having changed his prison dress for his old suit (rather mouldy smelling, by the way), and had cocked his pork-pie hat a trifle over his left eye, he sauntered backwards and forwards in one of the corridors, waiting for his order of release.

It came at length, as everything does come, from dinner-time to the time for giving up the ghost, and he was free.

The ponderous gate swung open, and he passed out.

"Good-day to you, sir," said he to Mr. Darbies.

"See you again soon, I suppose," said Mr. D.

"If I don't I shall always remember you," retorted Mr. Wag.

"You wouldn't have had the chance if I'd had my way."

"I can quite believe it. Thank you all the same."

"Come, get out, or I'll lock the door again."

"I won't trouble you. Good-day. Give my love to Mrs. D., if there is one.

"Get out."

He was out—he was in the street.

The world was before him where to choose.

XIV.—A Boy wanted.

THE world was, as I have told you, a very sunny-faced, smiling world upon this occasion, and Master Charles was very much pleased by the sight of it.

It cannot be denied that he felt a little uncomfortable at first in turning out of the gloomy prison gates into the glaring staring street, and rather ashamed of himself.

But he got over this after the first quarter of a mile.

After he had turned round the corner two or three times and made a plunge through several courts and alleys.

"I must have left all those behind, who saw me come out," he said to himself, "and now I can hold up my head with the best of them."

Still he had rather a gaol-birdish feeling hanging about him.

How can I describe it?

When he saw other boys playing innocently in the gutter at tip-cat, or mud-pie, or what not, he felt rather a contempt for them.

"Ah," he thought to himself. "If you were only up to half the things I am. If you had only gone through half what I have, you wouldn't amuse yourself with that sort of nonsense."

He was, you see, a boy of terrible experience.

You may think, perhaps, from the above remark of his, that his imprisonment had sobered him down, but there you are mistaken, he was quite as great a wag as ever he had been. It is a popular error to suppose that misfortune always takes the fun out of a person.

Of course it does out of some, but I doubt whether they would have been very funny in any case. With your right down wag there is nothing like sickness or poverty to sharpen him up. If they won't bring his fun out, why it's my opinion that there is no fun to come out.

Master Charley was very light-hearted and merry.

"If I had only got a penny in my pocket to get something to eat," he thought, " how jolly it would be !"

There is always a drawback to human happiness, as I believe several people have observed before. " I wish I had pegged away at that confounded old skillogolee this morning, only then I was so anxious, I couldn't eat anything.

He had not got a penny, so he tried to forget he was hungry.

It is difficult to forget an empty stomach, particularly when it keeps on rumbling.

About the middle of the afternoon he began to think it was growing serious.

Decidedly something must be done.

But what?

He had a great desire to go and see how Julia was getting on, but he conquered the inclination upon reflection. It would be much better if he were to try and look for some employment. When he was in a place, and earning a little money, would be quite soon enough to go and see his sweetheart.

Yes he must look after a place.

In what sort of shop?

He considered for sometime what track he would like best, and finally decided upon taking what turned up first.

After coming to this conclusion, he was not long before he saw in the window of a shop an oblong piece of paper, on which, in neat round hand, were the words :—

" A Boy Wanted."

" Hum !" said Mr. Wag to himself, stroking his chin, in a meditative way. " What's the business ?"

The business seemed to be limited, but extremely genteel.

In the window there were the week before last's *London Journal*, and a couple of copies of No. 1 (with which is presented gratis No. 2) of *Edith the Captive*, which did not seem to have gone off as well as could have been desired.

There were also several well-thumbed volumes opened at a picture, and displayed flat against the panes, with the notice that they were " Lent to read" on the top of them.

Then there were sheets of " nuts to crack," a sprinkling of tops, which looked as though they would not spin, and kites which, to a dead certainty, " had no fly in them."

There were besides a choice but limited collection of Dutch dolls at a penny, half-a-dozen sawdusters at sixpence, and one wax, with its eyes very wide open, at a shilling.

Besides this, the proprietor had dabbled a little in Berlin wools, and gone in extensively at one time for kettle-holders, which the public had not taken up; so that, like poor *Edith the Captive*, they were getting rather fly-blown, and beginning to curl up at the corners, under the influence of the sun, which had long ago effected the ruin of a bottle of bullseyes, and stuck them all of a lump.

"It seems to be an uncommonly genteel business, sich as there is of it," thought Mr. Wag; "and so here goes."

He opened the door, and entered the shop.

It was not one of those doors which, when opened, ring a bell, so that he entered the shop with scarcely any noise.

There was no one in it, and he knocked with his knuckles upon the counter.

He did this twice and nobody came.

"This is a lively sort of business," thought Charley, "any one might come in with a bag, walk off with the whole stock in trade, and sell it for—let me see—for I should say upwards of five shillings."

By the time that he had taken a mental inventory of the goods, and fixed a price upon everything down to the bullseyes, he thought he had better knock again upon the counter.

And this time he shouted out:

"Shop!"

"Dont make that noise, boy," said a sleepy old gentleman with gig lamps and a bald head both very bright and shining, "what do you mean by making that noise, boy? what do you want, boy? I ask you what you want, haven't you got a tongue in your head?"

"Well," thought Charley, "that's a nice way to answer a customer. How does he know I've not come in to buy something. I don't wonder at those old kettle holders not going off."

"If you please, sir, there's a notice in the window," began Charley.

"A what?" cried the old gentleman.

"A notice in about a boy."

"I don't know anything about boys, what do you mean?"

"About a boy being wanted, sir."

"Who want's a boy?"

"Well," retorted Charley, "I suppose you know best who want's one. Here's one if you do."

"Ah, you mean the paper wafered up in the window."

"Yes, sir."

"About a boy?"

"Yes, sir."

"To be sure. Why didn't you say so at first. Certainly, now I understand you."

"Well," thought Charley to himself, "its most time you did."

Meanwhile the old gentleman took a long look at him, and then scratched his head, and wandered to the window, apparently half inclined to take down the notice, but changing his mind as it seemed, he arranged the dolls and the kettle holders, fixing the former up into attitudes from which they immediately tumbled and lay upside down with their clothes deranged in the most unlady-like manner possible.

When he had pottered about in this way for some time, he looked up in a sleepy sort of way.

"A notice about a boy, eh?" said he, "to be sure, yes—certainly—I'll go and tell Mrs. Dormouse."

The old gentleman then went to the door by which he had entered the shop, and called out in a mild way as though he wanted somebody to hear, but was also afraid of waking somebody else—

"My dear—Mrs. Dormouse—my dear!"

"Well, Solomon," replied a subdued female voice, "whatever is the matter?"

"Will you come here a minute, my dear," said the old gentleman.

"Does somebody want something?" asked the old lady.

"Yes, my dear."

"Then can't you find it?"

"It isn't anybody wants to buy anything," the old gentleman replied. "It's somebody after the place."

"Oh, is it? Very well, I'll be down directly."

And in course of time down she came.

A very mild, not to say washed-out old lady, with a false front, and spectacles.

"After the place, eh?" said she, pulling her spectacles from her forehead, fixing them on the end of her nose, and then throwing back her head a little, to take a good sight at him.

"Is this the boy?"

"Ah, to be sure," said the old gentleman, the thought striking him suddenly: "boy, are you the boy?"

"Yes, sir," replied Charley; "I'm one boy, anyhow."

"And you want the place, eh?" asked the old lady.

"I want some place very badly, ma'am."

"What can you do?"

"I could make myself useful, I think, ma'am, in many ways."

"Do you understand the newspaper trade, now?"

"No, ma'am; but I could learn."

"Ah, well, perhaps you could."

Charley glanced at the feeble show of literature in the window, and thought to himself that there surely could not require much skill in purchasing such a stock.

The old lady asked him two or three more questions, and then came to the question of character.

Poor Charley. He had made quite sure of the situation, but now his heart began to sink within him.

"What was your last place, boy?" asked the old gentleman.

"My last place, sir?"

"Yes."

"I was—that is—this is the first time I have been out."

"Then where are your friends?"

"I have none, sir."

"Got no friends—what do you mean?"

"My poor mother, sir, was my only friend, and she is dead."

"When did she die?"

"Six months ago."

"And what have you done since then?"

Here was a puzzler.

What should he say?

He made up his mind to risk all. They were very kindhearted looking people, with a very motherly, fatherly, homely, or whatever you like to call it, look about them. Yes, he would tell them.

"I have been in prison, he said hesitatingly.

"Been where?" they both screamed out.

"In prison." •

"Solomon, did you hear that? He said he had been in prison. Run and look if there's a policeman anywhere. Oh, my goodness me! The idea of his impudence! In prison, too! Well I never! Perhaps his got some of the goods in his pocket."

"No I have not, ma'am," cried Charley, indignantly. No I have not. I'm not a thief ma'am, although I have been in gaol. I was wrongly accused. I'm an honest boy, and I beg of you on my knees to give me a trial and a chance of remaining honest."

"Stuff and nonsense," cried the old lady, "I don't mean to harbour no theives and vagabonds here, I can tell you."

"Oh, dear lady, do—do listen to me!" continued the boy, in accents of passionate entreaty. "Do give me a chance, and I will work hard, honestly, for you from morning till night. I am not a rogue, ma'am. If I had been, I should not have told you that I had been in prison. I should have told you a lie."

"I daresay what you are telling is quite true," said the old lady, a little softened, "but I'd rather not have anything to do with you."

"Most decidedly," said the old gentlman, "we'd rather not have anything to do with you."

"Oh. but sir—Oh, but ma'am—please—please listen to me. I will slave for you. Do not turn me away. Keep a watch on me. I am sure that you will be satisfied. Do but give me a trial."

"I can't," said Mrs. Dormouse, impatiently. I can't, I tell you, and I won't, there. Take an answer if you please, and take yourself off."

"Yes—certainly, exactly," observed Mr. D., who had been inclined at first to side with the boy. "Take yourself off, if you please. We won't have anything to say to you."

It was hopeless he could see. This Pig-headed old couple would not listen to him.

With a swelling heart he rose to his feet.

Then he took himself off as desired, and wandered on.

———

XV.—GIVE A DOG A BAD NAME AND HANG HIM.

HE wandered on for a long while without thinking or caring where he went.

He was thoroughly wretched, cast down and crushed by the reception he had met with.

Over and over again he cursed his folly!

Why had he told them that he had left prison?

But then, he thought, if I had not done so, what could he have said. He must have given some sort of explanation.

Well, who would say, perhaps he might have better luck at the next place. Anyhow, it was clear, that if he wanted employment he must sink the prison and deal a little with romance.

He had often heard the remark, that if you want to get on in trade, you must know how to tell a good twister. He wanted to do, so and so he began to manufacture a twister to suit the occasion.

Before long he came to another shop, where there was a similar notice to that which had before attracted his attention.

This was at a shoe shop.

He went in, and pulled off his cap to a grubby looking party in an apron.

"Now then," said the grubby one, "what's your order?"

"I have come about the place, sir."

"Oh, well, where have you come from?"

"From the country, sir."

"Have you got a character?"

"I haven't been out before."

"Not out before? Good Lord, what have you been doing all your life?"

"I have lived at home with my mother."

"Ah! so I should say. You look rather soft."

"I don't think I am soft, if I look it."

"Where's your mother?"

"She's dead, sir."

"How long have you been in London."

"Came up yesterday night, sir."

"What part?"

"Yorkshire."

"Whereabouts in Yorkshire?"

"Stavely."

"Where's that?"

"Near Chesterfield."

"Oh!"

He the shoemaker paused, and seemed to consider a while.

"The Lord forgive me for telling such crammers," thought Charley. "I wonder what he'll ask next."

"Have you any friends in London?" said the shoemaker, presently.

"No, sir—not one."

"Very well. I'll give you a trial; but take care what you're about. What are your clothes like?"

"Pretty good, sir, I think," replied Charley, quite cheerfully, for he thought the matter was settled."

"Come into the light, and let's have a look at you."

In accordance with this desire, Master Wag accompanied the shoemaker into the lightest part of the shop, which was. like most small shoe shops, very gloomy and crowded, and the grubby man took a very long and hard stare at him, beginning at his boots.

"They're not much account," he said.

"Then his eyes travelled upwards.

"You've had the wear out of them trousers," he remarked.

A little further up.

"That there weskit is more ornamental than useful."

A little higher again.

"What's that old rag round your neck?"

Still higher.

"Good God! what's the matter with your head?"

"My head, sir?"

"Yes, your head."

"Nothing sir."

"What do you mean by nothing?"

But Charley did not exactiy know what he did mean, nor what the shoe-maker was driving at, so he made no reply.

The grubby man stared at him harder than ever.

Then dragged him to the door and into a stronger light.

Then smiled in a very disencouraging way.

"Who cut your hair last?" said he.

"Cut my hair, sir?" repeated Charley, changing colour in spite of himself.

"You're hard of hearing," remarked the shoe-maker, sarcastically. "I said, who cut your hair, and I furthermore ask, how much did you pay for it?"

"I—I didn't pay anything."

"No I thought not. It was done by the government it strikes me, young gentleman. You've been to prison."

"Prison, sir?"

"Yes."

"I—I haven't been——"

"None of your lies here," roared the shoe-maker. "Get out of my shop you infernal young prig."

And I sincerely regret, as Master Charley's historian, to have to state that the shoe-maker enforced his command by a judicious use of his boot, which coming in contract with the seat of Charley's trousers, helped that young gentleman into the street, in an uncommon short space of time.

He did not try to retaliate, he was too much crest-fallen by his failure.

Like a dog that has been beaten he sneaked away, and only breathed freely when he put the length of two or three streets between the vendor of shoes and himself.

Then he sat down upon a door-step and had a good cry.

It was not very dignified, was it? or like what a hero ought to have done?

I draw from nature you see, and I have unfortunately no heroes handy to copy from, so I have to make mine do a brave thing one moment, and cry like a baby the next, just as it is probable anyone out of a book would do.

Well, we have agreed then Master Charley's behaviour was weak and undignified, only you see he was dreadfully hungry, and there is nothing like an empty stomach to take the pride out of a person.

However, when he had dried his tears, he began to think very seriously, and he came to a conclusion,

Which was—what?

That he must have something to eat.

What should it be?

And how should he get it?

He had soon made up his mind as to the ways and means.

He had got on a waistcoat, the ornamental one disparagingly alluded to by that beast of a shoe-maker.

He would eat that first.

As a preparatory step he of course took it off. He did this in a retired door-way.

When it was off he wrapped it up. Then put it under his arm and walked on.

It was not long before he came to the sort of shop he was in search of.

This was a rag and bottle shop, like Mr. Measles. Over the door dangled a little black doll. On the door-step stood a stout female, with a nose, which if it did not belong to a Jewess, most decidedly ought to have done so.

as it way by many sizes too large for a Christian lady.

"Vat ish it?" said this sweet creature to Master Charles.

"I want to sell this waistcoat," said Master Charles, producing his property. "Will you buy it?"

"Well, letsh shee it?" said the lady.

"Here it is."

The lady took it and turned it over, and turned up her nose at it, and did not seem to think very much of it.

"Vell!" she said, impatiently, "vat ish it to be?"

"How much will you give?" asked Charley.

"I don't want to give nothink. Fix a prish?"

"Half-a-crown, then."

"Half-a-crown, Moshish! Get out wid yer."

And the lady wrapped up the waistcoat and gave it back to the proprietor with a shrill laugh.

"Take it away!" she cried.

"No, but what will you give?" remarked Mr. Wag.

"Vell, shixpensh!"

"Make it a shilling."

"I couldn't, I should loosh by it."

"Lose by it, why its worth five shillings, at least."

"Five shillingsh! Stuff and nonshensh. Take it away."

"What do you say to ninepence?"

"No shixpensh."

"Well, I can't sell it, then."

Here he wrapped it up and put it away under his arm.

"You won't give me more, then?"

"No."

"Good morning."

He turned on his heel.

When about a yard from the shop the woman called to him.

"I'l give you sevenpence."

"Ninepence," replied Mr. Wag.

"Eightpence."

"Come, eightpence halfpenny."

"Vell, here it ish."

So he came back and laid the waistcoat on the counter.

Then the lady rummaged in her pockets for the money.

She rummaged a very long time, an a last produced sevenpence halfpenny.

"That's a penny short," said Charley.

"Vell, that ish all I've got."

"But you said you'd give eightpence halfpenny."

"Ah, vell, I cant that's all."

"Haven't you got a penny anywhere else?"

"No, not till Mr. Isnaacs comsh home."

"How long will that be?"

"Two hoursh."

"Two hours?"

"Yes, vil you vait?"

"Vait?" repeated Charley indignantly, "no, give us the rest of the money, and bad luck to you."

"Can't you spare the time?"

"No."

"I'm very sorry, I'm sure."

"Yes, I suppose you are."

Charley did not stop to bandy any more words, but took his money, put it into his pocket, and walked himself off.

What should he do with it when he got it? he asked himself.

Why, have a tightner.

What is a tightner?

Well, a plate of "a-la-mode," a piece of bread, and half-a-pint of porter, with perhaps to follow, a thumping good lump of pudding to fill up the spare corners.

How much would all that come to? Let us see. A-la-mode fourpence, bread a penny, beer a penny, pudding a penny—total sevenpence—balance in hand one halfpenny.

No, that was rather too extravagant. Upon reflection, he thought he would begin with the pudding and see how far that went. Then, if he could eat any more, he'd think of it.

He therefore bought his pudding, took a pull at the nearest pump, and with his stomach full, began to look at life from a more cheerful point of view.

He took a very extensive walk, fancying in a vague sort of way that something might somehow or other turn up.

Only nothing did.

He did not like the idea of trying any more shops just yet, so instead, he followed a punch show, and saw the performance twice through, then made one at an exhibition of tumbling, and had his coat collar cleaned gratuitously with some wonderful restorative mixture at a penny a cake, which a seedy man was selling in the street.

After all this he thought he would have something more in the way of refreshment, so he got a cup of coffee at three halfpence, and a roll and butter at twopence, which left a balance of fourpence in hand.

That's twopence for a bed, and a penny for sundries to-morrow, such as breakfast, and dinner, and tea and a drop of something to drink if I should want it particularly bad.

He was a dreadfully reckless young imp that Wag, and felt very little anxiety about the future.

He was one of those young men who believed that something might fall down from Heaven, and he had only got to keep his mouth wide open to catch it.

So he sat in the coffee-house drinking his coffee and reading one of the exciting romances which the proprietor supplied, free of charge, to those of his customers who were of a literary turn.

When he was tired of reading, that is to say, when he had twice fallen asleep over *Gentleman Jack*, and been remonstrated with by a young lady in attendance, he thought he had better go and look after a bed.

He turned his face towards Commercial Street, and steered on in the direction of Keate Street.

He stopped presently to read a handbill stuck upon a lamp-post.

It was the advertisement of such a lodging-house as he was in search of.

"Hookey's Home for the Traveller," it said, "where you can get a splendid lodging for the night and cook your steak or your bloater at the magnificent and roaring fires which are always going, and if desired, can obtain an unlimited supply of blacking and blacking-brushes and boiling hot water, for the ridiculously small charge of threepence. No connection with nowhere else. Ask for Hookey's. Everybody knows Hookey's. Hookey's is the place for everybody's money. Lodgings sixpence a couple. Single parties as above, with above advantages, threepence.

Underneath this was the address of the Hookey establishment. Charley made the best of his way to it.

He found that Hookey lived underground, and that you had to go down stairs to get to it.

On the stairs was a kind of watch-box, and in it a man to take the money, as though Hookey's was the legitimate drama instead of beds.

"Now then," said the man.

"How much?" asked Charley.

"Want to cook?"

"No, I want a bed."

"Twopence."

Charley gave his twopence, and proceeded onwards.

He found himself after a few more steps in a large kitchen, with a great fire, with an oven and boiler attached, a number of forms and tables, and a miscellaneous collection of blackguards, male and female, assembled.

Herrings seemed to be the popular food with the "regulars" at Hookey's, and the smell of them cooking was something terrific.

Charley sat down in a corner, as near the fire as he could get, and as he had no herrings to cook dozed off to sleep.

When the suppers were over, he followed some of the young gentlemen into the sleeping appartments, and laying down upon such an apology for a bed as Mr. Hookey's thought fit to provide for twopence, was soon in the land of dreams.

He woke up next morning very early and was soon in the street.

It was not very long, you may be sure, before he had spent his last penny in refreshment (a loaf of bread and a pull at the pump); and after that he began to look about him.

He looked about him all day without finding anytning which particularly repaid him for his trouble.

He made one or two feeble efforts to find a situation and applied at two or three shops but met with very dispiriting receptions.

He soon got hungry but he had no money.

He was too proud to beg, but he saw no chance of earning anything.

Once or twice he thought he might get a job by holding a horse and he ran after some one on horseback for a mile or two and then was disappointed.

As night drew near he was sick with hunger, foot sore and nigh broken-hearted.

He had no money for a lodging. Where should he go?

Accidentally he heard a ragged boy talking to another raggeder, about the Field Lane Refuge for the destitute.

"I'm destitute enough," thought Charley. "I'll try if they'll give me a berth for the night."

With this determination he set out in search of it.

XVI.—A Refuge for the Destitute.

THERE are some among our many readers whose professional duties demand that they should be out late at night, and who will require no aid of ours to recall to mind the crouching forms that sleep in doorways, under dry arches, or in niches on a bridge.

At that hour of night the time is past for impostors or beggars, and the outcasts who lie about, gathering for warmth into groups of two and three as autumn wanes and the night winds grow chill, are a peculiar class, who seldom beg and not more often steal.

Many must have noticed how these people gradually vanish in winter, though not entirely so, for even on the rawest nights small groups of two or three may still be met,—groups whose abject misery softens even the police, and they let them slumber on in doorways unmolested. These are members of, alas! too large a class, known as the homeless poor; and let those who wish to see both how they live and how they suffer, pass but one hour at the refuge for the destitute in Field Lane.

The way to it lies amid foul and noisome streets, where small and crazy tenements are crowded with many families, and where, amid even the scanty refuse which such a neighbourhood can afford to throw away, are groups of ragged infants, scarcely distinguishable save by their movements from the heap in which they search either for food itself or such small rubbish as rag dealers will give them bread for.

In such a vicinity, and close to the spot where Jonathan Wild's house once stood, is a large and cleanly whitewashed building, with lights inside, which at once distinguish it from the surrounding houses, where only rarely and at intervals is the dim reflection of a candle to be seen through the cracked and papered panes.

You have no need to be told that this one clean building among many is the "refuge," for long ere night has fallen the wretched claimants for its shelter have begun to assemble, and watch the door with that steady earnestness which only belongs to those who have no hope beyond its charity.

As the dusk deepens, they slink in from streets and byeways, old men of 60 and 70, young boys—ay, and even children, but all alike in misery—faint, wet, and weary.

They sit upon the sloppy ground in silence more impressive than the loudest complaints; or, if they speak at all, it is in whispers, for want and suffering have quailed their spirits, and they move with an abject deference painful to see from the paths of the very few who pass that way.

Gradually more and more drop in until the group is increased to 100 or thereabouts, and then the silence gets broken at last with hacking coughs from tall, meagre spectres, apparently in the last stage of decline, down to mere children hoarse with inflammation of the lungs, or paining the ear with their close suffocating whooping-cough.

Here are trampers, brick-makers, and labourers who have had no work since summer; some who have just come out of hospital, and are too feeble to labour; old men and little boys, street sweepers and orphans in every grade of misery and loneliness.

These are some, and only some, of London's homeless poor—the men and boys without a friend or place to lay their heads in all this vast metropolis—the Bedouins of England, who live no man cares how or where—who struggle through some years of bitter want and maybe crime, till they creep into a hole to die, and after lying in the parish dead-house a few days, with a placard on his breast marked with the touching word "Unknown," are given to the surgeons, and there's an end.

As soon as a moderate number have collected, the doors of the refuge are opened to its wretched tenants, and so remain open until the little cribs are filled with their full number of 300 outcasts, when the place is closed on all the many homeless applicants who come too late. The wants of grown men, though they feel cold and hunger like the rest, are apparently less severe than those which fall on little children, by whom, alas! nearly half the refuge is occupied.

Take the first who present themselves, and let them tell their own tale.

Here come four meagre little forms; they are mere children, all under the age of fourteen, all orphans, destitute, and living upon the streets, without a home or friend in the wide world.

One has a pair of tattered canvas trowsers and the remains of a grown man's fustian jacket hanging about his dirty limbs.

Dirt and sores disfigure his body, his eyes are swollen, his face is puffed and fevered-looking; for, though spokesman of the party, he can scarcely draw his breath from inflammation of the lungs.

They started two days since to see if they could gather some primroses to sell. They wandered through Tottenham, and thence on to Hornsey and Epping Forest, a lady giving them a penny by the way, with which they bought some bread, and shared it equally. They "couldn't get no posies," so they slept in a field, under a hedge, tramped back to London, and came to the Refuge, but it was full and closed, when one of the four went searching about the street for food, while the three other children slept in a doorway on Saffron Hill. Two of these four have newly been left orphans and destitute, but two have been upon the streets some time, the little spokesman having shifted for himself four years, carrying parcels, holding horses, minding vegetables in Covent Garden, or watching butcher's meat when left out in the summer nights to cool, but never stealing.

By and bye some little crossing-sweepers come in, eight in all—all children—all orphans—all destitute for years.

One has earned 2½d., which he has spent in a pennyworth of bread and a basin of coffee, keeping a halfpenny for some bread next day.

Another, a singularly handsome boy, also a crossing-sweeper, has lately walked up from Bristol, living on blackberries and "swedes" by the way, and getting a little work now and then at carrot-pulling. His mother, the only relative he ever knew, died four years since of cancer in the foot, and he himself has a similar disease forming, and now walks lame. He has been to an hospital about his foot, which pains him much, where they told him to rest it, keep it warm, and poultice it every night. Good advice this to a destitute child, speeping crossings, and without food enough to live on!

Another squalid, miserable child comes in, and his tale is so peculiar that we cannot refrain from giving it.

His father and mother are alive, and he is one of a family of twelve children. His two eldest brothers are nearly always in prison, "for they does hankerchers"—i.e., steal them—getting 2½d., each for them, or 3d. for very good ones. His eldest sister, now only fifteen, a thief in her infancy, has been much in prison, and is now in a reformatory. The father and mother and the rest of the children live in this peculiar way:—The whole family rise at two in the morning, and, quitting the wretched cellar in which they dwell, issue forth about the thoroughfares to tear down the posters and bills from paillings and dead walls.

Thus employed until daylight, the united exertions of the whole family in winter can collect a half-hundredweight of paper, for the sale of which they get 7¼d. But this is only during the long nights that even this pittance can be earned—in summer the father gets a little work, and the family scatter and shift in the fields, each as they can, for themselves.

It is useless, however, multiplying these painful instances. Let us pass to the female refuge.

It is part of the same charitable institution, though, for obvious reasons, not near where the outcast males are harboured for the night.

It is in another part of Field Lane, about half-a-mile distant, towards Saffron Hill, where all the Italian organ-grinders receive a wretched shelter from their masters, and where want and loathsome misery, of course, abound.

The refuge here is in a little yard off a narrow street, where a door near a coach-house admits the visitor up a steep flight of wooden steps to a very cleanly whitewashed and well-lighted room or loft, some forty feet long by twenty feet wide and high, along each side of which are five-and-twenty little cots, ranged on the floor.

A difference is very properly made between the treatment of the men and that of the women; the latter, instead of lying on the boards, have each a straw-stuffed mattress and extra rug, while, through the benevolent ministry of some kind ladies, a large cup of hot coffee is given to them with the 8oz. loaf provided by the refuge at night and morning. For obvious reasons, too, it opens to receive its hapless victims as soon as darkness falls.

At seven, therefore, they are mostly all assembled, and sit, women and children, in two long rows, drying their wretched garments near the stove; so worn and famished looking, that it wrings the heart to see them crouching moodily together, with the silence of exhaustion and despair upon them all.

At the first glance they seem to be all women of a middle age; but this is only the effect of care and hardship on their young frames, for a majority of them are under twenty, while but too many are mere children.

Others come in by and bye, in twos and threes, walking heavily and slowly, with their worn dresses—too light and cool for hottest summer—barely covering their poor thin forms.

The last comers have been working at the slop-houses, where, by incessant labour from eight in the morning till eight at night, they can earn 2½d. per day, finding their own cotton, needles, and tapes, and paying each 1d. a-week *for the use of the room they work in.*

Let us take the case of the girl who last came in.

She is sixteen, though she looks thirty; she has been a servant in two places, and had a good character from both, when she left the last to go into hospital for a long illness.

When she came out she could get no place; she pawned her clothes, endured starvation more or less severe for many weeks, till she had to apply for relief, and went the round of the casual wards of the Unions. She applied, she says, for admittance into Whitechapel Union, and was taken before the Board of Guardians, who told her the house was full, and they could "do nothing for her;" so she went away, and wandered in the streets another day and night, and next morning went to a magistrate, who told her her case was a hard one, but he could "do nothing for her." If she had given but one pert answer to any of those functionaries, miscalled relieving officers, the magistrate, whoever he was, would at once "have done something for him," and the girl would have gained a shelter, even though in a prison.

One person is there—a lady in manners and education, the daughter of an officer in the navy—who speaks French, understands German, and can teach music, and in whose face, worn and meagre as it is, can be discerned the traces of what once was beauty. Very little is known of her.

But it is needless to recapitulate such sad tales, from hearing the accumulated miseries of which our readers would shrink with heartfelt pain.

Let us return once more to the men's refuge.

It is past nine now, and all the rows of cribs are filled with occupants, and those who come too late—and there are always some forty or fifty such—must sleep in the streets, as those within the refuge now have done many hundred times before.

Among the 300 occupants not a word is heard; each has washed and sat down in his crib, and each receives, with grateful thanks, an 8oz. loaf, which is eaten almost before the man has done his work of distribution.

Prayers are read, in which all join.

Then each takes off his tattered clothes—though how they get them off, or, still more, how they are to get them on again, is almost a mystery—and, spreading them beneath them on the boards, cower under their rugs, and go quietly to sleep.

A watcher always remains up, though there is no need of him—there is seldom a movement among the poor thin forms around; worn out with hunger and fatigue, they sleep on as if the world had no cares for them, or the next day did not dawn on the same life of loneliness and misery as that which has just gone by.

Here Charley passed the night.

———

A CHOKER.

XVII.—SHEWS HOW CHARLEY GOES TO THE BAD, AND HOW MR. LARKINS LENDS A HELPING HAND.

NEXT day did not begin very brightly for the wanderer.

It rained, and was very chilly. Charley had several blisters upon his feet; he had got a bad cold, too; he had no money to get a breakfast, and was altogether thoroughly miserable.

He spent most of the day shivering under arches, and in doorways.

In the afternoon, he was told by a brother shiverer, apparently of long standing, that a job might be picked up down at the docks if a party looked sharp after it.

As want of victuals had imparted to Master

No. 24.

Charles a more than ordinary aptitude for looking sharp after everything, he determined to try what could be done.

Down to the docks he accordingly went; but on arriving there was informed by a young gentleman who seemed also to be looking out very sharp indeed, and to have got very thin during the operation, that he was a little too late.

"I'll come earlier to morrow," thought Charley, as he trudged away, gloomily chewing a bit of straw.

And then dismissing the subject from his mind, he resumed the consideration of a question which had been troubling him for some time past, namely, what was the good of anybody having a belly.

On and on he wandered in the weary streets;

[CHARLEY WAG, THE NEW JACK SHEPPARD.

the busy crowds hurried to and fro, while he loafed, and skulked, and sauntered, with a hopeless, vacant look upon his pinched face, and a gnawing within that made him feel sick.

That night he applied for shelter in a workhouse, was refused with much roundabout rigmarole from the beadle, and other great men in office, slunk about the Haymarket until two in the morning, earned twopence, spent it, and slept in the dark arches.

His head was aching and his limbs were stiff when he rose next day.

He was shivering with cold, but the wolf within was gnawing at him ravenously, and he ate his coat.

He did not go again to Mrs. Isaacs', but to a shop near Tower Hill, and he realized eighteenpence by the sale of this garment.

This was in its way quite a little fortune, and he managed to live upon it for the next two days, as the saying is, in clover.

But he could get no jobs to do, and he had now grown much too shabby to hope to be taken on at a shop, and he grew very hungry and wretched.

At last there came a time when he had been two whole days without tasting food, and every bit of pluck was entirely taken out of him.

He was sitting upon the door-step of a house down a quiet drowsy little street, and taking a nap in the sun.

He hardly knew how he had come there. He had crawled out of some hole or corner where he had passed the night, or had been ferretted out by the police, and had crept along the streets till he had reached this place, where, sinking down exhausted, he had fallen off to sleep, or rather, subsided into insensibility, under the influence of the warm sun.

Just opposite to where Charley was sitting, there was a little surgery with a couple of bottles in the window and a brass plate on the door.

On the brass plate was the name of Larkins, and a fat little man who had slightly run to belly, but who, nevertheless, retained a tolerable amount of youthful activity, came running out and in several times in the course of an hour.

Now the reason why he was thus kept upon the trot, was that no sooner had he done prescribing for one patient, and got on his hat and gloves again ready to go upon his rounds, than another was safe to drop in and require his services.

Then after this one was disposed of, another and another, so that there seemed to be no end to them.

He seemed to be an extremely fidgetty little man, this doctor, and besides the annoyance of being thus detained when he was in a hurry, he seemed also to have some other annoyance, in the fact of the non-arrival of some party or parties unknown, for every two or three minutes the little man toddled out to the door, and shading his eyes from the sun, peered into the distance in search of somebody who did not come, and after waiting thus two or three minutes, retired into the shop again, with some new expression of anger and disappointment after each journey.

Then, after he had been indoors for a few minutes, a young man with light curly hair and apron, rushed out to the door, or up to the top of the street, and gaze about each time with an expression of the most sanguine expectancy, returning presently in a state of the deepest despondency at his non-success, and betaking himself to the concoction of "mixtures as before," as though his life depended on it.

While Charley was watching these movements in a careless sleepy way, he wondered whom they could be looking out for, and whether it were possible that he had ever seen the fussy little gentleman before; and if so under what circumstances the meeting could have occurred, and where.

He fancied, too, that the name of Larkins was not altogether unfamiliar to him.

But then, he was too faint and weary to exert himself much about the matter, and while he was thinking of it, or thinking that he was thinking, he fell asleep.

At least, not exactly asleep, but into a sort of dreamy, half-senseless state, in which he was dimly concious of passing events.

From this he was suddenly aroused by a prodigious uproar.

He opened his eyes.

Out of the door of the surgery came the sound of blows, and of loud expostulation and lamentation.

Somebody was most certainly being thrashed.

And it was quite as certain that somebody did not like it.

Charley sat up and listened.

He also looked with all his eyes.

And this is what he saw—

Out of the surgery into the street, all of a lump, more like a bundle of legs and arms tied loosely together, than two human beings, came tumbling the doctor and the doctor's boy.

The former was slapping the latter's head.

The former was swearing and the latter was howling.

And they were both very much out of breath.

Decidedly something was the matter.

"You young villian, you incorrigible young villian, you audacious young villian, its scandalous, its outrageous, you ought to be hanged for it, you would have been hanged for it, if you'd been born a hundred years ago, and it's a great pity you weren't."

So far the old gentlemen, trying to get his breath, and wiping his head.

"I wish I had been born a hundred years ago," retorted the boy, "and then I shouldn't a know'd you, old bellows-to-mend."

"Oh, you awful young profligate! come out of that coat or I'll break all the bones in your skin. Oh, you ungrateful, graceless varlet. I wouldn't be your mother for a thousand pounds, for you'll break her heart to a dead certainty."

"I daresay I shall—O—O—O—O," bellowed the boy, who was crying as much from rage as from the smart of his recent chastisement. "I daresay—O—O—O—O—I don't care—O—O—O—O—I don't care for you, you big bully; hit one of your own size—O—O—O—O. That's more than you dare do—O—O—O—O."

"I shall warm your jacket directly," said the little doctor, "if you don't do what I tell you."

"Here's your old coat for you," replied the boy, divesting himself of his upper garment, "and I hope you'll get such another as I've been to you—that's all."

"I hope I shan't," said the doctor. "That's all I wish."

"There's nobody 'ud serve you as I have."

"Nobody would serve me out as you have."

"I don't want your stinking old six bob a week."

"You won't get it young gentleman."

"I'll tell everybody how you fills up their physic out of the pump."

"Go about your business."

"You've killed a tidy few in your time, and no wonder."

"Be off!"

"Yah! old rhubub!"

"Be off with you!"

And as the boy indulged in a very insulting gesture, the latter gentleman seemed to lose the last particle of patience which he had remaining, and rushed wildly after him up to the end of the street.

Not catching him, however, he came back panting after a minute or two, and stood leaning against the door-post, endeavouring to get his breath.

"This is a nice kettle of fish," said he, as soon as he could speak.

"Well, it is, sir," observed the curly-headed assistant with the apron, looking doleful.

"Who the dickens is to take out the physic?"

"Who indeed, sir."

"I can't."

"And I don't think I shall have time, sir."

"Certainly not."

"It's very awkward, sir, isn't it?"

"Yes, it is, Mr. Squills; but what's to be done?"

"I can't say, sir, really," replied the assistant, appearing to think with all his might, but not to think of anything in spite of it.

"That girl can't go with them," said the doctor.

"Of course not, sir."

"Why?"

"Well—yes to be sure. She might do," replied the assistant. Who wanted to agree with his employer if possible; and indeed, was equally satisfied, whatever occurred, as long as he himself did not get into hot water.

"The girls's so damned stupid!" cried the doctor.

"Yes, sir, to be sure!"

"She'd leave it all at the wrong houses."

"Of course she would, sir."

"But who can we get?"

"Who, indeed?"

"If we only knew of some boy."

"Some respectable boy."

"Damn the respectability, as long as he was sharp."

"And honest."

"To be sure!"

"We shall find one, perhaps."

"But then we want one this moment."

"Ah, that's the difficulty."

It was a difficulty that set both the doctor and his assistant scratching their heads.

"While thus ingaged the doctor's eyes fell upon Charley's recumbent figure.

Mr. Larkins walked up to him.

"Well my lad," he asked, "what are you doing here?"

"I'm doing no harm, I hope, sir," replied Charley looking up uneasily.

During the last day or two he had been "moved on" by the police, and had been generally stirred up and sent to the rightabouts, so that he was not quite sure that he had any right to anything or to be anywhere.

"You're doing no harm as I know of," said the doctor kindly, "though you don't seem to be doing much good. You're out of luck, my poor fellow, I should say by the look of you."

"Yes, sir, I am very much out of luck, indeed."

"Can you work?"

"If I could get it, sir."

"Ah, that's what you all say. Now if you're a honest lad, and you certainly look like one—I will give you a chance."

"Have you ever done any work before?"

"Yes, at home, sir, but I—"

"There, that will do; I don't want to know the family history. The work you'll have to do for me is easy enough, though there's plenty of it."

"I shall be very happy to do anything for a living."

"Yes, yes, yes. Now no cant, if you please. Can you read?"

"Yes, sir."

"Read writing, I meant."

"Yes, sir; I can write," replied Charley, proudly.

"That'll do. Now come in-doors."

Charley limped in after him, trying to walk as though he had no blisters.

"You're a dreadful scarecrow, my poor fellow," said the little doctor, looking him over.

He was a very kind-hearted man, this Mr. Larkins. (Our old friend Larkins, of course it was, as you supposed all along.) A very kind-hearted man, old, he had a funny way of expressing himself, as many kind people have.

"You look as though you were in training to go up a gas-pipe, as people say. When did you have your last victuals?"

"I haven't had anything for the last two days."

"Not for two days? Why, Lord bless us and save us, I never heard of such a thing! Do you hear that, Mr. Squills? What would you do for two days without your victuals?"

"I should do very badly, sir, I think," replied Mr. Squills, chuckling feebly, as he always did when Larkins joked with him.

"But, I say, Mr. Squills," the doctor continued, in a tone of facetious reproof, "you're a nice sort of fellow to call yourself a Christian, ain't you?"

"Me, sir? Why, sir?"

"Why, keeping the poor boy out of his food while you're gabbling there, like a pack of old women over a washtub. Ring the bell, if you please, Mr. Squills."

Mr. Squills did as he was desired, and presently a very prim servant made her appearance.

"This is the new boy, Fanny," said her master. "Take him down-stairs, and put a pint of soup into him, or some meat and bread."

"Yes, sir."

"He's rather shabby just now, but we'll brighten him up before we have done with him; so give him half-a-pound of yellow soap, and a scrubbing-brush, just to begin with."

"Yes, sir."

"And, Fanny, just keep your eye on him, and see that he doesn't burst himself. The victuals may be too strong a temptation, perhaps, for he hasn't had overmuch lately, by the look of him."

"Yes, sir."

Then, turning to Mr. Squills, the doctor continued :—

"When he's had his breakfast, and cleaned himself up a bit, send him out with the medicines. I can't stop any longer myself."

——

XVIII.—Shews how Charley resembles the Asp in the story book, and stings the hand that feeds him.

WHEN he was gone, Charley was taken down-stairs, and what seemed to him one of the most magnificent repasts that had ever been laid on a table, was laid on the table before him.

There was a most magnificent cold roast sirloin of beef, with a splendid new loaf, and a superb bottle of mixed pickles, let alone mustard and salt, and other luxuries, in a gorgeous cruet-stand; and the whole was washed down by some table-beer, which was, as regarded quality, as far beyond nectar as roast goose is beyond a-la-mode.

Charley put away slice after slice, and helped himself again and again to pickles—now trying a bit of cauliflower, and now an onion, and now a French bean, and then going in at random, and taking anything that came first.

But there must be an end to every kind of earthly enjoyment, the parsons tell us, and so in course of time this luxurious feast came to a termination, and Charley had a good deal of difficulty in swallowing the last mouthful; for he had had quite enough to eat by that time.

When it was swallowed, at Fanny's direction he set about cleaning himself.

When he was cleaned, he put on the coat which the other boy had taken off; he was also accommodated with a clean shirt, and his boots polished.

He was not a bad-looking young fellow, as I have before told you; indeed, when he was spruced up a little, he looked a very pretty little gentleman.

There was nothing common about him; his features were delicate, his carriage was easy.

Even in his raggedest moments, there was something distinguished about him.

Fanny, the cook, evidently thought so.

"Those things suits you capital," she said, gazing upon him admiringly.

"Do you think so?" asked Charley, with a good-natured grin.

One likes to have one's clothes admired, however old one may be.

I, the writer of this, who is probably old enough to be the reader's grandfather, have yet a weakness to hear myself praised, and like to hear how I look in my new spectacles—my last beautiful auburn wig.

"Yes, I do think so," replied Fanny; "you're quite the gent."

"Do you think I'm good-looking enough to be your sweetheart?" asked Charley.

"Lor bless me! I'm surprised at you."

"What for?"

"Why, for saying such things."

"Don't you like people to make love to you then?"

"No."

"Nor to tell you you're pretty?"

"No, because they'd be telling lies."

"Go on with you—you know better than that."

"No, I don't, young gentleman; and come, keep your hands to yourself, if you please, or I'll tell the doctor."

I don't believe she would have done so, you know, although she said so, and looked very angry.

Indeed she let Master Charles kiss her with less struggling than you might have anticipated by her ferocious expression.

There is no knowing, however, what liberty that young imp of a boy would have taken next; for now he had finished his beef and beer, he felt something like a great bashaw, and would not have much objected to have been able to call for his pipe and his harem after the eastern style, only instead, Mr. Squills called for him to take out the physic.

A great number of white paper parcels there were intrusted to him, and he was instructed as considerable length by the cheerful assistant at to where they should be left, and how he was to find the streets and houses; for the greater part of Mr. Larkins's patients were among the poorer classes, and resided down nameless alleys and unknown courts, not to be found upon any existing map.

When he was well primed with information, away he went, as blithe as any bird, carrying his well-stocked basket as though it were a feather, and wearing his hat of office jauntily cocked on one side of his head.

"This is a rather better fig-out than I've been accustomed to lately," said Charley to himself. "And though parties might be inclined to make disparaging remarks at the expense of a doctor's boy, yet who knows, before long I may be an assistant, and after that a practice of my own, perhaps. I always had a taste for cutting off legs."

Thus busy with his thoughts, this juvenile castle-builder went gaily upon his way, and sowed his physic, so to speak, to the right and to the left.

He was as happy as a king—supposing always that kings are happy. I do not know one intimately myself.

Anyhow, what I want you to understand is, that he was very happy.

It was a glorious thing, you must allow, to be thus snatched, as it were, from the jaws of death, and though in better times the young gentleman ought have been inclined to turn up his nose at so lowly an occupation, yet at the present moment the berth of a doctor's boy seemed more like that of Prime Minister than anything else, by comparison with the awful life he had been lately leading.

He was most particular in performing his

duties, and though the task was by no means an easy one, he acquitted himself with a great deal of credit, and Mr. Squills was loud in his praise of the boy's conduct when the doctor returned home that afternoon from his rounds.

For the last boy, besides being incorrigibly idle, was so careless, that a third part of the medicine was generally left at the wrong houses, and these mistakes sometimes occasioned a great deal of angry altercation, when the patients inside had been more than ordinarily disarranged by the internal application of lotions, inadvertently swallowed instead of draughts.

Mr. Larkins expressed himself much delighted at his *proteges* turning out so well, and as the next day and the next, there was no diminution in his good conduct, the doctor was so elated at what he was pleased to call his discernment of character, and knowledge of phisognomy that he narrated the circumstances to everybody who came fo the house, and pointing triumphantly to Master Charles, and exclaiming :—"There stands the very boy," as though that were an enormous fact, calculated to shut up everybody for ever.

A rather fine scene occurred one day after Charley had been at his place little less than a week.

Old Biles, a half-pay captain, and a great authority in parish matters, came grumbling into the shop for a pennyworth of black sticking plaster, having "cut a terrific hole in his chin," as he said, by using a rascally cheap razor some infamous blackguard had had the atrocious villany to sell to him.

When he had got his sticking plaster and was leaving the shop, his eye chanced to fall upon Mr. Wag.

"Eh! Hallo! What's that?" said he.

"What's what?" asked Mr. Squills.

"That boy—its a new one ain't it?"

"Yes, sir."

"And what's become of that other infamous scoundrel?"

"He's gone, sir."

"Gone where? Gone to be hanged I should think."

"Well, he was rather bad, sir, but you won't have to complain of this one."

"What do you mean? How do you know I shan't have to complain of him? He's a fool I can see at a glance. He'll most likely give me a great deal more trouble than the other did."

"I don't think he's a fool, sir."

"You don't think so. What do you know about it I should like to know? I say he is a fool, a confounded fool, I can see it at a glance, by the shape of the wretches head."

Just then the doctor came in.

"What's that your saying, captain?" he asked, "my boy, Charley, a fool. Oh, no. I assure you you're very much mistaken. Very sharp boy indeed, sir—remarkably sharp."

"Hump! perhaps he is, replied the captain, impatiently." Then if he isn't a fool, its my opinion he's a most remarkable rogue."

"No—no—no, my dear, sir," cried the doctor, in a deprecating tone; for he was rather annoyed at this unwarrantable attack upon his favourite. "Not at all—not at all, I assure you. You are entirely mistaken."

"Well I hope I am, sir. Where did you get him?"

"I picked him out of the street."

"So I should have thought."

"And I have strong reasons for believing that he has recently come out of prison."

"Just my impression."

"But I said to myself when I saw first him, That is the boy for my money. That's a boy that would do well if he got the chance, and he shall have the chance, so I gave it to him and he has done well."

"Ha, ha! it's as good as a play to hear yon. However it doesn't matter to me. I shall take my precautions, and have the chain put on the street door, when I see him coming. As for you, you'll be robbed, of course, and I shall look out for it in the morning paper. Good day to you doctor. Ha, ha! you'll excuse my laughing, but I never did hear anything half so ludicious !"

And away he went in a great rage.

"You hear what he says, Charley," observed Mr. Larkins. "You'll be a good boy I feel certain, if its only to spite that stupid old booby, who prophesies so badly about you."

"That I will, Sir! That I will," replied the boy, with tears in his eyes.

He felt that he would have worked the flesh off his bones for so good a master.

How cruel and unjust of the Captain to prophesy such a career of crime in store for him.

But he would be disappointed. He would find, that after all his knowingness he was not a very accurate judge of character.

Charley was really very happy in his place.

When he had done his work of a night he was allowed to sit in the kitchen and read a number of delightful books which Mr. Larkins had given him permission to borrow from the shelves in the library.

He kept up, too, a kind of courtship with Fanny, the cook; and as that young lady rather favoured his suit, he did not suffer much in consequence in the victualling department, as you may suppose.

Half-a-dozen times a day did Charley bless his good fortune at having fallen into such snug quarters, and deeply was he grateful for the doctor's kindness.

But, as we agreed a little while ago, there is unfortunately an end to all earthly happiness; and so Charley's happiness came to an end before he was much older.

And this is how it happened.

You are, of course, of opinion that little Doctor Larkins was a kindhearted old soul, and that he did the proper thing by young Master Wag.

So am I; but the worst of philanthrophy, it is so often misapplied?

Now the last boy he had had, he had picked up in some extraordinary fashion, and adopted, without making any inquiries into the youth's character. Before long he found he had caught a Tartar.

A great overgrown, idle, incorrigible young profligate, who was hand and glove with all the juvenile prigs of the neighbourhood, and was continually committing petty thefts in the surgery, or the houses of the doctor's patients, which Mr. Larkins had over and over again hushed-up and forgiven, upon promises of better behaviour for the future.

The boy had a mother, who professed to love him dearly; the doctor was a tenderhearted man, and so the lad triumphed.

At last, for some grievous offence, he was dismissed, as you already know, and Charley took his place.

But this was not the end of him.

First of all, Mrs. Gubbins, his mother, looked round the first evening, to ask when her poor boy was to come back; and, hearing that he was not to come back at all, had violent hysterics in the consulting-room, and broke a good many bottles by lungeing out with her legs.

Then, being put outside the door, she became even more violent, and was finally removed by the aid of the police.

Next day, upon being liberated from imprisonment, she returned to the charge, and was anything but complimentary to the doctor and his profession, at the top of her voice, to large audiences.

That evening, a stone thrown by a party or parties unknown broke one of Mr. Larkins's windows, and the beautiful blue bottle behind it.

The next day and evening, although no violence was resorted to, small gatherings of street-boys, hounded on, it is supposed, by the youthful Gubbins, gave derisive cheers outside the surgery door, demanded in shrill treble that "Old Rhubarb," and "Old Gooseberry," would come out, and, being treated with silent contempt by the besieged household, asked indignantly, "Who robbed the poor widder's son?" and "Who pizened the babby?"

After this, and as a policeman on that beat, for a consideration and a glass of spirits, promised to keep his "hi" upon "certain parties," the annoyances, as far as the doctor was concerned, began to subside.

But not so Charley.

At least half-a-dozen times did some hand unperceived fling a stone at him when he was going upon an errand.

Whenever he appeared in the street, his appearance seemed to be the signal for hootings and jeerings; and though upon several occasions he had slapped the heads of the boys who had called after him, still he could not quell the disorderly juvenile population, and it seemed that when he had overcome one, two more immediately rose up in his place.

To try and repeat here the annoyances which he suffered would but tire out the reader's patience, I will therefore go on to the climax.

One day, when Charley had been with his employer close upon a fortnight, the doctor, while at his dinner, was sent for in a great hurry to see some one who was said to be dying. So agitated was the messenger, that he could give Mr. Larkins no particulars about the case; and so the doctor told Charley to follow him, and set off as hard as he could run, accompanied by the person who had come to fetch him.

When they reached the house, it turned out that it was a case of suspected poisoning. A stomach-pump and some other little matters were required, and the doctor bade Charley run for his life back to the surgery and bring them.

The boy was always delighted to show how quick he could be, and like a greyhound he set off upon his errand.

There was some delay in finding the article when he arrived at Mr. Larkins's house; for the stomach-pump is not an instrument of every day use; but when at last it was found, he thrust it into his basket, and set off again as fast as his legs could carry him.

Now, Master Gubbins, who was a big bony resolute lad, of a very spiteful and unforgiving nature, had seen him pass into the house, had seen him return with the basket, and had made up his mind that he would, as it were, by accident, run up against Master Charles, or otherwise manage to overthrow him, so that the contents of the basket, whatever it might be, would be smashed.

He was standing at the corner of the street, and Charley would have to pass him, so it occurred to Mr. Gubbins that the best plan would be for him to stick out his foot in such a manner that it should trip the other boy up.

And so, without any further reflection, he did so.

Charley fell over it, made a very desperate effort to save himself, and went sprawling on to his nose in the gutter.

The street, where the doctor resided, was at all times a very quiet street, and one enjoying but very little traffic. Upon the occasion, no one was within sight but Master Gubbins.

There could be, therefore, very little doubt in Charley's mind that if anybody had thrown him down it was Master Gubbins who had done it.

Of course there was no doubt that he had done it, and so——

And so, all that remained to be done, was to ask Master Gubbins why he did it, and then to punch his head.

Charley rose to his feet, and rubbed the mud off his hands upon the seat of his trousers, as he spoke.

"What did you mean by that?" said he.

"By what?" asked Master Gubbins.

"By throwing me down."

"I could'nt help your falling down, could I?"

"Yes you could. You put out your foot."

"Your a liar!"

"Your another!"

"Am I?"

"Yes you are. Can you fight?"

"I'm not going to fight with you," replied Master Gubbins, contemptuously.

"Why not?"

"Because I don't fight with blackguards."

"Oh, you don't—very well. Then, do you know what I shall do?"

"What?"

"I shall give you a good kicking."

In pursuance of this purpose, Charley got hold of young Gubbins by the collar, and as Gubbins did not seem to be quite so desirous of being kicked as Charley was of kicking him, they struggled very fiercely for a few moments, and alternately battered one another's heads against the wall behind them.

But, though Gubbins would have stood no chance with the other in a fair stand-up fight—as, indeed, very few boys of his size and age would have done—yet he possessed much more strength than Charley had given him credit for, and he turned out rather a tough customer.

Besides that, Gubbins had no paltry notions about fair-play, and he not only stamped on his adversaries toes and kick him in the stomach with his knee whenever he had a chance, but he also endeavoured, in the American style, to gouge out his eye.

Who can blame Charley, if under these circumstances he lost his temper, and finding that he could not get the mastery over his opponent in any other way, he twitched his neckerchief round with both hands, and did his best to throttle him.

Not that he quite intended to kill him, as you may suppose, but he meant to give him a good hard pinch—a choker, in fact—just to teach him to be more respectful in future.

Charley got Gubbins's neckerchief in both hands, and gave it a great wrench.

Gubbins' eyes opened very wide, and his tongue lolled out on one side.

Charley was in a awful passion, and the uglier face Gubbins made, the harder Charley pinched him,

Soon he began to get very black and swollen.

But still he persisted in struggling.

" Will you beg my pardon ?" Charley asked through his teeth.

But Gubbins only gurgled, and expressed defiance in dumb-show.

" Very well, then, you shall have it."

And Charley went on squeezing tighter and tighter.

All at once the other ceased to fight against him. His hands fell down powerless, his head drooped on one side.

Charley left go his hold, and the senseless body of his foe fell at his feet.

Then, like a flash of lightning, the full horror of his situation burst upon him.

Was the boy dead? To all appearances such was the case.

What must he do? Fly most certainly, but whither.

Even now he heard the sound of footsteps coming round the corner,

The twilight was gathering thickly in the street, he could easily escape if he seized the moment and fled, but still he hesitated.

Could he go back to the doctor? No, he dare not. The stomach pump and the rest of the articles he had been sent for, lay smashed upon the pavement, His master would be furious. The loss must have been greater than he could hope to replace by his wages."

And who knows this fatal delay might have caused the death of the patient, to whom the doctor had been summoned. He was the cause of two deaths.

The footsteps approached. There was no time left to think.

He turned and fled.

XIX.—AT THE LAST EXTREMITY.

I HAVE come to an ugly chapter in Charley's life.

That be did a foolish act in running away, there is little doubt, but as he had run away, that the best thing he could do under the circumstances was to keep away, there can be but little doubt.

Again he wandered the streets.

Again he starved in holes and hid out of sight.

Again the police moved him on.

There was no hope for him now.

It seemed as though the brand of Cain was set upon his brow, for like a mangy dog he driven from every door. and hungry and footsore skulked out of night, afraid that even his wretched life should be taken from him.

A miserable, half-starved, ill-looking, lad, it was not likely that anyone would give him employment.

Once only did he get a situation for a few days, and then a policeman called upon his master and warned him that he was harbouring a released felon.

It was the same man upon whom Charley had played off that heartless trick about the play-bill boards.

When Charley saw him come in, he ran trembling into the back shop and hid himself for he made sure he was going to be taken into custody for murder.

However, when he ventured to make his appearance after the policeman was gone, the tradesman told him that his services could be dispensed with, and so with the balance of wages due to him, stowed away in his trowsers pocket he walked himself off.

Many, many days, he walked and walked.

In the same fashion that he had done before did he disposed of all the saleable part of his wearing apparel.

More and more lean and hungry did he grow.

More and more ragged and forlorn,

More wretched, more despairing.

There was no hope left for him.

How could he even hope to get into another situation. He was sick of trying.

Should he go back to the doctors? He dare not do so. He might be imprisoned for theft ; for had he not run away with the doctor's property in the basket, and the doctor's clothes on his back.

In his despair, he went down to Slogger's Alley, and tried to find out if anything was known of Mr. Toddleboy, but nobody had seen him there, neither had they seen him at Messrs. Bottle and Bung's.

He was so hungry and wretched, that he even swallowed his pride, and thought that he would go and beg Julia to assist him, but Julia had left Muggins' Music Hall, and, indeed it would seem that she had also left the profession, for nobody had seen her for some months, and her name was nowhere advertised.

All hope was over in those quarters.

No, he was left to his own resources, and his own resources failed him.

One night—a warm summer's night, when

all nature seemed to be hushed to sleep, and a happy lull of contentment soothed the troubled spirits of the ever restless, striving, battling, work-a-day world—a miserable outcast boy crept to the edge of London's murky river, and stood there gazing at it, in a vague, wondering kind of way, like a child might gaze at the green curtain which covers the coming wonders of the harlequinade.

Long and earnestly he watched the dark rippling surface of the black waters, which crept past him slowly and sluggishly upon its way to the open sea.

The church clocks near and far began to strike the hour of twelve; but though many of the London streets were thronged and busy enough with the traffic of nocturnal pleasure-seekers, the neighbourhood surrounding the spot where this lonely outcast stood was silent and deserted.

He stood by the water's edge, at the foot of Hungerford Bridge. He stood almost upon the very spot from which, a few months ago, he had sprang into the water to rescue a drowning duchess. He stood upon the spot from which a guilty mother had flung him, a helpless babe, bent on his destruction.

And why had he not died then?

Why had the officious old fool thrust forward his arm to rescue the miserable little nameless child, floating down with the tide to that haven where the weary shall rest.

What was in store for him?—what was left for him but to die now, as he might have died then? As it were, better he had died when he was young and innocent.

But now then, surely the time had come. Why did he linger?

He is going to spring. No, he is crying, this poor outcast; crying, it seems, as though his heart would break. But yet these are not tears of sorrow, or tears that bring relief.

They are rather tears of burning rage, and hate, and impatience.

Rage with the stonyhearted world; impatience with his hard lot, with his unmerited treatment and persecution at the hands of the cruel, unjust, and unsympathising men and women he has had to deal with.

No, there is no good in such tears as those. It were better not to cry at all than to cry as this boy does.

He has ceased.

He rubs them indignantly away. The time has come; he has made up his mind—one spring, and it will be all over.

Deadly still are the streets, heavy and thick the night air. There is a throbbing in his head as though of clockwork, and no other sound.

Then he peeps around him in a wolfish, murderous fashion, more like the manner of one who has a design against another's life than he who would fain take away his own.

A little closer to the water's edge he creeps, and makes ready for the fatal plunge.

There is yet time to save him, did some one see him from the bridge above, and, interpreting his purpose from that attitude of hesitation and stealthy terror, scream to him to stop.

In the bright moonlight his ragged figure stands out for a moment, gaunt and motionless, like some ugly phantom.

The next he has fallen into an attitude, as though he were about to dive, and then—

A sudden shout from the water makes him stagger back, and, like a hunted hare, stand panting in terror, with wide dilated eyes and twitching nostrils.

"Hallo, you there!" the voice cries out again; and from round the bridge, in an opposite direction to that in which the boy's regards had hitherto been directed, a boat, rowed by two sturdy fellows of a nautical turn, and containing besides on old man wrapped in an ample cloak, the collar of which covered his large ears, came rapidly towards him.

"What were you going to do, young fellow?" the old gentleman asked, not a little indignant, if one might judge by his tone. "Going to drown yourself, eh?"

"Well, if I was," the boy returned doggedly, "its no affair of yours, I reckon."

"No young man its not," the old gentleman remarked, as he stepped on shore. "And you might have done it for what I cared, and may do it now if you like, that is, as far as I am concerned, I shan't prevent you."

"Don't talk like that gov'nor," a rough, but kindly voice interrupted from the boat, and one of the seafaring men got out, and came up to the would-be suicide. "Look up!" said he, laying his hand upon the boys shoulder. "What's a-miss with you, mate, you look in a bad way."

"Yes, I am."

"Well, damn my eyes!" the nautical man continued. "I ought to know you. Don't I know you?"

"I don't know."

"You don't know. Don't tell me. You're name is Charley Wag. I'm George—we was lagged for the same crack. Here gov'nor, this ere's the lad we got into trouble. Lord love my pretty limbs, if I'm not as delighted to see you again, as though you was my own long lost baby, supposing I'd ever had one and lost it."

While he was speaking, Charley was scanning the man's features, as well as he could, for the other stood with his back to the light.

True enough it was George, and the old man was none other than the celebrated Mr. Measles, who kept the "Pigeons."

"What do you want with me?" the boy said at last.

"Want with you, my young chicken. I don't want to do you any harm, or else I shouldn't have called to you just now, when I see you on the pint of taking a header."

"I wish you had left me alone. I should be better out of the world than I am in it, for I can't make a living, and its hard work starving."

"Starve a fiddlestick. Why don't you come to the gov'nor? He'd have given you a job."

"What at?'

"Something in our line. Of course if you're too virtuous for the business, it would have been no good coming."

"What! you would have me steal!"

"Have you steal? we don't want to force you, my fine fellow. It seems to me its the only thing left for you. If you like now, the governor shall fit you out in a bran new set of

A QUIET PIPE.

togs, and give you a something to start with. I owe you a good turn, and, by God! I'll do the thing that's right by you."

"But I shall get into prison again.'

"Not if you go the right way to work. You must put your heart in it if you want to do any good. Why, you're the very chap that would make his fortune if you took to it kindly—you that can read and write, and such a pretty figure of a fellow too; you'd do the top sawyer sort of work. Come, now, what do you say?"

What should he say? He looked from George to the river, and from the river back to George.

It was that or death.

"I agree," Charley answered, giving him his hand.

No. 25.

"Hooray!" cried George, delighted; "spoken like a man, and may I never say another word in my life if what I say don't come true. You'll be a honour to your perfession."

———

XX.—IN WHICH LUCINDA'S INNOCENCE IS IN THE GREATEST POSSIBLE DANGER.

I LEFT four mysterious figures clad in white groping about in the dark outside the door of the bedchamber of a certain young lady.

I will leave them there a little longer, and, using the privilege of the novelist, penetrate into the sanctity of the maiden's sleeping apartment.

[CHARLEY WAG, THE NEW JACK SHEPPARD.

Lucinda had gone to bed.

Wearied by the unusual and exciting events of the day, she was not sorry to obtain a few hours rest; though when at last the opportunity arrived, her mind was so agitated by conflicting thoughts, that she was totally unable to sleep.

Yet at the same time her brains were so confused by the excitement she had gone through, and the quantity of wine which Mr. Leech and the clerical gentlemen had forced her to take, that she could not concentrate her thoughts for three consecutive minutes upon the same topic.

Most certainly there existed a great necessity for reflection.

She felt that she was standing upon the brink of an abyss.

What hands had she fallen into?

Surely, by what little she had seen, these men surrounding her seemed to be undoubtedly so many raging wolves disguised in innocent sheepskins.

Then as to the foreign nobleman. Although a remarkably soft sort of girl, Lucinda had very strong doubts about Mr. Leech's good breeding. He never in any way alluded to his noble birth or his property, which may be easily accounted for when it is considered that he had no idea himself what he was supposed to be.

Then did he mean marriage?

He said nothing about it. Persons whose intentions are honourable generally converse pretty largely upon the topic.

His conduct was not outrageously indecent to be sure, but his manners were rather free and easy.

He had a way of kissing which alone was likely to cause offence in any well regulated female mind.

No, decidedly the more she thought of Mr. Leech's conduct, the less confidence she felt in that gentleman's honour.

But what should she do? What course could she pursue?

To run away, she thought, would be a good plan, but then where could she run to? And might not she be running out of the fryingpan into the fire?

Besides, she was too sleepy to run.

Anyhow, she determined she would not go home again.

Her father would kill her at the very least. She had seen Mr. Hopley in a passion, and the recollection was not soothing.

And while thus she was pondering she began to feel drowsy.

She did not exactly go to sleep, but sank into a half unconscious state, in which she was dimly conscious of the ticking of a clock upon the stairs, and the flickering of a rushlight in a shade in the room.

While lying thus, she fancied that she heard the handle of the door move.

She fancied that she heard some one tampering with the lock, but such was the state of drowsy apathy into which she had fallen, that although she twice noticed the circumstance, she was yet too indolent to take any steps to see whether or no she had been mistaken.

Once in a dreamy kind of way, she wondered whether she had locked it or not, but the next moment she made up her mind to save trouble, that she had been mistaken, and closed her eyes again.

However, there was no mistake about it. The handle of the door slowly turned and turned.

Then the door gave a crack and opened.

An inch at a time, with the greatest caution, the intruder proceeded.

Gradually the breach widened.

Then, by slow degrees, a fat, bald, ugly head was poked into the room.

It was our reverend friend Mr. Swabb who was first in the field. Having well noted the position of Lucinda's bed-room on his way to his own, so that he could easily find it again in the dark, he waited a sufficient time after he had undressed, in a state of frantic suspense, for the house to become quiet, and then stole downstairs on tip-toe.

With the stealthy caution of a cat, and the expression of a hungry little boy in the company of a luscious plum-pudding, did this hoary old sinner creep into the young maiden's bed-room.

Burning with desire, and yet shivering with fright, he approached the bed where lay in all the voluptuous abandonment of unconsciousness the symmetrical and well-developed Lucinda.

Cautiously he crept towards her.

He listened for a moment, but could not hear her breathe.

"She must be asleep," he thought to himself.

In the position in which she lay he could not see her face, but he could see her plump bosom rise and fall in regular palpitations; for she had not seen him enter the room, and, as she was turning round at the very moment that the door creaked, neither she nor the intruder had been disturbed by the other's movements.

Then he crept nearer to her still.

He could trace the outline of her body beneath the clothes,—for she had thrown a portion of them off, feeling so hot,—and his lascivious imagination readily supplied all that was concealed.

Burning with impatience, he laid his hand upon the coverlid of the bed, and was in the act of drawing it down, when a noise at the door disturbed him.

Without reflecting for a moment, but in so awful a fright at the idea of being discovered in such a position, and irrevocably disgraced for life, did he even manage to escape the personal chastisement which his conduct merited, he bobbed down his head, and sat crouching in the shadow of the bed upon the floor.

The position he had assumed was, it must be owned, extremely ungraceful and undignified; but then he trusted not to be caught, and he was too much frightened to know what he was about.

On his hams, then, did the reverend gentleman squat.

With a palpitating heart did he wait.

His teeth chattered, too, a little, and he began to have the cramp almost immediately he stooped down, which by no means added to the comfort of his attitude.

Slowly the door opened as it had opened before.

Slowly and cautiously. Surely this must be another disturber of female innocence.

It was—it was Sleek.

Like Swabb had he waited impatiently for the rest of the house to go to sleep, and then stolen out on tip-toe, to seek the chamber of the unconscious object of his unlawful passion.

In the same cautious way, and with the same Tarquinish expression of countenance, did he open the door, inch by inch, and creep forward towards the maiden's bed.

But as he approached it, indeed was within a yard, as it seemed to him, of the possession of that which he so much desired, his hand, groping in the dark, fell upon some object at the side of the bed which both startled and surprised him.

And this was neither more nor less than Mr. Swabb's bald head.

Shiny, smooth, and hairless, he was utterly at a loss to account for its being there; and, to add to his dismay, while he stood transfixed and powerless, with his hand still resting on it, it began to revolve slowly under him, in a manner unspeakably horrible and supernatural.

So much so, that the miserable Sleek perspired at every pore, and every hair on his head bristled with intense terror, while his teeth chattered, and his knees knocked together as though he were momentarily in fear of falling to pieces, like a figure in a fantoccini show.

But still the awful object revolved beneath his touch, and still his teeth chattered, his knees knocked together, and his hair bristled.

Then, as if to add new terror to the scene, the mysterious globe began to rise. The Reverend Sleek's hand slipped from it, and in so slipping his finger fell into Brother Swabb's open mouth, the teeth of which immediately closed upon it with a snap.

For you must not suppose that the first reverend gentleman was not quite as much frightened when the second got hold of him as the second was when he accidentally did so.

For of course Mr. Swabb could not see in that uncertain light who it was; and he suspected that it was Leech, the lawyer, at whose hands he imagined he should receive an awful drubbing.

As for poor Sleek, he was so mortally terrified, he did not know whether to think that what he had got hold of belonged to this world or the next.

However, from a state of silent fright, the pain of Mr. Swabb's bite caused him to set up a dismal howl, which, commencing in a low guttural sound, became gradually shriller and shriller as it proceeded, and at length reached such an intensity of shrillness as the agony became unendurable, that the whole house heard it, and those who were asleep woke up in alarm, wondering what on earth could have happened.

Among the many whom Mr. Sleek's howl startled, you may easily suppose that the fair Lucinda was one; and when she discerned in the faint light shed by the moon through the window-blind, the two amorous shepherds in their shirts, struggling on the floor, she commenced a course of piercing shrieks, which would have led you to suppose, had you known their design, that the reverend gentlemen had been successful in their atrocious attempt upon her unsuspecting innocence.

But while these sounds of distress were issuing from the fat maiden's bed-chamber, on the floor above there arose simultaneously a loud shout-ing for help, and cries of "murder," "fire," and "thieves."

Thus it arose.

The Reverend Mr. Jack Pudding having retired to his bachelor bed, after partaking of a glass of hot rum and water by way of a nightcap, endeavoured to compose himself to sleep, but found it rather a harder job than he had expected.

In spite of all he could do, the thought of that pretty young lady he had had the pleasure of dining with persisted in creeping into his head.

What was Mr. Sleek's reason for wishing to know the number of the young lady's sleeping apartment?

Surely she could not be ignorant of his visit. She must have given him some encouragement. In that case, Mr. Pudding might try his chance. Who could say what might turn up?

Rum and water, and those sly kisses he had had at the revival in the kitchen, when the lights were out, combined to fire the Reverend Jack's imagination; and he sprung out of bed, and, without waiting to make an elaborate toilet, set out in search of the famous No. 6.

But scarcely had he passed the door of his room, when a creaking of the boards a few yards before him apprised him of the fact of there being another Richard in the field.

"That's Sleek, for a penny!" said he. "What an awful old rip! Never mind—I'll serve him out."

It was not, however, Mr. Sleek, as Pudding thought, but Mr. Ghastly Gash, who was bound upon a similar expedition to that of the three other gentlemen.

But Mr. Gash, either through want of recollection or rum and water, mistook the position of the chamber of which he was in search, and, instead of going down-stairs, he began to grope his way along the passage in which his own bedroom was situated, until he arrived at a door in a corner similar to that belonging to Lucinda's apartment on the floor below.

Making sure that he was in the right quarter, Mr. Gash proceeded with the utmost caution to open the door, and, having effected this with an infinity of trouble, advanced on tiptoe towards the bed.

What he supposed to be the beautiful Lucinda was snoring very comfortable in the middle of the couch.

The amorous parson approached the sleeping beauty, and took a hand which was lying on the counterpane between his own.

"Dearest love!" he whispered softly.

"Ugh!" grunted the object of his affection.

"Sweet maiden," he continued, "pardon the impetuosity of my passion in thus approaching you."

Here the supposed maiden sat up in bed.

"Oh, repulse me not, but grant my prayer," sighed the shepherd, and endeavoured to take her round the waist; but, greatly to his astonishment, he received a sounding smack in the face, which made him stagger back a couple of yards, at the same time that Leech the lawyer, into whose chamber he had accidentally intruded himself, roared in a gruff voice:

"Who are you, and what the devil do you want?"

But as Mr. Gash was too much astounded to make any reply, the lawyer continued to roar out at the top of his voice, and to call "murder," "fire," and "thieves," indiscriminately; at the same time he took the liberty of drubbing the reverend gent with his fists, until Mr. Gash began to bellow almost as loudly as the Reverend Mr. Sleek was bawling down-stairs.

The effect of this terrific uproar, arising on all sides at once, combined with the sudden appearance at each end of the passage of the disturbed inmates of the hotel, rushing to the rescue with lighted candles, was to cause a panic in Pudding's mind, and glued his feet to the floor.

The consequence was, that Mr. Gash, in his wild efforts to escape from the lawyer, ran full butt against him, and sent the unfortunate clergyman sprawling on his nose.

Just then a universal sally seemed to be made by everybody in the house to the scene of the disturbance, and at least a couple of dozen excited individuals of either sex, all in their night-clothes, and exhibiting a wild variety of styles in shirts and chemaises, made their appearance at their bed-room doors, and asked one another with white and awe-struck faces, what was the row.

"It's thieves!" said a commercial traveller, in blue jersey and flannel drawers.

"It's murder!" cried an old gentleman in his shirt and top-boots.

"Or worse," suggested an elderly spinster, in a scanty white slip, alluding to the sound of the woman's screams.

"It's them cursed parsons!" cried the landlord indignantly. "What are they up to now?"

The waiter and chambermaid could have made a shrewd guess, but for reasons of their own they remained silent; indeed, they did not wish particular attention to be drawn to the fact of them both appearing simultaneously from the same apartment.

As it was, and as it says in Ingoldsby's poem,

> "But these last two they created some scandal,
> By appearing together with only one candle."

XXI.—A Conversation between two Scoundrels.

BLOODYER, the workhouse master, and Faversham, the doctor, were talking together.

"I tell you, Faversham, we must be careful."

"Why?"

"Why? I should think you need not ask?"

"For my part, I am always careful."

"I know that. I did not say that you were not, but we must be more than usually cautious, I say. Things are going against us."

"What *has* gone against us?"

"The tale that that old mad fool Toddleboy told the magistrate has got noised about."

"It did not get into the newspapers, for as I told you, happening to hear from a friend who was present what had occurred, I straightway took steps to stifle the reports."

"Yes, I know that, but in spite of your precaution it has got whispered about. I have heard of it from several persons."

"Heard what?"

"Why, some tale about physicing the paupers and selling their bodies to the hospitals."

"But nobody believes such ridiculous nonsense."

"No. I don't suppose they do yet. It seems so unlikely. Only if we are not extra careful, any little slip might tell against us."

"Yes, I see, because——"

"Because there is no knowing where suspicions, once aroused, may end."

"For the present, of course, we will suspend operations."

"And lessen the mortality."

"Most certainly. We will let them enjoy their miserable lives a little longer. We shall get a good stock like that, and can send them to market after we've fattened them up a bit."

Here these two wholesale dealers in human flesh and blood chuckled grimly as though they were enjoying a joke of extra humour.

They were sitting one wild windy night in the workhouse master's room, where they had had a fire lighted, although it was the middle of July; for English weather is very uncertain, as everybody knows, and had you not known for a positive fact that it was summer, you might almost have been inclined to think that it was winter instead.

After a long pause, in which they had both been smoking in moody silence, the workhouse master looked up.

"That old man," said he, "did not get into the prison you visited, did he?"

"No, no," replied Faversham, in absent fashion; and then, his thoughts seeming to stray to some other subject, he muttered to himself,

"Curses light upon my bad memory," he said aloud; "I have quite forgotten the boy. He must be out by now."

"What boy?" asked Bloodyer.

"What boy?—oh, nobody. Nothing of any consequence. By the way, too, now I come to think of it, how has that man been going on; that—what was his name?"

"Whose name?"

"A man who had a locket. Don't you remember the night Cudder died he wanted to jump out of the window?"

"Yes—yes," replied the other, hastily; "I recollect—I recollect: you mean Horford."

"To be sure, Horford. How is he going on?"

"I don't know."

"What do you mean?" the other asked, turning hastily towards him. "Is he dead?"

"No—not dead."

"What then?"

"At least, he may be dead for what I know."

"What do you mean?"

"I mean that he is gone out, and so I know no more about him—that's all."

"Gone out?" cried Faversham, springing to his feet. "When did he go—where did he go? How came you to let him escape!"

His manner was wild and excited, and strangely unlike his usual composed and serious demeanour.

Bloodyer looked at him in astonishment.

He never yet had seen this mysterious and unscrupulous being so agitated, although he had

had many opportunities of observing him at very trying moments.

"What do you mean?" the workhouse master asked presently. "Why should I try to keep him. Business being slack, there was no particular point in fattening up a lot of stock, was there."

Faversham made no reply.

Presently, however, he asked :—

"How did he get out?"

"Some friend fetched him," replied the workhouse master.

"Friends, eh? I thought he had none, who was it?"

"Well, I can hardly recollect, though, by-the-bye, I should do."

"Who was it, then?"

"A lady fetched him?"

"A lady?"

"A party who was here on board-day—one of the overseers of the Westminster workhouse, told me that he knew her well."

"And she was—"

"A most respectable party from all accounts, a regular church goer, and gives largely to parochial charities—quite a model woman."

"Her name?"

"Is Mrs. Crow."

"You must find out where she lives if you possibly can do so," said Faversham, after awhile. "I want to speak to that man if I can. I think he may give me some information upon a subject connected with the Duke of Heatherland, which may put that nobleman into my power. Make some inquiries, will you?"

"Certainly! only I wonder you did not make them youself, when you had the opportunity."

"I had other things to think of."

"Very well, you may depend on me. By-the-bye, talking of the Duke, how did you find the young Duke?"

"You mean the boy?"

"Yes."

"He is at Lyons with his mother. He is much better, and will return in the spring,"

"Did you go to Lyons, then?"

"Yes, I have just come from there. And now I must say good-night. Get me what information you can upon that matter. And do nothing in the way of business for the present."

"No. Good-night."

"Good-night."

Thus they parted. The workhouse master bent his steps towards his bed-chamber, whilst Faversham strode rapidly away across the yard, and hailing a cab outside the gate, was conveyed to his own residence in Bayswater.

He had been, since the time when we last introduced him to the reader, despatched at the Duke's desire to Lyons, where the Duchess and the little boy was passing the spring.

He had found his late patient progressing favourably. He had also found that the Duchess was determined to remain abroad for several months, now that she found that her darling child was reaping so much benefit from the change of air.

If she persisted in this course, she would overthrow all Faversham's plans for the future.

Already had his schemes of vengeance been deferred by the Duchess's impetuous conduct.

The lamb had been snatched as it were from between the fangs of the wolf.

But not for long; he was determined of that.

Was the scheme of vengeance, which he had so long ago conceived, and through so many years been silently perfecting, to be abandoned now.

Not likely.

In the meantime he must wait, as he had done before, and bide his opportunity as he had done before.

He was not very long in arriving at his house in Westburnia. He had given his housekeeper a holiday about a fortnight back, and her time had not yet expired.

The house was left in charge of a young lad, who opened the door and answered questions, but whose chief duty was to sleep in the house at night, as a sort of protection to the property.

As it was then close upon midnight, the doctor thought, of course, that the boy would be gone to bed. He, however, expected to find some one else.

There was always somebody else in the house : somebody whom no other inmate of the house, besides the doctor himself, ever clapped eyes on.

A certain mysterious being, who was kept at the back of the house behind the surgery, in a room which the doctor called his laboratory.

Some people said this person so smuggled out of sight, was a poor half-witted relation of the doctor's.

In the neighbourhood, there had been from time to time, a great deal of curiosity manifested respecting him, but nothing definite was known by any but the doctor and the man himself.

It was close upon midnight, I say, when Faversham reached home.

As he put the key in the lock, the church clocks begun to strike twelve.

At first uncertain whether it was the hour striking, or the the three-quarters, he paused to listen, and listened until the last stroke.

Then he turned the key and entered his house

He closed the door behind him as noiselessly as possible, but the jar of the bolt echoed through the quiet and apparently deserted dwelling, awakening echoes in the upper rooms, as though a party of spirits had been disturbed by his approach, and were beating a hasty retreat.

Again he paused for a moment to listen.

When the echos had died out an awful, death-like silence succeeded them.

With an irrepressible throbbing at his heart, the doctor stepped forward into the grave-like darkness.

XXII.—THE LIVING DEATH.

BLOOD! Blood!! Blood!!!
  Crime upon crime. Horror upon horror.

Deeper and yet deeper still down the yawning abyss, where fiery torture awaited him.

No hope, no escape! around him darkness and misery. Before him darkness and despair, without a home that he dare call his own; without a place on earth.

Belonging rightly to the dead, yet lingering among the living.

Afraid to die, yet loathing his existence.

Such a life as this, was the life led by James Murdoch, the resuscitated murderer.

For near upon fifteen years had he been imprisoned, shut in, and hidden from the sight of every human being but one.

Near upon fifteen years had passed since he had dared to leave the place in which he was confined, and go forth into the streets to breathe the free air of heaven.

Near upon fifteen years had he been locked in the gloomy laboratory behind the surgery in Faversham's house.

The laboratory was a dark low-ceilinged room lighted by one small window, strongly grated, and covered with wire-work, so that in the day time it was quite impossible for any person outside to penetrate the gloom of the apartment, and distinguish what was going on inside.

But even if they had been able to do so, the window looked into a small cellar-like back yard, into which a door from the laboratory had originally opened, but which the doctor had had bricked up when first he came into the house, and as there was no other communication with it from without, no person was likely to endeavour to penetrate the mystery, whatever it was, which might have been hidden within the apartment.

The door which led from this laboratory into the surgery, was coated with iron, and fastened by two elaborate locks, of which Faversham himself carried the keys, and which, without the keys, it was impossible to unfasten from the inside, so that when locked up, the captive Murdoch was a prisoner until such time as the doctor chose to visit him.

Besides the door bricked up, and this door leading to the surgery, there was, however, another one which it would have been extremely difficult for any person to have found, even had they been aware of its existence, for there was no visible difference between it and the wall, and it was crossed by shelves covered with dusty bottles which wore the appearance of not having been disturbed for years.

It was seldom disturbed by Murdoch, never when he was there alone, for it *contained dead bodies.*

The corpses of Faversham's victims.

But though the wretched captive refrained from opening the door, how could he ever dispel the horrible consciousness of being within a yard of the decaying remains of those whom he had assisted to poison.

No; ever was the horrible thought present to his mind.

It haunted him by day.

It sat like a nightmare upon his breast, when he fain would have lost forgetfulness in slumber.

Yet he could not—he dare not fly from this hideous bugbear.

Faversham, for reasons of his own, had in the first instance exaggerated the danger of Murdoch's showing himself abroad.

Since then, for the same reason, whenever the miserable man had expressed his weariness and impatience, the doctor had invented some new lie to intimidate him, and hold him in check.

He told him the coffin had been dug up, and found to contain stones instead of bones, and that suspicion had arisen that all was not right.

A short time afterwards he came in, apparently in a state of great excitement, and bade Murdoch for heaven's sake keep close, and not show himself, for that he was advertised in the papers, and there was a general hue and cry after him.

In corroboration of this statement, Faversham showed him an advertisement, which he said he had cut from a paper published that day, and afterwards a paper from which he read, or pretended to read, a paragraph about his supposed escape from the gallows, and an account of the steps that the police were taking to find him.

As Murdoch could not read even his own name in print with any certainty, he, of course, had to take a great deal for granted, and though he secretly hated and distrusted his gaoler to such an extent, that had he dared, for his own sake, he would long ago have murdered him, yet he was obliged to believe him, as he had no one else to ask, and he dare not go out and put the truth of Faversham's statement to the test.

So from day to day, week to week, month to month, and year to year the time rolled on, and still he was immured in this dungeon, without air or light.

He grew grey, he grew wrinkled, he grew blind. There was nothing in the world one would have thought left to him worth living for, but still he clung to life with the desperate tenacity of a drowning man, clinging to the polished surface of a rock.

When Faversham was at home, he supplied him with his food by stealth, brought him in meat and vegetables to cook, wine and spirits and beer to drink.

When he went away for any time, as he trusted no one but himself to see the captive, he left him a large supply of such provisions as would keep until his return.

No one ever saw the captive, no one knew on what he fed, nor how he lived or employed himself.

A whisper got about in the neighbourhood that the doctor had something chained up, but nobody knew what.

A great many people were particularly curious about it, and among the number Master Joe Wickets, the boy whom the doctor had left in charge of the house, during the temporary absence of the housekeeper.

This Joe was the steadiest and most trustworthy of lads, with a five years' character for piety and sobriety, or else you may be sure he would not have been trusted in so responsible a situation as that which he now filled; but I suppose, like other sober-sided people, he had his "larky" moments.

If he had not, he would not have been human.

"I can't think what it means," said Joe to his mother one night at tea-time.

"It do seem curious, certainly," Joe's mother replied.

"Do you think it's a lunatic?"

"Lord bless us, Joe. He may get out and kill you."

"Oh, I'm not afraid of that; I only wish he would come out. That's all I want him to do."

"What beats me though, Joe, is this."

"Is what, mother?"

"…is what he eats."

"Well, I've thought that over several times, but I suppose he has his grub stowed away somewhere."

"What lives on dry things like they do on board ship?"

"Yes, I suppose so—but I tell you what."

"What?"

"I'll tell you where he gets his drink."

"Where's that?"

"I mean the water he drinks, you know."

"To be sure."

"He gets it from a pipe that runs through the surgery, because sometimes when I've been there, he's been moving in the other room I've fancied, and then there's been a gurgling in the pipe."

"Lor, Joe, how horrible! What did you do?"

"Do, mother? Don't be so foolish, I'll tell you what I mean to do."

"What will that be, Joe?"

"Why, I'll tell you; I shall knock at the door and ask him whether he didn't call, and if that wont do, I shall stop up the pipe and that must bring him out, you know, unless he can live without water."

"Gracious me, Joe, I hope you wont get into trouble."

"No fear of that, mother."

"Well, don't do anything foolish."

"Not if I can help it."

"And take care you don't excite this lunatic, if it is a lunatic."

"Trust me for that."

"Whatever you do, take care; and, Joe——"

"Yes, mother."

"Let me know what happens, I feel rather curious about it."

"All right, you may depend upon me for a full, true, and particular account of the whole proceeding."

With this, Master Joe swallowed his last morsel of bread and butter, and scampered back to his post.

He did not usually come out for his meals, but on this occasion he had done so, because he wanted to get a hammer to do the little trick he alluded to.

He slept in the house at night in a room on the first-floor, and kept a watchman's rattle behind his pillow in case of accidents.

But, perhaps after all, there was not much fear of thieves, for the upper part of the house was entirely empty, and the lower part was very poorly furnished.

The doctor kept no other servants besides the housekeeper, and though he had no use for so large a house, he objected to lodgers as likely to pry into his affairs.

When Joe came in, he straightway carried his project into execution.

He went to the iron door of the surgery: (it looked like the door of a safe more than a door leading into another room) and knocked.

He fancied that he had heard a movement within, which had ceased abruptly at the sound of his knuckles.

He waited awhile.

Then he knocked again

There was no answer.

Placing his ear against the door, he listened intently, but could hear nothing.

After a little while, though, there was a faint scuffling noise, as it were, creeping across the floor of the inner room, and the sound approached the door.

Still more intently did he listen.

What was it he heard?

Ah! he could not be mistaken; it was the sound of the captive's breath close against his ear upon the other side.

Like this he stood and listened to it intently, with a panting heart.

Summoning fresh courage, he knocked again.

Then with intense anxiety he waited, but there was no reply. He listened and listened.

The sound of the breathing still continued—all else was still.

The twilight was setting in, the house was unnaturally quiet, the whole scene lonely in the extreme, and a terror seizing upon the boy, he was more than half inclined to take to his heels and run for his life.

But this Joe was a brave young fellow, and he was as curious as any woman.

He was not going to give the matter up now he had got so far.

Looking down, he saw that there was a bolt outside the door, which would prevent the door being opened without his consent.

Having found this out, he felt much more courageous; so he shot the bolt, and determined "to give the beggar inside a good stir up."

He therefore knocked again.

As before, there was no answer.

"Very well, old fellow," said he to himself, "I'll serve you out."

Then he bawled at the top of his voice,

"Hallo! hallo! hallo! you inside there—what do you want?"

No answer.

"Perhaps he's dumb," thought Joe.

Then he shouted again,

"If you can't speak, knock."

He waited a long while, shouted once more, and again waited; but there was no reply.

"He's as obstinate as a pig," the boy said to himself; "but I'll bring him to his senses. I'll cut off his water."

So saying, he took the hammer which he had got on purpose, and banged away at the water-pipe until he beat it quite flat.

"That has quite cut off his supply," the boy thought. "Now he must come to terms."

Satisfied upon this point, Master Joe took himself off to bed, being, however, extra careful about locking his bed-room door, for somehow, in spite of himself, he could not help feeling a little frightened of this unknown and mysterious being, who seemed to live without food, and to hold no communion with its fellow men.

He went down to the surgery the first thing in the morning and listened at the door, then knocked about the articles of furniture in the room, so that the captive might hear him and make some signs if he wanted anything.

The captive, however, made no sign.

"Ah," said Joe to himself, "he hasn't wanted the water yet, but wait till he does, then he won't be so proud."

Twice during the course of the day he returned, and both times adopted the same course, but with the same success.

Next day again the same thing.

"He must have got some water some other way," Joe thought to himself as the evening drew near.

Once or twice he hammered at the iron door, but got no answer; he listened also, and although he felt confident that he heard as before the shuffling noise within, and the sound of breathing, there was no reply to his questions. Nothing but the same sullen silence that there had been before.

"Suppose, after all," said Master Joe with a shudder, "it shouldn't be a man, but some horrible beast shut up."

The thought gave him the horrors, and he did not come near the place again for another day.

XXIII.—BROKEN LOOSE.

MURDOCH inside was without water.

He did, as the boy had supposed, obtain his water through the pipe which Joe had flattened.

When in the morning he went to it wishing to draw some water to quench his thirst, he found in it only about half a tea-cup full, and most of this he carelessly spilt.

Of course he fancied that during the day the when water would come in.

He managed to go without until the evening, and waited with tolerable patience, cursing a little now and then, to be sure, but nothing out of the common way.

The next day it grew rather serious.

How long was it to last? How long would the doctor be away? What was to become of him?

A person can do without food for a long while but not without water.

Like a madman he took to drinking spirits the water failed him.

He felt that he was growing light-headed and that his wits were wandering.

Still it was necessary to concentrate his thoughts, and come to some determination as to what was to be done.

To die there, cooped up like a rat in a hole, was monstrous.

To die within reach of the necessaries of life, and yet debarred from them; the thought was maddening.

Although he felt delirious with thirst, he yet had sufficient presence of mind to know what steps must be taken first.

When night came, and all was quiet, he must get out and search the house for water.

As he had never dreamt of venturing out before, the very idea of it now filled him with fear. But he felt that his life depended upon the efforts that he made.

Of course, as you may suppose, he had no idea of effecting his escape by the iron door. From the inside it was an utter impossibility to have picked by an experienced cracksman, from the inside, however, it was quite impregnable, not only could it not be picked, but the door

fitted so tightly, that it was equally impossible to push back the bolts.

No, the only way out lay through the window.

Arrived at this conclusion, he lost no time in thinking about the matter, but set to work immediately.

With a strong screw-driver which he had in the room, he managed to loosen two of the bars from the casement, then concentrating all his strength in a pull, wrenched them out.

In like manner, he tore down the wire-work. The window frame was firmly nailed down (the room was ventilated by a cracked pane above) but the woodwork was old and rotten, and soon tore away.

Getting through at last after a couple of hours or so excessively hard work, he found himself in the little back-yard I have described.

By battering a brick out of the wall for a step, he managed to climb upon the top of the window above.

His case was so desperate, that he was entirely reckless of his personal safety, and this no doubt contributed to his success, for had he been timid and nervous, he would never have been able to keep his balance or support himself upon such narrow ledges as now he contrived to stand upon.

Having forced an entrance into the room above, he began to grope about in the dark to see what it contained.

He could find nothing, however, but some old lumber, and a broken bottle standing upon the mantlepiece empty.

It occurred to him, as most probable, that the water would be found down upon the ground or kitchen floor. He descended and commenced a search for it.

The house was pitch dark, and he groped about in the wildest manner, running his head against corners of walls, and hurting himself somehow at almost every step.

It was Joe's custom to lock up all the doors on the kitchen floor before he went to bed, and consequently the back kitchen, where Murdoch expected to find the water, was locked.

Driven almost mad with thirst, he now conceived the bold project of venturing out into the street in search of what he required.

He must find it, he thought, at some pump or spout in the neighbourhood.

No one was likely to meet him, and when he had obtained it, he could creep in again, and get back somehow to his lair.

At least, he had scarcely decided what he should do after he got the water. The first thing, and the most important, was to get it.

Feeling his way up-stairs again, he found the street door after a little trouble, pulled back the bolts, and undid the chain, and in another moment was in the street.

He felt strangely giddy and nervous, now he was in the open air.

It was near on fifteen years since he had been free.

The unusual sense of space and liberty confused him, and he felt lost.

However, the thirst that was gnawing at him again gave him courage, and he sped along the streets, looking eagerly to the right and to the left.

CHARLEY WAG, IN HIS POPULAR CHARACTER OF A SWELL OF THE PERIOD.

in quest of that in which he stood so greatly in need.

Thank God, he found it at last. There was a pump at a cab stand; a full bucket beside it.

Without in the least caring what the men might think, he plunged his head into the water and drank to his heart's content.

Then when his thirst was quenched he rose, and with a sensation of relief, which he never before recollected to have experienced, he gave himself for awhile to the full enjoyment of this new and delicious sense of freedom.

For more than an hour he wandered in the streets, snuffing ecstatically at the air, gathering leaves of trees and shrubs, through garden railings, lolling in luxurious ease upon the doorsteps of the portico houses in great squares.

No. 26.

His soul was filled with wild exuberance of spirits, his heart throbbed with joy, as though momentarily it was about to burst its bonds.

He was free.

Free from the stifling gloom of that accursed chamber—free from the oppressive sense of captivity—free from the murky closeness of the fœtid atmosphere, where for near upon fifteen years he had been inhaling.

Free—free once more.

A mad desire for motion seized him, and he bounded like a deer along the high road.

He shouted aloud for very joy.

The people in the streets, such few as there were, turned round amazed to look after him.

"He's mad," said some.

"Drunk," said others.

[CHARLEY WAG, THE NEW JACK SHEPPARD.

They all gave him as wide a berth as possible, and he rushed forward on his mad career, without a thought of time or space.

But his physical powers were not equal to these wild vagaries of his imagination.

Gradually he began to slacken his paces; his strength failed him, his knees bent under him.

Completely exhausted, at length, he sunk down upon the ground, and lay for a few moments pale and breathless, like a person in a swoon.

When he began slowly to recover, several people were standing round him.

Some one was raising his head.

"Hold up," he heard them say.

"Hold up, my poor fellow, what's the matter with you?"

Then presently.

"Where do you live?"

Where did he live, to be sure, madman that he was, would he ever be able to find the place again. The thought terrified him and he sprang up into a sitting posture, but then the idea occurred to him. But the idea occurred to him, did it matter? Why should he ever go back to slavery? Directly upon this thought, however, came the reflection that, bad as the place was, yet for fifteen years it had been his only home. How should he find a living elsewhere? Dare he show himself elsewhere?

As these thoughts were passing through his mind, he passed his eyes to the face of a person leaning over him, and as he looked, an expression of wild terror settled upon his features.

It was a policeman.

Unconscious of that fright which he occasioned, the officer, in an encouraging tone, bade Murdoch to hold up and never say die.

"Where do you live?" began he. "What's your name?"

"My name?" stammered Murdoch.

"Yes, try and stand up, and I'll see you home."

"No thank you," the other replied, shaking off the policeman's hold, and speaking with nervous haste. "I'm all right now, I can help myself."

But as soon as he was left to himself, he felt how helpless he was at the last, which he would have performed.

He could no more find the doctor's house than he could fly.

He had been running on in such a mad reckless style, that now he came to try to retrace his steps, every place seemed new to him.

Up one street and down another he wandered, until he was weary. The few persons whom he could find to enquire of, could give him no information on the subject. He must have got far away from the neighbourhood.

No, he reflected, the only way was to look at a post-office directory, but how was he to obtain a sight of one without having any money in his pocket.

And even when that difficulty was overcome, he must wait until the morning.

All night long he must wander in the streets without shelter.

He was cold and hungry and faint, and finding a door-step in a quiet corner, where he thought he could have an hour or two undisturbed, he coiled himself up, and sank into an uneasy fitful slumber.

XXIV.—Jack Rattan makes himself at Home with the Corpses.

MEANWHILE, inside the doctor's house, strange events were taking place.

Mr. Jack Rattan is an individual of so very amiable a disposition, that I feel sure the reader must be vexed at my having for so long a time neglected him.

It is necessary at the present moment that we should follow his fortunes, so with your leave we will take a flying jump from Bayswater to Westminster, and see how he is getting on.

On this particular evening, when Murdoch had broken out of his place of captivity, Mr. Rattan was sitting by the side of the fire in Mrs. Crow's house and was yawning so prodigiously with fatigue, that the upper portion of his head seemed in great danger of falling off altogether.

"What's the matter, Jack?" asked his mother.

"Oh, I don't know," replied Jack, surlily.

"Yes you do," said his mother. "What is it, dear? Can I do anything for you?"

"Do anything for me? No! What do you suppose you can do?" replied the dutiful son. "Shut up, will you, and leave me alone."

The only thing Mrs. Crow did for the amiable creature, was to keep him when he was out of luck; to feed him with the best; hide him from the police, and give him the lodging of a nobleman.

But that was nothing. There is a sort of ruffianly cur that always ill-treats the woman that is kind to him. Mr. Rattan was of that genus. He thought very little about banging his mother.

He was not even aware of the existence of a commandment, somewhat at variance with his sentiments upon the subject.

"I'm sure, Jack, you oughtn't to be unhappy," Mrs. Crow continued, presently. "Why don't you lie up, and make yourself comfortable? I'm sure I'll give you as much as ever I can, if you will only stay with me."

"Oh, ah, you're precious kind no doubt; and how the blazes is a cove to amuse hisself cooped up here, do you suppose. I wonder you can be so gallows unreasonable."

"Well, but Jack, what do you wish for?"

"Why I want a great variety, for one thing. It's devilish slow work, sitting here hour after hour staring at your old chops."

"Oh, Jack."

"Yes, it's, oh, Jack, I dare say, only you're not much of a beauty now, whatever you might have been. I reckon you don't set up for one."

He was a sweet specimen of a son, was he not?

Presently he began growling again.

"Why don't you let us have some tin, so as I can go out, and have a bit of a spree, instead of sticking here in this stinking old hole."

"Why, you have everything you can wish for?"

"No I don't?"

"What don't you have?"

"Why, I don't have no company. You won't even let me go up-stairs and see the gals."

"Of course I won't. What do you want with them; besides, I've told you over and over again they're accustomed to a different class of persons to you, Jack; they only see gentlemen."

"Oh, don't they?" said Jack, quite furious. "Very well, old woman, just you wait till you're in your box, and then I'll see if they'll turn up their noses at me; I'll keep a regular housefull, I shall, like a grand Turk, and spend your dirty old ha'pence."

"Yes, Jack, I dare say, only I'm not dead yet, you see."

"Ugh!" grunted Jack to himself, "It's time you was, though."

"What do you say?"

"I didn't say nothing."

"I thought you did."

"No, but I'm going to, now What'll you shell out—come?"

"Nothing; why do you want it?"

"Because I'm going out."

"What do you want to go out for?"

"I've told you, because it's so dull."

"Very well, then, go and get some money somewhere else."

"So I will," retorted Rattan, rising to his feet, "I'll get some out of your patron, the Duke, for one person."

"No, Jack, you won't. Not in the way you said. You promised me you wouldn't."

"Oh, damn promises; you give me some tin, then."

"I shan't."

"You won't."

"No."

"You mean it."

"Mean it."

"Very well, then, I'll do what I said."

"No—no, Jack," cried the woman, springing up and trying to stop him. "For God's sake, don't. You will ruin me."

But he heeded not her entreaties in the least, and forced his way past her out of the room.

For some time she called after him. She ran to the street door and called after him by name, and said he should have what he liked, but he took no notice.

He often treated her in this way. He thought it a very wise course to pursue. It brought her to her senses, he said, and showed her who was master.

Therefore, on this occasion he took no notice of her calling, but strolled along with his hands in his pockets, puffing of his pipe, and feeling very savage.

Things had not gone so well as usual with Mr. Rattan.

The horrible trade at the workhouse had been, as we have seen, temporarily suspended, and as nothing of a burglarious or murderous character had happened to turn up, Mr. Rattan found himself unpleasantly short of cash.

Something must be done, he felt that, and determined to act upon it.

He had not seen Faversham for a long while. He would go over to Bayswater and try and find him.

He knew the house well enough, for he had often been there.

Without any trouble he found it—he found it dark and apparently deserted.

Going up to the door, with the intention of ringing the bell, he was astonished to find the door open.

He had been debating with himself for some time with his hand on the wire, whether he should pull it because it was so late.

Then he reflected, that from what he knew of the doctor's habits, he would in all probability not have gone to bed.

"I'll work a trifle out of him," thought Rattan. "The deuce and all is in it if I don't. Well, here goes!"

He was just in the act of ringing, as I say, when the door attracted his notice.

"That's rayther rum."

Then he looked cautiously to the right and to the left.

Seeing nobody about, he stepped inside.

He groped his way cautiously down the passage, and into a room on the ground floor, the door of which was ajar, as Murdoch had left it.

Feeling about here he came upon a box of matches.

"That's my sort," said he, striking one. "Now I can see what I'm about."

After lighting the match, he was not very long before he saw an end of candle, and he lit it at once.

"Suppose I'm copped," said he to himself. "What'll happen to me?"

But then he reflected, the doctor was not likely to give him into custody, after their little business transactions.

No, he would stop there and make himself comfortable. Besides, somebody would come in directly, there was no doubt.

As he thought this he looked round the room, and at the same time could not help thinking that if he could lay his hands upon some valuable article, and get well off before anybody did come, that there would not be much harm done.

He, therefore, looked round him with an inquiring eye to meet what he could pick up.

He was in the surgery, which was scantily furnished. There was nothing there worth taking. His eye, however, fell upon the iron door.

"That must be where he keeps his money," said Rattan, "or anyways where he keeps something he thinks is worth locking up. I suppose it is locked up."

He tried it.

Yes, it was fast.

"Now for my keys," said Rattan.

He always carried some skeleton keys about with him. They were the most valuable property he had.

Besides, as he himself observed, there was no knowing what might turn up.

He took them out and began to operate upon the locks.

It was a great deal of trouble, and required some delicate manipulation, but at length they opened.

"Now for it," said he, thinking that he in another moment would be in sight of the money.

But greatly to his astonishment, instead of money he found the door open into another room.

After a few moments of surprise he stepped over the threshold.

"Well," said he, after looking round. "Why it should have been locked up like this, is more than I can tell."

He could see nothing very valuable.

Some shelves crowded with dusty bottles, seemingly containing the dregs of a variety of kinds of disagreeable physic, gone bad; a ricketty old chair and table, two or three cracked plates, and dishes, and nothing more.

Rattan looked round with rather a rueful expression of countenance. Decidedly there was nothing worth stealing there.

Now Rattan was thoroughly disgusted. To think that he should have taken so much trouble about nothing. It was very exasperating.

"Damn it, I won't go away without something," said he to himself.

There was a bottle on one of the shelves, which he fancied contained quicksilver. That would sell for something, anyhow. It was dear stuff, he had always understood.

He leant forward to get it.

To keep his balance, he rested his hand against the wall. When he had got the bottle, he withdrew his other hand.

Something gave a great "click."

"What's that?" said he, looking round in alarm.

But when he saw what it was he was even more frightened.

The shelves were moving — the wall was opening.

By slow degrees a black, yawning space was visible in the place of the dusty bottles.

"I've touched a spring," thought Rattan. "Well, I'm blowed—what's he got there?"

A rush of cold air came towards him, as though he were entering an ice-house.

With it a strange, sickly odour, which half suffocated him.

His candle flickered, and burnt dimly.

"What the devil is it?" he said, below his breath.

Then stepped forward.

Then started back, with an exclamation of intense horror, and dropped the candle from his hand.

"Good God Almighty!"

*   *   *   *   *

For some little time he was so stunned by what he had seen, that he reeled back several paces, and stood gasping, with his back to the wall, almost ready to faint.

Presently, when he had recovered a little, he began to reason with himself.

"What's there to be afraid of? I've seen lots of 'em in my time. I'll get a light again. Curse it, I should be a born fool not to have another peep at 'em. Besides, what's the doctor doing with 'em. I may get at his secrets."

Thinking thus, he groped upon the floor for the candle, and groped his way back into the surgery for some matches.

Having lighted his candle, he returned.

But though he knew beforehand what sort of sight he was going to see, he could not for the life of him repress a certain thrill of horror, which shot through his frame when he came into the presence of this hitherto hidden terror.

He found himself in a sort of vault, or sepulchre, crowded with dead bodies.

They lay round him on every side.

Some rotted on shelves, some dangled by their necks from the ceiling, some lay stretched —black and hideous—upon the floor, while others again, which had been reared in standing postures against the walls, had slipped down into grotesque and horrible shapes, and leered and grinned at him frightfully, with sightless eyes and fleshless jaws.

One terrible figure, rigid and twisted, was seated upon a chair in the middle of the room, with such an awful affectation of being at its ease, that Rattan for a moment was uncertain whether or not it was alive.

After a few moments of breathless and shuddering curiosity, the ruffian began to wonder what on earth it all meant.

"What's he keep 'em bottled up for like this?" said he. "Are any of these ere the subjects I've had from the workhouse, I wonder. I don't recollect none of 'em: but their mugs is so damaged one couldn't werry well recognize one's own family in sich a condition."

Here the coarse-minded ruffian chuckled.

After all why should he be afraid. He did not care anything about dead bodies, unless it was in the dark.

You didn't know what they were up to, when you didn't see them, he argued.

Then he was most afraid of the fresh ones; after they had been dead a month or two, they were very dead indeed, and as harmless as herrings.

But the fresh ones there was no trusting; they might come to life any minute, and he had never quite got over the shock old Toddleboy had given him.

Upon reflection he saw that it would give him an immense pull over the doctor if there was anything secret about this place, as most certainly there must be, or why should it be hid away in this fashion—for the doctor to find him there in possession of the secret.

"If he has stepped out anywhere," Rattan argued, "it will put him into an awful funk to come back and find me here."

He therefore determined to make himself as comfortable as possible.

The worst of it was, that the candle did not seem as though it would last much longer.

What was he to do then? He could not sit in the dark.

There was a fire-place without a grate in this vault, where the dead bodies and some wood lay heaped up in it. He thought he would light a fire.

"It will be rather fine for him to come in and find me sitting here, warming my feet and smoking my pipe," thought Mr. Rattan.

He, therefore, without any more ado, set light to the wood by the aid of some paper he found in the next room, dragged a stool up to the fire-place, and seated himself opposite to the dead body propped up in the chair.

Thus the ruffian sat and contemplated at his ease

He even thought it would be a piece of facetiousness were he to thrust a pipe betwixt the jaws of the corpse, and as there was an old pipe in the next room, he got it and did so.

Then he sat and waited. Chuckling to himself at the lark he was having.

The fire rose and fell, and the flames flickered in a ghostly way, and to the terror of the grim forms surrounding them, by throwing huge shadows against the walls, and twisting the profiles of the dead into fearfully appalling shapes.

Silently he sat and smoked, and the death-like silence of the place was broken only by the faint cracking of the wood, and the shivering of the ashes on the hearth.

* * * * *

When Faversham had closed the door behind him as noiselessly as possible, he proceeded with his usual cat-like tread towards the surgery, where he perceived a faint light.

When he arrived there he found the door communicating with the room beyond was standing open.

Without hesitating for a moment and pausing a moment to reflect, he stepped through into the inner room.

The light fell upon his face where he stood, and threw a red tinge over its ghastly pallor.

It worked in awful convulsions like the face of a poor wretch dying a death of strangulation.

He seemed writhed in mental agony.

The drops of sweat rolled down his pallid visage.

Who was it who had penetrated the mystery of that awful chamber.

Rattan sat with his back towards him. He, therefore, could not see the intruder's face, but he knew by his back and figure generally, that it was not Murdoch. He waited breathlessly for the man to turn.

At last Rattan shifted his face a little, so that Faversham could see his profile.

"The scoundrel," he muttered between his clenched teeth, "he has sealed his doom."

Noiselessly as a spectre he crept back into the gloom of the surgery.

Noiselessly he groped in a corner for a bludgeon which he knew to be there.

Having found it, he crept out again more stealthily still.

Like a tiger approaching its prey, with every muscle tightly strung, with his white dogs teeth firmly set, with his eyes gleaming like those of a rattlesnake, the murderer stole upon his unconscious victim.

Then raised his bludgeon in the air.

XXV.—In which Charley Wag, having broken the Ice, makes up his Mind to go in a "Buster."

HE was a curious fellow, that George. Don't run away with the idea that he was a tempter of innocence, for in the first place he did not believe in the existence of innocence; and in the second, he was not a man who would have given himself a great deal of trouble about anything, much more, what did not bring him any particular profit.

But the fact of it was, that George had taken a great fancy for our unfortunate hero, and was bent on doing him what appeared to his ill-regulated mind a deuced good turn.

He had no idea that anybody could be in a more enviable position than that of a successful thief.

As long has a cove don't get lagged, and as a tidy luck, there was no doubt about it being the best trade out.

This was what Mr. George said to Master Charley, and the latter gentleman with a good bellyful of boiled tripe and onions, and a stiff glass of something hot to top up with, was almost inclined to be of the same way of thinking.

Besides, what could the poor little beggar do. We have decided long ago that there was nothing else left for him.

He went to bed and slept better than he ever recollected to have done before.

The next morning, at George's suggestion, he went out and had a hot bath, though Mr. Measles. who did not waste much time in washing himself, and who said that he never knew any good to come of it, voting the proceeding rather an extravagant one.

When he returned, Mr. Measles looked him out a suit of clothes, George objecting to every article as it was produced, until, to wind up, a furious argument arose upon the old gentleman's shabby behaviour in trying to palm off on Charley a couple of half Wellingtons which were not pairs.

"You want him to wear two left-hand boots, do you?" said George, indignantly. "That's like you, that is; you never can do nothing above-board and straightfor'ard, like other folks."

"Well, I am sure," retorted Mr. Measles, "the turn-out is slap-up, and having to give them away, too—it is a five pound note out of my pocket."

"Nobody asked you to give them away, you horrible old man!" said George, indignantly. "I shall have one or two of the things changed for better, and then I shall give you fifteen bob for the suit."

At this Mr. Measles grumbled a great deal, as you may suppose; but, by dint of threats and entreaties, he was induced to bring out some very handsome clothes from some mysterious wardrobe, and Master Charley, putting them on, cut rather a distinguished figure.

"What are we to set him?" said George.

"Smashing," replied the old man.

"Don't you think he is fit for something better?"

"Well, whatever he is fit for, he must begin at the bottom of the ladder, like I did. I began with smashing."

"And see what you have rose to, guvnor. Smashing be it."

"Now, young man," said Mr. Measles, "my son's going to set you up, and you ought to be very grateful to him."

"I am grateful, sir."

"Ah, I hope you will prove yourself so. Now, look here—you see this card."

With these words, Mr. Measles produced a dingy piece of pasteboard, similar to that which Charley had picked up a long while ago.

"You can read, I believe," said Mr. Measles.

"I should hope I could," retorted Charley.

"Bravo!" cried George; "I can't no more nor a pig, and not so much as them ere pigs at the shows."

" There, just you hold your jaw," said the old man, " and let the boy listen to me. Read what's on that there card," said he.

Charley read :—

" Price List.

A Brum quid   .   .   .   .   4s. 6d.
A bull   .   .   .   .   1s.
Half-a-bull   .   .   .   5½d.

N.B. Not payable in same.

Nothing smaller made—Flimsies in great variety.

Ask for Measles, at the old place."

When he had finished reading this fine composition, Mr. Measles asked him what he thought of it.

" I don't know what it means," replied Charley.

" I didn't intend you should," said the old man.

" Then what was the good of showing it me ?"

" Because I am going to explain it. Do you know what a Brum quid is ?"

" No."

" Well, that means a Brummagem sovereign."

" And what's a bull ?"

" Five shillings; and a half bull is half-a-crown, of course. Flimsies is bank notes, as I suppose you know."

" What does it mean by not payable in same?"

" Why, that means that we don't take no duffers in payment for duffers; duffers is what I makes, and duffers is what I sells. You and other parties goes and passes 'em off, and makes your living out of them. That there price-list shows what I sells them at. Now George is going to give you half-a-sovereign's worth, and start you with five shillings besides of proper stuff. You goes and passes off the duffers, and then comes back here, and buys some more. In fact, your fortune's made, there is very little doubt about that."

" That is, if I don't get caught, you mean."

" If you are such a fool as to get caught, you deserve what you get."

" Well," said Charley, " I suppose I must take my chance."

" There's lots of my customers that's made a tidy thing by it," said Mr. Measles, " and been able to retire from the business. There is one now as keeps a glove shop in Regent Street; another is cashier at a bank; and one is waiter at one of the best West-end dining-rooms. He keeps his carriage, he does, and a couple of ladies in willas in St. John's Wood."

" But I should have thought that they would have got caught," said Charley.

" Not with my money," said Mr. Measles. " It would take a very cute hand to detect it, I can tell you."

Then, taking a half-crown out of his pocket, he said :

" Look here, you can ring it or bite it as much as you like. The only difference between it and another halfcrown is, that it is a precious sight better made. As for some of them new-fashioned ha'pence that's got about, I should be ashamed to put my name to them. But we don't go in for trash of that sort. I gave up bobs, too; they only sells at twopence-halfpenny."

As Charley was eager to go out and try his luck, George accompanied him immediately.

To give him confidence, George carried all the bad money except half-a-crown, and gave Charley the good five shillings; so that, if the bad halfcrown should be by any chance detected, he could immediately produce the good money, and allay all suspicion.

They went into a cigar shop, and each chose a cigar.

The shopman served them, politely thanked them, handed Charley two shillings and two-pence in change, and they walked away without the slightest stain upon their characters.

" Well," said George, when they had turned the street corner.

" Well," said Charley.

" You had better spit upon the money for luck, as it is your first. Let's have a look at it."

Charley handed it to him.

George looked at it, and burst into a loud guffaw.

" Well, I'm damned !" said he.

" What's up, eh ?"

" Well, I am blowed."

" What are you laughing at ?"

" Don't say anything to me, or else I shall bust."

And he leant against a wall, and fairly shook again.

Charley with some indignation waited until he had done grinning, and then asked him to be kind enough to explain.

" Why," roared George. " Ah, ah, ah, you jolly young muff, oh, oh, oh, he has given you, he, he, he, a duffing shilling in change."

" I don't see anything to laugh at," grumbled Mr. Wag. " Why didn't you look at them when we took them ? Suppose we go and take it back."

" Well, I'm blowed, if that wouldn't be a cheek too, and it is one of the guvnor's own manufacture; in fact, he does a little with us, and that's why I spotted the shop, thinking we might as well give him a turn."

" Cheek or no cheek," said Mr. Wag, who wished to come out grand, " I shall go back and get a good shilling. What does the blackguard mean by trying to cheat me ?"

" Ah, ah, ah," laughed his companion, " I told you how it would be; he will be a honour to his profession, will that young chap, or my name is not what it isn't."

But Mr. Wag, without paying much attention, retraced his steps to the shop, and indignantly requested to know what the shopman meant by giving him a bad shilling.

" A bad what ?" said the shopman.

" A bad shilling," said Charley, indignantly.

" I'm sure I did not know I had, sir. Would you allow me to look at it ?"

Charley gave it to him.

He rang it on the counter.

" It rings all right," said he.

Then he bit it.

" It bites all right," said he. Then he looked at it again.

" What's the matter with it ?"

" Well, I don't like it," said Charley, " and as you don't see anything the matter with it, you can have no objection to change it."

" Well," grumbled the man, " it aint customary to change money after it is taken from the counter, but as I see you are a gentleman, here is another shilling for it, and I am sorry it happened."

Charley took the new shilling, examined it critically, put it into his pocket, and walked off.

He found George waiting at the street corner.

"Well."

"Well, have you done it?"

"Yes."

"Has he given you another bad 'un?'

"No."

"Are you sure?"

"Yes, I am sure."

"Let's have a look."

Charley handed it to him.

"Why, what's this," said George, "it's one of the same breed."

"What do you mean?"

"I mean it's a duffer."

"Confound the duffers," cried Charley. "I can't tell a duffer from a good one."

"You are a pretty fellow for a smasher, you are," said George, with a roar of laughter; "you loose more money than you'll make."

"Just leave off grinning, then," said Mr. Wag, "and show us how I can tell the difference."

"Well," said George, "look here, the duffers have got rather a greasy appearance, and aint milled quite reglar at the edge, don't you see."

Charley looked at it hard.

"Well, dash my buttons!" said he.

"What now?" asked George.

"Why you awful cheat!"

"What do you mean?"

"Why that ain't the shilling I gave you."

George burst into another guffaw, louder than ever.

"Of course it ain't," said he; "no more was the one you took back to change. I couldn't help it, Charley, upon my soul I couldn't."

"Do you mean to say," asked Charley, laughing in spite of himself, "that you changed it?"

"To be sure I did. When you gave me the two shillings, I changed one for a duffer I'd got in my hand. I never see sich a spree. You've took a rise out of that old pickwick merchant, I'm jiggered if you hevn't."

"Well, you won't do me again; old fellow," retorted Mr. Wag. "I'm not caught twice by the same trick."

"No, no," said George, very seriously, "you're a downy young cock, you are. One would hev to get up precious early in the morning to take you in."

"Drop it," cried Mr. Wag, very irate; "you've had quite enough change out of me, I think."

"All right, guvnor," replied George; "let's get to business."

Then, as before, they proceeded on their way. In the same way that Master Wag had passed off the bad half-crown, he passed off a number of half-crowns during the day.

When evening came, he returned to Mr. Measles, with his pockets literally bursting with money.

Indeed, he not only paid back George what he had advanced, and paid Mr. Measles for the clothes, but, after laying in a large stock of base coin for next day, he stood a couple of bowls of punch, and five shillings worth of cigars.

"You're a goin' it, young cockywax," cried George, in ecstacies, slapping, first his own knee, and then the knee of his youthful companion. "You're a goin' it."

"I mean to go it," replied Mr. Wag, with his hands in his trousers' pockets, and a cigar in his mouth. "My motto in life has been, 'in for a penny, in for a pound.' What's worth doing at all is worth doing well."

"Brayvo, young un!" cried Mr. Measles. "Them's my sentiments."

"You'll excuse me, Mr. M.," observed Charles Wag, Esquire, with gravity, "but the term young un—as, indeed, is also that of cockywax—is extremely offensive."

"Beg pardon, Mr. W.," returned George, with a broad grin.

Then turning to the old man, he said, almost bursting with laughter:

"Blowed if I ever come across his ekel. I told you how it would be. He'll take the lead well, that chap. We shan't none of us touch him."

"You're about right there," said Charley, who was as tipsy as any nobleman in the United Kingdoms, "that's exactly what I shall do."

Although he was in a boastful mood when he said it, this turned out, in course of time, to be far from an empty boast.

The success of the young smasher was something incredible.

From being one of the most unlucky young wretches ever born of woman, he became one of the luckiest. Of all Mr. Measles' numerous customers, there was none who came for such large supplies, and got rid of them so easily.

He grew in time to be one of the most reckless, dare-devil young blackguards that it is possible to conceive.

There was no risk that he would not run, no act of effrontery and mad rashness that he would not commit, but still he passed unscathed through the fire.

He stuck to the smashing, as it was so lucrative, though he secretly pined for a bolder and more hazardous life.

Oh, he thought, if he could only make some great lump of money, conceive some gigantic fraud, execute some enormous piece of successful villany, and retire upon it.

Do something, in fact, that would make his name a town talk.

And he would, too, before he had done.

But although Charley, I regret to say, after his virtuous struggles, turned out eventually as great a rogue as ever went unhanged, there was still an immense difference between him and the other theives, with whom he was compelled to associate.

To begin with, he hated the society of those low-minded, ill-educated brutes, who spent their money in filthy debauchery and brutal excess.

Mind you, the young profligate had as nice a taste for debauchery as you could imagine, and where the other sex was concerned, quite carried out any promise of future impropriety, which his conduct in the opening chapter of our story may have led the reader to anticipate.

A perfect Sardanapulus was Mr. Wag in his small way, with all the vicious tastes of the aristocracy powerfully developed.

A taste for wine and women in a boy of fifteen, is likely to lead to the bad, as the most unprejudiced reader must allow, and there is, I fear, very little hope for the young profligate.

But still, would you believe it, there was lots of foolish persons, the softer sex particularly, who readily found excuses for him, as they will for all the villains, though the frail ones of their own sex they cannot be too hard upon.

The difference between him and the other bad characters I alluded to, will account for his.

Mr. Wag loved the fashionable vices.

So when he got drunk it was upon costly liquors, not upon three-halfpennyworth of gin, like his companions.

If he associated with the fallen sisterhood, he chose his sweetheart in the *cafes* of the Haymarket, at the Argyle, Casino, or in the Park, not at "a threepennny hop," or "a twopenny dust up,"* a penny "gaff," or a "twopenny duty."*

He soon got rid of Mr. Measles' wardrobe, and laid in a stock of splendid clothes.

He had double-breasted white waistcoats, extensive peg-top trousers, and blue Baltic coats elaborately braided.

You do not suppose, I should hope, that he would have worn a dress-coat on a Sunday in the street, like some common people.

Neither would you expect him to make any change in his dress at all on a Sunday. Why should he, when he was so magnificently dressed all the week. Why, the linen of that young man, the last thing on Saturday night was several degrees whiter than mine is when the laundress brings it home the first thing on Sunday morning.

There was no doubt about it, he WAS a swell.

He always had a taste for jewellery, even when he could not afford to buy it, and now that he could, his pins and rings were tremendous.

But there was one thing in which he cut everybody else out.

It was the more curious because everybody else might have imitated him so easily.

What do you think it was? I'll tell you.

HE KEPT HIS HANDS CLEAN.

It must be a mean spirited cur, poor paltry knave, who would be ashamed of the soil of honest labour, but is it not strange that those whose trade is known, cannot contrive to keep their long lazy picking and stealing fingers on better terms with soap and water.

Somehow, with all this success, Master Charley was not happy.

Something was weighing heavily upon his mind.

What had become of Julia?

He made the most minute inquiries at Mr. Muggins's Music Hall, and rather exasperated the door-keeper by the pertinacity with which he stuck to the subject.

Then he found out, with an immensity of trouble, the lodgings to which he had accompanied Julia on the first night of their acquaintance, and to which they had, as the reader may remember, been refused admittance.

"Does Miss Jenkini live here?" he asked.

"Miss who?"

"Jenkini."

"I don't know no Jenkinis."

"She used to live here."

"There was a baggage by the name of Jenkins, but she's gone."

"Where's she gone to?"

"Gone to the bad, I should say?"

"Should you?—and where's that?"

"I don't know nothing about her."

"But she left some property here?"

"Yes, and she left some rent unpaid."

"Now, look here, my good woman," continued Charley, fingering an imaginary half-crown in his waistcoat pocket, "I shall feel much obliged if you would tell me all you know about her."

But the old woman had nothing particular to tell. Julia had lodged there once, bore an indifferent character, and had left in debt.

So Charley, for the present, had to give her up, and give all his mind to smashing.

One night, when he was sitting, in a gloomy state of mind, over his quiet pint of sherry, in his rooms in the Temple, and wishing that it had been his luck to be born a lord, with a million a-year, instead of having to work so hard for his living, a knock at the door disturbed him.

It was George.

"Good-night, sir," said he, glancing round, and putting his hat down, in a bashful kind of way, behind the door, where it was presently squashed flat by Master Charles's servant coming in with some coals. "Good-night, sir; you seem pretty comfortable."

"I try to make myself so," replied Mr. Wag. "Don't stand on any ceremony, George, but take a chair. Will you liquor?"

"Will I do what?"

"Liquor."

"I don't mind taking a drop of something short, if you've got it handy."

Charley filled for him.

"Well," said he, "what brings you here?"

"Well," said George, "I've made so bold as to come and ask you to join me in a little crack. You're the pluckiest young feller as I knows on, and the only one I'd like to be mixed up with, only you're grown such an awful swell I don't know that you ain't got a cut above me."

"Never mind cuts, George, what is it?"

"Well, its neither more nor less than breaking into the vaults of the Bank of England. Are you willing?"

"Do you suppose there's much swag?"

"Sacks full. What do you say?"

"I'm on, George."

"It's a bargain, then?"

"And when's it to come off?"

"To night."

———

I will not trouble you with any longer description of this promising young gentleman. I have given you his picture in Rotten Row, so that you can see for yourself what sort of a fellow he looked in his fine clothes. In my next book, I shall commence the adventures of the most successful thief in London.

END OF BOOK THE THIRD.

———

* A dancing room.   † A gaff with a license.

CAUGHT IN THE ACT.

BOOK THE FOURTH.
THE MOST SUCCESSFUL THIEF IN LONDON.

I.—CHARLEY BREAKS INTO THE BANK OF ENGLAND.

"DO you suppose that the expedition will be very dangerous?" Charley asked.

"If it is," replied George, "you're not the boy to funk it, I reckon."

"I funk it? Not very likely, old fellow I want something, on the contrary, to wake me up a little. I'm devilish nipped."

"I tell you what it is," said George, presently. "I never in all my life see a young fellor as picked up like you have. Why it only seems like yesterday when I found you lying

No. 27.

on your back like a dying duck in the middle of that there road, that there night that you were shied out of that there trap."

"Yes, to be sure," replied Charley, with a laugh at his friend's style. "You mean when I was running away with that there girl."

"Lord love you!" continued George, without noticing Mr. Wag's humour. "You ain't the same fellor. There's nothink of your old self about you but the name. By the way, why don't you change it?"

"What! change my name?"

"Ah! Have a stunner, such as Clarendon, or Palmerston, or Yelverton."

"No, thank you. I'd rather stick to my own. I'll make it famous some day."

"Devil doubt you. If there ever was a

[CHARLEY WAG, THE NEW JACK SHEPPARD

young feller that I'd lay odds on for getting on in the world, you're the party. I alays had a fancy to you."

"Yes, you've said so before."

"Perhaps I have, and I mean it, too. The fust day when I found you, my mate was in favour of knocking you on the head, but I prevented him. Then again, the guvnor was in favour of turning you into the streets, but I put a stopper on him. I alays thought you'd got the right sort of stuff in you; and by gosh, when you got up the chimney that day, and hooked it, I says to myself, that there young cove was born to be a Jack Sheppard, and only wants the proper bringing up, to come out precious nobby; and I was right, wasn't I?"

"I dare say."

"You don't regret joining us—do you?"

"No!"

"You ain't got no squalms of conscience, as they call 'em."

"None, except that poor boy I gave such a choking to," replied Charley, looking very serious. "Your father told me that he died, but I trust to heaven it was not through my treatment to him."

"Told you he died, did he?"

"Yes."

"Then it's one of his twisters."

"What do you mean?"

"Why the old boy done it, I suppose, to keep you in a funk. He's an artful old tyke. But the fact of the case is, he sent me himself to make inquiries, and I found out, young what's his name, Gubbins, was getting on hearty, and had gone back to the doctor's."

"Gone back to the doctor's," cried Charley, in a rage. "Confound him, I'll warm his jacket for him, some of these fine mornings."

"Well, I like that," cried George with a laugh. "I thought you was sorry just now that you'd hurt him?"

"Well, never mind," Mr. Wag replied, conscious of some slight inconsistancy. "Let's talk about this crack you spoke of."

"What, into the Bank?"

"Yes; we can't have much time to waste, so I may as well tell you, that I overheard you and Measles talking about it, and I heard that you had hired a cellar in Princess street, and were working a way under the road into the cellar of the Bank."

"To be sure; and I've done it."

"What, broken in?"

"Well, not quite, but close upon it. I've only the width of a brick away."

"And you propose making a breach?"

"Yes; I propose breaking the crust to-night."

"By the way, how do you get rid of the dirt?"

"I've took the cellar as a wine cellar, you know, and to keep beer in. I'm supposed to be in the bottled beer line."

"I understand; and you carry the soil out in the boxes which are supposed to contain the beer."

"Yes, that's my game, and they imagine me to be doing a rare trade."

"Who takes it away?"

"Well, I generally do it myself, because I've let no one into the scheme besides you and the old man. I've got a waggon, as you know, and I've got a ware'us in the city."

"A warehouse?"

"Yes, i'll take you there some day. I keeps the goods there I pick off the boats on the river."

"What you steal?"

"To be sure. I'm what they calls a river shark. That's my trade."

"So I suspected; but about the plan at the bank?"

"We'll go now. I can give you full particulars as you walk along. By the way, jist put on your shabbiest togs, if you have any shabby ones, for its reyther dirty work we're going to do."

At this suggestion, Mr. Wag attired himself in the quietest suit of his wardrobe, and put on a turban hat.

"Should I not be armed?" he asked.

"You'd better," replied George.

And at this suggestion Charley thrust a brace of pistols, which he usually kept loaded at the head of his bed for fear of accidents, into his jacket.

"Well," said he, "are you ready?"

"Quite ready. Shall we start?"

They issued forth, without any more words, by the door of Charley's chambers, went down stairs, and threading their way through the intricacies of the Temple, stood at last in Fleet Street.

It was a wild and stormy night, and the wind swept by them with a shriek, and rattled the shutters of the shops, and made the windows clatter in their frames.

Every now and then, the rain, driven before the violence of the blast, was hurled into the face of the wayfarers.

The Autumn was far advanced, and the weather was bitterly cold.

Such few unfortunates who were compelled to be out, slunk along under the shadow of the houses, or cowered hopelessly in the dark arches and dry doorways screwed up in their rags.

A few miserable prostitutes still clung hopelessly to the street, their teeth chattering in their heads, and beating their poor wet feet together, to keep up the circulation of their sluggish blood.

Even the trotter-men had given it up as a bad job, and retiring to the warm shelter of some adjacent night-house, were giving way to reckless jolity, and twos of gin.

"The very night for the job," said George, in a low tone. "The wind will cover any noise we make. I wish this infernal rain would leave off. We shall a have reglar soaker if it don't."

"We had better have a cab."

"Ah, to be sure; perhaps we had."

Charley called one.

They drove in the direction of the Bank.

"Who is left in the place of a night?" asked Charley as they went along.

"There's a lot of guards there, well armed. You've seen them marching up there perhaps of an evening?"

"Yes."

"There's about twenty of 'em generally, and one or two officers. They has their grub provided, and they keeps watch all night."

"How do you expect to get in without their hearing you?"

"There's a risk, of course, but you know they think the place is so precious well guarded there's never no fear of nothing happening."

"I can understand that."

"Besides, they don't watch the vaults much, from what I understand, and I know pretty well where we shall come up."

"Where's that?"

"Why, just where the swag is kept; in one of the strong rooms, in fact—"

"The devil we shall?"

"If we hadn't managed it that way, there is no knowing but we might have got through the doors."

"Perhaps we should not have been able to get at the gold at all."

"Well, I don't know but that I've got my keys with me, and they'll nick pretty well anything."

By this time they had reached the corner of Princess Street.

George stopped the cab, and having discharged the man, they proceeded for some distance up the street, until they arrived at the wine cellar which Mr. Measles, Jun., rented.

On the door there was a zinc plate with the name of the supposed proprietor—Mr. Thompson, wine merchant.

George opened the door, and they entered the house noiselessly.

Then he struck a match, lit a dark lanthorn, and led the way below.

Evidently George had worked very carefully, and with a great deal of circumspection. Charley looked round, expecting to see a quantity of earth and stones piled up upon the floor, but there was nothing of that sort.

There was no litter or dust visible, and no signs of an excavation.

There were, instead, a number of empty bottles, and a few broken ones, and a quantity of old packing cases.

"I never made no litter," said George, with a grin. "The passage is through that door, which used to lead into a cellar beyond. I've always kept the door locked, for fear anyone might come down here and take a look at the premises; and for fear of accident, I cleared up always of a night before I went away."

"I was thinking how you managed when you got into prison. The people must have wondered what had become of you, and I should have thought they would have broken open the door."

"Not they, so long as the rent was paid."

"But then it wasn't."

"Oh, yes it was. I sent the old man with it. I wrote to him from gaol."

"Ah, I never thought of that."

So saying, George led the way through the inner cellar, and down a long passage bored through the earth.

Placing a lanthorn on the ground, he lighted another, which he gave to Charley to hold, and set to work.

With a sharp pointed crowbar he held in his hand, he began to prize at one of the bricks in the ceiling above them.

After a little trouble he loosened it.

"Catch hold," he cried suddenly; "don't let the brick fall, or it will make a row."

Charley caught it.

"That's right," whispered George. "We mustn't make a row, or we may be copped at the fust go off. Now for the next."

The next brick came out easier than the last.

Charley caught it in the same way as the last.

"We won't make a bigger hole than is necessary," whispered George. "You'll find a ladder just by your feet there. Do you see it?"

"I feel it."

"Have it ready to hand up there. I'll manage these bricks now."

Noiselessly George worked. In about ten minutes longer he had wrenched out four more bricks. He had made a square hole in the floor sufficiently large to squeeze their bodies through, for the mortar was old, rotten, and damp, and easily broken.

"I think you'd better make the place larger," whispered Charley, "because we will have to come down with a devil of a run if they hear us."

"No—no," replied the other. "It's quite large enough. And it will be all the harder for them to follow us. Don't you see. If one of them gets jammed in the hole it will stop it up. And if we are down below we can polish 'em off one by one quite easy."

"All right," said Charley, though not without a slight shudder at the picture of wholesale butchery which George words suggested.

"Now are we ready?" the other asked.

"I think so."

"No, stop."

"What is it?"

"I had forgotten the list slippers. I have them in my pocket. Catch hold. Have you got them?"

"All right."

Charley took them from him, and pulled them over his boots.

"Here's a match," whispered George; "and now for the ladder."

Charley handed it up to his companion, who fixed it at the hole and began to climb.

Next moment he had disappeared at the top. Charley followed.

The room in which they found themselves in was spacious but empty.

Some shelves on one side were filled with small bundles, tied up and labelled. Nothing else was there.

"What are those?" whispered Charley, looking towards the parcels.

Then advancing towards them he took one off a shelf.

"By jove!" he cried, "what do you think they are?"

"What?"

"Notes, every one of them."

"Yes; but they're no good."

"No good—why not? Let us take some. We needn't go any further. Why, we could carry away a million easily."

"Bosh! Just you listen to me. I tell you they are worth nothing."

"Why?"

"Because I know all about them. They're

the notes that are recalled from circulation, and they're all defaced. We couldn't pass them."

"Well, what are we to do?"

"Why, we must try the door. It's like our cursed luck to have come up here. There's gold in the next room, and we might have come up there instead. I expected we should; but you can't bore a hole in the dark to tell where you're going to with any certainty; and half-a-yard makes all the difference in life."

"And not touch the notes?"

"No; damn the notes! We'll leave them till the last anyhow—till we've got some of the gold. Come, now, and no more jaw."

As he spoke, George commenced operations upon the lock of the door.

With the first-rate tools he possessed, it was not a very difficult matter to open it.

When his task was done, he paused for a moment to feel in his breast for the plan of the building, which he had brought with him in case he should in his flurry forget the position of the various rooms, although he had studied it all over and over again, and pretty well knew it by heart.

"Yes, to be sure," he whispered, when they were outside the room in the passage; "if we'd only had the luck to come up half a yard nearer this way, we should have been all right. As it is, we've got to make a regular journey."

"Why so? Isn't the door of the room in this passage?"

"No; it's on the other side, in another passage, running in the same direction this does."

This accident obliged them to make a large circuit to arrive at the door of the strong room of which they were in search.

Every moment, as they crept along, holding their breath, they paused anxiously to listen, fancying that they heard footsteps approaching, or the sound of some hasty movement above.

Every moment, too, did George consult the plan he held in his hand, dreading to make some mistake which might prove fatal.

At last they reached the door, to their inexpressible relief, in safety.

It was, at first sight, quite impenetrable, and apparently coated with iron.

"There's a lock," said George; "let's operate."

This was not, however, quite so easily done as said.

The keys were useless.

"Blast the thing!" muttered the elder burglar, between his teeth. "I could soon open it if I could wrench out the brickwork at the side; but I haven't got the bar."

"Shall I fetch it?" asked Charley.

"No, no—I'll go. Stop quiet where you are."

George went away, and Charley remained. The silence of the place seemed perfectly awful, and the thumping of his heart quite audible, like the dull vibrating motion of a printing-press heard in the distance.

It seemed to him quite an hour before the other returned, though in reality George could could not have been away more than five minutes.

Returned, breathless and impatient, he began to work furiously at his task of taking out the bricks.

"Hush! hush! for God's sake!" cried his companion, in an anxious whisper; "you will alarm the guards."

George felt that more caution was necessary. His rashness would ruin all.

Using all his strength, but at the same time being as cautious and deliberate in his movements as a walker on a tight-rope, he prised out the bricks from the wall, until he was able to jam in the end of his crowbar, and force back the bolts of the lock.

So anxiously expectant were the two burglars, that, when the click did come, it sounded to them almost as loud as the report of a pistol.

"Hush!" they both whispered involuntarily.

Then they paused and listened.

All was still.

As yet they were safe.

"We've done the worst part of the work," said George; "and now for the swag."

As he spoke he pushed the door. It opened only a few inches.

It was fastened inside with a chain.

When Charley saw this, he was quite staggered.

He thought it was all over with them.

George, too, pulled a long face; but it was more with amazement than disappointment.

"Who the devil could have chained it inside?" said he. "I hope there isn't anybody there."

"What are we to do?" whispered Charley. "Can you file it?"

"There's no occasion to file it. It's as easy as sucking eggs to undo the chain on any door, as I will show you. People think when they've put up the chain that they've made their house quite safe."

In proof of what he said, George took a piece of string from his pocket, made it into a slip-knot, and, passing his hand in at the door, put the noose over the end of the chain, close to where the little knob is, then brought the other end of string outside, and pulled the door as close to as he could without bolting it.

Then, without any difficulty, he jerked the little knob out of its place, and the chain fell down by the side of the door.

Next moment they were in the strong room.

Their expectations were more than realized. There lay the gold, in little sacks, containing sums of a hundred to a thousand pounds.

They did not pause to look at anything else. They had no eyes for anything else. Quick as lightning they set to work loading themselves with gold.

Only for a moment did they delay their work, to look into the tops of the little sacks, to see that they really contained the most valuable metal. They were afraid that they might take away silver by mistake.

"What an awful fluke it would have been if we hadn't looked, and had taken away a bagful of dirty pennies by mistake," said Charley, who even now could not refrain from joking. "I wouldn't demean myself by carrying them—would you?"

"Hold your row!" growled George, gloating over the gold with savage joy.

Certainly there was no time to waste in cracking jokes; they must make the best of their opportunity, and get out of the place as soon as possible. George had brought some rope with him. This they fastened round their waists, and then tied as many sacks to it as they could possibly carry.

Of course George could take the largest load, but such strength did the thought of future enjoyment lend to our hero, that he managed to bear a much greater weight than, a day or two ago, he would have believed possible.

When they had both got as large a load as they could conveniently move under—and, indeed, then not without staggering—they moved towards the door.

"I wish I could have squared a hundred or two more," said George, panting with exertion as it was. "But there's no reason why we shouldn't come back again, when we've got rid of this load."

"None at all," said Charley. "I only wish we'd brought a wheelbarrow, if there wasn't quite so much risk; there is nothing I should like better than trundling it up and down all—"

Just at this moment they heard a sudden noise—a most alarming noise—approaching them.

It was the measured tramp of soldiers.

"Damnation!" cried George, "it is the guards going their round. We might have expected this."

"They'll see how you've been damaging the door outside."

"A thousand curses on them! But we'll keep them out. Push to the door as gently as you can, and put up the chain."

Charley obeyed.

"My head's going round so, I can hardly think. Which way does our passage lie? If it comes to the worst, while we keep them out I'll try and smash a hole through the wall, and, if we can, we'll get down again, and make our escape."

"Whatever we do, we won't leave the tin behind," said Charley.

While they were holding this conversation in low whispers, the low, measured tramp of the watch approached them. They could hear the clashing of the arms.

At the corner of the passage, however, they turned, to the listeners' intense relief, and pursued their course down the other corridor.

This relief was but momentary, for the thought rushed through their minds that the soldiers would find the door open leading into the room where they had just come up, that they would also discover the hole in the floor, and that then most likely it would be all up with them (the burglars).

With a heavy weight at their hearts—a much heavier weight than the gold, they listened as a prisoner might listen for the approach of the gaoler on the morning of his execution.

They listened breathlessly.

Ah! too true, it was as they expected.

A loud shout was raised.

The hole had been discovered.

"Help! help! thieves! thieves!"

The cries echoed through the vaults, and were rendered louder and more alarming by the cavernous structure of the building.

"Thieves! thieves!"

They heard the loud cries of the men above in answer to those below, and a hasty move-

ment of many feet, as they came flocking down the stairs.

"Thieves! thieves!"

The cry seemed to come from every side at once.

"We're caught," said Charley. "There's not much chance for us."

"Chance for us! Curse it, I don't see that there is any."

And, saying so, George flung down his load of gold, and folded his arms in resignation.

Meanwhile, the sound of footsteps approached the door.

Then stopped before it.

Then a cry of alarm arose.

"Some one has broken in here," they heard a voice say.

————

II.—CHARLEY WAG PROVES THAT HE HAS HIS WITS ABOUT HIM, EVEN IN THE MOST TRYING CIRCUMSTANCES; AND GEORGE HAS MORE REASON THAN EVER FOR BELIEVING THAT HIS PUPIL WILL PROVE AN HONOUR TO THE PROFESSION.

HARDLY were the words uttered, before there came a battering at the door.

The burglars within clenched their teeth.

George seized his crowbar, and stood ready to deal a deathblow to the first intruder.

Charley took out his pistols, and stood with one in each hand, waiting to see what might happen.

Who shall say what were the boy's feelings at this moment?

Was he again going to be taken into captivity? Was he again to be doomed to the awful incarceration of Spike Island?

When he thought of it, his young soul was filled with fury.

No, he would die first, rather than submit to such awful slavery again.

The battering at the door continued.

A voice asked loudly,

"Who is inside?"

But the burglars made no reply.

Then the battering continued.

But they did not seem to be forcing the door in a scientific style. Perhaps they did not intend to do it—perhaps they would go away.

Even now the noise grew weaker, and footsteps were heard retreating.

There might yet be a chance of escape.

But no.

A great glare of light filled the room.

A trap-door in the ceiling had been flung suddenly open, and some armed soldiers looked down upon them.

"It is no use struggling," said a man who was evidently in command; "escape is hopeless—surrender yourselves."

As the burglars made no reply, the soldier withdrew from the trap, and a ladder was let down.

Then he began deliberately to descend.

But hardly had he come down half-a-dozen rounds, when George seized the ladder with both hands, and, shaking it violently, managed to drag it into the room, and fling the soldier heavily to the ground, where he lay powerless.

But this triumph was of very short duration, for in another instant a man dropped down from the trap above, and then another, and another.

Hemmed in thus on all sides, George, with the fury of a wild beast, brandished his crowbar, and dealt blows at random to the right and to the left.

At the same time Charley let off his pistols in a purposeless way, without hurting any one.

As the soldier had said, there certainly seemed to be little use in struggling, although struggle they certainly did, and that with right good will.

But their struggles were brief.

One of the soldiers undoing the door, admitted half-a-dozen more of his comrades; and then, all flinging themselves together upon the captives, they secured them hand and foot, bound them with the ropes they themselves had provided, and dragged them helpless up-stairs.

Arrived on the floor above, they found the officer in command waiting for them.

The officer in command was, as is not very unfrequently the case with officers in her Majesty's army, a beardless, puny pale-faced youngster, not very long left school, and looking as unlike a man of war as it was possible for any he-creature to look.

This young gentleman had been sitting over his wine, and had fallen asleep, had woke up, and looked very frightened.

"Wha-a-at's it all about?" said he, coming out with a dinner napkin in his hand, and looking very frightened.

"These two fellers, sir," replied a corporal, who had taken the lead in the late proceedings —"these two fellers, sir, helping themselves to as much gold in the strong room as they could carry."

"Good gwacious!" cried the officer. "How much have they taken?"

"They haven't taken any yet, sir, that I know of, though they may have done before we disturbed 'em."

"I say, you fellaws," continued the young officer, addressing the culprits, "how much have you taken, aw? It's much better to say at once, and whether there are any more of you."

But George and Charley did not vouchsafe any remark.

"Well, sir," continued the corporal, "what shall we do with them?"

"Good gwacious," replied the officer, "I haven't the least ideaw."

However, it occurred to him that it was his place to make a suggestion; so, as he really was not capable of so much mental exertion, he asked the corporal, after a little pause, what he suggested.

The corporal, after a good deal of reflection, suggested that the director should be sent for.

The next step was to find out where the director lived.

His address was known to a porter who slept on the premises, and this having been obtained, a messenger was sent off directly to acquaint him with the facts of the case, and to ask his advice with respect to the steps which it would be necessary to take in the matter.

Now the director was a consequential fat little man (he has since departed this life, and deeply regretted, but it is to be hoped that his depar-

ture was in no way hastened by what had transpired on that eventful night). He was in bed at the time the messenger called, and he was awakened from a happy dream by a loud ringing of the bell, and a tremendous thumping at the knocker.

"Bless me!" said he to Mrs. Director, who was sleeping at his side in the biggest of frilled nightcaps, "don't you hear it?"

"Hear what, Samuel?" asked Mrs. Director.

"That dreadful disturbance outside."

"Yes. I hear it."

"Well, what do you think it is?"

"The sweeps, I suppose."

And the lady turned round upon the other side, and began dosing off again.

However, the bell continued to go tinkle—tinkle—tinkle—and the knocker to go bang—bang—bang.

"It's a very noisy sweep, if it is one," thought the director.

Then after another five minutes had elapsed.

"I wonder why the deuce some of those idle scoundrels of flunkeys of mine don't get up and let them in."

Then he begun to ring his own bell.

But as this plan seemed but to add to, instead of allaying the tumult, and as it was impossible to get to sleep again while the noise continued, the poor little gentleman came to the conclusion that the best thing he could do was to get up.

Therefore, as he slept inside, like all sensible men do who leave their wives to blow out the candle, and get up first in the morning; the little director puffed a good deal, for he was short of wind, managed to stride over his better half, and tumble out upon the floor with a great flop.

When there he went to the window, threw it up, and looked out.

To his great surprise he saw a soldier standing on the door-step.

"Hallo, you sir," said he, "What do you want?"

"I've come from the Bank."

"What's the matter?"

"Some one broke in."

"Good heavens!"

In went the director's head, down went the window; and next moment he was struggling furiously with his trousers, which having put on to his entire dissatisfaction, hind side before, he stumbled down-stairs into the hall, to hear more about it.

The man did not know a very great deal, but he told the director all that he did know, about the discovery of George and Charley in the strong room, and their seizure.

"Stop a minute there," said the director, "I'll come now directly, and go with you. Or, no,—stop a minute. Run and get a cab, and I'll go and put on some clothes."

Having done as he said, and with as much haste as possible, the director came toddling down-stairs again.

Then a cab being in attendance, they set off as hard as the man could drive, to the city.

The director lived some considerable distance from his place of business, and it was some time before they arrived at their destination.

As they crossed London Bridge, the director looked with a pale frightened face down the pool over which the first faint streaks of dawn were breaking, and saw the bank of black clouds extending sluggishly along the east, while the wind raised a chilly ripple on the river, the dark waters of which steamed along in muddy cheerlessness.

Arrived at the Bank, he found the young officer and his company waiting for him, with great anxiety.

The officer was pacing backwards and forwards, smoking a cigar he had not lighted.

"Oh! here you are," said he, on seeing the director.

" Yes, here I am."

" Will you step this way."

The director complied with his request.

When they were alone in a room, the director said.

" Here's a pretty kettle of fish, sir."

" Exactly so," replied the officer. " I'm quite of your way of thinking."

" What is to be done?"

" What do you propose?"

" I havn't an idea."

" That's exactly my case."

" So I should think," retorted the Director, with some indignation. " Now look here, sir."

" Well."

" This must not get public."

" I should think it most advisable, certainly."

" There's no knowing what might not result from it. It might ruin your prospects."

" For the matter of that, I don't suppose it would do you much good."

" What do you mean?"

" What I say."

" You intend to insinuate then, that this occurrence was not wholly and solely attributed to your negligence."

" I intend to insinuate that the building must have been in a very insecure state, or else it could have never occurred, and as you are responsible—"

" Well—well, sir," said the old gentleman, in great alarm. " It doesn't matter whose fault it was. One thing is certain, and that is—"

" That it must be hushed up?"

" Exactly."

" And how?"

" We will have the prisoners in and interrogate them."

At a word from the Director, George and Charley were brought forward.

The former looked very gloomy and down in the mouth at the want of success at his scheme. And he was calculating how many years penal servitude would be awarded to him for this little attempt.

He was not very great in inventive faculties, and a very little difficulty knocked him over. He thought himself hopelessly floored now, and having given himself up to despair, did not take any notice of what was going on around him, but maintained a moody silence, and frowned his hardest.

Charley was quite the reverse.

He was a volatile young man, and as elastic as india-rubber; press him down, and he jumped up the moment you took the weight off as brisk as ever.

Charley was thinking with all his might how he was to get out of the mess.

His first idea was to try and make his escape at all hazards.

Then as the time passed by without the appearance of a policeman, and without any active steps being taken for their conveyance to the nearest lock-up, his spirits began to rise a little.

He hardly knew why, but drowning men catch at straws, you know, and we are all of us hopeful—it is lucky that we are.

Besides this, there was one little circumstance which had occurred, and which seemed to him to suggest a loop-hole for escape.

One of the soldiers had said to another in his hearing, something to the effect of it being likely to prove a bad job for the young officer, such a bold attempt at burglary having taken place while he was there on guard.

It would not so much have mattered if they had caught the thieves the moment they had effected an entrance into the Bank; but the awkward part was to think that they had effected an entrance, made a journey half round the building, and were busily engaged sacking the gold in the strong room, before anybody found out their presence, and then only by the greatest chance.

Certainly it showed rather a bad system of guard.

When Charley heard this, he put one thing to another, and being a ready witted young dog, as you know by this time, he soon came to a conclusion.

When he was called into the room where the Director and officers were waiting for him, he had made up his mind what to do.

" I'll surprise their feeble understandings," thought Mr. Wag.

The Director put on his spectacles, and eyed the prisoners keenly.

Their masks were taken off, and he had a good view of their faces.

Charley stared just as hard at him.

" Well, young man," said the director, fixing Charley through his glasses, " you've done it this time."

" You mean we have not done it, I suppose," retorted the young man.

" Don't be impertinent, if you please," cried the director, angrily, " but attend to me. Do you know what punishment you have subjected yourself to?"

" No."

" Then you ought to have considered the question before. It's transportation for life."

" I did not think it was quite so long as that."

" But it is. You must also be aware, or, at least, you ought to be aware, that there is very little chance of escape. A government prosecution is not like another; a conviction is a certainty. There will be no escape."

" It will make a great stir in the papers, sir, won't it?" asked Charley, with a sly grin.

The director's countenance fell.

He, however, recovered himself directly.

" It is surely not possible that you have been weak enough to expose yourself to all this danger for the sake of gaining an unenviable notoriety."

" Well, sir, I won't deny that that idea has helped us up a little. Of course we did not want to be caught; but we thought to ourselves, when the worst comes to the worst, we shall be famous."

"Famous!"

"To be sure. There's a kind of emulation among burglars, just the same as there is among bankers. We have all of us our little ambitions."

"Your ambition, young man, is very likely to be gratified. But you have got to remember, that when your brief moment of pride is passed, that you will then have the remainder of your life to pass in miserable bondage, in chains and servitude. A poor gratification it will be to you, to be pointed out as the celebrated thief who broke into the Bank of England. No, no, young man—it's a mistake, I assure you."

"You haven't been brought up in the same school that I have, sir, and can scarcely enter into my feelings."

"Indeed I can't, young man, if they are as you lead me to imply by your words."

"I suppose not," said Charley, carelessly, and he began to whistle softly to himself.

The director was both surprised and annoyed at his behaviour. He had no idea that he should have found the young gentleman so independent.

However, he was not to be done in this way.

"Look here, young man," said he, after a pause, "I want to make a proposition to you. You seem to be a straightforward, honest young fellow, in spite of your being a thief."

"Thank you, sir."

"I mean to say, you don't look quite such a scoundrel as I should have expected."

Mr. Wag bowed.

"So I shall give you a chance of liberty. If you promise me, upon your word of honour, that you will mend your ways, I will set you free this time."

At these most unexpected words, George started from his reverie, and looked in a wild excited way from one to the other, scarcely crediting his senses.

Charley, too, was considerably astonished; but, with a great effort, he mastered his feelings.

Then, with an appearance of cold indifference, which was as wonderful a piece of acting as you could have met with at any of the theatres, he said:

"It's very kind of you to say so, sir, and there is only one drawback that I can see."

"A drawback!" cried the director, amazed. "What drawback? What do you mean, sir?"

"Why, you see," continued Master Charles, while George stood staring at him like a stuck pig, without understanding a syllable he uttered:

"Why, sir, you see," said Mr. Wag, "my friend and I had rather calculated upon this little job. It was to be, as the French say, our *chef d'œuvre*."

"Well, sir, never mind the French."

"Certainly not. We had therefore hoped to make a good haul by it. Having failed to do so, we shall not be able to meet certain liabilities we have incurred."

"What liabilities?"

"Well, we are both of us a good deal in debt, and we have made some heavy bets about this little affair coming off, so that, all things consi-

dered, it would really be worse for us to have our liberty than be locked up."

"Why, you unmitigated young impostor!" cried the director, indignantly, "do you mean to insinuate that you want me to give you some money to pay for your disappointment?"

"Exactly so," replied Mr. Wag, with all the coolness imaginable; "that's just what I do mean."

"Then I tell you what it is," said the director, "you're very much mistaken."

"Oh no, I'm not," retorted Mr. Wag. "Consider it over, old gentleman. The accommodation is mutual. I don't particularly care about being locked up, and you don't particularly care about locking me up. You don't want it to get into the papers; I rather do. Money or fame will suit me; either one or the other. Come, what do you say? Give us something handsome, and I'll promise to shut up, and say nothing about it."

The proposition was so astonishingly cheeky, that it quite took the director's breath away.

The young officer, too, had not a word to say for himself, but stood gaping at the burglars like a stranded codfish.

George, on the contrary, having slowly recovered from his fright, began to appreciate the situation, and to see his way clearly into a nice little sum of money.

"Well, sir," said the director, when he had recovered a portion of his breath, "and how much do you want?"

"Half of what I was going to take."

"How much was that?"

"Twenty thousand pounds."

"Pooh—preposterous!" cried the director, in a state of the most intense excitement. "It can't be done—it shan't be done. You shall go for trial."

Charley took a seat, and crossed his legs.

"I think not, old gentleman," said he, smiling blandly. "You'll change your mind, I haven't the slightest doubt."

"No, I shan't, sir."

"Oh yes, you will. Think it over. I and my friend here are in no hurry. Talk to the other gentleman about it; I'm sure he won't be so unreasonable."

Such was the outrageous impudence of our promising hero, that the two gentlemen with whom he was negociating were completely flabbergastered.

The idea of their bribing these vagabonds to remain quiet seemed absurd and monstrous; but still, what was to be done?

A long argument ensued, in which all the pros and cons were considered.

The morning was wearing on, and no decision had been come to. Some steps must be taken immediately. The clerks would soon be there, and then everything would be known.

"Look here," said the director at last, driven by sheer desperation and fatigue to propose some terms.

"Here's a check for five thousand; take it and go."

"We shan't take a check," replied Charley; "give us gold."

"I can't—I have no right to touch the gold."

"Well, take the right, old boy. You can pay it back again at your leisure."

THE PROPERTY OF THE DUKE.

After a little more disputing, the gold was produced, counted over, pocketed, and the burglars took themselves off rejoicing.

They did not say a single word to each other before they had put quite a mile between themselves and the scene of their late adventure.

Then says George:

"Would you have the kindness to pinch me; I can't believe that I am awake."

Charley obliged him.

"Yes, I am, though," George continued, rubbing his arm; "there's no doubt about it. I hope the quids ain't duffers."

"Not much fear of that, Georgie."

"Well, then, all I've got to say is, that you're the 'cutest young card I ever set my eyes on; and it's turned out exactly as I allays said it

No. 28.

would—you've proved yourself a honour to the profession."

"My dear fellow," said Mr. Wag, with calm dignity, "this is nothing; my talent lies in this sort of thing, and I shall surprise you before I've done."

"You've surprised me as it is."

"I shall surprise you a little more before Iv'e done with you, then."

"I haven't a doubt of it. I hope we'll do many another crack together."

"My talent, George, does not exactly lie in cracks, as you term them, but in negociation."

"What's that? Swindling?"

"Well, a species of swindling, perhaps." It's a term they use in the upper circles."

[CHARLEY WAG, THE NEW JACK SHEPPARD.

"Oh, indeed ; well it comes to much the same same thing, 1 suppose."

"It does."

"And pray what are you going to do with your tin ?"

"What shall you do with yours ?"

"Have a flare up."

"Ah, I shan't."

"What then ?"

"I shall put it into a bank."

"Go on with you."

"I mean it."

"Why, I should have thought what had happened would have broke your confidence in them institutions."

"To some extent, George; but I have a plan in my head that will rather astonish you, I'll tell you as we walk along."

I should not wonder if there was a disbelieving reader who thought this story all a pack of nonsense.

He would have heard of it if such an attempt had ever been made upon the bank.

Ah, my young friend, there are things happen every day which we never hear of, however wide open we may keep our ears.

———

III.—BURIED ALIVE.

JUST as Faversham raised the bludgeon in the air; just at that critical juncture, when another instant of time might have launched the blood-stained soul of Rattan into eternity, the would-be murderer arrested his hand and resolved upon another scheme of vengeance—more fiend-like and devilish than the preceding one, yet one which would be slower in its execution, though less deadly in its result.

The thought which occurred to the doctor's ever-busy brain, was, that instead of killing this man, he would shut him up in the vault with the dead bodies.

Then he would have time to reflect what steps should be taken by his victim.

If he determined to kill him, he had nothing else to do than to keep him there.

In vain would the wretched Rattan batter at the door and shriek aloud for help. It would all be useless.

Not a sound could be heard out of the vault.

The door was of iron, and fitted tightly. The chimney was so narrow that it was impossible for a child to have crept up it. It was also crossed with bars.

Besides this, it lay in Faversham's power to cover the top of the chimney with a block of stone which he kept there for that purpose.

Then would Rattan be literally buried alive.

All this flashed through the doctor's demon-like brain.

Silently as death he crept back.

Then slammed the door upon his victim.

Rattan sprang to his feet with a cry of alarm.

All the horror of his position rushed upon him at once, and like a madman he flew towards the dread portal and stove to tear it open.

But his efforts were futile.

Then he strained every nerve to listen.

Perhaps it might be an accident.

He had heard no one approach—he had seen no one. There was no reason to believe that any one had shut the door upon him.

No, no; he determined to persuade himself Faversham would presently return home, and release him.

When he had made up his mind to this conclusion, he felt for a short time tolerably comfortable. But it was only for a short time; doubts began to creep into his mind, and he endeavoured vainly to reason them away.

Surely no one could be such a monster as to lock up a human being with a dozen putrifying corpses.

No, it was too frightful to think of.

But then, on the other hand, from what Rattan knew of this awfully mysterious doctor, he seemed to be a man who would not hesitate at any crime.

Rattan did not know for a certainty that the bodies which he was employed to carry from Saint Starver-cum-Bag-o'-Bones workhouse to the houses of various doctors, and to some of the London hospitals, were the results of Faversham's murders, but he strongly suspected such to be the case.

He could not prove it, and he was in some measure doubtful, owing to the fact of no discovery of poison ever having been made by the many doctors who had been engaged upon their dissection.

Perhaps this was owing, he thought, to the medical men never having had any suspicion that poison had been employed in procuring their death.

He knew very well, by the newspapers, that when once the suspicion of poisoning is started, there are not wanting certain talented analytical chemists, who would find the thousandth part of a grain of arsenic, if it were required, and hang a man as comfortably as you please, without any fuss about the matter.

But then, he knew very well—at least, he was as good as certain in his own mind—that with a natural state of things, and no underhand work going on, paupers would never die off like they did die off at Saint Starver's.

Then, if a man could commit the wholesale murders which he suspected Faversham of committing, it was not to be supposed that he would hesitate about bottling Rattan up in the way we have seen.

To dispel this unpleasant notion from his mind, Rattan thought over all the suspicious circumstances connected with St. Starver's, and tried in some other way than by supposing that murders were committed ; but it was in vain, for, look at it how he would, he could in no way satisfactorily account for the mysterious way in which he had always had to fetch away the bodies at night.

Engaged with these considerations, time glided by, and Rattan was delighted when he came to reflect that perhaps he might have passed half-an-hour or more, and that very shortly that Faversham would return and release him.

"After all, it's not so very bad here, by the

fire," he said to himself, as he took his seat again.

But it was as though his imprisonment should appear to him at once in all its horrors, for as he spoke the fire began to sink, and on the flame dying out nothing but a handful of red embers remained.

I have before described what an objection Mr. Rattan had to being left alone in the dark, and what a dread of dead bodies he entertained when in that condition.

In the broad daylight he cared nothing for them, but in the dark, as he expressed it, he "never knew exactly what they were up to."

This dread seizing him now, he gave the ashes a vigorous stir.

They broke to pieces and died out, but he could not kindle a flame.

Again he tried, with like success.

He leant over them, stirring them round and round with a piece of stick, and blowing them, in the vain hope of getting them again into a blaze, and was in this position for several minutes.

Then they died out almost completely, and he turned to face the door.

That is, he twisted round without moving from the spot on which he had been standing.

Having turned, he paused, he knew not why, and a terrific dread of movement crept over him.

While standing thus, he listened intently, as though he expected to hear some movement among the bodies; at the same time he dare not for his life change his position, for fear that *they should hear him*.

It was a ridiculous notion, probably; but then, when one is in a fright, it is very difficult to reason calmly.

Therefore he stood, as we have said, stock still, and waited.

But every moment seemed like an hour.

His bones ached, and his limbs were cramped.

He must move, or he would die.

In what direction? He had forgotten where the door was.

Slowly he stretched forward his hands, and groped in the darkness.

His fingers came in contact with a corpse.

Starting back, with a thrill of horror similar to that which might be occasioned by the touch of some loathsome beast, he paused for a moment before he dare recommence his investigation, and then crept forward again.

But again it was with the same result.

Again he came in contact with the dead.

But still he persevered, and at last, groping round among the hideous inmates of this sepulchre, whose rotting flesh and crumbling bones encountered his touch on every side, he managed to make his way back to the door.

What to do then?

There could be no course to pursue than to remain there, crouching and waiting, with fluttering heart and wild staring eyes, until the door should be opened.

Thus did he wait.

Time rolled slowly on.

Hour followed hour heavily, wearily dragging on their leaden course.

Yet he crouched and waited.

At times driven almost frantic with terror, when he fancied that there was a movement among the bodies, or when to his distempered brain the faces of the dead seemed to be hemming him in, and half stifling him with their fearful proximity.

But the hope of escape in some measure sustained him, and he crouched and waited.

At length, all of a sudden, without a moment's warning, the door opened.

He was flung forward by the suddenness of the action, and lay sprawling upon the ground.

The next moment he was in the grasp of Faversham.

Then they were struggling fiercely together.

Then Rattan was imploring his mercy in a choking voice, and bidding him for the love of God, not to fling him back to that fearful place —that living tomb.

IV.—LUCINDA AGAIN.

I LEFT Lucinda in very bad company, although that company was chiefly composed of reverend gentlemen.

Since I had the misfortune, in a luckless moment, to introduce these clerical parties into my story, a perfect volley of letters from unknown correspondents has been fired at my offending head.

It seems, if I am to believe these ladies and gentlemen, that there really are no naughty parsons in existence, and even if there were that it is not the proper thing to represent them in their natural colours.

There are a great many people in the world who do not like to hear the truth, and a great many others who do not like the truth to be told, among these last are a great many good papas of families, who are up to a thing or two, but don't like the olive branches to be let into the secret; but dear heart, there can be but little harm in showing up these shallow knaves, or indeed in depicting vice in all its hideous deformity. I do not recommend any of my young subscribers to practice the sins I shew up.

On the contrary, I have told them over and over again, and here on this occasion tell them once more, that it won't do. No good comes of it. No happiness results from it. Nothing but wailing and gnashing of teeth, tears and anguish and the devil with his pitchfork at the end of the last scene.

I left Lucinda, as I have said, in some very queer company.

When the inmates of the hotel had in some measure recovered from the fright and astonishment at the alarming disturbance which had arisen in consequence of the amatory propensities of Messrs. Sleek, Swabb, Gash, and Pudding, everybody began to feel anxious to know how it had all come about.

The landlord, who was a godless old man, attributed it off-hand, to the reverend gents.

The landlady, on the contrary, laid it at the door of "that creature," Lucinda.

The greater part of the guests, on the other hand, were inclined to think that it must have been got up by Leech with some idea of robbing the house.

"It's a try-on to rob us, I'm certain," said the commercial traveller, in the blue Jersey and flannel drawers.

"We should all had our throats cut before we have had time to awake," said the old gentleman in the shirt and top boots.

"It's not so much murder that I am afraid of," said the elderly spinster.

At which everybody tittered, wondering what other cause for harm the poor old lady could possibly entertain.

"Somebody better go and look," said the old gentleman.

"Who will?" asked the landlord.

"You ought to."

"Who?"

"Why, you."

"Me?"

"Of course you ought!"

"John," said the landlord, shifting the responsibility on to the shoulders of the waiter, "go and see directly."

But the waiter seemed inclined to disobey.

"I wish I was not a woman," cried the spinster; "but a poor weak woman is at the mercy of every villian."

Here everybody tittered as before.

"What are you laughing at?" asked the lady, indignantly.

It was presently agreed that as nobody liked to go by themselves, everybody should go together, and so everybody went.

They found all the four reverend gentlemen sprawling in their their shirts, as I left them.

It was rather a difficult matter, of course, for the reverend gentlemen to explain how it had happened that they should all be wandering about the house in their shirts, but they found some sort of an excuse, and after a good deal had been said one way and the other, they were finally ushered back to their respective bedrooms, which they made believe to have lost in the dark.

When the commercial traveller, the old gentleman, and the angular spinster, who was so fearful of her virtue, were also induced to go back to their beds, and the landlord and the rest of the company followed their example.

The household dozed off to sleep.

The reverend gentlemen abandoned their amatory enterprises for the present, and affairs generally assumed a quiescent aspect.

Meanwhile, Mr. Leech, the lawyer, as he lay in bed, made up his mind to one thing, and that was that Lucinda should be his.

He had taken a great fancy to her when first he saw her.

Now that he found she was in such demand, it is not to be wondered at that his fancy increased.

Yes, he was determined to possess her; but he was also determined to wait until he reached London, and had her completely in his power.

He must wait until the morning and until the post-boy returned from his master, and the question of the post-chaise was finally settled.

Although he himself was safe enough, yet he had his doubts about Lucinda, and having taken so strong a liking to that young lady, he thought it best to take such steps as lay in his power to secure her safety as well.

As for Lucinda she hardly knew what to think.

She was not a young lady of very vast reasoning powers.

She was very pretty, and rather fat, and fat ladies, I am led to understand, like to take things as they come, and not put themselves very much out of the way about trifles.

As well as she could make up her mind about anything, she had made up her mind that she would not go back to her parents if she could help it.

But then, how was she to help it?

"Suppose they fetch me, and say I must go," she asked herself, "what shall I do then?"

But then, she reflected, there was Leech who would take care of her. She had a very great notion of Leech's sagacity, and she felt sure that he would protect her somehow, although she did not exactly know how.

And so she did not trouble her pretty head very much about the matter.

Once or twice she could not help asking herself:

"What is to become of me? What will he do with me?"

She was a very green young lady, was Lucinda, who had taken all her notions of life from circulating library romances, and stories in the penny journals, and she had really no idea how dishonourably it was possible for a man to behave towards a woman.

You will say, perhaps, that the conduct of those disgraceful shepherds was surely sufficient to have given her an insight into that peculiar kind of baseness; but then, Lucinda was so very green.

Very green indeed.

Consequently, when the disturbance was over, she dozed off to sleep again, and slept comfortably until the morning, without troubling her head with any troublesome reflections.

Very early in the morning, however, Mr. Leech knocked at the door, and bade her make all possible haste with her toilet.

She shortly found him in the breakfast-room.

The reverend gents had not got up yet, and they were quite alone.

"We are in rather an unpleasant position, my dear," said Leech.

"Yes," said Lucinda.

"You don't want to go home, I suppose."

"Indeed I don't."

"So I thought; but how to prevent it?"

"I thought you knew the law, sir."

"Exactly; and I know this much of the law, that preventative is better than cure."

"What does that mean?"

"It means that, though I might get you away from your father again, even supposing you fell into his hands, still, it would be a much better plan to keep you out of them altogether."

"Yer, sir, if you please; I should think that would be best."

"In that case, I will tell you what our plan shall be."

"I'm all attention."

"They will look to me in the hotel here for payment, and never suspect that you would go away and leave me; but you shall."

"Where shall I go to?"

"Straight to my chambers in town. Here is my address on this card. I have been looking at a time-table, and there is a train in half-an-hour. You turn out of the inn door to the right, and walk up the street until you come to the station on your left hand. Here is some money. Go in, and take a ticket; and when you arrive in town, ask your way to my place. Do you think you can manage all this?"

"I think so."

"Very well. Now you had better slip off at once. Nobody will suspect your object."

"But what will become of you?"

"Oh, I shall be all right. They can't touch me, you know, about the chaise. When they have been, I shall follow after you."

"Must I go now, then?"

"Yes, at once—you have no time to lose."

Lucinda waited for no more, but, slipping on her bonnet and shawl, watched her opportunity, at Leech's suggestion, and slipped out of the house.

Following his directions, she hastened up the street, and reached the railway station in the course of a few minutes, unmolested.

Then she took a ticket for London.

❦

V.—Mr. Leech's office, and what happened at it.

NEITHER was any one there when the train started who seemed particularly anxious about her.

She came up to town in due course, and made the best of her way to Leech's chambers in Clement's Inn.

He lived in Clement's Inn now, having moved away from his city office in Bevis Marks to a quiet third-floor, where he could be out of the way, and, at the same time that he was not brought prominently under the notice of every passer-by, it was not a very difficult matter for any of his old customers to find him out, if they felt so inclined.

Clement's Inn is a legal hostelry, as most of my readers probably know, already with an entrance which is remarkably imposing, in huge and massive pillars, a splendid carriage way, and a graceful arch, which are calculated to considerably astonish a weak mind.

But alas, the spell is broken when the portal is passed. It is just like the shows at Wandsworth fair, the outside is about the best part about them. When you have passed the door, you come upon a block of dingy buildings, narrow courts, tall gloomy houses, and narrow alleys: so very different to the column business outside, that you cannot understand it, but fancy that somehow the pillars have been put down in the wrong place by mistake, and ought to have gone to Buckingham Palace.

I suppose there are very few more attempts at a garden, than the garden in Clement's Inn.

As for the statue in the middle, surely nothing so abortive was ever conceived by artistical fancy. He might have had a great idea in his mind, but probably got drunk before he carried it out, and vacilating vaguely between several capital ones, he gave up making a statue to turn it into a fountain, and the water being cut off at a critical moment, he finally determined on a sun-dial.

Although it is very easy to find Clement's Inn from the Strand, it is not so from the north side.

To begin with, it is a matter of some small difficulty to find out the gate when you are in Lincoln's Inn Fields, and even if you do, the journey is of great enterprise, over apple and salad stalls, and through cabbage trucks, and between huge masses of fly-blown meat, and under barrows of rotting fruit.

There is a tremendous trade doing here, too, in toasting-forks, staylaces, and such like gimcracks, besides stupendous piles of hollow-eyed dried crabs, and avalanches of slimy sprats in winter time.

It is a chance if you escape being torn to pieces by the savage men of the district, who traffic in raw flesh, and it is more than probable that you would never find the gate at all, but wander about and loose yourself among the wild regions at the back of Dury-lane, until some friendly policeman in charge of the civilized world, left you there among the loins and briskets you had been compelled to buy during your voyage of discovery.

It was in the square in the middle of the Inn where Mr. Leech's chambers were situated.

He did a great trade, did Leech, with a very little show.

He was not a man who went in for appearances. His customers were of the genus commonly denominated, "rum."

They were dingy-looking and foul-smelling, and it was rather a trial to any one of sensitive nerves to pass one of Mr. Leech's clients upon the stairs.

They were usually to be found, too, there—one or two of them at least.

They were all great hands at waiting.

They never grumbled about the length of time they were kept there kicking their heels.

When they were told that Mr. Leech was out, and that there was no saying for certain how long he would be—it may be an hour, or it might be a minute, or it might be all the rest of the day—they usually said they would wait a bit and see, and then went on waiting quite contentedly until the evening if he did not come.

It may be judged from this, that Mr. Leech was a man of some importance in his profession.

He was.

The Slogger's Alleyites, and the gentry from Cop Court, and Bunker's Buildings, knew him as "a pretty hand at felony," and they would get you into a corner and tell you confidentially.

"Lokee here, Mister."

"Well, I'm looking."

"If you ever get into trouble about any little trifle, sich as a dawg, for instance, go to Leech's. Leech is the card, and if there's any one can get you off, why Leech is him."

Mr. Leech did not live in his chambers here. He only used them as an office.

He kept a clerk there in the day time. At night they were shut up and left to themselves.

Mr. Leech's clerk was a curious object. An overgrown boy, who had thrust his thin arms and legs so very far through his coat and trousers, that getting them out again seemed to be next door to an impossibility, they were so tight.

He was a dirty complexioned boy, evidently had a soul above linen, slept in his clothes and only washed at the beginning of the month, or on Christmas-day, or his birthday, perhaps—anyhow at very remote periods.

Sometimes upon rare occasions, this evil looking young gentleman slept on the premises, and then if he washed at all, as there was no other convenience that any one had ever discovered, it was supposed that he took a bath in a pint-pot, and wiped himself as well as he could on blotting paper.

He had not much to do when Leech was absent. He answered people put people off, and told lies to order.

At other times he read odd back numbers of exciting romances, bought cheaply at old book-stalls, or he played solos upon a wonderful instrument of his own invention, which he had constructed just inside the lid of his desk. But his great amusement was fly-catching, and by dint of great practice he arrived at a state of wonderful perfection, and scarcely ever missed his victim.

On the morning that Lucinda came to London this promising youth was all alone in his glory, but for want of some better employment, was engaged spitting out of the third pair front window, and endeavouring to hit a dog who was asleep upon the flags below.

He was so engaged when Lucinda came into the Inn.

Narrowly escaping one of his shots, she stepped into the door-way below, and began to read the names.

Then seeing that she had found the object of her search, she proceeded straightway up-stairs.

The clerk was still hanging out of the window. She knocked at the door, but as he did not hear her she came into the room.

Still he remained unconscious—still occupied with his gentlemanly posture, and talking to himself.

"That has you, old door-mats—I thought I should wake you up presently. There you are again, that's one in your eye—"

"Ahem—ahem!" coughed Lucinda.

"Hallo!" said the gent, looking round sharply

"If you please—"

"What do you want, eh?"

"This is Mr. Leech's office, is it not?"

"Well supposing it should be Mr. Leech's office," retorted the young gentleman, sharply, "not that I say it is Mr. Leech's office, but just supposing it is, what do you want with it? You ain't going to take it away with you, are you?"

"No," replied Lucinda, rather abashed; "Mr. Leech told me to come here, and wait for him."

"Oh, did he?" said the young man, incredulously. "Oh, he did, did he? And pray, if you please, where might he have happened to have been at the particular time that he gave you that there direction?"

"He was in the country."

"In the country, was he? Now may I inquire what particular part of the country he may have been in?"

Lucinda was going to have told him, when she reflected that perhaps Mr. Leech would not like it to be known for some reason or other.

She therefore replied, that, if he wanted to know, he had better ask Mr. Leech himself.

Thus discouraged, the clerk grinned horribly, and, twisting his mouth into a variety of hideous shapes, signified, by winks of vast import, that he would not intrude upon her confidence, but that he thoroughly understood all about it.

To a young lady of greater perceptive powers than Lucinda, this line of conduct must have been exceedingly distressing.

As it was, it somewhat embarrassed her.

For, having shown Lucinda into an inner room, where there were two chairs, a desk, a ruler, an inkstand, and a hatpeg, he assured her in a whisper that it was all right, and that she needn't be afraid of anything.

Then, scarcely had he shut the door, when he returned, and, putting in his ugly head, inquired how she felt herself by that time.

Lucinda replying that she felt "pretty well, thank you," he retired again, with the observation of, "that's hearty," as though a weight were taken off his mind.

But this was not all, for, in less than three minutes, she perceived him peeping in at her through a bleary glass eye in the wall, and felt intensely like a slave at a slave-market being ogled by the planters.

At last, with a sense of unutterable relief, she perceived that he had withdrawn his eye, though not for long, as he presently returned to the charge, and, opening the door, with an apology for disturbing her, said that he had come for the ruler.

"Though where it's got to is more than I can tell," said he.

As it lay in a remarkably prominent position, Lucinda saw it, of course, and pointed it out to him.

"There it is."

"Where, miss? Oh, there, miss—that is, mam. Thank you, mam; I'm much obliged to you. Could I get you anythink, mam."

Lucinda was dying with hunger, but had been afraid to go in anywhere by herself to buy anything on her way, and was now afraid of asking the boy.

"No, thank you," said she.

"If there had been, I should have been very delighted."

Lucinda thanking him, he retired, with a variety of grimaces, but presently returned, with profuse apologies, to fetch the inkstand.

After this, he came back with the ruler, and, in about five minutes or so, brought in the inkstand, apologizing every time for the intrusion.

Then he left her to herself for ten minutes, and then, poking his ugly head in at the door, observed:

"You're quite sure you wouldn't like to take anything, miss—that is to say, mam."

Lucinda summoned up courage.

"Could you tell me where I could get any breakfast?" said she.

"Oh, lor, goodness me, miss, why didn't you speak before, mam. I can get you anything. What will you have?"

"Some tea, if you please. But where will you get it?"

"There's a coffee shop under the pillars," he replied. "Prices moderate, and wittles filling.

Tea three-halfpence, round of toast twopence, egg twopence. Other luxuries at the same figure."

"I should like some tea, and toast, and an egg," Lucinda replied.

"That's right," said he; "I'll fetch 'em in a crack."

Lucinda pulled out her purse.

"Go on with you," said the boy. "Stick it up to the governor. He's got a tick there."

"Very well," said Lucinda, not understanding in the slightest what he meant.

He soon returned, however, with a waiter carrying a tray, containing the eatables he had enumerated, and Lucinda, having overcome some small amount of timidity, consequent upon the fixedness of the youthful clerk's regards while she was eating—ate away with a good appetite.

"It ain't often we have young ladies here," observed the clerk presently.

"Indeed," said Lucinda.

"No mam. Very seldom. At least, I may say, there's only one."

"Only one."

"Don't you be alarmed, Miss. It's all right down here,"

"What do you mean?"

"It's all on the square."

"I don't understand."

"Why, there's no flies."

"No flies."

"Don't you twig?"

"I'm sure I don't know," said Lucinda, laughing, "what a person does do when they twig, but I don't think I do."

"Ah, you ain't up to the moves in perlite society, I can see, Miss—I mean as far as the talk goes."

"No," said Lucinda, innocently. "I have always lived in the country with my father and mother."

"Lord, Miss, you ought to see the other one as comes here. But I was a going to tell you. She's a chant, she is, you know, so you needn't put yourself out of the way."

Lucinda stared.

"Because there's nothink betwixt her and the governor."

Lucinda blushed.

"She's somethink very tip-top I should say by the look of her, a reglar spanking swell, but bless you she's as sharp as if she'd lived all her life on the cross, and knows every move on the cards."

"Indeed."

"Yes, you're right, there's no mistake about her. She's an out and outer. She's the only swell as ever comes to this place, I can tell yer, and I knows one when I see one with one eye shut up."

While these two very opposite persons were talking together, and the clerk was doing his best to be agreeable to his fair companion, Mr. Leech came in.

It was now about three in the afternoon.

He had settled matters with Bob, had a storming interview with the proprietor of the chaise, and finally got the better of him; chaffed Mr. Hopley gently about his daughter, and recommended him to go and try and find her himself.

Then as the train happened to start in a few minutes time, he paid his bill and departed.

Lucinda was much more pleased to see him than was his precocious and grimy-faced clerk, who had began to be exceedingly marked in his attentions to the lady, much to the maiden's annoyance.

Mr. Leech inquired what had occurred during his absence, read his letters, kissed Lucinda, and proposed that they should go somewhere to dinner.

Lucinda being agreeable, they went to dinner in the Strand, and then adjourned to the play.

After which, Mr. Leech proposed a supper in the Haymarket.

Unsophisticated Lucinda yielded a willing consent.

They had a little private room and a bottle of wine. The repast was of a sumptuous character, and the wine was of the strongest.

Lucinda always said afterwards that she must have gone to sleep, but she could not exactly say when.

As the author of this story has an innate horror of impropriety, he does not intend to go into any further particulars.

Lucinda and Mr. Leech certainly did not leave the hotel until next day, and there certainly was a bashfulness about Miss Hopley on encountering the eyes of the barmaid and waiter, which, to a person inclined to think well of his fellow-creatures, like I am, is extremely difficult to account for.

VI.—CHARLEY WAG REMAINS OF THE SAME OPINION WITH RESPECT TO THE "BUSTER."

"YES," said Mr. Wag, as he and George rode towards the Temple in a hansom cab, each with his money in a separate bag, "I shall put my capital in a bank."

"Well, I shan't; I don't see the exact point of it," replied George.

"Oh, you don't, don't you?"

"No, I don't."

"Well, then, I'll tell you. I suppose you would see the point if, for letting it lie there for six months, you got as much again for it, wouldn't you?"

"Perhaps so; but I don't see how it's to happen."

"Well, I'll tell you."

"Go on."

"I shall begin by paying it all in, except a few pounds I may require for my amusement. Then I shall write checks on the bank for various amounts, so as to draw out about three or four small sums of from five to twenty pounds a-day. The day after, I shall pay them all in again."

"Well, I don't see much point in that."

"Don't you? The point is, give 'em a good deal of trouble."

"Why?"

"Because my object is to get my account well known, and my name well known."

"I don't see your game; but go on."

"When I have done this sort of thing for

about three months. I shall all at once let it drop."

"Let it drop?"

"I shall write no more checks, and pay in no more money; my balance, you understand, will therefore remain exactly the same. So many hundred pounds, so many shillings, and so many pence halfpenny."

"Yes, I see."

"Well, it is the custom in banks to call over the balances every morning. Every morning they will call over mine. It being always the same, if I let 'em call it over for six months, it is to be supposed that most of the clerks will know it by heart."

"Well?"

"Now comes the dodge.

"Go on—I'm getting excited."

"One day, when they're very busy, I and some other party will at the same moment, but at different ends of the counter, present two checks for the full amount, barring the shillings and halfpence."

"But they won't pay them."

"Won't they?—why not? Everybody is tremendously busy; and, besides, everybody knows what my balance is. They won't require to look at the book; anyhow, both of the clerks won't look. Besides, in a large bank they don't make the fuss about paying a large sum of money that a little tradesman does when you present a bill to him of five pounds."

"No, I should think not; but at the same time, don't you think it would make it more sure to go in for a smaller amount?"

"Bah! that's exactly the way that all you gentleman manage your affairs, and that is exactly why you never get on in the world."

"How so?"

"Why, because you are always frightening away your time over little peddling tricks, which are quite as much risk as large ones, and don't pay half as well."

"There's something in that, to be sure."

"Something in it, of course there is. There's everything in it."

"Well, I tell you what, Charley, you're nothing short of genius, you ain't, and so I don't deceive you, and I shall leave you to go your own way, though how you could have picked it all up the way you have bangs me entirely."

"Just so, and now here we are at the Temple, and so we'll go in and have a little nap, and then I'll give you a breakfast that will make a man of you."

"All right, governor, I'm on."

"But, although our young friend Mr. Charles Wag seemed upon the high-road to make his fortune, it must yet be borne in mind that he was a most extravagant young dog, and that he no sooner got a pound than he straightway found occasion to spend two.

One thing this hopeful youth had made up his mind about, was that he was going to see life in a large way.

He had, at first, some idea of travelling, but upon consideration he thought it best to use up his own country first.

With some of the money which he had so fortunately handled at the bank, he furnished his rooms in the Temple very beautifully.

He also started a little Tilbury, and a deminate tiger to ride behind

Of a morning he strolled in the park, appeared in the drive in the afternoon, or took a turn on the fashionable side of Regent-street, and a quiet dinner at Longs, which cost him from ten to fifteen shillings.

"But then, a fellow must dine, you know," he would say to George, who, being a vulgar fellow, thought the price was too high.

"Certainly," said George, and calculated mentally the difference between that sort of meal and "a good tightener of a-la-mode."

Of an evening you might see him in his stall at the Opera, or doing the Argyle with a cigar.

He also frequented the balls given by the young ladies in the ballet of Her Majesty's, or the soirees at Motts.

The swells who met him, were inclined to look upon him as a stuck up monkey, for one does not often see a boy of fifteen giving himself such airs, but such was the cheek and assurance of our young hero, and so nicely had he copied the manners of those he met with at the places he frequented, that he managed to pass muster, and, indeed, to come off with flying colours, and was never by any chance set down as a snob.

The ladies liked him, you may be sure; for he was as lavish with his money as an Eastern prince.

And there is nothing reaches a woman's heart sooner than money—is there?

One day, when he was lounging in the park, a lady passed him in an open carriage.

He was not paying attention at the time, but two young swells by his side were talking of her.

"Devilish fine girl that."

"Splendid creature. Who is she?"

"Don't you know?"

"No—tell us."

"It's the Duke of Hetherland's last. A regular beauty. Julia her name is."

Charley pricked up his ears.

"A dancing girl she was at one time, I believe."

"Indeed!"

"Yes, at some slum in the East-end."

"She's had a rise now."

"A rise—I believe you. To be kept by the richest man in England would be a rise a good many would like."

"Oh, fie! You don't believe in virtue, then."

"Well, not particularly."

"I'm ashamed of you."

"I suppose, then, that you are a believer."

"Well, to a certain extent."

"What extent, pray?"

"To a thousand or two pounds, perhaps. Every one has their price, I suppose."

"Yes, and some sell themselves cheaply."

"No doubt of it."

Charley did not wait to hear any more, but made the best of his way through the crowd of swells lounging upon the railings, or sauntering up the path, until he came in front of the carriage.

True enough it was she.

Julia Jenkini.

He stared at her very hard, and she in turn

ONE FOR HIS NOB.

stared at him, but apparently did not recognise him.

At that moment the carriage broke from the rank, and the horses mended their pace.

He was determined not to lose her.

But what could he do?

Seizing an opportunity, he rushed forward between the horses' heads, and, before any one could interfere to prevent him, vaulted lightly into the carriage containing his charmer, and took a seat by her side.

———

VII.—CHARLEY GOES LOVE-MAKING.

"WELL, sir," said Julia, "pray what do you want?"

No. 29.

"I want you," replied Charley.

"Me, indeed!"

"Why not?"

"Do you know whom you're speaking to?"

"Certainly I do."

"Who?"

"Julia Jenkini."

Julia stared at him very hard, opening her beautiful eyes in astonishment.

"I don't know you," she said.

"Oh yes, you do."

"I don't."

"Do you mean to say that that isn't your name?"

"Well, no, it isn't."

"You've changed it, then."

"I have."

[CHARLEY WAG, THE NEW JACK SHEPPARD.

" Are you married ?"

" Not altogether."

" Do you mean to say you don't remember me ?"

" How can I remember you, when I never saw you before ?"

Oh, the fickleness of women ! Charley felt awfully indignant.

" It was very presumptuous of me to suppose that you could remember so insignificant a person," said he, trying to be sarcastic.

It was a very fine sight to see this young gentleman, who could twist a bank-director round his fingers as easily as I could twist a morsel of thread, and who here, in the presence of a bit of a girl in a turban hat and a big crinoline, was positively nowhere.

He sat opposite to her, staring at her stupidly.

" Well, sir," said she, " if you have nothing else to say, perhaps you will have the kindness to jump out of my carriage."

" She shan't get over me in this way," thought Charley, making a desperate effort to appear plucky.

" Do you hear ?" she repeated.

" Hear what ?" he asked.

" Will you have the kindness to go ?"

" How can I ?"

" The way you came, I suppose."

" But the carriage is going so fast."

" I'll stop it for you."

" No, don't do that. What will the servants think ?"

" Why they have seen you."

" I don't think so. They haven't turned round since I have been in."

This was the case. The footman sat beside the coachman on the box, and, so rapid had been Mr. Wag's movements, that the servants had not observed him, but went on contentedly chattering about their own affairs.

" What do you propose doing ?" asked Julia, after a pause.

" Stopping," replied Charley.

" But you can't."

" If you will allow me."

" But I won't."

" But, Julia—Julia, I say—I never thought you would have treated me in this way."

" Didn't you ?"

" You said that you would never leave me."

" That is exactly what you said."

" But it was not my fault."

" Whose fault was it, then ?"

Charley explained at considerable length, and narrated his adventures until the time that he was about to throw himself into the water, and was rescued by George ; though he did not dwell for an unnecessarily long time upon the flogging he had received in gaol, as you will readily believe, for one does not generally like to tell those sort of things.

He told enough, however, for Julia to be deeply interested at the recital, and to sympathise with his misfortunes.

" Poor Charley," said she, laying her hand upon his arm, " how you must have suffered. I am afraid I did you more harm than good by coming to the police court."

" Oh, I don't know that. You did it for the best, I am certain."

" Yes. Did you see me and the cat in the crowd when you went into the van ?"

" To be sure I did ; and by the way, how is the cat ?"

" It's quite well. You shall see it."

" And its mistress."

" Well, I don't know how it is to be managed, the duke is so very particular."

" Oh, you will find a way."

" But I say, Charley, how is it you're such a tremendous little swell."

" Oh, because—because I have had some money left me."

He did not like to tell the truth and own that he had turned thief, because he was not quite sure how the lady would like it.

I have before pointed out the popular fallacy of supposing that when a young woman loses her virtue, she loses everything, and that every prostitute is necessarily a thief, so I need not enlarge upon the subject.

" You had better get down now," said Julia. " I am going home, and I cannot take you with me."

" When shall I see you again ?"

" To-night, if you like. The duke will not come to see me."

" Where do you live ?"

" Here is my address."

" What time shall I come ?"

" About nine. We will have supper together. Until then, good-bye."

" Good-bye."

Julia called to the coachman to stop, and Charley alighted, much to the servants' surprise, who now perceived him for the first time.

When the carriage was out of sight he walked away, turning over in his mind all that had occurred, and determining, if he possibly could, to obtain possession of this charming young lady, whom he considered the Duke had robbed him of.

He went away to dine, and to think it over.

In the evening at the appointed time, he took a cab and drove to the villa in St. John's Wood, where Julia resided.

Julia was waiting for him.

She had made great preparations, and was very beautifully dressed in a rich black velvet gown.

On her plump white arms were gorgeous bracelets of rubies and pearls, on her soft and delicate bosom were heavy necklaces of sparkling diamonds.

She wore pink silk stockings and tiny boots of white satin, with high heels tapered off to the size of a shilling.

Altogether she looked magnificent. She looked divinely beautiful.

To descend to matter of fact, she looked as if she cost somebody a good deal of money.

That was what occurred to Master Charles' mind, among other notions, and he said to himself,

" That's the sort of young person who would make a tidy hole in my little banking account."

He did not say so, however, but made her a variety of pleasant compliments, for he had a style of talking to the ladies which one would hardly have expected in a young man of his " bringings up."

It must have been owing to his parentage, if he really was born of noble parents, a fact by the bye, which I shall not, as yet, compromise myself by asserting, however much the curious reader might wish to know.

"Are you ready for supper?" asked Julia.

Charley replied that he was, and so without more ado they sat down to it.

There were usually two servants in the house, a man and a maid, but Julia had sent the man out that evening to amuse himself at the theatre, being rather fearful of his treachery. The duke was a very artful old man, and she more than half suspected that this servant was placed there as a spy over her actions.

Such, indeed, turned out to be the case.

The maid, however, was devoted to her mistress's interests, and would have been delighted had she had a hundred lovers.

All she cared about was for her own actions not to be questioned, and then she did not care particularly what her mistress did.

Charley and his lady-love sat down to supper.

They laughed and talked, and pledged one another in brimming bumpers of Burgundy.

Charley had told her several times that he loved her to distraction, and she, not being a very bashful young lady, had owned to a partiality for him.

They were getting on like the proverbial one o'clock, when a loud knock at the street door disturbed them.

"Hallo!" said Charley.

"Good heavens!" cried Julia.

"What's the matter?"

"It's him!"

"Who?"

"Why, the duke."

"The duke?"

"Yes."

"The devil!"

"Almost as bad, when he's put out, but he mustn't catch you here.

"Where am I to get?"

"Under the sofa."

"There isn't room."

"Try."

"I should break my back."

"Get up the chimney."

"I shall spoil my clothes."

"Don't think about your clothes; think of my reputation."

"Well, here's a cupboard," said Charley; "I'll get in here."

"Make haste, then. There, shut the door, he's coming."

Charley got into his hiding place, and screwed himself up into the smallest possible space.

Then the room-door opened.

It was the maid who came in, all breathless to say that the duke had arrived, and that she had detained him for a moment with some excuse below, so that her mistress might have time to stow her lover away.

The duke did not remain long behind. Hardly had the maid time to give notice of his arrival, when they heard his steps upon the stairs.

Charley darted out for a decanter of wine and bolted back again with it, to the dismay of the women, and then the duke entered the room.

VIII.—WHAT CAME OF CHARLEY'S LOVE-MAKING.

JULIA fancied that he cast his eyes round the apartment in a scrutinizing way, as though he were in search of some sort of evidence, but as he said nothing she came to the conclusion that she was mistaken.

She was a deceitful hussy—some of her sex are—so said she—

"You should have come a little sooner."

"Eh."

"If you had come a little sooner, you would have been in time."

The duke looked at her sharply.

"In time for what?"

"To meet a friend of mine, such a delightful young lady—dances in the ballet of Her Majesty's."

"Does she smoke?" asked the duke, with a dry cough.

Charley had been doing so.

"Yes," replied Julia, plumply, "she does."

"I don't like women to smoke."

"Why not?"

"Because it is a disgusting habit."

"Oh, indeed, that's your opinion."

Here there was a pause.

"Have you had supper?"

"Yes; will you have some?"

"No, I am tired, I shall go to bed."

"Are you going to stay here, then?" asked Julia, as pleasantly as she could.

"Yes, my dear, if you have no objection."

Charley hearing this from the cupboard, screwed himself up a little smaller than before, and wondered whether his grace was a light sleeper.

The bed-room opened from the room in which they had supper, and any one lying in bed with the door open between the two rooms, could command an excellent view of the door of the cupboard in which Mr. Wag was hidden.

The duke went into the next room, leaving the door wide open, while Julia remained behind, and pretending to be reading.

"Hallo," called his lordship, presently. "Aren't you coming?"

"Not yet, it is so very early."

"What are you doing?"

"I just want to finish a chapter in this book."

"Can't you finish it in the morning?"

"No, I have promised to give it back the first thing."

His grace had by this time divested himself of his wig and wadding, and retired to his couch.

Julia continued to read, hoping that he would soon drop off to sleep, although she was afraid that he had some artful design in wishing to go to bed so soon, seeing that he very rarely retired before two or three in the morning.

As for Mr. Wag, he noiselessly removed the stopper from the decanter, and took what is called "a good swig."

Thus the minutes past.

Charley began to feel rather cramped.

Julia had the fidgets.

The duke lay in bed with his eye fixed on the cupboard door.

"Haven't you nearly done?" asked his grace.

"I have only got another page to read ; you go to sleep.

"I'm not sleepy, I am only tired."

"This is a nice look out," thought Charley in the cupboard.

Julia turned over the pages and continued to read.

The whole scene began to grow to all the actors insufferably monotonous.

The duke in bed lay with his hand resting on a loaded pistol, expecting every moment to hear some sound in the house of the lover making his escape, for his servant, who had watched Charley enter the villa, and came to the duke post haste, to inform him of Julia's infidelity, in pursuance of a compact which master and man had entered into, with respect to the safe keeping of Miss Julia.

Julia, devoured by impatience, still kept up an appearance of being engaged with her book, but in reality scarcely able to control a burning desire which had possession of her, to jump up and slam too the bed-room door, thus, not only to escape the intense scrutiny with which she knew the duke was regarding her, but also to enable Charley to come from the cupboard, and beat a retreat.

Charley, on the other hand, was not only in great torture with the cramp, and suffering severely from want of air, but was also in no very pleasant state of mind, not only on account of the danger of his position, but the tremendous sell he had experienced in his love-making.

These sort of things could not go on for ever, as you may suppose.

Julia could could bear it no longer.

She rose, closed the book, and began to prepare her toilet for the night.

Once or twice she endeavoured to partially close the door between the two rooms, but when she did so the duke had always prevented her.

He felt so hot, he said, and she was obliged to desist.

"Poor Charley !" thought she. "There is no chance for him now, until the duke goes to sleep. I hope he won't be smothered."

But, besides her fears upon this head, it was exceedingly amazing to think that it should be Charley who was in the cupboard, instead of the duke. Julia fancied that she could have gone to sleep very comfortably if it had only been that ugly old man instead of her handsome young lover, who was being put to such inconvenience.

And she could not help thinking that there was something very noble in the young fellow, remaining there so quietly for her sake, for she imagined that if he had been discovered, she alone would have suffered, as is usually the case in such affairs, for her indiscretion.

However, Charley was there sure enough, and sure nnough the duke was very wide awake, and looking anything but sleepy.

Julia, on the other hand, began to feel unacountably fatigued, and could scarcely keep her eyes open.

She undressed as slowly as she possibly could, but although she loitered in every possible way, and made the process as long as possible, she could not tire out the duke, and after he had asked her full half-a-dozen times what made her so long, she was obliged to get into bed.

It was perhaps the over excitement, or a rather liberal supply of wine she had taken, combined with the fatigue of waiting and anticipation, that made her find it quite impossible, when once in bed, to prevent falling off to sleep, and so off to sleep she went.

She might have been, to the best of her calculation, asleep for an hour, when she awoke up at the sound of a pistol being discharged.

The duke had sprung out of bed.

He had another pistol in his hand.

Julia, collecting her scattered senses in the best way she could, rushed after him and flung herself in his way.

At the same moment there was a tremendous crash, for Charley in his flight had run full butt against the table, and dashed a quantity of glasses and dishes on the floor.

In an instant afterwards the boy threw up the window, and at the same time that he prepared to spring into the garden, the duke fired again.

Although there was a light burning in the room, Julia was too much frightened and confused by the events which were passing so rapidly before her, to be able to see exactly what was being done.

But she saw the duke fire, and she saw Charley drop from the window as though he had been shot.

IX.—A Strange Meeting.

THE spot which Murdoch chose for a resting-place, was, as I have said, a door-step in a quiet corner, where he hoped to be able to pass a few hours undisturbed.

It was in a little, dirty, damp street, or rather alley, at the mouth of which a gas lamp burnt dimly.

He could not have found a better place to slink into, he fancied.

No one was likely to disturb him there, he thought.

But he was mistaken.

Very shortly after he had taken a seat, and had screwed himself up in the smallest possible compass, he heard steps approaching him.

Ever on the alert, and anticipating danger, he pricked up his ears and listened.

The steps came nearer and nearer.

It was a dragging, shuffling, foot-sore kind of walk, like that of some one weary and in pain.

In the place that Murdoch sat it was impossible for him to see the new comer, for he slunk so closely to the wall; and it was the fact of not being able to see him, and yet hearing him creeping up so gradually, which presently threw him into an awful fright, and made him burst out into a cold sweat.

Meanwhile, the creeping sound advanced.

Murdoch strove to move.

He would have rushed forward to meet it, but some mysterious power had him spellbound.

At last the figure came suddenly upon him.

So suddenly that he sprang to his feet with a shriek, and then sank back again exhausted.

There was something in the new comer's appearance, apart from the suddenness with which he had come upon him, was almost sufficient to warrant the others alarm.

He was a thin, awfully thin, haggard and gaunt spectre of a man.

He wore a ragged, tangled, hideous, red beard, and a few wild locks of hair hung about his face, which was cadaverous and sickly in its hue, more like that of an inmate of a grave than the countenance of a living creature.

And he had large black eyes, which were so sunken, and so brilliant, and so savage, that one could not help thinking that they must belong to one of insane mind.

His apparel was of the most miserable and filthy description, and he seemed to be in a state of the most abject and sordid destitution.

As Murdoch gazed upon this unwelcome visitor, he could not help a shudder creeping through his frame.

"God grant I may never sink so low as that," he mentally and involuntarily exclaimed.

Then he crept nearer to his side of the door, and allowed the other more room.

The miserable outcast crouched opposite to him without speaking, and nursing his knees in a forlorn sort of way, stared out at vacancy apparently almost unconscious of the others presence.

But not so Murdoch; there was something so horrible in this silence, that he felt it impossible any longer to maintain it.

He, therefore, leant forward, and laying his hand upon the others arm, said :—

"Friend."

The man slowly turned his eyes towards the speaker.

"Did you speak?" he asked.

"Yes," said Murdoch.

"You called me friend."

"I did."

"I have no friends. I never have."

"You must have led a lonely life, then."

"I have."

They were silent for a few moments, then the stranger resumed—

"When I say lonely, I mean as regards friendship. I have had acquaintance enough. So many, perhaps, when I had money, I had little trouble in finding some one to help me squander it."

"You were rich once?"

"I was, very."

"Then you must have been unfortunate."

"It is fate. Fate was against me. I might as easily cheat the gallows, as cheat fate. Aye, easier."

Murdoch started, and was silent.

"No one could escape the gallows, I should think," he said, presently, "when the halter is round their neck."

"Why not. I know a man who could have managed it."

"But it never has been done."

"Perhaps not. He may never had occasion to do it."

"What was his name, if I may inquire?"

The other seemed to turn the question over in his mind, and consider whether or not he should answer it. Then he said :—

"He was a quaker. His proper name was Hezekiah Slink, but he has changed it since—"

"To what?"

"To Faversham."

If an adder had stung him, the start which Murdoch gave could not have been greater.

"Faversham!" he gasped.

"Do you know him?" the other asked.

"Yes—no—that is, I have heard of him."

The man stared at him for a few minutes.

"If you knew any bad of him," he said, "you might make your fortune."

"How so?"

"What do you know?"

"I know many things."

"Tell them to me."

"Well, not exactly," said the other with a grin. "How am I to know how you will use them?"

"I will use them fairly."

"Perhaps so; but like you, I have had few friends, and I am not over inclined to trust one who is a stranger to me. If I trust you, I shall trust you with my life."

"Indeed."

"And how can I tell that what I know will be of any service to you. It can be of service to none but one man, and he is dead."

"And he is Horford."

"He lives then. I am he!"

"Listen, then," said Murdoch, after he had recovered in some measure from his astonishment, "listen to what I shall tell you. I have been hanged, and have been brought to life."

"By whom?"

"By Faversham."

"And your name?"

"Is of no consequence."

"But your statement is rather improbable to commence with."

"Listen to me, then, and I will relate the details; you will then be able to judge whether or not it sounds like truth."

"Go on," said the other, "I am all attention."

Murdoch glanced round him to see whether any one was near them, and then began.

I have taken the liberty to alter the phraseology a little, but the substance of his statement was as follows.

X.—THE STORY OF THE RESUSCITATED.

"I WILL begin from the time that my wife and children left me, on the night before I was to be executed.

"It was four o'clock in the afternoon. As soon as they had left, everything appeared to be finished between this world and me.

"I should have wished to die then, on that very spot, and at that very hour, as the last action of my life, the bitterest of all, was done.

"As evening descended, my prison became more cold and damp, it seemed to me. The night was cold and foggy, and I shivered as I lay on my bed.

"My mind was becoming weaker by degrees, and my heart contracted beneath the misery and desolation that surrounded me, and little by little the thought of what would become of my poor little ones, banished little by little the thought of my own unhappy situation.

" This was the first time that I began fully to comprehend the sentence under which I was soon about to suffer; and while reflecting on it a horrible terror seized me, as if I had but just heard my sentence pronounced, and as if I had not understood before that I ought to die.

" I had eaten nothing for four and twenty hours. Near me, however, was plenty of food, but I could not touch it. I tried, but thought that it would choke me, and was obliged to spit it out again.

" I might have had any thing I liked. I I could not help thinking of the beasts of the field, and the birds of the air that are fattened in order to be killed.

" I felt that my ideas was not such as they ought to have been in such a moment. I believe that my wits were wandering.

" A sort of low buzzing, similar to the hum of bees, incessantly filled my ears. I thought it was night, bright luminous flashes passed to and fro before my eyes, and my mind became waste.

" I recollected nothing.

" I tried to pray, but I could not remember a single prayer. Only odds and ends of things I had heard when a child, when I last went to church, and it seemed to me that these words which I thus confusedly addressed to Heaven, were nothing else than so many blasphemies.

" Suddenly I thought all my terror was vain and useless, and it was madness thus to await death. Hope arose in my breast.

" The jailors were absent a moment from my cell, and I sprang up at the bars of my window, and seized them with the strength of a lion, and tried to tear them from their sockets. Then I carefully examined every part of the lock of the door and tried to raise the door itself with my shoulder, though it was heavier than the massive gates of a fortified town.

" Then I felt along the walls and in every corner of the prison, although I might have known, had I been in my right senses, that the walls were formed of massive stone, three feet thick, and that even could I have passed through a crack not bigger than the eye of a needle, I should not have had the slightest chance of escape.

" In the midst of my mad endeavours the jailers returned, and I sank upon my bed faint and sick, as though I had swallowed poison.

" But this did not last long, for my head swam, and the room appeared to turn, and, half awake and half asleep, I dreamed that it was midnight, that my wife had returned, as she had promised, and that they would not let her enter.

" It seemed to me that a heavy snow was falling, and that the streets were covered as with a white sheet, and that I saw her lying dead on the snow, in the middle of the night, before the prison door.

" When I came to my senses I was struggling for breath.

" In a minute or two I heard the clock of Saint Sepulchre's strike ten, and then I knew that I had been dreaming.

" The chaplain came to me presently, and exhorted me to think no more of the troubles of this world, but to turn my attention towards a future existence, and to try to reconcile my soul with Heaven, in the hope that my sins, though great, should be forgiven if I repented.

" When he was gone, I felt for a moment a little more collected. I sat down on my bed, and seriously began to examine myself, and prepare to meet my fate.

" I reflected that, under all circumstances, I had now but a few hours to live, and that there was no further hope for me, and that I ought at least to meet death bravely, and like a man.

" I then tried to recollect everything that I had heard said about death by hanging.

" It was but the struggle of a moment, it caused little or no pain at all, and produced instant death.

" Then I passed on to many other strange reflections; little by little again my mind began to wander.

" I carried my hands to my neck, which I clasped tightly, as if to see what strangulation was.

" Then I stroked my arms at the places the cords would bind them.

" I felt it pass round and round, until it was strongly fastened.

" I felt my hands tied behind me, one after the other.

" But what horrified me more than anything else, was the idea of feeling the white cap drawn slowly over my face.

" If I could have been spared this white cap —this wretched anticipation of eternal night— the rest would not have appeared so horrible to me.

" In the midst of these mournful ideas, the whole of my limbs were slowly seized with a general numbness.

" The giddiness I had felt was followed by a state of heavy stupor, which diminished the suffering attendant on my thoughts; and yet, even while I lay nearly unconscious, I still remained continuing to think.

" The church clock then struck twelve.

" I heard the sound, but it fell on my ears indistinctly, as if it had first penetrated through several walls, or come from a great distance. Then I gradually saw each object that filled my memory turn round and round, become less distinct, wander here and there, and at length entirely disappear, one after the other, and then I fell asleep.

" I awoke to find myself alone with Faversham.

" He told me he would save me.

" His words seemed like those of a magician.

" He proposed certain terms.

" I accepted them.

" He left me, and I fell back fainting on the bed.

" I slept to within two hours of my execution.

" At six o'clock in the morning, one of the jailers who had been sitting up with me awoke me from my slumber.

" I heard his voice as in a dream before I was thoroughly awake, and the feeling I first experienced was that of a man put out of humour by being suddenly aroused when tired out of a pleasant sleep.

" I was fatigued, and wished again to close my eyes.

" An hour afterwards the bolts outside my prison door were drawn back, and the governor and chaplain entered my cell.

" I looked up. A chilling shudder ran like an electric shock through my whole body.

" I felt as if I had just been plunged into a bath of icy water.

" One glance sufficed.

" I felt as though I had never known, nor ever again would I know, what sleep was. I cruelly felt my situation.

" The chaplain asked me how I had passed the night, and asked me to join in prayer with him.

" I huddled myself together on the side of the bed.

" My teeth chattered, and my knees shook, in spite of the promises that Faversham had made.

" ' It is more than a quarter past seven,' said one of the turnkeys.

" I gathered together all my strength, and begged them to leave me to myself as long as possible.

" I had forty minutes to live.

" I tried to make a second observation as they left the cell.

" But this time I could not articulate a single sound.

" My breath failed me.

" My tongue stuck to the roof of my mouth.

" I had lost, not my speech, but the power of speaking.

" I made two violent attempts to open my mouth, but it was all in vain.

" I could not pronounce a syllable.

" When they were gone, I remained in the same place on my bed. I was drowsy, and numbed with cold; probably on account of the cold air, which had penetrated through the open door, and to which I was unaccustomed.

" In order to keep myself warm, I remained huddled together with my arms across my breast, my head hanging down, and trembling in every limb.

" My body appeared to me an insupportable weight.

" The day became lighter and lighter, though dull and dingy, and gradually entered my cell, exposing in bold relief its black wall and flag-stones.

" Strange as it may seem, I could not help remarking all these puerile things, though death was waiting me an instant afterwards.

" I observed that a lamp which stood in a corner on a bracket, burnt very dimly, with a long wick, which seemed depressed and suffocated by the cold and foul air, and I recollect that this lamp had not been trimmed since the previous evening, and recalled the circumstances attending the trimming.

" I looked at the cold naked bars of the bed on which I was seated, and at the enormous nails in the door of my cell, and at some letters scratched on the walls by some former prisoners.

" I felt my pulse.

" It was so weak that I could hardly count it.

" But in spite of all my efforts I was unable to bring myself to think, to believe, to own to myself, that I was about to die.

" In the midst of my anxiety I heard them returning, and I inwardly said to myself—

" Oh, Lord, have mercy upon me, a miserable sinner.

" But no—no, it could not yet be time. But yet it was, they had come to fetch me.

" The cell seemed full of faces.

" They found me in the same place—the same position in which they had left me.

" They helped me up and took me out into a room, where the hangman awaited me.

" I seemed to be in a dream, and yet I knew what was passing.

" When they were going to pinion me I fell upon my knees, and like a madman prayed for mercy.

" I was about to faint, when Faversham, who was present and disguised, bent over me and whispered me to be courageous.

" It was all very well for him to do so, but how could I be sure that his plan would not fail.

" I tried with all my might to have faith in it, but in my heart I had none.

" My great difficulty was to prevent myself from falling.

" I felt that I had not a spark of courage left.

" Oh, God, I would have willingly suffered any amount of misery, shame, and humiliation, would have happily accepted any situation, had I but been allowed to keep my life.

" A nauseating faintness crept over me, and a feeling as though the floor was giving way beneath my feet.

" Soon they finished pinioning my arms and hands.

" I heard an officer of the gaol saying in a low voice to the chaplain.

" ' Everything is ready.'

" As we were leaving, one of the executioner's assistants put a glass of water to my lips, but I could not drink.

" The clock struck eight, and we began the journey to the scaffold.

" I heard the measured tolling of the bell, and the deep voice of the chaplain as he walked before.

" ' I am the resurrection and the life, saith the Lord, he that believeth in me though he were dead yet shall he live, and though after my skin worms destroy this body, yet in my flesh shall I see God.'

" It was the burial service.

" Prayers composed for those who are stretched lifeless in their coffins, which they were reading over us who were still alive.

" Till this moment I could live and see, but now all power of perception began to desert me.

" Yet I felt the sudden transition from the gloomy prison to the cold open platform I was being carried up to.

" Then I discovered an immense, dark silent crowd that filled the whole street beneath me.

" The windows of the houses opposite, and all the roofs were black with spectators.

" I saw the church of St. Sepulchre's through the yellow fog in the distance, and heard the tolling of its bell.

" I recollect the cloudy sky, the murky morning, the humidity that covered the scaffold, the enormous mass of all those black edifices, and the prison which rose at our side, and still seemed to cast on us its withering shadow.

"I still feel the cold fresh breeze, which blew against my face.

"I still see the whole sight, which pierces my heart like an arrow.

"The horrid perspective is stretched out before my eyes.

"The scaffold—the rain—the multitude.

"I hear the low hoarse murmur which rang through the crowd, when I came into sight.

"I never saw so many objects in one glance so cleanly and distinctly as I did then, but it was so soon over.

"From this moment my senses began again to waver.

"I was not altogether conscious of the prayers of the chaplain, or the adjusting of the fatal noose, though I know I shuddered at the hideous contact of the hangman's fingers and my neck.

"Then the white cap was drawn down over my head, and I gasped for air.

"The chaplain, I suppose, continued to read, though I could not listen to him.

"I was waiting.

"Waiting for the shock.

"Not long had I to wait, although to me it seemed an age.

"I stood with my shoulders shrugged up, with all my muscles quivering, though I endeavoured to hold myself well together; it was a mad hope that I should in this way break my fall.

"It came—I was down.

"With a jerk—a twist—a wrench, which clenched my teeth together, and sent the sparks dancing before my eyes,

"For a moment or so I thought myself dead, and I said to myself, 'is this all. Is it no worse than this!' But in a few moments I awoke to an intolerable sense of suffocation.

"I strove to tear the rope from my neck, but I could not reach it.

"The blood rushed up into my head; my brain seemed turning round.

"I lost my senses.

"When I recovered, I was with Faversham."

* * * * * *

"And your name?" said the man, who had called himself Horford, and who had been listening with wrapt attention throughout this recital "What was your name?"

Murdoch was silent.

After a while he replied.

"What reason have you for asking?"

The other made a gesture of impatience.

"Never mind," said he. "Keep your secret, I was wrong in asking it. When you know me better, it will perhaps be otherwise."

"You must allow," said Murdoch, "that I have sufficient cause for caution. You are, besides, a perfect stranger to me, except by name."

"Has Faversham, as you call him, ever told you how he and I were connected."

"Yes."

"He has told you how he urged me on to commit a thousand crimes and follies, and at last obliged me to commit the crime for which I have ever since suffered—which has made me an outcast on the face of God's earth."

"Yes."

"He has told you who was my victim?"

"He has told me all."

"And you are willing to be revenged on him?"

"If you will show me the way, and if—"

"If what?"

"There is not much danger."

"On the contrary."

"There is gain, perhaps."

"There is wealth."

"Give me your orders, then. Tell me what to do. Command me. I will be your servant."

"No," replied the other, "we will work together. But we must be cautious. We have one to deal with who is as crafty and as unscrupulous as Satan himself. We must wait patiently for an opportunity, and then strike the blow without fear or pity."

———

XI.—Which proves, if there was previously any doubt of the fact upon the reader's mind, that Charley Wag is an incorrigible young vagabond.

WHEN Charley fell out of the window, he lay for several seconds on his nose in the middle of the flower-bed.

The impression upon that volatile young gentleman's mind, was that it was all over with him.

He had been hit to a certainty.

The only question was where.

It seemed to Charley at first, that the pain was general. He was hit, as it appeared to him, everywhere at once.

After a few seconds he began to get his senses.

He was wounded in the left arm, and not very seriously. His arm was not broken, at any rate, for he could raise it up.

As soon as he had made this discovery, it occurred to him that he had better change his quarter.

The sound of the report of the pistol, had alarmed some of the neighbours. It seemed a wide straggling street, thinly populated, and that by detached villas, at about eighty or a hundred yards distance from each other.

The houses on either side was luckily to let, and empty, but the noise had alarmed the inmates of a house nearly opposite, and some one had thrown up a window, and was staring out.

The window above Charley's head was also open, but as Charley lay close to the wall, the people above could not catch sight of him, although for that purpose they were leaning out and waving a candle to and fro.

He heard the man-servant's voice say.

"I can't see him, my lord. Shall I go out and see?"

Then the duke answered.

"No. I don't want any disturbance. I have winged him, and that's enough. He just got the strength to creep off, I suppose. Let him go."

Then the window was shut down again.

But Charley said to himself.

"Mr. Wag, this is anything but a dignified position that I find you in. What do you propose to do, if you please? Suppose you take your nose out of that flower-pot, and consider."

A CRUSHER

He did so.

Then continued—

"If you try, young man, it is very probable that you will be able to stand on your legs, and take yourself off."

He climbed on to his feet slowly, and stretched himself.

"But will you do so," he continued. "What should I say about you—what would your friends say about you—what would the public say about you when your history comes to be written—if you were to pursue such a course? No, sir, it won't do. You have got a young lady into trouble, and you must do your best to get her out of it."

Then he brushed the dirt off his knees.

"The only question is, how.—Well we shall [CHARLEY WAG, THE NEW JACK SHEPPARD

see what turns up. One thing is sure, and that is, that there must be no running away."

Being determined upon this point, Master Wag looked fiercely up at the window and listened.

In the meantime the duke had dismissed his servants to their sleeping apartments, and was now alone with Julia.

"Well, madam," said he.

The young lady was very beautiful, but very disconsolate.

Very few ladies like to be caught tripping, however much they may be inclined to trip.

Julia did not exactly know what to say or do.

She wanted first of all to know how the duke was going to take it.

No. 30.

She was not very fond of the duke. He was such an awfully ugly old man, that it would be rather difficult to conceive the notion of anybody being fond of him.

But then he was enormously rich.

He was not the sort of protector that a woman with any sense would have abandoned easily, and without a struggle.

But what was she to say—what excuse was she to give?

There is no excuse for some things, and this seems to be one of them.

She therefore sat without saying a word, with her back hair hanging down, and her pretty face hidden in her hands.

As she had nothing to say, and as it is much easier, as every lady knows, to cry than to talk reason, she set to whimpering as hard as she could.

" Well," said the duke again.

She made no answer.

" Well," said he, for the third time.

Julia sobbed a little louder, but still made no answer.

" You don't suppose, I hope," continued the duke, " that I am going to look over this."

" Look over what?" asked Julia, between her tears.

" Over your conduct, madam."

" What conduct?"

" Don't talk folly, you know well enough to what I allude. To this young man."

" What of him?"

" What of him. Damnation! What was he doing in your room?"

" He wasn't doing any harm."

" Wasn't doing any harm, indeed. If he wasn't it was only because I did not give him time to do so."

" No it wasn't."

" Oh, then you pretend you are innocent."

" Yes; it was an old friend of mine who had come to see me."

" Oh, indeed, and what for?"

" To have supper."

" When I was out."

" He didn't know you were out."

" He didn't want to see me, that's very certain."

" Yes, he did."

" Oh, he did, did he, then, pray what made him get into the cupboard as soon as I came in. That was a funny way of behaving, if his intentions were honourable."

" He got in because I told him to do so."

" Why?"

" Because I thought you would be angry, and that perhaps you would go away again."

" Oh, you thought I would go away again."

" And then I could send him away quietly."

" But as I did not go away, why did you not tell me that he was in the cupboard?"

" Because I was afraid, and I saw how strange you would think my conduct."

" Yes, yes, this is all very fine, Miss Julia, but I'm too old a bird to be caught with chaff. 've only one objection to your story."

" What's that?"

" That I don't believe a word of it. '!

Julia began to cry louder than ever.

" There—there," said the duke, impatiently.

" There's quite enough of that. There is only one thing left."

" What's that?" asked Julia, with a sob.

" That's for you to go," replied the duke.

" Go," sobbed Julia.

" Yes," replied the old man sternly ; "you do not suppose that after this I am going to support you any longer. You must go—"

" Where ?"

" Where you like."

" When ?"

" Now."

" Oh dear, oh dear, oh dear !" cried Julia, " how cruel of you to send me away in the middle of the night."

" Look here, my dear," replied the duke, smiling savagely. " You don't suppose that I am going to keep you and your lovers to any extent. If you had chosen to behave well to me I should have behaved well to you; you didn't, and there is an end of the matter. Put on your bonnet and shawl, and here is five pounds. Now go and do what you like."

At this address Julia fired up.

She saw that no particular good was to be done by whimpering.

" You're a monster," said she, jumping up.

Then she dressed herself with energy.

When she was ready, the duke handed her the money, but she pushed back his hand.

" You'd better take it," said he.

But she refused, and as he still held it out towards her, she gave his hand a slap and sent the money spinning.

Then she flounced out of the room.

The duke laughed.

It would have been wiser had he not done so.

Women, as a rule, will stand a great deal of ill-usage, but they don't like to be laughed at.

They won't stand that at any price.

It was not to be supposed that Julia would either.

Up to now she had been rather ashamed of herself, and this little show of defiance was, in reality, only to cover a strong inclination she felt to burst out a crying.

But when the duke laughed, her indignation burst out.

" What are you grinning at, you ugly old wretch ?" she demanded, fiercely.

" At you," responded the duke.

" At me," she cried. " Then I'll give you something that will make you laugh the other side of your face.'

And so saying, she flew at his lordship more like a wild cat than a young woman, and catching the unfortunate nobleman by the two ears, shook him out of the flaxen wig which during the little dispute with Julia, he had been carefully arranging at a glass.

Then in spite of his shrieks for assistance, she kept on shaking him until the poor old profligate, opening his mouth very wide to bawl for mercy, let his beautiful double set of teeth jump out from between his jaws, like a great white frog.

You can imagine what were the old gentleman's feelings.

He always tried to keep those little secrets of his toilet inviolate.

He could hardly prevent her knowing about his wig, because it was such an evident wig.

A wig there was no mistake about.

A wig that seemed to say, in every curl and every twist,

"I'm an imposition and a sham,—I don't belong to this gentleman's head any more than his boots do—I don't grow here, bless you, any more than grass."

A wig which was altogether of so unnatural a cut and colour that its fraudulency was palpable at the first glance.

He had almost come to the same conclusion himself,—at least when I say that, I mean it had occurred to him as possible that any person living with him continually, and occupying the same bed, might in the course of a few years, ascertain its falsity, and so he put the best face he could on the matter, and owned it to himself.

But with his teeth and wadding, and complexion, it was different.

He never for a moment imagined that any one but Twiddle, his valet, knew how these little matters were managed, and you may suppose the liberty this passionate young woman had chosen to take with his grinders, he concluded altogether unpardonable.

It was certainly the most foolish thing she could have done.

The reader, thinking not, perhaps, fancies that in her place he would have like to have served out the horrid old scamp like she did.

But stop a bit. I will tell you why it was foolish.

The fact is, that the old duke really was much attached to Miss Julia. .

She had attracted his notice at Muggings' Music Hall, and he had gone to some considerable expense in establishing her.

Until now he had never been able to catch her tripping, and so confident had he become of her faithfulness, that he had in his exultation promised the servant a five pound note if he would let him know of the smallest frailty, and the booby had kept his eyes open, and run after the duke at the very first opportunity, though one might have supposed that he would have found it much more to his advantage if he had kept it a secret, as it might have been to his interest that the establishment should not be broken up.

Yes, the old gentleman most certainly loved her.

Even when he was, as it seemed, driving her out of the house in this indignant fashion, he in his heart intended that she should not go.

He meant to frighten her, that was all.

But now?

Now it was different.

She had outraged decency. She had hurt him in his most sensitive spot. She had shaken out his teeth, and he was determined he would have vengeance—nothing but vengeance.

Releasing himself with difficulty, the old man sat upon the floor where he had tumbled, and shook his fist at her.

"Chow-chow-chow," said he.

When his teeth were out he could not speak intelligibly.

"Do you want any more?" asked Julia.

"Chow-chow-chow."

"Because you shall have it."

"Chow."

"Oh, you do, do you?"

"Chow-chow-chow."

The old man waved her off in excited pantomime, though he could not make her understand what he wanted to say.

She, however, seemed to be satisfied with what she had done, and no longer desirous of inflicting further punishment upon his dilapidated old carcase.

She therefore desisted from any further attack, and, giving him a parting glance of withering contempt, flounced out of the room.

The servants were in the passage below, but they got out of her way as she came down stairs, and hid themselves in the dining-room.

Then she opened the street-door, and went out.

Before she had gone half-a-dozen yards, she met Mr. Wag.

"Hallo!" said he.

"Hallo!" said she in reply, very naturally.

"That isn't you, is it?"

"Well, if it isn't, it's you, anyhow."

"Where are you going?"

"I've no idea."

"Have you had a row with the old chap?"

"Slightly."

"Do you mean to say he has turned you out?"

"It looks very like it—doesn't it.?"

"What an old brute!"

"I quite agree with you."

"Why, it's monstrous!"

"So it is, but it can't be helped."

"Are you going away like this, then?"

"What would you have me do—go back?"

"Well, no—not exactly. I would rather you come with me. I can take care of you quite as well as he can, I'll be bound, only—"

"What?"

"Do you mean to say he turned you out of doors without a farthing in your pocket?"

"I don't want his money. Haven't you got money enough to keep me?"

"I don't say I haven't; but you ought to have had something out of the old screw. Not that I care a halfpenny about it, and as far as I am concerned, would rather you have nothing; but it's the principle of the thing I look at."

"Well, there's something in that."

"You see he has got all the laugh on his side."

"Well, he wasn't laughing when I left him, because I knocked it out of him."

"Did you hurray. Let me go and knock it out of him again."

"No, don't."

"Well, all right—but I say. Haven't you brought away any of those jewels you wore at supper?"

"No; I wish you had."

"It is a pity, certainly. However, it can't be helped. Let's be off."

She walked towards the gate.

Then Julia stopped.

"Charley," said she.

"Yes."

"I know you are courageous!"

"Pretty well, as times go."

"Would you mind running a little risk for me?"

"Name the risk, and I'll run it."

"I was sure of that, Charley. You are a brave fellow. How can I reward you?"

"Oh, you know how. I'll take a kiss on account."

"Be quiet—do. We haven't any time to waste."

"Well, what do you want me to do?"

"I'll tell you, if you'll be quiet."

"Go on, then."

"I want you to climb back in at that window —it's not very high up, you see—and get me my jewels."

"Isn't the old man there?"

"I don't think so, because, you see, the light is down below."

"Certainly it is. I did not notice it, though for that matter, I don't care very much whether he is there or not. I would soon settle his hash for him."

"Don't you hurt him though, Charley."

"No, you may trust me. Where shall I find the jewels?"

"I daresay they are all lying in the bed-room on my dressing-table. I put them there when I took them off."

"Will you wait here?"

"Yes."

The window he was going to get in at, was in the shadow of the house, and now the lights were extinguished inside, was scarcely discernable.

Charley was an astonishing climber, as you know already.

He was up like a bird.

As Julia looked after him, he seemed to be clutching at the wall by the extreme points of his nails.

To be hanging on, as the saying is, by his eyebrows.

He was up to the window-sill in less than three seconds.

Then balancing himself like another BLONDIN, he managed to get the window up, and presently crept into the room.

Julia stood gazing up at him.

Suddenly she heard heavy footsteps behind her.

She turned.

It was a policeman.

A policeman she knew by sight, one whom she had frequently seen as she returned from some place of amusement late at night, in company with the duke or her servant, upon his beat before the house.

She had, also, on one or two occasions given him a glass of spirits by way of conciliating him, and to induce him to keep a sharp look out upon the house, as it was so lonely a neighbourhood.

He, therefore, knew her well.

When she turned round to see who it was, the light from a gas-lamp at the edge of the path fell full upon her face.

"Good evening, ma'am," said he.

"Good evening," she replied hastily.

"Keeps warm, ma'am, don't it?"

"Yes."

"Can't you make them hear, ma'am?"

"Thank you. I don't want to."

"Not going in, ain't you, ma'am."

"No; I'm going out."

Anxious to cut short the loquacity of the fascinating policeman, who seemed to wish to prolong the conversation, she brushed by him and walked up the street.

But she did not want to go far, because of Charley, who she was every moment afraid would make his appearance at the window, or perhaps jump down into the garden.

She did not want the policeman to stop any longer on this account, and she did not want to go very far away, for fear Charley should miss her.

She, therefore, walked away, perhaps twenty yards, and then turned round.

The policeman was looking after her.

She proceeded ten yards further.

Then turned again.

The policeman was still looking after her.

Another ten yards.

Another look.

Same result.

What was to be done? She slowly proceeded on her way, turning every instant.

At last she lost sight of him.

But where had he gone? I will tell you.

If you must know the truth, this policeman was unlike the rest of his brethren, no more than mortal.

This policeman, was, in fact, susceptible to the allurements of the opposite sex. He had a weakness for the ladies, I am sorry to say.

I wish, for my part, that everybody in the world was good and virtuous, and that there were no bad characters, because, as I have often explained to you, I draw my people exactly as I find then; I have to show you them as ugly as they really are, because, if I were to touch them up, and make them as I should like them to be, you wide-awake ones would be calling out that they were unnatural.

Well, as I was saying, this policeman being something of a Don Juan in a small way, had conceived a ridiculous and presumptious passion for Julia.

He knew that that young lady was no better than she should be, and so, I suppose, he thought there was a chance for him.

He was a ruddy faced Yorkshireman, with mutton chop whiskers, and a big brawny chest, and he thought no small beer of himself.

"What's she up to, I wonder," said he to himself. "No good, I suspect. Where can she be going at this time of the night?"

Then, when he saw that she kept turning round every minute, he said to himself:

"She's waiting for some one, pephaps, and wants to get rid of me."

He began to puzzle his head for reasons to account for her singular conduct.

"She's up to no good, anyhow," he decided. Then,

"I'll hide somewhere, and wait till she comes back," he remarked to himself, with a grin. "When I know what is her little game, I shall have her in my power."

With this amiable motive he retired under the shadow of the house, close under the window where Charley had got in to steal the jewels.

Our young hero, while this was doing, was busy at work inside, as you may suppose.

He found the sitting-room and bed-room empty, and began to search for the jewels.

After a good deal of groping about in the dark, and a good deal of bumping and shin-breaking against divers articles of furniture, he came upon the objects of his search at last, as Julia had described, lying upon the dressing-table.

He gathered them all together, without being able to make any choice, and, cramming them into his pocket, began to think of beating a hasty retreat.

There was not a sound to be heard below.

Perhaps the duke had gone to bed in some other room, he thought; or he might be engaged in some way or other. Anyhow, there was not the slightest movement that he could hear.

He felt his way towards the window, which he had left open behind him.

Felt his way cautiously and noiselessly.

Then put out one leg, and then the other, and began to descend as quietly as a cat.

"This is the place," thought the policeman below. "She can't see me, and I can see her when she comes back, and I don't think I could have picked upon a better—"

SMASH.

Just when he got thus far in his soliloquy, Charley's foot alighted on the top of his hat.

It sent it right over his eyes.

A regular "crusher," and no mistake.

"What the devil's that?" cried the policeman.

XII.—THE PREMIER OF ENGLAND BEHIND THE SCENES.

WHEN the duke had sufficiently recovered from the effects of the shaking which Julia had given him, to be able to trust himself in the street, a condition at which he only arrived after the servant had administered to him a good stiff glass of brandy and water and a piping hot leg of deviled chicken; he took the man's arm and proceeded up the street, in quest of some vehicle which was to convey him to his mansion in Park Lane.

When he got outside the house there was nobody to be seen.

Neither Julia, Charley, or the policeman were visible.

Neither had the duke or the three servants within been disturbed by any noise outside.

Whatever had transpired had transpired noise-lessly.

What it was, and what has become of our hero, I must tell you presently.

In the meantime it is necessary that I should accompany my lord upon his travels.

They found a cab at the end of the road, and the duke got inside.

Then directed the driver to take him home.

Arrived there he was not long before he was tucked up in bed.

But he could not sleep.

The shaking he had had was sufficient to up-set him, and besides the infidelity of Miss Julia had considerably annoyed him.

Perhaps not so much because he had liked, or as because he did not like to be deceived, though he most certainly had had more than a passing weakness for the pretty hussy.

Altogether he was not sorry when morning came, and he could get up.

He was not in the habit of rising very early —eleven o'clock being his usual time.

Then Mr. Twiddle, his valet, waited upon him and served him with a new-laid egg beaten up in brandy.

About half an hour afterwards he got up.

Then his toilet commenced.

Allow me, ladies and gentlemen, to introduce you to a lord with his wig off.

For that matter, with every thing off, for he is going to take a bath.

The bath was always in readiness for his lord-ship, and his lordship looked an awfully skiny, yellow, wrinkled, and unnatural old goblin, when he stripped off his shirt and stood ready to step into it.

He had two baths every morning—one was beef-tea, the other rose-water.

Yes, reader, it is not a misprint, His bath was of beef-tea.

The doctors had recommended it as strength-ening.

It is sometimes used in cases where patients are unable to take nourishment in the usual way, not that that was the case with the duke, but his grace had led such a wild and profligate life, that he now required every imaginable stimulant to keep up what little life he had left in him.

He sat in the beef-tea bath for about half-an-hour.

Then he got out and got into a bath of rose-water.

After this he sluiced his mouth with CONDY'S DISINFECTANT, diluted with water. One of the most astounding cures, by the way, for that peculiar complaint called "hot coppers," which has ever been discovered, and not an expensive investment either, for you youthful profligates, seeing that you can get enough for fifty doses for sixpence.

After this his teeth was given him, after hav-ing been carefully washed and brushed.

Then his wig, beautifully curled and per-fumed.

Then his clothes, with all his pads, and the stays, and knee-caps, &c., which my lord's de-lapidated constitution required, before he could assume that sprightly frivolity for which he had been celebrated during the last sixty years or more.

When he was dressed all but his coat and boots, he put on a splendid dressing-gown of brocade satin, and had his breakfast, and the morning paper brought to him.

While he partook of some choice delicacy, which was almost worth its weight in gold, some hot-house fruit, or vegetable purchased in Co-vent Garden Market, a tiny morsel of boiled chicken, or some similar food and a bumper of sparkling Moselle, he read an account of the doings in the house the previous evening.

He read what he himself had said, and how some noble lord had agreed, or disagreed with him upon the subject under discussion.

He also read a leader or two praising or abus-ing his policy. Sometimes he saw himself styled a traitor, and sometimes the saviour of his country. He cared very little what he was called.

He was the premier of England, and the richest man in England.

He could afford to be hated, and he did not put himself much out of the way to be loved. However, of course, he had a certain position to keep up, and though he was, without exception, the most horrible old sinner unhanged, his villainies were mostly kept out of sight, and under the rose.

While taking his breakfast, and between the paragraphs in the paper, he contrived to carry on a little conversation with Twiddle, the valet.

"Has any body been this morning?" he asked.

"There has been a deputation of builders' workmen here, my lord."

"What, those striking fellows, eh?"

"Yes, my lord."

"What did they want?"

"They said a great deal, my lord, but I didn't take particular notice."

"Well, tell them I am always most willing to see them."

"Yes, my lord."

"Say that the interests of the working man are the interests dearest to my—what do you call it?—nearest to my heart."

"Yes, my lord."

"Say that whatever I can do for them I will do, but that they must give me time; I have so much on my hands."

"Certainly, my lord."

"Tell them to call again."

"When, my lord?"

"Whenever they like, and as often as they like."

"Will your lordship see them?"

"See them, Twiddle? Why what the devil do you suppose I want to see them for?"

"No, my lord—certainly not. I did not suppose your grace would wish to do so."

"Of course not. I never wish to see them, and never mean to do so; but you wouldn't have me tell them so, surely."

"No, my lord."

Here the duke went on reading his paper in indignant silence.

Looking up presently, he asked:

"Has anybody else been?"

"The Bishop of London called, my lord."

"What did he want?"

"He wanted your lordship to head a subscription for the destitute poor of the metropolis."

"Curse the destitute poor!—what are they to me? I didn't make them destitute. However, I suppose I must. Just find out what's the least I can give without looking shabby, and I'll send it."

Then he went on with his paper with a groan.

"Any one else?" he asked.

"Mrs. Crowe, my lord."

"Eh—indeed? Why didn't you keep her? I hope you were very polite."

"Yes, my lord."

"I've always said she is to come in whenever she calls, and that I'm always at home to her?"

"I thought you were so ill this morning, my lord."

"Ill!—who the devil says I'm ill? Ill!—what do you mean? What right have you—how dare you say I'm ill?"

"I don't say you're ill now, my lord," replied Twiddle, with great tact. "I never saw you heartier. I said, my lord, I thought that you were ill; but now I see that I was mistaken."

"Mistaken—of course you were. Don't make the same mistake again, that's all. And pray what did the lady want?"

"She said she wouldn't wait to see your lordship."

"Didn't she leave a message?"

"Yes, my lord, she left this."

So saying, Twiddle handed his grace a small note, written on pink paper.

The duke opened it, and read as follows:—

"Dear H.,—You always said that I might count upon you when 'up a tree.' Those intolerable donkies the parish authorities have taken it into their heads to indict me—at least, so I am led to believe.

"A word from you will silence them. I am sure that you will speak it.

"Awaiting your reply, I am yours till death,
            "'MOTHER CROWE.'

"P.S.—I have something delicious from the country, if you will give me a call."

After the duke had finished breakfast, and had been neatly packed in his blue frock-coat by the assiduous Twiddle, he walked down to the House and began business.

Throughout the day was his grace occupied discussing certain grave affairs of state. To see him so engaged, you would never for a moment have supposed that the same man could have been capable of the filthy attrocities which were attributed to him.

He was such a clear-sighted, far-seeing, meditative, contemplative, respectable gentleman.

Nobody would have supposed that the same man could have been the hero of the Haymarket, the patron of the brothels, the supporter of vice in every shape, which, in reality my lord duke of Heatherland was.

How it amuses me sometimes to hear, mind, middle-class families talk of such men as these. Long-headed, sober-sided fellow, they picture them giving all their minds, and a little more besides, to the arrangement of the affairs of the nation.

We men of the world know better, eh, my young friend Wildoats, we don't believe in these old fogies, do we? We know very well what the governor gets up to of a night after he has seen us home and said good night to us.

But after all the world is a very good world in its way, but you must not try to make it out better than it is, because we others know better.

When his lord duke had done his day's work, he turned his steps towards Mrs. Crow's mansion in Westminster.

He had settled the fate of several insignificant foreign states, he had voted in favour of a new tax, and he had suggested with his usual cheerful flippancy, some new and iniquitous scheme for oppressing and grinding down the already over-oppressed and ground down working classes, he had had a good dinner and a glass or two of good wine, and he felt—it is an awfully audacious thing to say of the primier of England, but it must be said, nevertheless—a little larkey.

Well, then, my lord lit his cigar and took his way towards Mrs. Crowe's establishment, anticipating considerable pleasure from what Mrs. Crow had promised him in the postcript to her letter.

XIII—The deserted Mistress—The Downward Course—The last Resource.

BUT before we accompany the duke to this abode of iniquity, we must go back to Miss Lucinda, whom we left with Leech the lawyer.

Leech, the lawyer, you must own, was scarcely the sort of person to whom one would have liked to have confided the destinies of an unsophisticated fat young maiden.

Poor Lucinda, how she came to listen to his seductive sophistry we will not enquire ; suffice it to say that she did lend a willing ear, and that, alas ! she fell.

This was bad enough, you will say, but yet worse remains to be told.

There was never, in all probability a meaner, nor a more sordid souled knave than this pettyfogging attorney. His unlawful desires were only equalled by his grasping avarice and dispicable meanness.

When first he had met her he had determined to possess her, and he had even some idea of keeping her afterwards for a short time as his mistress.

But having effected her ruin, he in the most cold-blooded fashion began to reckon up his halfpence, and to consider whether he was having proper value for his money, and whether he should tie himself to a woman, after he had gratified his passion.

Having well weighed the matter over in his mind, he came to the conclusion that in so doing he would be acting in a witless way.

He therefore determined upon throwing her up at the first convenient opportunity.

The opportunity occurred almost directly he had decided upon this shabby course of action.

Poor Lucinda, on the contrary, would have been very happy to have lived with him for the rest of her life.

She had at first laboured under some ridiculous delusion about his being a foreign nobleman, but having discovered her mistake, she soon settled down contentedly to her lot.

She was not really vicious, but she was very weak.

She had been brought up like the generality of girls, with a horror and dread of frailty, but in the strange position in which she found herself, she did not exactly see her way out of the dilemma into which she had fallen.

Leech had promised to marry her, and she hoped he would, only she did not like to bother him about it for fear he should change his mind, and she did not exactly see how she could compel him to abide by his word, should he see fit to alter his determination.

She therefore went on from day to day very happily, except at those moments when a misgiving crossed her mind that all was not quite as satisfactory as it should have been.

The fatal day soon arrived.

Leech was going into the country for a week or so about some legal business.

He thought it best not to make any formal leave-taking, but just quietly to take his departure.

He consequently went out one day after breakfast and never came back again.

He left directions with the boy at his chambers that he was not to tell Lucinda where he had gone.

He then took the train and went quietly down the line, smiling at his own scurviness, and reading the morning paper.

Poor Lucinda waited all that day and night very patiently.

Next day she became alarmed.

Surely something must have happened to him.

Then again she hoped that he might have been detained upon business somewhere or other, and obliged to sleep out.

She waited again as patiently as she could.

The landlady came up stairs in the middle of the day.

" Ahem ! I beg your pardon," said she. " Mr. Leech promised to settle for the rent this morning."

" He is out," said Lucinda.

" Dear me—is he ?"

" Yes."

" Hain't he been home all night ?"

" No—no."

" Lord bless me ! I hope nothing has happened to him."

" No, no," replied Lucinda, ready to cry. " I hope not—I should think not."

" Perhaps he has got into such pleasant company."

" I suppose so."

" Well, I hope he won't be long, for your sake."

" Thank you."

" What will you have for dinner, ma'am ?"

Lucinda felt in her pocket.

She had no money.

She had always been in the habit of paying beforehand for everything, and she was ashamed to ask for credit.

" I will not get anything yet," she said. " I will wait and see whether Mr. Leech returns."

" Very well, ma'am ; as you like."

The landlady left her.

Throughout the day she waited anxiously, but there was no sign of the missing lover.

She had had nothing to eat all day, and felt very sick and faint.

She must have some nourishment, however.

A thought occurred to her.

She would pledge something.

She had a ring on her finger, which she supposed must be worth something considerable.

She slipped on her bonnet and shawl, and left the house with a guilty glance behind her, as though she were about to commit a felony.

There was a pawnbroker's at the corner of the street.

Their lodging was in Pimlico, in the part nearest to Westminster.

She looked up at the three golden balls in a timid sort of way, then looked to the right and to the left, hesitated a moment, and finally decided that it was too near home.

She would try some more distant place, she thought.

With this idea, she walked on towards the Abbey, anxiously scanning the exterior of all the pawnbrokers she came to, and, one after the other, rejecting them for some reason, which she invented on purpose to delay the fatal moment as long as she possibly could.

At last, she began to feel fatigued with her long walk.

It was time that she decided upon a shop.

One was before her.

She would go in.

She therefore, with great caution, and much timidity, watched her opportunity, and slipped into the side door.

Then, after fumbling about a little time, found her way into one of the boxes.

The shopmen were at the moment engaged.

She waited silently until one chanced to notice her.

"What is it?" he asked.

"I want—that is—if you please."

"What is it?"

"To pledge this ring."

"It's too late."

"Too late?"

"An hour past the time. You must come again in the morning."

Poor Lucinda retired crestfallen, and went supperless to bed.

Next day, however, she returned to the charge.

This time she chose a shop a little nearer home.

In the same cautious fashion she had before adopted, she entered the side door, and opened the door of one of the little boxes.

"What is it?"

"This ring."

"What do you want?"

"How much can you give me?"

The man took it away and tested it.

Presently he returned.

Lucinda's heart fluttered with anticipation.

The man laid it on the counter with a smile.

"It's not gold," said he.

Lucinda felt ready to sink into the earth.

"What can you lend me on it?" she asked, faintly.

"A shilling," said the man.

"I will take it."

The man made out the ticket, and Lucinda, having given her name in great terror, retired with elevenpence halfpenny, the net proceeds of this little transaction.

When she reached her lodgings she had not had time to take off her bonnet before the landlady entered the room.

"Mr. Leech hasn't come back, I suppose?"

"No."

"I hope he will come."

"Of course he will," replied Lucinda, indignantly.

"Parties don't come back though, sometimes, when they go away. I've had lodgers as haven't before now."

"I do not understand you," replied Lucinda; "please to leave the room."

"If you comes to that," said the landlady, "I don't intend to wait much longer for the rent you owe me."

"As soon as Mr. Leech comes home, I will pay you."

"Oh, I don't know anything about Mr. Leech, as you call him, but I want my money by four this afternoon, for I have got my own landlord to settle with, and I don't want to keep other people out of their money, though other people don't seem to care how long they keep me."

Lucinda said nothing.

Her heart was bursting.

How could she reason with this vulgar wretch.

The landlady, however, was not satisfied with her silence.

"You heard what I said, I suppose?" she repeated.

Lucinda made no reply.

"You heard what I said?"

"Yes, and you can go."

"I will go," said the landlady, "and so shall you, my fine madam, if you are not ready with the rent when I come in again."

Left to herself, Lucinda tried to look her position in the face.

That mean scamp certainly did not intend to return.

She was then left upon her own resources.

What should she do.

She saw nothing before her but one course, at the bare contemplation of which she shuddered with horror.

"No—no—no," she cried, flinging herself upon her knees, "not yet—not yet."

She had only a little brooch.

The question was, would it turn out to be worth any more than the ring?

It was extremely improbable.

However she would try.

She had no other clothes than those she stood upright in, so she could not very well part with them.

She thought she had anyhow better try the fate of the brooch, and she went.

They lent her eighteen pence upon it.

Almost at her wit's end, yet still hoping that Leech might have turned up, she hurried back to her lodgings.

The landlady met her upon the threshold of the door.

"Can you pay me my money?" she asked.

"I hope to do so to-morrow," Lucinda replied.

"To-morrow, eh?"

"Yes, to-morrow, or next day at the latest."

"And where will you get it?"

"I will write to my friends."

"Oh, yes, I daresay; but I can't wait. I've let the rooms while you've been out; so you can take yourself off. And, what's more, you may thank your stars that you've got a tender-hearted person to deal with, or else you might have fared worse."

With this, the woman banged the door in Lucinda's face.

This cruel calamity reduced the poor girl to despair.

She turned away from the house, and wandered, without purpose, in the streets, utterly prostrated by her misfortune.

She had not eaten anything since the morning.

She was dreadfully hungry.

Night was coming on.

She felt chilled and wretched.

THE MYSTERIES OF THE PHOTOGRAPHIC BUSINESS.

But she had not a penny in her pocket. Nor did she know how she could get one.

The darkness increased.

The cold grew more intense, as she grew weaker and hungrier.

Hour after hour slipped by, and at length midnight was proclaimed by the iron tongues of Babylon.

She found, at length, a sheltered door-step, where she could sit and rest for a while, and here, huddled together as warm as she could make herself, she fell asleep.

She did not know how long she remained thus unconscious.

It might have been for a few minutes, she thought at first.

It was probably several hours.

When she awoke, she was lying in a strange bed, in a room with which she was totally unacquainted.

The daylight was pouring in upon her between the window curtains, and she could see that the apartment was magnificently furnished.

One circumstance certainly caused her some uneasiness.

The subjects of the pictures and statues ornamenting the room, were of a character which one would not have expected to find in any respectable house.

Where could she be?

Perhaps at some man's rooms.

On the table lay a half smoken cigar, and a half finished bottle of wine.

[CHARLEY WAG, THE NEW JACK SHEPPARD

When she was wondering about these and other matters, the door opened.

———

XIV.—WHAT BEFEL LUCINDA IN THE MYSTERIOUS HOUSE OF WHICH SHE FOUND HERSELF AN INMATE.

IT was a stoutish, showily dressed woman, who approached the bed.

"Well, my dear," said she, "how do you find yourself this morning?"

"Pretty well, ma'am, thank you," replied Lucinda.

"Well, you look a great deal better," said the stout lady, "than you did last night."

"Last night!"

"Last night, when me and my husband picked you up at the corner of the street. You looked as if you hadn't got half an hour's life in you."

"My dear madam," said Lucinda, her eyes filling with tears of gratitude. "How kind—how noble-hearted you must be, thus to help a poor homeless girl."

"Tut—tut," replied the stout lady, blushing slightly. "Not at all, my dear—not at all. I am always delighted to help any one who is in trouble. Come, dry your eyes, my dear, and tell me all your little story. How was it you were wandering about the streets last night alone?"

Lucinda was for a moment silent. She was ashamed of telling the real truth. But her hesitation was not of long duration. She had soon invented her story.

"I am an orphan, ma'am, and have just lost my place as Governess."

"How was that, my dear?"

"The family went abroad."

"But did they leave you destitute?"

"No; but I have been without a situation for a long while, and have parted with all my money and clothes."

"Then they turned you out of doors, I suppose, because you could not pay your rent."

"Yes, ma'am."

"And what is you name, my dear?"

Lucinda was just on the point of inventing a new one, when the recollection that her pocket contained a couple of pawnbroker's duplicates, with the name of Lucinda Leech upon them, flashed across her mind, and she gave that.

It might have been fancy; but she thought that she noticed the stout lady's eyes twinkle at the information, as though a weight were off her mind, and that some suspicion which she had hitherto entertained respecting the truth of Lucinda's story was completely cleared up.

She had no doubt, thought Lucinda, been examining the contents of her pockets.

This idea, at first, created some slight feeling of distrust in Lucinda's mind concerning the stout lady, but a moment's reflection sufficed to dispel it, for what could be more natural, than that the good lady should look into Lucinda's pocket to find some envelope or card, or something with an address upon it.

Luckily, the pawnbrokers ticket's had only the name of the street, but not the number.

"Well, my dear," said the stout lady, "make your mind quite easy. I will take care of you till you can get another situation, or until something else turns up, unless you would like to stop here and live with me."

"Oh, madam."

"However, that we can talk about presently. You must be dying for your breakfast, so you shall have it."

Saying this, the stout lady kissed her, and smiling very pleasantly, left the room.

"What a dear, kind creature," thought Lucinda as she lay back in bed.

Very shortly after the lady had left the room, a pretty servant-maid, who, however, looked rather pale and weary, and had untidy hair, as though she had been up very late the night before, and had not had too much time to spend upon her toilet, came into the room with breakfast.

This she spread upon a little table by the side of her bed, and poor Lucinda's mouth watered as she glanced at the delicacies, for of late she had been kept upon "short commons," as you know.

There was chocolate, buttered toast, sardines, marmalade, apricot jam, shrimps, and eggs.

Lucinda sat up in bed and did ample justice to the fare.

Meanwhile, the pretty servant stood yawning and looking at her.

"Will you take any more, miss?" she asked, when Lucinda had finished eating.

"No, thank you," the young lady replied. Then added:

"What is the name of the lady of the house?"

"Don't you know?" asked the girl.

"No," replied Lucinda, rather haughtily, "or I should not have asked."

"Her name's Crow."

"What is her husband?"

"Her husband?"

"Yes."

"Oh, he's a gentleman of independent means. Mrs. Crow keeps a boarding house."

Lucinda thought that the exhibition of further curiosity would have been ill-bred. She therefore asked no more questions.

When the girl had left the room, Lucinda lay back again in bed, and as she had not yet entirely recovered from the effect of the great fatigue which she had undergone on the previous day, she soon fell fast asleep again, and remained in this state for at least a couple of hours.

When she awoke, the stout lady had once more entered the room, and was standing over her.

"How do you find youself by this time?" she asked Lucinda with a good-natured smile.

"Thank you, madam," Lucinda replied. "Thanks to your kindness, I am quite recovered."

"You will get up, then."

"Yes."

"Your things were so damaged by the wet, my dear," continued the stout lady, "that you cannot possibly put them on."

"What shall I do, then?"

"Don't be alarmed. I have asked one of my young lady boarders—I have six—to lend you some of her things, and I have some others that will just suit you. So I want you to get dressed and come down to dinner, and I'll introduce you."

"Thank you, madam; but how can I repay your kindness?"

"Oh, I don't want to be repayed."

"But I cannot think of accepting these gifts."

"Ha, ha, ha!" laughed Mrs. Crow, merrily. "Now that's exactly what my husband said—he's the dearest man, is my husband; but you'll see him yourself soon, and can judge—he said to me, my dear, said he, you'll make Miss Leech uncomfortable, if you don't let her promise to pay you back. So there, what he says come true, and I'll tell you how you can pay me back."

"How?"

"Why, I know a lady who wants a companion, and you are, I can see, exactly the young lady to suit her, so when you get the situation, you shall repay me."

"I shall be most happy."

"That's all right, and so we shall make no mistakes. My husband drew me up a little paper, which you can sign, and then I will give you every thing you want, and find you in money and set you up."

"What shall I sign, madam?"

Mrs. Crow produced a slip of paper from her pocket as she spoke, and brought a pen and ink to the bed.

"I dont know, I'm sure," she said, laughing all the while. "Let me see, which is the right way up? That's it; put your name there, only give me a kiss first. Bless you!"

Lucinda was only too happy to show her gratitude in any way, so she took the pen and signed her name very readily.

It is true that she would liked to have read the paper; but that dear, good soul, Mrs. Crow, was kissing her all the while—was, in fact, literally smothering her with kisses, and she could not do so.

"You've just time to get dressed," said Mrs. Crow. "So I will leave you, my pet, and I will come back for you in an hour."

Lucinda, left to herself, commenced her toilet.

Some very beautiful clothes had been left for her. Perhaps the dress might have been a trifle too gaudy, and seemed more fitted for the stage than a drawing-room; but that was a matter of taste.

Lucinda dressed herself, and when she had arranged her hair, could not refrain from standing for a few moments to admire herself in the glass.

She had never before, to her thinking, been so beautifully apparelled, and she had never before looked so beautiful.

Most certainly she was beautiful. She was stout, it is true; but then mind you, it is only your bony maidens who dislike stout women.

Many gentlemen doat on them. Particularly the Turks, who, they say, fatten up their ladies with rice and rose leaves.

Yes, she was truly beautiful. She had dark, lustrous, languishing eyes, and rich, crimson,

pouting lips, full and moist like the inner folds of a rose-bud moist with dew.

And the curved neck, white as snow, rose from a soft-swelling bosom, of which the voluptuous fulness was lavishly displayed by the low bodied dress she wore.

"To think," said poor Lucinda, "that there are people who wear such clothes as these every day, and these beautiful necklaces and bracelets. These must be worth a great deal. Worth rather more, I should think, than those little jewels of mine."

Here she sighed at the recollection of the little broach and ring she had parted with.

"Never mind," she said. "It is not those that I value. I have not lost my locket."

As she spoke, she raised a golden locket from her bosom, which was attached to a tiny chain, and passionately kissed it.

"Yes, you are safe," said she. "And I will never part from you."

But while she was thus engaged, the door opened behind her.

She hurriedly hid it, and turned to meet Mrs. Crow, who entered at the moment.

"Well, my dear, are you ready?" asked the stout lady.

Lucinda assented, and they descended the stairs together.

In the room below dinner was laid.

The same profusion which Lucinda had noticed at breakfast was greatly exaggerated now.

Every description of delicacy was there, and the rarest wines.

The young ladies were introduced to her by Mrs. Crow. There were six of them, and they were all strikingly handsome, though to Lucinda's primitive notions — for you must remember, she had been brought up all her life in the country, and in great seclusion—their manners and language seemed to be of the boldest.

They partook, too, of the wine, in the freest possible fashion, and seemed to be used to drinking large quantities of it.

These things did not please Lucinda much, and when she came to glance round the room, the outrageous indecency of some of the oil paintings upon the walls shocked and alarmed her.

However, she endeavoured to persuade herself that it was more owing to her ignorance of the usages of polite society, than to any gross impropriety on the part of her new friends.

Meanwhile, the lady boarders became more and more free and easy, and the wine circulated, and conversation turning upon the tender passion, the lively creatures allowed certain words to slip from their lips which brought the blood in a hot rush into Lucinda's cheeks and neck.

Then as the conversation continued, and the profligacy of the speakers became more and more apparent, Lucinda fancied that the appearance of the young ladies, although they were all extremely beautiful, was very much against them.

They did not look modest.

They wore rouge, and excessively low dresses.

The youngest was perhaps fifteen, and the eldest twenty-one; but they wore a weary careworn look, something like what Lucinda had noticed in the pretty servant who brought up her breakfast.

What were they?

She asked herself again and again.

What were they?

They were too young, some of them, to be widows—at least, it was very curious if they were—and besides, they surely could not be widows.

If not, what else? How came they to live there together in this fashion?

I have told you before that Lucinda is a very green young lady.

Her companions all talked about their male acquaintances, and it appeared that a great number of noblemen and gentlemen were in the habit of visiting them there.

Shortly after dinner, there was a ring at the bell, and the servant announced that one of the young ladies was wanted, and a little while after that, several gentlemen arrived, and others of the young ladies were called out.

Lucinda, meanwhile, very unhappy in her mind, sat apart and tried to read a book, away from the rest, though with the noise that they made it was almost impossible.

Her suspicions by this time were seriously excited respecting the respectability of Mrs. Crow's establishment, though she tried to account for the strangeness of the " goings on " in every possible fashion.

At length, as the evening advanced, and Lucinda profoundly wretched, and greatly fatigued was still sitting alone, Mrs. Crow came in and announced that some young lords had come to supper, and would join them directly; then she came over to Lucinda, and said in a whisper :

"The most delightful young fellows, my love. All as rich as Jews, only a little wild. You must make yourself agreeable to them, my pet."

"But, madam," stammered Lucinda, "I am not accustomed—"

"Bah, child! that's all the better. You will get on well enough."

Lucinda would have wished to have made some objections to the intended festivities, but did not clearly see her way out of the dilemma.

While she was hesitating what she should say or do, the gentlemen entered the room.

Probably Mrs. Crow expected that she might not make herself quite so agreeable as could have been wished for, so she whispered something to the young men, which was no doubt a request that they would treat her with a little more respect than the other young ladies, as she was fresh at that sort of life.

Poor Lucinda scarcely noticed whether they treated her with respect or not; her fears of and her disgust for her companions increased every moment.

For some little time the supper party was conducted with some pretence of decorum, but as the wine circulated, all restraint was broken through.

Then followed a scene, which my pen is wholly incompetent to describe.

A scene of the most unbridled licentiousness.

A scene at which her soul revolted.

In the middle of it, and when it was at its height, when the company were screaming and howling, and mad drunk, dancing, and romping in the wildest and most hideous orgie, Lucinda sprang from the table, and tearing herself from the grasp of an intoxicated young nobleman, who, in a state of maudlin imbecility, was beseeching her to give an ear to his shameless proposals, she flew from the room, and locked herself in her own bed-chamber.

Here she lay trembling, and an in agony of fear until the morning.

———

XV.—In which His Grace the Duke of Heatherland feels rather ashamed of himself.

NEXT morning, when the girl brought up the breakfast, Lucinda asked to see Mrs. Crow.

"She's not up yet," replied the girl.

"I should like to see her when she does get up."

"All right, Miss. I'll tell her."

"There was a dreadful noise here last night."

"Was there? Not more than usual, I believe."

"When did those gentlemen go away?"

"Some of them's here yet, I believe."

"Oh."

Lucinda said no more.

She had quite made up her mind. There could be no doubt about it,

She was in a house of ill fame.

Poor Lucinda, when she was left alone, burst into an agony of tears and sobs, and tearing her hair, bewailed her unhappy lot.

What a horrible fate was this. How low had she fallen! But because she had become the victim of that despicable petty fogger, she was not altogether depraved. Yet it seemed as though now she had fallen, she must continue to sink.

There was nothing else left for her.

While she was yet crying, Mrs. Crow came into the room.

"What's all this about?" she asked.

Lucinda threw herself at the woman's feet.

"Oh dear, dear madam!" she cried. "Let me go—let me go while there is yet time. Oh, for God's sake let me go."

"Go where?" asked Mrs. Crow.

"To any where."

"To the workhouse, I suppose."

"Yes, rather than this."

"Oh, indeed, you're exceedingly grateful after all I've done for you. If it hadn't been for me, you'd most likely have been dead by this time."

"I know I should—I know I should, and I thank you."

"Well, then?"

"But it would have been better if I had died, than have lived for this."

"Oh, would it. Now pray what do want?"

"I want to go."

"You want to go."

"Yes."

"Do you?"

"Indeed I do."

"You know what sort of house you are in, I suppose?"

"Alas! yes."

"Alas? yes indeed! Why you're a little fool. Since you've found it out, it's all right. I didn't want to keep it a secret for ever. You made a great ass of yourself last night; but to-night you must do differently. I have promised you to an old gentleman, and so just don't be a booby."

"What?" shrieked Lucinda. "I will die first."

"Yes, I dare say; but I don't think so. You may die afterwards, when I have done with you, as soon as you like."

"Let me go," cried Lucinda, trying to leave the room.

But the woman pushed her back.

"If you leave here, you will leave for prison, my fine lady," said Mrs. Crow. "You forgot that paper you signed, I suppose?"

"What of it?"

"You'll find what of it, if I have much more of your cheek, so I tell you."

"But what claim have you against me? What have I signed?"

"You'll find that out all in good time, and now I warn you, don't make a fool of yourself when the old gentleman comes."

Lucinda said no more, but when the woman had gone, flung herself upon the bed and wept bitterly.

The day passed slowly by.

The servant came up several times.

Once to ask whether Lucinda would take some lunch; once to enquire whether she would not come down-stairs, and lastly, to say that Mrs. Crow desired that she would make her toilet, and make herself look as well as possible.

Poor Lucinda replied indignantly, that she would do nothing of the kind, and in a state bordering almost upon stupefaction, so terrible was her grief, she awaited what would happen.

She was lying weeping upon the bed, when Mrs. Crow again entered the apartment.

Lucinda had found the clothes which she had worn when she first came to the house in a cupboard in the room where she slept, and had put them on.

"Hey day!" cried Mrs. Crow. "How is it you're not ready?"

"Do you think, woman," Lucinda replied, "that I am going to assist at my own sacrifice?"

"Stuff and nonsense about sacrifices. Are you going to dress yourself?"

"No."

"You won't?"

"I won't."

"Then I'll have you dressed."

Then, Mrs. Crow, foaming with rage, left the apartment, and presently returned with an old woman, and a brawny ruffianly looking fellow, who was one of the bullies of the establishment.

Lucinda looked at them with terror, when Mrs. Crow again asked her whether she would dress herself.

As she replied in the negative, these wretches precipitated themselves upon the shrinking girl, and in spite of her screams and entreaties, stripped her of the clothes she wore, even to a state of nudity, and heedless of her struggles,

but with a variety of vile and brutal jests, arranged her in the softest linen and most costly satin the house could produce.

When her toilet was complete they left her alone.

An hour of suspense followed, and then she heard footsteps approaching the door.

Her heart beat fast with anticipation.

Then the handle turned, and the duke of Heatherland entered.

*   *   *   *   *

"Help, help, help!—Look at her—look at her, she is senseless—she is dead."

"No, it is only a fainting fit."

"She wants air."

"She wants water."

"Give her air, then."

"Let her smell my scent bottle."

"Chafe her hands."

"Has anybody some burnt feathers?"

It is Lucinda who is the object of all this solicitude. The most solicitous of the group, perhaps, the old man who has so brutally debauched her.

He leant over her and assisted the rest.

He laid his hand upon her heart, to ascertain whether it still beat.

A dull motion was dimly perceptible.

As he raised his hand again, however, his fingers caught in a tiny chain which she wore round her neck, and he dragged out a locket from her breast, where it had lain hidden.

"Great God!"

He had taken the locket in his hand, and was looking at it unconsciously.

Suddenly, his eyes dilated, his lower jaw dropped, his whole face changed to a leaden and ghastly hue, with intense horror.

"Great God!"

He started to his feet and reeled backwards, grasping wildly at the air, with his lean hands outstretched.

"My Lord—my Lord, what is the matter? What has happened?—are you ill?"

But he made no reply, only, sinking into a chair by the bed-side, shivered like one with the ague.

"Send for a doctor," cried Mrs. Crow in great terror.

She had not been the least alarmed by what had happened to Lucinda.

If she had died it would not have mattered very much—an obscure, unknown, friendless girl, like she was.

But it was different in the case of the duke —very different.

If the duke died, there would be a fuss about it, no doubt.

The manner and place of his death would certainly become public, and Mrs. Crow was far from being desirous of acquiring such a popularity for her house.

"Run for a doctor," she cried.

"No—no," replied the duke, faintly. "I am not ill. It is only a shock. Clear the room of all. I want to speak to you."

There was something awful in his face. He looked as though he had suddenly aged by twenty years.

In silent terror the women crept from the room.

None were left there but the duke, the

mistress of the brothel, and the wretched girl, senseless upon the bed.

"Tell me," Heatherland asked, in great agitation, "tell me where you found this poor child."

"I have told you, my lord."

"You have told me a pack of lies, woman," thundered the duke. "Now tell me the truth."

"Well, the truth is, then, I found her in the street."

"And what do you know of her?"

Mrs. Crow related all that Lucinda had told her.

"Nothing more?"

"Nothing more."

"Oh, my God!" the duke cried, wringing his hands in agony.

"Calm yourself, my lord," urged the woman. "What is there to make such a fuss about? It is not the first young girl by many that your grace has ruined."

"Peace, woman," the other replied.

Then raising his lean arms on high, he cried bitterly.

"Curses light upon me and upon this house, upon you and all such, for I have this day committed a crime which must blacken my soul for ever."

"What—what is it, my lord?" the woman asked with a white face.

The duke seized her by the arm.

His fingers pressed upon her flesh like the talons of a bird.

"Woman," he hissed in her ear. "I know her by the locket she wears. She is—"

"Yes—yes."

"She is *my own daughter !*"

As Mrs. Crow started back from him in horror, a knocking arose at the door.

The duke sprang to his feet.

"Keep them back—keep them back. Hide me," he cried, in a frenzy. "Do not let them see me."

But the hammering continued, and a voice cried :

"Some one wants to see the duke."

The duke fell down upon his knees, and his teeth chattered.

"My Lord—my Lord," whispered Mrs. Crow "Rouse yourself. Do not be afraid. Nothing will harm you."

But as he still remained upon the ground, and apparently bereft of all reasoning faculties, she turned and screamed for help.

Then the door opened, and the women came trooping back.

Among them was a sleek deferential individual in black.

"My name is Twiddle," said he ; "I am his grace's valet."

The duke looked up.

"What do you want, Twiddle?" he asked vaguely. "What's the matter, Twiddle? How is her grace, Twiddle? And my little boy—what has become of him?"

"Something serious has happened," said Twiddle, whose face wore a scared expression, and who had evidently travelled thither post-haste.

"What is it?" the duke asked.

He had risen to his feet, and seemed calmer, only that there was a vague frightened look upon him.

"My lady," returned the man, "as you left well and hearty at home two hours ago—"

"Well, what of her? Is she ill? is she—"

"Dead," replied the valet.

"Dead !" echoed the bystanders.

The duke stood entirely motionless, like a statue ; his mouth a little open, his eyes starting from their sockets.

Then he burst out crying feebly like a child, and, putting his hand through the valet's arm, was led from the room.

A mist came over his eyes, and he remembered or understood nothing of what passed around him.

He had an indistinct vision of people moving rapidly about him—of one grim face which was close to his.

Of passing down the staircase, of whisperings and rushings of groups around him, of the cool air of the street, of descending the steps.

Then of a bustling and pulling up of cabs and carriages close to the pavement, of horses plunging hither and thither, of faces which stared into his and then disappeared, of shouts, and loud calls, and the bustling of a crowd, of being lifted into a vehicle, and being carried away.

"What's the row?" he heard a voice ask.

"The Duchess of Heatherland's dead," replied another.

"What did she die of?"

"Poison."

"What ! murdered ?"

"Yes, so they say."

"Who's that old bloke ?"

"He's the duke."

"Was it him as done it ?"

"So I'm telled."

"Well, he'll get his neck stretched for that job, to a certainty."

Meanwhile, the carriage containing his grace drove onward, and he leant back in the carriage motionless.

Only his lips moved, and he repeated softly to himself,

"Murdered—murdered, and own daughter : it is the visitation of God."

XVI.—The commencement of the Plot.

IT is almost as difficult to get along with my *dramatis personæ* as it is to drive a flock of geese.

They are somehow such stragglers.

If I fetch one up to time, the others all lay behind. When I am doing justice by one, one or the other of the rest is being neglected.

We have left the duke in a very critical position, and we have left Charley with his foot on the head of a policeman. I feel inclined to go back to my hero, and should most certainly do so, did I not recollect that Rattan was being strangled several chapters ago, and that I have left him for an unconscionable time panting in the hands of his antagonist.

Therefore, upon mature reflection, and with

your kind permission, we will have a look at Rattan.

For some time did Faversham wrestle with him.

The other was as a baby in his arms.

In vain Rattan strove to maintain his ground against him.

Inch by inch he gave way, inch by inch he neared the door. Vainly he struggled and resisted, until at length, bruised and breathless, he loosened his hold upon the doctor's garments, and allowed himself to be dragged along in savage silence.

The other dragged him into the inner room, and, suddenly leaving go of him with his hands, flung him down upon his back with a stunning crash which half stupified him, and then planted his boot upon Rattan's breast.

"Now then," the doctor said coolly, "you're satisfied, I hope."

"Satisfied?" gasped the other.

"Satisfied that I am the master," continued Faversham. "Are you, or shall I give you a little more?"

"No."

"What do you mean?"

"I mean I've had enough," replied Rattan, surlily.

"Get up, then."

Rattan rose to his feet.

The other stood eyeing him attentively, although feigning an easy, careless manner.

He was making ready for a renewal of the struggle, if needed.

It was not. After a pause, Faversham asked:

"What brought you here?"

"Money," replied Rattan.

"You shall have it if you earn it. I want to act fair to you. Do you believe me?"

"I don't know."

"If you do not, you must be a fool. If I had wanted to harm you, could I not have done so a little while ago, when I had you shut up? There is no escape from that place. You might have rotted there with the rest, and no one been a bit the wiser. But I had no such intention. However, when I give you a chance, you try to escape, or to do me some injury I don't know what. Then, again, when I have you in my power again, instead of finishing you off, as most people would have done in my place, I give you your liberty."

"Yes," replied Rattan, rather impressed, "there's something in that."

"Something in it! Yes, I suppose there is. Now let me tell you, once for all, although I have let you off so far, by God I shall not do so if you play me false."

Rattan grumbled out something about wishing to act fair.

"I hope so," said Faversham; "I don't see why you should not. You want money, and I can give it you if you will serve me. First of all, answer me a question."

"Ask it."

"What has become of the man who was here?"

"What man?"

"Didn't you see one?"

"No."

Faversham looked at him for a moment or two.

"Well," said he, "I believe you. And now I will tell you what I want you to do. Take a seat."

Rattan did so.

"Have you ever heard of the Duke of Heatherland?" he asked.

Rattan's mouth and eyes opened, and he stared stupidly at the unmoved face opposite to him, behind which dim and awful thoughts seemed to move, thrilling through that warped and jarring, but awfully gifted brain.

There was a deep silence in the darkened room. At length Faversham spoke:

"You know him."

"No, I know nothing of him, except that he comes to my mother's house sometimes."

"What house?"

"Well, it's a little gay. It's in Westminster. All the nobs goes there."

"Is that all?"

"Yes."

"Then listen to my plan."

It matters little what the plan was at present, the reader will soon learn what was its effect.

Two days after it came into operation.

Two days after the duchess arrived in Park Lane, having travelled post-haste on receipt of a message by electric telegraph.

The message contained simply these three words,

HORFORD WANTS YOU.

XVII.—THE DRUG.

SHE travelled post-haste—she travelled express.

The fastest train went too slow for her; she was out of patience at the slightest delay. The fussy hindrances of the custom-house officials irritated her beyond all power of endurance.

But money can do a great deal. Money did do a great deal, and it brought her in an incredibly short space of time across the channel, across the country, and into town.

HORFORD WANTS YOU.

That was all the message said.

No answer was required, no address given; but it seemed that there was some mysterious magic in the words, for it brought her at once, without a moment's hesitation, without any delay, as fast as she could come by power of steam, to London.

Where was this Horford to be found who wanted her?

She knew not.

Perhaps at the railway station. She looked anxiously from the window, but saw no one.

She waited on the platform until the last, then ordered a cab, and drove to Park Lane. Yet Horford never came to speak to her.

But she supposed that he knew where to find her, and that he would come, and she waited patiently.

She had brought her child with her, for how else could she account for this mysterious and abrupt return?

She could not have come alone.

As it was, she ascribed it to a woman's fancy—a sudden desire for the duke's company.

The old man was rather flattered by it, and wished that he could have stopped at home with her. But he had business at the House (and at Mrs. Crow's) of great importance; so he could not.

Faversham, however, was there by some accident, and was delighted to see her.

He had dinner with her and his grace, and when the latter rose to go, the doctor, to her great dissatisfaction, still lingered.

She would gladly have been rid of his company, for he pestered her with endless inquiries concerning the reason of her sudden return.

At last, to her unspeakable relief, he took his departure, and she was left alone to her own reflections, and to the anticipation of some sign from the same quarter from which had come the message which had brought her home.

The evening was deepening fast, and a servant some time ago had lit the gas.

Despite of its gay furniture, the drawing-room in which she sat looked sad and gloomy by night. Her little boy had gone to bed fatigued, and she was necessarily left alone. She even more than once fancied, now that all was still, that low creaking noises proceeded from the wall, and that heavy footsteps sounded behind the panels.

She felt ill and depressed. Every moment she caught herself listening with suspended breath for the smothered noises which she fancied that she heard; then, with an emotion of impatience at her own childishness, she would rise, shake off the gathering feeling of lonesome awe, which she knew would fast deepen into fear, and, smiling at her own weakness, go stoutly on with some needlework on which she was engaged.

The dessert still lay on the table, and she filled herself a glass of wine.

After she had drank it a faintness seized her, as it had done before once that evening when she had tasted the wine; as it had done before, the feeling passed away.

She could not disguise from herself that she felt this evening more than usually timid and nervous.

Sometimes she almost regretted that she had not gone to the opera, or some place of amusement. She had almost made up her mind to go then, in spite of the sickly liquor, which oppressed her, and the desire she felt to hear more of Horford.

She thought of the gay house, the glitter of the lights, the peal of the music, and wished she was submitted to their inspiring influence.

Everything around her appeared to be more dark and luring than usual. The lamps burned dimly, shadows were piled within the corners of the room, and, as the curtains were moved by an occasional breath of wind from the half-opened window, she would shrink within herself, aghast and trembling at the light rustle of the damask.

An hour or more went slowly by.

Now and then the rumble of a passing vehicle struck with a dull force upon the ear, and anon the slight noises of the night floated into the room from the park.

Long and stoutly did the duchess struggle against the absorbing sensation of mingled fear and melancholy which seemed to encompass her as with a dim dark halo.

She had never before experienced so crushing, so overmastering a sensation, as that which now laid, as it were, a strong cold hand upon her spirit.

Dim forebodings—a restless, aching, indefinite sensation of dread, took possession of her.

Every moment she expected something awful or startling to happen, and yet what that something was to be she could not imagine or define.

In vain she racked her memory with vain efforts to recollect any similar attack of low spirits.

She could neither call to mind having ever before experienced her present sensations, or trace them to any reasonable cause.

She had frequently sat alone by night, where she sat now; but she had never before felt any fear.

She had sometimes felt a little nervous and excitable, perhaps; but on this particular occasion, everything like mental and physical energy seemed to have left her.

After a fruitless struggle, she surrendered to the over-mastering spell which bound her.

The work upon which she had been engaged, fell from her hands upon her lap.

Her eyes became dilated, and fixed upon the wainscotting opposite to where she sat, rigid and motionless. The evil spell which bound her seemed to have attained the height of its power.

All at once a low rumbling noise—faint, yet distinct—rolled through the room.

The lady heard it—for a slight start shot through her frame.

Her hands were clasped together with a convulsive energy.

Her eyes were glazed and dilated—her forehead damp, and her cheeks ashen white.

A minute passed away and the noise was heard again. A well oiled bolt was apparently shot back, and then the duchess saw, without any outward manifestations of terror, a slight longitudinal opening appear in the wainscot.

It gradually seemed to enlarge, and then the pannel slid quickly aside, showing a dark space behind, in which could be faintly discerned the forms of two men.

The foremost was tall and thin; his face was concealed by a black handkerchief twisted round his neck, and by a black crape mask he wore.

His companion carried a dark lantern, which flung a bright spot of light upon the opposite wall.

The duchess tried to scream, but her voice died in her throat.

The progress of fascination was completed by the intensity of the gaze which the foremost intruder flung on her from out his large, glittering eyes.

Step by step he advanced into the room.

"The preparatory portion has worked well," he muttered. "The system is in the state recommended for the success of the drug."

The man behind with the lantern remained motionless in the recess disclosed by the sliding panel.

THE STORM ON THE THAMES.

The duchess breathlessly followed the intruder with her eyes.

At length he stood opposite to her, and her bosom heaved, and her nostrils dilated, as she struggled madly against the torpor of fascination which was on her.

But the effort was fruitless.

The muscles relaxed, and she sank back, staring at the man before her.

Without moving his eyes from her, he slowly produced a phial from his inner breast coat pocket, and removing the ground glass stopper, poured the colourless contents into the wine glass which the duchess had used, and taking it up, said in low musical tones which thrilled through her frame, and somehow seemed strangely familiar to her:

No. 32.

"Drink this."

Then for the first time the intensity of fear combating successfully for a moment the effects of the potion which she now knew had been administered to her—though how or when she was not aware—she gasped:

"No, no, I cannot."

"You must," replied the other.

The duchess, by the effort of speaking, had for a moment partially broken the spell which clung to her. She waved her hand impatiently, and murmured:

"No, no, I will not. Leave me!"

The stranger crossed his arms upon his bosom, still holding the glass in his left hand.

Then, drawing himself up to his full height, he flashed his glaring eyes down into those of

[CHARLEY WAG, THE NEW JACK SHEPPARD.

his victim, while at the same moment, following a slight movement of his right hand, the duchess saw the glitter of a blade of steel shine out against his dark clothing.

It was either the tacit threat of violence, or the influence of the man's awful presence acting upon a nervous system artificially wrought into a state of confirmed excitement and weakness which again crushed the rallying energies of the hapless woman.

She shrank back, at the same time extending her hand for the glass by a mechanical motion; slowly, but with perfect steadiness she conveyed it to her lips, her eyes fixed upon those of Faversham.

His livid visage never stirred as she raised the draught to her lips, it showed not a trace of emotion or passion as she slowly drained the glass, but all the while the dreadful stare of his fierce eyes was never remitted until in about a minute after the duchess had swallowed the last drops of the potion, her face began to grow livid and to change its expression, and the muscles of the fingers gradually relaxed so that the glass first slipped into an horizontal position, and then fell and was shivered upon the floor.

At the same moment the head of the sufferer dropped upon her chest, and her limbs fell by their own gravity, in positions in which they either rested upon other portions of the body, or upon the chair.

Then Faversham uttered a low growl, and gazed with a look of passionate hate upon his victim.

All this time the accomplice stood within the recess, motionless.

Suddenly Faversham signed to him, and he flashed the lantern over the Duchess of Heatherland's face.

Faversham raised her head and placed it so as to be supported by the back of the chair.

He felt her pulse.

It had ceased to beat.

He placed a particle of down upon her lips, and not a feathery atom moved.

He passed his hand over her forehead.

It was cold and damp.

Then he carefully replaced the phial, the contents of which the duchess had swallowed, and produced another and a smaller one.

Glancing over the table, he selected a wine-glass, and half filled it with sherry.

Into the wine he poured about half-a-dozen drops of the colourless fluid contained in the phial.

Presently an acrid flavour, as of bitter almonds, rose into the room.

Faversham again looked round, until his eye caught an inkstand with paper and pens.

He took one of the latter and dipped the feathered end in the medicated wine and touched the lips of the lifeless woman with the fluid.

"In such a complete state of trance," he muttered, "there is no danger ere the absorbents can act, evaporation will have done their office."

XVIII.—THE TRANCE.

TO be dead in body—to be dead to all the usual tests of life—to be powerless, passive, cold, and yet to be alive to oneself—dimly and faintly, to be sure—but to be conscious of a torpid yet still lingering life, of a single spark-animating spirit, still glimmering, but unseen, unrecognised from without, glowing silently in the very depths of the physical nature.

Such were the horrible symptoms of the artificial state of catalepsy into which the potion swallowed at Faversham's bidding had flung the Duchess of Heatherland.

Outwardly and to others she presented all the phenomena of death.

Of all in the chamber, only she herself knew that death was not yet there.

The nerves of sensation still acted feebly and wearily, conveying, dim as it were, distinct impressions to the as feebly and wearily acting brain.

But the nerves of motion were utterly paralysed and dead.

One of the tearful attendants by chance lost her hold of the dead arm she was lifting.

It fell as so much wood upon the table, and only the seeming corpse knew that that arm fell against a will which still feebly existed in the inner tissues of the brain.

But that living spark of soul was like a wounded general without an army.

It could think and feel feebly and languidly, but could not act.

It could not by its operation signify its presence.

There was none to obey it.

It could only recognise itself—know itself—feel itself.

Outwardly all was blank, cold, dead, and those who stood terrified and weeping around would see before them but a moveless thing, from which the breath of life had gone out!

For some time after the administration of the drug, the duchess was utterly insensible—dead to the world—dead to herself.

A faint sound, like a distant scream, was the first sensation to cleave and stir the depths of her trance.

The cry appeared low, indistinct, raised by some one far, far away.

And yet it was loud, startling, piercing—uttered at her elbow—in her ear.

Then she was conscious of dark shapes rapidly moving round her, raising her from her chair, and placing her in a recumbent position.

Soon the dimly seen shapes became more distinct, for her eyes were yet open and staring.

They appeared men—strangers.

They hurried to and fro.

They mingled with female forms who thronged around.

There was a confused sound of whispering, and ejaculations, and sobs.

Hands were placed upon her forehead and her mouth.

A dim form bent long over her.

It seemed to place its head to hers.

It raised her hands, and then replaced them reverently by her side.

Meantime the other shapes stood around.

Then they turned to the table, and looked and lifted up glasses, which glimmered faintly, and the whispering arose again.

Presently the patient began to discern words and broken sentences.

At first they were but sounds distinctly heard.

Then a black shadow of meaning began to diffuse itself over her brain.

She began to comprehend that she was dead—gone away out of the world—that there was a gulf between her and the whisperings and the shapes.

These ideas rose up all shadowy, all incoherently, all dimly looming in spectral wreaths of thought.

But soon they began to take a certain order, a certain consistency, and she felt—she knew not how—that she was dead, yet alive.

It was a dark, indefinite, mysterious idea.

She could not understand it, she could not reconcile it, but there it was, overshadowing her as with a rent and disordered pall, through the holes in which she saw the world.

Then there was suddenly a movement in the now crowded chamber, and a shape she knew and a face she knew were over her.

She felt hot tears upon her face—she heard loud mournful sounds—she saw a circle of pale, woe-worn faces.

Then the hand of the shape she knew, gently closed her eyes, and all was darkness.

After this, the sounds and whisperings died away for a space, and there was silence.

Then came a half-understood consciousness that people were again around her.

She felt herself again raised and moved.

Busy hands lifted her limbs, and low voices sounded in her ears.

She could feel that some unaccustomed covering was being folded around her.

Then something soft and yielding, rose on each side of her head.

After a long interval of darkness and silence, the jaded and slumbering mind was aware that the passive form in which it dwelt was laid upon its bed.

Outward sounds soon attracted a feeble and disturbed attention, and at invervals the overthrown mind struggled faintly to hear them, and then to comprehend their meaning.

Sometimes it was low voices which would chime around the bed, and there would be a soft rustling, as though the curtains were gently drawn aside, and then the voices would sound more mournfully and more near.

The duchess often distinguished particular words as sounds familiar to her ears; but the more subtle meaning eluded the feeble grasping brain.

It was only occasionally that the mind was conscious of a general understanding, produced by these voices, after they had been, as it were, with a faint muffled noise at the portals of hearing.

Then she was conscious that those who spoke, spoke pitifully, sorrowfully, mournfully, tearfully.

But sometimes they would change their tone, and the idea would arise in the patient's mind that then, they spoke of some other object—spoke of it with anger and indignation, and strong abhorrence.

And when the voices spoke thus, there was often something suggested by a word they pronounced which made the sick mind thrill feebly—which lighted up, as it were, for a moment, into a more intense glow, the hidden spark of life—which seemed as if it would evoke sensation, indefinite and incoherent, yet sad and dear, and sweet, but which in a moment faded away and were gone—the word was HORFORD.

Then the duchess felt herself gentle lifted, and again laid down, the low deep voices still sounding over her, and this time without the rustle of drawn curtains.

Why, she knew not—how, she knew not; but there was a sensation of tightness around her which had not formerly been.

She thought she was in some narrow place.

Presently came a soft, sobbing voice, which she knew. Presently tears fell again over her face, and she thought that hot lips touched her forehead.

Then there was a brief silence.

It was broken by a grating sound, which seemed to be renewed at short intervals all round her.

Then suddenly the sense of tightness of restriction, and of darkness, at once increased tenfold.

The air got thick and heavy.

No puffs of wind passed over her—no sound of the world stole into the soul.

The sufferer could almost feel the thick darkness.

The veil which had hung between her and outer things grew imperious and thick, and hopeless in its grim intensity.

The Duchess of Heatherland knew that she was thought to be dead, and that she lay supine in her coffin.

———

XIX.—THE STORM UPON THE THAMES.

IT was a pitch dark night.

From time to time a hollow moaning gust would sigh through the air, and the dampening flag-stones would be spotted with the great splashes of huge rain-drops; but the tempest still hung aloof and above.

The tide is at its full, and the dark river brimming, when a wherry slowly approached Middlesex bank, making for the pier, which lies at the foot of Hungerford Bridge, to which I have already upon three occasions directed the readers' attention.

The boat was one built for great speed but yet not without regard to the comfortable accommodation of those who might be conveyed on board.

A low, broad seat stretched across the stene sheets, railed at the back and sides, and on the seat and on the bottom of the boat, before it was piled a mass of soft dark cushions.

The boat was pulled by two men, who worked noiselessly, and talked in whispers.

As the wherry approached the beach, they lay upon their oars, and one of them took a small lantern from beneath the seat on which he sat, and, turning round, held it up towards the shore.

Instantly a round star of light danced upon the ripples, which stirred the sand upon half-a-dozen slimy old piles, that formed part of an embankment, the greater part of which had long been washed away.

Having, by means of the dark lantern, ascertained their exact position, the boatmen turned the stern of the skiff towards the shore, and backed her almost to the beach.

Before landing, however, he who had pulled the stroke oar—a tall, gaunt, man—stood up, and gazed eagerly upon the dwelling before them.

Notwithstanding the darkness, he was near enough to perceive the dark square, formed by black, blindless windows of the house of which he was in search.

"Look look," he said in a hoarse whisper, "that is the room, in the left hand corner, just above the outhouse."

Then the oars were resumed, and in a moment the boat's stern touched the wall of the building alluded to, which, when the tide was at its full, rose from the water. It had probably been at one time a warehouse, but was now deserted and half in ruins.

The man who pulled the bow oar, dexterously shipped it, and catching up a short boat-hook, stuck it into the bottom, so as to anchor wherry in the position it occupied.

At the same moment, the tall man flashed the lantern upon the wall, and the glare showed a small door, apparently long disused, and green, and slimy, from the action of the water, which, in very high tides, rose a foot or more above the threshold, which in its turn was several feet above the level of the beach.

While the bowman held his boat-hook so as to steady the skiff, his companion, without a moment's pause, applied a small key to the door, which at once yielded, showing a space of pitchiest darkness beyond.

Making a sign which was promptly acknowledged by the other, he who had opened the door, stepped from the skiff upon the threshold.

The gleam of his lantern shot before him, and showed a cellar-like passage, the walls and roof formed of unplastered bricks.

Then the outer door closed behind him.

The man left in the boat, gazed eagerly up to the window which had been pointed out by his companion.

"This is reyther a ticklish job," he muttered to himself, when he was left alone; "but it is to be the last, and then off to Amerkey with a pocketful of browns."

As he spoke, a light gleamed from the window on which his eyes were fixed.

"He's at it now," muttered the man.

Meanwhile, the air appeared to become more and more stifling.

Not a breath of air stirred, and the ripples which the surging of the boat had produced, died away upon the dark waters.

Ten minutes elapsed.

Suddenly the light from the window was partially obscured, as if the lamp or candle had been removed to a corner of the room.

"He's worked the oracle," said the boatman.

Another minute elapsed.

The door opened.

The tall, gaunt man returned, bearing a burden—something large, heavy, and dark.

"Is it all right?" whispered the man with the boat hook.

"I've got her," was the reply.

And he who spoke deposited his burden carefully upon the piled-up cushions.

His companion eagerly gazed at it: he could distinguish but a mass of dark drapery.

Only once, for a moment, he saw something oval and white, and knew that it was the dead-like face of the entranced woman.

Meanwhile, Faversham—our readers have doubtless recognized him — piled round the unmoving form of his victim thick wreaths of shawls and cloaks, caught up, as it seemed, in the room from which he had borne her.

Then he lifted from the bottom of the boat what appeared to be a long bar, of a heavy substance, enveloped in some fleecy material, so as to be nearly a foot in diameter.

"It's about the same weight," he muttered. "At any rate, there can be hardly any difference."

Then he disappeared again by the side door he had before entered.

Rattan—for he it was who held the boat hook—gazed with a sort of gloomy fascination upon the dark mass in the stern sheets.

It lay as still as the metal bar which was to supply its place beneath the coffin..

In a moment, the light again streamed from the windward.

"He's using the screwdriver, and glutting down all close again," said Rattan.

A long quarter-of-an-hour elapsed; then the light was extinguished.

"There's the stars," said the watcher; "he's done it."

As he spoke, Faversham stepped into the boat. In a moment the door was flung to and locked.

In the next, the wherry shot down the stream as fast as the muscles of those who plied the oars could urge her.

The tide had turned, and as the boat flew onwards, Faversham looked up wistfully at the sky; the storm so long brewing gave indications that at length it was about to descend in its fury. The air became absolutely thick and sulphurous. A dim foreboding of impending danger took possession of those who watched the approaching conflict of the elements.

The silence was as profound as the darkness was intense.

All at once there fell a few scattered drops of rain, then there was a momentary pause.

Suddenly a stream of blue lightning tore across the darkness, and in an instant—and for an instant—the gleaming river, the piles of confused buildings rising upon its banks, the stately bridges, stretching their granite bulwarks from shore to shore, the hall spectral steeples, shooting up into the darkness, all appeared, and all vanished.

"Pull—pull hard and fast," shouted Faversham.

His voice was drowned in the thunder-peal which accompanied rather than followed the flash. It was not the usual hoarse roar of thunder; it was rather a sharp, ringing, crackling uproar, like the discharge of a volley of brass artillery.

In the midst of the tumult, the ashen staves bent, and the wherry flew fast and faster through the buzzing, foaming water. Another flash, as bright, as blue as the first. Two great portions of the sky appeared masses of lurid flame, and between them leaped a forked, jagged stream.

Again the river with its black waters shone and glared—again the thousand buildings of the great city stood out, more clear than by brightest sunlight, in that universal blaze; and again the thunder seemed to smite into the very brains of the listeners.

"Pull, pull! harder and faster—harder and faster," shouted Benosa. "We shall have it in a moment."

And as the last rattle of the thunder died away, a loud rushing sound came rustling through the air.

"The squall," cried Faversham; "keep her right before it, or we shall be over in a moment."

And as he spoke, the rushing sound waxed louder.

They heard the scream of the wind through the arches of Waterloo Bridge, which they had just passed.

A moment more, and spots of white foam gleaming all across the river, showed where the piers of the bridge stood stoutly out against the angry waters, as they flew headlong before the wind.

Then at last, driving before it a thick, sharp, whistling shower of mingled rain and spray, the gust caught the boat. But it was ably manned.

Shouting to Rattan to sit steadily, and keep his oar in the stream, Faversham partially rose as the wherry was borne on in the centre of a rushing ridge of foaming water.

The fury of the squall momentarily increased. The fierce wind tore up the troubled river, and scattered it in blinding showers through the air.

The whole tideway was a mass of foam, glistening as though the stream had been beaten with rods, while, howling above the water, shrieking through the vast arches of bridges, grasping and shaking piles of chimneys and high gables upon the banks, and bearing on in horizontal lines the pour of fast falling rain, the tempest sweeps the weak wherry before it, its crew deafened with the din, and blinded with the drift of flying water.

The black mass of Waterloo Bridge, with its crowning tiara of lights, loomed a moment ahead, and then appeared in the gloom behind.

Almost at the same moment, as appeared to Faversham, the arches of Blackfriars Bridge stood out in their colossal dimensions over the foaming flood.

The squall had reached its height; and almost at the culminating moment, as the wherry was shooting towards the centre arch, a wild flow of wind took her on the broadside.

What followed seemed the catastrophe of a wild dream.

There was a moment's violent tossing amid the white sparkling ridges of water—a moment when every sound was lost in the shrieks of the hustling wind; then a vision of massive masonry, an uncontrolable lurch of the tempest-beaten boat, a crash, a collision, a wild attempt to fend off the slimy, slippery piers, and, almost at the same instant, the wherry, leaking and half stove in, was swept downwards from the bridge between the crowded tiers of shipping in the Pool.

The storm was at its wildest as they shot the bridge.

Minute by minute it lulled from the full burst of its fury, settling into a blustering gale, which drove volleys of drenching rain before it, and urged to furious speed the race of the ebbing tide.

Not more than three quarters of an hour had elapsed from the time when the wherry quitted Hungerford, until it had swept up to a green and slimy stairs, which descended to the margin of a little creek beyond the bridge.

Arrived here, Faversham sprang lightly from the boat, and, steadying himself with difficulty, while Rattan with equal difficulty held the boat alongside the steps, leant over into the boat, and took the duchess's inanimate form in his arms.

"Come now," said Faversham.

"Shall I let the boat go adrift?"

"Yes—no. Fasten her, if you can, in case of accidents. Now follow me; the carriage is waiting above."

Rattan did as he was desired, and followed as quickly as the slimy and uncertain footing would allow of.

But suddenly, Faversham, who was a yard or two ahead, stopped abruptly, and listened.

"Hush!" he cried, in an agitated whisper—"hush!"

"What is it?"

"Don't you hear something above—a measured tramp?"

"Yes; it's the police going their rounds. They're coming this way."

"They're coming down the steps."

"Good God! what can we do?"

"We must take to the water again—quick!"

"No, no—we cannot."

"Why?"

"Our escape that way is cut off. Look—do you see that long boat full of men approaching? It is the river police."

"Then we are lost. Stand close to me; we will not be taken alive."

————

XX.—CHARLEY WAG TAKES TO HIS HEELS— THE POLICEMAN DOES DITTO, AND COMES IN FOR ANOTHER "CRUSHER."

I LEFT Charley with his foot on the head of the policeman.

You may be sure that he did not keep it there very long.

The "bobby" did not give him the chance.

Charley, little dreaming what sort of resting-place he had found, came down rather heavy.

The constable's hat went over the end of his nose, like an extinguisher, and the constable's knees giving way under him, he doubled up after the manner of a telescope; and Charley, losing his balance by this unexpected sinking of the support, left go of the window-sill, and fell down in a lump, spreading the policeman out flat beneath him with the force of the blow.

Arrived here, he was not very many minutes

considering what he should do ; but, scrambling to his feet, made for the garden-gate.

Then he looked eagerly round for Julia, whom he expected to find waiting there for him.

She must have gone up the street, he thought, but which way ?

While he was hesitating, the policeman having recovered a small portion of his lost breath, sat upright on the ground, and began to struggle desperately with his extinguisher.

The noise alarmed Master Charles, who, thinking that whichever way he went he would be acting wiser than by staying where he was, he took to his heels without more ado.

The policeman, scrambling to his feet, set off after him as fast as his legs would carry him.

Charley ran his hardest, and kept straight ahead, looking to the right and left as he went, to see whether Julia was anywhere in hiding.

She was ; and as Charley went pelting past; like a cannon-ball, she called after him.

" Charley, Charley."

" Hallo !" said Charley, pulling up short.

" Come in here ?"

She was in a doorway, and he popped into it by her side.

But he had no sooner done so, than he heard the steps of the pursuing policeman close behind.

Had he seen him ?—that was the question.

It seemed at first as if he hadn't, for the constable shot ahead. But next moment he turned.

" We'll be a match for him," said Julia.

" I'm not afraid," replied Charley ; " we're man to man."

" We're man and woman to man, you mean."

" What will you do, then ?"

" Oh, you'll see what I shall do. You get talking to him in front, and I'll get behind him."

" All right ; only, Julia, take care you don't get hurt."

" Don't alarm yourself."

While they were talking, the policeman came up.

" So you're here, are you ?" said he, talking as composedly as he could after his late exertions.

" Yes, I'm here," replied Charley. " What's there curious about that ?"

" Nothing very curious, perhaps ; but I shall take you into custody."

" Will you ?"

" Yes, I shall."

" What for ?"

" On suspicion."

" Suspicion of what ?"

" Of burglary."

While he was talking, Julia had got behind him. She had her veil down, and the corner where they were standing was none of the lightest ; besides, Charley was between her and the policeman, so that he could not possibly recognise her.

" On suspicion of burglary, young man," continued the officer, laying his hand upon Charley's collar. " You need'nt think to get over me, I can tell you. I'm not a man that's easily humbugged, and I can see in the dark as well as most folks."

" See, then !" cried Julia.

And, seizing hold of the brim of the policeman's hat on each side, she bonnetted him again for the second time that evening.

Simultaneously with this assault, Charley grasped him by the throat, and twisting his hand into his stock, almost strangled him.

Then together they pushed him back against some railings, and, muttering awful threats the while, tied him fast by the neck and arms, in spite of his struggles and half suffocated cries for help.

Having fastened him up securely, Charley turned round to his companion.

" We'd better be off," said he.

" Which way ?"

" We'll take a cab at the end of the street," replied Charley.

And away they went.

It was rather rash of them to talk so loud. The policeman had heard what Mr. Wag said, although he was so tightly bottled up in his hard hat.

" Oh, you will, will you ?" said he. " Wait till I get out of this infernal old goss, and I'll be after you, my chickens."

———

XXI.—George proposes a hazardous expedition, which Charley Wag agrees to.

TWO or three days after these events, the policeman called at Charley's rooms in the Temple.

Charley was out, and Julia answered him. He had come to serve Mr. Wag with a summons for the assault, but when he saw Julia established there, he was very much astonished.

She offered him a glass of wine, and asked him his business, and when he explained it, tendered him a couple of sovereigns, but he shook his head resolutely.

Then she offered him three. Eventually he took four, and departed.

She smiled to herself when he was gone, thinking that he was effectually silenced, but such was not the case.

The fact was, that the name of Charles Wag had struck him as being a rather remarkable one, and moreover, one with which he was familiar.

He made inquiries among the force, and found there was something about a goose against a young gentleman of that name. There was also a burglary.

" Can it be the same ?" he asked himself ; " how am I to find out. I must get hold of the party who had the charge."

With a little trouble he did so.

" Is he like him ?" he asked.

" As like as one pea to another."

" It's a very rum go, then ?"

" It is a very rum go."

" How does he get his living ?"

" He spends plenty of money, they say."

" He's up to no good, you may depend."

" We'll keep an eye on him, eh ?"

" Right you are, there may be pickings to be had."

*   *   *   *   *

Charley and Julia lived in blissful ignorance of these little arrangements.

For some time they lived very happily.

Charley had plenty of money, and Julia was a young lady who could help him to spend it.

She had quite a talent that way, in fact, and could make five pounds look very foolish in as many minutes, without having anything particular to show for it.

But Charley did not grumble; like the generality of persons who get their money easily, he did not care how easily it went.

The only thing that at all disturbed Miss Julia's serenity was the ignorance in which Mr. Wag kept her with regard to the quarter from which he drew his supplies.

He was so very young, that the idea of his being a man of property, living alone, and without any control, was to her mind exceedingly improbable. If he were a man of property how was it that nobody visited him? He had no friends or companions. People in the position in life which he pretended to occupy would not surely be so isolated from all society.

"I should very much like to know what it all means," thought Julia; "and I'll find out too, before I am many centuries older."

Oh, Julia, Julia! it was very unwise of you! I suppose you never read the story of Bluebeard!

Meantime, let us inquire, was Charley happy? Something, too, was preying upon his mind. What was it?

He was running through the money.

He had left a balance at the bank some months ago of nine hundred and ninety-nine pounds, nineteen shillings, and elevenpence halfpenny. The rest he had drawn out, and he had almost spent it.

Now he did not wish to touch the balance at the bankers, until such times as he could carry out the scheme about which he had spoken to George, the reader may perhaps remember, on his way home after a successful attempt upon the bank; but though sufficient time had not elapsed for an attempt to be made, he was loath to make it.

The fact was, he had become so lazy, and indifferent, and spritless, he could not collect sufficient energy to make an effort.

But an effort must be made, there was no doubt about that.

At the extravagant rate that he and Mrs. Wag lived, the money he had would not last much longer.

Then what was to be done?

He was a proud young fellow, and he did not like the idea of converting Julia's jewels into cash.

Besides, that could not be done without first letting her into the secret of his poverty, and to that he had even a still greater objection.

One night when Julia had gone out alone, to see some lady friend, Master Charles was left to his own reflections.

They were none of the pleasantest.

By way of amusing himself, he had been counting up his money. He counted it twice, to make sure there was no mistake. The amount of cash in hand was exactly sixteen shillings and a halfpenny.

"What shall I do?" said he to himself.

"Go back to the smashing?—no, that's paltry; and there's too much risk. The bad money business has been overdone lately, and the shopkeepers are so wide awake. And then it's such hard to mouth work. No, what I want is a good haul, and a good haul I must have—there's no mistake about it."

But the question was how the haul was to be had, and where it was to come from.

He lighted a cigar to help him to think about it.

After a pause, says he:

"Supposing I try this dodge on at the bank, who is to help me?"

Long pause and a good deal of smoke.

"Julia would do."

More smoke.

"But she's quite as well out of it."

A meditative draw a minute long.

"It doesn't follow that I should tell her what she's doing. She might be the innocent instrument. But then it wouldn't do either, because if anything came of it she'd be in a fix, and not know how to act. No, that wont do."

Here he considered so long without drawing that he let his cigar out.

Having lit it again, he continued:

"George is the man, but where is he?"

There is a certain individual of sulphurous notoriety of whom you have only got to speak, and——George knocked at the door as his name was mentioned.

"Come in!" cried Charley; and in he came.

When he was inside, he stood upon the mat for a moment, staring round him in mild astonishment at the occupant of the room and its furniture.

Master Charles had been spending a good deal of money, since he had last been to visit him, in decorations.

The room was furnished with luxurious magnificence, but with a careless absence of taste and harmony.

Vast mirrors gleamed upon the walls, extending from the rich cornices, heavily gilded, to the lusciously soft carpet.

Cabinet paintings of great merit were interspersed with vulgar prints of favourite ballet girls, coloured portraits of winners of great races, all very much alike, photographs of Tom Sayers and Mace in imposing boxing attitudes, besides several ugly representations of ugly bull pups, the property of sundry broken-nosed celebrities of the P. R.

Sofas, couches, chairs armed and unarmed, of every dimension and every pattern, were jumbled together without order or regularity. Costly ornaments, most of them broken, were strewed about on the side-tables.

Half a dozen clocks, pointing to half a dozen hours, stood about.

Splendidly bound keepsakes, Cider Cellar Songsters, Railway Library books, and back numbers of Mr. Reynolds's "plummiest" books lay pell-mell upon the sofas, chairs, and tables.

Everywhere was there this mixture of things good and bad.

If George had been of a reflective turn, which he most certainly was not, he might have compared the contents of the room to their owner. What a deal of good there was in him, but what a deal of bad mixed up with it.

On a magnificent couch, lined with Utrecht velvet, in a splendid dressing-gown of flowered satin, lay Charles Wag, Esquire, smoking a fourpenny cigar, and looking as though he were the very last person in the world to know what was the meaning of "skillogolee."

His feet were thrust into crimson slippers, embroidered with gold lace; and he had on a smoking cap, which was quite dazzling to look at.

He was a handsome young fellow.

His features were well cut, frank, and open; but his cheeks were deadly pale, and there was an air of languid and lazy indifference apparent in all his motions, which, in a lad of his years, seemed very ridiculous, not to say offensive.

I hate bits of stuck-up boys myself, and I suppose a good many other people do as well.

George, however, was not one of these.

He was a simple fellow, although an awful vagabond.

"Good evening, sir," said he, bowing low.

"Well, George, how are you?"

With this the young gentleman gave him a finger to shake.

George, having shaken it, observed:

"How's trade?"

"What trade?"

"Our's."

"I haven't been commercial lately."

"Playing the gentleman, eh? That must be a rare game."

"You think so."

"Think so? I should think I did."

"I can't agree with you."

"Well, you look as if you and it got on pretty well together, except that perhaps you're a trifle fine drawn like."

"I'm weary, George—I want something to do."

"Do you?"

"Something to stir me up, and set my blood in circulation." What do you say to breaking into the bank again?"

"Well, that won't wash, I'm afraid."

"Anything else can you propose?"

"Well, I can hardly say."

"Look here, now; are you man enough to come that dodge to-morrow I spoke to you about?"

"Which?"

"At the bank where I keep my money."

"What, drawing out the balance twice over, you mean."

"Yes."

"I'm not particular disagreeable to it."

"Will you do it?"

"It's running reyther a risk, aint it?"

"Of course it is."

"If you are found out in the trick, it seems to me there's not much escape?"

"No, not much."

"What will you stand?"

"I'll act liberally of course. We'll share alike."

"I'll tell you what it is," said George, "you're a young trump, and I always said it of you; but if you're agreeable, we'll put that bit of business off for a while. I've got another little matter to put to you."

"Put it."

"Well, then, I've got a crack in my eye."

"Good gracious, I don't see it."

"Now, get on with your chaff; you know fast enough what I mean—a burglary, of course. You're the party as can work it with me if you're agreeable. What do you say?"

"I say I'm agreeable if it's worth while."

"It's fully well worth while, I can assure you. It's at the house of an old miser."

"A miser!"

"A sort of money-lender he is. I've made lots of inquiries about him, and I've found out mostly everything that's necessary."

"Where does he live?"

"At Richmond."

"And when do you propose trying it?"

"To night."

"To night?"

"Why not, I thought you'd like it. That made me come. I've got all my traps with me, and some for you too."

"Well, George, you have your own way of doing business, you were in just such another hurry about the bank."

"And I hope we'll make as good a thing out of it."

"I hope so; has he money in the house, do you say?"

"A good bit, and no end of plate."

"Oh!"

"Yes, left in pledge with him, you know; and some jewels, too, they say, to a rattling tune."

"Does he live alone?"

"Not quite alone. There's a young man lives with him. A half-witted chap. We can easily manage him."

"Yes, there's nothing hard in that."

"Are you ready, then?"

"Quite ready. Let us look at the tools."

"Here they are, and as pretty a set as you could wish to see."

"What have you?"

"Here's a lantern."

"Yes."

"A pair of list slippers."

"Yes."

"A jemmy."

"Yes."

"A centre-bit."

"Yes."

"A knuckle-duster."

"Yes."

"And a crape mask."

"Now we're ready."

"Quite ready."

"A nip of brandy, then, and we're off."

As he spoke, Charley took a decanter from a cupboard, and filled two glasses with spirit.

"Here's luck," said George, tossing his off.

"Ditto," said Charley. Then they extinguished the light, and Charley having left a message with his servant for Julia, followed his companion out into the Strand.

"How shall we go?" asked Charley.

"I've got my boat waiting at the bottom of Essex Street."

"That's a slow way of going, isn't it?"

"Not very; I can pull if you can."

"I can do my share."

"Well, it's ten o'clock now. Say three hours for the journey, doing it quietly. We shall be down at one. Between one and two we must try the crack."

THE BLOODHOUNDS AND THE BURGLARS.

"Is the house near the river?"

"Close to it."

"Come on, then."

XXII.—THE NIGHT JOURNEY—THE BURGLARY—THE BATTLE WITH THE BLOODHOUNDS.

"IT'S very close to-night," said Charley, as he stood up in the boat, and loosened his neckerchief.

"We shall have a storm, if I don't mistake," replied George. "I hope it comes off after we have got there. I don't want to get a soaker."

"You seem provided, though," said Charley, looking at the other's thick over-coat.

"Oh, I shan't hurt," replied George. "I've

No. 33.

made provisions. There's some beer, too, in the boat, and a drop of something stiff."

"You don't mean that?"

"Yes, I do, though; and here's a trifle of cold rabbit-pie if we should feel peckish."

"I daresay we shall before we've done. We've a long night's work before us."

They settled down in their places, and began to pull steadily down the river.

The silent stars twinkled in the heavens above.

The lights on the river banks glimmered faintly.

There seemed to be no traffic upon the bridges, and all was hushed and still.

Presently a muffled rumbling sound and a faint splash were audible.

[CHARLEY WAG, THE NEW JACK SHEPPARD.

"Do you hear that?" whispered George.

"Yes; what is it?"

"The river police. Pull as quietly as you can. They know me."

"Let us get into the shade."

They were close to Waterloo bridge at the time, and another stroke of their oars brought them into the deep shadow thrown by the arch.

Here they lay silently until the police boat had passed.

Then they pursued their way.

As George had said that they had plenty of time before them, they did not hurry themselves, but stopped to rest upon the way, so that it was close upon two o'clock when they reached their destination.

The house which they intended to break into was upon the banks of the river. It stood alone in a large neglected piece of ground, which had once upon a time been a garden.

A high wall surrounded it upon the sides looking inland, but it was open towards the river.

Not but that there was some protection upon this side also, for the garden was at least seven feet above the water, and there was a smooth slippery brick wall underneath, to arrest the progress of the waves.

Under this the two adventurers rowed, and looked round for a convenient spot to moor their craft.

"Here's a bit of a hook that will do," said George, "though it's none of the strongest."

As he spoke, he attached the boat to the hook with a piece of string.

This done, they adjusted their black crape masks, and put on their list slippers, then scrambled up the wall the best way they could, at a spot where some thick bushes screened them from the view of the house.

"This way," whispered George. "We'll get in at a window at the back of the house. The old man sleeps in the front, and the boy in the kitchen. The window opens into the kitchen, so we must not make much row."

"If he wakes?"

"If he wakes, we scrag him."

"We won't use any violence if it can be helped."

"No, my boy; only look here—"

"Well?"

"We won't be took. That's understood?"

"Perfectly."

"Now, no more talking; walk as gentle as possible."

Silently they approached the house.

Their feet fell noiselessly upon the gravel.

George led the way, and paused before a small window about six feet from the ground.

"That's it," said he. "I tried it the other day. You can force the bolt back from the outside with a knife. Try it."

"Give me a lift up, then."

George stooped down and gave him a back, and Charley, raising himself thus to the window, began to work.

He was not very long before he was able to shoot back the bolt. It went with a loud click, and for a moment or two afterwards, the burglars remained perfectly still, fearing that the noise might have disturbed the young man who slept in the room within.

It seemed, however, that the young man had not been awakened, for he was quite quiet.

When they felt satisfied of this, the two burglars proceeded with their work.

Upon the road thither they had concocted a plan. George had described the interior of the house.

Charley being the slightest, was to squeeze himself in at the window, go round to the door and let his accomplice in.

Then, together, they were to proceed to the old man's room, which was at the top of the house, and where he was supposed to keep his money.

With the aid of George's back, Charley easily managed to make a lodgement on the window-sill, and then he flashed his lantern into the room.

On a truckle bed directly underneath the window, with his mouth very wide open, lay the old man's servant, fast asleep.

It was an affair requiring more than an average delicacy and dexterity to get down into the room without treading on the bed.

Charley looked long and wistfully at the bed and at the sleeper, and made up his mind that it would be next door to an impossibility.

Nevertheless, he must do his best.

With the greatest possible caution he introduced his legs one after the other, keeping his balance by nothing short of a miracle, and slid down as noiselessly as he could.

But still not altogether without noise.

Crick-crick went the bedstead, as his weight alighted upon the side.

The breathing of the sleeper was undisturbed.

Now if he only knew where to put his foot, so as to step over him.

He supported himself by the wall, and with the utmost caution, and holding his breath, he stretched out his leg. He wanted to place it upon the other side of the sleeper, but, afraid to use his lantern, and groping in the dark, he found it almost impossible to judge distances.

The consequence was, that he gave the young man an unfortunate kick with his heel.

"Hallo!" said the young man.

Then twisting over, he grumbled:

"Can't you keep your own side of the bed?"

He was dreaming.

Charley withdrew his boot with as much rapidity as if he had trodden upon an adder, and stood balancing himself on one leg, like a ballet dancer.

But the young man, after grumbling in an indistinct fashion for a moment or two, dozed off to sleep again, and Charley, wearied with the uncomfortable position into which he had thrown himself, determined upon making another move.

This time he would stretch out a little further.

The young man had got a little nearer to the edge of the bed, too, and he must take a much wider stride to clear him.

Feeling about with his toe in the air for a moment, he made up his mind, and putting all his trust in Providence, strode out.

But where to? What had he done? He felt his leg going and going; would his foot never reach the bed? No, it had passed the side. He had missed his aim. He had stepped too far.

He was falling.

Bump.

Right on the top of the young man he came with a flop, which for a moment or two, knocked them both breathless.

When Charley had somewhat recovered his wind, he felt the young man underneath him trembling violently.

The unfortunate youth, thus violently aroused from his sleep, was quite at a loss to account for the extraordinary assault.

"Perhaps," thought he, "it's a robber; but if it's not, it's most certainly the devil."

As Charley began to change his position, the young man recovered the power of speech, which had at first forsaken him.

"Wh—a—t—is it?" said he, faintly.

"Silence," growled Charley in his ear.

At the same time grasping his throat, and placing the cold muzzle of a pocket pistol against his head. "Silence, or I blow your brains out."

"Oh dear! oh Lord! There's no occasion to do that, sir," stammered the young man in an agony of terror.

"Will you lie still, then?"

"I'll be as gentle as a lamb."

"Beware, then," continued Charley, in a terrible voice. "Make the least noise, and you are a dead man."

"O—O—ooh," groaned the servant. "I don't want to make no noises. O—O—ooh!"

"Silence, then."

Thus awed into quiet, the young man's teeth were heard faintly chattering; but otherwise, he was quite still.

Charley then slipped off the bed, and carefully avoiding to throw any light upon himself for fear his appearance might decrease the dread with which his companion regarded him, he searched round the room for something with which he could secure him.

The young man at the sight of the bull's eye darting over him, behind him, before him, and all round him, lay and quaked.

But Charley could find nothing.

He therefore returned to the bed-head, and whispered in an awful voice:

"Young man."

"Ye—es."

"Do you value your life?"

"Ye—es."

"Do not stir an inch, then, or breathe a syllable. A pistol is being pointed at you from the window. Shut your eyes. If you speak or move, or open them in the slightest, you will be shot. Beware!"

With these words, Charley crept as noiselessly as possible from the room. The door had no key, so that he could not lock the young man in.

He, however, trusted to his terror to keep him quiet.

When Charley got out into the passage, one thing struck him as rather, indeed, as very singular.

And that was, that the inside of the house did not at all correspond with the description which George had given to him. The street door was on the left, instead of the right, as George had said. There were four rooms down-stairs, instead of two, and the staircase was in quite an opposite direction to that in which Charley expected to find it.

"Anyhow," thought he, "I've found out how things are; and now for letting him in."

But this was not such an easy job.

The street door was, bolted and barred, and chained.

So far so good.

The bolts, and bars, and chains, were easily undone; but that was not all.

It was locked, and the key was taken away.

"Well, I'm not going to be done like this," said Charley. "I'll let him in at a window."

He therefore undid one of the rooms on the ground floor, and entered as noiselessly as possible.

Then he advanced to one of the windows, unbolted it, and with some difficulty raised the sash.

It creaked horribly.

"What a devil of a row everything makes," said Charley, peevishly, and he paused to listen.

He fancied he heard a strange noise.

"It's that fool groaning," he said to himself. "I suppose he's in such a deuce of a funk."

Again the noise was heard; but this time Charley altered his opinion.

It was a strange, unearthly, moaning, melancholy sound, such as he never recollected to have heard the like of before.

His blood ran cold as he listened; and though he was a reckless, daring young blackguard, in spite of himself he trembled, though he knew not at what.

"Bah!" he exclaimed, and endeavouring to rid himself of this uncomfortable feeling. "It's nothing after all, but the wind in the key-hole. I'll bet a farthing."

Meanwhile, as George did not seem to come, Charley leant out of the window and whistled softly.

A soft whistle replied.

Charley turned his bull's eye upon the garden. Then George appproached.

"Come in," said the boy. "Where were you?"

"I was waiting at the door. What has made you so long?"

"I couldn't open the door."

"But the key was inside."

"No, it wasn't."

"Why, he always leaves it there."

"He hasn't done so now."

"Well, I was told he did."

"Where did you get your information?"

"That half-witted lad told me."

"He must have told you wrong. Nothing inside is at all like what you said it was."

"Then he must have gammoned me. Good God!"

"What is it?"

"Didn't you hear what a horrible noise?"

As he spoke, the same mysterious, awful sound was echoing through the house.

George's face became the colour of an underdone muffin.

"If it ain't something supernatural, I can't say what it is," he exclaimed in a frightened whisper.

"Never mind," said Charley, who was not of a superstitious turn. "It won't bite us, I'll be bound."

"Perhaps not," replied George; "but I don't half like it."

However, he agreed with his companion, that they had better set to work at once without any more delay. Delays were dangerous in these cases.

Acting upon this conclusion, they re-entered the passage and began to ascend the stairs.

But as they got higher up, the difference in the construction of the house to what George expected to find it, amazed him more and more.

The room which he expected to find used as a sleeping apartment by the miser, was empty. The rooms on either side were empty also.

Now as every door creaked awfully upon being opened, and as he felt convinced that they would finish by alarming the master of the house before they discovered his room, George voted that they should descend cautiously and question the young man.

Entering the room down-stairs, they found the young man still lying upon his back, with his eyes tightly shut, and drops of perspiration upon his brow.

When he saw them, the sight of their black crape masks, and sparkling eyes gleaming at him through the apertures, by no means tended to calm his fears.

"Speak, wretch!" cried George, clutching him by the throat. "Tell me where your master sleeps?"

"Right on the top of the house, sir," said the young man in a faint voice.

"What made you tell me those lies, then, the other day?"

"What lies, sir?"

George thought it useless to enter into the matter.

"Stop where you are," he growled, "or I'll cut your throat. What room is it, do you say?"

"The first on the left when you get up to the top of the house."

The robbers retraced their steps.

On reaching the top floor, they opened the door indicated with the greatest caution. The room was empty.

"A thousand curses light upon the lying fool," roared George, in a furious passion. "What does he mean by it?"

Just as he spoke, he heard one of the doors being opened on the floor beneath, and the voice of an old man crying:

"Who's there—who's there. Thieves—thieves!"

"There's two of them up-stairs," squealed the young man's voice.

"Ring the bell, then, and let loose the hounds."

"What's he say?" cried Charley.

"I didn't catch it," the other replied.

"Let loose something—"

"I think so."

But while they were speaking, there was a confused hurrying noise down below, like the scampering of many feet.

"Shine your lantern over the stairs," said Charley, "and see what it is."

"It's some wild beasts, I think," cried George, in mortal terror.

"What can we do?"

"We shall be torn to pieces."

"Not without an effort."

"We can do nothing as we are. We are regularly caged."

"Let us shut the door."

"No, let us go on to the roof by the trap-door. We'll fight the beasts there."

"But we cannot escape them, if we do."

"Why not? We can throw them over."

"But afterwards?"

"Get down by the ivy on the house side into one of the windows."

"We can never do it."

"Yes, yes. Come, there is no time to lose."

Indeed there was not.

A loud growl and a deep bay was heard below; then a furious tramp of feet upon the lower stairs.

Next moment George and Charley were straining every muscle to gain the door which led to the roof.

The next they were forcing it open.

The next they were out upon the tiles.

For one moment only they stood gathering breath. They were too much in one another's way springing out upon the roof in this violent hurry to be able to shut the door behind them, before the foremost of their pursuers, a terrific bloodhound, sprang out upon them, and throwing up his broad paws, uttered a hideous howl.

It sprang right upon George, with the furious silence of an assassin.

Then came another flying at his throat, and he fell to the ground beneath them with a piercing cry.

A third flew out at Charley, but providentially missed him; and as he ducked to escape, it went spinning over the side of the house down into the garden below, where, striking upon the flags, it fell dead beneath the windows.

But an instant afterwards, another bloodhound appeared to fill its place, and with an awful yell seized upon Charley by the breast.

The next moment they were mingled together, dogs and men, in the fearful struggle of life and death!

Charley could scarcely tell how long this horrible encounter lasted.

He felt himself grappling desperately with tawny monsters, and madly endeavouring to hurl them from the roof.

Now they sprang at his throat—now he threw out his arms to ward them off—now he thrust them fearlessly between their shining rows of fangs.

Then he was free again, and seizing a leg or a tail, or the loose flaps of the neck, he dragged a savage brute towards the parapet.

Then summoning all his strength, dashed him against it, and sent him howling over to certain death.

Once he lost his balance, and nearly staggered over himself.

At length, panting, bleeding, and exhausted, he fell to the earth.

He could struggle no longer.

He looked round.

George, torn and bleeding, leant against the door leading into the house, and held it shut.

"Whew!" cried George, wiping his head. "That's hot work."

"How many were there of them?"

"Half-a-dozen, I should say."

"Where did they come from? Didn't you know of the old man keeping bloodhounds?"

"Not a word. I've been regularly sold."

"What's to be done now?"

"We must do a bolt, if we can."

"Without the money?"

"Ah, I suppose so. Don't you hear that infernal row?"

"Yes—what is it?"

"It's the old man and the lad ringing a bell and springing a rattle. They think we're safe up here; but we can easily get in by one of the attic windows. Let me go first, and I'll show you how."

"What shall we do then?"

"Why creep down-stairs as quietly as possible, and get out of the house, and into our boat."

"All right—lead on."

There was such a tremendous noise going on underneath from the causes which George had named, that it was not very likely the originators of it would hear the noise which the burglars might make in escaping from the house.

George led the way up the slanting roof. When they reached the tilt, Charley stopped him.

"Why don't we go down the way we came up?"

"Because the old man, or that infernal young thief who told us them lies, has bolted it on the inside."

"Well, we can't, then, I suppose. Fire away!"

"I'll let you down first," said George. "Hold my hand, and glide down the roof steadily, till you get astride of the projecting part over the window; but, for God's sake, don't slip?"

Charley, though not without some misgivings of his power to do it, set about following George's instructions.

It turned out, though, not to be so difficult as at first it had appeared.

What was mostly wanted was courage and coolness.

Having managed to get astride of the slanting roof of one of the attic windows, it was not very difficult to stand upon the window-sill.

Then, breaking a pane, at George's suggestion, he managed to open the window.

So great a noise was being made by the old man and his servant, that the sound of the broken glass was inaudible to them.

Charley having got inside, George soon followed him.

Then drawing out his lantern, he flashed it round the apartment.

"By Jove!"

"What is it?"

"We've hit upon the place at last."

"What place?"

"The old man's bed-room."

It was as he had said.

"Now," continued George, "if I haven't been sold about this as well as the rest, the old man keeps his gold in that cupboard."

Drawing a small crowbar from his pocket, he thrust the pointed end between the door and the door-post, and with a wrench of his powerful wrist broke it open.

Then he threw back the door, and discovered a small chest.

He raised it, and shook it.

It was heavy, and emitted a dull chink.

"This is what we want," said he; "now let's be off."

"Can't you break it open?" asked Charley.

"No—not here. I'll do it in the boat."

"But can you carry it?"

"Yes—come on."

Following George, Charley hurried down-stairs.

At the bottom of the flight they met the old man with a pistol in each hand.

"Stand where you are, you villians!" cried he.

"Get out of the way, you old idiot!" retorted George.

"Give me back my money, then."

"Take it!"

Saying which, George flung the box right at the old man, and knocked him down flat.

"Good God!" said Charley, "you've killed him."

The old man lay perfectly motionless, bleeding from a wound in the head.

"So much the better!" retorted the robber. "It was in self-defence. Just wait a minute, while I touch up the other one."

Before Charley could stop him, George rushed in upon the servant, who was standing with his back towards them, and ringing a large dinner-bell with all his might.

George seized him by the neck, dealing him a couple of violent blows on the head.

Then, before his victim knew what had happened to him, the robber forced a gag into his mouth, which he had in his pocket, as it seemed, ready for any emergency. Then, tearing down a muslin window-blind, he contrived to tie the young man's hands tightly behind his back, and, locking him in the room, left him.

Returning to the stairs, he found Charley examing the wound of the old man, who still lay motionless.

"Come on," cried George; "we'd better be off."

"But you have killed him!" said Charley.

"Damn it!" replied the other, "I couldn't help it—could I? Come on."

"I don't like to leave him like this."

"If you don't like to come, you'd better stop behind," said George. "Listen—don't you hear that?"

"I hear nothing."

"Listen again."

"Yes, yes; there are shouts."

"To be sure; it is somebody coming to the old man's rescue. Let us be off. Stop—I'll take the box."

"Why the lid's broken open."

"By Jove, that's lucky! Here—shine your light. There are two bags full of something. The rest seems to be papers."

"Shall I help you?"

"No—I can carry both. Now for the boat."

XXIII.—A RUN FOR IT.

RAPIDLY descending the stairs, they got through the window where they had entered, hastily closed it behind them, and made for the boat.

Charley reached the spot first.

He gave a cry of surprise and alarm.

"What's the matter?" asked George.

"It's gone!" replied Charley.

"What, the boat?"

"Yes."

True enough, it had floated away.

What was to be done? The sounds of voices shouting reached their ears.

"There's nothing but a run for it," cried Charley.

"It's very fine to talk of running with these damned bags!" growled his companion.

"Give me one."

"No—go ahead."

"Stop—they are here."

A tramping of feet approached, and a confused murmur of voices.

"Hold hard, my lads," said some one; "I fancied I heard some one running up this way. They've hidden themselves in the bushes."

It was true enough; the two robbers were crouching amongst the fern and brushwood alluded to.

"Hush!" said George; "hush for your life! We'll bolt, if it comes to the worst."

The crowd pulled up short, and some one plunged into the bushes.

"Steady, Mr. Jones," cried another voice: "look out they don't hurt you."

"All right," was the reply.

But just as he was speaking, the man started back, having trodden on something that had palpably moved beneath his feet.

The next instant George's form rose from the fern, and, almost before the others could observe what had happened, darted across the road into a hollow surrounded by firs, which grew thickly together—thickly enough to exclude the moonlight entirely.

"After him! after him!" shouted several voices at once.

Mr. Jones dashed through the hedge, and the next minute was going helter-skelter down the hollow, along with the other pursuers.

Meanwhile, the object of their chase had crossed the shaw, and gained a gravel-pit, which was at the other side of it, some twenty feet steep.

With astonishing alacrity, assisted by the holes which the martins had made in its sides for their nests, he gained the top of this, which formed a sort of cornice, from being undermined, and skirted another thicket.

This he forced his way through, breaking down the nut-trees, and pulling away the long ten-feet brambles of the blackberries, which clung round his legs.

Then gained the open country.

The party, headed by the individual called Jones, tried to follow, and with some trouble contrived to scramble up the pit; not without the infliction of sundry injuries upon the heads, arms, and legs, of their followers.

When they gained the ledge, however, their combined weight was too heavy for it.

The cornice gave way altogether.

Eight or ten of them were precipitated to the bottom, surrounded by an avalanche of clattering pebbles loosened by the fall.

Jones had reached firm ground before this accident occurred, and now started off again, with one or two of those nearest to him, as they could see their game crossing a large corn-field on the slope of the hill.

George was hard put to it.

He knew that he was a good runner, though.

He had put his legs to the proof before now, and they had not failed him.

Therefore away he went in the moonlight across the corn.

By degrees his pursuers gave up.

The agricultural frame is rather adapted to slow, continuous labour than condensed energy, and their "wind" was no match for that of the well-trained thief, who was expert at every athletic exercise.

One by one they tailed off.

At last Mr. Jones, who was a postman, and consequently strong in the legs, found himself left with a red-headed yokel, who possessed lighter lungs and tougher limbs than his "mates."

"Dang un, he be a snorter though!" the rustic gasped. "Oi wonders if he can jump ony."

"Why?" asked Jones.

"Bekase he'll come to the bourne directly."

"How wide is it?"

"Seven foot, at least."

"That'll lick him, then. Come on."

They were not in a humour or a condition to waste more breath in talking than was absolutely necessary.

They kept on therefore in silence, one in the wake of the other, through the corn.

They vaulted over a rail at the bottom of the field, and then crossed the gardens of some cottagers, at one of which an awkward check took place.

George had found that he had met his match in point of speed.

In fact, that they were gaining on him.

He hit upon a bold scheme to detain them.

There were some beehives in the last garden he passed through to get to the bit of meadow that skirted the bourne.

Turning round for an instant after he had cleared the low turf wall, he took up a large stone, and hurled it at the nearest hive with so true an aim, that he immediately upset it.

Then, without pausing the fraction of a moment to see what effect the shock would have upon the enraged inmates, he darted off again.

"Don't ee go there, Mr. Jones," shouted the rustic, as the postman was rushing on to the very spot. "You'll be stoong to death, man."

"Which way can we go?"

"Round by the ditch."

"This way?"

"To be sure."

It was not the path, or rather the watercourse, one would have taken by choice; but there was no time to hesitate.

They skirted the garden, and came into the pasture, just as George, with a run and a leap, cleared the brook, in most steeple-chase fashion, and was off again, across another meadow.

His pursuers were less fortunate.

Jones, to be sure, got over; but the other trusted to a soft bit of ground to spring from, and so fell short of his mark, and came plump into the middle of the stream, with a splash that sent the water flying up all round him like half a dozen fountains.

What he could not leap, however, he waded through, and was soon by Jones's side again.

But now another object attracted their attention.

Far away in front they perceived a bright red light, and the noise of an approaching train was next audible.

George saw it, too, and directly changing his course, made at once for the point where the lamps betokened a railway-station.

Fancying that the train might stop there, and that perhaps he might get off by it, he rushed on.

Collecting all his energy for the last push, he doubled his speed.

The train came screaming on, and the bell announced its approach.

Then it slacked its pace. But it was not for long.

Just as he reached the station, it had begun to move up the line.

There was but one chance left.

It was a desperate one.

But it would not do to be taken now at the last moment, after all this chase.

Running to the end of the palings, that began at the station, and were continued a little way on each side of it, George vaulted over the rails, and gained the line.

The carriages were still moving slowly.

Clutching at a piece of the ironwork of the last one, which was a horse-box, he contrived to perch himself, although in a frightfully insecure manner, upon the buffer at the side of the rear light.

The porters at the station shouted to him, but it was no avail.

He was borne away, leaving his panting pursuers aghast at the perilous feat, which, coupled with his exertions, entirely took away what little breath remained in his body.

And now they were off, humming and screeching along with a ricketty, racketty noise, as the glowing cinders flew about in all directions, lighting up their course.

George held on with the grasp of a drowning man—more, however, to keep along with the train, than from terror of falling, since had he done so, the train would only have gone away from him instead of running over him.

As he began to put a greater and greater distance betwixt himself and his would-be captors, and began to feel much easier in his mind, the thought of his gold occurred to him.

He felt in his left hand pocket.

It was empty.

It gave him such a turn that it was all he could do to hold on to the carriage.

When he recovered a little, he felt in the other.

That was empty, too.

He had dropped every halfpenny on the way—most likely into the ditch over which he had jumped.

XXIV.—CHARLEY USES HIS WITS INSTEAD OF HIS LEGS, BUT HAS TO USE HIS LEGS AFTERWARDS.

WHEN George took to his heels in the manner that we have seen, Charley remained quietly where he was.

Seeing one man run out, the people never for a moment suspected that anyone else was left behind.

Perhaps Charley would have made a bolt of it, too, but where he had hidden he could not exactly see whereabouts the crowd was standing.

He delayed a moment to consider, and in that moment George rushed out, and everybody after him.

Charley, meanwhile, was left to himself.

He remained for some time concealed. Then he ventured out.

He thought very naturally that while the coast was clear he could not do better than make himself scarce.

But he had hardly got out of the bushes than he found himself face to face with five or six men, several of them looking like local constables.

Luckily he had not got on his crape mask, so there was nothing very suspicious about his appearance.

He might have been, for anything they could tell, some one who had been attracted to the scene of the robbery by the noise of the rattle and the bell. But a guilty conscience is, as the copy-books say, it's own accuser, and he made sure they took him for a thief; therefore he felt that he must resort to stratagem.

"What's the matter?" one of the foremost of the men inquired.

"I was coming for you," Charley replied. "Are you the police officers?"

"Yes, we are. What has happened?"

"A dreadful robbery!"

"Have the robbers escaped?"

"No, we have them safe."

"I'll get them in the house, and then be off as hard as I can," thought Charley.

"Where are the robbers?" asked the foremost constable.

"I'll take you to them," said Charley.

"Do so, my man."

And Charley, without more ado, led the way to the house.

He intended to have let them all in at the window where he had let in George, and then, instead of following, make his escape; but as they approached the spot, another idea occurred to him.

Close to the house there was a stable, above which was a loft, with the door opening outwards, standing open. A ladder stood against it.

He would get them all up there, he thought.

"Now then, which way?" asked one of the constables, seeing that he hesitated.

"Well," said Charley, "I'm thinking how you can get hold of them."

"What, are they loose?"

"They're not tied."

"Why the deuce didn't you tie them?"

"Because there was only me and the old man to do it."

"How many are there?"

"Two."

"Big 'uns?"

"Pretty middling."

"But where are they?"

"Up in that loft over the stable."

"I don't see them."

"They're at the back part. You don't expect them to be standing there, waiting for us at the top of the ladder; they're in the inner room."

"This is rather a nice affair, and wants consideration," said the chief constable. "How are we to manage them?"

"You'd better go up first, Mr. Nobbler, and talk 'em over a bit," suggested one of the assistant officers.

"Not at all, sir," replied Mr. Nobbler, who didn't exactly see it.

"It must be done, sir, by stratagem."

"How's that?"

"By a rush."

"What, altogether?"

"Yes."

"But we can only get up the ladder one at a time."

"I know that, but we can muster in the loft up at the top, and then all at once make a charge into the inner room."

"Don't you think some of us had better stop down below, in case of accident?"

"Case of fiddlestick. You mean to say you're afraid!"

"Me afraid?"

"Yes, you!"

Charley could not refrain from a grin. There was no doubt whatever that everybody was very much afraid, and would have liked to have backed out of the job altogether, if they had only seen their way clear.

But they didn't.

The chief constable took the lead.

"Follow me," said he, "and no shirking."

He did not, however, seem to be over confident. He led the way very slowly. Carrying a lantern in his hand, he held it over his head, and endeavoured in vain to pierce the gloom of the loft.

Charley, all in a tremble, waited for him to enter. If he discovered at the first glance that there was no inner room, or that if there was, it was empty, he would be immediately seized by those below.

Fearing this, he stood a little apart, and made up his mind for a run in case of need.

But chance favoured him.

The first constable disappeared, then the second, then the third. The whole company entered the loft.

He was left alone below.

He had not now a moment to lose.

Just as a shout arose within, he seized the ladder and dragged it to the ground.

Close by there was a well; without hesitating for a second, he pulled the bucket on one side, and dropped the ladder down.

Just as he did so, the head constable appeared at the door above.

"Why, there's no one here," he cried.

"Is'nt there," said Charley, with a grin. "Look again, to make sure of it."

"You young scamp, do you mean to say you've sold us?"

"Dead as nails, my old bantam," replied Mr. Wag.

"Then, by God, you shall smart for it!"

"Yes, when you catch me."

"Jump down," cried those behind.

"You'll break your neck, if you do," said Charley.

"It's too high," said the constable, looking down ruefully.

"Not a bit of it—jump!"

"Jump yourself."

But nobody liked to jump when it came to the point.

"Good night, gentlemen," said Mr. Wag. "Good night, and pleasant dreams!"

And the young vagabond took to his heels.

Two minutes after he had gone, some of the party who had been running after George returned.

"Catch him, catch him!" shouted the head constable, pointing. "Don't you see where he goes?"

But the persons he addressed, who were already sufficiently winded by their previous exertions, did not care about any more running.

"Let him go," said one.

"Be hanged to him," said another.

"I call on you in the Queen's name to assist me," shouted the head constable.

"Call away," retorted those below.

While they were talking, Charley did not let the grass grow under his feet. He put his best leg foremost, and was soon out of sight.

He ran towards the river, and kept along by the bank, because, as it was a beautiful moonlight night, he thought he might perhaps see his boat floating down the river, or lying somewhere among the rushes at the water's edge.

The latter turned out to be the case.

Wading through the water up to it, he scrambled in, and pulled out for the middle of the river.

Then putting his back into it, he was soon a good mile from his pursuers.

But he did not pause longer than was absolutely necessary to get his breath, but pulled away as hard as he could for London.

The tide was with him, and it was easy work.

"It's precious hot, though," said he to himself, as he pulled off his waistcoat, and fastened his braces tightly round his waist; "and looks very like as though we were going to have a storm."

Certainly a storm was brewing. As he spoke, a gush of wind swept past with a low, plaintive sigh, and rustled ominously in the trees upon the river's bank.

"We shall have it presently," said Charley, looking up at the sky.

XXV.—WHAT HAPPENED ON THE RIVER—LEFT ALONE WITH A CORPSE—CIRCUMSTANTIAL EVIDENCE.

IN course of time, and by dint of continual exertion, Charley Wag found himself nearing his destination.

When he had passed Westminster Bridge, he redoubled his efforts, hoping soon to be at home.

CHARLEY'S ESCAPE WITH JULIA.

As he came up to Hungerford, he was just thinking to himself that he might yet get housed in the Temple before the storm broke out, and was pulling his hardest.

So hard, indeed, was he pulling, and so intent was he on gaining his object, that he did not perceive the arch of the bridge until he was close upon it; and it was only by the most sudden and energetic shipping of his oars that he prevented himself from being capsized.

Having shipped them, and escaped the stonework of the arch by the closest shave, he glided on some distance noiselessly with the tide.

It was while he was thus passing out from under the bridge, that in the bright moonlight, he saw two men in a boat on his left hand side, close to the quay or pier from which he had

No. 34,

sprung that night when he rescued the duchess from a watery grave.

They were carrying what seemed to him to be a dead body.

One man was lifting it from the shore to another man in a boat.

"What are they up to, I wonder?" thought Charley.

These men, having laid the muffled figure down in the stern of the boat, rowed away.

It occurred to Charley that he might as well see what they were doing.

He held his boat back in the shadow of the arch, until they had gone on some distance.

Then, keeping well in the shadow of the river bank, he followed them.

[CHARLEY WAG, THE NEW JACK SHEPPARD.

Meanwhile the storm, which had been so long threatening, arose with terrible fury.

It was all he could do to keep the boat straight against the rush of water which swept him on towards the city.

Fairly in the current, it would have been impossible now, had he wished to do so, to have landed.

So violent was the strength of the waters dashing.

In spite of wind and weather, Charley, however, managed to keep the two mysterious men in view.

He felt desperately curious about them; and though he was very weary, as may readily be imagined, by his recent exertions, he was nevertheless sufficiently anxious to find out what was, as he termed it, "their little game," to resolve upon pushing forward to the end.

He saw their boat tossed to and fro before him. He saw how narrowly they escaped capsizing. At last he saw them land, as I have described.

But previous to this, a very disagreeable incident had occurred, which had for a time naturally diverted his attention.

While biding his time to pass through Southwark Bridge, he became suddenly conscious of the approach of a large boat in the rear.

He strained his eyes to see what it was, but it was at the instant hidden in the shadow of a barge.

In a momentary lull of the storm, he heard the steady plash of oars, and a low murmur of voices. It was evidently a boat wellmanned.

While he was wondering what it could be, it came out into the full moonlight.

It was the boat of the river police—a fouroared Thames Police galley, which had been lying in ambush in the deep shadow of a barge close under the corner arch of Southwark Bridge, and had been laying there a long while, as quiet as mice, waiting for the chance appearance of some river thieves, who might have thought the tempestuous night a favourable one for the exercise of their calling.

Charley knew very well that George's boat was no stranger to these guardians of the river; indeed it had once belonged to them, and had been stolen by the audacious thief from the old Thames Police Office at Wapping.

George had told him all about it before, and had described the various peculiarities of his calling, which was that of a river thief.

Perhaps, as the reader may not have had any opportunity of becoming acquainted with the features of this particular class of crime, a few words about them may amuse him.

There are various kinds.

There is the Tier Ranger, who silently drops alongside the tiers of shipping in the Pool by night; and who, going to the companion-head, listens for two snores: snore number one—the skipper's; snore number two, the mate's. Mates and skippers always snoring great guns, and being dead sure to be hard at it if they had turned in, and were asleep.

Hearing the double fire, down he goes into the skipper's cabin, gropes for the skipper's trousers—which it is the custom of those gentlemen to shake off, watch, money, braces, boots,

and all together, on to the floor—and therewith make off as silently as may be.

Then there are the Lumpers, or labourers, employed to unload vessels. They wear loose canvas jackets, with a broad hem in the bottom, turned inside, so as to form a large circular pocket, in which they can conceal, like clowns in pantomimes, packages of surprising size.

A great deal of property is stolen like this from steamers—first, because steamers carry a larger number of small packages than other ships; next, because of the extreme rapidity with which they are obliged to be unladen for their return voyages. The Lumpers dispose of their booty easily to marine store dealers, such as old Measles; and the only remedy to be suggested is that marine store dealers should be licensed, and thus brought under the eye of the police as rigidly as public-houses.

Lumpers also smuggle goods ashore for the crews of vessels.

The smuggling of tobacco is so considerable, that it is well worth the while of the sellers of smuggled tobacco to use presses to squeeze a single pound into a package small enough to be contained in an ordinary pocket.

Next are the Truckers, whose business it is to land more considerable parcels of goods than the Lumpers can manage.

They sometimes sell grocery to the crews, in order to cloak their own calling. Many of them have boats of their own, and make a great deal of money.

Dredgermen, under pretence of dredging up coals and suchlike from the bottom of the river, hang about barges, and other undecked craft, and whip away anything that may lay within reach.

Lastly, there are mild, harmless individuals, for whom barges are always drifting away of themselves, they having no hand in it, except first cutting them loose, and afterwards plundering them. Innocents meaning no harm, who have the misfortune to observe these foundlings wandering about alone on the Thames.

And now I have described all that is necessary about this genus of thief.

George was one, as I have said. The police knew him and his boat well.

When they came out from the shade, it was because they had recognized his boat pass by.

Charley at a glance saw that he was pursued, and plied his sculls vigorously.

"Hold hard there!" cried a voice from the police boat.

But Charley took no notice.

Only he pulled harder.

"Hold hard there! hold hard there!" repeated the voice behind, in louder tones; and this time several other boats swelled the chorus.

Charley, without in the least lessening his exertions, debated in his own mind whether or not he should stop, as desired.

He conceived it extremely probable that they had recognized the boat. The question was, whether they might not detain him in a mistake for George, or even as an accomplice of George's.

Anyhow, it was quite sure that if he managed to escape, he would be having the best of them.

On such a rough night as this he stood some chance of doing so.

Turning his head for a moment, he saw the two men whom he had been watching effecting a landing with their burthen.

If he could land at the same place, he would be safe.

He strained every nerve to do so.

He saw the men land just before him, and steering straight towards the steps, and in imminent danger of being capsized, he ran the boat alongside, and instantaneously sprang ashore.

No sooner had he landed, than he ran forward up the steps, and this without for a moment hesitating to see where they should lead, or whether there was any escape.

He was, however, brought very shortly to a sudden stop.

Some one seized him by the throat, and flung him back against the wall.

And while he was held thus for a moment, he heard a rapid conversation between two voices, one of which seemed not altogether unfamiliar to him, although that was hardly the time or place to think when or where he had heard it last.

It said:

"Damn him, he's not the police!"

"No, but they're here," said the other.

"What's to be done?"

"We have'nt time to waste in words. We must stand on the defensive."

"The defensive be hanged!—let's hook it."

"We cannot get away with the woman."

"Curse the woman!—leave her."

"I cannot."

"Then we shall both be taken."

"Yes."

"What's the point in that? Come on."

"I can't—there's no time."

"Yes, there is. Come on, and leave the woman with this young chap."

Next moment the gripe was removed from Charley's throat, and, recovering his breath, he found himself grasping, he hardly knew how, the insensible form of a woman, while he himself leant against the wall for support.

Rattan and Faversham meanwhile rushed down the steps to gain their boat.

But in their impetuous haste they flung themselves instead straight into the boat of the policemen, which was coming up at the moment.

The violence of the shock capsized it.

In another instant the four policemen, Faversham, and Rattan, were struggling in the water, like so many flies in a milk-jug.

The police shouted loudly for help, and some of the men scrambling on to the shore began to bellow loudly, "stop thief!" as well as "murder!"

These cries alarming the police on shore, who were going their rounds, they came running down the steps; and the first person whom they clapt their eyes on being Master Charley, they collared him.

But he shook off their grasp.

"What do you want with me?" he asked.

"Is this the party?" called out one of the policemen above to those below.

"Hold him tight, one of you," the other replied; "and come down here some of the rest to help us."

"Are you all out of the water?"

"All us four are; but what's become of the two parties that ran into and swamped us is more nor I can tell."

"Nor I."

"Nor I."

"Nor I."

"Where did they come from?"

"The deuce only knows."

"They didn't pass us at the top of the steps."

"We didn't see them land from the river, though they may have done so. In this squall one can't see half a dozen inches before one's nose. We were chasing a young swab who landed here."

"Has got a woman with him, hasn't he?"

"No; there was no one with him."

"There's a woman with him now."

"The dickens there is!"

Here the colloquy was cut short by the murmuring of voices in an excited state above.

The damp policeman who had been talking shook himself, and ran up the steps with the dry policeman he had been talking to, to hear what it was all about.

"The woman's dead," said one.

"Dead drunk, you mean," said another.

"No—dead."

"Fainted only."

"Feel her pulse."

"I have; it's quite still."

"And her heart?"

"Not a throb in it."

"Here's a go!"

"What's he been doing to her?"

"What have you been doing to the woman, young man?"

"I tell you again—" said Charley, in an excited voice.

"There—don't criminate yourself, young man; there's no occasion for that."

"I tell you again," repeated Charley, "I know nothing about her. I landed here, and was coming up the steps, when some men suddenly thrust her into my arms, and made their escape, before I could do anything to prevent them."

"Pray where do you say you had come from?"

"I landed here, I tell you."

"Where is your boat, then?"

"At the bottom of the steps, for all I know to the contrary."

"Whose boat was it?"

"How do I know?"

"You know who you got it from."

"Certainly."

"Who was it?"

"I hardly see why I should be called upon for an explanation."

"But you are."

"Well, I give you clearly to understand that I do not in the least acknowledge your right to question me."

"Indeed!"

"But I will nevertheless answer you."

"That's obliging."

Charley regarded him with a look of withering contempt, and proceeded:

"I hired this boat at the Temple Stairs, of a man who offered it to me; and my reason for doing so was because I wished to amuse myself by taking a row upon the river."

"Merely to amuse yourself?"

"Certainly."

"Perhaps the gentleman can give us his address," suggested somebody from the background.

"Of course I can. I live in the Temple. I have chambers there."

The police looked at him, and sniggered.

Charley had put on his coat again in the boat when it began to rain, but he had forgotten his neckerchief. When he set out upon this housebreaking expedition, he had selected the dingiest articles in his wardrobe, and, to tell the truth, he did not look very much like the young swell that he was trying to represent himself.

"I shouldn't have took him for a nob, at first sight," observed one.

"Not if he hadn't been pointed out to me," said another.

"Perhaps he ain't got his best things on."

"No, he thought we were going to have some rain, perhaps, and came out pervided."

Charley took no notice of these little sarcasms.

He was hardly paying any attention to them, for his thought were occupied by the inanimate form of the lady who lay beside him.

Where had he seen her before? They had met somewhere. Yes, now he recollected—she was the lady whom he had rescued from a watery grave that night that he was first locked up in the station-house.

Was he going to be locked up again now? The recollection of what he had suffered then brought back his thoughts to existing circumstances.

"What do you want with me?" he asked, turning to the men around him. "You do not wish to detain me, I suppose."

"Well, if you can't give us your card—"

"I can, if you like."

As he spoke, Charley plunged his hand into his pocket for his pasteboard; but he had forgotten that he had not got on his usual coat.

He found no card.

But a very unpleasant circumstance occurred instead.

In withdrawing his hand again, he jerked out an iron instrument, which fell with a clank upon the pavement.

One of the policemen stooped rapidly, and picked it up.

"Oh," said he.

"Aha!" said another, over his shoulder.

"Very much so!" said a third.

It was what is called a "jemmy."

"A gentlemanly sort of tool, that."

"Usually carried by the upper circles."

"A sweet thing in toothpicks."

Charley was confounded.

It was a most unlooked-for and unpleasant accident, and one which was not likely to inspire confidence in the most generous of natures.

For a moment or two he lost his tongue. Then finding it again, said he, innocently,

"What is it?"

"Come, that's rather too strong. You know well enough."

"I don't."

"Why, its yours."

"No, it isn't."

"How do you make that out, when you let it fall out of your pocket.

"It was in the pocket of this coat, and belonged to George, the owner of it, I suppose. I hadn't felt in the pockets. I only put it on first before I got out of the boat. What are you all gaping at? I'm telling you the truth."

"Well," said one policeman in confidence to another, "it might be so, you know."

"Not that its so very probable."

"Not by no means."

"Well," said Charley, "I will trouble you to allow me to pass."

"I don't know that," said the inspector of the shore police. "I'm afraid we can't."

"I know what I can't," said the head of the river police, with a shiver, "and that is, stop here in my wet clothes any longer, so we'll be off. You take charge of this young sprig and the woman. The woman you'd better take to the hospital."

"I've no objection to go with you," said Charley. "Why should I? I have my statements, which will bear investigation."

He knew very well that they wouldn't; but he thought it best to appear calm and collected.

What he had made his mind up for was a sudden bolt.

The river police were moving down towards the water. The shore police were five in number.

Four of them were stooping down to raise up the insensible duchess.

One only retained a hold upon Charley's arm.

This hold was not very firm, for the man was half twisted round, as his head was turned away intent upon watching his companions.

The river police had now almost reached the boat.

There was but one way of escaping, it seemed to Charley.

A desperate and wild chance presented itself. Should he try it?

If he did not, what would become of him?

Nothing might be proved against him. He might escape scot free. But then, was it wise to voluntarily undergo an examination?

Suspicions would be attached to him. His reputation already was not so wonderfully good that he could afford it.

No, he would risk all on the venture.

These thoughts flashed like lightning through his brain.

A moment sufficed for him to consider his chances.

The next moment he made the venture.

Collecting his strength—for you must bear in mind that Charley was but a boy after all, although a very precocious one, and was anything but a giant or a Samson—he drew from his pocket a little crowbar, struck the man who held him a violent blow on the head, and, wrenching his coat from the man's grasp, made a wild spring down the steps, scattering the police below to the right and left, with a series of wild random blows with his crowbar.

Next moment, before any one could recover from the state of intense astonishment into which this conduct had thrown them, he had gained the boat, and, pushing it violently from the shore, was floating out into the middle of the stream.

XXIV.—Escape—Not quite—Taking to the water—A close chase—Another plunge—Rescue.

THE police could not follow him, and for awhile stood paralyzed upon the bank, while he, waving his cap, gave a loud shout of defiance.

But his triumph was of short duration.

He looked round him in the boat for the oars, and found to his horror, that the jerk which he had given the craft in springing into it had thrown them overboard.

Two new causes of alarm then suddenly arose.

The police left behind were shouting loudly for some boat to come to their assistance.

The tide was drifting him rapidly back upon them.

Even if no boat was to be found, it was very probable that he would soon be landed again in their clutches.

When they saw his helpless position, they raised a shout of derision, and redoubled their cries for assistance.

Nothing was left for him but to take to the water.

He was a good swimmer, as the reader already knows.

He was not wanting in pluck, and his mind was soon made up.

The only thing he stopped to consider was, which way he should swim.

For the Middlesex or the Surrey shore.

Of course he did not intend to swim back on his pursuers; but he thought he could effect a landing on that side, a little nearer to the bridge.

The Surrey side would have been best, of course; but it was so far off. And he had tried his strength so much during the last two or three hours, that he hardly thought himself equal to the task.

Besides, the Middlesex shore was in deep shadow from the moon, as I have said before, and he had no doubt that he could land without being observed.

He was out of the shadow now, and in the broad moonlight.

He had his wits about him, and knew very well that it would not do to let them see him jump out of the boat.

How must he manage?

Ah, happy chance!

Close in front of him was a barge riding at anchor.

This would serve as a screen if he could reach it, and he was fortunately floating right upon it.

As he approached, he grasped the side, and then, with desperate efforts, for the tide was pushing him past, he managed to work the boat round the side; and as no one was on board, or if on board, they were fast asleep, he contrived to climb on board.

He did not intend to stop, of course. Though the police on shore, seeing him scramble up, and at the same time seeing the boat float past, made sure that that was his intention, and bawled for a boat to help them louder than ever.

Charley looked towards them and saw that one was approaching to their succour.

This decided him.

Creeping on his hands and knees, he crossed the deck of the barge, and taking off his coat, carefully descended on the other side, and took to the water.

He could hear that they had not noticed him by the words which reached him on the night breeze; and swimming round the boat, he made for a point which he had picked out upon the shore.

The storm had not yet by any means subsided, and it was a difficult matter to make any way through the boisterous waters, which surged and rumbled in his ears, and ever and anon closed over the swimmer's head with bounding fury.

But he swam on desperately, and diving as he approached the steps were the police stood, effected a landing a little further up.

Upon his hands and knees he crawled out of the water, crawled over the slimy stones and wood-work by the water's edge, and crept up some ragged steps, which led to a narrow passage between two dead walls.

At the top of this he hoped to find some egress.

Then he would get some conveyance, and go straight to the Temple; for decidedly it was no longer safe to remain in that quarter of the globe.

Having gained the top of the steps, he glanced round at his pursuers, and then made off as fast as he could towards Thames Street.

Still, he imagined he heard voices calling to each other, and the distant tramp of the police, and he continued running with all his might until he reached the top of the street.

Here he found that he had but been running into the lion's mouth, instead of away from it; for turning the corner sharply, he came plump on to the party of policemen carrying the duchess.

To spring back again into the narrow passage, and resume his flight, was but a moment's thought.

Still, his pursuers had evidently caught sight of him, and rushed after him with loud hallos.

Gathering together his fainting strength for a last desperate effort, Charley continued his course rapidly, and plunged down a long dark alley, and then through a tangled mass of lanes and courts, twisting to and fro, and doubling again and again to elude his pursuers, but in vain. They still kept behind him, and still shouted loudly in his rear.

Presently, a dark passage caught his eye. It was the one which he had come up, and at the top of which he had met the policemen.

Unconsciously he had twisted round until he had come, without knowing it, back to the starting-place.

Down this he plunged, and in an incredibly short space of time was by the water's brink.

But there was not any other escape this way than by taking to the water.

Yes, the balustrade leading to the river had a slight projection.

Behind this, although he thought it barely possible to remain concealed, he determined to ensconce himself.

Then he crouched down, and almost simultaneously a bull's-eye was turned upon the place where he had an instant before been standing.

One of the policemen had arrived at the summit of the stairs.

Glancing upward, he perceived three or four of them standing there, puffing and blowing with their recent exertions, and twisting their bulls-eyes to and fro in quest of the fugitive.

Their countenances expressed extreme vexation and surprise.

Charley saw that they paused, and entered into an eager discussion.

"He's drowned himself," said one.

"Most likely he's swum away, or dived like an otter."

"Where the devil did he come from, when he popped out on us at first?"

"I don't know, I'm sure. But that's not the question. Where's he gone to now? — that's what we want to know."

"Ah, that's the point."

"Well, let's go down and look."

"Lead the way, guv'nor."

"Blowed if I ever see such a slippery customer."

"He's more like a eel than a human being."

"I don't think he came down here at all," one suggested from the rear.

"Oh yes, he did," said two other voices, in contradiction.

"Come on, then—let's look."

Holding his lantern in front of him, and looking eagerly forward, the first policeman advanced.

The rest followed close behind.

Charley's heart beat quick, but he moved not a muscle.

At the first alarm they made, he intended to make a mad plunge, as he had done before to get to the boat, and spring past them into the water.

That he must be found, and that he would probably be caught, he made little doubt.

Just at that moment the dash of oars was heard, and figures approached through the darkness.

Then Charley heard a loud voice he seemed to know shouting,

"Charley Wag! Charley Wag! Give the beggars the double, and swim out. We'll pick you up!"

Charley had no idea who it was; there was not time to think.

He sprang to his feet, and shouted, "Here I am! Help! help! help!"

Then he sprang from his hiding-place, and took a header into the water.

The events of the next few moments appeared to him like a dream.

He felt himself struggling in the grasp of a policeman, who tried to hold him back.

He felt himself wildly buffeting the water, and furiously fighting his foe.

He felt that he had shaken him off.

Next moment he received a stunning blow on the head, and sank beneath the surface.

XXVII.—Mr. Jack Rattan does a good action, for a wonder—Mystery.

WHEN he recovered his senses, he was lying at the bottom of a boat which was rapidly approaching Waterloo Bridge; and looking up, he saw the well-remembered ugly face of Jack Rattan looking down upon him.

"Is that you?" said Charley.

"Who should it be?" retorted Rattan.

There was no great deal of love between these worthies, as you may suppose who recollect when they last met, and in how much Charley was indebted to Rattan.

Rattan probably saw what was passing in the boy's mind from the expression of his face, and, wonderful to say for so generally uncourteous a ruffian, he condescended to say a few words in explanation, and endeavoured to make them of a conciliatory character.

"You haven't forgotten me, then," said he.

"No," replied Charley.

"Well, as I never done you much good, I thought you might have done."

Charley was silent.

"It would have been quite excusable," continued Rattan. "However, I've done you a good turn this time—you'll allow that."

"Were not you one of the men who met me at the top of the steps, and thrust that lady upon me?"

"Well, yes, I was; but I didn't recognize you at the time."

"If it hadn't been for you I could have got away well enough."

Here the companion of Rattan broke in:

"How was she?" he said. "Where did you leave her?"

"She was in the hands of the police when I left her. I don't know how she was."

"We must see after her," said the man, who was, of course, none other than Faversham. "Let us make the best of our way to shore."

They rowed on for a little way in silence.

"Where do you mean to be landed?" asked Rattan.

"At the Temple Gardens," replied Charley.

They were close to the spot then, and Charley bethought him that it would perhaps be unwise to let his companions know where he lived. He therefore corrected himself—

"I mean at the bottom of Essex Street."

In another five minutes he had landed.

"When you floated out in the boat, and came in the moonlight," said Rattan, "I recognized who you were; and when we got hold of our boat, which had floated away, we came after you. We did the best we could for you, so tip us your fin, young feller."

Charley gave him his hand.

As he was walking away, Faversham called him back.

"You were locked up once in Stone's prison, I believe."

"Yes."

"I can tell you something that it would be greatly to your advantage to know. Will you call and see me? Here is my address."

And as he spoke he drew a card-case from his pocket, after a great deal of difficulty; for his clothes were all soaking with his recent immersion.

" Here is my address," he continued. " Come as soon as you possibly can. I can be of service to you."

" I will come."

" I shall look for you."

Thus they parted, and Charley made the best of his way towards the Temple gate.

Having rung the bell, the porter admitted him, with a good hard stare at his drenched habiliments.

" Is that Mr. Wag ?" said he, rubbing his eyes.

" Yes."

" Lor ! I hardly knew you."

" No ; I have been on the river, and had a ducking."

" So I should think," said the man, with a grin.

Charley did not stay to parley further, but made the best of his way to his rooms.

He regretted that he had owned to being on the river ; but then, when he came to think it over, his condition would have excited remarks and conjectures in any case. Perhaps, therefore, the wisest plan was to make no mystery of the matter.

He walked on, looking at the ground ; but as he approached his door, he raised his eyes.

As he did so, he fancied he saw a face suddenly drawn back into the door-way.

In his present frame of mind, any little incident like this was calculated to alarm him.

He hurried forward, and looked eagerly round and up the stairs.

No one.

" It must have been fancy," said he to himself.

He walked up-stairs to the first-floor, on which his chambers were situated.

Then fumbled in his pocket for the key.

While he was doing so, he fancied he heard a movement upon the stairs above.

Hastily undoing his door, he went inside, and fetched a lamp which had been left burning for him.

With this he walked up-stairs and looked round for the fugitive, whoever it might be, at the same time calling out loudly,

" Who's there ? Who's there ?"

But no one replied.

No one could he find.

While looking round in amazement upon the empty landing above, he fancied he heard a creaking below upon the stairs, and he ran hastily down ; but again his search was fruitless.

" It must have been fancy," he said again to himself ; but he did not feel at all satisfied.

However, resolving not to trouble about it any more, he went inside, and shut the door.

He turned to bolt it, and then turned round again.

XXVIII.—CHARLEY IS SUSPICIOUS—So IS JULIA —SHE RESOLVES TO FIND IT ALL OUT—EAVESDROPPING.

JULIA, in her dressing-gown, stood before him.

He could not help staring when he caught sight of her.

She seemed to come upon him so suddenly.

" Julia ?"

" Charley."

" Where you out on the stairs just now ?"

" No, dear."

He looked at her very hard.

" What makes you ask ?"

" Nothing, only I fancied I heard some one."

" Heard some one. Some one who lives upstairs, I suppose."

" No ; they did not go into any of the rooms, or I should have heard them close it to after them, unless—"

" Unless what ?"

" They had taken great care to avoid making a noise."

" Avoid making a noise ?"

" Yes."

" Why should they do so ?"

" So that I might not hear them."

" But why should they wish you not to hear them ?"

" I don't suppose they would want me to know, if they were playing the spy upon me."

" The spy ?"

" Yes, the spy—what makes you repeat every word ?"

Julia was silent.

She watched him uneasily as he pulled off his wet coat, and wrenched at his boots.

Then she came close up to him, and sat by his side upon the floor.

" Charley."

" Well."

" You're not cross with me about anything ?"

" No."

" What has happened to vex you ?"

" Nothing."

" How have you got so wet ?"

" By falling into the Thames."

" But how did it happen ?"

" I was out rowing with George."

" Rowing at this time in the morning ?"

" There, Julia, don't ask questions."

" Of course I won't, Charley, as you wish me not ; only I can see there is some mystery about it, and it makes me so uneasy, and so unhappy, to think that you won't take me into your confidence."

" There—there. Don't cry about it. Women don't understand these sort of things."

" Yes, they do," retorted Julia, crying more than ever. " Yes, they do ; and its very wicked, and unkind, and hard-hearted of you, Charley. It is."

But Charley was obstinate.

" I want to go to bed," said he.

" Why don't you tell me ?" pleaded Julia.

" Well, there, I'll tell you to-morrow," replied Charley, to pacify her.

And he thought he should have plenty of time, before the time came, to make up a good excuse to account for the singularity of his behaviour.

Julia, perhaps, believed him ; or, perhaps, thought that she might pump his secret out of him at a more fitting opportunity.

Whichever it was, she desisted from further

persecution for the present, and assisting Master Charley out of his clothes, which were all sopping wet, she gave him a dry shirt, and helped him into bed; and then got him a steaming hot glass of grog, for which she boiled the water herself.

The youthful tyrant was somewhat pacified by this little attention.

How could he help being so?

He asked Julia to kiss him, and as she would not, he begged in a humble way to be allowed to kiss her.

She granted this favour after a little very proper hesitation. Ladies should always be backward—though, for that matter, I suppose they know which is the best way to get over us poor male creatures much better than I can tell them.

However, though the warm bed, and the hot grog, and Julia's embraces had put him into a much better temper, he was still rather gloomy and uneasy, it seemed, on one point.

It came out presently.

"Why were you sitting up for me?" he asked.

"It was because I was so uneasy about you," Julia replied.

Charley was not long before he fell off to sleep.

The warmth and comfort, after the fatigue and misery which he had so recently suffered, had a most soothing effect upon him.

But Julia did not sleep so easily.

Her mind was a prey to various and conflicting emotions.

A dreadful suspicion haunted her; and as she tossed feverishly from side to side, she asked herself again and again what could account for her lover's singular conduct.

What indeed?

It was the first occasion on which he had thus left her.

Was it not mysterious that he should go out at such an hour, and give no explanation?

She was not jealous of him; her anxiety arose from a far different cause.

She had long asked herself how he obtained his means, but the answer had always been most unsatisfactory, for the simple reason that she could give herself no answer at all.

Then this about the spy.

Why should he suppose he was watched?

And why should he dread a spy?

Surely there must be some dreadful mystery.

All was not fair and above board.

Was he a thief?

When she looked upon him, sleeping there so placidly, with such an open innocent face—such a boy too, without a particle of an approach to a moustache or a beard, she could not believe him guilty.

"I'll find out all about it," said she, "before I am many hours older."

Then, after rolling about for half-an-hour longer, she fell asleep, and dreamt that Charley was the captain of a band of bandits, who had their head-quarters in a secret cave beneath Temple Bar, where they lay upon crimson velvet couches, and quaffed costly wine out of golden goblets.

All of which surprised her, she thought, very much, but did not grieve her so much as she expected it would, after she found upon what a very fine style they did their robberies.

Indeed, the only thing which excited her displeasure, was the discovery that in the secret cave there was another Mrs. Wag, at which she burst out crying, and woke up.

And was very glad to find that it was only a dream.

Charley slept late into the afternoon.

He was awakened by his servant, who said that some one wanted to see him.

"Who?"

"The party that was here last night, sir."

"Which one?"

"That went out with you, sir."

"Very well, I'll get up directly; show him into the sitting-room."

"Yes, sir."

"Where's your mistress?"

"Gone out shopping, sir."

"Shopping, eh?" said Charley to himself, rather ruefully. "How can she go shopping without any money? What the dickens am I to do for some money?"

Then he got out of bed, and began to dress himself.

"Yes, what the dickens am I to do for some money?"

He washed his face, and scrubbed it hard with the towel.

"Something must be done. But what? I've got something in my eye—"

Here he got the soap in, which made him swear a little.

"Well," he continued presently, "I shall see at last, I suppose. I'll hear what George has got to say."

George it was who was waiting, and who was beguiling the time with a strong pipe.

Charley made as much haste as possible, for he was most anxious to hear how his comrade had fared.

He also wanted his share of the money, which he supposed George to have.

He did not expect it was a very great deal, for the two bags which George had taken were not very large ones.

It might have been silver, or even copper, for what he knew, which they contained.

He was weary and disappointed whenever he thought of last night's expedition.

It was a poor trade indeed, if he was to go through all this misery to get five or ten pounds, supposing his share should be no more.

That was what had made him despondent just now.

He had a very good mind to cut the profession. Only one thing prevented him.

He was afraid that honest labour was harder work.

It's a great mistake to think so, my young friends. Only some of you bad ones, I suppose it is no good advising you.

He found George, having let his pipe out, growing rather impatient.

"Oh!" said he, "it's you at last."

"Yes."

Charley shut the door carefully, then came forward, and shook hands with him.

"How did you get on?"

George described what had befallen him at some considerable length.

" YOUR MONEY OR YOUR LIFE."

"And the tin ?" said Charley.

"The tin ?"

"How much was there ?"

"Well, that's difficult to say."

"Haven't you counted it yet ?"

"Well, no, I haven't."

"What the deuce have you been about, then ?"

"You may calculate young gentleman," said George, "that when I got up to London, after holding on to that there gallows old truck, I was pretty well ready to go to bed."

"Yes, yes, certainly."

"When I got up this morning, I began to think of it, and I went down again to Richmond to see where I had dropped it."

"Dropped it ?"

No. 35,

"Yes; I jerked it out of my pocket, you know, jumping over that ditch, I suppose."

"The devil you did !"

"So I searched everywhere to-day, and dragged the bottom of the ditch as well as I could, but I couldn't find nothink."

Charley sat for a few moments silent.

This was a clincher.

To think that he had gone through all that he had, and that nothing had come out of it.

He was more inclined than ever to give up the profession.

"However," thought he, " I'll give it one more chance."

He put it to George.

"George," said he, " your expedition turned out anything but trumps: that you must

[CHARLEY WAG, THE NEW JACK SHEPPARD.

allow yourself. Now what do you say to mine ?"

"Fire away."

"About this dodge, then, on my bankers ?"

"I'm on."

"We'll go then.—When ?"

"When you like."

"I don't think we can pitch upon a better time than this," said Charley. "It's now half-past two."

Here he looked at a clock upon the mantel-piece.

"That's a little slow, I think," observed George, consulting his turnip.

"Never mind ; so much the better. Now to work."

As he spoke, he went to a drawer and brought out a cheque-book.

He then filled up two cheques.

One for nine hundred and ninety pounds, the other for nine hundred.

The smallest he handed to George.

"My balance is, as I have told you before, nine hundred and ninety-nine pounds, nineteen shillings and elevenpence. We will present these cheques at the same moment ; and as everybody in the bank, in all probability, knows the amount of my balance, they will pay without a murmur or a doubt."

"But won't they take a long while to count it ? It seems an awful risk."

"We won't take it in gold, but in fifty pound notes. You ask for eighteen fifty pound notes. It is easy enough. They won't be a moment serving you."

"All right. I have no doubt but that it is all right, only the work is new to me, and I seem strange at it."

"Come on, then ; never say die."

Charley put on his boots, and his coat and hat.

They then each pocketed his note, and took their departure together.

"Has your mistress come in ?" Charley asked the servant.

"Ye—es—that is, no," replied he, with some hesitation.

But Charley did not notice his manner, and George and he left the house together.

No sooner, however, were they gone, than Julia, pale as death, and trembling, came out from a closet where she had hidden herself, and from which she had overheard all that had occurred.

She had come in from shopping while George was there, and hearing who it was, had bidden the servant say she had not returned, and concealed herself as we have seen, to listen.

"Poor boy ! poor boy !" she exclaimed. "What new crime is this he would commit ? It is as I feared—he is a thief. But I will save him if I can, if there is yet time."

And with these words she flew from the house in the steps of the two robbers.

She arrived in the yard below in time to see George and Charley getting into a cab.

At the same time two suspicious-looking individuals were pointing after them, and talking together.

As she approached, she heard one say ·

"That's the young feller as was lagged, and tother one's his mate."

"Well, we'll cop the pair on 'em."

"Ah, we'll put salt on their tails."

"Come on, then. They're up to no good, you may take your oath. Let's have 'em now, if we can. Let's see what their game is."

———

XXIX.—The Attempt at Fraud on Tinman's Bank, and its result.

TINMAN'S Bank is, as everybody knows, in St. James's Street.

It is one of the oldest established banking-houses in London.

Everybody knows Tinman's.

If you go in there any time between ten and four, you will see six young men, two middle aged men, and one old man, all wearing white chokers, and having their hair brushed smooth, and plastered down to the sides of their heads, and all attired in uncompromising black broadcloth.

All their pens are usually busy at work, chirping like so many birds, except at such times as they are engaged shovelling the Tinman gold across the counter to the greedy outer world waiting to take it away by the sackful.

They are staid young men, those six, far above young men's weakness, having no sympathy with profligates, tavern frequenters, and Sabbath breakers, and from their hearts despising and abhorring all manner of kind of carryings on, skylarking, and philandering.

The most correct of young men were they, who hummed hymn tunes as they walked home at night, entertained each other with mild repasts of tea and crumpets at their suburban homes, and discoursed windily upon things theological and sanctimonious, interspersed with the smallest of small secular jokes.

As for the elder clerks of the great house of Tinman, they were severe and upright men, who seemed as if the joints of their spines were glued together, and they were afraid of stooping, for fear that they should crack themselves.

In the bank, during office hours, you never by any chance saw any signs of levity. They might have been a company of undertakers instead of clerks, only undertakers are, as a rule, much jollier.

It was decidedly the most respectable and orderly of banks, and one where the widow and the orphan would find a safe asylum for their little property.

They did a deal of business, did Tinman's, in a smug sanctimonious sort of way ; and the widows, and the orphans, and the wealthy godly ones, crowded round the counter in great numbers, as Charley and his accomplice presented themselves with their checks.

Charley knew beforehand, because he had taken some trouble to ascertain the fact, that always just before shutting-up time was the busiest part of the day.

He had therefore chosen that time for making the fraudulent attempt upon their exchequer in which he was now engaged.

Both George and he were expensively dressed.

Charley with a good deal of good taste,

George in rather loud patterns and flaring colours, but both of them of very imposing exterior.

Charley walked boldly up to the end of the counter, and George chose the other end, close to the door.

They were thus as far apart as the length of the counter would permit.

Four clerks were at the counter, all busily engaged cashing cheques, and receiving money from customers to be placed to their credit.

Gold was passing to and fro across the mahogany with a loud rattle and chink. On every side was heard the flutter of bank-notes, and the chirping of busy pens.

Scarcely a word was spoken, and the two conspirators' hearts beat high, and seemed to themselves to be almost audible, as they stood waiting their turn.

Presently it came.

Charley passed his cheque.

"How will you take it?" asks the clerk, in a subdued tone.

Charley replied in the same way, speaking just loud enough to be heard.

The notes were flung upon the counter.

Charley counted them, and thrust them into his pocket.

The gold followed, and was stowed away.

The cheque was passed on to another table, and placed under a weight.

Charley, hardly able to contain himself, moved towards the door.

Meanwhile, George was being served.

"How will you take it?" a clerk also asked him, in the same subdued tone in which he had addressed the inquiry to Charley; but this time with a very different result.

Charley Wag had often presented cheques before, and knew what were the necessary forms to be observed under the circumstances.

He ought to have told George, too; but the cleverest people sometimes make these little omissions, and so mar the most elaborate plots.

Charley forgot to tell him what he was to do and say, further than that he was to to have the money in notes. So when the cashier asked George how he would take it, that booby did not in the slightest degree comprehend him.

He was in a great fright, for one thing, and had not half his wits about him; and for another thing, I think he was naturally a heavy, stupid sort of fellow.

"How will you take it?" asked the clerk.

"Eh?" said George.

"How will you take it?"

"Take what?"

"Take your money."

"Oh, I'll take it in my pocket."

"You seem a very queer sort of man," said the clerk.

"What's that to you?" retorted George. "I haven't come here to hear your opinion."

This was a most injudicious proceeding of George's, to be uncivil.

The clerk, offended, was determined to put as many obstacles in his way as possible.

He looked at the cheque very hard.

"What's the name?" he asked.

"Wag."

"Write yours at the back."

George fumbled about with his collars, and

looked very confused; for he could not have made a letter to save his life.

"Write it there."

"I can't."

"What do you mean?"

"I don't know how."

"Don't know how?"

"No."

"You're a very strange person for anybody to send for such a large sum of money."

"How much is it?" asked one of the elder clerks, coming forward.

The junior handed the cheque to him.

The senior put on his spectacles, and looked at it.

"Where did you get this?" he asked.

"From Mr. Wag."

"When?"

"An hour ago."

"Where is he?"

"At his chambers, in the Temple."

So far, so good. He had answered properly up to now. The senior was almost inclined to give it him.

There was nothing so suspicious about the case, after all; and if it had not been for George's clumsiness in the first instance, none of this scene would have occurred.

Charley, packing his money into his pocket, overheard the altercation, and was making his way as quickly as he possibly could towards the door.

If he could only manage to get outside, he made up his mind that he would take to his heels and be off.

The senior clerk, however, was still hesitating about the cheque.

"What's Mr. Wag's account?" he asked.

"Nine hundred and ninety-nine pounds, nineteen shillings and elevenpence halfpenny," said the other, glibly.

It was his duty to read up the balances in a morning; and he had read that one over and over again for many weeks, until he quite knew it by heart.

"Well, you can pay him."

"If you've any doubt about it," said George, insolently, "you'd better not do so. Give me back the cheque, and I'll tell Mr. Wag you haven't got as much in the bank."

"You'd better take yourself off, sir," said the senior clerk, "and we will keep the cheque here until Mr. Wag comes himself."

George looked a little blue at this; and he would probably have made a not very civil rejoinder, when the cashier who had just paid Charley happened to come up to the end of the counter where the senior clerk was standing with the cheque in his hand.

By the merest accident he chanced to look at the name upon it.

"Bless me!" said he, starting.

"What is it?"

"I've just cashed a draft for nine hundred odd upon the same account."

"When—to whom?"

"Just this moment, to that young gentleman going out."

"That?" said the senior clerk. "That's Mr. Wag himself. Run and stop him."

While they were speaking, the other cashier had opened a ledger.

"We should have overpaid the account if we had cashed the second cheque," said he. "It's a case of swindling, in my opinion."

George, who by no means liked the turn that things were taking, was making for the door.

The senior clerk saw the movement, and was in time to prevent it.

"Stop that man!" he cried to one of the door-porters. "Hold him fast, Thomas. You, Edwards, run out and stop that young gentleman who has just gone through."

Edwards did as desired; and finding Charley outside, just stepping into the cab, he brought him back.

George was looking already like a convicted thief.

A desperately hang-dog expression he was wearing.

He telegraphed clumsily to Charley as he entered, and this movement as well did not escape the eyes of the senior clerk.

Charley, with the slightest possible frown at his associate, sauntered unconcernedly towards the counter.

"What do you want?"

"Mr. Wag, I believe."

"That is my name."

"You have just presented a cheque, I believe."

"Certainly; I have the money in my pocket."

"This person says that you have also given him this cheque to present, which, had it been paid, would have exceeded your balance by nine hundred pounds."

"Allow me to look at the cheque," said Charley, in the most unconcerned fashion possible.

When he had looked at it, he handed it back, without changing a muscle of his face.

"Well," said he.

"Is that the case?"

"I never saw this man before that I am aware of," replied Mr. Wag, as cool as a cucumber; "and I have not written any other cheques but the one which I have just presented myself."

"We must detain this man, then. Will you appear against him, Mr. Wag?"

"I will give my evidence, of course."

Now you must not run away with the idea that Charley was going to betray his accomplice, and leave him altogether in the lurch.

He always had a long head, as you have seen before now.

He saw in a moment how matters stood. George was in a mess, and would have to be got out somehow.

That must be thought of later.

The first precaution which must be taken, was to pretend that they were perfect strangers.

That was the meaning of his frown at George.

But George, of course, dunderhead that he was, could not understand him.

He thought, of course, that Charley was going to "put him in the hole," as he termed it, and creep out himself.

Therefore, indignant at what he thought to be the other's meanness, he cried out,

"He knows me well enough. He's as bad as me, every bit. You know you did give it me. If I'm took, you ought to be as well."

Charley looked him up and down with unutterable contempt, and some little surprise.

"Perhaps he's acting," thought Charley; "but if he is, he is making an infernal fool of himself."

But George was not acting in the least. It was quite genuine, this foolishness of his.

"If I'm to be lagged, lag him too," he kept saying. And he began to launch into the lowest blackguardism, mingled with back-slang, in a way which, if any doubt existed in the clerk's mind respecting his honesty, must have rapidly dispelled it.

"Send for a policeman," said the senior clerk.

The porter stepped outside, and returned with one immediately.

He had met one at the door, who entered, accompanied by a person in plain clothes.

The same that Julia had seen and followed from the Temple.

"I want these parties," said the constable, laying his hands at once upon the arms of Charley and George, "on a charge of burglary."

"Good gracious!" exclaimed the senior clerk, "and they were just attempting the most impudent fraud upon this bank."

"Nothing more likely. They're two of the most hardenedest prigs to be found in or about London. There's a cab outside. Come on, both of you. You can attend against them, sir, if you please."

Without more to do, the policeman led his captives to the door, and, with the assistance of another policeman waiting there, helped them inside.

Just as it was going to drive off, Julia rushed forward.

"Oh, Charley! Charley!" she exclaimed; "where are they taking you? What have you done?"

One of the policemen pushed her rudely back.

The window was slammed down.

The other policeman called to the driver:

"Quod Street."

And away they went. Julia, with a scream, fell fainting into the arms of the policeman.

———

XXX.—IN WHICH JULIA MAKES UP HER MIND
TO DO IT.

"QUOD Street again," thought Charley. "I wonder what old Slang will say. I wonder whether I shall get off. If so, how?"

I need not describe the interior of the Police Court again, because I have already done so; neither need I enter particularly into the proceedings before the magistrate.

The policeman deposed, that from information he had received, he had for some time back, kept his eye upon the younger prisoner. That morning a friend of his, then present, a Richmond constable, had described the burglary, which had last night occurred at the money-lenders house, by the river side, and that he had followed after him, and taken him into custody.

The money-lender's servant than came forward, and stated that his master was lying dangerously ill, owing to the violence of one of the prisoners. And he swore to having seen George before, and having been questioned by him about the internal arrangement of the house.

He also stated, that he believed George had formed the notion, from his replies, that he was half-witted or soft.

He could not swear to Charley, as he had a mask on when he saw him; but he thought that one of the burglars was much about his build.

George, hearing him give his evidence so glibly looked thunderstruck. Charley, on the other hand, formed a still lower estimate than before of his accomplice's understanding.

The Richmond constable now came forward, and deposed that Charley was the boy who had inveigled him and his fellow-constables into the cock-loft, and then left them to their fate.

After this the banker's clerk stepped up into the witness-box, and stated what he knew of the prisoners.

By the way of a climax, another policeman stepped up, and gave both prisoners a bad character.

Mr. Slang, too, said he recollected them perfectly, and that they were a brace of unmitigated scoundrels.

He therefore committed them both to Newgate for trial; and the prisoners' van took them away, amid the cheers of the ragged mob which had assembled outside to see them depart.

What, think you, were Charley's feelings, at finding himself once more an inmate of a prison?

None of the most pleasurable you may be sure.

I will, however, leave him to the enjoyment of them, and return to Julia.

As soon as she recovered from her fainting fit, which happily was not of long duration, she made the most of her way home to Charley's chambers in the Temple.

Arriving at the bottom of the stairs, she was on the point of ascending, when a shrill whistle behind her caused her to turn her head.

Round the corner of the court at her back, she saw a hand beckoning to her.

Very much astonished, she stood still, looking at it.

"Whist!" said a voice.

She advanced a step.

"Whist!" said the voice again.

Another step.

Renewed pantomime.

Cautiously advancing to the corner, she was considerably surprised to find Charley's boy in buttons waiting for her.

More surprised was she still to find him in tears, with his livery half torn off his back, his face bruised, and his nose much swollen, as though he had had a good thump on it.

"What's the matter?" she asked.

"O-o-o-oh—o-o-h-o-o—b-o-o-h-o-o!"

"What's the matter?"

"Oh, missus!"

"What is it?"

"Oh dear, oh dear, oh Lord, oh my!"

"Speak if you can, you great stupid."

And she began to shake him.

This brought him to his senses, and he condescended to be a little more comprehensible.

"There's the police up in your chambers, mum. They've took everything. They pretty near took me, only I had a fight for it, and got away out o' window."

"What are they doing?"

"They're searching the place for stolen property, they says, mum. I told 'em there wasn't none, but they wouldn't believe me."

"I will go and see what they mean by such insolence," cried Julia.

And she made a step towards the chambers.

But the boy caught hold of her dress.

"No, mum. Don't, for goodness sake, don't. They said they wanted you, and asked me where you was to be found. They said they'd lock you up, too, along of master."

When Julia came to think it over, she came to the conclusion that much more unlikely things than that might happen.

She had better keep away.

"Here's half-a-crown," she said to the boy. "Go home."

The boy took the money, and made himself scarce.

Julia did ditto.

She passed out into Fleet Street, and walked along rapidly towards the city.

Suddenly she stopped.

An idea seemed to strike her.

She went into a public house, and had threepennyworth of hot brandy and water.

"I'll do it," said she, "if I die for it."

And she called a cab, and went to do it forthwith.

And this is what she did.

XXXI.—In which Julia does it.

SHE drove in the cab to a miserable locality at the back of Guildford Street, known as the Colonnade.

There was a very fusty greasy atmosphere about this neighbourhood; and it seemed a most unlikely place for such a dainty damsel as Julia, in her prodigious crinoline, brocaded petticoats, bronze boots, and pink silk stockings, to visit.

The dust from currycombs seemed to mingle with the sickly vapours of low, beastly cookshops; and the hot whiffs of soap-suds, and ironing, and mangling, which floated from the windows, struggled with the suffocating odour of dung.

The place was filled with washerwomen and stable-keepers, and they are most savoury trades.

Clothes-lines were to be seen everywhere; and the sound of ostlers whish-whishing to the horses they were rubbing down was on all sides audible.

Children of course abounded, clustering like flies round the windows of the cook-shops, pointing out to each other with their podgy little dirty fingers the luscious lumps of congealed flour and treacle, and speculating upon which tumbler of curds and whey they would choose, supposing they were ever lucky enough to get a halfpenny.

Out of the windows surly brutes with matted hair were lolling in their shirt-sleeves, smoking pipes, and spitting down below from time to time, very careless of the passers by, while shrewish women chattered to each other upon the door-steps, or screamed across the road.

Taking very little notice of these circumstances, Julia, hastening forward, and looking straight ahead, soon came to the object of her journey.

Then the cab stopped.

It was before a lop-sided, crazy tenement, in front of which was a large board, bearing a pictorial representation, in glaring colours, of a hardworking female engaged in busily turning a mangle.

Under this was the name of the laundress whose house it was—Mrs. Suds.

Under this, "Washing and Mangling taken in."

Under this again, "Clear-starching."

Leaving the cab at the door, Julia entered a close-smelling, dimly-lighted apartment on the ground-floor, reeking with the fumes of linen in the wash-tub, and linen undergoing the process of ironing.

By the wall stood a mangle; perhaps the same depicted outside, but now at rest.

A large table in the centre of the room was covered with many layers of shirts, more or less ragged, and chemises which the form of beauty had well-nigh worn to rags.

A pile of washing-baskets in a corner also appeared to prove that Mrs. Suds did a good trade, and had an extensive connection.

But it was Mrs. Suds herself that Julia wanted; and Mrs. Suds, a fat, red-faced woman, of the kind called motherly, was ironing at the table, and looking up as Julia came in, gave her "good-night."

"And law bless me! is it you, ma'am?" said she.

"Yes," replied Julia; "are you busy?"

"Pretty well, ma'am. Among the middlings, if I may call it so. There's plenty to do, ma'am, and more where that comes from, I dare say."

"I am glad to see you have so good a business."

"Thank you, ma'am, it's very good, I'm much obleeged to you. I can't complain."

"I'm happy to hear it."

"I suppose you called about your dress, ma'am. Do you want to have it ready before the time you said?"

"Oh no; on the contrary, you can keep it here until I send for it, and the rest of the things, too. Do not send them to the Temple."

"Very well, ma'am."

"It is not that I called about. I want you to do me a favour, Mrs. Suds."

"Me, ma'am?" said Mrs. Suds, astonished.

"Yes, you. You say you are busy; can you spare an hour or two to-night?"

"Well, ma'am, I have some things to do by to-morrow, which ought to be done."

"I know, Mrs. Suds, that you are a good kind soul, and you won't refuse me. Here's a sovereign. Get somebody to do your work, and come with me where I want you to go."

"Well, I'm sure I shall be most happy; only if its anywhere particular, I haven't got nothing fit to go in with a lady like you, ma'am."

"Tut, tut! Put on your bonnet and shawl; and, Mrs. Suds—"

"Yes, ma'am?"

"You must bring with you another dress like the one you are wearing. Have you one?"

"Well, no, ma'am—not the same pattern."

Julia reflected for a moment.

"Never mind, then," said she. "Come along as quickly as you can."

The present of a sovereign had imparted a more than usual activity to Mrs. Suds's movements.

She bustled out and fetched in a neighbour, whom she easily induced to take her place for awhile at the ironing-board.

Then, after a brief toilet, she declared herself ready.

"Let us go, then," said Julia.

Without more ado she led the way outside, and jumped lightly into the Hansom.

It took Mrs. Suds a little longer for two reasons.

One, because she was not used to Hansoms; the other, because she was in what is called an interesting situation. That is to say, there was some chance of the advent of an infant Suds, at no very distant period.

"Drive as quickly as you can," said Julia.

"Where to, ma'am?" says the cabman.

"To Holborn."

As they rode along, Mrs. Suds asked, with a diffident cough or two, what might be their destination.

To which Julia replied:

"You shall know directly—when we get to Holborn."

Arrived here, they stopped at a shop which Julia pointed out to the driver, and leaving Mrs. Suds in the cab, she went inside, and made some inquiries.

Mrs. Suds, who, from the cab, could see into the shop, saw that Julia asked for something which they had not got, and that the shopman was in doubt where to recommend her to go for it; and that he called in the aid of another shopman, who, after tapping his head and considering for awhile, looked in a book, and directed Julia to go to some other place which he found mentioned there.

At least, this is what Mrs. Suds believed was occurring, and what in the end proved to be the case, although Julia at the time denied it.

"What do you want to get, my dear?" asked the washerwoman.

"What do you mean?"

"Didn't you want to buy something?"

"No."

"Oh, I thought you did."

"I want to find out where some one lives."

"I beg your pardon, my dear."

Julia gave a direction to the cabman, and they rattled on as before.

Again they stopped. It was at the same sort of shop, as it appeared to Mrs. Suds, as that they had stopped at before.

Again Julia descended, and, as on the last occasion, Mrs. Suds was able to see inside the shop from her seat in the cab.

She saw Julia make some purchase, which was wrapt up in paper for her, and she returned to her place.

"What could make her tell this story, then?" thought Mrs. Suds.

Altogether the whole business was throughout extremely mysterious.

When she was in the cab again, the cabman asked:

"Where to?"

"To Newgate."

"Newgate, ma'am?"

"Yes."

"What, the prison?"

"To be sure."

The cabman let down the little trap, and whipped up his horse. He, however, was rather astonished.

So was Mrs. Suds.

She asked her companion presently, in rather a frightened voice:

"Is it to Newgate prison we're going, my dear?"

"Yes," replied Julia. "You're not afraid, are you?"

"No, my dear; that is, not particular. Only I hope to goodness gracious no harm will happen to us."

"Harm! not likely. All I want you to do, Mrs. Suds, is to come in with me. I want to see one of the prisoners."

"One of the prisoners?"

"Yes."

"Do you know them?"

"It is my husband."

"Good gracious!"

"You've never seen him, I believe."

"No, ma'am. Has he been there long?"

"He was put in to-day."

"Oh, indeed, ma'am. Might I ask, if there was no offence in doing so, that is, ma'am—"

"What is he imprisoned for, you mean."

"Yes."

"For libel, you know. Goodness, you did not think he was a common prisoner, did you?"

"Oh, no, ma'am. I'm sure he couldn't be. For what, did you call it?"

"For sedition."

"Seduction?"

"No, something quite different. For writing something in a newspaper—a political offence. Lots of distinguished people have been locked up for the same before now. Lord Brougham was in this very prison for the same thing."

"What, the Lord Brougham that there's the pictures of in the plaid trousers?"

"Yes, the same. But here we are."

As she spoke, they stopped at the Debtor's Door.

"What am I to do?" asked Mrs. Suds, in a great flutter.

"Do what I tell you," replied Julia, in a whisper, "and you shall have another sovereign for your trouble. When we go in—if we can get in—put your handkerchief up to your face, and hold it there, and pretend to be sobbing very hard. I am going to say you are my husband's mother, you know, and you must be very much affected."

"Yes; I understand."

"If you had not some reason for seeing him, you know, they wouldn't let you in."

"Wouldn't they?"

"No. I am going to say I am his sister.

Now don't let them see more of your face than you can help; and stop here till I fetch you,"

"Do you know any one here?"

"Yes; I know one of the gaolers. Now be quiet; I am going."

And with these words she tripped up the steps to the gaol-door.

"I don't half like it," said the old lady to herself, when she was left alone. "I must say I don't half like it. I hope no harm will come of it. I almost wish I was safe at home again, in front of my washing-tub. If it wasn't for the money, I wish I had never come; but in these hard times, two sovereigns are not to be sneezed at."

Julia approached the door.

A gaoler was standing there. Julia smiled her sweetest, and said:

"Is Mr. Jemmys in?"

"No, miss," said the gaoler; "he's over the way."

"Where?"

"At the 'Last Drop.' You'll find him in the bar-parlour. Shall I send for him, miss?"

"No, don't do that; I'll go for him myself."

She left the cab where it was, and crossed over to the public-house indicated.

At the bar she inquired for Mr. Jemmys.

"Mr. Jemmys, you're wanted," said the barmaid, calling over her shoulder.

And Mr. Jemmys came out.

"Who wants me?" he asked.

Julia beckoned him to the door.

Then, when they were alone, she raised her veil.

"Good Heavens!" exclaimed Mr. Jemmys. "Miss Jenkini, as I'm a Christian."

"Yes. It's Miss Jenkini sure enough. How well your looking, Mr. Jemmys. You're not a day older than you were, I'd stake my life."

"Go on with you. You don't mean it."

"Yes, I do. Well."

"Well, what is it?"

"Aren't you going to kiss me?"

"Oh, I thought you wouldn't like it. Your such a—"

"Such a what?"

"Such a swell."

"I've had a rise in life since you and I kept company; but you see I haven't forgotten my old friends."

"I never thought you would."

"Of course not. Kiss me again."

Mr. Jemmys did so.

"Thank you. Oh, you old duck!"

And Miss Julia took the goaler's head between her hands, and saluted him rapturously upon his rather red nose.

"I want to ask you a favour," said she, after a few more compliments had passed on either side.

"What is it?"

"I want to go into the prison, to see one of the prisoners."

"Have you an order?"

"Order? No—of course not."

"But you can't go in without."

"Pack of rubbish! You can take me in well enough if you like."

"Indeed I can't. It's as much as my place is worth."

"Oh, very well. You won't oblige an old

friend, won't you? Very well, Mr. Jemmys. I'll wish you good evening. Don't put yourself out on my account, I beg."

"No—no. I say, don't go away like that. Let's talk about it. Come into this room, and sit down; there's nobody here."

He led her into the coffee-room, and ordering a glass of hot brandy and water at the bar, took it in after her.

He had once in his time been desperately smitten with the lovely Julia, when she was a dancer at Muggins's Music Hall; and report did say, that he had squandered a good deal of money upon her.

That he was very much smitten with her now, there was no doubt.

When he brought in the brandy, and she had sipped a little, and he had sipped a little, he sat ogling her, like an old sheep, that he was.

"Don't it seem a long time ago?" said he.

"What?"

"Since we used to go out with one another."

"Have you ever thought of me since?"

"Many a time."

"You've never wished for those times to come again?"

"Haven't I?" with a great gulph at the grog.

"Nonsense. What do you care about me? You've got some other young lady now, I'll be bound."

"I don't care a button for any other young ladies. You're the only one I ever cared for, or ever will care for, Julia. The very sight of you as hput me all in a twitter."

"Oh, Mr. Jemmys—so it has me."

Here the deceitful hussy leant her head against the gaoler's cheek.

"What's to prevent us?" said he, in a whisper.

"Prevent us what?"

"Keeping company again."

"Nothing that I know of, if you would like to."

"You know I would. Where are you living?"

"With my mother."

"Where's she?"

"Outside."

"Outside?"

"In a cab."

"In a cab?"

"Yes; she's come here, and sent me in to beg of you to get us an interview with my poor dear brother, who is in that dreadful gaol, accused of a crime of which he is as guiltless as the unborn babe."

"Is he, my dear?" said Mr. Jemmys, who, although he was very much prejudiced in favour of the young lady herself, nevertheless placed very little faith in the innocence of her brother, whoever he might be.

"Your brother, did you say?" he asked presently. "What does he call himself?"

"Charley Wag."

"The deuce he does! He's a promising young blade, by all accounts."

"I'm sure he's the dearest fellow in all the world."

"I've no doubt; but he seems to be rather a precocious one."

"Why so?"

"Why they say he has chambers in the Temple."

"Well?"

"And that he keeps a couple of mistresses."

"It's a great story, for he only keeps one."

"Julia, Julia, I hope you're not the one."

"Me! What do you mean?"

"He is your brother, then."

"Come, I tell you what it is, Mr. Jemmys, if you think you are going to insult me with impunity, you're very much mistaken; for I'll claw your eyes out myself, and get some one else to punch your head afterwards."

"There—there, then; don't be so dreadful excited, my dear. Of course I don't want to insult you."

"What do you do it, then, for?"

"Come, give me a kiss, and I'll beg your pardon."

"Nothing of the sort. Keep your hands to yourself."

"But, Julia."

"I'll wish you a very good night."

"Julia, I'm very sorry."

"I don't care about your sorrow. Leave go of me."

"I'll take you into the prison."

"I don't believe you."

"I swear it."

"Come and do it, then."

"If I do—"

"Well?"

"What will you give me if I do?"

"Bless the man!—what do you want?"

Mr. Jemmys looked at her very slyly, and then whispered in her ear.

"Go on with you," said she; "I wouldn't think of such a thing."

"No—but why?"

"Why I'm ashamed of you."

"Well, we used to."

"Times have altered."

"Do, Julia, and I'll take you into the prison this minute."

"Take me, and I'll tell you afterwards. When I come out I will."

"You ought to promise now."

"There, then—I promise,

Mr. Jemmys seemed satisfied, and they crossed the road together.

Julia was very anxious to go back to Mrs. Suds.

She was desperately afraid that by this time Mrs. Suds would have got tired, and have run away.

To Julia's great relief, however, she had not done so; she had only fallen off to sleep.

Julia left the gaoler, and woke her up, telling her to get up, and to hold her handkerchief to her face, and sob; which the old lady obligingly did.

Mr. Jemmys then spoke to the doorkeeper for a few moments, and presently admitted the two ladies.

As the reader may suppose it would be far from an easy task, under ordinary circumstances, to obtain admission to Newgate:

As you perhaps know, when prisoners in that place are allowed to see their friends, it is only for a very short time, and from across a double range of iron bars, in the space between which sits a turnkey:

A THIEF IN THE DARK.

When they have interviews with their legal advisers, it is in a room with glass sides, round which walks a turnkey, who can see everything, but hear nothing.

But Julia and Mrs. Suds were privileged persons.

The governor happened to be out of the way, the other gaoler promised for a consideration to "keep it dark," and so Mr. Jemmys conducted the ladies through what at first seemed to be an interminable series of corridors and yards, yards and corridors, until they reached Master Wag's abiding-place.

At last, however, they entered a small paved court, two sides of which were studded by cell-doors.

Opening one of these with a resounding clang, Mr. Jemmys called out:

No. 36.

"Visitor, Number Forty-one."

Then he fell back, in order to allow the ladies to pass, closed the cell door again after him, and discreetly turned the huge key in the lock.

There was a "Judas," or small trap, open in the door itself; but this he also closed.

And having thus given them the opportunity to say all they wanted to say privately, but at the same time recommending them to be as sharp as possible about it, he took to walking backwards and forwards in the yard, whistling softly to himself, and probably thinking of Julia.

While he was thus engaged, a curious scene was occurring within.

When they entered the cell, they found Charley lying on his bed.

He woke and rose to his feet on seeing them.

[CHARLEY WAG, THE NEW JACK SHEPPARD.

" Julia !'' he cried.

He looked rather uncomfortable at the sight of her, and rather ashamed of himself, did this brazen young blackguard, in spite of his " cheek."

" Julia, have you come to see me ?"

" If I didn't, Charley, who should ?"

" But, do you—do you—''

" What ?"

" Believe me guilty ?"

She looked at him a moment steadfastly.

" Ask your own heart," said she.

He hung his head.

" I knew how it would be," he said ; " you despise me."

" No, Charley."

" What, do you love me still ?"

" I love you more than ever. I will always love you. I am come to save you."

" To save me ?"

" Yes."

" But how ?"

" By the aid of this lady. Take a seat on the bed, Mrs. Suds.''

Mrs. Suds, who had been listening in the blankest astonishment, did as she was desired directly.

Then Julia, advancing towards her, and fixing her steadily with her eyes, suddenly pushed her backwards upon the bed, and held her down by her arms.

" What are you going to do to me ?'' asked the old lady, breathless. " I'll scream if you don't let me get up."

" Listen to me," said Julia, between her teeth, and with an energy which astonished Charley almost as much as it did the old lady. " If you make any noise, or attempt to resist, I'll stick this penknife into you ?"

And as she spoke, she drew from her pocket a very murderous-looking little knife, and opened one of the blades.

The old lady shuddered.

" It's very cruel of you to treat me so, and me in the situation that I am. I don't know, I'm sure, what won't be the consequence."

" I can't help it ; I shall save my husband, whatever happens. Now listen : I want your gown, and bonnet, and shawl, for him to escape in ; then I shall tie your hands and feet, and bandage your mouth, and leave you. That will show them that you did not willingly assist. You won't be punished, so don't be afraid."

" Oh dear ! oh dear !"

" Sit where you are, and I'll take off your things."

" You aint going to undress me before that young fellow, surely. Oh dear, oh dear ! to think that I should have come to this, and me the mother of ten children, all boys. Oh dear ! oh dear !"

" Hold your stupid tongue !" hissed Julia in her ear ; " or I'll strangle you !"

This old lady was a very weak old lady. If she had had her wits about her, I have no doubt she might easily have given the alarm, and escaped without injury ; but she was too terrified to think of anything.

She therefore passively submitted, while Julia unrobed her.

Then, assisted by Charley, they gagged her with a handkerchief, and fastened her hands and feet.

Then Charley dressed himself, with Julia's aid, and Julia knocked at the door for Mr. Jemmys to let them out.

" Pretend to sob, and keep your handkerchief to your face," she whispered.

Mr. Jemmys opened the door for them. The whole affair had been so rapid, that he had not expected them yet.

" I brought mother away," Julia said to him. " If she had stopped any longer, there would have been a scene ''

She held the lamp in her hand which the gaoler had given her when they entered the cell, and as she handed it to him, she managed to get between him and the bed, so that he could not see the woman's figure upon it.

But he had to turn to shut the door.

Again it wanted stratagem.

Julia motioned to Charley to turn away, and then, turning to Jemmys as he pulled the door to, she put her arm round his neck, and pressed her lips to his, whispering at the same time :

" Will you meet me in half-an-hour's time over at that public-house, when I have given mother the slip ?"

" Yes, yes,'' replied the love-sick turnkey ; " mind you're there."

" Wait for me if I don't come to the minute."

" Yes, I'll wait till you come."

Several times on their way to the outer door Mr. Jemmys seemed as though he were inclined to criticise the appearance of Charley's mamma.

But upon each of these occasions the sly maiden intercepted him, distracted the amorous turnkey's attention by some playful dalliance which completely banished anything like vigilance from his mind."

So they at last reached the outer door, where the other turnkey was waiting for them.

XXXII.—In for it again.

WOULD they get by this turnkey also, was the question.

He was not blinded by love, like our worthy friend, Mr. Jemmys.

Would he not, then, be more likely to have his eyes about him ? and if so, would he not suspect the sex of the interesting elderly female, who went sobbing past him, squeezing a blue and white check pocket-handkerchief to her afflicted nose ?

Although Julia was acting her part with all her might, and making love as hard as ever she could make it ; she, nevertheless, found time to have an eye to Master Charley's deportment, and an eye to the behaviour of the other turnkey.

When they reached the outer door, she therefore bustled forward, spreading out her skirts to the very widest (which was very wide indeed), and taking up as much room as possible (which was a great deal), with her ample crinoline.

By these means she quite swamped poor Jemmys, and shut out all sight of Charley from the other gaoler.

Master Charley was sufficiently wide awake, in spite of being muffled up in clothes which did not fit him, and being obliged to cover his face with an atrocious rag, which smelt revoltingly of gamey red herrings; and he had his wits about him as usual, so that he could understand her object. And she need not have urged him as she did with a nudge, and a " Get along mother, do," to induce him to descend the steps into the street with the greatest possible celerity.

Taking great care not to trip himself up—for the skirts were rather too long in front—and at the same time being very careful indeed not to show his ankles.

However, after all, this great caution was not necessary; for Mr. Jemmys' fellow turnkey was far too eager too peep under Julia's bonnet, and catch a glimpse of the beautiful face of that bewitching young maiden, to care anything about the old woman on in front; while Jemmys in his turn, indignant at the other man's rudeness, was elbowing him up into a corner as much as possible, and endeavouring to thrust himself between Julia and him.

" You'll be sure to meet me," whispered Jemmys.

" Quite sure."

" You're not selling me ?"

" Do I look like it ?"

" I shall rely upon you, then."

" You can do so."

" While this brief conversation had been taking place, Charley had been scrambling as gracefully as he could into the Hansom cab.

Julia quickly followed him.

" You won't be long," whispered Jemmys.

" As soon as I can get rid of mother," responded the young lady.

The gaoler kissed her hand, and hastily retired.

" Down Fleet Street, as quickly as you can," Julia called to the cabman.

" Drive like the devil !" bawled Charley, through the trap.

" That's an energetic old woman," thought the cabman, as he whipped his horse into a canter.

As they rode along, Charley caught the girl to his heart, and kissed her passionately.

" Dear, dear Julia," he said. " What do I not owe you ?"

Julia replied with kisses.

Presently she said :

" I feel very faint, Charley. It is the excitement, perhaps. I wish I had a glass of water."

" Shall we stop for one ?"

" No ; we will get on as quickly as possible."

" By the way, where are we going ?"

" To the Temple."

" Will that be safe ?"

" I have got a reason."

" What reason ?"

" Have you any money ?"

" No."

" Well, then, what do you propose doing ?"

" My dear little girl, I haven't the least idea."

" I'll tell you what I propose, then."

" What's that?"

" That we go back there, and make an attempt to get my jewels."

" There'll be no particular difficulty in doing that. I suppose we shall only have to walk in and fetch them."

" I'm not quite so sure of that, if the police are there."

And Julia related what had occurred between her and the little boy in buttons, and what a risk she had run when she went there last time.

By this time they had reached the Temple, and Julia descending, paid the cabman with all the money she had remaining in her pocket, and in great perturbation took Charley's hand, and accompanied him into the Inn.

The porter at the gate looked at them very hard, but said nothing.

Julia had made up her mind at first to ask him whether Mr. Wag had returned; but there was such a contemptuous expression upon the man's face, that she had not the heart to do so.

Anyhow, she thought there was some small consolation in the fact of there being no policemen hanging about the lodge, or anybody else to interfere with them; and they hurried past, and were soon in front of the house in the court where they lived.

All was dark and quiet.

" Will you wait below ?" Charley said; " and I will go up-stairs and reconnoitre."

" That will be best ; but be careful."

As a first step, Charley pulled off the bonnet, and gown, and shawl which he wore, and which were rather calculated to impede his progress, if there arose any occasion for hasty movement.

No occasion, however, arose at present.

Taking Julia's key he went up-stairs, and let himself into the rooms, Julia remaining below to keep watch and guard against surprise.

Then he searched all round the rooms.

They looked very bare.

The police were evidently at work removing the goods.

Charley looked in all the drawers.

They were nearly all empty. The diamond-box had been removed.

There was scarcely anything whatever of any value which had not been removed ; and Charley, with a heavy heart and empty pockets, came down-stairs again.

Only one thing had he been able to secure, and that was a pistol, which had escaped the eyes of the authorities, and which he thought might, in his present desperate circumstances, prove of great service to him.

Coming down-stairs after his otherwise most unsatisfactory expedition, he found Julia seated upon the door-step, her head resting in her hands.

" What is the matter ?" he asked, anxiously.

Julia looked up to him with a faint smile.

" Oh, Charley," she said, " I feel so ill."

" Are you too ill to move ?"

" No, no—I shall be better directly. Hush ! do not you hear footsteps ?"

" Yes."

" Are they coming this way ?"

" They are running towards us, I think."

" Oh, Charley, let us fly !"

As she spoke, she rose to her feet, and made a step forwards; but a sudden faintness seizing upon her, she reeled, and would have fallen to the earth, had he not caught her in his arms.

At the same moment a couple of policemen made their appearance.

Charley did not wait to see whether they wanted him.

He caught up his Julia as though she had been a baby—for desperation lent him strength—and rushed off in an opposite direction.

If, however, he had had any doubt about the policemen's object, it was very soon dispelled.

"Stop! stop, Charley Wag!" the foremost shouted. "I call upon you in the Queen's name to surrender."

But Charley did not see it.

He continued running towards the river.

As he approached the water, they were close upon him.

"I hope I shan't have to swim for it again," thought Charley to himself. "I had rather too much of that last night."

As good luck would have it, a wherry was passing at the moment.

Charley hailed it.

"Boat, boat!" he shouted.

"Boat, boat!" shouted the police behind.

The boatman advanced, and pulled in close to the bottom of some stairs Charley was standing on.

Without a moment's hesitation, he sprang with his fair burthen into the boat.

"Stop him!" roared the police.

"Row for your life!" said Charley, presenting his pistol at the boatman's head.

"Deliver yourself up, you young scoundrel!" shouted the police.

"Come any nearer, and I'll blow your brains out!" bawled Charley.

The boatman, who would much rather have had nothing to do with the affair, but who had somehow got himself mixed up in it before he knew where he was, thought he had better obey his new master, and pull with all his might; so with this idea, he took two or three vigorous strokes.

But then it occurred to him that probably the police might know him again, and associate him with thieves, and that it might be his ruin; and so with this idea, he pulled up short.

"Go on," cried Charley.

The man remained motionless.

"Go on," he repeated.

Then, seeing that the other still hesitated, and knowing that there was no time to lose, he made a sudden start forward, and grasped the boatman by the throat.

He was luckily only a young man, and not much more than Charley's equal at a fair wrestle.

Being taken thus suddenly, he was no match for him.

Charley grasped him by the throat, and, throwing all his strength into the action, raised him from the seat, and pitched him head over heels into the water.

Then, with the boat rocking frightfully to and fro, he clutched at one of the sculls, and with it dealt the boatman a stunning blow on the head, as he rose and clutched at the boat side.

Then, dropping into his seat, and balancing the boat, which had dipped deeply at one side,

by a tremendous effort he pulled vigorously round, and managed to get hold of the other scull.

Then dashed boldly out into the stream.

XXXIII.—A RESOLUTION—HURRAH FOR THE ROAD—JULIA MAKES HER FIRST APPEARANCE IN TOP-BOOTS AND LEATHERS, WHILE CHARLEY IS, AS USUAL, A SWELL OF THE PERIOD—WHERE SHALL WE GET A SUPPER—THE OLD PROVERB, "THERE IS NOTHING LIKE CHEEK."

HE rowed on for five or six minutes, and then, seeing some steps where he could effect a landing, ran the boat in just by the Dark Arches, and stepping on shore, let it drift away.

Julia by this time had recovered her strength and courage, and she now proclaimed herself ready for anything.

"What shall we do?" Charley asked.

"We must live," said Julia.

"You wouldn't like to see me take a place as errand boy, even if I could get one."

"Well, not exactly."

"Then I'll tell you what, let's take to the road."

"The road?"

"Turn highwaymen."

"How can I turn highwayman?"

"Well, I'll tell you, Julia; I've been thinking it over. We've got two horses and a groom."

"I know that."

"Suppose we go straight round to the stables, and get them out. I don't mean the groom. We'll leave him; but you shall dress in his clothes. I'm sure they will fit you."

"Well?"

"Then we'll say good-bye to London for a season, and give them a turn in the country. Nothing could be more delightful than riding about from place to place, putting up where you choose, and leading a free roving life like that; could there? That is, providing you do not object to keep company with a highwayman.

"My dear Charley, as you are to be a highwayman, I suppose I must put up with it."

"But you don't despise me?"

"My dear Charley, you are a dear, kind, brave, lion-hearted fellow, and I could never despise you, if I were to find out that you were ten times wickeder than you are."

"And you won't leave me?"

"Never!"

The result of this conversation was great satisfaction upon either side; and the two lovers betook themselves without farther delay to the stables where Charley kept his horses.

It was not far off; indeed, close to Charing Cross. When they arrived there, the groom was out of the way.

"So much the better," Charley said. "We don't want him."

The groom lodged down a mews, in a house opposite to the stable where the horses were locked up. The man's landlady knowing Charley well, gave him the key without any hesitation; and Charley, lighting a small lantern, crossed the road with his companion.

Charley knew that the groom kept his best livery in a trunk in the stable, and with a spade thrust under the lid, he found it no very difficult matter to prize it open.

Then Julia undressed as quickly as possible, and donned the clothes; but not without a considerable amount of giggling at the comical figure which she insisted upon asserting that she cut in them; though Charley protested, with perfect truth, that they became her admirably.

When she was fully equipped, and had in the most heroic fashion slashed off a vast quantity of beautiful curly locks, she pronounced herself ready; and Charley having meanwhile saddled the two horses with new saddles, Mr. Wag and his "missus" mounted thereon, and rode up the mews into the street.

Then they turned their horses' heads towards Hampstead, and set off in a trot.

They were not long before they reached the Tottenham Court Road, and pushing on, soon came to Camden Town; then, still pressing forward, began the ascent of Hampstead Hill. In a little more than an hour from the time that they left the stable, they were standing still upon the Heath.

"Which way?" said Julia.

"What's it matter?" replied her companion. "All ways are alike."

"What do you say to straight forward?"

"I haven't the least objection."

"Come on then, and hurrah for the road!"

"But what's your opinion of the life of a highwayman, so far?" asked Mr. Wag.

"Well," said Julia, "as far as it has gone, it is highly satisfactory; though my motto is, anything for a change."

"Ah! but you might make a change for the worse, you know."

"Perhaps so; but as it is, I have always changed for the better."

"How is that?"

"I began life as a shirt-maker; and I used to earn threepence a day, if I stuck hard at it. Then I took to mantle-making, and made about ninepence a day. There was a rise, wasn't it? Then I thought I might do better, and went to sit as a model to photographers, at eighteenpence an hour, fastening my boot, or lolling on a sofa, showing my ankles. When I had a little more courage, I used to make a little more money. Indeed, the less clothes you have on, the larger price you get. I got up to three shillings; and I dare say you've seen me in lots of stereoscopic slides. They seized several thousands of me in Holywell Street, when Lord Campbell's Act was passed the other day. After a time I gave up that trade, and took to the music halls. That's where I first met you, you know. Then I picked up a swell who introduced me to the duke; and now I'm with you."

"And are you happy?"

"Don't I look like it? But I say, were not going to keep riding on like this all night, are we? I should very much like to have some supper, and go to bed. What do you say?"

"I'm the same way of thinking. I was anxious to make a start, and get out of London; but we won't go too far. Round about here is a capital neighbourhood. We might spend a night or two at Hampstead with advantage; though, as you say, I think supper is the first thing on the cards."

"Only we've got no money."

"Bah! what does that matter?"

"How do you mean?"

"I'll tell you. We'll go in a regular buster, you know. Order the best of every thing, and blow up the landlord. That'll make him think us respectable."

"To be sure."

"Then in the morning, I'll send you on with the horses, and I'll stop behind, and watch my opportunity of giving them the slip. Bless you, its easy enough. It only wants a little cheek."

"I say, Charley, there's one thing rather awkward."

"What's that?"

"You see, my being dressed as a groom, I shan't be able to have meals with you."

"Dash it, no; I never thought of that."

"No, and we shan't be able to—"

"To what?"

"To see one another, except when—That is to say, we can never—oh, it's disgusting!"

"Well, you shall have a suit of gentleman's clothes directly we can get some money, and then we will manage better. But here's the inn."

XXXIV.—A VERY IMPORTANT PERSONAGE—A TALKATIVE STRANGER—THE THIEF IN THE DARK—THE BITER BIT.

MASTER CHARLES and his groom alighted, and the former went swaggering into the hotel, whilst the latter held the horses outside.

"Hallo, landlord! landlord!" bawled the young gentleman.

And the landlord came bustling forward, and made a low bow; for he thought, of course, that no one but a young nobleman at the very least could have such lungs and such impudence.

"Can you accommodate me for the night?" asked Mr. Wag, in a very insolent and supercilious tone. "That is to say, have you got anything decent to eat, and a bed that it is possible to sleep in?"

"Well, I think so, sir."

"Think so, indeed! What do you know about such matters, I should like to know? I suppose you consider yourself a judge of what a nobleman's accustomed to—that's what you'd like me to believe."

"He is a nobleman, then," thought the landlord, who was a humble little man, and ready to truckle to any extent to anything like a title.

And as he spoke, he took a pair of wax candles, and led the way very pompously upstairs, anxious to show by his manners that he was accustomed to the best of society.

"I regret to say, sir," he remarked, with an apologetic cough, as he paused on the threshhold of one of the rooms, "that there is a gentleman already having his supper in the best apartment."

"Good heavens! do you suppose I'm going to eat my meals with a perfect stranger—a nobody knows who? What do you mean?"

"Oh, he's a perfect gentleman, I assure you, sir—"

"Well—there, there; I don't want to hear anything about him. Show me in."

Thus cut short on the brink of a long speech, the little landlord ushered Charley into the room, where the stranger was already seated at supper.

Charley then ordered the landlord to bring him the best that his house contained, and a bottle of champagne, and a bottle of port; and then, taking a toothpick from a glass upon a side-table, placed his back to the fire, spread out his legs, and became unconscious of the existence of anybody else but himself in the world.

The stranger, after glancing up at him for a few moments, dropped his eyes down to his plate, and went on with his supper.

Presently, however, after several stealthy glances at Mr. Wag, he coughed and spoke.

"A fine night to-night, sir."

"Pretty fair."

Then, with a glance at Charley's boots and spurs—for he had on an imposing pair—

"A pleasant night for a ride."

"Yes, not bad."

"Come far, sir?"

"Not very."

"A taciturn chap, that," muttered the stranger to himself, as he took a glass of wine from a decanter before him.

"Rather an inquisitive fellow," thought Mr. Wag, plying his toothpick.

"What's he call himself, I wonder?" thought the stranger. "He seems a swell."

"I should like to know who he is," thought Mr. Wag. "He has the air of a gentleman."

"After a little delay, the landlord made his appearance with the wine, followed by a waiter carrying the supper; and although he was very obsequious before, his behaviour now was several degrees more deferential.

The fact was, Miss Julia had been cracking up Charley sky high, and the landlord had become thoroughly impressed with his importance.

"He doesn't care what he pays," Julia had said, "so long as you give him the best quality; and he doesn't stint me either; so let's have some of the right sort, old fellow. Stick it down to the governor."

"Well," said the landlord to himself, "if that's the case, he shall pay well, whether he feeds well or not."

Master Charles was very fastidious. He objected to everything, and turned up his nose at everything, but managed to put away a tolerable quantity for all that.

The stranger eyed him attentively.

Once he left the room, and meeting the landlord upon the stairs, inquired who Charley was.

"Some young nob from town—a peer's son, according to his servant, and rolling in money."

"Indeed!"

"Got a beautiful pair of horses, I must say."

"Is he going to stop here to-night?"

"Yes, sir."

"Can I have a bed too?"

"Certainly."

The stranger returned to the sitting-room; but while he had been absent, Charley had been questioning the waiter.

"Know that gentleman?" he asked.

"No, sir. He seems a very nice sort of gentleman, though."

"Stopping here?"

"Came this evening, sir."

"How?"

"On foot, sir."

"Humph!"

"Beg your pardon, sir?"

"I didn't speak. You can leave the room."

When the stranger returned, Charley had done his supper, and was quietly discussing his wine.

The other gentleman returned to his decanter, and as they sat opposite to each other, they every now and then took sly glances at each other; and every now and then, when they happened to catch each other's eye, diving headlong into their respective decanters with more or less confusion.

At last, the stranger hazarded a remark about some public event; Master Charles, though a little under the influence of the wine, responded politely.

Then they got on to talk of events in town.

Master Charley began to launch out. He dearly loved bragging, particularly when in liquor.

He knew everybody, according to his account.

He mixed with the highest society, and was received into the very first circles.

If there was anyone who could at all surpass him in fashionable experience, it was the stranger.

Charley could mention nobody he did not know. Indeed, several persons with whom he himself had claimed acquaintance, the stranger claimed to be upon such intimate terms, that our hero, in some confusion, changed the conversation, for fear that he might be called upon for some explanations regarding them which he would have found it exceedingly hard to make.

I have told you that there was something about Charley which betokened gentle blood; a certain air of distinction, which the raggedest of clothes, and the dirtiest of faces, could not altogether obliterate.

Now that he was well dressed, he looked a thoroughbred young gentleman; and the stranger was evidently impressed with him.

They got on capitally.

Only once a little incident occurred to throw a gloom over the cheerfulness of the meeting.

"Have you seen the paper this evening?" the stranger asked.

"No," replied Charley.

"There was a curious case in the police."

"Indeed!"

"Yes; some young blackguard taken up for housebreaking, who called himself Charley Bag, or Rag, or Scrag, or something of that sort."

Charley looked uncomfortable, and lighted a cigar.

"An awful young scoundrel," continued the stranger: "kept a woman, and I don't know what all."

"You don't mean that."

"Yes, I do. By Jove, if I had my way with the likes of him—"

"What would you do?"

"I'd have them flogged at a cart's tail."

"Ah!"

But Charley could see that the other had not the slightest suspicion to whom he was talking, and quickly recovered his usual composed demeanour.

They presently had in a couple of glasses of hot brandy and water, after which they smoked several cigars; and at length Mr. Wag took himself off to bed, rather unsteady on his pins, and with an unusual thickness in his voice.

Then, having given a few instructions to his groom, he undressed, and tumbled into bed.

When there, he laid his head upon the pillow, where, as it seemed to him, he had a very great deal of difficulty in keeping it down, so tremendously did it throb.

"I'm very lushy," said Mr. Wag to himself, "and I shall have a splitting headache in the morning, or else I'm very much mistaken."

Then he shut his eyes again, and tried to go off to sleep.

Perhaps he did go to sleep, or perhaps he did not; he could hardly tell himself. If he had been sleeping, however, he was wide awake now.

Something had disturbed him; there was a movement in the room.

Some one was groping about in the room.

Ah! what was that?

The bulls-eye of a lantern dancing on the wall.

Charley rose upon his elbow, and felt under his pillow for his pistol, which he had placed there, he well remembered, before he went to bed.

Yes, it was there still. He took hold of the handle, and drew back the trigger.

The person in the room was evidently seeking about for Charley's clothes, and feeling in his pockets. It was a robber.

Charley drew back the trigger.

Click!

The thief heard the noise, and turned the bulls-eye full upon Charley's face.

The start had sobered him, and Charley felt that everything depended upon immediate action.

He sprang in an instant from the bed, and grasped the intruder by the throat.

"Who are you?" he said. "What do you want?"

The man struggled to get away, but Charley placed the cold muzzle of the pistol against his forehead.

"Move another inch, and you're a dead man!"

At the same moment, to his intense astonishment, he recognized the fashionable stranger.

"What do you want?" said Charley.

"Nothing. I've mistaken the room."

"What, with a dark lantern? That's a pretty story! You wanted to rob me."

"Well, I did; but, for God's sake, let me off —don't expose me."

"I don't want to. Did you find anything in my pockets?"

"Not a rap."

"No; I haven't got anything. I'm on the same lay as yourself."

"You're not a prig, are you?"

"Yes; and now I'll tell you something."

"What is it?"

"I want your purse."

"Mine?"

"Yes."

"That's very likely. If you're a prig, you wouldn't rob a prig, would you?"

"Why not? It's not so bad as robbing an honest man, surely."

"Damn that! There's honour among thieves, ain't there?"

"Bosh!" responded Charley; "I don't believe it. Here, hand us over your money. How much have you got?"

"Only half a quid."

"That's a lie."

"I swear it isn't."

"Look here," continued Charley; "if you don't shell out every halfpenny, I'll blow your brains out—I will, by Heavens! There is no reason why I shouldn't. You're a cursed scamp, and it would be doing society a good turn to shoot you. You have crept into my bed-room like a thief; I should be quite justified in killing you. No harm would come to me—do you see? Shell up!"

The thief very reluctantly pulled half a sovereign and some shillings out of his pocket.

"That won't do," said Charley. "I must have a little more."

After a great deal of argument, he produced another pound.

Then Charley, all the while keeping the pistol levelled at his head, ordered him out of the room; and the thief slunk away with his tail between his legs, like a dog that had been whipped.

After he was gone, Charley double locked the door, thrust a chest of drawers against it, and getting into bed again, went off to sleep.

XXXV.—How the Landlord was done, and how Charley fell in with an awkward customer.

NEXT morning Charley awoke with the lark, and was both surprised and gratified at finding that he had not got a headache as he expected. He had, however, got the money all right, which was exceeding gratifying.

Having unlocked the door, and removed the chest of drawers, he rang the bell.

A chambermaid answered it.

"Send my groom to me."

"Yes, sir."

When Julia came, he recounted the night's adventure.

"We shall have money enough to pay, then," said Julia.

"Yes," replied Charley; "but we won't."

When he had descended to the breakfast-room, he inquired after the stranger; but the stranger had gone.

When?

In the middle of the night, without paying his bill.

"The devil he did!" cried Charley. "I had my doubts about him."

"So had I," said the landlord.

"But you said you thought him to be a perfect gentleman."

"So I did, at first; but really appearances are so deceptive, one never knows who one has got to deal with."

"Well," observed Master Charles, "it will make you more careful for the future. By the way, can you tell me where there is a veterinary surgeon in the neighbourhood?"

"There's one less than half a mile off, sir, at the top of the hill."

"I want my groom to take the horses there. They have both got a cold somehow. Just direct him to the place, will you? and let me have breakfast."

The landlord bowed himself out of the room, and presently returned with the waiter and the desired meal.

"I shall most probably stay and dine here. If a gentleman calls for me, you can show him up. You know my name?"

"Yes, sir—the Honourable Mr. Berkeley Plantagenet, your servant said."

"That will do; let me have the morning paper, and my boots."

The servant brought what was required, and left him.

"Now," said Charley to himself, as he walked to the window, "how is it to be managed?"

The window was about eight feet from the ground, and looked out upon the garden.

"It would be easy enough to drop," he thought. "Only some one may be looking from one of the back windows, and see me. Besides, I should have to pass through the house. No, I'd better put a bold face upon it."

With this determination he went on with his breakfast.

After about half-an-hour had passed, he rose, put on his boots, and sauntered slowly towards the bar.

"Give me a cigar," he said; and stood smoking by the door.

The landlord came up to him.

"Hasn't my groom come back yet?"

"No, sir."

"It's very extraordinary. He's an immense time."

After this he stood for another twenty minutes impatiently.

"Do you mind walking with me towards the doctor's," he said to the landlord. "I want to send my servant with a message to Hampstead."

"Certainly not," replied the landlord. "I shall have much pleasure in doing so, sir."

The shabby trick which had been played upon him by the the other traveller, had made mine host rather wary, and seeing Charley so near the door had slightly aroused his suspicions.

"I shan't let him out without paying," he had said to himself.

But now that Charley proposed that he (the landlord), should accompany him, his suspicions were entirely allayed.

"Are you ready, sir?" he asked, when he had put on his hat.

"Quite."

Then they set off together.

At the bottom of a lane by the side of the house, they met Julia with the horses slowly approaching.

She had been waiting for them, by arrangement with Charley, of course.

"What has made you so long?" asked our hero, angrily, as he mounted his horse.

The landlord stood looking on.

When Charley was seated, he thrust his spurs into the horse's sides, and he and the groom started off down the road at full gallop.

The landlord, who for a moment was struck motionless with astonishment, began to run after them, and bawl "stop thief!" but leaping over a low hedge, they were now galloping at full speed over a grass field, and before he could climb over the hedge after them, they were out of sight.

"If this sort of thing goes on," observed the landlord, with a very long face, as he slowly retraced his steps, "it strikes me I shan't exactly make my fortune."

But Charley and Julia did not trouble themselves over much upon his account, but galloped on, laughing heartily at the success of their trick.

After they had gone some distance, they slackened their pace, and consulted together; and then it was determined that they should push on a few miles, and approach Hampstead again in the evening by a circuitous route. It was also determined that night they should make their first attempt as highwaymen.

It was a fine bright morning; but towards noonday the heat grew so oppressive, that they thought it advisable to seek shelter for a time.

The road where they found themselves, was skirted on either side by very rich meadows, and shaded by broad oaks and chesnuts; and Charley proposed that they should alight, and in a pleasant rural way rest themselves on the grass, in the shade under the trees.

They dismounted, therefore, and attaching the horses' bridles to the branch of a sturdy oak, let them feed upon the green herbage.

Then Charley, hearing the low bubbling of a stream at hand, penetrated a woody ravine to seek its cool water.

He had not advanced many yards, however, before he encountered a bony nag, tied by the leg to a crab-tree, and browsing with famished eagerness.

This made him look ahead, and he perceived not far off, a man stretched, either dead or asleep, upon the grass.

A few steps further, and the deep nasal snore which greeted him showed that the latter was the case.

Charley hesitated as to whether he should retire quietly, or take the society which chance offered.

The man was of a low, square, ill-built form.

His neck was short and thick, his arms disproportionately long, and terminated by large bony hands.

His visage and features were of a peculiar cast; for the mouth was in the centre of the face, and the disproportionate length of the chin gave him the look of a Gorilla monkey.

This natural ugliness, aided by an expression of low and diabolical cunning, which the features preserved even in sleep, made it one of the most disagreeable faces Charley had ever

WHAT HAD BECOME OF THE BOBBIES?

seen; yet, at the same time, it struck him very forcibly that he must some time or other have seen it before.

He was a poor, threadbare rascal, and wore a pair of battered old boots, from which the soles were struggling to get away, and the greater part of the heels had long since deserted.

He had been having his dinner before he took his nap, it appeared, by sundry fragments of coarse, broken victuals, lying littered about, an empty black bottle lying among them.

On the whole, Charley was inclined to leave him to his slumbers; but just then, Julia coming up, called to her lover, and awoke the stranger.

He jumped up with a low curse, and looked round with a pair of small vicious pigs' eyes, the

No. 37.

alarmed expression of which almost made Charley laugh; but he conquered the inclination and apologised for the intrusion.

Then, as the man muttered his acquiescence, Charley produced from his pocket a portion of a game-pie, which he had brought away from the breakfast table, and a flask of brandy, which Julia had provided at an equally cheap rate.

Observing that their new companion viewed these preparations with some anxiety, Charley invited him to partake, and soon found, that, whatever he had eaten previously, he had left off with a competent appetite.

He drank in proportion, and soon grew very talkative.

They talked about a variety of subjects, of more or less interest; but their new acquaintance was such a droll dog, that he managed to make the time pass merrily enough; and Charley was astonished on observing that the trees were shot with a deep crimson, and that the sun was setting.

"We must be getting on," he said.

"Which way are you going?"

"To Hampstead. Are we far off?"

"A goodish step."

"How much?"

"Ten miles, perhaps."

"Then we must have lost our way coming across country. Up these lonely roads there is nobody to ask."

"I'm going to London myself, as it happens, and I shall be proud to show you."

"Thank you. I shall be obliged to you. One wants company out in these country roads at night."

"You're right there; and there have been some rather ugly customers about lately."

"Indeed!"

"Yes; something in the Dick Turpin style come up again, they tell me."

"What! highwaymen?"

"Ah! for my part, I always carry a pistol."

As he spoke he produced it.

Charley took it in his hand and looked at it.

Then returned it to him.

"It's not loaded," said he.

He said so with an inward satisfaction, for there was something very ugly about his new friend; and it was also a great consolation to him, to think that his own weapon was a three-barrelled revolver, and that it was loaded in each.

He had got it in his breast-pocket, and he took it out and exhibited it.

But scarcely had he taken it from his pocket, when the other made a snatch at it with the quickness of thought, and at the same time presenting it at Charley's head, bade him give up his purse, or prepare to have his brains scattered on the grass.

As the other spoke, a thought flashed across Charley's brain, how well the spot was suited by its solitude for acts of treachery and violence.

For a moment he was terribly startled; but the next, recovering his presence of mind, which fortunately never deserted him very long at a time, he began laughing as if it were a joke.

"Come, none of your grinning at me," the other said, savagely. "I tell you, you are a fool, and in my power. I am a gentleman of the road. Your money or your life."

"You don't say so; and you are in earnest," said Charley, with imperturbable serenity.

"Never more so," replied the other. "I don't want to have to waste a bullet on either of you; so shell up."

"Don't excite yourself," replied Charley, with unruffled composure. "Do your worst. Fire away, if you like. The barrels are not loaded. Do you think that I was so jolly green, that I was going to trust a gent of your style of countenance. I let you get hold of it just to try you. The balls are drawn, my chick; so blaze away."

The man glanced for a moment at Charley, with a mixture of doubt and fear in his villainous eye, still leveling the revolver; but the unutterable coolness of Charley's manner produced the desired effect.

He burst into a laugh, and quietly returned the weapon, saying:

"Be Gad! you've a nerve young fellow, if ever anyone had. But bless you, you didn't think I meant you any harm, did you?"

"I should have found out what you meant, I expect, you damned scamp!" said Charley, clutching his pistol eagerly.

Then presenting it at the other's head, he continued:

"The barrels do really happen to be loaded, my fine fellow, as you shall see; and as a proof, here is a bullet through your old goss."

The rogue turned very pale.

Charley proceeded:

"And if you don't hand me up every farthing you've got about you, I shall take the liberty of sending the next ball through your ugly head."

Suiting the action to the word, Charley fired, and was somewhat surprised, knowing that he had not harmed him, to see the man drop to the ground as though he were dead.

After gazing upon him for a moment in astonishment, Charley gave him an energetic kick, and called upon him to rise.

The man, however, had the beetle's instinct, and feigned to be either dead or insensible.

For a moment Charley hesitated what he should do, so as to effectually disable the wretch from further wickedness.

A natural aversion to violence, and a loathing of the treacherous villain, deterred him from touching him more than was positively necessary.

Convinced, however, that he had a perfect right, setting on one side the right of being a highwayman, to help himself to the contents of the other's pockets, he began to ransack them with Julia's assistance.

After a great deal of rummaging, he found the gentleman's portable property to consist of two pounds, some greasy shillings, and four very bright half-crowns.

Charley eyed the latter attentively.

"I thought as much," said he.

"As much as what?" asked Julia.

"They're Measles make, I'll take my oath."

"What, bad ones?"

"Yes; our friend here is in the smashing business, I suppose. I fancied I knew his ugly mug when first I saw him. I suppose I must have met him at Measles's shop."

When they had emptied the man's pockets, and appropriated his pistol, they let his horse loose, and drove it away; and then, remounting, galloped off at a good speed.

"If we don't rob anybody but thieves," said Julia, as they dashed along, "we're not so much to blame after all."

"Perhaps not," replied Charley; "but all is fish that comes to our net. Only wait till tonight, and then we will begin with vigour."

"Hurrah for the road!" cried Julia.

"Hear, hear!" said Charley, "as you say—"

Then, taking off his hat, he shouted:

"Hurrah for the road!"

XXXVI.—How Mr. Bung, of the firm of Bottle and Bung, drysalters, of Garlic Hill, in the City of London, was robbed upon the Queen's highway, by a very celebrated highwayman.

"FIDDLEDEDEE!"

"What do you mean?"

"Bosh!"

"Don't you believe it?"

"Not a blessed syllable!"

"That's as good almost as calling me a liar!"

"Don't take offence, sir, I said nothing of the kind; only my observation upon your story, let it be true or false, is simply 'fiddlestick!'"

"I'll tell you what it is," said the tall man—

But stop a moment. Before we go any further, I ought to explain who is making these observations, and where they took place, and how they happened to take place, and, in short, all about it.

The reader, I can clearly see, is all in a fog; and well he may be.

Now, then, to explain.

A week after the events which I have been describing in my last chapter, a small, but exceedingly select circle of elderly gentlemen, chiefly connected with the parochial interest, were seated in the parlour of Jack Straw's Castle, on Hampstead Heath.

The conversation had turned upon highwaymen, and long Tom Popsle, the parish clerk, had been describing several daring robberies, which had lately been committed upon the heath at night; and had stated it as his opinion, that highwaymen were coming into fashion again, just as they were a hundred years ago.

To which observation, a stout little man, with a very bald and shining crown, had ejaculated, "fiddlededee," with which ejaculation I began this chapter.

Long Tom Popsle was speechless with indignation, as well he might be.

He was a great authority at Hampstead, as famous in the place as the ticklebats themselves.

And this stout little man was a stranger, whom nobody had seen before; but who, after listening to Mr. Popsle's observations for some time with a sarcastic expression of countenance, had thrown doubts upon them with the fiddle-de-dee aforesaid.

"Why don't the police catch 'em?" said the little man. "The police are paid to catch 'em, and they do catch 'em. Do you suppose that a highwayman could escape the vigilance of our London police? Stuff and nonsense!"

"But he does escape it, don't you see?"

"How many are there, pray?"

"Only one."

"What sort is he?"

"He's awfully tall."

"Well, no," interrupted some one else. "He's short Popsle, ain't he?"

"I've heard he was tall and stout."

"A red-haired man, I was told."

"No—very dark."

"About six foot high."

"I was told he wasn't more than four."

"Rides a black horse."

"No; a white one."

"Well," said the stout little man, with a grin, "if I meet him, I'll tell you all about him. I'm going to cross the heath to-night, and if he stops me I'll give him pepper, for I've got a pistol in my pocket."

As he spoke, the little man drew a large and murderous-looking weapon from his pocket, and laid it on the table before him, with an ominous frown.

"Good gracious me!" cried Mr. Popsle, backing away from it in great alarm; "it is'nt loaded, is it?"

"Loaded! I should rather think so," replied the stout little man. "It's loaded to the muzzle."

"Put it back into your pocket, then, for heavens sake, without you want somebody to get killed by it."

"You needn't be alarmed, sir," said a very mild, curly-headed lad, who was sitting in a dark corner by the fire-side, and who had not hitherto ventured to intrude himself upon the conversation—"because there's no cap on it."

And as he spoke, the mild-looking lad took the pistol into his hands, and drawing back the trigger to full cock, examined it very minutely, and as though he had been acquainted with the mechanism of fire-arms from his cradle upwards.

"Put it down, you young rascal!" shouted Mr. Popsle, who was by no means satisfied with the youth's assurance of their perfect safety. "Put it down, sir. This minute, sir. How dare you, sir? I'm positively astounded, sir. Put it down, will you?"

"With pleasure," replied the mild lad.

And he did as he was bid.

Then chuckled.

Meanwhile, the stout little man had been looking from one to the other, with a satisfied smirk; and when the excitement was over, he placed the pistol in his pocket, and rang the bell.

"Tell the ostler to bring my pony round to the door," said he to the waiter.

"Yes, sir," said that individual, and retired.

"You're bent on going, then?" observed Mr. Popsle.

"Certainly I am," replied the little man. "If there were a dozen highwayman."

"Well, I shouldn't like to be in your shoes, that's all I've got to say about it. It's tempting Providence, in my opinion."

"Fiddlededee, sir! fiddlededee! I've got some valuable legal documents in my pockets, which I must show to my partner to-night; and it's of the very greatest importance I should see him at once about them. Do you suppose I'm going to be frightened by a cock-and-bull tale, like you've been telling? Fiddlededee, sir, and good evening to you."

Thus delivering himself, the stout little man snapped his fingers at Mr. Popsle and company, and walked himself off.

"A most uncivil person," Mr. Popsle remarked, when the door had closed upon him. "It would serve him jolly well right if he did get robbed."

"That it would," chorussed the whole company. "That it jolly well would"

"And as for you, my lad—Hallo!"

"What's the matter?"

"Where's he got to?"

" Who ?"

" The boy."

" Why, he's there, isn't he ?"

" No !"

" The devil he isn't ?"

" The devil he is, you mean. Where's he got to, if he hasn't flown up the chimney ?"

It really was rather mysterious, the way in which the very mild lad had disappeared.

So very sudden, it seemed. And what made it odder still was the fact, that before he took up the pistol, nobody had noticed that he was in the room.

It was a very dark corner where he had ensconced himself, right behind the stout old gentleman's chair ; and he had been so very quiet, and they had been so much interested in the conversation which they had been having, that nobody noticed him at all until he took the pistol in his hands.

He was gone, however, and there was an end of him ; and the good company shortly after recovering from their astonishment, subsided into their pipes and parochial affairs, which the previous exciting talk had for a time interrupted.

The stout little old gentleman mounted his pony at the door, and took his way across the heath.

Although little and fat, he was strongly built and powerful. He was a courageous little man, too, and not easily frightened.

He was a stern little man, accustomed to command, and one who stood no nonsense from anybody.

His name was Bung ; none other, in fact, than our old friend Bung, of the firm of Bottle and Bung, drysalters, of Garlic Hill, in the city of London ; the second partner in the house in which poor old Toddleby was once a porter.

He rode slowly on for some time, whistling softly to himself, and smiling, as he thought of the ridiculous fears of the parish clerk and his friends.

It was a beautiful night, although there was no moon to light him on his way.

The church-clocks of Hampstead had struck eleven, and with the sound of their last stroke seemed to die out all other sounds, leaving nature hushed, as though to sleep.

And then arose a faint, far-off murmur in the air, and a smoky redness in the sky showed where lay the great ungainly town of London.

Here and there a light glimmered dimly from the window of some house upon the heath ; and as he glanced back at the tavern he had so recently quitted, he could see a lurid glow emitted from the closely-drawn red window-curtains of the bar-parlour.

Looking back again to the heath, the silent desolation of the scene before him, and the stillness of all surrounding objects, made him for the time half hesitate whether he should not return to the warm tap-room, or to a comfortable bed of Jack Straw's providing, and put off his journey until the morrow.

But a moment's reflection told him how very weak such a course would be, and to what ridicule it would expose him.

No, that would never do ; he could not bear to be laughed at. Of the two, he almost came to the conclusion that he would rather be robbed.

And then, after all, was it not in all probability, what he had called it himself—a cock-and-bull story ?

Somehow, now that he was out on the lonely heath by himself, he could not think it quite such an absurd tale as he had been inclined to do when at the warm fireside.

Once he tried to say " fiddlededee !" but the word stuck in his throat.

" Mr. Bung, sir," said he, addressing himself sternly, " this will never do. Anybody who did not know for a fact that such was not the case, would imagine that you were positively frightened. The idea ! Oh law ! what was that ?"

It turned out only to be a white cow, which, alarmed at his approach, rose up from some bushes. But the start it gave him made him perspire violently.

" Hang me !" he said to himself—" hang me if I haven't forgotten to put the cap on my pistol !"

And with that, he drew the pistol from his pocket.

But suddenly a thought struck him. Who could say ?—may be that mild lad had been tampering with it.

Such things had happened. He would make sure, anyhow. He would draw the charge, and load again.

With a chuckle at his own cunning, Mr. Bung did so.

He was perfectly right ; the lad had been tampering with it, but he had been rather too deep for Mr. Bung.

He had not touched the loading.

He had merely—

What do you think ?

Why, thrust a broken pin into the touchole.

Poor Bung ! He always fancied himself to an alarming extent. He thought himself one of the most knowing of old dogs. He believed himself to be one of the artfulest of old tykes ; only, you see, the worst of it was, that he wasn't.

However, he thought himself so to be ; and he rode on quite safe, according to his small notions.

Presently he came to a very lonely spot—a kind of hollow ; and he had dipped down into this, when suddenly he was startled by a voice close to his ear shouting,

" Stop !"

In his sudden fright—for the life of him he could not help being frightened—he sent his heels into his pony's side, and sprang up on to the level ground.

Arrived here, a man on a white horse sprang to his side, and presenting a pistol at him, cried, " Your money or your life !"

" Not a bit of it," replied Mr. Bung, drawing his own pistol from his pocket.

He presented, and drew the trigger—it snapped harmlessly a foot from the highwayman's head.

" Damn you !" shouted Bung, " you've got the best of me."

" I mean to have, old fellow," replied the highwayman, " before I've done with you."

Bung fancied that he knew the voice. He looked earnestly at the other.

Yes; it was the mild, curly-headed lad who had fingered his pistol at the public-house.

"Why, you infernal young vagabond!" roared Bung, "do you suppose I'm afraid of a lad like you? Stand out of the way!"

"A lad like I am can blow what little bit of brains you may have out of your stupid old noddle, old man; so try and be a trifle more civil."

"Take that!" replied Bung, flinging his pistol at the other's head.

The boy, however, ducked rapidly, as he saw the pistol coming, and, flying past him, it fell harmlessly among the furze.

But though he escaped thus without injury, not so poor Mr. Bung; for, losing his balance by the violence of his exertion, he came down with a heavy thump upon his nose on the turf.

While he lay there, asking himself mentally whether he was alive or dead, the robber sprang from his horse, flung Bung over upon his back, planted his knee upon Bung's throat, and began very coolly to rifle Bung's pockets.

"Lie still!" hissed the boy between his teeth in the old gentleman's ear. "Lie still, or I'll make cold meat of you, as sure as my name's Charley Wag."

"Oh, it's Charley Wag, is it?" said Mr. Bung, as well as he could speak for want of breath. "I've heard of you before, you young scoundrel! I hope I shall live to see you hanged."

"Thank you, sir; I shall be sure and send for you. But where do you keep your money? It isn't possible so respectable an old gent as you seem to be can only have fifteen shillings in his pocket. Why, you're a disgrace to your years!"

"Bad luck to you!" growled Mr. Bung. "I'm delighted that I brought no more out with me."

"Well," said Charley, "it can't be helped, I suppose. I'll take your watch, anyhow."

When he had relieved Mr. Bung of the family turnip, he still groped about in his pockets.

"What are you looking for now?"

"For those papers you spoke about."

"Papers!"

"Yes, papers. You heard, I suppose."

"What papers?"

"How should I know? Here they are. I shall take them."

"Give them back, you young blackguard! What do you want with them?"

"I want to keep them."

"What for?"

"To light my pipe with."

"Give them to me; they're no use to you."

"Are they any use to you?"

"Yes."

"Then you shall buy them of me."

"Buy them! Indeed I shall do nothing of the kind."

"Oh, you wont, eh? Well, let's see. They're all stamped. They must be worth something. Signed, too, as well; as I see here a B, and a U, and an N, and a G—Bung. Is that you?"

"Yes it is."

"So I should have thought. You look like it."

"What will you give me for them?"

"Five pounds."

"Too cheap."

"Ten."

"Can't be done."

"Twenty—thirty—fifty."

"I'll take a hundred."

"Oh Lord! oh Lord! Well, I suppose I must. Give them me back."

"Not so fast, old cock. I'll tell you how we'll manage it."

"How?"

"To-morrow night, at half-past twelve, bring the money to that shed you see yonder. Lay it under a large stone you'll find by the door; and an hour afterwards, if you come back again, you will find your papers waiting for you where you put the gold."

"But, you young blackguard, suppose you play me false?"

"You must take your chance of that, old fellow."

"Well, I hope you'll come to the gallows."

"Thank you."

"You young miscreant!"

"Good-bye, old cock. Give my love to your wife, if you've got one. Good-night to you."

Charley rose from the ground, and vaulted lightly on to his horse's back.

Then, touching his horse with his spur, he galloped away.

But just at that moment, Mr. Bung fancied he heard the sounds of horses' hoofs coming up from behind him.

Help was at hand, he thought.

Perhaps the papers might yet be saved without paying for them.

"Murder! murder!" he shouted; "help! help! help!"

Charley patted his horse's neck.

"Now for it. Now, my good steed, your master depends upon you. Away, away!"

As he spoke, he gave him rein, and spring after spring they went.

Soaring like the wind along the sloping heath.

Behind them thundered the clatter of pursuit, and the hoarse shouting of the chase lent wings to their headlong speed.

Soon he had crossed the heath; soon he came to a river's bank.

Then he rose in his stirrups, and looked back.

The mounted police were bearing down upon him. Bung, on his pony, was cheering them on.

With a wild shout he plunged into the water, sending it high in the air in glittering spray, while his enemies came dashing forward, spurring and shouting, like so many demons.

Some sprang in and followed; others fired their pistols after him.

See how he plunges through the water close to the opposite bank.

Two shots in quick succession!

See, he is down!

No, it was but a stumble.

"Ha, ha!" he shouts, and waves his hat in defiance!

Now up the steep hill he plunges and scrambles.

Another shot.

By heaven! it has knocked his hat off; but he turns in his saddle, and waves his hand with an exulting cheer; and in a moment more the rising bank had interposed.

Then he shouts again.

What is it he says?

"Take care, old cock, you don't forget the hundred pounds."

These are the last words of Mr. Charley Wag, for he a moment afterwards is seen galloping madly away in the far distance.

"You've done me this time, young gentleman," said Mr. Bung, shaking his fist at the boy's retreating form; "but I'll be even with you before I've done, or I'll eat my own head."

———

XXXVII. — Mr. Bung makes his mind up— He puts his case into the hands of the great Mr. Bucket—The Expedition — the Rude Boy — Waiting for the time — the time come.

ALTHOUGH that young vagabond, Wag, had escaped him for the time, you do not surely suppose, that Mr. Bung was going to let him escape altogether.

Oh, no—not at all. Quite the contrary, in fact.

Mr. Bung, when he could command a sufficient quantity of breath for so much exertion, took a very tremendous oath of vengeance.

He'd be even with that young man, he said, or else he would not only eat his own head, but he would pick his teeth afterwards with his own back-bone.

He didn't want anybody's chaff. That was the course he intended to pursue.

He went, first of all, to see his partner; and communicated to him the particulars of his loss.

"You'd better pay the money," Mr. Bottle advised; "but it's an awful swindle."

"As far as it goes, it certainly is."

"Why, what do you mean?"

"It is until I pay him out for it."

"How?"

"You leave that to me."

"Ar'n't you going to give him the money?"

"Not if I can help it."

"But how are you to help it?"

"Leave that to me."

Mr. Bung went up to town that night; but he arrived at his home so late, he thought it would be best to put off a visit which he intended to make to the police until next morning.

Next morning, as early as eight o'clock, he was at Scotland Yard.

He told his story to a policeman in command, who took all the particulars down in a large book.

"You see," said Mr. Bung. "I don't want to drop this money if I can help it."

"I can understand that," replied the policeman.

"How's it to be managed?"

"It requires consideration."

"But there isn't time for very much."

"Certainly not. I shall put it into Mr. Bucket's hands directly."

"What, Mr. Bucket, the celebrated detective?"

"The very same."

"And when shall I hear from you?"

"Not till to-night."

"Where?"

"Bucket must arrange all that. A letter shall be sent to you by eight to-night, with full instructions."

"Where to? To my house?"

"No; we may lose time like that. To Jack Straw's Castle."

"Very good."

Mr. Bung left the police-office, and betook himself to his affairs in the city. But when he arrived there, he began to wonder whether or not it would be necessary to provide himself with the hundred pounds.

He had not asked the officer in Scotland Yard.

He certainly did not mean to give it, if it could be helped; but then, perhaps it would be necessary in the first instance to give it, and he would be able, through the instrumentality of the great Mr. Bucket (for it was the celebrated detective, immortalized by Mr. Charles Dickens), who was engaged upon the occasion, to get it back again.

Acting upon this idea, he drew the money at his bankers; and stowing it into a little bag, took himself off to Hampstead in the evening, and repaired at once to Jack Straw's Castle.

There, at the bar, he expected to find a letter containing Mr. Bucket's instructions; but it all at once occurred to him, as he approached the door, that to make an appearance within would be a safe way of subjecting himself to unlimited chaff from Mr. Popsle and company.

"I'd better send in for it," thought he.

Then looking round, he saw a ragged lad, who came sauntering up at the moment.

"Here, boy," said he.

The boy approached.

"Go inside this house, and ask whether there is a letter for Mr. Bung."

"Bung, sir?"

"Yes."

"You ain't 'avin' a lark with me?"

"No—why?"

"'Cos it's such a rum name."

"Go, and do what you're told, will you?"

The boy obeyed, and brought him a letter.

He opened it. It contained these words:

"Sir,—I shall have a couple of the force with me, at the *Cow with a Crumpled Horn*—a little public just out of Hampstead. But I will meet you a quarter of a mile this side of the shed, at ten o'clock, among the furze. My men will come by different roads, and they and I will be in plain clothes.

"Be cautious; everything depends on you.

"We'll cop him beautiful.

"Yours respectfully,
"BUCKET."

"P.S.—Destroy when read."

Mr. Bung read this letter through carefully a couple of times.

"He's a cautious chap, this Bucket," said the old gentleman to himself. "If he manages this affair well, I'll stand something handsome.

An exceedingly cautious fellow. Now then, boy, what are you waiting for ?"

" Ain't you going to give me nothink ?"

" Ah, to be sure—I forgot. Here's a penny."

" Give us twopence."

" I shan't. Be off, sir, about your business."

" You won't give it me, then ?"

" No, sir—certainly not."

" Very well—take that."

And as he spoke, the ragged boy suddenly took a run, and dived head first into Mr. Bung's waistcoat, like a young battering-ram, totally depriving the worthy gentleman of his wind, and leaving him to gasp for a minute or two like a stranded codfish.

When, however, he recovered sufficiently from the attack, he gave chase, and called " stop thief" lustily ; but the boy dashed wildly on to the heath, and was soon lost in the darkness.

" Well, let him go," observed Mr. Bung, pulling up short after a sharp run. " Let him go, I don't want to have anything to say to him. Perhaps I ought to have given him twopence. I'd give him a good thrashing if I had him here. But I haven't, so it doesn't matter. Hallo ! bless me—well, I never !"

He began to rummage in his pockets.

" Lord have mercy upon me ! This all comes of that young vagabond. I was so dreadfully afraid of the money, that I never thought of the letter, which I was to have destroyed. Thank goodness, the gold is safe enough ; but I must have dropped that precious document."

He retraced his steps, and looked for it.

But could not find it.

" It's blown away, I suppose !" said he. " It's deuced awkward, and deuced careless, too, to all appearance ; but it can't be helped. Luckily the wording of the letter was so precious vague, that nobody who was not acquainted with all the circumstances of the case, would be able to make head or tail out of it. That's the beauty of a detective. He's so precious mysterious."

As it wanted almost two hours of the time when he was to meet Mr. Bucket, Mr. Bung took himself to a public-house near at hand, and ordered a good stiff glass of brandy and water, and the *Times* newspaper.

The former he drank, the latter he attempted to read ; but so excited was he by his expectations, or what was soon to occur, that he found it to be an utter impossibility.

In this frame of mind, he came to the conclusion that there was nothing in the paper worth reading ; and under this impression he threw it on one side, and ordered the *Globe*.

In the *Globe*, he found under the head of " The Claude Duvals of the Nineteenth Century," an account of the robbery he had sustained the previous evening, together with a variety of other acts of violence committed upon other persons.

The article wound up by expressing great astonishment that such things could occur, with the large and efficient staff of police that existed, and suggesting a variety of measures which should be taken to secure the offenders, supposed to be a band of desperate ruffians, very numerous and ferocious.

" We'll have 'em, sir, before long," observed Mr. Bung, addressing an imaginary editor ; " we'll have 'em, and then we'll touch 'em up."

It wanted yet an hour and a half of the time.

Mr. Bung had half finished his brandy and water, and he could find nothing more to read.

The coffee-room of the inn in which he was sitting was awfully dreary.

He was alone in it, and only one gas jet of the chandelier was alight.

It was a dark, gloomy sort of place, with a shut-up faint odour about it.

There was no fire burning in the grate, which looked black and miserable. A pile of spittoons stood in one corner, a large empty table filled the middle of the room, and on a great, black, ghostly sideboard, a single ale-glass stood by the side of a broken clay pipe.

To add to the general discomfort, and the dreary sameness of the scene, the rain began to patter against the window-panes, with a slow sleepy music.

" I feel very tired," said Mr. Bung, yawning and stretching. " I'd give a trifle if I were at home in my bed."

Here he yawned tremendously.

" I'm not accustomed to this sort of thing," he continued. " And it don't quite suit a man of my years. I like to have my dinner comfortably, and have a quiet nap afterwards. These irregularities, such as last night and to-night, regularly knock me up."

He sat a very long while after this, poring over the newspaper, and endeavouring vainly to discover something to interest him.

At last he found himself reading over and over the same line, or progressing slowly down the column, without understanding a single word that he saw before him.

It is weary work waiting for anybody. It is very curious, too, how sleepy one gets waiting ; though at other times, it would be easy enough to sit up twice the time.

Mr. Bung felt dreadfully sleepy.

He could not help it. For the life of him he could not help it. He was obliged to shut his eyes for just five minutes, and have a nap.

He shut his eyes first of all to rest them, thinking he could and would open them again in five minutes at the outside.

But it was such a delightful sensation to keep them shut, mortal man could not have struggled against or resisted it.

And so, of course, he kept them shut, and in course of time dropped off to sleep.

" Lord bless me !" he exclaimed, waking up with a start. " Whatever have I been about ?"

He sprang to his feet, and rang the bell.

The waiter came in.

" What time is it ?"

" Five minutes past ten, sir."

" By Jove !"

He was only just in time. Catching up his hat, he rushed out of the house.

It was a miserable night.

The rain was coming down heavily. The wind swept by in fitful gusts, dashing the water into his face.

He felt weary and dispirited, and his bones all ached, in consequence of having slept in an awkward position, in the hard Windsor chair in which he had been sitting.

He would willingly have given five pounds to have been well out of the affair.

Indeed, he felt half inclined to leave the

papers to their fate, and make the best of his way home.

But then, he thought how very weak such conduct would be, and whatever would the policemen say?

He might, perhaps, be put into prison. Who could say?

Filled with these thoughts, Mr. Bung hurried forward as well as he could, slipping and stumbling at every other step; for the rain had converted the heath into a vast collection of small puddles.

Twice he came down upon his hands and knees, and picked himself up swearing.

He was all over scratches from the prickly furze, and covered with mud from head to heel.

As he rolled along, wiping his hands upon his pocket-handkerchief, he cursed his luck for having got into such a scrape.

"When anything is stolen from you," he thought, "it is much the wisest plan to quietly put up with the loss; nothing but worry and vexation comes of trying to catch the thief."

It was a good long way from where he was to the shed were he was to leave the money, and by this time the rain had drenched him to the skin.

He had not brought his pony, because he thought that it might interfere with Mr. Bucket's plans; and as he was quite unused to such physical exertion, he was completely done up.

But he managed, however, to crawl along. The night was very dark, and he could hardly tell where he was going. At last, however, he thought he saw a human form a little a-head of him, among the furze.

It was a woman.

"That's not what I want," thought Mr. Bung.

It was an old woman with a crutch, who came hobbling towards him.

She seemed as though she were going to speak to him, and was looking at him very hard.

Mr. Bung hesitated, and paused.

The old woman approached.

"Is this the way to London?" she asked.

"Yes."

"You're from London, sir, ain't you?"

"Yes—why? What do you mean?"

"It's raining dreadful, isn't it?"

"It seems so."

"If we only had something to catch it, now —such as a *bucket*, for instance."

Bung stopped at the word, and looked hard at her.

"It would wash so beautiful, wouldn't it?"

"I don't know what you're talking about, my good woman," replied Mr. Bung; "but I'm in a hurry."

"Have you been to the *Cow?*"

"The *Cow!* What are you driving at?"

"Look here, sir; ain't your name Bung?"

"Why—a—yes, to be sure it is."

"Then my name's Bucket," said the other, suddenly changing his voice, and in a moment standing upright, without the assistance of the crutch. "I'm Bucket, the detective; and I've come to help you to spot Charley Wag; and we'll cop him beautiful, sir, if you leave it to me. Is that what's o'clock?"

Mr. Bung was very much astonished by the address, as well he might be.

"Goodness gracious!" he exclaimed, opening his mouth to its widest; "I should never have dreamt of such a thing."

"No," said Mr. Bucket, "I shouldn't wonder if you wouldn't. But you see, we have to get up betimes to salt the tails of these downy birds. They ain't caught by chaff, you know."

"I suppose not; and pray how do you propose catching this one?"

"My two mates are close handy," continued Mr. Bucket. "They're lying under cover, and watching. We must hide, too, and wait our turn."

"But arn't we very early?"

"We must be early. If we were to leave it to the last minute, we should spoil everything. We're not a moment too soon."

"No, but look here. What are we going to do?"

"Lie on the roof of the shed, and watch the bag."

"What are we going to do with the bag?"

"We're going to put that under the stone, as you agreed."

"Do you think that's any good?" asked Mr. Bung, doubtfully.

"Of course it is. Have you got it with you?"

"Yes."

"Give it me, then."

They by this time had arrived at the shed, and standing under cover, by what little light there was, the detective marked several coins with his penknife.

"What's that for?" asked Mr. Bung.

"To swear to on the trial."

"Ah, to be sure."

When he had done this, Mr. Bucket laid the bag under the stone.

"What's to be done now?" he inquired.

"To climb on to the roof."

"Bless me! I don't think I can do it."

"Oh, yes, you can if you try. I'll give you a leg up."

So saying, he began to hoist Mr. Bung, who panted and puffed like a grampus; and after several slips, which bruised the poor old gentleman considerably, he was helped up upon the thatched roof.

"I hope to goodness it will bear my weight," he said, fancying it shook a little under him.

"Oh, that's all right," replied Mr. Bucket; "you needn't be afraid."

However, poor Bung felt anything but comfortable.

"I don't quite see my way clear," he said. "What am I to do next?"

"You must lie down on your stomach, and remain perfectly silent."

"On my stomach?"

"Yes; not a word."

"No—but I say—"

"Everything depends upon your being quiet."

"Well, but dash it all—"

"Hush! hush! I hear footsteps."

They were silent for a few moments, and listened intently.

"I hear nothing," said Mr. Bung, after a while; "and it is awfully damp. I feel the wet soaking through me."

"Nonsense, nonsense!" interrupted the ener-

COCK'S LOT.

getic Bucket. "You'll never feel no hurt from it when you've got dry again."

"I shall catch my death of cold, that's all the harm it will do me."

"Lord, what a fuss you make about a drop of water!"

"I don't know what you call a fuss, young man."

"Well, I say," observed the detective, testily, "do you want to catch this fellow or not? because if you're going to keep on chattering like this, I shall give up the job altogether; for it's not no manner o' use."

"Well, well," said poor Mr. Bung, with a groan, "I'm not a going to say any more, only I wish to goodness I'd never spoken to you policemen about it at all."

No. 88.

"Here," said the detective, "take a sup out of this bottle. It'll waken you up a bit."

He handed Mr. Bung a small flask, and that gentleman took a pretty stiff pull at it.

He was dreadfully cold and wretched. The wind seemed to search the very marrow of his bones.

The contents of the bottle were very comforting under such circumstances.

He took a couple of "pulls," and presently a third just for luck.

"I shall be able to get on now," he said, cheerfully. "That stuff's put a little life into me. What do you call it?"

"It's a mixture."

"It's a deuced fine mixture. I should like the recipe."

[CHARLEY WAG, THE NEW JACK SHEPPARD.

"I'll give it you some day, with pleasure, sir; only just now we really must not talk."

"All right. I'll be still as a mouse."

Mr. Bung twisted about a little to make himself as comfortable as possible, and waited silently.

He waited, and waited, and waited.

Two hours afterwards they were still waiting. Mr. Bucket seemed as fresh as ever. Mr. Bung was completely done up.

They talk of people not having a leg to stand upon, I think we may almost say in this case that Mr. Bung had not a belly to lie upon.

He was tired to death. He was soaking wet. He had the cramp. He felt half drunk with his potations.

He began to get dreadfully drowsy.

You have heard of travellers ascending mountains, who were so overpowered with fatigue that they persisted in dropping off to sleep, although warned that sleep was certain death.

It was the same with the luckless drysalter.

No power on earth seemed strong enough to keep his eyes open. Cold, wet, and cramp—although he suffered from each and all—were yet not sufficient to banish the heavy and oppressive fatigue that was setting in upon him.

No, it would come. In vain he weakly struggled to resist the incursion of the drowsy god.

One eye and then the other slowly closed up. He opened them again with a jerk; he propped them open by turns with his fingers.

It was no good.

He counted high numbers, he tried to concentrate his faculties, and keep alive to the fact that everything depended upon his vigilance.

It was no good.

If the bag had contained all the wealth of the Indies, and losing sight of it would be losing countless riches—life—happiness—health—everything, indeed, he could not have managed to have kept his eyes open.

He fell asleep.

* * * * * *

How long he slept he had no idea.

When he came to himself, a faint streak of daylight was visible in the sky. He was as cold as ice, and aching in every limb, but he managed to scramble on to his hands and knees.

Mr. Bucket was no longer there.

What had happened.

With a horrible suspicion, he slid down the best way he could from the roof, and ran round to the stone.

It was raised, and *the money was gone.*

The money was gone, but there were no papers in its place.

What did it all mean?

What had become of the officers; was it possible that the great Bucket was in league with Charley Wag, and that together they had conspired to rob Mr. Bung.

The drysalter could come to no satisfactory conclusion, and he thought that, under the circumstances, the best thing he could do was to make the best of his way to the public-house called the *Cow with a Crumpled Horn,* and inquire whether anything had been heard of the police.

The public-house in question was a small beer-house, a little way out of Hampstead, and kept by an aged man, of intemperate habits who lived there altogether alone, and was supposed to consume himself almost as much liquor as he sold to customers.

Mr. Bung knocked at the door with all his might for some considerable time, but without receiving any answer.

Then he went to the window of the tap-room, and looked in.

The sight which presented itself considerably astonished him.

There were three policemen, all apparently dead drunk.

Hammering vigorously at the window-pane, he managed to arouse them from the uncomfortable slumbers which they were taking in divers uneasy postures about the room.

"Hallo!" said one of them at last; "what is it?"

Mr. Bung explained.

The policemen scratched their heads, and looked very sheepish.

"What is the meaning of all this?" said the drysalter, waxing very wroth. "You may rest assured that your conduct will be reported to the authorities. Where is Mr. Bucket? What has become of him? Has he been to you since he left me on the roof of the shed?"

"My name's Bucket," replied one of the men, with the ghost of a grin; "and I have never been on the roof of no shed at all."

Mr. Bung staggered back, as though he had been struck in the face.

"What do you say?"

Then the policeman explained.

Over night he, the celebrated detective officer, had come down, per omnibus, and joined the other two constables at the *Cow.*

They had not used any disguise, because they had counted that such was unnecessary, although they had taken care to pretend that their meeting was quite accidental, and to keep dark their object.

Before they had been long in the house, however, a young fellow, dressed as a groom, had made his appearance, and after getting into conversation with them, made himself very agreeable, and offered to stand treat a glass of hot grog round.

The grog was fetched from a neighbouring tavern, and he mixed it himself.

The policemen partook of it, and so did the landlord; and——that was all they knew.

"But who was that dressed as an old woman?"

They couldn't say.

"It must have been Charley Wag himself."

"Then I am swindled."

"It looks very like it."

I should have liked you to have heard Mr. Bung swear.

XXXVIII.—COCK'S LOT.

AT the present hour there exists in London a secret society of juvenile thieves.

Although a great deal has been said and written of late years upon the subject of metropolitan improvements, if the fair and rich readers of my story, who dwell in West-end mansions, far removed from the noisome and wretched abodes of poverty and crime, still doubt their existence, their eyes will any day convince them to the contrary, if they will penetrate the hideous labyrinths of courts and alleys to be found in that horrible neighbourhood lying on the east of the Southwark Bridge Road.

It may have been worse once. If there is any truth in history, it has been worse; but go and see it now, fair ladies. Go and look at the grimy denizens of this horrible locality, and then tell me, did you ever imagine that there existed, so near to home, so many unreclaimed savages? I have been reading lately, in Mr. Du Chaillu's book, his account of the human beasts he encountered in Gorilla land. One wonders how such things can be; and in spite of our determination at the outset to doubt nothing, can barely believe in some of these atrocities after all.

But if the description of some of the scenes which occur every day among the haunts of crime in this metropolis is true, we are not much better than our neighbours.

Supposing, now, we visit such neighbourhoods as that to which I alluded above, on Saturday night, in broad gas-light. If we watch the outdoor and public life of that portion of the London population which is then to be found, doing its marketing, in Blackman-street, High-street, Peter-street — any of those streets, in fact, round that vile quarter, what do we find?

The male population are, almost without exception, the lowest blackguards and ruffians; the woman, the shrillest tongued, most slatternly, and brazen-faced; the boys, slouching, hang-dog, evil-eyed; the girls, leering, bare-bosomed, and shameless.

But if this is their appearance in public, what is it in private life?

Down squalid courts and loathsome alleys are congregated the lowest refuse of a vile multitude. These foul-smelling, ill-lighted courts and alleys are the hot-beds of crime in all its most revolting shapes; and from thence issue every conceivable kind of revolting human deformity, mental and physical.

It is here, in a dingy den of a tavern, in a narrow, crooked lane, branching out of Mint-street, that the Juvenile Thieves' Society holds its meetings.

The police know it well.

It is called by its members, and by the force, and by the low, squalid rabble of those parts, "Cock's Lot."

Cock's Lot—it is a curious name. It is also a curious society.

The "Cock," or head of it, is the proprietor of the low "boozing ken" where the meetings are held, and the "Lot" consists of from fifty to sixty youths, between the ages of ten and sixteen.

These young gentleman are daily distributed over the metropolis, and employ themselves in every imaginable kind of theft and petty larceny.

The produce of their frauds and robberies are divided among all the band once a week. And there are receiving houses in various parts of London, where the stolen goods can be taken by any member of the community, and where a true and just account of all such transactions is regularly noted in a volume kept for that purpose.

If any member of Cock's Lot should come to grief in a police point of view, the society are bound over by solemn oaths to provide the necessary legal advisers and gentlemen of the horse-hair.

They also provide any number of witnesses, to vouch for the good character of the party accused, or to prove an *alibi*, if possible.

But if, in spite of these good offices, the accused should get into the "stone jug," then, during his incarceration, his share of the property is carefully put away for him, and on his release he is presented with it in a lump.

There is, therefore, every inducement for the "Lot" to be true to one another; and as any treachery is visited with the severest punishment, such a thing is almost unkown among these youthful desperadoes.

It is true that their existence is known to the police; but then, no stolen property is ever traced home to them, and so Cock's Lot flourish and grow fat.

Nightly meetings are held in the boozing-ken in the lane leading out of Mint Street, where every sort of excess and debauchery is practised. To one of these meetings we will, with your leave, accompany Mr. Bung and Detective Bucket.

It was a chilly, wet night without, but the inside of the club-room was stifling hot, and reeking with the perfumes of gin and beer, and rank tobacco. The company was of both sexes; the female portion in no case exceeding the age of sixteen, although the sunken eyes and bloated careworn faces of some of these poor little strumpets seemed more like those of old women than young children, like they really were.

The most frightful blasphemies, and the grossest obscenities, were heard on every side; and the hellish noise that the young wretches made over their drink, with their shrill singing, and bursts of imp-like laughter.

"I think I shall be able to show you a little life, sir," said the policeman; "and if we don't happen to spot this young cove Wag, you'll anyways spend a pleasant evening, supposing, that is, that you've got a taste for nat'ral curiosities."

"I don't know that I have much of a taste for this sort of curiosity," replied Mr. Bung. "But lead the way; there's no knowing what you can do till you try. Perhaps I may come to take a fancy to thieves and thieving. I've thought of nothing else these three days, ever since I had the misfortune to fall in first of all with that cursed young vagabond, and lose my documents."

"Are you ready, sir?"

"Quite."

"Then I'll lead the way."

"Do so."

A very peculiar "rat-tat," which must have taken a long while to acquire, easily obtained admission to Cock's Lot's head-quarters for Mr. Bucket and the drysalter.

It was Mr. Bucket, of course, who knocked at the door.

It was also Mr. Bucket who replied to a remarkably dirty young man in shirt-sleeves who opened it, and wanted to know their business.

"It's all serene," said Mr. Bucket, in a soothing sort of way, propping the door adroitly with his boot, and sliding in before the young man hardly knew where he was.

"Come on, sir," he continued, turning to Mr. Bung, and holding the door; "step forward."

"What do you want, both of you?" inquired the young man, rather irate.

Then, turning round, he began shouting:

"Here, I say, Bill—some of you, here's two coves—"

"Don't excite yourself, my young friend," continued the policeman, amicably. "Perhaps you don't know me."

"No, not partic'ler—unless you're a nose."

"I'm Inspector Bucket, of Her Majesty's Detective Police, my tulip; that's who I am. You're reyther a fresh hand, or you'd have known me by this time."

"Oh," grumbled the young man; "and what may you please to want?"

"Don't you flurry your cocoa-nut, my blossom. It ought to be a subject of great self-congratulation for you to think as you're not the party, else you'd have had the kibosk put on to you in reyther less than no time. I'm looking after another party this journey, my polyanthus. When I want you, I daresay I shall know where to put my hand upon you."

"Well," replied the young man, who was considerably awed by Mr. Bucket's observations, "if I'd knowed who you was, you wouldn't have got in, that's all."

The landlord had come forward by this time. Mr. Bucket took him on one side.

"We don't want none of your lot," he observed confidentially to this worthy. "We're after a party that's likely to look in here. Have you got anyone besides the reg'lar chickens below?"

"No, none. You can go down and satisfy yourself."

"Thank you, we will. Let's have two fours of hot gin, with a bit of peel in it, will you?"

Leaving the landlord to send down the drink after them, Mr. Bucket and the drysalter descended to the kitchen, where Cock's Lot were holding high festival.

Cock's Lot were not the sweetest to smell of any company that you can imagine. In fact, if you accused them of stinking atrociously, you would hardly be exaggerating to any great extent.

Mr. Bucket led Mr. Bung into a quiet corner, where they were not much observed, and for a while they listened to a popular song which one of the young gentlemen was singing.

"She was unfort'nate, and I was a thief,
   And we loved each other beyond all belief;
She lived in a garret, and me in the kitchen,
   And love it set our two hearts a itchin'.

"When she turned me up, to hide my grief,
   I borrowed my neighbour's hankychief;
And twelve kind friends as sat upon me,
   For change of air sent me over the sea.

"When I come back, in Reging Street
   My true love I chanced for to meet;
Her fig out, oh, never shall I forget,
   And on her carriage a coronet.

"My poor heart was a choking with love,
   Though me, I could see, she was miles above,
But a heavenly look upon me she threw,
   As she gave me a tract wrote by Mr. BELLEW.

"When my time comes to dance in the air,
   I feel quite sure that my love will be there;
And I'll make her a bow when her eye I've met,
   Sitting there in her coach with the coronet."*

When the loud applause which this ditty had elicited had somewhat subsided, one of the Lot getting upon his legs, apparently not without considerable difficulty, for he was horribly drunk, proposed that the company present should go what he termed "Tommy Dod" for half-a-quartern all round; but being overruled, he was induced to resume his seat, amid loud cries of "shut up," "lie down," "burke him," "shove him up the flue," etc.

Then melody set in again, and some lady obliged with "Home, sweet home."

"Sweet creatures, ain't they?" said Mr. Bucket.

"What are they all?" asked Mr. Bung—"thieves?"

"Thieves and prostitutes."

"God bless me! And so young, too. They all look very wretched. I suppose they don't make much of a living."

"Well, they don't," replied the policeman, confidentially. "They don't, and that's about the size of it. It's a precious hard life; but it's wonderful what some people won't go through, rather than earn their bread honest. It's the same as soldiering."

"How do you mean?"

"Why to escape military service; I mean. Bless you, I've come across the rummest things sometimes. Chaps who aren't able to buy their discharge often lame themselves horribly. Lots of people will gorge themselves with shell-fish, to give themselves the nettle-rash, and give themselves the itch by rubbing Spanish fly into needle-pricks, which is awful agony, you'll say; but I've known soldiers to put lime into their eyes, for the sake of getting them inflamed, or even prick their eyes with a needle, to get a cataract."

"Good heavens, how horrible!"

"You may well say so, sir; but I once heard of a case that beats them all hollow. It was a fellow who pretended to be in a death-sleep, and nothing they could do would make him make a sign that he was awake, though they felt quite convinced that he was only shamming; and so they took and cut a round piece out of his skull with a saw."

"But didn't he scream out?"

"No, he only groaned the least in all the world, so that he was one too many for them. Now these young dodgers are up to all sorts of hanky-pankies, pretending to be blind and such like, so that they may take their stand in the street and watch a house that the rest of the gang are robbing, or are going to rob. Some of them are very great at fits, and foam chewed-up soap at the mouth. In regular epileptic fits, you can't feel any pain you know. I have known beggars stand pins thrust into them

---

* I trust that Mr. OWEN MEREDITH will not suppose that it is I who have thus mangled his poem. The above is the version popular among Cock's Lot.—G. S.

without squalling; but what brings them to their senses is to flick them on the soles of their feet with a wet towel. If there is any shamming about them, they can't put up with that game very long, and have to cry for quarter."

"Bless me!" said Mr. Bung. "One requires to be very knowing to know when one of these beggars is shamming and when he is not."

"It's our trade to be knowing," said Mr. Bucket; "though sometimes we are taken in. I recollect, some years ago, there was a resurrection man found guilty of prigging the body of a young woman, the wife of a mate of mine. My mate identified the body, and so did the young woman's mother and father, not only by the features, but by the fact of one of her legs being shorter than the other; but after all they were mistaken."

"Mistaken?"

"Yes; for the body they all swore to belonged to quite another party altogether, and was taken out of another churchyard. By some wonderful chance they not only resembled one another very much, but they were both odd-legged. It's very difficult to swear to identity after death, for they change so; but it's rather difficult to swear to living people sometimes. For example: One foggy November night, three of the old Bow Street runners, who had been sent to search the neighbourhood of Hounslow, were in a post-chaise together, and were set upon by a couple of highwaymen. One of them went and caught hold of the horses' heads, and the other comes round to the window in the usual way, and demands their money or their lives."

"Well?"

"The night was precious foggy and dark, as I think I said before, but one of the officers swore positively that by the flash of two pistols which were fired at the robber at the window, he could distinctly see that the man rode a dark brown horse, between thirteen and fourteen hands high, and of a remarkable shape, having a square head and very thick shoulders; altogether, he said, a horse that he could have picked out from among fifty or a hundred. He did find the horse, according to his account, and the other two officers swore to the highwayman. They very nearly hanged him, sir; and I believe they would have done, if the judge himself hadn't stated in court that he thought it to be perfectly impossible to recognize a man under such circumstances; that he had made the experiment, and that the flash of a gun did not give sufficient light."

"Well," said Mr. Bung, "you don't mind telling a story against the force."

"That is not particularly against the force," replied Bucket; "at least I did not mean it to be so. Any one, besides a policeman, and other people much more probably, might have made the mistake. Besides, they were old Bow Street runners that I was talking of; stupid dogs compared to the police we have now, as everybody knows. By the way, with regard to identity, do you think you could identify this young lad who robbed you? How do you know it was Charley Wag?"

"How do I know it? Why I know it well enough. If it was by no other way, I know it because he told me that was his name himself."

"There's no believing these sort of gentlemen though, is there, sir?"

"Oh, stuff and nonsense. If I can come face to face with him again, I shall know him. Hadn't I got plenty of opportunity of seeing him, when he was handling the pistol, in the public-house, and then again, when the young vagabond was kneeling upon my breast, and emptying out my pockets. I had plenty of time to study his face; and as for his voice—"

"Well, sir, as to that, you see, when he was figged out as an old woman—"

"Nonsense! I don't believe it was the same."

"I can't help thinking it was myself, sir. Believe me, he's an artful young dodger, that way. I'd bet a pint it was him, too, dressed up as a ragged boy, that you sent into the *Castle* for a letter. It couldn't have been him as came to the *Cow* dressed as a tiger, because he couldn't be everywhere at once; but he's an awful deep card, depend upon it; and depend upon it also, that it's not a very large band which he belongs to, or they could not keep so close as they do, and a little more about their sayings and doings would creep out."

"Well, one thing's pretty certain."

"What's that?"

"That he must be making a pot of money at this highway robbery business."

"He certainly is at present; but it won't last very long, you may depend upon it. Hallo!"

Mr. Bung at this point of the conversation almost sprang out of his seat with astonishment. Mr. Bucket looked in the direction to which the other's eyes were turned.

Two men, shabbily dressed, and muffled up with comforters round their necks, had just entered the kitchen, and sneaked quietly into a dark corner, opposite the one where Bung and Bucket were sitting.

One of them, pushing his comforter down from his chin, had struck a match upon the table, and now held it to the bowl of a pipe, the stem of which was betwixt his teeth.

The light fell full upon his face.

It was a remarkable one, and one not easily forgotten. Not so much because of any peculiarity of its formation, or irregularity in feature, but because it was so ghastly white.

The man's eyes, too, were deep set, and very large; but their expression, perhaps, would not have been very unpleasant, if the extreme pallor of his face had not lent to them an additional glare.

"What's the matter?" asked the policeman, noticing his companion's face growing more and more astonished every moment. "What the deuce is the matter, sir?"

"Look, look!' whispered Mr. Bung, in great excitement; "don't you see that man?"

"Which?"

"The one lighting his pipe."

"Yes; what of him?"

"It's the most extraordinary thing. Do you know, he's a celebrated London physician. What on earth can he be doing here in that disguise?"

"Well, it's singular, certainly. Who do you suppose his friend is? He don't look much of a gentleman."

There was a good deal of truth in what the policeman said. The individual who was now the subject of remark, was probably as unprepossessing looking a scoundrel as you could well have met with in a summer's day in the wilds of Whitechapel.

"Who is the doctor, sir?" asked Bucket, after a pause.

"His name is Faversham. I have known him for many years. We used to deal very largely in chemicals at our warehouse some years ago, and he frequently came to us at that time to purchase large quantities of drugs, which he used in experiments, and which he could not purchase at retail chemists unadulterated. That's how I became acquainted with him. He was only studying then, but has since gone into practice, and has got a great name, I believe, in the fashionable world. He is family physician to the Duke of Heatherland."

"To be sure!" exclaimed the policeman, with a start. "How was it I came not to recollect it? A friend of mine is employed in an investigation of some very mysterious circumstances which have lately occurred in the duke's family. There's something wrong about that doctor, depend upon it. I must have my eye upon them."

While they were thus speaking, Faversham and Rattan—for those two were the persons under discussion—rose from their corner, and moved towards the door.

Letting them proceed a little in advance, the policeman and Mr. Bung followed them.

They went upstairs and approached the bar, where they met a young man, who wore a bandage over one side of his face, and his cap slouched over his eyes, with whom immediately began a conversation.

Bucket, drawing his companion on one side, was narrowly observing them, when his attention was distracted by the singular conduct of two other men, both miserably apparelled, who were trying to skulk out of sight behind some barrels.

"What are you afraid of, man? What harm can he do to you?"

"You know very well he can hang me."

"Pooh! rubbish! How many times am I to tell you that you are as safe as a church? Nobody would believe such a tale as yours; it is not probable. You've been hanged once, and there's an end of you. You've taken out a new lease of life now, and are somebody else. If you do something to get yourself hanged again, that's your look out: but you're all right as far as your old murder."

"Hush! hush! for God's sake—not so loud. Some one will hear you."

Mr. Bucket opened his eyes, and pricked up his ears.

"See," continued the man who had last spoken; see, Faversham is going. Let us follow cautiously."

"Follow, eh!" thought Mr. Bucket. "By Jove, it's a regular plot, of some sort or other, we've dropped upon. I shall keep my eyes open. There's something to be made out of this, or I am very much mistaken."

But just at that moment Mr. Bung pulled his arm, and pointed to the young man to whom Faversham had been talking.

He had raised his cap and was pulling off the bandage.

"It's he! It's he!" cried the drysalter, in great excitement.

"Who?" asked Mr. Bucket.

"Charley Wag!"

Mr. Bucket sprang forward to seize him, but the boy had heard his name pronounced, and in his turn sprang towards the door, while several persons lounging about immediately flung themselves between the officer and the object of his pursuit.

XXXIX.—THE DOVE BETWIXT THE CLAWS OF THE HAWK.

TIME rolled slowly on, and all was a blank to the entranced duchess, lying still as death in the awful sleep into which Faversham's drug had thrown her.

Yet, nevertheless, the sleeping soul began to sleep less sound.

Gradually she began to find the sensations produced by consciousness to grow sharper and sharper, and more defined.

The day seemed brighter through her closed eyelids, and the night, in turn, seemed darker.

Sharp physical pains, too, occasionally shot through her frame.

The consciousness of outward things began to grow more vivid. Sometimes she was conscious of the presence of some one by her side. She was conscious that she lay upon a bed.

She was conscious that she was visited from time to time by a man, who drew apart the curtains at the bottom of the bed, and gazed upon her.

At other times she was left all alone, and a stillness like that of the grave reigned undisturbed around her.

She asked herself again and again where she was, who could have brought her there, into whose power had she fallen, what did it all mean?

She recollected, as her brain began to work more clearly, all that had occurred just before the trance, and her thoughts reverted to her child left alone in a foreign country.

Then a sensation of terror and despair seized upon her, and she struggled desperately to shake off the heavy lethargy which oppressed her.

It was then that a sob burst from her breath, and with an enormous effort, which required all her strength, both physical and moral, she opened her eyes.

A burst of light opened upon her, sending a strange thrill of joy through her breast.

She looked wonderingly around, and thoughts of escape began to crowd upon her brain. But just at that moment she fancied that she could hear footsteps approaching.

It was her mysterious visitor, and she wisely determined upon exhibiting no signs of returning convalescence.

The footsteps approached.

She shut her eyes, and held her breath.

The door opened slowly and cautiously, and some one came on tiptoe to the bottom of the bed.

So intense was her suspense, that she could

scarcely refrain from screaming out and opening her eyes; but with an almost superhuman effort she mastered her emotions.

She heard the soft rustling of the curtains, and the low, deep sound of some one breathing.

Then the clutching of the person's fingers, as they seemed to hold the bed-post for support.

The long investigation which seemed to take place was to the duchess one of intolerable length; but at last the curtain fell again.

The footsteps retreated, the door closed, and all was again silent as before.

The duchess immediately opened her eyes, but for full an hour after the departure of the unknown she made no other movement.

At the end of that time, she became suddenly conscious of a strange and painful sensation pervading her whole frame.

It was what seemed to her the eruption of a burning heat, shooting downwards from the head to the extremities.

This was the circulation of the blood, so long stagnant, and the return of animal warmth.

The pain was horrible.

Every nerve and muscle tingled as though she were being roasted before a scorching furnace.

Those who have been recovered from death by drowning have described their sufferings as something similar. She recollected that when she had been rescued from such a death, that the reëntrance of air into the lungs had given her almost similar pains.

But at the same time, with these torments returned to her prostrate body some of the departed power of motion, and her muscles throbbed as though she were being held down forcibly in bed, and that they were all straining almost to bursting to get free.

At last the sufferer began to fling about her arms, and gasp for breath.

Then what seemed like a flood of molten lead poured from her head downwards, and, with a half-uttered scream of agony she sprang upright on the bed, her arms and fingers stretched out, and her mouth and eyes wide open.

But the next moment, overcome by weakness, which was the natural result of such a lengthy term of prostration, she sank back exhausted upon her pillow, and again wearily closed her eyes.

But this movement, however, was decidedly the turning point of the crisis.

The momentary pang was certainly as severe as the application of a galvanic battery; but it rapidly passed away, and at the same time the sensation of intense heat gradually gave place to a rich genial warmth, which flowed over the whole body.

Then followed a sweet sense of repose, and a gentle perspiration broke out upon the hitherto parched and feverish skin.

In less than half-an-hour afterwards, the duchess felt that she was able to rise from the bed; and though giddy and faint from the effects of her long stupefaction, still perfectly in possession of all her mental powers.

For some time, however, she endeavoured in vain to retain an upright posture, for her knees trembled under her.

The chamber reeled round before her eyes,

and staggering forward, she fell upon a sofa, which was fortunately there to catch her.

After a while, she summoned sufficient strength to regain a sitting posture; and being able to reach the window-curtain from where she sat, she drew it on one side, and looked out.

It was night.

The pale moon over head sailed serenely through the dark blue sky.

It was very still and quiet, and scarcely a breath of air came through the half opened window.

Dusky trees threw a shadow upon her face, and their higher branches shivered faintly in the cold light; and at the distance of about a hundred yards she could see the murky outline of houses.

Between her and them was a large garden.

She remained for nearly half an hour motionless at the window, inhaling the soft balmy air, which seemed to give her fresh life and spirits.

Presently she rose, and drawing up the blind, gazed at herself in a mirror upon a dressing-table.

She was deadly pale.

Arrayed in all the ghastly habiliments of the tomb.

Dressed in a winding-sheet.

It was, then, as she had supposed—they had believed her to be dead.

Who could say?—perhaps she had been buried!

She looked with an expression of wild alarm.

The moon was shining full into the chamber.

She sought for some sort of garment in which she could envelope herself, before she attempted to make her escape.

For to escape she was determined.

All at once, she saw a cloak lying upon the ground. It was the cloak in which she had been wrapped during her perilous journey in the boat.

With active though trembling hands, she enveloped herself in this mantle, and then stood for a few moments taking counsel of herself.

She could form no notion of where she was, or into whose hands she had fallen; but gradually as she pondered, a sensation of intense fear began to gain the mastery over her.

What horrors might she not still expect at the hands of those in whose power she then was?

All her hopes lay in escape.

Flight—instant flight.

Flight; swift and hidden flight was her only resource.

Flight anywhere—flight was all that would save her.

Would there be any safety for her until she was miles away from her present prison?

She paced the room eagerly, though with cautious footsteps, for she was fearful of making any noise.

She looked from the window.

There was a black gulf of unknown depth below.

Then she listened intently.

There was silence alike in the house and through the night.

Stepping with noiseless footsteps to the door, she examined the fastenings.

They were easily undone.

She swung the door open.

A dark corridor stretched away from it, ending in a flight of stairs, upon which shone the moonlight, through a small passage-window.

Groping her way along the wall, the duchess cautiously advanced in the darkness.

There was a thick carpeting laid down carelessly upon the floor. Probably it had been put there on her account; and she moved forward as noiselessly as a phantom.

She proceeded for some time in perfect silence.

Then, as she neared the head of the staircase, a low, muttering sound became faintly audible.

With suppressed breath, and a heart which beat until she sickened with the violence of her emotions, the duchess paused and listened.

The noise was that of the deep bass voice of a man, speaking in an excited and ferocious tone, though not very loud; in fact, with a kind of low, subdued ferocity of expression.

The peculiar sound of the voice the duchess felt convinced she had heard before.

She paused for a moment or two, and listened.

Then, as the sound still continued, she stole down-stairs, a step at a time, until she could lean over the balustrade of the staircase, and look below.

There, on the story beneath, she saw a faint gleam of light, evidently proceeding from a room opening on the stairs.

Partially supporting herself by the railings, she again descended step by step.

The staircase was of stone, and massive.

It made no sound beneath her feet.

As she descended, the sounds of the speaker's voice became more and more distinct; but as yet she could catch no word he uttered.

At length, she stood upon the landing-place at the foot of the stairs, and saw from whence the light proceeded.

It streamed from a small inner room, through an outer parlour, or antechamber, and along a small passage, until it fell upon the carved balustrade of the staircase.

The door of this outer parlour stood wide open.

That of the inner room was about three parts closed.

Through the small aperture thus formed the duchess saw ranges of books upon shelves, and part of a dark opening, which looked like a safe, with strong iron doors, in the further wall.

From this room came the light, and from this room sounded the voice of the speaker.

Impelled by a species of absorbing curiosity which had fascination in it, the duchess stole towards the inner room.

The low, savage voice proceeded in what seemed, to her unstrung nerves, to be a fearful and continuous malediction.

Suddenly she remembered the voice.

A shudder thrilled through her whole being.

It was Faversham's.

In another moment she had fallen upon her knees close to the partially-opened door.

She was within half a dozen feet of her enemy.

With strained brain and clenched hands she listened to his voice.

She listened and understood.

She knew him now to be her enemy, and she knew that he would be a powerful and deadly foe.

The more powerful and the more deadly, because hitherto he had nestled, as it were, in the bosom of the family without anyone for a moment suspecting that there was any harm in him.

But the mask had fallen off, and the hooded snake had thrust forth its venomous head.

Suddenly the voice ceased, and another and a rougher voice cried:

"Hush!"

"What is it?"

"I heard a step on the stairs, I thought."

"It must have been fancy. There's no one in the house that's likely to be walking about. She's as insensible as a log, or was when I saw her an hour or so ago; and the other thirteen—"

"Good God! do not talk about them walking about."

"They are not likely to do so in the body, though they hover round us in the spirit night and day."

"Well, the devil take me," growled the other speaker, "if I could talk like that. It gives me the horrors to hear you, and I'm blowed if I'm over particular. I don't mind dead bodies when they're all fair and above board. In fact, I think they're reyther fine company, but I can't stand 'em in the dark; and if there's another thing I can't stand, it's ghosts. I've never seen any ghosts, at least not to swear to, and I don't want to. I'd rather not; and if you can raise them up when you like, as you say you can, I'm be blessed if I admire your taste; for you must be precious hard up for company, I should think.

"Do you doubt my power, then?"

"No, I don't say I do."

"Because. if you would have proof, say but the word, and the spirits of one or all of those thirteen half-putrid corpses of the miserable victims to my vengeance, shall stand this moment by your elbow. Say but the word."

The duchess leaned, half fainting, against the wall.

She sought to realise the full meaning of the terrible words she had heard.

To a certainty she had fallen into an assassin's den.

Thirteen victims to his vengeance!

Was she, then, likely to become a fourteenth?

And a vengeance for what? What had she done?

Did she belong to a doomed race?

Never until this moment had she asked herself the question.

She did not do so now, in the words, or the order in which it is here set down; but in a confused crowd of half-formed phantom images.

The awful fact, at that moment, came strongly to her recollection, that there had been of late a mysterious and horrible fatality in the Heatherland family.

Every member of it had died in some way or other; all suspiciously sudden had been the deaths, now that she recalled the circumstances.

Also—most horrifying fact—all had been attended upon in their last moments by the wretch whom she heard now boasting of his thirteen victims.

CHARLEY AGAIN RESCUES THE DUCHESS.

What was, then, this man's object in wishing to exterminate her race?—for such would seem to be his intention.

What cause was there for the awful, deadly, and secret feud, pursued with a resolute ferocity to which the blood of the Saxon is ordinarily a stranger?

With a strong effort she roused herself, and listened again.

At the moment of her catching the sense of the words that Faversham uttered, he was exclaiming, with passionate vehemence:

"Yes, yes," he cried; "I have murdered thirteen of the accursed race; thirteen I have swept away like grass, and there now remain but three. For these three have I in store a deadlier vengeance than for all the rest. First

No. 39.

shall die the mother, then the son, and then last of all, that hoary-headed old wretch the duke, for whom I have in reserve the climax of my vengeance. For him have I invented the most exquisite and the most diabolical of retribution. For him I have imagined a death without parallel in the annals of fiendish atrocity, and I will execute it. Ha! ha! He shall writhe—he shall scream in my clutches; and as he begs in maddened frenzy for death to rid him of his torments, I will spit upon him, and jeer at him, and tell him the history of my wrongs, and that it was he who was the cause of them!"

A strange ghastly horror took possession of the listener's mind, and she trembled violently.

She was to be the first victim.

[CHARLEY WAG, THE NEW JACK SHEPPARD

Her abduction had only been the first step.

Some horrible fate awaited her.

The idea was too terrible to be endured.

Her heart sickened.

A species of despairing resignation took possession of her.

She bade a silent farewell to life.

Her head fell heavily upon her shoulder, and she sank into a species of torpor, supported in a half-sitting, half-leaning posture, by the corners of the wall.

But suddenly a change took place in her.

Her old pride, and courage, and daring returned to her.

She would not lie there, and submit passively to be slaughtered like a lamb, without making an effort to save herself.

Rising from the ground as though endowed with supernatural force, the duchess stood erect, her nostrils dilated, her eyes flashing, and her hair bristling on her head.

The feeble light shone upon her, and she was as a woman inspired.

Without pause or hesitation, and as though acting under the dictates of a species of instinct rather than of reason, she walked towards the staircase.

There was a degree of noiseless dignity about her motions.

She ascended the steps slowly, and with a mechanical certainty of footing, as persons walk in their sleep.

She passed along the corridor, reëntered the room where she had been confined, and advanced towards the window.

But at that moment the window was flung open, and a slim, graceful youth sprang into the room, and stood facing her.

The moonlight fell full upon his head, and the duchess reeled back with an exclamation of surprise and terror.

But her alarm had other foundation than that which might be supposed to lie in the suddenness of the youth's entrance, or a fear which she might have entertained that he would prove a bar to her escape.

Yes, there were other reasons; for all thoughts of escape for the moment abandoned her.

With wide-open, horror-stricken eyes, she glared at the intruder.

For a time she was speechless, and he remained motionless before her.

Then she said, in a low, husky voice:

"Who are you? What do you want? Where do you come from? Is it from the grave?"

"The grave, my lady?" replied the youth, cheerfully. "Not quite so bad as that. I'm Charley Wag, the celebrated highwayman and burglar."

"Yes, yes," said the duchess, the expression of her face changing from alarm to dislike; "I know you now. You are the boy who broke into my house."

"I have that honour, madam."

"And what are you doing here?"

"The old game again, my lady."

For a moment the lady was silent.

Then a thought seemed to occur to her.

"Do you expect to gain much by this robbery which you are about to commit?"

"Nothing worth mentioning."

"Would it be worth your while to relinquish your object for another?"

"What other?"

"To help me to effect my escape."

"Are you a prisoner here, my lady?"

"Yes."

"If I were to lose money by it I'd do it. I always make it a point to sacrifice myself for the ladies."

"What shall we do, then?"

"I have a rope-ladder outside the window."

"Come, then."

Without another word he took the lady's hand, and she trod upon the ladder.

It rocked to and fro unsteadily; but he descended at the same time, and managed to support her round the waist.

"Hold fast! hold fast!" he whispered softly.

In a couple of minutes more they had reached the ground.

"Where do you want to go?"

"To my house in Park Lane."

"I must help you over this wall, then."

He got down the rope-ladder, and helped her over the wall.

A cab was standing outside, and he assisted her into it.

The driver received the direction, and drove away.

But the sense of relief was too great for her already overtaxed energies.

Nature could endure no more.

She dropped upon his shoulder, and fainted.

And thus they travelled onwards.

*　　　*　　　*　　　*　　　*

They travelled on thus tranquilly.

The rich lady's head cushioned upon the heart of the low London thief.

Oh, Charley, Charley! had you known then what years afterwards you came to learn, what countless crimes might not the knowledge have saved you from.

But he knew nothing.

Onward they rode, as little dreaming what fate awaited them as though they were two innocent sleeping babes.

———

XL.—THE TIGER DRIVEN INTO A CORNER.

"HELP! help! help!"

A shrill cry rang through the house.

"Help! help! help!"

A wild, despairing cry; a cry at once of rage, of misery, of desolation.

"Help! help! help!"

Then, after a moment's pause, a loud, furious shouting of,

"Rattan, Rattan! Help! This way. She's gone. Quick, quick!"

Rattan, who was smoking a quiet pipe by himself at the bottom of the stairs, looked up alarmed.

"What the blazes is the matter now?" he asked himself.

Then, as it occurred to him that perhaps it would be as well if he went himself to inquire, he took the candle in his hand, and, with a discontented oath or two, he took himself upstairs, to see what could have occurred to cause all this disturbance.

But although he was prepared for something quite out of the ordinary course of events and every-day occurrences, Rattan did not for a moment expect such a sight as met his eyes upon entering the apartment.

There was only the doctor there—no one else; and he was not doing anything of a very startling character, although at the first sight of him Rattan, hardened ruffian as he was, staggered back and changed colour.

Surely never before did human face wear such a fearful expression of mingled malignity, ferocity, and despair, as that which the face of Faversham wore at this moment.

Usually very pale, his face was at this moment literally corpse-like, his jaw hung open, his lips were bloodless, his eyes starting from his head, and the whites turned to a dull yellow, streaked with red.

"What, in God's name, has happened?" demanded Rattan, eagerly.

The doctor rose silently from an arm-chair where he was sitting when the other entered.

"Happened!" he repeated, in a dull, hollow voice; "happened! She's gone."

"The devil she is! I thought that you had given her enough to keep her there for a day or two longer on her back."

"Yes, yes—I thought so. I must have made some frightful mistake. Fool, fool that I was!"

"When do you suppose she went?"

"I don't know, but recently."

"You saw her about three hours ago."

"Yes."

"How was she then? Did you notice?"

"I looked at her, as usual. She seemed to be insensible."

"But look here. What beats me—"

"Well?"

"Is where she's gone to."

"I can't imagine how she did it; but she must have gone by the window. See—it is open."

"Well, I don't know; perhaps she may yet be in the house. Shall we look?"

The doctor seemed to recover himself a little at these words.

He took the light in his hand, and followed the other down-stairs.

They searched through every room in the house, but without success.

Then they returned to the bed-chamber from whence they had started on their search, and Faversham again sank back despairingly into his arm-chair.

Rattan fidgetted about, and looked at him uneasily.

"What's to be done?" he inquired, after a while.

The other did not seem to hear him.

"What will be the consequences?" Rattan asked.

"Consequence!" repeated the doctor, looking up vaguely. "Consequence!"

Then, the meaning of the word seeming to occur to him suddenly,

"The consequence is, that I am ruined!" he shrieked out. "The consequence is, that the plots and schemes that I have brooded over night and day for these twenty years past, are all dashed to the ground—overthrown—de-feated irretrievably. There is no hope for them."

"Do you think it's so bad as that?"

"It is as bad, and worse. If we do not escape immediately, the police will be upon our track. Even now they may be coming. Hush! hush! did you hear nothing?"

"No, no," replied the ruffian, nervously; "I hear nothing. Do you think they'll be here so soon? If so, we'll get into a scrape if we're not off."

The doctor was examining the floor round by the window.

"It is here where she escaped."

"She must have been assisted by her friends. Then they've found out the whole rig."

"So it seems."

"By Jove, that's reyther serious. I didn't think of that at first. Why, I suppose it's a transporting job, this. And if they come and search the house, and find them stiff-uns—Lord, I feel a choking sensation in my throat already. I don't half like it."

While he spoke, Rattan was looking about upon the floor for foot-marks.

Suddenly he uttered an exclamation of astonishment.

"Hallo! what's this ere?"

He picked something up off the floor.

It was a black crape mask.

"Ha! ha!" said he; "this tells tales."

"What does it tell?"

"Why this must belong to our intelligent young friend, Charley Wag."

"Charley Wag?"

"None other. Why you was talking to him the other night, and telling him you wanted to see him. I told him, too, that you were as rich as a Jew. I saw his eye glitter at the time. I suppose the young gentleman thought he might as well try his hand at cracking the crib. It is that there circumstance, I expect, as we're indebted for the honour which Mr. Wag has done us. He's a plucky young chap, that, and a honour to my bringing up; for I done the first thing that put him in the way, like, of joining the perfession."

But while Rattan was speaking, the other was gazing out of the window, with a cold, stony, passionless expression, as though he had no ideas left, and that the flight of the duchess had so completely overthrown all his plans for the future, that he was unable to speak or act.

He was truly in an awful position.

If the duchess had gone back to her friends, she had, of course, discovered who it was who had given her the drug, and carried her away from her home.

All confidence was, of course, at an end between them.

He would, therefore, be unable to approach the family on whose destruction his mind had been so long bent, and for which he had been working, day and night, so many years.

However, he was not a man to be easily conquered; and though for a time prostrated by the greatness of the calamity which had befallen his nefarious projects, there was little doubt but that he would soon recover himself, as he had recovered himself before, and shake off these lethargic feelings, which for the moment overcame him, and rendered him almost as powerless as a child.

Even at that moment occurred a circumstance which caused a necessity for immediate action.

There came a terrific battering at the street-door.

Faversham rose to his feet, and trembled in every limb.

Rattan, pale as a sheet, stood staring at him.

Then, recovering his presence of mind, he went into one of the front rooms, and noiselessly opening the window, peeped into the street.

In another minute he returned to the doctor's side, several degrees paler than when he went away.

"What is it?" asked Faversham, in a hoarse whisper.

"It's the police."

"Many?"

"Five or six.   There is a great crowd, too."

"What shall we do?"

"Escape by the back."

"Is there time?"

"We will try."

They descended the stairs at once.   There was no time to take anything—not even their hats.

They went out into the garden by the window from a room at the end of the passage leading from the street-door.

They closed the window behind them, so that if shortly the police should force an entrance, they would not discover at first the direction the fugitives had taken.

With the aid of a small ladder, which Rattan knew how to lay his hands upon immediately, they scaled the wall, and dropped down into a quiet lane by the side of the house.

But here, as they touched the ground, a man ran forward, and laid his hand upon Rattan's arm.

The doctor immediately recognized him to be the duchess's coachman.

"Fell him to the earth," he said in a low tone to his companion.

The other wanted no second order.

Raising his powerful fist in the air, he dealt the man a terrific crushing blow in the face, which seemed to smash it, and caused the blood to spurt out violently from his damaged nose.

"Let's run for it," said Rattan, immediately afterwards, pulling his companion by the arm.

They easily made their escape, for there was no one else to stop them ; this servant having come round to the back of the house by himself.

After they had run about a quarter of a mile, they came to a stand still.

"What shall we do?" asked Rattan.

"Go your way," replied the doctor. "To-morrow morning early, I will meet you at that place in the Mint.   Until then, I will be by myself, if you please.   I want to think.   I want to be quiet.   Leave me."

Rattan left him as desired, and the doctor threaded the crowded streets alone.

He seemed to glide along like a dark shadow, or with the motion of an uneasy spirit, wandering alone by night round the churchyard, which contained its earthly tomb.

Like a shadow—a phantom—something supernatural, he passed along the crowded thoroughfares.

The people fell back from him as though he bore some infectious disease, and a lane was opened as he passed.

No one knew him, though he flashed his hollow eyes into theirs, and they sank back frightened in spite of themselves, and gazed after him in terror as he went upon his way.

Some thought him mad, seeing him thus without any covering on his head, and his lank, thin, white hair streaming in the wind.

Sometimes he heard exclamations of astonishment, and eager conjectures as he passed.

Sometimes he would turn round and look boldly, scornfully, and fiercely, at those who were struck by his wild exterior.

Again he would shrink and cower, endeavouring to escape from their regards, and quicken the long regular strides which bore him onwards.

Thus he traversed the Edgware-road, and the swarming market—for it was Monday night; thus he took his way, apparently unconscious of the multitudes which encompassed him, taking no notice of what passed around him; but staring when he did look, with something resembling the unintelligent fury of a wild beast.

Those who met his eye, and spoke of it afterwards, said that the mixture of glitter and bloodshed in it was truly awful.

And all the way he went he never once slackened his pace, but kept up the same hurrying stride, passing through groups who were conversing as though they did not stand there upon the pavement, and gliding onward like a black spectre past the crossings, amid the plunging of sharply-checked horses, and the hallooing of drivers and passengers, the savage interrogatories of irate Hansom cabmen, and the surly demands of savage omnibus drivers.

Many and many a time was there a cry of a man run over, and frantic rushes followed to the scene of the supposed accident; but nothing had occurred.

A chorus of hoarsely indignant coachmen explained to one another, in flowery language, how he had glided away, as they supposed, from underneath the very wheels, and was gone.

He wandered along, as it seemed, quite without purpose, and in course of time reached the East-end of London, and the Whitechapel-road.

Then he plunged into a horrible labyrinth of obscure and narrow streets, reeking with a thousand vile stenches.

At last, as it seemed, utterly fatigued and exhausted with his exertions, mental and physical, he seated himself upon a door-step, in a dark, quiet, bye-street, and rested for a while.

There was a dreadful change, which had taken place within the last hour or so, in this bad man's face.

He appeared to be quite prostrated, paralysed, and smitten down.

He looked about him in a vague, uncertain way, and his lips moved slightly ; while, from time to time, low muttering sounds came forth, as though he were communing with his own wicked thoughts.

His face still retained its demoniacal expression; but it seemed, too, as though the reasoning powers were entirely deserting him.

Was it possible that he was going mad?

Such an awful spinning feeling he felt in his head—such a strange, unstrung, exhausted, relaxed kind of feeling, he began to notice was creeping over him, that he clasped his forehead, suddenly struck with an overpowering horror of his impending fate, and sprang up with a scream.

Uttering an inarticulate cry of agony, Faversham rushed mechanically forward, caring not whither he went.

His heart beat quick and fast, his temples throbbed; and when he pressed them with his hands, he could feel how the burning heat of fever radiated from his brain.

The long lines of lamps began to dance madly before his eyes, the people in the streets seemed to caper wildly round him, to stand on their heads, and to indulge in a thousand grotesque antics, like the strange half-seen images in a nightmare.

The whole outward scene around him was somehow curiously mixed up and interwoven with a strange turmoil of thought within.

He could scarcely tell whether he looked upon realities, or upon the phantoms which his heated brain had called up; for, mixed with the faces of the crowd he every now and then could have sworn most positively that he saw the faces of the dead—the faces of the dead of the mysterious vault in Bayswater—the faces of his murdered victims, flitting to and fro before him, peeping at him over the shoulders of the living, and appearing suddenly at his elbow to jibe at and mock him.

He heard wild shrieks and bursts of fiendish laughter in the air, and every now and then a low idiotic snigger at his elbow, which again seemed to be drowned in the roar of the passing carriages.

In his madness he struck random blows at the hideous faces which encompassed him, and he shouted aloud, and raved at the top of his voice.

At last, suddenly he ran his head against a lamp-post, and fell backwards insensible.

Then followed a long blank.

When at last he recovered his senses in some measure, he found himself stretched upon a bench in the bar of a small tavern.

The landlord, landlady, and several other persons were bending over him, carefully excluding the air, as is customary upon such occasions.

The barmaid, a blushing young creature with a quantity of light-brown curls, was bending over him, and poking his nose from one side to the other with a scent-bottle.

A red-nosed gentleman, who was the "sticker up" from the skittle-ground, and who was smoking an uncommon long "churchwarden," was of opinion that it was a "tack of appleplexy."

But the barman contented himself by smiling sarcastically, and observing, with his finger upon the side of his nose, "lushy."

The policeman who had helped to bring Faversham there, proposed going for a doctor.

"It looks to me very like a case of pisoning," said the landlord; "and if so, we'd better have medical adwice."

"And a stomach-pump," said the landlady.

"Give him a pint of biling hot water to begin with," suggested the barman.

"Shut up," growled the gentleman from the skittle-ground. "You ought to be ashamed of yourself, you ought. I'd like to give you some biling water. I'd warm you."

"I haven't taken any poison," said Faversham, rousing himself a little. "I shall be better directly."

"I knew he would," said the barmaid, still knocking his nose about. "These salts always do it. I've never knowed 'em not to answer."

"He'd better have a glass of something," suggested the landlord, after a while; and the landlady went to get him one, remarking, though, at the time, that she was not too sure that the "party could pay for it; and if not, what was the good?"

It came, however, and Faversham having been raised a little by the sticker-up, a small quantity of the hot liquor was poured down his throat.

It to some extent revived him, and he was able to sit in a reclining posture, leaning back his head against the wall.

He was still unable to stir his limbs, and he felt deadly faint, as with closed eyes he lay listening mechanically to the conversation around him.

The policeman, under pretence of looking after the man in the fit, was having a little drop of beer with the sticker-up and a couple of other gentlemen, and they were listening to the policeman's experiences.

"Rum goes—I believe you," the officer observed. "There's lots of rum goes as is never heerd on. Some goes in for cunning, like, and some for cheek. Now this ere Charley Wag, that everybody's talking about, goes in for both."

"Have you seen him on your travels, policeman?"

"Well, me? No, I aint seen him myself; but he must be a rum un, if what they say is true."

"What do they say?"

"Well, there's that robbery, the night before last, of the lady on her way to the opera. Have you heard that?"

"No." (In chorus.)

"I'll tell you, then."

Respectful silence.

"She was some awful swell or another," began the policeman. "One of the tip-top nobility, you understand."

"Yes."

"And she was a-going in her carriage, you know, like the first-rate nobs goes, all togged out splendacious with diamonds and pearls, and gold and silver, and every other sort of jewels. Ever so many hundred pounds' worth. It was a very crack night on at the Opera, and there was some tremenjous foreigner doing somethink or other extry attractive, and so there was a precious long string of carriages before the door, and they had to go very slow acos of the letting down, you know, and had to keep a-stopping every now and then, as perhaps you are aware it is the custom."

" Certingly, gov'nor," replied the sticker-up, a little snappishly; for he could not help thinking that the policeman was entering into unnecessary particulars, with the idea that his audience were unfamiliar with the usages of good society.

" Certingly," he repeated.   " Go a-head."

" So this here lady was a riding along with another lady in their carriage, and it was dark, and the lamps was lit, and they was just a thinking of nothing at all particular, but talking quite cosy, like as you and me might be doing over this ere pint, when a chap bobs his head into them."

" Bobs his head into them ?"

" In at the windy, you know."

" Ah, to be sure.   Well, what did he say ?"

" He was dressed like one of them chaps as sells the nosegays, and he popped a nosegay in at the window."

" ' We don't want none,' said the lady.

" ' All right, mum,' says the young chap.

" ' We don't want to buy nothing,' says the lady, indignant, seeing he didn't go.

" ' I don't want to sell nothing,' says the young chap.

" ' Why don't you go, then ?' says the lady. ' What do you want?'

" ' I wants them there jewels you've got on,' says the young man. ' So hand 'em us as quick as you can.'

" ' You don't mean to say you're going to try and rob us here, in a crowded street, with our servants both within call ?' says the lady.

" ' Don't I, mum ?' says the young man. ' My name's Charley Wag, and this here's a pistol, and I'll shoot the first as makes the least sound through the arm.'

" You can fancy how the ladies was taken aback at these here awful words.

" ' I don't want to hurt you,' says Charley Wag, incontinuation, ' only I wants them there trinkets, and them there trinkets I must hev.'

" So with that he pops the nosegay which he was a holding straight up to one of their heads, and then the ladies sees for the first time that it wasn't no more a nosegay nor I am, but a pistol wrapped up in flowers, and as murderous-looking a weapon as you could well wish to meet with."

" A precious sight too much so for me," said the sticker-up. " And did he rob 'em ?"

" Ah, he robbed 'em, safe enough."

" And got off ?"

" Ah, and got off."

" Well, that's a rum go, as you remarked."

" It was a wery rum go ; but then it was a rum chap as done it."

" Blow me," said the sticker-up, " if I don't think the cheekier you are, the less risk you runs.   It's them timid bloaks as is nobbled directly."

" Ah," said the policeman, " they're all nobbled in time, and then it's all u r with 'em."

" You're right there," said the sticker-up, " Honesty's the best polisher, arter all."

The gossipers were interrupted by a movement of Faversham's, and turning round, they saw that he had risen.

He was supporting himself against the wall.

" I'll go now," he said.   " I am much better. I only want a little fresh air."

He therefore paid for what he had had, and took his departure.

" Are you quite sure you're strong enough ?" the landlady asked.

" Yes," replied Faversham, " quite sure, thank you.   It was only a giddiness—a fit which overtook me suddenly.   I had been very much put out about something ; but I am all right now."

He did not look quite the thing for all that. He, however, managed to walk pretty steadily out of the house, guiding himself a little by one hand leaning against the wall.

Almost before he knew it, he was in the street.

He was very faint, and felt dreadfully exhausted.

But the cool night air revived him to some extent, and he managed to walk along slowly.

His limbs shivered and shook beneath him.

Again and again he strove to bring his mind to bear upon the circumstances of his position, but it was impossible.

The overwrought brain refused to perform its functions of thought.

It received the images conducted to it by the organs of sense ; but it utterly failed to arrange, or classify, or retain them in any tangible sort of shape or order.

Afterwards he strove to recal the events of the night with some degree of distinctness, but it was impossible.

His efforts were in vain.

A dim haze seemed to hang over it.

The fog of fever was abroad upon his mind, and only the most broken and disjointed visions would arise at his call, like pinnacles above it.

He remembered standing at one time of the night under a pillared portico.

Lights flashed about him.

Carriages all glancing in the gaslight glare, dashed by.

Groups of gaily dressed company swept by him — women enveloped in rich cashmeres, and ermined drapery, with scented hair and fair bosoms, shining white in the lamp-light—men in all the elegancies of evening dress ; while, on every side of him there arose the rich joyous sounds of mirth and laughter, and the gaiety which accompanies the light-hearted and happy.

But suddenly, without any interval or space, as it appeared to him, he formed one of the company at a singing tavern.

There were lots of lights here, again, and rolling clouds of tobacco-smoke, and rows of red faces turned towards the platform.

It seemed to him, that a fat, foreign gentleman, was obliging the company assembled with some imitations of singing birds ; and to avoid any confusion—an arrangement which appeared to be very necessary to Faversham—he named the birds he was going to imitate before he began, and let it be clearly understood that this teetling was supposed to be like a " plackpurd," and that like a " trush."

In like fashion, those terrible persons who give imitations of popular actors, always kindly name the actor before they begin ; which is not, all things considered, such a very bad arrangement; though, even then, as it usually happens, most unfortunately, that you have never seen half the persons they strive to reproduce, a great deal of the effect is lost, in spite of your making up your mind beforehand that it must be exceedingly like them.

After the whistler was gone, or even before he was gone—for Faversham somehow was so confused, that his brain could not cope with the events occurring before him!—here began a rollicking chorus of small boys, with extremely pale, puddingy faces.

It was their opening day, these young goblins were saying. It was their opening day, and they called upon all the merry men then present to amuse themselves upon that account.

But even while listening to these, he had risen to take his departure, and was staggering through the streets again; and, as it seemed to him, in a few minutes' time, he was seated in another large, lighted, crowded room, looking at an exhibition of *poses plastiques.*

But why was he looking at them? What was he doing there at all?

It was very far from his custom to go to such places. Indeed, he held them all in horror. They were not according to his tastes.

But here, on this extraordinary night of nightmares, he wandered about from one to another, as though he could not have enough of them.

He was out in the Haymarket, and in two or three cigar-divans, drinking a wild mixture of unwholesome drinks, and smoking cigars as though for a wager.

Anon the scene changed.

He was alone in the streets.

They were almost deserted, and grey dawn was breaking over them.

Red streaks of light stretched along the Eastern sky behind the steeples.

A grimy group of men and women—the former muffled in great-coats, and comforters, and probably of the cab-driving interest; the latter, slatternly and thinly clad, and probably birds of the night—stood round the barrow of an early breakfast man in Drury-lane.

They were drinking, with drunken and riotous glee, sundry cups of the muddy compound, which the stall-keeper was pleased to designate by the name of coffee; and which Faversham was providing them with, for some reason or other, quite unknown to himself, at his own expense.

Then, gradually the sun began to fill the streets, and he was alone.

The air seemed to him as fresh and as pure as the air of the sea-side.

The far extending lines of roofs cut the blue heavens clearly and sharply.

The hum and buzz of the returning day commenced to sound.

Shops opened, and passengers began to press along the pavement.

The day had begun again.

Then, as though quite unable to retain the mere ordinary phenomena of common-place life, Faversham's memory was obscured by an utter blank.

He only remembered a sense of weariness—a sensation of dreary, purposeless wanderings—a dreamy, dreary vision of endless houses,

streets after streets, hurrying crowds, and some dim indefinite power, which drove him on and on.

At length he came, somehow or other, to green fields, and a dry ditch; and in the latter he laid himself down quietly to die.

XLI.—Fresh life—A new scheme of vengeance.

AH! far better would it have been for many then alive and happy, if this wicked man had thus ended his days; but it was not so to be.

He lay there until night set in, and the heavy dews began to fall; and then he arose, weak and trembling, but with his intellect almost restored to its only energy.

He arose, and tottered along towards his home.

The scene around him was full of peace and rest; but as he went, he clutched his thin fingers, and shook his fist in the air, cursing himself and his illness, for having so long delayed his schemes of vengeance.

"I have no time to lose," he muttered. "I have no time to lose. My plans must be at once matured. I have not time to wreak my vengeance upon the mother and child. I must proceed at once against the father. I must have him somehow or other in my clutches this very night. What has been doing while I have been sleeping away the precious hours? I must make inquiries."

He had purchased a hat the previous evening, I should have previously mentioned; and he now found out a quiet little shop, and bought a long cloak, and a thick comforter.

Thus provided, he was enabled to go to Bayswater, with very little chance of recognition; for his usual dress was very different.

To make more sure, however, he bought a pair of false moustachios, and a pair of blue spectacles.

"No one will know me now," he said to himself; and calling a cab, he bade the driver take him to the next street to that in which he had resided.

Here he entered a public-house, much frequented by the servants of the neighbourhood.

A policeman was talking across the bar to the landlord.

Faversham remained silent, and, without appearing to do so, listened intently to the conversation which was going on between them.

"And so you haven't caught him yet," the landlord said.

"Who?" asked the policeman.

"This 'ere doctor."

"No; we haven't got him yet."

"How does the matter stand? I haven't quite heard the rights of the case."

"Well, you see, he's been giving some drug or other, it's supposed, to the Duchess of Heatherland, making belief to kill her, or with the intent of killing her perhaps; anyways, he took her out of her coffin, and brought her to this house of his."

"It's a very rum start. What could he have done it for? I can hardly believe he wanted to kill her, if he brought her away like that out of her coffin. It seems more as though he wanted to revive her."

"Well I don't know, and I don't mind saying—"

"What?"

"That this ere case, from beginning to end—"

"Well?"

"Is more than I know what to make head or tail of."

There wasn't much information to be got out of this.

Only one thing Faversham felt the necessity of, and that was, to keep clear of his own house for the present.

He did not exactly know what could be the nature of the charge laid against him, but he knew that if upon any charge he got locked up in prison, he would not be able to proceed with the projects which at present filled his brain.

And the reader may ask, what had originally been his plan, when he gave the duchess the drug, and carried her away in the manner that we have seen.

His object was this.

He had found it to be quite impossible to do any mischief to the young duke whilst he was taken care of and watched over so anxiously by his mother. The only way that mischief could be effected, was to remove the mother first.

Then the child, left to the mercy of an Italian servant in the doctor's pay, might be disposed of easily.

It was his plan to have forced the duchess to have written for the child before he had murdered her, and it was for this reason that he administered to her the drug, and carried her away like we have seen.

It may strike the reader as extraordinary and improbable that he should have taken all this trouble, and gone about his business in such a roundabout way, when it would have been so much easier when he gave the duchess a drug, to have given her poison at once.

But that can be easily explained.

To a peculiarly constituted mind like that possessed by this extraordinary being, whose whole life was devoted to the hatching and consummation of deeds of the darkest atrocity, and whose every thought was centred in the accomplishment of the scheme of wholesale vengeance upon which he had been brooding for so many years, the departure from a laid-down plan seemed of much more importance than it can possibly do to a third person.

As yet, in his hellish career of blood, he had slain all his victims, one after the other, in the order he had laid down to himself.

Three victims now remained.

The duke, the duchess, and the little boy.

Now, as the duke was the object of his deadliest hate, he had arranged in his own mind that his murder should be the last of all.

The little boy he knew was fondly loved by the sinful old wretch who was his father.

Faversham, therefore, had well considered, that in killing the child he would be stabbing the father.

After the child was dead, the duchess should follow.

And then the duke last of all.

But now all his plans were changed.

He felt that he had no time to perfect his elaborate schemes.

Any moment he might be taken into custody. Who could tell? perhaps confined for a madman!

He might even go mad! He shuddered when he thought that his attack of yesterday might recur again, perhaps, with renewed violence.

His intellects, in that case, might altogether succumb beneath its effects.

Even now, he felt that his reasoning powers were in some measure impaired and weakened.

He would, therefore, if possible, obtain possession of the duke, and wreak his deadly vengeance upon him, without any reference to the others.

Yes; that would be the best plan.

Then afterwards he would have time to consider what course it would be best to take.

If he proceeded otherwise, and attacked the weaker and less important members of the family first, he might never have time to wreak his deadly vengeance upon the duke.

No; that would be the best plan. And as he sat here, huddled away in a corner of the public-house, he made up his mind what course he would pursue.

Meanwhile, the landlady and the policeman went on talking.

"A curious person that doctor," the landlady observed. "I've only seen him once, though. What do you think of him?"

"Well, I've not seen him myself," replied the policeman; "but he's a queer fish, according to accounts."

"Yes; so I've heard. What sort of a place, now, is it inside his house? Did you find anything out of the common?"

Faversham pricked up his ears.

"Well," replied the policeman, mysteriously, and as though he were imparting most important information, "I can't say as I did see anythink very much out of the common, at least, so far as I looked; but whether or not anythink will turn up remains to be seen."

Faversham, with a sense of great relief, rose from his seat, and presently went out into the open air.

He must waste no time.

If he was to have vengeance, it must be had at once, without delay

He must lay a plot to ensnare the duke.

His death was all that the doctor required. If he could get the others too, afterwards, so much the better. If he could slay all, as the next heir to the property their deaths would bring him a fortune.

But that he did not now consider.

The first object of all was vengeance.

Vengeance bloody and terrible.

Vengeance he would have.

He could not now, after the turn which events had taken, slay the duke in the way he had proposed to himself, and which he had spoken of to Rattan.

It must be done in some other manner.

But it should be done, and directly.

He walked along rapidly as he thought of it, and his busy brain began to hatch and hatch more and more hellish plots of blood and horror.

THE TEMPTER.

And now, reader, follow me, and we will see how they worked, and whether or not they were successful.

XLII.—THE POOR GOOSE IN THE NET OF THE DESTROYER.

IN Garlic-hill, as I have told you before, is the house of Messrs. Bottle and Bung.

The establishment occupies the ground-floor, and if you have any business to transact with the worthy firm, you must first of all enter a large, low-roofed room, lighted on dark days by gas, and behold half-a-dozen or so of clerks, No. 40.

scribbling as hard as they can scribble, and thumbing huge ledgers, or handing them about from one to another over the brass rails in front of their desks.

From this room, two doors of ground-glass lead to the private business rooms of the two members of the firm.

On the right-hand door is written the name of BOTTLE.

On the left hand-door you may observe the cognomination of BUNG.

If you were suddenly to open the door of the room of Mr. Bottle, you would probably find that gentleman turning over the pages of another ledger, steadily running his finger down the columns of figures, and pausing every now and then to make minute calculations upon

[CHARLEY WAG, THE NEW JACK SHEPPARD.

the corner of a sheet of blotting-paper before him.

If, on the other hand, you were to look in upon Mr. Bung, you would find him very similarly employed.

Perhaps he would be running up the columns instead of down them, or he might be making his calculations upon his thumb-nail, instead of on the blotting-paper.

Otherwise, there would not be a very great deal of difference between the occupation of the two gentlemen.

They were very well matched.

They took no interest in anything but pounds, shillings, and pence; and they made a rare lot of these from year's end to year's end.

It is, however, with the clerks, and not with the head men that we have now to do.

Eight o'clock is striking from a neighbouring church tower, and the clerks are hurrying in.

Each one as he comes, signs his name, and the time of his arrival, in a book kept for that purpose, and a porter stands ready with a pen in his hand, to draw a line below the last signature, after the five minutes of grace have expired, and thus expose the misdeeds of the lazy and lagging, when, woe betide them should either Mr. Bottle or Mr. Bung observe that the delinquent was in the habit of being behind his time as a rule; that is to say, that he had been late once before in the same week.

The five minutes had almost expired, when two young clerks, the youngest there, run in together and sign their names.

One is Mr. Thomas Twiddle, and the other is Mr. Robert Weazle; and having hurriedly scribbled these appellations in the book, they proceed at once to their places in a dark corner of the office; and, as they ply their pens with tremendous rapidity, these two young gentlemen, somehow or other, contrive to carry on a whispered conversation.

Mr. Thomas Twiddle is an open-featured, red-cheeked youth, the expression of whose face is, if anything, rather simple, ingenuous, and confiding; or, in fact, what is commonly called " green."

Mr. Weazle, on the other hand, is very pale and pinched, and dissipated, rather bilious, and somewhat blotchy.

" I say, Tom," whispered Mr. Weazle over his book; " I say, Tom."

" Hallo!"

" Did you go there last night?"

" Where?"

" To that place—you know."

" What, the theatre?"

" Ah."

" Yes; I went. It was first-rate."

" I'll get you another order some day, if you like."

" How do you manage to get them? I wish I could."

" Well, you could, I daresay."

" How, pray?"

" If you come and have your dinner along with me to-day, I'll show you."

" Can't you tell me?"

" Well, then, I get them from the old cove I told you of."

" What, the one you met at the eating-ouse?"

" The same. He told me I was to bring you some day."

" What sort of a chap is he?"

" A curious sort of old cove, I can tell you. He's an old gent. I don't know what his name is."

" He's taken a fancy to you, hasn't he?"

" Well, it would seem like it."

" How long ago did you meet him?"

" About three or four days. He goes there every day, just the same time I do. We sit in the same box very often, that's how I made his acquaintance."

" Is he a good sort?"

" I believe you. He often stands treat, custard pudding, and fruit tart, and such like; and it's him that gave me the tickets for the play; and he says to me the other day—' Is there any other young feller like you at your office?' says he. Then I says, ' Yes, there's Twiddle.' Then he says, ' Is Twiddle a friend of yourn?' Then I says, ' Twiddle's a great friend of mine.' Then he says, ' In that case, bring Twiddle along o' you.' And then I says, ' I will,' says I.'"

" What sort of a chap is he to look at?"

" He's a very white 'un in the face. Indeed, I may say, a most uncommon white 'un, and has eyes that reg'lar goes right through and through you, like a couple of gimblets."

" I've never seen him at the eating-house."

" No, 'cause you so seldom go there, I suppose, and because he don't happen to go the same time you do; but if you come to-day along o' me, you shall see him, and I will introduce you. You'll most likely get a jolly good blow out for nothing."

" I say, Weazle, old fellow."

" What now?"

" I hope there's nothing wrong about him, you know."

" Wrong? What should there be?"

" Well, there are such rum things goes on, one hears of, I don't know."

" If you're afraid, you'd better stop away; that's all I've got to say."

" I'm not afraid."

" Well, will you come?"

" Yes; I should like to."

" Well, then, don't say any more about it."

Indeed, had he wished, Twiddle could not have done so, for just then the chief clerk began to call out angrily:

" Now then, you two. I should like to know how long you're going to sit there magging. I shall separate you directly, if there ain't a little less talk. There can't be any work done with all that noise going on for everlasting."

The two young gentlemen, therefore, left off talking, and worked away in silence until dinner-time.

At one o'clock, having asked permission, they went out together.

At a little steaming cook-shop in the neighbourhood they found the subject of their discourse waiting for them.

For some days past, the elderly man whom they went there to meet had been a sort of puzzle to the other customers.

As most of the other customers were regular frequenters of the establishment, and as Mr. Weazle was a regular customer also, and as they knew to what house in the City he belonged, they had been all speculating among themselves, what the deuce the elderly man could have to say to Mr. Weazle, and what Mr. Weazle could have to say to the elderly man; and they had long ago come to the conclusion, that there could be no good in it at all.

When Weazle had bolted his dinner, which was usually a plate of meat and a pennyworth of cabbage, he would lend a willing ear to what the elderly man had to tell him; and it seemed as though he had a great deal to tell.

The pair would sit at the furthest corner of the most deserted box, and those who slily stole furtive glances at them, round the sides of the newspapers they made belief to be reading, and watched the couple, and watched the eager up-turned countenance of the lad, and the cold glistening eyes which were bent down upon him, and caught the low murmured tone of the elder's voice, which the boy appeared to drink in so eagerly—aye, as it were, with his very soul—the people who saw all this, day after day, could not help thinking somehow of the stories they had heard of the fascinations of a deadly snake, and remembered how the poor bird would flutter and scream from branch to branch, and fall at length helpless into the jaws of the hideous monster beneath.

To be sure, this steaming cook-shop was hardly the sort of place where one would have expected to hear of charms and enchantments.

It was not the sort of spot which you would have supposed the magician would have selected for the exercise of his black arts.

It was a very cheap dining-house, indeed, with a reeking atmosphere, redolent of over-cooked meat, and simmering watery vegetables, and crowded all day long with gaunt and hungry clerks.

Such huge masses of food did these persons put away, too!

Such plates—large and small—of boiled and roast, they got through, and such ceaseless demands for more bread and additional half-pints did they make; and so very particular were they about their potatoes being mealy ones, and their meat being half of it "out-side," and their plates being half filled with gravy.

It was truly a very vulgar sort of place; but there, nevertheless, day after day, the young clerk remained up to the very last moment he could devote to dinner, in converse with his unknown friend.

But the regular customers noticed something else more curious still before long.

After the day that Mr. Weazle brought his friend Mr. Twiddle to dine at the "slap bang," it was the latter with whom the elderly man held long conversations ever afterwards.

The elderly man came an hour later, at the time Mr. Twiddle usually took his dinner; for the regulations of the office, as a rule, prevented the two boys from dining together.

Then, after a while, the boy Twiddle went to other dining places to dine with the strange man; but wherever they went, the boy was always listening in the same earnest way that Weazle had been, and the elderly man was always talking.

And, in the meantime, a great alteration took place in Mr. Twiddle's manner.

He became gradually silent and pre-occupied.

The senior clerk of Messrs. Bottle and Bung's had no longer any necessity for checking his chattering propensities.

Mr. Weazle questioned him, and laughed at him, and chaffed; but he got nothing out of him.

Weazle told Twiddle all that the stranger said to him, or rather, as much as he could remember; but Twiddle told his friend nothing.

He was as close as he could be, and gave none but the briefest and driest of answers to the questions that were put to him.

Weazle bored away, though, for he could not make it out how the mysterious stranger should have dropped him so suddenly when he had introduced his friend; and he was a little jealous.

"What has he got to say to you so much?"

"Who?"

"You know who. Well, that chap at the dining-house."

"Nothing."

"He must say something."

"He doesn't come now."

"Don't you see him, then?"

"No."

"Well, I don't believe you. Whatever is the matter with you?"

"Nothing is; what should be?"

"The governor hasn't been blowing you up, has he?"

"No; why should he blow me up?"

"There," said Weazle, indignantly; "you can keep your secrets. I don't want to hear them."

"I haven't got any secrets," replied Twiddle. But he had.

The other boy, however, left him to himself, and waited patiently for his mood to change, concluding, either that his friend was labouring under an aggravated fit of the sulks, or that something very unpleasant had occurred at home or elsewhere, which he did not wish to communicate.

Something very unpleasant had occurred, as you will see.

Matters went on much in this way for about ten days from the first day that Mr. Twiddle made the strange man's acquaintance.

One evening after the office was closed, the stranger waited for him at a public-house by the water side.

The boy was low and out of spirits, which his companion observing, pressed him to take some hot spirits and water.

"Well, Tom," said Faversham.

Of course you knew it was the doctor.

"Well, Tom, you say you wish you were in a better situation?"

"You know I do."

"You haven't got money enough to spend on your little pleasures?"

"Not too much."

"And you want more?"

"I should like more."

"You shall have it."

The boy looked up.

The other's eyes were fixed upon him intently.

XLIII.—SHOWING WHAT WAS THE SOFT SPOT IN THE HEART OF THE DUKE'S VALET.

THE public-house where the boy and Faversham were seated in conversation, was close to the water's edge, and the water every now and then beat against the wooden side of the house with a dull thud.

In all London there is not a much drearier district than that which lies down near the river's bank in the City; particularly in the evening time, when the busy traffic of the day has drawn to a close.

Perhaps at one time the ground was a swamp, where the dull waters of the Thames soaked into the earth, and nourished rank crops of slimy bulrushes and creeping weeds; and still the place seemed to retain something of the noisome marshy stench about it.

The flags here, and the stones in the road, are covered with moisture when other streets are dry; and at high tides, water comes oozing through the grimy walls of slimy, faint-smelling underground vaults, where half-decayed goods are stowed away, apparently for the sole purpose of becoming speedily rotten.

The aspect of the whole neighbourhood is one of shabby, smouldering decay.

It does not appear to be so much dead as palsy-stricken..

The houses are irregular in structure, heavy, ghastly, and grim. Some of them have been handsome enough in their time, no doubt; for here are still to be seen ancient-looking porches, and massive carved lintels.

But mean, shabby dwellings stand side by side with these faded mansions, and low, cheap cook-shops, where unwholesome flabby meats simmer and sodden all day long in the steaming windows.

And again, low, gloomy public-houses, and rank-smelling chandlers' shops, lit up at night by feebly burning and energetically spluttering yellow tallow candles.

The streets are narrow, dark, badly paved, and half in ruins.

Thick mud incrusts the lower portions of the walls.

The windows are narrow, dusty, and mud-bedaubed.

There is neither stir, nor show, nor comfort about the place.

It looks as though there were a curse upon it.

If we wished for a haunted house—for a house where we should be likely to hear dim, rumbling noises in the dead of the night, and dull echoing taps against the mouldy wainscoting, and spectral footsteps creaking in dark, nailed-up rooms, and the nibbling and scampering of hungry rats in old cellars and half choked-up drains and sewers, and the beating of death-watches in dark crumbling walls—we should, I say, if we wished for such a dwelling, be likely to find one if we went to this quarter to look for it, and in all probability would most likely pick upon the very identical public-house at which Faversham and the boy were discussing their glass of hot gin-and-water.

The waning light of day shone faintly in at the dirty window upon the dark fusty-smelling little room where they sat, and upon the half-rotten matting and rickety chairs and tables.

The lurid sunlight coming through the panes of the window, imparted to the doctor's face an unusual colour, and, if possible, heightened the expression of his deep-set eyes.

The boy looked at him, as it seemed, uneasily and in terror, as a bird might look at a boy who held it in his hand, uncertain what was to be its fate in another moment—whether it was to be preserved or destroyed.

"Look you, my boy," Faversham said, coaxingly; "you surely don't suppose I should get you into a scrape willingly, do you? Is it at all likely, after all the kindness I have shown you up to now, that I should do so? I ask you, is it at all likely?"

"No, sir; I don't think it is."

"Of course it isn't. A week ago or more, I first made your acquaintance, through young Weazle. I came quite by accident to dine at your eating-house, and I made his acquaintance. He was a nice enough sort of boy, with plenty to say for himself; but nothing compared to you. I took a fancy to you at first sight. I am a queer old fellow, you know, and I do take these sort of sudden likings and dislikings, and always have done so."

He was silent for a moment, and the boy said nothing, being busily engaged in drawing lines upon the table with his fingers dipped in some beer which had been upset.

"I took a fancy to you, I say, because I liked your face, and your voice, and your conversation. We got acquainted in consequence, and we got to be very soon the good friends that we are. Is not that the case?"

"Yes, sir."

"You told me then all that you had to tell about yourself, and who you were, and what you hoped for; and then it occurred to me that I could help you."

"Yes, you suggested that I—that I—"

"That you should fill up a cheque for a hundred pounds, and sign it with Bottle and Bung's signatures. That's what I suggested."

"But—but," stammered the boy, "if I am found out, what will be done to me?"

"In the first place, I have told you a dozen times that you will not be found out, and that you may make your mind quite easy upon that account."

"Yes; but if—"

"There are no 'ifs' in the case. I have promised you that the cheque shall never be presented, and I have told you that my only reason for wishing to possess it, is that I wish to show it about among some merchants, to obtain credit for those speculations of which I have so frequently spoken to you, and the profits of which I have promised solemnly that you shall share with me."

"But suppose there are no profits?"

"In that case, there is no loss for you. Why, you spoke as though you doubted me, Tom, and that you thought that I would get you into some mess, and leave you there. Be a man, Tom. I thought much better of you than this. I thought you were a brave boy. Just consider, now; look the business fairly in the face. What great risk do you run in any way? Do not I run the risk in presenting the cheque, even if I were going to do so? But do you imagine that I should be such a fool? Why, I don't mind telling you, I don't at all believe in your power of imitating your employers' signatures; anyhow, I don't think it very likely that they would cash the cheque at the bankers, where they see lots of them from time to time."

"Why do not you write it yourself?"

"You know I cannot do so. You know I am unacquainted with the gentlemen's signatures; and even if I were not, my hands shake so abominably, it is as much as I can do to hold a pen, much more accomplish any feat of penmanship."

And as he spoke, Faversham held out his long thin hand, which trembled like a leaf.

"And you think that the speculations are sure to answer?"

"Certain. As far as human calculation can go, we are already rich."

"But then, human calculations are not infallible."

"True; but then, we must act upon the best calculations we can make. We might not be alive to-morrow, but that is no reason why we should not provide for to-morrow's dinner. If I have the cheque which you are to give me, I shall get the credit I require; if I have the credit, I shall make the money."

For some time neither spoke.

The boy was hesitating.

"I—I hope it will be all right," he stammered.

The doctor said nothing, only, unseen by his companion, made a gesture of violent anger, weariness, and impatience.

Meanwhile, the boy's face flushed, and he grew deadly pale.

The tempter eyed him narrowly.

At last the boy looked up; for he had been sitting for some minutes with his head buried between his hands.

He clenched his teeth, and struck the table with his closed hand.

"I will," he said, "whatever comes of it."

"That's right, that's right," said the other. "Spoken bravely, and like yourself. Now you will have money to spend, and be able to buy yourself whatever you may fancy. You won't have to pinch yourself now. Some day, and before long, too, when you have as many sovereigns in your pocket as you now have halfpence, you'll be ready to go down on your knees, and thank me for this. See if you don't."

Then, in a whisper:

"Have you got it with you?"

"Yes."

The boy looked round him furtively.

No one was looking, and he rapidly passed an envelope to his companion, and then looked round again, as though he expected the immediate arrival of a policeman.

Faversham, however, did not seem to be at all nervous.

He opened the envelope leisurely.

"Don't—don't let anyone see it!" cried the boy, in an agony of apprehension.

"There is no fear—none whatever," replied the other.

He glanced at the contents of the packet.

It was a cheque upon Messrs. Bottle and Bung's bankers, in Lombard Street, filled up in Thomas Twiddle's handwriting, and the sum named was a hundred pounds.

The signature was a very good imitation of that of the boy's employers, and it had every appearance of being genuine.

The boy looked up anxiously as Faversham perused the document, and asked, in a half-choking voice, as he wiped the perspiration off his forehead:

"Will it do?"

The other folded it up carefully, and placed it in his pocket, without making any reply.

The boy looked at him uneasily.

"Will it do?" he repeated.

But there was something about the doctor's manner which was anything but assuring.

The boy's looks grew more and more anxious, and at last, for the third time, he repeated the words:

"Will it do?"

"Excellently well," replied Faversham, with a curious smile. "It couldn't be better, young gentleman. You're an ornament to the age you live in."

The boy began to feel very uneasy.

There was so remarkable a change in his friend's manner.

"When will you give it me back?" he asked presently.

"What?"

"The cheque."

"Young man," said Faversham, "when you go to bed to-night, go down upon your knees, and thank Heaven that you fell into my hands instead of somebody else's. Are you aware that what you have done to-day is quite sufficient to transport you?"

"Ye—es," stammered Tom Twiddle, in a perfect agony of terror. "But then, you said, you know—that is, you asked me to—"

"My dear boy, if I were to ask you to commit a murder, and you were to commit it, and then afterwards you were caught, and put upon your trial for the same, do you suppose that the jury would think it sufficient excuse when you said that you were told to do it? I don't think so, my dear boy. I expect that you would be hanged by the neck until you were dead. That is what would happen to you, I expect."

"But, sir, you won't—you promised—"

"I shan't give you into custody, if you mean that; that is, not unless I am obliged to do so. I shall see your father; if he agrees to do what I shall ask of him, I shall have no occasion to avail myself of your cheque. However, don't give me any more trouble. I have had quite sufficient upon your account as it is. Your fate is in your father's hands."

But the boy could not understand him all at once. He was dumbfounded.

"Was what you said about the speculation not true?" he asked. "Have you urged me to commit this forgery only to have me in your power, so that you could work upon my father?"

"Yes."

"Then you are—you are a villain!"

"Don't call names."

"You are a villain! I repeat it, and I am not afraid of you. Give me back my cheque, I say. Give it me back at once."

" Shall I ring the bell, and send for a policeman ?"

" What have I done, sir? What have I done?"

" Will you have the kindness to ring the bell, if you won't allow me ?"

" Oh, sir, you would never have the heart to betray me! What have I done to you, that you should serve me so? What made you come to me, and tempt me to do what I have done, if it was only to betray me afterwards? Oh, sir—please, sir—"

And the poor boy clung to the doctor's arm, and tried to prevent him from leaving the room.

But the latter shook him off roughly.

" Leave me alone, you young fool !" he said, in a savage tone. " Keep your hands off. You've given me quite trouble enough as it is."

The boy, with the tears streaming from his eyes, flung his head upon the table before him, and covered it with his two hands, sobbing violently.

He remained in this position perhaps three or four minutes.

When he looked up, his mysterious companion had left the room.

He was alone.

*   *   *   *   *

The father of Tom Twiddle was the valet to the Duke of Heatherland.

The valet to the Duke of Heatherland was a hard, dry little man, between forty and fifty, wearing his hair cropped remarkably short and stubbly, and his beard shaved extremely blue.

To look at Twiddle senior, you would not have suspected him to be the possessor of much more heart than is to be found in a sardine, which is, I believe, a remarkably heartless fish.

But, in spite of his unamiable appearance, and his remarkably dry manners, there was no doubt in the world that Mr. Twiddle senior loved one person in the world with a love at once unselfish and unalterable.

He loved his son.

His son he had educated in the best fashion that he could afford—indeed, in a better fashion than he could afford; for among the duke's many vices might be reckoned those of niggardness and avarice, and the poor valet's wages were not half as large as they ought to have been, considering all the laborious and humiliating duties he had daily to perform in earning them.

Yes, this valet actually loved his son; and Faversham knew it, and upon the knowledge he intended to trade, as we shall see.

Since that awful night when the duke was upon the point of dying his soul with a terrible crime at the infamous house of old Mother Crow, and had only been rescued therefrom by the providential sight, at the very nick of time, of a locket which Lucinda wore round her neck; since that dreadful night when the duke had so suddenly received the intelligence of the duchess's supposed death, his grace's intellect had undergone a most decided and painfully observable change for the worse.

Up to now he had been most vigorously engaged in politics, though he had found time, as we have seen, to practice the fashionable vices for which he was always so celebrated. But now business seemed to have become suddenly distasteful to him.

He shut himself up all day in his own room.

He never moved out under any pretext.

He saw no one—not even the duchess.

The only person with whom he associated at all—if association it could be called—was the valet; though frequently he passed whole hours together in the man's company without saying a word.

Of course the news of the duchess's supposed death, and her miraculous restoration to life, got buzzed about town, though the particulars of her abduction were suppressed at her own desire.

People attributed the illness of the duke to the shock which his wife's supposed death had given him. The valet, who knew a little more, perhaps, than the general public about his master's private affairs, was inclined to attribute it to the scene which had taken place at Mrs. Crow's.

Both opinions might to some extent have been correct, but the real truth of the matter was, that the duke for some time past had been gradually breaking up.

Mentally and physically he was weakening. The horrible life which he had led for so many years—from the time that he was quite a child, in fact—had completely undermined his constitution. He was nothing but the wreck of the man he had once been.

It is true that for some years past he had been little better than a plastered-up old ruin, bewigged, padded, and painted; but then, he had had such excellent spirits, such a wonderful buoyancy and vivacity, that men of half his age envied him.

When his spirits gave way—directly he ceased to struggle against the invasion of his great enemy Father Time, he literally collapsed, shrunk up, broke down, fell in, as it were, like did his poor lank leathern jaws when his brilliant teeth were taken out.

He ceased to take any interest in politics; at the same time, he ceased to take any interest in anything else.

Since Faversham had left the house, he had refused to see any other medical man, although both the valet and the duchess had pressed him again and again to do so.

The duchess, when she had sufficiently recovered to travel, returned to France to fetch her child, fearful lest in her absence some calamity might befal him.

She felt certain now that Faversham had devised the artful scheme for bringing her to England.

His after conduct proved that but too clearly.

It was he who had sent that mysterious message about " Horford."

He was somehow or other acquainted with the strange secret of the duchess's life, in which Horford was so curiously mixed up.

He had profited by his knowledge of it to bring her to England, away from her child; and had she not been so providentially rescued by Charley Wag, there is no knowing how she would have fared, or what terrible fate might not have befallen her poor little boy.

Left alone, with no one else but the servants to speak to, in this great, rumbling, dreary Park Lane mansion, the old premier felt almost lost, and grew more silent and sad every day.

Dozens upon dozens, nay, hundred upon hundreds, of cards were poured in at the street-door upon his grace.

Charles Edward and Samuel Joseph had enough to do in taking them in and reading them, with a highly critical air passing their opinions every now and then upon the size and character of the type.

Shoals of letters, too, arrived by post and messenger.

All lay uncared for by their owner upon the table in his reading-room.

He would not look at them, or hear anything about them.

In vain did Mr. Twiddle plead for a moment or two of his grace's valuable attention for such and such a despatch, which its owner had sworn to be a matter of life and death.

He wouldn't look at it.

Those who had written wrote again and again, and called time after time.

What had become of the duke?

Was he at home?

Yes; but he was engaged.

Would be be engaged for long? Should they call again?

They could call again any time.

A permission which they availed themselves of to any extent, but without any better success.

Some, growing wearied, asked whether the duke had not gone out of town, but were assured to the contrary. Some asked whether he was ill, but the servants said no.

The public generally began to be very much astonished at his grace's behaviour, though they were hardly any more astonished than the servants in his grace's house.

Some said he must be ill; some said he was going childish; some said he was going "cranky."

The general impression upon the menial mind was, that what he wanted was a strait-waistcoat.

The great man who had no time to read his letters, nor to attend to affairs of state, sat doubled up by the hour together in his arm-chair before the fire.

The valet would prop him up with pillows every hour or two, and then he would slip down slowly, until at last he sank into a helpless position, and looked, as he sat there with his thin arms dangling over the arms of the chair, and his thin shanks twisted into a grotesque contortion before him, his chin resting on his breast, and his head garnished with a tasselled nightcap cocked over on one side—he looked, I say, when sitting in this ridiculous position, as though his backbone had been taken out, like they take the backbone out of a sole they are going to make a fillet of, and that they had not tied him up tight.

Hour after hour he would sit in this way, squawking out peevishly from time to time for Twiddle to put more coals upon the fire.

He persisted in saying that it was bitterly cold, although the weather was in reality close and hot; and he persisted in having an immense fire alight, and the room kept in a state of almost suffocating heat.

Unless he called for coals, he very seldom spoke.

Sometimes he had a book before him, as often upside down as any other way; but generally, as the valet said, he sat thinking.

The valet and the servants, though, did not think him to be in half such a bad way as he really was. But this is frequently the case. The generality of persons concern themselves but slightly with the ailments of their fellow-men. They are too careless or selfish—one or the other. There are many, I doubt not, who would not notice the sickness of another, until the other fell dead at their feet, supposing there was no complaint, and no extra trouble caused by his ailments.

The first time that the fact of the duke's rapidly approaching imbecility dawned upon the mind of Mr. Twiddle the elder, was when the following circumstance took place.

One of the numerous applicants for a few minutes of his grace's valuable time, after calling again and again, and writing quires of letters and volumes of petitions, became very furious indeed one day, and insisted upon having an interview.

Mr. Charles Edward said it was impossible.

Mr. Samuel Joseph assured him with a smile that it could not be done.

The petitioner was positive and peremptory.

He would see him. Indeed, I am ashamed to say, he even went so far as to say, that he would be damned if he wouldn't.

The two gentlemen in plush endeavoured to throw themselves in his way, and bar the passage.

Mr. Twiddle, in the background, waved him wildly off, and talked about going for the police.

"Let me go by," the petitioner cried.

"You can't, sir."

"Let me pass."

"You mustn't, sir."

"Really, sir."

"If you please, sir."

"His grace isn't visible, sir."

"Oh, sir! you really shouldn't."

But this most violent of persons, probably quite wearied out of all patience by dancing attendance at his grace's street-door, insisted upon coming in, and thrust Mr. Charles Edward and Mr. Samuel Joseph brutally to the right and to the left; and then, making a furious charge at Twiddle, caught that most fragile of valets by the collar of the coat, and with a vigorous twist, sent him spinning down the passage like a teetotum spins when in the state that is called "groggy."

Acting thus energetically, the petitioner managed to arrive at the sanctum sanctorum of the great man himself.

He thrust open the door.

Then entered, and looked round eagerly.

At first he thought the room was empty.

Had the duke fled at the sound of his approach?

But no, that was not very likely. Where was he, then? Where had he got to?

Ah! that must be him. Over the top of a large arm-chair before the fire bobbed the tassel of a white nightcap. The nightcap no doubt belonged to his grace the Duke of Heatherland.

The petitioner had never in his life seen the duke. He expected to find a tall, handsome, intellectual old gentleman, with a massive brow, and an eagle's eye; at least, that is the the notion he had formed of the nobleman.

He had come up from the country with a great grievance of some kind or another—no matter what—and he was determined to speak his mind about it, and, if necessary, tell the duke himself what his mind really was.

You can imagine his surprise when he caught sight of the nightcap, and the poor shrunken head in it, and the thin shanks, and the bony hands hanging helpless.

He turned towards Twiddle, who had entered after him.

"Is this—is that—" he stammered.

"Yes," replied Twiddle; "that's his grace."

"What, THAT?"

"Yes, sir."

The petitioner opened his eyes as wide as they would open.

That was a pretty good width, too, I can tell you.

"Oh!" said he.

Then he hesitated for a second or two, doubtful what he should do.

Mr. Twiddle took this opportunity of retiring quietly.

At last the petitioner, beginning to feel rather awkward in the oppressive silence of the room, which was broken only by the regular ticking of a timepiece upon a sideboard, and the metallic shivering of the half-dead ashes in the grate, advanced towards the old man, and coughed timidly behind his hand.

But the duke made no reply, being apparently unconscious of his presence.

"Your grace!" ventured the petitioner, in a mild tone, half supplicatory, half demonstrative.

No answer.

"Your grace."

Same result.

"I have ventured to intrude upon your grace," continued the petitioner, in a louder tone, determined that he would have his say, whether the nobleman deigned to look at him or not.

So, with a loud "ahem!" he went on:

"—Upon your grace's valuable time" (his grace was reading the *Lady of the Camelias,* upside down), "to call your attention to the existing state of the drainage and sewerage in the town of Twopennyton, a matter which your grace was kind enough to promise you would bring before the attention of parliament. Ahem, your grace. To expatiate lengthily upon the state of our flues, would be perhaps trespassing too much upon your valuable time, or, I may say, ahem, upon the time of the country. I will, therefore, with your grace's permission, proceed at once to what I may term the fountain head of our vexation—to, in point of fact, the main sewer. If your grace will allow me, I will read you a few rough facts, which I have gathered together with some considerable trouble, and no small amount of patient research, and put into a kind of framework of

my own, which I trust your grace will approve of. To begin—"

The terrible man pulled out a huge mass of papers from his coat-tail pocket, and cocking up one leg upon a chair, made a sort of table of his knee.

Then, carefully spreading them out, began again with—

"Ahem!"

But his grace was not listening.

If any subject was occupying his grace's mind at that moment, which from the extremely vacant expression upon the nobleman's sallow face, one would have been inclined very strongly to doubt, most certainly it was not the drainage and sewerage of the town of Twopennyton.

"Ahem!" said the petitioner, doing his best to catch my lord's eye.

But my lord did not look at him.

"The effluvia arising from the decomposed potato-peelings, deposited there by the domestic servants of Twopennyton—"

His grace spoke.

The petitioner pricked his ears, and listened.

"Chow—wow—wow!"

"I beg your grace's pardon."

"Chow—wow—wow!" (louder).

"I ask a thousand pardons," said the petitioner, straining every nerve to hear what the other said, and feeling convinced that he was doing his cause a great deal of harm by putting the nobleman to such unnecessary trouble; but for the life of him, he could not comprehend the duke's unintelligible mumblings.

"Chow—wow—wow!"

That was all he could make out of it.

But stooping down, and listening in a way that one might listen for a person's last words upon their death-bed, straining every nerve to hear, he made out at last the nobleman's meaning.

And what do you suppose it was?

Do you think that he was suggesting some extraordinarily clever mode of disposing of the surplus filth of the little town which this energetic petitioner had come to London to represent?

Not a bit of it.

Do you suppose that he was telling him, that he had not at that moment any time to go into the matter; but that he would very shortly, he hoped, have sufficient leisure to give it his full and undivided attention.

Not at all. What he was saying was this:

"Put some coals on, will you?"

The petitioner was flabbergasted. He looked up amazed, and looked round, and looked back at the duke, and then his eyes rested upon the coal-scuttle.

But his grace was growing furious.

"Damn you! put on some coals. Don't you hear what I say, you infernal blockhead?"

The petitioner grew purple. What should he do?—what could he say? He was quite alone with the old man. Nobody had heard the insult; should he pocket it quietly? If he did not do so, would he not be doing an injury to the great cause of sewerage and drainage?

Yes, he would do so. No one would know that he had so lowered himself—if it was lowering himself. When he came to think of it, he

MURDER.

felt convinced that it was a species of degradation, for the duke had addressed him just as though he were a dog.

But then he must conciliate the old man.

Yes, by heaven, he would do it!

"With pleasure," said he, and threw on the coals.

Then he opened his papers again, and began with another "ahem!"

But the duke roared out once more, this time louder than before, and more intelligible.

"Take yourself off," was what he said.

"Your grace—"

"Go about your business."

"Really, your grace—this language."

"Don't stand jabbering there; but go and get me my other slippers."

No. 41.

The petitioner picked up his papers one by one, staring at the nobleman as though he were a ghost. Then he took up his hat, but still stood hesitating whether to go or remain.

"He's out of his mind," said the countryman to himself. "There's no doubt about it."

But the duke, losing all patience, waved him away with his hand; and then, just as the other left the room, hurled one of his slippers after him, and hit him with it a tingling crack upon the side of the head, which made his great ear flush up red like a pickled cabbage.

But he did not remain any longer to see what might occur next. That his grace had gone out of his mind there could not be a doubt. By the next morning, everybody in Twopennyton knew the news, and was talking it over.

[CHARLEY WAG, THE NEW JACK SHEPPARD.

It got buzzed about at the clubs, and crept into the London newspapers before long, and everybody agreed in saying that it was just exactly what they had expected would be the end of him.

* * * * *

But there was one person who saw a way of profiting by the old gentleman's indisposition, or even by his death, did he happen to die now, while the duchess was away, and he was left altogether at his mercy. This was the valet, Twiddle.

He sat, one night, alone, in the room where the duchess had sat that night when Faversham came through the sliding panel and administered to her the noxious drug which plunged her into the mysterious trance, and out of which she had but just awakened.

He sat there alone, and plunged in thought.

His head was bent down, and his sharp pointed chin rested in the palm of his lean hand.

He bit the nails of his other hand from time to time, and doing so, looked up and round the room in an abstracted fashion.

The light at these moments coming from a reading lamp at his elbow, fell full upon his ugly face, and the shadow, thus thrown upon certain portions of it, increased the goblin-like aspect of his countenance. and gave it somewhat the appearance of a death's head.

"So," he muttered to himself, "it seems as though it were going to last. He gets no better. He even gets worse. It seems as though this imbecility had set in for good—if he does not die—"

At the word, he glanced round him timidly, as though he were fearful lest some unseen eavesdropper should have overheard it.

"If he dies," the valet continued, this time thinking to himself, instead of giving a murmured utterance to the dark thoughts passing through his brain.—" if he dies, how shall I be left, what will be my position?"

He rose from his seat, and paced the room slowly from end to end.

"If he dies—will he die—shall he die?"

He paused abruptly, and sinking into a chair close to where he had been standing, buried his face in his hands, and meditated profoundly.

So engrossed was he, too, with his thoughts, as to be unconscious of a slight movement in the room behind him.

First, the faintest possible creaking, as though of a hinge.

Then a slow whispering noise, as a secret panel slid open, and a man's cloak brushed slightly against the side of the passage.

In another moment, Faversham had stepped across the threshold into the room, and closed the door behind him.

At the next, he had placed his hand upon the valet's shoulder.

The latter sprang to his feet with a stifled cry of terror.

"Who are you? What is it? What do you want?"

"You know me," replied the doctor, grasping his arm tightly, and hissing the words into his ear. "I want to speak to you."

The valet stared at him, ghastly white, and trembling in his legs, so that he could hardly stand.

Then suppressing a choking sensation in his throat, as it seemed, by pressing his hand upon his throat, he said again:

"What are you doing here? How dare you come?"

"How dare I?" asked the other fiercely and indignantly. "How dare you question my right to go and come when I choose?"

"I only know that the police are after you, and that if you're taken—"

"But I shall not be taken."

"How do you know?"

"Because nobody but you knows that I am here."

"And if I—?"

"You won't."

"I won't?"

"No."

"Why?"

"Because you dare not.".

"I dare not—what do you mean?"

"Listen," said Faversham, quietly.

At the same time he took a chair himself, and crossed his legs.

"Take a seat."

The valet complied sullenly.

"Well?" said he interrogatively, after Faversham had eyed him several moments in silence.

"You are surprised at my words, I suppose?" remarked the doctor, in the same cool tone as before. "Rather astonished, eh? You thought that because I kept out of the way of the people here after it was discovered, that I was the principal agent in the abduction of the duchess; that I did so because I was afraid. That is your idea, I believe. Am I right?"

"Yes."

"Ha, ha! I thought so. Now did it ever strike you, Mr. Twiddle, that I had a good deal of influence in this family; and that I could twist—so to speak—the noble heads of this house round my little finger, whenever it suited me so to do? Did that ever strike you?"

"I thought you had influence."

"Therefore, it must have occurred to you that it was rather strange that I should play at hide-and-seek in this way. Did it not?"

"It did. But having spoilt yourself with his grace, I still do not think it very extraordinary that you should keep out of his way."

"You think, anyhow, that I must have played my cards very badly to get into such a scrape?"

"I do."

"Perhaps I have. There, I don't mind owning it, I have; but the best among us may make a slip sometimes. It is in human nature so to do. Even you might, Mr. Twiddle."

The valet eyed him, if possible, harder than before.

But his look was a very uneasy one.

"Now, Twiddle," continued the doctor, in quite a playful tone, at the same time tapping the valet upon the knee with one of his long bony fingers, "I want your help. Let's put our heads together."

"Eh?"

"We're rowing in the same boat, you know; and we're both of us waiting for the same ship to sink, so that we may board it."

"What ship?"

"You dull dog, Twiddle. You can't see a joke. I mean the duke."

"The duke! I don't understand you."

"Pooh! don't play the hypocrite with me. It's too old a game, and too stale a one. I had my opportunities of observing you, Mr. Twiddle, when I was so frequently in the house. You've suffered a good deal at the hands of that idiotic old wretch, who lies now almost at his last croak. It is quite time you were thinking of retiring, and living comfortably. Besides, you want to take a snug little business somewhere; and have your excellent son for managing man. Isn't that so? He's a very nice lad indeed, is Thomas. I have the pleasure of his acquaintance."

The valet looked up quickly. He had been looking down just now, and rubbing one hand over the other, listening intently all the while to what Faversham was saying but anxious not to let the doctor judge by the expression of his face, what were his thoughts, as he felt must otherwise have inevitably occurred, unless he could have kept a perfectly supernatural guard over himself, and prevented the slightest twitch of his muscles, which the other seemed to watch so eagerly.

Now he looked up in spite of himself, with an alarmed and anxious expression.

It was enough for Faversham.

He was right, then, in supposing that this valet, who was in every other way so worldly, selfish, mean, and covetous, loved his son with a pure devotion, which is to be found but in a parent's love.

"I have you, then," muttered the doctor to himself.

"You know my son?" stammered Twiddle.

"Oh, yes, intimately."

"Indeed! I was not aware of it."

"We have known each other for some time."

"He did not tell me."

"Perhaps not. Young men, for that matter, form many connections, of which they do not acquaint their relations. It's quite natural."

"I do not think it is the case with my Thomas."

"Ha, ha! don't you? Now that's not bad. I shouldn't have thought it of you, Twiddle. I should have fancied that you had formed rather a deprecatory opinion of human nature by this time, after your little experience of it; but it's always the way, the oldest birds are caught by chaff sometimes, whatever the proverb may say to the contrary. It's just exactly because they are such knowing old tykes, they never expect for a moment that it is at all likely anyone would try to take them in."

"What's all this got to do with my son?"

"Well, it has, as I will show you. The world is made up of coincidences. Did that ever strike you?"

"Really I—if you have anything to say—"

"Now," continued Faversham, in the same provoking style, seeing well how he was working upon the nerves of the listener, "one curious coincidence is, that the Duke of Heatherland banks at the same bank as Messrs. Bottle and Bung, Drysalters, &c., of Garlichill."

The valet looked at the other intently, and his breast heaved as though he were panting for breath; but he said nothing.

"Odd, isn't it? and odder still that I should know the cashier."

He paused here a moment.

"Well?" said the valet, hoarsely.

"Now," continued Faversham, changing his seat for a still more comfortable one, and taking a toothpick from his waistcoat-pocket, which he amused himself with by lazily picking his teeth. "Now, the cashier came to me to-day, and said, 'A rather ugly case at our place.' 'What is it?' I asked. 'Concerning your young friend Twiddle,' said he. He knew we were acquainted. 'What now,' I asked. 'A case of forgery,' he said. 'Forgery!' I cried. For you know I was rather astonished, as it was natural I should be. 'Forgery,' he answered. 'A forged cheque for a hundred pounds.'"

"It's a lie!" cried the valet, springing to his feet.

"What is?" asked Faversham, coolly.

"What you say. My son would never be guilty of such a thing."

"Take a chair, Twiddle. You're hasty. However, it is natural. Indeed, your warmth does you credit. Only your observation is uncourteous. In the first place, you surely don't suppose it likely that I should waste my time in coming here and telling you a pack of lies. It's not likely, you know. It's quite certain that it's not amusing. If I were in search of society, I would find it elsewhere, my estimable friend, depend upon it."

"Speak, then," cried the valet, who could bear the suspense no longer, springing excitedly to his feet. "Speak, man! if you are made of flesh and blood. What do you know about it? What has my son done? Where is he? Is he in prison?"

"Not yet. I thought I would keep him out till I had seen you."

As he spoke, he drew a pocket-book from his breast-pocket.

"The little effort at penmanship to which I allude, is this. You see a very tolerable imitation of the gentlemen's signatures. Are you acquainted with them? The rest is Master Thomas's handwriting."

"I see it is, or it looks very like it."

"Quite like enough to do for him, sir, I have no doubt; besides, the forgery has been proved in other ways. I'll trouble you for that back again, by the way, Mr. Twiddle. Don't put yourself out of the way so far as to destroy it. You will only make the affair worse. He can be convicted without the aid of that slip of paper."

The other sank back in his chair, and wiped his head with his hand.

"What do you want of me?" he asked. "If my son has acted so foolishly as to get into your power, what can I do? What is it to me?"

"It is a good deal to you, I should think, as his father; and what you can do is to save him, if you like."

"How?"

"By helping me."

"In what way?"

"I will show you."

As thus he spoke, Faversham entirely changed his tone.

He became in a moment stern and determined.

"I want to get some money out of the old man before he dies, as you have already. You have made him fill up many a cheque lately which he would not have done if he had been in his right senses. Don't interrupt me. I know that to be the case from my friend the cashier. Even supposing that the cheques are not like this I hold here, of which my friend the cashier has his doubts."

"Let him prove it."

"He does not want to. Now what I want of you is very little in return for the favour I do you. I want the duke to come, or to be brought, to a house, which I will give you the address of, to-morrow night."

"For what purpose?"

"I wish him to sign a document for me."

"But what can I do?"

"He is obstinate, I suppose. He always was. But you, if anybody does, know the way to manage him. You know some way or other—some inducement, or some threat, that will bring him there."

"I know of none," the valet replied.

Then, after a pause of a few moments:

"I think that perhaps something which occurred at Mrs. Crow's house may help you."

And so saying, he repeated all that he knew of what had happened on the night when the duke went to see Lucinda.

"That will do, that will do," said Faversham, as his face brightened. "You shall tell him that she wants to see him there at ten to-morrow night. If he does not get there by eleven, at twelve I shall be here to fetch him. You must help me then. Have the house free of servants, and keep all quiet. Your son's fate depends upon it."

"But why not make him sign the paper here?" asked the valet.

"Because I may have to use force. No matter why. In fact, that is my wish. Now leave me. I hear the bell ringing; some one may come."

"How will you get out?"

"The way I came. I am quite safe."

"And my poor boy—you will keep him out of harm?"

"Nothing shall happen to him if you do my bidding. If the duke comes to-night, to-morrow he shall receive back his forged cheque. There will then be an end of the matter."

"Can I—can I depend upon you?"

"You must; there is no help for you. Now go."

The valet left him, and then the mysterious being, with a smile of bitter malignity upon his ghastly face, slid noiselessly through the secret panel.

XLIV.—THE PREPARATION FOR THE CRIME.

TAKING the broad road from Aldgate Church to old Whitechapel Church, you may pass on either side about thirty narrow crooked avenues, leading to thousands of closely-packed nests, full to overflowing with dirt misery, and rags.

Many living signs of the hideous inner life behind the busy shops are always to be found oozing out on to the pavements, and into the gutters.

These are the wretched children from the back slums.

Their fathers and mothers mope in cellars or garrets.

Their grandfathers and grandmothers huddle and die in the same miserable dustbins; but the children dart about the roads with muddy naked feet, slink into corners to play with oyster-shells and pieces of broken china, or are found tossing halfpennies under the arches of a railway, or the dry arches of a bridge, or on some heap of rubbish among some unfinished buildings.

The stories of destitution, desertion, and cruelty, which these outcasts have to tell, if they would tell them, would be more harrowing than a hundred tragedies.

Most of them know no parents. One, perhaps, more lucky than the rest, may own to a mother in a drunken prostitute, who has disfigured his face with her violence, or dropped him in her drunkenness, and marked him for life, or caused him to hobble through the world a wretched cripple.

Poor little victims! what can they grow up for but the gallows, with no one in the world to love them or care for them?

Perhaps one of the worst of the horrible places is New Court, a nest of thieves, filled with thick-lipped, broad-featured, rough-haired, ragged women, and hulking, leering men.

The houses present every conceivable aspect of filth and wretchedness.

The broken windows are plastered with paper, which rises and falls when the doors of the rooms are opened.

The staircases always look upon the court, as there is seldom any street-door; and they are steep, winding, and covered with blocks of hard mud.

The faces that peer out of the narrow windows are yellow and repulsive.

Some are the faces of Jews, some of Irishwomen, and some of sickly-looking infants.

The ashes and filth lie in front of the houses, the drainage is thrown out of the windows to swell the heap, and the public water-closet is like a sentry-box, stuck against the pump in a corner of the court.

In most of the houses there are as many families as there are rooms, cellars, and cupboards in a single house; often as many as forty people huddled together in a small dwelling large enough for a dozen at most.

The lowest order of Irish, though, when they can get an opportunity, will take a room, and sublet it to as many families as the floor will hold. In a place called George Yard there are about a hundred families.

The inhabitants of these wretched dens are chiefly dock labourers and their families; but there are also a number of thieves, costermongers, professional beggars, rag dealers, and the smallest of tradesmen.

The rents charged for the holes called rooms in these dreary abodes of crime and misery vary from four shillings to ninepence a-week, which very often includes the hire of furniture, consisting of a round table, a couple of wooden chairs, a fender and poker (not much wanted), a turn-up bedstead, with a matting bag of straw for a bed, and a very dirty coverlet.

But this is for the first-rate rooms. For ninepence you have nothing; and even then, from those who hire these wretched sticks the money has to be collected punctually and incessantly, by small instalments, or it would never be paid at all.

The smallest of tradesmen, whom I alluded to, make desperate struggles to live in this poor quarter; though, as a rule, they do little else than starve.

Such mournful efforts do they make at trade. At some of the low dirty doors wet baskets are standing, full of a weak and watery kind of fish that they call "dabs." In some of the wretched parlour windows, under sickly yellow curtains, a few rotten oranges are displayed on a shutter for sale, along with a few very cheap toys, and a bottle or two of the softest, stickiest, and most unsatisfactory of "bulls-eyes." Children must have toys, you know; and as some cannot afford halfpenny dolls, and suchlike luxuries, they are obliged to put up with old saucepan-lids, and bits of broken crockery, picked up from the gutter.

Another tradesman takes some miserable front parlour, which seems to have been scooped out, and throws a quarter of a hundred of coal down in a corner, to show that he is a coal merchant. Another takes a front parlour, and opens in the cats' meat line. But the only regular shop is one of those small chandler's, which goes upon the weekly payment system, and where there are, I should imagine, a good many bad debts in the course of the year.

And this is a real picture of a real neighbourhood to be found to-day in London.

My story takes me to a public-house in this locality, which I will introduce to you, with your kind permission.

It is a curious public-house, where, during the day, no particular business in the liquor traffic seems to be doing.

Now and then there is a very drunken person, indeed, lolling on a bench outside the door, at whom the little boys of the neighbourhood jeer and jibe, as it is the custom of little boys to do.

But at night no doubt there is a good deal of hard drinking; and the landlord has other sources of revenue besides the regular ones, for the proprietor is a notorious dog-trainer, and has lived there for many years, and keeps a dog-pit for the gratification of his patrons.

His yard is often crammed with every kind of terrier and fighting dog; and an upper room, where the pit is built, is reached by a ladder passing through a trap-door.

When you enter this room, the ladder can be drawn up, and the trap-door let down, and so far you are secure from interruption.

The windows are boarded up behind the blinds, so that no noise within can reach the little street; and when a sufficient number of patrons are gathered together to pay the spirited proprietor of this den of infamy, dogs are set together by the throat, cats are worried and killed by bull-terriers within a certain time, to show the training of the dog, and rats are hunted screaming round the pit for the same purpose.

Here is it on record that the most awful atrocities have from time to time been committed by the inhuman monsters who frequent the house, and with the greatest impunity; for the celebrated Bill Rabbits, the proprietor, is not much troubled by the police.

On the night fixed by Faversham for the duke's visit to this awful neighbourhood, Faversham and Rattan were waiting at the public-house I have described.

A letter had been sent to the duke in a woman's handwriting, which ran as follows:

"Your daughter would like to see you for a few moments, as she has something of importance to communicate. She has been hoping to hear from you since that night when you met her at Mother Crow's. She now lies ill in a lodging in Whitechapel. A person will meet you at the *Crooked Billet*, in Shore Street, near New Court, who will conduct you to the lodging. Come, for God's sake, if you have any affection for your wretched child."

This incoherent and somewhat eccentric epistle was thought to have a genuine appearance, and be likely to effect its object, namely, to bring the duke to the place of rendezvous.

As the clocks in the vicinity tolled the hour of ten, Faversham rose from a seat which he had occupied close to a miserable little fireplace in the room at the back of the bar, and went, with an explanation of weariness and impatience, to look out of the street-door into the murky night.

A small drizzling rain was falling, and no one was about the street except a few slouching miserable beggars, who went by at intervals, casting an anxious longing look towards the warm lighted bar of the public-house, which was partially exposed through the half-opened door.

"He does not come," Faversham said, impatiently; "he does not come. How long am I to wait? Will he come at all? Oh, this suspense at the last moment is intolerable!"

He closed the door, and resumed his seat at the fire.

"There's plenty of time as yet," said Rattan, looking up from his pipe. "Don't be impatient, governor."

"Yes," replied Faversham, wearily, "there's plenty of time; but it's hard to wait at the last."

"What do you mean to do to the old bloke?" asked Rattan, between the puffs of his pipe.

"Kill him," replied the other, in a fierce whisper; "kill him to-night."

"Yes, so you said," observed the ruffian, coolly; "only I wanted to know how."

"You will know soon enough," the other replied, with a fiendish chuckle, "when he comes."

However, their intended victim seemed to be rather backward in answering the summons.

The rain began to fall heavily without, and the streets grew more and more deserted.

The finger hand on the dirty-faced little

cuckoo clock behind the bar was slowly progressing upwards towards the hour of twelve.

If he did not arrive directly they would be obliged to go and fetch him, according to the agreement.

What could detain him? Did he not care for his daughter? Did he suspect some trick? Or had he grown so imbecile that he could not understand the meaning of the note which had been written to him?

They were almost inclined to think that the last supposition was correct; and Faversham, who stood at the door wrapped up in his cloak, called impatiently to his companion, as the clock struck the three-quarters, that it was time for them to go.

But just at that moment the sound of wheels was audible in the street leading to the court.

Faversham peered through the darkness, shading his eyes with his hand.

"See! see! he is coming," he said. "The valet has brought him. Go forward to meet them, and bring him on to the house alone. Do not let the valet come with you; and see that you are not watched. I will go forward and wait for you."

"Do you suppose the old man has got any swag with him?" asked Rattan.

"No; I should think not. Only a trifle, most likely."

"You might as well have got him to bring some. It would have been just as well, you know. A word or two in the letter you sent him would have done all the business."

"No, no. You shall be well paid for the job, I tell you. But I don't want his money, I want his blood. I tell you, man, that old wretch's death has been my happy dream for years; and to-night he will be in my power."

"I should have thought you might have gratified your fancy long ago, if you'd wanted. You might have poisoned him over and over again, if you'd liked, when you had the handling of his physic bottles."

"Poisoned!" cried Faversham, with an expression of bitter contempt. "Do you think poison would satisfy me?"

But two figures were seen at this moment to approach slowly from the end of the street, the one assisting the other, as he hobbled along unsteadily.

Rattan walked forward to meet them, and Faversham plunged down a court at the back of the public-house where they had been waiting, and made his way through a tortuous mass of lanes and alleys to an old, neglected, half-ruined building, with broken and patched windows, blocked up with crazy half rotten shutters, and an old door with a portico, which looked dark and forbidding, like the entrance to a cellar.

Stepping within this doorway, after taking a hasty glance round to see whether he was observed, Faversham drew a key from his pocket, and with a great wrench forced it round in the rusty lock.

The door swung back with a great creak, and as Faversham stepped across the threshold, half a dozen rats scuttled away down the other end of the passage, apparently in great alarm.

Feeling, however, very little surprised or afraid upon their account, the doctor walked boldly forward; and pushing to the door behind him, but without closing it entirely, he took a dark-lantern from his pocket, and struck a light.

But the walls of the passage were damp, and this was a slow process, not unattended with failure.

Once or twice he struck the matches so violent, that he knocked off the phosphorus from the end of the little sticks; and when he had used three or four he had not yet obtained a light.

Thus was it that he was still in the dark when he heard footsteps approaching, and the sound of voices talking softly without.

Unwilling to meet the duke in the passage, Faversham thrust the lantern back unlighted into his pocket, and replacing the matches on a ledge in the wall from which he had taken them by the side of a coarse tin candlestick, he groped his way as silently as possible downstairs.

But the steps were so old, and the way so difficult to find in the dark, that he could not do so without making some considerable clatter.

When he arrived at the bottom, he paused and waited.

"It was not Rattan, then," he murmured to himself. "It was only somebody outside, I suppose, who has gone up the court."

Then he drew some more matches from his pocket, and struck a light upon the inside of the lantern.

When he had done this, he heard the sound of footsteps coming towards the house, and presently, the sound of feet in the passage.

But if his ears had been a little sharper, or the stairs had not creaked so loudly a few moments before, he would have heard that the steps which approached the house did not pass it and go down the court, as he supposed, but entered at the door, and cautiously stole upstairs.

A few moments before that, while Faversham was whispering upon the door-step of the *Crooked Billet* to his ruffianly accomplice, two miserably attired men crouching in a doorway opposite were watching them.

They were the same two men who had followed the doctor and watched him in the same manner that other night, at the public-house used by the association of juvenile thieves known as "Cock's Lot."

They were watching him still.

Who were they?

The reader has guessed, of course.

One was Murdoch.

The other, the mysterious being known as Horford.

They had been crouching there together, evidently making the most of such poor shelter as the doorway where they sat afforded. And one was dozing off to sleep, when the other aroused him by a rough shake of the shoulder.

"Here's some one we know," he said. "Get up—look!"

"Who is it?"

"Faversham."

"Where?"

"Looking out at the door."

"What mischief is he about now?"

"I don't know; but we must not let him,

slip again this time. He is so often in this neighbourhood, there must be some place he goes to close by."

"Let us follow him."

"Stop. Look, he is pointing up the street to those two men coming this way. One is an old man, leaning on the other's arm."

"Good heavens! it is the duke."

"The Duke of Heatherland?"

"The same. There is something in this more than one might suspect."

"Yes. See, Faversham is going away, and, seeming to creep out of sight, the other man goes forward to meet the duke. Come, let us follow the doctor. Quick—see where he goes."

Thus, then, they followed Faversham, rapidly but cautiously, hiding in the shadow of a wall while he unlocked the door of the lonely house, and then, seeing that he left the door open, advanced and peeped in, and finally entered the passage on tiptoe, and creeping forward, ascended a few stairs, and waited there to listen to the movements of the man they watched.

A very little while afterwards, the old duke arrived, under the guidance of Jack Rattan, who carefully closed the outer door upon them, and put up the chain.

Not a sound was to be heard in the house, and the two spies' hearts beat quickly as they listened.

* * * * *

"It's very dark here," the duke's weak voice was heard to say presently.

"Yes, your lordship," replied Rattan, trying to render his coarse tones as agreeable as possible, a task which was not without its difficulties; "it's rather dark; but I'll light up directly, when I can get hold of the blessed matches."

And he began to grope about, and then fumble with the candlestick.

Having got hold of the matches at last, and struck a light, with a good deal of scratching, and a choice variety of oaths, he held it up to light the duke on his way.

"It's a queer place you've brought me to," the latter said, as he glanced round him. "Does she live here? What a horrible place!"

"It's a good place enough," the other growled. "A better place by far than some of the poor devils about this part can find to sleep in. It ain't everybody that is a duke, and has a house to himself in Park Lane."

"Take me to her room, if you please. It's very curious that my servant did not come with me. I can't understand what could have made him go back. I told him to come."

"Will you go first?" said Rattan, a little impatient at the delay which the old man made, and the slowness of his movements.

"Which way?"

"Down-stairs."

The nobleman advanced as he was desired. The half childish manner which he had had for the last few days, seemed still to be upon him. Only this could have accounted for his so quietly following such a dangerous ruffian as Rattan into such an awful-looking den as the one he was now entering.

They descended a flight of ricketty steps together into what had once been a large kitchen, and through this they passed, Rattan closing and bolting the doors after them.

The duke looked somewhat uneasily at these precautions, which to the most unsuspicious person must have had something of the appearance of being done with the intention of cutting off any retreat in that direction; but he made no remark upon the circumstance.

Having passed through the kitchen, they came to a long low room, which had the look of a scullery or brewhouse.

At the end of this they came to another door, very thick and massive. Opening this, Rattan ushered his companion into a sort of low arched vault, from which there opened another door upon the opposite side; and through this could be seen a square black opening in the floor, which might have been a pit or a well, and over which dangled a rope, that a faint wind from somewhere or other waved to and fro gently.

Upon the other side of the pit or well there was a black door standing ajar, and perhaps the air which moved the rope came from here.

The vault they had entered had in the middle of the floor a round black hole, by the side of which lay a great stone, which might perhaps have been used to cover it.

By the side of the wall stood a rough wooden bench, on which lay a hatchet.

By the side of the bench, wrapped in a large dark cloak, stood perfectly motionless the figure of a man.

———

XLV.—THE SATURNALIA OF BLOOD.

I HAVE entered thus minutely into a description of the neighbourhood in which the house stood, the way to the vault, and the appearance of the interior of the vault itself, to give the reader as clear a notion as possible of the awful loneliness of the spot chosen for the commission of the crime, and the hopelessness of rescue.

Supposing that it were possible for the victim to make his shrieks for assistance audible without, was it likely that assistance would be lent by the residents of such a degraded locality?

Acts of violence and shrieks for help were not likely to meet with much attention here, for they were unhappily of too frequent occurrence. Women and children were savagely kicked and belaboured by brutal husbands and fathers at all hours of the day and night, and nobody particularly heeded their cries and lamentations.

If a wild shriek of agony rent the night air, there would be but little notice taken of it.

Some one was being robbed or murdered, perhaps. Well, what of that? It wasn't you or I, so what does it matter? Hand the drink this way, and oblige me with another pipe-light.

Perhaps now for the first time some notion of the danger of his position flashed through the duke's mind: for the old man looked round anxiously, and with a terrified glare in his usually dull and half-closed eyes, and he made a step back towards the door.

"What am I brought here for? Where is my daughter? What do you want with me?"

"I want you," said the man with the cloak; and as he spoke, he made a step forward, so that the light which Rattan carried fell full upon his face.

Then the duke, with an exclamation of surprise and terror, recognized Ralph Faversham.

"I want you," said the doctor, in a slow, measured tone, hollow and sonorous.

"I sent for you; I will tell you why."

The sudden terror which the sight of the doctor had given him, seemed to have aroused the duke suddenly from the weak and maudlin state into which he had fallen; and although he was still wanting in the energy and shrewdness for which when in good health he had been so celebrated, he still was sufficiently in possession of his reasoning powers to see at once the pit into which he had fallen.

He was in the hands of two unscrupulous and merciless ruffians, capable, for all he knew, of any atrocity.

What did they want with him?

He staggered back, and supported himself by the wall.

Then in a low voice said:

"Have you brought me here to murder me?"

Faversham fixed his lustrous snake-like eyes upon the old man's face, and a perfect demoniacal gleam of mingled hate and triumph lighted up his usually death-like countenance.

"I have," he hissed through his tightly clenched teeth. "I have brought you here to murder you, and I shall do so as certainly as there is a God above us."

The old man looked at him in wild terror, and his teeth chattered as though with intense cold.

"I have sent for you, Duke of Heatherland, with the intention of putting an end to your miserable and vicious life. I might have done so years ago, but the time had not then arrived. Even now I would have deferred it yet a little longer, until I have murdered your wife and child. I intended to have left you until the last of all your cursed race; then in the vault containing their crumbling and decomposed remains, I would have shut you up, and I would have bricked you in, and left you there to rot with the rest. That was my plan; but circumstances have occurred to make me change it to some extent. To change it, but not to forego my vengeance. No, old man; your blood I have sworn to have, and I will. When you are removed, your wife and your child will follow, and then your race will be extinct. Then, as you know, your property will descend to another branch of the family—to a Quaker in Cornwall of the name of Hezekiah Slink."

"Hezekiah Slink!" repeated the old man.

And as he spoke, an even more terrified expression than before passed across his pale face.

"Hezekiah Slink! He is dead long ago."

"Not so," replied Faversham, in a tone which was something between a howl and a shriek. "Not so," he cried furiously, whilst his whole frame trembled with the violence of his long pent-up passions, now all concentrated in the hate with which he addressed his victim. "He lives, old man. He lives to drink your blood. He is here. I am here!"

"God of heaven!" cried the duke.

And struck down, as it were, by the suddenness and horror of the communication, he fell down upon his knees before the other, and hid his frightened face in his hands.

"Yes," continued the doctor, almost screaming out his words, so great was his passion, "I have lived from years of misery and sorrow, of which you have been the cause—I have lived, buoyed up alone by the hope of some day repaying you for the wrong that you had done me. The day is come, and I triumph."

"Spare me—spare me!" cried the old man, wringing his hands. "Spare me for the crime I committed, and the injury I did you. But I have repented for it ever since. I have never ceased to repent. Oh! let me live, and I will do all in my power to atone for my youthful errors."

"Youthful errors! Do you call rape and murder errors? You miserable old wretch, the world calls them crimes—crimes for which the law would stretch your wretched old neck for you, although it is the neck of a duke. You remember well enough that I did my best to do so at the time, but that owing to your high position and influence you escaped. You escaped that time, and then I vowed before God, upon my knees, upon the spot where lay the ashes of my outraged, butchered wife, to have your dog's life."

The old man, into whose very soul each word seemed to enter like the thrust of a knife, crouched upon the bare damp floor at the speaker's feet, and seemed as though he would have bored his way, if possible, into the earth.

"Mercy!—mercy!" he sobbed.

"Mercy!" retorted the other, with a savage laugh. "Had you any mercy on me when you lashed me helpless to a tree to be a witness to the riotous outrages you committed in my dwelling-house? Had you any mercy on the poor screaming victim of your brutal lusts? No, none! nor will I have mercy on you. You will die, Duke of Heatherland. You shall die the death of a dog, as you deserve. I cannot murder you in the way that I had planned at first, but I have contrived another scheme of vengeance, and that I will execute to the letter. I have brought you here to die, where there can be no interruption—no help for you—no escape!"

"Oh! mercy! mercy! What would you do with me?"

"I have told you that I would murder you, and I have prepared for you a horrible death, worthy of your crimes."

"Oh, spare me!—spare me, if you are human. Oh, spare me, for the sake of my age. I am an old man, a poor old man, whose time is rapidly drawing nigh. I have at most but a very few years'—perhaps only a few months'—life left in me. Oh! spare me my life! Take anything else that you choose. You shall have all my wealth, down to the last penny. Leave me nothing to live upon—let me work for my bread—die in a workhouse—break stones upon the highway. Only let me live—oh! let me live!"

With a piteously supplicating expression, the old man crawled upon his knees to the other's feet, and tried to cling to his knees.

But the doctor shook him rudely off.

RETALIATION.

"Oh! if you had only told me years ago who you were," continued the duke, "I would have loaded you with wealth. I would have prayed for your forgiveness upon my knees, like I do now. But I did not know you, you had so changed, to what you were when I saw you last; and you had altered your name—your voice even. I never suspected for a moment that you were the Hezekiah Slink whom I used to know when a boy."

"Whom you went to school with—whom you made your fag, and obliged to slave for you, and lick your boots. Whom you afterwards tried to supplant in the affections of his betrothed bride. Whose wife you subsequently outraged, under circumstances of devilish atrocity, for which no punishment which human

ingenuity can imagine would be sufficient repayment."

"But, indeed—indeed, I am not so bad as you make out. I was drunk when I came to your house. I was urged on by my companions, who were worse than I was; and I never intended to have caused your wife's death. You cannot believe it possible that I could be such a villain. The house was accidentally set on fire in the riot, and we returned to the spot too late to rescue the unfortunate lady and servants, and be of any assistance."

"You lie!" roared the doctor. "The house was set on fire in cold blood. The whole brutal outrage was planned and concocted by you and your villanous comrades."

"I swear to Heaven it was not."

[CHARLEY WAG, THE NEW JACK SHEPPARD

No. 42.

"I know better, I tell you. I have heard as much from your accomplices. I have seen them all. I have seen all the choice companions of your youthful debaucheries. Stone, the governor of Spike Island; Jack Horford, the prison breaker; Rackstraw, the common hangman. I have seen all these choice spirits, and they have confessed the whole plot to me. They all point to you as the ringleader, and as the ringleader you shall suffer."

"But they were all as bad as I was. They were as much the ringleader as I was."

"Silence!" cried the other, sternly; "and prepare yourself for your fate."

The duke seemed to see that there was no hope for him, and he forbore from pleading; but half lying, half kneeling upon the ground, he rocked himself to and fro, uttering low, plaintive moans.

That his time had come, seemed certain.

But what was to be his fate?

What fearful death, devised by the Satanic malignity of the man into whose power he had fallen, awaited him?

The suspense was too horrible.

He looked up, and humbly besought the other to tell him his death.

"Come this way," cried he whom I have hitherto called Ralph Faversham, but whose real name appeared to be Hezekiah Slink. "Come, and I will show you the death that I have in store for you. You thought me dead and buried long ago, and that you had escaped. Ha, ha! I knew it; and many a time have I gloated over the anticipations of a sweet vengeance in store for me. I would have let you live a little longer; but the minions of the law, whom you have set upon my track, seem bent upon hounding me to death; and for fear that I should fall into their power, and that you in your rapidly approaching childishness and decay would sink into your grave before I could wreak my hate upon you, I determined to kill you at once, while I could make sure of you. The remainder of my vengeance I shall reserve for your wife and child, until you are gone."

"But why—why should you stain your hands with blood? Why not revenge yourself in some other way than by my murder?"

"Stain my hands in blood, do you say? Do you think that I care for the stain of blood, or that it will be the first time? Why, man, my hands are stained with the blood of all your accursed race. I have poisoned them all; and you, and your wife and child, remain alone to complete the list of my victims."

"Oh God! listen to him!" murmured the duke. "Can this be true, or can it be but the raving of a madman?"

"It is as true as that I am Hezekiah Slink, the Quaker, whom you wronged. Do you know me now?"

"Yes, yes; I seem to recognize you. I always noticed a slight likeness; but I thought you were dead."

"It would have been strange if there had not been a change in me after all that I had suffered; but I altered my appearance to some extent, on purpose that I might be near you, and so work out my plans."

"Oh, mercy! mercy!"

"Come," cried the doctor, whose patience seemed to be ebbing away; "come this way."

As he spoke, he grasped the old man by the collar, and dragged him, trembling and panting, towards the hole in the middle of the floor.

"Here, Rattan," he said; "your light."

Rattan until this had been a silent and astonished spectator of the strange scene enacting before him; for being unacquainted with Faversham's story (narrated in the Twelfth Chapter of the Second Book of this history), the doctor's remarks seemed more like the ravings of a madman than the long-determined, well-considered speeches which had been conned over and looked forward to eagerly for so many years.

Besides, the ruffian was rather curious to see what death was in store for the old man, and how it would be executed.

Rattan was not a person of a very sympathetic or tenderhearted disposition, and the scene enacting before him had all the attraction of an exciting tragedy at the theatre, without making him feel at all uncomfortable.

He therefore came forward as desired with the light, and held it in such a way, that the rays from it were reflected down the hole.

"See!" cried the doctor, dragging the duke still nearer to the aperture. "I shall throw you down there."

"Would you drown me?"

"No; the water is not deep; there is barely a foot of it. You will not die by the fall."

"How then?" asked the old man, with a shudder.

"Of cold, and starvation, and fatigue."

The duke looked at him, and then down the hole, with an expression of intense horror.

"There is just water enough to prevent your lying down. You will be obliged to stand all your time, or at best to rest yourself by sitting in the filth, or leaning against the slimy walls. You will find the water too beastly to drink. I shall keep you there until you die; and I shall give you a small portion of bread every day, gradually lessening it, till the supply ceases altogether. Then you will starve to death, unless you eat the toads and other vermin you find there, or you are worried to death by the savage rats, which will most likely be the case when your strength fails you, and you become too weak to ward them off."

The duke, in an agony of terror at this description of his impending fate, wrung his hands, and groaned aloud.

It was truly an awful place, this vault, into which the doctor proposed to fling him.

A faint stifling odour was emitted from the water lying at its bottom, as though there were rotting in it the dead bodies of departed rats.

In one corner could be seen the dark-coloured slippery form of a huge toad, which seemed to be making gigantic efforts to climb up the slimy brickwork at the side.

Something, apparently drowned, and swollen and distorted out of all shape, bobbed up and down in the water, as though it were being nibbled at by vermin underneath.

The horrible place was about ten feet deep, and from six to seven square.

To think of being condemned to pass the remainder of his life in such a hole was an idea so atrociously horrible and sickening, that the bare notion of it was enough to drive the old man mad.

If there had been remaining about him any enervating effects of his recent illness, the terror of the scene in which he found himself since he had been brought into the dreary vault by Jack Rattan had totally dispelled them.

Although weak and feeble, he was now in possession of all his faculties.

Indeed, his senses seemed, if anything, quickened by the necessity for their use.

He saw that unless he immediately made a great and desperate effort at escape, there would be no chance of escape left for him.

The doctor had got him by the collar, and was dragging him nearer and nearer to the hole.

"Get down," he said, "or I will fling you in."

The poor old man saw that now was the moment for the last effort.

He summoned all his feeble strength, and clung to the edge of the aperture.

The doctor dragged at him fiercely.

The old man tore at the side, and struggled against him.

Nearer and nearer he approached.

At last, just as the doctor was stooping to collect all his strength, and fling him over, the duke sprang to his feet, and dealt him a blow in the chest, which for the moment made him reel and stagger back tottering upon the brink of the chasm.

Then, without pausing to reflect or look round him, he rushed out of the vault.

But he did not go by the door at which he had entered.

That was closed behind him.

The way he chose was that which led to the other pit crossed by a plank.

As quick as lightning, and supporting himself by the rope, he ran across the plank, and thrust open the door on the other side.

The doctor, seizing the hatchet from the bench, instantly pursued him.

The old man hoped to have found some way of egress from the vault in which he now found himself, but all was pitch dark.

"Rattan, the light—the light!" he heard the doctor shouting.

The duke was as anxious for it as the other; for he knew that everything depended upon his getting out first, before the other had time to lay hands upon him.

In a moment the rays of the candle, which Rattan held above his head, penetrated the gloom of the cellar.

Eagerly the duke looked round him.

There was no way out.

He must turn and face his foe.

He had scarcely time to look round him, and to realize his position, before, with a wild yell of fury, the other had borne down upon him, and clutched him by the throat.

"What, wretch!" he hissed in his ear; "you would escape!"

And he began to drag the old man back.

But the desperation of his position lent the victim strength.

He pulled against his captor, twisted round, and wrestled with him.

The doctor seized him by the throat, and strove to drag him back.

"Come, come, or I'll murder you!"

"Rather that, than that I should be thrown into the hole."

"Come back, or I'll split open your skull."

He raised the hatchet he held in the air, as though he would instantly carry out his threat.

The old man crouched down upon the ground, and spread out his hands to ward off the coming blow.

But at that instant there was a sound of footsteps in the kitchen through which Rattan had brought the duke to the vault.

"Hush! hush!" cried that ruffian, holding the light above his head. "I hear some one coming."

"Which way?"

"Through the house."

"It must be fancy."

"No, no. Hark! don't you hear them?"

The doctor listened for a moment.

So did the duke.

Decidedly there were footsteps, and so there was hope, it seemed to the doomed man.

But, alas! there was none.

"If there is any one, by God he shall not escape!" Faversham cried.

And saying so, he swung the hatchet round his head, and brought it down with crushing force upon his victim's shoulder.

It seemed to split and sever the bone.

The old man, with a yell of agony, fell to the ground.

Then with shriek after shriek he rent the air.

But the murderer was bent upon his fell purpose. Again the axe swept the air; again it fell with a thud upon the victim's body.

The inhuman wretch, though bent upon his murder, wished, if possible, to prolong his agony to the utmost.

Again and again the blows descended, until the murdered man's screams were replaced by groans.

Then the murderer fell upon him with the fury of a tiger, and rained a perfect volley of blows upon his head, completely battering in his skull.

The axe fell again and again with a crashing, splintering, smashing sound.

Then, with a heavy, sloppy thud, for the bones were broken in, and the hatchet buried in the victim's brain.

He was stone dead and motionless, all save a tremulous quiver of his limbs, and a galvanic twisting in his bloody fingers upon the brickwork of the ground of the cellar.

He was stone dead; but still like a savage, or a maniac, or a demon, the murderer danced or capered round the corpse, and battered at it furiously with the murderous weapon, clotted with gore, reeking to the very handle in blood, and chipped and blunted at the edge by the contact with the victim's bones.

With wildly gleaming hair, set teeth, bloodstained hands, and ensanguined visage, the murderer paused at last, breathless, over the mass of bruised and bleeding flesh, and broken bones, which had once been the Duke of Heatherland.

But just then, Rattan, who until now had

been glaring at the butcher and the butchered with the fascination of horror and astonishment which such an act of savagery caused in the mind of even such a ruffian as he was, gave the alarm that they were observed, and the doctor, looking up, saw two faces staring down at him from a grating close to the ceiling of the outer vault.

By the light that Rattan held, he recognized them.

They were Horford and Murdoch.

With a frantic yell, such as might emanate from a wild beast springing upon its prey, Faversham waved the hatchet in the air, and called to his companion to follow.

Clutching the candle from Rattan, the better to be able to see where he was going, he caught hold of the rope dangling over the pit, with the other hand he threw himself forward to reach the other side, intending only to rest his foot in the middle of the plank to steady himself across.

But the violence of the shock was more than the rotten wood would bear.

It tipped over on one side, slipped, and fell with a crash into the pit.

At the same time, the fall of the plank broke the doctor's spring, and he fell short of the opposite side.

Clinging, however, with desperate tenacity, to the rope, he swang back through the air.

The beam above to which the rope was fastened, creaked with the unusual strain upon it, the rope seemed to stretch and crack with his weight.

Missing the side again to which he had swung back, and where he had hoped to gain a footing, he flew back again towards the centre of the pit, and spun round and round, like a bird roasting upon a spit.

The pain which he suffered in his arm by thus supporting his weight upon the rope, twisted round his wrist, was intense; and he could not forbear from uttering a hollow groan.

Then, unable to hold the candle in his other hand, which he wanted to use to support himself, he let it slip from his fingers.

They were in the dark.

Loud shouts were being raised by the two men who had played the spy upon them.

The doctor strove with all his might to reach the side of the chasm, for he felt that the rope was unfraying at the top, and in a few moments more would probably break asunder.

Rattan, helpless in the door-way, felt that he was caught in a trap.

At the same time, being, as we already know, an awful coward in the dark, a shuddering dread and horror crept over him when he thought of what was laying behind him, smashed, and chopped, and bloody, in the dark.

XLVI.—Shows what a slippery customer Master Charley Wag could be, and also how he could make himself agreeable when he liked.

"HE won't slip through my fingers this time," said Mr. Bung.

He made the observation as he rushed towards the door of the public-house, where were assembled Cock's Lot, and endeavoured to throw himself in the way of Master Charles Wag, in whom he was in pursuit.

"Stop him! stop him!" cried Mr. Bung.

"Hold him fast," shouted the celebrated Mr. Bucket.

But the people in the bar were undecided.

Some were for helping the boy to escape, and some were for stopping him.

The motive which prompted the first, was merely that desire to be in opposition to existing authority which one notices so much of among the lower class of English people.

The motive which prompted the second, was a desire to be witnesses of any kind of scene which could be witnessed at a cheap rate, and without much personal inconvenience, no matter what it cost the parties directly concerned.

But they were too long undecided which course to pursue. Although one or two persons made a feeble effort to throw themselves in the way, Mr. Bung and the policeman made a charge at them, and the latter laid his hand upon Charley's collar as he was slipping out of the door.

This attention Charley repaid by a great thump at the side of the policeman's head; but Bucket, not daunted by such rough usage, retained his hold, and dragged his captive back into the bar.

Then Mr. Bung coming to his assistance, they jammed Charley up against the wall, where Mr. Bung held him, while Mr. Bucket rummaged in his pocket for a pair of handcuffs he usually carried with him on all his thief-catching expeditions.

But the people round the bar, at once excited and astonished by these active proceedings, came crowding round.

Bucket felt with renewed eagerness for the handcuffs.

He could not find them.

Some one must have taken them out of his pocket.

There was, under the circumstances, now no help for it.

He was obliged to appeal to the people standing round him for assistance. It was what he had hoped to have been able to have avoided, for he well knew the disposition of the lower orders when assistance was required in such cases.

However, now he could not help himself.

He therefore turned round, and called upon those near to him to lend a hand.

"In the Queen's name," said he.

"Who the deuce do you call yourself?" asked a hulking fellow standing near, with his hands in his pockets.

"I'm Bucket, the detective officer," replied that worthy; "and I call upon you to help me."

"You may call, then," replied the hulking individual. "What's the boy done, that you're a throttling him in that style."

"Done!" replied Mr. Bucket. "He's Charley Wag, and he's done a highway robbery for one thing."

"He may do another for what I care," replied the man. "If he's the Charley Wag that there was that about in the papers, I'll be darned if I lend a hand to take him."

"That's right, old fellow," chimed in some one else, sitting close by; "them's my sentiments."

"And mine," added a third.

"If he is to be took at all," observed a fourth, "let the police take him themselves. It's what there paid for, ain't it?"

"Hear, hear," chorussed everybody.

"But look here, gentlemen," called out Charley Wag, as well as he could speak with the throttling gripe which the officer kept upon his throat; "but look here, gentlemen, why should I be taken at all? If you lend a hand, I can't be."

"Let anyone attempt a rescue at their peril," shouted Bucket, brandishing a staff, which he produced from his coat-tail pocket.

"Landlord!" shouted Mr. Bung. "It is your place to render assistance; it will be the worse for you if you don't."

"Well," retorted the landlord, "I should have thought that two of you was quite enough to take a bit of a boy like that there into custody."

"If you don't render assistance, you'll have to answer for it," said Mr. Bucket, who was quite out of breath, owing to Mr. Wag's desperate lunges and kicks.

The landlord looked round in an hesitating way.

It would not exactly do to stand there, after he had been formally called upon, and defy the law.

There was only one way to get out of it, and that he took.

He made a sign to one or two men near him to catch hold of his arms, and then he pretended to struggle to get away.

"Let me go and help the policeman," he cried, as though he wanted to do so. "Why are you holding me back?"

Then, Charley seeing the turn that affairs were taking, began to shout with all his might.

"Rescue—rescue!"

The noise disturbed Cock's Lot down below, and all the ladies and gentlemen came flocking up-stairs to see what was the matter.

"Who is it?"

"What's he done?"

"What are they up to with him?"

Sombody said: "It's Charley Wag."

"Charley Wag?" echoed some of the strongest of the young thieves. "Leave go of him, can't you?"

And they made a spring upon Bung and Bucket, and dragged them away.

"If it's Charley Wag, he shan't be nabbed."

"Are you the real Charley Wag?"

"Are you the Charley Wag that was in the papers?"

"Yes, yes," replied Charley. "Lend us a hand."

When Cock's Lot felt sure that they were going to assist the right person, and not a spurious Charley Wag who was famous for nothing, they entered into the business of the rescue with great vigour and energy.

Half-a-dozen of the Lot sprang upon Mr. Bucket, and half-a-dozen or more tackled Mr. Bung.

They got hold of these unfortunate gentlemen by the hair, and the ears, and the nose; and considering the pulling that all these parts were subject to, it was a great blessing that when it was over that they had any remaining.

Poor old Bung, flat upon his back, was bellowing a thousand murders, but in vain.

The unfortunate Bucket. Somebody had got hold of his ears and was banging his head against the wall, until the detective was half stupified.

A few moments sufficed, as you may suppose, to empty the pockets of the two victims; and though the greater part of the spoils went into the common till, yet you can hardly be surprised if a few shillings found their way into the purses of private individuals, who were lucky enough to be able quietly to appropriate them.

When they were entirely despoiled of all valuables, and had been drubbed out of breath by the desperate young ragamuffins, the unfortunate Bucket and Bung were taken down-stairs into the cellar, which was commonly called the club-room, where a grave consultation was held as to what should be their fate.

But first of all, it was unanimously voted that for the remainder of the evening Mr. Wag should fill the post of honour in the chair, and should give his decision upon all that should be done.

"Tie them in a couple of chairs," directed Mr. Wag, "and make 'em blazing drunk."

The proposition met with the loudest applause.

In a moment, half-a-dozen pairs of hands seized upon the obnoxious couple, and tied them hand and foot in two ricketty old armchairs.

"What shall we give them?" asked some one, when these arrangements were made.

"Some strong gin and water will do them good," said Charley. "Here, waiter, let's have a shilling's worth of your most turpentiny sort for those two gentleman, and half-a-dozen bowls of punch for the rest of us."

Then, seeing the waiter looked as though he thought the order a rather stiff one, Charley drew a couple of sovereigns from his pocket, and threw them upon the table.

"That'll do to begin with, old fellow," said our hero; "and there's lots more where that come from, when it's wanted."

Cock's Lot had all along been inclined to look favourably upon Mr. Wag; but this princely liberality raised him in their estimation to the highest possible pitch.

"Bravo, Charley," shouted some one.

And the rest took up the cry, and re-echoed it again and again, until the walls seemed to shake with the noise.

"Bravo, Charley! Hooray! Hooray!"

Again and again it was repeated.

At last Charley managed to make himself heard.

"I am very much obliged to you, ladies and gentlemen," said Mr. Wag. "I can assure you that this is the proudest moment of my life."

"Hear, hear," cried everybody.

"But before commencing our own liquor, I am sure you will agree with me in proposing that we first of all attend to our two guests, who really look as though they stood in need of something comforting."

Here Cock's Lot responded with a shout of approval.

" I don't want any," said Bucket.

" I'll be damned if I touch it!" said Mr. Bung.

" If they don't take it quietly, we must pour it down their throats with a funnel; but to begin with, try holding their noses."

This atrocious sugestion was, I regret to say, received with the loudest acclamation.

It was in vain for the unfortunate Bung to swear and protest that not a single drop of the liquor should pass his lips.

When you have your nose held, you know you can't very well help yourself.

It is the way they treat obstinate poodles who don't take kindly to their castor oil.

" I won't have it," cried Bung.

" You shall have it," said the party who had hold of his proboscis.

" I shan't."

" You shall."

" I'm damned if I do."

" I'm damned if you don't."

Then there was an awful struggle between Mr. Bung's nose and the young gentleman who had hold of it.

But, as I said before, it was no good struggling.

When he began to choke and to gurgle, and to grow very black and blue and swollen in the face, poor Mr. Bung gave up the unequal struggle as a bad job, and did what he might as well have done at first, without quite so much fuss.

That is to say, he gulphed down the liquid.

The young gentleman held his nose, and he swallowed for bare life.

Then when he had finished his shilling's-worth, and a sixpennyworth on the top of that, for what Mr. Wag was pleased to call luck, the unhappy old man began to feel extremely intoxicated.

The room began to spin round, and the young ladies and gentlemen took to standing on their heads, without any regard to the rules of propriety—or at least, so it seemed to the confused vision of the drysalter.

After awhile, he lost the power of speech; and shortly after he began to get very drowsy, and at last, if it had not been for the ropes which bound his arms, he would most certainly have slipped down under the table, and lain there, helpless, among the table legs.

Mr. Bucket was very much in the same way. He had drank as much as the old gentleman, but he had taken it quietly, and thereby saved his nose from a good deal of unnecessary tweaking and rough handling.

When these two were finally disposed of and seemed half insensible, Mr. Wag devoted his attention to the rest of the company.

They, too, were getting a little the worse for liquor, for they were not used to such a plentiful allowance of hot grog, as a general rule, as they had had to-night.

Mr. Charley's treat coming on the top of their other potations, and it being club-night, they had drunk rather deeply, and all their young brains were more or less muddled by the drink.

Indeed, they were extremely uproarious.

Some of them performed fantastic hornpipes upon the tables, among the pipes and glasses; others danced ; a great number sang choruses; one or two made speeches ; a great many more shouted at the top of their voices, just for the sake of making a noise ; and the rest quarrelled among themselves, and amused themselves a little by pulling one another's hair, and digging one another hard pokes in the ribs with their elbows.

But presently some young gentleman who had a little more to say for himself than the rest, balanced himself very unsteadily upon his legs, and in the most intelligible tone of voice which he could command, which after all was none of the plainest, he addressed the company at considerable length, and proposed Master Charles's health.

Mr. Wag, with the air of an emperor, rose and replied in a few graceful words.

He was proud, he said, to see so much youth and beauty assembled round him.

Here there was loud applause from the youth and beauty.

The way in which the honourable gentleman who had just spoken had expressed himself, was eloquence itself, Mr. Wag remarked ; but at the same time, he (Mr. Wag) was afraid that the honourable gentleman had been too lenient to his (Mr. Wag's) faults, and too eulogistic upon his (Mr. Wag's) merits.

Here there was tremendous applause from those who did not understand a single word that Mr. Wag was saying (this was the larger portion of the company), and cries of " No" from the rest.

Mr. Wag, holding out his hand with a bland smile to quell the tumult, proceeded.

He trusted that he might never do anything that in any way would tend to lower the noble profession to which he had the honour to belong.

Up to now he could proudly point to several small achievements which he had been able to perform, and he felt confident that there were those present who were of the same mind, and only lacked the opportunity of distinguishing themselves.

He made some further remarks to the same effect, and resumed his seat amidst thunders of applause.

Indeed, so great a hit did he make, that by universal desire one of the leaders of the band proposed that he should be their captain, and that in future they should go under the name of the United Wagtails instead as hitherto of Cock's Lot.

But Master Charley, in flowery language, and with many compliments to the assembled company, respectfully declined it ; and as he walked homewards, under the bright star-light, and the rank odours of gin and tobacco began to be blown away from his clothes by the night breeze, he smiled to himself as he thought of his new friends' enthusiastic reception of him.

" No, no," said he, shaking his head playfully at the moon, for he had had quite enough to drink as well as the rest, though he had gone away under the impression that he himself was as sober as a judge, but that everybody else was disgustingly intoxicated.

Indeed, they were all much further gone, and the landlord, at last quite tired out with their noise and disturbance, had turned the whole company into the street, and locked the doors on them, when those who could stand upright insisted upon seeing each other home, and advised one another sternly to be men, and hold up.

But I left Charley in the middle of a remark. "No, no," said he, addressing the moon. "I don't think I'll have anything to do with Cock's Lot. I've got a career before me that's chalked out, and Cock's Lot has nothing to do with it. I have a name to make, and must make it. I have adventures to seek, and must seek them. I feel sure that my life is intended to be an extraordinary one, and when it is published in weekly numbers and splendidly illustrated, as I suppose some day or other it will be, if I don't do two or three astonishing things, the ladies and gentlemen who take me in, won't think me interesting."

And so, reader, he did do something very extraordinary before long, which, if you read a few more chapters, you will come to.

XLVII.—In which a lady and gentleman, having nothing particular to do, make up their minds to go out of town, and enjoy themselves, and go accordingly. Also describes what befell them by the way, and what happened to them at their journey's end.

"I TELL you what it is," said Charley Wag, "we ought to be out of town."

"It's what I've been saying all along," said Julia.

"We want change of air."

"And scene."

"It isn't as though we had got no money."

"We've been doing so well lately."

"Making our fortune in a small way."

"And ought to rest ourselves."

"And spend it."

"Well, some of it, anyhow."

The conversation I have been recording took place, if you please, in a handsome apartment in Newman Street, Oxford Street.

A well-spread breakfast-table was before them.

There were tea, and coffee, and sherry, and bitter ale, lamb chops, and mushrooms, sweetbread, cold ham, anchovy toast, and sardines, potted shrimps, apricot jam, and preserved ginger. After that, some grapes, peaches, and pine apples. For Master Charley did everything in style when he did do it, as I have very frequently had occasion to tell you.

Mr. Wag was dressed in a magnificent brocaded dressing-gown, all gold and purple, which it quite dazzled you to look at; and a pair of slippers which were something astounding in embroidery.

Miss Julia had on a pale pink French merino wrapper, with pink satin slippers to match.

If you had seen them, and not known who they were, you must have supposed them to have been some royal prince and princess at the very least.

"Where shall we go to?" asked Charley, puffing at a fourpenny cigar as though it were nothing at all out of the common. "Which of the fashionable watering-places shall we patronize?"

"What do you say to Margate?" said Julia.

"Gracious me!" replied her companion; "we couldn't do it. It is several degrees too low. Why we might as well go to Gravesend. The idea, my dear, of Margate! Who goes there, but a set of third-rate people, counter-skippers, and such? No, my dear; we really couldn't. It would be letting ourselves down."

"Then what do you say to Brighton?"

"Ah! Brighton is the place. That's fashionable, if you like. Besides, it is too early in the year to go to any of the other sea-side places. Brighton let it be. And now, how shall we go?"

"I should like to go by the coach, if we could manage it."

"So should I, above all things; so I'll go and see when the coaches start."

For this purpose Mr. Wag presently walked down to the Circus, and made inquiries; but finding that the coaches were all gone for the day, he returned post haste to Miss Julia in a Hansom cab, and propounded a scheme which had occurred to him, he said, upon the way.

"And what is it?" asked Julia.

"That we should go down on horseback."

"To be sure."

They wondered that the notion had not occurred to them before, seeing how much they were out on horseback, one way and another.

If the distance was too great, they would sleep somewhere on the way, and they could have their luggage sent down by the rail.

They therefore, hot upon the scheme, packed up immediately, without any further delay, and sent round to the stable for their horses.

They set out at about two o'clock, and turned their horses' heads to the South.

They were in no very great hurry, and rode leisurely along, so that they had not made any very great way before evening began to set in.

It would have been far better for Master Charley and his fair friend if they had only made up their minds to go by the rail, like other folks do, or to wait until next day for the coach.

But so it was to be. They went on horseback, and fell in with the series of startling adventures which I am about to tell you.

Those who know anything of the environs of London must be aware, that within twenty or thirty miles of St. Paul's Cathedral there exist, not only rural spots, tracts of fields, and wood, and meadow, but even tiny villages, as perfectly isolated, lonely, and sequestered, as are the hamlets lying amidst the Devonshire hills, or the Westmoreland valleys.

To one of these little nooks of cosy country scenery our two travellers found their way as day was waning.

It was an old-fashioned, sleepy little place. The solitary street followed a bend in the road, and the houses had a quaint sort of irregularity. Prim three-story dwellings, with trees in front, jostle with ancient time-worn cottages, curiously

The afternoon sun was shining still with compounded of garrets and chimneys, and supported by irregular clusters of outhouses.
some considerable heat upon the little crooked flags in the pavement of the street, and the shopkeeping interest was lounging idly over their half-doors, and chatting to each other, most probably about topics of great parochial interest in their little world.

As the travellers passed by, they caught glimpses on each side of the street, through the cottage doors, open at the back and front alike, of green orchards and flowery gardens, and beyond, a vast space of open country.

In the centre of the village stood the village inn. Across the street was stretched a great white beam, from which dangled the signboard over the passenger's head; and the inn itself was a great, gloomy, overgrown looking building, which seemed as though it would, at a pinch, have accommodated a regiment of soldiers.

All round, for miles and miles, lay a great range of lovely landscape, woodland, and meadow.

The little place looked very sleepy.

There was a remarkably sleepy cat taking a nap on one door-step, and an uncommonly drowsy dog taking a nap on another; and the butcher's pony, the sleepiest of the three, was whisking his tail in a dreamy way at an unpleasantly wakeful fly who would keep pecking at him.

All else was still, and the travellers could hear the faint breeze rustling the apple-trees in the orchards.

But suddenly, as they were gazing upon the tranquil scene before them, they were startled by the sound of loud shouts in the distance.

They approached rapidly.

Immediately afterwards they heard the rattle of wheels.

Then the tramp of horses.

They grew nearer and nearer, and Charley and Julia reined in their horses by the roadside, to be out of the way.

They were only just in time, however; for a moment afterwards, amidst a whirlwind of dust, a runaway tandem shot down the street, the horses flying at a mad gallop, and the trap, with its contents, swaying awfully from side to side.

"Take care, Julia," cried Charley. "Pull in your horse, or they will run into us."

"They will certainly be thrown out."

"There's no doubt about that; they'll be spilt in a minute or two."

"Take care of the corner," shouted three or four people from the open shop-doors.

"Go easy," bawled as many more.

But the advice, though doubtless the best of its kind, was not of very great value upon the present occasion.

The horses had got the bit between their teeth. They galloped furiously on.

They turned the corner at railway speed.

The carriage rose upon one wheel, overturned, and the two occupants were flung with great violence into the road, where they lay stunned and motionless.

One of the horses fell with the gig, and lay entangled in the harness, lunging out desperately with its hind legs, every kick splintering and smashing the woodwork of the vehicle.

On the other hand, the leader reared and plunged in the traces, snorting and foaming at the mouth.

But Charley, dismounting quickly from his horse, threw the bridle to Julia, and while the small shopkeepers and open-mouthed rustics were staring stupidly at the scene enacting before them, rushed boldly forward, and without a moment's hesitation—for at such a moment hesitation would have most probably have been fatal—he seized the horse's head, and after a short but violent struggle, contrived to gain a mastery over the furious and terrified beast.

When this was done, several of the bystanders had recovered a sufficiency of presence of mind to come to the assistance of the two unfortunate gentlemen who had been thrown out of the gig.

They found them still senseless, and one, with his face covered with dust and blood, looked a most woful object.

But raising them carefully, they carried them into the public-house, and here, fortunately, happened to be the village surgeon, who promptly took means for restoring them to consciousness.

They were laid, one upon the sofa, and the other on the table, in the public room, and their coats, waistcoats, and neckerchiefs having been removed, cold water and other remedies were quickly procured to revive them.

Charley came in and looked at them while they were insensible.

They were neither of them very pleasant men to look at.

Although well dressed, Charley could see at a glance that neither of them were gentlemen.

One was decidedly an American; and had the long, lank jaws, and colourless cheeks, which are observable in most Yankees.

The other was a shouting, vulgar man, with moustaches.

The latter recovered first.

He opened his eyes, rubbed his head, and finally sat up, gazing round with a half stupified, half laughing, expression on his bloated face.

"By gosh," he said, "them stones had bones in 'em."

The surgeon, with a smile, expressed his satisfaction at learning this great mineralogical fact, and proceeded to chafe the temples, and feel the limbs of the young man who lay upon the table.

During this time, however, his companion, with many and odd contortions and twistings of his countenance, was hitting out his arms right and left, stretching his legs, and carefully patting himself all over, to make sure that none of his bones were broken.

Very little time was required to set his mind at rest upon this important point, after which he directed his attention to his fellow-sufferer, and observing that he had studied medicine for some time in New Orleans, as a specimen of his qualifications for practising the art of healing, prescribed a "brandy cocktail," or a "corpse reviver," both which drinks he assured the surgeon would bring round his friend in a brace of twinklings.

DUCHESS OF HEATHERLAND.

But as this curious medicine was not easily to be procured, he advised a little hot gin.

Before, however, any of these remedies could have been applied, the patient came to himself, and went through very much the same process, as to his arms and legs, as his friend had done before him.

Fortunately, with the same satisfactory result.

Both gentlemen were a good deal shaken by the tumble; but neither of them had otherwise sustained any injury from the mishap.

"I hope you are better, sir," said Charley, addressing the long-jawed Yankee.

The man looked up at him for a moment, with a hard stare, and then turned away his head without making any reply.

No. 43.

Charley thought that this was hardly polite, and was going to make some angry remark, when he reflected that probably the other had not heard what he said.

He therefore repeated it.

"I'm no worse," the American answered; "thought it is not your fault."

"What do you mean by that?" demanded our hero, somewhat imperiously.

"What I say."

"That I caused the accident?"

"Who else?"

"Come, come," interrupted the man with the moustache. "It wasn't the stranger, Jefferson. The trap must have upset, anyhow, when them devils of horses bolted like that round the sharp corner."

[CHARLEY WAG, THE NEW JACK SHEPPARD.

"If he had not stood where he did, they'd have taken a wider range."

"I could not help standing where I did," replied Charley. "Both I and the lady who was with me drew in our horses as much as possible, so as to be out of the way."

"Bah!" said the American, turning away his head contemptuously, with an ironical smile upon his thin, ill-natured looking lips.

"Sir!" cried Charley, blushing crimson.

But the man with the moustache interfered.

Taking Charley on one side, he held him by the button hole and whispered in his ear:

"A strange fellow, sir—a little flighty—a little touchy—a little touched (tapping his forehead). Don't mind him, sir; it's all manner."

"A very insolent manner."

"Perhaps so—no doubt. But don't quarrel with him, my dear boy—he's a dead shot."

"I don't care if he was the deadest shot upon record."

"Well, now don't, let me beg of you. I shouldn't like to see you picked off by my friend. It would be a pity. Don't provoke him, now. Take my advice."

While they were speaking thus in an under tone in a corner of the room, the man whom they had called Jefferson had lounged to the window, and was looking out into the street, smoking a cigar.

"We shall have to stop here, I suppose," said the man with the moustache. "I wonder whether there is any chance of getting anything eatable for dinner."

Charley, meanwhile, had gone to the outside of the house, where he found Julia had dismounted from her horse, and was talking to the landlady.

He had not heard that the two strangers had determined to stop there to dinner, and he now asked Julia whether she was agreeable that they (Julia and Charley) should do so.

Julia, whom the ride had made very hungry, willingly agreed to the proposition; and the chambermaid, at her direction, showed her to a room where she could effect some alteration in her dress before the meal.

When she descended to the dining-room, she found the two strangers seated at table.

The man with the moustache drumming his knife upon a tumbler, and so accompanying himself to an air he was whistling.

The other picking his teeth with a fork.

Julia gave them both a scrutinizing glance as she passed by.

Master Charley was standing with his back to the fire, and scowling rather gloomily at the strangers.

As Julia entered, they both looked up at her, and then looking at one another, smiled, in an insulting kind of way.

Or, at least, so it seemed to Mr. Wag, who scowled blacker than before.

"The right sort," observed one of the gentlemen.

"Slick," observed the other.

"An almighty screamer."

"An everlasting out-and-outer."

Charley's brow grew a little blacker still; but he said nothing.

There could be no doubt but that the men alluded to Julia. However, he thought that the insulting tendency of their remarks was scarcely evident enough for him to feel justified in taking the matter up; so he chewed the cud, as it were, and waited for an opportunity.

The opportunity was not long in coming, and it was not long before Charley had cause to quarrel with one of them.

The landlord presently entered the room, to see if the cloth was properly laid; and immediately afterwards the dinner made its appearance.

It was an excellent repast, which was owing to the fact of a great cricketing dinner having taken place at the inn the previous day, and a good deal of food being left, the cook with the fragments, was able to produce a very well laid table for the guests now assembled.

The village doctor joined the company, and proved himself a very jovial sort of fellow, full of jokes and anecdotes.

He was a middle aged man, and, according to his own account, had been a very gay dog indeed when he was younger.

He was full of stories of the fast places of amusement in town, when he was walking the hospitals; and it striking him that Master Charles was of rather a gay turn, and that the fair Julia was not over straight-laced, he drew Mr. Wag out, and asked him for the latest news respecting the fast life of London.

The opportunity for a quarrel with the American arose out of this circumstance.

Mr. Wag, as I have told you before, was very fond of boasting.

He never lost an opportunity of making himself out to be a great man.

They had been talking of various popular dining-rooms.

Mr. Wag launched out.

"The Wellington. Yes," said he, "it's not such a bad sort of place—or Simpson's in the Strand, or the London; but one dines much better at one's club than any of those places."

"Rather dearer, though, isn't it?" said the doctor.

"Dear!" said Master Charles, leaning back in his chair, and assuming the air of a millionaire. "Not particularly so. A fellow can get a very decent meal—plain, you know, of course, and half a pint of wine, for half a sovereign, or fifteen shillings; but men can't well expect to dine under that."

The surgeon looked a little astonished at this observation.

Up to now he had been accustomed to consider a shilling as a very fair price for a dinner.

The American and his companion said nothing.

They only looked at one another in a very significant fashion, and grinned.

"What does it cost you to dine, colonel?" asked Jefferson, presently.

"Fourpence, if I take soup," replied the man with the moustache.

And then they both laughed loudly.

Charley glared at them.

"What club do you belong to, sir?" asked the surgeon, presently.

"The Reform," replied Charley.

Here Jefferson cut in.

"What club to you belong to, colonel?"

"Cock's Lot, in the Mint."

Another roar of laughter.

Charley looked at them uneasily, and Julia changed colour.

Did they know who Charley was? Did they know that he was connected with the club of young thieves they had named, or was it merely a chance shot?

What was their motive in the former case? What in the latter?

However, as the case stood, Charley determined to pick a quarrel with and silence them.

"From your manner, sir," said Charley, addressing Jefferson, "I cannot suppose otherwise than that you want to insult me."

"Don't make any mistake, sir," replied the Yankee.

"What do you wish me to understand?"

"I have no wish upon the subject."

"What do you mean, then?"

"I mean, that I do not want you to run away with the idea that I was sufficiently interested in your existence to put myself out of the way to cause you either pleasure or pain."

"I do not suppose," said Charley, making desperate efforts to remain calm, "that you feel more interest in me than I do in you; although, after the trouble I took some time ago, in endeavouring to prevent a furious horse from scattering the contents of your head by a blow from its iron-shod hoof, I might almost have been led to suppose that you would have shown yourself a little more agreeable, if not grateful."

"Don't talk nonsense," retorted the American. "Who are you, pray, that I should be grateful to you? What did you do? I don't see it myself. Who are you, I say? and what are you? and how am I to know that all these fine stories you are pleased to tell us are not a pack of lies?"

"You know by this, that if they are, you are not at liberty to say so," replied Charley.

And as he spoke, he flung a tumbler at the Yankee's head with such violence, that the other fell to the ground as though he had been shot.

Next moment, however, he had regained his feet, and sprang forward to seize the boy by the throat; but the surgeon and the colonel both rushed upon him, and separated the combatants.

"I'll have his blood," roared the American, foaming at the mouth with passion, "I'll have his blood. He has insulted me. I'll cut his throat. I'll blow his brains out. I'll have his blood."

"No—no—no," interposed the surgeon. "It mustn't be. It would be murder. No harm was meant. It wasn't his fault. He's only a boy, and you provoked him."

"I'll have his blood," roared the American.

Julia clung to Charley's arm.

"I'm not afraid of him," cried that young gentleman. "I'll give him as good as he brings."

"What's the young blackguard's name?" shouted the American. "Here's my card. I'm Seth Jefferson of New York. I'm not afraid of my name. If he's a gentleman, let him give me his card."

"I havn't got a card with me."

"What do you call yourself, then?"

"My name," replied our hero, "is Charley Wag."

It was a very stupid thing to do, thus to deliver himself; but he was in such a passion, that he did not know what he was about.

The effect of the statement was electrical.

Charley saw in a moment what a mad act he had committed; but it was then too late to retract his words.

"The devil you are!" the colonel exclaimed. "I'm be blest if I didn't think it. I said you were one of the swell mob the moment I caught sight of you."

"Swell mob!" said the surgeon, feeling in his pockets. "You don't say so!"

"Swell mob!" echoed the landlord, who came in at the moment. "Have we got any of the swell mob here? Mary, come and count the spoons. John, run for the constables."

"Don't disturb yourself," said Mr. Wag, coolly. "I have money enough to pay for what I have had, and to give you something over for yourself."

"I'm sure I don't know whether it is safe or not," the landlord remarked. "I havn't been accustomed in my time to entertain this sort of company? But who was to know who they were by the look of them? Nobody would have took that there young gent for a thief, or that young person for a —— I don't know what."

"You'll be kind enough," said Charley, turning upon the landlord so fiercely that that worthy person stepped back in a great fright, and bumped the back of his head up against the wall. "You'll be kind enough to speak a little more respectfully, if you presume to speak at all of *this lady*, who, although I am a thief, and glory in it, was not aware of the circumstance until you kindly informed her. Accident has thrown us together; and although she is in such questionable company, she is deserving of every respect, which I shall take care is accorded her."

The landlord hearing this determined tone, began immediately to mend his manners, and to be much more respectful.

The man called Jefferson here broke into the conversation.

"I'm not surprised to hear that he's a thief," said he; "but, thief or no thief, I'm ready to fight him, if he's got the pluck to fight."

"I've got the pluck to fight you any way you like," retorted Charley; "and with any weapons you may please to choose."

"No—no," said the surgeon. "That won't do."

"You must go and fight somewhere else, if you want to fight," said the landlord.

"Why so?" cried the American. "By God, if you don't let me shoot the man I want, I'll shoot any other man who tries to prevent me."

"Certainly, that's fair enough," chimed in the colonel. "Let 'em have it out, all fair and straightforward. Who's got a right to put themselves in the way of what's proper?"

"If you want to fight," said the landlord, "I tell you you must go somewhere else to do it."

"Where can we go?"

"How am I to know?"

"Then we'll stop here."

"That you can't."

"Show us another place, then."

"There's a barn at the bottom of the yard. It's nothing to do with me if you fight there."

"Let's go to the barn, then."

"Let's choose the way we're to fight first," said Jefferson.

"I don't care a button," Charley observed.

A consultation issued thereon.

The landlord, who was a remarkably ill-looking savage fellow, and who, to judge from his countenance, was by no means averse to bloodshed, as he would have made them believe, suggested broadswords, informing the combatants that there were some to be had on the premises.

The doctor inclined to pistols.

Jefferson, however, objected to them, upon the score of them not being sufficiently dangerous.

The colonel suggested firing across the dining-table.

Jefferson said that was so soon over.

Charley made no remark.

"I shall be murdered somehow," he said to himself. "There's no other way out of it."

Julia clung to his arm. She was agitated by conflicting emotions.

She was afraid for her lover's life; but she was anxious for him to acquit himself bravely, and come out of the affair with flying colours.

"I'll tell you what," said Jefferson. "Let's fight a duel as they do in America."

"We'll fight as they do in Timbuctoo, if you like," replied Charley.

"How do they fight in America?" asked the landlord.

"In the dark," replied Jefferson.

"Yes; in the dark."

"What with?"

"With knives and pistols."

"How many pistols?"

"I have two double-barrelled revolvers."

"Two shots each, then."

"Yes; and a knife each."

"What knives?"

"I have got them."

"Do you agree to this?" asked the colonel.

"Have you the courage?" asked Jefferson.

"Yes," replied Charley, stoutly, "if you have."

XLVIII.—MATTERS GROW WORSE.

I DO not intend to try to deny that Master Charley felt a little uncomfortable.

Julia protested against such a horrible kind of duel. An exchange of shots at a reasonable distance, would be quite sufficient, she said, and insisted that Charley should decline the fight altogether.

The surgeon also said, that he thought they were going much too far, and that there was no occasion for such awful extremities. Still, he did not vote for the affair being dropped altogether; because, since it had been proposed, a strong desire to be a witness of the encounter had seized upon him.

The landlord most decidedly was strongly in favour of the meeting. To tell the truth, he was highly delighted; and nothing would have afforded him more pleasure, than to see these two slash and hack at one another, or blow one another's brains out, as long as it was done without any danger of his being brought within the pale of the law by so doing.

But it would never do to have the fight take place in the inn. What occurred outside he was not responsible for.

Let them fight in the barn, and he would be all right. He could go round quietly and see the fun, as he thought it, without being seen himself.

Besides, what harm need come of it?

Even supposing it terminated fatally for one of the parties, which was by no means the most improbable result to be anticipated, there was the surgeon, who could give a certificate of death, if he liked, and the affair might be hushed up quietly.

However the surgeon was pretty well of the same way of thinking as the landlord: he would very much have liked the fight to come off, only he was afraid.

Man is decidedly a cruel animal, whatever the lovers of their species may urge to the contrary; and the most tenderhearted amongst us find pleasure in causing pain somehow or another.

Jefferson would fight, however, and insisted that the duel should take place in the way that he had suggested.

"Mind you," whispered the colonel in Charley's ear, "you've a precious sight better chance that way than any other. The devil's a dead shot; and if he could see you, he'd pick you off as easy as I could hit a haystack at ten paces."

"In that case," said Charley, "perhaps it's as well that it came off in the dark."

"How's it going to be?" the landlord whispered to the colonel, when the latter had left the room, and gone to the bar for a light to his cigar.

"It's to be in the dark, sir; and it will be all right if we can only keep the place clear. Who is there about the house?"

"My wife has gone out to spend the evening. We must get rid of the waiter somehow."

"Yes; and this young woman that's with Wag? She'll spoil it, I feel certain."

"How's it to be worked, do you think?"

"The best way will be this," said the landlord, with a wink. "I'll take her on one side, and get her to go for the police."

"What do you mean?" the other demanded, angrily.

"Bah! don't you understand?"

"No."

"Why, we want to get her out of the way, don't we?"

"Yes; but we don't want the police."

"We shan't have them."

"But if you send for them?"

"She won't find them, for I shall send her wrong."

"Aha! that makes a difference."

"A slight difference."

"You're right. Send her, by all means."

A little time afterwards, the landlord took the opportunity of getting Julia for a moment by herself.

"This duel mustn't come off," said he.

"No, no," replied Julia, earnestly; "by no means."

"It would be murder."

"It would be horrid murder."

"You, then, are the only person who can prevent it."

"I?"

"Yes; by going for the police."

"But could not you? I do not like to leave my friend."

"You must go, I say. I cannot leave the house. Besides, surely it's more consequence to you than to me."

"Where shall I find the police? Are they close at hand?"

"Not very. They are about two miles off."

"Are there none in the town?"

"No. You must go to the nearest magistrate's. He lives about two miles off, straight up the road to the right. A large white house, on the top of the hill. You will easily find it."

"I can ask if I do not."

"No," said the landlord, hastily; "you mustn't ask. Go straight, and as quick as possible."

"Will you get me my horse?"

"Don't take it, miss, or they may hear you from the parlour, and prevent it. Them two foreign looking chaps are bloodthirsty enough for anything almost, in my opinion."

"But if I do not ride I shall be so long going. I shall be too late. The worst may have happened before I can return."

The landlord's object in thus sending her upon a wild-goose chase in search of the magistrate, whom he knew for a positive fact to be away from home, was to gain as much time as possible.

Julia fell in the trap, and without a word to anyone, slipped out of the house, and made the best of her way in the direction indicated.

She was in a few moments free of the town, and hurrying as fast as she could go up the hill leading to the white house.

When she had been gone about ten minutes, the landlord made his appearance in the parlour, pretending to be agitated and out of breath.

"If you want to have any fighting," said he, "you'd better get it over pretty sharp; for the young woman's bolted off on her horse for the police, and they'll be here in half-an-hour at the outside."

"That's a courageous trick of yours," said Jefferson, with a contemptuous laugh, addressing Charley. "I thought it of you."

"Do you suppose I sent her?" retorted Charley, in a towering rage.

"I haven't a doubt of it," replied Jefferson, coolly.

"You're a liar, then!" cried Charley; "and if you think so, let us fire now, across this table."

"No, no," said the colonel; "we'll have it in the dark, only let's look sharp about it."

Although Charley would have been highly delighted if he could have escaped from the contest with honour, yet feeling that he could not do so, he was determined to go through with it in a plucky way; for he was a courageous young fellow, as you know as well as I do.

The party, without further parley, went out to the back-yard, in search of the barn.

Over this was a loft, which they judged to be exactly suited for the purpose.

The shades of night had been falling upon the little village for some time past, and it was now quite dark. When the landlord and the colonel went up into the loft, and leaving the lantern outside, looked round them, to see if there were any chinks or openings through which the light could penetrate, the darkness was as profound as that of a closed tomb.

Pronouncing this to be exactly as it ought to be, the colonel led the way out to where the combatants were waiting for them.

He then suggested that they should take off their boots, so that they could walk noiselessly in the dark; but Jefferson voted that they should only wear a thin pair of drawers, and be otherwise naked, with a belt made of handkerchiefs round their waists, to hold the weapons.

This being agreed to, they had each a double-barrelled pistol and an American knife-dagger given to them. And it was determined that in case of either of the combatants being disabled by either pistol or knife, the other should shout out for the door to be opened, and the duel should be considered over.

The combatants assenting to this, they were carefully blindfolded by the landlord and the surgeon, and conducted to opposite corners of the loft, with instructions not to touch their bandages until they received a signal from below.

In dead silence they were taken to their places by the landlord and surgeon.

Then these two seconds retired cautiously on tiptoe, and closed the door carefully behind them.

The combatants waited a moment anxiously for the signal. It was three blows on the ceiling below.

Simultaneously they removed the bandages, and stood stock still in the pitch darkness, scarcely daring to breathe.

*   *   *   *   *

XLIX.—THE DUEL IN THE DARK.

THUS they remained for at least three minutes, neither daring to stir a limb, for fear of enabling his adversary by the action to judge of his position in the room.

When at last one ventures to glide a few steps along by the wall, he did it with the stealth and caution of a cat stealing upon a mouse.

The listeners below strained their ears to catch the faintest sound above, but heard nothing.

All was still as death.

They held their breath, like those above, and listened.

So intense was the anxiety and expectation of the listeners, that nothing like it can be conceived by anybody who has not assisted at a similar scene.

It was almost impossible to remain calm and patient in the state of dread suspense and expectancy in which they were thrown by the long prolonged silence; a silence which, the longer it endured, seemed to grow more and more ominous and terrible.

The listeners' hearts beat quickly, as they asked themselves how and when it would terminate.

But if the suspense of the listeners was thus intense, what must have been the feelings of the combatants?

Let us see how Charley fared.

When he had summoned up sufficient courage to move, and had glided on for about three or four yards, feeling his way cautiously by the wall, he paused all at once, with the horrible reflection that perhaps the other might be working his way round to him in a like manner from the opposite side.

At any moment they might meet—might touch—might feel their hot breaths upon each other's cheeks.

No, he would go no further.

The best and safest plan, if any plan in such an awful position could be considered to be safe, would be to stand still, and listen for the other's movements, and then to fire.

And Charley reflected with a shudder, that perhaps his adversary was then adopting the same plan, and listening for him.

He mentally thanked God that he had not stumbled in making the movement that he had, and that he had so noiselessly reached the spot where he now stood.

He listened—he listened intently.

Not a sound—not the faintest possible creak, or rustle, or crackling noise.

The darkness was as profound as ever.

It was thick, heavy, and choking, and seemed, as it were, to hem in and press him back.

To his excited imagination, there was a dull throbbing in the atmosphere, or in his head.

Every moment he felt as though he must cry out or die.

He felt as though the other's face was close up against his own, and that his eyeballs were glaring into his; and so strong was this impression at one time, that he stretched out his hand in the dark to feel whether such was not really the case.

But how long was this to last? Would it never terminate?

The protracted agony of fear was perfectly awful.

Charley's feelings were much like those of a man standing upon the drop of a scaffold, listening to the words of the chaplain, who is to give the signal for the withdrawal of the bolt.

Or of a poor wretch lying upon his back upon the guillotine, looking up at the glittering blade, which in a moment is to fall and slice away his head.

Or, worst of all, like the unhappy Indians, whom a humane and never sufficiently to be lauded British soldiery tied to the mouths of guns, and blew to pieces, during the Indian war.

It seemed to our hero that the silence had been of an hour's duration, but it in reality could not have been a quarter of that time.

By slow degrees his eyes became in some measure accustomed to the darkness, and he was able gradually to perceive tiny chinks of light in the walls.

An idea occurred to him.

To ascertain whether his enemy was moving, he would watch one of these right opposite to him intently.

Should it become darkened, he would fire straight at it.

When this horrible mode of duelling had been first proposed to him, he had not realized half its terrors.

Now he felt them. At first he had fancied that nothing but a harmless exchange of shots, or at most a scratch with the knives, would have terminated the affair in ten minutes' time.

But now he felt convinced that little short of Jefferson's death would save his life.

And how could he hope to be able to master the other, a dead shot, probably, and expert handler of the murderous knife—for all he knew, a professional duellist and butcherer.

He had neither the strength, or address, or experience of his antagonist.

When he came to think over what had happened, he felt convinced that he had been lured to his own destruction by these men, who probably took the same brutal pleasure in his butchery that some ruffians do in a dog fight, or the worrying to death of a poor cat.

When he felt the full horror of his position, he was at one moment upon the point of calling aloud for help, and so escaping from the almost certain death which awaited him.

But would he so escape?

Would not the sound of his voice rather be the sign of his whereabouts, which the American was waiting for, and his instant death result from his imprudence?

Then a ray of hope broke in upon him.

Would Julia return with the police?

Could he hope to live till then?

No; it was not likely. He felt that though the time had seemed long to him, probably but a very brief interval had passed since he first entered the loft. In a very few moments more he would probably be shot down.

And for what?

When he came to think over all the stupid quarrel from the beginning, he could not help asking himself in astonishment—what did it matter? Why should they fight? How was it they were going to fight?

With this thought came another—a horrible one. Had it all been arranged? Was it a plot—a plan—a plant, by which he had been ensnared, and from which his death would result?

Had Julia been sent out of the way? Was he there in a pit, in a hole, to be killed like a rat?

Then he asked himself, with a faint hope breaking in upon him: Why should he think that he was trapped? What had he done, that they should use him so? But next moment he reflected how foolish it was to argue thus with himself. Here he was, and there was no escape for him, unless in the death of his antagonist.

All these thoughts, though they have taken me some time to transcribe, occupied Charley's brain but a very small space of time.

When not engaged with them, he had enough to do to listen.

To listen for the awful tread of his destroyer in the dark.

He listened, and held his breath.

His heart throbbed as though it would burst his breast.

His nostrils quivered—his eyeballs throbbed —the veins rose up swollen and matted in his throat and on his forehead.

He felt as though something in his head would burst.

But this state of awful suspense was not to last long.

Suddenly he was startled by a movement in the room. Directly in front of him, and, as it appeared by the sound, at a distance of four or five yards, there was a faint noise, as though of a light footfall, or the rustle of some article of clothing.

He had not time to think about it, or come to any decision.

One thing seemed clear to him—his antagonist was at that spot.

Now, then, had the moment for action arrived.

Pointing his pistol at the spot from whence the noise had proceeded, he fired.

The flash of the pistol for a moment illuminated the apartment with the faintest flicker, but enough for him to see that his foe was not near the spot where he had expected to find him; but on the floor lay some cloth, which had fallen and made the noise he had heard.

Yes, he was sure of it.

The truth flashed upon him like stroke of lightning.

The American had thus thrown the cloth which had been used to bandage his eyes, in order that the noise might mislead his antagonist.

In this way, Charley firing, would be led to expose his position in the room.

The light would enable the American to take aim at him.

All these ideas had been perfectly correct. Charley fired, as we have seen, and the next moment the sound of the American's revolver rang through the apartment.

The ball struck Charley's arm, and by a sharp and severe twinge it gave him, he felt that it had entered the flesh, while he felt a hot liquid trickling down towards his finger ends, which he knew to be blood.

The mere fact of the darkness made his wound seem much more formidable than it would have done.

It is true he felt satisfied in his own mind that no bones had been broken; but then, might not the ball have cut some artery?

Perhaps he might bleed to death?

Then a greater danger occurred to him.

In spite of all his efforts to staunch the flow of blood, it poured through his hands and the handkerchief which he had taken from his neck, and with which he as noiselessly as possible endeavoured to tie up the wound.

In spite of all his efforts to prevent it, the blood fell with a dripping sound, faint, but distinct, in the otherwise unbroken silence of the room.

Charley would have fired at the other at once, but he felt that he could not have made sure of his aim.

When he had fired last, his eyes had been directed towards the spot where the cloth had fallen; and when he had been hit, he had not been able to tell from whence the blow came.

He had only one shot left, and it would not do to throw it away.

Therefore, he stood quite still, thinking it most likely that the other would think that he had changed his position, and used his utmost endeavours to stop the flow of blood.

But a death-like faintness began to steal over him.

He felt that he was beginning to grow dizzy, and he clutched at the wall to save himself from falling.

But the wall was at some distance, and he missed his aim as he tried to clutch it.

With an exclamation of alarm and pain, he fell heavily to the ground.

Next moment his antagonist was by his side, had placed his knee upon his breast, and had grasped his throat with his bony fingers, which closed upon it like a vice.

Then the boy, with a sensation of sickening horror, felt him groping about on his breast for his heart, and felt the cold steel of the cruel knife against his flesh.

———

L.—VERY NEAR TO DEATH—WHICH IS WHICH— A HORRIBLE SPECTACLE—JULIA'S RETURN.

BUT was he to die like this? Surely not.

Was no greater destiny in store for Charley Wag, after all he had gone through?

It perhaps was some mysterious monitor within which bade him make an effort, for his time had not yet arrived.

Let that be as it may, an effort most certainly he made. At least, he shook off the stupor of fright which seemed to be creeping over him; and seizing the pistol from his belt just at the critical moment that the Yankee was about to thrust the knife into his heart, and fired.

With a stifled scream the American sprang to his feet, and then fell forward again with a heavy groan, and lay a dead weight across the others body.

The blood from the gaping wound gushed out and deluged the boy's body.

Sick with horror and loss of blood from his own wound, Charley struggled for a while desperately, but unsuccessfully, to free himself of the loathsome burden which held him down.

But the efforts which he made grew momentarily weaker and weaker.

At length he fell back, his head striking heavily against the oaken floor.

Then he fainted.

The men down-stairs listened in the most profound silence for a length of time, after the sound of the boy's head upon the boards above had reached their ears.

Full ten minutes passed like this, and not a word was uttered on either side.

At length the landlord broke the silence.

"Well?"

"It's over," whispered the other.

"What shall we do?"

"We'd better go and look."

"Yes. Just peep outside that all's right, will you, while I strike a light?"

The colonel went as he was desired to the barn-door, treading cautiously, that he might not be heard.

Then screening his eyes, he looked out into the night.

There was no one within sight, and all was still.

He returned to his companion, fastening the door behind him.

The landlord was striking a match at the time, and the blue flame cast a livid light upon his strongly marked features, and upon those of the colonel.

They looked like two demons, as they stood there over that tiny light.

When the candle was lit, the landlord stood to listen again.

"There is no noise," he said, in a hoarse whisper; "let us go up-stairs."

Without any reply, the colonel made a motion with his hand for the other to lead the way, and they proceeded silently up the steep steps towards the loft.

When they reached the top, they both paused, as though by mutual consent, outside the door.

The awful silence had something portentous in it.

Neither of them liked to enter, for they knew not what dreadful sight might await them.

That they would find one dead body, they never doubted.

But perhaps there might be two.

And how would they be mangled, and where would they be lying?

Perhaps one, all stabbed, and torn, and bloody, might fall forward upon them as they opened the door.

The horror of finding one still quivering and writhing in his death's agony, seemed greater than to find them both dead.

It was, as they stood here at the door, that these two inhuman brutes, began to regret that they had been aiders and abettors in such a sanguinary encounter; and the anticipated horror of the bloody scene they were soon to see, entirely overcame the feeling of brutal, savage pleasure, which the notion of the fight had at first inspired them with.

However, they must sooner or later enter the room, and know the worst.

The landlord, therefore, without further delay, summoned up courage, and thrust open the door.

Then he held the light high above his head, and looked in.

"Good God!"

He might well make the exclamation, for the scene which his eyes fell upon was appalling in its horror.

The colonel pushed forward, and glared over his shoulder at the terrible spectacle.

There, on the floor, so bathed in blood as to be at first perfectly unrecognizable, lay the insensible body of Charley Wag; whilst across his breast, with a face hideously distorted, and breast torn and shattered in a dreadful manner, lay the body of the American.

The latter they raised first.

"How is it?" whispered the landlord.

The colonel laid his hand upon his friend's breast.

He started back.

The landlord looked towards him anxiously.

"Dead," said the colonel, in a faint voice.

"Sure?"

"Quite sure. He's stone dead."

"And the boy?"

"He seems little better."

"It's a case with him, too."

"It looks like it. This has been a bloody night's business."

"Stay, stay! Thank God the boy's all right, after all. His heart's beating feebly."

"Bring him on this way, then."

"How can I? I shall get my clothes all over blood. I don't exactly want to do that."

"It can be managed like this," said the landlord, after a little reflection. "Here's a piece of old sacking; we'll wrap that round him, and then I can lift him easily."

So saying, he took the boy up in his arms, wrapped round, as he had said, with an old piece of sackcloth.

The colonel held the light, and the other helped him down-stairs.

Then, laying him down upon the stones, they fetched some water from a pump, and dashed it over his face.

The cold liquid revived him, and presently he managed languidly to open his eyes, and gaze around him.

The landlord was just about to address some words to him, when the sound of voices in the house attracted his attention.

"What's that?" he cried, starting to his feet. "Come with me. It may be the police that woman has brought with her, or some other assistance. Bring the light. No; leave it there. Come with me."

The colonel did as the other wished, and they hurried into the tavern, leaving the door of the barn pulled to, but not closed after them.

"I wish it had been the other," said the landlord, as they went along; "at least, as far as I am concerned."

"Why so?" the other asked. "Jefferson was a devilish good fellow when he wasn't quarreling. But you did not know him."

"My reason is this," said the landlord. "That young prig's pockets were full of tin. I felt in them when the shindy was going on."

"The devil you did! Was it anything worth sticking to?"

"It was gold, I could tell by the feel."

"How much?"

"Fifty pound, I should say, at the least."

"Let's stick to it, then."

"But how can we?"

"Well, we can slit his wizen if he won't let us have it."

"To be sure. That is, if you're game."

"I'm game for anything."

Hardly had they entered the inn, when the door leading into the barn where Charley had been left was pushed open, and Julia looked in.

Next moment she was by her lover's side, kneeling on the ground, and supporting his head.

"Oh, Charley, Charley! You are, then, alive."

CHARLEY SAVES THE YOUNG DUKE.

"Yes," he answered, faintly; "I've got through it somehow. I can't tell you how it was managed."

"Dear love, you must come with me at once. Can you walk, do you think?"

"I'll try."

"There, there, I see you can't; you are so weak."

"What is to be done?"

"I'll manage somehow," she said, with determination.

"But how?"

"You shall see."

"Are the police here?" asked Charley, presently.

"No."

"I thought you had gone to fetch them. They said so."

No. 44.

"So I did; but the landlord directed me wrong—on purpose, I suspect. I found it out, though, before I had gone very far, and that determined me upon returning as quickly as possible. I learnt from a man in the neighbourhood that there was only one policeman within the next six miles, and that it would be a great chance if I found him. They don't have many police in these quiet country places, you know. Then, too, I came to reflect, if I brought the police, I should be as good as locking you up; so I made up my mind to return again alone, and try what I could do to save you myself. But come; where are your clothes? We must waste no more time."

While she had been speaking, Julia was busily employed bandaging Charley's arm with a small scarf, which she had worn round her neck.

[CHARLEY WAG, THE NEW JACK SHEPPARD.

She looked round now on all sides for his clothes, but they were nowhere visible.

Indeed, the landlord had quietly taken the opportunity, when the colonel was not looking at him, to hide them in a chest in a corner of the barn; so that, in case Charley should be killed, he could appropriate the contents of the pockets without any trouble.

"I can't find them," she said.

"But we cannot leave them," said Charley. "There is a lot of money in the pockets."

"We must, Charley. I hear them coming back. If we do not escape from these wretches you will be murdered. Here is an old rough coat belonging to some one; take this. There, let me help you on with it. That's it. Now let us be off."

"But, Julia, I cannot stand."

"Never mind that; I'll lift you."

"You lift me? You won't be able."

"Don't talk nonsense. You are not very big, or very heavy, Charley, although you are such a great man."

And so saying, the brave girl raised him in her arms, and bore him along towards a gate, which led out from the yard into a lane at the side of the house.

When she had got him here, she rested him upon the ground, and stopped to get breath.

"How are we to get along?" said she, considering, and addressing herself more than her companion. "You would not be able to sit on your horse, even if we could get the horses, which I am almost afraid would be impossible. No; we must get away in some other manner, and return for them afterwards. But how is it to be? I cannot carry you, that is quite sure. What is to be done?"

While she spoke, there arose a loud shout within the yard. It was the voice of the landlord she heard, saying:

"He's gone! he's gone!"

"Gone?" she heard the colonel reply. "Impossible! How could he have gone? He was next to dead."

"He's gone, I tell you. Come here, and look."

"He can't have got very far, though. We'll soon have him."

Julia did not wait to hear any more.

With a strength which desperation lent to her, she caught her lover again in her arms, and bore him resolutely forward.

About twenty or thirty yards down the lane she came to another which crossed it at right angles.

Here she was obliged to pause again for a moment for breath.

And doing so, she heard the sound of wheels approaching.

"Which way is it going?" she said to herself; and then, after a moment's reflection, "Well, it doesn't matter," she continued, "if they will only take us; it doesn't matter which way they are going, as long as we escape from here."

In a few moments the vehicle came up.

It was a cart, which looked like a butcher's.

An old man, wrapped up warmly with a sack across his shoulders, sat in front driving.

"Stop!" cried Julia, when the cart approached.

But the driver seemed inclined to go faster instead.

Julia, however, rushed forward, and caught hold of the bridle.

"Hallo, there!" cried the old man, greatly astonished. "What do you want?"

"I want a ride in your cart," she replied.

"You can't have one."

"I must. This poor boy I have with me is dying. Stop, I say."

"I can't take him; there's no room."

"Yes there is—plenty. Besides, I'll pay you well."

When the old man heard this, he grew less restive.

"I'll lift him in," said he.

"No," said Julia; "sit where you are; I can manage it. There, now make room for me. Thank you. Now drive as fast as you can."

"Where do you want to go?" asked the driver presently.

"Where are you going?" asked Julia, by way of reply.

"I'm going to a place just below Northfleet," said the man. "I've got something I'm taking to the captain of a vessel lying there."

"That will do," said Julia. "Drive on."

Just then, as they were going over a soft piece of road, Julia fancied she could hear the sound of horses' hoofs behind them.

"They're after us," she thought, and she covered up her companion, who lay at the bottom of the cart. "Drive as fast as you can," said she; "you won't lose by it."

The horses' hoofs sounded more distinct, then ceased.

"They have gone back," she thought. "Perhaps we are safe for a while."

"I am very cold," said Charley, with a shiver.

It was getting cold, and a wind was springing up; a few heavy drops of rain, too, were falling.

"We shall have a squally night of it," said the driver, "or I'm much mistaken."

LI.—The Flight.

A DREARIER drive of a dreary evening none need wish for.

As the night progressed, occasional showers were borne on the gusty wind, sweeping past as though hurrying to some elemental congress far away; while along the shore of the Thames, which they had now approached, the water beat with a sharp irregular plash, and the wind whistled across it with a low, mournful cadence, which made one think that there must be wild weather at sea.

The fitful moonlight rather heightened than diminished the dismal aspect of the scenery.

For miles the bleak marsh land stretched away, no headland or hillock marking the river's bank.

The spectral gable of a lonely church being the only object visible against the leaden sky.

The stunted brushes and rank grass round the poor graves rustling in the night wind sounded like ghostly whispers.

The driver looked half scared as he passed the ghostly spot, but Julia took no heed of it.

To wrap herself tighter in her shawl was all that the dreary scene exacted from her; and, except when a vivid flash of lightning made the horse swerve from the road, and dash down into the rough shingle of the strand, she made no remark, and adverted to neither way nor weather.

"There's too much wind here to get along," the driver said; "but we must stick to it."

They had entered now upon a low, sandy road, that traversed a wide and dreary tract, barely elevated a few feet above the river.

By degrees the little patches of grass and fern disappeared, and nothing stretched on either side but low sand hummocks, scantily covered with rushes; and by their side the water dashed upon the shore, and showered white spray around it like an angry ocean.

"There's a light ahead," the driver said. "That must be the boat. Are you going any further?"

"We'll go on to that public-house you spoke of, where you are going to put up."

"It's a rum thing," the driver remarked presently, "that you should have happened to meet me, if you was going this way."

"Yes," said Julia, shortly; "it is."

They lumbered forward again as well as they could, in the direction the driver had seen the light.

They floundered heavily on, the wheels sinking nearly to the axles, and the horse stumbling every step.

"Here we are at last," said the driver, pulling up at length before a low white house. "This is where I am to find the captain."

The captain was inside, and came out at the sound of the wheels to meet them.

"Oh, you're here at last," said he. "Have you brought the parcels with you?"

"Yes, captain."

"That's all right. Hallo! you've got company, haven't you?"

There were several more seafaring men in the public-house, who came out and stood there in the ruddy light flowing from the door; but the most conspicuous figure of the group was decidedly he whom the driver had designated "captain."

This was a Dutch-built old sailor, with a face browned and tanned by the suns and seas of every latitude, from the Line to the Antarctic Circle; for the captain, as Julia afterwards learnt, had led a tolerably roving life.

He had harpooned whales amid the icebergs, and shipped negroes from the Bight of Benin. He had groped his way through the Straits of Magellan, and smuggled opium in China.

The man had passed a long life, which was nothing but a series of escapes from death.

But the captain was tough.

The yellow fever could not kill him in Cuba, and he had weathered through the plague in the Levant.

He had once had a wonderful escape from being roasted on the white beach of a beauteous coral island in the South Seas, and had been all but snapped up by a shark in the middle of the surf at Madras.

Julia was not very long before she ascertained from the captain's yarns, that he had not only been a great traveller, but that he had travelled under many masters.

Many colours had flown over the grizzled head of this sailor of fortune.

When he was a man-of-war's man off the coast of Africa, he had chased slavers; and when he sailed as mate on board a slaver, he had evaded a man-of-war.

He had knocked about the Baltic under the glaring flag of the Hanse Towns.

He had hoisted the tricolor on board a Brest lugger very unfavourably known to the English revenue cruisers.

He had served the Spaniard west of the Horn, and the Dutchman amid the spicy islands of the Indian Archipelago.

The captain had battled with nor-westers on the banks of Newfoundland, in a clipper Yankee schooner, and seen white squalls amid the isles of Greece in a trim Maltese speronare.

There was no rig he did not understand, and he had a good spattering of the naval terms in most languages; and to hear him talk, you would have supposed that there was no cape which he had not doubled, and no roadstead in which he had not anchored.

Decidedly there was a nautical cut about the captain. He looked a regular T. P. COOKE.

He had a tremendous pair of gray whiskers, and a head of flowing wiry gray hair.

His coat was blown open, and as he stood there, the wind spreading out his loose canvas trousers, he looked something gigantic.

"You've got company, haven't you?" he repeated.

"Well, yes," the driver replied, with hesitation.

"Allow me to help you out, miss," said the captain, offering Julia his red fist.

"Thank you," said the young lady; "I'll jump down myself; but perhaps you will kindly help me with my husband, who is ill."

"Your husband!"

The captain looked round with a puzzled expression.

But the driver had mounted into the cart again, and was now busy helping Julia to assist Charley from the vehicle.

He had fainted, but several of the seafaring men came forward, and helped to raise him, and lift him from the cart into the house.

"Why, shiver my timbers!" exclaimed the captain, with a good sound nautical oath, "the boy's got no clothes on, and he's bleeding!"

"He has been bleeding," Julia replied, "but I have bound up the wound."

"Well," observed the captain, looking at Charley with a puzzled expression, and scratching his head the while, "there's been rum goings on, I should say, where this young gentleman came from."

"He has been almost murdered," Julia replied; "and would have been murdered, had we not escaped by the aid of this person, who has brought us on here, as you see, in his cart."

"And where may you be bound for, miss, if it's not an impertinent question?"

"I haven't the least idea, sir."

"Well, that's odd, too."

"We will stop here for the present, sir," replied Julia, "and move on to-morrow."

"The young gent's coming round," observed the captain, as Charley began to show signs of returning consciousness.

"Where am I?" asked our hero, faintly.

"You're in good hands, sir," replied the captain. "Don't be alarmed, and keep yourself quiet. You're badly hurt, I'm sure."

"No, no," replied Charley; "it's only a little bit of a scratch. It is the loss of blood that has made me weak."

The captain looked at him very hard indeed, almost as though he recognized him, or was endeavouring to call to mind where he had seen the boy before.

But upon reflection, Julia was inclined to attribute it to the fact of his wound, and his mysterious dress.

The other men, however, after staring at the couple for some little time, lounged out upon the beach to look after their boat, mumbling a little among themselves, but not seeming to take much notice of what Julia and her lover were doing.

The wife of the landlord of the little inn came forward very pleasantly, and offered her assistance in making Charley comfortable; and he lay presently propped up by pillows and cushions upon a large sofa in the room behind the bar, looking as easy and happy as, under the circumstances, you could well have expected to have found him.

But scarcely had all the things been thus arranged, than the tramping of a horse's hoofs became audible without.

Julia started to her feet.

"Good heavens!" she cried; "that must be our pursuers. Oh, protect my husband, sir! He is not strong enough to help himself in this state. Shut the door, for God's sake! and keep them out."

"Don't be afraid of them, whoever they are," cried the captain. "I don't know who your husband is, or what he's done, but keelhaul me for a lubber if I wouldn't keep out the devil and all his imps, if it was necessary, to get a smile from those rosy lips of yours."

Hardly had he time, however, to shut and bolt the door, when a loud shout arose without.

"House, there—house!" a voice cried, which Julia recognized as the colonel's. But she was much reassured to find he was alone.

"Now, then," responded the captain, through the window; "what do you want, mister?"

"You've got a young fellow inside that's committed a murder, and I want to put a pair of handcuffs on him—that's all."

"Oh, that's all," responded the captain, cheerfully. "Well, that's not much, certainly; and what's this 'ere murderous party's name?"

"He's a well-known thief," replied the other, "and his name's Charley Wag."

On hearing this, the captain staggered back as though he had been struck.

After a moment or two, he seemed to recover himself a little.

"There's no such person here," said he. "What made you think there was?"

"Well I made inquiries along the road, at the tollbar, a mile off, and they saw a cart pass containing a young woman, who, by the description, must be the same that was with him at the house where he fought and killed an American gentleman, in a duel with knives and pistols."

"He hasn't come on here, anyhow. Was it a fair fight?"

"As fair as those sort of things usually are. But are you certain he has not been here? Have you seen him pass?"

"No," said the captain.

"Very well," replied the colonel, after a pause; "I'll get on the road a bit. But I'll have him yet, or I'll know why; and if I do, by gosh he shall swing for it?"

So saying, the other galloped off up the lonely road.

When he was gone, the captain closed the window, and returned to Julia.

"Is he asleep?" he asked, motioning with his hand towards Charley.

Then, hearing that he was not, he went to the side of the sofa, and took his hand.

"Are you strong enough to be moved, do you think?"

"Quite," said Charley. "Why?"

"Because, if what that chap says is true, you mustn't stop here; it won't be safe. Have you killed a man in a duel, as he was saying?"

"I don't know," replied Charley. "I was very nearly killed myself. How I escaped was a miracle. He had me down, and was going to stab me, when I shot him."

"Going to stab you when you were down, was he? Serve him right, then. But, you see, you may come to grief if you stop here. You must both of you come with me."

"Come with you?—where?"

"Over the water, to France. I've got a neat little craft by the water side, that will sail in an hour's time, at the latest. What do you say?"

"I'm agreeable," said Charley. "But you are very kind."

"Never mind that," said the captain, with a strange sort of huskiness in his voice. "I ought to be to you."

"To me?"

"Your name's Charley Wag, isn't it?"

"Yes."

"And you're a thief?"

"I am," replied Charley, rather bashfully.

"Well, I'm a smuggler, which ain't much better; and my name is—what do you think?"

"Indeed, sir, I can't tell."

"Nonsense! Look at me. Don't you know me?"

"No."

"Don't you remember my voice?"

"I think I do, a little; and I almost fancy I know your face. But oh! it cannot be!"

"But it is."

"What, are you—"

"Yes, I am."

"You don't mean to say you are the same—"

"None other."

"Julia! Julia!" cried Charley, starting up, "what do you think?'

"What?" cried Julia, equally excited.

"Why, here is my dear old guardian and godfather come to life again. This is Mr. Toddleboy, that you have heard me talk about so much."

"Gracious goodness me!" cried Julia, throwing her arms round his neck. "I must kiss him, then, just for his kindness to you."

LII.—The Storm.

ROLLING and rocking, with a weary sickly motion, upon the successive ridges of a tumbling ground-swell, her timbers cracking and creaking as she wallowed in the deep trough of the ocean, and her canvas flapping in loud surges against the rigging which restrained it, there lay upon the stormy sea a small but strongly built cutter, with sharply cut bows, and a low, long, and elegant quarter.

The night had become more lowering and gloomier still.

The changeful breeze, which had blown in puffs in the earlier part of the evening, had subsided, and, with the exception of the slight movements and currents of air, partly, if not wholly, produced by the heaving of the waters, there was not a breath of air to agitate the heavy oppressive atmosphere which appeared to brood over the sea.

Above, all was pitch dark, except every now and then, when a star would peep out from the dark sky, and as quickly hide itself again.

All on board the cutter was hushed.

The tiller was lashed amidships, and the steersman, whose post in a calm is next door to being a sinecure, was sitting on the low taffrail, swaying his body backwards and forwards, as it were, to keep time to the swaying motion of the vessel, and occasionally looking anxiously out in the direction of the shore they had left behind.

Presently, a man joined him from below.

"She's all right now, sir," said the steersman, in answer to some question the other had addressed to him. "Her head is west by south now; but she's been boxing round for the last hour and a half."

The other man looked ahead on all sides. It was the captain, and he knew the Channel well, and from the lights visible on the horizon could fix at once the position of the vessel.

One bright light he knew burnt in the market-place of Calais, two lights, placed one above another, denoted the bold promontory called the South Foreland, and a low ruddy speck in the far distance was the harbour-light of Dover.

They were in the Straits of Dover, about ten miles off the English coast.

"It's going to be a rough night," said Captain Toddleboy, "or else I'm no sailor. Look at that there sea; it's beginning to comb white hair. We'd better take in a reef. We shall be plunging bows under, with three reefs in the mainsail and a storm-jib, before long."

"You're about right there, captain," said the other; "and I'd wager a jorum of grog, that before daybreak we'll be either lying-to under a trysail, or scudding under next to nothing at all, as if the very Old Harry was a punching of us behind."

The gale was not long in coming.

The wind was strengthening fast. A low hoarse roar—the mingled sound of the moving current of air and of the combing and breaking crests of the rough waves—made itself heard amidst the plunging of the cutter and the noisy flapping of the heavy sails overhead.

"Look out, there! look out!" bawled the captain, with all the strength of his lungs. "Stand firm—it's a coming."

He had scarcely time to utter these words, however, before a tremendous gust of bitterly cold air swept by them with terrific violence, filling out all the sails, and swaying the cutter down almost flat upon its side in the water under the violence of the shock.

But righting herself after a while from the shock, the cutter manfully struck her bows into the rolling sea, sending the stormy waters flying over her weather-bulwarks from the bowsprit pretty nearly to the mast, and then lifting herself up gallantly from the encounter, and flinging by a violent lurch the sea from her decks, the little vessel sped onwards towards the French coast.

What Captain Toddleboy had predicted about the weather turned out true enough. In less than an hour the cutter was bounding from sea to sea, driving her sharp bows into the rolling masses of water with occasional shocks, which caused her to tremble like a leaf, but still kept on upon her wild career, urged forward by the straining and crowded canvas.

It looked dangerous enough to an inexperienced land-lubber, but to a tar of some surprising bravery and coolness, as the redoubtable Captain Toddleboy seemed to be, there was nothing to excite alarm.

Above, all was dark as pitch.

The gale continued to increase in strength, the howling hurricane of wind coming heavy with the driving foam, which it caught upon its course in showers from the angry waters.

The captain, assisted by one of his men, took his place at the tiller, watching the run of the seas, and carefully easing off the cutter's bow, as each volume of the curving waves swept hissing past her cutwater.

Charley and Julia, who had come up from below to breathe the fresh air, stood upon the weather-quarter in a sheltered nook, and the boy's eyes sparkled with unwonted excitement, as the stubborn little vessel beneath him leaped, and bounded, and drove madly through the dark waters.

The excitement was new and strange to him, and he enjoyed it thoroughly.

The raging battle of the elements seemed to find an echo in the tumultuous yearnings within his own breast.

A strange presentiment had for some time past possessed him. He thought, somehow, that he had reached, as it were, a great climax in his life, or the commencement of some new career; a career of bolder, wilder, more daring adventure, and greater gain than he had hitherto achieved.

He could not tell what was coming, what was in store for him; but as the stormy wind howled aloud, and the wet canvas dragged and strained against the resistance of the tightly strung stays, and the labouring cutter walled with tremendous plunges into the frothing waves, his busy brain seemed to manufacture out of the deafening uproar a sort of bold rough music to accompany his thoughts.

"Is it not awful?" whispered his companion, gently pressing his arm, "are you not afraid?"

"Afraid of what?"

"Of being drowned."

"No," the boy replied, with a bitter laugh, which had but little mirth in it, and still very little bravado; "I was not born to be drowned."

The storm by this time had reached its fullest fury.

How long it was to last, who could say, or what damage it would do? How many aching hearts would it cause? and how many broken homes? How many rocky shores would it scatter with the evidences of its wrath.

About half-an-hour or so before daybreak, and when the darkness, as is always the case, was more impenetrably intense than at any other period of the night, Charley, who was peering out into the seeemingly solid blackness before him, fancied that he perceived something white.

Straining his eyes to the utmost, he imagined that he could faintly descry the form of some large square-rigged ship, which appeared to him to be bearing down upon them rapidly.

Could it be fancy? Did not the captain and the crew perceive it also? If so, why did they not alter their course? He spoke to Julia, and pointed it out to her; but she had fallen asleep, wrapped warmly in the captain's warm cloak.

Springing forward, he clutched hold of the arm of one of the seamen passing at the time, and pointed to it.

But at that instant the cutter sank into the deep trough of the sea, and the foaming waves rose high around them like a wall.

Immediately afterwards, when they again rose to the surface, they found that Charley's surmise had been but too correct, for, to their horror, they perceived close upon them, and threatening instantly to crush them beneath its weight, rose the towering black hull of a huge ship, urged onwards before the wind by the broad spread of double-reefed topsails, roaring through the water, and flinging a high double column of trothing waves from her ample bows.

There was not a moment to lose, for she was close upon them; at most she was not more than twelve yards from the cutter.

Charley could plainly perceive the bright copper shining, as she rose dripping and rolling on the top of a wave.

In another instant it seemed certain that the fearful mass would come toppling over, and crush the little cutter beneath it.

Everybody on board the cutter now saw it and their danger.

The captain with sudden energy seized a trumpet hanging by his side, and roared his commands in a voice of thunder.

Charley placed one arm round Julia's waist, and with the other steadied himself by grasping a rope.

Again the cutter sank between the waves—again the ship rose towering above them.

The captain's teeth were set; the men stood motionless as statues.

All eyes were turned upon the huge monster hovering above them.

It was in vain to use any efforts to turn their course.

They felt that their fate lay alone in the hands of an allwise Providence.

"The next moment will decide all," the captain muttered between his teeth.

The next moment came.

Then, within a fathom of the cutter's boom, hurling herself, as it appeared, upon the huge towering summit of a mountainous wave, there swept past them, amidst the loud roar and hiss of violently cloven water, the gigantic bulk of a great vessel, with her dripping sides, dusky bulwarks, and overhanging forest of masts, and spars, and tense rigging, and bellying, straining canvas.

Charley held his breath, and drew Julia still closer to his heart.

A moment afterwards, and the peril was past.

The ship was floating by to the leeward.

They were safe!

"Heaven be thanked," the boy murmured.

He looked down at his companion, who was slumbering by his side, all unconscious of the peril through which they had just passed.

"I tell you what, Charley," said Captain Toddleboy, tapping him on the shoulder, "I have had some devilish close shaves since I saw you last, but I can't say that I've had many to wop that one. It was what I don't mind terming a twister; shiver my timbers if it wasn't."

"How long is it since you took to the sea?" asked Charley, curious to hear something of his friend's adventures.

"I'll tell you all about it when we get over a glass of grog, young fellow," replied the captain. "It's as rum a start as you probably ever heerd tell on."

"Can't you tell me now? I'm dying to hear."

"I think we shall have something else to do for an hour or so," replied the captain. "You see, it's just upon daybreak, and I expect we shall have a bit of a parting squall before we've done with it."

While he spoke, the first pale grey streaks of morning began to be visible.

A heavy veil of rising mist swept across the white crests of the waves. No land was visible; but, according to Captain Toddleboy's opinion, they were not a great distance from the spot which they had occupied last night when the vessel from which they had had so narrow an escape passed by them.

It was not very long before the parting blow that the captain had anticipated reached them.

It was preceded by a brief lull, and then the mist driving away before the coming wind, the cutter, struck down as though by a powerful enemy, wallowed on her beam-ends, while the waves poured over her bulwarks in a foaming torrent, and the tempest hurled through the air with a loud hissing shriek, which rose high above the deafening thunder of the waves.

The captain shouted with all the strength of his lungs from his post in the rigging, when the water would allow him at length to get his breath, and the crew rushed hither and thither according to his directions.

If the cutter had not been a first-rate craft, there is every probability that it would have gone down bodily as it lay, and all on board would have shared a watery grave. But the captain and his crew placed implicit faith in her, and she certainly did her best on this occasion to keep up her character.

Recovering herself from the effects of the violent shock which she had received, and moving heavily forwards, she felt and yielded to the impulse of the rudder.

Then the bows fell off from the sea, and then her crew began to feel that they were riding smoothly and rapidly before the wind, over the fast subsiding though still agitated surface of the waters.

"That's better," said Captain Toddleboy, with an air of relief. "We shall get along now."

And the cutter, bounding along like a race-horse, flew on in the very heart of the squall, beating the foaming seas as though ship and waves were living things, and were in mere wantonness rollicking and frolicking together.

The fog was clearing away rapidly, and the captain began to devote all his spare energies to the very important business of sounding, which, at the part of the Channel where they were at the time, was a very necessary operation.

The wind was abating now, and their pace had slackened considerably.

Suddenly, the sound of a low, half smothered explosion came to them across the water.

Captain Toddleboy raised his head, and, standing motionless, listened intently.

In a few seconds it was heard again.

One of the men shouted from the forecastle.

"Boat ahoy! Boat on the starboard bow."

Charley looked in the direction indicated as well as the captain, and they could see a lugger-rigged boat, carrying a few yards of canvas on its foremast, rising over the foaming heads of the waves, and then sinking out of sight in the deep hollows betwixt them.

"What is it?" Charley asked.

"It's a vessel stuck on the sands," replied the captain. "That was what the firing was, I expect. That boat's going to her help."

Just then a third gun was fired, but this time the sound seemed to come from a different quarter to that from which the previous reports had proceeded.

"We must have passed her," said the captain. "Port the helm."

"There's a piece of floating wreck," cried Julia, pointing to the water.

The captain's eyes were turned in that direction.

"There is some one on it, isn't there?" said he.

A mass of broken spars and tangled rigging, as he spoke, rose upon the summit of a wave, so close to the side of the cutter, that any one on board might almost have stretched out an arm and touched it.

Julia uttered a cry as her eye caught the outline of a pale face on the surface of the water.

There, amidst the cordage and canvas, was the slender form of a fair-haired boy, about ten or twelve years of age.

The child seemed to be clinging with the tenacity of despair to the splinters of broken wood, though evidently its little strength was fast deserting it.

"He will be drowned," cried Julia.

"No," said Charley; "we can save him, surely."

"I doubt it, though," observed the captain. "He's floated past us now, you see; and I'm afraid we can't get alongside of him. No; it's all up with him, I fear."

"No, no, surely not," cried Julia. "Poor little boy, so young, and so beautiful as he looks!"

At that moment the drowning child raised a soft plaintive cry for help, which touched the listeners to the heart.

"If I were anything of a swimmer," the captain observed, "I'm dashed if I wouldn't risk it, although it's pretty near as much as anybody's life's worth, mind you."

"But I'll risk it, though," cried our hero, beginning to drag off his overcoat.

"You, Charley? Nonsense!" expostulated the captain. "You haven't the strength."

"No, no, Charley," pleaded Julia; "not you. You must not attempt it. Your arm has no power in it."

"Leave me alone," said Mr. Wag. "I shall be all right. I can swim like a duck."

"I know that, Charley," replied Captain Toddleboy; "but you mustn't venture it — you really mustn't."

But Charley was a self-willed young scamp, as you know by this time, and had a knack of never taking anybody's advice; so while they were showing him how very improper and imprudent it would be of him to try to do what he had proposed, he was very quietly measuring the distance with his eye, and making a little calculation.

By the time that they had made up their minds that it was perfectly impossible for him to do it, he had made up his mind how it was to be done; and suddenly he sprang upon the low bulwarks, at the same time winding the headline tightly round his arm.

Then, without heeding the cry which broke from everyone on board, he sprang with one tremendous bound into the stormy water beneath.

The waves closed over his head with a loud and angry crash.

A few moments of intense anxiety, and then he rose slowly to the surface.

The child whom he was bent upon rescuing was only a few yards ahead.

Half-a-dozen desperate strokes, and he had reached the wreck.

Then, with all that remained to him of his fast ebbing strength, he clutched at a confused mass of spars and cordage, and lifted himself out of the water.

The poor little boy lay insensible among the confusion, fortunately supported in a safe position by the ropes, which were twisted round his limbs in confusion by the action of the waves.

Charley as carefully as possibly released him from their folds, and took the child in his arms.

Then, clinging frantically to the slippery wood-work, he contrived, after several desperate and unsuccessful attempts, to wind the head-line, the end of which he had brought with him, round their two bodies in several folds.

Then he paused for a moment to take breath, and then, making a sign to those on board to draw in, he sprang back into the water.

The waves surged and boiled round Charley as he plunged onwards towards the cutter, half swimming, and half dragged along by those above.

Clutching the child in his arms, he still managed to retain his hold of the headline, and in a few minutes, amid the cheering of the men on board the cutter, and the loud thunder of the waves below, he found himself, panting and breathless, on the deck of Captain Toddleboy's ship, while the poor child lay wan, motionless, and insensible before him, his long fair hair streaming over his face and shoulders.

Yes, there he lay, cold and lifeless, the blue-veined lids of his eyes closed, his lips colourless.

To all appearances dead.

But such was not the case; for Julia, who had loosened the little boy's jacket, and placed her warm hand on his young heart, pronounced it to be still beating, though faintly.

"His clothes are very good," the captain observed. "He must be a young swell, I should say, when he is at home."

"Good heavens!" cried Julia, who had been looking fixedly into his face. "Good heavens! Charley, do you know who it is?"

"No."

"It is the son of the old duke."

"The old duke?"

"The Duke of Heatherland."

Charley remained a moment silent and thoughtful.

"It is strange," he muttered to himself, "how circumstances are continually occurring to bring me into conjunction with that family. At every turn of life I seem to meet them. Some strange fatality seems to connect us together, and to send me to their aid in moments of danger."

"Come, Charley," observed the captain at this point, breaking in upon our hero's meditations; "you had better go down below, and change your clothes, or you'll be catching your death of cold, that's what you'll be doing. Come, and let me mix you a good stiff glass of grog; and while you're drinking it the little boy will be coming round."

"To be sure, captain; and you've got to tell me your adventures."

"Certainly I have, my boy; and rum uns they are, too, as you will allow."

"They must have been curious to have changed you so wonderfully."

"Changed me, eh? Yes, I'm not much like I used to be, am I? Avast there! Shiver my timbers!"

And the captain swaggered down stairs before him with such a terribly ferocious air, that a little cabin boy who chanced to be coming up at the time was seized with a sudden panic, fled precipitately, and hid himself in a cupboard with the dirty dishes, quaking in every limb.

LII.—THE MURDERERS IN THE VAULTS.

I LEFT Faversham and Rattan in rather a critical position.

It is time that I should return to them.

But it is necessary that I should call to the reader's recollection the position in which I left them.

They were in the house where Faversham had just brutally murdered the Duke of Heatherland.

They were in the vaults.

The dead body of the duke, horribly mangled, lay in a cellar, at the door of which Rattan was standing, whilst Faversham was dangling by a rope over a dark well or pit, in endeavouring to cross which he had slipped his foot.

They were in the dark, and loud shouts echoed through the house.

The two men who had tracked the murderers thither were endeavouring to give the alarm, and attract the notice of the police.

Although a low neighbourhood, where cries of distress were not likely to meet with much attention from the ruffianly population there abounding, there was no doubt but that the energetic shouting of the spies must bring assistance before very long.

And with assistance Faversham knew very well that they would bring death to him.

His struggles now became perfectly frantic.

If he could only manage to reach the side of the pit on which lay the outer vault, he would be safe.

If he could secure his own escape, he cared very little what became of his companion in crime. Indeed, he did not give him a thought.

But struggling there in the intense darkness, and suffering excruciating pain from his strained and swollen arm, into the flesh of which the twisted rope seemed to be cutting like a knife, he began to lose all knowledge of the position of things.

In which direction lay the vault he would jump to? He had no idea.

He could not hear Rattan, who stood perfectly silent.

The rope was slowly unfraying, and giving way above.

He must spring.

Summoning all his courage, therefore, he seized the rope with his other hand, and released his almost useless arm; then, clutching the rope as well as he could with both hands, he gave himself a swing.

As he did so, he involuntarily clenched his teeth and closed his eyes, expecting the next moment to come with his head in violent contact with the stone walls or the edge of the pit.

But, to his unutterable relief, he found himself standing firmly on the ground.

Next moment he uttered a low curse, for he found himself standing side by side with Rattan, in the vault from which he had hoped to have escaped.

In jumping he had left go of the rope, which had swung back to its place in the middle of the pit.

There was no way of getting hold of it again, and no means of escaping by its aid.

But by what other means could they hope to effect it?

"How are we to get out?" asked Rattan.

"I see no way."

"We're nicely cooped-up by your clumsiness!" growled the ruffian, furious at the difficulties which surrounded him.

THE FLIGHT.

"Silence, fool!" growled the other, passionately, and in a voice which for the moment awed his companion into quiet. "Silence, and I will help you."

"How?"

"The only escape for us is to bar the door of this cellar, and break our way through the wall into the next house."

"Through the wall? Impossible—there is no time."

"There is plenty of time, if we work hard."

"But we cannot break through the brickwork."

"It is not all brickwork. If you feel, you will find wood above."

"And what tools have we?"

"There is the chopper. Feel for it on the floor."

No. 45.

Rattan, with a shudder he could not suppress, began to grope about upon the bloody floor for the implement of death.

"Have you found it?" asked Faversham, impatiently.

The other replied gruffly in the affirmative.

"Lend it to me, then. You guard the door."

"Can't we shut it to?"

"Yes; I will help you. Push with me."

With a strength which seemed to be almost superhuman, Faversham raised the heavy oaken door from the hollows of the brickwork of the floor, into which it had sunk and become wedged, and, with his companion's assistance, contrived to jam it back into its place in such a way, that from the outside it would be a matter of no small difficulty to push it open again.

"It's a pity that I haven't got something to

[CHARLEY WAG, THE NEW JACK SHEPPARD.

knock them down with, if they try to force an entrance," said Rattan.

"There's an old rotten bench in the corner; try if you can't break off a leg. We have no time to spare. I must begin on the wall."

And so saying, Faversham began to grope about for a weak place in the woodwork upon which to commence his attack, while the other used his best efforts to wrench away a leg from an old and half-rotten wooden form which upon entering he had noticed reared up in a corner.

Meanwhile, the shouts of the would-be captors grew louder and louder.

Faversham continued his work with vigour and precision.

He felt that his only chance lay in coolness and well-directed energy.

If he struck at random in the dark, nothing was more likely than that he would blunt or break the chopper against the brickwork.

To find a crevice between the planks was his first care. This done, to prize an opening large enough to allow them to creep through.

If this could be done, they might possibly pull the boards into their places in such a way as to cover their retreat for a time, if not altogether, and so give them time to get a good start of their pursuers.

Groping about, therefore, rapidly but carefully, he at last slipped the tips of his fingers into a small aperture.

Then, running his fingers along the plank, he felt for the place where it joined another plank; for he supposed, by what he recollected of the length of the wall, that there must be more than one plank employed in crossing it.

One end of the plank, he found, was fixed deep into the wall.

To the other he turned his attention.

Carefully working in the end of the chopper, he forced it as far down as the woodwork on the other side would allow, and then very cautiously began to prize it up.

The wood was very old, and much worm-eaten, and the nails burst out from their sockets from the strength of the pressure.

In a few minutes he had torn out the plank at one end. The other end yet fixed in the wall worked upon the old nails, fastening it like a hinge.

The plank he had chosen was low down, about the height of his knees; and he had not chosen it without due reflection. He had thought, that having got out the outer plank, he could then punch the inner plank into the inside of the next house with his foot.

While he was working, the sound of voices without grew louder and nearer; the voices now were much more numerous; the tramping of feet was easily distinguishable in the vault beyond the pit.

"Where are they—where are they?" the voices asked.

"Through that door."

"How are we to get in?"

"Jump across."

"It can't be done."

"Fetch a plank, or a ladder."

"You'll get one down the street opposite, at the timber-yard."

"Stop; there's one coming. Make way, there."

Faversham paused in his work for a moment to listen.

Sure enough there was some attempt going to be made to cross the pit.

Something was heard bumping against the walls.

It was a ladder they were bringing down.

"They won't be able to use much force," Faversham said. "But if you cannot hold the door against them, give way suddenly, and it will most likely throw some of them off their balance, and tumble them down the pit."

"Never fear. If they get their heads in here, I'll smash them for their pains."

The doctor said no more. He was working now with all his might, wrenching, and driving, and kicking at the planks, and endeavouring to thrust them back into the vault in the other house.

Under the repeated blows which he dealt it the woodwork soon began to split and crack, and at last a plank gave way altogether with a loud crash, and fell inwards.

It was all but the work of a few minutes. From the time that the doctor commenced his assault upon the wall scarcely three minutes had elapsed; but to Rattan, who was waiting, it seemed almost an age.

And those without were so eager to effect the murderers' capture, and so rapid in their movements, that they were already thrusting at the other side of the door at which Rattan was keeping guard.

Three or four men had crossed the ladder, and were all standing upon the door-sill, which was very broad and deep.

Here, balancing themselves and holding by the door-posts, they were pushing against the door with their united strength; but of course they had not room enough or sure enough footing to have much effect.

They could not use all their strength; and the door being so tightly jammed, and Rattan being so powerful a man, their efforts were of no avail.

Rattan easily kept them at bay as long as he remained there.

But Faversham called to him to leave the door, and follow through, at the same time creeping himself through the aperture.

Rattan considered for a moment.

He must not leave go of the door gently; he must not leave it shut against them, unless he could devise some means of effectually blocking it up, or they might push it open without his great object being gained, namely, that they should lose their balance.

And if they did not lose their balance, but effected an entrance without accident, they would in all probability seize upon him before he could get through the hole in the wall and follow Faversham.

No; although he barely gave a moment's thought to the pros and cons of the situation, he determined that the best way was, instead of pushing against those without, to suddenly yield; and not only yield, but assist their efforts by such means that they would fall forward and stagger.

Then, in the first moment of surprise, he would fling himself upon them with the weapon which he had contrived with the sharp-edged leg of the wooden bench, and, if possible, dash them back into the pit.

The moment came.

The pressure upon the door without had reached its utmost.

The resistance within which had at first met the efforts of the assailants, had given them courage; and now, not expecting the door to give way suddenly, as at first they had supposed that it might have done, they threw all their weight against it.

In a moment, without the faintest creak of warning, the door gave way.

Three men staggered forward with their arms out, trying to save themselves.

The fourth stumbled on the threshold, and saved himself from going into the pit by clutching at the woodwork of the door.

Rattan had placed himself in such a position, that when he flung the door wide open, he could escape into the shelter of the protecting wall.

He met the first of his assailants with a stunning blow on his forehead, which sent him reeling backwards as he uttered a shrill cry of pain.

In the next moment Rattan had struck the second with equal violence in the face, and at the same time giving the third of his assailants a terrific side blow, sent him sprawling against the opposite wall.

Leaving this one for the present, Rattan turned upon the other two; and, letting out furiously right and left, long before they could recover themselves, he knocked them backwards on to the top of the man who had been left outside, and the violence of the shock drove all three into the pit, down which they fell, vainly endeavouring to cling to the sides, and crying for help.

So violent an assault intimidated the rest of the murderers' would-be captors, and while some cried aloud for a rope, those with most presence of mind began to lower the ladder down the well to the assistance of the three men, whose cries for help were growing fainter and fainter, and more stifled in the noisome and stagnant water below.

No one, however, seemed to feel at all inclined to venture into the vault where the first four had met with so warm a reception.

Rattan, thus relieved for the present, stood for a moment, in expectation of an assault from the fourth man, whom he had knocked to the other side of the vault.

But evidently he had struck his head against the floor or wall in falling, and lay senseless.

Rattan did not wait long. Groping his way along, he strode over the bleeding corpse of the murdered duke, and groping his way to the hole in the wall, crept through with some difficulty into the vault beyond.

Here, he found Faversham struggling violently with a door, which as he arrived gave way before the doctor's efforts, and together they rushed through into another cellar.

As bad luck would have it, every door seemed to be closed and double locked.

A desperate wrench at the lock proved this second door to be securely fastened, and almost as firm as a rock.

The only way to freedom, as it seemed to them, lay through a narrow grating near the ceiling, leading out into some sort of court-yard at the back of the house.

But would they have time to tear away the bars before their pursuers were down upon them?

An attempt must be made.

Through the grating lay their way, and they must make an effort.

The doctor pointed out the fact to Rattan, and bade him assist.

The latter easily understood him.

He also saw their position, and understood it at one comprehensive glance.

Then, quick as thought, they approached the grating together, and simultaneously grasped the bars.

Rattan possessed the strength of a giant; the other was extraordinarily powerful, and with a mighty wrench they dragged the framework of the window from its rusty iron fastenings, and brought it lumbering down upon the cellar floor with a loud crash.

Next moment Faversham, taking the lead, had sprung up to the opening, and managed to work his way out to the open air.

He found himself in a small back-yard, on each side of which was a wall about six feet high, leading into the yards of the houses on either side.

Calling to Rattan to follow, he hastily scaled the wall leading to the house on the opposite side to the one where the murder had been committed.

Rattan followed him in almost less time than it takes to describe it, so rapid were his movements, labouring as he did under the dread of apprehension; for he knew well enough that if taken he would to a certainty be hanged.

"We will get through this house," said Faversham, pointing to the back-door, which stood ajar, and through the chink of which a light was shining.

As quickly said as done.

There was no one in the kitchen into which the door opened.

The person, whoever it was, who had been using the candle, which was left burning upon the mantel-piece, had deserted it to run to the front of the house, and ascertain the cause of all the disturbance.

They did not pause longer than a moment to bolt the door behind them, and then, taking the candle, ascended the stairs.

Scarcely, however, had Faversham, who led the way, placed his foot on the floor of the passage above, when a gruff voice saluted him with:

"Who's there? What do you want?"

Rattan's first impulse was to beat a hasty retreat the way he had come; and then, thinking of the hopelessness of their chance in that way—for the houses blocked up the yards at either end, so that there was no outlet but through the houses themselves—his second thought was to spring upon anyone who tried to stop him, and make the shortest possible job of them.

Faversham, however, although in his heart every bit as unscrupulous and bloodthirsty as the other ruffian, yet had much more presence of mind, and a greater command over his actions. He saw at a glance that there were a couple of powerfully made men in the passage, whom they would be obliged to pass to get out at the street-door.

He was already wearied by his exertions. It would be every way much better if they could effect their escape without incurring a struggle.

He therefore used his wits instead of his fists.

"What do you want?" repeated the man who had spoken before.

"It's all right," replied Faversham, coolly.

But the man did not seem satisfied upon that point.

He wanted an explanation.

"What's all right?" said he.

"I'm a police officer," replied Faversham, "and I expect you have got a man concealed in this house who has committed a murder."

"What murder?—when?—what do you mean?"

"What do I mean? Do you pretend to say you can't hear all that shouting outside, and haven't heard it for the last half-hour?"

"I've heard it plain enough."

"Then that is caused by the people trying to catch him."

"What's that to me?"

"Only this, that he has been seen to enter this house."

"How?"

"At the back."

"By Jove!" said the other man, speaking for the first time; "you left the door open, Bill. They may have done."

"If there had been anybody come in, we should have heard them."

"Perhaps not, with all that noise going on."

"We heard you."

"Well, my friend, I can't stop bandying words. He has come in. Have you been all the while at the door?"

"Yes."

"Then nobody could have passed out."

"Not likely."

"He must have gone by quietly, and got up-stairs."

"We should have heard him."

"Please not to be so obstinate. I tell you he is here, and up-stairs. You will find him, unless he has jumped out of the window. Hark! I hear a noise above, I am certain. Will you take the candle and look. We will stay here, and cut off his retreat. Or, if you don't feel inclined to assist, or are afraid to face him, we will call in assistance, if you will keep the door."

"Oh, I'm not afraid to face him, if he's there," replied the man who had been so doubtful. "Stay where you are, and I'll go and look."

Whatever suspicions he might at first have entertained of the truth of the doctor's statement, and the pureness of the motive which had led him to intrude himself into the house, —particularly as he came in company with such an unmitigated ruffian as Rattan was, both in manners and appearance—however, his doubts were now dissipated by the cool air of assurance which the doctor assumed, and perhaps in some small degree the taunt upon the subject of his courage might have had something to do with

it. In any case, be that as it may, he took the light from Faversham's hand, and ascended the stairs, in search of the imaginary murderer who was supposed to be hiding above.

The doctor, Rattan, and the other man, stood silently together in the passage, and listened to the sound of his retreating footsteps.

They heard him enter one room after another upon the first floor, and then ascend to the floor above.

They listened to his footfalls as he entered a room on the second floor, and then Faversham turned to Rattan, and whispered,

"Now."

The ruffian took the hint readily.

He required very little prompting in such cases.

Without a moment's warning, or any previous movement which might have aroused the victim's suspicion, he clutched him suddenly round the throat, and squeezing him with all his might for a few moments, the man became black in the face, and perfectly helpless, and slipped down when released upon a mat in the passage, without being able to speak or move.

But Rattan, fearful lest the punishment which he had inflicted might not be sufficiently severe, struck the unfortunate man a couple of terrific crushing blows in the face, which covered him with blood.

Then, plucking his companion by the arm, they made for the street-door.

However, though the struggle had been so very brief, and the noise which it occasioned so very slight, the sound of it had reached the ears of the man above, who might have been listening eagerly for some token of unfair play from below.

"What's the matter?" he shouted.

Then, receiving no reply, he came bounding down-stairs.

Rattan had got the door open.

They sprang with a bound into the street.

Just round the door it was deserted.

A considerable crowd stood a little further up, round the door of the house where the murder had been committed.

The windows of that house, too, were several of them wide open, and eager faces were looking out into the street below.

The light fell upon them, and they wore in its reflection a strangely ghostly effect.

There was a perfect Babel of voices, too; for everybody was asking everybody else why they did not take some more active steps than they were then taking to effect the capture of the murderers.

Faversham and Rattan stayed no longer than it took to glance momentarily at this scene, and then rushed off in an opposite direction, towards a dark and narrow alley which faced the house from which they had just made their escape.

But the time, brief as it was, was quite sufficient for some one leaning out of one of the windows to catch sight of them, and give a loud yell of recognition.

Faversham, attracted by the sound, looked back.

The man at the window was waving a lighted candle above his head, and gesticulating violently.

The light fell in fitful flashes upon his matted

hair, sordid apparel, and cadaverous and haggard face.

The doctor recognized him at a glance.

It was Murdoch.

As he turned, his former servant and slave saluted him with a savage howl.

"See! see!" he shouted. "There goes the murderer and his accomplice. There they go. Stop them! Stop—down that turning. Run for your lives, or they will escape!"

The doctor stayed no longer, but followed Rattan at the top of his speed.

The crowd behind, seeing the direction in which Murdoch pointed, and catching a glimpse of the retreating forms of the fugitives, with a wild shout set off in pursuit.

The two men ran for their lives, indeed, whatever the pursuers did.

But they were already greatly fatigued with the labours of the last hour.

They were not as strong or as fresh as the men who were trying to run them down.

They felt almost as though their hearts would break with the violence of their exertions, but they panted along, with bated breath and clenched teeth.

The sounds of their pursuers' shouts drew nearer and nearer, but still they pursued their wild career.

LIII.—CONTAINS AN EXTRAORDINARY NARRATIVE.

SURELY that Captain Toddleboy must have been the most wonderful of all living captains.

The little ship which he commanded was not of any extraordinary dimensions, although the crew consisted of twelve persons.

Ordinarily, so small a vessel is not so well manned; and ordinarily, so small a vessel does not carry so tremendous a captain.

For he was tremendous. I do not mean altogether in size, but in get-up, and in behaviour. There was such a flourish about him, such a smell of tobacco, and he was so extraordinarily demonstrative.

Now you who may be acquainted with Captain Stubbs, of the *Lively Peg*, or Captain Jones, of the *Frisky Fan*, know them to be very simple homely sort of men, rather given to an abuse of strong liquors, and, may be, to an objectionable habit of sprinkling their discourse with a few strong oaths; but they were nothing to Captain Toddleboy of the *Wasp*.

I have compared this noble commander to Mr. T. P. COOKE, the celebrated delineator of nautical characters; but Mr. T. P. COOKE at his best never did—or rather, I should say, over-did—the nautical business like our old friend Toddleboy.

He was more of a sailor than would have been half-a-dozen T. P. COOKES rolled into one.

He was tremendous.

There never was any sailor on the British stage who "hoisted his slacks" in the way that Captain Toddleboy did; there never was anybody who so frequently made use of the expression, "shiver my timbers;" and there never was anybody who got through so many quids in the course of a day, and did such a terrific amount of expectoration in the process.

Charley Wag, who had known him in former times to have been such a very harmless sort of old man—an old man, in fact, who was chiefly celebrated for muddling away a great deal of time, and imbibing a vast quantity of diluted alcohol, in front of various low taverns at which he was in the habit of calling during the day and night—could not believe him to be the same person at all.

What could have wrought so wonderful a change? How had it come about? How was it that he was captain of this vessel? And what sort of vessel was it? Had it no other trade than smuggling?

He was dying with curiosity; and no sooner did he find himself face to face with the captain in his snug little cabin, than Charley put the question to him.

"Charley, my boy," said Captain Toddleboy, with the usual allusion to the destruction of his timbers, "what do you think?"

"I don't know what to think," replied Charley.

At which the captain seemed to be so much tickled, that he fell back in his chair, and laughed for full ten minutes, until the tears rolled down his cheeks.

"You give it up," said he.

"Of course I do," replied Charley, rather out of patience.

"You've no idea what it means?"

"None whatever."

"And you can't guess?"

"No."

"Then I'll tell you. In the first place, what do you suppose is the particular trade of this vessel?"

"I've told you, Mr. Toddleboy, I could not guess; and if you don't want to tell me without so much fencing, you had better leave it alone altogether."

"But I'm going to tell you. This vessel, Charley, that you are on board, is nothing else than—"

Here he leant over, and whispered,

"A pirate."

"I thought you were a smuggler only."

"I'm a little of both. You've heard tell, perhaps, of the *Black Flag, or, the Pirate Fiend of the Secret Cave*. Well, I'm just such another, only, if anything, a little worse. Shiver my timbers, if I am not!"

"But how on earth did it happen that you became such a desperate character, Mr. Toddleboy?"

"It was a most extraordinary circumstance," replied his former guardian; "and while you're supping your grog I will tell it to you."

"Do so," said Charley, eagerly.

The captain then produced the liquor, mixed two glasses, lit a pipe, and, after a whiff or two, began with:

"There's very little doubt but that it was a most extraordinary circumstance—"

Mr. Wag politely intimated that he had said as much before.

Captain Toddleboy winked three times, took a gulph of boiling hot grog between each, and began again.

"The extraordinary circumstance which I

was a-speaking of, took place a short time after I had the pleasure of seeing you last. The circumstance happened about three months after I last saw you. In fact, I may say, it happened exactly three months after, to the very day."

" How is it you calculated so nicely ?"

" Well, I'll tell you. The last time I saw you was before that there estimable magistrate, Mr. Slang, of Quod Street. You may, perhaps, remember his giving me three months."

" Of course I do."

" Very well, then, it was on the first night that ever I came out that this ere extraordinary circumstance occurred to me."

" For goodness gracious' sake, what was it ?"

" I'll tell you. My time was up in the morning—a remarkably cold and wet one. When they opened the gate for me, the rain was coming down pretty tidy."

" ' I shall get wet through before I get under shelter,' said I to myself.

" ' Well, aren't you going ?' asked the gaoler.

" ' You haven't got such a thing as an umbrella to lend us ?' says I.

" ' I'm afraid you'll forget to bring it back when you come to see us again,' says he.

" ' I hope that'll be a long time first,' says I ; and I pulled up my trousers over the boots, and tramped it.

" I tramped it all day, looking for a job. At least, I believe I had some sort of idea that that was what I was up to, though I don't think that I had quite exactly made up my mind what the job was to be. You see, it wasn't as if I was a young chap who could turn his hand to anything. My joints were growing a bit stiff, and those infernal draughts at Spike Island had not very much improved 'em.

" As the evening came on, I was faint and hungry, and I hadn't the remotest idea where I was to go and get a bed, or what I was to do next day. I had been at Bottle and Bung's I don't know how many years, and I didn't feel that I could get along very well at any other place.

" I had wandered about all day long, and as it began to grow dark, I found myself among the back streets in the neighbourhood of Tower Hill. I was looking in a promiscuous sort of way in at the door of a public-house, when some good soul or other who thought I stood in need of a drop of something to warm me, stood a half-quartern. After I had had it, I curled myself up as comfortable as I could, in a corner where there wasn't quite such an awful draught from the chink in the door ; and as nobody took any particular notice of me, in course of time I dropped off to sleep, and snored away as happy as a king.

" But I was woke up after an hour or two, as it seemed to me, by the landlord, or the potboy, who said that sleeping was against the rules ; and if I wanted a bed anywhere, I had better go and get it.

" So I picked myself together the best way I could, and took myself off again on the tramp.

" It had left off raining now, the moon had come out, and it was precious cold and raw. I hadn't any particular way to go, and so, when I came out upon the open space on the Hill, I thought I might just as well cross over to the other side as stop where I was. It was too cold

to sit down and go to sleep, and so I thought I had better be walking than standing still ; but as I was in no hurry to go anywhere particular, I did not walk very fast, as you may suppose ; indeed, I was walking along with my eyes half shut.

" All at once, when I had got to about the middle of the square, I heard the sound of some one's footsteps behind me. I turned round sharp ; for they were coming fast up to me, and I was afraid that they might run against and knock me over by accident.

" The moon was hidden behind a cloud at the moment, and I could not see who it was distinctly ; only something very bulky in the shape of a man was running, or staggering, or lurching along, as it were, just like a chap who isn't used to the sea staggers across the deck in a gale of wind.

" He was close upon me when I turned, and, in spite of my dodging on one side to try and miss him, he ran full butt at me, and we went down in a heap together.

" I was uncommonly shaky, in those times, upon my pins, and a bit of a tumble used to knock me all to pieces, as it were, so that when I was down upon my back, I lay there ever so long, not caring particular to get up again, and not feeling very much as if I could have done so if I had wanted, for I had managed in tumbling to catch myself a very nasty wipe on the back of the head.

" However, after a bit, I did get up—at least, I got up into a sitting position—and I looked round for my rough friend.

" I had an idea that he must have knocked me over and gone stumbling on his way, and I expected to have seen him twenty yards off at least, which is perhaps the reason why, when I looked up and found him lying close against me, it gave me quite a turn.

" But there he was, lying quite still.

" ' He's lucky,' says I to myself.

" He was evidently a seafaring man, and dressed in sailor's clothes, and by the side of him, upon the ground, lay a thick pilot coat which he must have been carrying, and had let fall when he fell himself.

" ' Hallo, mate,' I cried out when I had looked at him for a minute or two.

" But he took no earthly notice of me.

" ' Hallo, mate,' says I again. ' Hold up, can't you ?'

" I began to get a little bit frightened, seeing him lie there so still, and never as much as moving a finger.

" Well, by a great effort I got up myself and went round to him.

" The moon was behind a cloud, and I could not at first get a good sight of his face, but I stooped down and knelt on one knee by the side of him upon the stones.

" Then, just as I got into that position, the moon came out and shined full upon his head.

" His face was deadly white, and there was blood up his nostrils, and from the corners of his mouth a thin stream had trickled down towards his neck on either side.

" He lay quite still, and his eyes were half closed.

" As I looked at him, a dreadful suspicion came over me that something was wrong with him—much more wrong than I'd supposed at first.

"I leant down and raised the lid from one of his eyes.

"There was no doubt about it.

"He was dead.

"It was a queer position for anyone to be placed in, you must allow.

"I jumped to my feet at the first fright, and was about to cry for help with all my might; but a circumstance checked me suddenly. And this was, that accidentally touching the coat lying by the sailor's side, I noticed that the pocket emitted a dull chink, as though there were a weight of money in it.

"At least, so it struck me, for it was not like the chink of keys, or of nails, or of heavy metal. It was not even as I fancied the chink of coppers, or of shillings, or of half-crowns. There was a most uncommon, musical, bewitching, intoxicating chink about it—it was the *chink of gold!*

"I touched it with my foot again, and I was certain of it.

"But I was more certain still, when, a moment afterwards, I knelt down again and felt the pocket with trembling hands, found a canvas bag, undid the string fastening the mouth, and brought forth a handful of bright glittering sovereigns into the light.

"A thousand thoughts came on me all at once. I hardly knew what I was about, or whether I stood upon my head or my heels.

"The distant outline of the houses seemed to be rolling from one side to the other, like the waves of a stormy sea, and the ground seemed to be trembling.

"I could scarcely keep my legs.

"But I seemed to master my feelings with an immense effort, and to think what I should do next.

"I had no intention now of calling for help. My only idea was to escape with safety, and unseen.

"There was no one about. It was past twelve, and the streets around for the moment seemed to be unnaturally still and lonely.

"Circumstances could not possibly have favoured me more.

"I hesitated no longer. Taking the coat carefully in my arms, I walked away at my most rapid pace—I was afraid to run, for fear that I might attract the notice of some late loiterer whom I had not seen, but who might have noticed me kneeling on the ground.

"When I reached the shadow of the houses, I put on the great coat, and walked on as fast as I could.

"I could not help fancying, somehow, that someone was dogging my footsteps, although, as it proved, such was not the case, and I kept plunging down every narrow court and alley that I came to, endeavouring by those means effectually to puzzle my imaginary pursuers.

At last, fancying myself quite safe, and being almost dead beat with my unusual exertions, I dived into a dingy, dark, little coffee-house, and slunk into the back of the gloomiest box.

"There was, however, no one there to notice me. Only one other person was in the place—a young sailor boy—who at the other end of the shop lay with his head upon the table, fast asleep.

"He was not very likely to interfere with me, and, indeed, where I sat he could not see me.

"I gave an order to the girl who came to see what I wanted, and it was not until she had gone away that it struck me that I had not got anything in my pocket but the bag of gold.

"I thought it would look very funny to change a sovereign for a pint of coffee; but it couldn't be helped, and so when she came back I handed it to her.

"She took it, and stared at it precious hard, and asked if I hadn't got anything else.

Then when I said I hadn't, she took it away with her to the room at the back, and there was an awful amount of banging and biting over it, I expect, for she was a good ten minutes before she brought back the change.

"All the while I was waiting in the greatest anxiety for it to come, for I wanted to see what my pockets contained.

"At last she came, and went away again, and I began to count over the money.

"There was a large bag full. I counted it as carefully as I possibly could, taking the greatest possible precautions against making any noise which might attract attention.

"It took me an enormous time, and cost me an enormous amount of trouble, and once or twice I lost count, and had to begin again; but I got through it at last entirely to my satisfaction, and I found that there were three hundred and thirty-seven pounds.

"What a fortune! I sat for some time in a wild transport of delight. I could not believe in my good fortune. I took out handfuls of the golden pieces and carefully examined them one by one.

"They were genuine. There was no doubt about it. They were all genuine. They were not all of the same date or make, but they were the proper thing. What should I do with them? How should I spend them? That was what I asked myself first.

"After that, I began to wonder who they had formerly belonged to, and how he had come by them. Had he gotten them as easily as I had?

"At last it struck me that I would look into the other pockets, and see what they contained.

"There was, to begin with, a mass of rubbish An old glove, a quid of tobacco, a bit of string, a broken pipe, some biscuit crumbs, and such like; and there was also a pocket-book.

"I opened this, and laid it before me.

"It contained several half worn-out letters, without any address, but bearing dates of several years back, and purporting to be from a mother to her son; and there was one letter from some one else, addressed to the same party, informing him of the mother's death.

"The first were all signed 'Hannah Cook,' and the last was signed 'John Welsh;' and they were all apparently written to 'Richard Cook,' a sailor.

There was nothing very interesting about the contents of any of these letters—at least, that could be interesting to a third party.

"I came to the conclusion when I had read them, that this Richard Cook was a hardhearted vagabond, and that he had deserted his poor old mother in her illness, and not only refused to assist her, but even to answer her passionate letters praying and beseeching him to write to her, if it were only half-a-dozen words, in reply.

"Besides these epistles, there were several scraps from newspapers, which I read through carefully, and which even left a worse impression upon my mind respecting the character of Richard Cook than I had had before.

"They all bore reference of my friend Richard's bad behaviour.

"There was an account of his committal for petty larceny, and an account of his committal for burglary, and an account of his trials for the same, and an account of his attempted escape from some jail.

"And there was, besides, a ticket-of-leave in the name of Richard Cook, and a number of the *Hue and Cry*, giving a very minute description of Richard Cook's person; and as well as I could judge, Richard Cook was the man who had fallen down dead by my side on Tower Hill.

"I don't mind owning to you, that before I had read these letters and scraps of paper, I had had one or two sharpish twinges of conscience respecting the appropriation of the dead man's money; but when I found out what an out-and-out bad 'un he was, I comforted myself a little by the discovery.

"'No doubt,' says I to myself, 'he came by it in some unfair way, whatever it was; and even if he'd been alive, it in all probability would have served him jolly well right to have taken it away from him. And as he's dead, of course it don't signify to him at all.'

"Then I thought of another argument:

"'Most likely Mr. Richard Cook has no living relation. By these letters he seems to have been the only living relation whom his mother had, at any rate; and there is nothing in these documents to lead one to suppose that he was a married man.'

"So I kept on persuading myself, or rather, I should say, trying to persuade myself, that I ought to stick to the money, and that I was quite justified in sticking to it. But the fact of the matter was, that I meant to stick to it, and so stick to it I did.

"Well, there I was, then, with my bag of gold, and my handful of silver—what was I to do next?

"I was dreadfully weary, knocked up, dead beat with the long day's tramping that I had gone through, so that what I would have liked to have done more than anything else in the world, would have been to have gone quietly to bed, and had a good night's rest.

"But this required consideration.

"I was in a coffee-house, certainly, and a coffee-house where they let beds; but would it be safe to sleep in them?

"Why not? you may ask. How was anybody likely to judge by my seedy exterior that I was the possessor of such a large sum of money? and still more improbable that I should be carrying it about in my pocket.

"You, sitting there with your legs crossed, quite at your ease, may be able to reason very coolly and sensibly about it; but then, you should just place yourself in my position, and it would make all the difference.

"Before I came into my property, I'd have slept among the awfullest thieves in London quite as comfortable as I should have slept in the strong room at the Bank of England; but that gold in my pocket made me awfully suspicious of everybody and everything.

"I considered a long while.

"I was, as I say, awfully tired. It had come on to rain rather heavily. I screwed up my courage, and determined to ask the girl whether I could have a bed there that night.

"Thinking thus, I raised my eyes quickly from the papers, which, while I had been thinking, I had been mechanically mumbling over; and as I raised them, I saw peeping at me, over the back of the next box, the young sailor who had been sleeping at the other end of the shop when I came in."

LIV.—THE CAPTAIN'S STORY CONTINUED.

"HE was a most remarkably ugly-looking young scamp, this young sailor, when you came to see his face.

"He had got an uncommon murderous sort of look in those squinting eyes of his, and his thin-lipped mouth.

"It gave me an awful start when I first caught sight of him, and I didn't by any means like it, I can assure you.

"For you see, I was not quite sure in my own mind how long the young blackguard had been watching me.

"The question was, had he seen me counting over the gold?

"I had not heard him get up or move from his place in the far corner.

"He must have done it very quietly on purpose, and crept up to the spot where I caught sight of him spying me like a serpent.

"Had he been attracted by the sound of the chink of the money, or what else?

"'Any how,' says I to myself, 'Toddleboy, my trump,' says I, 'will clear out of this in double quick time, with your kind permission.'

"I rose to my feet.

"The sailor had slunk back to his place, and was lolling back in something like the attitude that he had been when first I came in, and having his eyes half closed, was peeping out of the corners at me, I could plainly see, as I walked towards the street door.

"I passed out, and arriving outside, ran sharply across the road, and took shelter immediately in the dark entrance of a narrow alley opposite.

"No sooner arrived there, I had hardly time to turn round, than I saw the young sailor come out of the coffee-shop hastily, and at first making as though he were coming across to where I stood, stop in the middle of the road and look eagerly to the right and to the left.

"Evidently he was a good bit puzzled, and he ran down one way about twenty yards, and then came panting back and ran the other.

"I waited for some length of time, and as he did not return, I emerged from my hiding-place, and walking down the same side of the street for a little distance, turned up another

THE DUEL.

street, and pursued an opposite direction to that which I had seen the sailor take.

"I was in the neighbourhood of Shadwell; a dreadful locality, some of the little bye-streets and lanes and alleys of which are as bad as any to be found in London.

"In them you may meet with the most abandoned and desperate blackguards to be met with anywhere.

"Housebreakers, pickpockets, every description of thieves, escaped convicts, ticket-of-leave men, murderous, and assassins, English and foreign.

"The very scum of the city found a refuge in its confused wilderness of crooked streets and dismal dark passages.

"Down some of them there was scarcely any

No. 46.

gas-lamps to throw a friendly gleam along the path; everything was in perfect darkness, except when a faint ray streamed through the yellow blind of some filthy coffee-house, or through the partly closed door of some house of ill-fame, from which as often as not you might have heard shrieks and oaths, and the sound of blows, as though all those within were engaged in a deadly combat.

"There was a drizzling rain falling, and if it had not been for the thick pilot coat I was wearing, I should have been regularly wet through very soon.

"I should have been precious glad to have come across some respectable sort of place where I could have ventured upon getting a bed for the night without danger of being robbed, or

[CHARLEY WAG, THE NEW JACK SHEPPARD

having my throat cut; but I could see nothing that was at all likely.

"The only way was to get into a better neighbourhood; but how was this to be managed?

"The streets seemed to be almost entirely deserted, and such few who were about I did not much care about speaking to.

"Somehow, too, I got so muddled and confused by the labyrinth of dirty alleys, that I kept wandering about without being able to shake them off, as it were; and the more I walked, the uglier the place seemed to become.

"I got so precious blown at last, that I was obliged to sit down on a door-step for a while, and have a bit of a rest.

"While doing so, I heard the sound of heavy feet coming towards me.

"'It's a policeman, by the sound of him,' said I to myself.

"However, it was not. It was a man who looked something like a dock labourer, as well as I could see.

"I let him go by a bit, and then I gave him a hail.

"'Hallo, mate!' says I; 'which is the way to Tower Hill?'

"He came back instead of answering me, and looked at me very hard.

"There was not much light, but by such little as there was I could just see his face.

"It was most extraordinary!

"It was most extraordinary, but there was the strongest possible family likeness between that young sailor who had been playing the spy upon me at the coffee-house and this party.

"I asked him the question again, and then I noticed that he was paying great attention to what I said, although he made no reply.

"I took him to be a foreigner.

"He looked round him once or twice after he'd done taking stock of me, as if he were in search of some one; and then, turning to me again, said in a husky voice, like, and with a sort of foreign twist about his words:

"'Wait a minute, and I'll come back.'

"After that, he moved off in the direction he had come, leaving me standing there.

"He went on for about twenty yards or so, and then stood still, and seemed to be speaking to some one; I couldn't see for the darkness.

"Then it occurred to me all at once that I hadn't done the wisest of things.

"The man had evidently got some nasty game on by going back, and I was deuced sorry I had let him go.

"But then, after all, what was easier for him to do, if he wished, than to lead me just where he wanted? Perhaps he meant well!

"Only just then the sound of several voices talking together in a sort of loud whisper came up the quiet street.

"And I heard as well the sound of several feet.

"I felt awfully sick all at once, when I came to reflect that, if there was anything to be gained by it, they would think no more of wringing my neck than if it had been a cat's.

"Just as this idea struck me, I thought I might screw myself up pretty snug in the doorway, and perhaps not be seen.

"I'd hardly time to do it before the men came up—nine or ten of them.

"'Well, where is he?' says one.

"'It was somewhere here, wasn't it, you told us?'

"'To be sure,' said the man I had spoken to, and then added something foreign.

"Then he began to feel along the walls with his hands, and groped in the doorway of the house on the other side of the way.

"'Lord, how I did perspire!

"'Hallo!' he bawled, after a bit.

"'Shut up!' says one of the other chaps, or some word to the same effect.

"'Lie down!' says another. 'Don't do that. You frightened him, and he's hooked it.'

"'He can't have got very far by this time.'

"'He's hiding, most likely, somewhere about.'

"'Well, it's no thoroughfare, so he can't escape. Let's have a light.'

"One of the fellows then pulls out a match-box, and begins to strike a light.

"Every blessed flash seemed to show me some savager looking face than before.

"They seemed to be an awful crew.

"Some of 'em had clubs of wood.

"They were mostly foreigners, hungry, cut-throat looking wretches.

"I held my breath, and made up my mind to struggle as hard as I could; and, if they tried to kill me, to bawl out my loudest.

"The matches were damp, and they were a long while getting a light.

"But while they were trying, a hand was slipped round the pillar of the door where I was hiding.

"A long, bony, muscular hand crept round cautiously, and rested upon my leg.

*　*　*　*　*

"Slowly, slowly, slowly, the fingers crept upwards and upwards.

"Then it was still for an instant.

"Then slowly, slowly, it crept upwards again, and rested on my thigh.

"My heart seemed as if it left off beating.

"I felt just as if some loathsome reptile was coiling itself round me, fold after fold, griping me in its slimy embrace.

"Again it rested for a moment.

"Then was rapidly withdrawn.

"Then, before I could get my senses, and get over my astonishment, it fastened upon my throat with an iron grasp, and I was flung out into the road like an old shoe.

"A loud and savage yell of laughter burst from the rest of the men, and a lantern was thrust into my face.

"'You thought you'd dodged us, did you?' said the man whom I had first spoken to.

"Then they flung me violently backwards against the wall.

"'What have you got in your pockets?' one said.

"Then another interrupted him.

"'Hush!' he said; 'don't you hear? There's some one coming.'

"At the same time we heard the chorus of a number of voices singing together very musically, and the tramp of many feet approached us from the top of the street.

"'Do you hear them?' asked one of my captors of another.

"'Yes; they're going it again to-night.'

"'They won't go it like that very long, if I can have my way.'

"'You're right there. We'll put the stopper on them.'

"'Hush!' interrupted another of the party. 'Are they coming this way?'

"'No—be still! They've passed the end of the street. They've got their boats down at the bottom of the next turning.'

"Worse luck, it was too true. The singers, whoever they were, were going on their way, and my last hope of escape was going with them.

"But when I came to reflect how desperate was my situation—that I should be robbed of all my treasure, and in all probability murdered in cold blood, savagely and brutally—I formed a desperate resolve.

"Since I must die, I would at least die pluckily, and not be slaughtered like a fat pig.

"I made up my mind what to do in less than a second, and in less than a second I put it into execution.

"I stooped down, and gathered all my strength for a great effort.

"Then, taking a long breath, I struck the man in front a blow in the face, which toppled him over like a ninepin.

"Then, with ten times the rapidity which I would have thought my poor old bones capable of, 1 bounded up the street, and plunged into a long narrow alley leading from it in the direction which the singers had taken.

"You, Charley, who only remember me when I was in the employment of Messrs. Bottle and Bung, can't very easily realize my performing feats of this kind, I expect; but, you know, I had had a dose of Spike Island, and had given up dram-drinking for a considerable period; and the change had done me such a mighty deal of good, it seemed to have put another ten years on to my life at the very least.

"Besides, when a chap has a swarm of blood-thirsty vampires chiveying him, and swearing to cut his throat from ear to ear, if he doesn't find his legs then, I have very strong doubts whether he will ever find them afterwards, even if he gets the chance.

"Well, on I flew, and I could feel that I gained upon my pursuers at every stride.

"On I flew, clutching tight my bag of gold.

"But I dare not pause for a moment to listen how far they were behind me, nor to listen for the voices of the singers whom I was endeavouring to reach, and could only plunge forward recklessly in the darkness, trusting to Providence that I should come out all right in the end.

"Down and down the unevenly paved, steep, dark street I ran; and it seemed, as I proceeded further, to grow still narrower, and steeper, and more rugged.

"A faint light shone at the end, which, as I grew nearer, I found to be the moon shining on the gable end of a house, through an opening at the end of the street.

"It was not, then, as I had feared—'no thoroughfare.'

"Cheered by the hope of coming into a broad thoroughfare, where I might hope for protection from the thieves pursuing me, I plunged on even faster than before.

"But, reaching the end of the street, I drew up suddenly, and a weight like lead fell upon my heart.

"I had come to the river.

"The lane ended with it.

"The rapid current of the water lashed the massive wood-word that defended the bank with a deep, melancholy sound, like the moanings of a dying hound.

"I felt as though it were a death-chaunt being sung upon my account.

"A long way off, on the water, there trembled a solitary light, which probably shone from some barge anchored there.

"I fixed my eye upon it, and made up my mind in my desperation to take a plunge, although I was by no means certain that I should be able to swim, particularly with this weight of gold about me.

"But before I could jump from the parapet, with a loud yell my pursuers rushed out upon me from over a low wall by my side, and seized me again.

"In an instant they had knocked me down, and, in spite of my piercing shrieks—for I expected every moment to be murdered—they almost knocked me senseless by a shower of blows upon my head and face, which covered me with blood.

"'Let's have the money,' said one, speaking as well as he could for loss of breath. 'Strip his coat off, and fling him into the water. Blast him! he's given us trouble enough. He'll be past Sheerness by the morning. Heave him over.'

"They violently dragged off my coat, and then dragged me along the parapet towards the edge.

"My senses were as clear that awful moment as they are now, when I am sitting here telling you about it.

"My head was clear enough, though the blows I had had prevented me using my strength. Indeed, they seemed to have knocked it all out of me.

"I hadn't the power to resist, but I could calculate the precious little chance there was left me, when once I had been shied into the river.

"All this I was calculating, and at the same time I was mumbling over such two or three prayers as I could remember best, when all at once I heard a tremendous loud shout, and a piercing whistle ringing through the streets.

"The men about me sprang to their feet.

"The shouts grew nearer and louder.

"Most of my would-be murderers sprang to their feet, and were for taking to their heels.

"Most of them, too, managed to do so. With an awful imprecation, and vows of bloody vengeance, they darted off, with dreadfully scared looks, in a dozen different directions.

"Only one remained, and he stood alone busily engaged in making some sort of parcel.

"I looked up. The moonlight shone full upon him, and I saw that he was the man who had first spoken to me, and that he was rolling up a bundle.

"A bundle of what?

"Of my gold.

"Collecting all my strength, I wiped the blood from my eyes, and pushed back my matted hair.

"Next moment I had sprang upon him from behind like a tiger.

"I am an old man; his strength was double that which I possessed; but the thought that all I had in the world—the means of ease and happiness—was being wrested from me, lent me a power which was almost superhuman; and, closing with him, I dragged him to the earth.

"Then, next moment, holding him down, with my knee upon his throat, I battered at his head with a stone.

"But he freed himself by a tremendous effort, and flung me forcibly to the ground.

"I lay there half stunned, and unable to rise.

"Then I saw him spring to his feet, and seize the bundle under his arm.

"Next moment I saw him fall back heavily upon the ground, and, as it appeared to me, an instant afterwards I heard the report of a pistol, and then the hurrying tramp of men coming in my direction.

"Then half-a-dozen cheers broke out in the street above, as though some party had been victorious.

"I prayed to God at the moment that it should prove to be the other side.

"A loud voice called to me.

"'Is anyone hurt?' it said; 'or is anyone killed? If so, speak up.'

"I tried to call out in reply, but I had not the strength to do so.

"'Anyone hurt?' he sang out again.

"A window over my head opened as he spoke, and a man holding a candle looked out.

"The light fell full upon my head, and the person who had called out caught sight of me.

"'Come on,' he cried to some others behind him. 'Come on; he's down here.'

"Then, approaching me, and stooping over me where I lay, 'You're not much hurt, I hope,' said he. 'You're bleeding, I see.'

"'I'm only a little mauled,' I answered him. 'I shall soon get over it.'

"'Was there anybody else besides you?'

"'No—no one else.'

"'Can you walk?'

"'I'll try.'

"'No; don't exert yourself. We'll easily carry you. Here, mate, lend a hand; we'll get him along easy enough.'

"So saying, they raised me in their arms, and bore me along.

"But the motion made me feel faint and sick, and a weakness seeming to creep over me all at once, my head became dizzy, and I swooned away.

"When I came to myself, I was in a large saloon, on board of a ship, lying on a sofa, and surrounded by about half-a-dozen very jovial-looking red-faced men, all smoking large pipes, and pegging away at large glasses of steaming hot grog.

"When I came to myself a little bit, I sat up, and looked round me, rubbing my eyes.

"'Where have you brought me to?' I asked.

"Then I thought of my money, and asked after it anxiously.

"It's all right,' replied one of the company, and pointed as he spoke to the pilot coat lying on the table, and the bag of gold lying beside it.

"'It's all right, Captain Cook,' said he; 'so you can make your mind easy on that score.'

"'My name's not Captain Cook,' said I.

"'Don't be afraid of us,' replied the speaker, with a laugh. 'We shan't give you up to the authorities, so you needn't be afraid. Perhaps it's just as lucky you fell in with us, that's all. You'd have been robbed if you hadn't, to say the least of it.'

"'You're right there,' said I; 'and I return you my sincerest thanks.'

"'There, that's quite enough,' said my new friend. 'Make your mind easy, I say, and go to sleep.'

"I thought that perhaps it would be as well if I acted under his suggestion, and so I fell asleep at once, without any more ado, and I don't think I ever slept more comfortable in my life.

"When I woke up—however long I may have slept I have no idea—but all the company were drinking, and smoking, and chaffing, just as they were before.

"I sat up and looked about me with some considerable curiosity.

"A jollier set of dogs I don't think I ever clapt my eyes on.

"They were for the most part elderly men, and wore tremendous beards and moustaches. Most of them were very grey, and one was as bald as a billiard-ball.

"Their conversation, though mostly carried on in English, was sprinkled every now and then with French, and German, and Spanish; and one of the company had a tremendous Yankee twang.

"Their exceedingly free-and-easy way, and their curious dresses, the intimate terms with each other that they seemed to be upon, and various other little things that I noticed, made me inclined to doubt very strongly whether these gentlemen came by their bread and butter honestly; and I began to wonder whatever trade they could belong to. I took them at first to be highwaymen, but it turned out that they were smugglers.

"When I was sufficiently recovered to sit down and join the festivities—that is to say, the gin and water—I told them how I had found the money, and who I was, and all about it.

"You may say, perhaps, that it was a very green thing to do; but the fact is, they were such deuced good company, and the gin and water, and brandy and water, and drink generally, was so deuced good, I couldn't for the life of me keep any secrets from them.

"As it turned out, I lost nothing by being so communicative.

"I had always a turn for sociability, you know, Charley, and perhaps they took a liking to me. Anyhow one of them says at last—

"'What are you going to do with that money, Mr. Toddleboy?'

"'Spend it like a man,' says I.

"'But when its gone?'

"'Do without it.'

"'Ah, that's a poor trade. You'd much better invest it.'

"'In what?'

"'Buy a ship with it, and be a smuggler.'

"'A ship,' says I, 'I know a precious little about ships. I was a cabin boy when I was a lad, but I should say that must be close on forty years ago, and perhaps a little more. I'm too old to begin now.'

"'Not a bit of it. If you've ever been on the sea before it will all come as natural as two and two. There's a mate, too, on board that 'll put you up to all the capers. What do you say?'

"Well, I did'nt know what to say, so I listened to all they said first."

"The boat that was for sale had belonged to one of their friends who had recently died, leaving his widow and four young children behind him.

"The boat was to be sold for a couple of hundreds. The profits of the smuggling trade were said to be immense. It was a wonderful opening. It was something new.

"I determined to close upon the offer at once.

"Next day I went to look at the boat, paid the money, and started as Toddleboy, the pirate chief.

"And you've made it answer?" said Charley.

"First rate," replied the noble smuggler.

Both Charley and Julia, who had come down into the cabin during the latter part of Mr. Toddleboy's story, laughed heartily when he had concluded his recital.

"It's the last thing that ever I should have thought would have happened to you," said Charley.

And indeed it was. I suppose the reader scarcely expected it.

But while they were talking together over old times, a shout of "land!" arose upon deck, and the captain, leaving Charley and his mistress together, hurried up the companion-ladder.

He returned in a very few minutes, and with rather a long face said that he had found that his mate had been taken very ill suddenly with some kind of fits, and did not look as if he would get over it.

"I'm sorry enough on his account," said the captain, "for he was as good-hearted a fellow as ever wore shoe leather; but it's precious awkward at the present moment, because I counted upon his services in rather a delicate mission."

"What's that?"

"Well, in half an hour or so I was going to land him, and send him up the country with a letter, which it is of the greatest possible importance to me should be delivered to-night."

"Why can't I take it?"

"Do you know French?"

"No."

"Ah, there's the difficulty. My mate speaks like a native, and unless you could talk pretty glibly, I don't think you could manage it, though I am very much obliged to you, Charley, all the same."

"I tell you what, though," said Charley. "Julia, here—"

"Yes," broke in the young lady, "I can talk, and shall be delighted to do anything for you that lies in my power, captain."

"It's hardly a lady's errand, though," replied the captain doubtfully.

"Fiddlestick, what is there to do?"

"I'm afraid you'd have to—to put on—"

"What?"

"Men's clothes, you know. Coats and waistcoats, and such like."

"There's nothing I would like better. Tell me what to do, and I'm your man."

"I'm dashed!" cried Captain Toddleboy, delighted, "if you're not a stunner. I can't say I think much of women as a rule, but if I was only forty or fifty years younger, there's no knowing what I mightn't be saying."

The captain then explained that he had a packet which he wanted to be delivered to a lady living at a town some small distance from Calais, near to which they were going to effect a landing.

Julia was then to proceed by a road which he described to her, to a certain house on the outskirts of Calais, where she would be able to get the loan of a horse, upon representing that she had come from Toddleboy, and was the bearer of a letter for the lady aforesaid.

On this she would easily effect the journey, and after delivering the letter, bring back the reply that night or the first thing next morning.

Julia willingly agreed, and having learnt full particulars, and equipped herself in a suit of male attire, which a lad on board usually received for his Sunday best, she said good-bye to her lover, and set out upon her expedition.

———

LV.—JULIA SETS OUT ON HER JOURNEY.

THEY landed her up a little creek, and then the captain directed her the way she should go to find the house where a horse would be waiting to take her on her journey.

When she arrived at her destination, the person for whom she was to inquire was out, and was not expected to return until late in the day.

As, from the two or three hints she ventured to throw out, she saw very plainly that the other people about the place were not in the secret, whatever it was, she saw nothing else for it but to wait patiently until the person she had been sent to see, returned.

To pass the time, she put up at a miserable little tavern hard by, and leaving word that she was to be sent for if Mr. Bertrand returned, did her best to make herself comfortable.

But in spite of her most strenuous efforts to be jolly, the time passed miserably enough.

The rain had set in again, and poured down at intervals in torrents, making up for long hours of monotonous drizzling.

When night set in, she requested that a fire should be lighted, and a few damp sticks were heaped up upon the hearth, which hissed and smoked, but gave out no warmth.

Growing impatient, she sent over several times to ask whether Mr. Bertrand had come in.

Ever the same question and the same reply—

"Was he come?"

"No."

"Did they suppose he would be long?"

"They had not the remotest idea."

At last it got so late she thought she had better go to bed and wait until the morning.

The first thing in the morning he came.

"It's dreadfully provoking that it should have happened so," he said; "but the fact is, I expected you the day before yesterday."

"Indeed! The captain did not say so."

"He landed at a different place, too, I suppose, for I went to the usual spot and could see no sign of him. It's most provoking."

"Had I not better hurry on, then, at once, or shall I be too late?"

"I'm afraid you will find the lady out before you get there. She expected you yesterday."

"What shall I do in that case?"

"You must wait for her."

Julia could not help thinking that this promised to be a journey with a good deal of waiting about it.

She had barely time to swallow her breakfast before the Frenchman returned to tell her that he had the horse saddled and ready for the road.

She gulphed down the remainder, and announced herself at his disposal.

Then he gave her full directions how and where to find the lady she was in quest of; saw her mount her horse, and waved her an adieu politely with his hat.

If he had suspected her sex, he had not given her the faintest hint of it; but as he had from the first watched her narrowly to try and find out whether her disguise deceived him, she felt convinced that such was the case, and so was led to hope that she would be equally successful elsewhere.

There was no reason why she should not, as she always was successful enough in the various expeditions in England on which she had accompanied Charley Wag, dressed in man's attire.

The journey to the small town whither she was bound, was altogether without incident or adventure.

From a description which the Frenchman had given her, she easily found the house in which she was in search.

She rang the bell at the gate, and waited for some time before she got any answer.

At last an old man, having the appearance of a family servant, came to see what she wanted.

Julia looked for a moment at the address of the letter which she bore in her hand.

It bore the name of Madame Deschapelles.

Madame was not at home.

She was expected every hour, but it was very probable that she would not return until the evening.

Early in the evening?

It might be late.

Could she wait?

If she liked, most certainly.

She would find several excellent hotels in the town.

Julia went away crestfallen.

The reader may imagine that some of these details are rather unnecessary; but if he will only kindly have patience, he will see that we are coming to something presently which will atone for so much waiting and so many delays.

Julia began to canvas with herself how she could best escape from the prying inquisitiveness to which every stranger is exposed on entering a new community.

She might, however, very well have saved herself the trouble, for she found she was perfectly unnoticed in the motley throng in which she mingled.

It was market-day, and the streets were crowded by buyers and sellers, and herds of cattle and troops of horses blocked up every other thoroughfare leading to the market-place.

Her strong-boned, high-bred horse, indeed, called forth many a compliment as she rode along, but no one seemed to have any care for the rider.

At last, as she was approaching the chief inn, she beheld a small knot of men whose dress and looks were not unfamiliar to her.

Some of them decidedly were Englishmen— and in all probability, to judge from their appearance at first sight, English scamps.

One of them, however, she seemed to know very well indeed.

She had met him somewhere before, perhaps, in a different dress and under very different circumstances. She had met him, she felt quite certain.

When she came to look at him a second time, and a little harder, she felt she could not be mistaken.

No; he was the man whom Charley and she had met in the wood near Hampstead that morning when they bilked the landlord so cleverly.

There was no mistaking that apish face and that villainous expression.

But she trusted to escape recognition, not being by any means desirous of renewing the acquaintance.

While she was endeavouring to push her way between two carts full of vegetables, her ugly friend came up and laid his hand upon her horse's shoulder.

"How much for this?" he asked in bad French.

"He's not for sale," Julia replied, coldly.

But the other did not seem inclined to take "No" for an answer.

Without heeding her reply, he passed his hands along the animal's legs, feeling his tendons, and grasping his flesh.

After which he stepped back a pace or two, the better to survey him.

"Trot him a bit," said he.

Julia began to grow savage, for she was rather a hasty-tempered young lady at times.

"Excuse me, my good sir," said she, "but I do not want to sell it. I have come here to buy rather than to sell, if I can find anything to suit my fancy."

"But I'll give you a good price for it."

"I don't want to sell it."

"Your own price."

"I don't want to sell it."

"What's he say?" one of the horsey gents said to another.

"He won't part with the nag."

"Oh, he won't, won't he?"

"He says so."

"Josh 'll have it out of him yet. I'll bet a fi'pun-note to a sou."

With these observations the little company of "legs" drew on one side, and allowed Julia to pass into the inn-yard.

But Julia felt anything but comfortable.

If there was one thing she dreaded more than another, as likely to lead to detection of her sex, it was getting into a row.

She had wondered at first why the captain had thought it to be so necessary that she should wear male attire; but now, when she found what rough company she was likely to come in contact with, she wondered no longer.

However, she was in for it now, and thought she might as well put the best face upon that matter.

In spite of this resolve, I must tell you, all the easy assurance she could put on did not convince herself that her fears were not written in her face. She rode forward.

To be sure, she did make all possible noise and swagger as she flung herself from the saddle, and gave loud and imperious orders to the attendants, and she could see that she was put down at once for a young " milord."

She spoke very good French for an English-woman, for she had lived for some time at Paris, under the protection of the Duke of Heather-land, and she felt quite certain 'that she would be able to deceive the sporting gentleman with regard to her nationality, although she might not be so successful with Frenchmen.

Having commended her horse to the hands of the ostler, she entered the inn with all the swaggering assurance of a nabob, though, in good earnest, with anything but an easy heart at the vicinity of the sporting gents.

The public room into which she entered was crowded with country people, buyers and deal-ers, in busy and noisy discussion of their several bargains; and had she been a little more free'of personal anxiety, the study of their varied countenances, costumes, and manners, would probably have been amusing enough.

But, as it was, she only looked at them anxiously to see what they were like, and sought out the quietest corner.

She ordered a bottle of wine and such refresh-ment as the house afforded.

For she had not set out upon her journey, as you may suppose, without putting something in her pocket.

In the motley assemblage which the room contained she mingled unnoticed, and sat down to her omelette without even a passing obser-vation.

As she sat on, however, she was far from pleased by remarking that Mr. Josh and another had taken their seats at a table right opposite, and kept their eyes full on her with what, in better society, would have perhaps have been considered an impudent stare.

Miss Julia would, of course, have liked to have had a private room, but for this she would have had to have waited some time; and she had decided upon coming in here as being the likelier way to escape from her sporting friends than by hanging about round the door.

She could not, somehow, rid herself of an unpleasant sense of impending danger which seemed to hang over her.

Mr. Josh's ugly face wore an expression, half of doubt and half of conviction, as though he were trying to think whether he had ever seen her before.

Julia could see very well what was passing in his mind, or, at least, she fancied she could; and she resorted to little dodges, in the hope of putting him off the scent.

She wanted him to take her for a Frenchman, and she gave herself all a Frenchman's graces and grimaces.

But it wouldn't do for Josh.

He was not to be taken in.

She saw him sitting there, glaring at her uglier than ever, eyeing her most suspiciously.

Now and then he whispered something to his companions; and then, if possible, they seemed to stare harder than ever.

Julia's anxiety increased to a fever.

She could not stand it any longer, and she called the waiter to show her to a bed-room, hoping thus to escape.

She could not get one without a good deal of difficulty, and it was a poor place when she did get it.

Thank goodness, though, she was alone at last; and she threw herself on the bed, a great deal easier in her mind than she had been any time for this last couple of hours,

But she did not remain long undisturbed.

In less than five minutes there came a smart knock at the door.

" What is it?" she asked, in French.

" I want to speak to you," a voice replied, in English.

" I can't be bothered just now," she said, in French.

" You'd better open your door pretty sharp, or else I'll break it open," was the observation in reply.

———

LVI.—More danger still.

JULIA thought it best to open the door with-out any more delay.

She put on an expression of angry indignation to conceal a little bit of a tremble she could not help feeling.

" Whatever are you in such a hurry about," said she, " that you can't wait until I come down?"

" I want to speak to you most particularly."

" What do you want to say?"

" Let us shut the door first."

As he spoke, he suited the action to the words.

Then, having closed the door, he leant his back against it, and looked Julia hard in the face.

Then he smiled a little.

Julia drew herself up to her full height, and frowned in her severest fashion.

" Well, sir?" said she.

" You're very short with me, guvnor," said Mr. Josh; " and still,' we ought to be old friends."

Julia shook her head, to intimate that she did not understand what he was saying.

But Mr. Josh grinned broader.

" You know me well enough," said he. " Don't you recollect that little wood, where we had the pleasure of meeting last?"

Julia shook her head.

"Well, then, since you don't or won't speak English, I must talk the cursed lingo of this country, I suppose," said Mr. Josh; and from that time forward he talked the best French he was capable of.

"I want to buy your horse," said he.

"I won't sell it," replied Julia.

"But look here—you must. I've been having a squint at him as he stood in the stall. There's some races coming off here to-morrow. He's the very horse for my book. I can pull off neatly on him, I feel certain. Stop and share the swag, if you won't sell him. But anyhow, I must have the rise of him."

"I have told you," replied Julia, "that I won't let you have him. I want him myself. Really, your perseverance is astonishing!"

"It's because I'm in earnest, that's all. Now what do you say?"

"I say 'No.'"

"Well, don't say I didn't put it to you fair. If anything happens to the nag, it ain't my fault."

"There's law in the land, I suppose."

"Ah, there is so. I'm over here partly on legal business myself, after a young gent of the name of Charles Wag; and when I first dropped my eyes upon you, I thought you might have put me on to his traces."

"In what way?"

"You know best. When did you see him last?"

"I have never seen him."

"Come, come, there's quite enough of this sort of thing, you know. I want that horse, and if you don't let me have it on my own terms, I'll take it, and you along with it, my prisoner."

"You talk very largely, my fine fellow," replied Julia, pluckily; "but you must fancy that if I was Charley Wag I carried pistols about with me. Indeed, it strikes me you ought to remember—"

And as she spoke she drew a four-barrelled revolver from her pocket.

Mr. Josh looked a little startled, but he kept his countenance, in spite of the dangerous proximity of the murderous weapon.

"Put down your pistol," said he, "and let's come to terms."

"Talk politely, then, and don't bully quite so much."

There was just the faintest shadow of a smile on Mr. Josh's face, as though he did not think Julia was quite big enough to bully him; but he at any rate was a good deal more respectful than he had previously been.

"Can you let us have that horse?" he asked.

"No."

"Why not? I'll swap with you, or sell you another."

"I can't do it."

"But why?"

"Because it's not mine."

"Why the blazes didn't you say that at first?"

"Because I did not exactly see why I should put myself out of the way to acquaint you with my private affairs."

"Ah, that's true," observed Mr. Josh, whom the fact seemed to strike as something rather forcible.

"But can't you sell it all the same?" he added, after a smile.

"Well," said Julia, not knowing exactly what to say, "I'll think it over."

"Have a bit of dinner with me this afternoon. I'm here by myself. I'll give you a tidy spread."

"With pleasure. What time?"

"At six."

"Till then, good-bye."

As soon as the man had gone, Julia rang the bell and gave particular directions that no one should be allowed under any pretence to touch her horse, and then lay down to sleep.

"I'll be as sharp as they are," said she. "I don't think much harm can come to me now till I've delivered this horrible letter and got back to Charley."

But she had still a great deal to go through, as we shall see.

A very extraordinary adventure yet awaited her.

She got up much refreshed, after a couple of hours sleep, took a stroll down the town to see whether Madame Deschapelles had yet returned home.

She had not.

Coming back to the inn, she found Mr. Josh and dinner waiting.

Mr. Josh, over his wine, could manage, somehow or other, to make himself tolerable agreeable, and if he had not been so atrociously ugly, Julia almost fancied that it would have been possible for him to have persuaded her that he was not such an awful vagabond as she knew him to be.

He was a vagabond who had a pound or two in his pocket at any rate, for he not only ordered a most sumptuous dinner, but paid for it with a flourish, and gave some loose silver to the waiter when they had finished, with the air of a nobleman.

"There is a sort of dance going on down-stairs," said Josh, as the sound of violins reached them from below, and attracted Julia's attention.

"Shall we go down there and have our coffee, and smoke our cigars?"

Julia very much wished to do so, though she knew she should not.

Josh persuaded, and the waiter said that it was capital fun.

Therefore, the wine and their description had some effect, and, most unfortunately for her, she went.

LVII.—IN WHICH MISS JULIA'S BRIGHT EYES GET HER INTO A DEAL OF TROUBLE.

THE scene was extremely picturesque.

A trellised passage, roofed with twining honeysuckles, ran round the four sides of the building, in the open space of which the holiday folks were assembled.

Gay lamps of gaudily painted paper, and here and there flaring torches stuck in the walls, lit up the dancers, and imparted perhaps to the variously coloured and showy—though in most

THE FIGHT.

instances shabby, dresses of the ladies an elegance and brilliancy which the severer test of daylight might not have done the same for.

The dark complexions, the flushing black eyes, the graceful costumes, the inspiring music, the merry voices, the joyous laughter, —all were too many ingredients of pleasure to be easily resisted; and so Miss Julia thought that she would spend an hour very happily before she troubled herself by going about the letter for the mysterious Madame Deschapelles.

In a very lazy mood Miss Julia lit her cigarette, and lolling back upon a bench in an arbour, from whence she could see the merry-makings, you may be sure she began to scrutinize the dresses of the women around her.

No. 47.

There was one whom she very soon picked from the rest as being in looks and dress something much supior.

She was a slightly formed, graceful girl, whose dark eyes twice or thrice had met Julia's, and been withdrawn again with a kind of indolent reluctance, as Julia fancied, which if she had only happened to be of the sex which the young French lady naturally supposed, would have been highly flattering.

As it was, Miss Julia, who was as great an imp for mischief as any living—indeed, she was a fitting companion for Mr. Wag in that respect —thought she would have a little fun in a small way, and so she ogled the young lady in return.

There was an air of pride about this French

[CHARLEY WAG, THE NEW JACK SHEPPARD.

damsel, even in the position of her well planted foot, seen under the embroidery of her petticoat, which harmonized admirably with the erect carriage of her head, and the graceful composure of her crossed arms made her a perfect picture.

Nor was Miss Julia quite certain that she did not know this herself. One thing was quite certain: her air, her attitude, her attire, and her every gesture, were quite in keeping.

She was not very tastefully, though, perhaps, rather fantastically, dressed; but that might have been the last fashion.

She was not dancing. Several came to ask her, but she refused.

She stood among the lookers-on; and evidently she did not think much of the company she found herself amongst.

Her features wore an expression of passive indifference, changing even to a half smile of scornful contempt.

On one occasion some youthful swain took the awful liberty of twitching her shawl from behind, at which dire offence she turned upon him and boxed his ears in a way which might be heard above the noise of all the music.

"I like her," said Julia to herself; "she's my sort to a T."

Presently, after this little incident, and when the young man who had had "one for himself," had sneaked away dreadfully crest-fallen, a young man entered the enclosure.

He was a young, powerful built fellow, dressed in rustic smartness, very clumsily got up, it is true; but still evidently well to do, and with a well lined purse.

He was a surly-looking young man; indeed, a very surly-looking young man when you came well to observe him, and Julia took a great dislike to him, without knowing why, the first moment that she saw him.

He stood for a few moments looking round, and scowling at the spectators, as though he were looking for some one.

Then his eyes resting on the young French lady, he came straight towards her with a much brighter look and offered her his hand.

She, however, did not respond so cordially, for some reason or the other. Perhaps he had kept her waiting, and she did not like it. I believe very few ladies do; they think it a privilege belonging entirely to their own sex.

Anyhow, from whatever reason it was, does not so much signify—the fact is the same. He flushed up and scowled, and drew back, and seemed to be very bad indeed about it.

But to Miss Julia's great amazement, his glance was next bent upon her, and that with an expression of hatred there was no mistaking.

At first she fancied it might have been mere supposition on her part; but when she had looked at him again, she felt very certain there was no mistake.

She saw plainly that the insulting looks were meant for herself, and none other.

Let her look which side she would, let her occupy her attention how she might, the man's swarthy, sullen face, never turned from her for an instant.

Probably something in Julia's face must have betrayed to her companion what was passing within her breast, for Mr. Josh whispered in her ear very softly. "Take care, young fellow, you don't get it hot from the party over the way."

"What do you mean?"

"The scowling dark chap."

"I'm not afraid of him."

"Well, if you ain't, its all right, only you're very bounceable."

"What have I done to him, pray, that we should quarrel?"

"Well, it's his girl that's been looking over this way at you ever so long. I suppose you've noticed her?"

"Yes, I have; and why should she not?"

"Oh, I see no reason myself."

"It's a sign of her good taste, isn't it?"

"Oh, most decidedly."

And Mr. Josh subsided in silence with a kind of inward chuckle, which Julia, however, did not deign to notice.

His reason will, perhaps, become more apparent to the reader in a page or two.

"She's a devilish nice bit of goods," Mr. Josh remarked presently. "Why don't you dance with her?"

Julia was about to make some reply, when the young French lady came straight up to the table, and making a low curtsey before her, asked Julia to have a waltz.

There had been a good deal of wine going on, and a very great deal of brandy had been poured quietly into Julia's cup, when that young lady was not looking.

Perhaps this may in some way have accounted for Julia's conduct.

She ought to have known better, certainly, you may say; but then I ask you, what could she do, when a lady asked her, but accept.

She danced.

Springing from her seat, with the politest of bows, she put her arm round the other's waist, and the next moment they were whirling along in a waltz.

But scarcely had they time to make the round the circle once, before the ill-tempered looking young man rushed at them, and suddenly arresting their progress with his strong arm, seized Julia roughly by the shoulder and shook off her hold from the French girl.

The next moment Julia had seized a wine bottle from a side table, and struck the man a blow upon the head with it, which sent him reeling backwards.

Before he could recover himself, however, several men had thrown themselves between the combatants.

But the generality of the company were in favour of a row.

"A fight! a fight!" shouted out a score of voices.

"Make a ring."

"Clear a space."

"Stand back!"

"Give them room."

"Go on," and "leave off."

The crowd closed in upon the dancing space, and a hundred tongues mingled in wild altercation, although a few professed themselves indignant that a stranger should be thus insulted. The majority were with their countryman, whom they agreed in considering a most ill-used and outraged individual. Mr. Josh, to Julia's astonishment, took the same view of the matter, and was even more energetic than the others in reprobation of her conduct.

"A lark's a lark," said he; "but, damn it, that was going a little too far."

Julia was surprised; but still she was so savage with the man, that she demanded nothing better than to hit him again if she had not been held back.

"It must be a duel," everybody said.

"A duel!" cried Julia, astonished more and more. "Impossible, why I never—"

But here she checked herself, not liking to disclose her sex.

"A duel, decidedly," observed Mr. Josh. "It can't be got over any other way. I told you how it would be."

All this time the confusion and noise grew louder and louder, and from the angry looks which Julia met with on every side, there was no trouble in seeing how strong public opinion was against her.

Julia debated with herself hastily as to what course she should take. Should she run away? Would not it be sheer madness to stop? But then, again, how could she escape?

How was it going to end? Surely it was not possible that she was going to fight a duel. It seemed as though lately there was nothing now but duelling. It seems quite a farce—too ridiculous to be true. Two days ago Charley had been obliged to fight, and now she was in the same fix.

But why not say at once that she was a woman, and expose the absurdity of the whole affair? Well, somehow she did not like to do that. She had various very cogent reasons for objecting, though the writer does not attempt to explain them. Why should he? Were not they a woman's reasons?

Meanwhile Mr. Josh and the rest were disputing loudly.

Mr. Josh was determined to see fair play. Mr. Josh was not going to see his friend imposed upon, he could tell them that.

And the impression of the virtuous Josh's countenance when he imparted this information to his listeners, was something terrific in ferocity.

"Just look'ee, my fine fellow," Julia heard him saying. "I won't have the lad butchered, so you just understand me. If we are English, we're not going to be humbugged by you mounseers, so I tell you plainly. None of your bloodthirsty work with us, you know. There's a lovely little bit of ground behind the house, that looks as if it were made on purpose for the business."

A very noisy and excited discussion followed these remarks, to which Julia did not pay any very particular attention.

At the end of ten minutes or so, Mr. Josh came to Julia, and led her towards the hotel, saying that as soon as the necessary arrangements could be made, a little genteel sword practice was to come off between our heroine and the surly Frenchman.

"We've twenty minutes of time left," said Mr. Josh. "Let's have a drop of something. It will put a little courage into you, my lad."

"I've courage enough without that," replied Julia.

"By gosh, I know you have!" exclaimed Mr. Josh, with enthusiasm, and patting the young lady on the back. "You're not the boy to turn tail at the big words of an infernal frog-eating son of a gun like that is. I said you weren't. We may look like a girl, if they like; but, by Jove, I says, he's got the eye of a lion, and would be a match for any half-dozen of you —one down and the other come on."

It was always afterwards a matter of great uncertainty to Julia, whether or not her friend Mr. Josh was acting like the friend he professed to be.

One thing was very sure, and that was, that nobody alive could have been more careful of a friend's reputation; no one could possibly have shown a more chivalrous regard for Miss Julia's honour, or exhibited a more sovereign contempt for any danger which she might run in the coming encounter.

There must be a fight, he said. None of your bloodthirsty work, mind, but a gentlemanly exchange of thrusts, which would satisfy everybody, and make everything nice and comfortable.

He advanced almost an hundred reasons for a combat; and though Julia was inclined to think that the greater part of them were very far from cogent, still, this opinion did not seem to be shared by the crowd of indignant individuals who surrounded them, and who one and all seemed to be as much interested in the coming fight as the principals themselves.

Now, although a friend is everything in these cases, yet even friendship may be a little overdone, Julia began to think.

There appeared to be a kind of relish with which Mr. Josh expatiated upon the outrageous nature of the insult Julia had sustained, and the disgracefully open way in which it was done, that showed the very greatest appreciation of her position, allied to the most delicate sensitiveness upon account of her honour.

And perhaps it was upon this very account, and owing to the awful perversity of human nature, that the stronger and more powerful Mr. Josh's arguments became in favour of bloodshed, the harder did Julia struggle to refute them, and show that the best way under the circumstances would be to shake hands and make it up.

At last, apparently wearied out by Julia's arguments, Mr. Josh said, swearing a big oath, and thumping his fist upon the table,

"Do what the dickens you like. It will be a long while before I try any more to do you a good turn—you may take your oath of that."

"No, but look here, Mr. Josh."

"Oh, that be hanged! I'm sick of arguments."

"But I'll hear reason."

"If you prefer a knife in your ribs to the feeble chance of a sabre cut, I can't say I admire your taste, that's all."

"Do you suppose there's a chance of my being assassinated if I don't fight?"

"By gosh, I don't know anybody who stands a better. You don't surely suppose that the mounseer would let you cock it over him so quietly in the way you did, and take away his sweetheart from under his very nose, without wanting to have a cut at you, do you?"

"What am I to do then?"

"Well, I've been doing my best to explain for an hour or more. You must fight him, I say; and if you had never before had a sword in your hand, I think I could show you a trick in ten minutes that'll answer your purpose."

"What's that?"

"To run him through the body."

"Good God! I do not want—"

"No—exactly; I thought how it would be. Very well, then, let him skewer you instead."

"And if I do skewer him, what must I do afterwards?"

"Make yourself uncommon scarce, is my advice, and lose no time in doing it."

At last, quite overcome by Mr. Josh's arguments, and persuasions, and entreaties, Julia consented to take a lesson or two in sword practice; and although the result was of such a character that Mr. Josh almost cracked his sides with laughter, asking her who her fencing master was, and whether he would be willing to give a fellow a few finishing lessons at a small figure, Mr. Josh nevertheless pronounced her quite likely to cook the Frenchman's goose the first round.

Julia did not feel quite so certain of it, but she did her best to pick up what instruction Mr. Josh thought fit to give her; and, as she was extraordinary sharp at most things, it was wonderful what she did manage to learn in an incredibly small space of time.

While she was practising by herself, Mr. Josh had been very busy with a pen and ink and paper.

"What are you doing?" Julia asked.

"Just trying to map out a bit of a will."

"A will!"

"Aye; to settle that horse of yours, and your togs, and suchlike."

"Yes, but they'll go to my next of kin."

"Of course, if that's what you want," replied Mr. Josh, gloomily; "only I should have thought you might have remembered a friend."

"There, then," replied Julia, who was most anxious to conciliate him; "as you like. Let's have the paper, and I'll sign it."

And she suited the deed to the words.

Just then Mr. Josh pointed to a party of about a dozen or so of men taking their way silently through the tall grass at the bottom of the garden.

"That's the procession," said he. "It's time we were off."

I should think that the reader must own, in spite of all prejudice, that Miss Julia was a plucky young woman.

Whatever else she was not, she was anyhow courageous.

But it cannot be denied that the sight of those men stalking slowly and silently through the gloom, caused a most uncomfortable feeling to take possession of her.

There seemed, too, to be something so very purposely like and deadly in their regular plodding tramp.

There was a certain look of cold-blooded determination in their movements that chilled her to the heart.

They were mostly wrapped up in their long cloaks, and they mostly wore great moustaches and beards.

They all looked very terrible to Julia's eyes.

"I say," whispered Josh, as they walked along.

"Well?"

"I forgot to ask something."

"What?"

"It is, supposing anything should—"

"Well?"

"Should happen, you know?"

"Yes."

"Anything of an unpleasant character should result, you know?"

"I don't know. Speak plainer."

"Well, then, in case you should be popped off."

"Should be killed, you mean."

"Exactly. Have you any particular instructions to leave behind with respect to your covering up?"

"My covering up?"

"Your burying, you know," said Josh, in a whisper, sinking his voice very low, as it seemed, to make the unpleasant communication as palatable as possible.

"I've no instructions," replied Julia, with a little shudder.

"I thought you might have had," observed Mr. Josh, subsiding into a whistle.

Then they walked along together in silence.

Julia tried to keep her spirits up.

She was not thinking of the young lady who had been the innocent cause of this little misunderstanding.

Her reflections were simply limited to a few very selfish considerations. She was chiefly occupied in reflecting upon the construction of the human frame, and endeavouring to recollect everything that she had heard of the portions wherein a sword-thrust was likely to prove the most fatal, as also the portions where an individual could be cut and slashed at with the smallest possible amount of danger.

"Come along, young fellow," said Josh; "I've got everything ready for you. Your horse is saddled, in case of a bolt; and in case of the other thing, there's some bandages prepared, and a doctor sent for. What are you waiting for now?"

"Waiting?—oh, nothing. I'm quite ready," replied Julia, looking regretfully behind at the house she was leaving, as though it were an old friend.

"Well," said Josh, "anyone to see you would say you wanted to shirk off; but I know you've too much pluck for that, my lad."

"Oh, I don't want to shirk off," answered Julia, with a laugh; "and if I did, by jingo I should have a hard job of it with you at my elbow."

"Me! Well, I like that. What have I got to do with it, one way or the other? Damn me! what do you mean?"

"Don't excite yourself, sir. By the way, I've got a letter to deliver to a lady. I had forgotten it."

"Oh, that'll do afterwards."

"To be sure; only, if anything was to happen—you understand."

"Trust me—I'll see after it."

"Thank you; you're very kind."

"Don't mention it. It's only what every gentleman would do for another."

How Julia did hate Mr. Josh, in spite of all his kindness!

Human nature is so ungrateful!

"I wish it was his duel," thought the young lady to herself. "I could see him stuck with a great deal of pleasure."

As they walked along, Mr. Josh went on with his directions.

"Don't you go and forget what I explained to you about the guard for the face," said he.

Then, after a few seconds,

"Mind you always keep the hilt of your sword straight between your eyes, and hold your elbow down low."

This he repeated continually, until Julia found herself repeating the words mechanically after him, without hardly knowing what they meant.

"Now look here," Josh went on presently; "the mounseer has got a tremendous strong arm, you know. He could pretty well fell an ox. There's some of these mounseers are awful tough customers, as you can see for yourself, and have seen, I daresay. And perhaps his game may be to try and break down your guard. Now if that's the move, you must take a jump on one side, and let him have your point slap into his chest. That'll skewer him."

In this way Mr. Josh, with infinite relish and gusto, proceeded to discuss a thousand little niceties and tricks that good fencers are acquainted with, until at last, Julia could not refrain from saying that it was a very great pity Mr. Josh himself had not a chance of distinguishing himself, and asked him, in a sly sort of way, whether he did not think that it could be managed.

But Mr. Josh did not seem to see the fun.

"We'd better be getting on," said he.

And now, as they approached the scene of the coming conflict, Julia was debating with herself whether or not she should disclose her sex, and get out of this grossly absurd fight altogether.

But, improbable as it may seem, she decided to go on with the affair to the end, and preferred the chance of being killed to the exposure which she would otherwise suffer.

"I'll see it out, and God help me," said she.

"I say, are you listening to me, young man?" cried Mr. Josh, impatiently.

"What were you saying?"

"I was telling you about the cross-guard for your head."

'Ha! ha!' laughed Julia. "Don't be angry, but I haven't been paying the least attention."

"The devil you haven't! That's cool."

"You can't make a good hand of me, so it's no good taking any more trouble," replied Julia. "I must put my trust in Providence."

Mr. Josh seemed to be rather put out by this remark, and they plodded along in silence.

"It's not my fault if you're skewered," she heard him say two or three times as they walked along.

In a few minutes they had reached the appointed spot.

Half-a-dozen torches were stuck in the ground at regular distances, and at the same time that they threw a sufficient light upon the scene to enable the principal actors to see perfectly well what they were about, the lurid light imparted something awfully demoniacal to the faces and figures of the spectators, whose murky forms emerging from the red glare, looked like evil spirits in the shades of hell.

A party of men, among whom Julia perceived the individual with whom she was to fight, were seated at a table in an arbour; and, much to her astonishment, they were eating and drinking.

Yes, they were decidedly making a hearty breakfast.

Then she asked herself, when she came to think of it, why shouldn't they?

Once, when she had attended a public execution in London, she had noticed that the enlightened British public, or rather, that portion of it there assembled, seemed to treat the whole affair as an amusing drama, got up for their special edification; and, having paid for their places at the windows, they no doubt imagined that they were fully entitled to enjoy their money's worth; and that anything in the way of departure from his duties upon the part of the hangman, or the omission of any of the horrible and revolting details by any other official there employed, was a species of swindle upon them, and an attempt to defraud them out of their just rights, every bit the same as though a manager of a theatre, having announced a "host of talent" in his bills, comes before the curtain when the house is well packed, and informs the public that, owing to such and such a thing, Mr. So and So, and So and So, will be unable to appear; an announcement which he can scarcely expect to meet with much favour from the deluded ones who had dropped their shillings.

And so it was with these bloodthirsty Frenchmen, thought Julia. They had come there to have a bellyful of horrors, and if she did them out of it by refusing to fight, they might think themselves quite justified in murdering her on the spot.

She certainly was rather surprised to see the "other party" pegging away with the rest, as though he had nothing on earth upon his mind; and she could not help a certain vindictive feeling taking possession of her, as she thought that she would dearly like to have put something else into his stomach, besides his mess of stewed liver, bacon, and garlic.

"I say," whispered Josh.

"Yes," said Julia.

"They seem to be putting it away, don't they?"

"They do."

"So does that chap that you've got to fight. He don't look afraid, does he?"

"No."

"I think we ought to pick a bit of something."

"I'm not hungry."

"Nonsense, my boy; it'll put some pluck into you."

"I can't eat such mess."

"Go on with you. Suppose you try."

Without any more to do, Mr. Josh, who, it is to be supposed, was not so anxious about the issue of the fight as his companion, ordered a huge plate of some sort of abomination, and two stiff glasses of brandy and water.

Julia tried to affect an indifference, and to

appear well at her ease; but it was in vain.

The near neighbourhood of the other party, and more particularly of the principal member of it, who was sitting in a prominent place, and who certainly did not eat with the air of a man who is taking his last earthly meal, was quite enough to spoil her appetite, and quite put the stopper on any little airs of bravado which she would have practised.

Besides, there was Mr. Josh always nagging at her.

"You're not getting on," he said.

"Yes, I am."

"But you don't eat."

"Yes, I do."

"Look at that chap over there. He's tucking into his victuals, if you like."

"Let him tuck, then."

"He's not in a funk."

"No more am I."

"Well, I wish you wouldn't look as if you was, that's all. Just look how he is pitching into his prog."

"Damn him and his prog too!" cried Julia, in a passion. "If he's half as clever with his sword as he is with his carving knife, it may save him a whole skin."

"Bravo! bravo!" said Josh, smiting the table with his huge fist. "That's spoken like a man. By God, I'll tell him!"

And before Julia could prevent him, he had strode across the green to the opposite table, and communicated Julia's opinion.

LVIII.—THE DUEL AND ITS RESULT.

HARDLY had Mr. Josh had time to say what he had to say, than the whole party sprang to their feet with such a tremendous outpouring of "sacres" as Julia never before had heard in her life.

Mr. Josh returned to her side with a remarkably sinister grin.

"I thought that would stir them up," said he.

"Are we going to fight, then, at last?"

"Yes; everything is ready. Come along."

Without more ado Julia rose and followed her dear friend into the open space between the torches.

From certain marks, as of trampling feet, and other indications, she could not help thinking that the place had before been used for a somewhat similar purpose

The other party followed them directly afterwards, and began to take off their old shabby cloaks, and fold them as with a great deal of care, something after the fashion of certain of our comic singers at the music-halls, when they are called upon for an encore song.

One who seemed to be the best man of Julia's antagonist, came forward towards Mr. Josh, and began to enter into arrangements for the coming fight.

The rest lighted their cigars.

Julia thought it looked plucky, and lit hers.

While she was lolling against a tree, pretending not to be in the slightest degree interested about what was going on around her, she could not avoid listening to Mr. Josh, disputing with the other party's second.

"Don't tell me," Mr. Josh was saying, with a variety of the very strongest oaths. "Don't tell me, I say. It's quite the right length."

"I say it is not."

"Why not?"

"Because it's six or eight inches too long, at least."

"You mean to say, I suppose, that it's longer than your sword."

"Yes, I do."

"Well that's not our fault, is it. You shouldn't have brought your sword so precious short. We can't help it if you will put yourselves at a disadvantage."

"You oughtn't to use it."

"Oh! oughtn't we? That's what you think, you know. The worst of it is, that we mean to use it, and if your friend don't like it we won't fight him at all, so there's an end of the matter."

"Has it ever been used before?" the Frenchman asked.

"You mean for the same sort of purpose?"

"Yes."

"I should rather say it had, Mounseer."

"Oh, indeed. Often?"

"Rather too often for some parties tastes, Mounseer."

"What parties?"

"The parties it went through."

"You talk very big, sir. If you had only a witness to call to prove what you said, it might be rather more effective."

"Exactly. Only there's one drawback to the principal witnesses speaking—"

"And that is—"

"That they're buried."

Most certainly the Frenchman who had began this little dialogue, was a little bit shut up at its termination.

There is very little doubt but that he sincerely regretted having been so incautious as to commence it, and afterwards having commenced it, to lead it up to such a very mortifying climax.

Julia was delighted.

How she prayed to heaven that it might strike fear into the breasts of the opposite party.

That it might fill them with terror.

But was it so?

Alas, no!

The scowling wretch whom she was to fight, received the intelligence with a smile of contempt.

He stepped into the middle of the circle and rolled up his shirt sleeves, displaying an arm which, as Josh had surely said, could fell an ox.

As though he were anxious to give Miss Julia a notion of what she might expect, he with a mighty stroke clove down a stout branch from a yew tree standing near, with for all the world as much ease as though he were cutting a slice of butter upon a breakfast-table, preparatory to spreading with it a nice crisp piece of dry toast.

"Are you ready?" Josh whispered, noticing that his companion was eying the performance of this feat open-mouthed as though he were a conjuror.

"Quite ready."

"Here's your sword, then."

Julia for a moment felt half inclined to indulge Mr. Josh with half a yard of it right in the middle of his waistcoat, for she bore him as much ill-will as anybody else.

However, she mastered the inclination, and walked slowly forward with as brave a look as possible.

Her antagonist awaited her in the centre of the circle.

The rest of the men fell back to a little distance.

Julia's heart beat high; her head seemed to be turning round, and the company dancing before her.

She scarcely could hear the word being given to draw; but somehow mechanically she complied with it, and the flashing naked blades leapt forth from their scabbards.

Then came the sharp clang of metal, as the scabbards fell to the ground.

Then began the fight.

Who can describe that which had no system, and was not managed according to any prescribed rules?

The spectators looked on astonished and aghast, scarcely knowing whether Julia was not introducing some new and approved system of fencing, or whether she was not, as they were half inclined to suspect, a foolhardy novice.

Thrusts, parries, cuts, under and over advances, and retirings, feints and guards.

Through all this the loud and varied exclamations of the bye-standers, as they followed the success of the two combatants, and approved or disapproved of their movements.

Julia fought on.

She had not, to tell the truth, the least earthly idea how she was fighting, and whether or not she was getting the best or worst of it.

Suddenly, much to her astonishment, her antagonist uttered a faint cry, and staggered back.

The expression of his face was awful, and Julia saw him, without understanding what he meant, drop his sword to the ground, and clasp his two hands upon his side.

Then she saw the blood spurting out between his fingers.

A second afterwards, he had fallen heavily to the ground, and lay there upon his back motionless.

At the same time Julia sprang forward, and feeling a choking sensation at the throat, uttered a cry of horror, and with her fingers tore open her shirt at the neck.

An exclamation at the same time burst from the spectators.

What was it caused by?

The fall of the dying man?

No. All eyes were rivetted up on Julia.

What was it, then?

I will tell you.

When she had torn her shirt open at the neck, her soft white voluptuous bosom was instantly exposed to the wondering sight of those surrounding her.

A whisper ran round.

A whisper of astonishment and dismay.

"Gracious heavens, it is a woman!"

It was not until several moments had elapsed, that any one thought of the fallen man.

Then two or three Frenchmen came forward and helped to raise him.

One felt his breast, and shook his head.

Another raised the man's arm, and let it fall again.

It fell with a heavy thump upon the grass.

Julia's heart thumped almost as loudly.

Then they drew the body on one side, and covered it over with a cloak.

"Is he—is he dead?" asked Julia, whom the words seemed to choke.

"Dead as a herring," replied Mr. Josh, with a grin. "And I'm damned if it don't do you credit, miss."

"What must I do?"

"Hook it 's the best thing, with the least possible delay. There's no knowing what may happen else."

"Where shall I find my horse?"

"I'll take you to it."

On the way, Mr. Josh scarcely took his eyes off his companion.

He seemed to be filled with a great inward wonder.

"By jove," he said.

Then after awhile—

"By jingo."

Then in a minute or two, apparently more astonished than ever—

"I shouldn't have believed it."

"What are you cackling at there," Julia inquired angrily.

Mr. Josh explained. The discovery of her sex had been one too many for him.

"If you're not an almighty screamer," said he, "I'll eat my head. Talking of women! I don't believe there's two of the same breed as you. Sugar me if I do."

But Julia was not inclined for compliments.

A very angry altercation ensued between them—Josh insisting on her instant flight, and she refusing to comply with his desire.

But it ended at last by Josh, as you may suppose, getting the best of it.

Almost before Julia was aware that she had agreed to his propositions, and decidedly without knowing why she had, she found herself galloping along the road at a furious pace, as eager now for her own safety as before she had been careless about it.

And so she galloped on in anything but an enviable state of mind, and overwhelmed with terror at the approach of every horseman, fancying that they must be in pursuit of her.

At last, finding that the horse was getting blown, and had begun to limp as though it were lame, she dismounted.

Then for the first time she perceived that it was not her own horse, but some vile hack which Mr. Josh had taken the liberty of palming off upon her when she was agitated and harassed by other matters.

There was, as the saying is, no "go" left in it, and Julia, in not the best of tempers, let it loose by the way side, and determined to continue her journey on foot.

Suddenly the thought of the letter which she had undertaken to deliver, and which hither had escaped her memory, flashed upon it.

What must be done?

She had soon decided.

She would go back.

And instantly the courageous girl began to retrace her steps towards the fatal city.

Day was beginning to break, and the low marshy lands stretched out on every side of her, unspeakably lonely and desolate, filling her heart with a secret dread of she knew not what, and chilling her very blood.

———

LIX.—Shows how Charley Wag became a Prisoner in a very horrible sort of Prison.

CHARLEY and Captain Toddleboy were not very long before they began to grow extremely anxious for Julia's return.

"It's strange that she has not come back before this," the Captain said.

"She should never have gone," retorted Master Charles.

They were next door to getting to high words about it.

They had thought it more than probable that she would return the same night, or any how, next morning early.

But when next day began to pass away and decline into night, and still there were no signs of her, it began to grow rather alarming.

Nothing in the world is surely more fatiguing than protracted waiting.

Waiting maketh the heart grow sick.

Let it be either waiting for a lover, or waiting for money, waiting for the tide or waiting for the train; waiting for a place or waiting for promotion, the heart is likely to grow sick over any of these occasions, and the flesh to waste away.

At last Charley made up his mind to go in search of his sweetheart.

It was now the afternoon of the third day, and she had not returned.

Toddleboy proposed that they should still wait for her, but Charley would not hear of it.

He would set off himself.

As Toddleboy seemed to think that this was a very wild scheme, Charley thought that he would set off without saying anything to him about it.

Therefore when our friend the Captain was deep in a tumbler of grog, upon the evening of the third day, Charley took the mate on one side very quietly, and slipping some money into his hand, asked him to let get a boat and put him on shore.

The mate agreed, and in a quarter of an hour's time Charley was standing upon the dry land.

He waved adieu to the boatman, and promising to be back next day by noon, he walked rapidly away inland.

But he had not reflected very much upon the difficulties of the journey.

Now he was quite by himself, they came upon him rather strongly.

He knew no French—at least, not more than a word or two.

Two words he did know. One was the name of the place he was going to: the other, the name of the lady to whom the letter which Julia had taken was directed.

He made a great mistake, though.

He had been told by Toddleboy that the town was four leagues off. Toddleboy had spoken of the distance in French, and Charley had fancied that he said miles instead of leagues.

You can easily imagine what misery this mistake caused him.

When he had found out which was the road —and he only did this after making tremendous inquiries, and resorting largely to pantomime and dumb show—he walked on and on, wondering when the deuce he would be at his journey's end.

I shall not weary the reader's patience with a description of his journey.

He was very weak with his recent loss of blood, and many times during the night's tramp was obliged to sit down by the wayside to rest his aching bones.

Arrived at length at his journey's end, he halted at the gate of a large, gloomy-looking building, which he had been informed was the residence of Madame Deschapelles.

By dint of much knocking and a good deal of shouting, the gates were at length opened.

Faint, tired, and hungry, Charley was in hopes of soon coming to the end of his troubles.

He addressed the person who opened to him in English.

It was an old grey-headed negro, revoltingly ugly, and apparently half drunk.

"The devil take you, what do you want?" cried the black, in English.

"I want Madame Deschapelles."

"The devil take you. Why do you break our bell?"

"Is Madame Deschapelles within?"

"The devil take you. What's your business?"

"I want to see her or the young man who brought her a letter. Is he here?"

"The devil take you. What are you jabbering about? Go away. Get out. Be off."

"The devil take me if I do," retorted Charley in a rage, "without you give me a little more information."

The negro's reply was singular.

He gave a most diabolical grin, which showed all his fangs, gleaming like those of a dog.

Then he made a kind of hissing noise, something between a snake and an enraged ape.

Mr. Charley was very much irritated, and he did not love niggers like brothers, although he ought to have done so, most certainly.

So instead of trying to conciliate his black friend, Mr. Wag took the liberty of kicking him.

"Speak up, you surly black dog," said he.

The words, however, had scarcely been uttered, before the negro sprang upon him.

With a cry something like that of an infuriated beast, he clutched the lad's throat.

Charley struck out at him, and endeavoured to guard himself from attack with his arm; but the negro was too quick for him.

He bobbed down suddenly, and plunged a knife into Charley's side.

Charley staggered and groaned.

The assassin rushed out into the darkness, banging the gates to after him.

Charley in vain endeavoured to cry for help, and to catch at the bell wire.

His strength failed him, and he fell to the earth, and lay there weltering in his blood.

Again and again he strove to cry out, but his voice was too weak to be heard.

The blood run in a stream from the gaping wound.

A chill sickening sensation crept over him, that he mistook for death.

Then, as he lay there, half fainting, he thought of all the opportunities he had wasted, and what he might have done in the world if he had only rightly applied his energies.

And what he might and would still do, if he was only spared his life a little longer.

Then he thought how hard it was to die so young, and how little he was prepared for it.

This was the last effort of consciousness.

With it on his brain, he swooned away.

No. 48.

*　*　*　*　*

A strange and dreary scene must I now introduce you to, gentle reader.

We have already seen some curious sights together.

Probably this one will not be the least curious of the number.

Imagine a great rambling, gloomy, inconveniently built, foul smelling, filthy, dirty French prison.

Imagine a wretchedly emaciated creature, with sunken cheeks, deep-set eyes, shrivelled flesh, shrunken limbs, and shaved head.

Imagine that this is a prisoner, horribly dirty, lousy, helpless, and wretched, eaten up with filth and disease.

Imagine him squatted on his hams in a corner of his cell, among the loathsome straw,

[CHARLEY WAG, THE NEW JACK SHEPARD.

with a vacant idiotic look upon his thin gaunt visage.

Imagine this, and then allow me to tell you, that this is none other than the celebrated Mr. Charley Wag, the "New Jack Sheppard."

At least, this is all that is left of him.

This is the wreck of the celebrated Charley.

The ghost of the famous Mr. Wag.

Mr. Wag was attired in the dirtiest suit of flannel that it is possible to conceive, and looked altogether very much like a sea-sick monkey.

Mr. Wag has been very ill.

He has had the typhus fever, among other trifles, and he is coming slowly round the very best way he can without any assistance.

Most of the occupants of this hideous prison-house, with the exception of the gaolers themselves, seem to be suffering from the effects of some loathsome disease, which has left them emaciated, maimed, and crippled.

They squat about in the passages and yards wherever there is a faint streak of sunlight.

They chatted together in a weak feeble way, and some amused themselves by playing at snatch cradle.

They were all dreadful objects.

They all had a shambling gait, and many of them were cripples.

Some had twisted limbs, distorted into every frightful variety of lameness.

Some of them had no nose; some were blind ; some had lost their toes and fingers.

All of them were blotched, and scabby, and mangy, like neglected hounds.

Their voices, too, were weak and childish, or unnaturally gruff and husky.

But worse than anything else, was the madness and idiotcy which was but too evident upon the faces of three-quarters at least of the wretched captives.

And so poor Charley had got at last into such company as this !

Well might he give himself up for lost.

He was lost indeed !

The six weeks passed away, and then the seventh, and the eighth.

At last, in the middle of the ninth week, the visiting magistrates, having nothing else very particular to do, took it into their heads to pay the prison a visit.

The visiting magistrates were four in number, and were very snuffy old gentlemen, all wearing wigs, and all smelling more or less of garlic, which may be accounted for by the fact of their having laid in a heavy breakfast of savoury dishes, washed down by several bottles of good red wine, before they commenced their round of inspection.

And this was by no means an unnecessary measure, I can assure you, if you were anxious to avoid the infectious diseases in a place where every variety of loathsome complaint had its victim.

You may perhaps remark that it is rather curious in a prison which was visited by the magistracy that such a state of affairs should have x s ed.

But then, you know, I am writing of a foreign country, and not the land of liberty we have the happiness of belonging to.

Then, again, the head gaoler was on extremely good terms with the inspectors.

That is to say, the inspectors, when they called, found an excellent breakfast waiting for them, and plenty of good wine with it.

The inspectors came about once in three months.

The breakfast cost about a hundred francs.

The gaoler deducted the amount expended from his salary, and the balance left, though by no means too large, was large enough for him to live upon somehow.

Therefore, you see, having been well fed, the old gentlemen were not inclined to be too severe with their host, if they were to notice any little matters going on inside the gaol walls that they did not quite approve of.

The generous wine lent a generous tint to the scene, and they saw things *colour de rose.*

And that's how it was managed.

Charley Wag heard from the warder who brought his bread and water that the gentlemen had come.

His heart beat with joy.

"I'll speak to them," said he to himself.

Then he asked the gaoler :

"When shall I see them, do you suppose ?"

"See whom ?"

"The magistrates."

"Do you suppose they will come into this hole ?"

"Won't they?"

"Not likely—not if the governor knows it."

"Then how can I speak to them ?"

"What do you want to say?"

"I want to ask when my trial is coming on."

"You mean that you want to complain of the grub."

"No, I don't."

"Will you swear you don't ?"

"Yes."

"Then perhaps I shall put you out in the yard that they'll pass through, and give you a chance."

"Thank you—oh, thank you !"

The gaoler looked at him hard, and something seemed to cross his mind.

"The worst of it is—" he said.

Charley trembled.

"You're such a ragged beggar."

"I can't help that."

"Perhaps not; but you're a disgrace to the victuals."

"Oh, sir, do not forsake me ! I shall die if I remain here much longer."

"By Jove, I shouldn't wonder; but there's nothing uncommon in that."

"But you will not refuse me this opportunity ?"

"What will you give me ?"

"Alas, I have not a halfpenny."

"That's poor pay."

Charley gave himself up to despair, and burst into tears.

"There, don't blubber," said the man. "Come on, and I will see what I can do for you."

And he led the way into the yard.

"Now or never," said Charley to himself. "God give me strength."

———

LX.—How Charley fared with the four old gentlemen, and how he made up his mind to do something desperate.

AFTER what seemed to poor Charley to be several hours, the four feeble old gentlemen who were supposed to be upon their round of inspection came toddling round the corner towards the courtyard, in the sunniest portion of which our hero—or rather, I ought to say, as much as remained of him—was huddled up, waiting for them anxiously.

One of the old gentlemen, staring very hard about him, up above and on either side of the spot where Mr. Wag was sitting, almost tumbled over him.

Charley, with what was to him in his then exhausted state an almost superhuman effort, managed to scramble on to his legs; and when the other three gentlemen came up, was bobbing his head, and pulling his forelock, as much as to signify in dumb show that he was their most obedient humble servant.

"What's this?" says the first of the four old gentlemen, looking at Charley with very much the same sort of expression that a tidy housemaid might be supposed to look at a large spider which she had found dangling from the ceiling in the front drawing-room.

"What's that?" says he.

The other three old gentlemen did not offer any explanation.

They gathered round and looked on at the wretched prisoner, with a mingling of surprise and disgust in their wrinkled countenances.

Looked at him through their spectacles, and over their spectacles, and under their spectacles, and round their spectacles' sides.

Looked at him very hard indeed, and evidently did not think very much of him.

The first old gentleman, though, was growing impatient.

"What is it?" says he, for the third time. "Is it a human being, or a wild beast? Is it human or amphibious? Is it fish, flesh, or fowl?"

The head gaoler had been hanging behind, and came up at this moment.

"What is this?" says the old gentleman.

"One of our worst cases," replies the gaoler, hurriedly. "What are you doing out here, sir? Who let you out here? How dare you be out here?"

"He seems in a wretched plight," said another of the old gentlemen. "Has he been ill?"

"He is now, sir. He has a fever. Let me entreat of you not to go too near to him."

"Gracious heavens! is he infectious?"

"Very infectious, sir."

"What, the scoundrel! the villain! the audacious monster! What does he mean by endangering our lives in such a way?"

"Clear him away!" cried all the other three old gentlemen, getting as far off the prisoner as possible, and backing up all in a lump in a corner.

All this time poor Charley had been afraid to speak.

The reception he had met with had been such a staggerer, his knowledge of the French language was so extremely limited, and he felt so low and weak from his recent illness, and so unfit to cope with the circumstances of the case.

If he meant to say anything at all, he had not very much time to lose.

He saw that, and made up his mind.

"If you please, good gentlemen," said he, "will you kindly listen to me?"

The four old gentlemen all looked at one another, as though an earthquake had occurred.

"Keep your distance, sir! What do you want, sir? How dare you, sir!"

"I won't come near you, sir."

"You'd better not."

"If you will only allow me to speak, kind gentlemen."

"What does the vagabond want?" says one old gentleman.

"I can't imagine," says another.

"Shall we hear what he's got to say?"

"Suppose we do."

"Speak up, you young vagabond."

Thus kindly encouraged, the young vagabond spoke up.

"I have been in this prison more than six months," he said. "I do not know of what I am accused; I have had no trial. I want to know, gentlemen, when I am to be tried?"

"Is he a foreigner?" one of the inspectors asked of another.

"He speaks an extraordinary jargon. What countryman are you, vagabond?"

"I belong to a country, sir, where the meanest of the subjects has justice done him."

"Don't you have any of your impudence, sir. Are you English?"

"Yes."

"Why has he not been tried?" the old gentleman asked of the head gaoler.

"He has had the typhus, sir. We couldn't have sent him into court."

"There, prisoner, do you hear that?"

"But I am well now."

"He says he is well now—is that the case?"

"I shouldn't like you to have to touch him, sir," said the gaoler.

"Bless me, no. Let him be taken away; he is a very unpleasant object."

"And am I to have no justice, then?" asked Charley.

"You hear you're infectious, sir, don't you?"

"I am well enough to stand my trial."

"Don't be impatient, my fine fellow. There's quite time enough for you to be hanged; and that's what you'll come to, there's very little doubt."

And having imparted this soothing information, the old gentlemen walked away, and the wretched prisoner was left to his own reflections, such as they were—none of the pleasantest, you may be sure.

There was very little hope of justice here, he could plainly see.

His only hope lay in escape.

I said before that at certain intervals round the building there were sentries placed, to prevent the escape of the prisoners, with full permission either to shoot or brain with the butt end of their muskets any person who should be bold and rash enough to attempt it.

But in this there at first sight seemed to be

a good deal of unnecessary caution; for among those of the wretched captives who were no confined constantly in their dungeons, there were very few who were not in so helpless and hopeless a state, through the ravages of disease, as to render any active steps on their part almost if not quite an impossibility.

A few of the luckiest, perhaps, were able to creep about at a snail's pace, with the assistance of their crutches; but the greater part were utterly incapable of motion, and at most could only turn from side to side upon their filthy straw beds, or crawl a yard or so in their cells.

When assisted out into the yard, as occasionally happened when the gaolers were more humanely inclined than usual, they lay in a heap where they were placed, until the time came for them to be moved away again, just for all the world as though they were so many bundles of rags and rubbish.

Those with the most life in them—the active parties with the crutches—were just able to stagger up to the top of a sort of bank on the edge of the outer wall, and gaze down timidly into the stagnant moat beneath, a descent, perhaps, of twenty-five or thirty feet, but which, looked at from on high, seemed to be a most appalling depth.

Now whenever one of these miserable unfortunates was observed by the guards peeping over into the black water beneath, he was not driven away, as you might have supposed, because the guards thought that they could not do better than allow them to feast their minds upon all the horrors of a fall.

Charley had noticed this, and he had formed a resolution.

If he was to die, why should he not die in the moat beneath, or by a soldier's bullet?

Surely any death would be preferable to that of rotting slowly in the noisome dungeon where his days during the last six or seven months had been passed.

There seemed to be no chance of justice.

There seemed to be no other chance of escape.

No, this must be the way.

Then he reflected, supposing that the shock of the tumble killed him, which was, by the way, by no means an unlikely thing to happen, it would only be anticipating death for a few days.

And then, would that not be preferable even to life, when life was such an accumulation of horrors as that of this dread prison-house.

But then, although he reasoned with himself in this way, or rather, I should say, tried to persuade himself that these were his opinions upon the subject, do you suppose that they really were?

Not they.

Ever since that time when Charley was saved by George at the very moment that he was about to commit suicide, he had been thoroughly impressed with a sort of secret conviction, founded on I cannot say what strange romantic dreams, that he would live to be a great man—that he would soar high above all his present associates and associations—that a great future awaited him—that, in fact, he bore a charmed life.

He felt certain that he would shortly escape from his present thraldom.

He was by no means weary of life—at least, of the glorious free life outside the prison walls.

He felt, too, that this season of privation would but give a higher colour to his enjoyment of it, should he only be be happy enough to survive his present miseries.

And he would survive them; he felt certain of it—he made up his mind for it.

He was determined upon it.

And the time drew near for him to make an attempt for his life.

Gradually he was shaking off the pernicious effects of his long illness, and growing bolder and stronger.

The time came at last.

Charley made the attempt.

LXI.—A JUMP IN THE DARK—NIGHT ON THE SWAMP.

AS twilight set in, the prisoners—or rather, those who were allowed the privilege of walking on the battlements—were called into their cells by a bell.

Then parties of soldiers marched round, to see whether anyone chanced to have lingered behind.

The gaolers were also supposed to go round to all the cells, and see whether the prisoners had returned to them.

But this business was not very effectually performed.

An attempt at escape was almost unheard of and the soldiers had grown careless of late, owing to the fancied security of the charges.

When the bell rang, one particular evening, Charley lingered behind the rest, and hid himself, trembling, in a remote corner of the walls as evening began to close in.

With a beating heart he listened to the sound of the bell.

Was it the last time he should ever hear it?

Where should he be the next night at the same hour?

Should he be free? free to wander where he liked? free of chains and slavery and bondage.

Or should he be dead? Should he be lying a shapeless mass of wounds and bruises in some narrow bed beneath the prison flags?

Should he again be picked up dead, and drowned, and swollen, floating on the surface of the slimy moat?

What was to be his fate?

Alas, in any case it seemed to him that his departure from the world would cause but little excitement.

What was he there? Who would miss him? Who would grieve for him?

Alas, very few, he thought—very few. Why none, most likely.

Such a poor, sickly wretch as he was, was not very likely to leave many mourners behind him.

It was very sad to reflect upon this loneliness, and the poor lad felt half choking with his sorrow, as he stood there in the still twilight, gazing down from the battlement into the gloomy ditch below, which at that moment seemed black as ink.

Beyond the ditch, and into the far distance, stretched forth a low, mashy swamp, undrained and uninhabitable, and in all probability the noxious vapours arising from the damp ground contributed in no small measure to promote the prison fever.

Very, very far distant, might be seen faintly twinkling some tiny light, which indicated the resting-place of some poor farmer, who struggled to live in this most uninviting neighbourhood, and carried on an almost hopeless labour in tilling the uncultivatable land at the borders of the swamp.

Charley, with a cold shudder, which he felt quite unable to repress, strained his eyes to pierce the gloom overhanging the distant regions, from which a heavy exhalation seemed to be always rising.

However, determined upon making the best of everything, he tried to comfort himself with the reflection that the mist which enveloped the swamp might assist in some measure to shroud him from pursuit.

Would they pursue him? It was very questionable.

Would he require pursuit? Perhaps not, if he lay dead at the foot of the prison walls.

The bell had ceased to toll.

The moment was come.

For one brief moment he hesitated whether or not he should make the plunge.

One was life, miserable and wretched to a degree—but still life.

Before him, perchance, lay death—or liberty.

Liberty! The thought nerved him, and revived his waning courage.

He would make the spring.

Tramp, tramp, tramp.

The heavy roll of a drum.

The guard was coming that way.

He must be gone.

He heard their measured tread. The soldiers were not yet in sight; but he knew they must be near.

He had some vague idea of putting off the leap until another day.

But it was a thought dismissed as soon as conceived.

No; he must do it now or never.

The tramping of the men approached nearer and nearer.

He knew very well that if he were found out here skulking upon this occasion, upon all future occasions he would be narrowly watched.

Yes, this was his last chance.

He looked round him eagerly.

Then climbed to the edge of the wall.

He peeped down below, where all was dark as pitch.

It was impossible to see a yard, all was perfectly indistinguishable—unfathomable.

At most, the guards were now about twenty yards from him.

In another instant he would be seen and taken.

He would have given the world to have known whereabouts he would fall, and into what.

He clasped his hands and clenched his teeth. Then took a spring.

But at the critical moment his strength failed him.

He had miscalculated his power.

He tottered and fell.

Even at this awful moment he had sufficient presence of mind to know that he must not scream, or he would be lost.

He slipped his foot at the very edge of the wall, and fell.

He clutched wildly at the grass and ivy as he fell.

Down—down—down he went. It seemed to him miles. He suffered a martyrdom in the briefest possible space of time.

His mind seemed to give way. His consciousness deserted him.

Down—down he fell.

Down—down, until with a fearful shock he dropped into the green stagnant water of the moat, head over heels.

For a moment or two he thought himself dead; but it was not long before he had sufficiently recovered the use of his limbs and senses to scramble to the shore, and shake away the green duckweed which clung about and almost choked him.

It was the energy of despair which lent him an unwonted activity; for he had crawled out, and lay gasping upon the mud bank, almost before he knew that he had got there, and certainly before he had half convinced himself of the fact that he had broken none of his bones.

As he lay there, wet and flabby, and very much like a dead fish, he looked up languidly towards the top of the battlements, and felt that if they to have fire at him he could not move.

But all was still.

There were no signs of excitement within the gaol.

He could hear, as he lay there listening, the sound of the retreating footsteps of the guard, as they marched away upon their rounds.

He was then free, if he had but sufficient strength to crawl away from the spot, and hide himself in the swamp.

It must be done. With infinite labour and pain he managed to get into a standing posture, and then to totter away, dragging one leg wearily after the other.

After a while, he recovered sufficient of his strength to manage to creep along a little faster, and he struck out boldly across the waste.

It was most astonishing, though, how his strength seemed to come to him.

Before long he began to feel quite a giant, and, guiding himself by keeping his eyes fixed upon a twinkling light at a farmhouse far ahead, he tramped on and on, and before an hour was over, was walking almost as briskly as he had ever done in his life.

As he marched along, the fog seemed in a great measure to clear away. A fresh breeze had sprung up, which dissipated the heavy mists clinging to the damp earth, and refreshed the escaped prisoner's heated head.

Above him hundreds of bright stars peeped out and glittered, serving like lamps to guide him across the trackless marsh.

Now and then, when he felt fatigue creeping over him, the remembrance of the gaol and its horrible inmates soon nerved him to fresh efforts.

And sometimes even, so alarmed did he become lest the guard should pursue and drag him back to captivity, that he increased his speed, until it had almost become a run; and thus exerting himself to the very utmost, he made immense progress, considering the roundabout and zigzag course which the treacherous and boggy nature of the ground obliged him to take.

He found himself before daybreak at the margin of the marshes, and the commencement of an extensive though by no means dense forest, which he remembered to have noticed on his way from the sea-shore to the town where he had been stabbed by the black, and in a prison in the neighbourhood of which he had suffered so long and so fatiguing a confinement.

The change of scene encouraged the wanderer to fresh exertion, and he began to feel, that instead of being weighed down with fatigue, as one might have supposed, every additional mile but imparted more and more energy and determination, and that his strength seemed to grow with them in proportion as he left the hateful gaol farther and farther behind.

"Charley, my lad," said Mr. Wag, addressing himself.

It was a common habit with the young gentleman.

"Charley, my lad, good times are in store for you. There's not a doubt of it. Only keep up your pecker my pippin, and fate will turn up trumps before the game's played out."

At last, when he thought he had put sufficient distance between himself and the gaol authorities, he lay down under a tree, in a nice dry shady nook, and fell asleep.

It was a sleep so sound and deep, such a sleep as only a weary pedestrian can know, as he lay stretched under the shade of a spreading tree, dreamless and tranquil in mind and body.

So soundly did he sleep, that it was late in the day before he awoke.

The sunlight was slanting obliquely through the branches, and the golden rays of the sunset were resting upon the earth.

He rose slowly.

His limbs were rigid and stiff, and he felt very sick and weak.

After a time, though, his strength slowly returned, and he was able at last to step out briskly.

Keeping straight on, along a narrow path, he came before long to a little open spot, where he discovered the remains of a log hut.

Before the door of this was some charred fragments of fire-wood, indicating that there had been a fire lighted there at no very distant period.

Also were there two or three broken pieces of crockery, and some fragments of bread; and presently Charley found a large bone with some lumps of meat upon it.

Whoever it had been who had been supping here, they had not very long ago departed, it would appear.

However, it did not trouble Charley's head to wonder who they were, and where they had gone to.

What occupied him most, was the finding of some tit-bits to make a meal of.

He felt very grateful for the negligent abundance of their waste, and said grace thankfully.

Then he sat down, and with the aid of a tiny spring of clean water, the presence of which may have accounted for the choice of that spot by the pic-nicers, he managed to make a very hearty meal.

Night was coming on, and he determined on passing it where he was, in the tempting refuge of the little wooden hut.

He found some dry straw in a corner, and as it was a beautiful fine, mild night, he managed to sleep very comfortable.

Early next morning he set out again upon his travels, hoping during the day to come up with the party who had preceded him, and whom he supposed to be a party of gipsies, and whom he hoped to get into company with.

He would be safe with them, he thought, and he doubled his speed in the hope of soon coming up with them.

When he left the wood, he came upon a wild, open, dreary country, and he travelled on all day, scarcely coming within sight of any human habitation.

Once at a lonely cottage he begged for a morsel of bread.

The woman there gave him a dry crust, and a few scraps of very rancid bacon, upon which far from choice delicacies he managed, however, to make a most luxuriant breakfast.

Then he crept away, by this time foot sore and weary beyond belief, and wondering where he would rest his head next night, and the night afterwards, and for as many nights as this wandering life lasted.

After tramping in a vague and purposeless way, with no other object in view than a somewhat vague one of making towards the sea coast, he came at last on an open piece of land, even more dreary and uncultivated than any which he had come to yet. And here, utterly worn out and exhausted, he laid himself down upon a heap of stones by the road side, and thought that he was going to die, and would like to do so.

"The game is up," he said wearily. "The game is up, and it's no good trying any more."

His strength, which had buoyed him up for a long while against all fatigues and toils, had given way now, and he felt and hoped that the hour of release was nigh at hand.

He rubbed the cuff of his coat across his eyes.

There might have been a tear or two in the corner, although he would not have owned to it afterwards, I dare say.

When he looked up again, he fancied that in the far distance he could see the sparkle of flames.

He looked hard again.

Yes, it was a bonfire.

Could it be possible that he had at last come up to the gipsies?

The thought gave him courage and fresh strength. He would go on and see.

The stone heap that he was seated upon, was on a road which was about fifty or sixty feet above the ground where the fire was burning.

Charley immediately set about the descent, and by the moonlight which was now strong and clear, he was able to detect foot-prints in the clayey soil near the verge of the cliff.

A little after, he found a steep narrow path, and began cautiously to descend.

The descent was not only laborious in the extreme, but not without considerable danger.

The cliff was at some places almost perpendicular.

The path was very steep and slanting, and sometimes he had to cling to the weeds and tufts of grass upon the surface of the rock to save himself from falling.

Then again there were rough jagged blocks of rock, which he was obliged to scramble over, and which afforded him at best but a very unsafe and precarious footing, occasioning him more than one serious tumble.

Before he reached the bottom he had received many a severe bump and bruise.

He had hardly a bone in his body which was not aching.

His hands and knees were cut and bleeding, and his already ragged, threadbare suit, was so torn and ragged that it seemed fit for nothing but the dress of a scarecrow, or perhaps to be boiled down at a paper mills; but that even was questionable.

When he had looked at the fire from the road, it had appeared to him to be close at hand.

Now, as he approached the bottom, he found it to be at least half-a-mile distant.

He resolved, however, to go towards it, although he feared very much that he might not meet with an over kind reception.

He was so dreadfully exhausted, that during the journey he was obliged, more than a dozen times, to sit down and rest.

Hunger, weakness, and sickness, weighed him down, and he could scarcely drag his poor bones along.

Probably a more wretched object than he was, you have never set eyes on, although should you be a dweller in London, and accustomed to walk the streets, you must have seen some very wretched objects now and then.

That is, if you do not shut your eyes as you pass them.

The blood was oozing slowly from the wound in his side, which the unwonted exertion and violent shocks he had sustained in the descent, had partially re-opened.

Through the holes in his miserable rags, you might have caught much more than glimpses of his lean shrunken figure.

His hair was unnaturally long.

His jaws were gaunt, and blue with fasting.

His eyes were sunken; his nose drawn to a sharp point.

He had scarcely a scrap of shoe upon his foot. He had no stockings, and no particular shirt to speak of.

An awful object was he truly, as he crawled up towards the fire.

There was a large blaze when he had first seen the fire; but as he approached it had sunk very low that the figures (there were five or six), were scarcely distinguishable.

Noiselessly creeping on, he came at last to a little clump of trees, hardly more than six yards distant from the fire.

Here he lay down and peeped and listened.

They were talking French, whoever they were, and by an occasional jingle, or what seemed to be accoutrements, Charley fancied that they must either be soldiers or armed police.

As he listened, he heard a deep, hoarse voice say something which he fancied was English.

He strained his ear to listen.

Suddenly a piece of timber upon which he had been resting gave way with a sudden crash, and with a half stifled cry of fear he slipped, and fell heavily to the ground.

In a moment one of the party flung something into the fire, which blazed up and lighted all around with a strong light like day.

But the smoke, blowing towards Charley, and a heap of rubbish lying before him, hid him from their view.

This, however, clearing away, the party caught sight of the miserable object lying upon the ground.

Six men stood pointing their muskets towards him, with their fingers upon the triggers.

"Don't fire," cried Charley.

They did not fire; they seemed to be staring in horror and amazement.

At last they lowered their guns.

"What is it?" one asked.

"It's a monkey," said another.

"It's some sort of wild beast."

Unable to utter another word, from the various emotions he was suffering under, Charley could only scramble on to his knees, and gesticulate passionately to the men to spare his life, with his outstretched hands imploring their mercy, and bespeaking his own defencelessness.

One of the party presently caught up a firebrand from the blazing pile, and approached him.

"Hallo!" he cried.

"What is it?" asked the others.

"Well, I am dumbfounded."

"What is it?" they asked again.

"He's an escaped prisoner. He's got the dress on."

"Is he the one we're after?"

Here all the guns were pointed at Charley again.

The man who approached him, however, waved them back with his hand

"No—no," he said. "He's a poor devil with hardly a kick left in him. Get up."

Charley tried to stand upon his legs, but after a stagger or two fell down again.

Here he lay panting, and pressing his hand to his heart.

"God help me," said he.

The words were scarcely uttered, when the man holding the torch made a start, and threw the light more strongly into the boy's face.

"By God, he's English," the man cried, in Charley's own native language.

"English," repeated another man; and the whole party drew nearer round him.

"What's your name?" one asked.

Our hero raised himself as well as he could upon his elbow.

It was a most extraordinary thing, but he always was proud of his name, and delighted in the opportunity of its publicity.

"My name is Charley Wag."

He gave it out as well as his weak voice would let him, and looked as proud as he could under the circumstances.

"Charley Wag," echoed one of the men.

"Yes, he says Charley Wag."

" The Charley Wag we're after."

" Devil a doubt of it."

" Where's he turned up from ?"

" Tell us all about it, young fellow."

All these remarks were poured forth by half-a-dozen voices almost simultaneously—some talking French, and some English.

" I shall be able to tell you better when I've warmed myself a little, and had something to drink."

" Here, here ! Bravo !"

" Bring him nearer."

" Don't touch him."

" Mind what you're about."

" Why ?"

" Because he may have the prison fever."

" No, I have not," retorted Charley. " Let me come a little nearer the fire. I'm dying with cold and hunger—that's all that's the matter with me."

" By Jove, my lad," said one of the Englishmen, " it's bad enough complaint too."

And this man, in spite of the remonstrances of the rest, raised Charley in his arms and brought him towards the fire.

A little hot grog very carefully administered in the smallest of doses ; and also some nourishment in the smallest quantities.

Under the influence of which Charley revived slowly.

It was extraordinary, too, how lively he was when he had revived a little.

He began to chat and brag as hard as ever.

He told them how he had escaped, and what he had suffered since.

If anything, his adventures as he related them, were rather more wonderful than what actually occurred to him.

The policemen—for police they were—listened very attentively, and laughed very heartily at Mr. Wag's scraps of facetiousness.

When he had told his story and warmed himself well, he fell fast asleep.

Daylight was breaking when he awoke.

One of the men was shaking him.

" Get up." he said in a gruff voice.

" Hallo !" said Charley. " What's the matter ?"

" Get up, we want to be off."

" Where are we going ?"

" We're going to take you, my fine fellow."

" Take me—where ?"

" To prison."

" Not to that horrible place."

" Well, no ; you shall try another."

" Well, anything for a change," said Charley, ruefully ; but trying to put the best face upon it.

" Put on these handcuffs. Hold up your wrists."

" Rather unnecessary that, isn't it ?"

" It's customary."

" All right, then. Fire away."

The handcuffs were put on, and the party moved forward.

They marched all day long.

Towards evening, the wretched prisoner, faint and footsore, approached the gates of a strongly fortified town.

It looked gloomy and sombre in the twilight.

The sentinels challenged them as they approached.

" What have you there ?"

" A prisoner."

" What prisoner ?"

" An English prisoner,"

" His name ?"

" Charley Wag, the London thief."

" Take him on at once before the prefect."

" The prefect is away from the town," another soldier said.

" Then we will take him to prison."

The police marched on, and the gates of the town swang too heavily behind them and the prisoner

---

LXII.—A HUNTED MAN.

HOUNDED to death.
Set upon from all quarters!
Hotly pursued !

With the clatter of the pursuers' feet ever ringing through his aching head!

With the bay of the human bloodhound swelling sonoriously through the night and growing nearer and nearer, coming closer and closer upon him.

With the whole city, as it appeared to him, surging furiously around him, like angry billows in a stormy sea.

Thus Faversham dashed madly on through narrow courts and crooked alleys, flying the scene of the murder.

For some time Rattan ran by his side, and silently the two men strained every nerve and muscle to gain upon their pursuers.

But presently, without knowing why or how it occurred, the doctor found himself alone in a dark and narrow court.

Rattan was no longer by his side.

The sound of his pursuers' footsteps was not audible.

He listened, and held his breath.

No, he was free of them for a time at least.

Free once more.

The spot where he stood, with his vest and neckerchief torn open to admit the air, wiping his streaming face upon the cuff of his coat, was silent and deserted.

He looked round anxiously to see whether he was observed, for should there have been any person about who had observed him come panting down the court like a hunted stag, and then suddenly cease running and listen, they must, to say the least, have thought the circumstance was extremely curious.

But no one was observing him.

He sat down upon a pile of timber which lay in a corner by the side of a closed shop.

He was growing a little cooler and more collected than he had been for the last hour, but he could not yet sufficiently collect his scattered thoughts to decide upon any course of action.

Something, however, must be thought of.

What ?

The first and foremost consideration was surely the necessity for concealment.

Where should he go ?

Where should he hide ?

The world seemed closed against him.

He felt like one who, running towards his house to escape the fangs of a pack of furious

EVIL TIDINGS.

dogs, finds the gates locked at the critical moment, and is obliged to turn and face his pursuers.

He was shut out from help, and from concealment.

He was without a hole to hide in.

The first step to be taken, must be to get out of London, it appeared to him—to get out of England, perhaps.

And to do this he must lose no time, must delay no longer than possible.

But his brain seemed to be in a whirl.

He could not reflect. He could not look his position fairly in the face.

He felt something of the same sensations which he had felt that night when he had swooned in the street, and been carried, as the reader may recollect, into a little public-house.

No. 49.

As he sat in the dark corner in the court, he pressed his hands upon his throbbing temples, and tried to steady himself.

Suddenly a thought occurred to him.

He would go to the workhouse of Saint-Starver-Cum-Bag-o'Bones.

He would find the workhouse-master, Blood-yer.

He would ask for shelter for the present, until he was strong enough, his brains were sufficiently calm, and his wits sufficiently collected to think which would be the best way to escape, and where he should escape to.

Escape—escape! His mind now was set upon this object, and this object alone.

He had had his vengeance.

He was glutted with his feast of gore.

One might almost, without exaggeration,

have compared him to a leech sated with blood.

Rising to his feet, and scarcely able to see his way and support himself upon his weak and trembling limbs, he staggered up the court, and out into the busy thoroughfare.

He wandered on, hardly looking to see where he was going, as it appeared, but still bearing steadily onward.

It seemed as though he found his way by instinct—as though fate or destiny guided his footsteps.

Onward—onward. Across crowded streets, down narrow alleys, through labyrinths of intricate lanes and courts.

At last he came to a large open space in front of a gloomy ill-built building. It was Saint-Starver-Cum-Bag-o'Bones workhouse.

He was about to cross the road and enter the gate.

He had stepped from the kerbstone, when the sound of loud and angry voices startled him.

He looked up, and found that a large and noisy crowd surrounded the workhouse doors.

Instinctively he drew back into the shadow of the houses from which he was about to emerge.

Then he strained his eyes to see what was being done.

Two boys were talking together close to the spot where he stood.

"What's up, Bill?"

"It's a murder, for one thing."

"A murder! You don't mean it."

"Yes, I do."

"Who's done it?"

"I don't know the chaps name."

"It's not the workhouse-master, is it?"

"No, not this time. But it's a friend of his."

"What, the beadle?"

"No, no—a doctor; him as attends to the paupers there."

Faversham listened intently, but the boys crossed the road without any further conversation, merely remarking as they left the spot, that they might as well go and see "the fun."

What did they mean?

Was this doctor, whom the police were looking after, himself?

Of course it was; there could be no doubt.

He must not go there, then. He must escape. Where?

A thought came across him. He had formed a determination. He would act upon it at once.

Retracing his steps, and not without a chuckle as he thought how fruitless was the search at present going on at the workhouse, he called a cab in a bye-street, and bade the driver take him to a livery-stable he mentioned, in the neighbourhood of Waterloo Road.

"I will defeat them yet," he said, with a fiendish laugh.

LXIII.—FLIGHT.

WEARY and exhausted, Faversham lay back in the cab, and almost instantaneously fell asleep.

In another moment, as it seemed to him, he was awakened by the stopping of the cab in front of the gates of the livery stable-keeper. Getting out, he discharged the cabman, and rang the bell loudly.

The house was dark and silent. The echo of the bell died out after a lengthened series of tinklings, growing fainter and fainter.

In a few moments he rang again, with increased violence.

Then an extremely sleepy-looking ostler made his appearance, and asked what he was pleased to want.

"Why, you are shut up here as though it were the dead of night," Faversham replied.

"It is rather late."

"What time is it?" As he asked the question, Faversham consulted his watch; it was past one o'clock.

"I had no idea that it was this hour," he said in a surprised tone.

"Is the master in?"

"No, sir."

"I want a horse."

"What, to night?"

"To night—yes; now, directly. The best horse you have. The strongest and fastest."

The ostler grumbled a little.

"We don't usually let 'em out so late as this, sir," he said.

"You don't very often get a pound for your trouble, young man," replied Faversham.

And as he spoke, he placed the amount he had named in the groom's hand.

"All right, sir," this individual responded, with a grin; "we've got the nag to suit you, I haven't a doubt. Will you take the trouble to come this way?"

He led the way down the yard, and into a stable, at the end of which they found a powerful white horse in a stall by itself.

"That's the beast," the groom remarked. "How do you like it?"

"It will do excellently."

Without more ado, the groom brought the horse out and saddled it. He lighted a lantern, which hung upon a nail in a corner of the stable, to assist him in finding the bridle, that was stowed away in some adjoining apartment.

When the horse was ready, the groom brought it out into the yard, and holding the lantern aloft, so as to throw as much light as possible upon the horse to assist Faversham in mounting, he held the horse's head while he did so.

When the doctor had got into his seat in the saddle, he found that one of the stirrup-straps was too short, and he leant down and endeavoured to loosen the buckle.

Seeing what he was trying to do, the groom came forward to assist him, and in so doing, threw the light full upon his hand.

"Have you hurt yourself, sir?" he said.

"What?" asked the other, looking up.

"Have you cut your hand? It is bleeding."

"No," answered Faversham hastily. "No—that is, yes. I cut my finger, and it bled a good deal; but it's better now."

"The blood is all over your hand and wrist, and down your sleeve."

"I suppose I know that as well as you can tell me," retorted Faversham. "Just loosen this strap, if you please, and leave the blood alone."

The ostler, thus rebuked, applied himself to

his task, and soon succeeded in making the stirrup the desired length.

Then Faversham handed him a pound for himself, and left another pound upon the horse.

After which, and after the ostler had profusely thanked him for his liberality, he rode up the yard, and out into the street.

Arrived there, drew up suddenly.

"I want a spur," he said.

"You will find him go very well without, sir, I think."

"I want to have one."

"Certainly; I will fetch it."

The groom went back into the yard, and returned with the article demanded.

Faversham fixed it on to his boot.

"You've dropped the bandage off your hand," said the groom.

"I've done what?" asked Faversham, looking up angrily.

"Dropped the bandage, have you not?"

"What bandage?"

"You said that you had cut your hand, sir."

"Well! what of that?"

"Nothing, sir; I meant no offence, only I thought that perhaps the rag had fallen off."

"You're a stupid idiot!" said Faversham savagely. "It's a great pity that you can't mind your own business. Mark my words, if that jabbering tongue of yours does not get you into trouble before you're a hundred years older."

As he spoke, he wrenched the bridle from out of the groom's hand, and dealing him a smart blow on the side of his head with his clenched fist, he plunged the spur into the horse's flank, and galloped down the street.

The groom stood for a moment staring stupidly after the doctor, and rubbing his own head in a mournful and reflective sort of way.

"That's a bad lot, or I'm very much mistaken," said he. "He means no good, or I'm in error. He's been doing some bloody work of some sort or other, or I'm labouring under a fallacious delusion. Perhaps he's been committing a murder. Who knows? He looks like it. I shall look at all the newspapers to-morrow, and all through the week, and see if anybody's been cut up anywhere lately. Oh, Lord! it's a very horrible thing when you come to think of it, to be pulled out of bed at this hour of the morning, to see a man with his hands all over blood. Anyhow, here's a sovereign, that's one comfort."

Something unpleasant, however, crossed his mind at this moment.

"I hope he'll bring back that horse though, a pound won't pay for that very well."

And ruminating mournfully as he walked back to his bed, he shut to the door with a very long face indeed.

And the murderer pursued his way, unmindful of what the other might think.

He seemed to be very sure of the way he intended to go, for he rode on at a furious pace straight towards Kennington Common.

The few persons still left out in the almost deserted street ran screaming to the right and to the left, as the reckless horseman approached.

Once or twice, a more than usually energetic policeman rushed forward, and made belief that he was going to seize the horse's head, but

seemed to think better of it, and gave the notion up.

He passed Kennington Common, and galloped up the Clapham Road.

He passed Clapham, and still pursued his reckless course with unabated speed.

On—on he went.

The horse was soon in a lather.

A few miles further on, it began to slacken its pace.

It began to pant, and show signs of breaking down.

He was now in the open country.

He approached a pond.

And slackening his pace a little, allowed his horse to drink.

When it had refreshed itself a little, he pressed on again.

On—on. He had soon resumed his furious pace.

Was he riding without a purpose? If he was not, he must have been well acquainted with the road; for, though the day having by this time broke, it was quite light enough for him to read directions of the posts at the cross-roads.

He galloped on until broad day came, and still he hurried onwards.

At last, late in the afternoon, he came to a wide open place, without any other signs of vegetation beyond a scanty crop of burnt-up grass.

Not a house was to be seen all round.

The horseman drew up suddenly.

"I must be near the place," he said.

The horse could hardly crawl along, but its inhuman task-master still urged it onward.

It is true that he had been more careful of its welfare than he was of his own; for several times during the day he had halted for a few moments at some wayside house, and given the horse some refreshment, while he had neither tasted bit nor sup all day, nor, indeed, all the previous night, nor the previous day.

Now, at this period of the day, for the first time to-day, a weakness seemed to overcome him.

A giddiness seemed to seize upon him. Much of the old illness that he had felt before, last night, when he had just escaped from the pursuit of the mob in London.

Again, as before, he pressed his hand upon his throbbing head, and tried to collect his thoughts.

He had purchased a whip early in the day at a little shop in a village, and a sudden pain which had just seized him caused him to let it fall.

With a great deal of trouble and pain, for his head was aching fearfully, he descended from his seat to gather up the whip.

But his weakness increased when he was upon the ground.

As he stooped, an increased giddiness seized upon him, and losing his balance, he fell heavily to the ground.

For a few minutes he lay there, exactly as though he were dead.

He lay senseless and stupified for full a quarter of an hour. The horse, which he still held by the bridle, described a circle round him, as it fed upon the scanty grass, occasionally giving a sharp tug at his arm in its endeavours to free itself. But the bridle was twisted round the doctor's wrist, and the horse's efforts were fruitless. At the end of the period I have named, the prostrate man slowly opened his eyes with a heavy groan, and painfully and laboriously struggled into a sitting posture.

Again he pressed his hand to his head, and then, with a tremendous effort, gained his legs.

"I will not be beaten!" he muttered betwixt his clenched teeth.

"I will not be beaten yet. No, at this, the most critical moment of my life, I must have my wits about me. Ha! ha! They shall not get the better of me so easily as they think."

Here a violent pain seized him again, and seemed almost to tear his skull asunder—so severe was the agony.

Again he fell to the earth, and clasped his hands to his head.

Then rolling to and fro. he groaned aloud, the tears run from his eyes by excessive pain, trickling down his hollow cheeks.

"Oh, God! oh, God!" he cried, "I shall go mad—I shall go mad!"

But presently the paroxyism passed away, and he grew more calm.

"I want a little rest," he sighed. "A few hours' rest, and all will be well with me. Then I can meet them—then I can be equal with them. But I want rest; I must have rest. Courage, courage, and I shall soon be at my journey's end."

Then he managed to get upon his feet again, after half-a-dozen abortive efforts, and looked round for his horse.

In falling to the ground the second time, the bridle had dropped off his wrist. The horse, taking advantage of the circumstance, had wandered away to a distance of at least fifty yards.

It would not have been a very difficult task for any active man to have caught the poor jaded animal; for its powers of movement were so diminished by the fatigues of the journey, that it could do little more than crawl about.

But Faversham was himself in such a weak and exhausted state, and at the same time so giddy with pain, that the horse, slow as it was, was more than a match for him.

In vain did he follow it round and round, making every now and then a desperate clutch at the hanging bridle, and grasping only empty air.

In vain did he try threats and entreaties.

The horse most effectually baulked all his efforts to catch it, and eventually went gamboling away, in a clumsy, uncouth fashion, right to the farthest extremity of the common, and far beyond the doctor's reach.

Many times did the wretched man fall sprawling upon the earth, as he missed his footing; for he was so giddy he could scarcely see where he was going.

Many times he again crawled on to his hands and knees, and, with infinite pain and labour, obtained an upright position, only in a few moments to fall again.

At length, the horse twisting round at a moment when Faversham made sure that he had got it safely in a corner, suddenly sent out its hind legs, and striking its would be captor a violent and stunning blow with one hoof in the breast, sent him backwards near half-a-dozen yards, and left him at last motionless, and ghastly white, more like a corpse than a living man.

Thus he lay, stirring neither hand nor foot.

Hour succeeded hour, and the moon rose slowly in the heavens.

It was night. The hours crept on one by one, and he still lay there, in the middle of the dreary waste, without a single pitying soul to come and help him.

But he was not to die like this. His cup of bitterness was not yet full.

His list of crimes not yet ended.

Again would he awake, and again return to the life of vengeance and of blood, which he had marked out for himself.

This time the hand of God did not descend and strike him dead as he lay.

Again was he permitted to rise.

Again—more and still more crimes, hideous, demon-like, and infernal to perpetrate.

LXIV.—A CRY FOR VENGEANCE.

IN an old-fashioned country house, more than usually remarkable for the strength of its walls, and generally solid and substantial style of its architecture, it is necessary that I introduce the reader.

It is night. The clock upon the mantlepiece in the old-fashioned hall or "house-place," as it is usually termed, has just struck eleven.

Without, it is a bright moonlight night; within, a bright fire is blazing upon the hearth, and a bright lamp burning upon the table.

Two persons are sitting at the latter—a man and a woman, both past the middle age, the woman having a shrewish and dissipated look about her blotched and bloated face, and her dress is neglected and careless in the extreme.

The man is strongly built, muscular, and having rather a slouching gait when he rose to his feet, which he did do every now and then, for the purpose of going to the door to look out, up and down the road, shading his eyes, and waiting, as it seemed, for the approach of some one long expected.

When he returned to his seat, and sat for a short time at rest, he flung himself into awkward uncouth shapes which were curious to look at.

He was attired in the best broad-cloth. He most certainly wore the apparel of a gentleman; but a glance at him, was sufficient to convince any person capable of judging, that he was no gentleman.

They might have fancied as much by his rough boorish manners, his awkward movements, and the great disregard which he seemed to pay to the feelings of his companion, and the very little that he put himself out on her account.

For the woman was reading, or rather, I should say, trying to read, some old dogs-eared novel; and every time, which was about once every ten minutes or a quarter-of-an-hour, that he went to the door, he somehow always contrived to jog her elbow, or catch his foot in the legs of her chair, or to half upset the table on his way. All of which petty annoyances elicited a snappish, vixenish observation from the lady, and a request that he would try if he could be a trifle less clumsy.

But had not his manners been sufficient to convince you that this individual had very little gentle blood in his veins, or that his superfine broad cloth was rather out of place upon his gawky limbs, a good look at his face would have settled the matter without a doubt.

Very rarely could you have come across a more villainous face, even in the lowest haunts of the most depraved.

He was a scoundrel you could have sworn, with a very limited knowledge of phisology.

He was a savage, cruel brute, you could have guessed by the very lines about his thin lips.

Not to keep the reader longer in suspense, I may as well tell you at once, that he was all you could think of him that was bad. In short, he was none other than our old friend, Mr. Hopley, who, at the beginning of this history, distinguished himself for his inhuman behaviour to some wretched boys in his charge, and who was anxious to add Master Charley Wag to the number of his victims.

"What makes her so late?" the man said, coming back from the door for the tenth time in an hour. "Whatever can keep her?"

"Do sit down, and hold your noise," the woman retorted. "She'll come as soon as she can, you may be sure."

"She's a precious long while about it though," Hopley grunted.

"Perhaps the doctor was out, and she could not get the physic."

"Humph. Perhaps so. But she's more likely gossiping."

"It's not likely."

"She's most likely on to the old game, though."

"What old game?"

"You know well enough without my describing."

"You do her a very great wrong."

"Oh, do I?"

"You know you do. You have no right to say so."

"Very well. I don't want to say anything. I only want her to come back quickly, that's all."

He slunk back again in his lounging way to chair he had just vacated, and the couple were silent for some time.

Presently the old woman laid down her book, and listened intently.

"What is it?" Hopley asked.

"Hush—listen. Did you not hear a curious sound?"

There was such an expression of terror upon the woman's face, that a sudden alarm and dread seized upon the man, and he rose to his feet trembling excessively.

"What is it?" he asked.

But she said nothing, only appeared to listen more intently than before.

"What is?" he repeated.

"Listen, man—listen!"

Without another word she seized his arm and drew him towards the door.

They undid the lock, and threw it open.

Then looked out, and listened.

Yes, there was a sound—strange and mysterious it seemed at first. Strange—mysterious —inexplicable.

"Do you hear?" the woman asked.

"Yes; but I cannot understand it. What does it mean?"

"It is the sound of feet."

"The sound of feet?"

"Aye, the sound of the feet of a crowd."

"What does it mean, then? Where are they going?"

"They are going nowhere. They are coming."

"Coming? Good God! What for?"

"You know best. They have come to take you—to hunt you out—to drag you before the police. Who knows? Perhaps to tear you to pieces."

"Nonsense—nonsense. You exaggerate."

"Do I? You will see. Listen, there is some one coming across the Common. They are close at hand. Look, do you see?"

There were some tall trees close at hand, which threw a deep shadow across the road. In the shadow some slight object was seen approaching.

"Let us shut the door," cried Hopley, trembling from head to foot. "Come in, woman— quick—quick. Let's lock and bar the door."

But before they could do so, the white figure emerged from the shade, and came running towards them.

It was Lucinda—their daughter.

"Father—father," she cried, in wild and excited tones. "Save yourself, save yourself! They are coming—they are coming!"

"Who? What?"

"The villagers—the working people about —the police."

"The police!"

"They will have your life. They are furious. They know of the murder. They will have your life."

"What must I do?"

"Fly—fly at once. There is nothing else left for it. Fly while there is time, and while you can."

"Where am I to fly to? How you talk. No, by heavens, I'll stop and brazen it out."

"But they will kill you."

"Two can play at that game. Let us make the doors fast. Call to Rattan to come down. Is the servant better to-night?"

Lucinda ran to the bottom of the stairs, and called out Rattan's name; and the latter, who said that he also had been disturbed by the strange sound in the distance, came down-stairs hurriedly, and inquired what was the cause of the disturbance.

Hopley told him.

"They are after me, I expect," said he. "It is about that infernal boy."

Rattan was not so confident. He wished in his heart that such was the case; but he had his misgivings.

"Perhaps it's me," he said.

"Let's be off," he added, a minute after.

"No; there can't be so very many of them. Let's stop here, and give them a broadside from the window if they get troublesome. I have lots of ammunition."

"Are you mad? What's the good of that? If we keep them out, they will keep round the house until they tire us, and then take us al prisoners in the end. Come on, I say."

"We must leave Faversham, then."

"Yes; he can't run fast enough."

"And the women?"

"They won't be hurt, so it doesn't matter. Come on."

As he spoke, he stepped towards the door; but at the moment that he opened it, a couple of men from the outside flung themselves against the panels, and endeavoured to force it open.

As quick as lightning Hopley joined him, and throwing all their strength into a mighty effort, they dashed back the door upon the intruders, and managed to hold it thus until Lucinda had shot the bolts. Then, with equal rapidity, they ran to the windows, and made fast the shutters.

"We're caged now," cried Rattan, furiously. "Let us make the best of it. Have you any firearms?"

"Yes."

As they turned, they saw Faversham standing there in the doorway, deadly white, and looking more like a ghost than a human being; for he had just risen from a bed of sickness.

In his hand he held a gun, which he had just taken from its place on the wall; and he was engaged in examining the lock.

"What are you going to do?" Hopley asked.

"To sell my life as dearly as possible," he replied.

At that moment a loud and angry shout was heard, which must have come from at least fifty voices.

"Open the door! Open the door!"

"Can we hold out any time against them?" asked Faversham eagerly of Hopley.

"Yes, yes—if we go to work the proper way."

"Give the orders then. What must we do first?"

But before Hopley could reply, another shout arose, far louder and more angry than before.

It was a cry for vengeance.

LXV.—Set a Thief to catch a Thief.

BEFORE going any further, I must give the reader an account of the manner in which Faversham and Rattan arrived at Hopley's house.

Hopley had been for some years associated with the former, and his two accomplices, Rattan and Bloodyer, in that frightful scheme for murdering and disposing of the bodies of the wretched paupers at Saint Starver-cum-Bag-o'-Bones' workhouse, which I disclosed in the earlier chapters of this history.

Faversham had agreed with his accomplice Rattan, that after the murder had been committed, should everything go right, as they expected, that he would make at once for Hopley's house in the country, and there lie quiet for a while, until his plans were arranged and perfected for the perpetration of a final piece of villany and deceit.

But as the result of the murder had been so very different to what the two scoundrels had anticipated, and as they had both been obliged to run for their dear lives, and had not had a moment wherein to arrange what should be their course of action or ultimate destination, they had parted without coming to any determination as to where they were to meet next.

They missed one another somehow in a maze of crooked turnings, and Rattan pursued his course alone.

But when he, after a terrific run for it, found himself in what he considered a place of safety, he began to wonder what had become of his companion.

The place where he was—namely, one of the most frightful of all the frightful dens in the neighbourhood of Shadwell—was well known both to him and to Faversham; and Faversham might come to it, did he not carry out his plan of going down to the country, which, without taking Rattan, Rattan thought to be improbable; for, scoundrel as he was himself, he had every faith in the doctor's honour, at least that honour which is most fallaciously supposed to exist betwixt all rogues and vagabonds.

However, after waiting several hours without any result, Rattan determined to go the rounds of all the flash houses and low boozing-kens at which he and Faversham had been in company during the last few weeks of their peregrinations.

But at none of them did he find him.

Again and again he looked in at the different houses, fancying that the doctor might also be looking for him, and that they might by some chance have missed each other.

But, as he did not come, his accomplice began to grow alarmed.

What could have detained him? Had he fallen into the hands of the police?

In any case, there was nothing to be gained by hanging about in this way; and Rattan, thinking London a great deal too hot for him under the present circumstances, determined to make a bolt of it, and get down to Hopley's as soon as he could, where, if nothing went wrong, he would lie up quiet for a week or two.

Therefore, early on the day succeeding the murder, Rattan set off upon the tramp, having first made a few inquiries respecting the road.

He tramped on and on, laying in many a good pint of beer by the way.

He tramped from early morning until dusk, except at such times as he was lucky enough to get a lift in a waggon or cart.

As night came on, he took a long rest at a public-house, and had a good meal, and then set off again about ten o'clock, determined to walk all night; for he was most anxious to get to his journey's end as speedily as possible.

At last, by dint of tramping and trudging, he came to a great, open, desolate-looking common which was close to the place of his destination.

And here, having climbed over a style, and seated himself to rest for a few minutes on the top of it, casting his eyes upon the ground, at the distance of some twenty yards, he saw a sight which caused him to open his mouth and eyes to the widest.

*   *   *   *   *

Faversham lay exactly where he had fallen, for four or five hours at a stretch.

No one passed by that way—no one came

near him. He lay like one that is dead—cold and motionless.

It was a wild and barren part of the country, very thinly populated, in most parts, although at a distance of about a mile, or a mile and a half, there was a large colony composed of pitmen—savage, uncouth wretches, who spent more than half their lives under ground.

Close round the neighbourhood of the common, however, very few persons resided, and these only the poorest and most abject creatures, who struggled on with the greatest difficulty, living from hand to mouth.

There were not many policeman in the neighbourhood, as you may suppose. There was a clergyman, and there was also a church, it is true; but a very small congregation.

Neither the clergy or the police were very popular among the pitmen, and after a while, and after a good many rebuffs, they left them alone to their own evil courses.

The policemen, when on duty, gave the pitmen a very wide path, and did not include the colony in their rounds any oftener than was positively necessary.

Upon the morning of the day following the night on which Faversham fell insensible upon the common, one of the policemen was going on his rounds, and chanced to stumble across a young pitman, in the act of robbing the henroost belonging to a poor little farmer living on the borders of the common.

He was not a very ferocious or athletic thief, and so the policeman, who otherwise would not have meddled with him quite so readily perhaps, determined to make an example of this offender.

Therefore he stole up behind the lad very quietly, and suddenly pinned him.

"Now then," said the policeman.

"Now then," said the boy.

"I've got you," said the policeman.

"Have you?" said the boy, and twisted out of his gripe as easily as an eel would slip out of a pie-dish.

But the officer caught him again, after a little playful dodging round a pump, and then, with a rather smart struggle, managed to pop a pair of handcuffs upon his wrists.

"Now, come on," said he.

They proceeded together pretty quietly for some time.

Suddenly, however, they came to a dead stand-still, at the sight of something very dreadful lying on the grass right across their path.

"Wha—a—t is it?" cried the boy, his teeth chattering in his head.

"Stand up there, will you? Don't hang back."

"Oh, sir, I—I don't like to."

"Don't tell me. Step forward."

"Oh dear, oh dear."

But though the policeman thus insisted on his young friend proceeding, he nevertheless hung back himself very considerably.

The object which had attracted the attention and excited the fears of this zealous officer and his youthful charge was this.

Upon the grass, turned up towards the sky, a still white face, looking awful in the calm moonlight.

The human form to which it belonged—if human it were—was hidden from their sight in deep shadow.

Only the face could be seen at first from where they stood.

Only the face, with its fixed and rigid features, its sunken eyes looking like holes.

A black gaping slit where the mouth was.

"G—g—good heavens! what is it?" the policeman cried, in abject terror; for he was much too frightened by the terrible apparition even to think of keeping up his dignity before the young thief whom he had captured.

"G—g—good heavens! what is it?"

"It's a man," the boy said, with a long breath, as he got at last a better view of the object which excited their fears.

"It's a man, to be sure," said the policeman.

"What man?"

"A drunken man, most likely."

Then, recovering himself altogether with this comfortable suggestion, he pulled his captive along with him, and advanced towards the spot where the body lay.

"A drunken man, of course. Most likely one of them mining chaps."

"No, it's not," retorted the boy. "Look at his togs."

"To be sure, he's well dressed."

"He's a gentleman."

"What's up with him, then?"

"He's drunk, I should think."

"Not likely. It's only you miners that get drunk. You don't suppose a gentleman would?"

"I wouldn't take my oath that they didn't."

"You're a disrespectful young cur, that's what you are. Just lend a hand, and try and get him up."

"How can I?"

"Why not?"

"Because of these darbies."

"Oh, very well, then; leave it alone. You won't get them off, young fellow, so you needn't think it."

"I didn't think it."

The policeman, not feeling inclined to bandy any more words about the matter, devoted himself to the task of raising the head of the prostrate man, and endeavouring to find out what was the matter with him.

"He's very ill. It seems as if he had had some sort of fit. He's quite insensible. I wonder who he is."

"Why don't you feel in his pockets?"

The policeman took the hint, or perhaps the notion had occurred to him at the same time; however, he began to grope among Faversham's pockets.

He selected the waistcoat pockets first.

There was nothing in them.

The trousers.

Same result.

Then he came to the breast-pocket.

In this he placed his hand, and felt something hard.

He turned it out.

It was a pocket pistol.

"Hallo!" said the policeman; "he's a desperate customer when he's up. But arms are wanted in such a lonely place as this."

"Ain't there nothing more?" asked the boy,

who was interested in the result of the investigation.

"Yes; there's something."

"What is it?"

"I can't make out."

The policeman had plunged his hand again into the pocket, and was struggling with some other hard substance, which, having got crossways, refused to be pulled out without a great deal of difficulty.

"Let me try," said the boy, growing eager.

"You stand back, will you?" retorted the policeman.

And began to struggle again.

Suddenly the object of resistance gave way, and it came out unexpectedly.

It was a little bag.

In coming out the end came undone.

A shower of golden pieces fell around them.

Both the policeman and the thief were astounded.

"Well, I never!"

"Did you ever!"

"Who'd have thought it?"

"Here's a go!"

And a dozen more exclamations of a like character.

After which the policeman set to work collecting the sovereigns which were rolling about, at the same time, by the way, refusing all aid from his young friend, who in this work was most particularly anxious to assist him.

It took some time to find them; for several of the pieces had fallen down to the roots of the long grass, and required a good deal of patient investigation to discover them.

The policeman, however, searched for them diligently, and groped and groped for yards round.

It is rather a pleasant occupation, mind you, looking for sovereigns; only when "findings is keepings," as the children say, perhaps it is rather better still.

This idea may have occurred to the officer.

"Why should I pick them up for him? Why shouldn't I stick to them? Why should I have all my trouble for nothing?"

There was a good deal in this, you know, when you come to consider it. Why should he have all his trouble for nothing?

In fact, the more he thought of it, the more convinced was he that he ought to keep it.

When he had made up his mind that to give up the money would be a most absurd proceeding, he began to consider what was the best way of getting hold of it.

You may say, why did he not help himself to it, when he had it there under his hand.

What was to prevent him?

Well, you see, there was the presence of the thief.

You would not surely have a member of the force commit himself.

No, I am sure that you would not.

For that matter, knowing, as I do, that you have such a high opinion of their integrity as a body, I more than half suspect that you are inclined to look upon the whole affair as very improbable.

Still, you know, there are some policemen who forget their duty. I have read of such in the newspapers. Indeed, for that matter, I know

persons who have had instances come under their own personal observation—undoubted instances, that there was no mistake about.

The policeman, therefore, was in a bit of a fix. He was not quite sure what he should do.

If he took the money, and there was any row about it, everybody would suspect him, should the thief state, as he no doubt would that they together had seen the body and found the money.

The way, then, was to square the thief, and that must be done.

"Tom," said the policeman, "this is a tidy bit of money."

"There's no doubt about that."

"A little fortune, eh?"

"A big 'un to some folks."

"Pity it aint ours, eh?"

"A great pity."

"Half of it would set you up."

"A third of it wonldd't hurt me."

"That is, if you had your liberty."

"Yee."

"It wouldn't be much good to you as it is."

"No, not particular. Unless it was when I come out again."

"Yes. But if it was found on your person, there would be an inquiry, and you'd get into hot water, I'm thinking."

"Very likely. They're very hard upon us poor coves."

"Now if you'd only come on here instead of trying that hen-roost."

"I wish to goodness I had."

"You'd have made a good job by it."

"You're right there.

"Now the only way to help you that I can see—"

"Yes, sir."

"The only way to give you a chance of doing better for the future, is to set you at liberty."

"It would be the making of me."

"If I was to do such a thing you ought to be very grateful."

"I should be."

"And you ought to be willing to do anything on earth by way of return which lay in your power."

"So I should."

"Well, I want to be liberal with you if I can. You're a nice young fellow, and if you had had better bringings up, you'd have turned out better, I have no doubt."

"I'm sure I should."

"Now, if I was to give you your liberty, and five pound of this money, you'd be jolly well pleased, I should think."

"I certainly should, sir, though I'd be more pleased with ten."

"Now just keep civil, if you can, or else you won't have any. Listen to me. These are my terms. There, I'll make it seven. Pocket the money, and keep a quiet tongue in your head, and you'll be none the worse for it."

"I'm much obliged to you, sir," said the thief.

"Kneel down, then, and I'll take off the handcuffs."

So he did kneel down as desired, and the policeman liberated him.

Then he counted out the money, giving the lad seven pounds, and keeping the remain-

THE ATTACK.

ing twelve — there were nineteen in all — for himself.

They were engaged in the division, and were very intent about it, when Jack Rattan happened to come up.

"What are they up to?" said he to himself, looking on for a minute or two very quietly.

"They're dividing the swag," he said, when he caught sight of the body lying beside them.

"They've slogged some one, and emptied his pockets."

Then listening a moment to the chink of the money,

"It's gold," said he, "by all that's lucky. I'll go snacks with them."

But as he prepared to bawl out to them lustily, and ask "what was their game," his eye alighted upon the policeman's uniform.

"There's a bobby," said he. "What does it mean?"

At that moment the policeman spoke.

"That's your share. Now, mind, you've taken your dying oath you won't tell anyone a word about it."

"I've sworn I won't."

"By Jove!" thought Rattan, "it's as I supposed. They are dividing the swag, after all."

Then he made up his mind to have a share of it, and that that share should be the lion's share.

He therefore stole up behind the couple of robbers, without their for one moment suspect-

No. 50.

[CHARLEY WAG, THE NEW JACK SHEPPARD.

ing that anyone had observed them, or that anyone was approaching.

When behind them, he raised his two hands, and with a mighty blow bonnetted the pair.

So very sudden and so violent was the movement, that the policeman was sent sprawling in one direction, and the boy in the other.

The money going anywhere.

Mr. Rattan picked as much of it up as he could in the smallest possible space of time, and thrust it into his pockets.

By the time that he had done this, the policeman and the boy had in a measure recovered themselves.

When they saw that the stranger was pocketing their money, they were as much enraged as at first they had been frightened at his appearance.

" What do you mean, you vagabond ?" cried the policeman.

" Mean by what ?"

" Do you suppose that you are going to stick to that money ?"

" I should rather think I did."

" But it's not yours."

" No, nor yours either."

" Give it up."

" I shan't.

" Give it up."

" I tell you I shan't."

" Very well, then, we'll make you."

But Rattan was not a man to be easily overcome.

He possessed, as I have said before, a lion's strength.

He was a match for any ordinary two men.

Aye, and for that matter, for any four.

The policeman and the young thief made a rush at him.

He received the officer first with a terrific blow in the mouth, which sent him sprawling head over heels like a snowball, until he came at last plump into a ditch, in which he presently sat up, looking remarkably sheepish, and grasping his jaw, which for a minute or two he supposed to be broken.

But the fight was not over yet.

There was still the boy to be disposed of.

This young gentleman, furious at his loss, ran forward and grappled with the robber.

" Give it up ! give it up !" he screamed.

But Rattan was not very easily persuaded.

The boy made a spring at him like a young bulldog, and sticking to the robber's neckerchief, allowed himself to be swayed to and fro violently without loosening his hold.

" Damn you !" the ruffian cried, between his clenched teeth. " Damn you ! You shall smart for it if you don't leave go !"

But the boy seemed determined to cling to him, as though to a last chance.

" Give me back my money !" he cried ; " give me back my money !"

Rattan grew furious.

" You will have it, then."

And he grasped the boy by the throat.

" Give me my money !" the lad gasped, choking. " Give me my money !"

" Leave go of me, you cursed young varmint ; or, by God, I'll smash you !"

Then, as the lad still clung to him frantically, he grasped his windpipe with one hand, and

raising the other high in the air, brought it down with a felling smash upon the poor boy's face, which in an instant became covered with blood.

It was a cruel, cowardly act.

An act which only a savage ruffian such as Rattan could commit.

The boy fell to the ground with a deep groan. Then the ruffian, seeing the coast clear, turned to fly.

The policeman, being desperately frightened, and fancying very truly that he was much safer where he was, did not venture out.

Only when Rattan looked towards him, he ducked his head, so as to escape notice as much as possible.

He had not any particular desire to get another " one in the mouth," such as Rattan had just accommodated him with.

Rattan, however, catching sight of him, most unfortunately for the policeman, he advanced towards him, and dealt him a terrific kick, which almost knocked all the little bit of breath remaining out of his body.

Then he returned to the scene of the struggle, and looked out for the rest of the money which might be lying about.

While thus engaged, he had his back to Faversham.

He was stooping down.

Suddenly he felt a cold hand upon his throat, which tightened as he tried to remove it.

" Is it you again ?" he said, as he turned round his head, expecting that it was the boy returned again to the charge.

" Is it you ?"

" It is I," a voice he knew replied.

His jaw dropped, and his eyes opened.

" You ?"

" I."

" Good God ! I thought it was a ghost."

It was Faversham.

" No ; it's myself in flesh and blood—at least, as much as is left of me."

" What has happened to you, then ? Have you been knocked down and robbed ?"

" I have not been knocked down—"

" I thought you had."

" Though I have been robbed."

" Who by ?"

" By you."

" What do you mean ?"

" What I say."

" Why, it is I that rescued you !"

" Oh, I misunderstood your motive. You were picking up my money for me."

" Exactly."

" Thank you."

LXVI.—Shows how Charley grew to be a monstrous favourite with the French ladies.

DRAGGED back to prison, securely ironed, and cast into a cell without being allowed to say a word for himself, good, bad, or indifferent, poor Charley Wag, almost fainting from fatigue and hunger, gave himself up for lost.

But he was too sleepy to think much of his

melancholy condition; and, after one or two fruitless attempts to concentrate his faculties, and look his case steadily in the face, he gave the matter up in despair, and rolling himself up as comfortably as he could upon the heap of straw which the prison authorities had kindly allotted to him, he was not very long before he was in that happy land of dreams wherein the poor and wretched find relief from their troubles.

He slept very soundly through the night, and, except that he felt rather stiff and sore when he awoke in the morning, he was not so very uncomfortable, all things considered.

There was a tiny grating to a hole above his head, which did duty as a window; and through this a very homœopathic dose of sunshine was stealing into his cell.

However, what little there was of it was sufficient to cheer our young friend's spirits.

"Who cares?" said he to himself. "I shall be out of this before I am many months older. I wasn't born to rot away in a prison. It's not my destiny. I'm meant for better things, or else I'm very much mistaken. So keep up your pecker, Master Charley; the prison isn't built yet that can hold you. I believe a party of the name of Sheppard made a similar observation; but Mr. Jack was a clumsy sort of thief, whatever our friend Harrison Ainsworth may try to make out to the contrary. He hadn't the style and polish of the professional gentleman of the present day. He couldn't touch us."

And as he spoke, Mr. Wag looked down at his ragged wardrobe as complacently as though he were surveying the most finished *chef d'œuvre* of the most stylish of West-end tailors.

"Mr. Wag, sir," he continued, "there's no disguising the fact—you're a gentleman, sir—you're a gentleman, every inch of you; and though you may be depressed and kept down at the present moment, you will rise, sir—mark my words—you will rise and cut a figure in the world yet before you have done."

But at this moment his soliloquy was interrupted by the arrival of a warder with a basin of thin soup for the prisoner's breakfast.

"Good morning to you, sir," said the warder, politely, and in English.

"Good morning, sir," responded Mr. Wag, with great courtesy. "I hope I see you pretty middling. How's all all your family?"

But the warder, whose knowledge of the language was extremely limited, only bowed and grinned, and said,

"Yes."

"You seem to be a jolly old cock," pursued Mr. Wag, still talking in his own tongue. "I'm sorry I can't offer you a chair; but there don't seem to be any provision for company. And I suppose you've had your breakfast."

"What?" said the Frenchman, who did not understand a word that Mr. Wag was saying.

"Because," continued Charley, "I can hardly recommend what I've got."

The Frenchman stared and smiled.

"It's flavoury, sir," said Mr. Wag, "without being heavy; it's peppery, sir, without too much grease; it's the sort of soup that wouldn't disagree with a sick blue-bottle. What's your opinion, sir?"

"I don't understand you," said the Frenchman.

"Then why didn't you say so at first?" asked Mr. Wag, in French.

"Oh," said the other, "you can talk, can you?"

"Like a native," replied Mr. Wag, who, by the way, made a most woeful hash of it.

"Well, then," said the Frenchman; "and so you are Monsieur Charley Wag."

"I should rather say I was."

"The celebrated Charley Wag."

"Ah, that's my description."

"And so you've been breaking out of one of our prisons."

"Exactly."

"And what were you in for?"

"That's just what I should like to know."

"Don't you know?"

"No; and if you come to that, I don't know what I'm in this one for."

"For getting out of the other."

"Humph, there's something in that, perhaps. It did not occur to me. But supposing it is proved that I did nothing to warrant my former incarceration, what do you suppose will be the result?"

"It's extremely difficult to get out of one of our gaols when once you get in."

"You mean, I suppose, if the prisoners don't adopt the method that I did."

"Ah, but you won't get the chance again."

"I will wait for it."

"You will probably wait a long while, my young friend, unless you can gnaw a hole through the walls with your teeth."

"Well, but what am I to expect? Am I to lie here and rot?"

"If you've done anything very bad, you will most likely be sent for fifteen years to the galleys."

"That's cheerful."

"If you haven't done anything—"

"Ah, there's a chance for me."

"In that case, you'll probably be handed over to your own government—"

"Oh!"

"And hanged."

"Certainly."

"Or else—"

"Another chance?"

"You may be left here to wait your trial, and will probably be polished off by the prison fever in a year or so."

"Then my best plan will be to gnaw a hole through the wall with my teeth, as you suggested."

"I should think so. Set about it."

With this the gaoler turned upon his heel, and went away, laughing.

Master Charley began to fancy that his position was rather an unpleasant one.

"But I won't be downhearted," said he to himself. "I'll keep my pecker up, in spite of them all."

During the morning Mr. Wag was removed from the cell where he had slept into a better one; and he was considerably pleased to exchange his miserable rags for a warm suit of clothes, even though those clothes were a convict's dress.

He had a tolerable allowance, too, of wholesome food ; and, indeed, his condition, as compared to that of the other prison, was infinitely superior.

One thing he very soon noticed, and you who know Mr. Wag can easily imagine how the circumstance gratified that young gentleman's vanity.

He was regarded by everybody as an object of curiosity.

"That is the famous London thief," he heard them whispering.

"That is the celebrated Charley Wag."

"That is the great prison-breaker."

"That is the boy who did the trick."

Mr. Wag overhearing all this, and pretending that he did not, was a very fine sight indeed.

The lad strutted about like a young bantam, up and down the prison yard, and glanced sideways at those who stood, open-mouthed, admiring him.

"There's no doubt about," he was thinking to himself, "I am a very fine fellow indeed ; and they know it, too."

The arrival of our hero most certainly created a very great sensation in the gaol, and in the town surrounding it.

Visitors came flocking in every day, not only from the town itself, but from the adjacent villages, and even from villages ten miles off.

The celebrated Charley Wag held little levies.

Beautiful young ladies, redolent of sweet violets, jockey club, and Frangipanni, came rustling into the gloomy gaol in wonderous gowns of the richest silk, in splendid mantles, in costly shawls, with delightful little gloves which fitted them like their own skin ; with glossy stockings of flesh coloured silk ; with dainty little boots with pointed heels that fairies might have worn, came in to see him and went into ecstacies about him.

Thought that he was so romantic—that he was so noble looking—that his air was so grand.

Some went so far as to say, so " God like."

And all this did Master Charley take as quietly as you please, fancying in his heart, I have no doubt, that it was only the praise which was due to him as one of the heads of the thieving profession.

So he strutted about, and threw himself into imposing attitudes, and exerted himself to make sharp replies to the questions addressed to him, and gave himself altogether some wonderful airs, all of which, however, met with public approval.

For some time he was the lion of the little French town in which the prison stood.

I believe that if he could have had his liberty just at this time, he would rather have given it up than have sacrificed the delightful sensation of being a hero.

There were even verses made about and addressed to him by the enthusiastic lady visitors; and one young maiden wrote him a most impassioned love-letter, telling him that she loved him more than all the world, that she should die without him, and that he must burst his bonds and fly to her.

But it is a good deal easier to talk of bursting bonds than to do it.

The walls were too thick, and the iron bars too strong.

It could not be done, and so Charley, although he would have been only too happy to do a little love-making, did not exactly see his way clear to get out of his present lodging.

Many presents of money were made to him, and as the system of bribery was pretty extensively practised in this gaol, he was enabled by its means to procure a great many luxuries and indulgences, which without it, he would have had very little chance of getting.

And so, for some time, Mr. Wag enjoyed himself very well, although he was only an unfortunate prisoner.

However, worse luck, there is an end to most good things in this world, and there was very soon an end to Master Wag's popularity.

In course of time, something—it does not very much matter what—say a coronation or a poultry show—a great fire—an awful murder—a heartless seduction, or a disgraceful intrigue—anyhow, something occurred in the little town which caused poor Charley to be forgotten.

He and his wonderful adventures were put upon the shelf.

There was an end of him.

The interest died out little by little, and three months after he came to the gaol, he was quite forgotten.

And he was not only forgotten by those faithless young ladies in the rustling silks, so daintily gloved, with such delicate little boots, and such divinely fitting silk stockings ; but he was also forgotten by other people, which was worse.

He seemed to be altogether forgotten by the authorities.

There had been a very long and wearisome correspondence between the English Consul and the English Government.

The English Government had advertised for Mr. Wag, and had set a high price upon his capture.

He was now captured, and they would not have him.

Interminable letters flowed from either side ; but nothing particular came of it at all.

Time wore on, and poor Charley lay in gaol, and began to get very sick of it.

When his popularity as a pet prisoner began to be upon the wane, the governor of the prison ordered him to be placed in a cell with two other prisoners, instead of the cell which he had occupied alone.

Mr. Wag very much objected to this, because he now sunk to the level of the rest of the prisoners, and had to work like they did; but before long he found cause to rejoice in it, for it was the means eventually of his effecting his escape.

LXVII.—Shows how Charley broke out in a fresh place.

THE immense strength of most of the new criminal prisons in England and France, renders any effort to escape from them almost utterly hopeless.

Not so, however, this particular prison in which Master Charley was confined.

It was originally intended for a barrack, and was for the most part built of bricks.

It had subsequently, and with a great deal of difficulty been converted into a gaol, and at this time contained within its walls more desperate characters than could be found in the same circumference in any other part of the globe.

The classification of these, therefore, was a very important part of the duty of the warders.

They very soon mark out the men who are likely to endeavour to get away.

Then they at once adopt measures, not only to frustrate their attempts, but also to recapture them if they are successful.

Thus the haunts of every felon likely to break his bonds, are as well known to the gaol authorities as the man himself.

Besides this, they are most carefully watched.

The room in which Charley and his two companions slept, was one upon the basement story.

From this an iron ventilator in the wall communicated with a cellar beyond.

At half-past eight in the evening the hammocks in the cells were let down, and by a quarter to nine all the prisoners were in bed.

An open grating in the door allowed the sentry to see that every man was sleeping.

Once or twice in each night the cells themselves were visited and examined.

The reader may see by this, that there was a good deal of difficulty in the way of any one who should attempt to escape.

But attempt to escape, these three most certainly did, as you shall see.

Let me first of all, however, introduce Charley's two companions.

One was a melancholy fellow about thirty years of age, a banker's clerk, who had committed forgery, and been caught in the act.

He was very morose and taciturn, this individual, and very rarely volunteered any remark to his companions.

He kept himself to himself, only if he got a chance he ate more than his share of black bread and soup.

The other was an old offender, a frightful ruffian. A man condemned to the galleys for life, and who was waiting there until the trial of some other prisoners was concluded, that they might be all transported together to their future place of incarceration.

His last little offence was that of chopping a man in two with a spade.

How it was that his own head was not cut off in return, was very difficult to say.

Probably because it should have been.

This is France, you know, which I am describing, where there is much unjust justice dispensed.

We do these things much better in England, don't we?

We don't hang the wrong man in our country, and we always hang a man when we ought to do.

Our jury is a fine institution, as everybody can testify.

But to return to our trio.

Master Charley did not get on very well with his two companions. They did not hit it, as people say. They could not pull together.

Therefore, for some length of time they were all three as uncomfortable as they well could be.

Silently they sat and glared at one another, never speaking a word. It was a great trial for Master Charles, who so dearly loved to hear himself talk. And after being such a hero, after being so courted by the ladies, it was really dreadful to subside in this sort of style into a monotony, and cooped up here with two silent wretches, looking as gloomy and miserable as a couple of old hens with the mumps.

Master Charley resolved to make an attempt at escape.

It had been his first thought upon arriving at the prison.

For a brief period it had been abandoned, it is true—this was the period when he had been the object of so much curiosity and admiration—but now all the old desire had been revived in his breast.

His heart throbbed for liberty.

How was it to be obtained?

He set his wits to work, and in course of time, the opportunity not only arrived, but he readily availed himself of it.

There had always existed between himself and that warder, who, the first morning he was in the prison had brought him his soup, a curious kind of friendship and good feeling.

One day when he was taking his exercise in the yard, and when nobody was near to observe them, the gaoler came up and gave him a hail.

"Well, young fellow, how are you getting on?"

"As well as can be expected," replied Master Charley.

"You don't seem very lively."

"No, it's one of those feathers out of my bed that has stuck in my throat, and made me a little poorly."

"You were always a merry fellow."

"It's a poor place to show off my humour in, though, Guvnor. You should come and see me when I'm at home; that's the time I come out in my true character."

"Ah, I hope you'll get home soon."

"I see very little chance of it, worse luck."

"No, you haven't gnawed your way out yet."

"But I could do so in time."

"Why don't you?"

"I will, if you'll lend me some teeth."

"Aha, Master Wag, you're getting on to ticklish ground."

"Not at all—there's no risk. You know how to do it."

"What! risk my place? And what for?"

"For friendship to me."

"But, my dear young friend, what is friendship?"

"Then there is gain—Does that tempt you?"

"What gain?"

"I have forty francs put by."

"A mere trifle, my dear young friend. It really is not worth the risk."

"You would'nt put much faith in my word if I were to promise to pay you well for it afterwards, when I have recovered my liberty."

"Well, there's no knowing. I'm a soft-hearted sort of a fellow. I might be tempted."

"Can I tempt you?"

"Hist! is there any one coming?"

"I think not."

"Tempt away, then."

"I am rather a popular thief in my own country," Charley began.

"So I have heard," said the warder.

"You may suppose, then, I make a good bit of money. You've heard of my breaking into the Bank of England, I suppose?"

"I have heard you tell the story."

"There was a trifle hanging to that, as you may suppose."

"Yes, I should say so."

"I have had several other uncommonly lucky hits. I have made a good round sum every month for some time past, and was in full swing, when I was foolish enough to think of making a journey into the country, and then had the ill-luck to come over to this precious country of yours."

"Well, it is to be reasonably supposed that if I once get back again, I shall go on as before."

"There's a chance of it."

"Then what I am going to promise is, that the first hundred pounds I land I will send to you from England, in return for the loan of your teeth."

"Will you swear to do so?"

"I will promise to do so, upon my honour, which is a greater security than all the oaths. Are you content?"

"I am. I accept the compact."

"When shall I have the tools?"

"To-night, at eight."

"I depend upon you."

"Until then, good-bye."

"Good-bye."

At eight that night the warder kept his promise by bringing the tools.

He slipped them quietly into the boy's hand without saying a word, or without a soul seeing the action.

Charley silently thanked him by a glance.

Then when he was left alone with his companions, he reflected whether or not he should let them into the secret.

He had laid down a plan of escape, in which their assistance was necessary.

He determined that he would tell them, although he disliked them so much that he had almost decided upon thinking of some new plan which he might try alone.

When they were all in bed, and the jailor, whose duty it was to do so, had peeped at them through the grating in the door, Charley spoke up.

"Are you two awake?"

Neither of them made any answer at first.

He repeated the question to each.

To the old offender:—

"Are you awake, Michael?"

"Yes; of course I am."

Then to the clerk:—

"Are you awake, Duborg?"

"What's that to you?"

"You're two nice amiable sort of chaps, you are," retorted Master Charley. "I've a very good mind not to tell you what I was going to tell you; but I'm of a philanthropic turn, and return good for evil."

"Well, what good are you going to do us, pray?"

"Going to open the doors of this prison for you, that's all."

His two companions suddenly became lively. They sat up in bed.

"What do you say? Are you mad?"

But Charley repeated his statement very calmly, and then, at their request, entered into lengthened particulars concerning his scheme.

I will not, however, weary the reader by recording them, neither will I lengthily decipher their progress.

It was a long and weary work.

To make the description of it as short and concise as possible shall be my object.

This, then, was what they did.

It took them many weeks before they had managed it.

The first thing they did, was to dress up a dummy out of their own clothes, and to place upon its head a nightcap—they all three wore night-caps, according to prison regulations.

This dummy, then, was put into one of the hammocks, so that the man who looked through the grating, if he were to come and look without their having been able to hear his approach, would see the three beds occupied, two by real men, the other by a dummy, which he would suppose to be the third man.

The man whose place the dummy occupied, would then be at work.

The next thing that was to be done, was to remove the bricks round the ventilator.

The operation was a very long and tiresome one, for the tools which the gaoler had supplied were by no means first-class.

The wall also was very thick, and even that was not the worst of it.

To enable the sentries to detect any attempt of this kind, the walls were whitewashed.

What was to be done in that case?

Why, the three prisoners imitated the whitewash, and when the bricks were replaced in the inner hole every morning, they made a composition to resemble mortar, whitened it all over with some whiting which they had supplied them for the purpose of cleaning and polishing their tins.

So beautifully was this done, after a little practice, that in the day the most careful scrutiny failed to discover any signs of the manipulation.

Not a trace of an opening in the wall was discernable.

As soon as an entrance into the cellar beyond had been effected, the men only worked from one o'clock in the morning until about four.

In the cellar beyond was another ventilator, leading out into the prison grounds, though still within the walls.

The prisoner working at removing the bricks round the ventilator had a strap fastened to his waist, the other end of which was held by one of his companions in the cell.

Thus, whenever they heard anything unusual, or thought that the sentry was coming to enter the cells, they pulled the string, and the prisoner at work instantly returned through the narrow hole in the wall, replaced the ventilator and piece of brickwork, and was in his hammock again in a minute.

Much practice had made them expert, and the rapidity of their movements upon one of these occasions at last grew to be something marvellous.

In the course of time everything was complete, and they determined to try the experiment.

During the day they were employed in making up soldier's overcoats for the Government, and had contrived by little and little to get together a vast quantity of string, which they plaited into a long rope ladder, and hid away in the cellar.

They also contrived in the most artful way to secrete three of the overcoats, in which they were to dress themselves when they made the attempt.

One night they fixed upon at last.

The time chosen was between half-past eight and nine o'clock.

The time that the men were sent to their cells for the night.

At nine o'clock sentries were posted all round the outer walls, so that the men knew that they must be away before that hour, or not at all.

They accordingly went to the cell, let down their hammocks, and two of them put in the dummies with night-caps on under the clothes.

But at this juncture, the heart of the third failed him.

It was the banker's clerk.

"You don't mean to say you are going to turn tail?" said Charley.

"Yes I do."

"Why?"

"Because mine is only a three year's sentence, And it is not worth the risk."

"Don't you think that we shall be successful?"

"No."

With this opinion to comfort them, Charley and the hardened offender commenced their work.

They were determined to risk everything for the chance of liberty.

They accordingly got through the wall into the cellar and put on their great coats.

With the aid of their thin twine ladder, they quickly scaled the inner prison wall, and then the outer.

In ten minutes at most, from the time that they left their cell, they were standing safe and sound in a dark narrow lane outside the prison walls.

"We are free," cried Michael.

"Yes," repeated Charley, though his heart was so full he could scarcely speak, "we are free."

"Where shall we go?" asked the other

"You choose your path," replied Charley, "and I will choose mine."

"Shan't we go together?"

"We shall be safer apart."

"But for the sake of company."

"My friend," said Charley, "I hardly think that we were cut out for one another. We have never been over amicable. We have been tolerable good friends while we have been working this job together, it is true. The job is finished now. Our object is gained. I will wish you good-bye."

"Oh! as you choose."

"Good-bye, then."

And Charley went to the right, while his late comrade went to the left.

Three days after that Michael was recaptured, and a week afterwards went to the galleys, where he remained all the rest of his life.

Charley pursued his own course.

He had forty francs in his pocket. He managed to get a coarse suit of clothes with this to hide his dress. He managed to find his way to Calais, and then to find a merchant vessel laden with goods for England.

And it set sail and bore him home again.

How his heart beat as he once more gazed upon the old familiar river shores.

The sight of the tower and London Bridge, was to him a far more glorious vision than anything in fairy land.

England once more! London again, with its dear old streets, its vices and its follies.

How he longed to go again to some of his old haunts, to plunge once more into that wild, reckless life which he had led before; but above all, he longed to meet again with his dear Julia.

As soon as he landed on shore he ran as fast as his legs would carry him—for any earthly conveyance was much too slow for him—to their old lodgings.

Was she in?

In? No. She had gone away months ago.

Gone away! He staggered back as though he had been struck, and would have fallen had he not clutched at the door-post.

Gone away—months ago!

Where to?

They could not tell.

She had come there with a strange gentleman, and they had fetched away the boxes and things which belonged to her.

Charley walked away from the door.

He was hungry, and thirsty, and sleepy; but he had not a halfpenny in his pocket.

There was nobody in London to welcome him. No one.

Stay, should he go to Cock's Lot, and get a bed there; there would be a welcome there.

But then the old dislike which he had always felt of associating himself with other thieves came over him.

No, he would not go there.

But he must have money.

Should he beg?

An old lady came toddling up at the time.

He asked her for a few coppers.

She said that she would call the police.

"I must have something," said he to himself. "And since she won't give it, I suppose I must take it."

He, however, chose a bye-street, where there was very little light, and very little traffic.

Hidden here in a door-way, he waited.

He did not wait long before an old gentleman came down the street. He was a stout gentleman who walked very slowly. He had a fine gold watch, two sovereigns, and some silver in his pocket.

At the police station that very night, that very same old gentleman made a statement to the effect that he had been garrotted and robbed of all his valuable property.

He had no idea who did it, it was done so suddenly.

There were no witnesses.

Only one person in London could have named the thief, and that was the thief himself.

Mr. Charles Wag supped in the Haymarket that night, and stood a bottle of champagne to a couple of nice young ladies, who also partook of a few dozen of oysters at his expense.

LXVIII.—SOME ACCOUNT OF THE GREAT MILL BETWEEN TOMMY COBB AND BILL THE SLOGGER.

WHEN the celebrated Tommy Cobb, through the medium of *Bell's Life*, challenged the well known Billy Brains, *alias the Slogger*, to fight him in seven or eight months, for any sum from fifty pounds up to a thousand, the fighting world was quite astonished at Tommy's temerity.

Every night the bar at Nat Langham's was noisy with the discussions upon Tommy's foolhardiness. It seemed to be the general opinion that Mr. Cobb had over-rated his powers, as he would find out by the awful licking he would get when the fight came off.

Billy Brains was the champion of England—a man above six feet high, with a fist like a sledge-hammer, and a frame like Hercules. He was only sixteen when he fought his first battle, and he was considered to be the most precocious boy of the day.

He continued to fight to gain himself a name, until he was pretty nearly knocked out of all recognition; and, indeed, it was difficult to tell if ever he had a nose or any other feature.

At last he gained the height of his ambition, and became champion of England.

He was famous for striking tremendously hard with his left, and if he hit "home," the blow was invariably the cause of a coroner's inquest to follow soon afterwards.

Indeed, to use fistic parlance, it was a case of "cold meat and pickles," with other pastry.

Tommy Cobb, on the contrary, was shorter and lighter than his antagonist, and every one wondered why he took so great a fancy to fight Billy Brains, alias the Slogger, as it was a contest in which he was almost certain to get the worst. All his friends knew he was the gamest little chap out; but did not for a moment suppose he had the slightest chance of gaining the victory.

Tommy Cobb, it is true, had done plenty of "bruising;" for many a straight nose he had spoilt, and many an eye "bunged up," and was looked upon generally as a plucky one; but, as one of his "pals" remarked,

"It was backing a tomtit against a gamecock. What chance," he asked, "can eleven stone have against fifteen? Why no more than a shop-front against a paving-stone.

"If Tommy should get a good 'smeller,' it will spoil his 'daylights,' and it will be all *up* with him."

The place of meeting for all those who wished to see this wonderful fight was the railway station; and as the clock struck the hour appointed, Charley Wag and his friends drove up to the terminus with a great flourish; and

being well known among the "fancy" as a patron of the ring, Master Charles was received with much respect by the profession generally.

There were between five and six hundred men, all dressed in a very extraordinary manner, wearing caps of every colour, neckerchiefs of shawl-patterns, and some with velveteen shooting-coats.

There was dreadful pushing and squeezing to get the tickets, and the uproar was not diminished when those behind began to shout out to their friends, "Tom, get four for us, will yer?" or, "Jack, just collar a dozen, will yer? I'll make it all square."

Master Charley Wag was here, of course; and when he and his friends had secured their places, they passed the time in walking about the platform, and reading the advertisements, and watching the people Charley quickly pointed out to his friends.

"Where's our man?" asked one of his friends, and he was informed that, in order to keep clear of the police, they had been "forwarded" over-night.

It was an ordinary train by which they travelled, and among the passengers were a few women, who could not for the life of them imagine why all the carriages should be full of such ugly-faced men with broken noses.

Some of them were afraid to trust themselves among such a savage-looking crew, and as much alarmed as if they had suddenly tumbled in with a lot of wild Indians.

Charley Wag, who knew the country well, endeavoured to beguile the three hours' ride by chatting and smoking, although smoking was strictly prohibited by the railway company; but Charley, as the reader knows, never cared for rules.

"It's a bad country for hunting," he observed, with the air of a man who kept a pack of hounds of his own; and he seemed able to enlighten them on any subject. He could point out farmer's houses, and tell them long yarns about each house; and when they came to a little secluded wooded spot, he would describe at great length a picnic he once had there, and relate a very curious adventure, in which a very young and lovely lady acted very imprudently.

Those in power had arranged it—so as to avoid the tag-rag and bobtail who always find out and go to such meetings—that the train should go some eighty miles along the coast, where they would join a steamer, which was in waiting to convey the select party to the place of combat. At every station there were a number of policemen, ready to seize the combatants if they made their appearance.

At one of the stations they saw a crowd hurrying along the platform after a brown-faced man

"There's Billy Brains!" cried Charley, with great excitement, at the same time springing to the window. "What a fellow he is, to be sure! He seems to have more strength in him than ever. If Tommy only has one of his gentle taps on his nose, he will be done for."

"Yes, that's Billy, sure enough," said a stranger in the same compartment with Charley and his friends; "and the best-hearted fellow in England. You might almost spit in his face, and he wouldn't hurt you."

USEFUL INFORMATION.

After a while, another man, quite as brown, but not so tall or so stout as Billy Brains, passed along the platform, and everybody recognized Tommy Cobb.

"How well he looks, curse him!" said Charley. "Who's coached the beggar up like that, I should like to know?"

At this moment there was a great noise, and confusion, and talking, occasioned by a man running from carriage to carriage, offering to bet five to two on Cobb.

After everybody had evinced great anxiety to know how much farther they had to go, the terminus was reached, and there was a general rush to get to the steamer.

The two prize-fighters had already been taken out, and were seen trudging along far ahead,

accompanied by their seconds and backers, at the same time concealing them as much as possible, for fear of the police.

There were boats of every description at the water's edge, waiting to take the raff to the steamer, which was in waiting some distance from the shore.

Tiny boats, only intended to carry four persons, were crammed with ten or twelve; and the waves tossed them about in such a fearful manner, that you expected to see them sink every moment. But none of the small craft, from the "Emily Rosa" and the "Frisky Kate"—neither scarcely larger than a good sized ottoman—to the "Pretty Julia," a large fishing-smack, met with any accident.

There was a deal to be gone through before

No. 51.

[CHARLEY WAG, THE NEW JACK SHEPPARD.

they could get on board the steamer; for every one had to pay two guineas and a half, and some of them were trying to climb up the sides, in order to avoid that expense.

"Show your ticket," shouted the man in the gangway. "You can't come up here without it, so I can tell yer; so yer needn't try it on."

"Pay the two pun' ten, then, you sir!"

"Here, take this gent's money in."

The men were all more or less in a rage during these disputes. Some shook their clenched fists in the other's face, and some threatened to give the other a good "ducking."

There is no telling what might have occurred, had not an order been given to call some of the gentlemen of the ring to establish peace.

These gents hurled some of them back again, at the risk of death by drowning; for when they have got a chance of exercising their strength, they do not stand upon trifles. But luckily no one came to much harm; and all those who would pay and could, came on board, and then the boat started.

Both the combatants were on board.

The man with the ropes to make the ring was also there. The fighters were in splendid condition, and amused themselves by walking to and fro upon the deck.

Tommy Cobb was as brown as an Indian, and his flesh was shining as brightly as though it had been polished with bees-wax and turpentine. His hair was cropped close to his head, and the scars of ancient bruises acquired in former "mills" were dimly visible upon his flat square face.

Billy Brains was also there—a prodigious brawny giant. He lay sprawling upon his back in the sun, with his cap laid across his eyes to protect them from the glare.

There were a great number of young swells on board besides our esteemed friend Mr. Wag. A great deal of eating and drinking was being done by them, too, in a quiet way.

Some awful compounds, facetiously termed salads, and some fowls which ate like so much india-rubber, were being sold at fabulous prices. Bottled ale was to be had at half-a-crown and three shillings, and liquids, called by the vendors gin and brandy, were sold at all kinds of rates, according to the purchaser's gullability.

To beguile the time, there was a good deal of gambling got up, and the sharps picked up the flats to any extent, in a way that was perfectly astonishing.

A row arose out of these little winnings and losings every now and then, and occasionally there was a little hustling and shoving; but nothing more serious occurred than the loss of a few sovereigns by those who were so green as to stake them.

At last they disembarked, and after a short tramp across country, with a stiffish leap or two across dykes, and an ugly tumble or two for those who could not jump, they arrived at the place which had been fixed upon for the fight.

This was a field, in the rear of an empty farm-house, and a spot where they were not at all likely to be interrupted.

As soon as the combatants had reached the ground, stakes were driven into the grass, and all those among the swells who had tickets took up their places close to the ropes, where they sat down, so as to enable those behind to have a good view over their heads.

The boxers stripped to the waist, and came into the ring dressed only in their corduroys, stockings, and ancle-boots.

It was wonderful to see how pleasant and smiling they were. You would almost have fancied that they could not have found it in their hearts to hurt one another.

They began by shaking hands, after they had tossed for corners; and after eyeing one another all over, they fell into attitudes, and commenced sparring.

There was a great deal of betting when the spectators got their first full view of the men. The betting was mostly in favour of the Slogger, though the backers of each seemed to be pretty well divided, and whenever either man did anything effective, the loudest cheers and yells of encouragement burst from his side.

On the other hand, hisses, and groans, and execrations greeted the success of the other man from his opponents; and thus, some encouraging, some hooting, the battle was fought amidst a din which was at times perfectly demoniacal.

But Tommy Cobb and Billy Brains did not seem to care for, or even to notice, their noisy admirers. They kept their eyes steadily fixed upon each other's faces, and steadily worked their fists up and down, waiting for a good opportunity to go in and win.

There was a wonderful amount of sparring and dodging, of feinting, and sliding, and dancing backwards and forwards, and round and round in half circles, until at length, all of a sudden, Tommy made a spring upwards, and planted his right upon the Slogger's "tater-trap," sending him flying half-a-dozen yards, as though he had been a feather instead of a six-foot giant of ever so many stone weight, until he dropped down in a sitting posture under the ropes, looking very much surprised and very foolish.

Tommy's friends raised a tremendous shout at this success.

The mob behind grew very excited, and would have broken down the ropes, had not the rope-keepers butted at them like bulls, and drove them backwards with kicks and cuffs.

"Curse you! can't you keep in your places? You dirty blackguards, get behind your betters, will you?"

Presently time was called, and the combatants came up again, smiling as before.

The Slogger tried to look as though he had quite forgotten that little affair at the end of the last round, but was nevertheless a trifle savage.

Tommy Cobb, being a leery little card, had come to a conclusion as regarded the way the battle must be fought.

What he had to take care of was not to catch one of the Slogger's thumpers full-face, or it most probably would make an end of him.

"I'll squelch the beggar, by God!" the Slogger cried, with a fearful oath, as they were rincing out his mouth in his corner; but after that he came up smiling, as I have said, like an innocent babe.

There was something very deadly, though, about Bill's eye; and if he could have caught the other one, it would, there is very little doubt, have been a case with him.

But he didn't.

Round and round the nimble Tommy danced, the big man following him slowly, and lunging at him with his long arms like the sails of a windmill.

Then again, as he had done before, Tommy went in with his right, and gave the Slogger a terrific smeller, which covered his face with blood.

"That had you," said the roughs.

The round is over again, and the combatants retire to their corners.

Time is called, and again they are at it.

Bill is determined to carry all before him, and rushes on his antagonist like a man-mountain; but Tom dodges him, and lands this time in the Slogger's eye.

The yelling of the roughs is terrible.

Those in favour of Tom bellow out:

"That's shut up your daylights, Billy!"

And:

"You'll want a dog and string before he's done with you!"

While the Slogger's backers roar in indignation:

"Why don't you stand up to him like a man, you cursed jumping-jack? Where are you running to now? It's a blessed wonder he don't hook it altogether!"

Tommy and Billy, however, fought as before, without taking any notice of these insults; and the Slogger, as before, got some tremendous wipes in the face from his active little foe.

He was rather too slow, somehow, and too heavy for Cobb, who danced about him like a fawn, and dropped in his telling blows quick as lightning, before the other man knew where he was, or before he could recover himself after the wild lunge in the air which he himself had made in one of his fruitless attempts to fell his antagonist.

Again and again did Tommy strike home, effectually closing the Slogger's eye, and cutting a fearful gash in his cheek, by the side of his nose.

Bill, furious to think that as yet he had done nothing—for the other had not a scar upon his face, and no bruise anywhere but upon his arm, with which he guarded off the Slogger's blows—ran at him, gnashing his teeth; but the other managed to slip out of his way, and miss the intended floorer which the other would have bestowed upon him.

It was not until the tenth round that Bill got a blow at young Cobb.

That time they had come up smiling, as usual, but both of them a little out of breath.

As usual, there had been a good bit of fencing until Cobb managed to touch his antagonist slightly upon the chin. Without waiting to guard himself, the Slogger struck out with all his might and main, and Tommy Cobb was felled with a blow which might have been heard a quarter of a mile off.

They carried Tom into the corner almost senseless, and sponged him, and squirted water in his face, and rinsed his mouth, and did all they could to revive him: but time was called twice before he could come up to the scratch.

Then he came tottering, and looking as though he were half asleep.

Again the Slogger struck him; but this time Tom dodged his head a little, and he went down lightly.

The next round Tom fell again.

The roughs were in a frenzy of rage and delight.

Those who had at first been backing the Slogger, but who since had become fearful for the fate of their stakes, now were in the highest glee.

Tommy's friends began to look very glum.

But Tommy was not beaten yet.

After his third downfall, he came into the ring apparently as fresh as ever.

One of his eyes was closed up, it is true, and one of his cheeks was a little puffy; but he was not nearly such an ugly object as the Slogger, who was cut and slashed out of all recognition.

At it they went again.

Some terrible blows were given and received upon either side, but Tom had decidedly the advantage.

The Slogger—a hideous mass of bruised and bleeding flesh, which was sickening to behold—came reeling out from his corner at the twentieth round, and receiving a stunning blow on his already smashed and shapeless nose, fell back and lay like a log.

Every one thought it was all over, for both his eyes were by this time bunged up.

But he came groping out again, and sparred at random, hitting desperate blows at the air in his blind rage and fury.

Again and again, with fearful violence and frightful punishment, Tommy's iron fists fell upon the victim's face, now beaten to a mass of jelly and pulp. Again and again, with a dull splash which was most revolting to listen to.

Once or twice he managed to get a blow at the other by chance, but none of them had much effect; therefore every time he came up, the other fetched him down again as flat as a flounder, and he was carried away again to his corner, bleeding and stunned.

The yells of the mob grew more and more ferocious, the insults heaped upon the beaten champion more and more insulting, galling, and irritating; but happily the poor wretch was unconscious of them.

He came staggering out again, and would have done for half-a-dozen more rounds, although now his eyes were completely closed, and he was as blind as a new-born kitten; but the more respectable of the spectators shouted indignantly to his backers to force him to give in.

Still, however, the frightful scene continued.

His backers still had some faint hope that he might yet plant one of those celebrated blows which had so often upon other occasions proved fatal, and that even now he might gain the victory.

But it was all in vain.

At last the *coup de grâce* was given by Tommy, who, with a terrific stroke full from his shoulder, shattered the other's jaw, and the miserable creature, groaning pitifully, was taken away for good.

Then the sponge was flung up, and Tommy Cobb was Champion of England.

Charley Wag, who had been an anxious spectator of the fight from the commencement, and who had lost a heavy sum of money upon it, was turning to leave the ground, when a man touched his arm.

" You're the party I want," said he.

" What is it ?" asked Charley, throwing himself directly upon the defensive, and determining to sell his liberty dearly if it should be in danger.

" Who are you ?" he asked.

" Oh, I'm not a police-officer," the other replied, with a sinister smile. " You needn't be afraid."

" I don't want your advice upon that point," retorted Charley, angrily ; " and I did not ask you what you were not. Who are you ?"

" It doesn't matter very much who I am, young man. I've something of importance to communicate to you, if you will give me the chance."

" Speak on, then."

'· I can't speak here, where I am being pushed to the right and to the left every moment."

" Let's get out of this. We'll talk as we go along."

The crowd was rapidly dispersing.

The unfortunate Slogger had been carried away, an awful object to contemplate.

Tommy Cobb, who, having washed his hands and face, looked very little the worse for the mill, was walking away rapidly towards the railway train, chatting and laughing with a group of admirers, who pressed round him, anxious to associate themselves with the hero of the day, and proud of the slightest recognition from so great a man. The ropes had been taken up.

The roughs were discussing the leading points of the fight, and were in some cases apparently rather desirous of rehearsing one or two of the effects.

Here and there on the grass some energetic gentlemen, anxious not to lose a chance of " besting " their fellow-creatures, were busily engaged in that famous old three-card trick ; and little groups surrounding them, evidently having an interest in the affair, were very loud and energetic whenever any stranger approached them. But, unfortunately, everybody seemed to be more bent on catching the train to town than upon " spotting the Jack," and trade was very slack indeed.

In vain did the gentleman working the oracle shuffle and reshuffle his three cards, in vain did he patter in the old familiar style.

" I bet anyone here present they can't tell me which is the face card. Here it is ! there it goes !—now, then, where's it got to ?"

" That's it," says the the inevitable country gentleman in the top-boots who is always to be found upon these occasions assisting at such a scene.

Then, in a great state of excitement,

" Don't move it ! See he don't move it. I know which it is. Who'll join two pounds to my three ?"

And then, if an unfortunate green one was weak enough to do so, thinking that he, too, knew which was the card, as he had seen the corner of it turned up, down went his two pounds, and it turned out—most wonderful to relate—that that was not the card after all, and the money was lost.

But somehow to-day the green ones were either not very numerous, or they had not got much in their pockets ; for very few came forward to make up the required amount, and trade was very slack.

Charley, without heeding these gamblers, or the operations of the light-fingered gentry around him, gave all his attention to the gentleman walking by his side.

He was a thin, wiry gentleman, with rather a sneaking appearance, and rather a sly and cunning expression about his eyes, which was not agreeable to look at.

" My name is Leech," said the gentleman ; " I am in the legal profession. My offices are in Clements Inn. You may have heard of me."

" I have had that pleasure," replied Charley. " You go in for the police-courts a good deal, don't you ?"

" Precisely, sir ; that is the business I have taken up."

" I have often heard of you. If a scamp with a shaky case can be got off at all, you are the party who can manage it for him.''

Mr. Leech bowed.

" I am extremely flattered, sir, by your good opinion. If any of your friends should require my professional assistance, I shall only be too proud to do my best for them."

" I will mention it, sir," said Mr. Wag. " They will esteem it a great honour."

" A recommendation from such a quarter will carry great weight," said Mr. Leech.

Here Mr. Wag bowed.

Then both gentlemen smiled, and each one looked as though he did not exactly believe what the other was saying to him.

At last Charley said,

" I suppose you've got something else to say besides this ?"

" I have something very important to say," replied the other ; " but, as I told you, this is not the sort of place to say it. When we get to London, if you will come to my chambers, you shall hear all about."

" Very well ; only if there should be some plant in this ?"

" What do you mean ?"

" If it is some dodge to give me up to the police."

" My dear sir, if you doubt me do not come."

" Is it any information by which I shall benefit ?"

" It is information by which you will acquire a considerable fortune, if you take my advice."

" Acquire a fortune ! Is it some crack you are going to recommend ?"

" Not exactly."

" Can you give me any hint that will put me on the scent before I come ?"

" It is concerning your parents."

" My parents !" cried Charley, turning hot and cold.

" You know that while you were with Miss Williams I supplied her with money for your support."

" You supplied her with money—"

" Yes."

" I never heard of it."

"You will hear all about it if you come and see me."

"When shall I come?"

"To-night,"

"At what time?"

"At ten."

"I will be there."

———

LXIX.—THE SICK WOMAN IN THE DARKENED ROOM.

WHEN Julia recollected that she had not executed her commission in the town from which she had just fled, and that in seeking her own safety she had entirely forgotten all about the letter which Captain Toddleboy had been so very anxious should be delivered, she determined, as the reader may recollect, to return and do so.

It may be said, and not without reason, that this was an act which, under the circumstances, was very foolish, and that it would have been better even to have broken her word than to have gone back to the fatal city, and faced the danger afresh.

But Julia was a courageous, lion-hearted girl, and nothing daunted her.

She had promised that the letter should be delivered, and it should be, let the fine of doing so be what it might.

How could she, she asked herself, show her face to Captain Toddleboy, and, after such a lengthened absence, tell him that she had not only lost the horse, but had not executed her commission after all?

No; she was determined that she would do it, and she set off bravely upon the road.

The poor beast of a horse was too weak to carry her, and she left it behind without any regret.

She did not suffer much inconvenience by so doing; for she had not proceeded very far upon the road before a countryman's cart overtook her.

The driver stopped, and asked politely whether she would like "a lift."

"Yes," she said, thanking him, and took her place by his side.

They arrived at the town in a much shorter time than it had taken her to come; for she had taken the longest road, it seemed, and had mistaken Mr. Josh's directions.

Seeing a blue blouse or smock-frock lying at the bottom of the cart, in company with a large slouching cap, Julia inquired whether the countryman was willing to part with them.

They were his Sunday best, he replied, but he was open to an offer.

Julia therefore made the offer, and, after a little haggling on both sides, the bargain was concluded, and Julia became the owner of the articles in question.

She thought it would be the wisest plan to disguise herself in this way before going through the streets, for fear she might meet any of the company of the previous evening.

She therefore put on the cap, pulling it over her forehead as much as possible.

She then put on the blouse, and tied a comforter round her face.

There was consequently very little to be seen of her.

"You seem to be wrapping up," the countryman said.

"Yes."

"Are you afraid of meeting somebody?"

"Yes."

"What have you been doing?"

"Nothing very serious, sir. A little love affair."

"Ah, you young rascal, I thought as much."

"Yes, and I am afraid of meeting the young lady's papa."

"To be sure. He's not favourable to the courting, eh?"

"Not very. He's promised to break my head as soon as he claps his eyes on me."

"Does he?—that's kind of him; and that's why you are trying to look as little like yourself as possible."

"Certainly. How have I succeeded?"

"I don't think I should know you again."

"That's as I wish it to be."

By this time they had reached the town.

The market seemed to be going on as on the previous day. Probably it was of daily occurrence. There seemed to be a large traffic in vegetables, fish, flesh, and fowl. The affairs of the market, however, were not conducted in a place so called, but up and down through the streets.

These ambulatory markets during the hours of household preparation for the day, gave to the town the aspect of a great tumultuous fair.

Sometimes there came a donkey pattering slowly along, heavily laden with panniers, piled sky high with all kinds of golden produce, and driven by women with high white caps shining in the sun, lemon-coloured shawls, blue petticoats, and wooden shoes.

Immediately after the donkey would come trailing up a great puce-coloured horse, toiling between shafts of such inordinate length, that, being in advance of the wheels by at least four feet, the draught is thrown to a considerable distance behind him, while the shafts continue to run back to an equal extent beyond the wheels.

In the centre of this rude contrivance was raised a kind of basketwork, bearing aloft a whole garden of flowers and fruits, or millinery work, or hardware, or the contents of the butcher's shop, or select extracts from the live and dead stock of the farmyard.

These carts were usually escorted by men in blue check frocks and dark trousers, furnished with enormously long and powerful whips, and blowing cows' horns with most discordant energy to announce their approach.

Within the car was usually seated a woman, perched upon a bundle, ready to serve the crowd, through which the lumbering machine moves at a snail's pace.

Then comes a young man (sometimes a girl) with a semicircular basket, built up flat to his back, and ascending to a considerable height above his head, displaying an attractive variety of articles: geraniums in pots, flowering out tier above tier, crisp brocoli, turnips, beetroot, salad cabbages. Nor is he satisfied with the ponderous weight he balances so dexterously on his back, but he must needs increase his toil by shrill, ear-splitting cries, describing his whole cargo in minute detail.

He was not singular in this respect. All the itinerant merchants cry their goods, and their name is legion. It is easy to imagine the prodigious uproar of the scene — the braying of donkies, dull recipients of kicks and cuffs—the rumbling of the long carts — the cracking of whips, like irregular volleys of small arms—the Babel of cries—the shricking of the cows' horns, and the din of voices bartering, cheapening, clamouring, throughout the length and breadth of the procession.

But, happily for the peace of the inhabitants, it lulls a little towards noon. By that time the townspeople have laid in their stores for dinner, and the occupation of the perambulatory venlors is over for the day

A few of them with a surplus stock on hand still straggle about, like drops of rain after a shower, hoping to catch some late customer, or to tempt others, already supplied, with a bargain 'rom the refuse.

But the riot is comparatively exhausted, and, with the exception of the clatter of the wooden shoes, the reverberations of voices down the narrow streets, or an incidental whip or horn dying away in the distance, the town is tolerably tranquil for the rest of the day.

It was at the busy time that Julia and her conductor arrived at the market-place.

Thanking him, and at the same time presenting him with a piece of silver in return for the ide, Julia left her friend, and set out alone in quest of the house.

It was very early in the day, and the street where Madame Deschapelles house stood was yet silent and deserted.

Julia approached the house, and after a moment's hesitation and a glance round, rang the ell.

For some time the summons was unanswered.

There was not much wind about, but what little there was faintly sighed and whistled amid the leafless branches of the old chestnuts. Perhaps the invisible spirits of the night air were still lingering round the house, and mourning for the departed darkness.

After waiting a short time she rang again.

Then she heard the sound of steps approaching.

The gates slowly opened, and the black man who stabbed Charley in the way we have seen looked out his head, and asked her gruffly what he wanted.

"I want to see Madame Deschapelles. Is he in?"

"Yes."

"I must see her directly."

"Were you here before?"

"Yes—yesterday."

"Come in."

So saying, the black led the way.

They crossed the threshold of the door, and the black closed the door after them, slamming it to with a force that awakened a dismal echo in the large and apparently empty house.

Julia could not refrain from feeling a faint uneasiness at the loneliness of the place, and the very questionable companionship in which she found herself; but she did her best not to allow it to be seen.

When they had entered, the black bolted and barred the door behind them, and then took up a lamp which stood upon a bracket fixed in the wall.

Julia, while he did so, stood a few paces from him, and could not refrain from listening intently to the strange stillness of the house.

As she did so, and as she strove in vain to pierce the darkness which enveloped all the distant objects beyond the immediate sphere of the faint lamp the black was holding, she fancied that she heard a noise.

It was a very curious one—a flapping, sliding noise.

A moment afterwards, dash against the lamp came something black and large.

"Curse you!" the negro growled. "Isn't there room enough for us all, stupid?"

Julia stood in amazement, not unmixed with terror.

It was a large bat whirling to and fro in an uncertain flight in the old hall, and ever and anon dashing its leathery wings against some object with a hollow sound.

The negro, with numerous curses, relit the lamp, which had been extinguished, and led the way.

Julia followed, watching for the approach of the bat with some anxiety, and involuntarily shrinking back when, appearing suddenly from strange angles, it whirled round and round her head.

They mounted an old wide staircase, with broad short steps, and a rich old oaken balustrade.

It took a wide sweep to the floor above, terminating in a kind of corridor, from which opened many rooms.

The door of one of these rooms he opened with a key which he took from his pocket.

It was with some difficulty that he turned the key; but at last he succeeded, and with a harsh grating noise the lock yielded.

The door creaked open an inch or two, and they entered a room which was in a state of dim obscurity.

"Wait here a minute or two, young man," the black said, and left the room.

Julia sat there for a long while in perfect silence.

At last the negro, poking his head into the room,

"She will see you directly," he said.

"Thank you."

At the end of another quarter of an hour she fancied that she heard a faint coughing in the distance.

Then an elderly woman made her appearance at the door, and said, in so low a tone that Julia could scarcely hear what she was saying,

"Will you come this way?"

Julia rose and followed her.

They traversed a broad corridor, and entered a room, the door of which was ajar.

The apartment was enveloped in dim obscurity. Two candles alight upon the mantelpiece shed a faint light around.

On one side of the apartment stood a huge four-post bedstead, upon the four corners of which were plumes of black funereal feathers, that in the draft from the door nodded to and fro in a ghostly fashion, which to Julia's excited fancy suggested the horrible idea that a corpse inside was shaking them.

Julia looked round for the occupant of this apartment.

There were several lumbering pieces of furniture, of dark wood and ancient fashion.

There was a table crowded with physic bottles, and there was a huge wardrobe.

At last she saw a female figure, very much muffled up, and with a face that was ghostly in its whiteness.

A face that was still of a striking beauty, although the hair upon the smooth brows was broadly streaked with grey.

A faint voice as Julia entered said:

" Come hither."

Julia approached.

" You have been here to see me before."

" Yes, madam."

" I was out."

Julia looked at her very hard. She did not seem much like a person capable of travelling.

The lady noticed it.

" I was taken ill when I returned. I have been in search of my son. He left me the other day. I traced him to Calais. I found that he had taken a passage for England. He was a bad, disobedient child. I forbade him to go; and the ship has been wrecked, and he—he—oh God forgive me! he is dead;"

So speaking, the lady fell forward with her head upon the table, and burst into an agony of grief.

The woman who had summoned Julia ran forward, and, with Julia's assistance, raised the invalid, who seemed in a fainting state, and laid her back in the chair.

" God forgive me! God forgive me. God has punished me for my crime. I would have slain one—He has taken the other."

Julia looked in amazement at the speaker, but said nothing.

The woman assisting her appeared not to understand what the lady said.

" She's a little delirious; she's had a dreadful shock," she whispered.

" What is it?" asked Julia.

" She's lost her son. Hush! don't talk so loud. He would go to sea, and has got drowned. Dreadful, isn't it? Don't speak to her about it. She's coming to again."

The lady, slowly recovering, languidly opened her eyes, and looked round her.

" Give me the letter," she said to Julia.

Then, turning to the servant,

" Leave us, Martha."

The servant went away with rather a sulky air, and Julia was left with the invalid.

The latter took the letter, and breaking the seal, scanned the contents with an anxious expression.

Gradually, as she proceeded, the expression changed into one of intense anxiety and horror.

" My husband!" she cried suddenly; " my poor husband! He is murdered—he is murdered! My child is drowned—I am alone. I am the last. I shall be pursued, and tracked, and hunted down. He is upon my track now—even now. Our race is doomed!"

Julia endeavoured to calm her.

But the sick woman shook her off.

" Keep back—keep back!" she screamed.

" You have come from him—you are one of his tools! There is blood upon your hands!"

Julia, with a shudder that she could not repress, glanced at her own fingers. There might have been blood upon them—she did not know.

There was nothing, however; it was but the excited fancy of the invalid.

" Calm yourself, madam, calm yourself," said Julia, kneeling by her side, and using every effort to induce the other to be quiet.

But in vain.

" Oh, my child, my child!" she kept repeating; " my poor child, why did you disobey your poor mother? There is no one in the world left to love me!"

Then she rolled her head from side to side, groaning, until she seemed as though she had lulled herself herself to sleep.

Julia was uncertain what she should do.

The scene was so strange a one.

She was so excited by what she had seen and heard.

She was so anxious to be gone.

Upon the table by the lady's head lay the letter which she had brought, open.

Julia involuntarily cast her eyes upon it.

A few words at the bottom of the page caught her eye, and for a moment transfixed her with astonishment.

Then with horror.

They were these:

" *Your husband, his Grace the Duke of Heatherland, was murdered.*"

Julia started back.

Was this, then, the duchess?

The wife of the man of whom she had been the mistress.

A thousand conflicting emotions agitated her, and for some time she was unable to do or say anything.

Then suddenly a thought entered her brain.

This was the mother of the boy whom Charley had rescued from a watery grave.

Should she keep the mother in ignorance of the child's rescue?

No, not another moment.

Her kind heart already rebuked her for her momentary neglect.

She fell upon her knees by the invalid's side, and gently arousing her, broke the joyful news cautiously and delicately, like only a loving woman would have done it.

" Oh, bless you, bless you!" the lady said, as her head fell upon the other's shoulder, and the tears rolled fast down her pale cheeks.

Then, after she had thus been lying for a moment or two, she raised her head, and placing one hand upon each of Julia's shoulders, looked fixedly into her face.

" You are a woman," she said.

The other made no reply, but her blush answered the question.

* * * * *

Hour after hour passed, and still Julia remained by the duchess's side.

She had changed her clothes for garments belonging to her own sex.

She had thrown back the shutters, and let some sun and air enter the hitherto gloomy apartment.

Hour after hour passed away, and the invalid lay there, tossing her head uneasily upon her hot pillow, and raving in a wild and startling manner of her past life.

Julia sat by her side, listening in amazement and in horror.

It was a dreadful story which the sick woman unconsciously revealed as she lay there in her wild delirious ravings.

A strange and terrible secret was revealed.

But this is not the place that I must tell it.

Charley Wag has just gone to meet Leech, who is to tell him the same story.

It is there that we must hear it.

Not until then.

_____

LXX.—The Attack.

BUT now we must return to Faversham and Rattan, and to the Hopleys, whom we left in the old country house belonging to the latter, at the moment when a crowd had assembled round the house.

For nearly three weeks had Faversham been an inmate of the establishment.

For nearly three weeks he had been confined to his bed, day by day lingering on, although burning with impatience to be about and stirring.

At the time when the alarm took place which I have before described, he was slowly recovering, though rarely able to leave his room.

The cause of the alarm was at first a mystery to the Hopley's, though Hopley strongly suspected that some violence was intended towards himself.

When first he was introduced, the reader, it may be, recollects that he kept a very curious kind of seminary for young gentlemen—an establishment where young men were " done for" upon reasonable terms, and where they were " finished" in more senses than one.

One of these unfortunates had been " done for" and " finished" to such an extent, that all the little breath was knocked out his miserable little body.

It had been knocked out, in fact, by Mr. Hopley's walking-stick.

The little accident had got wind.

There had been an inquest, and a good deal of unpleasantness of one sort and another.

Mr. Hopley, upon making his appearance out of doors, had been a good deal hooted.

One day, when he had ventured as far as the miner's village before alluded to, there had been a good deal of ill-feeling exhibited by the mob.

There had been cries raised of,

" Who beat the boy to death?"

After that some one had contributed a brick-bat, and sent Hopley's hat a-flying.

After that, some one else had presented him with a piece of plate—that is to say, he had taken a cockshy at him with a piece of cracked willow-pattern.

Mr. Hopley not unnaturally took these as hints that he might expect something a little worse presently; and so, without waiting for anything further, he took to his heels, and ran as though a mad bull were after him.

It was a wonder that he escaped the horse-pond. However, he did somehow, and got clear away, with only a little spattering of mud upon his back, and a bruise or two about his head.

Since then he had been rather shy of showing himself out of doors.

When anything had been wanted, Mrs. Hopley had gone out to fetch it; and even she had been received by the rustic population with hisses and hootings of anything but an assuring character.

The servant having deserted them, and their two guests—Faversham and Rattan—not being over desirous of showing their heads out of doors, the Hopley's had been compelled to go out themselves, and do such marketing as they required.

There were even rumours that the magistrates were going to have the body disinterred, and enter into a regular investigation of the circumstances attending his death; and this evening, when Lucinda had gone down the village, she was alarmed by seeing groups of men gathered together, and angrily discussing some topic in which the name of Hopley frequently occurred.

She had also noticed an unusual excitement among the rustic constabulary, and in other respects certain indications which led her to suppose that something serious was about to take place.

No sooner was she convinced of this fact, than she fled back to the house, as we have seen, and the approach of the mob immediately afterwards proved that she had not been very far out in her calculations.

But the motive which prompted the miners to surround the house was not exactly that which she had supposed.

The fact was, that the policeman whose appropriation of Faversham's money had been interrupted in the way which the reader already knows, returned to the spot after Rattan and Faversham had departed, and groped among the grass for such stray corns as might have escaped Rattan's notice.

He, however, sad to relate, found only three, after a most patient investigation.

But he found something else.

It was a letter directed to Faversham.

It contained nothing of importance.

It was a letter written by some patient, and directed to him at his house in Bayswater. A mere trifle, to which no value could be attached, as the policeman thought when he thrust it into his pocket.

But next day he changed his opinion.

Next day he saw Faversham's name and description in the Hue and Cry.

Next day he made up his mind to see what had become of the wounded man and his pugilistic companion.

Surely in the state that Faversham was he could not have gone very far.

Where had he crept to?

Was he the Faversham described in the Hue and Cry?

Most certainly — there could be very little doubt about it.

The policeman determined to find him out if he were in the neighbourhood.

He had had orders to keep his eye upon the Hopleys' establishment for other reasons, and keeping his eye one evening fixed upon a win-

dow at the back of the house, he was considerably astonished to see the head of Mr. Jack Rattan.

"By jingo!" said the constable to himself. "That's where you are, is it?"

When he had made the discovery, he resolved to let as little grass grow under his feet as possible.

But at the same time he was also anxious to keep the little business snug.

He was an ambitious young man, and it occurred to him that if he were to manage the capture by himself his fortune would be made.

He would be a marked man in the force.

He would be a couple of hundred pounds the better for it; for that was the price fixed upon Faversham's head.

No. 52.

Then, when he came to reflect upon the matter, he did not exactly see how he could manage it all by himself.

He had desperate customers to deal with.

He knew that very well; for his face bore proof of it, which stuck by him with provoking tenacity.

He must have assistance, and who should he choose?

Just when he had come to this difficulty in his projects, two strangers turned up and helped him.

One of these was—for why should I make a mystery out of it, and keep the reader for ever so many pages in suspense?—James Murdoch, the resuscitated murderer; the other was Horford, the man who had joined him in endea-

[CHARLEY WAG, THE NEW JACK SHEPPARD.

ouring to hunt down Ralph Faversham upon he night of the assassination of the duke.

These two men, with untiring patience and sleepless energy, had succeeded in tracking Faversham to Hopley's house; and coming across the policeman in the course of their inquiries, they all joined together in an attempt to take him.

They would not, however, agree to take the policeman's advice about the way in which it should be done.

He would have attempted it with their aid alone; but they called in the aid of at least fifty miners, who, excited by promises of a handsome reward, and the stories of Faversham's hellish crimes and cruelties, swore that they would go through fire and water to catch him.

Upon the night that we have already described the plan was laid and put into immediate execution.

Faversham's guilty conscience told him that it was he whom they wanted, and he resolved to sell his liberty only with his life.

"We will keep them out," he said. "If you only do as I direct, we can easily keep them at bay for hours. Besides, the smell of powder will most likely send them all about their business, as fast as their legs can carry them."

It was agreed, as the first and most important measure, that they should well blockade the bottom of the house, and then retire to the first floor, and fire down on the mob, if necessary, from the windows.

The operations were immediately commenced, and in less time than it would take to describe them, all the necessary preparations were made.

They then retired to the first floor, and loaded their guns.

Mrs. Hopley, who had fainted, was assisted up-stairs by her daughter, who afterwards assisted the besieged party in any way which they could suggest; for though her heart revolted at having to help such wretches as Faversham and Rattan, and even such a man as her father, still there perhaps remained, in spite of brutal ill-treatment and outrage, a filial love which nothing had been able entirely to crush.

The tenderhearted reader may thus account for Miss Lucinda's conduct if he so chooses, though for my part, knowing the young lady better, and recollecting how she behaved when she deserted her parents' house with Master Charley Wag, I am inclined to think that she must have decided upon this occasion to remain with her parents and assist them only because she did not see how she could get away.

Meanwhile, from the dark ferocious mass of heads now ranged in front of the house came forward a single person, who appeared to act as their leader.

It was Murdoch.

Calling loudly to Hopley by name, he summoned him to give up to them the two men they were harbouring within.

Hopley would have faced them, and bade them do their worst, but Faversham prevented him.

"I'll talk to them," said he.

Accordingly he flung up the sash, and standing before the mob, unshrinkingly declared himself to be the person in search of whom they had come.

"There are two hundred pounds on my head, if I am taken alive," said he. "But don't think that any of you will reap a pennyworth of benefit by me, for, by God! I'll blow my brains out before you can take me."

The crowd stood a moment, struck dumb by his energetic manner and desperate words.

"Besides," he continued, "why should you be led by the nose by the police? If they want to take me, let them do so if they can. Why should you risk your lives to help them? You will gain nothing by it. Why, men, it is sheer madness!"

The miners listened to him, and muttered among themselves.

"There's something in that."

"He says right."

"He talks fair enough."

"He's a plucky one."

"Let's leave him to it. We ought to give the chap a squeak for his life. It ain't as though he were a sneaking lubber. Look at him; he's got the spirit of twenty in him at least."

In fact the quietness, firmness, and coolness of Faversham's manner was striking.

It produced an obvious effect.

A waverig and hesitation was observable among the mass of heads.

Even Murdoch himself retired to consult with the police.

There is every reason to believe that his address would have been successful, had not a figure, who had hitherto kept entirely in the background, now crept up, and mixed with the outlying stragglers, who were unable to hear what was said.

"Hoot him," said this figure to a lad. "Why don't you hoot him—a murdering thief?"

"Ya—ah!" bawled the boy directly.

"Ya—ah!" joined his neighbours.

And the clamour once commenced, in a few moments the contagion seized the whole body, and an infernal din and roar arose.

It drowned all that Faversham had to say.

He saw that his attempts to get the miners on his side were now useless.

He made signs, but in vain.

In spite of the noise, however, he continued to stand firm and unmoved, waiting for an opportunity of obtaining another hearing.

Even a mob can't hoot for ever.

Though the favourable impression was quite extinguished for the time by the physical excitement which had been raised against him, he hoped once more to have gained an audience.

But the figure in the background, who seemed impatient of delay, once more crept into the crowd.

"Why don't you have a shy at him?" he said to the same boy. "Here's a bit of brickbat."

Next moment Faversham heard the pane of glass over his head shiver into atoms.

It was like the single big drop which brings down the whole torrent of the thunderstorm.

No sooner was the sound heard, than there arose from the dense mass of heads a yell twice as fearful as before.

"Down with him—down with him!" was the cry.

A volley of stones followed, which shattered every window in the front of the house.

"Down with him!"

"Tear his heart out!"

Faversham saw that all was now over.

He had been struck on the head with a flint, and his face was bleeding.

"Let us fire on the beggars," said Rattan.

"No, no—not yet," replied the doctor.

"You're growing particular in your old age," said the other, with a sneer.

Faversham answered with a scornful laugh.

"If a sea of blood filled the place where they stand, I would wash my hands in it and smile," he cried. "What are their lives to me? I'd cut them down like grass, and I will if there is any occasion. It is our own safety I am careful about."

"Oh, all right," said Rattan. "I misunderstood you."

Faversham, during a momentary lull, again addressed the mob.

"I warn you, now," he said, "that we are all well armed—thoroughly prepared to shoot the first man who proposes to enter the house; and I call Heaven to witness, that if you still persist in this outrage, your blood is on your own heads."

But before he could finish the sentence, a pistol was fired from the crowd.

A ball whizzed past Faversham, and grazed his ear.

"Now then," said he to Rattan, "let's get to our posts."

He drew his head within the window, closed down the sash, and helped to put up some mattresses against it, so as to leave a space from which, with his own pistols, he could command the entrance.

It was the only window in the house where this was possible.

"Now go to the side walls," he said. "For God's sake don't fire promiscuously, or you will waste your shot. Take a good aim, and kill whenever you hit."

Meanwhile, the firing of the pistol was the signal for the first attack.

Twelve huge savage miners, each wielding an enormous crowbar, with which they break open their furnaces, detached themselves from the front of the mob, and advanced to the door.

Two blows were levelled on it, but failed to demolish it.

But as the third man was poising his bar, and levelling it against the lock, three tongues of flame leaped out of the side walls, amidst a volume of smoke and a vibrating report.

The smoke cleared away.

Two of the ringleaders were lying dead upon the ground.

One other had been wounded.

Amidst a yell, partly of terror and surprise, and partly of fury, the whole mass of assailants had recoiled, and left the space in front of the house quite clear.

LXXI.—THE FIGHT CONTINUES—THE FIRE— THE FRIGHTFUL DEATH.

"I WILL speak to them again," said Faversham, and he approached the window.

Perhaps he thought that the exhibition of the decisive measures the besieged party intended to adopt would induce the majority of the miners to side with them; for he knew very well that the police were not the most popular parties in the world with this rough class.

He threw up the window, and endeavoured to make himself heard.

But the moment he appeared, the uproar became terrific.

Several shots were fired at him, amidst a volley of stones.

Rattan dragged him back into the room.

"Are you mad?" cried he, indignantly. "Do you want to have your brains knocked out? Do you suppose that you can quiet them now, after what you have done?"

Faversham had no time, however, to say more if he had desired to do so.

The assailants had consulted together, and, gathering themselves in a dense column, they rushed with a hideous cry up to the front of the house.

Once more the fire from the flanking walls opened upon them, and every shot told.

Faversham himself, from his post at the window, fixed upon the most conspicuous of the assailants, and his aim very rarely missed its object.

From the attics the old woman—Mrs. Hopley—hurled down bricks and stones, which, with Lucinda's help, she managed to tear from the parapet in front of the window, upon a mass of heads, on which every missile did execution.

Indeed the women, now kindled with excitement, joined vigorously in the defence, and arming themselves with kettles of boiling water, and pails of scalding liquid from a brewhouse at the back of the house, poured them upon the upturned faces of the besiegers, until they shrieked and writhed in their agony.

Body after body fell, and was trampled down by the advancing crowd, who, untouched as yet by the fire of the musketry, were not aware of the danger of approaching until they were close to the house, and there, excluded from retreat, aimed their ineffectual blows at the doors and windows, and then sank and were trodden down in a mass of carnage.

Pressed and jammed together, they were unable to use their arms or receive orders.

Everything was confusion and uproar: howlings of the wounded and dying—shriekings and horrible imprecations, as the torrents of boiling stuff were poured suddenly upon their heads—blasphemous outcries, which none but demons would have uttered; and, rising above all, threats of the most horrible vengeance against Faversham and his companions.

At last their efforts succeeded. The panels of the door were smashed to atoms; the windows, the shutters, framework—all were demolished.

A breach, it seemed, was made into the house, but, to the disappointment of the attackers, both the passage and rooms below had been so filled with mattresses, drawers, chests, and light chairs, piled up to the ceiling, over which it was impossible to climb, that they were as far removed from their object as at first.

Murdoch, furious when he found himself thus baffled, at last succeeded in forcing his men back from an unavailing attempt, in which life after life was sacrificed without their being able to touch the defenders of the little fortress.

Once more the mass recoiled—the space before the house was cleared; and as Faversham looked down upon it again, now piled with corpses, and heaps of mutilated and wounded bodies groaning with pain, a fiendish smile flitted across his demoniacal face.

There was a pause—a silence as awful as the dead—a breathless calm, like that which occurs between the bursts of a hurricane.

Rattan was out of breath with his recent exertions; Hopley was in a similar condition. They were both wiping their streaming faces with their pocket-handkerchiefs.

"Is it over?" asked Hopley.

"It ought to be," replied Rattan. "We've given them pepper enough in all conscience surely."

But Faversham thought differently.

"Over!" said he, with a scornful laugh; "it has only just begun."

Just then they heard, and they caught distinctly by intently listening, the sound of a large body of men approaching at a brisk run.

Faversham looked out again from his loophole of observation. The same dark figure of Horford, which had so frequently before stolen into the outskirts of the crowd, and directed their movements unperceived, when he saw the determined resistance of the little garrison, had hastened to a hut which stood on the top of an eminence over the town. From this immediately a rocket shot up, which was a signal for another large body of miners and police to come up from the other village; and the wild hurrahs of the assailants now hailed the arrival of a strong reinforcement from that quarter. Only a few minutes of suspense were given, but even these moments were as hours. Faversham gave fresh directions; they held a brief council of war, and then descended to the lower part of the house.

As they hurried down the stairs, the whole mass of assailants rushed with horrible yells towards the house

Instead of attempting the door as before, they divided themselves into two parties, and, provided with such means as they had been able to procure, they climbed upon one another's shoulders, and proceeded to scale both the walls at once.

Wave followed on wave; the openings made in the mass by the fire from the loopholes were filled up as if none had fallen. Heads, shoulders, whole bodies, appeared on the summit of the wall along the whole line, some hanging lifeless across it, as they fell under the shots of the besieged.

Others thrust forward by the advancing mass, and thrown headlong into the court. Others dropping down in the intervals, between the line of defenders.

The struggle was fearful.

But Faversham saw that it was hopeless; and while it was yet possible to give the signal for retreat, they made a rush for the back-door.

That is to say, Rattan and Faversham. One man was missing. It was Hopley.

"He's in the loft, there, across the yard," said Faversham, "and will be cut off."

And plunging across the yard, he had all but brought him to the steps of the door, when a fresh body of men burst through the garden-gate.

They fell on him with fury.

"Save me!" cried the miserable man; "save me!"

One of the foremost, however, seized and tore him from Faversham's grasp.

Faversham threw himself upon the body, and with a sabre swept a circle around him, and placing the unhappy man behind him, he endeavoured to cover his retreat into the house.

But it was in vain.

The walls were scaled, the yard filled with the mob, and, after a tremendous effort, Faversham found himself driven up to the steps, and was dragged by Rattan inside the door.

"Open the door!" he cried, excited, as Rattan pushed him roughly back. "We can save him if we try. They'll tear the poor devil to pieces!"

"Devil a doubt of it," said Rattan, and slammed-to the door.

There was no hope for Hopley now. Midst the roar and outcry they heard one fearful scream.

From a window above the distracted wife of the miserable wretch saw a figure hurled down to the ground by a group of fiend-like faces, who fell on it like cannibals on their prey.

And this was the last known of the unhappy man. When the morning dawned, and the field of slaughter was examined, a limb was found with a fragment of dress on it which was supposed to be his, but all the rest was undistinguishable.

The old woman, sick with horror, fell swooning back upon the floor.

"We're all right, I think, for another half-dozen hours, if we wanted to hold out," said Rattan. "But if we can only get a chance, and see the coast clear, we'll get out of window at the back, and slope across country."

There was near to, but not actually adjoining, the north gable end of Hopley's house, a long low range of building, which had been attached by degrees to the main fabric, and served the purpose of scullery, brewhouse, washhouse, and other useful offices. Seemingly, there was an open passage between it and the house, and externally it presented no means of access to the interior. It had therefore not been marked as a point of attack; and as no window opened from the gables, it lay out of sight of the besieged.

Some one, however, in the crowd now led the way to it, and at his directions, the rest began to remove a pile of old packing-boxes and hampers which were lying loosely in one corner.

"Underneath," he said, "you will find a trap-door. That door is the outer entrance to the cellars, which lie under these low buildings. From the cellars a flight of stone steps leads to the kitchens. And I will venture to say that no one has thought of blocking up that passage; it is hardly ever used."

The man who gave the information had been employed upon some occasion carting coals into Hopley's house, and it was through this opening he spoke of that they had been carried.

And while this fresh attempt was being made

to break in upon them, Rattan and Faversham were consulting together. Rattan had heard Hopley speak of some powder which he had kept down in the cellar. They had by this time almost exhausted the supply above stairs, and they determined to avail themselves of the temporary lull in the fight to go and fetch some more from below.

They went down-stairs together, and just as they reached the door, which opened from the kitchen at the top of the stone steps, they heard voices, a rush, and a shout on the other side, within the cellar; and before they could recover themselves, a crash followed, the panels of the door fell in, and they found themselves confronting ten of the most savage of the gang, armed with pickaxes, crowbars, hatchets, and pikes, and their clothes and faces smeared with filth and blood.

Murdoch was at their head.

Each party recoiled for a moment at the unlooked-for encounter.

But it was only for an instant.

The next a furious conflict commenced.

The stairs were narrow, steep, and without any protection on the sides; and the communication between them and the vaults beyond was through a dark, narrow archway, which admitted only two persons abreast.

But for this all must have been over at once. It gave Faversham and Rattan an opportunity to stop their progress.

Two of the assailants were hurled off the steps by a tremendous blow from the butt end of Rattan's gun. Murdoch had aimed a thrust at Faversham, but it was parried by a side blow from the same weapon, and a deadly shot from Faversham's gun drove back the rest for a moment.

There was a moment's respite.

"Let us block up this doorway," cried Rattan. "Here are tubs and boxes. Roll that hogshead to the entrance, and we are still safe."

But before their purpose could be effected, the whole range of cellars behind was filled with armed men.

They rushed forward like demons, some of them bearing torches, which threw a lurid glare on the horrible faces of the throng; others staving some casks which they found there full of beer, and gorging themselves with their contents—all thrusting and forcing on each other in an irresistible torrent.

The foremost, who had retired within the narrow archway, were driven on by the rear, whether they would or not.

There of them were struck down. Four more fell under the fire of the besieged party, who had stationed themselves on the stone steps.

But the crush carried everything before it. Faversham was driven back, and thrown down just on the other side of the archway. Rattan was grasped and hurled from the steps. But suddenly, amidst the din and clamour of the conflict, all at once, without a moment's warning, the whole body, besieged and besiegers, were wrapt in a whirlwind of fire. There was a deep, rushing, quivering shock, like an earthquake. A burst as of thunder, a crash, gusts and volumes of smoke, chimneys tottering, roofs splitting, walls opening and closing again

in huge rents from top to bottom, the ground rocking under their feet.

Then came a pause.

Then over their heads the showering down of beams and stones, and fragments of roofs, and mangled limbs.

Then all was silent.

When Faversham opened his eyes, he looked up, and saw the grey sky just paling with the approach of dawn, and visible through a yawning chasm, which had been broken in the roof of the vault.

A large stone was hanging over his head, and seemed ready to fall and crush him. And stunned and bewildered as he was, he endeavoured to move himself; but a heavy weigh was lying across him.

It was a body apparently lifeless, his face to the ground, and by his rough pea-jacket, it was evidently one of the assailants. Faversham drew himself from beneath him, and raised himself to look round.

The vault was shattered, black volumes of smoke were curling round and round within it, and issuing from the now shapeless aperture which had formed the narrow entrance to the cellar.

The stone steps were covered with a pile of mangled, scorched, and blackened bodies, among which he recognised Rattan stretched upon the ground, but still breathing, and half burned, under a mass of rubbish.

Faversham made an effort to move from the spot. Having been thrown behind the wall through which the archway opened, he had been secured from the blast and the crash of the explosion.

He now remembered the barrel of powder, and was satisfied that the assailants, in their fury, having begun to stave the casks, had fallen on this one; and the torches which had glared within the cellar was sufficient to explain the rest.

Now was the time for escape, he thought; but at that moment he heard the sound of voices again approaching.

Scrambling through a hole in the wall, and rushing up-stairs, he looked from an upper window.

Then he saw a glare of light rising up over the roofs of the adjoining houses. On came the mob—once more the assailants rushed into the square.

Leaping, dancing, shrieking, howling, more of them bearing in their hands fragments of burning wood than weapons, and resembling little but a herd of wild savages in some mad and bloody revel—tossing their torches into the air, and hurling imprecations upon all who should resist them, mixed with obscene jests and blasphemous curses, they rushed upon the house.

He ran up the stairs, and shouted to the women; but there was no reply. Then he shouted to Rattan.

"Are you killed?" he asked.

By way of answer, Rattan came crawling up through the aperture in the wall.

"What are they going to do to us now?" the ruffian asked. "Are we going to be roasted?"

"I suppose so, if we cannot escape."

"There is no chance of that. Let us block up the aperture, and keep the flames out if can."

Without wasting any more time in useless talk, they set about blocking up the hole with stones and bricks, and fragments, and rubbish.

They had not long completed their task, when the mob had surrounded the house, with loud shrieks, and yells, and hootings.

"Help me to tear down this part of the staircase," said Rattan. "There is a cistern below. We may be able to get at the water-pipe, if we want it."

They renewed their exertions to keep the aperture of the staircase well blocked-up with wet carpets. Apparently their efforts were successful. The flames roared beneath their feet, vast whirlwinds of smoke gushed out of the lower windows, and swept round them, at times almost suffocating them; but their position was still tenable.

But before long they heard a loud crash below. A portion of the outer wall was giving way. It had been shaken by the explosion, and now was falling. There was a lull in the fury of the flames, and then they burst forth with redoubled violence.

The smoke began to find its way through the crevices of the planks.

The heat became intolerable. Huge flakes of fire swept up into the air, and fell again upon the roof, threatening to kindle that.

The four walls seemed to tremble and rock to and fro like a ship at sea.

It was evident that all was over—that before long the house would fall.

The men spoke not a word to each other. There was no escape for them, as it seemed.

Rattan approached the window and looked out. Beneath him lay the cistern. He would drop into that.

But, no; as he looked down, his eyes lighted upon a sight enough to appal the stoutest heart, for the water had run away, and the bottom of the cistern was boiling lead.

Even that sight, however, did not daunt this courageous ruffian.

He would make a spring.

From the window-ledge he would be able to clear it.

If he did, he might escape with life. It was an even toss-up. He would try it.

He leaped upon the window like a maniac, with a wild beast's roar. But his foot slipped.

He strove to recover himself in vain.

He tottered—he staggered—he clung to the window-ledge.

Then he fell into the cistern.

There was a yell, such as few present had ever heard.

A cry of such unutterable horror, that for years afterwards, some who heard it, would wake up in the middle of the night, as they fancied they heard it in their dreams; and the cold sweat would stand in drops upon their foreheads.

The miserable wretch had fallen upon his hands and knees in the pool of molten lead. He shrieked to the mob to save him. "Take me out—take me out! It is hell—it is hell!"

Just then, with a deafening crash, the house toppled over, and came down in ruins to the earth, burying the cistern; and the scalding, howling, agonized creature in the fall.

LXXII.—CHARLEY GOES TO HEAR THE SECRET.

IT was a wild, tempestuous night.

The rain descended in torrents, or, as the vulgar and unpoetic say, came down in bucket's full.

Nobody was about the streets who could keep out of them.

The birds of night put up for shelter in the roomiest porticos, and peeped out in a bird-like fashion to see if luck was coming their way.

In the quiet suburbs of London, such as Clapham, Holloway, and North Brixton, there was scarcely a soul to be seen.

Every now and then, mayhap, you might by chance encounter some rosy maiden, scudding, beer-jug in hand, before the biting blast, her striped petticoats fluttering and flapping like the loose sails of a boat, and her shapely calves, stocking encased, gleaming whitely in the gas-light.

She had been sent out for the supper-beer, and was so blown, and tousled, and tumbled by the rude romping of the boisterous elements, that it were not safe for any luckless youth, amorously disposed, to try and stay her course.

There was much more likely than not a tingling slap on the head in store for such as ventured on undue familiarity.

For she was savage at being sent out "trapesing in the wet upon so bad a night; and not at all inclined to put up with no impudence whatever."

The brightly lighted blinds at the houses of the wealthy told a story of domestic happiness and comfort highly exasperating to the shuffling outcast, doomed to foot-it long miles in the mud and rain, and to them seemed to make the outer coldness more cold and harder to bear.

In the low and poor neighbourhoods, the public-houses were crammed chock full, and the reeking, steaming mass of gin-drinkers crowded the bars of the palaces, and exhaled rank pestiferous vapours, like flocks of sheep jammed together and smoking in the pens of a cattle-market.

These wet nights the public-houses in the Whitechapel wilds did a rare stroke of business.

One person was there in London, however, who would have faced any weather, rather than not have kept his appointment.

And this was Charley Wag.

Ever since the lawyer, Leech, had told him that he had something of importance to communicate, bearing reference to the secret of his birth and parentage, the lad had been burning with an inordinate impatience and anxiety to learn the particulars.

Curious as it may seem, until the present time, the reckless never-do-well had never troubled his mind with any conjectures upon the subject, except, perhaps, in a careless, off-hand, unconcerned sort of fashion, when Julia had alluded to it.

In most novels and romances the heroes are depicted as burning with anxiety to find out who they are. Most indefatigable are they in their endeavours. Indeed, if I recollect rightly, I have come across several instances of the hero making quite a trade of it.

Charley Wag, however, had of late had other things to think of. He was not a very sentimental young gentleman; and yet, mind you, he was not devoid of feeling.

He said to himself, when the subject chanced to occupy his thoughts for a few minutes,

"There's very little doubt but that I was meant for a gentleman, if I had my rights. There's a superior cut about me which there is no mistaking. If I'd only had the luck, and the bringings up, I should have come out A 1 there isn't a doubt. Only I haven't. I've been a changeling, most likely—been swopped for some other baby—been changed at the wash. It doesn't matter particularly how it has happened. It has happened, and that's certain."

But the question which naturally arose in Master Charley's mind was, if he managed to regain his lost position in society, would he be able creditably to fill it?

Had his schooling in courts, and alleys, boozing-kens, flash houses, brothels, and jails, made a gentleman of him?

It is certain that there was something about the young fellow, in spite of his brazen-facedness and depravity, which bespoke gentle blood; but there was, of course, a want of breeding, and a certain coarseness in his manners, which we must allow could hardly have been avoided, when we come to consider what sort of company he had spent his youth.

Still, again, there were hopes for him, because he had never willingly associated with other thieves.

Their tastes and habits did not suit Mr. Charles.

You may say, perhaps, that Master Charles's tastes and habits were coarse and depraved upon my own showing.

That is true; but still, there was a great striving after the grandly voluptuous in Mr. Wag's small endeavours.

There is no denying that he was in his heart an enormous profligate. But then, profligacy is fashionable. The vices tolerated, nay, even smiled upon, fostered, and encouraged, by a licentious, heartless, and unprincipled aristocracy, are condemned and reprobated with the most violent loathing and contempt when they are found to be practised by a poor hard-up devil in a Whitechapel back-slum.

If the boy had only had the luck to be brought up a swell as well as born a swell, there is no doubt that he would have made a name in the world, and that, though most likely he would have been a most outrageous young rogue, and rake, still, I am not quite sure that he would have lost caste in consequence.

However, you see he was not a swell, although he practiced a swell's vices; and so by rights we ought to be very much disgusted with him."

But return to the night, and the storm, and the story.

Charley Wag took a cab from the hotel where he was stopping, and bade the driver take him to the Strand entrance of Clements Inn.

Arrived there, he made a plunge through the rain into the porter's lodge to make inquiries.

"Does a gentleman of the name of Leech live here?"

"Yes, sir."

"What number is it?"

"I'll show you, sir, if you will allow me."

Charley naturally thought that the porter was eager to earn a small gratuity, and as he had no change in his pocket, he said:

"I will find it myself, thank you."

"It's no trouble, sir.',

"I won't bring you out in the rain."

"I'm going out, sir."

"Oh! well."

"I'm going to the house itself."

Charley, seeing it could not be avoided, agreed, after a little murmuring.

As they walked, they talked.

"The fact is," said the porter, "I'm going to see a mysterious old party as lives on the ground-floor of the same house that Mr. Leech does."

"Oh, indeed!"

"You may well say so, sir—a regular rum-un."

"Is he?"

"He is, sir."

"Oh, indeed!" said Charley again, not feeling the slightest interest by the way.

However, the porter was determined to be comunicative,

"A most mysterious individual, sir. You'd hardly believe it, he's been here these six weeks, and never left his room. Nobody has ever been inside, and hardly any body has ever seen him; at least only two, that is, me, and the woman with the bloaters."

"The woman with the bloaters?"

"A woman who called regular every day with a couple. He never asked to have anything else to eat, that we could find out. Bloaters and cold water. It don't sound filling, do it?"

"Not particularly."

"A most extraordinary card, sir."

"A miser, I should think."

"You're right, a miser; there isn't a doubt. His room's full of money, I expect."

"What makes you think so?"

"Well, I've heard him chinking his cash sometimes of a night, when the place has been quiet, and I have happened to be passing his door. I dare say he has millions, and no one to leave it to. That's the worst of it."

"Has he no friends?"

"None that I know of. He has no letters."

"How hold is he?"

"Close on eighty, I should say; though by the look of him, he might be three hundred. For he is so filthy dirty, there's no catching a sight of his skin."

"A horrid old wretch!"

"And most likely he'll be turning up his toes some of these fine days, and no one here to own him. For that matter he's very near it now."

"Is he ill?"

"He's very bad, I should think; but I get to see him. He won't open the door."

"What makes you think he's ill?"

"Why, because he's left off his bloaters."

"Oh!"

"Yes, for a good fortnight he ain't bought none."

"He must be living on air, like the thingembob you read of in the book about wild beasts. Now and then, when I pass the door, I hear him groaning awful, and I give a tap or two; but he'll never show. And I've asked him if he wasn't ill, and whether I should fetch him a docter, but he screamed out, 'No!' in the savagest way, as though I wanted to rob him. Oh! he's a rum-un, sir, there's no mistake."

"He's most likely out of his mind."

"To be sure, and he'll die there, is his own obstinate way, when a bottle of doctor's stuff would probably set him up again as right as a trivet."

They had by this time reached the house that contained the curious specimen of humanity, whose oddities they had been discussing.

The staircase was very dark and narrow, and Charley was obliged to mount it cautiously.

He was, therefore, some time before he reached the first-floor.

He heard the porter tap three times at the door of a room upon the basement story.

Then he heard a weak and squeaky voice reply—

"Who's there?"

"How are you, to-night, sir?" responded the porter.

"What does it matter to you how I am?" the voice replied. "Go away."

"Don't you want anything?"

"I don't want you."

"Don't you want anyone else?"

"Go to the devil!"

The porter, however, did not go, at least, not immediately; but he took his departure in high dudgeon at the uncouth reception he had met with.

Charley continued upon his way up-stairs.

He knocked at Leech's door, and the lawyer himself came forward to receive him.

"You are punctual," Leech observed, as he led his visitor into an inner room.

"Yes," replied Charley; "the clock is now striking the hour."

And as he spoke, St. Clement's sent forth an iron clang.

Leech placed the lamp upon a table, and motioned his friend to take a chair by the side of the fire; then he drew his own chair to the other side, and sat down opposite to him.

A slight pause ensued, in which the two eyed each other, something like the two prizefighters whom they had been watching that morning, eyed each other before they commenced hostilities.

Charley first broke the silence.

"You said that you had something to tell me," he observed.

The other nodded.

"I have come here to hear it."

"Certainly."

Again there was a pause

Leech seemed to be considering how he should begin.

"I am waiting for you, sir," said Charley.

"Look here," said the other, opening upon

him suddenly; "let us understand one another."

"With all my heart."

"You are in want of money."

"I am."

"I can get it for you."

"I am obliged to you."

"But—"

"Yes."

"I must be paid for doing so."

"To be sure. That's fair enough."

"You must, therefore, sign me a bond which I have here, promising to pay me a certain sum for my trouble."

"Yes,"

"The bond is for twenty thousand pounds."

"Twenty—how much?" cried Charley, opening his eyes as wide as saucers.

And then, before the other could reply, he had burst into a loud laugh.

But Leech did not move a muscle of his face.

After Charley had finished grinning, the lawyer observed drily,

"You seem amused."

"I'm rather astonished, sir. That's all."

"You fancy, probably, that there is very little likelihoods of you ever being able to meet such a sum."

"Very little indeed, sir, I should say."

"You probably think me extremely green, when I say I am willing to invest some hundreds of pounds, in endeavouring to place you in such a position as will enable you to do so."

"I should be inclined to think that you were."

"Indeed! Now, Mr. Wag, I should like to give you a word or two of advice. Don't you run away with the notion that you know everything. You know a thing or two I haven't a doubt; but you're young—you're very young, I may say."

"I have that disadvantage."

"Yes, and another, that you are eaten up with conceit of yourself and your fine doings. But, my dear fellow, let me impress upon you the fact, that what you have done up to now is very little to your credit."

Mr. Wag smiled; but felt foolish.

"What are you?" pursued Mr. Leech, leaning back in his chair, and contemplating his companion at his ease; "what are you, but a low, London thief, in spite of your fine dress and flash airs?"

"Sir!"

"Take a seat. I ask you—what are you else? If you ask me what you shall be, I reply simply, a duke, with close on half a million a year to spend for pocket money."

"You are mad."

"Not very; not mad enough to lock up. And now you shall see, my friend.'

———

LXXIII.—What became of Lucinda.

YOU don't suppose that Lucinda was dead, do you?

Or blown up?

Not at all.

SENSATION CAUSED BY THE PRETTY BOY.

With the first grey tint of morning she was flying away from the appalling scene of the fire. She had escaped out of the back-door just before the explosion, leaving her father and mother and the rest to their fate.

She was not an affectionate girl.

Anxious to escape recognition, she avoided the frequented lanes in the neighbourhood, and made her way across some fields in the direction of a village on the road to London.

Panting and breathless she hastened onwards, the dread of falling into the hands of an infuriated mob urging her to almost superhuman exertions, and by five o'clock she had placed many miles between her and the exasperated creatures who would have delighted in capturing and perhaps maltreating the daughter of the man whose blood they were thirsting for.

At last, through fatigue and the want of food (for she had tasted nothing since the dinner-hour of the day before), nature, supported as it had been by unnatural excitement, could hold out no longer, and she fell fainting under a tree, a short distance from a little cottage, the diminutive proportions of which, together with the combined air of rustic neatness and poverty, betokened the dwelling-place of an agricultural labourer.

The good man was just starting for the farm on which he worked, when he discovered Lucinda in the state just described.

He raised her in his arms, and placed her with her back against the tree; then, fetching some water in the crown of his hat from the brook which flowed close at hand, he dashed it in her face; but failing to restore her to consciousness, he carried her bodily into the house, and shouting to his dame, who was busily engaged in her domestic duties, speedily brought that individual to his assistance.

"What is the matter?" cried she. "Poor dear!" and without waiting for the good yeoman's reply, which might not have been satisfactory, inasmuch as he knew no more of the cause of her indisposition than his wife, she prepared some tea, and, with considerable difficulty, succeeded in getting some of that refreshing beverage down Lucinda's throat.

The honest yokel in the meanwhile was assiduously chafing her hands, and alternately applying vinegar and other abominations to her nostrils.

In a short time these had the desired effect. She opened her eyes, and gazing round with a bewildered look, faintly exclaimed,

"Where am I?"

Our good dame, whose womanly curiosity was aroused, speedily informed her, and hoped that she would communicate the circumstances which had brought her into their neighbourhood at that hour of the morning.

A fine opportunity now presented itself for the exercise of the virtue of patience; but in this, as in many other cases, the virtue was a necessity.

Her patient, who had been by this time placed in their own bed, but slowly recovered, and was then so weak as to be unable to sustain a lengthy conversation, such as her kind though garrulous attendant seemed inclined to carry on.

Ill as she felt, Lucinda could see that the good woman was anxious for some explanation of what seemed to her a complete mystery, and in reply to her numerous questions, briefly related the events that had driven her from home, and her intention to go to London.

"You will not betray me?" said she, tremulously.

The poor woman, astonished at her story, for a few moments did not answer, and Lucinda feared she had fallen in with those who might be induced to give information to the very persons she wished to escape from.

She was mentally reproaching herself for having told the exact state of her case, when her companion seemed suddenly to recollect that she had not answered the poor girl's question.

"No, no, poor child; you have done no harm. Rest here, and when you are well it will be time enough to think of going on your journey. Now go to sleep."

Lucinda felt assured by this answer, and was not long before she fell into a deep slumber.

When she awoke, she found that it was past midday. She had ample time to mature her plans for the future, and determined to trust entirely to these sympathising rustics.

In the midst of her reflections the door opened, and the good-natured hostess appeared, like another good Samaritan; only in this instance, a basin of hot broth usurped the place of the corn and oil which the celebrated party in good books is said to have had with him when he fell in with the unfortunate who had been so roughly handled on his road to Jericho.

Lucinda partook of this with relish, for her long rest had restored her to almost her usual strength.

She insisted upon getting up, and, notwithstanding the opposition of the bearer of the broth, carried her point.

She had her reasons for doing so.

In the first place, she was anxious to get away from people whom she knew could not keep her without feeling the inconvenience, however much they might feel the inclination. Secondly she wished to procure a suit of men's clothes, as she had determined to adopt them on her road to town.

She therefore took these good people into her confidence, and in the evening had the satisfaction of trying on the attributes of the sterner sex.

They consisted of a felt hat, together with coat, waistcoat, and trousers, of a decidedly country cut.

These had been purchased at a village store, at which could be obtained everything that was necessary to the existence of the humble villagers.

Thus attired, she surveyed herself in a fragment of a looking-glass which graced a corner of the room, the honest countryman declaring she "wor a beautiful boy."

"I am glad you think so," said she, cutting short her hair.

This done, she took one more look in the glass. The transformation was complete.

Her style of features were admirably suited to the disguise she had chosen. She now looked a very good-looking and rather saucy boy.

She came to the conclusion it would be wise to take advantage of the "shades of night," and pass through the village after the fashion of the young gentleman of "Excelsior" notoriety.

Her first care was to look to the state of her finances; and she was rather dismayed at discovering that, after paying for her clothes, she had not more than two pounds left. She could not leave without offering these kind-hearted people some remuneration, but it was refused with honest pride.

She therefore left her female attire, and begging their acceptance of a few trifles which she had carried in the pockets, took an affectionate adieu of this worthy couple, and set out on her journey.

The night was dark, and Lucinda passed through the village, and on to the road to London, without exciting observation of any kind.

Indeed, so perfect was her disguise, that it would have been a matter to be wondered at had she done so.

She felt this, and she determined to carry out the character, and boldly opened fire upon a carrier whom she overtook going the same way as herself.

"Will you give us a lift, guv'ner?" said she.

"Yes, my lad; jump up. Where be going?"

Lucinda hardly knew what to say, for her geographical knowledge of the neighbourhood was extremely limited; but she answered him by saying that she was going to London.

"You've many miles before ye, boy. What be ye going there for?"

"I should like to get some work to do."

"Have you got any friends there?"

"No," said she.

"Then don't go."

Lucinda told him that if she could get work elsewhere she did not so much care about going to London.

"I want a boy of your sort myself, to help me with the parcels and things. You look honest. If you like, I'll give you your grub and summut a-week."

Lucinda hesitated, but finally agreed to his proposition, which for the present suited her well enough.

For some time at least, Lucinda Hopley will be known to the reader as "John Burton," for that was the name she assumed when her new master made inquiry as to the same.

John Miles was the carrier between Barton and Nettleborough, which places were about thirty miles apart. It was to the latter town he was now journeying.

The night was rather cold, and our heroine not having as yet to enter upon her new duties, asked permission to lie down, as she felt very tired.

This was speedily granted, and she crept under the tilt, rolled herself in some horse-rugs, and was soon in the arms of Morpheus—in other words, went fast asleep.

It was just daybreak when our friend John awoke, and they were entering the town of Nettleborough.

"Jack—Jack, my lad, get up. You'll be wanting some breakfast, I'm thinking, eh?"

Jack at this summons sprang up, and it certainly did occur to him that he could do justice to the meal mentioned by his master.

At this moment they pulled up at the *Bull*, a little roadside inn much frequented by men of Miles's class.

A hot breakfast was soon before them, and in a short time both master and man were in a state of great sensual enjoyment.

After this meal, Jack accompanied Miles on his round through the town, where his particular duty was to deliver the smaller packages.

This was amusing enough, for the servant girls of the various establishments were quite captivated with the good-looking boy the carrier had brought with him.

After a few days envy, hatred, and malice, together with all uncharitableness, filled the hearts of the butcher's boy, the baker's boy, and all the other boys of the town who had experienced the first emotions of love for these "spider-brushing" divinities.

The butcher's boy swore a mighty oath, that if he caught our hero at any of his games, "he'd punch his —— head, he would!"

The baker's boy seconded the proposition of this ferocious youth, and the other boys carried it unanimously.

But, unfortunately for the gratification of their cold-blooded conspiracy, Jack did not give them an opportunity of carrying it into execution, notwithstanding the significant hints from these "area belles" that the next would be their "Sunday out," and that it was "such a beautiful walk to Blitsford Wood;" and many other little temptations, which our friend Jack carefully avoided seeing.

For well he knew (and so do we) that any attempt to assuage the pangs of these warm-tempered damsels would be attended with highly unsatisfactory results to both parties.

A week passed in journeying backwards and forwards between the before-mentioned places.

On getting into Barton, Jack never failed to visit the yeoman and his wife; for he remembered their kindness on the memorable day of escape from Hopley's house.

On one of these occasions he was returning to the village, where he expected to meet Miles, but was rather surprised at seeing that individual running in the direction of the yeoman's cottage.

Jack was soon up with him, and inquired,

"What is the matter?"

But as honest Miles was somewhat fat, and as violent running is not at all suited to corpulent people, it was with some difficulty that he gasped, in a disconnected manner,

"You—must—leave—here—Miss Hopley—at once!"

Lucinda sank into a chair, unable to answer.

She had been discovered, and it was high time for her to be off.

Miles had put up on this evening at the *Barton Arms*, the house he frequented when in this part of the country, and had heard a conversation between some men that were drinking there about the events that had driven Lucinda from home.

He gathered from their remarks that they were anxious to get hold of her, and having cause to remember a service that Mr. Hopley had done him in former days, the grateful carrier was soon interested when he heard that his daughter was a fugitive from home.

One of the men declared he believed she was in Barton then, and that the clothes which Jim Bailey down at the shop had sold some days ago had been for her; and that Jim had told him that very night that "he had see 'em on the boy as Miles the carrier had got."

Poor Miles fortunately could hear all that passed without being seen by these worthies, not one of whom would have been a desirable companion for a dark lane.

Feeling convinced that Lucinda Hopley and John Burton were one and the same, he started off to prevent Jack's joining him at the *Barton Arms*, as he assuredly would have done, had it not been for his timely discovery.

To serve the daughter of his former benefactor was all that Miles now thought of; the packages of the good villagers never entered his head.

He started for the inn once more to get his horse and cart ready, but not before arranging that Lucinda should meet him at some cross-roads which he indicated, and which were known to her.

Half-an-hour after found Lucinda in his cart, and on the road to Nettleborough again.

Miles kept his horse at a slashing pace, for he was not without some apprehensions of pursuit.

Nor were his fears groundless.

——

LXXIV.—THE PRETTY BOY GETS INTO DIFFICULTIES.

THEY had proceeded some miles upon their road, when, in one of the most secluded parts of it, Miles could see two figures ahead of them; and by the light of the moon, which at the moment shone out brightly, he recognized the men who were vowing vengeance against Lucinda should she fall into their clutches.

The stout-hearted carrier was now puzzled how to act; not that he entertained any fears for his own safety, although in all probability he should be a sufferer in an encounter so unequal.

It was the fear of Lucinda falling into the hands of these monsters in human shape that made him hesitate, knowing how little consideration she might expect from them.

In the meanwhile Lucinda continued to sleep, for Miles thought it would be useless to awaken her.

He drove on steadily, anxiously watching the movements of the two men, one of whom was tall and largely proportioned, with a felt hat slouched over his face; the other was a man of the middle height, with the most villainous expression of countenance ever beheld.

These two worthies were now at the side of the cart, and keeping pace with it, when a few hastily uttered words from the taller caused the other to spring at the horse's head.

The effect of this was to make the poor animal stop, and the tall ruffian, with an oath, jumped at Miles, and endeavoured to pull him from the cart, shouting to him to " give the girl up; they know'd she was inside."

This Miles resolutely refused to do, and the man had drawn a knife from his pocket, with which he soon would have terminated the poor carrier's existence, when, in trying to open the blade with one hand, the other grasping his intended victim's throat, who now struggled harder than ever, the blade closed upon his fingers!

He tried hard to shake it off, but could not.

He now shouted for assistance to his comrade, who had plenty of occupation in holding the horse's head, but was answered by that individual:

" You ought to be enough to tackle the carrier, and he an old 'un. If I left the beast he'd bolt."

This answer made the maimed wretch howl with rage and pain, and Lucinda, startled at it, woke up.

She comprehended the state of things at a glance, and seizing a hatchet that was close to her, dealt her friend's assailant a violent blow on the head, which brought him to the ground with a low groan.

Miles, on finding himself free, caught hold of the reins, and administered a smart cut to the horse, who, suddenly plunging forward, knocked down the man at its head.

He fell under its hoofs, the near wheel breaking his leg.

His shriek of agony pierced the hearts of Lucinda and Miles, but as their safety depended on flight, the latter made his beast " hum along," regardless of the fate of their late opponents.

This exciting occurrence had effectually deprived Lucinda of any inclination to sleep; she therefore insisted upon the worthy carrier taking a little rest, which he sorely needed after the recent struggle, which had exhausted him in no small degree.

After she had seen him comfortably settled inside, she took his place, and drove for the rest of the way, until they came near Nettleborough.

This occupied some hours.

On their arriving at the entrance of the town Miles again took his place in front, his object being to pass through Nettleborough without exposing Lucinda to recognition.

As it was not yet light, this was an easy task; and in a few hours more their jaded beast had arrived at its destination.

The place fixed upon by Miles was called Ashbury, and was about forty miles from London.

He had a relative residing here, who kept a shop, besides being the village postmaster.

It was to this person and his wife's care that Lucinda, under the name of John Burton, was consigned, after some explanations from Miles, to the effect that she was the son of an old friend, who had died rather suddenly, leaving him totally unprovided for; that he, John, was fit for " something better than carrier's work;" and that as he would want some sort of a character to get another situation, he would write him one.

This he did, and lodged it in the hands of his relative, who promised to get John a good berth.

Our heroine's parting with Miles was extremely affecting. The tears she shed would have excited no surprise had she been habited as young ladies usually are; but the impression created by them in this instance on the minds of the postmaster and his wife was, that their charge was a blubbering booby of a boy.

Subsequent events that we must not anticipate proved to these good people how much they had been mistaken.

John assisted the Watkinses in their shop, and his aptitude for business, together with his willingness to make himself generally useful, soon gained him their goodwill.

About this time it became known to Watkins that the page at the hall was going to leave; and thither did Watkins, accompanied by John, wend his way, to solicit the situation for his young protégé.

Some little objection was made at his not having filled a similar place before. But this was soon got over by the butler, a friend of Mr. Watkins, saying, " that he would teach him himself."

The magnanimous proposal from this august personage settled the matter, and on the Monday following, John Burton was duly invested with the buttons pertaining to the office of page to the Norton family.

Lucinda had now to carry out the most difficult part of her assumed character.

The Norton family consisted of the squire—a fine specimen of the English gentleman—three daughters, and a son. His wife had been dead about four years, and his eldest daughter, Laura, presided as lady of the house.

She was a plump, good-looking girl, with large black eyes, of the ripe age of eight-and-twenty.

Being rather overbearing in her manner towards the servants of the hall, and, in fact, to all those she deemed her inferiors, she was not a favourite with them; and it was through her instrumentality that John's predecessor had been dismissed.

The other two daughters, Fanny and Emily, were girls just escaped from the trammels of boarding-school, with their heads full of the latest Paris fashions, their first militia ball, and the other *et ceteras* which usually predominate in the minds of young ladies from the age of sixteen to twenty-five.

After that age, women are apt to banish the idealities of girlhood, and to enjoy the realies of the present—at least, such is the case if we may judge from the conduct of Laura Norton.

Lastly, we have to describe Frank Norton, a fine, handsome young fellow of four-and-twenty, who had just left Oxford, and taken up his abode at the hall, to use his own expression, "to do the rural."

"Doing the rural" with him, consisted in hunting, fishing, and shooting, in their proper seasons.

He had an extensive acquaintance with the neighbouring gentry and ladies; was a great favourite with the former, and a greater with the latter.

It was not to be wondered at, for few could know him without liking him; in fact, some of the rustic beauties carried it to even greater lengths.

Idolized in the servants' hall, where he was a frequent visitor, the housemaids were flattered at his "impudence;" and their sweethearts, whether coachman, footman, or groom, were not offended at it—perhaps, not jealous.

It was on one of these visits that he first paid any particular attention to John.

"Well, my lad, what's your name?" said he: "John, of course."

"John Burton, sir."

"John Burton, is it?—and a deuced good name, too. Well, John, and how do you think you will like being buttons?"

"I think I shall like it very well, sir."

"Do you? Well, you'll have to be smart here, or Miss Norton will give you the sack."

"I mean to be, sir."

"Then you'll do. "And whistling merrily, he was leaving the room, when recollecting something, he shouted:

"Buttons!"

"Yes, sir."

"Run to my dressing-room, and you will see a small paper parcel on the table. Bring it to me."

"Yes, sir!" replied John, and started off upon his mission.

She was soon back; but in the place of the small parcel he had described, she bore one of the opposite dimensions.

"Here it is, sir," said our friend John.

"Blockhead! I told you a small parcel, and you bring me one as big as yourself."

On being so harshly spoken to, for what she did not deserve, for it was the only parcel there, the tears started involuntarily to our heroine's eyes as she told him so; for be it known, she had with the most inconceivable stupidity, allowed this rollicking young squire's image to make a deep impression upon her feelings, already too susceptible to these tender influences.

Frank saw the tears, and remarked,

"You stupid cry-baby. You're big enough to know better. You are as bad as any girl. There, take it back again."

At this Lucinda blushed crimson, and turned her face away, as though to conceal it.

This action was not lost upon Frank, who being a rather keen observer, immediately detected a fullness in the chest, that others ascribed to the padding in the jacket of our page, but which Master Frank ascribed to some other invisible agency. "Aha! aha! my fine fellow," said he to himself, "we must penetrate this little mystery."

Nor had he long to wait for a confirmation of his surmises.

——

LXXV.—STILL IN HOT WATER.

LAURA NORTON had from the moment of John Burton entering their service, treated him with a kindness so unusual to her, that the other servants had noticed it; and many were the jokes cracked in the servants' hall about "missis" and John.

She had observed his partiality for reading, and lent him books; and unobserved, and under a promise from him that he would not mention it to his fellow servants, had affected to teach him drawing.

These lessons took place in her boudoir—a room into which not even her sisters came uninvited.

The intention of these lessons was evident to poor John, for with the help of Byron, which she insisted upon explaining to him in its fullest sense, she made the most unmistakeable advances to him. And one fatal morning, after having made a quotation from Don Juan, which she deemed "telling," she drew him to her, and impressed a kiss upon his rosy lips.

Lucinda started back, the blood mantling to her fair forehead.

"I think I had better leave the room, Miss Norton," said she.

"Leave the room! how dare you attempt such a liberty with me? I'll acquaint your master of your conduct on his return. Begone, or I'll ring, and have you removed!"

Lucinda left the room, but not without a strong inclination to let such an amiable mistress know the mistake she had made; but stifling this feeling, she resumed her duty, and waited patiently for the return of the old squire, who was out hunting with Frank.

On entering the house, a servant met him with a message from Miss Norton, saying she would be glad to see him at once in her boudoir.

The old gentleman went, and found Laura apparently much agitated.

"What is the matter, my dear?" said he.

"Oh, papa! I can hardly tell you," commenced this virtuous and much to be sympathized with damsel; "but that page, John, has this morning had the audacity to kiss me!"

"Eh! what? Where's my whip?" Saying which he dived under the table to reach his whip, which had rolled there. Not being able to do so had only increased his rage.

"Let him be sent for! Let him be sent for!" shouted he. "Confound that Watkins! I'll—I'll——" but seeming at a loss how to conclude this speech, he sat down, and looked savagely at the door, as if meditating a spring at the unfortunate page the moment he came in sight.

Miss Laura objected to his presence in her boudoir, and suggested the propriety of her papa seeing him in the library.

The old gentleman, nothing loth, took his way to that apartment, and thither the wretched "buttons" was directed to follow him.

On his entrance the storm of abuse was something terrific, and could easily be heard outside the door.

By degrees it got less, and in a short time was reduced to a subdued conversation, which lasted for nearly half-an-hour.

After which, the squire and Lucinda came out; the former looking very grave and wiping his spectacles, saying in his kindest tones:

"You must leave here, my child—you must leave."

Lucinda could not restrain the tears which flowed from various causes.

Leaving the hall was one, undoubtedly, for the gay-hearted Frank had but that morning caught her in his dressing-room, and taxed her with being a girl.

She had confessed to it—begged him to keep her secret—and he had sworn on her pouting lips to do so.

Leave the hall she must. So packing up her scanty wardrobe—for she knew not how soon she might require male attire again—she prepared to depart.

Frank contrived to have a few minutes' conversation with her, in which he insisted upon being allowed to take apartments for her, until she could settle something for the future.

This he did in an adjoining town, a few miles from Ashbury, not thinking it prudent to do so in a village where he was so well known; and on the same evening, Lucinda, once more a girl, was sitting by her "ain fire side," with Frank's arm around her waist.

Important business in London at this time called Frank away from Ashbury, but it was here that the "important business" was transacted.

It was a happy time for poor Lucinda, after all she had gone through.

But her happiness was doomed to be of short duration.

In the same house, on the floor above them, lived a Frenchman, a professor of music. Being a very gentlemanly man, Frank and he had exchanged little civilities on the staircase in passing.

By degrees they became familiar, and Monsieur was invited to supper one evening. This led to a visit next morning.

After a while these visits became of frequent occurrence, and the professor falling into the error that so many of his countrymen are in the habit of doing, fancied that he had made a conquest of the "belle Anglaise."

He presumed upon this hallucination, and Lucinda informed Frank, who meeting him on the stairs, knocked him down, and then told him his reason for so doing.

"You shall give me the satisfaction due to un gentilhomme, you shall, sar, by gar! I have your life, sar!"

"Oh, all right! whenever you like," said Frank, and left him.

He thought little of the Frenchman's threat until the evening, when a Monsieur de Brondt (a tutor from a neighbouring academy) called on "the part of his ami ze professeur."

He gave Frank clearly to understand that an apology would be accepted.

This Frank would not give, and requested Monsieur de Brondt to give an address, and that he would send a friend to him if possible that night.

Monsieur did so, bowed, and took his departure.

Frank immediately penned a few hasty lines to a friend near Ashbury, and sent a messenger with them.

In less than an hour and a half, Arthur Graham was with him.

"Well, old boy," said he, on entering a private room at the "Crown," whither Frank had gone to meet him; "so you've got into a mess with a Frenchman."

Frank related the circumstances, and Arthur started to call on Monsieur de Brondt, with a request that he would name an early hour for the meeting in the morning.

This being arranged the two young men supped together, and parted about eleven o'clock.

The morning was cold and grey, and Frank, and Arthur with the pistols under his cloak, walked briskly to the rendezvous, the professor and Monsieur de Brondt arriving about the same time.

There was no unnecessary delay. The distance was measured, the handkerchief dropped, and Frank Morton fell, with a ball through his heart!

A fly was waiting for them at a short distance, and with the assistance of the driver, Arthur placed the body of his unfortunate friend inside, and seating himself by it, ordered him to drive at once to Ashbury, from which place he immediately wrote to Lucinda, acquainting her with the fatal termination of the affair. By this time the professor had collected his limited stock of linen, which only a Frenchman knows how to economise, and was some distance in the direction of Dover, in company with his friend De Brondt.

The early departure of the professor removed any doubt she might have entertained as to the truth of Arthur Graham's announcement.

She wept bitterly at the loss of one who had been so kind to her. And now came the awful reality, she was alone, without a friend.

Whither should she go?

———

LXXVI.—CHARLEY AND THE LAWYER.

RETURN we now to Charley Wag, whom we left seated in Mr. Leech's room at Clement's Inn, whither he had gone to hear the story of his birth.

When that ornament to the legal profession abruptly informed our hero that he should be a duke, with close on half a million a-year to spend, he very naturally thought that Mr. Leech had suddenly taken leave of his senses, and in the purest Saxon told him so.

His remark did not seem to offend the lawyer, who was searching in a bureau for a paper which he could not find.

He only smiled—a quiet and meaning smile.

Although astonished, and extremely incredulous, Charley could not help building a series of castles in the air; and it was evident when Leech spoke to him that he had to make his descent from the highest of these ethereal structures.

He had, however, when " up there," lighted a weed, and was now fully prepared for Mr. Leech's communication.

The moment had at last arrived when the darkly shrouded mystery of his birth and parentage was to be solved to him.

He fidgetted in his seat, and finally became very impatient.

Mr. Leech again sat down, and said :

" Mr. Wag, you are here this evening to hear what may materially affect your future career. But before I proceed, I want to know whether you agree to my terms—whether you will sign the bond I have already mentioned ?"

" What, for twenty thousand pounds ?"

" Yes, Mr. Wag, for twenty thousand pounds," said Mr. Leech, with the coolest air imaginable. " You will be pleased to remember, that if you obtain the dukedom, that sum would be but a trifle from such a princely revenue."

Charley communed with himself for a period, took three whiffs at his cigar in quick succession, and then spoke.

" I'll sign it," said he.

Mr. Leech produced the formidable document, which had been evidently drawn up with care, and was in Mr. Leech's own handwriting.

It was to the effect, that upon Mr. Charles Wag's succeeding to the title and estates of the Duke of Heatherland, that gentleman was to hand over the sum of twenty thousand pounds to Mr. Leech.

In his present frame of mind Charley would have signed anything, so anxious was he to get at the bottom of the mystery.

Mr. Leech, seeing that he had achieved his point, went in search of a grimy individual he called his clerk (not the facetious party who had received Lucinda on her visit to Clement's Inn), to witness the signature.

Having secured this personage, he tendered a pen to our hero, and the name of Wag was duly affixed and witnessed.

This done, the " grimy one" having retired to the privacy of his own apartment, which was small, and not encumbered with useless furniture—there being a coal-box, on which he slept, and a sink, on which he took his meals—Charley and Mr. Leech were once more alone.

The latter, having fastened the door of the room in which they were sitting, commenced the tale, which our hero was anxiously awaiting.

" My dear Mr. Wag," said he, " you have of course heard of the man Faversham, who murdered the Duke of Heatherland ?"

" I should like to know who hasn't," quoth Charley.

" Good. This man, a Quaker, had been deeply injured by the duke, with whom he went to school. The persecution commenced when they were boys together. He was the duke's fag, and was subjected by him to every indignity which that scion of the aristocracy could heap upon him—forced up the chimney of a winter's night, and on one occasion held before the fire until he fell fainting with the heat, burning himself severely in so doing.

" As they grew up, Heatherland thwarted him in every conceivable manner, trying to supplant him in the object of his affections, and to crown all, broke into his house with a party of young men, ravished his wife, and finally, after setting fire to the premises, left his dishonoured victim to perish in the flames.

" While this diabolical outrage was being enacted, the wretched Faversham was lashed to a tree, with his face towards the house, and could hear the voice of his beloved wife imploring him to come to her assistance, and he powerless.

" He could hear the shouts of the hellish crew as they ransacked his house, and then— oh, horror !—he saw his wife literally burnt before his eyes.

" This is why Ralph Faversham determined upon a bloody vengeance."

Charley had been listening attentively during Mr. Leech's narration about Faversham, but could not for the life and soul of him imagine what it had to do with him.

* * * * *

We shall take the liberty of using our own phraseology in relating the circumstances connected with Charley Wag's birth, and in describing the manner in which Faversham carried his deeply laid scheme of vengeance into execution.

LXXVII.—A THRILLING NARRATIVE.

RALPH FAVERSHAM had indeed determined upon a bloody vengeance. It was to attain this end that he devoted his powerful energies.

Chance threw him in the way of the handsome Jack Horford, who was then the boon companion of the Duke of Heatherland.

Faversham resolved to make this man the instrument of his terrible scheme.

Horford, being a younger, his fortune was small, and, as a matter of course, his habits extravagant.

About the time Faversham made his acquaintance he was a ruined spendthrift, and his prospects were, to say the best, gloomy.

Faversham had marked him for his prey, and for this purpose cultivated his friendship, proffered his advice, and lastly, in a most disinterested manner, volunteered the discharge of the majority of his liabilities.

This was accepted by Horford (after a very becoming show of reluctance)

There were still many of his debts unpaid, for it was no part of Faversham's policy to set him entirely free.

Any one of these creditors could consign him to a prison, and it was in dread of this fate that Horford now lived.

He felt the immense obligation under which he was to Faversham, and sometimes regretted having placed himself so entirely in the hands of that mysterious man; for well he knew that it would never be in his power to discharge his enormous debt. Nor did Faversham wish him to do so.

On an intimation from this worthy the remaining creditors of the wretched Horford took steps for his immediate arrest, and he was served with three writs in one day.

Faversham knew all this, and felt that the time had now arrived for him to make the unfortunate man a participator in his guilt; and on the day following the serving of the writs he called on Horford.

He found him in a most desponding state, and on inquiring the cause, Horford silently pointed to the terrible slips of paper on the table.

Faversham took them up and examined their amounts, then turning to his companion, said,

"Horford, if you will do me a service, I will make myself responsible for the remainder of your liabilities!"

"Do you a service, Faversham! What would I not do to serve you?—you, who have treated me as no other man living would have treated me! tell me how I can serve you, and I swear before God that your bidding shall be done!"

A ghastly smile fitted across the features of the arch plotter Faversham as he narrated the injury the duke had done him, and he looked more devil than man when he told Jack Horford that the service he required of him was none other than the ravishing of Maud Allingham the Duke of Heatherland's betrothed bride!

At this diabolical proposal, Horford groaned, He had to choose between a prison, and the committal of an act at which his better feelings revolted.

The struggle was however short, and Faversham left him, after having made him swear the most solemn oath to perpetrate the horrible deed whenever he should call upon him to dô so.

Faversham had laid down a plan of operations, the success of which he was most sanguine, and on receiving Horford's oath to assist him, he proceeded to put it into execution.

About four o'clock he bent his steps to the Great Northern Railway Terminus, and having ascertained at what hour the express left at night for the north, he made his way to a public-house close at hand, which was much frequented by the railway officials.

On entering, he called for a glass of brandy-and-water, and inquired if he could be shown into a private room, and supplied with writing materials.

Being answered in the affirmative, he asked the barman if he thought it likely that any of the porters could tell him where to find the guard of the evening train.

"I should think they could, sir—but here comes one of the guards—he might know."

On inquiry, this man proved to be the identical person, and being "off" for a few hours, had found his way hither to beguile the time with a pipe and glass—say several.

Faversham was seated at a table writing a letter when the man entered, which he did, bearing with him the everlasting attributes of a railway guard, viz., two or three different coloured flags, rolled up, a small lamp, a flat tin bottle with a cork in it, and a key—the key Faversham intended having.

He easily recognized it by its peculiar shape —like the letter T.

"You wanted to see the guard of the down express, sir?"

"Yes."

"I take charge of the 8.30 down, sir."

"Are you in a hurry now?" said Faversham.

"No, sir; I'm just going to smoke a pipe for a little while."

"Very well, then, I will finish my letter; and I want you to take charge of it, and post it at Bradford. Have what you like to drink, and come to me in a few minutes," said he, at the same time putting five shillings into the man's hand.

On receiving this amount, the guard deliberately placed the whole of his accoutrements on a chair, and made a dive for the bar, where he was soon undergoing "a course of gin" with some of his particular friends and acquaintances.

Faversham, on seeing the coast clear, immediately secured the key, congratulating himself upon having obtained it with so little trouble.

Having occupied sufficient time with the letter, which bore a fictitious address, he rang the bell, and requested the guard might be sent to him.

This worthy entered, and was soon engaged in gathering his property together, after having received Faversham's directions.

The quantity of "blue ruin" that he had imbibed had rendered him somewhat uncertain as to what things he had left in the room, and he was in that happy state when the loss of a trifle does not make a deep impression upon the mind.

Having succeeded thus far, Faversham returned home, and soon after he might have been seen absorbed in the occupation of copying the printed portion of a telegraphic message.

This was completed after some hours' labour, and the deception was so accurate that it would have been difficult to detect the fraud.

Indeed, it would have been almost impossible, and unless some one suspected the genuineness of the message, and examined it with a view to its discovery, its purport would be answered.

Faversham then considered what was best to be inserted in the message, and ultimately decided upon the following, as most likely to cause Maud Allingham to fall into his snare. It ran thus:

Lady Allingham was taken suddenly ill last night, and wishes to see you as soon as you can come to her. I consider her in a very precarious state. A train leaves London at 8.30. The carriage will await you at the station on the arrival of that train.

ARTHUR HAMPTON, M.D.

HORFORD AND HIS VICTIM.

Faversham had calculated every obstacle that was likely to operate against his deeply schemed vengeance.

In choosing the name of the family physician of the Allingham's, he foresaw that the summons would be attended to immediately, and he had every hope that Maud would travel unattended. His next slip was to write to Horford, requesting him call on him the next morning, intimating also, that he wished him to hold himself ready for a journey on the following evening.

More than this he did not say.

When he had despatched the letter, he seated himself before the fire, and gazing into it, the fiendish smile we have so often noticed, gradually stole upon his face, as he muttered:

"And to-morrow I shall be revenged!"

No. 54.

He sat gloating over his projected vengeanc until late in the night, and when he sought hi pillow, it was but a troubled sleep that visited him.

He dreamt that he was a boy again, and at school with his hated enemy, Heatherland!— that he was forcing him into the fire! Then the scene seemed to change, and he was witnessing Maud Allingham's struggle with Horford, and could hear her cries for mercy! And then another and more terrible change took place, for again his beloved wife was martyred before his eyes—he could hear her agonized shreaks as she implored his assistance, and he unable to render it. And lastly, he saw her perish in the flames!

Faversham here awoke, and the cold perspiration was streaming down his face.

[CHARLEY WAG, THE NEW JACK SHEPPARD.

This terrible dream was so impressed upon him that for a time he could scarcely believe that it was only the fantastic vision of his heated brain.

Until day-light he remained tossing about, so thoroughly had rest been driven from him by his fearful dream.

At an earlier hour than usual he arose, for on this day he had much before him.

The first thing of importance, was forwarding the telegraphic message to Maud Allingham; and Faversham went out in search of one of the many boys attached to the various telegraphic offices.

On nearing one of the central stations he espied a lad leaving it, and making up to him, addressed him with—

"Here, my boy, do you want to earn a couple of shillings?"

"I should't mind, sir. What is it to do?"

"To leave this letter in Park Lane," said Faversham.

"I must take a cab," said young hopeful, with an eye to an extra shilling.

"Very well," replied the other, "do so. There's the fare, and here's half-a-crown for yourself."

The youth pocketed the money, and inwardly determined to wait till he had to take some other message in that direction, and so appropriate the extra bob.

The consequence was, that Maud did not receive the message till nearly five o'clock.

She had been out for a drive with her friend, Lady Alice de Courtenay, with whom she was staying in Park Lane, and on her return the message was placed in her hands.

"What will you do, dearest?" said Lady Alice. "You cannot go alone."

"I do not mind that at all, Alice," said Maud. "I can engage a compartment to myself. And I would not on any account postpone going. Poor dear, mamma, she was so well when I left," continued Maud with a sob.

Lady Alice here tried to comfort her by saying :

"You know what a fidgetty person Dr. Frampton is: perhaps it may not be so bad, after all."

But this did not seem to appease Maud's apprehensions for her mother, whom she loved as sincerely as she was capable of loving.

The two friends, with the assistance of Lady Alice's maid, were soon busied in making the hasty preparations for the journey, and Maud made her appearance at the dinner-table in her travelling dress instead of the usual attire.

After this meal, which she scarcely touched, she took her farewell of her friends, and was soon seated in their carriage and bowling along as fast as the horses could go towards the Great Northern Railway terminus.

*   *   *   *

We shall now return to Faversham, whom we left after having engaged the services of the telegraph boy.

On his return home he found Horford awaiting him. He was looking pale and wretchedly ill.

Faversham noticed it, but abstained from making any remark relative to it.

"You sent for me," said Horford, in a low sepulchral tone.

"I did," said Faversham, "and am glad to see you so punctual."

And then a pause.

"I sent for you," continued Faversham, "to tell you that I have discharged the remainder of your liabilities; and to claim the performance of your promise to-night."

At this announcement Horford started as though he had been shot. His teeth chattered, and he trembled in every limb.

"You will leave town by the express that leaves London at 8.30 to-night," said Faversham. "In all probability you will see Maud."

"Oh! spare me this terrible task!" almost shrieked Horford, on whom the fearful reality of the service imposed upon him now seemed suddenly to dawn.

Faversham regarded him for a few moments with a look of supreme contempt, and then said in a low, but fearfully distinct tone :

"May I enquire the cause of your present weakness,"

Horford glared at him and replied, "It is because I shrink from the committal of the crime you have imposed upon me!"

"Oh! I suppose you would cry ' off ' at the last moment," said Faversham with a sneer. "Honorable—very."

This allusion to his honour aroused Horford's spirit, and in a firm and haughty voice, he made answer to the biting remark of this double-dyed scoundrel.

"Mr. Faversham, you have paid my debt, and I in a weak moment, swore to aid you in a transaction which may consign me to a felon's instead of a debtor's prison. Do not now taunt me with any mention of honourable feelings, for I must be too great a ruffian to understand it."

Faversham saw that the game was his, and the devilish smile again passed over his features.

Horford continued: "You have performed your part of the compact. I must do mine, and may God forgive me."

"Spoken like a man, Horford," said he.

"Or rather, devil," said Horford; "for none but a demon would execute anything so terrible."

"Well, devil, if you like," said Faversham, with a fiendish laugh. "And now my Satanic friend, here is the key that is to introduce you to the presence of the fair Maud Allingham. You know the rest."

Horford seized the key, and imprecating curses on the head of Faversham, rushed from the house.

His walk home had somewhat calmed him, and after a little while, calling in the aid of two or three glasses of brandy, he began to console himself with the notion that it was his fate and resolved to abide by its decree—in short, to keep his oath to the arch-fiend, Faversham, who was at this moment anticipating the result of his hellish design, and speculating upon the probability of Horford being taken into custody on the charge.

"Ha! ha!" laughed he, "the fool, let him be—it cannot effect me—it will only make my vengeance the more complete! My martyred wife, in a few short hours, by the aid of God or Devil, you shall be avenged. Avenged did I say? No, not until I am sure the accursed

Heatherland is in hell with all his brood, can you be avenged."

Thus the blasphemous wretch continued.

* * * * * *

It was now time for the wretched Horford to be taking his departure for the railway station. He had applied himself so frequently to the brandy bottle, that he felt in that happy state which makes a man brave in spite of himself.

At the same time that he arrived at the terminus, a carriage drove up, and from it stepped Maud Allingham.

She was looking rather pale, and her face wore an anxious expression; but, notwithstanding, she looked surprisingly beautiful.

Horford almost chuckled when he thought that in a short time she would be his!

He watched her movements from a distance, and saw her enter a carriage in the centre of the train, and shortly afterwards the guard came up and affixed a small board with the word "Engaged" on it, to the door of the compartment.

Horford saw this, and rightly conjectured from it that she would travel alone, and had taken this precaution to prevent intrusion.

Poor Maud Allingham, she thought that by avoiding the companionship of other passengers who might have shared the carriage with her she was secure from insult—she even felt at ease, and without timidity.

Was she secure?

Time will show!

It was nearly time for the train to start; but Horford had purposely delayed getting into his seat until almost the moment of starting.

He had fixed upon the coupe adjoining the compartment which Maud Allingham had engaged.

As the bell rang, Horford stepped in, and the guard being near, he called him, and placing some small silver in his hand, said,

"Don't you put any one in here. I want to smoke, and don't want to be disturbed."

"All right, sir," said the guard, blowing his whistle and jumping on the side of the carriage; "we shan't stop till we get to Bradford, and that's a few miles yet."

Saying this, he left the moving carriage with the ease peculiar to railway officials, and leaped into his box at the end of the train, which was in a short space of time some miles upon its way towards the north.

Horford had now plenty of time to consider how he could best act to insure the success of this accursed project of the fiendish Faversham.

In his present state, "half cocked" as he was from the quantity of brandy he had taken, Horford felt quite interested in the undertaking, which he looked upon in the light of an adventure more than any thing else.

For the time he forgot that he was simply the hired instrument of a villain's bloodiest vengeance, and the anticipation of his guilty pleasure filled his brain with the most voluptuous sensations.

The wretched man had now fairly given himself up to the intoxicating influence that was slowly but surely composing him.

He thought not of the law he would be transgressing, for at that moment neither the laws of God or man would have swayed him.

It was in this frame of mind that Horford continued for the first two or three hours of the journey. As midnight approached he felt that the most favourable time for the execution of the damnable deed was at hand.

He lowered the windows and reconnoitred the steps of the carriage, and his observations seemed satisfactory.

A wooden platform ran from one end of the carriage to the other, and the only fear that entered Horford's head was that the guard might see him, and thus thwart him at the last moment.

He therefore determined to delay making the attempt until they had entered a tunnel, from which he knew they were then only a few miles distant.

Meanwhile Maud slumbered, little fancying that a terrible deed was shortly to be enacted, and she the victim.

She had thrown off her bonnet soon after taking her seat, and was now comfortably settled for the night.

She had drawn the hood of her travelling-cloak over her head before going to sleep, but it had fallen back with the motion of the train, and her rich golden tresses fell in luxuriant masses over her shoulders.

Thus she lay, calmly sleeping, unconscious of what fate had in store for her.

By this time they had reached the tunnel, in which Horford determined to carry out his infamous design.

He clutched nervously at the key, and with it opening the door, he swung himself on to the wooden platform; then closing it carefully, he stretched out his hand, and grasping the handle of it, found himself at the door of the compartment in which the fair Maud was sleeping.

He gazed along the long line of carriages, and his heart beat with pleasure at having succeeded thus far without discovery.

He applied the key, and the door opened, and he was face to face with the beautiful girl he meant to wrong.

Involuntarily he exclaimed, "How lovely!" and seating himself at her side, he took hold of one of her small hands, and pressed it in his own.

She started up with a shriek at seeing a man at her side, and with a voice trembling with terror she asked him what he wanted.

"Yourself, Maud Allingham!" said he, looking with a libertine glance at the shrinking creature before him.

She at once comprehended her perilous position, and could see how futile her efforts would be against this desperate man, but inwardly resolved to sell her honour with her life.

She dared him to approach her, and for a moment—a moment only—the villain quailed before her; and then, seizing her in his powerful grasp, swore that she should be his.

The struggle was long, for bravely did this heroic girl strive to defend what was dearer to her than her very existence. But of what avail was the strength of a weak female against a man inflamed with brandy, and maddened with the lust that the sight of this beautiful woman had excited.

In vain did she struggle and shriek piteously for help.

In vain did she sue for mercy, imploring and threatening in the same breath; and in spite of her screams, which were drowned in the uproar of the train passing through the tunnel, and the crashing noise and shrill whistling of the engine, the deed of violence was committed!!

*　　*　　*　　*　　*

Horford left the train on its arrival at Bradford, about three o'clock in the morning.

Making his way at once to the refreshment room, in search of more brandy, he found that establishment closed. He therefore considered what he should do with himself until six o'clock, the hour at which the first train would stop there on its way to London.

He left his portmanteau in charge of a porter, who stared when he told him he was going to return by the six o'clock train, and walked out in the gray morning through the streets of Bradford, in search of the stimulant which he felt he needed now more than ever.

He had walked many miles, when looking at his watch, he found it time to retrace his steps to the station.

This he did.

He was beginning to feel a fearful depression stealing over him.

His guilty conduct appeared in all its hideous reality.

Again he heard the shrieks of his victim ring in his ears; he could see the agonized expression of her face as she fainted in his arms!

He strove to banish the thoughts that would keep uppermost in his mind, but could not.

Then he thought of his old friend Heatherland, and how irreparably he had injured him.

And for what?

To gratify the vengeance of a man he now abhorred, and to save himself from a debtor's prison.

But how willingly would he have endured, aye, for life, the horrors of a prison, could he have wiped from his conscience the crime of which he had been guilty.

He was pale and haggard when he entered the station again; so much so, that the porter to whom he had consigned his portmanteau noticed it, and exclaimed to a brother official:

"Dash my wig, Bill, if I don't think that fellow that came down by the express, and gave me his portmanteau to take care on, is bolting from the bobbies!"

"Do ye—why?" says Bill.

"Because he looks in such an awful funk, and so white. He's a thief, or summut worse, you may depend on't."

"Well, don't let us say anything about it," said Bill, who was of a soft-hearted turn of mind, and had seen one or two fellows tapped on the shoulder in the course of his experience as a railway porter.

"No," said the other; "give the poor devil a chance. It's no more than we'd like ourselves."

The train coming up cut short this interesting dialogue.

Horford took his seat, and the porter placed his portmanteau under the seat at his feet, saying as he did so, in a confidential and mysterious manner.

"Have it there. You can be off at once when you get to the station you're going to, better than waiting at the luggage van for it."

Horford did not seem to comprehend the man's remark at the time; so placing a shilling in his hand, which the good-hearted fellow appeared unwilling to take, the train started with him and his conscience, which at present was pricking him pretty considerably.

And well it might.

The mysterious manner of the porter awakened a thousand terrors in his agitated breast.

Perhaps she had given information, and he should be arrested on his arrival in town! But that could not be, as he had watched, and she did not even show herself at Bradford.

And then he thought, and it almost drove him wild—perhaps she was dead!

One idea chased away the other, after giving birth to another, which in like manner propagated its species, until his brain was racked by a thousand groundless fears.

Indeed, it was easy to see that a severe inward struggle was going on, if the face may be accepted as the index of the mind.

He certainly did look very much "like a thief, or summut worse."

And he was worse than an ordinary thief, who is not always such a mightily guilty person; for his offence may be committed from an erroneous impression that property should be equally divided, and that by some mistake he hasn't got quite his share.

It not to be wondered that the porter at Bradford made the remark to his mate that he did, for a guiltier looking wretch than Horford was is not often seen.

After the departure of the train, the two porters could not help speaking of him.

The resumption of their conversation was as follows:

"Well?" says Bill.

"Can't make it out," said the other, scratching his head.

"He did look a good deal in the same way as the cove as was taken here last year—you remember," said Bill, musing; "but then he hadn't got such a gallus look about him as that fellow had."

"He gave me a bob when I put his portmanteau in the carriage to him," said the other.

"Did he though?" said Bill, suddenly convinced. "He's a gen'lman, you may take yer davey. What are you going to stand?"

"Well, we'll have so'thing warm, I think. It's coolish this morning."

Leaving these worthies to enjoy their tipple, we shall now return to Horford, who on his arrival in town went at once to Ralph Faversham, for the double purpose of acquainting him of the result of his mission, and of his intention to leave the kingdom.

Faversham on his entry grasped his hand in a manner unusual to him, for he could see by Horford's face that the deed was done before he asked a question.

Horford cast his hand away, and in a vehement manner exclaimed:

"The deed is done, Ralph Faversham, and I stand before you a guilty wretch. But for you I might have remained free from crime. May God's curse light upon you and yours for having tempted me with your gold to commit such an acrocious action !"

At this latter remark, Faversham said to his companion, in a bitter tone of voice :

"God's curse will rest upon you equally, my friend, I'm thinking !"

"Had it not been at your devilish instigation, I should never have committed an act which must drive me from the society of my fellow men."

"You were easily tempted, I admit," tauntingly replied this monster in human shape.

Horford could stand this no longer, and rushed upon Faversham, who being the stronger man, grappled with him, and held him down in a chair until he was calmer.

Horford literally foamed with rage as he writhed in the grasp of this devil incarnate, who, without seeming to exert himself, kept the wretched man firmly in the chair, and in a posture that he could not be dangerous.

"This weakness is unmanly, Horford. You have done me a service, and to prove to you how much I appreciate it, 1 will enable you to leave the country, although I must say, an unscrupulous man like you would be invaluable to me."

At this cruel speech Horford strove to rid himself from Faversham, who held him firmly, notwithstanding the tremendous exertions he made to get free.

His fury soon cooled down, and Faversham released him ; then, going to his desk, he took out ten five-pound notes, and placing them in Horford's hand, said, in a calm and unruffled voice :

"Now go. Your life is not safe while you remain in England. Go to Australia, assume another name, and all may yet go well. And now I have business to attend to, so good-night."

With this he turned to the table, where lay his writing materials, and Horford took his departure.

On his way home he carefully avoided the crowded thoroughfares, and the glare of the gaslight. As it was, he fancied that everyone he met, even in the wretched slums through which he skulked, knew of the crime he had committed, and looked upon him with detestation for it.

Arriving at home, he at once commenced the work of packing, and preparing for a passage to Australia.

This occupied him nearly all night, and when he sought his couch his dreams were terrible.

He could hear his victim's shrieks, and again heard her imploring for the mercy he would not grant.

In the morning when he got up, and it was then early, he went and purchased the few things that he deemed necessary for the voyage. At the outfitter's he saw the advertisements for the ships' sailing, and finding that one would go on the following day he engaged a steerage birth—his limited means preventing him going in superior class.

For the rest of the day he was in a fever of excitement.

He was longing for the morrow, that would see him borne far from the associations of his brutal deed.

The morrow came, and the close of it saw Horford down Channel on his way to Australia.

* * * * *

Three months after the perpetration of Horford's villanous act, Maud Allingham was married to the Duke of Heatherland.

She was as beautiful as ever—perhaps more so ; but still a keen observer might have noticed a shade on that fair brow, as though a weight were resting on the mind.

She was unhappy !

Not but what she had all that wealth could procure, and the world could give ; but she lacked " that peace of mind which the world cannot give."

She had been married four months or so when she found it impossible to conceal the state she was in much longer.

How she had done so hitherto I am at a loss to conjecture.

(I dare say some of my fair lady readers could tell me.)

However, to proceed, she felt that it would be necessary for her to manage his grace the duke so as not to excite his suspicions. She therefore opened the ball by being slightly indisposed, and of course the medical man who attended her thought change of air would do her good. It was her suggestion to him, and he being a wise disciple of Æsculapius, and knowing upon which side his bread was buttered, to use a very vulgar expression, furthered her grace's suggestion as to change.

By a most curious coincidence, Lady Alice de Courtenay, the duchess's most intimate friend, to whom she had confided her secret, wrote a most affectionate letter, begging, that if she did take change of air, she would come to her.

This letter the duke saw, and approved of the scheme, as he was very much engaged in his ministerial capacity, and, indeed, would be for several months to come.

Maud, therefore, joined her fair friend in the country ; and the two lovely heads were soon laid together, to know what could be done in her Grace's critical situation.

It happened, fortunately, that Mauds' nurse was still living, and residing in a little cottage near Hampstead.

To this old woman Maud wrote, telling the good soul all that had happened to her, and was enchanted at having, by return of post, a reply of the most satisfactory nature.

She should be ready to receive her dear young mistress whenever she came.

(Most useful old parties, these nurses ; a little given to gin and strong tea ; but none the worse for that.)

As the duchess expected her confinement very shortly, she proceeded to Hampstead, accompanied by her friend Lady Alice.

She had been there rather more than a week, when the long looked for but dreaded event took place—for it brought to her none of those blissful feelings attributed to young mothers.

This boy was a child of sin and shame ; and although she consoled herself with the idea that the *sin* did not lie at her door, she could not rid herself of the obtrusive fact that the *shame* did.

In due time she got better, and returned with Lady Alice ; but not before placing the child with some poor but honest people in the neighbourhood.

In the first instance, she paid for his support through the old nurse, and from her used to receive the intelligence (gratifying or not), that the young tyke throve wonderfully well.

Being now sufficiently recovered, Maud returned to town; and as the London season was at its height, she was soon in a vortex of fashionable gaiety; but amid the whirl of excitement, the thought of her shame was always before her, and one night she resolved upon taking a dreadful step to rid herself of the infant she had given birth to.

She dreaded discovery—the thought of her husband knowing of the child's existence almost drove her mad.

And the world's scorn.

Maud was a woman of the world, and like a sensible person, had a respect for its opinion.

And this is what she did.

Leaving her home one fearfully stormy night, when the rain was beating heavily against the window-panes, and the wind sweeping in fierce and fitful gusts along the deserted streets, she hired a cab, and drove to Hampstead. Then entering unseen the dwelling of the poor people to whom she had confided the care of the child she stole it from them, and drove back to town.

She discharged the cabman at the Nelson monument, and with hurried footsteps went in the direction of Hungerford Market.

Her deadly intention might have been seen from her flashing eyes and set teeth; but who was likely to observe her on such a night as this?

Her dress was not likely to attract attention, for it was torn, wet, and draggled.

She hurried along, unheeding the blinding rain, until she came to the steps leading from the market to the quay below. Down these she ran, and creeping along the slippery stonework, she gained the extreme point; and here the unnatural mother tore her little one from the bosom in which it nestled, and giving one fearful, shuddering look around, she cast her baby into the black and struggling waters gurgling at her feet.

"Thus perishes the record of my sin and folly," she murmured, as she saw the water close over the baby's face, which to the last seemed turned reproachfully towards her.

She saw it as a flash of lightning illumined the terrible darkness of the place she had chosen, and fancied she heard through the raging storm its last stifled wail.

And then she turned and fled!

No one had seen her, no one had witnessed the crime.

She almost flew up the steps by which she had descended, and passing along the covered way of the market, through another passage to the right, turned into Villiers-street, and into the Strand.

The infant did not appear to have been born for drowning—perhaps he was born for hanging; indeed, some of his subsequent exploits would richly entitle him to that polite attention on the part of Mr. John Ketch.

As it is already known, he was rescued by Mr. Toddleboy and Joe Cudder, who had been having a drain "t'other side of the water," and

were returning home to seek the retirement of their virtuous couches, when they lighted upon the half-drowned brat.

After many adventures, which my readers know more about than I can tell them, he found a home with Sarah Williams, a poor dressmaker, who lived in the same house as Mr. Toddleboy, and had just lost her own baby.

"Heigho!" sighed she, on hearing that Toddleboy intended going to the workhouse about it. "I wish I was not so poor, that I might keep it altogether."

And she did keep it.

A lawyer called upon Toddleboy and Miss Williams one day, requiring to see the baby.

It was shown him, and in rather a rough manner he began to examine its apparel, as though in search of marks. Then turning round, he inquired for a ribbon that had been about its neck.

On being told that they did not know what had become of it, he appeared anxious.

But a diligent search being quickly instituted, the ribbon was soon found.

"I will take charge of this," said the lawyer; "and here's the money."

First—five pounds was paid to Mr. Toddleboy for rescuing it, and five more for its keep for a certain time; after which the lawyer again supplied them with money, and continued to do so as long as the boy remained under their care, which was till the death of his foster mother, Sarah Williams.

The lawyer's name was Leech.

How he came to be concerned in the matter is rather a roundabout story.

It will be remembered that Horford, after committing the brutal deed that Faversham had instigated him to do, was so stung by remorse for what he had done, that he engaged a passage in a ship bound for Australia, and left the country in which he had committed his crime.

Years rolled on, but still the recollection of his misconduct was before him.

He could not shake it off—it haunted him like a hideous nightmare.

After toiling and suffering every privation that can be conceived, he worked his passage to England in one of the homeward bound ships that had been lying in port short handed.

On reaching his native land once more, he found himself friendless, and without shelter for his head. He journeyed to London from Liverpool as a tramp, begging his way, and sleeping in any barn or shed that chance threw in his way.

There were days upon which he scarcely tasted food, and had to sleep at night with no other protection than that which his rags afforded him.

And thus he entered London; the very town in which, years before, he had moved in its best society, and now had not bread to eat!

He walked about the streets until the cravings of hunger became insupportable, and then, driven to desperation, he rushed into a baker's shop, and stole a twopenny loaf.

This was a sin crying to Heaven for vengeance, and vengeance very shortly made its appearance in the shape of an active and intelligent officer (as he was next morning called) of the A division, who was soon on the track of his guilt-stained wretch!

He was taken into custody, and his captor thrust his knuckles into his throat as fiercely as he could have done had his prisoner been taken in the act of assaulting Sir Richard Mayne himself.

He was taken to Quod Street, and in a filthy cell awaited the punishment due to his heinous offence.

Mr. Leech happened at that time to be prowling about, seeking whom he might defend, when his attention was drawn by some circumstance or other to the unfortunate Horford.

He tendered his services for the following morning, when his case should come on, but the starving wretch declined.

The fact is, the poor devil had taken it into his head that he should look tolerably well in a suit of " dandy grey russet," and had come to the conclusion that he might be doing worse than " getting up-stairs" all day long.

His refusal rather astonished Mr. Leech, who had not met with many such cases as this in the course of his police-court practice; and curiosity in the first instance led him to make some inquiries of Horford relative to his past life.

The unfortunate man, mistaking this for genuine sympathy, thought he had now found one into whose bosom he could pour the story of guilt which so weighed him down.

He felt if he could unburthen his mind, if only to a stranger, he should feel easier.

Leech listened to him attentively, and inwardly determined to make a good thing out of the startling revelation made to him.

He felt by this information he had the Duchess of Heatherland completely in his power; for although he had been employed to make all the payments from her to Mr. Toddleboy and Sarah Williams for the child's maintenance, and might have had his suspicions as to relationship, he did not know the actual circumstances which led to the birth of our hero, Charley Wag.

It was thus that Mr. Leech discovered that Charley was the son of the Duchess of Heatherland, and born in wedlock, which made him the heir to the title and immense property of the duke.

*　　*　　*　　*　　*

Mr. Wag, during the story of his birth, had interrupted Mr. Leech in a variety of ways.

And as a specimen of his interruptions, we shall give his remark on its conclusion.

It was, " Well, I'm blowed!"

" You do not now object to the bond you have signed, my dear Wag?" said Leech, smiling blandly. " It is a mere nothing from the princely fortune that will be yours."

Notwithstanding this last remark, which Leech thought would show things in a different light, Mr. Wag had still serious objections to the bond, which he had signed for the express purpose of hearing what Mr. Leech had to say to him, and that alone.

Not being affected with any maudlin qualms of conscience, Mr. Wag in the meanwhile determined to render his bond " null and void."

With a view to this, he asked Mr. Leech if he thought his claim to the title and estates was indisputable.

" Without doubt, my young friend."

" And you think there would be no difficulty in establishing it?" said Charley.

" Not the slightest," said Leech, producing a piece of faded ribbon from an iron safe in the corner of the room. " This was taken from your neck by myself, when I went to pay Toddleboy and Miss Williams for rescuing and taking care of you."

Charley didn't quite see how a bit of ribbon could make him a duke. The bond was uppermost in his mind, and on receiving Leech's reply to his questions, a sudden thought entered his head.

He pocketed the ribbon, much to Leech's surprise, and before that worthy could cry out had seized him by the throat with one hand, and with the other pitched the bond into the fire.

As he saw it burn, he tightened his grasp upon the lean throat of the scoundrelly lawyer, nor did he loosen it till he saw his face get to the desired phase of blackness.

Then flinging him back, he left the room as calmly as if nothing had occurred.

LXXVIII.—Something about a Ghost, and a great deal about Dirt.

AFTER having so roughly handled the exemplary lawyer Leech, Charley came to the conclusion that the best thing he could do was to leave the premises as soon as possible, as he had not the slightest inclination to be waited upon by a deputation of the A division.

On quitting Leech's rooms he found himself at the head of the staircase, which was as dark as pitch; for the dim gaslight which flickered faintly on the landing up to a certain hour had long since been put out by the night watchman, or something of the sort, who lived in the attics above by day, and prowled about the Inn by night.

I suppose the " ancients" are connected with the gas interest in a manner which makes them look rather sharply after the supply on the landings, for which the occupants of each set of rooms have to pay.

Or perhaps the venerably grizzled old nigger who hangs out above with the watchman may do it with a malicious feeling for his white " brethren."

Be this as it may, the lights are put out at an hour when many young swells are returning home, and find it extremely difficult to insert their latchkeys in their keyholes; and Charley, although not having to put this trying process into operation, felt that making the descent of these infernal stairs was bad enough.

But make it he must, and he groped his way down them cautiously enough, but not without having now and then taken two steps at a time instead of one as he intended, which was extremely unpleasant, as it brought him up with rather a sudden jerk.

At last he got to the bottom, thanking his stars that he had not broken his neck in doing so, and was making his way to the outer door, when his attention was called to the fact of the sick man's door on the ground-floor being open.

Charley, who was always of an inquiring turn of mind, determined to see if there was any truth in what the porter had told him about this mysterious old party as he walked from the lodge with him, and was upon the point of entering the room, when a faint though hollow moan startled him.

He turned round, and saw——shall we confess that Mr. Charles Wag, in spite of his experience, was weak enough to think it was a ghost? and considering what our friend had been up to on the floor above, it is not to be wondered at, that when he positively heard a moan, at no great distance from him, and saw the terrible " something white," that a thousand vague thoughts should suddenly enter his head, and cause him to perspire not a little, and rather coldly.

His first impulse was to run away, his second to remain where he was, although I should be sorry to assert that it arose from the conviction that " second thoughts are best," inasmuch as Mr. Wag was not calm enough to employ his thinking powers at all.

Some irresistible feeling rooted him to the spot, from which he might not have " moved on" even had the deputation of the A division that I have mentioned before, and for whose address Mr. Charles was not at all anxious, made their appearance, requesting him to do so.

It is useless to disguise it from my readers, who are doubtless not to be gulled by everything they hear, but may implicitly believe me when I say that Charley Wag was frightened.

He was always afraid of being in the dark. At Spike Island it had a powerful effect on him; only there it was for some hours at a stretch, while here it was very different.

He stood staring in the direction of the ghostlike figure, and his eye getting accustomed to the darkness, he soon found that it was flesh and blood that he was gazing at.

Perhaps the less we say about " flesh" the better. Another groan from the figure made Charley (who had by this time settled that it was not a ghost) go towards it.

He found it was the old man of whom the porter had spoken. The poor wretch had left his room, apparently with the intention of going down below; but had not strength to get there, and had fallen down where Charley found him.

He was speechless when Charley raised him in his arms—he was as light as a child—and carried him into the room, the door of which was open as our hero was passing out, where there was just enough light from a lamp opposite for him to discover a wretched little truckle bed. and upon this he laid the old man.

After doing so, Charley carefully fastened the door and was soon engaged in a voyage of discovery, the objects of which were matches and a candle, He moved about as carefully as he could, for fear of disturbing the old man, who still remained quite quiet and insensible to all around him.

" If he should hear me, and sing out before I can get a light and talk to him a bit, I shall be in a mess, and no mistake," said Charley to himself, as he came upon a cupboard, which he opened, and commenced groping about in.

" At last I've found 'em," and his hand rested on a match-box. " I shall be able to find a candle when I've got a light."

" Well, I'm damned!" remarked Mr. Charles, in a subdued tone; " here's a pretty go."

The box was empty.

What was he to do?

To remain here in the dark was useless, to get assistance from the porter he did not feel inclined, and to leave the poor old man in his present state without aid would be very brutal.

The latter thought he dismissed at once; for be it known that Charley Wag, although a loose and reckless young fellow—perhaps a a *trifle* too unscrupulous in some [matters—was not wholly destitute of feeling.

In fact, he was rather kind-hearted than otherwise.

He therefore determined to renew the search for the matches, and had he been hunting for the fabulous amounts that the porter had ascribed to the old miser, he could not have exhibited greater zeal and perseverance.

He tumbled over one thing and another, barking his shins frequently ; but he bore these little annoyances with the fortitude of a martyr, and was not long before he reaped the reward of his labour.

This time, on a sideboard, as he conceived it to be, his hand came in contact with a candlestick, and in it a morsel of candle.

He secured this, and passed his hand along the sideboard, when, to his delight, he found two or three lucifers scattered about.

Having procured a light, and that was all you could say for the wretched glimpse of a rushlight — value one farthing—he next looked about the room, which attracted his attention even before he thought of doing anything for the relief of its miserly tenant.

The place was filthy beyond description, and the scanty furnitrue that it contained had accumulated dirt enough to render it in every respect fit for the rooms in which it did duty, and harmonized so well with.

The wretched occupant of these chambers was evidently not a clean man, for on the floor snugly embedded in the dirt, which was literally an inch thick, lay bits of candle, looking very much as though they had been gnawed and thrown away until they were again required either for satisfying the cravings of hunger or shedding a gleam over the disgusting spectacles the room contained.

Thickly interspersed with the above were bits of herrings, heads and tails of that delicate and much sought after inhabitant of the briny deep being one of the principal features in the patterns of the floor-cloth.

These and every other abomination which the fertile minds of our readers can suggest, but which it is entirely out of the power of the poor penny romance writer to depict, met the eye at every step.

The stench in the room was fearful, and saluted Master Charles's nostrils on entering, not prepossessing him in favour of the dirty old wretch in whose company he now was.

" Then there is some truth in what the porter said," murmured Charley, glancing round this wretched scene, and stopping his nose with his finger and thumb, for he had unconsciously discovered a snug little heap of heads and tails,

THE DISCOVERY.

with his feet, and the smell arising from them was decidedly nasty.

"Well! this is a jolly place, and no mistake!"

"I should think the old gentleman doesn't pay much for scrubbing and cleaning, and if he does he's woefully cheated."

And thus Charley might have continued, had not the old man at this moment given a low moan similar to the one that frightened Master Charles outside.

"Poor old devil!"

"What the deuce can I do for him?"

"He ought to have something, and I strongly suspect that deuced little I shall find here for him in the way of nourishing food and drink; but I suppose I must look about, and I'll commence with this cupboard," said

No. 55.

Charley, taking the light from the table.

"A very pretty assortment, indeed, though not quite as handsome as some of the old china I've clapped my eyes upon."

"The contents of the cupboard chiefly consisted of bottles (empty), a large array of gallipots (ditto), and a few other et ceteras, that were neither useful nor ornamental."

"Dash my buttons if I know what to do," said Charley, after rummaging away among the gallipots, which were in great numbers, and rendered it rather difficult to get at anything that might be behind them.

"Tea! by jingo!" exclaimed he, pouncing upon a little japanned tin canister which was carefully placed in one of the pots with a small plate over it.

[CHARLEY WAG, THE NEW JACK SHEPPARD.]

"I'll make him some."—that's sure to set him on his pins if anything will.

So saying, Charley secured the canister, and placed it on the table while he went in search of a kettle.

"I don't know whether the old fellow indulges in such a luxury—it involves the necessity of fire to make it useful," remarked Charley facetiously.

He then passed into the inner room, which rivalled the other in filth.

This elegant apartment answered the purposes of kitchen, coal cellar, and general repository,

"It strikes me forcibly that the old dog is not troubled with any superfluous articles of furniture," said Charley, routing in a corner, "or with an over dose of kitchen utensils," producing from a heap of lumber a small kettle which appeared to have been on the retired lid for some time.

The spout of it happened to catch Charley's eye as he was turning over the rubbish, or it is probable our hero might have been put to some greater straits than he was, to make the old man's tea.

The kettle was small, and of the bachelor order, and Master Charles was rather puzzled how to proceed, without a "wheel" for the same.

He grubbed about until he came upon a fragment of one, and a few sticks of wood.

"They'll do gloriously! I shall have it boiling in a brace of shakes, and if the tea doesn't effect as much as a physician, I shall give it up as a bad job, and be off."

Returning to the front room, he had a look at the old man, who was lying on his back, with his mouth partly open, and looking very much as though he would "shuffle off this mortal coil" before our hero had time to get some tea unto him.

"If I don't look sharp he'll be turning up his toes before I can give him his dose of bohea," said he, "and now for a tea-pot."

In search of this, Charley made another descent upon the cupboard which had yielded the tea, justly anticipating that the pot might be stowed away behind the bottles, &c., in the cupboard.

Not the slightest approach to a tea-pot was to be found.

What, what was to be done?

Give up the tea making?

Oh! dear, no!

How was it to be done then?

This was a poser.

There is an old, though somewhat hackneyed saying—which my readers, or at least the lady portion of them, will forgive me for using—it will fill up a line or so—a consideration to romances—it is "necessity is the mother of invention."

We must allow that in this case the necessity was great, and Mr. Wag's inventive genius proportionate.

"Well! may I be sugared! if this isn't the rummiest go! making tea without a tea-pot."

I've hit it, said he, taking the largest and the cleanest (they were all very dirty) of the gallipots out of the cupboard, and wiping it out with a cloth he had found on the back of

a chair, after washing it well at the tap from which he had filled the kettle.

"I'll make him a drink that shall astonish him."

The old man here breathed heavily, and Charley, in a soothing voice, told him to lie quiet for a little while.

This was thrown away upon the miser, who appeared miserable to all around him.

By this time the kettle boiled, and Charley prepared to make tea.

For my own part, nothing annoys me more than to see a man make tea—to see his lanky arms wandering over the table in the most ungraceful fashion, not to say anything of the vice-like grasp with which he clutches the handle of the tea-pot—then you see him diving into the sugar basin—overturning the milk, of course—oh! it puts me in a fever of excitement—which I dare say will prove fatal when I leave the paternal roof and have to do it myself, unless some of my fair lady readers come to the rescue, by volunteering to make it for me.

But I am digressing, and must now return to Mr. Wag, whose inventive powers had been sorely tried, but he had surmounted the difficulty.

Placing the gallipot which he had just washed on the table, he opened the little canister which contained enough tea for one dose.

Then deliberately drawing his handkerchief out of his pocket, he placed it over the gallipot, and put the contents of the canister into it.

Into this he poured the hot water, and then let it stand!

"What a disgusting idea," I can hear some one exclaim; "the writer of Charley Wag must be a nasty fellow, or he would never have thought of such a thing."

Well! dear reader, perhaps it *is* a nasty idea, but if I had not had it, the old miser would not have had his tea, and a portion of Mr. Wag's adventures would not have been written!

I give you my word of honor the handkerchief was a clean one.

When Charley considered that it had stood long enough, he removed the tea leaves, and then the gallipot answered the purpose of a cup.

"I hope the old boy is not fastidious, and can drink his tea without milk and sugar."

He then went to the old man's bedside, and raising him up, placed a little of the hot tea to his lips.

The effect was magical!

He started up, and glared at our hero in a wild and excited manner.

He then tried to shout out, but his voice was too feeble.

"Easy, old gentleman, don't you make a row or I shall hook it," said Charley.

"The tea seems to have warmed him a bit, I'll give him some more," again pouring a small quantity down the wretched man's throat.

And then the delirious old man began to rave.

"What have you done with it? What have you done with it, I say? Give it me back! You have stolen my gold!"

"Go to blazes, will you," said Charley, "I haven't stolen your gold yet, old boy!"

Exhausted by his exertions, the unfortunate man lay back moaning, and Charley began to turn over in his mind the way to get at the money, which he now felt quite certain the miser must have stowed away in some place or other.

He determined to listen to his ravings, and from them learn where it was.

Nor had he long to wait, for the man began to rave again.

"I will not give it up! I will not! it is mine! —mine!—my darling gold!"

Then his mind seemed to wander, and he fancied it was stolen.

"It is gone, gone—what shall I do?" he exclaimed piteously.

Then, changing his tone, he laughed, and said—

"Ha! ha! it is safe enough—safe down below!"

"Oh! *is* it?" said Charley, "I'm extremely obliged for the information. I'll dig it up."

At these words the miser started up and seized Charley, who had just given him some more tea, by the throat! shouting—

"You shall not dig it up, I tell you. It is buried safe enough, and you cannot get at it."

And then he laughed at the supposed security of his hoard.

Charley, who did not approve of being throttled altogether, quietly disengaged the old man's claws, which were rather too sharp to be in close proximity with one's flesh—and placed him back on the pillow, saying—

"I tell you what it is, old fellow, I won't have any of your little games, I don't like them—

"Talk as much as you like, but keep your paws off."

The old man was still raving and talking in an unconnected manner, and it occurred to Charley that it was the tea that made him so violent.

"I won't give him any more, perhaps its too strong for his nervous system."

And then he sat down on a ricketty old chair, and gave vent to the following expression of his feelings :—

"I wish the old buffer would die or get better, or hold his row—or he'll be attracting some one here with his infernal chatter, and then I shall be up a tree."

The old man moaned as if in pain, and Charley went to him to see if he could do anything for him, when the wretched man started up, his eyes glazed, but staring wildly, and stretching forth his arms, essayed to shriek out, but a gurgling sound in his throat prevented him, and he fell back—dead!

Just at this moment Charley heard footsteps, and a confused hum of voices outside.

LXXIX. — LEECH RECOVERS, AND CREATES SOME EXCITEMENT IN CLEMENT'S INN.

IT is high time for us to return to Leech, whom we left seated in a chair, and very

black in the face from the effects of Master Charley's fingers.

He remained some while in a happy state of insensibility, for the squeeze had been severe.

He slowly recovered himself, and was sensible of a very unpleasing sensation, similar to what one feels on returning consciousness after a fainting fit, but by several degrees worse.

His first act was to seize hold of the poker, and commence a vigorous attack on the ceiling of his room.

This was for the purpose of arousing the nigger who lived above.

That grizzled old party crawled down stairs, and, presenting himself at the door, inquired what was the matter?

Leech told him as much of the circumstances as he deemed necessary, and requested him to fetch a policeman, and Scipio (such was the venerable darkey's patronymic) hurried down to the lodge as fast as his shaky old shanks would allow him, to communicate with his friend the night watchman, who in turn roused Mr. Garnett, the porter, and by him sent off in search of a policeman, and it is an astonishing fact that one was found in Boswell Court, and brought to Clement's Inn immediately.

By this time the place was all excitement.

The news of the "attempted murder" had spread in an incomprehensible way.

Scampy lawyers popped their heads out of many of the windows inquiring "what was up? while their "lady housekeepers" showed in great force, exhibiting a great deal of curiosity, and some sweet things in night dresses, et cetera.

The whole inn knew of it, and were looking out.

Down at the lodge the excitement beggars description.

Mrs. Garnett and the servant were bustling about, for poor Garnett was sure to require "something warm" after having to turn out so suddenly.

Miss Garnett was also exhibiting in her robe de nuit at her bedroom window, looking curious as ladies do sometimes, and awfully "used up" as she did always.

The policeman was at once conducted to Mr. Leech's rooms, who in a few words related what had occurred.

This member of the force had hardly arrived at the dignity of being called an "active and intelligent" officer.

To tell the truth he was rather a clumsy sort of fellow, and certainly not intelligent.

He was "from the country," and it is not to be wondered at that he perhaps did waste a little more time in standing open-mouthed, with a "stuck pig" expression of countenance, than was actually necessary.

He wasted a great deal of time, and Mr. Leech felt rather angry.

It was fortunate for Mr. Wag that the "bobby" was rather green.

On hearing the noise of their arrival he decided that as they had come in he would go out!

But how?

Trust Charley Wag for finding the way.

He went to the back room and tried the window.

It was so encrusted with dirt that he could not open it.

It had evidently not been used for letting in air for years,

What should he do—escape he must!

He seized hold of a piece of iron, and with it prised open the window.

This was something towards it.

Then, running into the front room, he took the coverlet off the dead man's bed, and tearing it into strips as noiselessly as possible, fastened one end to a staple near the window, and commenced lowering himself down. Just as he heard the policeman trying the door of the miser's room, the noise of his opening the window having attracted his attention.

Alighting in the court beneath, Charley mounted a shed, got on to the wall, and dropped into Clement's Lane, and so away down the Strand.

LXXX.—AT THE BACK OF CLEMENT'S INN. THE CELLAR.

WHEN the "bobby" found the miser's oak opposed to him, he suddenly conceived the notion of cutting off our hero's retreat at the back, but as he took rather too long a time to carry this brilliant thought into execution, Charley was off before he got into the lane.

Here our policeman met with a brother constable—an old stager—who was up to a move or two.

This enlightened officer of the A division suggested searching the houses in the lane, some of which bore anything but a first-rate reputation.

The old stager "spotted" one house at once, and they both entered it.

In this house there were syrens—syrens who immediately made a conquest of the heart of the susceptible young "bobby." As it may be imagined, the search was not carried on with the vigour that it might have been, for the elder bobby was soon seated, with cold meat and strong drink before him, and the younger one went off to inform Mr. Leech that his search had been unsuccessful.

Leech heard him in silence, and then dismissed him.

The youthful bobby, burning with impatience, hurried back to the house where he had left his more experienced brother in blue.

He was expected by these fat damsels, who were also burning with impatience—but it was to hear all about the attack upon the lawyer.

The innocent "peeler" was perfectly happy in the idea that they were anxious for his presence from other causes, and was only too delighted at being able to reply to the various questions relative to the communication Mr. Leech had made to him about the attack.

The weak and guileless preserver of the public morals told his curious companion all he knew, mentioning our hero's name in so doing.

A smile might have been seen to pass over the face of this female divinity on hearing Charley Wag's name.

It will be hardly necessary for me to say that Mr. Wag was well known here, and the young ladies of the establishment—as well as the male portion of the household—were rather surprised at his having been so near them without favouring them with a call, after so long an absence. Mr. Charles, while getting out of the way for the present, remembered his friends up the lane, and resolved to make their home his head-quarters during his attempt on the old miser's cellar.

In their locality he was likely to obtain the implements necessary for the undertaking, besides being close to the scene of his operations—in fact from their upper windows he should be able to survey the approach to the cellars—which he had been unable to do during the hasty retreat from his pursuers.

His pursuit, as we already know, was not a hot one, and after making his way in the first instance into the Strand, he shaped his course to that gloomy refuge for the destitute—the dark arches of the Adelphi.

Then he was safe for a while, and although the society was not the most refined, Charley being able to suit his manners to his company, was well received, and remained with the motley crew here assembled for more than an hour, when he thought he might venture to return to the house in Clement's lane without being detected by the police, who had not seen him during his escape.

For this purpose he passed into the Strand, and crossing Wellington and Catherine streets, found himself in Drury lane; then diving into some of the blind alleys, which were well known to him, he reached Clare market, and from thence got into Clement's lane.

On arriving, Master Charley began to think he had acted somewhat foolishly in going there without knowing whether his old friends occupied the house still, but as we all know he was not to be daunted by a trifle, he determined to make the attempt.

If they lived here still—well and good—if not, he must go somewhere else.

Such was the philosophical view that Mr. Wag took of his present precarious position.

Before proceeding, I shall have to introduce to my readers, as they have not appeared before, the family in whose house Charley was about to seek an asylum.

It consisted of Mr. William Mugford, the master of the house, and two buxom daughters, Patty and Jenny. We must also reckon the numerous female acquaintances that these young ladies had, and who lodged in the house, and were *almost* like Mr. Mugford's daughters.

Mugford, who was by profession a shoemaker, was a snuffy-looking little man, with foxey-coloured hair, and ferrety grey eyes, with a peculiar indentation in his nose, and of a restless irritable temper, which had caused him some years previously to stab his wife with an awl, of which stab she died, Mr. M. escaping hanging from want of evidence. This little secret did not serve to increase the regard of his neighbours, who always fought shy of this cantankerous cobler. The Misses Mugford, who followed no decided occupation, were a pair of fat slommacking-looking girls, who seemed to pay little attention to their outward appearance, and were decidedly of opinion that "charms unadorned were adorned the most," for they followed this maxim out almost to the letter.

The other young ladies in the house appeared to agree with them in this respect, and perhaps they carried their ideas on the absurdity of dress to even greater lengths than the Misses Mugford.

As it may be supposed, the worthy maker of shoes was not without enemies, especially among the female acquaintances of the late lamented Mrs. Mugford—for that unlucky "prod" which made Mrs. M. a ghost, and her husband a widower, was not likely to be forgiven or forgotten by her sorrowing companions. The unfortunate occurrence was always alluded to by one of the party whenever fresh comers settled in the lane, and gossiping had commenced. Then the tale would be told, and poor little snuffy Mugford would be held up to the execution he so justly merited.

In fact he was looked upon as little better than a monster in human shape by these gin-tippling matrons, who would enact the bloody scene over and over again, carefully suppressing the circumstances which led to it, and which, I think, in fairness to the much-abused cobler, should be known to the readers, so that some allowance may be made for him; and I think that when they have heard how it occurred, they will agree with me that his act was *almost* justifiable.

Mrs. Mugford was a large, stout woman (her daughters take after her in this respect), who had a weakness for imbibing—to tell the truth she was often drunk—and when in this state she would return home, and heedless of her husband's expostulations, she would beat him severely—and what could he do? He was a small man, and a big woman is no mean opponent. Her treatment was very exasperating.

On the fatal occasion, I am sorry to say, she was furiously drunk, and entering the little room where "snuffy" was at work, she assailed him with a pewter pot, and succeeded in breaking his nasal organ! And was it to be wondered at that the cobler should jump up in a rage, and let the daylight into his misguided spouse,

I think not, dear reader, and I can only pray that I (being very small), may never be so situated.

These malicious gossips even dared to asperse Mr. Mugford's character, and openly insinuated that he was not as honest as he might be!

To tell the truth he *did* sometimes, when the shoemending was slack, dabble a little in stolen property—that is to say, he would never trouble the vendor with unnecessary questions relative to the way in which he became possessed of his articles of merchandise, nor would he insist upon seeing his license to deal in the same.

In purchasing the little articles that were brought to him every now and then he did his friends a service, and that was what Mr. Mugford principally aimed at, at least so he said; and although the same little articles were not of the slightest value to him. it did occasionally happen the merest chance in the world that he realised by their sale ten times as much as he had obliged his friends with in exchange for them!

From our knowledge of Charley Wag, we may conclude that there *was* some truth in the insinuations of the ladies of the neighbourhood, or Billy Mugford would never have occupied a position in the mind of our hero, who always took care to select those that he knew and could trust when engaging in an affair that was likely to be attended with risk of any sort.

As I have given the reader a pretty accurate sketch of the interesting family into whose bosom Charley was about to rush. I shall therefore return to our hero whom we left at the top of Clement's-lane hesitating whether he should seek shelter at Mugford's home, or go elsewhere, and the conclusion he came to was a wise one.

He determed to see if his old friends lived in the lane still.

He looked about him to see if the coast was clear, and finding it so, walked quietly towards the house, and knocking three distinct blows on the door with his knuckles (this was an old signal), it was soon opened, and Patty Letchford, in defiance of the prescribed rules of maiden modesty and reserve—flung her arms round his neck, and kissed him heartily. As soon as Charley recovered from this sudden attack he was about to ask some question, when his fair companion made a sign for him to be silent, adding in an under-tone.

"the 'bobbies' are here—the pair after you!"

"The devil!" irreverently muttered Mr. Wag; "I'll be off."

"That you won't," said Patty, "now you are here we'll keep you," So saying, she put her arms within Charley's, and drew him into the house.

"You're safe enough here," she continued. "We'll soon get rid of the peelers."

Charley did not make any violent opposition to the pressing invitation of the fair Patty, who soon had a blazing fire in the room, into which she had dragged our hero. She then went to acquaint her father of Charley's arrival, and to get rid of the policeman if possible, who having stowed away a large quantity of meat and strong drink, were by this time very happy. They were enjoying the society of the lady-lodgers, and indulging in "churchwardens" when Patty entered the room.

Seeing them thus engaged she decided upon letting them remain as long as they felt inclined, for any attempt to get them out of the house might only awake their suspicions. and as the house did not bear a *first rate* reputation this was not at all desirable.

Patty soon returned to Charley, who was being regaled by Billy Mugford with the best that the house contained

Charley was a great favourite of Billy's.

"Well!" said Charley, you didn't expect to see *me* here to-night.

"No! indeed!" said Patty, "but the bobbies told us what you've been up to!" Saying this she left the room.

"Ah!" said Charley, "they're clever fellows, those 'babies,' but they don't know everything, do they Billy?"

Billy seemed highly delighted that they did not, and replied to Mr. Wag, by saying, with a chuckle.

"No, they don't—they don't know as Charley Wag is in the same house with them, or I reckon they wouldn't smoke their pipes so quietly up-stairs.

Here the two indulged in a hearty laugh at the expense of the "blue bottles" up above.

"I say, govo'ner, said Charley, with a wink, how's shoemaking at present? Slack! Eh!"

"Well! it is slack, reyther, and I shouldn't mind a job of some sort just to fill up the time," observed Billy, knowingly. "Have you got anything in hand?"

"Something for to-morrow night if you're game!"

"Done!" said Billy, "what is it?"

Charley then recounted to him what the porter had said about the old miser, and how he had heard him raving about his gold before his death.

"I'll bet there's a swag down in the cellar, for I've see'd him with a light there almost every night—curious that I shouldn't have thought of the thing myself—but when shall we crack it?"

"Oh! to-morrow night—I suppose you've got tools that'll do—use 'em for shoemaking, of course," ha! ha! ha!

"Yes! I've got the tools I'm thinking."

"Then that's all right. I suppose the old fellow has buried his tin, and we shall have to dig for it!"

And thus this worthy pair settled the affair for the ensuing night.

Charley was rather anxious that they should be successful, for he was at present in a state of insolvency, and this was a state our hero was not constituted to bear for any length of time.

It was now nearly five o'clock, and would soon be getting light, so our policemen, whom we left enjoying their pipes, once more returned to their respective "bates," as though they had been zealously w tching the safety of the public for the last hour or so, instead of gorging or guzzling one against the other.

Charley and Billy, although they had not made a night of it, as the saying is, had certainly "had their morning," and as our hero and snuffy had plenty of work before them when night came, they were of opinion that bed would be the best occupation for the day.

And to bed they went.

Charley slept until late in the day, and when he awoke felt quite refreshed and eager for night.

He got up and dressed, and after playing first knife and fork to a feed of the fair Patty's preparing, seated himself by Billy, and was soon enjoying a pipe with that respected maker of shoes.

Billy Mugford's thoughts were engrossed with the idea of the miser's gold, and, without any other prefatory remarks, commenced—

"How are we to get over that cursed wall, Charley? it's twelve or fourteen feet high."

"Over the wall! You don't think I'm going over that wall, do you? Because if you do you're very much mistaken, and I'm sorry for you," exclaimed Mr. Wag; I shall walk into the inn through the side entrance.

"But how will you get to the cellars?" suggested Billy,

"How do the people that they belong to get at 'em? You ought to know you've lived here long enough, Billy, eh? They goes down the stairs?."

"Yes! I suppose they do to get to a cellar," interrupted Mr. Wag.

Mr. Mugford laughed feebly at this sally, and continued—

"The doors is always open, or else how could the old women as attends to the rooms get at the coals when they're wanted?"

Mr. Wag seemed satisfied: for after the conclusion of Billy's remark he remained silent for some time, and then suddenly turning to his companion told him to get the things ready.

Billy did as he was desired, and Charley, putting on an Inverness cape, placed them under it and moved off, after having told Billy to follow him in a short time. It was now getting dusk, and Charley felt the necessity of taking up his position before it got later, when the door might be fastened.

He entered the gate without meeting a soul, and making straight for the house walked in as boldly as possible, and descended the stairs which led to the cellars.

He looked about him with the aid of his dark lantern and discovered one without anything in it—this was exactly suited for their hiding place as no one was likely to enter it.

He now waited anxiously for Billy's coming for without him he should be uncertain which had been the old miser's cellar.

He sat quietly awaiting the arrival of his snuffy little friend, whose low whistle he presently heard.

He turned the light of his lantern in the direction of the sound (the signal agreed upon) and Billy Mugford was by his side.

"We're all right," said Billy, "shall we have to stay here long before we commence?"

"Till midnight, I should think, the place will be quiet by that time."

"It's a deuce of a time though," growled Billy in an under tone, "so I shall take a nap." With this he curled himself up on an empty chest that happened to be near him and dosed.

Charley, meanwhile, sat and listened.

All was still, and he began to think that they might as well begin then as later.

It was now past ten o'clock and the task before them might prove a long one. Reasoning in this manner, Charley aroused Billy and told him that they would get to work immediately. This announcement had the effect of making the snuffy little fellow "shake off dull sloth," and, jumping to his feet, he exclaimed excitedly——

"What's the time though, Charley?"

"Oh! never mind that, the great thing is the place is quiet, so we ought to get to work while it is.

"I hope no one will come down here for coals while we're at it," said Billy, with some degree of trepidation in his manner.

"If they do, I shall treat them to some 'nubbly' bits on the head!"

"Well! that would be the best thing to do," acquiesced Mr. Mugford in a cold-blooded fashion; "and now I'll show you the cellar where I used to go to him with a light at night, if I can find it; it ought to be about here somewhere—opposite my place—I should say this was it," said Billy, spotting a solid looking door which seemed in better condition than the others, for it had a lock; and, although a lock would strike many of my readers as a very proper thing to have upon a cellar-door in which coals were kept, it was evident that the idea of a lock had only been carried out by one of the persons who had the use of these cellars.

"You may take yer davey it's here," whispered Foxey, "or else there wouldn't be a lock—there ain't none to the others."

Charley was of the same opinion, and in a trice had picked the lock and entered the cellar.

It was empty.

"I expected this," said Charley, seeing that Billy's face had rather a blank expression—"it's not likely he'd been so green as to leave it out here—it's buried;" as he said this, he kicked against a shovel which rather confirmed him in the idea; he stooped down, and then saw that the earth had been freshly turned up, near it and indeed all about it appeared to have been dug over.

"Damnation! that's a go! we sha'n't know which spot to commence at!" observed Billy, savagely.

Charley, although taken aback rather by finding the ground dug over in a manner which did not afford the slightest clue to what they were in search of, soon recovered his equanimity, and fixed upon what was best to be done.

"It's a good job we began early, for we shall have a regular hunt for the old ghost's swag," said Charley, taking up a shovel and beginning to dig at one corner. "You, Billy, take the other which the old gentleman so kindly left for us, and peg away at the next corner."

And at it they went.

After digging to the depth of several feet without discovering anything, Charley began to swear.

What he said I shall not repeat, but leaving the corner he had commenced at, he tried another.

Billy was growling away, over the hole he had made, in a discontented manner, when Charley said in an under tone—

"You take the other corner now—leave that—you've gone deep enough there for the present."

"All right," said Billy; "anything for a change," shifting his quarters to the corner of the cellar that had not been touched by them, and digging away there in a manner that threatened the foundation of the structure above them.

Charley was working steadily at the hole he had made, and had been rather disappointed on one or two occasions, when any obstacle came in the way of his spade, to find they were only brickbats.

At a time like the present they made him savage, as the ringing noise the spade made in coming in contact with them might lead to their discovery. He, therefore, felt for them cautiously, and removed them with his hand whenever he came across them.

In the like manner Billy was toiling away, only ceasing to stand upright, for not being quite so young as Mr. Wag, and subject to pains in his bones, it is not to be wondered at that on this occasion he should find his occupation rather trying to his back, and Billy found great relief in standing up straight, for then he could growl at their ill luck without difficulty; whereas, when digging, he could only engage in a faint and disjointed grumble' which was extremely annoying to Billy, who was, if anything rather in advance of his countryman in this national peculiarity.

Charley bore this severe trial of his patience like a martyr; for, if anything put him out, it was grumbling.

He, however, allowed Mr. Mugford to continue his irritating whine out of consideration for his years and infirmities—only warning him, now and then, when Billy's feelings caused him to growl in a louder key than was necessary.

In a short time, they had made four holes each big enough to bury a man in, when Charley proposed that they should work to the centre of the cellar from each corner.

"The old cock may have buried it in the middle after all, Billy!"

"Well! I hope he has, for my back's aching like the devil," growled the cross-grained little cobbler, in as quiet a tone as he could command under the circumstances.

Charley now commenced a trench crossing the cellar diagonally, and directed Billy to make a similar one.

This he did, and after digging until the whole of the ground was turned up, Mr. Charles hinted that the cobbler might have been mistaken as to this being the place where he had seen the old miser come out of at night.

Billy seemed struck with the probability of such being the case, and proposed they should immediately go to another of these cellars which was next to it.

"There was another one as we seed when we came in, but it's such a broken down looking place—and no lock on it—he wouldn't have been such a flat to leave his tin without a lock on the door."

"I don't know," replied Charley; "locks are not much of a protection."

"Not when some people's concerned!" said Billy, with a grin.

Charley silently gathered up the tools they had brought with them, and directed by Billy, moved towards the other cellars.

They entered one or two of them, and Charley found there nothing but—diamonds!—but they were black ones!

Making use of some very improper language, he turned from one door to another, and, at last, fixed upon one which was closed, and of a very mouldy exterior.

To enter was a work of some difficulty for, although the door was not locked, it had been fastened in a puzzling manner. This fact raised our hero's hopes and, with the assistance of Billy, who for a short time had ceased grumbling, prised it open, making as little noise as possible in doing it.

On entering, Mr. Charles' experience in smells upstairs, convinced him that they were now on the right scent—and a very nasty one it was too.

The filth in the rooms above could not be mentioned in the same breath with that which met their view when Charley turned his lantern upon it.

It must have been the dirty old wretch's custom to convey the heads and tails of the herrings, together with the other beastliness that we have already noticed, down here when the supply became more than he deemed necessary for the preservation of his floor-cloth.

This proceeding was not at all calculated to improve the atmosphere of the cellar, which was considerably smaller than the one in which they had been digging so unsuccessfully.

It was filthy.

On one side of it was a cat-trap, and in it a cat in a very advanced stage of putrefaction.

"This is not pleasant," thought Charley, as he put his foot on something soft which, to his horror, proved to be another cat already skinned and minus a couple of legs!

The old wretch had lived upon them! For on a stove stood a pot with the amputated limbs and a few potatoes in it half cooked!

"Ugh! what a disgusting old brute," said Charley.

"Ah! that'll account for the row the poor devils made when he cotched and skinned 'em, for I daresay he sold the skins—they're always better skinned alive," added Billy, in a confident tone, as though he had had some experience in that sort of thing himself at one time or other of his life.

"There! hold your jaw, or you'll make me sick," said Charley, "it's bad enough to be in this stinking hole, without your making it worse."

Billy was sillent.

"Now, let us get to work, or we shan't get at the swag to-night."

Charley had settled upon the spot in which the old miser must have buried his money, from the appearance of the ground which in this corner had been dug over within a day or two, and from which the filth had been removed.

To work he went, and after a good deal of labour he had got to a debth of about two feet, when he told Billy to take a spell. And Billy accordingly took a spell, but it was one of a short duration, for before long his back began to pain him again, and he was obliged to give in.

"There," said Charley, "let me come, you're not half a fellow!"

Billy murmured somthing inarticulately, and gave up the shovel to Mr. Wag, who went at the work with spirit and determination.

After turning up a few more spadesful he came in contact with something that offered resistance.

It was evidently a box.

He stooped down, directing Billy to hold the lantern, and cleared away the ground with his hands and discovered a box about eighteen inches square.

He removed the ground around it, and placing the spade underneath raised it.

It was about a foot deep and was very heavy.

Billy was so delighted that he could only look at the box, without attempting to hand Charley a chisel that he had asked him for several times without receiving any reply.

At last Billy spoke.

"Are you going to open it?" said he.

"Why, of course you don't think I'm going to walk off with a lot of rubbish perhaps!"

This idea had never entered Billy's head before, so he immediately handed Charley the chisel who forthwith undid the lid of the box.

It was the miser's gold!

And a good round sum there was.

Charley refastened the lid, and telling Billy to gather up the tools, prepared to move off when they heard footsteps coming in their direction.

As the consequences of detection would be anything but pleasant, our hero and Billy remained quite quiet, having darkened their lantern on hearing the first intimation of a visitor's approach.

It was fortunate for Billy, that on entering one cellar he had taken the precaution of placing a piece of crape in true burglar style over his face, and otherwise disguising his usual appearance, for the new-comer proved to be the porter with whom Billy was slightly acquainted.

This worthy fellow's curiosity had been excited by the extraordinary tales about the miser, added to which the fact of our hero on the previous night, having let himself out of his window had given rise to the idea in his mind that he might have walked off with his gold at the same time, or would do so at some future period.

But he little dreamt that if not already done, that the attempt would be made upon the following night, before the excitement caused by the attempt to murder Mr. Leech, had worn off.

It was on the strength of this notion and a feeling of intense curiosity that made Mr. Garnell pay this visit to the miser's cellar.

It was simply to see if the gold was gone.

He had satisfied himself that it was not in the old man's room into which they had broken in pursuit of Charley, and the next likely place was his cellar.

And on this night down he came.

He had a lamp in his hand by the light of which he could be plainly seen as he stopped for a few moments examining the various doors.

Billy recognised him, and was rather frightened.

Charley said nothing as the porter approached, but waiting until he was near enough, sprang at him, and bore him to the ground, placing his handkerchief over his mouth.

THE LIEUTENANT IN DIFFICULTIES.

This attack was so sudden and unexpected, that the poor fellow had not time to sing out.

It might have fared badly with him had he done so.

As it was, Billy in the most blood-thirsty manner, suggested in a whisper to Charley.

"Hadn't we better tap him on the head—he can't tell any tales then."

But Charley didn't see the necessity for this extreme measure—so taking a piece of the rope they had brought with them, he securely bound the unfortunate porter hand and foot, at the same time warning him, that if he gave any alarm or information his life would pay forfeit.

Then closing the door of the cellar they made their way into the court.

No. 56.

Charley's plan was to get over the wall himself and make Billy lower the box down to him.

And this he did.

Billy contrived to drop from the wall in a manner which did him infinite credit, and elicited a low "bravo" from Master Charley, who now felt very jolly, and determined to "make a night of it," as the saying is.

Having arrived at this conclusion, and the door of Mugford's house simultaneously—they entered.

<hr>

LXXXI.—LUCINDA AGAIN.

THE vicissitudes of Lucinda's life had done much to remove the sentimental and

[CHARLEY WAG, THE NEW JACK SHEPPARD.]

romantic turn of that young lady's mind.

She was now a sensible girl, with a pretty face and facinating manners.

As we already know she was not an affectionate girl.

Frank Norton, who had made the greatest impression upon her, that she was capable of feeling, was now dead, and although she bewailed his loss in a very decorous fashion she did not allow her grief to interfere with her arrangements for the future.

She resolved to remain where she was for a short time, and to give lessons in singing, an accomplishment she was rather great at.

She was not without money, for Frank had supplied her liberally, beside giving into her charge the key of his desk the evening before the duel.

In this desk she found a hundred pounds and an affectionate little note from him, requesting her to use it in event of anything happening to him.

This additional mark of his kindness caused Lucinda's tears to flow afresh, but soon drying them she went out with a view of obtaining a piano on hire, which would enable her to carry her scheme of teaching the young idea how to sing into operation.

Having ordered one, she also requested the proprietor of pianos to place an advertisement for her in his shop, and gave her name as 'Linley,' with "Mrs." affixed.

Her reason for pretending to be a married woman was rather a good one.

This was the name that Norton had asumed on taking the apartments, and of course Lucinda had been Mrs. Linley *pro. tem.*

For some days she heard nothing of pupils, and in the innermost recesses of her heart she hoped she might not at all—when to her dismay a pupil appeared.

This was a long, lanky, bony girl, accompanied by her mother, to whom she bore a surprising likeness.

Lucinda received them courtiously enough, stated her terms, which were approved of, and an engagement was entered into to teach the "bony one" singing.

Wearily passed the days spent in attempting to make this *she* raven croak melodiously.

Lucinda was bored to death, and one day after feeling more than usually, disgusted with the step she had taken, wrote a polite note to the young lady's mamma, declining to give any more lessons, sent back her piano and prepared for a journey to London.

And what was she going to do there? you will say.

She did not know herself.

She only felt that she would change, and like many other obstinate young ladies—she would have it.

And have it she did.

The town in which she had been staying was not many miles from London, and the railway station was only a few minutes walk from the house.

Had this station been some miles off, perhaps she would not have taken it into her head to go to the great city—but with the trains passing several times in the day, the temptation was too much for her to withstand.

And she gave into it.

Having packed her luggage (and she had a pretty considerable quantity, for which poor Frank had suffered), she paid for her lodgings and took her departure in a fly for the railway station.

Here she took a ticket for London.

In a few moments the train came up, and Lucinda took her seat in a carriage, in which sat a gentleman, he was a good-looking young fellow, in the undress uniform of a naval officer.

They were soon engaged in an animated conversation—in the course of which he told her that he had lately returned from China, and had come up from Portsmouth about his promotion.

Lucinda liked the look of this jolly Jack Tar—some of the startling romances she had read contained the wonderful adventures of naval men—and she could not refrain from asking this young " Salt" whether he had had many adventures during his naval career.

"Oh! yes! some wonderful escapes!" he replied, delighted at having an opportunity of "spinning a twister" to so fair a listener.

"On one occason I was sent with a party to attack some forts at Ching-ran-whung. You might have seen the picture in the Illustrated News and after getting close under them we were going to land, not seeing any of the enemy, when a masked battery opened upon it, and sank the boat I was in command of. We were all struggling in the water, and two of the men could not swim.

I took them both in tow and swam to the ship, a distance of five miles!

"You must be a good swimmer, said Lucinda.

"Well! I am a pretty fair one, considering."

"I suppose you have been able to save a good many lives through it," suggested Lucinda, inquiringly.

"Yes! I have a few—but the most curious thing that ever happened to me in the way of saving a man's life was when I was a midshipman on board the 'Grumpy' screw corvette."

"Some of the hands had been sent out on the flying-jib-boom to stow the sail—the wind was on the quarter, and we were going through the water at the rate of twelve knots an hour —when one of these men missed his footing and fell. I was on the quarter deck at the time when I heard the cry of 'a man overboard,' and I immediately jumped down into the starboard main chains—luckily on the side the man passed—and, notwithstanding the rate the ship was going, I caught him by the hair! You'd hardly believe it!"

"Dear me," said Lucinda, "how very fortunate!"

And thus this son of Neptune rattled on, amusing her with his exploits, the majority of which were like the one already related, of *rather* an impossible character.

After a very pleasant journey they reached London, and here the sucking Nelson insisted upon escorting her to her destination.

She was rather "taken aback" at his proposal, as she had not as yet fixed upon any home.

The only one she knew was the one at which Mr. Leech and she had stayed, and she did not feel inclined to go there.

She told her companion that she was going to an hotel, but did not know of any quiet one.

"Oh! if that's all, there's one in Norfolk Street, in the Strand. Shall I tell the cabman to drive there?" said he.

Lucinda offered no objection; so, having told cabby, he jumped in himself, and they rattled over the stones towards Norfolk Street.

It was about six o'clock when they left the terminus.

It was raining violently, and the streets wore a deserted and miserable look.

This was not calculated to raise Lucinda's spirits, which were now at rather a low ebb, and had it not been for the incessant chatter of her companion, she would have indulged in a "good cry.

It would have done her good, but she felt that she must postpone the pleasure till she retired to rest at night.

The cab drew up at the hotel, and this amiable sea-monster was profuse in his polite attentions to her. After seeing her comfortably located he took his departure, but not before having requested permission to call and see her during his stay in town.

This Lucinda readily accorded, and her nautical friend went off in a state of happiness easier to be imagined than described.

A frolicsome youth was this—his name was Horatio Spanker Duffy, a junior lieutenant in the navy.

His father was a retired something who had settled in the country, when, by some means or other, he had a good deal to do with electioneering matters.

Chance threw him in the way of Captain Spanker just before the birth of a child—it turned out a boy—and was christened Horatio Spanker.

Horatio, after the immortal Nelson—and Spanker, of the captain of that name.

The captain and Mr. Duffy had dealings together—dealings about votes—which proved so satisfactory to Captain Spanker that one day over their port (they were both fond of it), he (the captain) said:—

"Duffy! my boy, when young 'shiver the mizen' is old enough, he shall have a cadetship in the navy! He shall by G——, if Jack Spanker's alive!"

Jack Spanker did live, and, what is more, lived to be an admiral.

As the youthful Duffy grew, he became a great favourite with the old admiral, who used to "tip" him whenever he visited him during the holidays.

When he was eleven he placed him at a celebrated school at Portsmouth, from which young gentlemen invariably pass, and in a short time he was a naval cadet on board the "Grumpy."

Horatio Spanker Duffy had remained in the service ever since, and had now received his promotion through the influence of the old admiral.

And to the admiral, who lived in one of the swell squares, he was going to pay a short visit, his exchequer being in a low state.

Lucinda, after he left, indulged in her own reflections and dinner, winding up with the "good cry" she was longing for in the sanctity of her own room.

After this she went to bed, and enjoyed a good night's rest.

The next morning she arose refreshed in mind and body.

She did justice to a very excellent breakfast, and had hardly finished it when Horatio Spanker Duffy made his appearance, smiling all over his face.

"Good morning, Mrs. Linley," he began rather awkwardly, "I fear I am intruding."

And indeed it was rather soon to pay his visit; but then consider his feelings!

Lucinda, however, did not think him intruding—in fact she was rather pleased to see him.

"Not at all," said she, "I'm delighted to see you. Had it not been for your kindness yesterday I should not have found such a comfortable hotel."

Mr. Duffy mumbled something to the effect that he was "delighted at being of service, &c."

Lucinda asked him if he had breakfasted.

He thanked her, and replied that he had, some time ago; and then with a mighty effort, and with astonishment at his own presumption, he asked her if she had any engagement for that day!

(He had paid a visit to the old admiral on the previous evening, and strongly hinted that his purse was low. The good-natured old fellow, who had been a bit of a rake in his own day, saw the state of the case in less time than you could say "luff," and came down pretty handsomely.)

This so elated Horatio that he resolved to pay a visit to his fair travelling companion at once, so, hailing a Hansom, he was off to his god-father's bankers, cashed his cheque, and from thence drove to Norfolk Street, and found Lucinda, as we have just described, sitting over a very late breakfast.

Being in funds, our nautical man was bold, and pressed his inquiry relative to Lucinda's engagements for the day.

Had she been a very strait-laced young lady she might have questioned the propriety of his inquiry, and of her answering it.

But she was not.

She told him that she had not any engagements—that her time was her own.

And then this audacious fellow absolutely asked if she would honour him with her company to an opera concert at the Crystal Palace?

"I have a couple of tickets, and should be delighted if you would go," said this wily tempter, in his most persuasive tones.

"I shall be very happy to accept your offer, for I have never seen the Palace, and I hear the grounds are very beautiful," said Lucinda. "At what time do you think of starting?"

"Well! I have to go to my rooms in Jermyn Street first. I will be back here in an hour—will that suit you?"

"Oh! yes," said Lucinda, "any time will suit me."

And this happy youth jumped into the Hansom which he had kept waiting, regardless of expense, and bowled away to his rooms in

Jermyn Street, where he was soon occupied in getting himself up to a greater extent than he was at present.

Having attired himself to his own satisfaction, he sent for a cab—this time a fourwheeler—and returned to Norfolk Street within the hour.

He found Lucinda awaiting him.

She was very handsomely dressed, and looked very beautiful.

Altogether, she turned out in first-rate condition, and Horatio thought so, as he caught a glimpse of her pretty little feet, which were encased in natty boots, and terminated a pair of plump but exquisitely formed legs.

All this he saw as she was getting into the cab.

And then he told the cabman to drive to the London Bridge Terminus, and in less than twenty minutes they were there.

They fortunately found that a train was about to start, and, taking tickets and seats, they were soon whirling towards Sydenham.

They arrived at the Palace in time for the commencement of the concert, in which Lucinda heard, for the first time in her life, some of our first-rate singers.

She was in raptures, and again and again thanked Horatio for bringing her to such a delightful place.

Then they walked through the courts, the Egyptian Pompeian, and all the other courts, Horatio, in the meanwhile, treating her to the most wonderful descriptions of every thing in them.

And then they rested in the Alhambra.

Here Lucinda's ecstacies knew no bounds, and Horatio (knowing dog) knew that he had done the correct thing in proposing the Crystal Palace.

After resting here some time Horatio looked at his watch, and found that it was nearly dinner-time, and then, linking her again in his, piloted her to the Terrace dining rooms.

Here this youth regaled her with a repast that must have shaken his purse not a little, if we may judge by the wine they both put away.

Champagne was rather a novelty to Lucinda and she certainly thought it was THE tipple.

She did not vulgerly express her feelings in words, but was contented to do so by deeds.

She *did* drink several glasses of champagne and became very merry.

It has this effect on young ladies sometimes.

Horatio proposed a walk through the grounds and Lucinda feeling so happy that she could do anything, agreed—

And in these beautiful grounds they strolled about until it got very late, so late that they only had time to save the last train and then had the utmost difficulty to get seats.

It was a splendid night, very dry and the moon shining brightly, and on alighting at London Bridge, Lucinda who was in high spirits suggested walking to Norfolk Street.

Horatio did'nt much like the idea, he would have preferred a cab on this occasion but a lady's will, was law to him at times,

And as this chanced to be one of the times in which he acknowledged the supremacy of womans will, her proposal met with his ungratified approbation.

So they walked from the Terminus to the Hotel.

And here, as it was rather late, Lucinda wished Horatio good night, positively "hoping to see him to morrow.

Horatio promised to do so.

Indeed it was his intention to see her every day during his stay in town.

And then this naughty young man went off to supper—supper in the Haymarket!

Into Scott's—did Horatio Spanker Duffy go and here his generous nature prompted him to stand glasses of wine to several, and supper to one of the young ladies there assembled.

At what time he reached Jermyn Street, on the following morning, I haven't the slightest idea.

I suppose it was after the milk by several hours.

But this I know, he went in for large doses of soda water dashed with brandy, on his return before he ventured to make his appearance in Norfolk Street.

It was nearly two before he got there, and Lucinda who had felt rather seedy from the effects of the wine bibbing of the previous day, was doing the lazy on a lounge, in which she lay half buried, in the cushions, when he entered the room.

She greeted Horatio warmly, and expressed the pleasure she felt at seeing him again.

" But you are late to day "? said she.

Horatio was about to account for it, when Lucinda, who then noticed the state of his complexion added before he had time to speak.

" How very pale you are! are you ill?"

" Oh! dear no! never was better in my life" replied Mr. Duffy in a very feeble fashion.

" You certainly are unwell " proceeded Lucinda, let me get you some brandy. "

" Duffy did not refuse. "

He thought that this was about the best medicine for his complaint and took three glasses one after the other, much to the astonishment of the waiter, who looked at him—but said nothing.

" What the devil are you staring at ? exclaimed the redoubtable Duffy,

" Beg pardon Sir! nothing at all Sir! said the waiter leaving the room.

Horatio turned to Lucinda, who looked rather surprised at his speaking so sharply to the unfortunate waiter, and in an explanatary manner remarked.

"You can have no conception, My dear Mrs. Linley, of the difficulty we gentlemen have in preventing these waiters from being impertinent "

Lucinda who knew nothing of this difficulty—very properly said.

" I daresay "

Horatio to his own satisfaction accounted for his little display of irritability to the waiter he essayed to account for his slight indisposition and here the three glasses did good service for they restored him to his wanted vigour, and in his usual spirited style he began:—

I have never been right since I had the fever and ague in China, I took it soon after the attack on the fools at Ching-rang-whung, when

I was in the water so long, and saved the three men that could'nt swim I think, I told you.'

"Three men!" said Lucinda.

"Yes! three!

I thought you said two.

"Well, I ought only to say two for the third man after sinking twice caught hold of my pea-jacket—I had it on at the time—and so saved himself."

"I think it was the water that did it."

"Did what?" innocently enquired Lucinda.

"Gave me the fever and ague, my dear Mrs. Linley, and I can assure you when ever I go home into Essex I have an attack which lasts for days."

"You have been there lately?"

"Yes, and I don't think I shall go again in a hurry—its precious slow there—now I like something exciting—something to call forth our energies! Now I should like a war with France."

"Oh! I should prefer peace instead of the horrid war you wish for," said Lucinda.

"Ah! but, my dear Mrs. Linley, if you were in the navy you'd think differently, and be delighted when a war did break out—I long for it, and then let them but give me the opportunity, and I will undertake to destroy 'La Gloire,' and all the other iron cased vessels of the French navy!"

"But, how?"

"Well! you will excuse me, my dear Mrs. Linley, when I tell you that I cannot divulge my plan, although my regard for you would induce me to do almost anything."

Lucinda blushed, and said.

"I beg pardon for asking—it was very rude of me.

"Not at all! I should be delighted to tell you, but really the fact is—and——

The great Duffy feeling rather foggy as to the excuse he should make for not explaining his system, determined to take advantage of it, and to impress Lucinda with the regard he had for her by entrusting her with his plan for annihilating the iron clad vessels of our neighbours, should occasion require it,

To tell the honest truth, Master Duffy had no royal road which would lead to the destruction of these celebrated novelties, whether he was up in the subject or not, but he was like many other youths, he liked to talk—to talk largely, but only to those who was totally ignorant on what he was speaking.

And certainly on the subject of iron-clad ships, Horatio Spanker Duffy, although a lieutenant in her Majesty's navy, was no where at all!

But then Lucinda knew less—infact she had not heard of them.

A fine chance was before Mr. Duffy, and he had settled himself in an easy-chair opposite his fair companion's sofa, preparatory to commencing the explanation, when a long drawn breath from that young lady caused him to pause before doing so.

That young lady had fallen asleep!

And through this occurrance the British public were deprived the benefit of hearing Mr. Duffy's scheme, as explained by himself.

"Well! may I be scuttled!" said he, "here's a space. By Jove, I'll go to sleep myself!"

And curling himself in the chair, he now slept soundly.

His rest had been disturbed the night before, so it is not to be wondered at, and poor Lucinda's jaunt to the Palace had had a powerful effect upon her.

She too, slept well, and they snored harmoniously.

Their siesta was a long one, and it was four o'clock when Lucinda awoke, and then her astonishment was great at beholding Horatio seated in the chair close to her, and snoring like—pork,

She did not disturb him, but retired to her bed-room for a short time to arrange her tumbled appearance before he should awake.

After having "arranged" herself in a very becoming manner, she entered the sitting-room, and it would almost seem intentionally, knocked over a chair which made a crack that caused poor Horatio to jump up with a start.

Lucinda had picked up the chair and seated herself in her lounge, before the unfortunate could tell where he was or what he was doing.

When after a stretch and a yawn the reality of his position dawned upon him, he felt very much confused, for Lucinda did not look at all as though she had been dosing, while he knew that he looked awfully wretched.

He was profuse in his apologies, and the fair lady to whom he made them was too wide-awake by this time to recall the fact of her having been asleep herself.

The nap had done him good, and although his hair did want brushing and his whiskers combing out, still he looked almost himself again and certainly felt so.

And this being the case he began to talk.

"Have you been to see the Colleen Bawn?" said he.

"Yes! I went the last time that it was performed, and was very much delighted with it—it is well worth going to—have you seen it?"

"No!" he replied, "I had engaged tickets for to-night, but as you have already seen it, I don't care about going."

"Oh! pray don't let me hinder you!"

"Would you think it too great an infliction to see it again?"

"On the contrary, I think it is well worth seeing a second time."

"And you will go?"

"With pleasure."

"Then I'll be off," said Mr. Duffy, in great glee, "and will call for you about seven."

Lucinda once more left to herself, hurried herself in selecting a suitable dress from her extensive wardrobe for going to the theatre in the evening.

She soon fixed upon one, and was not long before she was deep in the mysteries of the laces, ribbons, &c., necessary to a young lady's existence.

The dress she had selected was one that she used to wear on red-letter days, during the latter part of the time she was at school.

But since that happy time, Lucinda had grown perhaps not in length much, but certainly a trifle in width.

The skirt fitted her to a nicety, but the body notwithstanding the tremendous efforts of a chamber-maid summoned to her assistance at this trying moment, obstinately refused to meet round her plump form.

Then came the work of alteration—letting out a seam here and putting in a gore there, but all to no purpose, for what fair lady can endure an altered dress?

I never met with one in the whole course of my experience.

The "horrid thing" was always thrown aside and of course Mamma suggested the property of the girls having new ones, they looked perfectly disgraceful in the shabby things they had worn for ages! In this way papas are victimized

With the young married ladies it is different they watch their oppotunity and plead the dress cause at a time when their most extravagant requisites are irrisistable, for they are perfectly aware that there are times when the dear partner of their affections is lost to all sense of economy nor deigns to think of the little accounts in that invariably follows any weakness of this kind.

Unfortunately, for Lucinda she had neither a bullied papa, nor a loving husband to provide the substitute for the dress she was vastly endeavouring to alter, to suit her full blown figure.

She stamped, and would have sworn, had it been usual for ladies to do so, and then throwing down the offending garment burst into tears—tears of passion!

Now this was wrong I admit, but I am sure that her sympathising sex will make every excuse for her doing so.

It was very trying—the only dress she could wear as she thought would not fit her!

Troubles never come singly,—the dress question was not the only obsticle—she had no opera cloak!

And how could she do without one?

Poor Frank Norton had by some oversight omitted this elegant addition to her wardrobe —The little town in which they resided did not boast of a Theatre or in all human probability, Lucinda would have been the happy possessor of this absolute necessary.

And in a moment she resolved upon getting one.

With an opera cloak she could hide, the little defect in the body of her dress well enough—She would have one.

And without more ado she had a cab sent for and jumping into it, ordered the driver to St. Pauls Church-yard, and to make haste.

Thither he went making his wretched steed go over the stones at his usual jog trot pace and obtaining an extra shilling from Lucinda, for fast driving.

She alighted at one of those shops where "an awful sacrifice," and "less than prime cost!" was pretty lavishly pasted up.

Here she had seen opera cloaks on many occasions, but the idea of purchasing one had never entered her head until this day, and now she stood before the very shop window intent upon doing so.

And in this window she saw them marked at fabulously low prices. "The Fashion, 13s. 9d."—"Elegant, 15s. 7d."—and "Real Cashmere was only 19s. 11d."

Lucinda gazed at them, and speculated upon the one she should have, when a tall "counter skipper" came out to her, and, handing her a

"tract" on his establishment, inquired what he could have the honour of doing for her, and begging her to enter the shop and inspect their stock.

Lucinda entered, and was immediately pounced upon by a legion of zealous assistants, each bearing a roll of something, and chattering like so many magpies.

She at once stated her wants, and then the tall counter skipper shouted to a myrmidon!

"Opera cloaks!"

Away sprang the individual addressed, and from the back of the premises appeared staggering under a heap of these elegant articles of female attire.

And then he spread them out temptingly before his victim.

"Beautiful article, madam," said the tall wretch (and the lesser ruffian echoed his words), "Beautiful article, madam, feel the quality. This article we can sell you at 28s. I can assure you we make no profit on it!"

Lucinda turned them over, but did not see one she liked so well as one in the window, and expressed a wish to see it. "It is marked up at 18s. 9d." said she.

"A very inferior article, madam, or we should not place it in the window! Allow me to show you some others we have fresh from Paris."

Lucinda declined, and in a firm tone requested to be shown the one she mentioned or none at all.

The tall shopman glared savagely at the unoffending assistant, who quailed before him. Then, turning, said blandily,

"We shall have to disarrange the window entirely, madam."

Lucinda did not seem to see that it was any concern of hers, and the wretched assistant was detached upon this service.

During his absence Lucinda looked round the shop, and saw various articles that arrested her attention.

Among others there were dresses—skirts I should say—but my fair lady readers will excuse my ignorance, as I have not had much experience in these matters.

Skirts for evening wear were placarded at 14s. 11d. ready to put on!

This was the very thing to suit her, for she had not the slightest inclination to sit with her cloak over her shoulders—which were very pretty—all the evening, on account of that horrid body which did not fit her.

One of the knights of the counter saw her eyes resting on these dresses, and in a trice a large number of them were displayed before her.

She admired them very much, but then how about the body?

I suppose shopmen divine the thoughts of customers, for this one seemed to do so, and I have met with others during a "shopping" excursion with ladies, who seemed to be gifted in a similar manner.

"We can make up the body immediately, madam," said he.

"But how long would you take to do it?"

"We can send it home in an hour."

Lucinda was enchanted, and selected one

which, instead of it being 14s. 11d. as it was marked, turned out to be a pound.

Being determined to have it, she did not haggle at the price, and was forthwith handed over to the care of a young lady who was seated in a little room at the back of the shop.

This young lady having taken our fair friend's dimensions, and promised that the dress should be sent home in time, Lucinda returned to the counter where the tall counter skipper was standing, with the opera cloak she had chosen before him.

"We are very sorry, madam," commenced this buyer up of bankrupt stock, "we are very sorry, but by some mistake this cloak has been wrongly ticketed; it should have been 22s., but in consideration of your having purchased other articles, and as it was entirely our fault, we shall say 20s. It is a loss to us, indeed, madam."

"Allow me to send it with the dress."

Lucinda declined, and one of the "young men" was desired to fetch a cab, which bowled her back to Norfolk Street, where she fortified herself with dinner.

This over, she retired to her bedroom, to try on the dress which had been sent home during dinner.

It was getting late, and she had to be ready by seven, so she commenced the operations of her toilet at once.

She did not take longer over it than most young ladies do, and when Horatio arrived, she entered the room fully accoutred.

Her dress fitted her to a nicety, and showed her figure to the greatest advantage.

Horatio, who was looking considerably better than he did in the morning, was in high spirits.

"Do you know, my dear Mrs. Linley, I feel so awfully jolly I could do almost anything!" said he, placing Lucinda's cloak, a scarlet one with a white hood and tassal, over her snowy shoulders. "How well you look to-night."

"Do I?" innocently inquired Lucinda, who knew very well that she did. "I'm glad you think so."

Then, with her arm in his, he escorted her down stairs, and into the cab that was waiting for them.

And off they went, rattling down the Strand in great style.

Reaching the theatre, they found an immense crowd assembled, and it was not without some difficulty that they made their way to the stalls, for which Horatio had taken tickets.

Lucinda had never been in such grand state to a theatre before, and felt immensely grand herself.

When she went with Leech it was only to the boxes, and now she felt a proper contempt for the respectable people she saw occupying them.

After the first piece, and between the acts, Lucinda found amusement in looking about the house, which was thronged.

Her good looks soon attracted the attention of many of the gentlemen portion of the audience in her vicinity, and a fair sprinkling of glasses were pointed at her.

She felt rather confused at this, but was certainly not displeased—she knew she was being admired—and where is the woman that objects to it?

Horatio noticed the attention she was exciting, and mentioned it to her, but she replied "Nonsense."

"Indeed you are though," said he, "look at that young gentleman in the stage box, he has evidently lost his heart."

Lucinda had seen him, and thought him very handsome, but did not say so to Horatio, whom she now thought positively plain.

This young gentleman, who had been looking at Lucinda from the moment of her entering the theatre, was standing at the side of the box, and leaning against one of the pillars.

He was tall and slight, with delicately formed features, had light hair and a budding moustache, and altogether a very aristocratic and superior animal.

Lucinda thought him the handsomest creature she had ever seen, and at the same time thought the poor lieutenant at her side the ugliest.

Now this was not kind, for the good natured tar had been particularly civil to her; but then ladies are very fickle, and Lucinda was certainly no exception to this rule.

She gave poor Horatio cuit answers to his remarks, and sometimes when he addressed her, was so intent upon her admiration of the youth in the stage box, that she did not notice him, and would frequently say "yes" or "no" at a time when the question required an elaborate answer.

Duffy felt wrath, but controlled his temper, and secretly vowed that if that young gentleman came "athwart his house" as they left the theatre, he would tread upon his toes to say the very least.

"How do you like the Colleen Bawn," ventured he, with a great struggle for coolness, after having asked Lucinda, who was occupied in thinking of this handsome young party, the question three times without getting a reply.

Again he asked it, and his fair companion replied snappishly

"I've seen it before."

Here was a shut up for our son of Neptune, who longed for the conclusion of the piece, that they might go, and he might find some pretext for attacking this unsuspecting youth.

At last it was over, and they rose to depart. Horatio felt fierce and anxious to be out, and Lucinda felt a regret at leaving.

On their way through the crush she saw the object of her admiration standing near them, and looking at her with all the intensity of devotion.

He had evidently waited for them, for when he saw them pass he followed quietly.

Lucinda was delighted, and Horatio, on whom his movement was not lost, was rather pleased than otherwise.

He should be able to get him outside as he thought—it would not do to kick up a shine in the theatre.

With this cold-blooded resolve he moved towards the door, and, as luck would have it, not a man could be seen to get a cab.

It usually happens that there are too many

of these fellows about the theatre, but on this occasion not one was to be seen.

Fate had decreed it.

Horatio saw there was no help for it, and had to go himself. He did so, notwithstanding the proximity of Lucinda's youthful admirer.

During his absence in search of the cab, Lucinda remained under the portico awaiting his return.

While doing so, by some means or other her cloak got adrift, and fell off, and the youth, who was now close at hand, sprang forward, and, picking it up, placed it on her pretty shoulders.

She could only thank him with her eyes, which were very expressive, for utterance at the moment seemed impossible.

The youth made some common-place remark, and Lucinda managed to reply to it.

This led to other remarks, which were being exchanged when Horatio returned with a cab.

He was furious, and, striding up to Lucinda, pushed rudely against the delicate-looking youth, making some insulting remark in doing so.

This fragile-looking creature, much to his astonishment, shot out with his right, and Master Duffy was sprawling!

Lucinda, of course, screamed, but not until the prostrate Duffy had arisen, and prepared to do battle against this young stranger, who seemed to be very confident, and, from the attitude he struck, appeared to be a master of the noble art of self-defence.

Horatio, although a pretty good bruiser found that he had plenty to do with this active youth, who kept skipping about and delivering his blows with marvellous rapidity much to the annoyance of his opponent, whose intended vengeance did not seem in a fair way of being wreaked.

The affray did not last long, for just as Horatio was putting himself together after a smart tap upon the noise, followed by another between the eyes, which had caused him to see a greater number of stars, than one usually observes in the heavens on a frosty night, and was collecting his energies, preparitory to administering a blow which might have done his youthful adversary some grievous bodily harm, a member of the A division seized him —he had seen him in the act of striking, or about to strike a blow, and therefore took him into custody.

In vain he protested against this proceeding; the officer was inflexible—so flagrant a breach of the public peace could not pass unnoticed and unpunished.

The youngster in the meanwhile was delighted at seeing the wretched Horatio hurried away in the vice-like grasp of the unyielding constable, who seemed to have forgotten that there were two persons concerned in this breach of the peace.

Lucinda stood by and saw Horatio dragged away without saying a word to comfort him— in fact she looked very severely at him.

When he had been fairly taken off the youthful Adonis, who was now coolly drawing on his gloves in a most unconcerned fashion, and looking nothing the worse for his late encounter—approached her, and in the most respectful manner enquired if he could be of any service to her.

"If I might trespass on your kindness to procure me a cab," said Lucinda, in her sweetest accents.

Away bounded the delighted youth to do her bidding, and in two minutes returned with the cab.

"May I have the honor of escording you home"? ventured he

Lucinda blushed, and thanked him for offering, but replied that she lived close at hand.

This announcement did not seem a refusal, and handing Lucinda in, this presumtuous boy, after enquiring where to direct the driver, seated himself in the cab with her!

The fair lady did not seem at all offended, and the boy grew bolder.

"I must apologise for behaving so before you this evening my dear madame, but really your friend treated me rather roughly"

Lucinda agreed that his conduct was infamous, and that she was heartily sorry that anything of the sort should have occured.

The fact is she was not at all sorry.

The arbiture of this evening had amused her, although for a short time only a most agreeable companion.

She was dying to know his name, and who he was, but how to find out she knew not.

She found that even now she should know nothing more about him, and perhaps might not see him again.

As they neared Norfolk Street, she asked him what he thought Mr. Duffy would be done to.

"Oh! nothing at all" he replied, pay a fine and be sent about his business—but if you will allow me I will go to the police court to-night and do myself the pleasure of calling on you in the morning with whatever information I may get"

This was precisely what Miss Lucinda was driving at, so thanking him for his kindness she gave him her name with an intimation that she should expect him in the morning.

The cab drawing up at the Hotel they alighted and she wished her young companion good night.

And then she hurried to her room and surveyed herself in the looking-glass,

She did look very charming and she knew it, and felt convinced that she had made a conquest of this handsome youth.

And flinging herself into an easy-chair, she wondered who he was—and what was his name, and then she thought of his politeness— so different to Horatio, who, although a very civil, good-looking, good-natured fellow, could not be compared to this elegant young stranger.

And thus she ran on puzzling herself about this youth, till at last she felt sleepy, and as the chair was very comfortable, she went to sleep, and, then she dreamt of him—she saw him fighting with Horatio—saw the blood streaming from his face—then he was lying fainting in her arms, and she was upbraiding Horatio with his cruelty, and that monster revenged himself upon her, by exposing her

IN THE PARK.

partially undressed to the inclemency of the night.

This unheard of piece of barbarity had the effect of waking Miss Lucinda, who discovered that she was very cold, and that her opera cloak had slipped off, and her shoulders were bare.

She undressed as quickly as possible and jumped into bed, where she felt infinitely better than she did on awaking after her sleep in the chair.

To get to sleep after her long snooze was no easy matter, and she remained awake for some hours, still thinking of her boyish admirer. Sleep at last wooed and won her eyelids, and Lucinda was once more in the land of dreams.

LXXXII.—QUOD STREET—A MORNING CALL FROM A SON OF MARS.

AFTER leaving Lucinda, young hopeful made the cabman who took them to Norfolk Street drive to the Quod Street police station.

Here he inquired for a gentleman who was charged with fighting at the Adelphi Theatre during the evening, and was shown by the Inspector, who thought he had come to bail the prisoner out, into a room in which he was sitting, looking very crestfallen.

"What the devil do you do here?" shouted Horatio, who looked very much inclined to renew the attack.

No. 57.

[CHARLEY WAG, THE NEW JACK SHEPPARD.]

"Well! the fact is my good fellow, I came here to see what they were going to do with you," said the youngster.

"The devil, you did!"

"Yes! I was rather curious myself, besides which your friend Mrs. Linley wanted to know, and I promised to call and tell her in the morning."

Horatio muttered something which could not well be heard by the other. I am inclined to think it was very improper language that he made use of—then added in a louder key, with a dash of a growl in it,

"I shall be bailed out presently, and can tell her myself."

"Oh! pray don't trouble yourself—I shall be most happy to call on her with the news," said this cool hand—"and now as the Inspector has told me that you'll only be fined, and will not be transported for life for your offence, I'll wish you good night."

"Damn his impudence," said Horatio, when he had left the room; "If this doesn't top everything I've been shipmates with I don't know what does,"

And yet Horatio did not feel so wrath against his rival as he had previously to this visit.

He rather admired him now, and thought he should like to make his acquaintance.

While he was thinking of the unpleasant events of the evening, the friend arrived that he had written to to bail him out.

They went off together, supper was proposed, and they shipped their course to the only likely spot to get anything to eat at that time of the night, or rather morning—the Haymarket.

Here Master Duffy soon forgot that he was only a prisoner on parole, and enjoyed himself as well as any free man could.

After leaving Scott's, Duffy proposed coffee, and into a cafe they went, and here seated, enjoying his weed and sipping his coffee, was the redoubtable youngster that had given him so much trouble a few hours previously.

They recognized each other at once, and Horatio, whose wrath had now entirely departed, involuntarily put out his hand, which was grasped in a most cordial manner by the other, who said,

"Glad to see you out again, old fellow! vile places to sleep in those station-houses—I've tried them myself once or twice."

"Yes! devilish glad to get away," said Horatio, "good joke my being taken off after getting such a lacing up as you gave me."

"Well, I hope I haven't damaged you much."

"Oh! not at all, I think it did me good."

"Ha! ha! ha! there's no accounting for taste, but my idea on *that* subject is "that it is more blessed to give than to receive.""

They rattled on in this style till the small hours were getting larger, and then they separated, but not before exchanging cards, but this was with a view to a friendly and not a hostile meeting.

Horatio was delighted with his new acquaintance, and the new acquaintance certainly thought that he had met with many worse fellows than Horatio Spanker Duffy.

Duffy felt exceedingly small when his thoughts reverted to Mrs. Linley; she was so manifestly displeased at his conduct, that the very idea of it made him hesitate whether he should call in Norfolk Street again.

At least he would not for a day or two, and perhaps not until he was going to leave town to join his ship at Portsmouth.

The other young gentleman's reflections were of a different order, he saw plainly that he had made an impression on pretty Mrs. Linley, and he intended to make the best of it.

With this resolve the young dog on the following morning rattled down Norfolk Street in his own cab, with the tiniest little tiger behind that could be warranted to hold on.

His advent created quite a sensation with the waiters, for they twigged in a moment that he was a tip-top swell.

Lucinda had risen early; after bestowing more than ordinary care upon her toilet she had breakfasted, and was now reclining in an easy chair, indulging in day-dreams. She was beginning to feel romantic again, and this youth was the hero of every thought.

At one time she would picture him a lord, and then, suddenly descending the ladder of social position, she would fancy him a poor artist or poet.

These harmless surmises served to fill up the time between breakfast and the youngster's arrival.

She was reclining in an easy chair as we have already said, reading, or rather pretending to read, "Great Expectations" which Horatio, in the essence of good nature, had procured her from Mudies, when the cab and tiger rattled down the street, and in a few moments a waiter entered and handed her a card—her heart beat fast as she took it—who was he?

CAPT. ARTHUR FITZROY GABION,

1st Batt. Grenadier Guards.

.

She seemed bewildered. "That boy a captain in the army! impossible!"

Now, I daresay many of my lady readers might know of the special favours granted to the chosen regiments in point of rank, &c., but then we must remember Lucinda was from the country, and her only opportunity of seeing the guards was in the park, at eleven o'clock, when Mr. Leech had taken her one morning to hear the band, and then had not thought more of them than she would of any other regiment—volunteers included.

She was lost in thought, twisting the card over and over in her hand, when its late owner entered.

He looked, to use her own expression afterwards, "very sweet,"

He certainly was very handsome, and his appearance would have led a weak-minded person to believe that he had literally been taken out of a band-box.

Lucinda rose murmuring something very indistinctly, and motioned him to a seat.

"I have done myself the pleasure of calling to tell you, Mrs. Linley, that your friend, Mr. Duffy, was let out of 'durance vile' last night upon bail," said he.

"Is that all his punishment," said Lucinda with surprise.

He smiled at this remark, and replied that he would only have to walk to the court this morning and pay a fine.

"I think he richly deserved whatever punishment he may get, for I'm sure his attack upon you was most unwarrantable," said Lucinda, blushing.

"I am sure you will exonerate me from any ungentlemanly conduct towards you, Mrs. Linley," said this knowing young blade.

"Your conduct was most considerate, Captain Gabion, and I cannot conceive what made Mr. Duffy behave in such an extraordinary manner."

The young guardsman thought he could give a very shrewd guess, but said nothing on the subject at present.

"I met Mr. Duffy after I had seen him at the station-house—I think he seems a very amusing fellow."

"Indeed, you met him? may I inquire where?"

"At some supper place at the west end," said this youth, with the utmost composure. "Yes! we smoked the calumet of peace, and I hope I shall meet him again," he added.

Lucinda did not seem best pleased at this, for she had determined to give poor Horatio his *congé* that morning, but now if his opponent had forgiven his attack, what right had she to do otherwise?

This was not exactly her reason for passing his offence over—the fact is, it would be rather absurd for her to be unbending, when the principles in the affair had amicably met—and after all there was no actual necessity for getting rid of Horatio, who might prove very useful, in order to enjoy the society of this enchanting young soldier.

I'm very much afraid that Miss Lucinda was getting very depraved, for she fancied a thousand things that would have shocked the propriety of many young ladies.

Circumstances over which she had had no control, had rendered her anything but straitlaced, and beside which she was not troubled the conventional ideas that frequently prove and insuperable barrin to the unrestrained enjoyment of many of the pleasures of this wicked world.

She had met this youth by chance, his appearance at first, and now his fascinating manners, had made a conquest of her heart, if such a thing were possible, and she determined to encourage any advance that he might make.

Do not for one moment, young ladies, run away with the idea that Lucinda meant in any way to exceed the prescribed bounds of maiden modesty, at least such was not her intention in encouraging the advances of this pretty boy.

We must admit that it is *possible* to experience a platonic feeling for those of the opposite sex to ourselves, but at the same time think it our duty earnestly to warn our young readers from attempting anything approaching it as this highly dangerous, and with few exceptions has hitherto proved a decided failure.

Of course Lucinda had great confidence in her own strength, or she would never have given way to this highly dangerous amusement.

The morning passed very pleasantly, and the leading topics of the day were reviewed and discussed in the most animated style by this charming pair.

At last our young guardsman, thinking that he had stayed long enough, besides having other engagements rose to take leave of the pretty Lucinda, who felt quite avoid on the left side after his departure.

In the course of his visit the conversation had turned upon the parks, and he had expressed the pleasure he should feel at taking her for a drive.

And Lucinda had accepted his offer, the Monday following was fixed for it, and the young rip felt as joyous as though he had been just gazetted to a colonelcy.

After his departure, Lucinda took herself to task pretty severely for having allowed this boy to make such an impression upon her—she blamed herself for having accepted his offer to take her for a ride in the Park; but, then, what harm could there be in going?

It was a very innocent way of passing a few hours, and she saw no reason for denying herself the pleasure.

Should she go or not?

It would appear so strange after having said she would—to refuse when he called for her on the following day.

It is almost unnecessary for me to say that she ultimately made up her mind to go—at the same time vowing that this should not lead to any greater intimacy.

Indeed, Lucinda had suddenly taken it into her head to be religious and 'go in' for church three times a day, and as the following day would be Sunday a fine opportunity offered for her to put this exemplary resolve into operation.

She intended to reform and amend her ways, which had been rather too fast of late, if we may judge of her exceedingly reprehensible conduct with the late Mr. Frank Norton.

To pray for strength to resist the temptations that assail we poor mortals, was now her first consideration.

She would conquer her weakness, and henceforth lead an irreproachable and virtuous life.

This was a very praiseworth course to pursue, and did her infinite credit.

Then she weighed the pleasures of this life against those of absolute retirement from its busy scenes, and tried hard to persuade herself that it was preferable to lead the life of a nun if necessary, to the life of pleasure, which sensible are too much in the habit of enjoying.

Somehow or other her ideas were very unsettled. There would be rides in the Park for her if she were to assume the robe of a sœur de charite; but, then, suppose Arthur (for she positively *thought* of him by this name) were ill or wounded she could, a la Theresa Longworth follow him to the seat of war, and nurse him—and, oh! how tenderly she would do so!

Now this was not at all a proper thought to enter the brain of a young lady who conceived the notion of retiring from the world to avoid its temptations.

This certainly was not the way to do so; but her reflections had their charm, and she indulged in them.

They were interrupted, however, by the announcement of Mr. Horatio S. Duffy, who had found it impossible to adhere to his resolution of not calling upon Lucinda until the day previous to his leaving for Portsmouth.

He came with a very penitent and crest-fallen-look, and abjectly apologised to the offended lady for his barbarous behaviour before her at the theatre.

Lucinda heard him without interruption, and then said,

"Your conduct did appear very strange, and I may add ungentlemanly, but as you request my forgiveness I can only accord it."

Horatio's countenance cleared up almost immediately, and his tongue was soon wagging at its usual rate.

He related to her his having met Captain Gabion, and having discovered that he was the son of a friend of Admiral Spanker's—he then went on to express the pleasure he felt at having made the acquaintance of the young captain, and added, that " he should not forget him in a hurry."

Lucinda thought to herself that it was hardly probable that he would, at least for some time to come, as his new acquaintance had give him something to remember him by, in the shape of a little cut between the eyes.

The portion of his cheeks that were bruised had been carefully painted, at the trifling charge of half-a-crown per eye—(a very common operation for young gentlemen to undergo, whose reputation might suffer, were they to exhibit black-eyes to the public gaze.)

Lucinda felt quite pleased to here Horatio speak so well of the young soldier, and for the rest of the time that the good-natured "Salt" stayed with her, she was very gracious to him, and he related many of his startling adventures during his service in China.

About this time it began to rain violently, and Lucinda, who had intended going out was very much annoyed at it, and allowed her annoyance to exhibit itself so palpably that the poor lieutenant, who feared that her wrath might eventually turn upon him, beat a hasty retreat, notwithstanding her invitation to him to remain to tea.

This he construed as merely an effort of politeness on her part—so he declined it.

Lucinda really wished him to stay for she felt lonely by herself, but did not press him to do so, thinking that he might have some other engagement that prevented him.

" I shall see you again soon I hope," said he on leaving; "shall you be at home on Monday?"

"On Monday I am engaged," replied Lucinda, with a conscious blush.

Horatio grumbled out something, and bowed himself out. "Ah!" said he to himself, "I can twig—she's going out with that youngster."

And then he hailed a Hansom and drove to Jermyn-street, where he arrived in a very savage mood.

Lucinda was soon seated over her tea in the cosy little sitting-room she occupied at the hotel.

Being alone, she made herself comfortable by drawing her chair close to the fire, placing her feet on the fender, and lifting her dress almost to her knees, sat gazing into the fire, with her bohea close beside her.

And here we shall leave her for a time—as our readers are doubtless anxious to here something more about Master Charley Wag and his doings.

LXXXIII.—What Charley Wag Did with his Share of the Miser's Gold.

AFTER the successful attempt on the miser's cellar Mr. Mugford and our hero felt they were justified in spending the rest of the night in as jolly a fashion as possible, and to this end Mr. Wag, in his usual reckless manner insisted upon champagne, being the tipple.

This little festival in honour of their luck was strictly confined to the Mugford family, as it was not deemed expedient to publish their doings to their neighbours—some of the middle-aged female portion of whom, would have "blown" upon them in a trice—so much did they detest the little cobbler for the perpetration of the crime that had robbed them of the sainted Mrs. Mugford.

The night passed merrily, and if guzzling constitutes happiness, Charley, Snuffy, and the two blooming daughters were as happy as kings and queens could possibly be under any circumstances.

The pint bottle upon bottle of champagne down their throats, and in due time the effect was possible.

The ladies were first attacked, but their symptoms were not alarming, they simply grew very merry, while Master Wag and their respected parent who had changed their liquor and gone in for hot grog, passed through the various stages, and finally settled themselves for sleep, with their arms round each others necks.

This the young ladies would not permit, so gently disengaging Charley's arm, they left their parent in a most undaughterly and inhuman manner to "knock it out" on the floor, and being a pair of powerfully-made damsels, they actually carried their favourite up-stairs, undressed him, and put him to bed!

Here Master Charley slept until the middle of the following day, when he awoke, and his first call was for brandy and soda.

And brandy and soda was brought him by Patty Mugford—who chaffed him upon his getting "tight," and I believe she mentioned something about having undressed him!

After taking his "pick me up" he arose, and Billy and himself sat down to breakfast.

This meal concluded, the two proceeded to business.

This business was the counting of the miser's hoard—the back was a long one for the amount exceeded Charley's most sanguine expectations!

At last it was finished—and if Mr Mugford's unprepossessing physiognomy was to be taken as the index to his innermost thoughts, our hero had acted very liberally towards him for his share in the undertaking.

Charley was now in possession of a large sum, and he determined upon giving up his dangerous profession for a time and leading the life of a swell.

For this purpose he engaged a handsome suite of chambers at the west end, started a cab and tiger, besides having a superb animal for riding in the Park.

He soon had a large circle of acquaintances, and these young bloods voted Charley a "regular brick."

Charley had money, and like most other wild young men spent it pretty freely—his young friends having no delicate scruples in helping him do so.

I suppose there was no swell on town got rid of his fortune in an easier manner than our friend Charley Wag did the miser's money.

He joined a Club, one of the best in town, but how he escaped blackballing I cannot imagine, and in fact, plunged into every excess that offered any inducement to a young gentlemen of his age and taste.

He led a jolly life, but still there were times when he felt bored by his own society and that of his numerous acquaintances.

The desire to find out Julia grew stronger than ever.

But how to do so was a puzzler.

Now, as we all know Mr, Charley was of a very determined disposition, and whenever he had the will to do anything, he invariably forced the way.

But in his search after Julia he seemed doomed to disappointment.

To curse Toddleboy and himself for allowing her to undertake the delivery of the letter, was a daily occurrence.

Why did he not accompany her?

Why did he allow her to expose herself to danger for old Toddleboy or a thousand letters?

And then the green-eyed monster would glare at him, who was the strange gentleman with whom she had left her lodgings?

Could she have been false to him?

He thought not.

Charley daily visited the Parks in hopes of seeing her as he had once before done, in fact he should almost feel satisfied even if he found she was living under another protection, for he felt pretty certain that it would require but little persuasion on his part to make her return to him.

But his daily rides were useless.

In them he saw the same carriages, the same horses, and the same faces.

Where could she be?

Was she still in England?

Charley was growing desperate.

He would find out Toddleboy—from him he might gather some tidings of his missing Julia.

For this purpose he placed himself in the train and was soon whirling on the way to Northfleet.

It was not until six o'clock in the evening that he left London and by the time he reached his destination it was quite dark.

He at once made for the little public house to which he was taken after the fight with the Americans, and at which he had met Captain Toddleboy so unexpectedly.

He recognised it without difficulty and entered it.

At the bar he found a woman to whom he addressed his enquiries relative to the old captain.

"Has he been here lately?" said Charley.

"We've seen nothing of him for the last three or four months, sir."

"Do you know where his vessel trades to now."

"Well! I don't know as I do—exactly—I heard my husband say that he had bought a larger vessel and went to South Amerikey and them parts, but whether it is so I can't say" replied she.

Charley saw that there was little hope of finding anything out about Julia, in this quarter.

All that he could look forward to was Toddleboy's return but when that might be Mr. Charles had not, of course, the most remote conception.

All that he could do was to wait patiently.

This, a very easy thing to talk about but not such an easy thing to put into practice, but wait, he must, whether patiently or not.

This was the result of Mr. Wag's reflections over a stiff glass of hot brandy and water in the tap-room, whither he had retired after arranging to sleep at the house that night, the last train having left for London.

He was solacing himself with a cigar and a second edition of brandy and water, when the landlord came into the room and saluting our hero with "good evening, Sir," seated himself opposite to him and lighted his long clay.

Charley looked at him and felt convinced that the face was quite familiar to him, but where he had seen it, he could not for the life of him recollect.

The landlord, who was a seafaring man to judge from his appearance, soon opened the conversation by making the following remark.

"You was enquiring after Captain Toddleboy, Sir, my wife tells me. "Yes," replied Charley eagerly what do you know about him good fellow?"

"I think I've seen you before" said the man without heeding Charly's question.

"Very likely" said our hero, rather snappishly, what the devil has that to do with Toddleboy, I should like to know?"

"Well, it *has* something to do with it," replied the old sailor good humouredly, I was one of the crew aboard the cutter when you and the young lady went over to France with us—you was wounded at the time"

This was conclusive, Charley saw that the man really knew him, and Mr. Wag felt that he had a better chance of getting authentic information about Toddleboy and perhaps Julia than ever.

" I did cross over to France with a young lady and I think I remember your face," said Charley, "but what has become of the Captain now?"

" Well! as you're a friend of his, I don't mind telling you."

" Fire away then " said master Charles, lighting another weed, and requesting to have his glass replenished.

" You remember the day the young lady left us to take the letter for the skipper?"

" Well "?

" And I daresay you know when you went after her?

" I should think I did."

" That very night the damned French Custom House fellows got scent of where we were lying, and we had to get under weigh and run for it "

This remark alone, proved to Charley that Julia could not have returned to Toddleboy.

" We steered down Channel " the man continued, and was not long before we made the hand that's *set* us all up."

" What do you mean?" said Charley in astonishment.

" Why, a homeward bound barque from Australia " said the man.

" And what of it " inquired Mr. Wag.

" Gold dust " said the other putting his finger to the side of his nose in a very knowing manner.

" Oh! I understand—but you have not told me yet, what has become of my old friend Toddleboy."

" I'm just a going to " observed his companion taking a great gulp at his grog.

After we made the haul of the dust we thought it would'nt do to shew in any of our old quarters again in a hurry, so we decided upon getting as many of the crew to join us as possible, and, putting the rest and the pilot in irons down below, there was only two or three as would'nt, so we had'nt much trouble with'em. We put the barque about and got out to sea, but this sort o'craft was not what our skipper wanted—but how to get rid of her safely we did'nt know. At last Toddleboy made up his mind to abandon her, giving those who wanted to, and choose to risk it, leave to go home in her—I was one of them, and here I am as jolly as I can be.

" But did'nt the fellows that had been kept in irons kick up a bobbing?" enquired Charley.

" Not a bit of it they were'nt bad shipmates at all, and not one of them preached on us, but then our skipper got to wind'ard of them by giving them all a little of the dust before parting company—" That was knowing wasn't it?"

" Yes," said Charley, " now let's hear about Toddleboy himself? what became of him "—

" Well he and the crew got to Baltimore somehow or other and there he bought a clipper, a scooner between two and three hundred tons, a regular out and out craft, so he wrote and told me, and fitted her out first rate with four heavy guns, and in fact every thing that was wanted for the slave trade, or, as he said, " for anything else as might come in his way "

" What was the name of his vessel?" said Charley.

" The Scud " replied the other.

" And where do you suppose he is trading?"

" Oh! on the coast I should think—it's the best place for that sort of thing, only he must mind he doesn't get taken into Ascension some fine morning."

Into Ascension?

" Yes, they generally take the slavers in there and break 'em up."

" Much better sell them," said Charley.

" Well, you see they ain't built much for selling neither—they're very lightly knocked together—for if a fellow can run one or two cargoes of niggers his fortune's made—so he don't care much about the vessel as long as she's fast."

" I should think not," said Mr. Wag, "but I dare say our friend Toddleboy's is a good one."

" You may depend on that, for she's intended for more than a slaver."

Here the landlord was summoned to the bar for some purpose or other, and Charley, feeling sleepy, asked for his bed candle.

The landlady handed it to him, and Mr. Wag marched off to his room. Here he undressed, and was soon on his pillow in a sound sleep.

Perhaps some of my lady readers may blame Master Charles for sleeping, instead of pacing the room with very little clothing on him, and raving about his lost Julia.

But Mr. Wag was too sensible a young gentleman to descend to such an absurdity. For it is an absurdity after all. If the loved lost one could witness the exhibition of her demonstrative adorer there might be some reason his conducting himself like a maniac—he might even add to his display by tearing his hair and beating his breast in the gorilla fashion.

But as young ladies do not generally see their deserted lovers after they have retired to their bed-rooms for the night, the pranks of their love-sick youths are literally thrown away.

I suspect that Master Charles was very much of this opinion, for he slept on till the following morning.

Then he awoke.

His first act was to consult his watch, a splendid English lever—gold of course--which he had obtained some time previously for almost next to nothing—and found by that useful and elegant appendage that it was time to get up.

And out of bed he jumped, and commenced the operations of his toilet.

He swore a little at not having a bath—it would have freshened him up he felt—and then he was very much disgusted with the soap he found in his wash-stand. Had it been the old-fashioned yellow soap our hero might not have grumbled so. Instead of which the compound that supplied its place was a mottled abomination, off which flaked great pieces of beastliness each time that it was passed through the hands. Added to this, the supply of water was very small, and Charley, who was like a duck in his love for it, was very much inclined to ring the bell, and abuse the first person that should appear for all the shortcomings of his bed-chamber.

Looking about, Charley came to the conclusion that bells were not used in this small establishment—so it was impossible to ring for the person he had destined to abuse.

"After all perhaps it is better not to kick up a rumpus here, or perhaps I shan't get news of old Toddleboy when there's any, and beside I'm not going to stay here."

Thus Charley very properly argued, and went on with his dressing.

When this was completed he went down stairs, where he found the jovial landlord awaiting his company to breakfast in their little sanctum the back parlour.

Charley accepted his invitation to join him, without hesitation, for on the table was a spread to which our hero felt quite able to do justice.

Down they sat, and were both soon engaged in feeding.

"You won't forget to let me know if you should hear from Toddleboy?" said Charley, after breakfast, while they were enjoying their pipes over some of the best "bitter" the house contained.

"Let you know at once," replied the landlord, blowing a cloud, "only you must let me know where to send to."

Charley pulled out his card and handed it to his companion, who pocketed it, and continued—

"I think it very likely the captain may come home for a little while—he seemed very anxious about a letter that young lady friend of yours took to deliver in France. He said something about it in the letter he wrote me. I wanted to show it to you, and looked for it after you'd gone to bed last night, but couldn't find it—it's got adrift somehow or other—I daresay I shall get hold on it after you've gone, but I'll send it you."

"All right," said Charley, " do, and if that young lady should call here to inquire about Toddleboy, tell her my address."

"I will so," said his companion, refilling his glass, "and send her to you ' double quick' as the sojers say."

Charley felt quite satisfied about old Toddleboy, he knew that he was not now in England, and he also knew that when he arrived he should be informed,

This was as much as he could expect.

From what he had gathered from his companion he felt that Toddleboy knew no more about Julia than he did himself.

This had the effect of making our hero rather down-hearted, not that he had for one moment supposed that she was with Toddleboy, but still he trusted to the old captain knowing something about her.

The morning passed in conversation, with pipes and bitter ale, and it was after dinner at the little inn, which did for Charley's lunch, that he took his departure from the abode of this jolly retired smuggler.

He arrived at the Northfleet station in time to catch a train for London, and, jumping in, found himself in company with a young gentleman who appeared to be his senior by two or three years.

This young gentleman, who had rather a nautical look, was smoking, in open defiance of the company's bye-law, which prohibits the use of tobacco in their stations and carriages.

On Master Charley's entering the carriage the smoker looked at him, and asked him in a manner that clearly intimated the alternative.

"Do you object to smoking?"

"On the contrary," said our hero, "I smoke myself."

"Will you allow me to offer you a cigar," said he, offering a well-filled case.

"Thanks," said Charley, selecting one.

"You will find them rattling weeds," said his companion presenting a light, "I've brought them from Manilla myself."

"Indeed," said Charley.

"Yes, my ship was on the station for a short time, so I took care to bring a few of the best home with me."

Charley, who was a pretty good judge of weeds, pronounced these excellent, much to his companion's delight, who seemed to derive great satisfaction from hearing his cigars praised, and from seeing them smoked.

And Charley was just the sort of person to please in this respect.

They smoked furiously all the way to town, and by the time they reached London Bridge they felt as intimate as though they had known each other for years instead of hours,

Charley insisted upon his newly-made acquaintance dining with him, and this young gentleman, not having any other engagement for the evening, accepted his pressing invitation.

To his club then Mr. Wag marched his fellow-traveller, and there regaled him in the most lordly fashion.

An opportunity of doing a thing of this sort Master Charley never missed. He loved to impress strangers with the idea that he was "somebody," but, who, he never exactly explained to them. He talked of his swell acquaintances with an ease that was astounding, and his companion, who was rather great at boasting, felt entirely shut up on this subject, and regarded our hero as a tip-top swell himself.

If Charley could have known this how delighted he would have been.

His great ambition was to be thought a swell, and if his sayings and doings did not convey the idea of his being so, at least to the verdant portion of his circle of acquaintances, and to strangers when he met them, it was no fault of his.

Certainly he had succeeded in making his present companion believe that it was with a nob, although an untitled one, that he had the honor of dining. And this is not to be wondered at when we consider that Charley's guest was a naval man.

Naval men, I think as a rule are very innocent. They have not the time to see much of *the* world, their world for several months of the year, being limited to one of H. M. ships of war, perhaps on the China station. So they take in all the yarns that are twisted them when they get ashore, and believe them as implicitly as could be wished.

It so happened that this young gentleman had been stationed in China, and when he found that he was "no where at all," when Mr. Wag began to talk of *his* aristocratic friends this youth threw a new element into the conversation and went in for anecdote, and told some of his startling adventures in China.

Charley listened, but I am sorry to say, for the sake of the young gentleman, who was doing his best to entertain him, our hero did not believe one half of what he heard!

Charley could, and frequently did draw the long bow, and he had had so much practice in the art, that he could generally tell when any one else was at the same game.

He allowed this youth to run on however, just to hear what he would say, and his forbearance was rewarded, by hearing some of the most wonderful and improbable adventures ever emanating from a sailor.

They invariably commenced with "When I was in China," &c., and as Master Charley was beginning to feel bored by this never-ending string of unpublished adventures, he suggested a move to the smoking-room.

"With pleasure," said his companion, "as I was saying when I was in the "Grumpy"—

But Charley cut him short, and hurried him towards the place of smoke, where he hoped with the aid of a cigar to stop his relating his adventures.

And in this he partially succeeded.

Our readers have doubtless recognised in Mr. Wag's railway acquaintance the naval man who was so polite to Lucinda during her journey to London and subsequently.

It was, indeed, the great Duffy—Horatio Spanker—whose plan for the destruction of the iron-cased ships of our neighbours, we were so near hearing on one occasion, but which place circumstances, have prevented the inventor from getting noticed in the proper quarters.

Duffy had been to Chatham, having been appointed to a ship fitting out there, and was on his way back to town when he met with Master Wag.

He was in his usual good spirits at the time, for he rather liked the idea of the change from Portsmouth to Chatham, beside which he had met with one or two nice fellows down at Chatham—clerks in the Dock-yard—who had been very much delighted with his experience in China, and who had after some little persuasion partaken of lunch at his expense at the "Sun."

All this was calculated to make Horatio very jolly, added to which he had again been "tipped" by his god father—Admiral Spanker, and whenever this was the case, he was in a good humour with all his fellow-creatures.

Charley and he smoked away manfully, our hero diving into the generous Duffy's cigar-case in a most alarming manner.

After consuming an immense quantity of smoke Charley proposed that they should go for a stroll.

"Where shall we go?"—then consulting his watch, he added, "It is too early to go anywhere—what do you say to a game of billiards?"

Horatio was delighted, and as he played very badly, Master Charles had no great difficulty in winning a little of the Admiral's tin.

They had several "quiet fifties," and after the last, which our hero allowed Duffy to win, Charley suggested that they would now go out.

"Well," said Mr. Wag, on getting into the street, "what shall it be?"

"What do you say to the Canterbury." said Mr. Duffy.

"Oh! hang the Canterbury—such a low hole," said Charley. "You do meet with such horrid cads there."

"Weston's?"

"That's as bad."

"Suppose we try the Argyll?" said Charley.

But Mr. Duffy did not seem to see it at all, perhaps he had some reason for not going to that celebrated place.

"Or the Alhambra?"

"We'll toss up for it," said Charley, taking a coin from his well-filled pocket—'heads' for the Alhambra—'woman' for the Argyll."

"All right," assented Mr. Duffy, 'sudden death' or best two out of three."

"Oh! best two out of three, there's more excitement, and the one that wins the toss shall have the choice, that'll do."

"Very well, you cry to me," said Duffy, and up went the copper.

"Head," said Charley.

It was so.

"That's one to you," observed Mr. Duffy.

"Up she goes," said Mr. Wag.

"Woman!" sang out the gallant Duffy, and woman it was.

"This time settles the hash," observed Charley, as Horatio sent his copper spinning into the air, "Woman!"

"It's a head," said Duffy exultingly, "and I have the choice."

"Well! what do you say?"

"Oh! the Alhambra for a change."

"Done," said Mr. Wag, "let's have a cabriolet," and he accordingly hailed one from the stand close by.

Into the Hansom they jumped, and were soon in the Alhambra, seated at a little table in the stalls, indulging in hot grog, and more of the celebrated Manilla cigars.

They got in here in time to witness the performance of a mountebank on bottles—to hear a famous female comic singer encored rapturously for "Aunt Sally,"—and to see another woman with her neck upon a wire stretched across the upper part of the building.

All this Mr. Duffy thought very amusing, and in all probability would have remained for hours, had the performance continued.

Mr. Wag had seen these wondrous feats and heard the self-same songs too many times to be enchanted by their repetition.

He had evinced an inclination to go once or twice, but Horatio had begged him to stay in such a manner that our hero had not the heart to refuse.

At last it was over, and Horatio and Charley once more in the street.

It was past twelve o'clock, and as the two young sparks began to feel peckish—or fancied they did—it was proposed by one, and agreed to by both of them, that they should get some supper at Scott's.

Now Scotts, as we all know, is in the Haymarket, and I daresay you may have heard that the Haymarket is a very improper place.

BLIND MAN'S BUFF.

It is quite a matter of opinion whether it is, or is not, and I should like to hear the *private* opinions of the promoters of the midnight meetings on this subject—for my own views are very unsettled upon this point.

However, it is no affair of mine whether the Haymarket is a nuisance or otherwise; my object is simply to tell my readers that are ignorant of the fact, that such a place exists, and if they are country readers and have never visited this great city, they must not imagine that it is actually a market for the sale of hay that we are describing.

Oh! dear, no! nothing of the sort, fair ladies. It is a market for——. But it is just as well not to describe it, I darsay you will know what I mean, when I tell you it is a very naughty place.

And to this naughty place Horatio and our hero turned their footsteps in search of supper —supper to men who had only dined a short time previously seems rather unnecessary, but nevertheless it is as usual here as drinking is without feeling thirsty.

I am sorry to say, that Master Duffy had every inclination to " go on the tiles," but Charley was not of the same way of thinking, he wanted a spree of some sort, and communicated his feelings to Mr. Duffy, who immediately gave up his immoral intentions, and agreed to " make a night of it" in the way our hero proposed, instead.

No. 58

And supper over they sallied out—out into the glare of the gas-light, which renders the Haymarket as bright as day.

Here Mr. Duffy almost forgot his engagement with Master Charley, to make a night of it in his company, which meant every species of known mischief, and as much more as that talented young gentleman could invent on the spur of the moment.

Charley saw his danger, and succeeded in getting him away from a syren in pink, with her dress looped up for the purpose of displaying her shapely calves and well-fitting boots. She had placed her arm enticingly within the young lieutenant's, and was whispering the words which might have lured him to Trevon-square, Brompton, or to some part of Pimlico perhaps, when our hero Charley came to the rescue, and saved the unstable Duffy from encouraging the social evil.

At this unwarranted interference, the young lady in pink and boots grew infuriated, and I grieve to tell it, made use of some expressions, which were, I to repeat, might horrify a few of my readers, and certainly would not add to the character, that this publication has hitherto enjoyed.

Mr. Wag paid little or no attention to this ebulision of the young lady's feeling.

This irritated her more and more, and at last, allowing her wish to avenge herself on such a monster as Master Charley appeared in her eyes, to overcome her interest, she bonneted our hero, and incited some of her lady-friends, who had been attracted to the spot by the violence of her behaviour—to join in his persecution.

There was a terrible scrimmage.

It seemed to excite the young ladies collected, to the highest pitch and woe be to any unfortunate young gentleman, who happened to stop for the purpose of witnessing the shindy, should he have been spotted by any of these out-raged females, as a person devoid of honour as regarded some of his little debts.

One wretched youth, who was recognized as a defaulter escaped with hardly a vestige of clothing left upon him.

Charley struggled with his fair assailants manfully, and Horatio followed his example.

They were in the most pitiable plight when she looked and longed for number of the A division, made his appearance. Master Wag's hat had been knocked off and smashed in, and was now amusing a select party, who were making use of it in the place of a foot-ball.

His coat was torn into ribbons, and had it not been for the opportune arrival of the "bobby," I am under the impression that his inexpressibles might have suffered in a like manner.

With the wretched Duffy—it was almost as bad.

One exasperated damsel burning to avenge the wrongs of a sister, but hardly knowing how she had suffered, and certainly not caring at whose hands—rushed upon the unlucky Horatio, and forcibly drove his hat over his eyes.

In vain did he try to get it off again—it had passed his nose and remained immoveable! Now was a glorious time for his persicutors.

He was hustled from one to the other, each young lady, literally picking holes in his coat whenever he was pushed in their direction.

When the policeman came up he was struggling in a most helpless fashion, deprived of his coat tails and the seat of his trousers!

This was a trying position for a young man to be in during the small hours in the Haymarket!

What say you, my gentlemen readers? You may have witnessed a similar scene, for they are by no means uncommon occurrences in that much-frequented locality.

The solitory policeman rushed in between the combatants, for the row was now general, every gentleman that had had his oysters, and a sufficient quantity of stout joining in it—striking out right and left, and avenging the imaginery insults heaped upon them by the gentlemen nearest to them.

This was the state of things when the solitary "bobby" aforesaid, made his appearance.

He was rather a wise "bobby," and seemed fully aware of the fact, that young gentlemen in this excited stage of intoxication are rather rough customers.

So he confined himself to the capture of an "unfortunate," who was at this moment pegging away at the miserable Horatio.

This happened to be our friend in the pink and boots.

As soon as she became cognisant of the "bobby's" intentions she let fly a tremedious rasper, which caught that enlightened member of the force, full in his dexter goggle. This little fact elicited shouts from the bystanders, and sealed the fate of the young lady.

Two other constables rushed up, eager for the fray, one assisting his brother "bobby" to secure the violent young female, and the other pouncing upon a mild-looking youth in spectacles, who happened to be looking on at the time.

In vain did this youth protest against this inflexible "bobby's" conduct, in vain did he account for his being in that most improper place at that particular time of the morning, having just left a midnight-meeting, with which he was connected.

"Oh! yes! I daresay—you won't gammon me, young feller—I knows you—I've seen yer before to-day. Come along!"

The policeman's remark seemed to arouse the dormant spirit of this youth, and he absolutely struggled, and refused to be dragged along the streets in such a disgraceful manner.

This was quite enough for the "peeler," who now, thrusting his knuckles into his victims throat in the approved fashion peculiar to the force, "moved him on" towards the Station-house by dint of superior strength.

Through one street and another he hurried him until they were not very far from the station-house, when a thought suddenly seemed to enter the head of the prisoner, and caused him to say a few words, which had a visible affect upon the policeman.

"Well, what'll yer give?" said this corruptible "bobby."

"If you will let me go," said this terrified mortal. "I will give you a sovereign!"

"All right—just wait a bit till we've got a little higher up here."

And he turned with his captive up a passage—rather dark, but light enough for this guardian of the peace to see that it really was a sovereign, and not a "duffer," that was tendered as the price of his prisoner's liberty—for that matter, he had fingered so many of the genuine articles in his time, that he could generally tell whether they were good or not in the dark.

But it is as well to be on the safe side at this time of the morning, thought the bobby.

"Don't you go back to the market, young feller," said he, after pocketing the sovereign, "I'm a going there myself."

With this admonition they parted company, and the youth went on his way, rejoicing that he had escaped, even though it had cost him a pound.

After all, it was worth it, for this young man held an appointment in a Government office—Diddleset House—and it would have caused him rather an unenviable notoriety in that building, had it got wind that he had been mixed up in a fight with prostitutes in the Haymarket, at two o'clock in the morning—and how scandalized would his friends the midnight meetingites have been—what would the Rev. Jack Pudding and the Rev. Ghastly Gash (of the revival celebrity), both models of piety and virtue—have said? Oh! it was horrible even to contemplate.

So he went home.

All this while I have been neglecting Messrs. Wag and Duffy, who had jumped into the nearest four-wheeler they could find, without troubling themselves about the fate of the high-spirited young lady in pink and boots, who had caused the shindy.

"Well! this has been a spree," said Charley, "never had so much fun before in my life."

Now this speech is not calculated to impress our readers with the idea that Mr. Wag was as sober as a judge is usually represented as being—on the contrary, he was rather "tight" as the saying is, (but not passed the jolly stage)—and Horatio Spanker was decidedly slued, to speak nautically.

Perhaps they had eaten too many oysters, or drank too much stout.

It must have been something of the sort.

To Charley's remark about the spree, Mr. Duffy muttered—

"Yes! it's very cold."

"What the devil are you talking about," said Charley, who was not so drunk as not to know what he was saying.

"It's a' right, old feller! it's a' right! but it's very cold!"

"What's the matter with you? what the devil is it?" again said Charley, endeavouring to lift him up from the bottom of the cab, where he had slipped down.

Our hero now discovered that his companion was minus the seat of his trousers, and judged from his remark on being placed on the seat, that this little fact made him complain of the cold.

"Tha's better, old boy, tha's better," settling himself against Charley.

"Come, hold up," said that young gentleman, "and tell me where you hang out."

Here the cabby put his head in, and grumbled out—

"I can't stay here a month, if yer don't say where you're going to yer must git out."

"You go to ——!" said Charley, shaking the sleepy Duffy, "wait till I find out where this gentleman lives."

"Where do you live, old boy," again asked our hero.

"It's a' right," replied Duffy, "Jermyn Street."

"Yes! but what number?"

"Straight up, straight up."

"Here, cabby," said Charley, "drive to Jermyn Street."

As soon as they began to rattle over the stones, Master Duffy began to sing, and from this Charley argued that he might be induced to talk a little more, so he propped him up, with his head near the window for the benefit of the air, and again asked him the number of the house at which he had rooms in Jermyn Street.

"I wish you'd shing, Wag—not—half fellow!"

"Oh! damn the singing," sharply observed Charley, "what's the number of your diggings?"

"Diggingsh?"

"Yes! where you live—you know."

"Yesh! I know," was the exasperating answer.

And now the cab neared Jermyn Street, and Charley felt that he must either find out where this tipsy "Salt" resided, or take him home to his own chambers.

This latter course he strongly objected to.

We all know that a drunken companion is not desirable, and I daresay this was Mr. Wag's idea at the time, for he made another attempt to find out the number of this helpless youth's abode, and this time the tipsy one mumbled "shixty-shix."

"Oh, all right," and putting his head out of the window, sung out to the John

"Sixty-six."

Charley thought that now all he had to do was to get him in, and, when the cab pulled up, he jumped out and knocked at the door himself.

It was some time before it was answered, but after repeating his attack with the knocker several times, and old woman with very little clothing on her came to the door.

"Does Mr. Duffy live here?" said our hero.

"Duffy—no—I don't know no Mr. Duffys, and don't want to neither—scandlous knocking anybody up at this time of the morning—you ought to be ashamed of yerselves."

"Well, my good woman, this is sixty-six, and my friend says he lives here."

"Where's yer friend?—in the cab—I s'pose he's drunk."

"He is rather intoxicated," said Charley, "and the sooner he goes to bed the better."

"You'd better go next door, that's sixty-six an' a 'arf—p'r'aps it's there," said the elderly party, in a slightly modified tone.

Charley thanked her for the information.

and said he would try, at the same time pla-cing a two shilling piece in her hand.

"Get a toothful of gin, old lady, and see if you can't be civil to the next fellow that knocks you up in mistake."

At this the old lady got indignant, and be-gan to abuse Master Charles, who had by this time made his second attempt on the knocker of sixty-six and a half.

"Now shut up old scarecrow, and go to bed," said that young gentleman, tauntingly.

To which rude remark the enraged female vouchsafed no reply, but closed the door vio-lently.

Charley was about to give his third rat-tat-tat when the housekeeper made her appearance.

"Does Mr. Duffy live here?" said our hero, in a sort of despairing tone.

"Yes, sir, on the ground floor."

"The Lord be praised! for I don't know how you'd get him up-stairs."

"Had a little too much wine, sir," I sup-pose?"

"He's had a great deal too much of some-thing, and it's made him very drunk."

"Dear me!" said the respectable party that looked after the rooms, "what a pity! such a nice gentleman as he is."

"Now, then, my tulip, come along!" Here, cabby, lay hold of him on the other side."

After some pulling and hauling they con-trived to get the unfortunate Duffy out of the cab and on to the pavement, where he showed strong symptoms of obstinacy, by clinging on to the area railing, and bellowing out in a de-cidedly intoxicated voice, "Rule Britannia," with a hicupping accompaniment.

Charley tried all that he could to get him to go in.

"Sha'n't!—won't go home till mor—ning!"

"Come along, there's a good fellow," said Charley, after having exerted his strength to no avail, "I want to go to bed myself."

Duffy seemed to consider this proposal of Mr. Wag's as rather a good one.

He let go his hold and made a dive for the door, propped up by Charley and the cabman —the respectable female showing them his bedroom, and holding a light.

Charley guided him to, and shot him into an arm chair, where, after seeing his boots taken off, and saying that he would call and see Mr. Duffy during the day, he took his de-parture for his own home.

After jumping in and directing the cabman, Charley felt rather sleepy, and settled himself for a snooze, and remained in this state till the cab stopped at his chambers.

"Now then, wake up," said cabby, shaking our hero rather roughly.

"I sha'n't," that young gentleman replied, in a drowsy tone.

"You must, or I'll damned soon 'ave yer hout o' this."

"You'd better try it on," murmured Charley.

"Vell, I vill then," said the cabby, and suiting the action to the word, commenced lugging at Mr. Wag in a most rough and ob-jectionable manner.

This had the effect of thoroughly rousing Master Charles, and as he was in the habit of losing his temper if awoke suddenly, it is not to be wondered at that on this occasion his good humour deserted him.

"Curse your impudence, what are you doing?" said he, starting up in a rage.

"Vy getting yer hout o' this here—that's vot I'm a doing! Yer not going to stay here all day."

"I shall stay here as long as I like, you thundering sweep!"

"I'm no more a sweep nor you are, and if yer don't come hout o' that I'll give you such a dusting as yer won't forget in a 'urry."

Thus appealed to, Charley looked about him, and discovered that he was at his own door.

Then he got out of the cab, but not to avoid the dusting cabby had promised him if he did not, but to take it if the Jehn could give it to him.

"What's your fare?"

"Five shillings" said the cabman, with his arms akinbo.

"I sha'n't pay you," said Mr. Wag, in the coolest possible manner. "I'll see you damned first, and then I won't."

"Von't yer," said the enraged cabby, "then I'll take it out of yer!"

When the man said this, and began squar-ing up to Charley, that youth divested him-self of his tattered coat in the twinkling of an eye, and threw himself into a position that rendered it extremely difficult for the cabman to get a blow at him.

Cabby danced about, lavishing some of the choicest abuse upon his antagonist each time Charley planted a blow that told.

After several rounds cabby came up again, looking very viciously at our hero, who, watching his opportunity when Jehn made a violent blow with his left, bobbed his head on one side, and cross-countered him.

Down went the unfortunate fellow under his own cab wheels, and there stood Mr. Wag with hardly a scratch.

This tremendous blow had nearly knocked his head off his shoulders, and for a few mo-ments the man did not move.

"Now, then, aren't you going to take some more out of me?" said Charley, tauntingly. "Get up."

The man groaned.

Charley stooped down and assisted to raise him, politely inquiring "whether he would like any more?" and "what was his fare?"

"I don't want no more," said the man, holding a handkerchief to his head, which was bleeding through falling on the curbstone, "and my fare's two bob."

"Well," said Charley, "considering what you have taken out of me, and the damaged state of your own crown, there's another for you," handing him a five shilling piece, "and now I wish you a very good morning."

Cabby pocketed the five bob, after thanking Charley for all he had given him, and mount-ing the box, drove off.

Mr. Wag, with his tattered coat under his arm, applied the latchkey to his oak, and en-tered his rooms.

It was now past five, and Charley thought the best thing he could do was to go to bed.

And to bed he went, and was soon asleep.

About nine o'clock his servant came to his bedside bearing a tray, on which was a cup of the strongest tea and a bloater.

This is a favourite remedy for hot coppers I believe.

Master Wag seemed to expect it—in fact he knew that his well-trained man never omitted it when his master was out late at night, or came home very early in the morning.

After this dose Charley felt better, and sprung out of bed, and into his bath room, which he left as fresh as a lark.

Then he dressed himself, and in another hour or so was seated at breakfast, with the morning papers before him.

He read and re-read their contents from the date at the top to the printer's name at the bottom.

Then he yawned and looked at his watch.

It was past twelve.

What should he do?

It was almost too early to find Horatio up, after the state he was in the previous night, but as the morning was fine he thought he would saunter down to Jermyn Street and see.

Having settled upon this, he lighted a cigar and walked out.

He found a greater number of people about than usual, and it suddenly occurred to our hero that it was the first day of the cattle show, and Charley decided that he would visit it that night.

"I daresay Duffy would like to go," said he to himself, "at all events I'll ask him."

After strolling quietly in the direction, he found himself close to Horatio's rooms, so he knocked and inquired whether he was visible.

On being answered in the affirmative, Mr. Wag entered his newly-formed acquaintance's sitting-room.

And there he found him looking very seedy, seated at table before an untasted breakfast, with a very woe-begone expression of countenance.

"Well, Duffy, how are you this fine morning," said Charley, briskly.

"To tell you the truth, my dear fellow, I feel rather seedy."

"You look so."

"Do I?"

"What have you been taking?"

"Brandy and soda."

"Oh, that's no good, only makes you sick."

"What's your remedy, then?"

"Strong tea and a bloater, and I'll answer for it; you'll tackle your breakfast after it, and then you'll be all right."

"I'll try it."

"Do, and you'll try again the next time you want anything of the sort," said Charley, confidently.

Horatio rang the bell, and the respectable party that let them in the night before answered it.

"Mrs. Gubbins, be good enough to make me a very strong cup of tea, and get me a bloater!"

"A bloater, sir?"

"Yes, a bloater."

"Yes, sir."

"I think your old slavey seemed rather astonished," said Charley.

"She did look rather surprised I think," replied Duffy.

"She'll know another time," observed Mr. Wag.

"How did you get home?" asked Duffy, "All right."

"I should think so," replied Charley, "but I had a bit of a mill with the cabby."

"The devil, you did? How was that?"

"Oh, he began pulling me about in rather a rough manner when I was asleep—then got very cheeky—wanted five bob for his fare—and was going 'to take it out of me' as he said; so I jumped out and slipped into him."

"Did you lick him?"

"Rather!"

"Served him right," said Horatio.

"The last crack I gave him put him under the wheels, and he cut his head open on the curbstone."

"What did you pay him after all?"

"Oh! I asked him what his fare was then, and he said, two 'bob,' but I gave the poor devil five, for I must have mauled him frightfully."

"About the best thing that could happen to him—a good drubbing is the only thing to teach those fellows to be civil," said Mr. Duffy.

At this moment the bloater and the tea made their appearance, and Horatio prepared to attack them.

He made rather an ugly face on sipping the strong tea without any milk in it, and said to Charley,

"It's deucedly like senna."

"Never mind that," replied Mr. Wag, "senna will do you good sometimes. You peg away at the bloater and you'll relish the bohea fast enough."

"That may be your idea, but it's not mine just at present," said the sceptical Duffy, who nevertheless took our hero's advice, and went into the bloater in fine stile.

Then he took a little more tea.

"Well, after all it's not so bad."

"I should think not," said Charley, "nothing goes so well together after being 'tight' over night, as tea and herring; I seldom take tea at any other time, though"

"Soda-water and brandy's not a bad thing sometimes," observed Duffy.

"It depends a good deal upon what you get screwed," said Mr. Wag, with an experienced air; "for my part I have given it up lately, for it makes me feel inclined to cascade."

"To what?"

"Why to cat—you know."

"Oh! I understand."

"That's why I do not take it," said Charley, "and I don't suppose you will do so in a hurry again."

"I don't think I shall," said Duffy, pushing his plate from him. "Now that's in me, I think I feel better, and shall be able to do some breakfast presently."

"Some fellows recommend bitter-beer, but I don't like it myself," said Master Wag.

"I fancy that would suit me better than tea—I'm half a mind to have a bottle myself—bye-the-bye, will you have one with your cigar?"

"Thank you, I will." said Charley, "but I shouldn't advise you to take any so soon after the tea."

"Perhaps it wouldn't be as well—I won't."

Mr. Duffy then rang for the beer, and Charley showed his companion that he did not fear the effects of it himself, for he was not long in reducing a quart bottle of the best Bass to a state of emptiness.

Duffy in the meanwhile breakfasting, for the tea and bloater had effected all the good that Charley had prophecied.

Mr. Wag was rather at a loss to know how to spend this day, for like many other young gentlemen, who have nothing else to do but to amuse themselves, he had exhausted all the known sources of pleasure, and oftentimes felt bored with leading the life he had so frequently longed for, that of a swell with nothing to do, and lots to spend in doing it.

Charley had anticipated that Mr. Duffy would not be fit for much during the day, and was rather agreeably surprised at being asked by that youth, "what he was game for that morning."

"Anything you like, said Charley; "but what the deuce is there to be done?"

"I hardly know—suppose we go for a walk?"

"That's about the *last* thing *I* should think of doing," said Mr. Wag, who had a very proper contempt for walking, as a way of amusing oneself. "I don't mind going for a ride into the country, or having a trap for the day, if you like."

"I'm not much of a figure outside a horse—suppose we say the trap."

"Agreed, I'll be off, and get one and be back here as soon as I can," said Charley, putting on his hat and going out.

By this time Duffy had finished his breakfast and retired to his dressing-room to conclude the operations of his toilet, which he had not completed when our hero first came in the morning.

This occupied him for nearly half-an-hour, and he had only just put the finishing touch to his 'get up' when Charley dashed up in a stylish looking dog-cart.

Mr. Wag jumped down, handing the ribbons to the servant, who was very correctly attired, and in keeping with the trap in every respect.

"Now, then," said Charley, as he entered, "are you ready?"

"Yes," as soon as I've filled this other cigar-case."

"Ah! that's right, let's have plenty of smoke, where shall we go to?"

"Well, I don't know—anywhere, I shall leave it to you to decide," said Horatio, cramming his cigar-case into his pocket.

"Let me see, where's a good place to go, what do yuo—say to Bexley or the Crays? tha t'lldo as well as any other."

"All right," said Horatio; "now come along—I think I have everything needful."

And the two took their seats. after lighting their weeds.

"Will you drive, or shall I?" said Mr. Wag.

"You, by all means," replied Duffy. "if I try my hand at all, it will be when we're out of town."

Charley laughed, and administered a smart cut to the horse, and away they went in gallant style.

"I think, Bexley is as good a place as we could have chosen," said Charley, "we shall get down there soon enough for lunch, and after a drive be back in town in time for dinner.

"That's glorious," observed Mr. Duffy; "I ordered dinner at six. You'll dine with me to-day?"

"Most happy," replied our hero, "and after feeding we'll go to the Cattle Show."

"I should like it amazingly" said Horatio, "for I have never seen it."

"You won't see much of the beasts—but you'll see some deuced swell women, said Mr. Wag,

"That's a consolation anyhow."

Yes, but I'll tell you something else—they won't have anything to say to you.

"Why not?"

"Because this week they are dead on to the farmers, in fact, every body that has the look of "young men from the Country."

"I don't think I look much like a Londoner, I'm rather too brown"

"You have a decidely nauticle cut about you as well—I daresay you will be seized upon as a jolly jack tar"

"The women certainly do give us the credit of being open fitted "said Duffy"

"Yes—but I think that's a very popular delusion."

"What?"

"That sailors are such a generous hearted disinterested set of fellows."

"Dont you think so?"

"Hardly—but I ought'nt to say anything against them, for one of the best friends I have ever had, is a sailor, an old fellow named Toddleboy"

"Toddleboy!—why that's the name of the skipper of the "Skud" a craft that's been dodging our cruisers on the Coast of Africa, for months—she's a slaver or a pirate, I should think the latter, for a friend of mine who is after her, wrote and told me that she is heavily armed."

"The Captain of her is my friend" said Charley, sinking his voice so that he might not be overheard by the servant.

"The devil! you dont say so?

"I do though and a better hearted creature never lived."

"Well, the ships I've joined is ordered to that station. and if I come athwart him I'll mention your name to him " said Horatio with a smile.

"I will ask you to do more than that, should you succeed in taking the vessel—Will you deliver a letter to him, and if your power aid the old man to escape?

"The first part of your request is reasonable enough," said Duffy, "but by Jove! the latter—why it would cost me my commission!"

"If discovered?"

"Yes. and I don't see well how one could avoid being discovered in such an affair as that."

"Where there's a will there's a way," said

Mr. Wag, in a mildly reproachful tone.

"By Jingo! Wag, I'd do a good deal to oblige you, but——"

"You don't feel inclined to in this matter," broke in Master Charley.

"Indeed I do though, and if it's to be done I'll do it."

"You promise?"

"On my word of honour."

"I believe you," said Charley, "and will entrust you with the letter before your departure—when do I sail?"

"In about a fortnight—I've got to go down to Essex for a week or so, but shall return to town before I leave England."

"Good," replied our hero, "I shall have the letter ready for you."

During the conversation, which had lasted some time, they had been going at a rapid pace, and after keeping this up for another half hour, in which they chatted and smoked, they neared Ellham, where Mr. Duffy, feeling hungry, again proposed lunching.

Charley readily agreed to his proposition, for he began to feel peckish himself.

"But where the deuce shall we find a place fit to go to," said Master Wag, who was rather fastidious at times.

"The first public we come to," replied Duffy, who was by no means so. "We shall get bread and cheese if we can't get anything else—that will keep us from starving until dinner."

"After all, bread and cheese if it's good, is not to be sneezed at when a fellows hungry," said Charley "and I am frightfully."

"Here we are then" said Horatio as Mr. Wag drew up at the "Greyhound" and jumped out, "now we shall see what they've got fit to eat.

"I shouldn't think much more than the popular bread and cheese" said Charley,—then directing the servant to give the Horse a feed, they entered the House and were shown into the best room it contained.

"I say landlord, have you anything to eat in the house—anything fit for a Christian?" said Mr. Wag facetiously.

"Christians are very well satisfied if they get bread and cheese, sometimes, sir, observed the landlord with a dash of solemnity in his tone,

"Ah! well, I suppose they are when they can't get anything superior"—but do you happen to have a cold joint in the house"?

"I am sorry, sir, but I haven't so much as the bone of a joint,—for a club as is held here weekly, met last night and they cleared the house.

"Well, what have you got?"

"A nice home baked loaf and cheese, gentleman, and some of the best ale in Kent, and when you've tried it you,ll say so."

"Let's have it, then, as soon as you can"!

And away the landlord went to order it to be sent in.

In a few minutes it made its appearance and Charley and Horatio pigged away in a most alarming manner at the home baked bread and the delicious butter and cheese.

"By Jove!" said Mr. Wag, after a long draught, "this is rattling ale."

"It is so," replied Horatio, with his mouth full of bread and butter, "I don't think we could have lighted on a better shop—do you."

"I think we've done very well," said Mr. Wag, "but I want some more beer."

"So do I," said Horatio, "just order another supply."

Charley rang, and in came the landlord.

"We want some more of your excellent ale."

"Ah! I said you'd like it, sir. How much will you 'ave, sir."

"Oh! another quart."

"Yes, sir."

"And now," said Charley, "we've eaten as much as we conveniently can—we'll give our minds to drinking and smoke—where are your weeds. I'll trouble you for a choice one."

Horatio produced his case, and the pair went at it with as much vigour as they had evinced in their attack on the bread and cheese a few minutes previously.

"I say," said Duffy, suddenly, "we mustn't starve the man—I'd quite forgotten him."

"I hadn't though—I told him to have whatever he could get, and if he's fared as well as we have, he hasn't done badly."

"That's all right," said Duffy, "and now whenever you're ready we'll get on the road again. I want to see something of this part of the globe."

"Very well, you go and look after the trap, and I'll square with the landlord," said Charley, ringing for that obese personage.

Horatio went to look after the dog-cart as Charley requested, and found the man quite ready and waiting for them, beguiling his time with a long clay.

Charley soon followed, and the trio mounting the trap, were once more rattling along in the direction of the Crags.

"The day was cold but bright, and Horatio enjoyed the ride amazingly.

"How about time?" said Charley, "will you look at your watch?"

Duffy did so, and told our hero the time o' day.

"Then I think we had better turn our heads in the direction of London, if we are to get there before six," said Charley.

"Yes, we had better," assented Duffy.

Charley then took the shortest and most direct route which led into Lewisham, and after a steady drive passed through it, and so on to New Cross and the Old Kent Road.

"This is about the most disgusting part of our drive," said Duffy, as they passed the Bricklayers' Arms.

"Yes, this is bad enough, but it's nothing to the Borough—there you're almost choked with the stink of cheese and every conceivable beastliness."

"We shan't have to pass through it—shall we?" said Duffy.

"No! we shall go over Waterloo Bridge," replied our hero, "we shall be in Jermyn Street by half-past five.'

"That's all serene then," said Horatio, "we shan't have the dinner spoilt."

"I hope not, for I'm getting peckish again," observed Mr. Wag.

"I'm glad to hear it, for I feel in the same state. I think it must be the drive."

"Or the tea and bloater this morning," laughed Charley, "I did not think you would have been fit for so much when I saw you first this morning—you did look awfully seedy."

"I did feel very queer—it must have been that cursed stout we drank such a lot of."

"It was something of the sort you may depend upon it."

"What a lot of yokels there seem to be about," said Duffy, after a pause.

"Visitors to the cattle show, a good many of them."

"I daresay."

"I've been thinking of a devilish good spree for to-night," said Charley.

"Well! what is it? another fight in the Haymarket?"

"No!—let us go to the cattle show like two countrymen, we,re sure to have some fun with the women!"

"But how about the togs?"

"Oh! that's easy enough."

"But how?"

"Why, cords and boots, with a long scarf and one of those little round hats, that will do gloriouly."

"But I've neither cords nor boots here in town, said Duffy, dolefully.

"Oh! we'll manage that somehow," said our hero. "I've a pretty good supply of these articles, and we're much about a size. We must get dinner over as soon as possible, and get up to my place, and I'll undertake to rig you out in less than no time."

Horatio was delighted and enjoyed the fun they were likely to have, in anticipation.

It was now about a quarter to six, and they were close to Jermyn-street.

"We were not very far out," said Charley as he pulled up.

Out they got, and Charley after dismissing the man with the trap, followed Horatio into the house.

They found the cloth laid, and everything ready for dinner.

"This is stunning," said Horatio, "we shan't have to wait— won't you wash your hands?"

"I was just going to propose doing so, said Charley,

"Come into my bed-room then," said Duffy, leading the way, "and then you can do so."

"Charley followed him, and having performed the operation, they returned to the sitting-room, and dinner was served immediately after.

There was very little time wasted over this meal, both the young gentlemen being very hungry, and not inclined to chat, and eat at the same time.

As for Duffy, he was dwelling upon the mighty joke they were going to play that evening, and said very little except such phrases as "make yourself at home, old boy." Don't spare the wine, old fellow—there's lots more where that came from.

At last, dinner was over, and Horatio proposed that they should smoke their weeds, as they walked to Charley's chambers.

That young gentleman being of the same opinion as Mr. Duffy, the weeds were produced, lighted, and away they went.

LXXXIV.—GETTING THEMSELVES—YOUNG MEN FROM THE COUNTRY—THE CATTLE SHOW—BLINDMAN'S BUFF.

ON reaching his chambers, Charley at once commenced routing out his stock of tools, cords, &c., which was anything but limited, in search of the necessary attire for the evening's spree.

"What the deuce do you do with so many different rigs?" said Duffy, as Charley in looking for a pair of boots likely to fit his companion, opened a cupboard, wherein were all kinds of dresses, from a Life Guardman's down to a costermonger's.

"Oh, they are only some of my masquerading togs," replied Charley, shutting the door.

"And a jolly lot you've got of 'em," observed Mr. Duffy.

"Yes, a few—will these fit you?" said Charley, pitching him a pair of Bedford cords.

"I can't say, but I'll try—they look about the thing. If they don't we shall be all up a tree."

"Not at all—I've others that I daresay will if those won't."

"I'm blessed if they're not too tight here," said Duffy, placing his hand upon his posterior. "If I have to stoop down I shall crack them."

"That wouldn't do at any price," said Charley, with a grin, "we should have you carried off by a brace of peelers for &c,, &c.—try these, they're larger."

"I should fancy by the look of them that they were almost as much too large as the others were too small."

"Well, never mind, try them on—and if they don't do we must find the happy medium," said Charley, producing another pair.

"I'm hanged if I know what you can want with all these things—what the devil use do you make of them?" again asked Duffy.

"Oh, they come in handy at times, especially when my friends come to see me," said Charley, with a laugh." "Well, what's the result?"

"Oh! damn it, they're too big."

"Then here you are then—these will ft you to a nicety, or I'm very much mistaken."

"These do, gloriously," said Duffy, delighted.

"That's one difficulty got over," said Mr' Wag; "now then, if you will choose one of these scarves you can put it on while I'm getting the boots. You'll find the sort of pin to wear on my dressing-table; I think there are two or three—you'd better use one, your's is too small."

"I will," said Duffy. "Ah! this is a stunner, and no mistake," added he, taking up a large gilt horse-shoe, "this is about the correct thing."

Charley in the meanwhile, was hunting for a particular pair of boots for Duffy, whose foot was a trifle broader than our hero's.

"Damn the things—it's always the way when you're in a hurry. You can never find them.

"What's the row," sang out Duffy from the adjoining room.

"Oh! nothing, much—I've found them now, and here they are," said Charley, exhibiting

A RUFFIAN.

a pair of boots to Mr. Duffy—"if you can't get into these, I'm hanged if I know what we shall do."

"I'll manage it somehow," replied Horatio; "but haven't you a pair a size larger?"

"The only ones I have beside are three times as big as those, and they wouldn't do."

"I must try these."

"Do, and while you're at it I'll get myself up."

Charley at once commenced his toilette for the evening, and Duffy made preparations for getting into the boots—that is to say—he took his coat of, and drew a long breath.

Then he took the right boot in his hands and inserted his foot—down, down it went as far as the instep, without the slightest difficulty, and there it met with a little opposition.

Duffy tried to persuade himself that it was simply the opposition one always meets with when putting on a pair of boots for the first time; but after one or two violent efforts, the damning truth flashed upon him, they were tight! and it would be some time before he got them on.

"I'm blessed, if I think they'll go on at all!" said he to Charley, as he paused to wipe the perspiration, which had been caused by his exertions, from his forehead.

"What the devil is to be done?"

"Oh! try again, man," said Charley, "per-

[CHARLEY WAG, THE NEW JACK SHEPPARD.]

haps your foot is a little warm—here try this."

"What is it?" inquired the rueful looking Duffy.

"French chalk, and if that won't help them on, nothing will," observed our hero, handing the box to Duffy, who seized hold of it and emptied half its contents into the boot he had been so vainly endeavouring to get on.

"And now for another trial," said he, thrusting his foot in again.

But it stuck fast at the same place in spite of the chalk and his mighty efforts!

"What in the name of heaven are you puffing and blowing at?" said Charley.

"Why—this cur—sed bo—ot—I—can't get on."

"Put your strength into it." said Charley.

"Strength be damned—here have I been pulling and hauling, and I can't gain an inch."

"You'll have to give it up then as a bad job."

"Will I though?—not without a struggle anyhow!"

"But you can never walk in them."

"If I could get them pass the in—step—I —think they'd do."

A tug.

"Blast the boots."

Another tug.

"I won't try any more."

But notwithstanding this resolution, Duffy continued to try. "I think it's moving a little," said he to Charley, who entered the room fully attired in his cords, boots, &c., looking a great deal more like a countryman than a young gentleman who lived rather fastly in London.

"A *very* little—I should say," remarked that youth.

"By Jove! how well you are got up?" said the admiring Duffy, between his paroxysms. "You look first rate!"

"You'd look equally well if you'd get on your boots—it's getting late," said Charley, consulting his watch.

"But, my good fellow, what am I to do? I can't get this infernal right boot on—and on the left foot I've got a thundering great bunnion!"

"It's no good trying," said Duffy, pitching the offending boot away from him; "I must go in my own, and he commenced putting them on and lacing them up."

"I've hit it!" said Charley, and away he went into the next room, in which he kept his stock of ready-made clothing.

In a few minutes he returned with a pair of gaiters.

"Will these suit you?" said he, holding them up.

"Do you think they'll do?" said that individual.

"Capitally."

"Then let's have 'em."

"Catch," said Mr. Wag, throwing them to him.

Duffy took no time in buttoning them up, and to his intense satisfaction, they fitted him in a manner which showed his symmetrical calves to the greatest advantage.

"I like this rig better than boots," said he, and I think they'll do equally well.

"Every bit," said Charley, "and now if you'r ready, we'll start—will you have a stick?"

"I think it would be an improvement."

"Yes! and if we get into a 'difficulty— as the Yankees say, it may be useful."

"Just so—but what are you going to take?"

"Oh! I shall take this whip—it has a bit of lead in the top—feel it."

Duffy did so, and came to the conclusion that it was heavy enough to crack the thickest skull.

And away they went.

Hailing a cab at the end of the street, Charley and Duffy were soon on their way to the Cattle Show.

As they approached Baker-street they had to slacken their pace for the numerous vehicles and omnibuses, which seemed to be running from all parts of London, and conveying at this point, completely blocked up the way.

On the footpath it was worse if anything, for the inhabitants of the metropolis showed in great numbers as well as the yokels.

All around the Bazaar it was like a fair, on both sides of the way were wonderful illuminated advertisements with unpronounceable names, intended to gull the green ones from the country.

Horatio, who was very much amused by the outside show, was most impatient to get in, but this was a work of time. He was for getting out and pushing his way through the crowd, but Charley objected to this proceeding as undignified.

"Hang it, no, we'll drive up to the door— its better than walking," said he.

"Just as you like—but, I say, suppose we get talking to any yokels—where the devil shall we say we're from?"

"I'm jiggered if I know," replied Mr. Wag, "it must be somewhat from the other side of Jordan."

"Look here," said Duffy, "suppose we settle on Somersetshire, I know something about the country—leave the rest to me; but remember we came from Banwell—that's our nearest railway station. You won't forget?"

"Not a bit of it—Banwell—I shall remember it right enough."

"All right then," said Duffy; "here we are at last—what's the damage cabman?"

"Four shillings."

"Four shillings!" said Master Wag, forgetful of his character as a countryman, and feeling very much inclined to tip the man eighteen-pence after damning his eyes.

"Yes! sir," said the man, touching his hat.

"You infer——," began Mr. Wag, but controlling his feelings with a mighty effort he innocently inquired the fare from a policeman standing by.

The "bobby" was evidently deceived by their outward appearance for going up to the cabman, and 1 suppose winking at him in a manner that cabby understood as "brandy and water," he turned to the two young gentlemen and said.

"Vell" you see gentlemen, is fare hi three and six, but at the show time, they will stick on a hextra sixpence or so!"

The young gentleman thus addressed did not deem it wise to dispute this authority for many reasons, so cabby got the fare as decided by the policeman—who—muttered as they passed into the Bazaar—Vell! they are green, and no two vays about it!

"Vot time are you hoff? enquired the cabman of his accomplice, the bobby.

"In 'arf an 'our"

"I'll meet yer at the "Spurgeon's Head" down by the stand at 'arf past nine".

"I'll be with yer, my tulip" said the policeman,

After making this appointment the cabman drove off in search of fresh victims, leaving the policeman to adjudicate in an eminently succesful manner on fresh cases of extortionate fares.

We must now follow our friends Charley and Horatio into the show.

As yet, they had only succeeded in paying their shillings and getting little round cheques in exchange.

The entrance was crowded, and it was not the easiest matter in the world to get through it.

However, by struggling manfully, they contrived to make their way towards the beasts,, to view them with any degree of comfort was totally out of the question.

As for the beasts themselves it mattered little to our friends Charley and Duffy, whether they saw them, or not, as the object of their visit to Baker Street, was to see Prize Cattle of another description.

They went with the crowd down one row of the pens, and up by another, and when, by any chance they got close to a splendid beast, the pressure caused by enthusiastic countrymen anxious to get a sight, was something tremendous.

On one of these occasions when Charley felt almost suffocated, he turned round sharply to the person close behind and in a savage tone enquired "where the devil he was pushing to?.

The man who had incurred our hero's displeasure by the awkward use he made of his elbows, to say nothing of his feet, was a good natured, broad shouldered young fellow—a fair speciman of the yeomanry of this country.

On being addressed by Mr. Wag, he replied with a grin.

"I'm afraid it was against you, Sir! but I beg your pardon."

"This is an awful squash," said Horatio, who had stuck close to Charley.

"It is so" replied the young farmer, who had been visited by Charley's anger, "and you don't catch me coming here at night again."

"It's not much use, for you can't see the beasts" said Horatio,

"Well! as for that matter, many comes here, as know very little about cattle, though they may live in the country—besides it's a treat for us to come to London once a year—particularly at this time."

"I always look forward to it myself"—in fact, I think all we country fellows do, said Horatio.

"What part do you come from?" asked the farmer.

"Somersetshire."

"Well to be sure so do I"—l live near Bridgewater"

"Oh! indeed" said Horatio—"I'm some distance from that, my place is near Banwell"

"I don't know the neighbourhood at all myself, but a friend of mine's been staying a few miles from it."

Here Charley broke in with "damn me if I think we shall ever get out of this infernal crush."

"I suppose we must grin, and bear it then, said the farmer with a smile."

"Bearing it is one thing, but the grinning's another" said Charley, in by no means an amiable manner.

The farmer seeing that our hero's temper was short, resumed his conversation with Duffy, notwithstanding the difficulty of carrying it on in the crowd.

After several unsuccesful attempts they extricated themselves from their unpleasant position, and made their way upstairs to where the Agricultural Impliments were exhibited.

Here they had more room, and the farmer and Horatio could talk at their ease.

Charley was having a conversation with some friend of Horatio's companion, and the astonished expression of the rust'c youth's countenance clearly proved that Mr. Wag was indulging the guileless one with some of his own reminiscences—whether of town or country life, it is impossible for me to say.

Duffy feeling rather tired seated himself on a portion of some wonderful machine, (for what purpose intended I haven't the slightest idea) and his companion followed his example, and then they began to chat again.

"Did you ever meet with a farmer down your way of the name of Grill?"

"No—I can't say that I have" replied Horatio "I may have heard the name and that's all."

"I thought to be sure you'd have heard of him, for my friend that's been staying down there, tells me he's the rummiest old fellow in the county.

"Indeed" said Duffy, what's he famous for?"

"Why he's got a Museum, in which he has something of everything.—he's got the stone with which David killed Go—the Giant, you know who I mean."

"Goliah"—yes—walker!"—

So say I, but I hear there's a good many of the people about as believes it."

Well! what else has he got—any of Pharoah's chariot wheels?.

"No, but something almost as good, if not better."

What is it then?

The identical charger in which John the Baptist's head was served up!"

"Ha! ha! ha! that tops everything," said Horatio.

"Then he has no end of curios beside—skeletons of beasts, birds and fish, Indian bows and arrows, and the devil knows what else"

"He must have an odd collection"

"He has, and no mistake—why he has

snakes of every description, and while he was shewing my friend round the room, they came to where the snakes were, after telling him all about them he pointed to a bottle with something white in it and asked him if he knew what it was—my friend didn't—so old Grill says, "that's my thumb!"

"His thumb!" said Horatio, "what the deuce did he mean?"

"Why he'd lost his thumb by a gun bursting—he's got the barrel in the museum—and then nothing would do but he must keep his thumb—and there it is sure enough bottled up."

"Good God! what an idea."

"Yes, and he tells a wonderful story about the number of pieces it was blown into, and how many yards off it was found."

"What, his thumb?"

"No; I mean the stock of the gun."

"Oh! I was going to say——"

"He's a devilish good-hearted old fellow they say—that museum's his only weakness."

"When I get back I think I shall look him up," said Horatio.

"I should advise you to—he's got some rattling good cider."

"I'll work it then you may depend."

Here Charley once more joined them, and this time he was accompanied by two very pretty girls. Having introduced them, Horatio relieved him of one of them. and wishing his farmer acquaintance good night, that worthy asked Horatio with a wink, if he should be at Scotts' in an hour's time? as he (the farmer) would to a dead certainty.

Duffy was about to reply—it might have been yes, or it might have been no, it is entirely out of my power to decide—when the young lady on his arm answered for him.

"Yes," said she, "we're going to Scotts' now—you'd better get a friend and come with us."

"Ah, do," said the young lady who was with Charley, "we shall be a jolly party."

"I shall follow you," said the farmer, "I daresay I shan't be long after you."

"All right," said Charley, "we'll look out for you, and keep places for you and your friend."

"That'll be rather a hard matter to-night," said the young lady in the blue silk that was leaning on his arm.

"Why?" asked Mr. Wag in the most innocent manner imaginable.

"On account of the cattle show," replied the goddess in blue; "it's bad enough on other nights, but during this week it's always crammed."

"We had better go somewhere else then," suggested Horatio, but his proposition was negatived by the lady at his side.

"Oh! no," said she of the yellow silk and black lace flounces, "let us take our chance at Scotts', there's more fun there than at any other place."

"Agreed," said Charley, "now let's try and get out of this infernal hole, for I'm pretty nearly sick of it, besides being awfully thirsty."

"And so am I," said the fair lady on his arm.

"Well! then we'll moisten our clay when we get outside."

To do so they had to pass through the crowd again, which, notwithstanding it was nearly the time for closing, continued as dense as when they first came in.

After a frantic struggle they found themselves near the pens in which the pigs were, and here the crowd chiefly consisted of an inferior order of chawbacons.

While hemmed in here our party were very much amused at some of the remarks made by these judges of pigsflesh.

"Bill," said a Yokel, who looked as though his idea of happiness did not extend beyond the possession of an unlimited supply of bacon, "Bill! look'ehere!" pointing with one hand to the card with ther age, &c., above the pen, and with the other to the porkers wallowing in the straw, "three months and thirteen days! what d'ye think o' that?"

Bill evidently thought a great deal, but the result of his cogitations was only manifested by his placing both hands on the pen, and gazing first at the pigs, then at the card above, and down at the pigs again—then he exclaimed deliberately, with a fixed look at the pork before him—

"Well! I'm damned!"

This highly improper remark was all he made use of—but if there is any language in the eye, and I am inclined to believe that there is—Bill's eye, while gazing at the pigs, expressed enough to have filled my next week's number.

Leaving Bill still rooted to the spot, Charley and Duffy, with their fascinating companions, contrived to gain the place of exit, but this was not effected without some difficulty, loss of breath, and a considerable quantity of lace off the young ladies dresses.

It will be hardly credited that this trifling misfortune caused the wearers of the said dresses to use some very appalling language—indeed the young lady in yellow was so indignant with some unfortunate rustic who happened to be driven against her rather forcibly, that Horatio had to exert himself to prevent bloodshed.

Don't misunderstand me, dear reader, I do not apply the word as it usually used—I simply refer to the bloodshed likely to be caused by an infuriated female party, drawing her nails smartly down the face of one of the sterner sex.

That is what I mean, and I should fancy it was one of the most unpleasant ways of being bled.

However, Horatio happily prevented this deed of blood, and succeeded in soothing the young lady anxious to perpetrate it, much to the delight of the terrified countryman, who looked during the shindy, as though he verily believed his last hour had come.

When it was over, and the young lady pacified, the good-natured joskin wanted to stand something, and politely inquired if the young lady would do him the honor of drinking with him, in token of her forgiveness.

The young lady was not bashful, and expressed her willingness to do so.

This settled, the whole party adjourned to a

highly respectable public close at hand, where the facinating females did lemonade and sherry, and the gentlemen did something stronger.

While they were here, in walked the young farmer, who had promised to meet them at Scott's.

"Hullo!" said he, in imitation of some of our most celebrated clowns, "here we are again!"

He was accompanied by a very showy damsel, gaily attired in pink satin, who proved to be a friend of the young ladies with Charley and Horatio! infact they lived in the same house.

"By jingo! this is jolly, we shall be able to stick together," said the farmer.

I suppose the honest knight of the hayfork had heard some of the marvellous tales of the frightful traps laid for the unsuspecting in some of the questionable establishments of the great metropolis; or perhaps he had been reading the tracts on the awful doings in Granby-street, and anticipated nothing less, should he get alone into one of these dens, then some such terrible occurrence as the bed sinking beneath him, and taking to itself wheels bearing him in triumph down the main sewer!

Whatever were the thoughts passing in his mind, he seemed very pleased at having met Charley and Horatio again; and after they had liquored pretty considerably at each others expense, he proposed that they should make for the Haymarket, and get some supper.

The young lady in the yellow silk, who had lost a part of her lace-flounce, for which loss she had felt that blood, alone could atone, now took an affectionate adieu of the despoiler of her raiment, who had been standing unlimited treat to all her friends.

She begged him to accompany them to supper, he was sure to find a friend at Scotts; but the man was married, and affected to be virtuous, so he refused.

"Bosh!" says some old stager, "as though married men never went to those places. Why, it's an acknowledged fact that the married men are the worst."

"Very true, most sapiant, observer of the manners and customs of the married portion of the British public; but, then perhaps our worthy countryman had reasons for not joining this supper-party, that you and I know nothing about."

"Why he refused I can't say; but he certainly did, perhaps he really was virtuously inclined."

"Oh! come," exclaims my reader, who doesn't believe that much virtue exists in the married state, that's rather too good."

I suppose I must humour him, and as he will undoubtedly admit, that there is no rule without an exception; with his permission we will consider our married friend, one of the exceptions to the rule he has laid down relative to the existence of virtue in wedded life."

"Now for a cab," said Charley, as they left the public, "we must have a four-wheeler, and that won't hold us all."

"We must squeeze in someway or other," said one of the goddesses.

"Oh! yes there'll be room, I'll get outside with the driver," said the young farmer.

"I'm hanged if there is a cab disengaged, now we want one," said Horatio.

"Let us walk till we get one," suggested the yellow silk divinity.

"Not if I know it," said Duffy, "walking's not to my taste, when I can ride, at least not in town; but here we are—sir! Cab and a four-wheeler drew up close to the curb."

"'Aymarket, Sir?"

"Yes! Scotts, and get there as soon as you can" said Horatio from underneath a press of crinoline, having kindly accomodated the young lady in yellow with his knee.

Away went the cab bearing its living freight towards that popular locality,—the Haymarket.

On arriving at their destination, they found the celebrated supper rooms crowded to excess every seat occupied.

"What the deuce shall we do?" said Horatio "we shan't get places to-night,"

"Oh! shan't we" said Cearley "I'm not quite of your opinion—there's a small party in the corner, squaring up, so we can nail their seats."

"There are others on the look out for them as well as we are."

"You stick close to me" said Charley, "and tell our friend to do the same,"

Horatio did as Charley suggested, and the whole of them kept together awaiting the departure of the occupants of the seats mentioned by Mr. Wag as likely to be soon vacant.

At last the party got up to go, and one of the gentlemen of it, a stout burly fellow, seeing our friends prediciment, very kindly assisted them to slip into the seats vocated, much to the annoyance of some other hungry people who had been waiting for the same opportunity but were not fortunat eenogh to profit by it when it occured.

They must of been leary individuals indeed to take advantage of any circumstance where Mr. Wag was concerned—he was too knowing for the majority of his fellow creatures.

It was to this superior tact that he owed his success in some matters, and to it also, may be attributed many of his misfortunes—but as a rule he was a crafty youth—never sleeping with more than one eye closed, and the other ready to open on the slightest occasion.

After a little trouble and a great expenditure of Patience, our party succeeded in getting some supper—then they became very merry and the young ladies got rather noisy, and called for whatever they fancied—It must have been *rather* an expensive little repast for the number of bottles with lead paper round their necks that the indefatigable waiter uncorked, was prodigious. It might have been goosebury or champagne, or—but at all events whatever it was, it was charged for at Champagne price and paid at that, by the gentlemen.

Supper over, the thoughts of the party turned homeward. but do not run away with the notion, my verdant reader that Messrs. Wag and Duffy had the slightest idea of passing the rest of the morning at their own residences—certainly not—they escorted these young ladies home to Trevor Square, Bromp ton, and with this polite intention they made a move.

Again did Horatio hail a cab and accommodate the beauteous being in yellow with his knee and again did the young farmer who accompanied them up his position at the side of the Juhn.

Away they dashed down Piccadilly and towards Bromptom at a pace that must have astonished the very beast that drew them, considering the hard day's work the poor brute had already done.

But what is the beast's astonishment to us? what does his hard days work, or his driver's hard day' s work signify to us?

They were made for it, and we pay them,—that is quite sufficient. We are not going to make ourselves miserable by troubling our heads with the hardships of others. We are on our way gay Trevor Square, so of course we must be jolly.

And a jolly party they were, in that four-wheel cab, rolling on to that most celebrated square of Brompton—They laughed and sang, and I really believe that Horatio would have treated them to a hornpipe had he not laboured under the impression that in a cab with four other persons beside himself (three of whom were of the sex that indulge in crinoline) he should hardly have space enough to execute the complicated steps of that most elaborate dance the young farmer on the box was not a whit behind them in merriment—he and the cabby went in for harmony, drumming an accompaniment with their feet against the splash board. an altogether succeeding tolerably well in "making night hideous though by the by it was now morning.

Trevor Square was reached at last, cabby dismissed with a double fare, the door of one of the most respectable houses opened with the latch key of one of the silk draped goddesses, and our hero, together with Horatio, the young farmer, and the young ladies inside.

On entering they found themselves in a large and handsomely-furnished drawing-room, hung with pictures perhaps not of the order you would find exhibited at the Kensington Museum, or the Louvre, or even at the Royal Academy over the water, but certainly of an order appreciated in establishments of this kind. I must not shock the feelings of the young ladies who may read this by any attempt at their description—suffice to say that had these works of art been displayed in any window of Holywell Street, the committee would have been down upon the unfortunate vendor of pictures in the twinkling of an eye, and the day after the name of the miserable wretch would have figured in the *Times* charged with having &c., &c., and fined accordingly.

Holywell Street has very little to do with Trevor Square, so our fancy must take its flight from the former back again to the latter, where we shall find a right merry party assembled—several gentlemen from the country and as many ladies—the ladies residents in the great metropolis.

Into this select circle they were introduced by the young ladies they had so politely escorted home—soon after, as a matter of course, everybody felt thirsty, and as a necessary consequence everybody must drink.

After the drink the fun grew fast and furious, the playful kitten in blue silk, to whose peerless charms our hero had surrendered, insisted upon that youth's divesting himself of his coat and boots, preparatory to having a handkerchief bound over his eyes. Then the whole party engaged in a game of blind man's buff, but as they were not intimately acquainted enough to know each others names, the game subsided into a most exciting romp.

You young ladies all know what is usually termed romping, though your idea of it, dear virtuous girls, is very milk and watery, compared to the romping that goes on in Trevor Square.

You would like to know all that takes place—would you not? Perhaps like to play at such a game yourselves?

But really I must not tell you anything more about these highly improper doings, or you will be inundating me with a host of letters, directed to the publishers, containing invitations to amateur performances of your own.

And now for a short time we must say good bye to Charley Wag and his friends, leaving them to enjoy their game and all that followed, about which you inquisitive darlings, I must not tell you any more than I did about the romping.

———

LXXXV.—SERMONS AND GOOD RESOLUTIONS—CAPTAIN ARTHUR FITZROY GABION—THE RIDE IN THE PARK, AND WHAT IT LED TO.

WE shall now pass on to the Sunday following the visit of Captain Gabion, and it found Lucinda still strong in her purpose to go in for church.

I am not quite certain she fancied that hearing three eloquent discourses in one day would render her proof against the temptations likely to assail her on the next, or whether she was simply anxious to see the latest thing—bonnets.

To tell a young lady's thoughts is rather a difficult matter at the best of times—they may be good, or they may be bad—I am rather inclined to believe that young ladies are not often possessed with the naughty thoughts that many of my own sex are continually imputing to them.

Whether these young gentlemen have been jilted, and have conceived a bad opinion of the fair sex in general, accordingly, I know not—but they certainly do rail very furiously against everything in petticoats.

As I said before, I am not inclined to think harshly of young ladies, and ascribe bad motives to all they say and do. On the contrary, I believe that good motives generally actuate the dear creatures, and the only thing that I find fault with them for, is—that they do not make much of a struggle to avoid temptation when it comes in their way.

This frequently arises from a very false notion of their own strength, and perhaps an erroneous impression of, and a misplaced confidence in, the honour of we of the pegtops.

With regard to Miss Lucinda, I am almost

at a loss to know what sort of influence was at work with her. She went to church three times on the Sunday, and in these sacred edifices heard three most eloquent sermons, all of which seemed preached for her especially. At least so she imagined, and the consequence was that she returned home fully resolved to flee all sorts of temptation, and to lead a new life.

Now this was just as it ought to be, and had it not been for that stupid trusting in one's own strength, for which I have just been abusing young ladies, a very different future might have opened to her.

A Protestant nun would have been rather slow for her, it is true, but then she might have taken an active part in the missionary mania, become a lady visitor, read by the bedsides of the dirtiest old parties she could pounce upon in the filthiest localities of the metropolis, or preside at the tea meetings got up by the good-looking clergymen.

All these and thousands of other equally innocent pleasures passed in review before the mind's eye of this unstable young lady, and I am sorry to say that what she thought would be the best fun were the tea fights with the parson.

This was the last thing she should have thought about, but somehow or other it would keep uppermost.

My idea on the subject is, that Miss Lucinda had not yet been " converted," and to tell the truth I think she was still some dis tance from it.

It was after her third sermon, and in her snug little sitting-room, that she determined upon the irreproachable life she intended leading for the future. As for a theatre, she would never enter such a place again (the reverend gentleman had had a shy at them in the sermon.) " No—never again" she exclaimed, "how I could have been so lost to do so before I know not."

This was one of her good resolutions, and another was not to see Captain Gabion on the morrow.

This latter resolution was made on her retiring to her bedroom for the night. It was made, and as quickly broken! This sudden change may be accounted for very easily—for on entering her room she saw her bonnet which she had hastily thrown off on her return, lying near, and the sight of it immediately recalled to her memory—not that I think she could have forgotten it—a certain bonnet she had seen that day at church, and at church she had resolved upon having a similar one if Regent Street could supply it.

While undressing she very improperly pictured herself, with such a becoming head-dress, seated by the side of the young captain, enjoying the ride in the Park.

And what was the result, think you?

The result was, that the pretty Lucinda laid her head od her pillow, and came to the conclusion that she would have jsut this one ride, and then——. Oh! there would be time enough to think of the new line of life afterwards.

The reader may be anxious to know something about this young gentleman—Arthur Fizroy Gabion, who had made such an impression on the susceptible Lucinda.

He was the only son of a baronet of that name, and at the time of his making the acquaintance of our plump young friend, held a commission in the Guards, and was altogether a fast young gentleman. His resources were decidedly good, but at the same time he had drawn upon them to such an extent that he was frequently hard up, not as hard up as you, or I might be—but there were days when he could not place his hand on fifty pounds without first putting it to a little slip of paper, in which he promised to return eighty for the loan of the same for a limited period.

This is really not what you can call being hard up. The correct difinition of the term is, when you haven't a copper, and not a soul that would lend you one. That's my notion of being at the last gasp.

This had never been the case with young Gabion. He found no difficulty in keeping up a very dashing appearance; but as he was rather involved he found that his means would not enable him to continue in the Guards, and at this time he was thinking of exchanging into a line regiment.

He first thought of the plungers, but that would never do, he should require as much tin in a cavalry regiment as he did in the guards. There was only one alternative, and this was to become a liner.

" Damnation!" said he, seating himself before a table in his rooms, covered with the applications of importunate duns—" what the devil shall I do—saw bones?"

This observation was made to the surgeon of the regiment, who happened to know the state of Captain Arthur's finances, as did most of the other officers, who were with few exceptions, in a similar state.

" What the devil shall I do?" repeated the youth.

" Do," replied the docter, " change into a marching regiment, to be sure, and go abroad, that's the only way to pull up—you can't do it here."

" No, curse it! that't the worst of it."

" Well then, you must do the next best thing, and that is exchange."

" It's all very well for you to talk so coolly of exchanging, but it goes against the grain I can tell you, to leave the guards."

" I can perfectly understand that, my dear fellow! but to revert to your own question— ' what the devil are you to do?' "

" I'm hanged, if I know—I suppose I shall have to do as you suggest, after all."

" The only course," said the surgeon, lighting a cigar.

" There are some awful cads in the line— aren't there?" said Gabion.

" There are so," repled the doctor, who had been in the line, and felt nettled at this remark, " and almost as many gentlemen as there are in the guards."

" That's one consolation, anyhow."

" I daresay you'll like the line as much as do the guards now," said the doctor; at all events in your position it's worth trying, and the sooner you do it the better."

"So I think, and I shall set to work about it at once."

"Do, and let's know the result," said the saw bones, looking at his watch. "By Jove! it's late—I must hook it."

This conversation took place some time previously to Gabion's meeting with Lucinda at the Adelphi, and the day on which he had appointed to take Lucinda for a drive, he was gazetted to an Indian regiment, the depôt of which was at Chatham.

Monday came, and with it, in a handsome trap, with a pair of servants behind, came Arthur Fitzroy Gabion, looking as charming as ever.

Lucinda had been watching for him for more than half an hour, although he had mentioned a particular hour, and that had hardly arrived when his carriage drove up to the door, and he bounded up stairs.

She had scarcely time to settle herself in an elegant posture, with her book upside down, when he was ushered in.

"How do you do, my dear Mrs. Linley?" said he, squeezing her pretty hand with all the warmth of an intimate friend—and it is just possible that this youth was not mistaken in fancying that he felt the least little pressure in return—"I hope I have not kept you waiting?"

"Oh, not at all! I have only just returned from a shopping expedition—(she had not been out since ordering that bonnet in the morning, and it was now nearly four)—"what a magnificent day it is."

"It is indeed, we have had some splendid weather this year."

"I must not keep you waiting," said Lucinda, "you will excuse me, I shall not be long," retiring to make her toilet for the drive.

Left to himself, the youthful Captain thought upon the beauty who had just left his presence, and his thoughts were somewhat in the following fashion.

"By Jove she is a screamer! and if I'm not very much out of my reckoning she squeezed my paw! She is a beauty, and when I go to Chatham she shall go with me. At all events I'll try it on with her, and if she won't why it can't be helped—and I shall save by her virtuous refusal.

I think the reader will agree with me that this proposal, if accepted, was likely to blow all the youth's idea of retrenchment into thin air—but I am led to suppose that young gentlemen, when they take a gig of this kind into their heads, are not troubled with the consequences any more than young ladies are when they throw themselves recklessly into the way of temptation.

The young soldier's reflections about Lucinda were at this moment interrupted by the appearance of that young lady, very tastefully dressed in a rich *moiré antique*, and wearing one of the prettiest bonnets that could be obtained in Regent Street.

"I'm afraid I've kept you a long time," said she, with a sweet smile, "but I'm sure you'll forgive me."

"Don't mention the time, Mrs. Linley, I'm sure you have not been half the time that most ladies are."

"I think there is more time wasted before the looking-glass than is actually necessary."

"You may think so, perhaps, because your glass has told you so often that you are beautiful, that you do not see the necessity for consulting it to the extent that others do," said this youthful flatterer.

"Oh! Captain Gabion—you are laughing at me," said Lucinda, her face crimsoning with pleasure at his admiration.

"Laughing at you! impossible!" exclaimed this impetuous youth taking her hand, "I only tell you what I feel—I think you the most beautiful woman I have ever seen!"

They were seated on a sofa, and Lucinda allowed him to draw her gently towards him, and here, with her head resting on his shoulder, she listened to his protestations of regard, and then told him that she loved him.

"Your very wishes shall be anticipated, dearest," said this youth in his most seductive tone, trying to soothe Lucinda, who was now weeping violently.

Here then, were all her good resolutions scattered to the wind, for when a young lady begins to cry, the victory is achieved.

*   *   *   *   *

It was nearly five before they started for their drive, and it was getting dusk as they entered the park.

During the drive, which was necessarily short, Lucinda said little, her happiness was too great for words, and Gabion felt exceedingly jolly for the prospect of going to Chatham, did not now seem half so dreary.

"Are you tired, dearest?" said he, as they left the park, and were proceeding rapidly in the direction of Norfolk-street.

"Oh! no, but I'm so happy." He pressed her hand silently, and she returned the pressure, this time unmistakeably.

The high-mettled horses were not long in accomplishing the distance between Hyde-Park corner and Norfolk-street, where they arrived about a quarter to seven.

"You will dine with me, dearest Arthur?" said Lucinda.

Arthur acquiesced with a kiss, and so the matter was settled, and Lucinda tripped into her bed-room to make some slight alteration in her dress. This effected, she returned and the two sat down to dinner.

Over the dessert, they chattered and arranged their plans for the future.

Gabion told her of his exchange into the line, and of his being ordered to Chatham.

"It's a frightfully dull place dear," said he.

"Oh, never mind that, dearest Arthur, we shall see more of each other," replied Lucinda, who felt very happy and willing to follow him to the most objectionable part of the habitable globe.

It was late before this billing and cooing was over, and Gabion did not leave until propriety obliged him to.

"Confound the hotel," said he to himself, as he walked home, "the sooner I get her away from it the better I shall be pleased."

Having to join at Chatham on the following day, he determined upon getting leave of absence, and looking about him for a suitable house for the pretty Lucinda.

This he had communicated to her, and as a matter of course it had met with a blushing approval.

I daresay that the reader may condemn Lucinda's apparent weakness in giving way to what she had so resolutely resolved to shun, but they must make allowances for her, and remember that her finances were getting extremely low, for her residence in town, to say nothing of opera cloaks, bonnets, and other articles purchased, necessary to the existence of a young lady, had made a frightful inroad into the sum bequeathed her by Frank Norton.

In fact she was beginning to tremble for the future, and the thoughts of being again as destitute as she was on Leech's desertion of her, made her at times perfectly wretched. It is therefore, not surprising that when Arthur Gabion told her that he loved her, and delicately hinted that he would place her in a desirable position (in a pecuniary sense), that she should hail the proposal with delight, and like a sensible girl, as she had now grown, accept it.

I think there are few young ladies in her position that would have done otherwise.

Perhaps it might have been better had she embraced the life of piety she had laid down for herself after hearing those sermons, but somehow or other she forgot all about that, with Arthur's first kiss.

[CHARLEY WAG, THE NEW JACK SHEPPARD.]

And allowing that she had gone in for piety, how would it have supported her, and found those dear little boots for which she was so famous?

The idea was simply absurd—preposterous.

LXXXVI.—AFTER THE GAME OF ROMP OFF TO THE COUNTRY, BACK AGAIN TO TREVOR-SQUARE—A BALOON ASCENT—GIVING YOUR FRIENDS THE SLIP.

IT was late on the following day before Messrs. Wag and Duffy took leave of the goddesses in Trevor-square—indeed, had it not been that Horatio was to go down that night into Essex, they might have remained there until now, for ought I know to the contrary.

The two young gentlemen at once proceeded to Duffy's rooms where they dined, after which Horatio commenced his preparations for his journey into the country. During this operation Mr. Wag was enjoying a nap on the sofa—his previous night's rest having been a very broken one.

"Come! rouse up here, old fellow!" said Duffy, when everything was ready, and it wanted but an hour to the time of the train's starting, "rouse up!"

Charley sat up and rubbed his eyes in a very infantile fashion with his knuckles, after which proceeding, coupled with a shake or two, he appeared thoroughly awake.

"Why, hang it, man, you haven't been long getting ready," said he.

"You've had a jolly snooze, that's what makes you think I haven't been long over it."

"There's something in that," said Mr. Wag, with a yawn; "what time do you start?"

"At once, and not any time to spare," replied Duffy, rolling up a railway rug; "there's the cab I sent for now," added he, as the respectable woman who took care of the rooms tapped at the door.

"I shan't offer to see you off," said Charley, stretching himself, and putting on his hat, "I'm too tired, and shan't be sorry to get out of these boots and breeches."

"Now I'm off," said Duffy, shaking hands with our hero; "good bye—you'll come down by the four o'clock train on Christmas Eve—I'll be at the station to meet you," sang out Duffy from the cab, as it rolled away.

Mr. Wag had been invited by Horatio to spend Christmas Day at the paternal mansion in Essex, where a large party were expected, which included Horatio's good father, Admiral Spanker, and several county families.

Duffy had told our hero that he had frequently mentioned him during his last visit at home, and assured Charley that he would meet with a hearty welcome from his governor and the rest of the Duffys—and Charley had accepted the invitation.

After Horatio's departure, Mr. Wag went straight home to his chambers and retired to bed at a much earlier hour than he was in the habit of doing usually.

On the following morning Charley felt the absence of his friend Duffy, to a most alarming extent.

They had seen so much of each other lately that our hero experienced almost a feeling of loneliness without him.

The days wore heavily away, until the time came for Charley to go down to Essex to join Horatio.

Charley had been making his preparations for this visit on a grand scale, if we may judge from the extensive orders that were given to his tailor about this time, and from the various suits sent home, from which Mr. Wag selected those most likely to create a sensation.

Christmas Eve came at last, and after seeing everything in readiness for his journey, Mr. Wag placed himself in a cab, and forthwith proceeded on his way to the railway terminus, where he arrived about a quarter of an hour before the time for the train's starting.

He found some difficulty in getting his luggage looked after, but as he was a young gentleman who _would_ be attended to, he succeeded, where many other less energetic people failed.

To see his luggage labelled in accordance with the printed notices of the Company, was all that Mr. Wag was anxious for. This done, he took his seat in the most inviting-looking first class carriage he could find.

Some time elapsed before the train left the station, but at last the whistle sounded and they were off.

During the journey Charley speculated upon the sort of reception he should meet with, and wondered whether the Misses Duffy were pretty girls.

A sad youth was this Charley Wag, always thinking of the women, and I'm sorry to add, that many of the audacious minxes gave him every encouragement.

"It will be infernally slow if they're ugly," said he to himself, "and if they are I shan't stay long."

Mr. Wag occupied himself with his thoughts for many miles of the way, and was only interrupted by the stoppages at the different stations where they took up or set down numbers, who like himself were going out to spend Christmas.

During these delays, Mr. Wag found plenty to amuse him, for should any pretty girls happen to cast admiring glances towards the face of the young scamp he would immediately kiss his hand to them, and by other telegraphic signs, express his desire that they would come into the same carriage. And from the giggling that went on between the young ladies on these occasions, I really believe that had it not been for stern papas and mammas that many of these merry girls would have availed themselves of his invitation.

At last the station was reached that Horatio had mentioned to our hero as being the one at which he was to alight, and at which he had promised to meet him on the arrival of the train.

Charley got out, and had hardly done so, when that individual dashed up to him and seized his hand.

"How are you, old boy?" said he, still shaking away at Mr. Wag's hand in the most demonstrative and unnecessary fashion, "how are you?"

"First rate," said Charley, "but devilish cold."

"Well, we'll go to the refreshment room and have a toothful of something to warm us—come along."

Charley followed him in after seeing his luggage taken out, and there they partook of a glass of brandy each.

"Have another," said Duffy, "we've got a long drive before us, and it's snowing like the very devil."

And they had another.

"This your luggage, sir?" said a porter, as they emerged from the refreshment room.

"Yes," said Charley.

"This way my man," shouted Horatio, leading the way to a dog-cart which was waiting in readiness to convey them to the mansion which sheltered the illustrious members of the Duffy family.

Charley's portmanteau was soon stowed away, and then the two young gentlemen took their seats on the trap, the servant jumped up behind, and away they went.

"You have learnt to drive then," said Charley, as they bowled along the snow-covered road.

"I should rather think I had," replied Duffy, "by jingo it's the only thing to be done by anyone staying long in this God-forsaken place."

"How far do you reckon your place is from the station?" asked Charley.

"About two miles and a half."

"As much as that!"

"We shan't be any too soon for dinner, and I'm infernally hungry," said Horatio, "your train was a long while behind its time to-night"

"It was—I thought we were never going to start."

"We must make up for lost time now," said Horatio, giving the horse a tickler under the flank.

"This is what I call going at the rate of knots," added our nautical friend shortly afterwards, when they were rattling along at a great rate.

"It's a good pace," observed Charley, from under the folds of the great coat in which he was wrapped, "keep it up old fellow, and we shan't be long over the two miles."

Horatio did not require urging to do this, for he tucked it into the unfortunate animal to such an extent, that it bounded along at the top of its speed.

"What have you been doing in town since I left?" asked Horatio, during one of the intervals between administering the doses of whipcord to the horse.

"Nothing at all."

"Haven't you been down to Trevor Square since?"

"Not I," said Mr. Wag.

"We must dig them out on our return to London," said Duffy, "I promised to take my yellow-robed damsel down to the Palace during the Christmas holidays."

"What palace?" asked Charley.

"The Crystal Palace."

"Oh!——"

"Yes, there's something going on there more than usual, so I said I'd go with her."

"I think you're a muff for doing so," said Mr. Wag, "It's a stupid game taking women to those sort of places."

"I'm sorry you think so, I had calculated on you taking the syren in blue and going with us."

"Oh! if that's all, I'll go, but I don't think we can have much fun down there."

"Well, we shall see—then you'll go?"

"Yes."

"That's all right then—steady old chap."

This latter remark was addressed to the horse, who had at this moment given some indications of anything but steadiness, as they passed through the lodge gates, and entered the avenue which led to the house.

"Here we are at last," said Horatio, as they alighted, and the servants walked off with Charley's luggage.

"We shall just have time to dress before dinner, and that's all."

Saying this, Horatio led the way up stairs, and conducted Charley to the rooms appropriated to him, and, having seen all our hero's wants attended to, he retired to his own room to make his toilet for the evening.

Gentlemen are not usually so long over this operation as ladies, and a few minutes only had elapsed between Horatio's leaving Charley's dressing-room, and his return to that apartment, attired for the dinner table.

He found Charley nearly ready—a few moments later and he was quite so.

"Now, old fellow, I'm your man," said this inimitable youth.

The dinner party, which was small—being confined to the Duffys, Admiral Spanker, and two other intimate friends of the family—were all assembled in the drawing-room when Horatio with our hero entered it. Charley was first presented to the Duffys père et mére, and was received by them most cordially—after which the old admiral did ditto; he was then introduced to the Misses Duffy and the two intimate friends.

The aged Duffy was a short fubsy man, with a port winey nose, and a decided air of pomposity about him which was anything but agreeable at first, but, as it was subsequently demonstrated to our hero, that air of pomposity was only assumed to impress strangers with the fact of his being a gentleman, and a rich one to boot.

The admiral was of a much larger build than Duffy senior, and only resembled him in one particular feature—and that was his nose—which certainly did not add to the appearance of his otherwise good-looking countenance. It was what is termed a "jolly nose," and the proprietor of it seemed to be a very jolly fellow.

The two intimate friends played so insignificant a part during our hero's visit, that I shall not bore the reader with any description of them—suffice to say that they ate and drank, but, notwithstanding all this, were anything but merry.

And now for the ladies. Perhaps you will

say that it is very ungallant of me to leave them till the last?

It is, I admit, but then I have my reasons for doing so.

One of these reasons is a natural timidity on my part to enter into any particulars where ladies are concerned, and another is my total inability to do justice to their charms when the description of them falls to my lot.

This failing of mine generally makes me leave the ladies till the last, and, if I can possibly get out of it, I eschew their description altogether.

In this case unfortunately, I was weak enough to mention the gentleman individually, and if I neglect the ladies of the house of Duffy, I shall deserve to be called a bear.

The ladies themselves and the fair readers of these pages will, I am sure, make every allowance for one who is not well up in the subject, on which he is obliged to write—so here goes—To begin with Horatio's mamma—she was rather a ponderous woman, several inches taller than her lord, with large features and a high colour indicative of temper, her hair, or at least the hair she wore was a wondrous structure, and would certainly have astonished any person less cool than our hero Charley, it was braided and stooned in the most architectural manner, and was surmounted by a powerful head-dress, that was terrible in its gorgeousness—add to this a flame coloured dress and you may form some slight idea of the imposing appearance of Mrs. Duffy—The youg ladies were three well grown, handsome girls, with merry, twinkling, dark eyes, which suggested a certain spice of devilry in their compositions that at once prepossed Mr. Wag in their favour, and led to that young gentlemen becomming very thick with them during his stay.

Horatio seemed a great favorite with his visitors and Mr. Wag, as a particular friend of their dear brother, was made welcome by every possible attention that these lively creatures could show him.

At dinner these young ladies kept our hero engaged in conversation, which was only broken by a challenge from the host, who still kept up as a good old custom that most objectionable practice of taking wine with his guests.

Then would follow a similar attack by the admiral and the two intimate friends. Horatio, like most young men of the peesent school, had a very proper contempt for this sort of thing, and would not acknowledge the necessity for this senseless observance, much to the disgust of his honoured parent.

Charley bowed with as much dignity as a courtier when any of the oldsters " requested the pleasure," but carefully avoided the discussion which ensued subsequent to Horatio's declining in the most obstinate manner to nod to his papa as he gulped down a glass of wine.

To keep out of this argument would have been no easy matter for our hero, had it not been for the tact of the three young ladies, who very judiciously grew animated in the extreme, so much so that Master Wag had as much as he could possibly do to reply to their delightful chit-chat.

In due time the ladies retired, and the gentlemen are left, as the saying is, " over their wine"

" Fill up, my boys " said Duffy senior to Charley, " fill up, and lets be jolly "—he was beginning to grow familiar with our hero and that young gentlemen felt a great deal more at his ease as the pomposity wore off, with every glass of good old port.

" Now let's hear what you two boys have been up to lately?" said the old admiral, draining a bumper of the ruby, " what have you been up to?" asked the old dog, digging Charley in the ribs, and winking at him in a most expressive way.

" There's not much going on, now, sir," said Charley innocently.

" I suppose not," said old Spanker, " you youngsters like the Opera and such trash," then turning round to Horatio who sat on the other side of him, he added " now let's have your account, young Skyscaper? What have you been doing in the sweethearting line—eh?"

Horatio's reply was evasive, and as the old gentleman saw that there was nothing to be got out of his godson or his friend—at least while the father of the former was present—he let conversations drop, and devoted himself to the task of colouring his nose by applying himself to the old port for which Duffy was famed.

Horatio feeling this must be rather slow for Charley, proposed joining the ladies in the drawing-room.

This proposition met with Charley's decided approval, and they immediately made a move notwithstanding a sleepy enquiry from the aged Duffy, as to what they were up to.

The two intimate friends who had concluded in chorus after a feeble fashion whenever any joke had been made by the admiral or the elder Duffy, deemed it a duty to follow the example of these worthies in every respect, and in pursuance of this duty had comfortably settled themselves in their chairs for a nap.

This was the happy state in which Charley and Horatio left them, and joined the ladies.

These charming young creatures had been anxiously waiting for our hero's appearance in the drawing-room, where they had been criticising that young gentleman's looks in the manner usual to ladies.

" Isn't he divine?" said Maggie, the eldest, a plump and pretty maiden of four and twenty summers, with dark hair and blue eyes with a figure that would have made a small fortune for the proprietors, had she exhibited in flesh coloured tights at the El Dorado in Leicester Square, or at any other establishment where young ladies are employed to show themselves with the least possible amount of drapery.—" Isn't he a darling," exclaimed this warm hearted creature, " oh, I could——"

" For shame! Maggie, I'm surprised at you," said her second sister Fanny—" you really oughtn't——"

" But I can't help it," said Maggie, rising and endeavouring to shake out some perverse fold in her dress, " I really believe I'm in love."

" But Maggie, dearest, he's very handsome,

but he's so slight," said Fanny, whose affections were fixed upon a very broad-shouldered young gentleman in the neighbourhood.

"That's just what I admire so much," replied the infatuated Maggie; "I hate to see a gentleman with shoulders like a farmer."

"That's your taste," said Miss Fanny, in a mildly affended tone, "I like to see a man look like one."

"Upon my word, your conversation is anything but what it should be—it's positively indecent," said their youngest sister Matilda.

"La! dear, do you really think so?" asked Miss Fanny.

"I do, indeed—and I think you might talk of something else, and not waste your time on such silly subjects."

Miss Matilda Duffy was a young lady who went in largely for propriety, and was given to missionary meetings, tea-meetings, and meetings with the curate to whom she was engaged.

This gentleman belonged to a party in the church, recognised by the hang-dog look of its ministers, who delight in showing a great deal of white neck-cloth and shirt front, are voracious consumers of tea and buttered toast, and endeavour to impress their flock with the notion that salvation depends upon the number of tracts that those deluded people read, and the amount given towards the support of their pastor.

This was the sort of animal Miss Matilda held at the apple of her eye, and this will account in some measure for her outward show of propriety.

But Maggie and Fanny cared little for her remarks, and the latter who was rather of a nagging turn of mind, observed, "It was better talk about Mr. Wag in this way than to kiss him, as somebody did the parson."

This speech made Miss Matilda wince again, for she was the self-same somebody, and this proof of their intimacy had led to her engagement to this amourous ecclesiastic on the suggestion of Old Spanker, who had seen the clergyman impressing kisses upon the girls lips, and had kicked him out of the house for so doing. And it was soon after determined that matrimony was necessary for the young lady, and the ceremony was to come off soon after Christmas.

Their little differences on the point were abruptly brought to a termination by the entrance of Horatio and Charley.

"We thought you were never coming to us," said Maggie to her brother, but looking at Charley in a manner that sent a thrill through that young gentleman's waistcoat on the left side, and making room for him at her side—into which seat Charley subsided, and was immediately covered by the ample crinolines of the pretty Maggie and Fanny. Matilda sat apart deriving spiritual nourishment from a book that had been sent to her that morning by her clerical admirer, the Reverend Guzzle Gush.

This worthy divine was himself the author of it, and had realized a tidy sum by its publication, for it had gone down with the faithful in a most astounding fashion.

The title of this work was "What's your

Game? or The Right and the Wrong road to Abraham's bosom." The object of it was to point out to the sinner the course that should be pursued in event of the said sinner at any time wishing to be saved.

It strongly recommend him to turn from his wickedness and go to the Right road, upon which it mentioned the spiritual posting houses, amongst which the establishment of the Reverend Author figured as one of the most respectable.

Such was the book that the youngest Miss Duffy was perusing when our hero took his seat between her two elder sisters. Miss Matilda, either anxious to make a convert, or attracted by Charley's good looks, called his attention to this precious volume, and after quoting several of the grandest fpassages, which the Rev. Guzzle had marked, she asked our hero what he thought of them.

Here was a fix—it would be necessary for Mr. Wag to tell a lie, for it would never do to tell a lady, and that lady engaged to the perpetrator of the work, that he (Mr. Wag) thought that all he had heard quoted of it, was most arrant bosh—no that would never do; so Charley replied most demurely that he considered it "very beautiful."

This remark of his caused the pretty Maggie to laugh to such an extent, that it appeared doubtful whether she would ever cease. Horatio was also infected and Fanny.

"Really," said Miss Matilda, controlling her wrath with a mighty and most admirable effort; "really I see nothing in Mr. Wag's reply to laugh at."

Mr. Wag saw a great deal himself, but succeeded in keeping his face as long as a juvenile Jackass's.

"Oh! the deuce take Guzzle, and his trash as well," said Horatio in a pet when he saw the young lady preparing to renew the subject, when Maggie's mirth had in some measure subsided. "Let's have some music."

This request was seconded by Charley, and the fair Maggie rose up to comply with it.

Our hero handed her to the piano, and stood by while she played an overture, in a most brilliant style.

This concluded, she turned to Charley, asking—"Do you sing, Mr. Wag?"

"I'm sorry to say I do not," replied Charley, who for once in his life positively felt what he said.

"I wish you did, I have some charming duets that we might have praeticed together, and that stupid brother of mine will not take the trouble to learn them."

"No, I should think not," replied that youth, "not when I can hear you and Fanny, but come Maggie, he added, slapping her white shoulders, let us have one of your favourites."

And Maggie after a very pretty display of hesitation, and pleading a severe cold, which somehow or other did not affect her voice in the slightest degree, sang in a clear soprano, that favourite air, "Balli, Balli," from Don Giovanni

Her singing won the applause of Mr. Wag, who at the conclusion of it was most impressive in his thanks.

The naughty Maggie seemed perfectly delighted at having pleased our hero if only in this respect.

This idea made her sing away merrily, and she was in the middle of an Italian song when Admiral Spanker, having finished his nap, entered the drawing-room, and, after backing and filling for a short time near the door, to see exactly where they were, made a tack for the group at the piano.

His entrance caused Maggie to cease her Italian ballad immediately, for the old gentleman, who reigned supreme in the house of Duffy, had a very English notion, and dislike to anything foreign.

He was in a very merry mood, and insisted upon the pretty Maggie playing a hornpipe to which he intended to dance, but this little exhibition was over-ruled by his God-son, Horatio, who dissuaded the venerable Spanker from such a rash proceeding.

Then he would sing, and commenced —

The parson went a fishing by the light of the moon,
And he caught a craw-fish by the back-bone,
By the back—— bone—— by—— by——

What the rest of the ditty was I have not the slightest idea, but I suppose it was not fit for ears polite, for Horatio seized hold of his respected sponsor, and forcibly dragged him away from the piano, notwithstanding his struggles to remain.

Out of the room he would not go, but as he promised not to sing any more he was allowed to return, and was handed over to the tender mercies of Miss Matilda, by whom he took a seat.

"Well, my dear, and how are you?" said he, mopping his forehead with his pocket-handkerchief, "how are you, ' Tilly.' "

"Thank you, my dear admiral, I am tolerably well."

"You'll be all right next week—Mrs. Gush—Eh?"

Miss Matilda made no reply to this old rip's impudence, but after no end of exertion contrived to pump up a blush, which was, however, thrown away on the old admiral, who was not just then in a state likely to appreciate any such a display of modesty.

"What's that book you're reading?" he asked, after some minutes silence.

"I fear it is not one that would interest you, dear sir," said Miss Matilda, in a tone decidedly expressing her opinion that Admiral Spanker was a lost sheep.

"What's the name of it?" said he this time, rather gruffly.

Matilda, after some little dodging about to evade doing so, told him.

"Abraham's Bosom," sneered he, with the most profound contempt—"Abraham's——," Here he stopped suddenly, as the idea faintly gleamed upon him that he was talking to a young lady.

"It's beautifully written," said Matilda. "If I could persuade you to read it, dear Admiral, Spanker, it might——"

"Well?"

"If I could only persuade you."

"But you can't," replied the old gentleman, placing his thumb to his nose, and out-spreading his four fingers—" Walker !"

This conclusive expression did not have the effect of silencing Miss Matilda, for she again opened fire on the even-tempered old sailor.

"Oh! Admiral Spanker, if you could be brought to see the folly of your present life— if papa and you would go to church, and give up consuming such an unnecessary quantity of wine——"

"Eh!—what!—go to church and get drunk! Does anybody dare to say I get drunk?"

"Mr. Gush——"

"Did he? by G—— !" shouted the old admiral, now perfectly furious. "Did he? guzzle guts!—then I'll——," added he, glaring round for something to break, and his eye resting on an elegant little table at his side, until then unnoticed, "I'll smash him!" and bringing his ponderous fist down upon it with a bang, the table was shattered.

His loudly uttered vow of vengeance, together with the crash of the table, soon brought the rest of the party round them, and there in the centre of them stood the admiral, brandishing a piece of the table, and roaring out the most terrible threats against the unfortunate clergyman whom he fancied had accused him of getting drunk in church.

"I'll brain him!—I will," he roared, "the first time I meet him, if it's ten years hence."

This blood-thirsty remark caused Miss Matilda to dissolve into a most passionate flood of tears, for the devoted Gush was to dine with the party on the following day.

It was some time before Horatio could pacify the outraged old gentleman, but at last he succeeded, with the assistance of Fanny, in getting him out of the drawing-room, the angry old tyke still retaining the piece of the table, with which he intended executing the deed of blood, firmly tucked under his arm.

Master Wag and the pretty Maggie were now left alone, for Miss Matilda had retired before the admiral's wrath.

Notwithstanding Charley's love for music, I may venture to say that during Horatio and Fanny's absence not a song was sung, and very little said—Maggie, in the most improper manner, gazing into Charley's eyes, and that young gentleman fancied he saw something in her bright orbs that hinted if he took her soft little hand in his own, and imprinted a kiss upon her lips, that she would not be indignant.

Charley as we already know was a bold fellow, and made the experiment and I grieve to say for the sake of the sex, the young lady did not resent his impertinents.

Mr. Wag felt that the ice was broken, but was not sorry when they heard the sound of voices warning them to resume the singing and to place a respectable distance between them, for the chance of discovery was anything but agreeable to contemplate.

"Well! old fellow" said Horatio on entering the room with Fanny "I hope that good-for-nothing sister of mine has been amusing you—I didn't hear the piano going.

"I have been shewing Mr. Wag some of those beautiful prints of your—he's a great admirer of them" said the artful Miss Maggie.

"Indeed! I did not know you cared for

those sort of things," said Horatio, "we have some rattlers—you shall see them to-morrow."

"I shall be very glad to see them," said Charley, who had suddenly to take an interest in things that he had never thought of before.

Mr. Duffy and the two intimate friends having finished their nap, marched into the drawing-room, and the party was soon after joined by Mrs. Duffy, who had concluded her evening devotion.

She was one of the Guzzle Gush flock, and it was mainly to her instrumentality that the Rev. Guzzle had obtained a footing in the Duffy family.

The party now assumed the formal air, which hung about it on Mr. Wag's introduction, for Mrs. Duffy was grave (the Gushites always look miserable), and her worthy spouse had wrapped himself up in his mantle of pomposity once more.

This was invariably the case when he and the admiral had been as "jolly" as they had been that evening.

The Admiral had gone to bed, still vowing vengeance against the wretched Gush, and actually placed the piece of the broken table under his pillow, to be "at time," as he observed the first thing in the morning.

The young ladies, after the addition to the party, not feeling much inclination to remain, soon retired.

Mrs. Duffy doing ditto to her boudoir, whither she was joined by the sweet young creature Matilda, who now had an opportunity of conversing upon the beauties of "What's your Game?" and telling her mother many other little things, which were intended for her mamma's ears, and hers alone. Here in the sanctity of this retreat we must leave the mamma and her daughter calculating months to the number of nine, and winding up with a pious chuckle at something or other, which we *know* very little about, but may guess a great deal.

Our hero and Horatio soon sloped after the ladies had left, and retired to the latter's room, where they indulged in smoke until they separated for bed.

After breakfast on the following morning the ladies arrayed themselves for church. The gentlemen of the party did not manifest any great anxiety to undergo the same infliction, and although Mrs. Duffy looked reproachfully at her lord for not accompanying them, that gentleman did not heed it in the slightest degree, for very good reason—the Admiral was not addicted to church going, and had only expressed his dislike to it at the breakfast table. So Mr. Duffy intended to remain at home and keep him company.

Mrs. Duffy turned her eyes heavenward at her husband's heathenish conduct, and addressing Charley, said in a solemn tone.

"Would *you* like to hear Mr. Gush preach this morning, Mr. Wag?"

Mr. Wag felt very much inclined to say, that he would rather be excused; but at the moment he was about to reply, his eye caught Miss Maggie's, and his reply much to the astonishment of the old Admiral and Horatio was expressive of his delight at so doing.

"You don't mean to say you're going to church!" said Horatio, in accents of astonishment.

"I told Mrs. Duffy I would," replied Charley.

"Oh! well, if you do—I will, but I think it's a foolish way of spending the morning."

Charley would have thought the same had it not been for Maggie's glance, which settled the business for him.

"Mind they don't convert you, youngsters," sang out old Spanker, as Charley and Horatio left the room.

The old sailor was in a high good humour, and relinquished his cold-blooded design upon the Reverend Mr. Gush, much to Miss Matilda and her mamma's satisfaction. Horatio and Charley accompanied the ladies to the church, but on their arrival the former gentleman pleaded an engagement that he had made and forgotten, as an excuse for not attending the service.

It turned out afterwards that the scamp went to visit a pretty little country girl, who lived in the neighbourhood, and with whom Master Horatio was exceedingly intimate— so much so that he was reputed to be the papa of two bouncing babies that, that young party occasionally wheeled about in a perambulator. Mr. Wag was not sorry for losing Horatio's company on this occasion, for it would enable him to pay attention to Maggie, which he would not do before the vigilant eyes of an affectionate brother.

Sitting by the pretty damsel's side in church, he bore the sermon, a frightfully long-winded and trashy composition, with the fortitude of a Martyr.

Not that it mattered much, for had it been one of the most eloquent discourses that ever emanated from the lips of the celebrated Mr. Bellew, the same amount of attention would have been paid by this well assorted pair. Indeed, it is to be questioned whether they paid any attention whatever, except to each other.

At last the sermon came to an end, and Charley had the pleasure of walking home with Maggie and Fanny—Mrs. Duffy and the pious Matilda staying to hold sweet converse with the Rev. Guzzle.

"Well, Mr. Wag, what do you think of Mr. Gush?" said Fanny.

"To tell you the truth, Miss Fanny, I think him an awful monster," said Charley.

"He's so horridly vulgar," put in Maggie, "and seems to have the most profound contempt for the letter H."

"He makes use of it very often though," said Fanny.

"Yes, but in the wrong place," replied her sister—"but you will have an opportunity of seeing more of him this evening—he's coming to dinner."

"Is he?"

"Yes."

"Then he'll spoil my appetite."

"Why?" said Fanny.

"Because my gaze will be rivetted on his exceedingly ugly mouth all the while."

Ha! ha! ha! "what a funny idea," said Fanny.

"It is," said Maggie, "I only take a pleasure on looking at what I admire (here she cast a glance at our hero), and not at ugly things.

"You are speaking of what you take a pleasure in (the young lady blushed at this remark), but have you never felt an irresistable inclination to look at anything horrible?"

"Oh! often, Mr. Wag—I know the feeling you allude to perfectly well—it has induced me sometimes to look at the most hideously deformed people, and the sight, perhaps, has haunted me for days after."

"I hope the sight of this Reverend Gorilla will not haunt me for days," said Charley.

As they neared the house Horatio came in sight. He had seen them, and was advancing towards them.

His fisrt enquiry, after skilfully evading Maggie's questioning, as to where he had been, was—" Well, Wag, how do you like Gush?"

"Like him—did you say?"

"Yes! why not?" said Horatio, with a grin.

"Mr. Wag thinks him an awful monster," observed Fanny, "and he is not far out when he calls him so," she added.

"That's about my opinion," said Horatio, "and Matilda will have a delightful husband when she has him; but then, they're birds of a feather, so it doesn't matter much."

"You'll have a charming brother-in-law," suggested Fanny.

"It's deuced little I have to say to him now, and I shall say less when they're married."

"You don't seem to approve of the rev. gentleman," said Charley.

"Not at any price—what say you, Maggie?"

"I haven't much regard for him, myself," replied that young lady, "and certainly have not any anxiety for such a brother-in-law."

"Brother-in-law indeed!—why, Wag, scamp as he is, would make a better one."

This very unnecessary eulogium on Charley made Miss Maggie blush—only her veil fortunately concealed it, and she inwardly thought that she should not at all object to being the cause of Horatio's finding a brother-in-law after his own heart. Unfortunately for the young lady herself, she had mistaken the drift of Mr. Wag's attentions, or she would never have allowed that young gentleman to go to the lengths she had on the preceding evening. She was under the impression that he meant matrimony, and he was under the impression that she meant anything but——As it was, they enjoyed each other's society without troubling about the future in any way whatever.

After a short stroll they returned home, and the old admiral at once began chaffing them about the sermon.

"Well, what was the text, Wag?" said he.

"I really don't know," replied Charley, "but I daresay Miss Duffy may know."

"Indeed I do not," said that young lady, "I know as little about it as Horatio does, and that is nothing at all—for he did not go to church, and will not tell where he has been to all the morning,"

"Not been to church!" exclaimed old Spanker, "not been to church! what a heathen to be sure. I say, youngster, where the deuce have you been to?—out with it."

"I went for a long walk," replied Horatio, who mentally consigned the old gentleman to a much warmer climate than he had ever visited before.

"I daresay," observed Fanny, "you are so very fond of walking."

"I can assure you all I did go for a walk, and you may believe me or not, as yon like," said Horatio, who was getting rather confused at their remarks—then, turning to Charley, asked him if he would go for a drive after lunch.

"Yes, if you like," replied Mr. Wag, although he would have preferred remaining at home in the society of the pretty Maggie, but did not like to refuse going, for fear of its exciting attention.

During lunch, to which Mr. Gush had been invited by Mrs. Duffy, the conversation assumed rather a grave turn, the reverend gentleman quoting great pieces of "what's your game," whenever he was not engaged in consuming the good things before him.

"Have you read any portion of the work my young friend?" said he, in his usually oily tone of voice, to Horatio"

"I beg your pardon, Mr. Gush," replied that youth, "what did you say?"

"I asked you whether you had read any portion of my new work, what's your game?" said the Rev. Guzzle Gush in a mild tone.

"I have not," said Master Duffy, in a mock tone of solemnity—"is it good? what's all about?"

"You should read it, my young friend, and judge for yourself,—I must not give any opinion, but your estimable mamma and Miss Matilda have read it, and I believe they were charmed with it."

"Oh! oh! I daresay, I shall be so, as well, when I read it."

At this remark of Horatio's old Spanker gave a low chuckle and turning to Charley who was seated close to him, said—

"When that boy reads it, you and I will go in for it, and I daresay it will do us as much good as it has done Mrs D. and her daughter."

Charley replied that if they waited until Horatio read it, he feared that it would never come off, as that young gentleman was not given to that sort of reading any more than himself.

"I should think not," said the admiral, "when I was your age I liked something in penny numbers better, and so I do now, better than the trash that fellow writes. I'll tell you what I should like to do with the rogue."

"What?"

"I should like to take him across the line with me for the first time in his life."

"What would you do with him?" inquired Charley, who forgot about the shaving.

"Do with him? why I'd have the skin scraped off him, and ducked until he was half dead!—that's what I'd do."

"I should like to assist," said Charley, "I'd take that ' Newgate frill' off his chin."

"It would be a good joke to pretend being drunk, and pitch into him."

A HARD HIT.

"Glorious," said Charley, "why don't you carry your threat into execution?"

"What—last night's?"

"Yes!"

"And break his head with the leg of the table, as I swore I would?"

"Yes!"

"It would be a good joke—suppose I pick a quarrel with him—I think I'll do it to-night."

"Do—it will be great fun," said Charley, "and you might easily get it up."

"I will, and we'll have a spree with him," said the old boy, chuckling, "I hate the brute, and should like to give him a shaking."

By this time lunch was concluded, and Ho-

ratio joined Charley and the admiral, and was by them let into their plot.

"By jove it will be glorious," said Horatio, "mind you hit him hard."

"Trust me to that," replied old Spanker, with a grin.

"And now Wag," said Horatio, turning to Charley, "are you coming with me? for I want to be off."

"I'm ready whenever you are," replied that young gentleman.

"Then come along, the trap's waiting."

"You boys are up to no good, I know," said the old admiral, as they left him.

Neither of the boys paid much attention to this remark. Charley did not hear it, and the only notice that Horatio took of it was to place his finger to the side of his nose in a very knowing manner, and then made his exit.

Charley and he were soon bowling along towards an adjoining village, where Horatio told our hero that he would show him as pretty a girl as he had ever clapped his eyes on.

"Oh! that's your game, is it?" said Charley, "I thought there was something of the sort up when you left us this morning"

"You weren't far out."

"But who is she?"

"I'll tell you as much as I know myself, and then you'll be satisfied?"

"I'll try to—only let's hear all about it?"

"During the time I was down here after my return from the Mediterranean, nearly two years ago, I went into the town to make some purchases or other, and was returning to the place where a friend was waiting with the trap. When passing through one of the slums which led to it, I heard a devil of a row and screams up a court. Of course I ran to see what was going on, and found a man beating a girl in a frightful manner. I immediately took her part, and then the fellow turned on me, and we had a tussle, and I licked him, much to the girl's delight, although it was her own father I pounded. Well! this girl was very grateful, and obliged me with the particulars on the spot. Her story was soon told. She was an artificial flower maker, and was then out of work, and whenever that was the case, she had to stand by for a dressing from her affectionate papa, who was rather given to intoxication. On this occasion he had been imbibing pretty freely, and on his return home met the unfortunate girl, who had been out seeking for employment. He at once began pegging into her, and he was busily engaged at it when I made my appearance."

"I see what followed," said Charley, "you took advantage of the poor maiden's position, and——"

"No, I didn't," interrupted Horatio, "just the reverse."

"What do you mean?"

"Why, that she took advantage of my good nature, and settled the matter that way."

"Oh! ah!"

"She did—and I'll tell you how. After the shindy, and when her gov'nor had gone into the house, I had a long chat with her, and she expressed her fear at living under the same roof with him. It was then that it came out about the artificial flower business, and she strongly hinted at apartments of her own, where she could live respectably."

"And you took them?"

"Exactly so."

"And seduced her?"

"No."

"No!" Mr. Wag was going to add "what a muff," when Horatio replied—

"I'm sorry to say that she had been weak enough to allow some unprincipled ruffian before my time to do her that irreparable injury."

"Oh! that alters the case," said Charley.

"I took the rooms for her in the place we are getting to now, and she has lived there for some time—ever since."

"By jove!" said Charley, "she must be rather constant."

"She has never forgotten my saving her from the latter portion of that towelling."

"She *must* be grateful, and I suppose is very affectionate?"

"Yes."

"Too much so at times?"

"That's according to taste—she always makes a great fuss when I go there, and has the youngsters- —"

"Eh!—what? youngsters!"

"Twins."

"Twins!" almost shouted Charley, "you don't mean to say——"

"I do though, unfortunately."

"That's too much of a good thing, I couldn't stand that," observed our hero, who, like most of his sex, had a great aversion to squalling brats.

"What the devil are you to do?"

"Do? why cut the connexion to be sure," replied Mr. Wag, in a most heartless manner.

Our friend Charley had none of the absurd notions that one hears continually put forward when any matrimonial squabble has taken place, and the male party is anxious for a separation—then we hear such pious ejaculations as "what! leave the mother of his children?" "scandalous," &c. But in this case you may say there was no matrimony, and any connexion, without that ceremony having previously been gone through and paid for, should be broken off without hesitation. I am not of opinion that Mr. Wag advised Horatio to break with this girl on the ground that the celebrated marriage service had not been mumbled to them, and that it was exceedingly wrong to dispense with it. His only reason, I feel convinced, was his horror of babies. He positively dreaded entering any house celebrated for them, and generally made himself scarce when the brats made their appearance. He was still thinking of them when he said to Horatio

"Will they be exhibited?"

Under the impression that Duffy must be thinking of them also, he asked the question, and was not a little surprised at Horatio's inquiring who *they* were?

"The cursed kids to be sure."

"The kids! yes, to be sure they will. Patty is very proud of them."

"And so are you, from the happy way you speak about them," growled our hero, who had no patience with a fellow that could take an interest in a brace of babies—his own into the bargain.

"Well, I can't say that they make me anything but proud—you'll say you never saw finer youngsters."

"I don't pretend to be a judge," said Charley, puffing away at his cigar desperately, for Horatio had pulled up at the door of a cottage at which appeared a good-looking woman, with a baby in her arms.

"Here we are, old fellow, get out." Then turning to an apple-faced boy who was playing close at hand, Horatio told him to hold the horse.

"Yes, sir," said the boy.

"Don't you leave him for anything," said

Duffy, "or I'll break every bone in your body."

The boy grinned, and replied—

"I shan't leave him—don't you be afraid, sir."

Horatio and Charley then entered the house and proceeded up stairs to the young lady's apartments, at the door of which they were met by the fair creature herself.

Charley thought her a very pretty girl as she stood at the head of the stair-case welcoming them. He thought that Horatio might have *done* much worse than to befriend the young creature who was now introduced to him.

Mr. Wag conceived a very good opinion of the young lady, and had expressed it to Horatio when she left the room, and immediately after returned with the twins !

Charley had for a time forgotten them, but their sudden appearance, coupled with the fact that there were more babies below, made him say to himself—

"Good God ! why the house is full of them !"

At this moment one of the pair of babies commenced yelling, of course the other joined in the chorus, and the effect was tremendous, In vain did their mamma try to pacify them—they refused to be comforted, at least for some time.

Charley was upon thorns, and cursed Horatio, the brats, and their mother, over and over again. He had the good sense, though, to do all this to himself, or the chances are that the great Duffy might have offered to do battle with him, could he have heard all that our hero thought.

"What the devil did he bring me here for at all," said he to himself, "the girl's pretty enough to be sure, but what's that to me, I can see lots of pretty girls in my wanderings, and I would sooner have passed the afternoon with his pretty sister a thousand times rather than hearing this cursed yelling."

Fortunately the yelling alluded to gradually subsided, and our hero felt a great deal happier when it ceased entirely, and the causes of it were removed.

Horatio did not part with them until he had dandled them about in the most approved fashion of simple-minded papas—in fact he made himself as ridiculous over these two little pests as any respectable married man might have behaved over his legitimate offspring.

This was very absurd of him we must all admit, but then, when a young gentleman becomes a papa for the first time, it is not at all an unusual thing for him to make a great donkey of himself where the little olive branches are concerned.

Perhaps this was not actually the first time that Master Duffy had been a papa, but it certainly was the first time that he knew of the circumstance, and heard the pipes of the little devils that owed their existence in this world of lights and shadows to him.

His antics with the brats had continued for some time, and his attempts to excite Charley into admiring them having failed, the little innocents having once more commenced squalling, were bundled off to another room, to the intense relief of Charley.

Horatio, deprived of the dear little ones, now turned his attention to their mamma, who had been vainly endeavouring to engage Charley in conversation.

To tell the truth, the young lady was rather taken with our hero, and Master Duffy's nose might have been put out of joint very easily had Charley given the damsel the slightest encouragement. But if our hero had the slightest inclination for anything of the sort, the thought of the twins effectually settled the point for him, and the settling was not in the lady's favour.

If Mr. Wag thought at all on this matter, I daresay his idea was, that a young lady that had commenced with twins, might indulge in them yearly.

Whatever he thought, it is certain that he did not reciprocal any of her polite little attentions; this was rather unusual for Charley, but consider Horatio was his friend, and then ——the twins——.

Duffy certainly had not noticed the dead set Miss Polly had made at Charley, or perhaps he would not have been so lavish of his caresses to that young lady. Their billing and cooing might have continued much longer had not our hero evinced signs of great impatience and anxiety to be off.

At last Charley determined to take the trap and go for a drive, feeling that his room must be more desirable than his company.

He bade adieu to the fascinating Polly, who hoped that she should have the pleasure of seeing him again, and mounted the trap, after dismissing the apple-faced youth with a sixpence, which had the effect of making him open his eyes to a greater extent than he had ever before succeeded in doing.

Away he drove at a slapping pace, for it suited his present mood which was anything but amiable. He considered that he had been shamefully chiseled out of a pleasant afternoon with Maggie, and for what?—to hear the pipes of a pair of squalling brats.

A long drive in the frosty air, and a good cigar had the most beneficial results upon our hero's temper, and when he returned for Horatio his humour was just the reverse of what it had been on his leaving.

"I thought you weren't coming back at all," said Duffy, "you've been a devil of a drive, 'look at the nag,' added he, with a glance at the horse, which was steaming not a little.

"He is rather smoky," replied Charley.

"Where did you drive to, Mr. Wag?" enquired Miss Polly.

"I really can't tell you—I've been up one road and down another, and it was by the greatest fluke imaginable that I found my way here again."

"I'm deuced glad you did, though, for I should have been nicely in for it without the trap to get home in."

"It is no great distance to walk from here to your place," said Charley.

"More than I like, when I can ride," replied Horatio, "and as it is getting late we'll be off—so good-bye, Polly, dear—merry Christmas to you—mind you don't get tight."

With this admonitory remark, which called

forth " how can you talk so?" from the young lady, our hero and Horatio started for home.

Charley undertook the management of the steed, for the animal exhibited symptoms of restiveness, with which Horatio's abilities as a Jehu, were not of an order to cope.

Mr. Wag was a famous charioteer, and they arrived at home safely in spite of the many efforts of their steed to do them some grievous bodily harm.

It was getting near the dinner hour, and they had barely time to dress.

When the two young gentlemen joined the company in the drawing-room, the Admiral made up to them and addressing Charley, said that he did not think it would do to carry his scheme against the parson into effect that night.

" Why not?" asked Charley, who was rather disappointed at his crying off after settling it so recently.

" Because there's no chance of Old Duffy being slued to-night—so it won't do for me to pretend to be."

" No—that wouldn't do at any price—it would be twigged at once."

" I'll do it though before he marries that stupid girl Matilda, and that's to come off next week."

" The devil it is—as soon as that?"

" Yes! as soon as that—and not a bit too soon," grumbled the admiral in a lower tone to himself, as he walked off to speak to some one else.

" I say, Duffy," said Charley, as Horatio came up to him, " Old Spanker is going to postpone his attack on the rev. gentleman."

" You don't say so?"

" I do."

" What a nuisance!"

" Are you thirsting for his blood?" said Charley, with a smile.

" Yes, nothing would please me better than to see the cork of his claret drawn, unless I had the doing of it myself."

" Why don't you?"

" It wouldn't do for me—now Spanker can do what he likes; besides I don't get screwed here, and he does."

The two separated after this little conversation and were not thrown much together until after dinner.

Dancing had been going on merrily, and Charley had been enjoying one or two round dances with the pretty Maggie, when Horatio came up to him and told him that he had just received a telegraphic message, which would oblige him to go to London on the following morning, and perhaps oblige him to remain there for a day or more.

" What's it about?" asked Charley.

" It's a question of pay I want settled before I leave England."

" Oh! but must you attend personally?"

" It's not absolutely necessary for the success of the application, but as I asked for an interview on the subject I must. You'll run up with me—won't you?"

" Yes, if you wish it, I will."

" Well, I should like it old fellow—it would be awfully slow if I have to pass a day in town alone,' and for that matter it would be frightfully slow for you here without me."

Charley would not attempt any reply to the latter portion of this speech, but inwardly anathematized everything and everybody that prevented his intimacy with Maggie being carried to the extent that he wished it to be.

Horatio settled that they should start by the early train on the following morning, and Charley gave his consent as reluctantly as possible without exciting the notice of Horatio, who was at this moment about to choose a partner for a waltz.

" You secure my eldest sister Maggie," said he to Charley, " she waltzes beautifully."

Master Charley had discovered that Miss Duffy was a very desirable partner for this sort of thing, so without the slightest regard for " what people might say," (he had danced with her twice already) he was soon whirling round the room with the charming Maggie.

" Is it a fact that you are going to leave to-morrow?" said she, as he handed her to a seat.

" I'm going to town with Horatio."

" I'm afraid if you once get to London you will not care to come down here again."

" Indeed, my dearest Miss Duffy, you are much mistaken—if I consulted my own inclination I should not go at all."

" Why do you?—why not stay here until Horatio returns?"

" Because he is under the impression that I should find it slow here without him," said Charley, smiling killingly, " and I do not see the necessity for undeceiving him."

" Perhaps you do find us tiresome," said the beauty, assiduously picking her bouquet to pieces.

" Maggie!" said our hero, reproachfully, " how can you hint at such a thing? Have I not——"

" Now then, Wag, how is it you are not dancing?" said Old Spanker, close at their elbows, " here is a partner for you, and Maggie you must dance with me this time, I think I can walk through a quadrille."

The old gentleman's untimely interference prevented Master Charley making a very telling speech to his pretty companion. Charley was annoyed at it, and if we may judge from the manner in which the admiral's proposition to walk through the quadrille with her, was received, Miss Maggie was decidedly suffering from the effects of suppressed passion.

Charley's partner was a pretty, fair, timid-looking little girl, with a profusion of light hair; she was most becomingly dressed in blue, which suited her complexion admirably, and our hero thought after all she was not a bad substitute, as far as appearance went, for the handsome Miss Duffy.

That young lady glared savagely at the unoffending little lady in blue, who seemed to look very guilty whenever Mr. Wag spoke to her, which he did pretty often, for he rather admired his little partner, and it was very evident, from Miss Maggie's spiteful glances, that she noticed it, and did not half like it.

And what was calculated to excite her ire to a higher degree. Charley did not seem at all anxious to relinquish the young lady when the quadrille was over, but remained at her side, when, according to Miss Maggie's notion, he should have been at hers.

His neglect had the effect of making that young lady exceedingly waspish to all around her, and some of her old admirers were quite at a loss to know what had caused such a radical change in the temper of the usually amiable Miss Duffy.

"What the deuce can be the cause of it?" said one of the snubbed ones to a sympathising brother.

"I believe she's sweet upon that fellow, Gush, that her sister is going to marry," replied the jealous youth.

"Is it possible," said the other, "I should not have given her credit for so much taste," he added, affectionately smoothing a very dirty tuft of hair upon his chin.

"It's either the parson or the old admiral— I'm rather inclined to think it's Spanker—did you see how unceremoniously he took her away from that good-looking young fellow that her brother brought down with him?"

"I didn't see it, but I should think it very likely that old Spanker's the man—he's got plenty of tin, and I daresay they'd like to keep it in the family."

"I daresay."

Mr. Wag found that his little partner in blue was very well to dance with, and was pretty, but was nowhere at all in a flirtation, and as our hero was rather great at this sort of thing, and enjoyed it immensely, he came to the conclusion that Miss Duffy was more in his style. Having arrived at this decision, "he sought her side, whispered low, and led her forth to dance." This dance happened to be a gallop, and it is a curious fact that at its conclusion Miss Maggie's face beamed again with her usual smile. What that artful dog Charley had contrived to say to her during the gallop, I know not—the effect alone was visible.

"I say, Wag," said Master Duffy, when the last of the guests had departed, and the ladies had retired to their downy couches to dream of their late partners,

"What is it?" said Wag.

"Come up to my room and have a pipe, and then we'll get to bed—the infernal train goes at nine, and we shall have to leave here by a quarter past eight at the latest."

"What a bore," replied Charley.

"It's the only train that will suit me, and I shan't get to town a moment earlier than I could wish."

Charley accompanied Horatio to his room, and after smoking a pipe with him, retired to his own room, and to bed.

On the following morning Duffy got up before six, and most unmercifully entered Charley's room, and aroused him from a very sweet slumber.

"Get up!" cried the fiendish Duffy, "get up, it's very late,"

"All right, I'm awake," replied Master Wag.

"Yes, but I must see you get out first," said the unyielding youth.

Doubtless he had some experience with his sleepy nautical brethren, and knew the necessity for preventing the drowsy one from taking one turn over, which generally leads to the second or third edition of a sound sleep.

"Oh! go to blazes!" said Charley, jumping out, "ugh! how cold it is."

"It is my boy, and you'll find it colder when you tumble into your bath."

"You're a Job's comforter."

"Now you're out, I'll go and dress—don't be long, for we shan't have any time to spare."

"I shall be ready as soon as you are." replied our hero.

In less than an hour they were both dressed, and shortly after seated at breakfast. This meal was soon despatched, and the trap ready to convey them to the station.

The train was due when they reached the station, for the frost during the night had rendered the road so slippery, that they could not go at the pace they usually did. They had just time to take their tickets and get into their seats when the train moved off.

"This is very jolly," said Horatio, refering to catching the train.

"You may think so, but I don't," grumbled Charley, thinking of the loss of his night's rest, and Miss Maggie's society, "I shall go to sleep." So suiting the action to the word, he ensconsed himself comfortably in the corner of the well-cushioned carriage, and snored harmoniously for the whole of the journey.

Horatio indulged in a little of nature's soft nursing, but only by fits and starts between the stations.

On their arrival in London, they proceeded to Duffy's rooms in Jermyn-street.

Here Master Wag was to remain until Horatio returned from Whitehall, whither he went immediately.

Charley was quite refreshed by the snooze in the train, to say nothing of another on the sofa during Horatio's absence, and when that individual returned our hero was as game as ever.

"Damnation!" said Duffy, on entering the room, "I can't get an answer till to-morrow. If I had expected this I wouldn't have lugged you up here, for I can't go down to-night, as I am to see the fellow again in the morning."

"Well, it can't be helped now, we must make the best of it, and try to amuse ourselves as well as we can," said Charley, philosophically.

"How the devil can we amuse ourselves," snarled Horatio.

"In the first place-let us have something to eat, for this is about a rational time for breakfast."

"I am rather peckish myself, so agitate the tinkler."

Breakfast being prepared and served up in a marvellously short time, the two sat down to it, and then began to talk over what they could do that day.

Horatio was looking at the *Times*, and the Crystal Palace advertisement caught his eye.

"By jingo! the Christmas Revels down there to-day will do."

"What do you mean?" asked Charley.

"The Crystal Palace."

"Oh! hang that place—you're always for going there

"I must say I like it, and besides you agreed to go with the Trevor Square girls and myself."

"Oh! ah! so I did," said Charley, in a resigned tone.

"Then we'll go to-day."

"If you like—anything," observed Master Wag, in an abstracted manner, with his mouth full of ham and eggs.

"We shall get down to Brompton by a little after twelve, if we make haste."

"But I don't feel very much inclined to hurry," said Charley, "perhaps the young ladies may not be up."

"That be hanged," said Horatio.

"It was nearly twelve when they started, so they did not arrive at Trevor Square so early as Master Duffy had predicted. They found the young ladies at home, and disengaged—their proposal to go to the Palace accepted immediately, and the young ladies at once retired to don the silk-dresses, in which they were so gorgously arrayed on the evening our friends visited the cattle show.

The damsel in yellow was rather astonished to see Charley and Duffy dressed, and looking like a pair of Piccadilly swells. It will be remembered, that on their first meeting Messrs. Wag and Duffy were got up to represent countrymen, so the young ladies astonishment at the transformation is not to be wondered at.

The blue-silked goddess, however, had never entertained the idea that Charley was a countryman, and told him so on the following morning.

After a good laugh at the joke, and the fun they had, they set out for the Palace, and reached there about two o'clock.

Our hero was rather disgusted than otherwise at all that was going on. It certainly did seem more fitted for children than grown persons, but the young ladies seemed pleased, and that was everything.

Charley was beginning to feel awfully bored with the place, and all that it contained, when it was announced through a brazen trumpet that the baloon ascent would take place at four o'clock. This seemed to be the great event of the day, for the people flocked to the spot where the machine was already inflated and secured by ropes.

The damsel in the yellow silk had expressed a desire to go up in the baloon, and as they were issuing tickets for a partial ascent, at the trifling charge of half-a-crown, Mr. Duffy had purchased his fair friend a ticket; but just before the first ascent, the young ladies had left our friends for some purpose or other, which they informed our hero and Horatio, would not detain them long.

Their backs being turned, Mr. Wag thought it would be fine fun to give them the slip, and communicated the idea to Duffy.

"But I've taken a ticket for the balloon."

"Oh! never mind that—give it to me—I'll soon get rid of it."

Duffy did so, and Charley seeing a good-looking girl standing near, politely offered the ticket, which was accepted with thanks, and Mr. Wag handed the young lady to a seat in the car.

This young party certainly had never studied the art of entering or leaving a vehicle with grace, or perhaps the liberal display of her well-formed legs would not have excited so much admiration as they did on this occasion.

After seeing her take her course upwards, our hero and Duffy made all possible speed away from the spot, to which the blue and yellow-dressed syrens were to return.

Away they went through the gardens, towards the station, and as luck would have it, a train came up shortly after they reached the platform.

"I was getting tired of it myself," said Duffy, as they went off.

"I'm glad of that—I always feel so when I go there," replied Charley.

"You won't go home to your diggings tonight?" said Horatio, "you may as well stop at my place—I have a spare room."

"It's hardly worth while, as we're going down to your gov'nor's again to-morrow," said Charley. "I think I'll accept your offer, and I shall go to bed deuced early, I can tell you."

"Not sooner than I shall," replied Duffy, who was more than half asleep now.

"Now for a Hansom," said Charley, as they got into the terminus.

A cab was chartered, and the two young gentlemen were soon in Jermyn-street, where at an early hour they retired to roost.

LXXXVII.—THE COUNTRY AGAIN—HOW A PARSON GOT A RAP ON THE HEAD—CHATHAM—AN UNEXPECTED MEETING, AND WHAT IT LED TO.

TO keep his appointment at Whitehall was the first thing Horatio did after breakfast on the following morning.

Charley had not even risen when Duffy went out, and as there was no necessity for him to get up, the lieutenant did not "rouse him out," as he was in the habit of doing to his friends after his nautical fashion.

On his return from Whitehall, about one o'clock, he found Charley up, and enjoying a cigar while perusing the morning papers.

"Well, what news," said Charley, as he entered the room.

"Good—my application has been successful—so we can get back to our place whenever you feel inclined."

"I'm ready this moment," said Charley.

"Ah! I don't mean as soon as all that, one of the afternoon trains will do. Just dive into that Bradshaw at your elbow, and see when there's a train."

"There's one at 3.15."

"That will do, first-rate, and if I telegraph they'll get it in time to send the trap to meet us."

"I should think so," replied Charley, "if you do it at once."

Horatio was not long about it, and as there was an office close at hand the message was soon dispatched.

They passed their time between lunch and their departure for the terminus at billiards, and had played several games, when Horatio looking at his watch, said that it was time for them to be off.

Their journey was a weary one, for the train stopped at every station; but a railway journey, like everything else, must have an end, and at last their destination was reached.

And on the platform, awaiting their arrival, stood old Admiral Spanker.

"What have you done up in town, my boy?" said he to Horatio, after warmly shaking hands with him and our hero.

"All that we wanted to," replied his godson.

"That's all right, then—now I'll tell you what brought me here, beside my anxiety to know how you had got on at head quarters.

"We'll get into the trap first."

"Not till I've had a drain of something to keep out the cold," said the old tar, with a wink at Charley, "come along, we shall all want it, for it is rather cool to-night."

After the trio had "freshened the nip" as the old admiral termed it, they started for home, and on the way the old gentleman told them that Gush had been invited to dinner, and that he (the admiral) meant to have his spree with him that night without fail.

"Never have such a chance again, peehaps —nobody there but ourselves," chuckled this old rip, "nobody to prevent it—I don't think you boys will—ha! ha! Eh?"

"I don't think there's *much* chance of our interfering. Eh, Wag?"

"Not the most remote chance of my doing so," said Charley, "I should rather approve of seeing the beast get a dressing."

"You shall see it, my boy, or my name's not Jack Spanker."

The intended lark with the Rev. Guzzle Gush was about the only topic of conversation on the road home.

They arrived at the hospitable mansion of the Duffys in time to witness the young ladies Maggie and Fanny doing feats on skates before dressing for dinner.

The Rev. Guzzle and Miss Matilda were standing aloof, holding a serious conversation on "the pomps and vanities of this wicked world," and Gush was pointing out a frightful instance of the devil triumphant in the persons of her two sisters, who were innocently enjoying themselves upon the ice.

To Admiral Spanker and these girls he dealt out hell and damnation unsparingly. He seemed to avoid abusing the male portion of the family, although he exhibited every inclination to backbite one and all, and hinted his fears that his young friend Horatio had gone astray lately, and that he grieved to say he feared Admiral Spanker was the cause of it.

His simple companion had to leave him to dress for dinner, and the rev. gentleman went in for a little pomp and vanity on the ice by himself.

His boots were not as thin as worldly-minded men usually pass the evening in, so the rev. gentleman tried on a pair of skates, but in less time than his clerk could have said "amen," the learned divine had come to grief. As he landed with a thump upon his posterior, the Rev. Guzzle so far forgot himself as to say—and rather loudly—"Damnation!" and it was not used in the way that the clergy generally employ it when they are dealing it

out to the uncontroverted, but it was made use of after the fashion of degenerate people, who never go to church, and, as a necessary consequence of the omission of this duty, make use of bad language, and otherwise misconduct themselves on the slightest provocation.

The rev. gentleman did not appear to be at all sorry for what he had said, for at first he did not think any one was near, but unfortunately the gardener (one of his flock) was close at hand, and must have heard him.

The shepherd remained in a sitting posture on the ice, with his hands on his knees, and when the gardener rushed to his assistance, the Rev. Guzzle looked calmly around him, and in his most impressive tone said

"All is vanity."

"And mortally unpleasant your pertickler vanity was, sir, to bring you down such a bump, sir!"

"I can only repeat what I have already said, my worthy man, "all is vanity."

"You're quite right, sir, and if you take my advice you'll take them damned vanities off your feet, or you'll be cracking your nut shortly."

"My Christian friend, as you value my esteem, never let me hear you make use of such highly improper language again."

"I'm werry much mistaken if I didn't hear him let out a little stronger than I did just now, when he came down on his starn," said the gardener to himself as he unstrapped the skates, and took them off the rev. gentleman's hoofs.

Mr. Gush looked round him in a dreamy sort of way, and again murmured "all is vanity."

This time the gardener did not venture any reply to his observation on the subject of vanity in general. It is rather a difficult matter to imagine what the rev. gentleman did intend to convey by it, and the writer of these pages is under the impression that Mr. Gush was rather foggy upon the point himself.

Be this as it may, the rev. divine retraced his steps to the house and entered the drawing-room, where Maggie and Fanny were chatting with Charley and their brother.

He moved about uneasily, for that rap on the ice had made him rather sore, and disinclined to sit down. He was at last picked up by the old admiral, who brought himself to anchor at his side, and boarded him about *Essays and Reviews.*

The old Salt watched his confusion, for the Rev. Mr. Gush knew very little more of them than Nana Sahib might be supposed to know of *La dame aux Camelias,* perhaps not so much. What he might have said, had not the dinner bell prevented it, there is no knowing.

As it was, the admiral left him in a brown study, considering what to reply, and after the fashion of the landlord mentioned in Tom Tiddler's Ground, taking a comprehensive view under a half-closed blind.

After dinner Mr. Gush retired with the ladies to the drawing-room, and the rest of the gentlemen remained at table.

Mr. Duffy had not been let into the secret of the evening's fun, for fear that he should get rid of Gush before the time settled, as being most favourable for the affair to take place.

The evening passed away rather slowly to those who were looking forward to the fun. Maggie and Fanny, who knew nothing of the plot were remarking how long their papa and the admiral stayed over their wine, and were hoping they would not get tipsy.

The young ladies knew their parent's propensities, and the admiral's also, but then he was a seasoned old dog, and could keep his head clear, when the aged Duffy, as Old Spanker, who had been reading "Great Expectations," facetiously called him, would be drunk, and incapable of the slightest mental or bodily exertion.

It grew late, but still the admiral did not join them.

"He will be very tipsy," said Maggie to her sister Fanny, "but he's generally good tempered, even when in that state."

"It will be very annoying if papa is in a similar condition," said Fanny.

"He is sure to be," replied Magge; "but then he never shows it here."

"It will be the second time since Mr. Wag has been down—what can he think of us all?"

Miss Maggie did not attempt to reply to the latter portion of her sister's remark, for, being rather selfish, she cared very little about what Mr. Wag might think of the family, if he made her an exception.

Charley and Horatio had been for some while enduring the conversation of the Rev. Guzzle, who elated with the quantity of wine he had drank at dinner (as it was Mr. Duffy's custom, the rev. gentleman made a point of taking wine with every body at table) was entertaning them with some wonderful exploits of his own, when a missionary in Africa, and the successful result of his endeavours to convert a female Gorilla!

When the rev. shepherd had concluded this interesting account, he looked round to see the effect of it, as depicted on the physiognomies of his hearers, and, to his intense horror, observed Admiral Spanker amongst them.

The old gentleman, instead of merely pretending to be drunk, was really, but, notwithstanding, was as cunning as a fox, and had his purpose steadily in view.

On leaving the dining-room he had gone to his bed-chamber, and possessed himself of the broken piece of the table, which he had shattered a day or so previously, and having found it in the place where he had hidden it, had made his way into the drawing-room without the fact of his presence being known to the unfortunate divine, behind whom he was standing when that gentleman was recounting the conversion of the Gorilla.

None of the party had felt inclined to address the old sailor on his entry, for he looked dangerous—thus he had remained some time in the room before Mr. Gush became aware of his proximity. The aged tar was still glaring at the devoted parson with a savage expression, when the luckless minister, thinking to propitiate him, offered him *The Gorilla; or a call to the unconverted*—a little tract of which the rev. gentleman was the author.

This polite attention on the part of the Rev. Guzzle the admiral considered an insult, for the hints that Miss Matilda had thrown out with reference to the anxiety of Mr. Gush for the spiritual welfare of the hardened old tar, were still sounding in his ears, and this present of a tract roused him to a pitch of fury better imagined than described. With a roar which must have painfully reminded the rev. gentleman of that intelligent link (in its unconverted state), between man and beast, the admiral was upon him.

"You devil—dodging thief! I go to church and get drunk—do I?" he bellowed out, shaking him with one hand, and with the other grasping his piece of wood in the most threatening manner. "Answer me, you son of a lubber! or I'll scuttle you without mercy!"

The shrieks of Mrs. Duffy and Matilda seemed only to exasperate the old fellow the more, for when Horatio and Charley approached him, in a manner which appeared to indicate interference, he struck out right and left with his piece of wood, after a fashion calculated to do a grievous bodily injury to the unfortunate who should happen to come within its reach. Our hero and Horatio very properly kept back, and contented themselves with shouting to the admiral to desist, who, however, paid not the slightest attention to their request.

"Will you answer me or not?" again roared old Spanker, "Do I go to church and get drunk?"

"No—o—o," howled the terrified wretch, "I'm su—re you wouldn't."

"Then take that!" shouted the infuriated old boy, "for saying I did," and down came the piece of wood on the head of the wretched Gush, who fell beneath the blow stunned and bleeding.

Mrs. Duffy, with a yell, flopped down at the side of the roughly-used clergyman, calling him "a blessed martyr," "a slaughtered lamb," and other endearing names which she deemed appropriate.

"Come along, you boys, and we'll have some grog," shouted old Spanker, throwing away the weapon with which the deed of blood had been committed, with a force that sent it to the further end of the room, smashing a mirror. "Come along! and I say, Maggie! just play 'Rule Britannia' as loud as you can, and I'll give you five pounds and a kiss!"

"Or 'The cries of the wounded from the battle of Prague,'" suggested the mischievous Fanny."

"Yes, yes, that'll do—run and play it!" said Old Spanker, but the young ladies, although anxious to please their old friend, had a wholesome regard for their mamma's anger, so abstained from indulging the musical whim of the old gentleman, who, finding that "the boys" would not accompanying him to partake of grog on the strength of the affair, and that the young ladies would not celebrate his feat with music, took himself off and joined Duffy, senior, who had been enjoying a nap, and who, although still hazy, was game for some grog, and Old Spanker related the affair that had just occurred, to the infinite amusement of his companion, who detested the Rev.

A FIEND.

Guzzle as much as his friend, but did not dare evince his dislike on account of his wife, who, as it is not unfrequently the case, figuratively wore the inexpressible attributes of male attire.

That lady was still at the side of the injured person, and was mopping up the blood, which was trickling from a cut on his head, with her laced pocket-handkerchief. He was still insensible, for old Spanker's arm came down heavily, and our hero and Duffy proposed his being sent home, but this Mrs. Duffy would not hear of—he should be placed in bed, and a surgeon sent for.

During the discussion relative to his disposal. Miss Matilda had been lying on a sofa, having fainted just before the blow was struck. She recovered from her swoon just as the old admiral called out to Maggie for "Rule Britannia," and hearing Fanny suggest the "Cries of the wounded," she immediately concluded that her darling Gush was wounded—perhaps killed—and the kneeling figures of her mother, Mr. Wag, and her brother, confirmed her in the latter erroneous impression. Why, it is difficult to say, for a wounded man invariably requires more attention than a dead one.

This idea could not have entered Miss Matilda's head, which she moved a little in acknowledgment of a glass of water dashed violently in her face by the sisterly hand of the young lady who proposed the "Cries of the wounded" when the Rev. Guzzle was struck down. Believing that the spirit of the loving Gush had winged its flight, and taking the notion from the barbarous musical proposals of the admiral and Fanny, she whispered solemnly to the latter, who stood beside her, " The Dead March in Saul."

" Fudge!" replied that young lady, and added, in an undertone, " it's too soon for that, unfortunately."

" He's gone! and I care not how soon I follow," said she, kissing " The Gorilla," and pressing it to her bosom.

She had picked it up when Admiral Spanker had thrown it at the terror-stricken Gush, and now looked upon it as the cause of his martyrdom.

" To think that that deluded man should have slain my gentle Guzzle. Oh! Guzzle! Guzzle! I will not survive you," she cried.

The rev. gentleman hearing this exclamation, and judging from it that he was considered dead, and would, perhaps, be buried alive, made an effort, and gave vent to a yell that must have quickly undeceived Mrs. Duffy and her sorrowing daughter on that point.

Horatio and Charley had plaistered up his broken scalp, so well, indeed, that it was not thought necessary to send for a doctor—and thus let that professional gentleman into more of the secrets of the house of Duffy than he was already possessed of.

After the reverend sufferer had been conducted by our hero and Master Duffy to the room prepared for him, where everything was done that could possibly conduce to his comfort, and allay the pain of his broken poll, these two youths joined Admiral Spanker and Mr. Duffy, the young ladies and their mamma having, during their absence with the damaged ecclesiastic, retired to bed.

The entrance of the two young gentlemen was hailed with shouts by old Spanker, who had been engaged brewing punch in anticipation of their joining them. Horatio's papa also expressed (though somewhat thickly) the pleasure he felt at seeing " his dear boy" and his friend on such an occasion. It was very evident that Mr. Duffy considered this an occasion to be celebrated, for he insisted upon Charley and Horatio drinking to the admiral's good health for what he had done that evening. Neither Mr. Wag nor Horatio had the slightest objection to do this, for the parson was not a favourite with the latter gentleman, and Charley had not been prepossessed by his appearance in the first instance, and certainly not by his conversation subsequently.

" Bumpersh!" shouted old Duffy, whose articulation was beginning to grow indistinct, " sta'd up!" The young gentlemen addressed immediately complied with this request.

" My tear Spanker, your cond'ct 'night h's been mosh adm'rable—from what you tell me, 1 think you've killed him—and—and allow me—us—for doing sho—to dri'k your 'ealth."

After making this speech, which clearly indicated the state of his feelings for his future son-in-law, Mr. Duffy drained his tumbler of grog and sat down.

The formal manner in which his health had been drank, coupled with the speech made by

Mr. Duffy, seemed to impress the admiral with the idea that it would be necessary for him to return thanks, and with a view to this, he essayed to rise, but being by this time rather unsteady on his pins, he sank back upon his seat, cursing the table for moving away from him. He was soon up again, and after see-sawing backwards and forwards several times, at last succeeded in holding on by the table in almost an erect position, and commencing what he, doubtless, imagined to be a most coherent and appropriate return of thanks for what had been said by Mr. Duffy in proposing his health. Some of his remarks were totally irrelevant to what had occurred that evening, and to what Mr. Duffy had mentioned respecting the affair, but, considering his state, his reply was not so bad as might have been expected under the circumstances.

With a preparatory grunt to clear his throat, and after another series of sways backwards and forwards, during which he exhibited remarkable tenacity in his hold upon the table, he began his wandering and unconnected return of thanks.

" My friend Duffy—I've known—many years—many glass grog 'gether—have many more—your son there—my god-son, and 'll have all my money—which God forbid—when I die—and dri'k Misteter Wagsh 'ealth—damn that Gushle Guz—I—I—gave him a rap—and no mishtake—sorry to hear he's tead, Duffy—but it can't be 'elped—a'd much 'bliged to you all—a'd—jolly good fellows."

With this the old admiral sat down, quite overcome by his emotions. The aged Duffy, during his old friend's speech, had been mixing him a glass of grog such as his soul loved—strong and hot—and the admiral took it down with a rapidity, for his emotion was great, and he required something of this kind to prevent his giving way to tears. It had the desired effect, and the admiral did not cry, but instead of which he settled himself very firmly on his chair, and went fast asleep. Horatio's papa, after partaking of a similar settling potation, followed his example.

When they were both snoring away merrily our hero and Horatio left them, and sought their own couches.

On the following morning letters arrived for Horatio, directing him to join his ship immediately.

" What an infernal nuisance," said that young gentleman, on reading the official communication, " and we shall sail at once."

" So much the better, my lad!" said old Spanker, bringing his hand down on the youth's back with almost as much weight as it had descended on the Rev. Guzzle's head on the previous night, " so much the better, you'll get your promotion quicker, and then look at the prize-money to be picked up on the coast after slavers."

" Yes! that's very well now and then, but you don't always catch them."

" In ninety-nine cases out of a hundred you do," replied the admiral.

" Now look at the *Scud*, she's been dodging our cruisers for months, and they can't catch her, and Jack Piper, of the *Turk*, thinks that they never will."

"Ah! but then you must recollect that the *Scud* is an exception—it's my belief, from what I've heard from my old friend Bunk, who commands the *Turk*, that craft is more than a slaver! and, what's more, she's armed as heavily as any schooner in the service—now slavers don't go in for that sort of thing."

"So Jack wrote me word," said Horatio.

"And she has shown fight on one or two occasions, but got off after all!" observed old Spanker, excitedly.

"I only hope we may come athwart her," said Horatio, "if she doesn't become our prize, Billy Tack, of the *Dodger*, is not the man I took him to be."

"I should like the fun myself, old as I am," said the admiral.

"Cursed nuisance," grumbled Horatio, "I shall have to go up to town first, and down to Chatham to-night."

"Oh! that's nothing to a youngster like you," said old Spanker, "I daresay your friend Wag will go with you."

The admiral had hardly got the words out of his mouth when Charley made his appearance.

"Well, Duffy, so I hear you are off to-day," said he.

"Yes! I am, worse luck—I suppose you'll see a fellow as far as Chatham."

"Of course I will—but you won't go till to-morrow—shall you?"

"I must be off to London at once, but I hardly think I shall have time to settle everything there, and get down to Chatham to-night."

"I don't think it could be done."

"I shall try it, however, and we must leave here by twelve to catch the next train."

All was bustle and confusion in the house of Duffy in consequence of the sudden departure of Horatio.

The young ladies were most active, and, between the violent bursts of grief which they could not control, at losing their dear brother for three years, were also very useful. Everything that young gentleman could require, these affectionate girls saw that he was supplied with. In fact he had more than he actually stood in need of, as he discovered some few months after he had been at sea, for the thoughtful Matilda had secreted in one of his numerous packages a large bundle of some of the choicest things in the way of tracts, all written by the broken-pated clergyman upstairs.

In due time Horatio's preparations were completed, and the time for parting had arrived.

The old admiral, after giving his god-son some very good professional advice, tipped him very handsomely, and roughly wished him good-bye. Mr. Duffy, although incapable of imparting professional advice, was not backward in saying what is usual for papas on such occasions as the present—his "tip" was moderate, but his adieu was fatherly.

Then ensued a most maternal display of grief on the part of Mrs. Duffy, who was in reality rather glad at her son's departure, for Horatio, not knowing exactly how matters stood between them, was a most violent oppo-ser to the marriage of Miss Matilda with the Rev. Guzzle Gush.

The sincerity of his sisters grief was beyond doubt. They were all much attached to him; even Matilda, although she partook of her mother's sentiments, had an affectionate regard for her brother, and before Gush had deluded her with his trash, and poisoned her mind in the manner he had, Matilda was rather a pet of Horatio's, but latterly the hypocrisy which had been so systematically instilled, and which had exhibited itself so palpably, had disgusted him, and caused him to treat her very differently to what he had been in the habit of doing. But at this moment all was forgotten, and Miss Matilda came in for her share of the hugging and kissing incidental to a leave-taking of this kind.

Maggie's grief was even greater than her sisters, for be it remembered that with Horatio she was taking leave of Charley, and, if the truth be told, this parting was more painful to her than the separation from her brother. The poor girl had fostered the idea that Charley Wag loved her, whereas the young blade had been simply indulging in a violent flirtation at her expense—such a one that he would have carried on with any pretty girl that had given him the slightest encouragement; and it must be admitted that Miss Maggie Duffy had not acted as discreetly as she might have done, on the first evening of our hero's being at the house. She had brought all this upon herself by her own indiscretion, so that we must not pity her, but leave her to indulge in the flood of tears which came to her relief when the trap, which contained our hero and the young lieutenant, rolled away, and was lost to her view.

After assisting Horatio to make all his arrangements in London, where they arrived about three o'clock, our hero sat down to write the letter to Toddleboy, which, it will be remembered, Horatio promised to deliver, in event of his ship falling in with the *Scud*. The longing to discover his missing love, which he had not felt so much during his stay in Essex, now that he was writing about her, returned as strong as ever—when should he see her handsome face again? he thought Master Wag was rash enough to think that could he find her out he would willingly part with the wealth he was now possessed of and be content to live as they had in other times. This was a very foolish idea to enter the head of a young gentleman of Mr. Wag's age and opportunities, and had he not very properly dismissed the thought as the height of absurdity, I should have been inclined to believe that his brain was softening.

He was very fond of the fascinating Julia, and her bright vision, that his imagination conjured up while writing to Toddleboy, put poor Maggie's charms woefully in the shade. It was rather a lengthy epistle he wrote, and Horatio had settled everything that he could think of, and was talking about dinner before our hero had finished it.

"That's a twister you've tipped the old pirate," said Horatio, as Charley was sealing it.

"Yes—rather," replied Mr. Wag, who did

not seem inclined to explain the nature of the letter, although he might have seen that Horatio was anxious to know what sort of a communication he was to be made the bearear of.

Charley had noticed this, and assured Horatio, as he handed it to him, that there was nothing in it that could affect him in his position, in the slightest degree, as it was relative to a private matter entirely.

This explanation of its contents was perfectly satisfactory to Duffy, who immediately placed the important epistle under lock and key, promising faithfully to deliver it, should they capture the *Scud*, and also to assist the old skipper to escape if possible.

"Thank you!—thank you, my dear fellow, I shall never forget your kindness."

"That's all right then, I shall have somebody to think of me then," laughed Horatio, "but now we must feed, it's getting late, and our train goes at eight."

Dinner was soon over, and the two friends had a short time, after settling one or two matters that Horatio had forgotten, to smoke and chat before leaving for the railway terminus.

"I think I've done pretty well to get everything ready so soon," said Horatio.

"You've not been long certainly, taking into consideration your call in Norfolk-street," replied our hero.

"Confound it all, that was lost time, for the lady I went to see had left the hotel she was staying at, and they did not know where she had gone."

"Devilish provoking though," said Charley, unpathetically.

Horatio had been out after there arrival in town, to call upon Lucinda before he left England, but on inquiry he found that she had left the hotel a few days previously, without giving them any address whatever.

On the whole, it was rather fortunate for Master Duffy that she had gone, for had he found her at her old quarters, in all probability he would not have completed his arrangements, and would have postponed his departure for Chatham until the following day. As it was, they were off almost immediately.

"I think I have all my traps," said Horatio, glancing round the room, when the cab was announced.

After a very few minutes delay the luggage was stowed, and they were not long before they reached the station and were on the road to Chatham.

They arrived at Strood at about a quarter past nine, and chartering a fly, they drove into Chatham and put up at the "Sun."

Charley felt rather tired with his day's travelling, and did not at all relish Mr. Duffy's proposal to go for a stroll at that time of night in such a very slow place, as Mr. Wag imagined Chatham must be after London. However, this being the last night of Horatio's being on *terra firma* he acceded to his request, and they sallied out into the high street.

"Which way shall we go?" asked Horatio when they were outside.

"You know the place best," replied Charley—"I'm hanged if I care which way."

"What's it to be, Chatham or Rochester?"

"Let's prowl, first one way and then the other," replied Charley.

"As you like—but, just give me a light to my weed before we start."

Charley did so, and then the two moved off in the direction of Rochester.

After walking some distance, without seeing anything attractive, Horatio proposed that they should turn about and try Chatham.

And this they accordingly did and had reached the "Sun," when Horatio espied on ahead one of the young gentlemen who had lunched with him at that hotel on his last visit to Chatham.

Horatio at once made up to this individual, who was a long, lathy kind of creature, who certainly presented no appearance of having been fed upon Thorly's celebrated Food for cattle, for he was as lean as a ghost, and a good deal like one about the legs—no perceptible hair on his face, but in lieu of this, nature had blessed him with a curly poll, on the top of which, and rather at the back, was perched a tiny cap, which seemed to have been made for him when he was several feet less in height than at the time this was written.

The lathy one immdiately recognised Duffy, who introduced Mr. Wag to him, and the trio walked on in the direction of Brompton, whither this lanky speciman of humanity was bound in pursuit of billiards.

"You may as well look in and have a game," said he to Duffy.

"What do you say, Wag?" asked Horatio of Charley.

"I shall be most happy to play, if you wish to," replied Mr. Wag, and so the affair was settled.

Before proceeding with the occurences of the evening, I may as well introduce the spinkle-shanked individual to the reader.

He was a junior clerk in the Dockyard, on a salary of something less than a hundred and fifty-pounds per annum, upon which small sum, Master Bilkly (such was the name he rejoiced in) had to keep his rabid duns quiet, and latterly to pay for the support of a little come-by-chance, of which a designing spider-brusher had the audacity to declare he was the papa. Whether Master Bilkly ever admitted the truth of the slavey's assertion, or whether he considered himself a victim to circumstantial evidence, I am not prepared to say; but whatever were his own convictions on the subject, he had to pay up—which he did with the same good grace that characterises most young men in a similar position.

Such was the young gentleman with whom our hero and Horatio were going to pass the remainder of the evening.

"Will you liquor?" said he, "I'm going to," and he stopped before a little public.

"I shouldn't be sorry to do so, for I feel rather thirsty," said Charley.

"Then, we'll go in here," said Mr. Bilkly, "and you shall see three screaming girls."

"That'll be quite refreshing," replied Duffy, "for I'm hanged if I've seen one in Chatham yet."

They entered, and Mr. Bilkly immediately began talking to a very nice old landlady, whom he addressed as Mrs. Etagwood.

Charley and Horatio ordered cold brandy and water, and their lengthy companion went in for hot gin. While the old lady was serving them, two of the young ladies emerged from the little bar-parlour at the back, from which they could see, and be seen by all who were called to the bar, either for the purpose of slacking their thirst, or from a desire to see the three pretty Misses Etagwood.

The writer of these pages has visited this celebrated public for *both* purposes, and is thus enabled to pay a just tribute to the excellent tipple to be obtained there, and to the good looks of the three charming daughters, two of whom had just made their appearance in the bar, after no end of telegraphing from Mr. Bilkly. One of these young ladies was a fine handsome girl, plump and fair, and the other was a vivacious little party, with dark hair and sparkling eyes, which she knew how to use to the best advantage.

Miss Jenny, the last mentioned damsel, after replying to Mr. Bilkly's kind enquiry, relative to the general state of her health, asked that young gentleman how it was that they had not seen him lately. To this the lathy one replied that he lived at New Brompton now, and did not go out so often in the evening.

" We thought you had deserted us entirely, Mr. Bilkly," said the nice old lady, handing him another glass of hot gin.

"Not the slightest chance of that, Mrs. Etagwood," and in a lower key added, "never could leave you, Jenny, could I ?"

The young lady very properly paid little attention to his remark—in all probability our long friend had said the same thing to her on many previous occasions.

While Mr. Bilkly was putting away his hot gin and water, and chatting to Miss Jenny, in which Duffy assisted him, our hero was talking to the plump *blonde*, who seemed rather taken with the young gentleman—indeed her expressive eyes said as much, and she was carrying on a lively conversation about London amusements (she sometimes went to stay with friends in town), when her vigilent mamma, perhaps a little frightened by the rather fast air of our hero, called from the little bar parlour, " Emma !"—and Miss Emma vanished.

" I think we may as well make a move now," observed Charley, with a smile.

The other young gentlemen agreeing to this, the three bent their steps towards Brompton.

" It's deuced little time we shall have for billiards to-night," said Charley, stopping under a lamp-post to look at his watch.

" What's the time ?" asked Bilkly, who did not possess a pocket chronometer, or at least, had not it with him.

" Half-past eleven," replied Charley.

" It is too late, and I think the best thing we can do is to back to *t'other side*" said Bilkly.

" Where the devil's that ?" said Horatio.

" Why the public we've just left—we call it so down here.

" Oh."

" What do you say to it, Wag ? Do you feel inclined to renew your chat with the fair damsel ?

" I haven't the slightest objection, I can assure you—she seems a very jolly girl."

" Then we'll do so," said Duffy, and they retraced their steps to the public they had just come out of.

On their arrival they found the little bar filled with the friends and brother clerks of Mr. Bilkly. Horatio and Mr. Wag were presented to these young gentlemen, and in one of them Horatio remembered the youth who had lunched with Mr. Bilkly and himself at the " Sun."

This individual, who was called Bob, was not an elegant looking creature, being rather heasy in his build, with broad shoulders, surmounted by a head and ears, bearing a striking resemblance to one of the plaister of Paris casts one sees of celebrated murderers—no matter which in the shop windows of " burnologists." He was an extremely good-natured fellow, and appeared to be a great favourite with his companions, in spite of the head and ears.

" Jerry," said he, addressing Bilkly, in rather a beery voice, " I'm going to have a cab home—I'll give you a ride."

" Don't be in such a devil of a hurry, and I'll go with you," replied Mr. Bilkly.

" Oh ! all right, tell me when you're ready, then."

Jerry then went in for a little more hot gin and conversation with Mr. Wag, and Horatio was delighted at having found a diminutive gentleman, who happened to have been in China, and was always in the seventh heaven when talking of it.

To this little fellow, Horatio related his most startling adventures, but the small party, who was up to a thing or two, believed as much of them as he deemed probable, and no more.

Of course, Horatio was under the impression that his companion credited all that he stated ; but I am sorry to say, that Mr. Duffy was really mistaken. It mattered little, however, for the diminutive one was not backward in gulling him on several points, and fancying that it had been done too cleverly to be seen through. Horatio felt rather uncertain, whether to take in one or two things or not, but ultimately swallowed everything.

At last, the young gentlemen had to leave the public, as it was time to shut up.

" Now, I vote we get home," said Charley, who thought this rather a weak way of passing the hours, which ought to have seen them in bed and asleep.

" Very well," replied Horatio, " we'll wish these fellows good-night, and hook it."

After saying good-night to our hero and Horatio, the lathy one and the diminutive gentleman availed themselves of the offer of the head and ears, and were soon seated in a cab, and driving up the Military Road, yelling out, " Peter Gray," and other popular melodies, in a most discordant and gin and water fashion.

Horatio had promised to meet these youths on the following day, and the Mr. Bilkly had asked him to dig him out at his rooms in the evening, should the "*Dodger*" remain any longer before sailing.

The diminutive gentleman, who was looked upon as rather an authority in these matters, had told Duffy that he would not leave Chatham for a couple of days at least. This information had rather elated him, and he returned home, anxious for the morning to come, that he might go down to the yard and learn how matters stood.

"Good night, old fellow," said Charley, as they separated for the night, "I shan't be up very early to-morrow, I promise you, I'm as tired as a dog."

"And so am I—good night."

Neither of these youngsters were long in getting to sleep, and it seemed to Horatio as though he had only dozed for a few minutes, when the bright sun, streaming in at his window, warned him that it was time for him to be up and down to the dockyard to inquire about his ship sailing.

He jumped up, and hastily dressing himself in his uniform, went into our hero's bed-room. That young gentleman was asleep of course, so Horatio ruthlessly woke him, and informed him that he should be back by the time he was up to breakfast.

Mr Wag grumbled out a sleepy "very well," and turning himself over, slept again soundly.

It was now ten o'clock, and Horatio walked briskly from the "Sun" to the Dockyard, which he reached in a few minutes. He went direct to the captain's office, where he found a hairy youth (the lathy one had not yet arrived), who could tell him very little about the matter upon which he made his inquiries.

Horatio then thought he would go on board and report himself, although not at all anxious to be considered on duty. Hazarding this, he made his way to where the "*Dodger*" was lying, and went on board of her.

The officer then in command, who to Horatio's surprise happened to be known to him, received him very politely, and to his inquiry, informed him that it was not at all certain on what day they sailed, they were expecting to be moved down to Sheerness every tide.

"The deuce you are! said Master Duffy, "I wanted a couple of days leave of absence."

"If you join at Sheerness to-morrow night I should think that would do," said the officer, "but you must see the captain superintendent first."

"The devil!"

"He's a very jolly fellow, so you need not mind."

"Where does he hang out?"

"You'll see him up at his office in the yard."

"Then I'll be off, and if I do not return you will know that I have succeeded in getting my leave."

Mr. Duffy immediately on landing, walked over and had an interview with the captain. The result of it was satisfactory, and Horatio was about to leave the yard when he met Mr. Bilkly.

"Hullo! old boy—how are you, this morning? You're not going to leave Chatham to-day?" said the tall youth."

"No, I've just got some leave?"

"How much?"

"Until to-morrow night."

"You'll come up to my diggings to-night, then?"

"Yes."

"Bring your friend—he seems to be a brick."

"We shall be with you, at some time or other this evening—bye, bye, till then."

Duffy hastened back to the "Sun," where he found Charley up and waiting breakfast.

"What a cursed while you've been," said Mr. Wag, who was very hungry.

"Well, my dear fellow, I made all the haste I could to get back, and I only wonder that I returned at all!"

"How's that?" asked Charley.

"They are expecting to be moved down to Sheerness every tide—so the lieutenant said."

"Then, what will you do?"

"Join at Sheerness," replied Horatio.

"When?"

"To-morrow night, if she leaves Chatham, but it's my opinion, that she will not," said Duffy.

"Curse that infernal waiter!" said Charley, "I told him to have breakfast ready on your return."

Mr. Wag had hardly uttered the words, when the infernal waiter and breakfast put in an appearance.

The two friends immediately fell upon the latter, and Mr. Wag's anger vanished under the soothing influence of a breakfast fit for a queen.

"Now that I have it, I'm hanged if I know what to do with my leave," said Horatio, when they were smoking their cigars,

"It is rather a difficult matter to decide."

"There's nothing to be done in a place like this during the day," observed Master Duffy.

"And devilish little at night—I think we may as well pass the day in playing billiards."

"So we will "

Having determined to spend the day thus, the two walked up to the rooms at Brompton. Horatio knew the way to them, having been there with Mr. Bilkly on a former occasion, and thither he piloted Charley.

They engaged the room for the whole day, and commenced playing soon after. They had game after game, only pausing to rest their legs, after walking miles round the table. The quantity of bitter beer and tobacco consumed by them was something fabulous, and at luncheon-time, instead of returning to the "Sun," the infatuated Horatio insisted upon feeding on whatever the billiard-marker could obtain for them in the way of eating and drinking.

Mr. Wag was rather averse to this, but did not violently oppose his friend's proposal, and when the brace of mutton chops and a fresh supply of bottled ale arrived, our hero thought it was about the best thing that could have been arranged, and put away his chop and bitter accordingly. Their lunch over, and their weeds lighted, the two went at their game again, and by the time they ceased playing, in order to dine, several of Mr. Duffy's sovereigns had found their way into Mr. Wag's pocket, and very few of them had been re-won by the unlucky Horatio, who was not such a practised player as our hero Charley. This did not seem to trouble our nautical friend much, he had still a good round sum left, and he was not the sort of person to say die, when there was a shot in the locker.

About six o'clock they returned to the "Sun," and dined, after which Master Duffy proposed an adjournment to Mr. Bilkly's rooms.

"What's up there to-night?" inquired our hero.

"Haven't the slightest conception—only a drunk I should think."

"That's not very entertaining, but I suppose we must go."

"I should rather think so; indeed we may as well do our 'baccy in one place as in another," said Horatio, who was decidedly anxious to be moving, "let's be off."

As it was a fine night, the two young gentlemen walked over the lines to Brompton.

Mr. Bilkly lived at Vile Terrace, and had told Horatio his address, which that individual had forgotten.

"How the devil shall we rook him up?" said he, after telling Charley the state of the case.

"Oh! easy enough," replied Mr. Wag, "ask at the public."

"Ah! that's a good idea," said Horatio, to whom the thought of doing so had never occured.

"Do you happen to know at what number in Vile Terrace Mr. Bilkly lives?" inquired Horatio of the landlord at the public.

"Oh, yes, sir, he lives at No. 97—my boy is going there at once with some beer, he'll show you the house."

Horatio thanked him, and they followed the boy, who took them to Mr. Bilkly's door in less than no time. On nearing the house they heard a terrible din, and the boy, answering Mr. Wag's remark of "what the devil are they doing?" replied—

"Oh! they're 'aving a concert, sir! it's first rate sometimes."

Once inside the room, the noise was easily accounted for. The lathy one, divested of his coat, was stretched upon a sofa, blowing away at a flute; the little gentleman who had been to China was sitting in a corner, beating a brass drum, gazing at nothing particular, and looking very serious on the matter; and near him sat a brickdusty-coloured party, with rather a wiry terrier look about him, playing a bag-pipe accompaniment on a stick. The effect of this combination of sound was very striking, and our hero was of opinion that a little of it went a long way. The room was rather crowded, so the lanky youth was obliged to coil up his legs in some incomprehensible manner, and accommodate our friends with part of his sofa. After supplying them with beer, Mr. Bilkly showed signs of blowing again upon his flute, and the little gentleman in the corner once more restored his features to that serious expression from which they had relaxed for a short time, and gave one or two preliminary taps to his drum. This caused the wiry party to re-place the pewter on the table, and pick up his stick, which he tuned,

and then remained in readiness for the others to begin.

Our friend Charley did not at all relish this state of things, so he engaged, as he thought, the principal instrument, Bilkly, in conversation, and thus fancied he should put a stop to their harmony. He was mistaken, however. The little drummer glared at him, and unbraced his drum, evidently disgusted at such a want of taste on the part of our hero; but the brick-dusty one, not to disappoint the rest of the company who had been invited to the concert, favoured them with a solo on his stick.

The applause which followed this rather lengthy performance was too much for the gentleman of the drum, who commenced "bracing up" as quickly as possible. The lathy one was also sensibly affected, and his fingers played nervously with the keys of his flute. Charley saw all these symptoms with dismay, and knew it would be impossible to restrain their musical inclinations, so, mentally cursing the whole party, more especially the wretch with the drum, our hero plunged his beak into the pewter. This was an opportunity not to be lost, and before the unfortunate Charley had finished his draught, the instrumentalists broke out with a gush of harmony.

Mr. Wag came to the conclusion that the best thing to be done, under the circumstances, was to hook it, and communicated his idea to Horatio, but, alas! that individual had such a passion for music that it was immaterial to him whether it was good or bad, so long as he heard it.

"Go!" said he, "I should think not—I call this great fun."

"God help your taste then," muttered Charley, as he filled his pipe again, after seeing that his efforts to induce Duffy to leave this place would be futile.

Trios, solos, and choruses, went on till the music began to grow wearisome to the performers themselves (amateurs though they were), and it was proposed by one of the party that they should go to the "Tin Can."

Our hero and Horatio, having been informed that it was a singing shop, agreed to go, Charley being only too delighted for a change of harmony.

The young gentleman who was known as the P. M. G. happened to be in funds on this occasion, hence the reckless extravagance of going to a music hall.

As many of the young gentlemen as could conveniently spare the price of admission from their floating capital, joined the party for the "Tin Can."

This establishment was rather a select one, being constructed with a due regard to the different grades of society. There was a balcony "for officers," another for gentlemen, and here the ladies of their acquaintance were admitted—and last of all, intended for that grade of society which never pays more than a penny for any sort of entertainment, was the pit.

Our party went in for the balcony where the ladies were in the habit of congregating, and after squeezing through a tremendous mass of crinoline near the door, brought up a short distance from it.

Mr. Bilkly seemed to be known to all the

young ladies present, some of whom, however, regarded him with anything but favourable glances—but others, on the contrary, seemed to be on very good terms with him.

Our hero and Horatio soon got into conversation with the fair ladies about them, and stood various glasses of hot and strong to the thirsty ones.

While they were thus engaged, a lady who seemed to know, and be known to by the whole party, entered the balcony.

"Hullo!" said Mr. Bilkly, "here's the P. J.! this way, Polly! we'll make room for you."

The lady was not handsome, but she was decidedly good-looking, and, to judge from her appearance, thoroughly good-tempered. The writer of these pages had the pleasure of chatting with her one evening at the celebrated "Tin Can," and he believes that he is not far out in judging this lady's amiability, by her appearance and engaging manner. If he is wrong, he trusts that some of the gentlemen who may know her intimately will read her a severe lecture on the impropriety of her conduct, and present her with a bundle of tracts.

"What are you going to have, Polly?" asked Mr. Bilkly.

"I'll have some brandy and water, Jerry—hot."

Jerry winced a little at this order, and felt in his waistcoat pocket to see if his funds would run to it, and finding that he should have a surplus of two pence halfpenny to keep him till pay-day, summoned the waiter, and gave the order like a man.

"How long are you going to stay here?" said Charley to Horatio, who was holding, in conjunction with the gentleman who was at the "t'other side" with them on the previous evening, called Bob, a most animated discussion with a young lady styled Martha.

In reply to Charley's question, Horatio told him he did not know. Our hero grumbled a little at this, but began chaffing a little damsel, named Alice, who was sitting near him, partaking of hot grog at his expense. This young lady was very engaging, and Master Wag was rather pleased with her than otherwise, staying much longer at the singing shop than he intended doing, on her account. The entertainment was over at last, and the gentlemen separated for the night, and each went his way. Horatio accompanied Miss Martha home, and I am sorry to say Mr. Wag followed his example, and did not return to the "Sun" after escorting Miss Alice to her residence.

It was past two o'clock on the following day before these young gentlemen met again, and then they mutually entertained each other with their adventures after parting company the night before. Thus passed the remainder of the day, and soon evening came, and Master Duffy had to prepare for going on board the *Dodger*, which had not left Chatham yet, and would not until the next morning.

"It is an awful nuisance having to join to-night," said Horatio, "I half promised Bilkly to go with him to a sort of dancing crib, 'The Five Bells,' but, of course, shan't be able to."

"But will you sleep on board to-night?"

"Yes."

"And what time will the tide answer to-morrow?"

"About eleven."

"Oh! then I'll go and see you off—so look out for me."

"What will you do with yourself to-night without me?" said Horatio, who had conceived an erroneous impression that his presence was absolutely necessary to the existence of our hero.

"Tolerably well I daresay," replied Charley, smiling.

"You'll go out with Bilkly and the rest of them."

"Not if I know it—one night a week is enough of that sort of thing. Another of these concerts and I should be a corpse."

"Then for heaven's sake don't go to any more of them."

"Don't you run away with the notion that I shall. After you leave I shall say good-bye to Chatham for one while I promise you," said Master Charley, in a manner which plainly showed the state of his regard for that garrison-town and its inhabitants.

The cab which was to convey Horatio and his luggage to the dockyard was announced during the discussion, and after seeing everything carefully stowed, took his seat with Charley, who was going to ride with him as far as the yard gate. On their way Mr. Wag puffed away at his weed in silence, which was only broken by Horatio's reminding him to be on board early the ensuing morning.

"I'll be with you, my pippin! so look out for me."

With this injunction Charley alighted, as the cab pulled up at the dockyard gates.

"Well, good bye, old fellow, till the morning," said Mr. Wag, shaking his friend's hand warmly, and then walking slowly back to the "Sun," where he read a little, smoked a little, and then retired to bed.

The *Dodger* was to leave Chatham at ten o'clock, and Horatio had asked Charley to be on board early in the morning, as he should have but little time to spare when they were getting under weigh. Mr. Wag had, therefore, to get up much earlier than he thought necessary, as a general rule, and after cursing the cold water in the roundest terms, he dressed himself, and hurried to the ship. Horatio was delighted to see him, and after introducing him to some brother officers, invited him to breakfast. Our hero accepted this invitation, and remained on board until the last moment, then taking leave of Horatio, reminding him not to forget the letter to Toddleboy. Charley jumped into a boat alongside, and was landed at the dockyard stairs. In walking up to the gates his attention was attracted by a gang of convicts, who were employed in removing timber from one part of the yard to the other. Mr. Wag stopped for a short time to look at them, and perhaps he was congratulating himself on having nothing to do, and being elegantly attired, instead of having to toil like these unfortunate fellows, and having to wear the "dandy-grey russet." It might have been his lot, on more than one occasion. He had had enough of Spike Island

A NOBLE SPORTSMAN.

when rather younger, and his remembrances of it were decidedly unpleasant.

Mr. Wag could not help allowing to himself that these gentlemen in whitey-brown were an ill-looking set, to say they most for them, and was about to turn away when his gaze rested upon one of the convicts, who came out from behind some timber, Charley recognised him immediately.

It was George Measels!

The reader may recollect, that after the attempted fraud on Timnan's bank our hero, through the devotedness of Julia succeeded in making his escape; but George was not so fortunate, he was convicted and was now serving his time. Charley was rather puz-

zled how to act, for should George treat him to any open sign of recognition the consequences might be very disagreeable.

"What the deuce was to be done?" thought our hero, whose immediate resolution on seeing Measels was to aid him to escape.

But how was it to be done?

"If I could only catch his eye and drop him a little piece of paper, that would do famously," said Charley to himself; "but then, there's that damned driver." Our hero was fearful of exciting the attention of this individual, by remaining so long observing the uninteresting movements of a gang of convicts, so he strolled away to another part of the yard and wrote on a slip of paper to the

[CHARLEY WAG, THE NEW JACK SHEPPARD.]

effect, that George was to attempt his escape that night, by concealing himself when the gang knocked off work, and that he (Charley) would be down by the prison at midnight.

In writing these directions to George, Charley had made use of as few words as possible, for he had calculated the difficulty that George might have in finding an opportunity for reading it. Having finished this, he was strolling about, and for a wonder was not interfered with by the policemen of the yard, who are generally very inquisitive with reference to strangers, when he saw the lean shanks of Mr. Bilkly approaching.

"How do you do, Mr. Wag? What are you amusing yourself with?"

"I'm just looking about your dockyard—it's a very large one."

"Not so large as some of them," observed shanks.

"I suppose there is a great deal of machinery here."

"Oh! yes—would you like to see the copper-mills—it's a great sight, and if you don't mind a row——,"

"Thank you," said Charley, remembering the concert of the previous evening, "I had rather not—I'm not particularly fond of a noise of any sort."

Of course Mr. Bilkly did not see this, and they walked on together through the yard, till they came in sight of the gang of convicts, in which was George Measels.

Charley wished his companion at the devil, for his presence might prevent him carrying out his scheme with George, but as our hero's wishing did not have the desired effect with Mr. Bilkly, it would be necessary to pursue some other course.

Charley was not long in deciding upon one, and it was bold and impudent, and worthy of the youth who devised it.

As they neared the gang, our hero said to Mr. Bilkly, as he pointed out George.

"That fellow was a servant of mine."

"Indeed!" said his companion, "how did he get here?"

"He was accused of forging a bill by a tradesman of mine, and as the circumstantial evidence was strong against him he was convicted, notwithstanding all I could do for him, for I have'nt the slightest doubt of his innocence. In fact, the judge told a friend of mine afterwards that *he* was convinced of the man's innocence, and said that it was all the doing of the jury."

"What a damned shame!" said the lathy one indignant, that such a flagrant act of injustice should be enacted in the nineteenth-century.

"It is, indeed," observed Mr. Wag. "I want to tell the poor fellow how his wife is, but I don't exactly see the way."

"I should advise you not to try it—there's a heavy fine for anything of the sort—and the others are so likely to split of it, if even you could do it without the keeper's knowing of it, but I shouldn't advise you to try it on."

"If I could only catch his eye, I'd drop a little ball of paper, on which I've written and rolled up."

Charley and Mr. Bilkly were sitting on a baulk of timber close to the convicts, but for all that, Mr. Bilkly did not know that while they were talking together, Charley *had* caught the man's eye, and had dropped the little ball of paper without its being noticed by any, but the one for whom it was intended.

After seeing George pick it up, at the same time he did a shovel which was lying by it, our hero seemingly with much regret gave up the idea of communicating with his unfortunate servant.

"Come away," said he, "it's no use tantalizing the poor devil by showing myself."

"You'r quite right in not trying to convey anything to him—I wouldn't for a trifle."

They had reached the pile of buildings used as offices, and Mr. Bilkly felt it his duty to return to work, of which he had done very little that morning—feeling rather seedy after that "Tin Can" affair.

Charley, glad to be quit of him returned to the "Sun," and did not go out for the rest of the day.

He packed his portmanteau, and had everything in readiness to be off that night, having ordered a cab to call for him at eleven.

————

LXXXVIII.—The Escape—Murder—Mr. Wag suddenly takes to Whiskers and Moustaches, and goes in for good Society—How Charley adopted a pretty Little Girl.

WHEN George picked up the paper, so artfully dropped in his way by Charley Wag, his first difficulty was, as our hero anticipated, to find an opportunity to read it.

By dint of a little tact, he contrived to surmount this obstacle and made himself master of its contents; but then, how could he escape? The thought of doing so, had often occurred to him, but he had always abandoned it as a useless attempt, and one that would only subject him to even severer treatment than he already experienced.

The few lines that Charley had written nerved him to the task.

It was worth the risk, and he well knew that Charley was one that could be depended upon in the hour of danger.

He would make the attempt if it cost him his life.

About this time the convicts had manifested a mutinous feeling, which had caused the guards to treat them with a greater degree of severity than usual, but as George had never taken any active part in these riots, he was not kept under such restraint as many of the others.

On the day that our hero had proposed his attempt at escape, the gang returned as usual to St. Mary's Island, but on their arrival so great a disturbance was going on with the refractory convicts, that it was deemed prudent to keep the gang to which Measels belonged separate from the riotous portion of them.

For this purpose they were marched into a hut close at hand, and the guard entered with them. They had been here some hours, and it was past eleven when it was proposed by one of them, who was anxious to join his riotous brethren, that they should suddenly attack and overthrow the guard. The proposal was considered a good one, and the ruffian who made it volunteered to take a most active part in its perpetrations.

He had secured a short heavy piece of wood, and with this he crept up behind the unsuspecting guard and dealt him a crushing blow on the head! So sudden had been the attack, that the man fell without a cry, and then the convicts rushed upon him and gagged him.

This will account for the ignorance of those outside as to what had occurred in the hut until the mischief was done, and all the convicts with the exception of George, had marched out in the most orderly manner. Measels remained behind, on pretence of assisting the wounded man.

Some of the convicts derided him for it, and the man who had struck the blow was anxious to serve Measels in the same manner to prevent his peaching on them ; but this was overruled by the others, who left him, after making him swear under the most terrible threats of vengeance not to betray them. Immediately they were gone, George stripped the senseless man and assumed his uniform, then walking boldly out of the hut, made at once to a place where a little boat was always kept fast.

Into this he got, and was soon on the opposite shore, at no great distance from the prison, and where Charley had appointed to meet him.

He sauntered about until he heard footsteps approaching, and then the dread of being recognised by any of the prison officers, made him cock the revolver he had taken with the rest of the accoutrements from the person of the injured warder.

"He's by himself, anyhow," said George to himself, as the figure, whose footsteps on the hard frozen ground he had heard so distincly advanced towards him, "and if he's after me, I'll settle his hash—or he shall mine."

In spite of this courageous resolve, Measels felt how critical was his position, for should he be retaken in his present attire, he knew what he had to expect.

But the thought of this only served to make him desperate, and when Charley (for it was he) came up George received him with his revolver levelled, but seeing his mistake, notwithstaning the darkness of the night he lowered the pistol and grasped our hero's hand.

"What the devil do you do with that dress on?" said Charley, after his astonishment at seeing his companion in the uniform of a prison warder, had somewhat subsided.

"Took'em off a fellow we knocked on the head," replied George.

"Well! you must change 'em, and as soon as you can," said Charley, producing from a small carpet-bag, some clothes, which he had obtained during the evening at one of the outfitter's in the town.' He had made a tolerable guess at George's size, and the things fitted him well enough.

"Now, throw those cursed togs into the river, said Charley, after George had divested himself of the warder's clothes and had dressed himself in the others, and let's be off."

Measels did as he was directed, and the two moved away to where Charley had ordered the cabman to await him.

On reaching the cab, which Charley from prudential motives had kept at some distance from where he was to meet George, our hero directed the driver to take the road to Maidstone, promising to pay him well for his night's work.

The man relished this fare amazingly, and they soon left Chatham far behind them.

They had proceeded some distance on their road when Charley, for some reason or other put his hand in his pocket for his purse, and to his dismay found that it was not there.

"By G—— I've lost it !" he exclaimed, after vainly searching for it in all his pockets, "what the devil could I have done with it ?"

"Perhaps you left it at the crib you were staying at," said Measels.

"No—I remember having it after I left there," said Charley, still rummaging in his pockets, from which he took a sovereign and nearly a pounds worth of silver, adding as he did so, "It's devilish lucky I've enough to pay the cabman—if he were to ride rusty we might be traced."

"We'll chance that," replied Measels.

"But, how the devil are we to get to London ?" said our hero, who had no notion of making the journey in an uncomfortable manner, if the means of doing it luxuriously presented themselves, "unless we meet with any one on the road."

The same idea had struck Measels, as the only course to be pursued under the circumstances, and he replied to Charley's remark, by saying, with a broad grin on his unprepossessing countenance.

"I'm afraid we *shall* be obliged to borrow a trifle from the first likely-looking customer we comes across."

"Yes—so we'll get rid of the cabby in Maidstone, and take to the road at once— though I shouldn't fancy there was much to be picked up in this part of the world," said Charley.

"It's a bad time o'day for the best of places, but we must make the most of it— we're not far from the town."

"Getting close to it—I should fancy," said Charley, as the cabman twisting round, inquired where he should drive them to.

After hastily consulting with his companion, Charley directed the man to drive on through the town to a little road-side inn, the landlord of which was a particular friend of Mr. Measels, and had been at one period of his life the possessor of a very becoming suit of whitey-brown, which he had worn for a lengthened period in the neighbourhood of Chatham.

To this gentleman's establishment our hero and Measels proceeded, notwithstanding Charley's objections at doing so.

Although ready enough to relieve any

person they might chance to meet, of their surplus cash, he was not at all anxious to extend his circle of disreputable acquaintances, which he considered to be large enough already; indeed, had it not been for that sense of honor which has existed among thieves from time immemorial, the probability is, that Mr. Wag would not have renewed his acquaintance with Mr. Measels, and that worthy would have remained, clothed in dandy grey russet, until he had worked out the whole of the time, for which he was sentenced. But fate, and the sense of honor just alluded to, had the entire arrangement of the matter, as far as our hero was concerned, and Charley remembered that Measels had suffered for an offence, of which he was equally guilty, and of which he was the proposer. Then the sense of honor for which prigs are even more famous, than respectable people, came into play, for on seeing George, working with the rest of the gang he felt that he ought to make some effort towards restoring him to liberty, and the reader is already aware of the steps he took, and the manner in which Measels effected his escape.

Our hero objected to going to this house on the ground that he did not wish to meet a lot of prigs, who might recognise him in London.—

"If that's all, come along then—you won't meet any body there in our line, I'll warrant, Billy Knuckles as keeps the house, got nabbed for killing a man in a prize fight—that's all" said George.

Oh! I understand—"

"But you're cutting an awful swell, Charley—what's your game, Tinmans?',

"No, I've given up the profession, and am living on some property that has been left me" replied our hero who did not see the necessity for letting his companion into the secret of his present affluent circumstances.

"Whew! I thought you'd turn out a gentleman in the end, Charley?" said measels.

To this complimentary remark our hero did not vouchsafe any reply, as the cab stopped before the little inn, and they got out.

After paying the cabman, who immediately drove back towards Maidstone, our hero found the balance of his cash was trifling in the extreme, and mentioned this fact to George who was of opinion that Billy Knuckles would not be hard upon them for the want of it.

"He and the guv'ner have been chums too long for him to want any tin for what we shall get here," said he, thundering at the door.

For some time no notice was taken of his knocking, and in a little while he repeated it—perhaps a trifle louder than before—this last attack was followed by a window being flung open, a night capped head being popped out and a surly voice enquiring "what the devil they wanted disturbing a man's rest,"

"Is Billy Knuckles at home?" asked George.

"Knuckles be——he's left here months ago" when the night cap disppeared and down went the window with a bang.—

"Well! said Measels" this is a pretty go, we shall have to tramp it till daylight."

"Confound it all" said Charley "I hate walking."

"I'd rather ride myself."

"Here, take a nip of this" said Chaaley, handing his companion a flask of brandy "it will keep out a little of the cold,"

George held out his hand for it, and then took a long swig at it.

"By jingo!" said he "that's the sweetest toothful I've tasted for months."

"And deuced big teeth yours must be to require such filling," said Charley, when putting the flask to his own lips he found it nearly empty, "its develish lucky I've another."

"I did have a good pull at it, and its done me more good, than a week's allowance of skillagalee would have done—taken all at once.

"I believe you my boy, and now let's be moving for its infernally cold standing about, but which is our road?"

"The one we're in now is the direct road to London," replied George.

"Then we'll take to it at once."

And in a few minutes they were walking briskly on their way.

They were not more than four miles from the place from whence they commenced their walk, when they heard the sound of carriage wheels and saw the lamps of a vehicle which was coming up behind them at a rapid pace.

"Now's our time" said Measels, there's something to be had here—are you game?"

"Of course I am" replied our hero indignantly, but at the same time Charley felt rather annoyed at having to relapse into highway robbery again.

In the meanwhile the carriage approached. It proved to be a brougham, and the only servant in charge of which was the coachman on his box.

"Now look out," said George, as the brougham came up, "you make for the horses head, and I'll see to the rest."

Charley clenched his teeth and waited, and then made a spring at the bridle—the animal reared and plunged under the lash, which the old man applied furiously, immediately the nature of the attack became manifest to him.

Measels seeing our hero's danger rushed to his assistance, jumped upon the box, and seizing the old man in his arms, he dashed him down under the very hoofs of the plunging and kicking horse! the servant disposed of Measels, at once presented himself at the door of the carriage, and shaking its occupant a gentleman about thirty, who was asleep, demanded his money, the gentleman seemed to comprehend his position in an instant for seizing a sword cane, he prepared to defend himself, but before he had time to use it Measels had dragged him out of the brougham, into the road, here the stuaggle was fearful, at one time Measels being uppermost and at another the stranger, both were striving to strangle each other, and Charley looked on, hardly knowing how the apparently equal contest would end.

At last the superior strength of Measels triumphed, and he succeeded in once more getting above the unfortunate man; then raising his revolver with one hand, while with the other he retained his hold upon his adversary's throat, he made a blow at the prostrate man's head—the dull thud with which the weapon descended, announced that it had taken effect, as indeed it had, having struck the unfortunate man on the temple and deprived him of life. !

"Curse him" said Measels, kicking the lifeless body "he nearly throtled me "! then stooping down he commenced rifling the pockets of his victim, but the search did not prove satisfactory for he only found a few shillings and some bundles of papers—"him it was not worth the trouble of tussling with him for " he added in a rage.

"The best thing we can do" said Charley, who was still holding the horse " is to take the trap and be off. "

"Yes, but we must first get rid of these dead 'uns " returned George.

"But how"?

"Oh! in the ditch, but in the first place as I suppose I'm to be coachman I'll trouble the old gentleman for his coat and hat "

"The poor old man was quite dead, having received a kick which had killed him while Measels and his master were struggling on the ground.

George was not long in divesting the corpse of his attire and assuming it himself, and as he did so, he chuckled at the changes he had made within the last few hours. In an incredibly short time he had thrown the two bodies into the ditch at the side of the road when sinking under the filth which it contained, they were covered and hidden from view.

This task completed, Measel's, at Charley's suggestion extinguished the lamps which only rendered their equipage more conspicious than was desirable.

"We shan't have to tramp it, that's one consolation," said Measels, mounting the box, and taking the reins, "now, Charley you jump inside—give me a bob or two for the pikes—and I'll drive you to town in as fine a style as you could wish for."

Our hero got in after giving him some silver, and away they went. Charley felt very sleepy, and, encouraging the feeling, he lolled on the luxurious cushions of the brougham, and slept for hours.

They were not far from London when he awoke, for George had driven on without making any stoppages.

Not knowing Mr. Wag's present residence, George alighted, and in the most natural and professional manner touched his laced hat, and inquired whither he should drive.

Charley directed him—away they rattled—and in less than half an hour our hero was at his chambers.

On his arrival he at once had the portmanteau of the murdered man taken out of the brougham and carried to his rooms, and here, in the presence of Measels, Charley opened it in search of the money his companion was so anxious to obtain. Much to that worthy's disappointment the portmanteau contained nothing but articles of clothing, and a quantity of letters and papers.

"Well! I'm damned," said Measels, discontentedly, "if it hadn't been for the ride it would not had been worth while knocking him on the head."

"There's the horse and trap," said Charley, "that shall be your's if you can get rid of it."

"I should rather think I could," replied Mr. Measels, who knew of places at which he could dispose of anything that he might fall in with without being troubled with inquiries as to how it came into his possession.

"Very well then, George, here's a five pound note for you, and now take that cursed carriage from my door."

George pocketed the note, and thanking our hero for all that he had done for him, took his departure, without receiving any intimation from Mr. Wag that his company would be desirable on futu.e occasions.

This little omission on the part of our hero did not seem to hurt Mr. Measel's feelings. He was too much delighted with his liberty to care for much else, and he drove off to sell his brougham and horse with a lighter heart (in spite of the crime he had just committed), than many an honest man.

Charley was not at all sorry to see the back of him, and at once ordered his breakfast, for he was beginning to feel very hungry.

While this was preparing he occupied himself with reading some of the letters of the murdered man. From these he gathered that their late owner was a Frenchman, and had just left Calais, and was proceeding to London when he fell into their hands. For his being in the direction in which they met with him Charley could not account.

After turning over several letters, our hero's attention was attracted to one in a lady's hand addressed to the Duchess of Heatherland. For some time he could only gaze at the envelope, without daring to look at its contents, but at last his curiosity was too much for him. He opened it, and it proved to be a letter of introduction to the Duchess from an intimate female friend in France. It recommended the bearer, Monsieur Adolphe de Bessac, to the favourable notice of the Duchess, alluding to the fact of his being a perfect stranger to English manners and customs, although speaking the language tolerably well; and concluded by begging the Duchess, for the sake of their long-standing friendship, to do all she possibly could for the young Frenchman.

"An introduction to my—— yes! that I will—I'll personate this Monsieur de Bessac, and pay her a visit," said Charley, after reading this letter.

The idea of gaining the entré into good society had been a pet scheme with Charley for a long time, and in this letter of introduction he fancied that he had found a royal road to what he so earnestly longed for—a position. It must be allowed that his present one was a very equivocal one, and his anxiety to establish a footing with the upper ten thousand was very excusable.

Mr. Wag loitered away the entire day in speculating upon the probable success of his attempt to pass himself off as Monsieur de Bessac, and he resolved that he would put it into execution on the following day.

After having dined, his next step was to go in search of a hair-dresser and wig-maker, whom he had been in the habit of employing professionally whenever a "make up" was necessary. This individual lived in one of the innumerable courts leading out of Drury-lane, and thither Charley proceeded.

He had some little difficulty in finding the residence of this knight of the curling-tongs, but at last he pitched upon it, and entered. Mr. Wag was not long in stating his wants, nor was the hair-dresser slow in comprehending the nature of his requirements, and it was finally settled that our hero should be with the barber on the following morning by eleven o'clock.

Charley was very well satisfied with the result of this visit, for he feared that the accommodating wig-maker might have died, or left his present abode and become lord mayor, since the last time our hero had found it necessary to employ him.

"By jove!" said he to himself, on leaving the shop, "there's some good to be got in a French prison,—I've got the lingo like a native, and shall make up gloriously."

Perusing his thoughts thus, he was making his way out of the court, when, passing the open door of one of the most wretched hovels that abounded in that neighbourhood, the piteous shrieks of a child, mingled with the harsh notes of a woman's voice, saluted his ear. As he stopped to listen he heard another shriek, so prolonged and agonising in its tone, that it made him positively shudder. Again he heard it, and this time some irresistable impulse urged him to seek from whence the cries proceeded.

He sprang up the narrow staircase, and, guided by the sound, reached an attic, where a fearful spectacle presented itself.

Crouching in a corner of the room was a little girl, apparently about eight years of age, with scarcely a vestige of clothing upon her emaciated body, which bore the traces of the most brutal treatment. Her shoulders were bruised and bleeding from the punishment recently inflicted by the fiendish old hag who was standing over her in the most threatening attitude when our hero fortunately rushed into the room, and prevented her from carrying her diabolical intention into execution. This monster, in the shape of a woman, had seized a pair of pinchers she had heated, and, yelling with rage, swore that she would tear the flesh from the child's bones! Charley made his appearance at this critical moment, and the hag being thwarted in her intended vengeance upon the defenceless little creature, turned upon our hero with the ferocity of a tigress.

Charley dodged the hot pinchers with which she made a blow at his head, and wrenching them from her hand, and seizing her lean throat, dashed her senseless to the ground.

"Lie there, yon cursed brute!" said Charley, as he threw her from him, and turning to the little girl, who was now crying bitterly, he raised her in his arms. The poor child trembled violently as she nestled close to him, looking with a terrified glance at her persecutor, who had recovered from our hero's grip sufficiently to sit up, and gaze savagely at him and the victim of her brutality.

"You thundering old hag," said Mr. Wag, in a passion, "I've half a mind to settle you!"

"You'd better try it," retorted the woman.

The child was fearfully excited at the recovery of her tormentor, and clung to Charley, begging him to protect her.

"Oh! take me away, take me away—she will kill me—she said she would," exclaimed the terrified girl.

"Yes! you little wretch I will kill you! I'll tear you limb from limb !" screeched the brutish woman. "If it hadn't been for him I'd a done so just now, but I'll do it yet—curse you, you little devil !" added she, shaking her clenched fists at the girl, who begged frantically that Charley would take her away, and not leave her with the woman.

Charley felt sorely puzzled—what to do he knew not. If he went for a policeman, or even left the room in search of the other people whom he supposed lived in the house, the infuriated woman would assuredly kill the poor little innocent.

"If you dare to touch her while I am away I'll smash you !" said Charley.

"I'll kill her, or my name's not Madge !" returned the woman, gnashing her teeth with rage.

"Then I shan't go, old devil-skin"

"Oh! do go, and take me with you," implored the child, turning her beautiful little face up to him, "I will love you so, and be so good."

Charley was not a lover of children, but this one's pleasing blue eyes seemed to affect him in a marvellous fashion. He smoothed back the flaxen hair which hung in tangled masses on her shoulders, and, wondrous to relate, imprinted a kiss upon her forehead, and told her that she should go home with him !

The reader will hardly credit this, but it is true nevertheless.

The child hearing that she was to go with him, grew as frantic with delight as she had previously been with terror.

She leaped from his arms in spite of the bruises and cuts her poor little frame had sustained, and running to one end of the room, and pointing to a small casket which stood upon a shelf, she exclaimed—

"That is mine, so she says, but I'm never to have it."

"Oh! we'll soon see about that, little one," said Charley.

The woman, hearing his reply to the child, made a dash for the shelf, but Master Wag was rather too quick for her, and possessed himself of the box before she could do so. With a yell like a wild beast she turned on him once more, and this time Charley did not hesitate to use his fists, for the crone wielded an iron bolt which might have proved fatal had it descended on our hero's head, instead of on the floor, as it did, however, for Charley darted at her, and struck her down like a ninepin. Then taking the little girl in his arms, and wrapping her tenderly in his inverness cape, he left the house, and as soon as possible got into a cab.

The child stuck very close to him during the ride, but said very little. Mr. Wag, therefore, had ample time to consider what he should do with the little creature.

"By Jupiter!" said he to himself, "I must be an awful idiot to saddle myself with a brat in this manner, and what the devil I'm to do with her, I can't say—send her to the workhouse I suppose."

But just as this workhouse alternative entered his head, the poor little soul raised herself up and kissed his cheek.

"No, damn it! that I won't," said he, answering his own thoughts aloud, much to the child's dismay at first, for she thought she had done wrong and he was angry, but Charley's manner soon re-assured her, and she began to prattle and talk just as they were reaching home.

"I say, Mrs. Harris," said he, addressing his house-keeper, whom he had summoned on his arrival, "This is my adopted daughter—what can be done for her in the way of washing and dressing?"

"Well, sir," said the redoubtable Mrs. H., looking at the little child as only a woman who has ten of them herself can look, "well, sir, I should say a great deal can be done for her in that way."

"I shall hand her over to you, and if you know where to get her any togs at this time of night she must have them."

"I think you'd better put the dressing part of it off till to-morrow."

"You don't mean to say you'd have her go without clothes until to-morrow."

"Oh, sir!" replied Mrs. Harris, pretending to be very much confused, but in reality never more collected in her life, "you know what I mean, sir, my little 'Melia is just about her size, and she can have one of her frocks till you get her some things."

"Ah! that'll do, stunning—there, run along little Tippetywichet—and, Mrs. Harris."

"Yes, sir."

"Have the little room off my dressing-room got ready."

"Yes, sir."

"This is rather a rummy gig for me to take into my noddle," thought Charley, "I suppose I'm growing soft. What the deuce I'm to do with her I don't know—put her to school is about the only thing,"

Mr. Wag had been left to himself, his thoughts, and his cigar, for nearly three quarters of an hour, when Mrs. Harris, with the child, returned to the room.

The little lady was wonderfully improved by the washing and combing processes, so much so that Charley could not help being struck with her beauty. Her golden hair was brushed back from a perfectly-formed forehead, and confined in a net behind, and her dark blue eyes seemed a deeper blue, now that the fairness of her complexion was visible. The frock in which Mrs. Harris had arraigned her was too short for her by several inches, but this only served to display the exquisite shape of her little limbs, which were encased in a pair of 'Melia's best stockings.

Charley kissed the little fairy, and asked her if she were tired.

"I am—a little."

"Then you must have your supper and go to bed," said Mr. Wag, in the most fatherly manner.

Carving a chicken, which he considered the lightest for a young lady's supper, it suddenly occurred to him that he had never asked his adopted daughter her name, and he did so immediately.

"What is your name, dear?"

"Amy."

"Amy what?"

"Amy Pelton—so Madge says."

Mr. Wag, satisfied on this point, saw that his little friend made a good supper, and after making her drink a glass of wine, which he considered she required after the brutal treatment she had been subjected to, handed her over to Mrs. Harris, by whom she was undressed and put to bed.

On the following day Charley paid his visit to Richmond.

LXXXIX.—LUCINDA AND THE CAPTAIN.

A young lady of our acquaintance has been shamefully neglected, but then she has adopted a line of life which we all affect to think very improper. This may in some measure account for my not wishing to bring her prominently before the reader's notice, but as it is absolutely necessary that she should not be entirely forgotten, I shall relate, in the shortest chapter that I have ever perpetrated, some of her doings since we last had the pleasure of her society in Norfolk Street.

It may be remembered that Captain Gabion was gazetted to a line regiment, the depôt of which was at Chatham.

Immediately on joining, that young officer applied for leave of absence and at once commenced looking for a house.

In due time he found one in Gillingham, furnished it elegantly, went up to London, and returned to Chatham with the blooming Lucinda—but not as his wife—dear reader—not as his wife—it is a sad tale altogether, and one that I had much rather say nothing at all about. Miss Lucinda Hopley was Miss Lucinda still, and what is worse, she had actually been foolish enough to confess to her dear Arthur that the name of Linley with the Mrs. prefixed was all bosh—

Does it not make one's blood boil to think that any living creature should be so silly as to disclose anything which might induce another person to think lightly of them? I hear the strong-minded reader say yes, it does—but another (and this one a lady), exclaims—ah, you neevr loved!

Does this fair lady mean to insinuate that because a mortal loves, he or she must necessarily be devoid of common sense for the time that the fit continues? I think she does, and I verily believe she is right in doing so.

Lucinda loved this youthful soldier, and was imprudent enough to tell him so, and not content with this, she must entertain him with the history of her past life, mentioning one or two little occurrences that might just as well have been kept to herself. It was very silly of her, and I can only account for it in one way. She had h rd some twaddle to the effect that there coul be no love without mutual confidence, and as she was particularly anxious for Arthur's love, she considered it a duty to confide ALL her secrets to him, while he, knowing dog, obliged her in return with a few fictitious ones.

The disclosures relative to her past life were not at all agreeable to Gabion, and he took her to live with him in a business-like and cold-blooded manner, and Lucinda's life was anything but the kind of existence she had pictured to herself on Arthur's avowal of his love for her.

She had everything she could wish for, but still she was not happy—Arthur had changed. Their evenings were dull to both of them.

Sometimes Lucinda would ask him whether she should read to him, and not unfrequently he would growl—

"No! I can read myself."

"Shall I sing to you, Arthur, dearest?" she would say, placing her hand on his arm endearingly.

"Singing be ——. I don't want to hear you squalling."

"What *shall* I do to please my darling?"

"There, go to the devil!" the darling wc*ld say, getting up and going out to play billiards with a few of his acquaintances, in whose company he often remained until breakfast time the next morning.

Poor Lucinda would thus be left alone for hours together, and she found it dull enough. And as the reader, doubtless, finds this chapter the same, we will conclude it, and leave the young lady to brood over her vanished dream of love.

———

LXL.—SHOWS HOW TWO YOUNG PEOPLE MET, WHO HAD NOT SEEN EACH OTHER FOR A LONG TIME.— WHAT THEY SAID, AND A LITTLE OF WHAT THEY DID.

THE visit to Richmond had taken place, and Charley Wag, as Monsieur Adolphe de Bessac, had been received most kindly by the Duchess of Heatherland, at whose res dence he was always a welcome guest, for t) young duke, her son, infinitely preferred (.r hero's society to that of their only other fiequent visitor, the doctor, Mr. Bellamy, a gentleman who had lat.'y taken a house in the neighbourhood, and established a practice through the influence of the duchess.

Charley Wag was now the chosen companion of a duke, and in a fair way to establish the footing he had so longed for among the upper ten thousand.

* * * * * *

"But Charley, dear, what made you come here?"

"To look for you to be sure."

"Yes! I know—but how could you tell where I was?"

"I looked for you in every other conceivable place and could not find you—so came here."

"Dear, dear Charley, how I love you and always shall."

"And you will leave here and come home to me again, dearest?"

"How can I, Charley, after all that has happened?" said the young lady.

"What the deuce is to hinder you?" said Mr. Wag, rather sharply.

"How could I leave the duchess after all her kindness to me?"

"Oh, hang it, I think you might study me as well."

"But what excuse can I make to her?"

"That's easily done, I'll settle something by to-morrow,"

"Do as you like, Charley," said the pretty girl, leaning confidingly on his arm, "and I will never part from you again."

"I should rather think you wouldn't," replied Mr. Wag, impudently, "but I must leave you, though, for if that youngster the duke finds me here on his return, I shan't get back to town to day."

"But Charley, you have not told me why you are so disguised—what necessity was there for it?"

"A great deal, my dear, I'll tell you why another time—and now good bye," said he, putting his arm round the waist, and kissing her pouting lips, "good bye, Julia."

"Good bye, Charley," said the young lady, returning his kiss passionately, "I shall see you to-morrow?"

"Yes."

"*Au revoir.*"

This conversation took place one day when Charley had paid a visit to Richmond, and had found the duchess and her son out. Our hero was not sorry at their absence, for it enabled him to have a *tete a tete* with his dear Julia.

The reader will ceollect that when that young lady left the vessel which Toddleboy commanded, it was to deliver a letter to the Duchess of Heatherland, relative to the murder of the duke. After meeting with many startling adventures she accomplished her mission, and from that time had resided with the duchess and her son, as a friend and companion.

This explanation will serve to remove some portion of the improbability of the meeting between Charley and Julia Jenkini.

The young lady had emained some lengthened time in Fra: with the duchess, and had accompanied aer on her return to England.

Having once more brought the pretty Julia before the notice of the reader, we shall pass on to Mr. Wag again, who had returned to London to look after his little adopted daughter.

———

LXLI.—MR. WAG MAKES PURCHASES FOR A LITTLE LADY, AND LOOKS OUT FOR A FIRST-RATE ESTABLISHMENT AT WHICH TO PLACE HER.

ON his return to London, Charley found the little girl looking out for him, and s it was yet early he chartered a cab, and,

CHARLEY AT THE CASINO.

taking Amy with him, proceeded in search of suitable attire for the little lady.

Charley felt that he was tolerably well up in matters which concerned young ladies dress, so he set off on his errand with no small amount of confidence.

Even the most unexperienced would find little difficulty in such a task, were they to place implicit reliance on the young ladies who superintend the ready-made department of the shops where the olive branches can be rigged from top to toe at a trifling cost.

Our hero made his way to one of the many establishments of this kind, and in a short time Amy was provided with an outfit worthy of an alderman's daughter. Mr. Wag returned home, and consigned Amy to the housekeeper.

"Now, Mrs. Harris," said he, "be good enough to make Miss Amy as smart as you can."

"I shan't have much trouble in doing that, sir," replied Mrs. H., "for she's a pretty creature—bless her."

"And as soon as she is dressed we'll dine."

"Yes, sir."

The little lady ran off with the good-natured housekeeper, who was as proud of her as if she had been one of the ten which the prolific Mrs. Harris had presented her spouse with during the eleven years of their married life.

No. 64

[CHARLEY WAG, THE NEW JACK SHEPPARD.]

"I'm sure, miss," said the good woman, putting on an extensive crinoline, "you look like a little fairy."

"Do you think so, Mrs. Harris?"

"Yes, miss, and you must be very good, and very fond of Mr. Wag, for buying you so many beautiful things."

"And so I am, and always shall be," replied the young lady, arranging her beautiful golden hair in a handsome net.

"Now, dear, let me put on your frock."

Amy allowed the old lady to attire her in a very becoming dress, which had been selected by the young lady, who had provided all that was necessary for the young lady's outfit. "There, Miss Amy, now I think you are quite ready."

Amy immediately tripped off to join her papa, as she termed our hero. With a bound she was in his arms, kissing him, and thanking him for the "pretty things" he had bought her.

After Charley had had enough he made her sit down by him.

"Amy," said he, "wouldn't you like to be a little lady?"

"Oh, yes, papa, and ride in a carriage, and have lots of money!" replied the child.

"Ah! I daresay you would," said Charley, with a grin at her idea of what constituted a lady, "but you must go to school first."

"And leave you, papa," said the child, sadly,

"For a little while, dear."

"And never see you?"

"Oh! I shall come and see you often, if you are a good girl."

"I'll be very, very good—but I'd much rather stay with you."

"Well, my dear, we'll talk of that at some other time, but now dinner is ready."

After dining the little lady went to bed, and Charley passed the rest of the evening in arranging some scheme for Julia's leaving the duchess without appearing ungrateful for the many kindnesses shown her by her grace.

His inventive powers, as we are already aware, were great, and he was not long in concocting a plan which he deemed the best under the circumstances.

He rose early the next morning, and after breakfast took up the *Times*, and pored over the advertisements headed "Education."

"I'm jiggered if I know which is best out of such a lot," said he to himself. "I wish Julia was here, she'd tell me in a twinkling." Then he went over them again, and at last lighted on a seminary in Westbournia.

"It won't be too far off, and I can go and look after her now and then."

Having settled upon this establishment as a likely one, Charley summoned Mrs. Harris, and requested her to dress Amy, as he was going to take her out.

The housekeeper was not long in arraying her, and in a short time the little girl was ready.

She was delighted at the idea of going out with her papa, and prattled away merrily during their ride to the seminary upon which Charley had fixed.

Our hero was most courteously received by a gentleman and lady, who, although not related, seemed to be the joint principals of the establishment.

Charley introduced the little Amy as his adopted daughter, whom he was most anxious should be thoroughly educated and accomplished, and expressed his readiness to pay pretty handsomely to secure this for her.

The lady and gentleman seemed to understand him perfectly, and it was finally settled that Amy should become a pupil at the half-quarter.

Mr. Wag left perfectly satisfied with the reception he had met with, but not without feeling some unaccountable dislike for the gentleman principal. He returned home with Amy, and was about to pay a visit to the wig-maker in Drury-lane, previous to going down to Richmond, when a young swell, the Hon. Percy Rufus, with whom Charley had contrived to scrape acquaintance at the club, looked in to see how that young gentleman was thriving.

"'Morning, Wag—what's up—haven't seen you anywhere lately."

"I've been in the country for a few days, beside having some business that has kept me pretty close."

"Oh!—that one of yours?" asked the Hon. Rufus, pointing to Amy, who was seated near the window, reading a book of fairy tales.

"No—she's a ward of mine."

"Of course," said the hon. with a smile.

"Fact, I assure you," said Charley, who understood his incredulous look, and calling to the little girl, he introduced her to Mr Rufus, and then sent her out of the room.

"She's a pretty little thing."

"She is," replied Charley, "and now I'll tell you how I came by her," and he related the circumstances which led to his adopting her.

"By Jove!" said Rufus, as he concluded, "quite romantic—but what are you going to do with her?"

"Put her to school."

"Ah! there's something in that—but the difficult matter is to find one."

"There are plenty of them."

"Heaps—but some of them are devilish queer places. I heard a funny story about one a few months ago while travelling on the Great Western line. I was going down to Somersetshire, and had for a travelling companion a very pretty girl, who was bound to Bath; somehow or other we got into conversation touching upon school days, and she told me several little things that had happened to her. She had been at a school in Westbourne —— something—I never remember streets or terraces—where her treatment had been anything but what I should like a sister of mine to experience."

"How do you mean?"

"Why the infernal masters were in the habit of kissing the prettiest of the girls."

"How about the lady principal?"

"She didn't care—and the singing master had a weakness for putting his head rather closer to the neck of my pretty companion than she admired. I suppose he did it by way of stimulating her to get out the high notes."

"Rather a novel way," said Charley, with

a laugh. "Do you know who she was?"

"No, hang it—she lived at Notting Hill though, but at what part I haven't the slightest idea. She was an awfully pretty girl, and I should amazingly like to see her again. I think I shall go the round of the churches at Notting Hill, and see if I can find her. I hope there's not a number of the sacred edifices in the neighbourhood."

"I can't say exactly," replied Charley, "I only go in for church now and then—but you must have been an awful muff not to find out all about her, and her whereabouts when at home, during the ride down."

"It was not the want of opportunity that prevented me, for we had an hour's walk at Didcot."

"Alone?"

"No—there was an organ grinding wretch that stuck pretty close to us."

"Organ grinding! what do you mean?"

"Why an organist to be sure—so he described himself."

"Oh! that alters the case entirely."

"He seemed to be a very entertaining fellow, and I was rather sorry when he left us."

"But then was your time to make way with your pretty companion."

"Yes—but I didn't."

"By jingo you ought to have been scalped didn't you find out her name even?"

"No—I got out to see to her luggage at Bath, and just as I had it pointed out to me the cursed whistle sounded, and I had hastily to bid her adieu, and jump into my seat again without even reading the name on her boxes."

"But did you not find out where she was going to stay at Bath?"

"No—she was going on to Weston-super-Mare the following week, and I did drive over one day from where I was staying, but could see nothing of her."

"You didn't deserve to. I never heard such a muffish business before. But bye the bye you have not told me the name of these people who keeps the school where these pranks are played with the girls?"

"I'm hanged if I remember."

"That's infernally annoying—for there happens to be a gentleman at the place I've hit upon for Amy, that I don't entirely like the look of."

"I don't see that it matters much in her case, she is a mere child—now my little railway acquaintance was, I should say, about seventeen, and as enticing a girl as you could meet with."

"I think you're right— it can't matter, at least for the present."

"What a beastly nuisance," said the Hon. Percy, "my watch has run down—what's the time, Wag?"

"A quarter past one," replied Charley.

"The deuce! then I must be off. I have to meet a fellow at Tattersall's, and shall hardly get there in time."

When this young gentleman had departed, Charley at once proceeded towards Drury-lane, with the intention of having the moustache and imperial, which he wore as Monsieur de Bessac, affixed by the obliging little barber,

for which purpose our hero now paid him a daily visit.

His journey to Richmond was postponed, however, till a later hour in the day, by an occurrence over which our hero had not the slightest control.

XCII. — An old acquaintance in the legal profession.

AFTER Charley's escape from Clement's Inn, on the night that he nearly throttled Leech, he had very wisely kept out of that individual's way, not being at all anxious to figure at Quod-street on the charge. Hitherto he had succeeded in avoiding him, and might have continued to do so had it not been for his visits to Drury-lane. On the previous morning Leech had been in that neighbourhood, and had seen Charley enter the court in which the wig-maker resided, and from this court he had seen our hero emerge with a heavy moustache and pointed beard.

"What the devil's his little game now?" said Leech to himself, as Charley entered a cab.

The lawyer entered another.

"Follow that cab," said he to the driver; and away they went in close pursuit of the vehicle which contained Mr. Wag.

"Going to the railway station," said Leech, as they passed over Waterloo Bridge—"well, my fine fellow, I've nothing particular to do to-day, I'll take a trip into the country myself, and see what you are up to,"

With this intention he followed Charley to Richmond, and after seeing the doors of a handsome mansion close upon our hero, the indefatigable lawyer set to work to discover in whose family, and under what name, our hero had established a footing. To a man of Leech's stamp this was an easy matter.

A few half-crowns judiciously applied to the itching palm of an over-fed flunky put him in possession of all he was anxious to learn, and he returned to town rather disappointed than otherwise at the discovery he had made.

But Leech was not a man to be cast down by a trifle, and, as he sat in his chambers that night, he looked calmly at the affair in every light.

"He must be exceedingly intimate, to be there almost every day" thought Leech, "I wonder whether he has made himself known to the Duchess,—if so, my little game's up— it cant be—I must have a little quiet conversation with him on the subject, and this time I'll be on the look out for his fingers, as I'm not particularly anxious for another tightener on my throat,—here the hard featured limb of the law, gave vent to a chuckle as hard and dry as his own parchmenty skin, and he rubbed his bony hands gleefully in anticipation of what he should make out of Charley.

"Let me see" said Leech, "if he goes down there every day, he must pay the barber a visit, to have that moustache and Billy goat put on!—yes—to-morrow I'll watch him in, and wait till he comes out a la Francais, and then I'll address him as Mr. Wag,".

On the day after Mr. Leech stationed himself in a position which commanded the entrance to the court, where Charley was in the habit of going daily, and at about two o'clock that young gentleman stepped out of a cab, which he discharged, and walked up to the wig makers door.

Leech had waited for nearly half an hour when Charley made his appearance again with the moustache and beard.

"Now's my time" said Leech "he dare'nt attack me in the streets."

Consoling himself with this notion he followed our hero down the lane, and just as he was about to turn into the Strand, this talented lawyer stepped up to him.

"How do you do, Sir!" said he, I'm glad to see you looking so well."

Charley knew him at a glance, but affected not to understand his remark, replying in french to the effect that he did not know him.

"Oh! come Mr. Wag, a joke's a joke, did'nt you nearly throttle me the last time we met?"

"Yes! damn you, and I'll settle you the next time I get old of you, if you dont leave me to myself" returned Charley, fiercely.

"My dear Sir, you misunderstand me, all I want is an hours conversation with you,"

"I'm in a hurry now, and can't wait."

"It is important that you should hear what I have to say" said Leech in the most insinuating tone he was capable of using.

"If it's about the title, I don't want to hear any more about it."

"But, my dear Sir, I have something else to communicate, beside."

"Well! out with it, as soon as you like, or keep it to yourself, which ever you choose."

"Let us step into this coffee shop" said Leech "we shall be free from interruption."

"Would'nt your chambers be better?" said Charley, savagely.

"I think this will do, equally well" replied Leech, blandly, for he saw the drift of Charley's remark, and did not feel at all inclined to place his life at that young gentleman's disposal a second time,—Charley followed him into the coffee shop and throwing himself into a seat, said.—

"Now then, what have you to say to me?"

"My dear Mr. Wag" began Leech, perhaps you are not aware that I have heard of your frequent visits to the Duchess of Heatherland at Richmond?"

"Well?"

"Also the name you have assumed."

"What of it?" thundered Charley.

"Hush! my dear friend, you will be attracting attention,

"I don't care replied Charley, doggedly, "what else do you think you know?"

"That you are personating someone" said Leech, in a lower tone.

"What the devil are you driving at?"

"Simply this, Mr. Wag, unless you pay me well, to remain quiet, I will expose you to the duchess, by letting her know that your name is no more De Bessac, than it is Leech."

"You cursed scoundrel!" said Charley, as he suddenly sprang up and thrust his hand

kerchief into the lawyer's mouth in a manner which prevented him from uttering a sound.

"Give the slightest alarm and I'll murder you, if I swing for it!"

The wretched man saw that he was completely in the power of one whom he knew never threatened in vain, so he remained quiet.

"Swear that you will never interfere with me, or my doings again" continued our hero, taking up a table knife Do you hear me" he added in a low but very distinct voice, shaking the writhing Leech, who found it impossible to speak, and rather hard to breathe with Mr. Wag's handkerchief in his mouth. He contrived however to nod his head, in a manner which seemed to satisfy Charley, who at once removed the gag.

"You perfectly understand me?" said he, "interfere with me again in any way, and I'll have your life."

After this little understanding had been arrived at, Charley summoned the waitress and paid for the coffee grounds, of which neither of them had partaken—then motioning to Leech to follow him, he left the house.

They separated at the corner of Drury Lane, Leech betaking himself to his chambers and Charley to the railway terminus at Waterloo Bridge.

XCIII.—A little more about Chatham,— An unprotected Female.

THE Author has been greatly astonished at receiving through the publisher several letters from Chatham, of a most insulting and threatening nature, relative to the number of the week before last, how he can have given offence to the good people of that town, he is at a loss to understand, as he is not aware that he is known to a single person in the place; the sketch he made with reference to it, was purely imaginary, but this harmless flight of fancy it seems has caused a perfect *furore*, for one of the epistles, just alluded to, contains a threat, that bloodshed will ensue, unless the allusions to Chatham cease immediately, the only impression that these effusions create in the author's mind, is, that the characters he conjured up under the influence of weak gin and water, must positively exist. The gin and water *may* have rendered him *clairvoyant*, hence the faithful delineation, had he known that his production would have given rise to such an amount of indignation, he certainly would not have indulged in that last glass of grog to which he ascribes all the mischief.

The bloodshed business, which the author feels convinced must have emanated from the diminutive gentleman, for having been called "the wretch with the drum," will not deter him from relating what occured to Miss Lucinda Hopley, whom we left at Gillingham brooding over her vanished dream of love,— vanished now in every sense, for Captain Arthur Fitzroy Gabion had taken his departure from Chatham, to join his regiment in India.

Notwithstanding his beastly behaviour, the young soldier felt as much regard for her as could be expected, and before leaving England he made her a present of five hundred pounds, as the most substantial way of expressing his feelings towards her. Lucinda really suffered at losing him, for she still loved him passionately, and for some weeks after he left she was so ill that she was unable to leave her room.

During her convalesence her thoughts turned upon religious matters and she strongly inclined to the Protestant nun notion, which had entered her head about the time she met with Arthur—but matters took a very different turn after the first day on which she ventured out.

She was returning home from Brompton, whither she had been to purchase some sacred music, with which to beguile the weary hours, and was crossing the lines on her way to Gillingham, when she was accosted by an individual of a decidedly unprepossessing appearance—he was rather stout with a flabby white face, the roses having deserted his cheeks, and taken up a position on his nose,—he was clothed in rusty black, and wore a napless hat on his head, and a very dirty white handkerchief tied in a slovenly manner round his bull neck.

On addressing Lucinda this worthy tucked his umbrella, which was of sairey gamp proportions, under his arm, and thrusting a bundle of tracts before the young lady, said, in a snuffy tone,

"Accept of these young woman," at the same time leering under her bonnet in a most lascivious and unclerical manner.

Lucinda took them, and, as she did so, stole a glance, as young ladies will, at her companion.

The face seemed familiar to her.

She certainly had seen him before—but where ?

The reverend shepherd was walking her way, and kept up a very edifying discourse about nothing in particular, and to which Miss Hopley paid very little attention. She was, apparently engrossed with the tracts, but in reality was thinking where she had seen the man before.

Where had she seen him ?

Suddenly it occurred to her, and the remembrance of the circumstances connected with the last sight of this person made her blush in spite of herself. This gentleman was one of the three shepherds who made their way in the most unaccountable manner into her bedroom when staying at the inn with Leech, after her escape from home with Charley Wag.

The shepherd recognised her again, and, in a fat voice, mentioned the fact to her.

"Have we not held converse together before to-day ?"

"I think not," replied Lucinda, who was busily engaged in looking over the tracts the reverend party had given her, and was deeply interested in " Jesus wept, and well he might," and " How are you off for soap ?" when her companion returned to the charge by saying—

"But were you not with a gentleman at the inn at Coddlethorpe, where we din.d after a very successful revival meeting."

"I think you are mistaken," said Lucinda, quite convinced that this was one of the shep-

herds who had entered her room in the mysterious manner on that night.

" Ah ! yes I must be—and yet——"

Here the worthy minister gave her a leer which seemed to indicate his incredulity as to her statement.

Lucinda again dived into the tracts.

" I trust, my dear young lady, those little books may do you good," said the shepherd, seeing that she was going into them in great style—" I shall make it my duty to supply you with them, and may they——"

What this devout man was about to say it is impossible to suggest, but his remark was nipped in the bud by Lucinda, who had by this time arrived at her own door.

" Will you not walk in, sir ?"

" You are kind," said the shepherd, as the spider-brusher opened the door and they entered—" Oh that it may be my task——buttered toast by all that's glorious," added he, in a lower tone, sniffing it immediately.

Miss Hopley was not long in taking off her walking attire, and on her return to the sitting room she found the shepherd seated, with his hands upon his knees, and his hat and umbrella placed at a convenient distance from him on the floor.

" Oh ! this is heavenly," said he, as she entered the room, but to what he alluded, unless it was the smell of the toast, is a matter of speculation.

He was evidently meditating.

" Ah ! my dear madam, we do indulge our carnal appetites to an alarming extent—gluttony for instance."

A sniff.

" And lust "

Another sniff.

" How immoderately have I seen Brother Pudding eat of buttered toast."

Here the reverend gentleman was quite overcome at the brother's weakness, and gave way to a violent fit of nose-blowing, during which operation Lucinda rang for tea.

The servant entered with the tea-things, and Lucinda, turning to the shepherd, inquired whether he would take tea with her.

She felt so lonely that even the society of this person, unprepossessing as he was, was acceptable. " Will you stay and take tea with me, Mr.——"

" Swabb—the Rev. Oyley Swabb, of the New Bethel—I shall be most happy."

Lucinda presided in her usual graceful manner at the tea-table, and the shepherd, entranced by her beauty, combined with the buttered toast and bohea, could only peg away and be silent. When the last piece of toast was disposed of, and the butter was still visible at the corners of his ugly mouth, the Rev. Oyley began to talk again. His conversation was chiefly upon theological matters, of which Lucinda knew very little, and, if the truth must be told, the rev. shepherd knew still less.

But this knowledge is quite immaterial, if a man can read—not necessarily like a Bellew— it stands to reason he is eligible for the clergy. And in Chatham, which is the head-quarters of the great Smash and Splinter Association of the United Unitarian Baptist Devil Dodgers, the system works admirably. The worthy

Swabb had been at one time a mender of boots and shoes, but having received a parochial education, he felt that he had a soul above leather, and gave up his all for the good cause, in which he had laboured for the last ten years with great success.

Such are the men to whom the *reasoning* portion of the elect look for spiritual aid.

And why not?

Are not they as capable of imparting it as the well-educated?

Is it because the purse-proud priests of the establishment, to say nothing of the bloody-minded Papists, hold that ordination, a cere-money performed by a person they designate a bishop, is necessary to entitle a man to be-come a minister of the Gospel, that we should despise those who deem it unnecessary?

What if some of our shepherds *do* come of the dregs of the people? Are they not as good as *any* member of that bloated and unprinci-pled aristocracy which is striving to ride rough shod over all our privileges as Britons? They are, I say, and, as a member of the great Smash and Splinter Junction of Coddlethorpe, (where I had the good fortune to meet with Brother Swabb), I call upon you, brethren, to uphold and liberally contribute to the support of our beloved shepherds.

The Rev. Oyley Swabb is a brother in whose praise too much cannot be said, and Miss Lu-cinda found him of infinite service to her, in settling in the most reasonable manner some knotty points which she never fully compre-hended before. She therefore confided all her doubts to the rev. gentleman, who promised to go more fully into the subject on the following evening.

The events which followed their discussion will be set forth in the next chapter.

———

XCIV..—A REV. GENTLEMAN'S NIGHTCAP—
SHOWS HOW LUCINDA LISTENED TO THE REV.
OYLEY SWABB, AND WHAT WAS THE RESULT—
BROTHERS PUDDING, GASH, AND OTHERS—
BAPTISM WITH THE CHILL OFF.

THIS was Saturday night and the good shepherd did not remain long with Lucinda after the buttered toast and bohea had disap-peared,—in fact, he thought her conversation which touched upon religious topics, rather slow, beside which he felt he required a little stimulant, in the shape of rum and water, so bidding the young damsel, adieu, in the warm-est possible manner, after entreating her to attend the morning buster, at the New Bethel on the following day, he took his de-parture, and deliberately walked down into Chatham, and into the public known to a chosen few at "t'other side."

And here the artful swabb put away several glasses of rum and water by way of a night-cap.

His principle object in visiting this house, next to rum and water, was to leer at the pretty daughters, who on this occasion kept close in their little sanctum at the back of the bar, for the rev. gentleman when under the influence of six glasses of hot and strong, was more like a wolf than a shepherd.

After paying for his tipple, Mr. Swabb made his way home in a fearfully zig-zag and un-parsonlike fashion.

He tumbled into bed with his boots on, and and without saying his prayers—and by sleep sought to prepare himself for the duties of the following day.

Lucinda had promised the Rev. Oyley that she would attend the "Buster," at the New Bethel, and after breakfast on Sunday she arrayed herself most bewitchingly and made sail for the chapel of the worthy shepherd.

On her arrival, she found a large muster of seedy looking brethren, with gouty umbrellas hanging about the entrance.

She was hesitating whether to pass through this host of the elect, or to turn back when the Rev. Oyley Swabb espied her and coming forward offered his arm which she accepted, and thus conveyed, she passed the crowd of admiring Bethelites and entered the Chapel, here Mr. Swabb introduced her to the Deacon Goggles, a facetiously pious brother, who contrived to give the shepherd a dig in the ribs, saying, as he thrust his tongue into his cheek and closed his left eye.

"Plummy," and then went off whistling one of the hymns; (it was his duty to give them out) to the tune of "Old Bob Ridley."

Lucinda had not been seated long, when two brother shepherds made up to Swabb and requested him to present them to the "young vessel."

Brother Swabb seemed rather annoyed at their request, and with rather a bad grace, acceded to it.

"The Rev. Jack Pudding" said he, and the Rev. Ghastly Gash."

To her horror, Lucinda saw that these were the other two shepherds who dined with them and behaved subsequently in the same extraordinary manner that Swabb did.

They evidently remembered her, for the nods and winks which passed between them, said as much.

By this time the building was filled, but still the three shepherds were purring about Lucinda.

Although this was a grand occasion at the Bethel, and Brothers Pudding, and Gash had come down from London expressly to take part in the affair, neither of the worthies see-med inclined to leave the young lady's side; and the eyes of the elderly portion of the elect, were directed to them.

The Deacon, Brother Goggles saw the state of the case, and at once proceeded to remind the amorous shepherds that the con-gregation were getting impatient

Walking up to within a short distance of where the rev. gentleman were seated, Brother Goggles screwing his lips together gave vent to a sound which might be spelt, thus,—

"Sfit!"

But this failing to attract the attention of the trio, Goggles placed his two forefingers in his mouth and gave a short sharp whistle.

This had the effect of making Brother Swabb turn round.

"Hullo! said he, "what's up?"

"Damn it, Swabb—lets get to prayers."

Thus appealed to the Rev. Oyley communicated with the other shepherds and the result was that they bundled out of the seats they were occupying, which were quickly filled by three of the faithful who had been standing close by, waiting for these gentlemen to commence the service.

This began by the Deacon's giving out the first verse or two of a hymn, which was sung to the tune of "Old Bob Ridley," (a great favorite at the New Bethel) and which was encored by the delighted congregation.

"After this the Rev. Ghastly Gash went in for one of his peculiar orations in the blood and murder line, but notwithstanding his praiseworthy efforts, in the true hell and damnation style, his success was not so great as it had been on many previous occasions, perhaps his failure might have arrisen from the constant repetition of the words "hell" and "damnation," which are always intensely offensive, when dealt out to us from the pulpit and the applause which followed this gentleman's address, was not of a thundering nature, Indeed, there were several unmitigated heathens in the gallery, who were profane enough to hiss at the conclusion of it, which so enraged Brother Gash, that he slapped his posterior in a manner which clearly indicated the contempt he felt for these miscreants, and immediately made for the little private room, devoted to the use of the shepherds, where he consoled himself with a long clay and a pot of "dogs nose."

The Rev. Oyley Swabb then put up an *extempore* prayer for the good of the great Smash and Splinter Association, on the behalf of which Brother Jack Pudding had kindly consented to appeal to the charitable feeling of the congregation then assembled. The latter portion of the shepherd's announcement, relative to collection, did not seem to meet with the unanimous approval of the congregation, several of whom got up to go before the appeal should be made, but the vigilant deacon was up to this little dodge, and had taken the precaution of having the doors closed, with the exception of one, to which he rushed, plate in hand, on the first demonstration of a move.

"Shell out, old cock!" said he, to a stout comfortable-looking gentleman, who might have been the skipper of a barge—he had a nautical cut—who was endeavouring to evade contributing. "Shell out! or the Recording Angel will pop you down in the defaulter's list."

"I wer'n't a going yet," growled this individual, who saw it was no go, "who's a going to spout? I wanted to know."

"All right, commander—Jack Pudding's his name—no offence, guv'nor, only you see," and here the speaker closed his eye and put his tongue in his cheek, "we *must* look after the brads."

In this way the indefatigable deacon prevented the egress of many of the shabby ones, and at last they gave up trying to escape.

The Rev. Jack Pudding, the great comic Baptist from the Obelisk, some of whose doings have been mentioned in a preceding chapter, now ascended the pulpit. His appearance elicited shouts from all parts of the chapel, and after bowing right and left to the congregation,

he suddenly disappeared at the bottom of the pulpit, from whence, after a lapse of a few minutes, during which the silence was profound, he sprang up in the skin of a gorilla. Then, perching himself on the edge of the pulpit, he went through many astounding antics to an accompaniment on the organ, after which he made a facetious appeal to the generosity of the congregation on the behalf of the Smash and Splinter Association, also a branch society for supplying an unlimited number of copies of "What's your Game?" "What are you up to?" "Who kissed Maria," "Come out of the Cupboard," "How the little boy went to hell for whistling on a Sunday," and many others too numerous to mention, but equally conducive to salvation, to the benighted gorillas of the interior of Africa.

During this address, Deacon Goggles, with Brothers Gash and Swabb, had been making a collection in aid of the above societies.

At the conclusion of his appeal the Rev. Jack again dropped to the bottom of the pulpit, and again silence reigned, broken only by the clinking of the shillings, as they fell from the hands of the faithful into the plates of the collectors.

The excitement was tremendous when Brother Pudding again appeared, divested of the gorilla's skin, but attired in a large leathern apron, a broken down hat upon his head, and a pipe in his mouth; for the congregation knew by this that he was going through his highly humerous representation of an argument between the deity and a drunken shoemaker, in which the latter was supposed to have the best of it.

This representation, although only figurative, never failed to elicit the warmest applause, and on this occasion it was eminently successful, "bringing the house down," and concluding the "buster." Then the congregation marched out in the most orderly manner, the organ, in the meanwhile, playing "The other side of Jordan."

Before Lucinda left, the three shepherds and Goggles joined her, earnestly expressing their hopes that she had been edified by what she had heard, and trusting she might "be converted," and become a "vessel of holiness."

From the deacon she received a pressing invitation to dinner, when she would meet the shepherds, whom he was going to entertain.

Lucinda declined this kindness on the part of Brother Goggles, as she infinitely preferred passing the rest of the day to herself—that is to say, until Brother Swabb came in the evening.

On her way home she pondered upon what she had seen and heard. How this service appealed to the senses, and how different were her feelings when listening to the monotonous and never- varying services of the Church of England. At the "New Bethel" the thoughts of her neighbours bonnets never once entered her head—she had given her whole attention to what was going forward.

And was this to be wondered at? Certainly not.

She had been kept in a state of religious excitement the whole time. The wonderful performances of the Rev. Jack Pudding appealed to her senses in a forcible manner, and she reached her home firmly resolved to lead a new life and be baptised. This resolution she communicated to Brother Swabb when he came in the evening after prayers, accompanied by the other two shepherds.

"Ah! my beloved sister," said the Rev. Oyley, taking one of her plump little hands within his own beefy paw, the Rev. Jack Pudding seizing the other, to the intense *chagrin* of Brother Gash, who contented himself with rubbing his knees against hers, as he sat opposite to her. "Ah! my beloved sister, how happy shall I be to receive you into my flock."

Gash and Pudding echoed their brother's sentiments, and expressed a determination to remain and assist at the ceremony, at which the Rev. Oyley did not seem greatly delighted.

"And when do you propose to undergo this solemn rite, my dear sister?" asked Brother Gash.

"As soon as possible."

"Is there any objection to-morrow, Brother Swabb?"

"That's rather sharp after conversion," returned Swabb, who was in hopes that his brother shepherds could not stay over the next day.

"It is to save a soul alive, Brother Swabb," said Gash.

"And as you very truly said in your beautiful discourse of this evening, Brother Gash, life is uncertain," chimed in the Rev. Jack—"but for my part I am in no hurry, and would remain for a week to see this lamb made one of the fold."

Swabb seeing that in any case his brethren were determined to be present, concurred with the remark made by the Rev. Jack relative to the uncertainty of human life, and agreed that the ceremony should take place on the following evening.

Having settled this point, Lucinda hoped that they would go, as she felt very tired, and was anxious to get to bed. But, unfortunately for her, the rev. shepherds evinced no signs of moving, each man seeming determined to outstay his neighbour.

At last, when she felt so sleepy that she could scarcely keep her eyes open, and hinted to the rev. gentlemen her intention of retiring for the night, they rose simultaneously and took their departure.

In a place like Chatham, and, indeed, in every town that boasts its "Ebenezers," "Bethels," and "Salems," the announcement of a baptism invariably attracts the attention of the male or female portion of the community. Should it be one of the softer sex who is about to be "dipped," the lords of the creation appear in great force, and should it happen to be one of the said lords about to undergo a similar process, I blush to say the ladies are always powerfully represented.

But, fortunately for our friend Lucinda, she was not to be exposed to the gaze of "outsiders." Her dipping was to take place in the presence of a very select party of the elect, chiefly shepherds and deacons.

As the evening approached she began to grow quite nervous, and at one time thought of giving up the idea of being baptised altogether. She had almost settled the matter when the rev. gentleman, who anticipated from past experience some such weakness at the eleventh hour, drove over from Chatham to fetch her.

At the sight of the brethren her fortitude returned, and in a short time she was ready, and the four drove back to the New Bethel, where everything was prepared for her reception—even to two huge kettles of hot water which stood ready on one side of Jordan, to be soused in just to take the chill off, unknown to even the elect visitors on the other side, who were not supposed to be up to *all* the hanky panky arrangements.

In a short time everything was complete, and the Rev. Oyley Swabb emerged from behind a curtain, where he had been superintending the undressing of the fair Lucinda, and where he had wasted a great deal of time unnecessarily in making his own toilet, and gloating over the buxom proportions of the young lady about to be dipped. He was attired in a costume, if it may be so dignified, very similar to the attendants at a Turkish bath, and one that was admirably suited, as it turned out, to the ceremony about to be performed.

At once commencing the usual prayers, he stepped into the water, and soon after Lucinda, led by Brothers Pudding and Gash, attended by Deacon Goggles, made her appearance with nothing on her but her chemise! This was a very appropriate garment for such an occasion, being very mattily trimmed with real Honiton lace, at least two inches in depth, and, but for one circumstance, would have answered the purpose admirably.

I have been given to understand that it is usual for ladies to run a tape through the top of their chemises, and thus prevent their falling down. Now that tape in poor Lucinda's garment had, I firmly believe, been cut by the Rev. Jack Pudding. She came forth exposing a great deal more of her bosom than she ought to have done, and when Brother Swabb came to the part of the service where she should have advanced to him, the two shepherds, who had each hold of an arm, did not seem at all inclined to part with her, but remained gazing at her uncovered charms in the most lawless manner. Brother Swabb, who was growing impatient, walked towards her, and, taking her hand, drew her into the water.

At this moment they were left in utter darkness, the gass having been off! The elect visitors began to move, and in less than no time Brothers Pudding and Gash, together with Deacon Goggles, were floundering in the water with Swabb and Lucinda! What went on there I shall not attempt to deficit, suffice it to say, that when a light was brought, Brother Goggles was discovered sitting, without his spectacles, on the banks of the Jordan, supporting the half-drowned Lucinda, and the three rev. shepherds were engaged in an indiscriminate mill about something or other which had happened in the middle of the stream!

Order was at length restored, and then the question arose, was Miss Hopley's baptism valid or not?

CHATHAM ON SUNDAY.

XCV. — A MIRACULOUS ESCAPE. —MOTHER AND SON BURIED ALIVE.

THE reader will, doubtless, remember that the chapter which contained the account of the attack upon Hopley's house and the terrible death of Jack Rattan, terminated somewhat abruptly, without mentioning the fate of Faversham, who was close to the unhappy man when he fell from the window into the cistern of boiling lead.

After this fearful catastrophe, and while the shrieks of the agonised wretch were still ringing in his ears, Faversham contrived to reach a part of the building which remained untouched by the fire, and completely secured from its further ravages by the ruins with which it was almost covered. Here he remained in breathless expectation. At every sound he heard, he fancied that the infuriated creatures who were howling for his life had found out his hiding place, and would shortly be upon him.

In this frightful anticipation he remained for hours. At last the shouts of the mob, who had seen the fate of Rattan, and had concluded that the others must have met with their death under the falling ruins, died away, and all was quiet. Cautiously creeping out, Faversham looked about him, and seeing no one, he at once made his way across the fields that Lucinda had passed through after the falling

[CHARLEY WAG, THE NEW JACK SHEPPARD.]

of the ruins. Striking at once into the road, towards the nearest railway station, he arrived in time to catch the first train for London. There he felt himself comparatively safe, for his experience had taught him the most secure haunts of the metropolis.

Notwithstanding his temporary security, he determined upon another step for evading the course of justice. With this intention he paid a visit to his mother in Cornwall, and with her assistance put his scheme into execution.

In the course of his mysterious studies he had discovered a mode of feigning death so perfect, that it defied even the detection of medical men. The trance produced by the preparation administered enabled the person taking it to remain without air or food for several days. This was the idea upon which Faversham founded his plan of operations.

His first step was to cause his mother to give out, as though inadvertently, that her son, who had been known as Ralph Faversham, had returned to her in a dying state. This announcement had the effect of bringing the police down upon them—but too late. The apparently lifeless body of Faversham was all that met the view of these officers when they entered the house for the purpose of taking him into custody. By exerting her influence, which was considerable with the authorities of the place in which she lived, she succeeded in having the circumstances of his death thoroughly circulated.

His burial took place soon after this fact had been established, and on the same night he was disinterred, and again in London, after having been in the trance for four days, and under ground from midday till midnight, when he was secretly conveyed to his mother's house, and there restored to consciousness by the remedies he had directed should be employed on the occasion.

For weeks after this had occurred he remained concealed, and during this period he devised fresh schemes of vengeance against the duchess and her son.

With the death of the duke, his old enemy, much of his vengeful feeling had departed, but still two of the race he had doomed to destruction were alive, although at present out of his reach. Indeed he did not even know to what place the duchess had retired with the young duke since the murder of her husband. This was a mere trifle to a man like Faversham, and he decided that his first step should be to discover them, and then the rest would be an easy matter.

With the exception of the duke, his victims had perished in the order he had laid down, and the deviation from his original plan was in consequence of the sudden attack of illness which seized him on the night he escaped with Rattan from his house in Bayswater, when the police came to apprehend him for the abduction of the duchess.

This deviation, as the reader is already aware, arose from a fear that his own intellect, taxed as it had been, might give way before the time came for the murder of the duke, who was to have been the last victim of the blood-thirsty Faversham.

While concealed in his mother's house, this mysterious man was engaged in altering his personal appearance as much as possible, and for this purpose he caused certain chemicals to be procured, which he prepared and applied to his features. Their effect was miraculous; not only altering the complexion, which before had been pale and cadaverous, to a ruddy and healthy look, but apparently the features themselves! His hair, which was naturally black, together with a large moustache, he had succeeded in changing to a light brown.

The transformation into a totally different looking person was so complete, that after a time he did not hesitate to make his appearance in the village, and join in the society to which his mother introduced him as an intimate friend.

His reception by those who had seen him before his pretended death convinced him that his disguise was impenetrable, and that he should never be recognised as Ralph Faversham.

Thoroughly satisfied on this head, he resolved to return to London, and commence his search for the duchess and her son, and with this intention he left Cornwall about two months after his burial and disinterment, and again entered London in pursuit of the innocent objects of his vengeance.

———

XCVI.—A VISIT TO RICHMOND—CHARLEY AND THE DUKE IN LONDON—LET DOGS DELIGHT TO BARK AND BITE—A HOP AT THE ARGYLL —A YOUNG LADY HEARS SOMETHING TO HER ADVANTAGE.

OUR hero was not long before he was at Richmond, after separating from Leech in the manner mentioned in the last chapter relating to their meeting. He found his pretty Julia anxiously awaiting his arrival, and it was very evident from her looks that she was expecting to hear from Charley's lips his plan by which she might leave the Duchess without appearing to be insensible to the many kindnesses her grace had lavished upon her from time to time.

"Here's a pretty go," said Charley to himself, "what the deuce will she think of me for not arranging something after all?"

As the duchess had not yet made her appearance, our hero and Julia were left alone for a short time, much to their delight.

"Well, dearest," said the young lady, after kissing him affectionately, "what have you settled?"

"The fact is, my dear Julia, that I have not settled anything. The task is one of such a delicate nature that I really do not see how it can be done."

"Oh! Charley."

"Well, my love, I was saying that I do not see how it can be done hastily."

"I thought you meant not at all," said the young lady, flinging her arms round Charley's neck.

"You made a grand mistake then I can tell you."

"But when can we arrange something?"

urged the young lady, who was now most anxious to join our hero again.

"As soon as I can possible hit upon something—but why not make a bolt of it?"

"I don't want to do that, but——"

"But if there's no other way you will."

"Oh! yes, Charley, I'd do anything."

"All right—but I don't think I shall call upon you to proceed to extremeties."

"No? What do you think of doing then?"

"An idea has just entered my head.'

"What is it?"

"To advertise for you."

"Advertise—what do you mean?"

"For the next of kin of Victor Jenkini!—will that do?"

"Capitally—only you mustn't forget saying 'will hear something to her advantage.'"

"I shan't leave that out you may depend."

"And when will you do it?"

"To day, and then it will be in the paper the day after to-morrow."

"How I long for the day to come," said Julia, who was about to repeat the demonstration with her arms round our heroe's neck when the young duke entered."

"I say monsieur" said that young gentleman "I want to go to London, to the theatre, and mamma says she wouldn't mind me going with you."

This was a tolerably strong hint, and our hero who was not at all averse to being seen by the British public, in the company of a live duke, notwithstanding the fact of the said duke, being of the tender age of fourteen, replied that he should be "delighted to accompany him."

"That's jolly," said the boy "at what time must we leave here, Monsieur de Bessac?

"I have to get back to town rather early to-day, you may as well return with me, and we can dine together at my club."

"Oh! that will be ripping!" said the youngster, who had an idea that belonging to a club, was the correct thing for every man to do, and intended joining one himself, as soon as he was a little taller."

"What theatre do you want to go to?" asked Charley.

"I'm not particular to a theatre—I want to see a little of life, you know, before that horrid tutor of mine comes—have you seen him?"

"No."

"Then you've lost a sight, I can tell you."

"Is he so frightful?"

"No—but he's such a grim looking fellow, with a large moustache, not like yours, and a great scar across his forehead."

"Who is he?"

"He has been an officer in the Austrian Army," said Julia "he certainly has a very military appearance," then turning to the young duke, she said with a smile, "and I think you'll find him very strict."

"He'd better not be strict with me, or I shall get him the sack" replied the boy in a tone which proved him to be rather a determined young gentleman, and one with whom the tutor might expect a little trouble.

"But where did this fellow spring from?" asked Charley, of Julia who seemed to know more about him, than the boy did."

"I can't say—he was recommended by Mr. Bellamy."

"The doctor."

"Yes."

"And when is he going to take of your grace?"

"Not yet, if I know it."

Just as the young gentleman had said this, the duchess made her appearance.

"How do you do, Monsieur de Bessac? has that fickle son of mine been asking you to take him to London?"

"Well, now your grace mentions it, I think he did say something of the sort" said Charley smiling.

"If you have no objection to looking after him for a day or two, I should not mind his going."

"It would give me great pleasure, I assure you."

"He wants to go to a theatre this evening, are you disengaged?

"Yes—and I proposed that he should return with me this afternoon, as I have some business to transact, after that I shall be entirely at his disposal."

"I'm sure it's very kind of you, Monsieur."

"Dont't mention it, I'm only too happy to be of service to your grace."

"Then you will return with him the day after to-morrow," said the duchess.

"Certainly."

"And you will look after him," said the mother, anxiously.

"I will remain at the same hotel."

After luncheon which was at this moment announced, Charley with the young duke and his servant returned to town.

Having seen them settled at an hotel our hero next proceeded to the "Times" office, where he paid for the insersion of the advertisement he had spoken to Julia about, then he removed his moustache and beard, and went to his chambers where he packed a small portmanteau, and after visiting the wig maker to have his hair affixed again, he returned to the hotel, too late as he told the young duke, to go to the club to dine.

He had mentioned the club inadvertently forgetting that there he was known as Charles Wag Esq., without a vestige of hair on his face, and at Richmond he was Monsieur Adolphe de Bessac, with a very large moustache and imperial.

The young duke seemed rather disappointed at not going to the club, but made a very excellant dinner at the hotel in spite of it.

This, concluded, the question was, where were they to go?

"Where the deuce shall we go, de Bessac? said the youngster (he had dropped the 'Monsieur' directly they left Richmond.

"Anywhere your grace wishes," replied Charley.

"Oh, hang it, drop the grace," said the youthful scion of Heatherland, "let us be jolly sociable, and go somewhere for the evening."

A theatre was at length fixed upon, and the two sallied forth. Charley sustained his character admirably, and his questions, asked with a well-assumed air of ignorance, would have convinced persons of a far more suspicious nature than the young duke, that he was actually a stranger to the ins and outs of the great metropolis.

Charley was frightfully bored by the "domestic drama of thrilling interest" which his young companion was listening to with great attention, for he knew full well that the virtuous heroine would triumph alternately over all her enemies, and as heroines in plays always, and in real life never, do.

When the curtain at length fell, our hero, repressing a yawn, proposed an adjournment to some other place of amusement, but it was not consistent with his assumed character to be acquainted with any of the popular places of resort in London.

"Shall we go to the Argyll?" suggested his companion.

"The Argyll—what is that?" asked the innocent Charley,

"Why the Argyll Rooms, a dancing place," replied the other.

Now, in case it may appear unnatural that one so young should be acquainted even with the name of such a naughty place, let me explain that, although he had not been educated at a public school, where it is not at all an uncommon thing among the scholars, for those who can afford it, to give their masters the slip in the evening, come up by the express to London, spend a few hours in some of the festive scenes which abound in the west end, and then take the last train down, and steal quietly into their room, yet the young duke had heard of them, and had picked up the names of some of the "fast" places in town. Now the opportunity seemed to present itself to him of becoming acquainted with those scenes he had so often heard described.

Charley expressed his readiness to accompany him to the Argyll, and the pair were soon bowling along the streets in a Hansom, on their way to the rooms dedicated to the goddess of saltatory movement. The cabman, of course, asked treble his fare, and Mr. Wag's first impulse was to settle with him in the same way, my readers may remember, he settled with another of his race a short time since; but prudence saved the cabby's head, for Charles remembered that in his present character he knew nothing of the ways of London, and, moreover, that few of the nation to which he now belonged understood anything of the "noble art of self-defence."

The rooms were moderately full when they entered. Perhaps the less said respecting the company the better.

There was the average sprinkling of fast men, blackguards, and lawyers clerks, on the male side; while the female —— well, if the ladies characters were as good as their dresses, very little fault could be found with them.

The young peer was soon captivated. A syren in a blue dress, which she raised sufficiently to display part of a well-formed leg, seemed to him to possess all the charms that could be desired (and certainly she was not niggardly in displaying them.) Charley soon recognised some of his numerous female acquaintances, and as he had no fear that they would identify Monsieur Adolphe de Bessac with Mr. Wag, he surrendered his youthful

charge to the damsel in blue, and, selecting his own partner, was soon whirling a pretty girl with black hair and sparkling eyes, round and round in the most approved style.

My readers will agree that Master Charles was quite able to take care of himself—not so, however, with the noble young sprig who had accompanied him.

Led away by the charms of the enchantress, he had partaken pretty freely of the wine, which, coupled with what he had already drunk at dinner, and the close hot rooms, had the effect of making him rather unsteady in his gait, and confused in his speech.

He was not the only one in this state.

A youth apparently equally affected with himself happened to tread upon his partner's dress, and tore it considerably.

The lady's words are best not recorded; let it suffice that they were not of the description generally used in polite society. Her cavalier, however, took up her cause.

"D'you mean to insult th lady?" he asked of the delinquent.

The reply was coarse, though forcible, and had such an effect upon the young duke, that he seized the nearest weapon—a decanter—and hurled it at the object of his wrath. It merely grazed him, however, and expended its full force against a looking-glass. The uproar soon became general, and Charley, fearing evil, hastening to the spot, found the future member of the House of Peers struggling valiantly with two waiters, who had seized him, while his late partner stood by, pouring forth a volley of vituperation on the cause of the mishap.

A well-directed blow from Charley's fist rid the duke from one of these shilling-seeking miscreants, and had a wonderfully calming effect upon the other; but war, in the enemy's country, could not be successfully carried on long, and the two would have stood a good chance of passing the night in "durance vile," but for the production of sundry sovereigns from Charley's pocket.

"Well," said Mr. Wag, as the pair drove rapidly away from the scene of the scrimmage, "what do you think of your first experience of London life?"

"That it's one of the jolliest larks I ever heard of. By jove how that waiter went down when you struck out—we are well out of it though," added he, after a moment's reflection, "I should have scarcely liked my name to figure in the newspapers under the head of 'murderous outrage by a peer of the realm.'"

"No—it would not be pleasant," said Charley, thinking that the lyne-eyed policemen might have peered through the disguise of his beard and moustache, and have brought about a rather unpleasant exposure.

"What is the order of things for to-morrow?" asked the young seeker after pleasure, "I hear there is to be a dog-fight. Have you ever seen one?"

Charley was too cautious to admit having ever been present at any such spectacle, but expressed his readiness to accompany his grace to that, or any other amusement he chose.

On their arrival at the hotel, Charley at once proceeded to bed, but the duke, feeling inclined for something more before retiring to rest, ordered some refreshment. It is not to be wondered at that when Monsieur de Bessac *alias* Mr. Wag, proceeded the following morning to his companion's room, he found him lying on the bed, with his hat by his side, and boots on.

"Wake up," he cried, shaking him violently, "confound the fellow, he sleeps like a top—wake up!"

Is it to-morrow morning?" asked the young rake in sleepy tones, partially raising himself but all to no purpose, in a few minutes he was sound asleep again.

Muttering something uncommonly like a curse, Mr. Wag gave up the attempt, and descended to a solitary breakfast.

Nothing is more trying than waiting for another person, Mr. Wag found it so—he eat his breakfast, read the morning paper, smoked his cigar, and there ended his resources! for although as Charles Wag Esq., he was never at a loss for companions, or amusement; as Monsieur de Bessac, he was without friends in London and entirely dependant on his boyish companion.

He however employed part of his time in ascertaining the particulars of the dog fight which his young friend was so anxious to see, and secured admittance for himself, and the Duke of Heatherland as the "noble patrons" of the entertainment.

At length the young nobleman appeared bearing unmistakeable signs upon his face of the previous nights excess.

Brandy and soda water applied internally, and plenty of cold water externally, soon brought him round, and, although in a less eager tone, he broached the topic of the day's amusement.

Late as it was when he made his appearance, there were still some hours to pass before the time for the dog-fight, and how they were to be passed became the all important topic, Billiards, were at length resorted to.

I fear the game they played have to answer for very many suppressed naughty words thought, but not uttered by Charley Wag.

I have already said he was a first-rate player so my billiard playing readers may imagine his discomfort at having to play game after game, with one who was, to say the least, a wretchedly bad one, at length the time arrived to start for the canine combat, so, chartering a cab, behold the pair on their way to the far east.

The dog-fight was to take place in one of the sporting publics "down Whitechapel way," and in due time they were set down at the "Champion's Head."

The bowing landlord received his "noble patrons" with great respect, and showed them into a little parlor previous to the commencement of the sport, a great clattering, shouting and stamping rendered talking a toil, the landlord however explained it was only the mode adopted by the anxious backers, to show they were impatient for the combat to commence, the two were presently ushered into a large room, lighted by flaring jets of gas, in the centre of which a space had been boarded off for the fight, round this enclosure were gathered a motley group of sporting men, all eager for the fray.

The arrival of the two "Swells" was the signal for the introduction of the dogs, and the respective trainers appeared, carrying the animals.

If I were a reporter to "Bell's life," I should be able to give an account of the battle in sporting phraseology, and discribe in glowing terms each onset, and struggle between the dogs, encouraged by the shouts of their respective trainers and backers; but not being anything of the kind, I must necessarily curtail the description, and recommend those who wish further particulars, to buy the Sporting paper which contained the full account of it.

The Duke of Heatherland was not so much gratified as he expected to be, and the close room, scented with bad tobacco, sawdust and spirits, did not tend to cure the head-ache which had resulted from his last night's spree. On emerging from the house into the fresh night air, he proposed to Charley that they should walk some part of the way back. To this de Bessac acceded though with rather a bad grace for walking, when a vehicle was obtainable, seemed to our hero the height of folly. However, to humour his young friend he complied, but he soon repented of his goodnature, for they became involved in a labyrinth of streets, the inhabitants of which scowled at them as they passed for being well dressed.

Charley began to feel uneasy, not for himself, for he was accustomed to all phases of society, and knew very well how to extricate himself from every species of scrape, but for his young companion, for he had to bear in mind that to his grace he was Monsieur de Bessac, a stranger to London and its customs.

By mistake they turned down a narrow street which had not any outlet, and they were forced to retrace their steps; they had not proceeded many yards before their way was barred by a party of dirty scowling ruffians, who, without using violence, seemed determined to prevent their passing.

Charley's first thought was to knock down the nearest, a brawny costermonger, and then run for it, but a moment's reflection convinced him such a course would be useless. He and his companion were the two white sheep among the black, and any attempt at escape would certainly be ineffectual, and he knew from experience that such men as those in whose company he now found himself would have little compunction in enforcing silence upon them in the surest way.

His acquaintance with thieves "*patter*" came to his service, and drawing one of the men aside, he whispered a few words in his ear. The man looked astounded, and exclaimed—

"Blow me, Sam, this 'ere foreneering cove talks patter like a prig."

I do not wish to shock any of my readers, so omit to record the strong adjectives which emphasized his speech.

The Duke of Heatherland had been an astonished but passive spectator of all that had passed, and his astonishment was not lessened when Charley whispered hurriedly in his ear,

"Do not be alarmed; we must go with them, all will soon be right."

"But——" commenced the young duke.

"Hush!" said Charley, "take my arm and walk boldly on—you will see a phase of life neither of us expected this morning."

The fact was, the gang were uncertain how to behave. They wished to keep to the old proverb of "honour among thieves," and Charley's words conveyed the impression to their minds that he was one of them, but still all seemed suspicious of allowing two "swells" to escape without deriving any pecuniary benefit from them, so it had been decided that the two should be politely asked to supper, the materials for which they were to contribute. The young duke resigned himself quietly, and, in fact, rather enjoyed the prospect of seeing the English costermonger "at home." Charley however, cursed his unlucky stars for bringing him into such a scrape, for, although their ultimate escape was a certainty, still Mr. Wag feared that his companion might gather from the conversation that Monsieur Adolphe was not the person he passed for.

The pair were conducted by their captors to a large cellar, partially lighted by guttering tallow candles, and flaring oil lamps. A party of men and women talking, laughing, and drinking, looked up at their entrance. A few words from one of the party accounted for the presence of the duke and Charley, and our heroes were greeted with a loud derisive cheer. The funds for the proposed supper were extracted from the pockets of the gentlemen, and soon the already stifling atmosphere received the additional odour of cooking.

In a short time the table, which was formed by laying three planks upon some old barrels, was covered with eatables and drinkables—the latter predominating. Knives and forks were luxuries despised by the community, who evidently thought fingers were not given them for nothing. The eating, however, was nothing to the drinking, every minute the bottles, containing spirits, were raised to the mouths of the duke's self-inviting guests, who swallowed gin as ordinary mortals would bitter beer. No wonder that, towards the close of the repast, the fun grew fast and furious. Songs were sung which were certainly never heard in Exeter Hall, and speeches were made which, for force of expression, rivalled any ever heard at St. Stephen's.

The ladies became excited, and as they swallowed draught after draught of "blue ruin," expressed their determination for a dance.

"A dance!" cries the young lady reader. Yes—but not the sort, my pretty innocent, you picture to yourself, where flowing dresses, abundant crinoline, and a garden of flowers at the back of the head, constitute the toilet. Not the solemn quadrille walked through in the approved fashion, nor even the giddy waltz. For while, inpolite society, ladies spend some hours in dressing for a dance, those in question spent only a few minutes in doing the reverse. And then arose a scene of indescribable confusion and uproar—the men, inflamed with liquor, rose to join the giddy throng of groggy seraphs, but, unfortunately, few were able to keep their feet, and the whole company soon measured their lengths upon the ground.

In the midst of all this hellish noise Charley signed to his companion to follow him. Picking their way over the prostrate forms of the votories of Bacchus, they reached the place of exit unobserved, but here a difficulty to their egress presented itself. The ladder which led to the trap, through which they had descended, had been removed.

"What the deuce are we to do now?" asked the duke, "we shall have to stop here all night.

"Whilst any means of escape remain untried," said Charley, "we must not despair—can you climb a rope?" added he, after a moment's reflection.

"I should think I could; but where can we get a rope? and where can we fix it when we have got it?"

Charley did not reply, but, casting his eyes about, he espied a syren, overtaken by intoxication, in the act of undressing. Her dress lay near her, so, without hesitation, Charley purloined the garment from the "sleeping beauty," and hastily tore it into strips; these he knotted firmly together, and succeeded in casting this impromptu rope over a hook which his quick eye had observed near the trap. A running noose made it firm, and after a few trials of its strength, Charley mounted it, only to find a fresh disappointment.

The trap was securely, but secretly fastened, and resisted all his efforts; at length, as he was on the point of relinquishing his efforts with a hearty curse, he touched the hidden spring, and to his joy he saw the means of escape open to them.

He let himself down the rope, and assisted the youthful nobleman to mount, and saw him safely reach the street.

All this had taken place in one corner of the cellar, partly hidden from the others by a projecting wall.

Some noise however, aroused the men's suspicions, and five of them came up in time to see the duke get through the trap. Charley was on the point of following when the men rushed forward.

"Run," cried he to the duke, "for heaven's sake run," so saying he faced his assailants.

"I can make sure of settling two of them," thought Charley, "but it's long odds."

Watching his opportunity, he rushed upon them, dealing blows right and left, and, as was shown at Waterloo, numbers gave way to determination, Availing himself of the cofnusion occasioned by his onslaught, he seized the rope, and nimbly mounted it, and close upon him followed the most vindictive of his pursuers.

Charley waited behind the trap till his head appeared, when, exerting his strength to the utmost, he threw down the heavy covering with all his force. He heard it close, but before that sound, a heavy dull thud proved it had taken effect on the man's skull, as he had intended.

Which way to take, Charley had no idea, but to get away from the neighbourhood was all he desired at present, and great was his delight to find himself at length in a frequented street, and now he had leisure to think of his companion.

Supposing however, that he had taken a cab to the hotel, he was about doing the same himself, when a crowd at a little distance caught his eye; what was his dismay to see in the centre of it the Duke of Heatherland, held tightly by the collar by two policemen.

Now Charley had a very justifiable antipathy to the guardians of the peace, and never courted their society, but still he could not leave his young friend in their hands. Of course he could have freed him by giving his custodians a sovereign, and his card; but he had no desire to appear voluntarily in a court of justice.

Catching the Duke's eye, he made him a sign not to recognize him.

"What's the row?" asked he of one of the policemen. "Don't drag the gentelman along like that."

"*Gentleman!* why he's one of the werry wussest pickpockets in London—we knows him and 'as been a looking out for him this ever so long."

Charley whispered something in the policeman's ear, which had the salutory effect of making him touch his hat, and look more earnestly at the speaker, and as he turned Mr. Wag recognised in him a well known character. In fact Charley had done a little business with him in the cracksman's line some time previously.

This at once gave him the whip-hand.

"Let this gentleman go," said he, in a low voice, "or perhaps it may reach your superintendant's ears, that there is some one in the force who could give intelligence respecting the Eaton-square robbery."

The policeman made no answer, but presently suggested the gentleman might like a a cab. One was called forthwith, and our two adventurers entered it, accompanied by the policemen. A satisfactory remuneration got rid of the latter in the next street, and Charley and the duke drove on to the hotel. As they went, Charley asked,

"How was it the Peelers got hold of you, Heatherland?"

"Why, you see, after cutting about those infernal dark streets, I got out into a broad well lighted one, but just as I turned the corner I knocked against an old fellow passing, and cannoned off against the lanky peeler, who seized me by the collar and swore I was a prig."

"Well," said Charley, "you have had a little more adventure than you bargained for, old fellow, but all's well that ends well."

"I say, de Bessac, how did you manage to calm those blood-thirsty ruffians."

As this was a subject Charley did not care to enter upon, he answered only with a yawn, and composed himself for sleep in one corner of the cab.

Tobacco, wine, late hours, and stirring adventures, do not generally improve the personal appearance of those unaccustomed to such excesses, and even dukes are not exempt from the laws of nature, so when the young Peer presented himself the next morning, no won-

der he looked most decidedly seedy, following Charley's advice of a Turkish Bath, he became more presentable, and, after a substantial luncheon, the pair proceeded to the Waterloo Station.

"When they will let me, we'll have some more larks together in London," said the Duke, on their way down to Richmond "only we had better not try down east again, I think."

"Oh!" said Charley "we have not seen half the wonders of London yet, and I should like much to see some more of them.

"I say though, old fellow, you never told me how you got over the roughs, and the policemen."

"Oh never mind that—I would do much more to serve you in any way."

"Well guv'nor," said the duke as they alighted at the Station, "I must say you're a brick, a regular trump; and I'm very much obliged to you, it was nearly four o'clock when Charley and the young duke reached Richmond.

On their arrival they found that Julia was making preparations to leave for London, whither she was going relative to the advertisement Charley had put in the paper which she had seen that day, for the next of kin of Victor Jenkini.

"But are you going to town this evening, Mademoiselle?" asked Charley.

"Yes, Monsieur I shall lose no time."

"Monsieur de Bessac will kindly escort you, I'm sure, my dear," said the duchess.

"I shall deem it an honor," to do so," replied Monsieur who was delighted at the success of her arrangement.

Then the duchess retired with Julia to conclude her final preparations during which time Charley and the duke were left together.

"I'll tip you an epistle, when I can get away again," said the youngster where shall I send it to?"

Charley felt rather posed for the moment, but soon recovered himself and replied.—

"I'm going to shift my quarters in a day or two, but send it to this address—it will be forwarded."

And he gave him the direction of a place to which he frequently had letters addressed, and from whence they were forwarded to his chambers.

"All right, guv'nor—I wish that beast of a tutor was not coming at all."

"When are you to commence with him?"

"On Monday."

"That's close at hand."

"Mind you're disengaged when I send to you."

"I'll try to be."

Julia and the duchess here entered the room the former arrayed in a travelling dress in readiness to depart.

"You must write to me constantly, my dear," said the duchess kissing her ,, and let me know how the affair is going on."

Julia promised, and after an affecting leave taking the carriage conveyed her and Monsieur de Bessac to the Railway Station, and in a few short minutes they were whirling along on the road to London.

During the journey the pair talked over their plans for the future, for as the duchess had begged Julia to return to her after the business was settled, it would be necessary to invent some excuse for her not doing so.

"She expects me back in a week Charley—what can we say?"

"Oh! there's lots of time to think about it, and when I once commence, I shall settle upon a plan as soon as I did the advertiseing."

"But you must have planned it, before you spoke to me about it, Charley."

"Not a bit of it—to tell you the truth, I was dispairing of arranging anything when the idea came into my noddle."

"You dear, clever creature!" said Julia, kissing him—"Oh! that nasty moustache!—do take it off, Charley."

"I will my love, before we get home, but it's rather a painful operation without water, I can tell you."

I daresay it is, but why do you wear such a horrid thing—tell me, Charley?

"Well, you see my dear, it's rather a long story."

"Oh! never mind, we have plenty of time."

"I doubt it."

"Go on then as far as you can."

"To begin then—do you remember anything about Tinman's bank?"

"I'm sorry to say I do."

"You remember the man that called upon me the day before?"

"Yes—a low-looking wretch."

"Just so. That man got nabbed, and I——, but you know this part of the story—escaped from that cursed prison through you, dearest," said Charley, placing his arm round her waist, and kissing her heartily.

"But what can that have to do with your disguise?"

"We shall come to that presently."

"Make haste then, I'm all impatience."

"Since our separation in France I have been through a great deal."

"And so have I," said the young lady, "my adventures would make you laugh."

"I must hear them."

"After I have heard yours you shall, perhaps—but go on."

"To make a long story short, I lighted upon some gold in a miser's cellar, after the old fellow turned up his toes, and this set me up."

"You didn't kill the poor man," said Julia, anxiously.

"Kill him!" I should rather think I didn't —I kept him alive ever so long—but I'm going from my story. This money enabled me to cut a swell, and I made the acquaintance of a lieutenant in the navy, named Duffy. I met him one day when I was returning from Northfleet, where I had been to inquire after you, you good for nothing puss."

"After me!"

"Yes—at the little public where we met Toddleboy."

"I remember."

"This meeting with Duffy resulted in our becoming very thick, and I had been to Chaham to see him sail. When passing throug the dockyard, after seeing him off, I saw th

'low-looking wretch,' as you expressively term him, working in a gang of convicts."

"And you helped him to escape?"

"I did—and we had nearly reached Maidstone when I discovered I had lost my purse, and had only enough to pay the cabman."

"Whatever did you do?"

"Took to the road, and fell in with a brougham."

"Well?"

"The fellow inside showed fight, and Measels tapped him on the head with the butt end of his revolver."

"Killed him?"

"Dead as a nail."

"And the servant?"

"Died also—verdict 'accidental death,' from the kick of a horse."

"Good God! how awful—and you assumed the murdered gentleman's name?"

"And letters of introduction."

"And as this man you made the acquaintance of the duchess?"

"Exactly so—but of course they know nothing of this name at my chambers, or the infernal moustache and beard either."

"But how do you manage?"

"I go to a little shop out of Drury-lane."

"Every time you go down to Richmond?"

"Yes—trying, isn't it?"

"What a nuisance."

"And it's an awful bore to get it off," said Charley, "but it must be done before we reach home."

"In the cab."

"Yes—and now to charter one," said Charley, as the train entered the terminus at Waterloo Bridge.

This was soon settled, and they rattled off to Charley's chambers.

"I think you've taken them off capitally," said Julia, as our hero wiped his face after removing his moustache and beard, "and you deserve a kiss."

"Then I'll trouble you for it at once," said the young gentleman, "for here we are at home."

XCVII.—How FAVERSHAM ONCE MORE BECAME ASSOCIATED WITH THE DUCHESS AND HER SON.

ON discovering that the Duchess of Heatherland and her son had taken up their abode at Richmond, Faversham immediately set to work, and obtained a tutorship at a school in the neighbourhood. During the short time that he filled this post he contrived to make the acquaintance of Mr. Bellamy, the surgeon who attended the duchess, and who was also a constant visitor at her house. With him Faversham was soon on the most intimate terms, for the worthy doctor, a bachelor, was quite charmed with his new friend, and it was no unusual occurrence for him to walk over to the school, to ask Faversham to look in and pass the evening with him.

Faversham invariably accepted his invitations, which were frequent, and it was on one of these occasions that his expressions of disgust

THE ESCAPE.

at the life he was leading at the school, caused the doctor to think of bettering his friend's position.

"But, would you not prefer being a private tutor?" asked Mr. Bellamy one evening, as they sat together chatting.

"Infinitely—but then there is such a difficulty to obtain a tutorship in a good family, and unless you have friends, it is next to an impossibility," replied the artful Faversham, who was simply pumping the doctor, to find out the extent of his influence with the duchess.

"Ah! yes—so you think," said the surgeon responsibly, but ultimately agreed to undertake it, but declined leaving the school,

much to Mr. Bellamy's surprise, until the end of the quarter.

This came at last, and on the Monday following, the day that the duke returned from London after seeing "a litte life" with our hero, Charley Wag, Faversham joined the household of the duchess as tutor to her son.

———

XCVIII.—LUCINDA AND THE ELDERS.

AFTER the gas had been turned off (which practical joke was the work of an unregenerate clerk in the dockyard, who had

No. 66

obtained admission to witness the ceremony through the influence of Deacon Goggles), poor Lucinda became the object of a frightful scrimmage for the three shepherds, all of whom were most anxious to render her their assistance at this trying moment, endeavoured to seize her in their arms and bear her safely to the bank's side. But this very anxiety on the part of the reverend gentlemen, only rendered their attempts furtile.

Brother Swabb, who had hold of her by the hand when they were left in darkness, instantly threw his arm round the plump form of the lightly attired young lady, and with his great greasy lips, left the impress of a kiss upon her snowy neck. This, the young lady did not approve of, so twisting herself out of his embrace, she dealt him a box on the ear. As this took place, the rush was made, which precipitated Brother Pudding, Gash, and Goggles into the water.

Brother Jack Pudding was not particularly annoyed at his ducking—infact when the lights went out, he contemplated jumping in, and his object in doing so may be seen from what took place a few minutes subsequently. On his immersion the Rev. Jack commenced groping about him, and at last came in contact with what he inconsiderately concluded was the object of his search.

"Be of good cheer, daughter," snuffled he, employing the same treatment that the baptising brother had already employed unsuccessfully with the fair Lucinda.

"Cheer be——! what are yer a doing of?" said the indignant Swabb, striking out at the worthy shepherd, who had thus saluted him.

"Cheer up for Chatham!" shouted the Rev. Jack, who, after lovely woman, liked a jolly mill as well as anything else. "Come on—you cobbling son of a——, and I give you such a hiding as ain't been heard of since the time of Joshua!" at the same time hinging out furiously, his blow taking effect in the face of the Rev. Ghastly Gash. "Stand up! you cursed cobbler, and I'll welt yer!"

Brother Pudding frequently alluded to the fact of the Rev. Oyley Swabb having been, previously to his assuming the more lucrative calling of shepherd, a mender of boots and shoes. This allusion arose from the contempt which Brother Pudding felt for the low-bred Swabb—above whom he felt he towered immensely in an intellectual point of view, having been educated for the profession. He had received his education at the public school, of the parish of St. Saviour, Southwark, and subsequently went to college—that is to say, the professor under whom he had studied elocution, at nine-pence per lesson, resided in *College-court*, Union-street, Borough. This was all the collegiate education that the Rev. Jack had received, but it sufficed to render him, as we are already aware, a most popular preacher, and certainly placed him in a higher position in the social scale, than many of his brother shepherds could adorn, who had not had his peculiar advantages.

But to return to the encounter, Ghastly Gash, although decidedly a man of peace, and an intimate friend of Pudding (Gash did the

blood and murder business at the Obelisk) was terribly enraged at what he considered a wanton attack upon the part of the Rev. Jack, who was now shouting, "Yah—hoop!" and striking out right and left.

One of the these random shots happened to catch the Rev. Ghastly a second time, and toppled him over like a ninepin. Up he jumped again, and in a trice, had seized upon the wretched Swabb.

"You accursed vessel of wrath!"

A frightful rap on the Oyley's nose.

"To attack a brother——" another crack— "in the faith!"

This second edition seemed to arouse the British lion in the bosom of the suffering shepherd, who swore roundly at his assailant, and planted one from the shoulder, full in the nose of the Rev. Jack Pudding, who was close at hand, seeking for an opportunity of putting in 'one' to the account of Swabb and Co.

The effect of this was, that they all closed, and the indiscriminate mill alluded to in the last number was going on when lights were produced and order restored.

It was then discovered that Lucinda had been rescued from the water by Deacon Goggles, who being actuated by a similar feeling to that of the shepherds, had searched diligently, and had discovered Lucinda half-drowned.

He lost no time in seating her on the bank, where he exerted himself in a praiseworthy manner to restore her from her fainting fit.

"By Jove!" said he, as he placed his arm round her waist, in his endeavours to restore warmth, "By Jove she is pluming—ah! what would my Betsy say if she could see me now? oh! wouldn't there be a bobbery, and no mistake!

"Where am I?" said Lucinda, faintly.

"Hush! my dear young lady, you are in the arms of one who will——, a married man, my dear—who knows——."

"Who are you?"

"My name is Goggles—Deacon Goggles."

"Gog-goggles," murmered Lucinda, again resting her head on his shoulder.

"My dear young lady, rouse yourself," said the worthy deacon, who was growing frightened for his reputation, which might suffer in the eyes of the elect, to say nothing of his beloved Betsey, who didn't quite approve of her spouse attending the dippings, when the converted parties were young and pretty girls. "What the devil shall I do? If any of those cursed chaps outside hear of it, there'll be the devil to pay! And damn it there's——."

His unfinished remark, which was interrupted by the appearance of lights, had reference to the young gentleman, for whom he had procured admission, and who had acted in such a scandalous manner, by turning off the gas when Lucinda entered the water.

This youth *did* see the deacon tolerably close to the plump young lady, and for months after the occurrence chaffed him most unmercifully about taking off his spectacles on the occasion.

"Hullo! Goggle!" said a stout portly looking shepherd, who was close at hand, "what the devil are you up with that young vessel?"

The wretched Goggles, trembling like a

leaf, suffered the insensible girl to slide gently from his arms, and then commenced wiping his spectacles with his pockethandkerchief preparatory to putting them on and replying to the stern demand of the indignent father of his spouse.

"I'm not doing anything."

"Oh! gammon—I know better than that."

"She was nearly drowned."

"And you picked her up?"

"Ye-es."

By this time a crowd had gathered round the still senseless girl carefully excluding the air, in the usual fashion pursued in fainting fits.

"Bring her this way," said the stout shepherd. "And I say," continued he, "you see what you can do for her."

This latter observation was addressed to a mild-looking young gentleman—an apothecary, who seemed to be known to the shepherd and Goggles.

"I shall be boast happy," replied this individual, who spoke as though suffering from a severe cold; but this however, was not case.

Lucinda was then carried to the little room, to which the Rev. Ghastly Gash had retired to do his long day and dog's-nose, after preaching his unsuccessful sermon on the morning of the "buster" at the New Bethel.

Here she was surrounded by a few of the elect, who were privileged to enter this retreat of the shepherds.

Deacon Goggles stuck very close to the medical man, and as a matter of course, very near the object of their solicitude.

The portly shepherd, who had censured Goggles for his behaviour on the banks of the stream, had disappeared.

He had gone with the intention of making peace between Brothers Swabb, Pudding, and Gash, who had retired to a court behind the chapel, where the Rev. Jack Pudding had offered to fight the pair of his brother shepherds, one down and the other come on.

The portly brother only arrived in time to see Brother Pudding's last rounds with Swabb, (he had already settled Gash) and as they appeared prettily equally matched he did not deem it necessary to interfere. Indeed he rather admired the sport.

Two or three rounds followed, and Pudding was at last declared victor; the unfortunate Swabb, not being able to come up when time was called by the portly shepherd, who, with his characteristic love of fair play, had constituted himself timekeeper.

The result of this mill was highly satisfactory, for the three combatants shook hands with each other, and accepted the invitation of their jolly timekeeper to spend the rest of the evening at Brother Goggle's.

During this unclerical demonstration the deacon and the few of the elect, who remained with Lucinda in preference to witnessing the fight between the shepherds, had succeeded in restoring her to consciousness, and were engaged assisting at her toilet when the portly shepherd, with the pugnacious brethren entered the room.

"Well! Brother Goggles—and how is ou

suffering sister?"

"I am delighted to say she is better—Brother Smug."

"Let us return thanks," said that individual.

The portly party then commenced a long-winded prayer of thanksgiving, after which the deacon gave out the hymn—"Oh! let us be joyful," which was sung to one of the popular melodies of the day.

This took place in the little room before alluded to—and by the time it was concluded, many of the elect had sloped, and Lucinda was about to follow their example when Brother Smug and Deacon Goggles begged her to return with them to supper.

After some little hesitation she accepted the invitation to join the party.

Brothers Smug and Pudding, with Deacon Goggles, found room in the fly with Lucinda —the Rev. Ghastly Gash, Swabb and Brother Herd, the apothecary who assisted in restoring the young lady after her dipping, taking their seats in another carriage.

A short ride brought them to Deacon Goggles's residence, where after Lucinda had been introduced to the worthy deacon's spouse, they sat down to supper.

For a short time conversation was not indulged in, for the shepherds all seemed too intent upon the feed to waste time in words.

At last Brother Jack Pudding was done up in the eating way, and announced this to his host, who pressed him to take something more.

"Chuck to the bung! old boy—couldn't if I stood up."

"Brother Herd, can I have the pleasure of assisting you to a little pigeon pie?" said the deacon.

"Doa—don't like bie," said the brother, helping himself to some cold roast beef.

"Now, then, Gash," said the hospitable Goggles, "peg away old chap."

By this time Ghastly was also done up, and Swabb alone remained hard at.

Lucinda had been taken care of by Mrs. Goggles, who was quite charmed with the young vessel of piety, but in her heart felt that she should have liked her a great deal better if she had not been so pretty.

In due course the table was cleared, and Lucinda retired, a fly being procured for her by one of the servants.

After her departure the shepherds and Deacon Goggles went in for hot grog to an alarming extent, and had it not been for the mediation of Brother Herd, who abstained from spirituous drinks, and thus remained sober, a second edition of the fight that had so recently occurred would have inevitably been enacted in the deacon's house, in all probability to the detriment of his furniture.

He succeeded in pacifying them, and assisted Brother Smug to ply them with a sufficient quantity of grog to render them harmless—then, with his assistance (Smug was a seasoned old cask), and that of the deacon, they got them out into the street, Brother Herd kindly expressing his "habbiness to see them hobe."

XCIX—Home again—Julia recounts her adventures in France—Necessity is the mother of invention.

JULIA was delighted with the domestic arrangements of Charley Wag.

When our hero had possessed himself of the miser's treasure, he determined to live in the finest style, and, consequently, furnished his rooms in a most luxurious manner.

"Ah! Charley," said she, "this is, indeed, splendid. I did not think you had such a nice place."

So saying, she threw herself upon a sofa, and proceeded to take a deliberate survey of the whole apartment.

"Very nice, indeed, Charley," continued she, "I should almost have thought you had had a lady's help to make your room so nice, but you are such a dear clever fellow you can do everything."

Charley thanked her for her compliment, and prevented her paying him any more by the simple process of closing her mouth with a kiss.

"Now dearest, let me hear all about your adventures after leaving me."

"You monster," playfully replied the lady, "you will not be satisfied till I have told you all I see; but I shall not gratify your curiosity yet—you must wait."

It was not very long, however, before Julia's pretty red lips opened again, and she began to relate what had happened to her.

"You recollect the trouble I had to get a horse," said Julia.

"How the deuce should I know?"

"When at last I obtained one, I set off on the road I had been directed, but, although I flatter myself on being a very fair horsewoman——"

"That you are, by jove!" exclaimed Charley.

"Now, don't you interrupt me, or I won't tell you anything."

"Go on," said Charley, "I won't balk your run."

"Well, I pushed on as fast as I could, but failed to reach the town that night—at least it became so dark that I was afraid of missing my road if I continued on my way, so I put up at a road-side inn, where I was very kindly received by the buxom landlady. She seemed in fact to pay me particular attention."

"And no wonder, dear—you made one of the prettiest boys I have ever seen."

"Well, after supper she showed me to a bed-room, where I slept very soundly."

"And what took place the next day?"

"All my adventures."

"Then let me hear them, there's a darling."

"Well, after Toddleboy landed me up the creek I had to make to a place where a horse was to await me."

"Yes."

"And of course met with a great deal of difficulty in obtaining the beast."

"Did you get one at last?"

"Oh! yes, but I went through a great deal before I did though."

"You had a fight with a Frenchman—hadn't you?"

"Yes!—I think I told you of it when we met down at Richmond."

"Yes, and I think you killed him if I remember rightly."

"I'm sorry to say I did, Charley, but I couldn't help it."

"I think it's a deuced good job he didn't kill you."

"So, think I—but at the same time I wish I hadn't."

"You never told me what it was about."

"Oh! nothing at all, I just looked at his sweetheart, and he grew nearly frantic with me, and challenged me."

"And how did you get away after the fight."

"I managed it somehow—and after some little difficulty found out Madame Deschapples, and delivered my letter to her, but not before I had given up discovering her, and had returned to where I left the cutter, which I found gone."

"And then you went to look after the duchess again?"

"Yes, and this time I found her, and now you know how it came to pass, that I stayed with her and afterwards returned to England."

"Yes, and I also know that she will be very glad if you return to Richmond and continue to reside with her."

"I shan't though, unless you turn me out Charley; but what excuse to make for remaining away from her."

"I have it," said Charley, "Victor Jenkini was an Italian of course, so you must go to Italy where he resided to settle the matter."

"Oh! you dear clever fellow!" and the young lady presented her pouting lips, which Charley took the opportunity of kissing.

"There will be plenty of time for thinking about it a week hence," said Charley, "as she cannot expect you back for a fortnight or so."

"No, I suppose not."

"But in the meantime, my love, we'll mature our plan—I think it's a good one."

"I'm sure it is, Charley."

"All you say and do, is clever."

"That's more than some of my friends say for me."

"Well, never mind Charley, I think so, and you ought to be satisfied."

"Oh! very well, my love, I'll try to be, and now I am going out for a stroll, just going to look in at the club—I haven't been there for ages."

"Don't be a long while Charley, for I want you to give me a drive in the park, if you have nothing better to do."

"Well! I'll think the matter over—but I shan't promise."

"Oh! you monster!"

"Ta! ta! my love—au revoir."

———

C.—A Private Tutor — Murder most foul—Vengeance—A Love Passage.

THE consummation of Faversham's vengeance might now take place at any time. In the character he had assumed, as the tutor to the young duke of Heatherland, his facilities for carrying out the great aim of his existence were unequalled.

He was the instructor of the boy, and the constant companion of the mother.

He styled himself Captain Leopold Ralph, and related the history of his past life in the Austrian service, in a manner, which deeply interested the still beautiful duchess.

He stated that he was the son of an English general officer, but that he had offended his father by entering the service of a foreign power, and the result had been, that at his father's death he found, that the considerable property, which he anticipated would revert to him was willed to a distant relative, and that he was a beggar, having overstayed his leave of absence.

Then he told her how he had supported himself; how he had striven to gain his daily bread in various ways; how he had obtained the turtorship at the school in the neighbourhood, which he had lately left for the purpose of entering her household as the tutor to her son.

The intimate footing which he soon established, would enable him to commence his diabolical scheme against the lives of the duchess and her son at any time.

The young duke was to be the first victim.

And to this end the blood-stained Faversham devoted himself.

He had scarcely been a month with him when the duke was taken ill, and Mr. Bellamy attended him.

Faversham was most attentive to the young sufferer, with whom he was a great favourite.

The wily wretch had foreseen the necessity for securing the boy's regard, and had succeeded in doing this, as he did in almost everything he undertook.

The young duke could not bear him to leave the room, such was the magnetic influence with which the mysterious Faversham had fascinated him, nor would the youthful sufferer allow any hand but Faversham's to administer his medicines.

In this instance the crafty murderer had not acted with his usual caution.

He saw his error, and lost no time in correcting it.

The intimacy between Bellamy and Faversham had continued, and the latter's visits to the doctor were as frequent as ever.

In the meanwhile the young duke got better.

The duchess was for removing him to the sea-side for change, but this Mr. Bellamy did not consider necessary.

In fact he was anxious that the boy should be near him, for his case puzzled him.

Some weeks after his partial recovery, the patient had a relapse, and again Faversham's services were called into requisition.

Again he sat by his bed-side, and again he administered the medicines prescribed by Mr. Bellamy.

"Upon my soul, Ralph!" said the doctor one evening in his snug little sitting-room at the back of the surgery, "if I did not know that you were the only person from whom that boy takes his medicine, I should swear that he was suffering from the effects of a mineral poison."

Faversham involuntarily started.

"His case is certainly similar," said he.

This speech of Bellamy's convinced the arch-plotter that it would be necessary to remove the doctor from his path.

"A *post mortem* examination might prove something, and the circumstantial evidence would be strong," thought Faversham.

He must be removed.

Every hour's delay was dangerous.

He might have already mentioned the same thing to some one else!

The thought was terrible.

His long sought vengeance might be thwarted even now.

Bellamy must die!

But how?

Without the slightest warning, Faversham was upon the unfortunate wretch who had befriended him, and, seizing him by the throat, before he could utter a cry he poured the contents of a small vial into his open mouth. The victim gave a convulsive shudder—all was over—and one more crime added to the many Faversham had already committed.

After arranging the murdered man in a natural position in the arm-chair he usually occupied, the perpetrator of this dark deed went into the surgery, and procuring the vial labelled "*prussic acid*," and from it re-filled the one the contents of which had deprived the doctor of life, and placing the empty bottle in the right hand of the murdered man, left the house, and returned to the bed-side of the young duke, who had been sleeping heavily during his absence.

The duchess was bending over the sick boy's couch when he entered the room, and, for a moment—a moment only—the guilty, blood-stained Faversham experienced almost a feeling of tenderness for both mother and son.

But this feeling he quickly banished.

The son, who bore the same title as his detested enemy, must die; and Faversham resolved that this should occur during the night, for the suspicions of a new doctor might be as easily aroused by seeing him give the medicines to the young duke, as Bellamy's had been, and it might not be in his power to remove the new-comer in a similar manner.

Bellamy had paid his visit for the night, and had pronounced the young nobleman rather better, though in a most critical state.

This opinion accorded with the poisoner's views admirably well, and he determined that the unfortunate boy should pass from sleep to "that sleep which knows no waking."

The result of a *post mortem* examination Faversham did not fear; and his only object in murdering Bellamy was to prevent him analyzing the medicine he was then giving to the duke.

In that stage the presence of poison might have been detected; but previous to death ensuing all traces of it would be removed from the stomach by administering the preparation, the discovery of which had cost the black-hearted Faversham so many years of study and toil.

*　　*　　*　　*　　*

The dawn of the morning found the duchess

and Faversham at the side of the bed upon which rested the earthly remains of the young Duke of Heatherland.

The mother's grief at the loss of her beloved boy was fearful in its intensity, and for a while she seemed almost frantic.

There followed a fainting fit, which continued for many hours, and which was followed by a severe illness, which lasted for many days. During this period the love for the Duchess, which Faversham had secretly nursed in his bosom, could no longer be hidden, and he exhibited his feelings as plainly as his mysterious and stoical nature would permit.

———

CI.—How the young idea is taught to shoot—The green-eyed monster appears.

JULIA regarded Amy at first rather suspiciously, thinking she was, perhaps, a pledge of affection from some of Charley's numerous female admirers, but her age, and the account Mr. Wag gave of finding the little girl, which was fully corroborated by Amy herself, set her mind at ease, and she grew very fond of the little adopted one.

Caressed and petted by all, no wonder Amy disliked the idea of being sent away to school, but on this point Charley was firm, for he saw that if she remained at his lodgings she was likely to prove rather an incumbrance to his movements, which were forced very often to be rather hurried.

Accordingly, one morning Charley accompanied Julia and the little Amy to the school he had selected in Westbournia.

They were very politely received by the lady principal, who professed the greatest willingness to receive the pretty little girl under her charge.

"The terms," she said, "you will, perhaps, consider rather high, but when you take into consideration the innumerable advantages obtainable at this establishment, not to be found anywhere else, you will not consider them exorbitant. In fact," continued she, quoting the advertisement, "to those who want a home for their daughters, where the strictest morals are combined with the best diet, and the most excellent tuition, the present opportunity is not to be neglected."

Charley, as in courtesy bound, made a polite answer, but if the truth must be told, the one word uppermost in his mind was "Walker!"

As for Amy, she eyed the lady principal with undisguised disgust.

She had hoped, after her rescue by Charley, always to live with him, for the extreme kindness she had experienced since she had been with him, seemed doubly kind when compared with the great cruelty she had been subjected to, and she dreaded leaving her benefactor.

Charley did all in his power to console her, whilst Julia settled various details with the lady.

He had, though I fear not without sundry curses, forced two bags, the one containing cakes, the other sweetmeats, into his pockets, and now produced them for the little Amy.

But even cakes had now no charms for her:

she was really very much attached to Charley, and grieved at the idea of separation.

The lady principal proposed to Julia to view the bed-rooms of the establishment, and the two ladies left the room, followed mechanically by Charley and the little Amy, who refused to leave his hand.

A broad hint from the principal, however, told Charley it was not customary for gentlemen to peer into the mysteries of ladies' sleeping apartments.

Julia, with difficulty, enticed Amy from our hero's side, but at length she succeeded, and Charley was left kicking his heels on the landing outside the bed-rooms.

A giggling up above made him look up, and there he saw ——; well, perhaps it would be better not to enter into particulars—but at the top of a rather steep flight of stairs stood a group of pretty girls laughing and quizzing Mr. Wag. They were attired in the prevailing fashion of crinoline, and what, with pressing together, and their being above our hero, rather less was left to the imagination than should have been.

Now, perhaps one of Charley Wag's greatest failings—if failing it be—was his unbounded admiration of pretty girls, consequently, without thinking, Charley flew up the stairs, the girls flying, laughing and shrieking, in all directions at his approach.

He caught one of the prettiest, and was in the very act of making her pay the forfeit for laughing at him, by imprinting a kiss upon her lips, when a harsh voice at his elbow exclaimed—

"Heavens! go to your room instantly, miss."

Our hero for once in his life was disconcerted on turning round, to find the gentleman principal looking at him with stern reproach.

He was not a very prepossessing-looking man. His receding brow and projecting lips gave him a far from intellectual appearance, nor was his unfavourable countenance improved by the blotchy, unhealthy appearance of his skin.

"Can I have the honour of a few minutes conversation with you, Mr. Wag?" he asked.

"Certainly," replied our hero, who had entirely recovered his self-possession although been caught in the act, he saw no way to lessen his offence.

The pair proceeded down stairs, and entered the parlour.

"I should prefer waiting until the lady principal and your wife are present," said the proprietor of the select establishment for young ladies.

They did not keep them long in suspense, and when Julia and the lady appeared, they were both requested to seat themselves.

When they were arranged in anxious expectation he rose, and placing one hand elegantly beneath his coat-tails, and grasping the back of a chair firmly with the other, he delivered himself of the following speech :—

"I regret to say, ladies, that during your absence this gentleman has grossly misconducted himself—I repeat it—grossly misconducted himself. It is with deep regret I bring myself to utter the words, but when the morals of this establishment are openly and wantonly insulted in broad day light, it is my disagreeable duty to express the unwelcome truth. In short, I regret to say, I found Mr. Wag kissing one of our pupils on the landing!"

The lady principal looked properly horrified, but Julia, who had suspected something of the sort only looked reproachfully at "her Charley."

"Of course," said the lady, "after what has passed it will be quite impossible for us to receive your little girl. The sort of education she has received at home must have necessarily unfitted her for associating with the superior class of young ladies she would meet with here. And I do not feel justified in allowing my pupils to run the risk of contamination."

"All very well," said our hero, "but there is one small question I should like to ask this worthy gentleman. Can he account for his presence in the young ladies bed-room satisfactorily?"

The naturally red countenance of the gentleman principal became still redder at this question, and he stammered forth some excuses about his duty, his age, his respectability, &c.; but this shot of Charley's had hit the mark, and as soon as the principal recovered himself, he asked Charley,

"What the devil do you mean to imply by your insinuation."

"I mean to insinuate nothing, but to state simply my belief, that I had quite as good a right to be where you found me as you had."

"Such scandalous imputations shall not pass unnoticed, sir. You shall hear from my solicitor, sir. And sir, you may thank your stars that I am a man of peace, or I should certainly take your punishment into my own hands."

"D——," exclaimed Charley.

"Oh! dreadful! ejaculated the lady principal, "to think that I should be subjected to such awful language in my own house. Turn him out somebody!"

The gentleman principal took two or three steps towards Charley, who waited to receive him, while Julia rose and hurried towards Mr. Wag. When the principal was within a short distance of our hero, finding he showed no symptoms of flinching, he seemed to think it better he should keep his distance, and enlighten Charley with another moral discourse.

"I fear, sir, you are not displaying a Christian spirit; instead of professing repentance, you add insult to the injury you have inflicted upon the moral tone of this establishment, and make use of disgusting and improper language in the presence of a lady. I have, therefore, only to request that you and this female will leave the house instantly, with your unfortunate child, and our united prayers will be that you may be shown the error of your way, and may bring up this infant in the way it should go."

"Damn it all," broke out Charley, "I can't stand this."

So saying, he seized hold of a music-stool and hurled it at the principal's head, then, taking the astonished little Amy in his arms, and directing Julia to precede him down stairs,

he only waited himself to see the worthy pedagogue topple over into the thunder-struck lady principal's lap.

Luckily a cab was passing as they emerged into the street.

Charley hailed it, and the trio gladly got in, and were driven away as fast as the wretched old hack could carry them.

"What a disgusting old brute," said Charley.

"Yes—we are well out of the whole affair. But yet, Charley, I don't see that you had any occasion to kiss that girl."

"Pooh! nonsense. There's no reason why I shouldn't kiss a pretty girl whenever I get the chance."

"You may call it nonsense if you like, but after all I have given up for you, I think you need not neglect me after three days."

"What nonsense you talk," said Charley, for much as he loved Julia, he did not feel disposed to have his right to indulge in other loves, when he was so disposed, questioned.

"When you were the admired danseuse at Muggins' Music Hall, and exhibited your charms to all who could afford to pay three pence for their entrance fee, did I ever object to any of those puppies that were always hovering round you. You let them kiss you often enough I'll be bound."

"If you mean to make love to other girls before my eyes, and then expect me to approve of it, you are mistaken, sir, and if that is the course you intend to pursue, I shall return to the Duchess of Heatherland as she expects."

"Confound it, Julia, this is childish—what can I do for you. I don't want to pain you, but still I must say that you are making yourself jealous without the least occasion."

"You do love me then, Charley?"

"My darling, I dote upon you."

"And you won't ever love me less?"

An eloquent look from Charley's magnificent eyes succeeded in re-establishing the confidence of the charming Julia, and the two were soon locked in a close and loving embrace.

Amy had been astonished at the violence of this short conversation, for though she could not understand it all, still the purport was evident; but, when the speaking embrace told her they were reconciled, she stole quietly up to Charley's side, and placed her hand quietly in his.

"I am not to go to school?" asked the little one.

"No—I think on the whole we had better all keep away from that neighbourhood for the present," replied Charley.

"And I am not to go to school at all?" continued the little innocent, highly delighted.

"Well, I don't know," said Charley, "how we can manage, besides, you must be taught something."

"Let me teach her," pleaded Julia, "at least for the present."

Thus it was settled, and Amy remained the happy little inmate of Charley's lodgings.

CII.—FAVERSHAM.

THE reader may have been rather astounded at the conclusion of the last chapter relative to the doings at Richmond.

That Faversham really loved the Duchess of Heatherland there could be no doubt; that he had spared her life when he might have taken it easily, there was no denying; but then, it has been stated on that occasion his reason for sparing her was for the purpose of making her instrumental in his scheme of vengeance. This might have been, but still Faversham had conceived a passion for the beautiful woman, who was at one time so completely in his power.

His love for her was increased tenfold when he saw her looking even more beautiful in her tears, by the bed-side of her murdered child.

Should he spare her?

Should he spare the last of the race he had sworn to exterminate?

Yes.

But only for a time.

The severe illness which immediately followed the death of her son, nearly proved fatal to the sorrow-stricken duchess, and for a time her life was despaired of.

With judicious treatment she slowly recovered, and during her convalescence Faversham first breathed the words of love, which were fully reciprocated by the duchess, who had conceived a regard for the *soi-disant* Captain Leopold Ralph soon after he had become a member of her household. His evident partiality for the late duke had much to do with the matter, and she had felt, previous to her son's death, that in uniting herself to this man she should be securing the guidance of a valuable mentor for her beloved boy.

The young duke's death did not alter her sentiments towards the man on whom she had placed her affections; indeed his conduct during the young sufferer's illness, and more especially subsequent to it, had only served to increase the regard she already felt for him, so that when Faversham spoke of his love for her, it is not to be wondered at that she admitted that she loved him, and was willing to be his.

*　　*　　*　　*　　*

A few days after her consent to his proposal, the Duchess of Heatherland was privately married to Ralph Faversham, the murderer of her husband and her child. The wedding, which, from the recent death of her son, was strictly private, took place at the residence of the duchess. No blushing bridesmaids graced the scene; no wreath of orange blossoms decorated the placid brow of the still handsome duchess; there she stood, her pale face bearing the traces of her late sorrow, and pronounced the vows which bound her for life to the destroyer of her husband's race.

For a while Faversham lived happily in the society of the amiable duchess, who sought by every means in her power to render herself dear to him, and to banish the gloom which would frequently steal over this mysterious being.

Her influence over him became almost as great as that of his former wife, and at times Faversham felt that the vow he had made to destroy the duchess must be broken.

CIII.—Leech Again—A Race for Life.

CHARLEY, one day, sauntering down to his club, saw his old enemy Leech lurking about opposite it as he entered.

At the time he scarcely bestowed a thought upon the circumstance, but he might have known from experience, that this malicious old party would not be idling about for his pleasure, but must have some sinister design in being in the neighbourhood. He was not a man who would leave his den in Clement's Inn for the sake of looking at the club-loungers, unless he had some motive for so doing.

After reading the papers, and conversing with his friends who happened to be at the club, different to his usual practice, Charley left. We know the reason. At his lodgings was "metal more attractive" than any his club could furnish, for though his affection for Julia was not so strong that the pleasure of her society could induce Mr. Wag to forego his old custom of spending part of the day at his club, still, he did not now pass so much of his time there as he had been accustomed to do. It is always a pleasing and gratifying thing to a young man to be worshipped by a young and beautiful girl, and certainly Julia carried her devotion to our hero to the greatest extent.

To resume, however, Charley, on quitting the building, was surprised at the impudence of Leech, who boldly crossed the road and made up to him.

This excited Charley's wrath, for, saying nothing of the hatred Mr. Wag had for this mean little wretch, which he had fully shown at their last meeting, a handsome well-dressed young man does not feel over and above flattered at being addressed at the door of his club by a seedy, disreputable-looking individual, with trousers too short for him, and a shocking bad hat, too large for him.

"Curse you," said Charley, "what brings you here?"

"Is that the way to speak to an old friend, Mr. Wag?"

"Friend be ——," said Charley, "what is it you want with me? Look sharp or I shall give you in charge."

"This is all very fine, Mr. Wag—it was your turn when last we met, it is mine now—you are my prisoner!"

So saying, the little pettifogger placed his hand on our hero's collar.

Charley was, for the moment, completely taken aback, and on looking round him perceived that a couple of policemen had stolen up behind Leech, and only awaited his signal to take him into custody. The fact is, Charley had considered himself safe from any desperate measures from so despicable a little brute as Leech, and considered the intimidation which had closed their last interview would effectually close his mouth.

Mr. Wag saw that "deeds not words" were his only chance of escape, so, watching for a moment, he seized the unfortunate Leech by the throat, and hurled him, with all the force of which he was capable, from the curb-stone on which he was standing directly under the

AN INTERVIEW WITH THE DUCHESS.

wheels of a cab which was passing rapidly by.

A cry of horror burst from the crowd as the wheel passed over the wretched man's head, spattering those nearest with the blood; their attention thus, for the moment, distracted, Charley saw his opportunity, and dashed rapidly through the crowd, which, for the minute, were so paralysed by the deed and the daring of the attempt at escape, that they opened and suffered him to pass unmolested.

This only lasted for a few seconds, and then the police, followed by a large mob, were on Charley's track.

Quick—quick he ran—it was a race for life.

Onwards—onwards—the hounds were at his heels.

He turned down some of the narrow streets, and rushed on as only one who runs for life can speed.

Beware how you attempt to stop him, rash man. You must pay the penalty.

Up one narrow street, down the next, onwards ran our hero.

What means that wild exultant shout from the mob? Is Charley a prisoner?

No—but they make sure now of their prey. The alley he has just entered has *no other outlet than that now blocked by the pursuing throng*!!

Charley perceives his error, but it is now too late to retrieve it.

What will he do? He cannot hope to hide

No. 67

in any of the houses from the searching eyes of the police.

Can he turn to bay, and defy his pursuers? No—that idea is madness. He would be torn to pieces by the mob in a few minutes.

He looks round and sees the surging, heaving mob tearing on towards him. He hears their cries, and knows that to surrender himself would be but to give his life to the miscreants who are following and hollaoing after him.

The only chance is to take refuge in a house, and, rapidly turning an angle, Charley rushed in at the first open door—he hoped unobserved. No!—again cruel fate was against him!

The panting mob saw the house and marked it! Upwards ran Charley. Hardly had he reached the first floor when the rabble were at the door.

Up—up—still he ran; a ladder led on to the roof. Quick as thought he mounted it—reached the top, and flung the means of ascent down, in order to retard his pursuers.

Again the fates were against him; scarcely had he proceeded over the roof a dozen yards when a howl from the street told him he was seen by the infuriated crowd.

How was he to escape?

For the first time a feeling of despair flitted athwart his mind.

The idea of losing Julia so soon after he had re-gained her came across him, but it did not unman him—it nerved him to use his best endeavours to escape.

Cool courage, great strength, and a firm mind, were all Charley's, but even these qualities seemed useless when opposed to the numbers who were on his track.

Still mechanically he pursued his way over the tiled tops of the houses. Slipping every minute in his dangerous career, and in a position where a single false step would precipitate him into the street below, where, should he escape an instantaneous death, only a more horrible one awaited him—the roof behind him already swarmed with his pursuers.

The one in advance was less sure of foot than Charley. He slipped. Nothing could save him, and, with horror-stricken countenances, those behind saw his body fall into the street below.

The less venturesome stopped in their pursuit, but many bolder continued their course, and the question Charley had so often asked himself, " *How* shall I escape?" was changed to the more despairing one of "*shall* I escape?"

CIV.—A NAVAL ENGAGEMENT—A MOST UNWARRANTABLE CAPTURE—TODDLEBOY ONCE MORE.

THE *Dodger* had been cruising about the Coast of Africa for some time without falling in with the *Scud*, the celebrated slaver and pirate, which had for its commander the redoubtable Toddleboy. Our friend Lieutenant Horatio Spanker Duffy was beginning to despair of having an opportunity to deliver the note confided to him by Charley Wag, and

had almost given up the idea of being able to serve our hero, when one day the welcome cry of "sail ho!" greeted him from the man on the look out.

" Where away ?"

" On the lee bow."

Horatio sprang up the rigging, and into the " top," and with the aid of his glass soon made out the stranger.

" That's the *Scud*, I'll take my davy," said the weather-beaten tar who was on the lookout, " I've seen her afore to-day."

Horatio felt perfectly satisfied from the appearance of the craft that it was the identical one they had been looking after so long; he quickly descended, and at once proceeded to report his conviction to the commander, who was at this moment enjoying a nap in his cabin.

The worthy officer was soon on deck, all hands were piped and sail made, a stiffish breeze was blowing at the time, and the *Dodger* flew through the water under the press of canvas which her anxious commander insisted upon being carried on.

" Blow me tight! Bill, if she'll stand much more," said one of the crew, as they were setting the top-gallant studding sails, " and if we don't lose some of the sticks to-night, why I'm werry much out o' my reckoning."

It's a werry dirty night and squally—but I s'pose the skipper knows what he's about."

" Oh! he knows fast enough, Bill, but for all that I shan't be sorry when it's our watch below."

Well as to getting below, it don't much signify, we shall be roused out when we get along side that ere *Scud*, or to shorten sail, or something else you may depend."

The man had hardly concluded these words, when a violent squall struck the brig, making her heal over, until her yard arms were only a few feet from the water.

" Take in the studdn't sails !" shouted the officer of the watch, but ere the order had been fully given, the studding sails had taken themselves off, and were now some distance to leward.

" Clew up the top-gallant sails !"—stand by the top-sail haulyards ! was then shouted in quick succession, and in a short time the *Dodger* was running before the gale under a reefed fore course and double reefed main top-sail.

The strange sail was no where to be seen, and the gale which blew during the night she was almost forgotten.

The *Dodger* had been " hove to " for some hours, when the first grey streaks of the morning appeared. The gale had lessened considerably in violence, and the strange sail was once more visible, and from her position she must have been " hove to " at the same time that the brig was.

She was still on the starboard bow, some few miles to leeward of the *Dodger*, when the order to make sail was given.

It was evident that the stranger was trying to get away from them, for she had spread every available inch of canvas ; but the commander of H. M. S. *Dodger* was not a man to be beaten where carrying on was concerned. The brig was once more under a cloud of canvas, with the wind well on her quarter, and again in hot pursuit of the rakish schooner, which was now easily recognised as the celebrated *Scud.*

Horatio felt quite excited as to the result of this chase.

Should they capture her, there would be prize money decidedly, and that was a consideration ; but then how about his promise to aid her skipper to escape ?

Duffy felt puzzled.

How to see his way out of this, he knew not.

His rumuneration were interrupted by the commander.

" Don't you think, Mr. Duffy, that schooner sails faster than we do ?"

"She can decidedly—but. --"

" What ?

" She doesn't."

" Doesn't ?

" No—she is continually shortening sail, and then we gain on her."

" He really can't have the impudence to want to fight us."

" It wouldn't surprise me in the least—it wouldn't be the first time he had had a brush with her Majesty's cruisers."

" So I've heard," said the commander, " but this will uhdoubtably be the *last* time he'll have that honour."

In the meanwhile the brig was gradually drawing on the schooner and after a chase of several hours they were within gun shot, the brig still being to windward.

A blank cartridge was fired across the bows of the schooner, but without having the effect of bringing her to.—

This so exasperated the commander of the *Dodger,* that he gave orders for firing into the schooner and this time the guns were shotted.

" By jove ! I'll sink her !" said the enraged naval officer as the schooner returned the fire with one of her long brass guns—the shot tearing away the bulwarks on the quarter deck and sending an unfortunate midshipman into the next world in the most unceremonious manner.

"I'll sink her, or my name's not Bunk" roared the commander ; but some how or other the crew of H. M. S. *Dodger* did not seem to be first rate at the gunnery practice necessary to a running fight ; their shots whistling harmlessly through the schooner's rigging or at the most only passing through a sail.

It was equally evident that the *Scud's* men had played at this game before, for every shot told—and several of the brave crew of the *Dodger* had been laid low by them.

" Damn'em !" shouted Bunk, totally unforgetful that this was not an expression for an officer and a gentleman to make use of, " Damn'em, I'll yard-arm every mother's son of 'em !"

This was a terrible threat, and one, which I haven't the slightest doubt, Jack Bunk would have carried into execution, if he had had the opportunity.

But he had'nt.

It would be necesary ¦for any officer in H. M. Navy to get up considerably earlier in the morning than he was in the habit of doing, if he felt the slightest idea of getting figu- -ratively to windward of our old friend Toddleboy, and even Commander John Bunk of H. M. S. *Dodger,* was not the man to do it !

" By G——, I'll board him !" roared the said commander ; but this little attention Toddleboy did not seem to approve of, for as the *Dodger* approached he sheered off.

Commander Bunk was anxious to come to close quarters for various reasons, the first and foremost being, that the *Dodger* had lost her fore-yard—one of the shots from the *Scud* having carried away the truss. Secondly, the bowsprit had received some rough usage ; and if this affair continued H.¦M's. brig was in a very fair way to become unmanageable. In fact she was so at present, and Commander Bunk felt that the schooner would escape, when to his intense surprise she backed her fore-yard and ceased firing.

" Man the boats! bear a hand !" sang out the astonished officer.

The order was soon obeyed, and every available man from the brig was sent to assist in the capture of the celebrated *Scud.*

After a long pull they approached her, Duffy's boat leading. He was soon alongside, and springing on board, called upon the captain to surrender.

He had hardly done so, when he was seized from behind and his sword taken from him. He shouted to the men who had followed him, but who in the meanwhile had been pushed over the bulwarks, much to their indignation after what they imagined had been the surrender of the vessel.

But as I before observed, it would be necessary to get up excessively early to do Toddleboy. His only object in brining to, was to get the crew from the *Dodger,* while he made off. This was hardly necessary in the crippled state of the brig ; but still, it was the old gentleman's idea, and he carried it out.

Beside which, perhaps he might have anticipated capturing a British naval officer, just for the fun of the thing.

After the boat's crew, which Duffy commanded, had been repulsed, and before the others could come to their assistance, Captain Toddleboy had shouted, " starboard fore-brace !" And again, the fore-yard was filled, and the *Scud* was upon her course, leaving the brig's boats astern, and bearing upon her decks the astonished Duffy.

———

CV.—A Critical Position—How Charley Escaped—Westward ho !—The Police at fault—M. de Bessac.

WE left our hero in a rather critical position. His escape seemed almost impossible, but the good fortune which had hitherto attended did not now desert him.

Charley saw, that if he remained on the roof much longer he would most assuredly be captured. In the street, which the houses faced a howling and infuriated mob were awaiting him, consequently his only chance of escape lay in descending on the opposite side of the houses, into some little back-yards, so getting a fresh start of his pursuers. It was much easier to say get down into these back-yards than to do it, for accomplished as Charley was in gymnastic exercises he was not clever enough to climb from the roof of a four-storied house to the ground, down a perpendicular brick-wall.

His quick eye at last caught a crazy looking water-pipe, which he thought would aid his descent. The idea no sooner entered his head than it was acted upon.

Down—down he went the dilapidated old pipe, bending and creaking as he descended.

His pursuers arrived at the edge of the parapet when he was about half way down, and were at a loss to know how to act, to attempt to descend after him was certain death, for even with Charley's weight the pipe was bulging out in a most dangerous way, and any additional strain upon it would assuredly snap it in two.

While some of Charley's huntsmen ran quickly down through the house to intercept him on his arrival on terra firma, others remained on the roof to watch his movements. He was still some distance from the ground when the crazy pipe, unable any longer to bear the strain upon it gave way, and Charley still firmly grasping the tube was precipitated to the earth. To anyone else this fall would have been certain destruction, but Charley's luck had not completely deserted him for he alighted like a cat upon his legs, and after the first surprise was over, he was ready for a fresh start, and lucky for him he was, for the officers of justice were close upon him. He was over the wall in a moment and into a narrow dark alley, and luckily for him in a neighbourhood, with which he was acquainted. He ran quickly on, hearing with pleasure his pursuers steps, growing fainter and fainter in the distance, till they ceased entirely. No time he felt was to be lost, so quickly through the back streets he continued his way until he was close to his lodgings, there he feared that the police might be watching for him.

But no—they were either unaware of his place of residence, or else had made so sure of arresting him in the street, that they considered the precaution of watching his rooms unnecessary.

Was it not too bold for him to go home? he asked himself, and for the moment he thought it was, but the recollection of Julia, and all she had gone through for him, made him spurn the idea of escape without her. So watching his opportunity he darted across the road and let himself in.

"Have you come to take me for a drive, Charley?" asked Julia, as he ran up the stairs, but a moment's glance at his torn and mud bespattered clothes showed her that something dreadful had happened.

I am fully aware that most heroines in her situation would have fainted, but she was a strong-minded girl, and never even thought of such a thing. Her dearest Charley was in danger, and her only thought was to assist him in any way that lay in her power.

In a few minutes Charley had briefly recounted his adventures, and a quarter of an hour had not elapsed before she and Charley, the latter completely disguised, were rattling along in a cab to the Euston Square railway station, and within two hours of the time Leech had first accosted him, they were flying rapidly along the iron rails to Liverpool.

"My dearest Charley," said his companion, "what are you going to do?"

"Escape my love."

"But how? Are you going to leave the country?"

"I am going to take places in the packet for America."

"Shall we be able to get away do you think?"

"Certainly not; therefore I do not intend trying. The police will trace us to Liverpool, and detectives and telegraphs will be brought into work to stop us."

"Then what is it you mean to do?"

"Play a bold game, which, if I win, will enable me to return to London without fear, but which, if I lose, will——," and Charley finished the sentence by making a sign round his neck.

Most people have visited Liverpool, so it is needless to describe it. The wharves, the quays, the warehouses, are all well known. The busy Mersey thronged with ships from every part of the world, the bustling, snorting little ferry-boats have been seen by nearly all.

It was getting dusk when Charley and Julia reached the busy port, and after leaving Julia at one of the waterside hotels, Mr. Wag proceeded to one of the numerous shipping offices to inquire respecting ships bound for New York. The *Fire King* was to sail that evening. Nothing could have been more fortunate for our hero's plan than this. He thanked his informant and left the office. Shortly afterwards he presented himself there again, only this time undisguised, and took a berth under the name of Arthur Smythe.

Julia was curious to know the particulars of the plan of escape, but Charley preferred not wasting time in words, and asked her to get ready at once to go with him. She had implicit confidence in her lover, and felt certain that he would be sure to select the best way to ensure their united safety. With little attempt at secrecy, they made their way to the docks. It was quite dark, and the *Fire King* was lying out in the middle of the stream, with Blue Peter flying, and steam up. They took a boat off from the wharf to the ship, and were safely landed on board. They were only just in time, and the bell was ringing for strangers to leave as they mounted the side.

Charley had already said that it was not his purpose to leave the country, so my readers will not be surprised that during the confusion which ensued on the departure of friends and relations from those who were starting for the far west, he assisted Julia into an empty boat, which was fastened by a rope to the vessel, and, cutting her adrift, the two were soon drifting down the stream.

"Now, dearest," said Charley, "exert your

strength to the utmost, and endeavour to keep the boat's head straight down the stream, while I alter my dress a little." So saying, he abstracted some articles of dress from a small portmanteau, and in a few minutes was so changed in appearance, that no one would have recognised him. Even Julia, accustomed as she was to our hero in all dresses, was astonished at the great change a few minutes had made in him.

She had exerted herself bravely to do as Charley had bade her, and, the change of dress complete, Mr. Wag sculled the boat quickly over to the Cheshire coast, and after helping Julia out, pushed the boat adrift into the stream.

"Now," said Charley, "we must make for Chester, and so back to London."

"But Charley," said Julia, "what is the use of taking your passage for America? We could have got over here, and so to Chester, quite as easily without doing that."

"True—but then the police would have soon been after us; as it is, they will be down to Liverpool on the chance of hearing tidings of us."

"Will they overtake us, Charley, dear?" said the beautiful girl, clinging to our hero's arm, and looking up into his face with an expression of earnest solicitude.

"I think not, my love," and there was a shade of triumph in his tone as he added—"You see the first thing they will do will be to make inquiries at all the shipping offices, and they will hear that a gentleman, whose description resembled Mr. Wag, and who gave his name as Arthur Smythe, had taken a passage out to New York."

"I begin to see now. Oh, you dear, clever Charley." and Julia, emboldened by the darkness, actually stood on tip-toe and kissed him.

"Well—then they will make inquiries of all the boatmen, and will learn that the gentleman in question was taken on board the *Fire King* by one of them, and that the vessel sailed shortly afterwards. They then will have very fair presumptive evidence that Mr. Wag has escaped, and will, in about a fortnight, be walking the broadway of the United States capital."

"But why did we not go to New York?"

"Because there is much more to be done in London."

"What will you do?"

"Go down to Richmond."

"As Monsieur de Bessac?"

"Precisely."

"And what am I to do. Shall I return to the duchess?"

"No, I think it would be better not."

They had walked on during this conversation, and reached a small railway station. Charley took tickets for Chester, and they were soon whirling along in a comfortable carriage towards the ancient town.

Arrived there, they stopped for the night at an hotel. No wonder, that after all he had gone through Charley slept well.

The following afternoon saw them back again in London.

———

CVI.—CONTAINS SOME ACCOUNT OF A CONVERSATION BETWEEN TODDLEBOY AND HIS PRISONER.

WHEN Duffy had somewhat recovered from his surprise at being seized in the manner alluded to in a former chapter, he ventured to ask Captain Toddleboy, who was seated on some spars looking at him, what he intended doing with him.

"Do with you?" replied Toddleboy—then pointing in the direction, said,—"You see the fore-yard arm?"

"I do," said Horatio, "but not without losing a little of his colour, and naturally enough, as it is not a pleasant thing to anticipate swinging from the yard-arm. Then a thousand tales of the wanton barbarities practised by pirates, crowded upon his imagination, and he nerved himself to prepare for some of the most terrible.

"Well! you see it?" said old Toddleboy, who noticed the effect the mention of the fore-yard-arm had made upon his captive.

"I do," replied Horatio, calmly, for he had resolved to die as a British tar, should—

"You do?"

"Yes."

"Then it's very likely I shall send you out there the next time we reef topsails," said Toddleboy, with a grin, "that's all."

Duffy was perfectly astounded, "what the devil can he intend doing with me," thought he.

"Come into my cabin, sir," said the old pirate, interrupting Horatio's reverie on his present position.

The astonished lieutenant followed old Toddleboy.

"This doesn't look much like hanging, or having my tongue cut out," thought he, as his companion sang out to him, "to bring his stern to an anchor," and then sat down himself, producing from a locker close at hand, a case of spirits which he pushed towards Duffy.

"Liquor up;" said he "and let's know who you are and all about you."

Duffy helped himself.

"I am lieutenant Horatio Spanker Duffy of H. M. S. Brig *Dodger*.

"Horatio Spanker Duffy—and a damned fine name it is," said the old skipper.

"I'm glad you think so, Captain Toddleboy."

"Eh! how the devil did you know my name?" said the old fellow jumping up—"how the devil did you find it out?"

"You are tolerably well known in these waters."

"But not by that name."

"Well! perhaps not—but you see I wasn't wrong in calling you by it."

"No—but who the devil are you!"

"I've told you."

"I don't believe you heard my name, in these latitudes."

"I am not aware that I said I did," replied Horatio, who could not suppress a smile at the old sailors astonishment at being addressed by his right name by a stranger.

"Come now," said the old fellow coaxingly

"let's know all about you, and where you sprung from—have some more grog."

"I have already told you my name and rank."

"Ah, but——"

"And now I'll——"

"Go on then."

"But what I'm going to tell you will astonish you not a little,"

"What is it—out with it?"

"I've been wanting to see you for a long while."

"Wanting to see me?"

"Yes."

"You're joking."

"I'm not."

"But what for?"

"Ah!"

"Damn it! man, spit it out—what for?"

"I've got a letter for you."

"Who's it from?"

"Read it."

Horatio here handed the letter which Charley Wag had confided to his care, and which he had placed in his pocket previous to leaving the *Dodger*.

Toddleboy read the note, and, on concluding it, sprang up and seized Duffy's hand.

"And you are a friend of his?"

"Yes."

"God bless you, my boy! where can I land you—what can I do to serve you?"

These questions followed so rapidly one after the other, that Horatio felt puzzled how to reply to them, and Toddleboy once more spoke—

"If I had only known this before."

"Well, what if you had?" asked Horatio.

"You should have gone back in your boat."

"And you would have struck to the *Dodger*."

"Struck! not while the magazine was full, I can tell you."

"The devil!"

"Sooner than do so I'd blow the *Scud* out of the water!"

"By Jove! then, all I can say is, that I hope you may not fall in with another of our cruisers while I'm with you, for I haven't the slightest inclination to be settled in that fashion."

"We must chance it."

"Where are you bound to, now?"

"Home."

"England!"

"Yes—I've had enough of this sort of thing, so mean to cut it and go in for quiet the rest of my days—I'm getting too old."

"You look hearty enough," said Horatio, as he regarded the old man, who certainly did look the very picture of good health and strength."

But Toddleboy felt that he had arrived at that age when rest is so necessary to old people, and he had determined to give up piracy, slave-dealing, and the *Scud*, and to retire into private life.

Indeed, his resolution is not to be wondered at; the reader is aware that Toddleboy was not a young man, when he was instrumental in saving Charley Wag from the watery death, to which his unfortunate mother would

have consigned him; and as that was a thing of some years past, it will not be but supposed that the old sailor was getting in the "sere and yellow leaf."

"It's all very well, Mr. Duffy, but I can't stand it much longer, there's the gout and one or two other things just as unpleasant always hanging about me now, so you see it's very necessary I should get home."

"But how the devil will you get into any English port without its being found out, who and what you are?"

"Oh! the easiest matter in the world."

"You may think so."

"I know it."

"You'll find yourself 'up a tree,' as the saying is."

"Not a bit of it—I've done it before."

"You have?"

"Yes! and then I had the guns stowed away in the hold, but this time I was thinking of pitching them overboard."

"What a pity!" said Horatio, who could not help remembering their telling effect upon the *Dodger's* spars and bulwarks; "but can't you stow them away in that manner again?"

"Yes—I could, but I want to take in a cargo of oranges at the Azores."

"Ah! that's a nuisance."

"And I don't fancy it would be safe to have them stowed away while the cargo was being put in."

"It seems an awful pity to throw the guns overboard."

"I think so myself, but——"

"What are you going to do with the *Scud*?"

"My first mate is going to have her, and the crew will remain with him."

"Then, why not take your passage home in one of the packets, then there would be no necessity to take in a cargo, and the *Scud* might be off after landing you."

"A devilish bright idea!" and one that my chief officer will be delighted at, he didn't like the idea of losing those guns, they are stunners, and no mistake."

Here the the old captain clapped his hands, and a little negro boy appeared.

"Send Mr. Gasket here."

"Yes, massa capting."

In a few minutes the mate made his appearance.

"You sent for me sir?" said he.

"I did—this gentleman—allow me to introduce you. Lieutenant Duffy, Mr. Gasket. This gentleman," continued Toddleboy, "happens to be a friend of a son of mine."

"Indeed!" exclaimed Horatio, "I was not aware of that."

"Not exactly my son either, though at one time I was almost persuaded into believing that he was."

"The deuce, you were?"

"Yes—but that's not much to do with what I was going to say to you, Mr. Gasket. This gentleman has suggested a plan by which we may save the guns."

"Indeed!" said the mate, his eyes glistening with pleasure. "I shall be very glad to hear it."

"How the devil it was I didn't think of it myself I can't tell."

"But what is it, sir?" said Gasket, who appeared anxious to hear it.

"Simply that you should land Captain Toddleboy at the Azores, and be off, without waiting for a cargo of oranges or anything else."

"First rate—but how about the commander's getting a passage home?"

"In the same way that I shall—in one of the packets."

"So he can—how the devil it is we didn't think of this plan is a puzzler to me."

"And to me—so now we'll drink his health for saving the guns. Come, fill up."

The other officers were summoned, and invited to drink the health of our friend Duffy, which they did most cordially.

"I say, Bunt," said Toddleboy to the second mate, "have a sharp look out kept—I don't want to come athwart anything between this and the Azores."

"All right, captain, it shall be attended to."

"And Mr. Fid."

"Yes, sir."

"To-morrow you will see that the guns are stowed in the hold, in the usual manner."

"Very well, sir."

"It would have been a thousand pities to have pitched them overboard," said Gasket to Duffy.

"You seem to have quite an affection for them."

"I know what they can do."

"They carry a devil of a way."

"I should rather think they did—what did you think of them on board your craft."

"Think of them—why they licked ours out and out."

"They're the right sort—rifled—but good, old-fashioned muzzle loaders, none of the hanky-panky breech-loading contrivances about them."

"Don't you think the breech-loaders good?"

"Not one of them—they're always getting out of order, and require no end of attending to."

"What are you two fellows yarning about?" said old Toddleboy, who had just returned after giving some directions to the officer of the watch, "what's the yarn about?"

"We were talking about the guns," said Duffy.

"Ah! they astonished you on board the Dodger, I'll swear."

"They did so. I've been telling Mr. Gasket that their range was greater than our breech-loaders."

"Of course it is."

"If it's a fair question, how did you come by them, Captain Toddleboy?"

"Well, one fine morning, not many miles from this coast, we fell in with a little Spanish brigantine—man-o'-war—and after a sharpish fight, in which I lost my arm, she surrendered, and we took her guns."

"But what had you before?"

"Only four 32-pounder carronades; they weren't bad, though, for a marine-store dealer's."

"Marine-store dealer's—you don't mean to say you bought them at a place of that sort?"

"I did though."

"But where?"

"In Shadwell—handy for us we could send our boat up and fetch them, one at a time."

"By jove!"

"I got most of my stores there—powder, shot, and shell."

"The devil! shell?"

"Shell! sir—you'd hardly believe it, would you?"

"I shouldn't have thought it."

"People would be rather astonished if they knew that at some of these places they keep shells charged, already for use—why the cellars at the crib I bought the carronades were full of them!"

"You don't say so?"

"Yes—and what is more, the people in the neighbourhood knew nothing about it."

"And you bought your guns at this shop."

"And they were rattling good ones of their sort—I was rather sorry to part with them, but then, the brigantine's guns were a devilish sight better."

"What became of her crew?"

"That, I'm sorry to say is not in my power to answer."

"How's that?"

"Why, you see, after she struck to us, I determined to have her guns, and set my men about getting them on board the Scud, after pitching the carronades overboard."

"But what's that to do with her crew."

"I was going to tell you. After my fellows had got the last of the guns on board my little craft, I intended letting the brigantine's crew be off about their business, but——"

"Well! what became of them?"

"Don't you intterrupt. Just as the last few of my men were leaving the brigantine it was discovered that she was on fire, fore and aft."

"Well——"

"The infernal Spaniards had set fire to her after getting the boats ready."

"But how was it you didn't prevent them doing all this?"

"Oh! I didn't care what they did, I only wanted the guns, but I didn't bargain to be blown up in their dirty craft."

"I should think not."

"So I made my fellows get away from her as soon as they could—and by jingo! before we were four boat's length from her she blew up, and I suppose every one of her crew perished, for we couldn't save one."

"Good God! you don't mean to say they were all killed."

"The devil a one was alive that we picked up, so I conclude none of them escaped, for the wreck of the brigantine went down almost immediately after the explosion."

"What a frightful thing for the poor devils."

"Awful, wasn't it, but I couldn't help it."

Just at this moment, Mr. Bunt came into the cabin and reported a strange sail to windward, bearing down upon them.

"I'll be on deck in a trice, Mr. Bunt,"

said Toddleboy, " keep her on her course— how's her head?"

The mate replied to his question, and then returned to his duty.

" I hope this infernal stranger is not one of your cruisers looking after me."

" You'll show fight—won't you ?"

" You remember what I told you about blowing up the *Scud* sooner than surrender, eh ?"

" You did, but I hope it won't come to that."

" Let's go on deck and see what she's like, and afterwards we'll have supper."

" By Jove! she's evidently on the same course as we are," said Duffy to old Toddleboy.

" She is," replied he, " and she's a man-o'-war, or I'm a Dutchman."

Duffy took the glass which was offered him and at a look at the stranger.

" What do you make her out?"

" A brig."

" Yes, I can see that."

" She's the *Banger*, or I'm very much mistaken," said Duffy.

" You know her then ?"

" Rather."

" Heavily armed ?"

" A ten-gun brig."

" How many hands ?"

" About the usual compliment."

" Then she may have a slap at us, and welcome—I shan't alter my course for her."

Evening was approaching, but still the stranger was discernable, and Toddleboy with his officers and Duffy remained watching her.

" Clear the decks! shouted the old commander prepare for action."

The order was sharply given, and as sharply executed, and when supper was announced everything was in readiness for the engagement.

CVII.—AMY—MRS. HARRIS EXPRESSES HER
OPINION ON POLICEMEN.

IT may possibly have occurred to the mind of some deep-thinking reader that in all the hurry of flight Charley's pretty little adopted daughter had been forgotten.

That, indeed, had been the case. She had been employing herself, as little girls of her tender age like to employ themselves, in dressing and undressing a large doll that Charley had bought her, and so absorbed had she been in this occupation, that she had not heard Charley's footsteps in the house, and had continued her amusement until even she was tired of it.

Into the sitting-room in search of Julia she went. She was not there. The room was untidy and disordered.

' Mrs. Harris." shouted the little one over the banisters, " where is mamma ?" for so she had learnt to call Julia.

" Don't know, darling—gone out I suppose."

" She said I should go with her and papa for a drive."

" Well, I daresay they will be in in a few minutes."

Poor little Amy looked disappointed, and tears dimmed her eyes, but the good-natured Mrs. Harris soon drove them away, and, finishing up her conversation with " well, dear, don't cry no more, and come and see me make a pudden," completely restored the little one to happiness, and sent her skipping down the kitchen stairs."

Mrs. Harris strove hard to amuse the child, and to answer all her questions, but when it grew late, and Mr. Wag made no appearance, neither did Julia return, she felt a little uneasy.

A loud single knock at the door made her pause in a delightful story she was relating to Amy, all about ogres, fairies, princesses, and demons, without number.

" Bless us," said the old woman, looking up through the area railings, " it's a bobby !"

" A what ?" asked little Amy, innocently.

" A peeler, my blessed love, one of those blue-coated lions who go about seeking whom they may devour—least-ways, take up and fine five shillings."

Amy looked mystified, and Mrs. Harris quietly seated herself again, and not until the knock had been several times repeated, did she condescend to bawl up from the bottom of the area to ask what was wanted.

" Open the door my good woman," said the policeman, in an authorative tone.

This Mrs. Harris refused to do, unless she knew his business.

" Open in the name of the law."

" Drat the law ! I shan't let you in unless you tell me what it is you want."

" We want one of your lodgers."

" Then devil a one will you have, for they're not at home."

" We'll soon see that. Open the door woman."

" Woman !" shrieked Mrs. Harris, getting excited, " who are you a calling woman ? Let alone coming and wanting my lodgers. If I could get at you I'd make you remember the day."

" We shall force the door unless you open it immediately."

Now, as there was little doubt in the worthy housekeeper's mind that they would do what they said, she preferred saving her property, and accordingly, with an unwilling hand, withdrew the bolts, and admitted the officers of justice.

They asked questions as silly and useless as as their own capes, and opened a tea-caddy in their search for Charley, but it is needless to say their hunt was unsuccessful, but as we know that our hero was about arriving at Liverpool at this time.

" Well," said Mrs. Harris as they at length took their departure, " my opinion of peelers is that they are the uselessest stupidest lot of blackguards as ever eat cold mutton off a lady's dresser, drat 'em all.

THE DUCHESS.

CVIII.—THE SHEPHERDS AGAIN.

AFTER the supper given by Deacon Goggles on the evening of Lucinda's baptism it will be remembered that three of the shepherds were slightly fatigued with drinking, and the duties of the day, and required some little assistance to reach their lodgings.

Brother Herd had volunteered this; but after getting Brother Swabb, Pudding, and Gash, into the Street, he found that the task he had undertaken was a prodigious one.

Swabb was very helpless and leant heavily on his supporters arm, while Pudding and Gash were for a time in a most excited state.

The Rev. Jack commenced, by renewing his attack upon Swabb, and Brother Herd had to exert his strength to prevent his maltreating the unfortunate shepherd who was now totally incapable of defending himself."

" Yah—hoops ! you damned cobbler—stand up, and I'll warm you " shouted the Rev. Jack.

" Brother Puddig, I'm surbrised at you."

" Are you Squirt—if you don't look out I'll give you a pop in the eye !"

This intimation from the Rev. Jack, had the effect of making Brother Herd hold his tongue, as he was not at all anxious to get one of the Rev. Shepherds " raspers,"

Pudding then turned to Gash, who was delivering one of his tremendous orations to the winds, steadying himself by a lamp-post, under which they had brought up.

"Come along, old chap," said Jack, "let's have a race?"

"Done," replied Gash, letting go his hold of the lamp-post, and starting off at a break-neck pace, closely followed by the Rev. Jack.

The road was wide, and for the first fifty or sixty yards they went on well enough, Jack Pudding being some distance in advance of Gash, who was certainly not so good a runner as his reverend brother shepherd.

Gash felt that there was no chance for him, and slackend his pace; but had the Rev. Ghastly known the consequences of this rash act, the probability is, that he would continue running until the next morning, or at least until he was sober.

Immediately he slackened his pace, he began to swear about in a most alarming manner, first tacking to the right and then to the left.

Unfortunately for her, a respectable middle-aged female chanced to be crossing the road first at this time.

To do Brother Gash justice, his intention was to avoid her, but somehow or other he miscalculated the time for tacking, and came with a smash against the woman, who was sent sprawling with the Rev. Ghastly rollnig over her!

Not knowing at first that Gash was a little tight, and seeing him make so deliberately towards her; the woman naturally concluded that his upsetting her was intentionally.

"You wretch," said she, seizing hold of the unfortunate Gash by the hair, and shaking him, as he lay helplessly in the road, "I'll teach you to come your impudence to a respectable married woman—the mother of six—I will!"

"Quite 'n accident," said Gash, who felt somewhat revived by her treatment.

The Rev. Jack Pudding now returned to where the collision had taken place, and shortly afterwards Brother Herd made his appearance, propping up Swabb, who was still unable to walk by himself.

"Hullo!" shouted the worthy Jack Pudding; "what the devil's up?"

"We were down, Brother Jack," said Gash.

"Ha! ha! ha!" laughed Pudding.

"You laugh! you ugly brute—if my husband was only here—he'd soon——."

"My good woman 'sure you 't was quite 'n accident—my friend—runs—very fast—race of hundred yards—beat me—but didn't mean — it — 'sure you — very sorry," said Gash.

"It's evident you're drunk—the whole lot of you—pretty clergymen, indeed!"

"By good woban—I deed dot dell you, id was ad accident," observed Brother Herd, soothingly.

"What do you doa about it?" said the woman, imitating the unfortunate brother's peculiarity in speaking.

"By good woban——," began he; but here he was interrupted by the arrival of one of the county constabulary, who happened by the merest chance in the world to be strolling up the road.

"What's all this about?" said the constable.

"I'm a very good mind to give you in charge—I am," said the woman, "knocking down a respectable woman—you ought to be ashamed of yourselves!"

"All right, old lady—give me in charge," said the Rev. Jack Pudding.

Brother Herd attempted to give some sort of explanation as to how the accident occurred, but was interrupted by the indignant female, who persisted that he could not have seen anthing of it.

During the dispute, the constable had recognized the Rev. Oiley Swabb; this was not the first time that he had fallen across the worthy shepherd in a similar state to what he was on this occasion, and seeing that the delinquents were friends of this worthy minister, the enlightened member of the county constabulary determined to espouse their cause in preference to that of the assaulted woman.

Perhaps his determination was the result of conviction; but the writer is inclined to believe, that a brace of half-crowns slipped dexteriously into his hand by the Rev. Jack Pudding, had a great deal more to do with the matter than conscience had.

Be this as it may—the policeman immediately declared that he had witnessed the whole affair, that it was quite accidental, and wound up by saying, that if the woman did not "move on," he'd lock her up

"Move on—indeed!" she exclaimed, passionately—"you'd better lock me up—yes, lock me up—I'll go to the station-house——."

"I'll tell you what it is, missus, you'd best step it—I don't want to lock you up, but if you stay here a-kicking up a row about nothing at all—why you'll nab it, and no mistake."

This speech had the desired effect upon the unfortunate female, who took herself off, but not before she had abused the whole party in the roundest terms.

Brother Herd felt immensely relieved at her departure, for he was now able to devote his energies to Swabb, who still required a deal of propping up.

"Stad ub," said he, as he made a dive at the Rev. Oiley, who evinced a strong disposition to curl down in the mud for the rest of the night. "Ad boliceban, you bust 'elb be hobe with this gendleban."

"All right, sir," said the bobby, "come along, Mr. Swabb—hold up."

With some little difficulty they succeeded in getting the wretched Swabb home. The Rev. Jack Pudding and Ghastly Gash had gone off on the spree into the town.

This fact may be hardly credited by some of our readers; but "the flesh is weak," as Brother Pudding often observed.

The shaking that Gash had received at the hands of the exasperated woman he had knocked over, served in a great measure to sober him, and then he became aware of the fact of his being smothered in mud, and mentioned it to Pudding.

"Oh! that be damned," said the Rev. Jack, "it doesn't matter a bit—come along?" and the Rev. Ghastly was led unresistingly through the streets by his brother shepherd, in spite of his dilapidated appearance.

It was very late, and much to the disgust of the reverend pair, all the publics were closed.

"This is rather dry work, Brother Pudding," suggested Gash, "couldn't we look out for a place to wet our whistles at?"

"I'm hanged if I know of any about here—by jove! I wish we were in town, we shouldn't be long in finding a crib."

"By jingo! we'll be off there to-morrow morning—it's no good staying any longer down here."

"Now that we've seen that plummy vessel dipped you mean?"

"Yes."

"It strikes me that if we went the right way about it we might see her dipped again."

"The devil!—how?"

"How? Why by saying that the baptism did not actually take place to be sure."

"I don't quite understand," said Gash, who was still rather foggy.

"Don't understand?"

"No."

"You're drunk."

"And so are you."

"You're a liar."

"You're another," said Gash, valiantly.

"You have got an awful lot of cheek to tell me so," observed the Rev. Jack, "why if I was to hit you just one (here Brother Pudding made a demonstration illustrative of the blow), I should send you into space."

Gash seemed to see the force of his brother shepherd's remark, for he abstained from using any more abusive language, and meekly asked for an explanation relative to the subject of their conversation.

"Why you see," explained the Rev. Jack, "the baptism did not actually take place."

"Ah! that's what I can't quite understand."

"Then you must be a fool."

"Brother Pudding," said Gash, solemnly, "remember the Scriptures."

"Oh! the scriptures —— you know devilish well what I mean—or if you don't you ought to."

"I really cannot recall any circumstance which could affect the validity of Miss Lucinda's baptism."

"You can't?"

"I cannot."

"Then you are a greater idiot than I took you for."

"Amen, Brother Pudding."

"How about the gas being turned out?"

"Oh! damn it! I forgot all about that—the ceremony was only just commenced. Oh! yes, decidedly invalid—we must have it over again."

"It's all very well to say so, but I'm of opinion that the young party will object."

"You don't think so?"

"She evidently didn't relish it last time, and twigged the humbug, when that infernal Swabb kissed her in the dark."

"As you very properly say, Brother Jack,

'the flesh is weak,' and I daresay Brother Swabb felt the temptation was great."

"Of course he did; but that was no reason that he should frighten a lamb just received into the fold—a damned stupid thing I call it —the gal's got money."

"Really?"

"I was told so."

"Well, Smug was particularly civil to her."

"I should rather think he was—she's first chop you may take your davy."

"But, Brother Pudding," said Gash, with a leer, "don't you think we might manage to persuade this lamb to become one of the congregation at the Obelisk?"

"And cut the Bethel?"

"And cut the Bethel."

"I don't think it's a bad notion—but how to set about it is a difficult matter."

"Not very."

"What do you propose?"

"Call on her to-morrow morning."

"Well?"

"And we must tell her that we were grieved to see that she had been made the subject of one of Brother Swabb's practical jokes."

"Capital."

"Then we can gently touch upon her leaving the fold of such an immoral shepherd, and at the same time we can poke in a word or two in favour of the Obelisk."

"I like the scheme; but remember, Brother Gash, if she comes to our shop, we'll have no caterwauling after her, it 'ud spoil the little game about the tin."

The reader will not for one moment suppose that when the Rev. Jack Pudding said that there was to be no "caterwauling" after the pretty Lucinda, that he included himself— oh! dear, no. It was simply to impress his fellow shepherd, the Rev. Ghastly Gash, with the idea that in this instance he (the Rev. Jack) intended to act with the strictest propriety.

This intimation was quite sufficient for Gash. Jack Pudding in the field, there would be little chance for Ghastly. This the latter knew from experience, for on a previous occasion he had evinced a partiality for a young vessel who had excited the Rev. Jack's admiration, and the result of it was that the unfortunate Gash was beaten by his brother shepherd to within an inch of his life.

This will in some measure account for his resigning the prize so easily.

Jack saw that the game was his, as far as Gash went, and the only difficulty to contend with was getting her out of the clutches of the Bethelites.

"That's the rub, Brother Gash."

"They'll cut up rough, but we mustn't mind that."

"Mind it, not I—only let that Swabb say a word to me about it, and I'll give him a bigger larruping than I did to-night," said the Rev. Jack, shaking his fist, and looking savage.

"Well, we'll go and see her to-morrow morning, Brother Pudding, and for the present we'll drop the conversation."

They had by this time arrived at that part of Chatham known as the Brook, and, as Brother Gash was concluding his remark, he was suddenly slapped on the back by a corpulent young lady, who called him "ducky," and asked him to "stand something to drink."

"I should be delighted, if I could only get some myself," replied Gash.

"Oh! come along then, we'll show you where to get lush—come on, Sal!"

This latter remark was made to a stout young lady who had taken the Rev. Jack in hand, and the two worthy shepherds, not being over particular, followed them up a blind alley, and into a house.

In this anything but aristocratic neighbourhood we shall leave the rev. pair, to wet their whistles and otherwise amuse themselves.

———

CIX. — SAINT STARVER-CUM-BAG-O'BONES — HOW PAUPERS ARE TAKEN IN AND DONE FOR —BLOODYER AND FAVERSHAM.

THE workhouse of Saint Starver-Cum-Bag-o'-Bones has already been described in one of the early chapters, and its master, Bloodyer has also fallen under the notice of the reader. This worthy personage still presided over the establishment, which continued to bear the reputation of being one of the best regulated workhouses in London. Its inmates never had any complaints to make—at least they never made them, or if they did, the said complaints never came to the ears of the parishioners.

Bloodyer still bore the best of characters.

Still he continued the leading man in parish politics.

Improvements which he had suggested, with a view to ameliorating the condition of the poor, had been carried out ; the recipients of parochial relief were as numerous as ever, and Bloodyer was as popular as ever.

The aged people of the parish had no dread of going into " the house"—not they. They were sure of kind treatment. They would be cared for in every respect—there wants supplied when living, and when death should—but stay, dear reader, has it never struck you that the paupers at Saint Starver's died very soon after their admission?

Of course it has, and the revelation made by the unfortunate Joe Cudder was perfectly true.

This Bloodyer, who had always a kind word for the miserable wretches, whom Fate had decreed, should pass their latter days under the roof of that last refuge for the destitute—the workhouse; this man trafficked in their carcasses! Nor did he hesitate to hasten that death, which would have come soon enough, should the demand for bodies be great at the time!

Then, would a wretched pauper be taken suddenly ill, and in a few days, or perhaps hours, would be a corpse !

Such was the fate of the unfortunate creatures, in nine cases out of ten; but still this Bloodyer remained master of the workhouse—the destitute flocked to its shelter—died off—and their places were filled by others, who in due time " shuffled off' this mortal coil," and went the way of their predecessors.

But how could this wholesale murder be carried on by one man?

How could such atrocities be permitted in his enlightened age?

And how could they remain undetected?

This wholesale murder was *not* carried on by one man. Several were engaged in it, and the first great cause was Faversham !

Upon the paupers at Saint Starver's he had made all his experiments in poisons, and thus for the attainment of the one great purpose of his existence—revenge, he had sacrificed the lives of dozens of his fellow-creatures !

Some of these poor wretches he had deprived of life in a manner so sudden, that their sufferings must have been slight. Others had died writhing and screaming under terrible effects of strychnine.

One pauper would be suffered to die easily, and almost unperceptibly, while another would experience all the horrors of a lingering and painful death.

Latterly Bloodyer's victims had died very easily and naturally.

This can be readily accounted for.

Bloodyer cared very little for the result of Faversham's experiments. The workhouse master's sole object being to dispose of the bodies profitably without being detected in his nefarious practices, had therefore employed a poison, which killed those to whom it was administered in a short time, without leaving the slightest trace of its presence behind.

Thus, the paupers of Saint Starver-Cum-Bag-o'-Bones appeared to have died a natural death ; and as relatives and friends of paupers are not, as a rule anxious to bear the expense of burying the dear departed one, Bloodyer was seldom troubled about the interment of the bodies.

Indeed, had he been so troubled, he would soon have found ways and means to evade the inquiries.

With such an invaluable beadle, as he possessed, it was next to an impossibility that any troublesome friend of the ailing or deceased paupers could gain admittance into the sacred precincts of Saint Starver.

With this assistance Bloodyer had carried on a thriving trade—the beadle of course, sharing the profits.

It was this worthy beadle's duty to submit the application for relief to the master, who invariably allowed his subordinate to detect the most *likely-looking* of the tribe of applicants, without the slightest reference to their being the most worthy of parochial assistance.

And this trafficking in human bodies, went on, day after day, month after month, year after year, but still no suspicion attached to Bloodyer, no suspicion rested on the man, whose very hobby was the poor.

But how was this?

How was it that these terrible doings were allowed to go on in these days of detectives, to say nothing of Private Enquiry Offices?

To this I reply—because no one was aware of these doings, but the perpetrators of the atrocities themselves.

Yet, I am wrong—there is one, who,

although many miles from Saint Starver's is aware of the workhouse master's evil doings, and will one day most assuredly take steps to bring the miscreants to justice.

But I am anticipating.

Bloodyer's trade is still thriving.

The workhouse is very full, the applications for admittance as numerous, and the demand for bodies greater than ever.

It was on one evening, when Bloodyer was sitting in his private room, congratulating himself upon the good stroke of business that had been done during the week, a stranger was announced.

"I can't be—be bothered—I'm not at home—anything," said Bloodyer to the beadle.

"He sez he must, and will see you," returned the man.

"The devil! what sort of looking fellow is he?"

"A tall, thin man, with a sunburnt face and moustachers," said the beadle, "like a furriner."

"Does he speak like me?"

"No—not a bit."

"What the deuce can he want with me?"

"You'd better ask him," suggested the beadle, "and not keep him waiting so long—he don't look much like a friend of a pauper come to kick up a shine," added the worthy functionary, with a grin.

"Well, if you think it's all right, show him up."

"Right as a bank, I should say," said the beadle, as he left the room.

In a few minutes he returned, and ushered in the stranger, whom he announced as Captain Leopold Ralph.

Bloodyer received his visitor politely enough after apologising on the plea of being busily engaged, for having caused himself to be denied to him.

"But may I enquire the object of your visit?" said the workhouse master.

"I have called with reference to the death of a pauper——"

"Sir! I really——"

"Will you allow me to proceed?" said the stranger.

"Certainly," gasped Bloodyer, wiping the perspiration from his forehead.

"As I before said, I have called relative to the death of a man who died here some years ago."

"Oh! indeed," said Bloodyer, somewhat relieved by this statement, for some of the latter cases which had fallen under his especial treatment had been rather awkwardly "worked off." Indeed, the suspicions of some of the paupers had been aroused by the circumstances attending the deaths of the others.

But this only made Bloodyer redouble his kindness to them, and the pauper mind was soon set at rest.

"Will you favour me with his name?" asked Bloodyer, blandly.

"Cudder—Joe Cudder."

The face of the workhouse master became ghastly in its expression, and dropping the book he was about to search, made no reply.

"You are ill," said the stranger.

"No, no, only a little faint—the heat of this room is oppressive—allow me to offer you a glass of wine," and, staggering to a cupboard, Bloodyer produced glasses and two decanters. Filling his own glass from one, he pushed the other towards his companion.

"Help yourself," said the master of Saint Starver's in the most cordial tone he could assume. But the reader may judge his surprise and terror when his visitor said, looking him full in the face,

"I'll trouble you for the decanter you are using, Mr. Bloodyer, I don't like the look of the other."

The glass of wine which the workhouse master had raised to his lips did not make its way down his throat, but in lieu of this it ornamented his shirt front.

"Well, how about this Cudder, Mr. Bloodyer?"

Mr. Bloodyer had dropped his glass, and was looking at his companion with a most terrified expression.

"He died here," said the other, coolly, filling his glass from the decanter the workhouse master had used.

"The circumstances attending his death."

"What do you know of his death?" shrieked Bloodyer, starting up suddenly.

"As much as you do—you fool!"

The voice in which this was said seemed to affect Bloodyer powerfully. Placing a chair between himself and this mysterious stranger, he gazed at him for some time without speaking.

"In the name of heaven who are you?" said he at last.

"Who am I? Look again—do you not know me?"

"No-o-no!"

"You do not?"

"No—no."

"You don't remember me?"

"I have never seen you before—who are you?"

"Faversham!"

Bloodyer started back, looking if anything more terrified than he had when he supposed his visitor had come to accuse him of the murder of Joe Cudder. Then summoning what little courage remained in him, he ventured to speak to this inhabitant of the grave, for so he deemed Faversham.

"But you died in Cornwall," stuttered he.

"Was buried and rose again," replied Faversham, in a sepulchral tone.

"But your face is entirely changed."

"It is——"

"But how did this occur?"

"Never mind about that, it can matter very little to you—first of all, let me warn you not to betray yourself again in the manner you did to me, any stranger to the facts would have been convinced of your guilt," said Faversham, in a severe tone.

Bloodyer remained silent, and the mysterious doctor continued.

"And now to business. In the first place, you must get me appointed doctor here—do you understand?"

"Yes."

"After that we will proceed as usual—but

again let me warn you to do away with any such weakness as you have exhibited this evening."

"It *must* be Faversham," said Bloodyer, musingly.

"It is."

"But, what became of you after leaving London?"

"My adventures would fill pages, and would weary me to recount—but to make my story short—I went to Cornwall to my mother, there I employed the sleeping medicine, and was buried after it had been well circulated, that I had died—my body was taken up and returned to London."

"But your features are changed, they are not the same."

"I succeeded in altering them, and believe no one would recognise me."

"Unless by your voice."

"Which I alter also," replied Faversham, in a totally different voice to his natural one. "And now you know all that is necessary for you to know," added he, "and the sooner we get to business the better."

"I will procure your appointment to the post of doctor as soon as possible—but there may be others in the field—I believe there are."

"They must be removed."

"But, how?"

"The best way you can."

"I will do my best to serve you."

"I am satisfied—and now for the present shall leave you—any communication you may have to make can be sent to that address," said Faversham, taking a card from his pocket and giving it to Bloodyer—"and now good-bye—I shall anxiously await your letter."

In this manner these guilty wretches separated—again to meet, and again to plunge into a fresh career of crime.

———

CX. — Julia and Amy — The Arrest — Despair.

CHARLEY and Julia arrived safely at Euston Square after their exciting adventures, and as it was out of the question for them to return to their former lodgings, they proceeded in search of others. As Charley would, necessarily, be obliged for some time, at all events, to live quietly, they took up their new quarters in a quiet street in the north-west postal district.

It was a very quiet street, for, as it was no thoroughfare, the road was undisturbed, save at intervals the rattle of wheels warned the careful housekeeper of the butcher's approach. It was a great street for organs. From an early hour in the morning, to a late one at night, organs ground out their strength in gruff unmusical tones. Sometimes two contended together, and by these means a far more melodious duet was produced, for, good as the musical merits of the "Old Hundredth," and "Aunt Sally," may be, they do not harmonise well together.

The first thought of our hero and his companion, after they had settled down a little, was about poor little Amy.

"How are we to get her to us?" asked Julia.

"Well, I don't see exactly how it's to be managed. I'm afraid we must leave her just at present where she is."

"You naughty, cruel man! how can you talk so?" said Julia, for she was really very fond of the little Amy.

"Well, as you always manage to get what you want, young lady, I suppose I had better yield at once, and go and fetch her."

"You kind, stupid, rash old darling, do you think I will let you risk your precious life in going to your old lodgings? Some policemen will be sure to be lurking about and see you."

"More than probable. But then I'm equal to six policemen any day."

"Very likely darling, but *you* are not going and *I* am," said Julia, fetching her bonnet, "now good-bye, Charley," said she, kissing him, "they will be sure not to suspect me, so I shall be safely back in an hour or two with your little adopted daughter. Bye, bye, Charley."

Julia hailed a cab, and was soon in the old neighbourhood. Leaving the vehicle a street or two away from the house, she walked to the well-known doorway and knocked. Mrs. Harris answered it in person, and welcomed her back very warmly, but, nevertheless, not quite so cordially as when she thought her the grand lady of a great gentleman.

Amy heard her voice directly, and came running along the passage.

"Ah! mamma, dear mamma, where have you been. Come in—why do you stand in the passage?"

"Because I am going directly dear—and am going to take you with me, so put on your hat and cloak."

Amy looked rather surprised at hearing this, and asked where they were going to; but when she heard she should be taken to her dear papa, as she called Charley, her countenance brightened up, and she soon came running down stairs fully equipped for walking, and bearing in her hand the casket which she had been so anxious to bring with her when Charley rescued her from the old hag.

Julia had in the meantime fully satisfied Mrs. Harris in a pecuniary way, and when Amy was ready, the two walked quietly down the street to where the cab was left. They had just reached it when two policemen stepped forward, and almost before Julia could utter an exclamation, they had lifted her into the cab, and in another moment she was being conveyed rapidly to Bow-street, while the poor little Amy was left standing amazed in the street.

Her kind protector snatched away from her directly she had regained her!

Surprize soon gave way to consternation, and consternation to fear, and the poor little thing burst into a flood of tears, as a feeling of utter desolation came over her, and she wandered about in a helpless way, till worn out with fatigue, she sank to sleep upon a door-step.

Charley had passed the first hour of Julia's absence well enough, but when the second, third, and fourth passed, and still she did not return, he grew uneasy, and at length he became so restless, that in spite of the imprudence of the step, he determined to set out in search of his Julia himself.

The worst of it was, he had no good disguises at hand, but muffling himself up as well as he could, and hoping in that way to avoid recognition, he proceeded by back streets and little frequented alleys, to the neighbourhood of his former lodgings.

He scarcely dared inquire at the door himself, for fear that Mrs. Harris should recognize him, and while he was hesitating what he should do, the flaring gas-lamps revealed to him a troop of policemen marching down the street. Now Charley had no desire to risk their eyes, so he drew himself up in a low door-way, and in doing so trod on something soft, and a low moaning cry rose from the previous occupant of the step.

Stooping down he found it was a little girl, and when the police had passed, and he lifted her out into the light, he recognised to his great astonisment his little adopted daughter.

"Amy!" he cried, "for God's sake, speak, Amy, and tell me how you came here. Where is Julia? Why don't you answer? Good heaven, she is in a swoon!" continued he.

Little Amy soon recovered from the swoon, brought on by fear and exhaustion, and was then able to give Charley an account of Julia's arrest.

Charley's anger was frightful, but he contented himself with swearing one or two deep oaths, that he would either rescue her or perish in the attempt.

———

CXI.— PREPARING FOR AN ENGAGEMENT.

THE strange sail was still some distance from them when Duffy sat down to supper with Toddleboy and his officers.

"What do you propose, Gasket?" said the old commander, "shall we fight or run away?"

"I don't like the idea of running away, captain, but at the same time we don't do much good by tackling men-o'-war."

"There is'nt much change to be taken out of them," replied the old fellow, with a smile, "I daresay our friend Duffy here, would be a tough'un to fall athwart, if he were in command of one H. M. cruisers on this coast."

"I should fight as long as I could, you may depend," said Duffy.

"I believe you, my boy—and I like you all the better for it," replied the old man as he filled his glass, and proposed Duffy's health, which was drank with the utmost cordiality by the three officers.

"And now, gentlemen, we must hold a council of war—I want to get home if I possibly can, without being taken there in one of her Majesty's brigs—but at the same time I don't quite approve of going out of my course—no! not for all the brigs in her Majesty's navy!"

"Hear! hear!" shouted the mates, knocking most lustily on the table with their glasses.

"Let's fight," said Mr. Fid, the junior of them.

"But as I before observed, continued old Toddleboy, "I am not at all anxious to take my passage home as a prisoner on board the craft that's after us now."

"We'll blow the Scud out of the water sooner than you should be taken," shouted the same enthusiastic young officer who had voted for the fighting.

"All very well, my dear Fid, but you seem to lose sight of the important fact that in blowing the Scud out of the water, you will blow me up with her—now that is what I am anxious to avoid. You all know me better than to imagine for one moment that I would surrender under any circumstances; at the same time I am not without my anxieties as to the result of this action."

"We shall win it," again broke in the courageous young Fid.

"I hope so," said Toddleboy, with a smile, "and now gentlemen, my proposal is that we 'go about,' as you are all aware it will not suit us to fight in the dark;" then, turning to Duffy, he added, "we like to see what we're about when we have such customers as these to deal with."

"Quite right, sir, I agree with you perfectly," said Mr. Gasket, the chief officer. "It is just as well we should keep out of the brig's way until daylight."

The captain's proposition having been assented to by the mates, the matter was settled.

Supper concluded, the officers returned on deck.

The darkness of the night, which prevented them from seeing the brig, was favourable to their tactics, and when old Toddleboy came on deck, he lost no time in giving the necessary orders.

"Mr. Gasket, see all clear for going about."

"Aye, aye, sir."

Everything was in readiness, waiting the commander's order.

This was smartly given, and round went the Scud, and away upon the other tack.

After seeing everything prepared for action at a moment's notice, Duffy and Toddleboy again returned to the cabin, and shortly afterwards retired to their berths.

At daybreak the officer of the watch went into the captain's cabin, and informed him that the stranger was again in sight.

"In what direction is she now, Mr. Bunt?"

"On the weather quarter, sir."

"Damnation! then she must have ' gone about' at the same time we did!"

"About that time," replied Mr. Bunt.

"Very well—carry on as much sail as you think proper, Mr. Bunt, and see which has the best pair of heels—the Scud or the Banger—and I'll be on deck as soon as I can."

"The stranger certainly sails faster than we do."

"She does?"

"She is gaining on us."

"Then don't carry on any more—let her come within range, and we'll knock the sticks out of her."

The officer went on deck again, and Toddleboy went into Duffy's berth.

"Rouse out, Duffy," said the old fellow, shaking the lieutenant, who was sleeping soundly, "rouse out—here's that infernal *Banger* close upon us."

"You don't say so?" said Horatio, sleepily.

"I do, though—and there'll be a devil of a smell of powder presently."

This latter speech had the effect of making Duffy jump out of his berth.

"Is she far off?" asked he.

"Close at hand—she must have gone about almost at the same moment we did."

"By Jove! how odd."

"And what's more, Bunt tells me she sails much faster than we do."

"She's famous for it, I know—and if I had been your adviser, I should have suggested avoiding her altogether if possible."

"Our only chance now, is to play the devil with her spars."

"There's just this to be considered——"

"What?"

"She *might* play the devil with yours."

"I'm not much afraid of that—I'll back my crew against any, at gunnery practice. Your fellows don't have one half the drilling at it that mine do—you see we lose no opportunity."

"That's true, but a lucky shot from one of the brig's Armstrong's may prove rather unlucky to you—perhaps knock away your browsprit, and then, where are you?"

"Let us hope that they'll miss it, but now we'll get on deck and have a look at her."

Duffy followed the old sailor up the companion.

"By Jupiter!" said old Toddleboy, "she's not far off—Mr. Gasket, get the men to their quarters!"

"Aye! aye! sir, shouted the mate, and immediately after the boatswain's shrill whistle, piped the crew to their relative positions—the decks were cleared—the men stood to the guns, and all was ready for action.

In the meanwhile the *Banger* drew nearer, her superiority in point of sailing being evident. She was soon within range, and running up her ensign she fired a blank cartridge for the *Scud* to bring to.

This being unnoticed, the *Banger* treated the pirate to a round shot, which whistled harmlessly across her bows.

"Now, then my lads—be steady!" said old Toddleboy, "steady, till I give the word."

Each man waited breathlessly for their commander's voice, which rang out clearly and distinctly.

"Fire!" shouted he, and away went the messengers of death and destruction.

One of the shots told in a most alarming manner upon the brig's cutwater, and another played Mag's diversion with the main-topgallant yard—the wreck of which came thundering down on deck.

"Lie down my men—keep close!" said Toddleboy.

The men did so, and it was fortunate that they did—for the brig's guns at this moment boomed forth, and the shot passed over the *Scud's* bulwarks, tearing away part of the rail above them.

"Give it her again!" said the old Salt, who looked the beau-ideal of a pirate as he stood on the quarter-deck of the schooner, grasping his cutlass in one hand, and a revolver in the other.

Before the *Scud's* men repeated their fire, the brig's gun's belched forth again, and the *Scud* lost three of her crew by the discharge.

Again Toddleboy gave the word, and again the shot told—this time evidently dealing death in its course.

During the exchange of shots, the brig had been drawing gradually closer, and the confusion on her decks could be plainly seen by those on board the pirate.

"Keep her away, Quartermaster — we mustn't let that craft come too close to us. Mr. Gasket," shouted the old boy through his speaking trumpet.

"Yes, sir," said the mate, running up to him.

"Just lay that gun on the quarter-deck yourself, and see if you can't damage her bowsprit or something for'ard."

"I'll do what I can, sir," answered Mr. Gasket, and immediately walked aft to carry out the order of his commander.

The brig fired shot after shot, but, fortunately without doing more mischief than riddling the *Scud's* sails.

Toddleboy saw that it would be necessary to do something towards crippling the brig as soon as possible, and with a view to this walked aft to where Gasket was, and assisted him in laying the gun that was to do the brig some serious injury.

"That's about it, sir," said the mate, and the two stood by to see the effect of the shot which was fired at the moment, most favourable to its correctness.

With a crash the fore-topmast came down, and the shout, which rose from the crew of the *Scud*, at their success, must have jarred upon the ears of the discomforted *Bangers*.

The brig was now rendered less dangerous by this accident, and Toddleboy congratulated himself upon his skill in gunnery.

"I'm hanged, if I shouldn't like to have a shot myself," thought Horatio, looking longingly at the long brass guns, which had done such service.

"What do you think of that last shot, my boy?" said old Toddleboy, who came up to him at that moment.

"Think of it?—why it's one of the finest I have ever seen."

"If it weren't for my commission I'd like to have one myself."

"You can if you like—but I don't think it would *quite* the thing for you to do."

"Nor do I—now you fellows, are fighting for your lives."

"Exactly so, and I'm very anxious to save my neck, I can tell you."

FAVERSHAM AND BLOODYER.

This conversation was carried between the discharges of cannon.

"There's only one more lucky hit wanting now to cripple her entirely," said Duffy—"if you can manage to knock away her bowsprit, she's done for, and you may be off when you like,"

"It's to be done, my dear fellow, and I'll do it, or my name's not Toddleboy."

Saying this, our friend the captain went up to the gun, with which he and Mr. Gasket had succeeded in bringing down the *Banger's* fore-topmast.

"I'll make you a bet, Duffy, that I don't," said the old boy, laying the gun, and taking the lanyard attached to the lock in his hand. "Will you bet?"

But, Mr. Duffy not having anything with him on board the *Scud*, worthy of staking declined to speculate.

Well, then—here goes!" said Toddleboy, at a favourable moment. Bang went the gun, and true to its aim, the shot carried away the devoted bowsprit! "There! I told you so," said the old pirate, triumphantly. "And now, Mr. Gasket, the sooner we're off the better, she can't follow us—that's one consolation."

"I'm very much of the same opinion, for this sort of fighting is a losing game—there's no swag to be had out of it."

Having delivered himself thus. Mr. Gasket went off to see all clear for "going about."

"On second thoughts," said Toddleboy to

his chief officer, "I don't think we'll go about until we're out of sight of that cruiser."

"Very well, sir."

"As we are out of the range of her guns we can make sail, and get out of sight as quickly as possible. And let me know our list of casualties."

Mr. Gasket went below to inquire.

"Well, how many ?"

"Three killed and four wounded, sir — Mr. Bunt is hurt very badly."

"But, who are killed ?"

"Poor fellows," said Toddleboy. The mate mentioned the mens names. "Three of my smartest lads. Mr. Bunt wounded, did you say ?"

"Yes, sir, with a splinter from the bulwarks."

"Come along, Duffy, we'll go and have a look at the wounded—I always like to cheer 'em up a bit," said the good-hearted old sailor.

The two then went below to the portion of the *Scud's* hold, which served as a cockpit on these occasions.

Here were the four poor men who had been wounded by the fire of the *Banger's* guns. One was minus an arm, which had been fearfully lacerated by a round shot, and which had been amputated by Mr. Fid, who was acting as surgeon, as having been a medical student previous to becoming a pirate ; the others were more or less injured by the splinters from the bulwarks. Mr. Bunk lost a portion of his right-ear, and his face was sorely damaged by one of these fragments.

"Well, Bunt, my boy, how are you?" said the cheering voice of old Toddleboy as he entered the cockpit, where the wounded were lying, groaning with pain.

The unfortunate officer's reply was almost in audible, and after his attempt to speak he fainted away.

"Poor fellow," said the captain, "look after them, Fid."

"I'll do all I can for them, sir," said Mr. Fid, as he proceeded to dress the wounds of another wounded sailor.

For the present we must leave Captain Toddleboy and his crew, and take the reader a voyage upon dry land, and into the latitude of Cock's Lot.

CXII.—IN WHICH CHARLEY TAKES TO COCK'S LOT.

COCKS lot were having a row,
It was all about herrings,
Buffing Jim had destiously exchanged one of his own purchase, which was stronger than himself, for a mild fish he had marked on Wapping Well's half a plate, and while the latter lind turned away his head, to look after Nagging Sall, who was supposed to be slighting wapping will, for the Bermondsey Swasher Wapping Will soon smelt the difference when he once more turned his attention to his half plate and he at once roared out.

Who's been a vinin on charges.

Why, the peeler has rung the hairy bell, answered Duffing Jim.

Any how I'll punch his high, if I catch him, says Wapping Will.

"What's the row," says Cork, the proprietor of Cock's lot—gentlemen and ladies' can't be disturbed with no row."

"Mine was a hard roe, and this yere's a soft," says Wapping Will.

"Well, you're soft lot," says Duffing Will "and so there's a pair on you."

Whereupon Wapping Will, having his back up, made no more to do, but smacked the unoffending herring right into duffing Jim's eye, his right eye, which was always the weakest,—

"Take that," says wapping Will,

"He's got it," says Cocks.

"An won't he," says duffing Jim, who immediately took a header over the lake to get at wapping Will, who haved a deal of fight though he was shaking in his shoes,

Why was he shaking in his shoes?

Because his hair was short.

Well but why wys he shaking in his shoes, because his hair was short? for this simple reason—his hair had just been cut short by the goverments hair-dresser, that is to say the jail barber, and therefore he was not strong as he had just had a course of skillagalee and crack—tooth chump (prison biscuit) through there mouth so was not equal to meeting duffing Jim, who had not been quodded for six months and had had a steak in him every day at twelve,

However he was determined to show fight and hit out before duffing Jim could get at him.

A scream immediately followed, for Nagging Sall had rushed forward to protect her Bill, and she had caught it on the nose, or as she termed it "the smeller," but she is not to be condemned for this expression, her godfather and godmother had taught her to call her nose a smeller.

Wopping Will was so horrified to see Nagging Sall suddenly fly backward, flung up her legs and show more of her stocking that even the young person at Cox's are in the habit of displaying, that he was off his guard, and before he was on it, again duffing Jim had hit him such a stunner between the eyes that his head seemed all lightning.

The blow knocked him back upon old mother O'Rafferty who was trying to eat a tough chop with the only tooth she had in her head, the old lady was naturally not in a very good temper over this business, and therefore when wapping Will came crash on her and knocked her, and her chair and her chop right into old Miggles lap, she set up such a willaloo that Cock's said—Danny—we shall have every bobby about come, droppin down on us.

Oh. when a—where a—where's me chop ye blaygard says Mrs, O'Rafferty, catching up a plate and breaking it on Wapping Wills head ye dirthy villun—wheres my tooth.

And thereupon she plumped down on the ground and looked for both of them.

Well, I may as well say at once that whether she herself had swallowed both tooth and chop, under the force of the blow, or whether old Miggles swallowed them without knowing it, or whether Cock's cat swallowed them up, this is certain that old Mrs. O'Rafferty never set the only eye she had left to see with (the other looked alive but it was not), upon either of those articles again.

I have said O'Rafferty fell into old Miggles lap and thought he had both his eyes to see out of, he was unfortunately paralytic, and the consequence was that whenever he wanted to go to the left he found himself blundering towards the right, and whenever he wanted to go to the right he shot straight ahead, if he wanted to sit down he could'nt do it, and if he wanted to get up he had to be pulled out of his chair, wrenched out for all the world like a tooth, he swearing meanwhile as though he did'nt want to be moved.

"Well, old Miggles saw perfectly well she had plunged into his lap, and immediately hit out at Mr. O'Rafferty, *as he thought*. But instead of doing so he struck that old Indian, who goes about with the Indian drum, and singing a song that frightens all the horses.

"Tum, tum—ki—ki," said the old Indian, and immediately caught up a stool to send the old nigger into kingdom come. But the legs caught in the frizzled cuts of Cut-away-Bess, who without more ade wrenched all the old niggers white music right away from his body."

"Oh, ki—ki," said the Indian, "doanty, coldy, givey backy cloey."

But all Cocks who was not fighting were too delighted with the fun to let the ki—ki, as he was called, regain his arm once more, so he stood shivering near the fire, everybody roaring about him—even those who were fighting could not help roaring, and covering himself into a state of decency with an old broken plate he held before him.

"Horde—r—r," at last called out Cocks, as he saw Nagging Sall and Cut-away-Bess, just begining a set-to, for he knew by experience that if those two pretty creatures began a row that there was no knowing when it would end, for every man or boy at Cock's who was not ready to fight, for Nagging Sall was only prevented from so doing by reason of the fact, that his fists were at the service of Cut-away-Bess; and as the admirers of these two beauties were pretty nearly equal, the fight at Cocks', in which they were engaged were sweet things.

Poor Cocks, his plates lay heavy on his mind, for they always got smashed within five minutes of the commencement of a row. He had tried tin plates once, and then the parties at Cocks' had beaten these tin plates together till the neighbours sent for the police, who walked Cocks himself off to quod. Then Cocks had tried pewter-plates; but these the company had doubled up into half-moons, and so back at last Cocks came to crockery, and he bought his plates by the hundred, and looked upon them as dead loss, for strange to say, in a scrimmidge, though every blessed piece of crockery was smashed, everybody denied having had a hand in it. It was a practical joke at Cocks' to lay all these smashes on the "cat," but Cocks would

reply, "that's nonsense, for my cat's a wise cat, and when there's a row on allers bolts, and Lor a mussey me! I wishes I could bolt to!"

"Horde-r-r," shrieked out Cocks-"let dogs delight To bark and bite, but boys and gals should never fight."—HORDEBE.

But the row only got the stronger.

Within two minutes the row was general.

Cocks rushed at the tables after his plates, and soon got a pile of chairs ready for removal into a safe corner, that he might as well have saved himself that trouble, for he had only got half way up the room with his burden when the ki—ki's Indian drum came down on his nose, knocked him down, and sent his plates into fifty thousand pieces.

"Yere goes them," says Cocks, getting up, "and I'm blowed if I don't have my whack, and catching the ki—ki, who naked as he was, was flying after his drum, a fine fister in the bread-basket (stomach), down the native went, and about a dozen the next moment fell on top of him.

Things came to this pretty pass—everybody was swearing, including Cocks' cat, who was doing if safely from the top of a very high cupboard, and the Indian gentleman was screaming out — "Oh! ki — ki—getty uppy, or me shall be squashy—squashy. When the door leading to Cocks' was opening, and a young gentleman of highly wide-a-wake appearance stood upon the threshold of that field of battle.

"Nix my dolly pals, fight away," said the new-comer, putting the back of his hands on his hips, "have it out, I'll see fair play, and when you've quite done, say so—go it!"

A sudden silence became evident.

"Ha!" said the new-comer, "you may stare; it *is*—you know."

But not a soul spoke.

"What, can't nobody blab at Cocks'! and the young gentleman knocked all the wind out in yer?"

"Why its, its——," said Cocks, still on the ground, which he had for a second time reached in consequence of a vigorous kick Cut-away-Bess and Nagging Sall, agreeing for once in their lives, had at one and the same moment given him—one on each side of his seat of honour.

"It is——," said Cocks, getting up and rubbing the seat of honour aforesaid, "it is, and these yere old eyes aint a deceiving this yere old body—it is him, and it aint not nobody helse."

"No, that it aint," said the new-comer—"I never, never change—you'll never find not no change in me."

"Why—why—why!" said Cocks, flinging his cap up to the ceiling with one hand, while he still continued to rub his seat of honour with the other, "why its CHARLEY WAG."

Whereupon Charley, to show that it was himself, turned head over heels three times right into the centre of the company, suddenly leapt to his feet, put his right arm round Nagging Sall's neck, his left round that of Cut-away-Bess, kissed them almost in the same second, and then, crowing like a clown, bawled out—

"Oh, yes, yere we are again—how deye do to-morrow?"

The way in which they grew good-tempered in a moment at Cocks', after the arrival of Charley Wag, was something to marvel at. To be sure Cut-away-Bess was inclined to "have at" "Nagging Sall" in consequence of that sweet young creature being the first who had received the kind kiss of the returned Charley, but Charley soon put an end to the dispute by bestowing two more kisses on the chaste young females, and beginning this time with Cut-away-Bess.

"I'll warm yer," said Charley, as he took her hearty kisses, "an' as often as you like—this is the chap for both of yer when and where you like, me angel of Cocks' Hall."

"I say," said one of the company, "Charley's been playing the wag—ain't he."

"Don't you go a wagging your tongue," said Mr. Wag, "Charley's been a waggin for some purpose—he's been a waiting for the waggon, has Charley—and I can tell you he's been riding like a lord; but Lor' a fellow must come back to his true-love."

Here he first chucked Bess under the chin, and then did the like for Sall, then he began singing—

How happy could I be with either,
Were 'tother dear charmer away,
But while yer both tease me together.
To neither a word will I say.
Tol lol de lol, lol diddy oldy, &c.

"I wasn't a teasing yer," said Cut-away-Bess.

"Then I wish you was," answered Charley, with a laugh, "for I like to be teased by a voman—so go it, my charmer."

"Oh, ki, ki, drummy smashy," here a voice moaned piteously.

"Hullo," said Charley, "aint that ki-ki?" and looking round, Charley Wag burst into roars of laughter as he saw ki-ki tied up in one of Cocks' aprons. "What? Drummy Smashy, there, taky thaty."

And as our hero spoke he flung down a bright gold sovereign.

"Oh, ki-ki, cooley—cooley, ki-ki," said the Indian, running with such a zest upon the glittering coin that he did not care for the consequence, and, therefore, exhibited a good deal of that which with much better taste might have been concealed.

Cocks' was once more silent.

Hadn't Charley been lucky they all thought, and it is a dismal fact that no sooner had Charley done the liberal with a real sov, and not a "brum," that Sall and Bess seemed to pay him more and more attention, and in the midst of their smiles, look at each other with more and more venom.

"Aint I been up to larks," says Charley, putting his arms round Bess and Sall.

"Have you my fancy?" said Sall.

"Oh, ah, you may think so, Sall," said Bess, "your fancy hindeed—don't go for to fancy any sitch thing."

"I shall fancy whatever tning I like marm," returned Sall, and no doubt she would have taken a fancy to scratching Bess's eyes out but

happening at that moment to smooth Charley's cheek, a new object of interest attracted her.

"Oh, pals," said she, "if Charley aint got whiskers a coming—oh, plummy."

This discovery on the part of Sall, whom he immediately squeezed closer, caused Charley some queer sensations. His breast seemed to open and shut, and he felt a queer tingling sensation all over him, from the crown of his head to the nails of both his great toes.

"Charley's almost a man," continued Sall, and thereupon such a shout rent Cocks', that Cocks shrieked out with such alarm, "ki, take care of the roof," and Cocks' cat, which had come down from the top of the cupboard, immediately leapt to that place of safety again, in the full belief that a worse row than ever was going to begin.

"Yes, pals, I begin to feel a foot and higher," said Charley, "and I say, Cocks, yere's the needful—no flash—send out for six gallons o' beer," and thereupon Charley pitched out a half sovereign to the table.

"Ki-ki," said the old Indian, making for that coin, but thereupon the fair Bess administered to him such a slap on the plumpest part of the old beggar's person, that it gave him such a jerk that the sovereign he had received for his "drummy smashy" was jerked out of his mouth, which he had used as a purse, on to the table, and the next moment a score of hands rabbed at it, and though the old nigger ki-ki'd this conduct, it was no use He never saw his sovereign again.

"I say Charley—what have you been up to?" asked Cock.

"What haven't I? I've been doing everything and everybody almost since we met last," and Charley proceeded to recount some of his adventures. He was wide awake, was Master Charles and knew exactly what to tell and what to hide and in relating his adventures he managed to amuse and interest the company, without revealing anything which could compromise himself

But I fancy I hear the reader exclaim, how is it that Charley Wag, the gentleman, the friend of the great and well born, has voluntarily sought this strange society? what has become of Julia? what has he done with Amy? patience reader, patience, Charley I have already said was wide awake and never did anything without a purpose, no one was better qualified by nature to play the gentlemen and we have seen his manners enabled him to pass unquestioned in the best society, but there again, Charley had a miscellaneous acquaintance and his hand which at one time might be guilty pressed by lads of rank, a few hours afterwards might be round the waist of one of the frequenters of Cocks' as it was now, his language too which when he chose to make it so, was good and refined would, if always similar to the specimen just given, have hardly passed muster in polite society, but he understood the art of suiting himself to his company for although he would by appearing among his former comrades as a great "swell," perhaps have won from them more respect, still he would not have been treated with so much cordiality for they looked upon him in his shabby clothes and his incorrect English, as one of them.

But why should he wish to ingratiate himself with them ?

The reason is simple, he wished them to do him a service, when he had learnt from the little Amy the particulars of Julia's arrest his passion knew no bounds for he really was very fond of her and the determined on her escape, but how ?

Every plan which suggested itself to his angry mind appeared quite impracticable when viewed calmly.

He knew he had himself only just escaped from the hands of justice, and that for him to venture within the precincts of a police court was literally putting his head into the lions mouth, but what was he to do ?

The remembrance of Cocks' and his old companions came across his mind, could they help him, and if they could, would they do to ? Charley thought it at all events worth the experiment, so having little Amy in a place of safety and muffling himself up to avoid recognition he made his way to the east and at length made the triumphant entry we have seen into Cocks'

Hence the presence of our hero in his old haunts and his desire to conciliate those of whom he had thought he was quite independent.

Charley's jovial nature, his manifold adventures, and his free expenditure of money above all soon raised him as a hero in the eyes of the others.

He did not deem it prudent to relate everything that had occurred to him in England, so confined himself more to his French adventures, to which he added not a little for, he knew pretty well the sort of incidents which were likely to raise him in the estimation of his hearers, and accordingly invented when his true adventures failed.

The liquor he had furnished, together with his pleasing adventures procured him great applause, and he felt almost sure of being able to enlist the sypathies of all the ruffians in Julia, and by their means to procure her escape from prison His only doubt was whether they would take the trouble for a woman, if it had been a man who got into the mess, he knew that they would have pulled down the walls of the prison rather than suffer his pal to remain in durance vile. In the meantime the conversation continued.

" What have you been up to during the last year or so ?"

" I have been living a swell, and living so quiet, that none of my old acquaintances have heard a word about me. I have not been up to any tricks, not my old fame. I have been living a quiet and honest life *out of England*. Infact I have been living in France, and have been supposed by the people amongst whom I have been living to be a young English gentleman."

Then he continued with a slight touch of humour.

" To be sure it was a mystery as to who stole the pine-apples growing in the conservatory of the French prince's palace, and the Emperor himself lost a quantity of splendid

peaches from his country-house, situated in the town in which I was living, but nobody ever dreamed about the young Enlishman being the guilty youth. Then again, there was the care of that pretty girl, who——, but never mind the particulars. *She* didn't know who did the damage—*she* didn't hear the window of her room opened, and when Charley Wag heard of this affair, he said he hoped the police would find it out, and inquired whether the mother of the young person was ' out' herself."

Then Charley launched out into invention, and said that suddenly the supplies which had kept him out of arm's length of the new police stopped—utterly and wholly, and he was without any means of living, so as his landlord had always "stuck it in," in the bills, stuck it off again, by relieving that greedy old gentleman of his cash-box, and so that he might be quite unaware of the "time of day," he relieved him of his "ticker," but finding it was only an old copper trump he dropped it into an old lady's pocket, who by the way, announced that a saint miraculously put it there, and she was only quite sure to the contrary, whereas the being shown as something wonderful, the Mr. gentleman owner, who had not yet discovered the loss of his cash-box, came with the rest to look at it, and found it was his own property.

He gave the old lady in charge for stealing it, but she was liberated, and the stingy old gentleman had to pay her four hundred francs (£17) for having dared to assert the watch was hers. And the old lady giving it to the priest of her church, he retained it to this day, though inconsequence of Charley having poked his penknife into the works, and then jerked it round it, doesn't go very well.

" *Who was it who* supported you *during these two or three years ?*" asked one of the damsels.

" It was a duchess."

However great, radical men may be a title always, produces a sensation among them, and that Charley had a friend amongst the nobility, and still consorted with his old comrades, raised him still higher in their eyes than he had been before.

The fact, that Charley had been supplied with money by the Duchess of Heatherland, was not altogether a fabrication, at least he had often thought of applying to her for money, and settling down to lead a quiet honest life, but he did not see his way quite clearly.

If, he agreed I tell her I am her son, will she not be more inclined to get me ont of the way altogether than to pension me for keeping the secret. She tried it once, and were I to reveal myself to her, the hold I have upon her, would very likely make her still more desirous of putting me out of the way than she was before.

He had been, it will be remembered, put in full possession of the secret of his deplorable birth by the lawyer Leech, and reflections as to the use he could make of the knowledge were continually crossing his mind.

Now Charley you know, after all his faults, which are none of his own, for had he been brought up properly he would have been a very good fellow, and a credit to any father and mother, and to society. Charley, I say was a capital hearted fellow. He saw as far through a mile-stone as most men, and he could see a deal farther through anything than seven-eights of the men and women he came across.

He was a sharp fellow was Charley, and he felt that if he chose he could turn three-fourths of the people he met round his little finger.

And at heart he was an honest fellow was Charley Wag, though he *was* a thief.

So he determined that the Duchess of Heatherland should never know that he was aware he was her son. He also determined that she should never learn that the child she had attempted to slay with her own cruel hands still lived to reproach her with his life.

No—he would keep this secret, and be an honest man in this one act of his life, come what would of it.

Yet the temptation was sore.

He had been born at the expiration of six months from the date of the marriage of the duchess with the duke her husband. Six months children are not impossible, and, therefore, as he was born in wedlock, he could claim the title and estate of the murdered duke.

Ha! it was true Faversham, the man who had hated him, had paved the way to the thief wearing a coronet and a ducal robe, if he were so minded.

Such is often the destiny of sin. It is turned back upon itself!

But Faversham he thought was dead, and he would therefore do him no more harm.

Was Faversham dead?

Do not those we most dread often rise again to plague us when we least expect it?

Charley resumed the account of his adventures to the delight of his auditors, who listened to his hair-breadth escape with unfeigned delight, and applauded his plan of putting the police on a wrong scent by making them believe he had gone to America; and by his pleasing manner, and the generous way in which he had treated all around him, so won their hearts, that he had little doubt that they would all assist him in regaining his lost Julia.

He waited patiently for the right time, and as the men's enthusiasm arose, so rose his hopes of again clasping his beloved Julia in his arms. The account of his pursuit by the myrmidons of justice so roused the natural antipathy all his auditors had for the police, that he saw it only required a spark to fire the train, and most probably produce the result he wished.

He therefore commenced.

"Mates!" said he, "I want your help and advice."

"'Ear, 'ear!" said Cocks.

"I've told you how precious nearly I've been quoded myself, but I didn't say that a friend of mine had been nabbed, and had up afore the beaks. Now just look here. I've made up my mind that my pal shall be released. Will any of you help me?"

A confused chorus answered in the affirmative, mingled with questions of who is he?

"It is not a he," said Charley, "its a *she*."

Murmurs of dissatisfaction followed this announcement, and Charley began to fear it was no go; but he determined to appeal to them again.

"Pals!" said he, "do you mean to say you will refuse to help a woman? One who has gone through many of the adventures I have told you, with me. Come," continued he, "are our women to be torn from us and we to take no steps to recover them?"

"No, no," cried Cocks, "go it Charley—go it—go it."

"Revenge on the bobbies," cried one.

"Come on then," shouted Charley, waving a formidable-looking stick, "we're in for a —— row."

"Hoorah!"

"Damn the peelers."

"No cages, no prisons, no nothing."

"Where to?"

"Bow Street."

"Come on mates. give way to no one."

The whole uproarious mob swept through the streets, scattering everything before them,

Charley, with a select few, had rushed on in front to obtain tidings of Julia.

Will he rescue her?

———

CXIII.—BLOODYER AND THE BEADLE OF ST. STARVER-CUM-BAG-O'-BONES.

"WELL, guv'nor, who was it?" asked the beadle of Bloodyer immediately after the departure of the *soi-disant* Captain Leopold Ralph.

"Faversham!"

"Oh, come, that *is* a good 'un—*that* won't do."

"I tell you man that it *was* Faversham, or his spirit."

"I don't believe it was either—if it was his sperit it weren't much like what he used to be—besides sperits don't have moustarchers."

"I know not," replied Bloodyer, gloomily, "if it were not Faversham it was his ghost."

"A very bad imitation, if so be it was his ghost, but I'm inclined to think you've been gammoned master, and want to gammon me now."

"Nothing of the sort——"

"Honour!"

"I tell you I do not feel inclined to joke."

"But look 'ere guv'nor——"

"Well?"

"You've been gammoned."

"I have not—I again repeat that my visitor was Faversham."

"It's all very well to say so to me, but I know Doctor Faversham when I see him as well as you do—and for you to tell me that the cove as has just left was Faversham—why——"

"And what of it?"

"A leetle too much of the monkey."

"If you disbelieve what I have already stated, I have nothing more to say."

"Don't get shirty over it guv'nor, only just tell us—wouldn't you think me devilish queer if I took in all you've been a telling me?"

"I think you a fool for not taking it in as you call it," replied Bloodyer.

"But that cove's face was different to Faversham's."

"It was, but——"

"And I say, guv'nor," said the beadle with a leer, "you wouldn't have put out that decanter for Mister Faversham I reckon."

"It was by doing so that I accidentally discovered him."

"How d'ye mean?"

"I mean that by offering him that decanter he discovered himself."

"How? let's hear."

"He first commenced by making inquiries relative to the death of a pauper——"

"Yes."

"And then he mentioned the name——"

"Whose?"

"Joe Cudder."

"Well?"

"I thought that a glass of wine wouldn't hurt any visitor at this stage of the conversation, so I took out both the decanters, and pushed the doctored one to him."

"You did?"

"I did, and you may imagine my terror when he looked me full in the face, and said that he didn't like the look of it, and would trouble me for the other."

"You did feel a little queer, I'll be bound."

"Queer—I thought I should have fallen off my seat."

"But, how did he let out who he was?"

"He began by questioning me about the circumstances attending that fellow Cudder's death and I."

"You did'nt let anything out, I hope," interrupted the beadle.

"Not I—I asked him what he knew about it, and to my surprise he started up and said, 'as much as you—fool,' or something very like it."

"I don't see guv'nor as that proves him to be Faversham."

"You would not have doubted it if you had heard the voice—his voice—not at all the same that he now assumes as Captain Ralph; but you shall judge for yourself the next time he comes."

"Is he coming again?"

"Yes, and what is more he wished me to procure his appointment as doctor here again."

"The devil! and are you going to do so?"

"I think I shall, we have had some rather awkward escapes lately with these cursed paupers, they don't die so easily as they might."

"And, you think he'll be useful?"

"Exactly so."

"Then get him the berth by all means."

"I mean to," replied Bloodyer. And now you can be off, I'm going to bed."

"Well, good night, guv'nor."

"Good night."

———

CXIV.—A Breeze springing up—The Burial at sea—A little conversation between Toddleboy and Duffy.

WE left Captain Toddleboy and Duffy in the cockpit of the *Scud*, looking to the unfortunate fellows who had been wounded during the engagement with the *Banger*.

After seeing the poor fellows carefully attended to, the old sailor proposed that they should return on deck.

And on deck they went.

"It strikes me, it's going to blow to-night," observed Toddleboy.

"It looks a good deal like it."

"It does, and I think the wisest thing is to shorten sail before it begins."

"There's plenty of time for that," said Horatio, who was of opinion that now the schooner was on her course again, "you couldn't carry on too long."

"Yes, my friend, there's heaps of time I know, but I'm thinking of my lads."

"Well, what of them?"

"They've been fighting, and I daresay won't be sorry to turn in."

"And what's to hinder them?"

"There's nothing to hinder them turning in, that I know of—but if we have to shorten sail in a hurry, there'll be something to make 'em rouse out, I rather reckon, and that's what I want to avoid, so I shall shorten sail before supper."

"And bury the dead?"

"Yes, that must be done as well. Mr. Gasket, what do you think of the weather?"

"I think we shall have it presently, sir—it looks very dirty to windward."

"That's just my idea, Gasket, and I think the best thing we can do is to shorten sail before the hands turn in."

"Well, sir—shall we do so at once?"

"Yes, and after doing so—we'll bury the dead, poor fellows."

The chief officer, Mr. Gasket was not long in seeing the commands of Captain Toddleboy carried out, and in a very short time the schooner was tearing along under very little canvas, the breeze having freshened considerably already.

"We shall have a rough night of it—you may depend," said old Toddleboy; "there's one consideration at present, the wind is fair."

"I hope it may last so," replied Duffy, "though I have my doubts."

"I don't feel at all certain that it will last myself; but here comes Gasket."

"All ready for the burial, sir, when you are."

"Be good enough to send to my cabin for a prayer-book, Gasket."

The officer went off, and Toddleboy and Duffy went towards where the bodies were lying. They were placed near the gangway on a grating, and were now covered with a large flag—the black flag of the pirate.

It may seem rather absurd for the captain of a pirate to read the burial service over men who have been killed in action.

The author is of opinion that it is not a habit indulged in by many skippers who sail under the black flag; but in this case it may be accounted for. Toddleboy was not one of those lawless buccaneers whose object next to plunder is blood—not he. With the exception of taking what did not belong to him from other vessels, Toddleboy wat guiltless. His crew had to a man the same idea on the subject that he had, and thinking as he did, they never sought lives of prisoners, after the fashion of other celebrated pirates, who go in largely for bloodshed and cruelty.

Notwithstanding his profession, Toddleboy still maintained a great respect for the service of the church in which he had been brought up. In fact he had attempted to introduce prayers on Sunday mornings, but this his crew thought was rather too much of a good thing. Men may be very willing to spare the lives of their fellow-creatures when they fall into their power, but expecting men to sit out a morning service on board a ship is a totally different affair.

Toddleboy had to give this up; but with regard to the burial service there was no opposition.

On this occasion, therefore, he armed himself with the book of Common Prayer, and proceeded to the gangway, where the whole of the crew were mustered.

Standing on the bulwarks, and holding on by the lee rigging, Toddleboy began the service. The wind howled and moaned through the cordage, so that his voice at times could be scarcely heard.

But when he came to that part, "we therefore commit their bodies to the deep &c." a sudden lill enabled every one to hear the words distinctly, and the splash of the bodies, as they were consigned to their last resting place—the mighty deep.

The solemn ceremony concluded, the crew went forward again and Toddleboy with Duffy and the officers went below to supper.

This was soon over and Toddleboy and Duffy were alone.

"If this breeze lasts we shan't be long before we get to the Azoris," said the old skipper.

"Not many days sail now," replied Duffy.

"I shan't be sorry to see old England once more," said Toddleboy.

"I daresay not," remarked Duffy, "but you must be deuced careful, or you may get spotted by some one or other, and that would not be agreeable."

"I shall take very good care of that, you may depend," replied the old boy with a chuckle.

"It is not an easy matter, I can tell you, if the police once get scent of anything."

"Isn't it—look at Charley Wag."

"Charley Wag! what do you mean?"

"You are his friend——"

"I am—but I don't know what you allude to."

"Now, come Duffy thats too good.

"I really do not know what you mean."

"The devil!"

"I don't—what is it?"

"If you're his friend you wouldn't peach."

"Not if he'd committed murder."

"I don't know that he has ever done that, but——"

"But what?"

"He's the most successful thief in London!"

"You don't say so?"

"Yes."

"And that is how he lives?"

"Or rather exists—for you can't call that living."

"Can't you though—I only wish I could live—honestly—in the style he does."

"Good?"

"Good! like a lord! and a great deal better than many lords that I have met with, I can tell you."

"Poor boy," said the old sailor, "a thousand pities that he should have gone to the bad—he was a fine little fellow."

"Did you know him when he was so young?"

"I had charge of him when he was a baby."

"You had?"

"Yes."

"But how was that?"

"Oh! it's a long story."

"I should like to hear it—for Wag's a fellow I have taken a great liking to—but I didn't think he was a thief. Why damn it he spent Christmas at my guv'nor's down in Essex."

"You mustn't think the worse of him for being a thief," said Toddleboy.

"Well, I don't know—I don't *think* I should have introduced him to my sisters if I had known what he was—but let me hear his history."

"Fill your glass, and I'll tell you all I know about him."

———

CXV.—The journey in the cab—The cell —Surprise.

It will be remembered that when Julia was torn from the side of little Amy she was forced into a cab by two men dressed as policemen, who took their seats by her side.

She heard directions given to the cabman to drive to Bow-street, and she had fully made up her mind that she had been seized as Charley's accomplice, and would as such be handed over to the tender mercies of—so called—justice.

She was tolerably well acquainted with her way about town, and was surprised at being so long reaching the far-famed metropolitan police court.

On, on went the cab, and presently the rows of houses on each side of the road began to be broken by fields.

What can it mean?

On, on still rolled the cab, and the shades of evening spread quickly over them, and deepened into black night.

Her guardians refused to answer any questions put to them, only moving when Julia

JULIA IN A POLICE CELL.

made a rush at the cab window, apparently for the purpose of calling for help when they both simultaneously stretched out their arms like machines, and pulled her back with some violence, while one of them taking a gag from his pocket showed it to her with a significant gesture.

"How will it end? What does it mean?" asked Julia of herself mentally, until she grew tired of the unsatisfactory repetition, and by necessity resigned herself to her fate.

"Charley—poor Charley," she thought," "what will he think. Heaven forbid his doing anything rash."

Charley was about that time in Cocks' Lot

with each arm round a blotchy syren's waist. Perhaps if Julia had known this her thoughts mights have taken a rather different turn.

The cab suddenly stopped, and before Julia could observe anything of the place or neighbourhood in which she was, her eyes were blindfolded, and she was lifted from the cab and carried along by the two men who had first seized her when coming from Charley's old lodgings.

It seemed to her a very long time passed before she was put down.

"Have you succeeded?" asked a voice.

"Yes."

"Is she here?"

"Yes."

"Help—help!" called Julia.

A chorus of mocking laughter answered her, and the bandage was removed from her eyes.

She was alone.

Where?

She was in a cell.

Was it a prison cell she asked herself.

It looked like it, but the extraordinary mode of proceeding adopted by her captors made her doubt that her seizure had been made by the authorized gentleman in blue, with names represented by figures and all the letters of the alphabet.

For what reason she should have been conveyed away in this mysterious manner, if not to serve the ends of justice, she was quite at a loss to imagine.

She proceeded to inspect her place of confinement.

It was a circular cell with stone walls. She could see no door, but high up there was a small grated-window.

Could she but reach it, she thought, she might be enabled to ascertain her whereabouts, but it was impossible. The most she could see through it was a few stars.

Light and food she had none, and courageous as she was, she almost gave way under this mysterious occurrence.

"Oh, where was Charley? would he not rescue her?"

Charley was drinking half-and-half in Cocks' Lot.

At length she lay down, and sank into the sort of dreamy unconsciousness which precedes sleep.

Was she dreaming?

Had she fallen asleep, and in her thoughts fancied those sweet strains?

No—she was awake.

She raised herself and listened, as a sound of soft gentle music came sweeping and dying away through her place of confinement.

What could it mean?

Policemen are not in the habit of serenading their prisoners.

Was it Charley?

Her earnest wishes could not make her fancy that, for Charley had not a cultivated taste for music. Indeed, whistling "God save the Queen," was about as much as he could do in the musical line.

What could it be, then?

Again as she pondered the same sweet strains struck upon her ear, and again died away.

Was it fancy, or was the cell lighter than before?

She looked at the solitary window.

No—the light did not come from there. The few stars even she had before seen were now clouded over.

The light increased till a pale rose-tint lighted up the cell, contrasting strangely with the bare stone walls.

Was she dreaming?

She even went the length of pinching herself to be sure she was awake.

She had heard of table-moving, and she had seen a hat spin wound, but she had never heard of a stone-cell being moved.

Yet it did move.

She was sure of it.

Yes, she was sinking—down—down. She surely could not be fancying it. Was the cell actually moving?

No—it was only the floor which was sinking with a gradual steady movement.

Had she any enemies that sought her death? She knew of none. She had heard of traps something similar, by which victims had been let down into the river, and as she remembered all the dreadful stories, a thrill of horror ran through her frame.

The light every moment became brighter, the music enchanting.

Could she believe her eyes?

The cell had vanished. She stood in a splendidly furnished room, furnished in a most luxurious style. Heavy crimson curtains hung across the windows. In the centre of the room was a table spread with every conceivable delicacy. No lamps were visible, but still the same rose-coloured hue, which had amazed her in her confinement shed a soft glare through the apartment.

A young handsome man was the sole occupant of the room, and as Julia stood amazed he advanced towards her with a cheerful jaunty air. Julia shrank back in horror, but with a smile he followed, and placing his arm round her waist, said,

"My dear, it is of no use to struggle, you are in my power, and nothing can disturb us. Sit down, and we will have some supper."

Nothing can disturb them.

Is it so?

What are those confused noises outside?

"Help—help!" shrieked Julia. What does it mean? What is the noise?

It is help for one who sore needs it.

"Help—help!"

We shall see what the cause of the disturbance was.

CXVI.—A CONVERSATION IN WHICH TODDLEBOY TELLS DUFFY, CHARLEY WAG'S HISTORY.

DUFFY filled his glass as Toddleboy desired, and then waited patiently for the recital.

After taking a good pull at the grog, Toddleboy commenced as follows:

"I had been out one night, and was returning home, when I picked up Charley in a most marvellous manner."

"Picked him up!"

"That's how I came by him—I was crossing the water in a little boat with my old friend Joe Cudder—poor Joe he's dead now; but I'm forgetting my story—I was crossing the river as I before observed, and had nearly reached the Middlesex side, when I saw something in the water——"

"Any distance from the shore?"

"No, close to it, but deep enough to drown a baby, as you may suppose."

"But how came it there?"

"That's the strange part of the story—the

baby, as I have since learned was thrown there by its mother!"

"What an unnatural wretch!"

"She must have been at that time—but poor soul, I suppose her shame drove her to it, but I must tell you all that happened to me with the youngster."

"But I want to hear about its, mother, who was she?"

"That's just what I'm not going to tell you until you have heard a few of my adventures with the little Wag."

"Your adventures?"

"Yes—mine, for I had no end ot to trouble with him."

"Fire away then, I'm so anxious to hear about his mother afterwards."

"But you won't pay much attention to what concerns me."

"Oh! not at all, I want to know all about the whole affair."

"After picking him out of the water I took him to a public I used to frequent, and the landlady and the barmaid soon recovered the poor little fellow, who was very nearly dead when I got hold of him at first—well, after recovering him they began chaffing me about its being mine, but I denied it of course, and told them how I came by it."

"And they wouldn't believe you of course?"

"Believe me—not they—and to make the matter worse, Joe Cudder who was with me at the time, was *rather* 'tight,' and he agreed with them that it must be one of mine I wanted to get rid of."

"Well, how did it end?"

"Oh! the end of it was, I got put out of the house."

"Did they keep the baby?"

"Not they, I wandered about with the little thing for hours, till at last I found myself in the Haymarket."

"A nice neighbourhood for a respectable middle-aged gentleman and a baby—what did you do there?"

"Why, I turned into a tavern, where it turned out there was a supper being given by some medical students."

"Why didn't you sell the youngster to them—they would have given something for it—to cut up."

"I didn't sell him, but I did them."

"How?"

"One of them asked me if I would lend them the baby for a little while, for which he was to give me a trifle and some grog, I accepted his offer readily as you may suppose, and after drinking my grog I bolted!"

"Exactly so—I expected as much."

"That's not all."

"As far as you're concerned I suppose?"

"Not a bit of it."

"Then let's hear the rest," said Duffy, who was getting impatient to hear about the mother of Charley."

"Have some more grog?" said old Toddleboy, helping himself.

Duffy followed his example, and then waited for his companion to begin again, which he did after swallowing another tumbler of hot and strong to clear his throat.

"In the house in which I resided th er lived a young woman of the name of Williams—Sarah Williams."

"Not a very aristocratic name."

"Not very—but to go on—she was a dressmaker, and on the morning that I got rid of the baby in the Haymarket."

"Morning!"

"Yes, morning—why it was getting late before I succeeded in palming the youngster off on the chirpy-cock robins."

"Chirpy cock-robins! what the devil do you mean?"

"These medical students called themselves so, or something very like it."

"A queer name."

"Rather—but such it was. It was getting late, or rather early when I left them."

"But, what has Sarah Williams to do with?"

"Every thing—she was going to her work in the morning when she came across the baby—somewhere near the Park."

"Which park?"

"Hyde Park."

"But how came the poor little devil there?"

"It's a roundabout story, I can tell you."

"Did the chirpy, what d'ye call'ems put the youngster there?"

"No—but this is what they did—one of them had left his lodgings, but hadn't given up the key."

"Well?"

"Give a fellow time—well, this fellow proposed that they should take the little one there and leave it."

"A good joke."

"The landlady was a virgin, about forty-five years of age, and that is why they thought it would be a good spree to leave it in her house. They got in without making any noise, and finding a basket with some dirty clothes standing in the hall, they popped Master Charley into it, and made off."

"I can't see how Sarah——"

"It's as clear as mud, my dear fellow."

"It may be to you, but I'm jiggered if it is to me."

"The old spinster comes down in the morning and discovers the child. Then ensued a mutual recrimination between the spinster and the servant—the latter having first seen her mistress nursing it, accused her of being the mother of it, and then the spinster accused the girl, and the end of it was, that the servant undertook to take it away and leave it somewhere."

"But, how came you to know all about it's history after it left you?"

"Oh! from one source and another—but to continue—the girl left it in the park, and it was there discovered by Sarah Williams on her way to work."

"Ah! I see now."

"Well, at this moment a 'bobby' comes up and accuses her of deserting her child. Of course she told him that she had found the poor little thing, but the policeman wouldn't believe her."

"It didn't look very probable, did it?"

It was true. The 'bobby' went home

with her, and then it was proved her baby had died some time previously—a very short time though.'

"Her baby—was she a married woman?"

"I'm sorry to say she wasn't—she had been seduced."

"Oh! that does happen at times."

"She proved that it was not her baby, and the 'bobby' was satisfied."

"And so were you when you found the brat again, I should say."

"I was perfectly bewildered—but now you know how I came, as much as I do of Charley Wag's early history."

"Who named him?"

"We did."

"And now, about his mother?"

"I'll tell you that another time, I'm getting sleepy, and shall turn in."

"I must do the same I suppose, so good night to you, I shall expect to hear the rest to-morrow morning."

"All right—good night."

CXVII.—In which Toddleboy Astonished Duffy with the particulars of Charley Wag's Birth and Parentage.

"NOW Captain Toddleboy, I must remind you of your promise, to tell me all about Charley Wag's mother," said Duffy on the morning following his conversation with the old suitor, on the subject of Charley's early history.

"You shall hear it—and as it's a fine morning we can't do better than smoke our cigars on deck, so here goes—I'll just trouble you for a light," said Toddleboy, producing a well-filled cigar-case, and offering it to Duffy.

The two were soon seated, and then Toddleboy began

"Did you ever hear of a man called Faversham?"

"I can't say that I remember the name."

"This man and the Duke of Heatherland went to school together."

"Well?"

"And at school the duke made this Faversham his fag, and ill-used him in every possible manner."

"Every fellow must expect that, if he goes to a large school."

"To be made a fag—yes, but not to be so brutally treated as this poor devil Faversham seems to have been."

"What did the duke do to him then?"

"Poked him up the chimney."

"Oh! 1 daresay."

"It's a fact—and held him inside the fender till the wretched boy fell fainting against the bars; what do you say to that? it's not every boy that has to put up with that."

"What a brute! But has this anything to do with Charley Wag and his mother?"

"Everything."

"Then go ahead, captain."

"This state of things between the duke and Faversham continued all the time they were at school, and when they left the nobleman thought fit to persecute him in every possible manner."

"I wonder Faversham didn't murder him."

"It is strange—isn't it?"

"I should have felt a great inclination to do so, I can tell you."

"Well, later in life, when Faversham was engaged to a lady, this duke tried all he could to cut him out—but he didn't succeed."

"And Faversham married her?"

"Yes, and his grace was kicked out of the church at which the wedding took place, by Faversham's orders."

"By Jove!"

"And now comes the most terrible part of the affair. Some time after Faversham and his wife had been settled in the country, the duke determined to be revenged for the insult offered him at the church—now guess what he did?"

"Carried off the other's wife I suppose."

"Guess again—but there, you'd never guess correctly, so I'll tell you."

"That's better—but before you begin this 'terrible affair' as you call it, give me another weed."

"Help yourself."

"Now, I'm all attention again."

"The affair was a terrible one, and so you'll admit when you've heard it. This duke, with a party of friends, went down to where Faversham was living, and succeeded in getting him out of the house on some errand or other."

"After which they——"

"Stop a moment—not so fast. They seized the unfortunate man and bound him to a tree just in front of his own dwelling, and then they entered the house. The wretched Faversham could hear the screams of his beloved wife, as this villain of a duke violated her! and, finally, *saw* her perish in the flames!"

"You don't mean to say——"

"I do—these wretches, after destroying everything in the house, sacking the cellars, where they made themselves mad drunk, set fire to the house which contained Faversham's wife and the servant girls they had debauched!"

"Good God! how horrible!"

"You may well say so. Such provocation might be deemed a sufficient excuse for the atrocities Faversham has committed."

"He has committed atrocities then?"

"Done things which would make the blood curdle. I've a long account to settle with him myself; but I'll tell you about that another time—and now I'll go on with what particularly relates to Charley Wag. The Duke of Heatherland was going to be married, and Faversham conceived the diabolical idea of having his graces affianced bride dishonoured."

"Incredible!"

"True, my dear sir."

"Is it possible that a man can be such a scoundrel?"

"And then this monster pounced upon an unfortunate creature to carry his plot into execution."

"As great a scoundrel as himself I should think."

" No, I believe not. Faversham took steps to place this man entirely in his power, and then dictated his terms to him."

" But how did they succeed in carrying out this devilish scheme?"

" Oh! easily enough, as it happened, Maud Allingham, the lady the duke was going to marry, was at this time staying with some friends in Park Lane, and Faversham thought this would be a favourable opportunity for the execution of his plan."

" In Park Lane?" Not quite the place I should have chosen for such an affair."

" Nor did he——"

" I thought you said——"

" You won't let me go on in my own way, you're in such a deuced hurry."

" Well, fire away, captain."

" Faversham's scheme was to induce this young girl to proceed on a journey."

" Ah! now I begin to twig."

" And for this purpose he forged a telegraphic message, purporting to come from the family physician of the Allinghams."

" Recalling Maud I suppose."

" Exactly so—it stated that her mother, Lady Allingham, was dangerously ill, suggested that Maud should return, and even went so far as to mention the train by which she could do so, and on the arrival of which the carriage would be awaiting her at the station !"

" What a designing scoundrel !"

" Then the villain summoned the wretched man whom he had bound by an oath to assist him in anything he should have to do, and communicated to him the service he required him to perform."

" I should think Mr. Faversham met with an indignant refusal for his pains."

" He did at first ; but the wily ruffian taunted his victim in various ways, hinting that to break his solemn promise was as dishonourable as committing the crime proposed."

" The fellow was surely never led away by such reasoning ?"

" Perhaps not so much by Faversham's reasoning on the subject, as by the powerful influence he exerted upon everybody that came in his way—added to this the unfortunate Horford."

" Horford !"

" Yes, Horford—do you know him ?"

" No, I can't say I do—but I've heard my godfather, Admiral Spanker, speak of him very often, and wonder what had become of him. Was his name John or Jack ?"

" Yes—he used to be called Handsome Jack."

" The same fellow—how strange ! why he used to be, I've heard the admiral say, the Duke of Heatherland's most intimate friend."

" He was one of the party that went down to Faversham's house in the Country and took part in the frightful affair I have already told you about."

" Is it possible ! and that he should have been chosen by Faversham as the instrument of his vengeance !

" It might have been intentional on Faversham's part, picking him up—at all events, he's deep enough for anything. This wretch-

ed Horford at last consented to the perpetration of this attrocity upon the unsusbecting Maud Allingham."

" Then he must have been as great a scoundrel as the other."

" Not quite—brandy had a great deal to do with it."

" Brandy. What do you mean —did he get drunk."

" Not exactly—but, for all that, brandy had a great deal to do with it ; and you would be astonished at the effect of some sorts of brandy upon people—doctored brandy especially. I experienced the influence of Doctor Faversham's doctored brandy once, and I know that its effect is most powerful."

" Faversham's been dosing you—the devil ! let me hear all about it ?"

" Not now—that must come in when I tell you why I have an account to settle with him ; but to continue about Horford—I've every reason to believe that Faversham had plied the unfortunate man with some of his cursed stuff, and in that state had made him promise to commit the crime. At all events the promise was made."

" But was it performed ?"

" It was. Maud Allingham fell into the snare, and took her departure for the North ; and at the London terminus Horford met her. watched her into a carriage of which she had engaged a compartment, and then took his seat in the adjoining coupe."

" Well, what followed ?"

" You may guess."

" But how the deuce did he get into the carriage?"

" You, a sailor, and ask such a question. Don't you think it would be easy enough to pass from one carriage to another along the wooden platform which runs along the side?"

" Yes, but to get in at the door is another thing, they are often locked in express trains I believe."

" Yes, but only on one side—but to make sure, Faversham had in someway or other possessed himself of one of the keys, and so Horford had not the slightest difficulty in letting himself into the very carriage Maud Allingham had engaged—and now to pass over the most horrible part of it, and to make a long story short, Horford ravished her !"

" Good Go ! ! how terrible."

" He then left the train at Bradford."

" But did she give no alarm on reaching the station ?"

" Not the slightest, the poor girl had fainted, and was insensible when the train stopped at Bradford, where Horford alighted."

" Then of course he escaped undetected."

" Yes, and returned to London, and shortly after sailed for Australia—in a few days infact."

" And what became of Maud Allingham ?"

" Oh ! she married the Duke of Heatherland."

" After what had happened ?"

" Yes,"

" How long after ?"

" A month or so—I can't say possitively."

" And Charley Wag was her first son ?"

" Exactly so, she contrived in some comprehensible manner to hide her state from the duke, and on the plea of ill-health, went into the country on a visit to a friend, to whom she confided her secret."

"That was some months after her marriage, I suppose?"

"Yes, and the duke being very much occupied with his ministerial duties, rather approved of the step she had taken, than otherwise."

"And did not accompany her."

"Not he, he found plenty of amusement in his young wife's absence in Westminster."

"A matter of taste—but I must say, I should have preferred the society of a pretty woman to the companionship of all the peers of the realm."

"Very likely, but how about the peeresses?"

"Oh! that's another thing entirely."

"Well, I can't say that his grace created any public scandal in his own circle, but this I know, he was the support of the house I have just mentioned in Westminster."

"Who kept it?"

"A woman named Crow—Mother Crow, as she was familiarly termed by her patrons."

"And what sort of place was it?"

"First rate."

"You've been there yourself, and speak from experience. Eh? old gentleman, That's how you amuse yourself when you're ashore—is it?" said Duffy, poking the old salt in the ribs."

"No, you're on the wrong tack, youngster, I only know the place by name, though I daresay I could find it if I wanted to do so."

"I daresay you could, but you don't mean to say, that the Duke of Heatherland patronised such a place, and so soon after his marriage with Maud Allingham."

"He certainly did, and has continued to do I'm told."

"He must be old now."

"Yes—and now I've told you all I know about Charley Wag."

"You've astonished me not a little I can tell you."

"And I hope given you an appetite for tiffen, which this youngster is about to announce," replied Toddleboy, as a little negro approached.

"I feel as hungry as a hunter."

"Then come along," replied the old sailor, as he led the way to the cabin.

"You must tell what your grudge is against Faversham," said Duffy, as they descended the cabin stairs.

"When we return on deck will be time enough for that—I must wet my whistle first, or I shall be as hoarse as a raven after the jawbation of this morning."

CXVIII.—TODDLEBOY TELLS DUFFY A LITTLE ABOUT FAVERSHAM AND HIS GOINGS ON AT SAINT-STARVER-CUM-BAG-O'-BONES.

"YOU must know," said old Toddleboy, as soon as they returned upon deck and were again seated, "that I was not always a pirate."

"I didn't suppose that you were."

"In fact I did not occupy so good a position as the commander of my own ship."

"Indeed! but you were brought up to the sea—were you not?"

"Certainly not. I was intended for the church—but somehow or other it didn't come off, and after a great many occupations, none of which were suited to me, I found myself a light porter to Messrs. Bottle and Bung, drysalters, of Garlic Hill. Do you know Garlic Hill?"

"Never heard of such a place that I know of."

"And next door to Messrs. Bottle and Bung's is a milliner's establishment," said the old sailor, with a wink at his younger companion, "where I passed the best part of a night once, and a little of the morning."

"A knowing old dog, I'll be bound."

"You won't say so when you hear how I came there though."

"Let me judge for myself, so spit it out as soon as you like."

"It's a part of my story, so you won't hear it until I come to it. As I have already told you my last occupation was that of light porter."

"At Bottle and Bung's, next to the milliner's; pity you couldn't get employment there," said Duffy.

"I shouldn't have objected; but Miss Gusset was not the sort of person to employ a man about her premises."

"Too knowing, I suppose."

"Yes, well you may fancy my acquaintances were not of the arristocratic order—indeed, they were anything but swells, my most intimate companion being a boatman, named Cudder. Poor Joe—he's dead, and it's about his death that I have the grudge against Faversham and his accomplice Bloodyer."

"That's a good sort of name."

"Too good for the scoundrel, who rejoices in it."

"Who may he be?"

"The master of Saint Starver-Cum-Bag-o'Bones workhouse."

"What had he to do with your friend the boatman."

"What had he to do with?—killed him, that's all—but no, that's not all."

"What the deuce more did he do?"

"Sold his body."

"The devil!"

"You'd hardly believe it—but I've been told this sort of thing is by no means an uncommon occurrence in most of the workhouses—one of the master's perquisites."

"By jingo, clear profit—but let me hear about this unfortunate Codger."

"Cudder."

"Ah!—Cudder."

"Poor Joe was taken ill—not very bad, but too ill to work, and as Joe hadn't any private property to keep him in idleness, he was obliged to avail himself of the generosity of the rate-payers of the parish of Saint Starver."

"Turned pauper in fact."

" Yes, Joe went into the workhouse, and there I went to see him. The poor fellow was but a shadow of what he had been a short time previously." .

" Had they starved him ?"

" Doctored him to within an inch of his life."

" The workhouse master ?"

" And Faversham—but just let you into what happened to me there. I had some difficulty in getting to see Joe Cudder, but at last I succeeded. The poor fellow was almost insensible when I entered the ward in which he was lying, but when I went to his bedside—he recognised me. When Bloodyer and Faversham saw this, they wished me to retire, saying that it was against the rules of the workhouse to allow strangers to remain so long, and I don't know what else beside."

" You didn't go, I hope."

" Not a bit of it—poor Joe was now raving and screaming in my ear about them murdering the paupers and selling their bodies."

" Faversham and Bloodyer standing by ?"

" Both of them, Joe continued to rave, till at length Bloodyer seized hold of me and dragged me away from the bed. I was not so strong then as I am now, but I struggled with him—it was useless, however ; but this I know, that Joe's screams ceased directly we were outside the door of the ward."

Here Toddleboy paused.

" What do you think happened, Captain ?"

" Faversham gave him a dose which finished him. That's my opinion, and I'm not far out I reckon."

" How did you get on with Bloodyer ?"

" He asked me into his private room, and began to soap me down a little, and hinted that all I had heard was nothing more than the raving of a maniac—not a vestige of truth in his statement. Then he touched upon the injury it would do him should the mention of such an affair get about, and concluded by asking me to take a glass of brandy, as he felt sure I must require it after the scene I had witnessed up-stairs."

" And you drank the brandy ?"

" Yes—I have always had a weakness for it. I think it was my partiality for it somehow operated against my entering the church, for which, as I have already told you, I was educated. Well, to go on, I had another glass when the doctor joined us."

" Faversham ?"

" Yes, and then I began to feel queer."

" What, after two glasses ?"

" Yes, my dear fellow, you must remember that the brandy was doctored."

" That's another thing."

" And then the room seemed capering about with me. But here comes Gasket, I must attend to him, and go on with my yarn afterwards."

___

CXIX.—A CONVERSATION AS TO HOW TODDLEBOY AND DUFFY SHOULD RETURN TO ENGLAND.

" WELL, Gasket, what's up ?" said Toddleboy, as the mate joined them."

" The land's in sight, sir. What do you and Mr. Duffy propose doing when we get to Fayal ?"

" Go ashore to be sure, Gasket, what would you have us do ?"

" You misunderstand me, captain : do you think it will be safe for you to land there ?"

" I should think so, and, what is more, I feel very much inclined to try it on," returned the old sailor.

" I was going to say, sir, that we should all be delighted to take you home in the Scud."

" I wouldn't hear of such a thing—the risk would be too great my dear Gasket. I appreciate your kindness, and the kindness of the crew, but at the same time I cannot consent to your exposing yourselves so recklessly for my convenience."

" It would be all up with you before you reached the Channel I'm afraid," said Duffy, who was rather anxious to take his passage to England in a steamer.

" I don't think we should escape myself," said Gasket.

" Then, under the circumstances, I don't think we'll avail ourselves of your kind offer, Gasket, but land, as I before proposed, at Fayal, and take our passages home in a steamer."

" It would be rather awkward if one of our cruisers happened to be there and spotted the Scud," said Duffy.

" Devilish awkward I admit, but we must chance it," replied Toddleboy. " There's one good thing no one knows me, and we may land with impunity, besides we can describe ourselves as prisoners. You are a prisoner, and your story can be vouched for, and no one will know the truth of the twister 1 can spin them."

" Then you will not let us give you a passage home in the Scud," said Gasket.

" Not further on our way than Fayal," replied Toddleboy.

" Very well, captain ; you know that we are willing enough to go home with you if you wish it."

" I'm sure of it, Gasket ; but you will see the reason of my refusal to accept your kind offer."

" What do you propose that we should do then, captain, when we get into the harbour—drop anchor, or only lay to ?"

" I should suggest your laying to—just long enough to put us ashore, and no longer."

" But the mischief will be done, should one of the cruisers be in there when we get in," said Duffy."

" Well, it can't be helped," said Toddleboy, " we must make the best of it—and now, Gasket, I should like you to go about, so as not to go in until the evening."

" It shall be done, sir," said the officer.

" And now come along, Duffy and I'll tell you the rest of the yarn about my experience in the workhouse."

Saying this, old Toddleboy again seated himself, and Gasket went off to give directions for putting the Scud about."

The men were soon at their quarters, everything was in readiness, and at the word from the chief-officer, who had now assumed command of the *Scud*, went round on the other tack, and stood away from the land.

———

CXX.—In which Toddleboy continues the Narrative of his experience at Saint-Starver-Cum-Bag-o'Bones.

"I THINK I left off at where they gave me the brandy?"

"Yes, two glasses of which served you up."

"Exactly so, well, the room went round and round with me, and I felt my head in a whirl, I could see two Favershams and two Bloodyers."

"In short you could see double."

"That I did, and at last, I think, instead of four faces I saw four hundred."

"I should think you felt rather astonished."

"I did, as long as my senses lasted, but I was not in possession of them long."

"What did they do with you?"

"I'm hanged if I know, for I remember nothing more until I recovered, and then I found myself in a sort of dead-house!"

"By Jove!"

"And I'll tell you something else."

"Well, what?"

"I had nothing on me but my shirt."

"Was the night cold?"

"It was devilish cold, and so I found it wandering about."

"You contrived to escape from the dead-house, then?"

"Yes—but how I can never clearly recollect, I have some faint idea of a row with a policeman and a ride with a drunken swell in a cab, but beyond that I haven't the slightest notion."

"Did you get insensible again?"

"No, but I still remained in a hazy state."

"And don't you remember where you went to with the drunken swell?"

"No, but it's my firm conviction that it was his intention to turn me adrift in the Haymarket!"

"What a spree!"

"It might have been a spree for the lookers on, but certainly not for me."

"And where did you eventually find yourself?"

"After wandering about for some time I found myself not very far from my employers warehouse."

"Aha! old gentleman, close to the milliner's without your——, but there I'll spare your feelings."

"Close to the milliner's, and as I couldn't get into Bottle and Bung's place, I contrived to secret myself in a cupboard in the millinery establishment!"

"How the deuce did you manage to get in?"

"The girls were just arriving—it was getting late—so I slipped in after them, and took up my position in the cupboard."

"Lucky that none of them caught you in there."

"Unfortunately they did."

"And there was an awful shindy I suppose."

"Frightful—they were going to give me in charge, and the devil knows what else beside. I don't think the girls were so much horrified as the proprietress of the establishment herself."

"A sour old spinster I suppose."

"Just so—Miss Gussit, for such was her name, affected to be frightfully shocked, and to make the matter worse, one of the girls suggested the probability of its being Miss Gusset's young man who was in the cupboard. You may suppose this riled the ancient maid, and the unfortunate girl would have been dismissed in a twinkling had the others split about it."

"And you were still without anything on you."

"I covered myself with some of their cloaks and shawls, and came forth."

"Did you get locked up?"

"No—I got into Bottle and Bung's place after all, and there I had some old clothes, with which I quickly arrayed myself, and then went home. I think I've told you now why I've a grudge against Faversham, and that other scoundrel, Bloodyer, not only for killing poor Joe Cudder, but for trying to get rid of me as well."

"But you have not told me how it was that you became a sailor."

"I'll tell you that some other day, on the passage home."

"Very well, captain, I'll take care and keep you to your promise."

"By jove it's getting late—how the time passes when a fellow's yarning—we must be getting our traps ready for going ashore."

"Our traps—unfortunately I didn't bring a large supply on board with me," said Duffy, with a smile.

"So much the better, for I've too many—that is to say, if I have to describe myself to the authorities on shore as having been plundered by the pirates who have just landed us, so a portion of my luggage will go down as yours."

"A bright idea."

"And now let's go below."

Toddleboy and Duffy then left the deck together, and the former was soon engaged in his preparations for going ashore.

The day passed away slowly to our friend Duffy, who was most anxious to set his foot on dry land once more, and he was not at all sorry when the shades of night began to fall, when the order to "'bout ship" was given.

———

A DISCOVERY.

CXXI.—The Landing at Fayal.

BY the time the *Scud* neared the harbour it was quite dark, and Toddleboy prepared to leave the ship and crew he had so long commanded.

As a measure of precaution, the *Scud* was "hove to" at some distance from the land. The boat which was to convey the late captain and Duffy ashore was lowered, and manned by six of the crew, who had drawn lots for the honour of escorting their old commander; the luggage was all carefully stowed, and the men already seated awaiting the skipper, who was busily engaged in bidding adieu to his old shipmates, from whom he could not part without the most sincere feelings of regret.

There were still remaining in the crew a few of the men, who were on board the ship in the Thames, to which Toddleboy was conveyed after he had been attacked by the men who tried to rob him of the gold which he had found upon the sailor, who, as it will be remembered, ran against Toddleboy in Shadwell, and cannoned off the old gentleman—a corpse.

To these men the old sailor had much to say at parting, for to them he felt he owed everything. To each he made a handsome present as a mark of his gratitude, beside which, every one in the ship's company,

No. 71

from Mr. Gasket, or, as he was now called, Captain Gasket, down to the little negro boy, who officiated as captain's steward, received some memento of the kind old man, who was about to leave them.

"Good-bye, my lads," said the old sailor, as they crowded round him, each man grasping his hand in their own horny and tar-stained paws. "Good-bye, my lads, continue to believe as you have always done with me, and Captain Gasket will never have any cause to complain. Do this—if only for my sake."

"We will! we will!" shouted the brave fellows in chorus.

"And above all things, my men," continued Toddleboy, "never shed blood uselessly, and I need not add—never surrender the *Scud*."

"Never! never!" shouted the crew as one voice.

"Once more, I bid you farewell," said old Toddleboy, in a husky voice, as he passed over the side, followed by Duffy, and the good wishes of his late crew. The oars were shipped, and the brawny arms of the stout fellows in the boat were stretched to their work, and soon the *Scud* was lost in the darkness, and the shore approached.

"Now, my fine fellows," said Toddleboy, as they neared the landing-place, "we must bid you all good-bye, for it won't do for the shore folks to see us shaking the slippers of a pirate boat's crew—they won't believe the yarn I may have to spin 'em."

At this speech the men jumped up, and again the old commander was grasping the horny palms of his faithful shipmates.

At the conclusion of this demonstration of mutual affection, the men resumed their seats and oars, and the boat was laid alongside the landing-place.

A short time only was occupied in transferring the luggage to the quay; after which, by the brave fellows, who had conveyed Toddleboy and Duffy, they made off again as fast as possible to rejoin the *Scud*.

"It's to be hoped we shall find some one to carry these traps for us, or by jingo we shall be in a fix," said Toddleboy."

"Sure to," replied Duffy."

He had hardly said the words when a posse of porters pounced upon the luggage, and commenced bearing it off, followed by Toddleboy and Duffy.

"We had better let them go, they know the way to the hotels better than you or I," said the latter to the old salt, who was about to lay violent hands on the nearest of these officious fellows, for daring to touch his worldly possessions without his permission.

"After all, perhaps you are right, but we may as well ask them where they are taking us to."

"You can do that if you like, replied Duffy.

Toddleboy did so, and one of the men having given a satisfactory answer, the substance of which was, that they were going to the best hotel in the island, our two friends followed close in their wake, and were not long before they found themselves located in very comfortable quarters in (as the porters had already said) the best hotel the island boasted.

It was late when they got ashore, and our two friends were not long before they turned in, but before doing so Toddleboy inquired when the next packet would sail for England, and learning that it would leave the following day, he dispatched the commissionaire of the hotel, late as it was, to engage berths for himself and Duffy.

In a short time the man returned with the announcement, that all was arranged.

"That's satisfactory," said Duffy, "now we can sleep soundly," he added, when they were alone, "and as we shall have to be up early, I think the sooner we get to bed the better."

"So do I, I'm awfully tired."

"Then to bed we'll go," said the old boy, putting out his huge paw for Duffy to shake, "I'll rouse you in the morning."

"At what time does the steamer leave?"

"Eight o'clock."

"By jove! that's early."

"So much the better—the sooner we get away from here, the sooner I shall feel secure."

"As for that matter I don't think there's the slightest cause for apprehension."

"I'm not so certain about that myself, we landed in a very mysterious manner last night. It's not as though we came from a ship at anchor in the harbour. We shall have to tell the tale of the pirate on board the packet after all."

"I think the way in which I was captured will startle a few of them."

"I think I'll leave you to spin the cuffer—you bring me in somehow or other, and what you say I'll swear to."

"That'll top it—now I'll turn in, and don't you forget to rouse me out early, captain."

"About four bells?"

"That'll do gloriously."

CXXII.—BLOODYER AND HIS BEADLE—How TWO RESPECTABLE TRADESMEN ALLOW THEMSELVES TO BE BRIBED—FAVERSHAM ONCE MORE THE DOCTOR AT SAINT STARVER'S.

WHEN Faversham and Bloodyer separated, the latter was undecided whether to procure his companion in guilt the appointment as doctor to Saint-Starver-Cum-Bag-o'-Bones workhouse or not; but subsequent reflection on the matter convinced him that it would be to his advantage to secure so able a colleague. "It is true," said Bloodyer to himself, "I have done a long while without him; but at the same time, I *might* make a mistake, and then——"

Here the idea of the gallows struck him, and this it seems decided the matter.

"Yes!" continued he aloud, striking the table with his hand. "Yes! he shall have the appointment, as sure as my name is Bloodyer."

"Beg pardon, guv'ner, what did you say?"

This question was asked by that important personage, the beadle of Saint Starver, who had at that moment just looked in to see how the master was, and to get a toothful of brandy, having been engaged in disposing of a few paupers corpses a short time previously.

"What did you say, guv'nor?"

"Nothing."

"That's a crammer, for I heard you say it."

"Say what?"

"Or else my name ain't Bloodyer—that's what you said."

"Well, what more have you to say—you want some brandy, I suppose."

"Yes, and I was a going to say——"

"Out with it—what is it?"

"You're mighty short with a fellow to-nigth guv'nor—what's riled yer?"

"Nothing that I know of."

"A billious attack I s'pose—well, take my advice, and that is—s'posing you 'ave a billious attack—a bull-dog and a driver."

"I'm in no humour for your jokes, if you have anything to say to me on business, say it, and go."

"That's uncommon perlite, I must say—well, how about the brandy?"

"Help yourself."

"That's better, and now guv'nor, I'll get to business—one of the two as you are a dosing of at present is uncommon bad jist at present, leastways he was 'arf an' our ago—but p'rhaps he's kicked it by this time."

"Which one do you mean?" asked Bloodyer, anxiously.

"The young'nn, he's terrible tough, and don't seem noways inclined to die heasy."

"Let him die in his own fashion."

"That's all wery well, mister, but you see one of the nusses jist said to me—

"'Mr. Grimes,' sez she, 'I'm blest if I don't think that 'ere pauper's taken pison. The devil! says I, why? 'Cause he's just like a chap I seed die in the 'ospital as had taken pison, sez she."

"Of course you said she was mistaken in the symptoms."

"'Course I did; but she didn't seem to pay much regard to what I said about it—leastways, she said gammon."

Bloodyer seemed agitated at the information of the beadle, and for some time he remained silent, during which interval his companion occupied himself in consuming brandy.

At last the workhouse master broke the silence.

"I'm afraid, Grimes, we have dosed these two last injudiciously; I would not use the quick medicine at once, for fear of exciting the suspicion of the nurses, and the very thing I wanted to avoid has happened. Who is the woman that made these remarks to you?"

"Sarah Spriggins is her name."

"Where did she come from?"

"One of the hospitals; but I don't know who recommended her."

"It doesn't much matter who did—she's too knowing for us—she must go before she finds out anything—you must bring a charge of some sort or other against her."

"I can easily do that, for all the nurses breaks the rules every day, and I can catch her on the hop."

"Don't be too hasty, or, perhaps, she may blab the very thing we want kept dark."

"Well, I'll see as she goes on some charge or other, and let me advise you, guv'nor, get Mister Faversham back as soon as you can, or I'm blowed if we shan't get into a mess, and no two ways about it."

"As soon as I can get his appointment settled I will—the two others can easily be beaten out of the field—that is to say, if there is anything known against their characters."

"I think it would be a werry 'ard case, if so be, in a parish like Saint-Starver-Cum-bag-o'-Bones, we couldn't find one or two as was willing to say something against their charactus on a pinch," said Mr. Grimes, with a leer, which seemed to convey its meaning pretty clearly to his intelligent companion.

"Certainly it would be very hard indeed," chuckled Bloodyer, who forthwith determined to act upon the suggestion of his unscrupulous accomplice. "Who would be the best person to undertake this affair think you?"

The beadle considered for a short time, and then replied—

"I should think about the best person as could be put upon this 'ere matter is Bullock—he's a churchwarden, and carries weight in the parish; and next to him there's Measurem, the undertaker—he's always ready to serve a friend living or dead."

"You think these would be the men to employ?"

"Certainly—'cause why? they've both men under 'em, which they can make say anything—twig?"

"I understand. I will write to both of them at once—you can either wait for the letters, or return for them presently."

"Then I'll be back in 'arf an 'our."

Bloodyer immediately sat down, and penned the letters to the two worthies mentioned by the beadle, as fitting persons to be employed to blacken the characters of the medical men who were candidates for the appointment of surgeon to the workhouse of Saint Starver, in opposition to Faversham.

In less than an hour the beadle had delivered and returned with satisfactory answers to these letters. The churchwarden and the undertaker would do all that laid in their power to serve their friend Bloodyer, and, of course, friend Bloodyer would be expected to serve them in some way at another time.

A few weeks after found Faversham once more assisting in the wholesale murders at the workhouse. The victims were once more scientifically deprived of life, and not in the bungling manner in which the business had been executed lately.

The chances of detection were now lessened considerably. Bloodyer felt this, and rejoiced in his own fancied security.

But beware!

The avenger is drawing nigh.

And Faversham was again in his element.

Again sacrificing the lives of dozens of his fellow-creatures.

And for what purpose?

God knows.

CXXIII.—THE PASSAGE HOME—TODDLEBOY TELLS DUFFY HOW HE BECAME A SAILOR.

ON the following morning Captain Toddleboy and Lieutenant Horatio Spanker Duffy found themselves on board the steamer homeward bound. There were several passengers beside themselves, to whom Duffy found it necessary to spin the yarn about his capture by the pirate, at the same time carefully avoiding to mention the vessel's name; but Toddleboy was not so discreet. To a nervous lady who appeared to be very much terrified at the idea of pirates, the old rogue spoke of the commander of the *Scud* as a most blood-thirsty ruffian; describing him as a man who had been known on one occasion, when a lady who happened to have twins fell into his clutches, to have treated her with the most unheard-of barbarity, and, finally, to have lashed the babies to the fore-yard, one at the starboard-yard-arm, the other at the port, and then coolly fired at them with a double-barrelled shot gun, until their blessed little bodies were riddled!

"Good heavens! sir, you really do not mean to say that such an atrocity was committed in the nineteenth century?"

"Nineteenth century! ma'am—not nineteen months ago!"

"Oh! dear, oh! dear, what a monster! Indeed what you have told me has quite alarmed me."

The poor lady was evidently frightened, and Toddleboy thought it would be only right to inform her that this barbarous captain was not in the habit of frequenting the waters they were then in. This served to allay her fears a little, but still every ship she saw she fancied must be the celebrated *Scud*, and went into hysterics accordingly.

"I shan't say any more to her about it," said old Toddleboy one day, after a terrific attack of hysteria, "I shall devote my energies to that plummy piece of goods with the roguish eyes."

The lady alluded to might have been from five-and-thirty to forty years of age, a widow, and, as the old gentleman expressively termed her, decidedly a plummy one. She seemed greatly to admire the fine old sailor, who might have passed muster as an admiral—indeed he looked a greater swell than most admirals, who, as a body, are rather a seedy-looking race.

The end of all this was, that the old Trojan proposed, and was accepted by the buxom widow.

"If I don't board the captain I shall never hear how he became a sailor, and I'm rather curious to know," said Duffy to himself, one day when they were not many day's sail from the chops of the Channel. "I'll be down upon him this very day, and by jingo! there he is, and for a wonder Mrs. Dewberry is not with him."

"I say, guv'nor, when are you going to tell me how you became a gallant Jack Tar?"

"Ah! my dear boy, I have had so little time lately, that I really haven't had time for anything."

"That comes of love-making you see."

"Ah! well! old fools are the worst of fools —but really I might do worse—she's a monstrous fine woman."

"Yes, she's all that, and I admire your taste; but I very much want to hear your story, and I don't thank her for monopolising you."

"She won't annoy you to-day, she's had a bad headache, and is confined to her berth."

"Dear me, I'm very sorry to hear it—then you'll be able to spin me the yarn to-day?"

"At once, if you like my boy."

"Be it so," replied Duffy, "no time like the present, so begin."

"I don't think I told you I had three months for that little affair at the milliners."

"Three months! you don't mean to say——"

"But I do though, sure enough, at Spike Island."

"But you told me that you got into Bottle and Bung's place after all, put on your clothes, and then went home."

"Very likely I did tell you so—I hadn't made up my mind to tell you all I knew then. I do spin twisters sometimes, but now I'll make a clean breast of it."

Duffy here seated himself, and prepared to listen to the old man's narrative.

"You'd hardly believe that they would have given me three months for such a trifling affair as being found in a cupboard?"

"I don't know about three months—it was rather stiff—but I must say the circumstances were rather suspicious. A man with only his shirt on in a cupboard remember."

"Well, to continue, after I came out of 'chokey' I didn't know what the deuce to do with myself. I was getting old, and, beside which, I had been so long at Bottle and Bung's that I didn't feel fit for much else. After wandering about the whole day without having tasted anything, I found myself somewhere in the neighbourhood of Tower Hill."

"What the deuce took you down there?"

"One place was just as good as another to me then, and, as it turned out, I couldn't have chosen a better road. You may fancy that I stood in need of something to cheer me up a bit, and you may imagine how comfortable half a quartern made me."

"Had you any tin to get it?"

"Devil a copper. A good-natured fellow who saw how miserable I looked stood a treat. The gin warmed me up first-rate, and after a little while I dropped off to sleep. But the infernal landlord didn't let me stay there long, though I should think, between you and I, my snooze lasted for two or three hours. Sleeping was against the rules, and if I wanted a bed anywhere I had better look after one at once."

"You did not find it particularly pleasant I should think in turning out of the warm bar into the street?"

"It was frightful, but then there was no help for it—so I gathered my poor old bones together, and set off on the tramp. I walked along, more to keep myself warm than for any other reason—the night was terribly raw and cold, to say nothing of the rain, which came down considerably every now and then. I had got on to the open space just on Tower Hill, and was going to cross it, as the other side of the way looked a trifle more inviting than the side I had been walking on, when I heard footsteps coming up behind me. I turned round quickly, for I didn't feel anxious to get knocked over I can tell you."

" And as a motter of course——"

" I did get knocked over. This fellow came full butt against me, and down we both went—and, what is more, I got a very ugly crack at the back of my skull when falling.

" Did you two fellows come to blows about it ?"

" Blows ! bless you, no. The blow I got was bad enough in all conscience, and the rap which settled him must have been a trifle harder."

" Settled him ?"

" Yes, settled him. When I recovered my senses, which were rather scattered, I looked round, though not expecting to see the fellow, but judge how astonished I must have been to find him close alongside me lying quite still."

" By the piper ! you did feel queer I reckon."

" Queer's no word for it. I shook him, but he didn't answer; I shouted to him, and it's a wonder I didn't bring the bobbies round me by doing so ; but, as luck would have it, they were all out of the way at the time."

" He wasn't dead then ?"

" Dead as a door nail. I was awfully frightened, for it was rather an awkward position for a fellow to be placed in ; and you may depend if they had found me alongside this dead fellow, I should have had some little difficulty in proving that I hadn't murdered him."

" Your friend at Quod Street would have done his best to have you strung up I reckon."

" It wasn't to be, and no one interfered with me or the unfortunate man who had just kicked the bucket."

" He really was dead then ?"

" Oh ! yes—the blood had trickled from his mouth and nose, and altogether he looked a very ghastly object."

" I think I should have bolted."

" And so I should but for one thing."

" What was that ?"

" In trying to raise the man a coat, which was hanging on his arm, fell, and something chinked."

" Money ?"

" Gold ! there was no mistaking the sound of it."

" What the devil did you do with it ?"

" I touched it with my foot, and then I was certain of it. I don't know whether you will call it robbery or not, but the end of it was, that I put on the coat with the bag of sovereigns in the pocket."

" I think it was a devilish near share to robbery, to make the best of it," said Duffy.

" I think so myself, but then what the deuce could I do ? I had no place to shelter me, and, until then, no means of obtaining so much as a loaf."

" Well, we'll call it robbery under extenuating circumstances."

" Exactly so."

" And so your conscience was easy on the matter—but go on."

" I made off with my prize at a rapid rate, for I couldn't help fancying some one was dodging me. At last, being awfully tired and worn out, I dived into a dingy little coffee shop up a slum, and slunk into the gloomiest of the boxes."

" And did no one interfere with you ?"

" Not a soul, at least not then—there was only a sailor boy in the place, and he was lying with his head on the table fast asleep. I ordered some coffee of the girl, and then it struck me I should have to change one of the sovereigns to pay for it. I thought it would look funny, but there was no help for it."

" Not so very funny either—I've often changed a sovereign for a cup of coffee."

" For a cup of coffee at Verey's, but not for a pint of slops at a crib not many miles from Shadwell."

" Well, I can't say that I have."

" You seem quite to forget the difference, my dear Duffy. The girl seemed perfectly astonished when I handed her a piece of gold in payment. She opened her eyes wide enough at any rate."

" She changed it I suppose."

" Yes, after trying it for about a quarter of an hour, first with her teeth, and then by ringing it. I wished her at Jericho for being so long, for I wanted to count my money, and I did not care about displaying my wealth to her. At last she came and gave me my change, and then left me to myself again."

" Then you began to count the tin."

" I did, and found myself the possessor of rather more than three hundred pounds."

" A deuced good haul."

" Pretty fair—though I don't think much of such a sum now."

" I should think your late profession was a paying one."

" At times—latterly it has been very good—so good that it induced me to give it up while I was a rich man. That three hundred pounds laid the foundation of the large fortune I have since realised."

" Could you find out who the fellow was who tumbled down dead alongside you ?"

" His name was Cook, Richard Cook, at least so I made out by some letters and papers I found in his pocket. There was also a ticket-of-leave in his name—so Mister Cook had been no better than he ought to be. This rather pleased me ; I felt confident that he came by his gold in an unfair manner, so that my scruples at appropriating it were not so violent as they might have been, had I found out he was a respectable member of society ; added to which I meant to stick to the tin, blow high, blow low, and stick to it I did."

" I think you were perfectly justified in doing so, considering your circumstances at the time."

" The next thing to be thought of, after counting my tin, was to get a bed, and this was an awful puzzler."

"Didn't they let beds at the coffee shop?"

"They might have done so, but something prevented me asking. I told you that there was a sailor boy sleeping with his head on the table, when I entered the coffee shop."

"Yes, I remember."

"Well, to my dismay I saw this ugly young scoundrel watching me."

"Had he seen you counting the money?"

"So it turned out. I had determined upon asking the girl if they let beds, when I saw this fellow looking at me."

"And then I suppose you thought it better to slope?"

"Which I soon after did."

"How about the sailor?"

"He followed; but to make a long story short he must have communicated with some pals, and before I had gone very far I was attacked, and might have been murdered but——"

"But you weren't."

"No, or you wouldn't have been captured by me. I might have been murdered had it not been for the timely assistance that was rendered me."

"By whom?"

"By a party of sailors who were attracted to the spot by my cries. I was terribly mauled by the blows I had received from the murderous villains they had just rescued me from, and as they carried me along I fainted away."

"And where did you find yourself on your recovery?"

"Now comes the commencement of my career. I found myself in the cabin of a vessel lying on a sofa, surrounded by several very jovial-looking fellows, who were all smoking large pipes, and pegging away at large glasses of boiling hot grog."

"Rather better company than you had been in, a short time previously."

"So I thought—but to go on with my yarn, the first thing I thought of was my money, and I asked after it. 'It's all right,' replied one of the men, as he pointed to the pilot-coat on the table, and the bag of gold lying beside it."

"You weren't sorry to hear that, I'll swear."

"I felt delighted, and returned my preservers my sincerest thanks, after which I acted upon their suggestion, and went to sleep, and I think I never had a more comfortable snooze in my life."

"Not even in the public after the half-quartern."

"Ah! that was a sweet sleep."

"But, who were your friends with the jovial faces?"

"Smugglers, and a jollier set of dogs I never clapped my eyes upon."

"And were these the fellows who first initiated you into the mysteries of boxing the compass?"

"Yes, these were the very men who first made a sailor of me, putting me up to getting a vessel, and volunteering to serve under me."

"A mutual accommodation."

"So I found it—and thus, I became a sailor, Duffy, and from smuggling in a small way, I got on by degrees until I purchased the *Scud*, and turned pirate."

"I'm blest, if you're not one of the most extraordinary birds I have ever come across," said Duffy at the conclusion of the old sailor's yarn.

"And so you would say if you could have seen me a few years ago—why I was a mere bag of bones, with a gin and watery constitution, not worth twopence."

"You look hale and hearty enough now, I shall see you the father of a small family yet."

"Exceedingly small, I should say. By the bye, that reminds me, I must go and inquire after Mrs. Dewberry," said Toddleboy."

"I hope the poor lady is better," observed Duffy; "but at the same time I hope she wont monopolise you for the rest of the day, I want you to tell me some of the curious scenes you have witnessed during your piratical career."

"I want to have a little conversation with you, but not about my past exploits."

"What is it about then?"

"When we arrive in England I intend to bring those infernal scoundrels, Faversham and Bloodyer to justice, and I think you may aid me materially in doing so."

"I'm at your service, my dear Captain Toddleboy."

"Thanks, my friends, you and I will go on a voyage of discovery together."

"After Bloodyer and the other?"

"No, I think I can always put my hand on Bloodyer, and finding him, I shall be able to get at the whereabouts of Faversham."

"Then, who are the fellows you want to hunt up?"

"Two men—one named Horford—Jack Horford, and another of the name of Murdock; but I'll tell you all about it another time; and now I'll pay my fair friend a visit. I shall be on deck again soon, and then I'll let you know my reasons for wanting to find these two men."

———

CXXIV.—GOES BACK TO MISS LUCINDA AND THE REV. SHEPHERDS.

SO long a time has elapsed since Miss Lucinda Hopley's name has been mentioned, that the author feels that some sort of an apology is due, both to that young lady and to the reader.

It may be rembered, that we left the two worthy shepherds, the Rev. Jack Pudding and the Rev. Ghastly Gash in a very questionable part of Chatham, whither they had wended their way after the supper, given by Brother Goggles on the occasion of Lucinda's baptism, by the Rev. Oiley Swabb.

These two shepherds had determined upon bearing off Lucinda in triumph to the Obelisk, and for this purpose they called at her house on the day following their little spree in that quarter of Chatham—caleld Brook.

It was rather late in the day when they arrived at Miss Hopley's residence, and much to their annoyance they were informed that the young lady was not "at home," although Brother Gash said, "be damned if he didn't see her at the window, before the slavey answered the knock."

"What's to be done?" said Ghastly.

"Suppose we say we'll wait till she comes home?"

"She doesn't want to see us—it's plain, and if she doesn't, why it's devilish little good trying to get her to come to our shop."

"I feel very much inclined to stay, whether you do or not," said Gash, meekly.

"I'll be hanged if you do, though fiercely retorted Pudding, "none of your mousing after her. Mind, I warn you, if I hear of any of it, I'll break every bone in your cursed body."

"Realy, Brother Pudding, I cannot see the necessity for your being so exceedingly violent."

"Then I do, and I warn you Mister——"

"Brother——"

"Brother be damned—I tell you what it is, Mister Gash, if you don't immediately slope from Chatham, I'll kick——"

"Brother Pudding, control your wrath."

"If you don't slope, I'll give you a hiding—go back to the Obelisk—damn you. There's a collection to-night, and if no one is there, by G—— we shall be bilked of every copper by those cursed deacons."

"I will accede to you your request, Brother Pudding, although I believe it would be better for both of us to be present this evening—you carry a great deal more weight than I do."

This seasonable piece of flattery had the desired effect, viz., it appeared Brother Jack's wrath, although it did not for one moment cause him to swerve from his intention to remain and see Lucinda if possible.

"Perhaps you are right, Gash about my influence with the congregation; but at the same time, when they hear that I have delegated you to act in my absence, I daresay they'll shell out pretty handsomely. And there's one thing I would particularly impress upon you, Brother Gash," said the Rev. Jack, in a severe tone, at the same time casting a penetrating look at his fellow shepherd. "Just you, you keep a correct account of the swag, you know what I mean, none of your sniping."

"I am grieved at your insinuation," began Gash.

"Insinuation, be bothered! I mean in plain English, don't you get a fingering the cash."

"My conduct has hitherto——"

"Gammon," observed Pudding. "You be off as soon as you can—the station's no distance from here, and I'll send your traps after you to-night."

Brother Gash was about to expostulate, but Jack cut him short, and again warned him to be off."

"It's no go," said Ghastly to himself, "there's not a ghost of a chance for me, so I'll make a virtue of necessity, and hook it."

Thinking thus, he bade Brother Pudding adieu, and left him.

"Now, I'll return," said Jack, when the other was out of sight, "I'll return and wait till she comes home."

Walking up to Miss Lucinda's house, he knocked at the door, and inquired at what time that young lady was expected back.

To this the servant replied, that it was quite uncertain whether Miss Hopley would be home that day or not, that she had gone to London."

"Damnation!" muttered the rev. shepherd between his teeth at this announcement.

"Then, it is uncertain whether she will be at home to-morrow morning or not?" he asked.

"Werry uncertain, Missus said she mightn't be back for days."

"I'll write to her then, give her this card."

"Yes, sir."

Had the Rev. Jack known that at this moment the pretty Lucinda was peeping at him from behind the window-curtains, the chances are that his wrath, which was great enough at present, would have exhibited itself in some very unclerical form. He might have spared himself the trouble of his walk, had he believed Gash when he asserted that he had seen Miss Lucinda's head at the window; but the Rev. brother, like Saint Thomas, was rather incredulous, and refused to pay any attention to what the Rev. Ghastly said.

After having left his card, the Rev. Jack turned away from the house, and took his way to Brother Swabb's lodgings.

Here he deliberated upon what was to be done and finally determined upon returning to London, where he deemed his presence would be necessary as a check upon Brother Gash's pilfering propensities.

"That infernal Ghastly is not going to chisel me, I can tell him," thought he to himself—"I'll return to London myself to-night. After all I'm sure to have a spree there, and that's something after this deadly-lively place."

With reference to Lucinda, the Rev. Jack felt that he should have some trouble; but nothing daunted at this, he sat down on his return to Swabb's lodgings, and penned her a tremendous epistle, in which he denounced Swabb as a most immoral shepherd, and wound up, by begging her to cut the Bethel and patronise the Obelisk in future.

After finishing this letter, Brother Jack consulted a time-table, and finding that a train would shortly leave for London, he packed up his traps and took his departure for the Great Metropolis.

Lucinda's behaviour to these rev. shepherds may be easily accounted for.

In the first place, Brother Swabb's unmistakeable advances to her during the ceremony of her baptism, displeased her considerably, and in the second place, the heavy pulls that had been made upon her purse by the rev. shepherds, on all occasions that she had patronised their entertainments, were anything but agreeable to her.

After a little consideration, she resolved to leave Chatham, and with a view to this, she wended her way to Hammond Place, where after an interview with one of the numerous Israelites, who abound in the neighbourhood, she arranged the sale of her furniture, receiving for it something less than a fourth of what Captain Gabion had given for it at the same Jewish establishment a few months previously.

This was arranged, she gave up her house, and set off for London, where we shall find her located, when again we bring her—perhaps for the last time—before the notice of the reader.

———

CXXV.—THE NEW DOCTER AT SAINT-STARVER-CUM-BAG-O'-BONES.

THE result of Bloodyer's endeavours to blacken the character of the two medical men who had offered themselves as candidates in opposition to Faversham, for the appointment of surgeon to the workhouse of Saint Starver, had the desired effect. On the day before the election several dark hints were thrown out against the two unsuspecting men. Messrs. Bullock and Measurem were ready with *facts* which could be proved by several of their own workmen. The matter was discussed. The facts were proved after a fashion which satisfied some, but not others, and Faversham was, in consequence, duly elected to the post.

Nor was he long before he entered upon its duties.

On the evening of the day upon which he was elected, he was closeted with his companion in guilt, Bloodyer. With him he arranged a new plan of operations with reference to the disposal of the bodies of the paupers, which had been done lately in a fashion which Faversham did not approve of.

"But what is to be done with them," asked Bloodyer, "I have them removed to the dead house as soon as they are dead, or devilish soon after."

"I do not consider that safe," replied Faversham, in his usual cautious tone.

"What would you advise, then?" asked Bloodyer.

"I should suggest that they are sent to a place I will name."

"Where is that?"

"To a place of mine in Bayswater."

"And you fancy that is a secure place?"

"I am sure of it."

"You speak from experience, I presume."

"I invariably do," said Faversham, coldly."

"If we are to work together, I must have my own way in everything."

"I don't object to that in the least," replied Bloodyer, who felt that his companion was a man in whom he could put the most implicit

confidence in the matter, which interested them both so deeply.

"Then, now to business," said Faversham. "Have you any doctored ones in hand."

"Yes, three, and one of them evinces the greatest disinclination to die quietly."

"Then lead me to him at once, but stay—it's late, and his death occurring so soon after my visit might create a bad impression."

"There's something in that you might see, though there's no occasion for you to physic him yet."

"Let me see him then," said Faversham.

"This way then," said Bloodyer, leading the way from his own room to the ward, where the unfortunate pauper was lying, to all appearances in great bodily agony.

Faversham gazed at the poor young fellow, who was thus being sacrificed to the rapacity of the workhouse master, but said nothing.

Having felt his pulse, and given some trifling directions to one of the nurses, he turned to Bloodyer, and the two visited the other men, who had been dosed.

They were aged and did not appear to suffer much.

"Let us return to your room," said Faversham, in a low voice.

Bloodyer immediately obeyed.

On their return, Faversham closed the door and, turning to the workhouse master, said severely,

"Never—during the time that I remain doctor to this workhouse, never do you dare to physic any of these paupers."

"What is the matter?" gasped Bloodyer.

"Only that you have used medicine, that, in all probability, will excite the suspicions of the nurses."

"Good God," said Bloodyer, "you do not mean it."

"Do I often jest?"

Bloodyer remained silent.

At this moment the beadle made his appearance, and to him Faversham turned, and inquired whether he had heard anything mentioned about this particular case by the nurses.

"Well, sir," replied that functionary, "I did hear one of 'em say as how that young man was jist like another she had seed die of pison in the 'ospital."

"You are convinced now I hope," said Faversham.

"I could not help it," moaned the terrified workhouse master, "I gave him the right medicine as I thought."

"Give him nothing more except nourishing food until I come in the morning," said the mysterious doctor, as he took his departure.

"I thought you'd put your foot in it guv'-nor. The best thing we can do now is to settle Mrs. Sarah Spriggins, and with this suggestion the cold-blooded beadle hurried after Faversham, for the purpose of letting him out at the little wicket at which our old friend, Toddleboy, many years ago, had stood with our hero, soon after he hed been ejected from the public-house to which he had taken the infant Charley, after he had rescued him from a watery grave.

———

CHARLEY AND THE DETECTIVES.

CXXVI.—CHARLEY DISCOVERS WHERE JULIA IS CONCEALED — THE ATTACK — JULIA IS KILLED—HOW COCKS' LOT SERVED THE TITLED RUFFIAN—A LITTLE AFFRAY WITH THE POLICE.

HOW Charley Wag and the illustrious members of Cocks' Lot discovered the place to which Julia had been conveyed, the writer has not the slightest idea. Suffice to say—they *did* discover it, and headed by our hero at once, surrounded the house, and proceeded to attack it.

The windows were speedily demolished, those opening on to the lawn being first destroyed. Through these, Charley rushed, followed by host of his companions.

Ransacking the premises, appeared to offer greater charms to many of his followers than the rescue of the unfortunate Julia; and when Charley, after continuing his search for some time, at last found himself at a closed door of rather suspicious appearance, he had only a couple of the Lot as a support.

In the meantime, the rest of the young gentlemen of that association were engaged in a desperate fray with the servants of the establishment.

The struggle was short, however, for the flunkies, although pluckier by far than the ordinary run of gentlemen in plush, were but poor adversaries for Charley Wag's band.

Perhaps the lot did not do battle, in the proved fashion of the P. R. ; but certain it is, that they attained their end, viz., victory, and the flunkies, who were not rendered helpless from the severe treatment they had received at the hands of their youthful assailants, were securely bound and locked in a room with one of Cocks' lot to guard them.

After the knights of the pluck had been disposed of Charley was joined by the rest of his band of trusty followers.

With their assistance, the door, the only obstacle to his reaching the chamber, from which he fancied he heard the sound of voices, was quickly removed, and Charley once more pressed his Julia in his arms.

"Saved! dearest!" said he, as he kissed her repeatedly. "And now, where is the scoundrel who has detained you?" The blackguard has bolted I'm afraid.

"Oh! no," replied Julia, as she clung to Charley, "he has gone for his pistols."

"But how the deuce did he get out? We came in by the only door that I can see. By Jove! he must have gone through the floor." Didn't you see him go, Julia?

"I was looking anxiously at the door by which you entered—when he spoke about his pistols, and never noticed how he went out."

"Now, my lads," said Charley, turning to the youths, who were standing near him, lost in admiration of the fair Julia—"now my lad, stand by, and look out for the bullets when this fellow pops up from the floor,"

His remark elicited a laugh from the surrounding gentry, to say nothing of several forcible expressions, highly detrimental to the eyes and limbs of the individual who was expected to make his appearance through some Jack-in-the-Box contrivance in the floor.

Much to the surprise of Charley and his friends, who imagined that they had engaged and routed the entire staff of the domestics, the gentleman who had left Julia so suddenly and mysteriously, made his appearance—not through the floor—but through a secret panel in the wall of the room—and not alone —but followed by at least a couple of dozen retainers, all armed in some fashion or other.

The flunkses, who had been bound and left in charge of one of the lot, had been released by some of the other domestics, who had overpowered, and nearly murdered the guard set over their fellow-servants. This will account for the strong party, by which the proprietor of the mansion was accompanied.

On his re-entering the room thus attended, the lot immediately commenced the attack, and in a few moments the fight became general.

In the midst of all this, Charley singled out the man, who had for the gratification of his unreciprocated passion arranged the forcible abduction of the pretty Julia.

It will be necessary to explain to the reader before going any further, that during Charley's temporary absences from home, Julia had been persecuted by the attentions of a noble-man, who had made her the most princely offers. Now, it may appear somewhat strange, that Miss Julia did not accept these offers. We all know she had lived under the protection of a nobleman ; and why should she not again?

Why not?

Because she was still very fond of her dear Charley.

It will hardly be credited—but she positively entertained a love for him, so absorbing, that she resolved to be faithful to him in spite of the princely offers of this designing peer.

In vain did my lord entreat her to fly with him to Paris, Venice, or anywhere else. Julia remained firm, and at last threatened to inform Mr. Wag, if he did not instantly cease his attentions. But the noble lord didn't seem to see it; and at last resorted to the means we have already described as the only way to obtain possession of the handsome girl, who had made so complete a conquest of him.

We shall now return to the noble lord and Charley, whom we left just as the latter, was about to spring upon the former.

A terrible struggle was taking place.

Charley was strong and active, but he found the nobleman no mean antagonist. With stunning violence they both came to the floor, and now Charley found that he must exert himself to the utmost or be defeated.

Julia saw her lover's predicament, and, like a brave girl as she was, rushed to his assistance.

Her heroism cost her her life.

The baffled nobleman, enraged at this act on her part, succeeded in disengaging his right hand, and grasped a pistol which he had concealed in his breast, deliberately aimed the unfortunate girl and fired !

With a scream she fell backward, the blood flowing from a wound in her bosom.

Charley, like a mad man, struggled to free himself from his opponent, but in vain.

The report of the pistol quickly brought the other combatants round the prostrate form of the wounded Julia.

The flunkies even were horrified at the dastardly act of their master.

Cocks' lot were furious, and, rushing with a wild yell upon the prostrate peer, they *literally tore him limb from limb !*

Charley at once flew to the side of the bleeding Julia, but, alas! the ball had passed through her beautiful bosom, and life was fast ebbing away.

"Get a cab one of you," said Charley, quite unmindful of their being some miles from Charing Cross.

Two of his companions at once started in search of a conveyance, and the rest of them evinced an inclination to sacrifice the wretched flunkies to their wrath; but the sympathy which these fellows openly exhibited, now that their master was no more, saved them from a similar fate.

The two young gentlemen who had gone in search of a carriage returned without one. In all probability their appearance operated greatly against their obtaining one by fair means, so, summoning the aid of the rest of their brotherhood of the Lot, the sallied forth to obtain a carriage by foul means.

And this time they were successful; returning with a brougham, after a terrific tussle for it at a neighbouring livery stable.

One of the young gentlemen also thought a doctor might be of some service to the wounded girl, so on their way back to the house they pressed a mild-looking medical man into their service, pushing him into the brougham they had appropriated in the most unceremonious manner possible.

Unfortunately his services were not required, for on his arrival life was extinct.

"Come away my friends," said Charley, sadly, as he lifted the lifeless body of the once beautiful girl in his arms, "it is useless remaining here any longer."

Some of the Lot demurred at this.

"Let's settle the flunkies first!" roared one blood-thirsty individual, and again the lives of the wretched serving men bring tremblingly in the balance.

"Tie 'em up, and set fire to the 'ouse," shouted another.

"Kill 'em anyhow," said another, who was not at all particular as to the mode of their death.

"It is now time we were moving," said Charley, "and those who wish to stick to me had better say so."

"We all means to stick to you in course, Charley, but what we want to do fust is to pull this 'ere 'ouse down."

"Or set fire to out," suggested another young gentleman.

"And roast the coves in plush."

"My eye! won't their calves just 'iss and no mistake!"

"No useless cruelty," said Charley, in an authoritative voice, "set the house on fire if you like, but spare these poor devils."

"Yes, set the 'ouse on fire!" and away rushed the whole of the Lot to set about doing so, with the exception of a couple who remained to assist Charley in placing his Julia's lifeless body in the carriage.

The incendiaries had completed their work; the flames were breaking out on every side of the handsome mansion, when a cry of police arose, and a small body of the force appeared, headed by a sergeant.

The people at the livery stable had despatched a messenger for them soon after the brougham had been carried off by Charley's lawless companions.

It was suggested by one of the young gentlemen that Charley should make his escape with the brougham, but this our hero would not hear of; so, marshalling the Lot, he prepared for the onset of the police.

With a shout the two parties closed.

The Lot had to fight for bare life.

Charley, wielding a formidable cudgel, brought down two or three of the bobbies, who were also using their truncheons most unsparingly

The conflict continued for some time, and fortune smiled upon the Lot, for the greater part of the bobbies were disabled—when, to their inexpressible dismay, a reinforcement of peelers could be seen approaching.

The order to fly was given. One of the Lot jumped on to the box of the brougham, and Charley jumped inside. "Run for it, my boys! separate—at the old quarters to-night."

———

CXXVII.—HANGING OR WORSE—FAVERSHAM THREATENS BLOODYER WITH HIS VENGEANCE—THE WORKHOUSE MASTER IS ANXIOUS TO CEASE SPECULATING IN DEAD PAUPERS; BUT GETS DEEPER INTO THE MIRE THAN EVER.

WHEN Faversham returned to the workhouse on the morning following his visit to the paupers who had been dosed by the ignorant Bloodyer, he found the young man still alive, but apparently suffering intolerable agony.

Bloodyer had obeyed the doctor's directions to the letter, and had provided his wretched victim with wines and jellies to an extent that had never been witnessed in the workhouse of Saint-Starver-Cum-Bag-o'-Bones before.

His kind treatment served to allay the suspicions of the wretched paupers around, and some were even foolish enough to express a wish to have a little of the sufferer's complaint, and so come in for a share of the good things which the master was so liberally showering down upon the three sick men.

These unsophisticated paupers little knew, whatever they might have imagined, that in a few short hours the men they were envying would be corpses, thrust away in a dead-house, there to remain until the time came for them to be hacked to pieces in the theatre of some hospital or other.

"Have you carried out my directions," said Faversham, on entering the workhouse master's room on the morning in question.

"I have, and the man is better."

"Then now I will visit the paupers professionally."

Bloodyer accompanied him through the various wards, stopping here and there to say a kind word at the bedside of the sick and ailing; but his primary object being to pick out the best subjects for his own experiments.

"That one will do," said he, pointing to one man whom he thought a fit subject, and who certainly did look precious tough, and likely to stand a great deal of killing.

"There are one or two better than that fellow in the other wards," remarked Bloodyer, walking forward in their direction.

"Not half so well suited to my purpose," quietly replied Faversham, as he glanced at the unfortunate men who were doomed to a violent death at a future period, either at the hands of the doctor or Bloodyer.

"Now let us return to the young man you have been dosing like a fool as you are," said Faversham.

A few steps brought them to the sufferer's side. Faversham felt his pulse, and examined him in various ways, and then turned away satisfied with the result of his inspection.

"That man is now free from the effects of the poison you gave him—leave him to me—he must recover now."

"I'm very much afraid that the nurse who has been discharged may do us a great deal of mischief notwithstanding."

"Explain yourself man—I don't see what you are driving at."

"I mean the nurse who threw out hints about the poisoning."

"And you have discharged her?"

"Yes."

"You miserable dolt! do you not perceive that this looks blacker than ever against you?"

"It's all very well, doctor," said Bloodyer, with a sickly attempt at a smile, "it's all very well to say it looks blacker than ever against me. How about the finger you have had in the pie, doctor?"

"You would have some difficulty in implicating me in this affair even if you dared," said Faversham, "and if I believed you capable of such treachery I would slay you this moment!"

Bloodyer was, evidently, uneasy at what he had said, for he knew his companion was not one to be lightly trifled with. His remark had aroused Faversham's suspicions.

"Mark you! Bloodyer, if ever you play me false, no power on earth shall save you from my vengeance—the bloodiest vengeance tho mind of man and devil can invent."

"Why damn it, doctor, one would believe you fancied me guilty of deceiving you," said Bloodyer, as he tossed off a glass of brandy.

"I do not for one moment believe you have already been guilty of any treachery towards me, nor do I think you will have the courage to play me false at any time; but should you, I warn you look to the consequences."

"Really, doctor, you make a fellow feel quite uncomfortable—and just when we are doing so well, as if I should ever betray you."

"It would be an exceedingly foolish thing to do; for if you are accused of having committed the murders it would be as well to confess it as your own doing,"

"And be hanged, while you——"

"You seem to forget what I have already said," replied his implacable accomplice. "Should you implicate me you would die assuredly, and not so easily as you would under the hands of the hangman."

"Good God! doctor, you don't mean to say you——"

"I have already said, that I would destroy you, and in a manner you little dream of."

Bloodyer covered his face with his hands, and groaned at the idea of becoming a victim to the shedder of blood, who sat near him.

"What can I do? what shall I do?" said the wretched Bloodyer.

"Keep your tongue between your teeth, and make up your mind to be hanged, in case you are found guilty."

"But I have not been accused yet."

"Not yet—but of course you will be."

"Oh! no, perhaps it may never be found out."

"If it is—prepare for the worst."

"But, would it not be better to discontinue our trade entirely—I will—I would rather lose all than die. No! not another pauper shall be sold while I remain master of this workhouse."

Faversham laughed, his low scornful laugh, at this speech of Bloodyer's, then coldly said:—

"You may be the master of Saint Starver-Cum-Bag-o'Bones—but you seem quite to forget that I am your master."

Bloodyer stared wildly at his companion, but could say nothing more.

"I have not the slightest intention of giving up trading in bodies, if you have—if you refuse to share the gain—well and good, you cannot shrink the guilt."

"But, if I give it up entirely?" gasped the wretched man.

"It is too late, in event of any discovery, you must die."

Bloodyer saw that he was doomed, and inwardly resolved to fly the country on the first intimation of anything unpleasant.

Faversham occupied himself in reading some papers which he drew from his pocket, and for a time he left Bloodyer to his reflections.

At length Faversham broke silence.

"What do you intend doing?" said he, "to give up your share in the profits, or share them with Grimes and myself? Remember hanging or death at my hands!"

"I will share them," replied Bloodyer, faintly."

"Then once more we will get to business," said Faversham. "How many dead have you? and where are they?"

"Four."

"And where are they?"

"In the old place."

"They must be removed."

"But, when—and how?"

"To-night, and in a manner I shall suggest."

"You will want two men, and there is only Grimes."

"And ourselves."

"Oh!"

"Too proud to assist in carrying a body—are you, my fine fellow—I'm sorry for you—but you'll have to do it?"

"I don't much like the idea, I admit, but——"

"But, you must do it, in spite of your dislike. It will never do to trust our secret to any one beside Grimes. We must carry our own dead."

"But, what place have you for them?"

"A cellar, that I had built specially for the kind of thing at Bayswater."

"Were you not afraid of the workmen mentioning that such a place was in existence?"

"Dead men tell no tales."

"But they might have mentioned being employed upon such a place while living."

"No."

"How do you know?"

"I promised the man who built it, a large reward if he would remain on the spot until it was completed. It was finished, and he was *its first inmate!*"

"You will be here to-night—at what time?"

"A quarter before twelve—have everything in readiness. I will provide a conveyance," said Faversham.

Bloodyer promised that every thing should be done according to his wishes; and the two separated.

CXXVIII.—TODDLEBOY MAKES LOVE—WHAT PASSED BETWEEN THE OLD CAPTAIN AND DUFFY RELATIVE TO CHARLEY WAG.

CAPTAIN Toddleboy passed some time in the state room of the fascinating widow, Mrs. Dewberry; indeed the old boy felt young again, and chatted away to his companion (who was now much better), in as lively a strain as he could possibly command.

The old gentleman positively went in for poetry to please his fair companion, and he quoted Moore and Byron until he thought he was only sixteen.

There were several very naughty little bits of the last great poet's effusions which the old captain repeated more than once, and Mrs. Dewberry only called him a wicked man, and did not appear at all shocked.

And why should she be? She was a widow, and widows are not often horrified at a simple quotation.

Toddleboy continued to quote, first from one poet, and then another, much to the amusement of Mrs. Dewberry, who certainly thought the old sailor one of the nicest fellows she had ever met with.

The late Mr. D. had been a sickly, puling creature, not at all a fit mate for the pretty woman who now wore weeds for him, and had consented to become the bride of our old friend the pirate.

While the captain was making fierce love to the widow, Duffy was pacing the deck, thinking how jolly glad he should be to get home, and congratulating himself upon having fallen in with old Toddleboy. His pleasing reflections continued until rather late in the day, or rather evening, when he was joined by Toddleboy.

"Here you are at last then," said Duffy, as the old sailor seated himself near him. "well, when is the splicing to take place?"

"Oh, damn it! you know my dear boy it won't do to urge her very much on that point. She has only buried her husband very lately."

"And what of that?"

"It wouldn't be decent."

"Oh! that's all gammon. I know a fellow who married a few weeks after his guv'nor's

death, and I think that's a denced site worse."

"Well, perhaps it is, but——"

"You ask her to name the day, and you see if she doesn't blush, and mention the lamented Mr. Dewberry, and finally fix a day, a month at least, earlier than you could have expected in your most sanguine moments."

"I hope it may be as you suggest, my dear boy, but whenever it comes off you shall dance at my wedding. Yes! and so shall Charley Wag, or my name's not Toddleboy."

"Charley Wag!"

"Yes! Charley Wag. You look upon him as a thief I suppose, and nothing more. What am I but a thief—a sea thief?"

"That's all very well—a pirate is a thief; but you will allow it's a higher grade in the profession."

"Yes."

"Housebreaking, for which I believe our friend is famous, is not to be named in the same breath with piracy on the open sea."

"There's a good deal of truth in what you say, young shiver-the-mizen."

"Of course there is. Why there's as much difference between a pirate and a housebreaker as there is between the man who boldly robs you on the highway, and the sneak who picks your pocket in a dark slum."

"Shiver my timbers! but you're about right Duffy; but damn it! going to the bad hasn't been the fault of the boy himself."

"He might have been honest I suppose if he had had the slightest inclination that way."

"Not a bit of it—he was made a thief."

"I must say the little you have told me about him has astonished me rather."

"Ah! he's a good lad spoilt; but I'll reclaim him, or I'll know the reason why, and he shall dance at my wedding—keel haul me if he sha'nt!"

"But what will Mrs. Dewberry say to it do you think?"

"She might not like to hear thieves patter talked in her drawing-room."

"Did Charley Wag ever behave himself otherwise than a gentleman should do when you had him staying with you in Essex?"

"I must say he conducted himself as a gentleman and an honourable fellow," said Duffy, who knew nothing at all about our hero's love passage with Miss Maggie Duffy, when they were alone in the music room.

"Then why the devil do you think he would behave otherwise in my house," said Toddleboy, who was quite indignant at the idea of such an insinuation.

The fact is, when Horatio Spanker Duffy invited Charley Wag to his father's residence, he had not the slightest idea that our hero derived his income by laying violent hands on the cash of his neighbours. He believed him to be a well-conducted, wealthy youth; he knew he was a very jolly companion, who spent his money freely; and, as such, invited him to spend the Christmas with the Duffy family.

While Horatio remained in ignorance of the true state of the case, Charley was treasured in his memory as the jolliest fellow he knew;

but now that he had heard that he was a common thief—a low London thief—the reaction was terrible. This is an everyday occurrence. Billy Jones is our dearest friend until Tommy Brown blackens his character to us, for some purpose or other (an interested motive generally), and then we discover that no greater villain ever existed than Billy Jones, and blame ourselves for having been blind to the atrocities committed by him so long.

And now that Duffy knew that our unfortunate hero was a thief, he felt that he could abuse him right royally. He did not, however, proceed to these lengths, for the savage demeanour of the old pirate awed him a little.

"But, my dear Captain Toddleboy," said Duffy, after a pause, "don't you think that Mrs. Dewberry might object to associate with thieves?"

"My wife, sir, will not object to associate with any person I may introduce to her," said Toddleboy, with great dignity; indeed the old gentleman felt quite a thrill pass through him as he said "my wife."

"Well, if she doesn't kick at it, its all right you know."

"I feel confident that Mrs. Dewberry will not 'kick,' as you so elegantly term it."

"So much the better; but now, captain, you won't call me impertinent for asking the queston——"

"What is it?"

"Does the fair lady below know that you have been a pirate chief?"

The old gentleman winced a little at this question, and well he might. People in love don't like confessing everything, and, least of all, telling a third person how far their weakness has carried them.

Toddleboy *had* told Mrs. Dewberry that he was a pirate chief, and, as the novelist knows everything, he is aware of the fact of Mrs. D.'s liking her gallant old sailor all the better for it, and telling him so. There was a spice of the romantic about it which pleased the dear lady of four-and-thirty summers amazingly, and in her heart she regretted that she had not been taken prisoner by the pirate chief, lodged in a sumptuously fitted cabin in the oriental style, with a black slave to attend upon her, &c., &c.

But as this did not take place, Mrs. Dewberry consoled herself with the fact of having the pirate-chief sighing for her hand, in a state room of the mail-packet, with an occasional visit from the stewardess in lieu of the polite attentions of the black slave.

To Duffy's question, Toddleboy, after a good deal of beating about the bush, replied, that "he *had* told Mrs. Dewberry, and that that lady had expressed no disgust at the news.

"Then, by Jove, she must be a trump!" said Duffy."

"She is, my boy, and so you'll say when you know her better," remarked Toddleboy, now thoroughly restored to good humour. "Don't you fancy, Duffy, that I would introduce her to Wag if he still continued his present mode of life. He must reform and become a respectable member of society before I introduce him to my wife."

"Of course I shouldn't mind knowing him if he gave up prigging, but damn it! you know——"

"I know exactly what your feelings must be on the subject, and I can account for your being rather astonished when I told he was a thief."

"'Gad, I never was taken so aback in my life."

"Poor boy, he has that cursed Faversham to thank for most of the evil that has attended him from his birth."

"By the bye—what were you going to tell me about Horford and another fellow, I forget the name."

"Murdock."

"That's it."

"Then I'll tell you what I intend doing when I get to England; but first let me go below and get my pipe."

"Shall I go for it?" asked Duffy, who was afraid if once the old fellow got into Mrs. Dewberry state-room again, it would be one while before he made his appearance on deck again."

The old captain saw his young companion's meaning, and replied with a grin, "that he knew where to find it, and wouldn't trouble him."

"He's good for another half hour at least," said Duffy, as Toddleboy's head disappeared down the companion.

CXXIX.—THE DUCHESS MAKES A DISCOVERY

FOR some time after his marriage with the Duchess of Heatherland, Faversham had led an altered life, and the duchess had been happier that she had been for many a long day. The dark mysterious man had become a loving husband, no longer subject to those gloomy fits which used to steal upon him at times—no longer planning the consummation of bloody vengeance. Faversham for a short time—a very short time was happy.

And who would not be happy in the possession of such a woman as the Dutchess of Heatherland?

No one knew her without speaking well of her.

Whenever she went forth, it was to do some good action—to realise some needy family—to visit some sick couch.

The husband of such a woman, how could Faversham be otherwise than happy?

And yet there came a time when he grew weary of leading a similar life, and again pined for his old pursuits.

It was about this time that he paid his visit to Bloodyer, and proposed to take the appointment of doctor to Saint Starver's workhouse.

The reader is already aware how he succeeded in obtaining it, and for what purpose.

His absences from home were now long and frequent occurrence.

He again grew reserved, and it was useless for even the duchess to attempt finding out where he went or what he did. This might have remained a mystry had it not been for a mere accident, which threw a glimmering light upon the subject at the time, and years afterwards explained it.

Faversham had been away from home a week without a soul in the establishment having the slightest suspicion of where he had gone to, with the exception of one person.

And this was the butler.

This man had picked up a few days after his master's departure, a small strip of paper, upon which was written—*Bloodyer*.

The man's astonishment was great at this discovery for the name was his own, although he passed by the humble one of Joseph Perry.

On the same evening this man was seated in close confab, the housekeeper to whom he was engaged, and from whom he had no secrets.

"I'll tell you what, I think Jenny—it's my belief the captain goes to see that brother of mine at Saint Starver's."

"Lor—you don't say so—do you?"

"Yes! and I'll tell you why, Jenny—just you look what I found in the hall after he left tee other day."

Saying this, he handed her the strip of paper, upon which the name was written, and then waited for her remarks upon it.

"But what can he do there?" inquired the housekeeper.

All this while the duchess was listening outside the door of the room in which the butler and the housekeeper were sitting.

Start not, dear reader, at what may be considered a dishonourable act.

The duchess was a wife, and like other women, was of course very curious.

Happening to pass the housekeeper's sanctum, of which the door was ajar, she heard the butler express his belief, that the captain (Faversham) visited his (the butler's) brother during his long absences from home.

"What can be his object in visiting the master of a workhouse?" again asked the housekeeper.

"That I can't say, all I know is, my brother is an awful scoundrel, that wouldn't hesitate to commit any crime."

"I shouldn't think it's a very likely thing the captain would have anthing to do with such a man," said the housekeeper.

"Bloodyer's not a common name, and what the devil that strip of paper meant I can't say."

"Perhaps he may have found out your right name."

"He might have."

"Is that name in the captain's handwriting?"

"No—and it's so many years since I have seen my brother's writing that I could not say whether it is the blackguard's signature or not."

"I should think it had been torn off the bottom of a letter," said the housekeeper, again examining the strip of paper.

"Yes, it must have been, and here is part of an initial—it looks something like an I."

"Let me see," said the butler, grasping at the piece of paper."

"What do you make of it?"

"It must be my brother's signature, he's name is Jacob."

"And you really think the captain goes to see him—what can they have to do with each other?"

"The captain's a very scientific man, always making experiments."

Here the butler sank his voice, and the duchess held her breath, and listened eagerly to what he said.

"Perhaps," he continued, "he tries his hand on the paupers—my brother was once, very nearly charged with getting rid of the paupers before their time."

"Good heaven! for what purpose?"

"It's my belief, he used to sell the bodies to the doctors."

"But look at the terrible risk."

"But then, Jenny, the pay, I suppose was good—bodies sell well even now."

"Was your brother tried for murder?"

"Oh! bless you—no, there was a wonderful fellow, a doctor in partnership with him, I suppose that proved, that no poison had been given, and insisted that the bodies of several of the dead should undergo a medical examination."

"It must have made a great stir at the time."

"Only known to a few in the parish, kept deuced snug, I can tell you."

"Who was the man who spoke up for your brother?"

"The fellow who murdered the Duke of Heatherland—Faversham."

The duchess stayed no longer, for at this moment the butler rose from his seat. She returned to her boudoir, and then pondered over the conversation she had just overheard.

"Is it possible," said she to herself, "that my present husband is associated with an accomplice of that wretch Faversham! Good Good! how terrible!"

———

CXXX.—TODDLEBOY TELLS DUFFY HIS PLAN FOR CONVICTING BLOODYER AND FAVERSHAM.

IT will be hardly necessary to state, that Captain Toddleboy was at least an hour looking for his pipe. He hunted in every improbable place for it, and at the expiration of five minutes searching, he bethought him, that he might have left it in Mrs. Dewberry's state-room, and thither the old rogue went to look for it. He found his pipe immediately, and found the lady asleep, or "foxing" on a sofa. What could an old gentleman do under circumstances, but bend over her and kiss her? And this, Toddleboy did, and the fair lady awoke, and I am not quite certain that she did not kiss him in return!

Toddleboy did not return to Duffy before the expiration of an hour, and when he did the young gentleman chaffed him most unmercifully about looking for his pipe, which the old boy had forgotten after all.

" Now we really must talk seriously, Duffy—I've a great deal to tell you, and I want your advice," said Toddleboy, when he thought his young friend had gone far enough with his facetious remarks about Mrs. Dewberry."

" have lighted my pipe," replied Duffy, with a grinn, " and I'm listening."

" I told you I wanted to hunt up two men."

" You did—Horford and Murdock, I think you said was the other fellows name."

" Horford and Murdock—right—now I'll tell you for what purpose I want to get hold of them."

" you have never told me who Murdock is?"

" I don't know very much about him myself—but what I do I'll tell you. When I used to do a little in the light portering line, business one day took me to some chambers in the same place that Faversham was living. I had to wait some time, and began amusing myself by looking about; but to make this part of my story, I peeped through a window, and saw Faversham with what was, apparently, a dead body. He first put the man in a bath, then he rubbed, then galvanized him, and lastly restored him to life!"

" He had never been dead of course," said Duffy, with something like contempt at what he supposed to be his old companion's ignorance.

" He had been hanged though, young gentleman, and if that's not calculated to take away a fellow's life, I don't know what is."

" By jingo! I should be devilish sorry to try it—but go on with the yarn, it's qu'te exciting."

" As I have already said, the man was restored to life, although rendered hideous for life, by having his mouth twisted, and his other features by no means improved by the rough treatment he had received at the hands of justice."

" Was this man a friend of Faversham's that he took so much trouble to restore him to life?"

" A friend, no—but he made him swear to be his slave—and the oath he administered was the most terrible I ever heard, to say nothing of what I saw."

" What you sew! What was it?"

" I can hardly tell you—you'll call me superstitious."

" No, I won't let's hear it?"

" If ever a spirit, or ghost, or shadow, or whatever you like to call it—if ever such a thing was seen, I saw one at the moment the terrible oath was taken."

" The spirit of a man or woman?"

" A woman—Faversham's murdered wife, perhaps."

" What did it do?"

" To tell you the truth I didn't stop to see. I was too much frightened, and scudded away at the rate of knots."

" But what became of the Murdoch?"

" That's precisely what I want to find out. I know that he remained with Faversham up to a certain time, but that's all I know. If he is still alive we shall find him in some of the cribs in London, and if we can only hit upon Charley Wag, he'll point us out the most likely spots in a brace of shakes."

" And what are you going to do with the Murdoch when you get hold of him?"

" He shall give evidence against Faversham, and the other, Horford, shall say all he knows about that scoundrel, Bloodyer. He was in the workhouse of Saint Starver once."

" Poor devil."

" You may well say that," replied Toddleboy, " it's a sorry place for any one to take refuge in. I saw quite enough of it when I went to visit poor Joe Cudder."

" Ah! that's where you got your dose of brandy by Faversham and Bloodyer."

" Yes! and for that dose of brandy I'll make Mis'er Bloodyer and the doctor pay pretty dearly."

" If any of these murders are brought home to them, they'll get hanged to a dead certainty."

" I mean them to be," replied old Toddleboy, calmly, " for if ever a man was murdered poor Joe was, and I think myself lucky that they didn't settle my hash at the same time; it was their intention I feel confident."

" It's so long ago that you may have some difficulty in proving these things."

" I expect it will be a difficult matter, but I'll try it on—keel-haul me if I don't. And what we must do when we get home is to set about it at once."

" Before your marriage?"

" Ah! that depends you see, but——"

" As soon after as possible I suppose."

" Exactly so. The first thing I shall discover is whether Bloodyer still remains master of the Saint-Starver-Cum-Bag-o'-Bones workhouse, and the next thing I shall do will be to hunt up Faversham. After that we'll go on a cruise of discovery in search of the other fellows Horford and Murdoch."

" Having found them, what will be your next move?"

" I shall immediately communicate with the police, and charge Bloodyer and Faversham with the murder of Joe Cudder."

" How about your witnesses?"

" I suppose they'll take me as one. I was at Joe's bedside and heard what he said about the codies—beside I shall tell them how I got dosed myself—that's pretty conclusive I think. I shan't mind telling the public how Mr. Slang treated me on the occasion of my being found in the cupboard at the milliner's."

" I hope you'll hang the blackguards."

" I'll try all I know to do it, shiver my timbers if I don't," replied the old fellow, savagely, " but we must wait patiently. Now I've told you my plan of operations—let me hear whether you stick by me?"

" Like a leech, guv'nor, and we'll go

together to see the beggars hanged."

"Ha! ha! ha! a devilish good idea, and have one of the best windows opposite."

Toddleboy and Duffy's conversation closed here. The old man went to pay another visit to his lady love, and Lieutenant Duffy gave his arm to a young lady passenger who had been unwell, and had only made her appearance on deck that evening.

———

CXXXI.—In search of Charley Wag— The Policeman's vengeance, its consequences, and what it came to.

AFTER the dreadful occurrence with Charley Wag and the nobleman, who the unfortunate Julia fell by, in giving help to Charley, it having been rumoured that Charley had set fire to the house, the police were dispersed in all directions.

After three weeks searching and no bottle for them, they turned it up, for Charley disappeared, he had gone, and nobody knew where.

When some time had elapsed, one of the bobbies informed his superior officer that he had received information to the effect that Charley was concealed in one of the houses in Slogger's Alley, Westminster. He was despatched there immediately. Having arrived there he knocked at the door, when a poor young woman appeared in black, with pale cheeks and sunken eyes, who seemed horror-stricken at the arrival of a policeman.

Almost dropping to the ground with fatigue, she exclaimed, with her hands clasped tightly together—

"Oh! sir, pray what may you want?"

"What do I want do you say? I'll let yer see what I want It won't do for me I can tell yer—you have got a man concealed here."

"Oh! mercy, sir, I declare I have nobody here but my poor dying child."

"You have I tell you, his name is Charley Wag."

The instant she heard this said the poor woman fell in a fainting state on the ground. On recovering consciousness she exclaimed poor Charley, I hope there is nothing wrong. He was my only friend.

"Get away with you I tell you once more. If you do not let me pass I will strike you to the ground."

"You would, sir, you would strike a poor dying woman. No, no, sir, if you were a man with an honest heart you would never have made use of such an expression," said she,

kneeling and looking up to heaven, as a picture of death praying to God for mercy.

The hard-hearted bobbie at this moment gave a rush by her into her apartment, and was paralyzed at the sight. There laid the poor child in one corner of the room, half naked—it was about seven years old, but looked about one.

Now, my dear reader, it must have been a most horrible sight. There was no fire, and only a stool and a basket for their use, and a few more little things not worth a penny.

The policeman, looking at her first, and then at the child, until the tears rolled down his cheeks, could not answer her for some time.

"Cheer up, cheer up, my good woman, forgive me I know I have done wrong, but I'm sure you will not be angry with me. It was my duty to obey my officer. Now, come, give me your hand old gal and be friends."

To this she replied, with a little smile on her countenance—

"Thank you, sir, I do forgive you with all my heart."

Putting his hand into his pocket, and pulling out a five shilling piece, he put it into her tiny hand.

Dear reader, to make the long story short, we will not go into the scene that ensued between them at that moment—it was the most pitiable occurrence I have ever seen. We left the broken-hearted policeman bidding her good-bye, and declaring that he would never see her want.

———

CXXXII.—Miss Lucinda Hopley gets settled in life.

IN one of the cosiest little habitations in the most respectable part of Brompton, occupying the first floor which was furnished elegantly, dwelt a young lady—a young lady who has borne a prominent part in this work. She is still pretty, rather too stout to please some fastidious people, but still a most charming and facinating creature.

The reader is, of course aware, that we are alluding to Miss Lucinda Hopley.

It will be remembered that she left Chatham soon after the two Rev. Shepherds Pudding and Gash paid their last visit.

Finding that her finances were far from being in a flourishing condition on her arrival in the metropolis, she resolved upon obtaining employment of some sort. The advertisement columns of the *Times* were consulted, but in them our fair friend could see nothing likely to suit her.

"As for being a governess," said she, "I'd sooner be a housemaid," and then she turned to other advertisements.

"A young lady required in a light fancy business" caught her eye, but that did not seem to suit.

"Catch me serving out Berlin wool and crotchet cotton to a lot of middle-aged spinsters—not if I know it," said she, as she threw aside the paper in a rage, and, seating herself at her piano, rattled off a brilliant fantasia, by way of stifling the inclination to use bad language.

Her playing and singing had often attracted the attention of a musical professor who lived in the house, and one evening, soon after Lucinda's determination to "do something for herself," this gentleman had paid her a visit, and, in the course of conversation, he had expressed his astonishment at her not turning her musical talent to account.

"I should only be too happy to do so, signor, but how am I to go about it?"

"Nothing easier. I will introduce you to my friend Beagle, the proprietor of the * * * Music Hall, and I think your engagement is almost certain."

Lucinda expressed her thanks, and it was arranged that she should see Mr. Beagle on the following day.

To become a public character of some sort had been a favourite idea with Lucinda, and now that her hopes were about to be realised, she felt decidedly happy.

The next day came, and with it the Signor and Mr. Beagle. With our fair friend's singing, the latter gentleman was perfectly enchanted, and immediately concluded an engagement with the young lady at about one half the salary he had paid another young lady, whose services he had dispensed with that day to make way for Lucinda, who was to make her first appearance that very evening.

This was really alarming, but the professor who resided in the house assured her that she had but to sing one of her charming little ballads "to bring the house down."

Evening found our fair friend singing to a "crowded and delighted audience," and it is not exaggerating to say that her performance elicited "thunders of applause."

And thus Lucinda Hopley settled down to the profession of a public singer. She soon left the * * * * (in spite of the entreaties of Beagle, and the offer of double pay), for another and more profitable engagement, and is now starring it—the first favourite of the London audiences.

Beagle went every night for three weeks to the hall at which she was singing, to beg of her to return to the * * * * but in vain. At the expiration of the three weeks the * * * * went to smash, and Beagle was found drowned!

CXXXIII.—Treats of Vengeance, Matrimony, Murder, Mystery, and Maniacs, and concludes the story of Charley Wag.

FOUR years passed, and during this period numerous changes had been wrought by the hand of time.

On Toddleboy's return to England, he had, with the assistance of Lieutenant Duffy, succeeded in fishing up sufficient evidence against Bloodyer, the master of Saint-Starver-Cum-Bag-o'-Bones workhouse.

Found guilty, the wretched Bloodyer contemplated implicating Faversham, but the warning received years before rang in the condemned man's ears, and deterred him from naming his accomplice. On the morning of the execution our old friend Toddleboy might have been seen calmly seated at a window directly in front of the scaffold, from which elevated position he witnessed the death of the man who had murdered his old friend, Joe Cudder, and had attempted his (Toddleboy's) life. At his window the old pirate remained until the body was cut down, then he returned to breakfast with Mrs. Dewberry—I beg her pardon, Mrs. Toddleboy I should say —for the old fellow had indeed married her.

"I should be perfectly happy, my love, if I could but find out that unfortunate fellow, Charley Wag. It's most extraordinary I never can hear anything at all about him—perhaps he's dead," the old man would say.

"Not at all impossible my dear. Have another cup of coffee. When shall we go Brighton, Captain?"

"Whenever you like dearest."

Then the lady would get up and kiss the old fellow, and positively he had been heard to exclaim that he had never been so happy before in his life.

In one of the handsomest mansions in Park Lane a ball given in honour of some foreign princes was taking place. In the brilliantly lighted saloons were assembled the élite of England's aristocracy. All seemed to partake of the gaity around, and the host, a handsome young man, was about to lead the lovely daughter of the Earl of Dumbledore to join the dancers, when a tall, grave-looking man approached, and requested a few moments private conversation. The host conducted his fair companion to a seat, and complied with the stranger's request. The stranger proved to be a detective, and the gentleman whom he came to apprehend upon a charge of murder, and with whom he had requested the few minutes private conversation, was our hero, Charley Wag!

A verdict of guilty was found, and our hero was condemned to death. The sentence was to be carried into effect the following morning, when, to the astonishment of the officials at Newgate, the prisoner was respited, and afterwards pardoned. The Duchess of Heatherland had saved her son's life. On the day before the execution was to take place she had an interview with the Home Secretary; to him she had explained all, and to him she proclaimed our hero, Charley Wag, as the heir to the dukedom and estates of Heatherland. This will, in some measure, account for Charley's respite and subsequent pardon.

Feeling that the position he had succeeded in establishing in society was gone for ever, our hero determined upon going abroad, where he passed the rest of his life in strict retirement.

.   .   .   .   .   .

After justice had overtaken Bloodyer, Faversham had altered visibly, and latterly the duchess perceived that his mind was affected. She seldom permitted herself to lose sight of him; but on one occasion he succeeded in evading her vigilance, and set off for London by the last train at night. The duchess discovered his absence soon enough to catch the same train. Curious to know where he would go, she did not interfere with him, but kept him in sight from the moment of leaving the terminus at Waterloo Bridge. Striding onwards, Faversham made his way to his old house in Bayswater.

At the back of this house was an old cellar which Faversham rented—in this he had, years ago, caused a bricklayer to build him another or inner cellar. In this place were the bodies of all Faversham's victims! To this cellar the madman bent his steps.

Entering the first cellar, the door of which he left open while he procured a light, Faversham passed into the other chamber without observing that he was followed by the duchess.

Here a sight presented itself which curdled the blood of the shrinking woman. Lying about in all directions were the bodies or skeletons of the unfortunate who had been murdered by Faversham; and in a corner, over a few bones, the madman was crouching down, and muttering incoherently. The duchess, unable to control her feelings at the ghastly spectacle, gave vent to an exclamation of horror. Uttering a yell, the maniac sprang to the door, and closed it. The unfortunate woman was shut in with this infuriated demon. Vainly did she beg of him to spare her life, and return home with her. The madman heeded her not. She must die. *His vow must be fulfilled.* Again giving the terrible yell, he clutched her by the throat, nor did he relax his grasp until his victim was a corpse. Then, flinging the lifeless body from him, he sat chattering by the bones in the corner until late in the night, when he fell asleep. When he awoke he was sensible of the horrors of his situation! His wife, murdered by his own hand, was lying a corpse at his feet. The bodies of his victims around him, and—oh! horror! escape impossible!

The door of the inner chamber closed with a spring, and thus the madman, in his frenzy, had sealed his own death-warrant.

For days the wretched man remained fully alive to a sense of what his fate must be; but at length, worn out and exhausted from want of food, and his efforts to make his terrible position known to the outer world, death came to his relief, and the charnel-house of those he had murdered became his own tomb.

THE END.